Dear Bert, ... thank
you for the gift of your
friendship.

Always,

Tony.

January 1987.

GREAT AMERICAN SHORT STORIES

GREAT AMERICAN SHORT STORIES

Longmeadow Press

This volume first published in 1984 by

Octopus Books Limited
59 Grosvenor Street
London W1

This edition published 1985

Copyright © 1984 Introduction and arrangement

Octopus Books Limited

ISBN 0 681 31925 9

Printed in the United States of America
by R.R. Donnelley and Sons Company

CONTENTS

Introduction

THE AMERICAN SHORT STORY is as old as the United States itself, and is probably unique in the completeness with which it reflects the spiritual and material history of the nation. For over two hundred years these stories have revealed not only the profundities of American life but also its great diversity. Until recent times, European writers have more often than not been gentlemen, divines or scholars – breeds of which America has certainly had her share; but almost from the beginning there have also been individuals with a wider experience of American life who have succeeded in turning themselves into authors. There have been author-sailors like Melville, author-hobos like Jack London, author-convicts like O. Henry, and author-riverboatmen like Mark Twain; the list could be extended for pages. This has been America's good fortune, since only writers with such a breadth of experience could do justice to the vastness of their land and the crowded, epic tale of its people, who have known migration and settlement, democracy, industrialization, war and world power with the span of half a dozen lifetimes.

As a result, the American short story has a sheer variety that is unmatched in any other national literature. Alongside the subtleties of high society, as chronicled by Henry James and Edith Wharton, we may set the savage, elemental struggles for existence narrated in Jack London's tales of the Klondyke and the South Seas, and the realities of poverty and prostitution described by Stephen Crane in 'Maggie'. Edgar Allan Poe's heroes, their refined sensibilities shuddering with horror within the curtained rooms they never leave, were the countrymen of Bret Harte's gamblers and gunmen and Herman Melville's obsessed, peg-legged Captain Ahab, who roamed the oceans in his mad quest to slay the whale Moby Dick. Hawthorne and Melville, with their powerful symbols and troubled metaphysical consciousness of evil, were contemporaries of Mark Twain and such cracker-barrel philosophers as Josh Billings. And Scott Fitzgerald, poet of Jazz Age cocktails and kiss-and-tell, was the close friend and rival of Ernest Hemingway, who created unforgettable images of intense physical life in the woods of Michigan and on the battlefronts of war-torn 20th century Europe. It is one of the cardinal virtues of the short story genre that all these riches can be crammed within the covers of a single volume.

However, a distinctively American tone and stance did not develop at once after the revolution that made the United States. In fact it is one of the paradoxes of literary history that the earliest American short stories of real importance were published and acclaimed in Britain. Their author, Washington Irving, was a cosmopolitan who spent much of his adult life in Europe, and most of his famous *Sketch Book of Geoffrey Crayon, Gent.* (1819–20) consists of little pictures of English life, written in a fluent, whimsical style reminiscent of British authors like Oliver Goldsmith. Even the most famous stories in Irving's collection, 'Rip Van Winkle' and 'The Legend of Sleepy Hollow', were largely taken from German sources and transferred to American settings. Nevertheless Irving's achievement was no mean one: he gave enduring myths to a new nation that sorely needed them, and he was the first American writer to gain a truly international reputation. He put American literature 'on the map'.

In the decades leading up to the outbreak of the Civil War in 1861, that literature came into its own. As well as major figures such as Ralph Waldo Emerson, H. D. Thoreau and Walt Whitman, three masters of fiction appeared: Edgar Allan Poe, Nathaniel Hawthorne and Herman Melville. All three were products of the Romantic movement at its most intense. Hawthorne and Melville were New Englanders and, as such, heirs to the high seriousness of Puritanism and Transcendentalist philosophy. Poe, a more raffish figure, was Boston-born but a Southerner by upbringing and a vagabond by literary destiny and personal misfortune. Though condemned by poverty to spend much of his energy on hackwork, he put his genius into stories, poems and essays. His tales are macabre and often morbid – fearfully effective when their gruesome events take place within the narrow walls of the mind, as in 'The Cask of Amontillado', or on the uncertain margins of life and death, as in 'The Fall of the House of Usher'.

Poe's life was a struggle, and he died miserably; his fame was posthumous, and at first owed more to French than to American readers. By contrast, Nathaniel Hawthorne was famous in his own lifetime. Most of his stories, in *Twice-Told Tales* and other collections, appeared before he turned to novel writing and devoted the powers of his puritanical mind to an examination of puritan motives in his classic *The Scarlet Letter*.

Melville's career had a more ironic pattern: he made a substantial reputation with *Typee* (1846) and other books based on his experiences at sea, then quickly lost most of his readers when his genius flowered in *Moby Dick* (1851) and other mighty allegories. 'Benito Cereno' and the other *Piazza Tales* (1856) met with the same indifference as Melville's novels, and in the last years of his life he wrote little and was utterly forgotten. The rediscovery of Melville is one of the indisputable triumphs of 20th century criticism.

The greatest events are not always the most memorably recorded, and apart from Whitman's verse and Lincoln's speeches, the literature that came out of the Civil War tends to be disappointing. The best short stories about the war by a contemporary were written by Ambrose Bierce, who served through it with distinction while still a very young man. Later, as a highly successful San Francisco newspaperman and author of the popular *Devil's Dictionary*, Bierce wrung a wry laughter out of his confirmed pessimism; but in war stories such as 'Occurrence at Owl Creek Bridge' and 'A Horseman in the Sky' the incidents of civil war are shown in an entirely tragic light.

The Civil War proved to be a watershed. After it, the United States was transformed by a long continuous surge of energy that flung railroads across the continent and put commerce, manufacturers and cities at the heart of a new American culture. Ruthless speculators and 'robber barons' made the headlines in the early years of the new era, known (after the title of a book by Mark Twain and Charles Dudley Warner) as 'the Gilded Age'. The dominance of 'the money power' was widely resented – by aristocrats of the old order such as Edith Wharton as well as by sturdy products of semi-rural small-town America like Mark Twain.

Twain is, of course, still known above all as a humorist, whether chronicling the nefarious doings of Tom Sawyer and Huck Finn or writing a story such as 'The Celebrated Jumping Frog of Calaveras County', in the tradition of the 'tall tale' beloved of the Westerner. He was also intensely conscious of the new forces in American society, which he viewed with a strong streak of pessimism that grew more marked with the years. The miraculous, life-transforming properties of money, displayed admiringly in 'The £1,000,000 Bank-Note', eventually come to be seen in his work as totally evil, notably in such late stories as the relentless 'Man That Corrupted Hadleyburg'.

Fortunately, there were writers to celebrate the old America before it passed away. The 'Wild West' found an unlikely historian in Bret Harte, a bookish Easterner who went out to California, worked as a teacher, drug store clerk, Wells Fargo messenger and magazine editor, then struck it rich with his stories (*The Luck of Roaring Camp*, 1870) and left for good as soon as he was assured of a literary career in a more 'cultured' environment. If Harte's miners, gamblers and saloon ladies now seem rather sentimentalized figures, his importance is undeniable: he created what may be called the 'Hollywood' image of the West, which dominated the American imagination for almost a century.

In Harte's day the frontier was still a reality, though its disappearance was already imminent. Many later writers (for example Sarah Orne Jewett and Willa Cather) lamented good, gracious days that had gone for ever, and their dominant literary emotions were nostalgia and sense of loss. For the literary sensibility that winced at the materialistic, thrusting society of late 19th century America, however, there was another solution: flight from the New World to the Old. This was the course adopted by Henry James, who found in Europe the restrained manners, refined culture and complexities of feeling that his art required. Not that James abandoned his Americanness; on the contrary, it was an essential component of his great 'international' theme, which arose from the confrontation between America, virtuous but crass, and a civilized but corrupt Europe. James's artistic rigor and somewhat rarefied view of life are arguably most effectively expressed in his stories; and not just those devoted to manners and morals. In the famous 'The Turn of the Screw' he trespasses on the territory of Edgar Allan Poe, substituting for Poe's hair-raising happenings a set of entirely mental, elusive, ambiguous horrors that are all the more disturbing in that they may only be a figment of a governess's inflamed imagination.

In the 1890s and early 1900s several writers took a still more critical and unflinching look at American society. The most important of these, Frank Norris, Stephen Crane and Theodore Dreiser, were all naturalist writers, seeing men and women as beneficiaries or (more often) victims of a huge social machine which they were powerless to control. Crane's Maggie, for example, is less an individual than a social statistic – one of a set percentage of casualties typically produced by the interaction of poverty, public morality, lust and commercial values.

Writers such as Crane and Norris undoubtedly felt a kind of grim satisfaction in detailing the brutal realities with which they shocked their readers. This can also be sensed in the writings of Jack London, whose stories are usually based on a conviction that the Darwinian struggle for existence – savage, and unmodified by ethics or feeling – applied to human beings as completely as it did to the animal creation. London managed at one and the same time to be a socialist and an admirer of the Nietzschean Superman, but in his short stories the emphasis is generally on the heroic individual, who is often imbued with naively romantic virtues in sharp contrast to the remorseless narrative of events. London's Klondyke tales came out of his experiences in the Gold Rush, in which, it has been justly said, writers like London and Robert W. Service struck the richest of all the mother-lodes.

By the time Jack London died in 1916, reality had begun to surpass the horrors invented by imaginative writers. The First World War had claimed millions of casualties even before the entry of the United States in 1917 – an event that began America's terrible baptism of fire as a great power. In the circumstances it is understandable that Americans preferred to forget their new status almost as soon as the war was over. Isolationism and unprecedentedly prosperous 'business as usual' at home led to a change of social climate; in the big cities, at least, pleasure was sought more openly and unashamedly than before (stimulated rather than repressed by Prohibition), women achieved a degree of emancipation, and some social taboos seemed to be on the way out. Francis Scott Fitzgerald christened this the Jazz Age, and claimed to have – almost – invented the Flapper. Fitzgerald and his wife Zelda became emblematic figures of the age, jumping into fountains, dancing on the tops of taxis and pioneering the South of France beach holiday – facts that tended to obscure the moral perception behind Fitzgerald's best fiction. The Jazz Age ended with Black Friday on Wall Street and the Great Depression; Fitzgerald, like so many others, was badly hit, and in 'Babylon Revisited' he ruefully counts the cost of a moral and material binge that had gone on for ten years.

In the 1930s – the decade of the dole queue and the New Deal – writing tended to be socially aware and 'committed'; John Steinbeck's novel *The Grapes of Wrath* is a singularly powerful example of this stance. However, the dominant figure of the period, Ernest Hemingway, was to some extent unrepresentative, and had actually published many of his best stories in the 1920s. Although *For Whom The Bell Tolls* is concerned with the struggle against Fascism in the Spanish Civil War, the characteristic Hemingway hero is more of a loner, even in war; he is a man who seeks intensities of personal sensation in deep-sea fishing, big-game hunting, bullfighting and battle. He is, in fact, a thoroughly American and Romantic individual, living on the only remaining 'frontiers' where it was still possible to experience adventure, freedom and the simple certainties of action. The famous Hemingway style, the apparently artless, terse speech of the 'tough guy', influenced several generations of American writers.

The contemporary American short story is outside the scope of this volume, but it is clear that its vitality is as great as that of its predecessors and that future generations will undoubtedly have the pleasure of reading further and as aptly-named collections of 'Great American Short Stories'.

WASHINGTON IRVING
1783-1859

Washington Irving was born in New York City in 1783. As a young man he studied law, but abandoned it in favor of a career in writing. During his travels in Europe in the early part of the nineteenth century, Irving encountered the great British novelist Sir Walter Scott. Encouraged by Scott's enthusiasm for his writings Irving published his first and most successful collection of stories and essays, *The Sketch Book*, in 1820, under the humorous *nom de plume* of 'Diedrich Knickerbocker'.

All three of the following stories first appeared in *The Sketch Book* and their warmth and humor, combined with Irving's great descriptive gift and superbly dramatic narrative power, have ensured their continuing popularity. The tale of 'Rip Van Winkle' in particular, in content presaging the later time travel fantasies of H. G. Wells, has attained wide recognition and been adapted many times for the stage.

The Legend of Sleepy Hollow

FOUND AMONG THE PAPERS OF THE LATE DIEDRICH KNICKERBOCKER

'A pleasing land of drowsyhead it was,
 Of dreams that wave before the half-shut eye;
And of gay castles in the clouds that pass,
 For ever flushing round a summer sky.'

Castle of Indolence.

In the bosom of one of those spacious coves which indent the eastern shore of the Hudson, at that broad expansion of the river denominated by the ancient Dutch navigators the Tappan Zee, and where they always prudently shortened sail and implored the protection of St Nicholas when they crossed, there lies a small market-town or rural port, which by some is called Greensburgh, but which is more generally and properly known by the name of Tarry Town. This name was given, we are told, in former days, by the good housewives of the adjacent country, from the inveterate propensity of their husbands to linger about the village tavern on market-days. Be that as it may, I do not vouch for the fact, but merely advert to it for the sake of being precise and authentic. Not far from this village, perhaps about two miles, there is a little valley, or rather lap of land, among high hills, which is one of the quietest places in the whole world. A small brook glides through it, with just murmur enough to lull one to repose, and the occasional whistle of a quail or tapping of a woodpecker is almost the only sound that ever breaks in upon the uniform tranquillity.

I recollect that, when a stripling, my first exploit in squirrel-shooting was in a grove of tall walnut-trees that shades one side of the valley. I had wandered into it at noon-time, when all nature is peculiarly quiet, and was startled by the roar of my own gun as it broke the Sabbath stillness around, and was prolonged and reverberated by the angry echoes. If ever I should wish for a retreat, whither I might steal from the world and its distractions, and dream quietly away the remnant of a troubled life, I know of none more promising than this little valley.

From the listless repose of the place, and the peculiar character of its inhabitants, who are descendants from the original Dutch settlers, this sequestered glen has long been known by the name of SLEEPY HOLLOW, and its rustic lads are called the Sleepy Hollow Boys throughout all the neighbouring country. A drowsy, dreamy influence seems to hang over the land and to pervade the very atmosphere. Some say that the place was bewitched by a high German doctor during the early days of the settlement; others that an old Indian chief, the prophet or wizard of his tribe, held his

17

pow-wows there before the country was discovered by Master Hendrick Hudson. Certain it is, the place still continues under the sway of some witching power that holds a spell over the minds of the good people, causing them to walk in a continual reverie. They are given to all kinds of marvellous beliefs; are subject to trances and visions; and frequently see strange sights and hear music and voices in the air. The whole neighbourhood abounds with local tales, haunted spots, and twilight superstitions; stars shoot and meteors glare oftener across the valley than in any other part of the country, and the night-mare, with her whole nine fold, seems to make it the favourite scene of her gambols.

The dominant spirit, however, that haunts this enchanted region, and seems to be commander-in-chief of all the powers of the air, is the apparition of a figure on horseback without a head. It is said by some to be the ghost of a Hessian trooper whose head had been carried away by a cannon-ball in some nameless battle during the revolutionary war, and who is ever and anon seen by the country-folk hurrying along in the gloom of night as if on the wings of the wind. His haunts are not confined to the valley, but extend at times to the adjacent roads, and especially to the vicinity of a church at no great distance. Indeed, certain of the most authentic historians of those parts, who have been careful in collecting and collating the floating facts concerning this spectre, allege that the body of the trooper, having been buried in the churchyard, the ghost rides forth to the scene of battle in nightly quest of the head, and that the rushing speed with which he sometimes passes along the Hollow, like a midnight blast, is owing to his being belated and in a hurry to get back to the churchyard before daybreak.

Such is the general purport of this legendary superstition, which has furnished materials for many a wild story in that region of shadows, and the spectre is known at all the country firesides by the name of the Headless Horseman of Sleepy Hollow.

It is remarkable that the visionary propensity I have mentioned is not confined to the native inhabitants of the valley, but is unconsciously imbibed by everyone who resides there for a time. However wide-awake they may have been before they entered that sleepy region, they are sure, in a little time, to inhale the witching influence of the air and begin to grow imaginative—to dream dreams and see apparitions.

I mention this peaceful spot with all possible laud, for it is in such little retired Dutch valleys, found here and there embosomed in the great state of New York, that population, manners, and customs remain fixed; while the great torrent of migration and improvement, which is making such incessant changes in other parts of this restless country, sweeps by them unobserved. They are like those little nooks of still water which border a rapid stream, where we may see the straw and bubble riding quietly at anchor, or slowly revolving in their mimic harbour, undisturbed by the rush of the passing current. Though many years have elapsed since I trod the drowsy shades of Sleepy Hollow, yet I question whether I should not still find the same trees and the same families vegetating in its sheltered bosom.

In this by-place of nature there abode, in a remote period of American history, that is to say, some thirty years since, a worthy wight of the name of Ichabod Crane, who sojourned, or, as he expressed it, 'tarried,' in Sleepy Hollow for the purpose of instructing the children of the vicinity. He was a native of Connecticut, a state which supplies the Union with pioneers for the mind as well as for the forest, and sends forth yearly its legions of frontier woodmen and country schoolmasters. The cognomen of Crane was not inapplicable to his person. He was tall but exceedingly lank, with narrow shoulders, long arms and legs, hands that dangled a mile out of his sleeves, feet that might have served for shovels, and his whole frame most loosely hung together. His head was small and flat at top, with huge ears, large green glassy eyes, and a long snipe nose, so that it looked like a weather-cock perched upon his spindle neck to tell which way the wind blew. To see him striding along the profile of a hill on a windy day, with his clothes bagging and fluttering about him, one might have mistaken him for the genius of famine descending upon the earth, or some scarecrow eloped from a corn-field.

His school-house was a low building of one large room, rudely constructed of logs, the windows partly glazed and partly patched with leaves of old copy-books. It was most ingeniously secured at vacant hours by a withe twisted in the handle of the door, and stakes set against the window-shutters, so that, though a thief might get in with perfect ease, he would find some embarrassment in getting out, an idea most probably borrowed by the architect, Yost Van Houten, from the mystery of an eel-pot. The school-house stood in a rather lonely but pleasant situation just at the foot of a woody hill with a brook running close by, and a formidable birch-tree growing at one end of it. From hence the low murmur of his pupils' voices, conning over their lessons, might be heard on a drowsy summer's day like the hum of a bee-hive, interrupted now and then by the authoritative voice of the master in the tone of menace or command; or, peradventure, by the appalling sound of the birch as he urged some tardy loiterer along the flowery path of knowledge. Truth to say, he was a conscientious man, and ever bore in mind the golden maxim: 'Spare the rod and spoil the child.' Ichabod Crane's scholars certainly were not spoiled.

I would not have it imagined, however, that he was one of those cruel potentates of the school who joy in the smart of their subjects; on the contrary, he administered justice with discrimination rather than severity, taking the burthen off the backs of the weak and laying it on those of the strong. Your mere puny stripling, that winced at the least flourish of the rod, was passed by with indulgence, but the claims of justice were satisfied by inflicting a double portion on some little tough, wrong-headed, broad-skirted Dutch urchin who sulked and swelled and grew dogged and sullen beneath the birch. All this he called 'doing his duty by their parents,' and he never inflicted a chastisement without following it by the assurance, so consolatory to the smarting urchin, that 'he would remember it and thank him for it the longest day he had to live.'

When school hours were over he was even the companion and playmate of the larger boys, and on holiday afternoons would convoy some of the smaller ones home who happened to have pretty sisters, or good housewives for mothers, noted for the comforts of the cupboard. Indeed, it behoved him to keep on good terms with his pupils. The revenue arising from his school was small, and would have been scarcely sufficient to furnish him with daily bread, for he was a huge feeder, and, though lank, had the dilating powers of an anaconda; but to help out his maintenance he was, according to country custom in those parts, boarded and lodged at the houses of the farmers whose children he instructed. With these he lived successively a week at a time, thus going the rounds of the neighbourhood, with all his worldly effects tied up in a cotton handkerchief.

That all this might not be too onerous on the purses of his rustic patrons, who are apt to consider the costs of schooling a grievous burden, and schoolmasters as mere drones, he had various ways of rendering himself both useful and agreeable. He assisted the farmers occasionally in the lighter labours of their farms: helped to make hay, mended the fences, took the horses to water, drove the cows from pasture, and cut wood for the winter fire. He laid aside, too, all the dominant dignity and absolute sway with which he lorded it in his little empire, the school, and became wonderfully gentle and ingratiating. He found favour in the eyes of the mothers by petting the children, particularly the youngest; and like the lion bold, which whilom so magnificently the lamb did hold, he would sit with a child on one knee and rock a cradle with his foot for whole hours together.

In addition to his other vocations, he was the singing-master of the neighbourhood, and picked up many bright shillings by instructing the young folks in psalmody. It was a matter of no little vanity to him on Sundays to take his station in front of the church gallery with a band of chosen singers, where, in his own mind, he completely carried away the psalm from the parson. Certain it is, his voice resounded far above all the rest of the congregation; and there are peculiar quavers still to be heard in that church, and which may even be heard half a mile off, quite to the opposite side of the mill-pond, on a still Sunday morning, which are said to be legitimately descended from the nose of Ichabod Crane. Thus, by divers little make-shifts, in that ingenious way which is commonly denominated 'by hook and by crook,' the worthy pedagogue got on tolerably enough, and was thought by all who understood nothing of the labour of headwork to have a wonderfully easy life of it.

The schoolmaster is generally a man of some importance in the female circle of a rural neighbourhood, being considered a kind of idle gentleman-like personage, of vastly superior taste and accomplishments to the rough country swains, and indeed inferior in learning only to the parson. His appearance, therefore, is apt to occasion some little stir at the tea-table of a farmhouse, and the addition of a supernumerary dish of cakes or sweet-meats, or, peradventure, the parade of a silver tea-pot. Our man of letters, therefore, was peculiarly happy in the smiles of all the country damsels. How he would figure among them in the churchyard between services on Sundays! gathering grapes for them from the wild vines that overran the surrounding trees, reciting for their amusement all the epitaphs on the tombstones, or sauntering with a whole bevy of them along the banks of the adjacent mill-pond; while the more bashful country bumpkins hung sheepishly back, envying his superior elegance and address.

From his half-itinerant life, also, he was a kind of travelling gazette, carrying the whole budget of local gossip from house to house, so that his appearance was always greeted with satisfaction. He was, moreover, esteemed by the women as a man of great erudition, for he had read several books quite through, and was a perfect master of Cotton Mather's *History of New England Witchcraft*, in which, by the way, he most firmly and potently believed.

He was, in fact, an odd mixture of small shrewdness and simple credulity. His appetite for the marvellous and his powers of digesting it were equally extraordinary; and both had been increased by his residence in this spell-bound region. No tale was too gross or monstrous for his capacious swallow. It was often his delight, after his school was dismissed in the afternoon, to stretch himself on the rich bed of clover bordering the little brook that whimpered by his school-house, and there con over old Mather's direful tales until the gathering dusk of the evening made the printed page a mere mist before his eyes. Then, as he wended his way by swamp and stream and awful woodland to the farmhouse where he happened to be quartered, every sound of nature at that witching hour fluttered his excited imagination: the moan of the whip-poor-will[1] from the hill-side; the boding cry of the tree-toad, that harbinger of storm; the dreary hooting of the screech-owl; or the sudden rustling in the thicket of birds frightened from their roost. The fireflies, too, which sparkled most vividly in the darkest places, now and then startled him, as one of uncommon brightness would stream across his path; and if by chance a huge blockhead of a beetle came winging his blundering flight against him, the poor varlet was ready to give up the ghost, with the idea that he was struck with a witch's token. His only resource on such occasions, either to drown thought or drive away evil spirits, was to sing psalm tunes; and the good people of Sleepy Hollow, as they sat by their doors of an evening, were often filled with awe at hearing his nasal melody, 'in linked sweetness long drawn out,' floating from the distant hill or along the dusky road.

Another of his sources of fearful pleasure was to pass long winter evenings with the old Dutch wives as they sat spinning by the fire, with a row of apples roasting and spluttering along the hearth, and listen to their marvellous tales of ghosts and goblins, and haunted fields, and haunted brooks, and haunted bridges, and haunted houses, and particularly of the headless horseman, or Galloping Hessian of the Hollow, as they sometimes called him. He would delight them equally by his anecdotes of witchcraft and of the direful omens and portentous sights and sounds in the air which prevailed in the earlier times of Connecticut; and would frighten them woefully with speculations upon comets and shooting-stars, and with the alarming fact that the world did absolutely turn round, and that they were half the time topsy-turvy!

But if there was a pleasure in all this, while snugly cuddling in the chimney corner of a chamber that was all of a ruddy glow from the crackling wood fire, and where, of course, no spectre dared to show its face, it was dearly purchased by the terrors of his subsequent walk homewards. What fearful shapes and shadows beset his path amidst the dim and ghastly glare of a snowy night! With what wistful look did he eye every trembling ray of light streaming across the waste fields from some distant window! How often was he appalled by some shrub covered with snow, which, like a sheeted spectre, beset his very path! How often did he shrink with curdling awe at the sound of his own steps on the frosty crust beneath his feet, and dread to look over his shoulder lest he should behold some uncouth being tramping close behind him! And how often was he thrown into complete dismay by some

---

[1] The whip-poor-will is a bird which is only heard at night. It receives its name from its note, which is thought to resemble those words.

rushing blast howling among the trees, in the idea that it was the Galloping Hessian on one of his nightly scourings!

All these, however, were mere terrors of the night, phantoms of the mind that walk in darkness; and though he had seen many spectres in his time, and been more than once beset by Satan in divers shapes, in his lonely perambulations, yet daylight put an end to all these evils, and he would have passed a pleasant life of it, in despite of the devil and all his works, if his path had not been crossed by a being that causes more perplexity to mortal man than ghosts, goblins, and the whole race of witches put together, and that was—a woman.

Among the musical disciples who assembled one evening in each week to receive his instructions in psalmody was Katrina Van Tassel, the daughter and only child of a substantial Dutch farmer. She was a blooming lass of fresh eighteen, plump as a partridge, ripe and melting and rosy-cheeked as one of her father's peaches, and universally famed, not merely for her beauty, but her vast expectations. She was, withal, a little of a coquette, as might be perceived even in her dress, which was a mixture of ancient and modern fashions, as most suited to set off her charms. She wore the ornaments of pure yellow gold which her great-great-grandmother had brought over from Saardam, the tempting stomacher of the olden time, and, withal, a provokingly short petticoat to display the prettiest foot and ankle in the country round.

Ichabod Crane had a soft and foolish heart towards the sex, and it is not to be wondered at that so tempting a morsel soon found favour in his eyes, more especially after he had visited her in her paternal mansion. Old Baltus Van Tassel was a perfect picture of a thriving, contented, liberal-hearted farmer. He seldom, it is true, sent either his eyes or his thoughts beyond the boundaries of his own farm; but within those everything was snug, happy, and well-conditioned. He was satisfied with his wealth, but not proud of it, and piqued himself upon the hearty abundance rather than the style in which he lived. His stronghold was situated on the banks of the Hudson, in one of those green, sheltered, fertile nooks in which the Dutch farmers are so fond of nestling. A great elm-tree spread its broad branches over it, at the foot of which bubbled up a spring of the softest and sweetest water, in a little well formed of a barrel, and then stole sparkling away through the grass to a neighbouring brook that bubbled along among alders and dwarf willows. Hard by the farmhouse was a vast barn that might have served for a church, every window and crevice of which seemed bursting forth with the treasures of the farm; the flail was busily resounding within it from morning to night; swallows and martins skimmed twittering about the eaves; and rows of pigeons, some with one eye turned up, as if watching the weather, some with their heads under their wings or buried in their bosoms, and other swelling, and cooing, and bowing about their dames, were enjoying the sunshine on the roof. Sleek unwieldy porkers were grunting in the repose and abundance of their pens, whence sallied forth, now and then, troops of sucking pigs, as if to snuff the air. A stately squadron of snowy geese were riding in an adjoining pond, convoying whole fleets of ducks; regiments of turkeys were gobbling through the farmyard, and guinea-fowls fretting about it, like ill-tempered housewives, with their peevish, discontented cry. Before the barn-door strutted the gallant cock, that pattern of a husband, a warrior, and a fine gentleman, clapping his burnished wings, and crowing in the pride and gladness of his heart—sometimes tearing up the earth with his feet, and then generously calling his ever-hungry family of wives and children to enjoy the rich morsel which he had discovered.

The pedagogue's mouth watered as he looked upon this sumptuous promise of luxurious winter fare. In his devouring mind's eye he pictured to himself every roasting-pig running about with a pudding in his belly and an apple in his mouth; the pigeons were snugly put to bed in a comfortable pie, and tucked in with a coverlet of crust; the geese were swimming in their own gravy; and the ducks pairing cosily in dishes, like snug married couples, with a decent competency of onion sauce. In the porkers he saw carved out the future sleek side of bacon and juicy relishing ham; not a turkey but he beheld daintily trussed up with its gizzard under its wing, and, peradventure, a necklace of savoury sausages; and even bright chanticleer himself lay sprawling on his back in a side-dish, with uplifted claws, as if craving that quarter which his chivalrous spirit disdained to ask while living.

As the enraptured Ichabod fancied all this, and as he rolled his great green eyes over the fat meadowlands, the rich fields of wheat, of rye, of buckwheat, and Indian corn, and the orchards burthened with ruddy fruit, which surrounded the warm tenement of Van Tassel, his heart yearned after the damsel who was to inherit these domains, and his imagination expanded with the idea how they might be readily turned into cash and the money invested in immense tracts of wild land and shingle palaces in the wilderness. Nay, his busy fancy already realized his hopes, and presented to him the blooming Katrina, with a whole family of children, mounted on the top of a wagon loaded with household trumpery, with pots and kettles dangling beneath; and he beheld himself bestriding a pacing mare, with a colt at her heels, setting out for Kentucky, Tennessee, or the Lord knows where.

When he entered the house the conquest of his heart was complete. It was one of those spacious farmhouses, with high-ridged but lowly-sloping roofs, built in the style handed down from the first Dutch settlers, the low projecting eaves forming a piazza along the front capable of being closed up in bad weather. Under this were hung flails, harness, various utensils of husbandry, and nets for fishing in the neighbouring river. Benches were built along the sides for summer use; and a great spinning-wheel at one end, and a churn at the other, showed the various uses to which this important porch might be devoted. From this piazza the wondering Ichabod entered the hall, which formed the centre of the mansion and the place of usual residence. Here rows of resplendent pewter, ranged on a long dresser, dazzled his eyes. In one corner stood a huge bag of wool ready to be spun, in another a quantity of linsey-woolsey just from the loom; ears of Indian corn, and strings of dried apples and peaches, hung in gay festoons along the wall, mingled with the gaud of red peppers; and a door left ajar gave him a peep into the best parlour, where the claw-footed chairs and dark mahogany tables shone like mirrors; andirons, with their accompanying shovel and tongs, glistened from their covert of asparagus tops; mock oranges and conch-shells decorated the mantel-piece; strings of various coloured birds' eggs were suspended above it; a great ostrich egg was hung from the centre of the room, and a corner cupboard, knowingly left open, displayed immense treasures of old silver and well-mended china.

From the moment Ichabod laid his eyes upon these regions of delight the peace of his mind was at an end, and his only study was how to gain the affections of the peerless daughter of Van Tassel. In this enterprise, however, he had more real difficulties than generally fell to the lot of a knight-errant of yore, who seldom had anything but giants, enchanters, fiery dragons, and such like easily-conquered adversaries to contend with; and had to make his way merely through gates of iron and brass, and walls of adamant, to the castle keep, where the lady of his heart was confined; all which he achieved as easily as a man would carve his way to the centre of a Christmas pie, and then the lady gave him her hand as a matter of course. Ichabod, on the contrary, had to win his way to the heart of a country coquette, beset with a labyrinth of whims and caprices, which were for ever presenting new difficulties and impediments, and he had to encounter a host of fearful adversaries of real flesh and blood, the numerous rustic admirers, who beset every portal to her heart; keeping a watchful and angry eye upon each other, but ready to fly out in the common cause against any new competitor.

Among these the most formidable was a burly, roaring, roistering blade of the name of Abraham, or, according to the Dutch abbreviation, Brom Van Brunt, the hero of the country round, which rang with his feats of strength and hardihood. He was broad-shouldered and double-jointed, with short curly black hair and a bluff but not unpleasant countenance, having a mingled air of fun and arrogance. From his Herculean frame and great powers of limb he had received the nickname of Brom Bones, by which he was universally known. He was famed for great knowledge and skill in horsemanship, being as dexterous on horseback as a Tartar. He was foremost at all races and cock-fights, and, with the ascendency which bodily strength acquires in rustic life, was the umpire in all disputes, setting his hat on one side, and giving his decisions with an air and tone admitting of no gainsay or appeal. He was always ready for either a fight or a frolic, but had more mischief than ill-will in his composition; and, with all his overbearing roughness, there was a strong dash of waggish good-humour at bottom. He had three or four boon companions, who regarded him as their model, and at the head of whom he scoured the country, attending every scene of feud or merriment for miles round. In cold weather he was distinguished by a fur cap, surmounted with a flaunting fox's tail; and when the folks at a country gathering descried this well-known crest at a distance, whisking about among a squad of hard riders, they always stood by for a squall. Sometimes his crew would be heard dashing along past the farmhouses at midnight, with whoop and halloo, like a troop of Don Cossacks; and the old dames, startled out of their sleep, would listen for a moment till the hurry-scurry had clattered by, and then exclaim: 'Ay, there goes Brom Bones and his gang!' The neighbours looked upon him with a mixture of awe, admiration, and good-will, and when any madcap prank or rustic brawl occurred in the vicinity, always shook their heads, and warranted Brom Bones was at the bottom of it.

This rantipole hero had for some time singled out the blooming Katrina for the object of his uncouth gallantries, and though his amorous toyings were something like the gentle caresses and endearments of a bear, yet it was whispered that she did not altogether discourage his hopes. Certain it is, his advances were signals for rival candidates to retire, who felt no inclination to cross a lion in his amours; insomuch that, when his horse was seen tied to Van Tassel's paling on a Sunday night, a sure sign that his master was courting, or, as it is termed, 'sparking,' within, all other suitors passed by in despair, and carried the war into other quarters.

Such was the formidable rival with whom Ichabod Crane had to contend, and, considering all things, a stouter man than he would have shrunk from the competition, and a wiser man would have despaired. He had, however, a happy mixture of pliability and perseverance in his nature; he was in form and spirit like a supple-jack—yielding but tough; though he bent, he never broke, and though he bowed beneath the slightest pressure, yet, the moment it was away—jerk! he was as erect, and carried his head as high, as ever.

To have taken the field openly against his rival would have been madness, for he was not a man to be thwarted in his amours, any more than that stormy lover, Achilles. Ichabod, therefore, made his advances in a quiet and gently-insinuating manner. Under cover of his character of singing-master he made frequent visits at the farmhouse; not that he had anything to apprehend from the meddlesome interference of parents, which is so often a stumbling-block in the path of lovers. Balt Van Tassel was an easy, indulgent soul; he loved his daughter better even than his pipe, and, like a reasonable man and an excellent father, let her have her way in everything. His notable little wife, too, had enough to do to attend to her housekeeping and manage her poultry; for, as she sagely observed, ducks and geese are foolish things, and must be looked after, but girls can take care of themselves. Thus, while the busy dame bustled about the house, or plied her spinning-wheel at one end of the piazza, honest Balt would sit smoking his evening pipe at the other, watching the achievements of a little wooden warrior, who, armed with a sword in each hand, was most valiantly fighting the wind on the pinnacle of the barn. In the meantime, Ichabod would carry on his suit with the daughter by the side of the spring under the great elm, or sauntering along in the twilight, that hour so favourable to the lover's eloquence.

I profess not to know how women's hearts are wooed and won. To me they have always been matters of riddle and admiration. Some seem to have but one vulnerable point or door of access, while others have a thousand avenues, and may be captured in a thousand different ways. It is a great triumph of skill to gain the former, but a still greater proof of generalship to maintain possession of the latter, for a man must battle for his fortress at every door and window. He who wins a thousand common hearts is therefore entitled to some renown, but he who keeps undisputed sway over the heart of a coquette is indeed a hero. Certain it is, this was not the case with the redoubtable Brom Bones, and from the moment Ichabod Crane made his advances the interests of the former evidently declined; his horse was no longer seen tied at the palings on Sunday nights, and a deadly feud gradually arose between him and the preceptor of Sleepy Hollow.

Brom, who had a degree of rough chivalry in his nature, would fain have carried matters to open warfare, and have settled their pretensions to the lady according to the mode of those most concise and simple reasoners, the knights-errant of yore, by single combat; but Ichabod was too conscious of the superior might of his adversary to enter the lists against him. He had overheard a boast of Bones that he would 'double the schoolmaster up and lay him on a shelf of his own school-house,' and he was too wary to give him

an opportunity. There was something extremely provoking in this obstinate-
ly pacific system; it left Brom no alternative but to draw upon the funds of
rustic waggery in his disposition, and to play off boorish practical jokes upon
his rival. Ichabod became the object of whimsical persecution to Bones and
his gang of rough-riders. They harried his hitherto peaceful domains, smoked
out his singing-school by stopping up the chimney, broke into the school-
house at night in spite of its formidable fastenings of withe and window
stakes, and turned everything topsy-turvy; so that the poor schoolmaster
began to think all the witches in the country held their meetings there. But
what was still more annoying, Brom took all opportunities of turning him
into ridicule in presence of his mistress, and had a scoundrel dog whom he
taught to whine in the most ludicrous manner, and introduced as a rival of
Ichabod's to instruct her in psalmody.

In this way matters went on for some time without producing any material
effect on the relative situation of the contending powers. On a fine autumnal
afternoon, Ichabod, in pensive mood, sat enthroned on the lofty stool whence
he usually watched all the concerns of his little literary realm. In his hand he
swayed a ferule, that sceptre of despotic power; the birch of justice reposed
on three nails behind the throne, a constant terror to evil-doers, while on the
desk before him might be seen sundry contraband articles and prohibited
weapons detected upon the persons of idle urchins, such as half-munched
apples, pop-guns, whirligigs, fly-cages, and whole legions of rampant little
paper game-cocks. Apparently there had been some appalling act of justice
recently inflicted, for his scholars were all busily intent upon their books, or
slily whispering behind them with one eye kept upon the master, and a kind
of buzzing stillness reigned throughout the school-room. It was suddenly
interrupted by the appearance of a negro in tow-cloth jacket and trousers, a
round-crowned fragment of a hat, like the cap of Mercury, and mounted on
the back of a ragged, wild, half-broken colt, which he managed with a rope
by way of halter. He came clattering up to the school door with an invitation
to Ichabod to attend a merry-making, or 'quilting frolic,' to be held that
evening at Mynheer Van Tassel's; and having delivered his message with
that air of importance and effort at fine language which a negro is apt to
display on petty embassies of the kind, he dashed over the brook and was
seen scampering away up the hollow, full of the importance and hurry of his
mission.

All was now bustle and hubbub in the late quiet school-room. The scholars
were hurried through their lessons without stopping at trifles; those who were
nimble skipped over half with impunity, and those who were tardy had a
smart application now and then in the rear to quicken their speed, or help
them over a tall word. Books were flung aside without being put away on the
shelves, ink-stands were overturned, benches thrown down, and the whole
school was turned loose an hour before the usual time, bursting forth like a
legion of young imps yelping and racketing about the green in joy at their
early emancipation.

The gallant Ichabod now spent at least an extra half-hour at his toilet,
brushing and furbishing up his best, and indeed only, suit of rusty black, and
arranging his looks by a bit of broken looking-glass that hung up in the
school-house. That he might make his appearance before his mistress in the
true style of a cavalier he borrowed a horse from the farmer with whom he

was domiciliated, a choleric old Dutchman of the name of Hans Van Ripper, and, thus gallantly mounted, issued forth like a knight-errant in quest of adventures. But it is meet I should, in the true spirit of romantic story, give some account of the looks and equipments of my hero and his steed. The animal he bestrode was a broken-down plough-horse that had outlived almost everything but his viciousness. He was gaunt and shagged, with a ewe neck and a head like a hammer; his rusty mane and tail were tangled and knotted with burs; one eye had lost its pupil, and was glaring and spectral, but the other had the gleam of a genuine devil in it. Still, he must have had fire and metal in his day, if we may judge from the name he bore of Gunpowder. He had, in fact, been a favourite steed of his master's, the choleric Van Ripper, who was a furious rider, and had infused very probably some of his own spirit into the animal; for, old and broken down as he looked, there was more of the lurking devil in him than in any young filly in the country.

Ichabod was a suitable figure for such a steed. He rode with short stirrups, which brought his knees nearly up to the pommel of the saddle; his sharp elbows stuck out like grasshoppers'; he carried his whip perpendicularly in his hand like a sceptre, and, as his horse jogged on, the motion of his arms was not unlike the flapping of a pair of wings. A small wool hat rested on the top of his nose, for so his scanty strip of forehead might be called, and the skirts of his black coat fluttered out almost to the horse's tail. Such was the appearance of Ichabod and his steed as they shambled out of the gate of Hans Van Ripper, and it was altogether such an apparition as is seldom to be met with in broad daylight.

It was, as I have said, a fine autumnal day, the sky was clear and serene, and nature wore that rich and golden livery which we always associate with the idea of abundance. The forests had put on their sober brown and yellow, while some trees of the tenderer kind had been nipped by the frosts into brilliant dyes of orange, purple, and scarlet. Streaming files of wild ducks began to make their appearance high in the air; the bark of the squirrel might be heard from the groves of beech and hickory nuts, and the pensive whistle of the quail at intervals from the neighbouring stubble field.

The small birds were taking their farewell banquets. In the fulness of their revelry they fluttered, chirping and frolicking, from bush to bush and tree to tree, capricious from the very profusion and variety around them. There was the honest cock-robin, the favourite game of stripling sportsmen, with its loud, querulous note; and the twittering blackbirds flying in sable clouds; and the golden-winged woodpecker, with his crimson crest, his broad black gorget, and splendid plumage; and the cedar-bird, with its red-tipped wings and yellow-tipped tail, and its little montero cap of feathers; and the blue jay, that noisy coxcomb, in his gay light-blue coat and white under-clothes, screaming and chattering, nodding and bobbing and bowing, and pretending to be on good terms with every songster of the grove.

As Ichabod jogged slowly on his way, his eye, ever open to every symptom of culinary abundance, ranged with delight over the treasures of jolly autumn. On all sides he beheld vast stores of apples, some hanging in oppressive opulence on the trees, some gathered into baskets and barrels for the market, others heaped up in rich piles for the cider press. Farther on he beheld great fields of Indian corn, with its golden ears peeping from their leafy coverts and holding out the promise of cakes and hasty-pudding; and the yellow pumpkins lying beneath them, turning up their fair round bellies to the sun, and giving ample prospects of the most luxurious of pies; and anon he passed the fragrant buckwheat fields, breathing the odour of the bee-hive, and as he beheld them, soft anticipations stole over his mind of dainty slap-jacks, well buttered, and garnished with honey or treacle, by the delicate little dimpled hand of Katrina Van Tassel.

Thus feeding his mind with many sweet thoughts and 'sugared suppo-sitions,' he journeyed along the sides of a range of hills which look out upon some of the goodliest scenes of the mighty Hudson. The sun gradually wheeled his broad disc down into the west. The wide bosom of the Tappan Zee lay motionless and glassy, except that here and there a gentle undulation waved and prolonged the blue shadow of the distant mountain. A few amber clouds floated in the sky, without a breath of air to move them. The horizon was of a fine golden tint, changing gradually into a pure apple-green, and from that into the deep blue of the mid-heaven. A slanting ray lingered on the woody crests of the precipices that overhung some parts of the river, giving greater depth to the dark-grey and purple of their rocky sides. A sloop was loitering in the distance, dropping slowly down with the tide, her sail hanging uselessly against the mast; and as the reflection of the sky gleamed along the still water, it seemed as if the vessel was suspended in the air.

It was toward evening that Ichabod arrived at the castle of the Heer Van Tassel, which he found thronged with the pride and flower of the adjacent country. Old farmers, a spare leathern-faced race, in homespun coats and breeches, blue stockings, huge shoes, and magnificent pewter buckles. Their brisk withered little dames, in close crimped caps, long-waisted short gowns, homespun petticoats, with scissors, and pin-cushions, and gay calico pockets hanging on the outside. Buxom lasses, almost as antiquated as their mothers, excepting where a straw hat, a fine riband, or perhaps a white frock gave symptoms of city innovation. The sons, in short square-skirted coats with rows of stupendous brass buttons, and their hair generally queued in the fashion of the times, especially if they could procure an eel-skin for the purpose, it being esteemed throughout the country as a potent nourisher and strengthener of the hair.

Brom Bones, however, was the hero of the scene, having come to the gathering on his favourite steed, Daredevil, a creature, like himself, full of mettle and mischief, and which no one but himself could manage. He was, in fact, noted for preferring vicious animals, given to all kinds of tricks, which kept the rider in constant risk of his neck, for he held a tractable, well-broken horse as unworthy of a lad of spirit.

Fain would I pause to dwell upon the world of charms that burst upon the enraptured gaze of my hero as he entered the state parlour of Van Tassel's mansion. Not those of the bevy of buxom lasses with their luxurious display of red and white, but the ample charms of a genuine Dutch country tea-table in the sumptuous time of autumn. Such heaped-up platters of cakes of various and almost indescribable kinds, known only to experienced Dutch housewives! There was the doughty dough-nut, the tenderer oly koek, and the crisp and crumbling cruller; sweet-cakes and short-cakes, ginger-cakes and honey-cakes, and the whole family of cakes. And then there were apple-pies and peach-pies and pumpkin-pies, besides slices of ham and smoked beef; and, moreover, delectable dishes of preserved plums, and peaches, and pears, and quinces, not to mention broiled shad and roasted chickens, together with bowls of milk and cream all mingled higgledy-piggledy pretty much as I have enumerated them, with the motherly tea-pot sending up its clouds of vapour from the midst—Heaven bless the mark! I want breath and time to discuss this banquet as it deserves, and am too eager to get on with my story. Happily, Ichabod Crane was not in so great a hurry as his historian, but did ample justice to every dainty.

He was a kind and thankful creature, whose heart dilated in proportion as his skin was filled with good cheer, and whose spirits rose with eating as some men's do with drink. He could not help, too, rolling his large eyes round him as he ate, and chuckling with the possibility that he might one day be lord of all this scene of almost unimaginable luxury and splendour. Then he thought how soon he'd turn his back upon the old school-house, snap his fingers in the face of Hans Van Ripper and every other niggardly patron, and kick any itinerant pedagogue out-of-doors that should dare to call him comrade!

Old Baltus Van Tassel moved about among his guests with a face dilated with content and good-humour, round and jolly as the harvest moon. His hospitable attentions were brief but expressive, being confined to a shake of the hand, a slap on the shoulder, a loud laugh, and a pressing invitation to 'fall to, and help themselves.'

And now the sound of the music from the common room or hall summoned to the dance. The musician was an old grey-headed negro who had been the itinerant orchestra of the neighbourhood for more than half a century. His instrument was as old and battered as himself. The greater part of the time he scraped on two or three strings, accompanying every movement of the bow with a motion of the head, bowing almost to the ground, and stamping with his foot whenever a fresh couple were to start.

Ichabod prided himself upon his dancing as much as upon his vocal powers. Not a limb, not a fibre about him was idle; and to have seen his loosely-hung frame in full motion, and clattering about the room, you would have thought Saint Vitus himself, that blessed patron of the dance, was figuring before you in person. He was the admiration of all the negroes, who having gathered, of all ages and sizes, from the farm and the neighbourhood, stood forming a pyramid of shining black faces at every door and window, gazing with delight at the scene, rolling their white eyeballs, and showing grinning rows of ivory from ear to ear. How could the flogger of urchins be otherwise than animated and joyous? the lady of his heart was his partner in the dance and smiling graciously in reply to all his amorous oglings, while Brom Bones, sorely smitten with love and jealousy, sat brooding by himself in one corner.

When the dance was at an end, Ichabod was attracted to a knot of the sager folks, who with old Van Tassel, sat smoking at one end of the piazza, gossiping over former times and drawing out long stories about the war.

This neighbourhood, at the time of which I am speaking, was one of those highly-favoured places which abound with chronicle and great men. The British and American line had run near it during the war. It had, therefore, been the scene of marauding, and infested with refugees, cow-boys, and all kinds of border chivalry. Just sufficient time had elapsed to enable each story-teller to dress up his tale with a little becoming fiction, and, in the indistinctness of his recollection, to make himself the hero of every exploit.

There was the story of Doffue Martling, a large blue-bearded Dutchman, who had nearly taken a British frigate with an old iron nine-pounder from a mud breastwork, only that his gun burst at the sixth discharge. And there was an old gentleman who shall be nameless, being too rich a mynheer to be lightly mentioned, who, in the battle of Whiteplains, being an excellent master of defence, parried a musket ball with a small sword, insomuch that he absolutely felt it whiz round the blade and glance off at the hilt: in proof of which he was ready at any time to show the sword with the hilt a little bent. There were several more that had been equally great in the field, not one of whom but was persuaded that he had a considerable hand in bringing the war to a happy termination.

But all these were nothing to the tales of ghosts and apparitions that succeeded. The neighbourhood is rich in legendary treasures of the kind. Local tales and superstitions thrive best in these sheltered long-settled retreats, but are trampled under foot by the shifting throng that forms the population of most of our country places. Besides, there is no encouragement for ghosts in most of our villages, for they have scarcely had time to finish their first nap, and turn themselves in their graves, before their surviving friends have travelled away from the neighbourhood; so that when they turn out at night to walk their rounds they have no acquaintance left to call upon. This is perhaps the reason why we so seldom hear of ghosts except in our long-established Dutch communities.

The immediate cause, however, of the prevalence of supernatural stories in these parts was doubtless owing to the vicinity of Sleepy Hollow. There was a contagion in the very air that blew from that haunted region; it breathed forth an atmosphere of dreams and fancies infecting all the land. Several of the Sleepy Hollow people were present at Van Tassel's, and, as usual, were doling out their wild and wonderful legends. Many dismal tales were told about funeral trains and mourning cries and wailings heard and seen about the great tree where the unfortunate Major André was taken, and which stood in the neighbourhood. Some mention was made also of the woman in white that haunted the dark glen at Raven Rock, and was often heard to shriek on winter nights before a storm, having perished there in the snow. The chief part of the stories, however, turned upon the favourite spectre of Sleepy Hollow, the headless horseman, who had been heard several times of late patrolling the country, and, it was said, tethered his horse nightly among the graves in the churchyard.

The sequestered situation of this church seems always to have made it a favourite haunt of troubled spirits. It stands on a knoll surrounded by locust-trees and lofty elms, from among which its decent whitewashed walls shine modestly forth like Christian purity beaming through the shades of retirement. A gentle slope descends from it to a silver sheet of water, bordered by high trees, between which peeps may be caught at the blue hills of the Hudson. To look upon its grass-grown yard, where the sunbeams seem to sleep so quietly, one would think that there at least the dead might rest in peace. On one side of the church extends a wide woody dell along which raves a large brook among broken rocks and trunks of fallen trees. Over a deep black part of the stream, not far from the church, was formerly thrown a wooden bridge; the road that led to it, and the bridge itself, were thickly shaded by overhanging trees which cast a gloom about it even in the daytime, but occasioned a fearful darkness at night. Such was one of the favourite haunts of the headless horseman, and the place where he was most frequently encountered. The tale was told of old Brouwer, a most heretical disbeliever in ghosts, how he met the horseman returning from his foray into Sleepy Hollow, and was obliged to get up behind him; how they galloped over bush and brake, over hill and swamp, until they reached the bridge, when the horseman suddenly turned into a skeleton, threw old Brouwer into the brook, and sprang away over the tree-tops with a clap of thunder.

This story was immediately matched by a thrice marvellous adventure of Brom Bones, who made light of the Galloping Hessian as an arrant jockey. He affirmed that, on returning one night from the neighbouring village of Sing-Sing, he had been overtaken by this midnight trooper, that he had offered to race with him for a bowl of punch, and should have won it too, for Daredevil beat the goblin horse all hollow, but, just as they came to the church bridge, the Hessian bolted and vanished in a flash of fire.

All these tales, told in that drowsy undertone with which men talk in the dark, the countenances of the listeners only now and then receiving a casual gleam from the glare of a pipe, sank deep in the mind of Ichabod. He repaid them in kind with large extracts from his invaluable author, Cotton Mather, and added many marvellous events that had taken place in his native state of Connecticut, and fearful sights which he had seen in his nightly walks about Sleepy Hollow.

The revel now gradually broke up. The old farmers gathered together their families in their wagons, and were heard for some time rattling along the hollow roads and over the distant hills. Some of the damsels mounted on pillions behind their favourite swains, and their light-hearted laughter, mingling with the clatter of hoofs, echoed along the silent woodlands, sounding fainter and fainter until they gradually died away—and the late scene of noise and frolic was all silent and deserted. Ichabod only lingered behind, according to the custom of country lovers, to have a tête-à-tête with the heiress, fully convinced that he was now on the high-road to success. What passed at this interview I will not pretend to say, for, in fact, I do not know. Something, however, I fear me, must have gone wrong, for he certainly sallied forth, after no very great interval, with an air quite desolate and chop-fallen. O, these women! these women! Could that girl have been playing off any of her coquettish tricks? Was her encouragement of the poor pedagogue all a mere sham to secure her conquest of his rival? Heaven only knows, not I! Let it suffice to say, Ichabod stole forth with the air of one who had been sacking a hen-roost rather than a fair lady's heart. Without looking to the right or left to notice the scene of rural wealth on which he had so often gloated, he went straight to the stable, and with several hearty cuffs and kicks roused his steed most uncourteously from the comfortable quarters in which he was soundly sleeping, dreaming of mountains of corn and oats and whole valleys of timothy and clover.

It was the very witching time of night that Ichabod, heavy-hearted and crest-fallen, pursued his travels homewards along the sides of the lofty hills which rise above Tarry Town, and which he had traversed so cheerily in the afternoon. The hour was as dismal as himself. Far below him the Tappan Zee spread its dusky and indistinct waste of waters, with here and there the tall mast of a sloop riding quietly at anchor under the land. In the dead hush of midnight he could even hear the barking of the watch-dog from the opposite shore of the Hudson; but it was so vague and faint as only to give an idea of his distance from this faithful companion of man. Now and then, too, the long-drawn crowing of a cock, accidentally awakened, would sound far, far off from some farmhouse away among the hills, but it was like a dreaming sound in his ear. No signs of life occurred near him, but occasionally the melancholy chirp of a cricket, or perhaps the guttural twang of a bull-frog from a neighbouring marsh, as if sleeping uncomfortably, and turning suddenly in his bed.

All the stories of ghosts and goblins that he had heard in the afternoon now came crowding upon his recollection. The night grew darker and darker; the stars seemed to sink deeper in the sky, and driving clouds occasionally hid them from his sight. He had never felt so lonely and dismal. He was, moreover, approaching the very place where many of the scenes of the ghost stories had been laid. In the centre of the road stood an enormous tulip-tree, which towered like a giant above all the other trees of the neighbourhood, and formed a kind of landmark. Its limbs were gnarled and fantastic, large enough to form trunks for ordinary trees, twisting down almost to the earth, and rising again into the air. It was connected with the tragical story of the unfortunate André, who had been taken prisoner hard by, and was universally known by the name of Major André's tree. The common people regarded it with a mixture of respect and superstition, partly out of sympathy for the fate of its ill-starred namesake and partly from the tales of strange sights and doleful lamentations told concerning it.

As Ichabod approached this fearful tree he began to whistle: he thought his whistle was answered—it was but a blast sweeping sharply through the dry branches. As he approached a little nearer, he thought he saw something white hanging in the midst of the tree—he paused and ceased whistling, but, on looking more narrowly, perceived that it was a place where the tree had been scathed by lightning and the white wood laid bare. Suddenly he heard a groan—his teeth chattered and his knees smote against the saddle: it was but the rubbing of one huge bough upon another as they were swayed about by the breeze. He passed the tree in safety, but new perils lay before him.

About two hundred yards from the tree a small brook crossed the road, and ran into a marshy and thickly-wooded glen known by the name of Wiley's swamp. A few rough logs, laid side by side, served for a bridge over this stream. On that side of the road where the brook entered the wood a group of oaks and chestnuts, matted thick with wild grape-vines, threw a cavernous gloom over it. To pass this bridge was the severest trial. It was at this identical spot that the unfortunate André was captured, and under the covert of those chestnuts and vines were the sturdy yeomen concealed who surprised him. This has ever since been considered a haunted stream, and fearful are the feelings of the school-boy who has to pass it alone after dark.

As he approached the stream his heart began to thump; he summoned up, however, all his resolution, gave his horse half a score of kicks in the ribs, and attempted to dash briskly across the bridge; but instead of starting forward, the perverse old animal made a lateral movement, and ran broadside against the fence. Ichabod, whose fears increased with the delay, jerked the reins on the other side, and kicked lustily with the contrary foot: it was all in vain; his steed started, it is true, but it was only to plunge to the opposite side of the road, into a thicket of brambles and alder bushes. The schoolmaster now bestowed both whip and heel upon the starveling ribs of old Gunpowder, who dashed forward snuffling and snorting, but came to a stand just by the bridge, with a suddenness that had nearly sent his rider sprawling over his head. Just at this moment a plashy tramp by the side of the bridge caught the sensitive ear of Ichabod. In the dark shadow of the grove, on the margin of the brook, he beheld something huge, misshapen, black, and towering. It stirred not, but seemed gathered up in the gloom, like some gigantic monster ready to spring upon the traveller.

The hair of the affrighted pedagogue rose upon his head with terror. What was to be done? To turn and fly was now too late; and, besides, what chance was there of escaping ghost or goblin, if such it was, which could ride upon the wings of the wind? Summoning up, therefore, a show of courage, he demanded in stammering accents: 'Who are you?' He received no reply. He repeated his demand in a still more agitated voice. Still there was no answer. Once more he cudgelled the sides of the inflexible Gunpowder, and shutting his eyes, broke forth with involuntary fervour into a psalm tune. Just then the shadowy object of alarm put itself in motion, and with a scramble and a bound stood at once in the middle of the road. Though the night was dark and dismal, yet the form of the unknown might now in some degree be ascertained. He appeared to be a horseman of large dimensions, and mounted on a black horse of powerful frame. He made no offer of molestation or sociability, but kept aloof on one side of the road, jogging along on the blind side of old Gunpowder, who had now got over his fright and waywardness.

Ichabod, who had no relish for this strange midnight companion, and bethought himself of the adventure of Brom Bones with the Galloping Hessian, now quickened his steed in hopes of leaving him behind. The stranger, however, quickened his horse to an equal pace. Ichabod pulled up and fell into a walk, thinking to lag behind—the other did the same. His heart began to sink within him; he endeavoured to resume his psalm tune, but his parched tongue cloye to the roof of his mouth, and he could not utter a stave. There was something in the moody and dogged silence of this pernicious companion that was mysterious and appalling. It was soon fearfully accounted for. On mounting a rising ground, which brought the figure of his fellow-traveller in relief against the sky, gigantic in height, and muffled in a cloak, Ichabod was horror-struck on perceiving that he was headless! but his horror was still more increased on observing that the head, which should have rested on his shoulders, was carried before him on the pommel of the saddle. His terror rose to desperation; he rained a shower of kicks and blows upon Gunpowder, hoping by a sudden movement to give his companion the slip, but the spectre started full jump with him. Away then they dashed through thick and thin, stones flying and sparks flashing at every bound. Ichabod's flimsy garments fluttered in the air as he stretched his long, lank body away over his horse's head in the eagerness of his flight.

They had now reached the road which turns off to Sleepy Hollow, but Gunpowder, who seemed possessed with a demon, instead of keeping up it made an opposite turn, and plunged headlong down the hill to the left. This road leads through a sandy hollow, shaded by trees for about a quarter of a mile, where it crosses the bridge famous in goblin story, and just beyond swells the green knoll on which stands the whitewashed church.

As yet the panic of the steed had given his unskilful rider an apparent advantage in the chase; but, just as he had got half-way through the hollow, the girths of the saddle gave way, and he felt it slipping from under him. He seized it by the pommel and endeavoured to hold it firm, but in vain, and had just time to save himself by clasping old Gunpowder round the neck, when the saddle fell to the earth, and he heard it trampled under foot by his pursuer. For a moment the terror of Hans Van Ripper's wrath passed across his mind, for it was his Sunday saddle; but this was no time for petty fears, the goblin was hard on his haunches, and (unskilful rider that he was!) he had much ado to maintain his seat, sometimes slipping on one side, sometimes on the other, and sometimes jolted on the high ridge of his horse's backbone with a violence that he verily feared would cleave him asunder.

An opening in the trees now cheered him with the hopes that the church bridge was at hand. The wavering reflection of a silver star in the bosom of the brook told him that he was not mistaken. He saw the walls of the church dimly glaring under the trees beyond. He recollected the place where Brom Bones' ghostly competitor had disappeared. 'If I can but reach that bridge,' thought Ichabod, 'I am safe.' Just then he heard the black steed panting and blowing close behind him; he even fancied that he felt his hot breath. Another convulsive kick in the ribs, and old Gunpowder sprang upon the bridge; he thundered over the resounding planks; he gained the opposite side; and now Ichabod cast a look behind to see if his pursuer should vanish, according to rule, in a flash of fire and brimstone. Just then he saw the goblin rising in his stirrups, and in the very act of hurling his head at him. Ichabod endeavoured to dodge the horrible missile, but too late. It encountered his cranium with a tremendous crash, he was tumbled headlong into the dust, and Gunpowder, the black steed, and the goblin rider passed by like a whirlwind.

The next morning the old horse was found without his saddle, and with the bridle under his feet, soberly cropping the grass at his master's gate. Ichabod did not make his appearance at breakfast—dinner-hour came, but no Ichabod. The boys assembled at the school-house, and strolled idly about the banks of the brook; but no schoolmaster. Hans Van Ripper now began to feel some uneasiness about the fate of poor Ichabod and his saddle. An enquiry was set on foot, and after diligent investigation they came upon his traces. In one part of the road leading to the church was found the saddle trampled in the dirt; the tracks of horses' hoofs deeply dented in the road, and evidently at furious speed, were traced to the bridge, beyond which, on the bank of a broad part of the brook, where the water ran deep and black, was found the hat of the unfortunate Ichabod, and close beside it a shattered pumpkin.

The brook was searched, but the body of the schoolmaster was not to be discovered. Hans Van Ripper, as executor of his estate, examined the bundle which contained all his worldly effects. They consisted of two shirts and a half; two stocks for the neck; a pair or two or worsted stockings; an old pair of corduroy small-clothes; a rusty razor; a book of psalm tunes, full of dog's ears; and a broken pitch-pipe. As to the books and furniture of the school-house, they belonged to the community, excepting Cotton Mather's *History of Witchcraft*, a New England Almanac, and a book of dreams and fortune-telling, in which last was a sheet of foolscap much scribbled and blotted in several fruitless attempts to make a copy of verses in honour of the heiress of Van Tassel. These magic books and the poetic scrawl were forthwith consigned to the flames by Hans Van Ripper, who from that time forward determined to send his children no more to school, observing that he never knew any good come of this same reading and writing. Whatever money the schoolmaster possessed—and he had received his quarter's pay but a day or two before—he must have had about his person at the time of his disappearance.

The mysterious event caused much speculation at the church on the following Sunday. Knots of gazers and gossips were collected in the churchyard, at the bridge, and at the spot where the hat and pumpkin had been found. The stories of Brouwer, of Bones, and a whole budget of others, were called to mind, and when they had diligently considered them all, and compared them with the symptoms of the present case, they shook their heads, and came to the conclusion that Ichabod had been carried off by the Galloping Hessian. As he was a bachelor, and in nobody's debt, nobody troubled his head any more about him: the school was removed to a different quarter of the Hollow, and another pedagogue reigned in his stead.

It is true, an old farmer, who had been down to New York on a visit several years after, and from whom this account of the ghostly adventure was received, brought home the intelligence that Ichabod Crane was still alive; that he had left the neighbourhood partly through fear of the goblin and Hans Van Ripper, and partly in mortification at having been suddenly dismissed by the heiress; that he had changed his quarters to a distant part of the country, had kept school and studied law at the same time, had been admitted to the bar, turned politician, electioneered, written for the newspapers, and finally had been made a justice of the Ten-pound Court. Brom Bones, too, who shortly after his rival's disappearance conducted the blooming Katrina in triumph to the altar, was observed to look exceedingly knowing whenever the story of Ichabod was related, and always burst into a hearty laugh at the mention of the pumpkin, which led some to suspect that he knew more about the matter than he chose to tell.

The old country wives, however, who are the best judges of these matters, maintain to this day that Ichabod was spirited away by supernatural means, and it is a favourite story often told about the neighbourhood round the winter evening fire. The bridge became more than ever an object of superstitious awe, and that may be the reason why the road has been altered of late years, so as to approach the church by the border of the mill-pond. The school-house, being deserted, soon fell to decay, and was reported to be haunted by the ghost of the unfortunate pedagogue; and the plough-boy, loitering homeward of a still summer evening, has often fancied his voice at a distance, chanting a melancholy psalm tune among the tranquil solitudes of Sleepy Hollow.

POSTSCRIPT

FOUND IN THE HANDWRITING OF MR KNICKERBOCKER

The preceding tale is given almost in the precise words in which I heard it related at a corporation meeting of the ancient city of Manhattoes, at which were present many of its sagest and most illustrious burghers. The narrator was a pleasant, shabby, gentlemanly old fellow, in pepper-and-salt clothes, with a sadly humorous face; and one whom I strongly suspected of being poor—he made such efforts to be entertaining. When his story was concluded, there was much laughter and approbation, particularly from two or three deputy aldermen, who had been asleep the greater part of the time. There was, however, one tall, dry-looking old gentleman, with beetling eyebrows, who maintained a grave and rather a severe face throughout, now and then folding his arms, inclining his head, and looking down upon the floor, as if turning a doubt over in his mind. He was one of your wary men, who never laugh but upon good grounds—when they have reason and the law on their side. When the mirth of the rest of the company had subsided, and silence was restored, he leaned one arm on the elbow of his chair, and, sticking the other a-kimbo, demanded, with a slight but exceedingly sage motion of the head and contraction of the brow, what was the moral of the story, and what it went to prove?

The story-teller, who was just putting a glass of wine to his lips, as a refreshment after his toils, paused for a moment, looking at his enquirer with an air of infinite deference, and, lowering the glass slowly to the table, observed that the story was intended most logically to prove:

'That there is no situation in life but has its advantages and pleasures—provided we will but take a joke as we find it;

'That, therefore, he that runs races with goblin troopers is likely to have rough riding of it;

'Ergo, for a country schoolmaster to be refused the hand of a Dutch heiress is a certain step to high preferment to the state.'

The cautious old gentleman knit his brows tenfold closer after this explanation, being sorely puzzled by the ratiocination of the syllogism; while, methought, the one in pepper-and-salt eyed him with something of a triumphant leer. At length he observed that all this was very well; but still he thought the story a little on the extravagant—there were one or two points on which he had his doubts.

'Faith, sir,' replied the story-teller, 'as to that matter, I don't believe one-half of it myself!'

D. K.

Rip Van Winkle

THE FOLLOWING TALE WAS found among the papers of the late Diedrich Knickerbocker, an old gentleman of New York, who was very curious in the Dutch history of the province, and the manners of the descendants from its primitive settlers. His historical researches, however, did not lie so much among books as among men; for the former are lamentably scanty on his favourite topics; whereas he found the old burghers, and still more their wives, rich in that legendary lore so invaluable to true history. Whenever, therefore, he happened upon a genuine Dutch family, snugly shut up in its low-roofed farmhouse, under a spreading sycamore, he looked upon it as a little clasped volume of black-letter, and studied it with the zeal of a bookworm.

The result of all these researches was a history of the province during the reign of the Dutch governors, which he published some years since. There have been various opinions as to the literary character of his work, and, to tell the truth, it is not a whit better than it should be. Its chief merit is its scrupulous accuracy, which indeed was a little questioned on its first appearance, but has since been completely established; and it is now admitted into all historical collections as a book of unquestionable authority.

The old gentleman died shortly after the publication of his work, and now that he is dead and gone, it cannot do much harm to his memory to say that his time might have been much better employed in weightier labours. He, however, was apt to ride his hobby his own way; and though it did now and then kick up the dust a little in the eyes of his neighbours, and grieve the spirit of some friends, for whom he felt the truest deference and affection, yet his errors and follies are remembered 'more in sorrow than in anger,' and it begins to be suspected that he never intended to injure or offend. But however his memory may be appreciated by critics, it is still held dear by many folk whose good opinion is well worth having; particularly by certain biscuit-bakers, who have gone so far as to imprint his likeness on their new-year cakes, and have thus given him a chance for immortality almost equal to the being stamped on a Waterloo medal or a Queen Anne's farthing.

RIP VAN WINKLE
A POSTHUMOUS WRITING OF DIEDRICH KNICKERBOCKER

'By Woden God of Saxons,
From whence comes Wensday, that is Wodensday.
Truth is a thing that ever I will keep
Unto thylke day in which I creep into
My sepulchre—'   —*Cartwright.*

Whoever has made a voyage up the Hudson must remember the Kaatskill mountains. They are a dismembered branch of the great Appalachian family, and are seen away to the west of the river, swelling up to a noble height, and lording it over the surrounding country. Every change of season, every change of weather, indeed every hour of the day, produces some change in the magical hues and shapes of these mountains, and they are regarded by all the good wives, far and near, as perfect barometers. When the weather is fair and settled they are clothed in blue and purple, and print their bold outlines on the clear evening sky; but sometimes, when the rest of the landscape is cloudless, they will gather a hood of grey vapours about their summits, which, in the last rays of the setting sun, will glow and light up like a crown of glory.

At the foot of these fairy mountains the voyager may have descried the light smoke curling up from a village, whose shingle-roofs gleam among the trees just where the blue tints of the upland melt away into the fresh green of the nearer landscape. It is a little village of great antiquity, having been founded by some of the Dutch colonists in the early times of the province, just about the beginning of the government of the good Peter Stuyvesant (may he rest in peace!), and there were some of the houses of the original settlers standing within a few years, built of small yellow bricks brought from Holland, having latticed windows and gable fronts, surmounted with weather-cocks.

In that same village, and in one of these very houses (which, to tell the precise truth, was sadly time-worn and weather-beaten), there lived many years since, while the country was yet a province of Great Britain, a simple good-natured fellow of the name of Rip Van Winkle. He was a descendant of the Van Winkles who figured so gallantly in the chivalrous days of Peter Stuyvesant, and accompanied him to the siege of Fort Christina. He inherited, however, but little of the martial character of his ancestors. I have observed that he was a simple good-natured man; he was, moreover, a kind neighbour and an obedient henpecked husband. Indeed, to the latter circumstance might be owing that meekness of spirit which gained him such universal popularity, for those men are most apt to be obsequious and conciliating abroad who are under the discipline of shrews at home. Their tempers, doubtless, are rendered pliant and malleable in the fiery furnace of domestic tribulation, and a curtain lecture is worth all the sermons in the world for teaching the virtues of patience and long-suffering. A termagant wife may, therefore, in some respects be considered a tolerable blessing; and if so, Rip Van Winkle was thrice blessed.

Certain it is that he was a great favourite among all the good wives of the village, who, as usual with the amiable sex, took his part in all family squabbles, and never failed, whenever they talked those matters over in their evening gossipings, to lay all the blame on Dame Van Winkle. The children of the village, too, would shout with joy whenever he approached. He assisted at their sports, made their playthings, taught them to fly kites and shoot marbles, and told them long stories of ghosts, witches, and Indians. Whenever he went dodging about the village he was surrounded by a troop of them hanging on his skirts, clambering on his back, and playing a thousand tricks on him with impunity, and not a dog would bark at him throughout the neighbourhood.

The great error in Rip's composition was an insuperable aversion to all kinds of profitable labour. It could not be from the want of assiduity or perseverance, for he would sit on a wet rock, with a rod as long and heavy as a Tartar's lance, and fish all day without a murmur, even though he should not be encouraged by a single nibble. He would carry a fowling-piece on his shoulder for hours together, trudging through woods and swamps, and up hill and down dale, to shoot a few squirrels or wild pigeons. He would never refuse to assist a neighbour even in the roughest toil, and was a foremost man at all country frolics for husking Indian corn or building stone fences; the women of the village, too, used to employ him to run their errands, and to do such little odd jobs as their less obliging husbands would not do for them. In a word, Rip was ready to attend to anybody's business but his own; but as to doing family duty, and keeping his farm in order, he found it impossible.

In fact, he declared it was of no use to work on his farm; it was the most pestilent little piece of ground in the whole country; everything about it went wrong and would go wrong, in spite of him. His fences were continually falling to pieces; his cow would either go astray or get among the cabbages; weeds were sure to grow quicker in his fields than anywhere else; the rain always made a point of setting in just as he had some outdoor work to do; so that though his patrimonial estate had dwindled away under his management, acre by acre, until there was little more left than a mere patch of Indian corn and potatoes, yet it was the worst-conditioned farm in the neighbourhood.

His children, too, were as ragged and wild as if they belonged to nobody. His son Rip, an urchin begotten in his own likeness, promised to inherit the habits, with the old clothes, of his father. He was generally seen trooping like a colt at his mother's heels, equipped in a pair of his father's cast-off galligaskins, which he had much ado to hold up with one hand, as a fine lady does her train in bad weather.

Rip Van Winkle, however, was one of those happy mortals, of foolish, well-oiled dispositions, who take the world easy, eat white bread or brown, whichever can be got with least thought or trouble, and would rather starve on a penny than work for a pound. If left to himself, he would have whistled life away in perfect contentment; but his wife kept continually dinning in his ears about his idleness, his carelessness, and the ruin he was bringing on his family. Morning, noon, and night her tongue was incessantly going, and everything he said or did was sure to produce a torrent of household eloquence. Rip had but one way of replying to all lectures of the kind, and that, by frequent use, had grown into a habit. He shrugged his shoulders, shook his head, cast up his eyes, but said nothing. This, however, always provoked a fresh volley from his wife; so that he was fain to draw off his forces, and take to the outside of the house—the only side which, in truth, belongs to a henpecked husband.

Rip's sole domestic adherent was his dog Wolf, who was as much henpecked as his master; for Dame Van Winkle regarded them as companions in idleness, and even looked upon Wolf with an evil eye as the cause of his master's going so often astray. True it is, in all points of spirit befitting an honourable dog, he was as courageous an animal as ever scoured the woods—but what courage can withstand the ever-during and all-besetting terrors of a woman's tongue? The moment Wolf entered the house his crest fell, his tail drooped to the ground or curled between his legs, he sneaked about with a gallows air, casting many a sidelong glance at Dame Van Winkle, and at the least flourish of a broomstick or ladle he would fly to the door with yelping precipitation.

Times grew worse and worse with Rip Van Winkle as years of matrimony rolled on; a tart temper never mellows with age, and a sharp tongue is the only edged tool that grows keener with constant use. For a long while he used to console himself, when driven from home, by frequenting a kind of perpetual club of the sages, philosophers, and other idle personages of the village, which held its sessions on a bench before a small inn, designated by a rubicund portrait of his Majesty George the Third. Here they used to sit in the shade through a long lazy summer's day, talking listlessly over village gossip, or telling endless sleepy stories about nothing. But it would have been worth any statesman's money to have heard the profound discussions that sometimes took place, when by chance an old newspaper fell into their hands from some passing traveller. How solemnly they would listen to the contents, as drawled out by Derrick Van Bummel, the schoolmaster, a dapper learned little man, who was not to be daunted by the most gigantic word in the dictionary; and how sagely they would deliberate upon public events some months after they had taken place!

The opinions of this junta were completely controlled by Nicholas Vedder, a patriarch of the village, and landlord of the inn, at the door of which he took his seat from morning till night, just moving sufficiently to avoid the sun and keep in the shade of a large tree, so that the neighbours could tell the hour by his movements as accurately as by a sun-dial. It is true he was rarely heard to speak, but smoked his pipe incessantly. His adherents, however (for every great man has his adherents), perfectly understood him, and knew how to gather his opinions. When anything that was read or related displeased him, he was observed to smoke his pipe vehemently, and to send forth short, frequent, and angry puffs; but when pleased, he would inhale the smoke slowly and tranquilly, and emit it in light and placid clouds; and sometimes, taking the pipe from his mouth and letting the fragrant vapour curl about his nose, would gravely nod his head in token of perfect approbation.

From even this stronghold the unlucky Rip was at length routed by his termagant wife, who would suddenly break in upon the tranquillity of the assemblage and call the members all to naught; nor was that august personage, Nicholas Vedder himself, sacred from the daring tongue of this terrible virago, who charged him outright with encouraging her husband in habits of idleness.

Poor Rip was at last reduced almost to despair, and his only alternative to escape from the labour of the farm and clamour of his wife was to take gun in hand and stroll away to the woods. Here he would sometimes seat himself at the foot of a tree and share the contents of his wallet with Wolf, with whom he sympathized as a fellow-sufferer in persecution. 'Poor Wolf,' he would say, 'thy mistress leads thee a dog's life of it; but never mind, my lad, whilst I live thou shalt never want a friend to stand by thee!' Wolf would wag his tail, look wistfully in his master's face, and if dogs can feel pity, I verily believe he reciprocated the sentiment with all his heart.

In a long ramble of the kind, on a fine autumnal day, Rip had unconsciously scrambled to one of the highest parts of the Kaatskill mountains. He was after his favourite sport of squirrel-shooting, and the still solitudes had echoed and re-echoed with the reports of his gun. Panting and fatigued, he threw himself, late in the afternoon, on a green knoll covered with mountain herbage that crowned the brow of a precipice. From an opening between the trees he could overlook all the lower country for many a mile of rich woodland. He saw at a distance the lordly Hudson, far, far below him, moving on its silent but majestic course, with the reflection of a purple cloud, or the sail of a lagging bark, here and there sleeping on its glassy bosom, and at last losing itself in the blue highlands.

On the other side he looked down into a deep mountain glen, wild, lonely, and shagged, the bottom filled with fragments from the impending cliffs, and scarcely lighted by the reflected rays of the setting sun. For some time Rip lay musing on this scene; evening was gradually advancing; the mountains began to throw their long blue shadows over the valleys; he saw that it would be dark long before he could reach the village, and he heaved a heavy sigh when he thought of encountering the terrors of Dame Van Winkle.

As he was about to descend, he heard a voice from a distance, hallooing: 'Rip Van Winkle! Rip Van Winkle!' He looked round, but could see nothing but a crow winging its solitary flight across the mountain. He thought his fancy must have deceived him, and turned again to descend, when he heard the same cry ring through the still evening air: 'Rip Van Winkle! Rip Van Winkle!'—at the same time Wolf bristled up his back, and giving a loud growl, skulked to his master's side, looking fearfully down into the glen. Rip now felt a vague apprehension stealing over him; he looked anxiously in the same direction, and perceived a strange figure slowly toiling up the rocks, and bending under the weight of something he carried on his back. He was surprised to see any human being in this lonely and unfrequented place, but supposing it to be someone of the neighbourhood in need of his assistance, he hastened down to yield it.

On nearer approach he was still more surprised at the singularity of the stranger's appearance. He was a short square-built old fellow, with thick bushy hair and a grizzled beard. His dress was of the antique Dutch fashion—a cloth jerkin strapped round the waist—several pairs of breeches, the outer one of ample volume, decorated with rows of buttons down the sides, and bunches at the knees. He bore on his shoulder a stout keg that seemed full of liquor, and made signs for Rip to approach and assist him with the load. Though rather shy and distrustful of this new acquaintance, Rip complied with his usual alacrity, and, mutually relieving each other, they clambered up a narrow gully, apparently the dry bed of a mountain torrent. As they ascended, Rip every now and then heard long rolling peals, like distant thunder, that seemed to issue out of a deep ravine, or rather cleft, between lofty rocks, toward which their rugged path conducted. He paused for an instant, but, supposing it to be the muttering of one of those transient thunder-showers which often take place in mountain heights, he proceeded. Passing through the ravine they came to a hollow, like a small amphitheatre, surrounded by perpendicular precipices, over the brinks of which impending trees shot their branches, so that you only caught glimpses of the azure sky and the bright evening cloud. During the whole time Rip and his companion had laboured on in silence, for though the former marvelled greatly what could be the object of carrying a keg of liquor up this wild mountain, yet there was something strange and incomprehensible about the unknown that inspired awe and checked familiarity.

On entering the amphitheatre new objects of wonder presented themselves. On a level spot in the centre was a company of odd-looking personages playing at ninepins. They were dressed in a quaint outlandish fashion; some wore short doublets, others jerkins, with long knives in their belts, and most of them had enormous breeches, of similar style with that of the guide's. Their visages, too, were peculiar: one had a large head, broad face, and small piggish eyes; the face of another seemed to consist entirely of nose, and was surrounded by a white sugar-loaf hat, set off with a little red cock's tail. They all had beards, of various shapes and colours. There was one who seemed to be the commander. He was a stout old gentleman, with a weather-beaten countenance; he wore a lace doublet, broad belt and hanger, high-crowned hat and feather, red stockings, and high-heeled shoes, with roses in them. The whole group reminded Rip of the figures in an old Flemish painting in the parlour of Dominie Van Shaick, the village parson, and which had been brought over from Holland at the time of the settlement.

What seemed particularly odd to Rip was, that though these folks were evidently amusing themselves, yet they maintained the gravest faces, the most mysterious silence, and were withal the most melancholy party of pleasure he had ever witnessed. Nothing interrupted the stillness of the scene but the noise of the balls, which, whenever they were rolled, echoed along the mountains like rumbling peals of thunder.

As Rip and his companion approached them they suddenly desisted from their play, and stared at him with such fixed statue-like gaze, and such strange, uncouth, lack-lustre countenances, that his heart turned within him, and his knees smote together. His companion now emptied the contents of the keg into large flagons, and made signs to him to wait upon the company. He obeyed with fear and trembling; they quaffed the liquor in profound silence, and then returned to their game.

By degrees Rip's awe and apprehension subsided. He even ventured, when no eye was fixed upon him, to taste the beverage, which he found had much of the flavour of excellent Hollands. He was naturally a thirsty soul, and was soon tempted to repeat the draught. One taste provoked another, and he reiterated his visits to the flagon so often that at length his senses were overpowered, his eyes swam in his head, his head gradually declined, and he fell into a deep sleep.

On waking, he found himself on the green knoll whence he had first seen the old man of the glen. He rubbed his eyes—it was a bright sunny morning. The birds were hopping and twittering among the bushes, and the eagle was wheeling aloft and breasting the pure mountain breeze. 'Surely,' thought Rip, 'I have not slept here all night.' He recalled the occurrences before he fell asleep. The strange man with a keg of liquor—the mountain ravine—the wild retreat among the rocks—the woebegone party at ninepins—the flagon—'Oh! that flagon! that wicked flagon!' thought Rip; 'what excuse shall I make to Dame Van Winkle?'

He looked round for his gun, but in place of the clean, well-oiled fowling-piece he found an old firelock lying by him, the barrel encrusted with rust, the lock falling off, and the stock worm-eaten. He now suspected that the grave roysters of the mountain had put a trick upon him, and, having dosed him with liquor, had robbed him of his gun. Wolf, too, had disappeared, but he might have strayed away after a squirrel or partridge. He whistled after him and shouted his name, but all in vain; the echoes repeated his whistle and shout, but no dog was to be seen.

He determined to revisit the scene of the last evening's gambol, and if he met with any of the party, to demand his dog and gun. As he rose to walk he found himself stiff in the joints, and wanting in his usual activity. 'These mountain beds do not agree with me,' thought Rip, 'and if this frolic should lay me up with a fit of rheumatism, I shall have a blessed time with Dame Van Winkle.' With some difficulty he got down into the glen: he found the gully up which he and his companion had ascended the preceding evening; but to his astonishment a mountain stream was now foaming down it, leaping from rock to rock and filling the glen with babbling murmurs. He, however, made shift to scramble up its sides, working his toilsome way through thickets of birch, sassafras, and witch-hazel, and sometimes tripped up or entangled by the wild grape-vines that twisted their coils or tendrils from tree to tree, and spread a kind of net-work in his path.

At length he reached to where the ravine had opened through the cliffs to the amphitheatre; but no traces of such opening remained. The rocks presented a high impenetrable wall, over which the torrent came tumbling in a sheet of feathery foam, and fell into a broad deep basin, black from the shadows of the surrounding forest. Here, then, poor Rip was brought to a stand. He again called and whistled after his dog; he was only answered by the cawing of a flock of idle crows, sporting high in air about a dry tree that overhung a sunny precipice; and who, secure in their elevation, seemed to look down and scoff at the poor man's perplexities. What was to be done? the morning was passing away, and Rip felt famished for want of his breakfast. He grieved to give up his dog and his gun; he dreaded to meet his wife; but it would not do to starve among the mountains. He shook his head, shouldered the rusty firelock, and, with a heart full of trouble and anxiety, turned his steps homeward.

As he approached the village he met a number of people, but none whom he knew, which somewhat surprised him, for he had thought himself acquainted with every one in the country round. Their dress, too, was of a different fashion from that to which he was accustomed. They all stared at him with equal marks of surprise, and whenever they cast their eyes upon him invariably stroked their chins. The constant recurrence of this gesture induced Rip, involuntarily, to do the same, when, to his astonishment, he found his beard had grown a foot long!

He had now entered the skirts of the village. A troop of strange children ran at his heels, hooting after him and pointing at his grey beard. The dogs, too, not one of which he recognized for an old acquaintance, barked at him as he passed. The very village was altered; it was larger and more populous. There were rows of houses which he had never seen before, and those which had been his familiar haunts had disappeared. Strange names were over the doors—strange faces at the windows—everything was strange. His mind now misgave him; he began to doubt whether both he and the world around him were not bewitched. Surely this was his native village, which he had left but the day before. There stood the Kaatskill mountains—there ran the silver Hudson at a distance—there was every hill and dale precisely as it had always been—Rip was sorely perplexed—'That flagon last night,' thought he, 'has addled my poor head sadly!'

It was with some difficulty that he found the way to his own house, which he approached with silent awe, expecting every moment to hear the shrill voice of Dame Van Winkle. He found the house gone to decay—the roof fallen in, the windows shattered, and the doors off the hinges. A half-starved dog that looked like Wolf was skulking about it. Rip called him by name, but the cur snarled, showed his teeth, and passed on. This was an unkind cut indeed—'My very dog,' sighed poor Rip, 'has forgotten me!'

He entered the house, which, to tell the truth, Dame Van Winkle had always kept in neat order. It was empty, forlorn, and apparently abandoned. The desolateness overcame all his connubial fears—he called loudly for his wife and children—the lonely chambers rang for a moment with his voice, and then all again was silence.

He now hurried forth and hastened to his old resort, the village inn—but it too was gone. A large rickety wooden building stood in its place, with great gaping windows, some of them broken and mended with old hats and petticoats, and over the door was painted: 'The Union Hotel, by Jonathan Doolittle.' Instead of the great tree that used to shelter the quiet little Dutch inn of yore, there was now reared a tall naked pole, with something on the top that looked like a red night-cap, and from it was fluttering a flag, on which was a singular assemblage of stars and stripes—all this was strange and incomprehensible. He recognized on the sign, however, the ruby face of King George, under which he had smoked so many a peaceful pipe; but even this was singularly metamorphosed. The red coat was changed for one of blue and buff, a sword was held in the hand instead of a sceptre, the head was decorated with a cocked hat, and underneath was painted in large characters: GENERAL WASHINGTON.

There was, as usual, a crowd of folks about the door, but none that Rip recollected. The very character of the people seemed changed. There was a busy, bustling, disputatious tone about it, instead of the accustomed phlegm and drowsy tranquillity. He looked in vain for the sage Nicholas Vedder, with his broad face, double chin, and fair long pipe, uttering clouds of tobacco-smoke instead of idle speeches; or Van Bummel, the schoolmaster, doling forth the contents of an ancient newspaper. In place of these a lean, bilious-looking fellow, with his pockets full of handbills, was haranguing vehemently about rights of citizens—elections—members of congress— liberty, Bunker's Hill—heroes of seventy-six—and other words, which were a perfect Babylonish jargon to the bewildered Van Winkle.

The appearance of Rip, with his long grizzled beard, his rusty fowling-piece, his uncouth dress, and an army of woman and children at his heels, soon attracted the attention of the tavern politicians. They crowded round him, eyeing him from head to foot with great curiosity. The orator bustled up to him, and, drawing him partly aside, enquired 'on which side he voted?' Rip stared in vacant stupidity. Another short but busy little fellow pulled him by the arm, and, rising on tiptoe, enquired in his ear: 'Whether he was Federal or Democrat?' Rip was equally at a loss to comprehend the question; when a knowing self-important old gentleman, in a sharp cocked hat, made his way through the crowd, putting them to the right and left with his elbows as he passed, and planting himself before Van Winkle, with one arm akimbo, the other resting on his cane, his keen eyes and sharp hat penetrating, as it were, into his very soul, demanded in an austere tone: 'What brought him to the election with a gun on his shoulder and a mob at his heels, and whether he meant to breed a riot in the village?'—'Alas! gentlemen,' cried Rip, somewhat dismayed, 'I am a poor quiet man, a native of the place, and a loyal subject of the king, God bless him!'

Here a general shout burst from the by-standers: 'A tory! a tory! a spy! a refugee! hustle him! away with him!' It was with great difficulty that the self-important man in the cocked hat restored order; and, having assumed a tenfold austerity of brow, demanded again of the unknown culprit what he came there for, and whom he was seeking? The poor man humbly assured him that he meant no harm, but merely came there in search of some of his neighbours, who used to keep about the tavern.

'Well—who are they?—name them.'

Rip bethought himself a moment, and enquired: 'Where's Nicholas Vedder?'

There was a silence for a little while, when an old man replied in a thin piping voice: 'Nicholas Vedder! why, he is dead and gone these eighteen years! There was a wooden tombstone in the churchyard that used to tell all about him, but that's rotten and gone too.'

'Where's Brom Dutcher?'

'Oh, he went off to the army in the beginning of the war! Some say he was killed at the storming of Stony Point—others say he was drowned in a squall at the foot of Antony's Nose. I don't know—he never came back again.'

'Where's Van Bummel, the schoolmaster?'

'He went off to the wars too, was a great militia general, and is now in congress.'

Rip's heart died away at hearing of these sad changes in his home and friends, and finding himself thus alone in the world. Every answer puzzled him too by treating of such enormous lapses of time, and of matters which he could not understand: War—Congress—Stony Point;—he had no courage to ask after any more friends, but cried out in despair: 'Does nobody here know Rip Van Winkle?'

'Oh, Rip Van Winkle!' exclaimed two or three. 'Oh, to be sure! that's Rip Van Winkle yonder, leaning against the tree.'

Rip looked, and beheld a precise counterpart of himself as he went up the mountain: apparently as lazy, and certainly as ragged. The poor fellow was now completely confounded. He doubted his own identity, and whether he was himself or another man. In the midst of his bewilderment the man in the cocked hat demanded who he was, and what was his name?

'God knows,' exclaimed he, at his wits' end; 'I'm not myself—I'm somebody else—that's me yonder—no—that's somebody else got into my shoes—I was myself last night, but I fell asleep on the mountain, and they've changed my gun, and everything's changed, and I'm changed, and I can't tell what's my name, or who I am!'

The by-standers began now to look at each other, nod, wink significantly, and tap their fingers against their foreheads. There was a whisper also about securing the gun, and keeping the old fellow from doing mischief, at the very suggestion of which the self-important man in the cocked hat retired with some precipitation. At this critical moment a fresh, comely woman pressed through the throng to get a peep at the grey-bearded man. She had a chubby child in her arms, which, frightened at his looks, began to cry. 'Hush, Rip,' cried she, 'hush, you little fool; the old man won't hurt you.' The name of the child, the air of the mother, the tone of her voice, all awakened a train of recollections in his mind. 'What is your name, my good woman?' asked he.

'Judith Gardenier.'

'And your father's name?'

'Ah, poor man, Rip Van Winkle was his name, but it's twenty years since he went away from home with his gun, and never has been heard of since—his dog came home without him; but whether he shot himself, or was carried away by the Indians, nobody can tell. I was then but a little girl.'

Rip had but one question more to ask; but he put it with a faltering voice: 'Where's your mother?'

'Oh, she too had died but a short time since; she broke a blood-vessel in a fit of passion at a New England pedlar.'

There was a drop of comfort, at least, in this intelligence. The honest man could contain himself no longer. He caught his daughter and her child in his arms. 'I am your father!' cried he; 'Young Rip Van Winkle once—old Rip Van Winkle now!—Does nobody know poor Rip Van Winkle?'

All stood amazed, until an old woman, tottering out from among the crowd, put her hand to her brow, and, peering under it in his face for a moment, exclaimed: 'Sure enough, it is Rip Van Winkle—it is himself! Welcome home again, old neighbour! Why, where have you been these twenty long years?'

Rip's story was soon told, for the whole twenty years had been to him but as one night. The neighbours stared when they heard it; some were seen to wink at each other, and put their tongues in their cheeks, and the self-important man in the cocked hat, who when the alarm was over had returned to the field, screwed down the corners of his mouth, and shook his head, upon which there was a general shaking of the head throughout the assemblage.

It was determined, however, to take the opinion of old Peter Vanderdonk, who was seen slowly advancing up the road. He was a descendant of the historian of that name, who wrote one of the earliest accounts of the province. Peter was the most ancient inhabitant of the village, and well versed in all the wonderful events and traditions of the neighbourhood. He recollected Rip at once, and corroborated his story in the most satisfactory manner. He assured the company that it was a fact, handed down from his ancestor the historian, that the Kaatskill mountains had always been haunted by strange beings. That it was affirmed that the great Hendrik Hudson, the first discoverer of the river and country, kept a kind of vigil there every twenty years, with his crew of the *Halfmoon*; being permitted in this way to revisit the scenes of his enterprise, and keep a guardian eye upon the river and the great city called by his name. That his father had once seen them in their old Dutch dresses playing at ninepins in a hollow of the mountain, and that he himself had heard one summer afternoon the sound of their balls like distant peals of thunder.

To make a long story short, the company broke up and returned to the more important concerns of the election. Rip's daughter took him home to live with her; she had a snug, well-furnished house, and a stout, cheery farmer for her husband, whom Rip recollected for one of the urchins that used to climb upon his back. As to Rip's son and heir, who was the ditto of himself, seen leaning against the tree, he was employed to work on the farm, but evinced an hereditary disposition to attend to anything else but his business.

Rip now resumed his old walks and habits; he soon found many of his former cronies, though, all rather the worse for the wear and tear of time, and preferred making friends among the rising generation, with whom he soon grew into great favour.

Having nothing to do at home, and being arrived at that happy age when a man can be idle with impunity, he took his place once more on the bench at the inn door, and was reverenced as one of the patriarchs of the village, and a chronicle of the old times 'before the war'. It was some time before he could get into the regular track of gossip, or could be made to comprehend the strange events that had taken place during his torpor. How that there had been a revolutionary war—that the country had thrown off the yoke of old England—and that, instead of being a subject of his Majesty George the Third, he was now a free citizen of the United States. Rip, in fact, was no politician; the changes of states and empires made but little impression on him; but there was one species of despotism under which he had long groaned, and that was petticoat government. Happily that was at an end; he had got his neck out of the yoke of matrimony, and could go in and out whenever he pleased without dreading the tyranny of Dame Van Winkle. Whenever her name was mentioned, however, he shook his head, shrugged his shoulders, and cast up his eyes, which might pass either for an expression of resignation to his fate, or joy at his deliverance.

He used to tell his story to every stranger that arrived at Mr. Doolittle's hotel. He was observed at first to vary on some points every time he told it, which was doubtless owing to his having so recently awakened. It at last settled down precisely to the tale I have related, and not a man, woman, or child in the neighbourhood but knew it by heart. Some always pretended to doubt the reality of it, and insisted that Rip had been out of his head, and that this was one point in which he always remained flighty. The old Dutch inhabitants, however, almost universally gave it full credit. Even to this day they never hear a thunderstorm of a summer afternoon about the Kaatskill but they say Hendrik Hudson and his crew are at their game of ninepins; and it is a common wish of all hen-pecked husbands in the neighbourhood, when life hangs heavy on their hands, that they might have a quieting draught out of Rip Van Winkle's flagon.

NOTE.—The foregoing tale, one would suspect, had been suggested to Mr. Knickerbocker by a little German superstition about the Emperor Frederick *der Rothbart*, and the Kypphaüser mountain; the subjoined note, however, which he had appended to the tale, shows that it is an absolute fact, narrated with his usual fidelity:

The story of Rip Van Winkle may seem incredible to many, but nevertheless I give it my full belief, for I know the vicinity of our old Dutch settlements to have been the very subject to marvellous events and appearances. Indeed, I have heard many stranger stories than this in the villages along the Hudson, all of which were too well authenticated to admit of a doubt. I have even talked with Rip Van Winkle myself, who, when I last saw him, was a very venerable old man, and so perfectly rational and consistent on every other point that I think no conscientious person could refuse to take this into the bargain; nay, I have seen a certificate on the subject, taken before a country justice, and signed with a cross, in the justice's own handwriting. The story, therefore, is beyond the possibility of doubt.   'D. K.'

POSTSCRIPT.—The following are travelling notes from a memorandum-book of Mr. Knickerbocker:—

The Kaatsberg, or Catskill Mountains, have always been a region full of fable. The Indians considered them the abode of spirits, who influenced the weather, spreading sunshine or clouds over the landscape, and sending good or bad hunting seasons. They were ruled by an old squaw spirit, said to be their mother. She dwelt on the highest peak of the Catskills, and had charge of the doors of day and night, to open and shut them at the proper hour. She hung up the new moons in the skies, and cut up the old ones into stars. In times of drought, if properly propitiated, she would spin light summer clouds out of cobwebs and morning dew, and send them off from the crest of the mountain, flake after flake, like flakes of carded cotton, to float in the air until, dissolved by the heat of the sun, they would fall in gentle showers, causing the grass to spring, the fruits to ripen, and the corn to grow an inch an hour. If displeased, however, she would brew up clouds black as ink, sitting in the midst of them like a bottle-bellied spider in the midst of its web; and when these clouds broke, woe betide the valleys!

In old times, say the Indian traditions, there was a kind of Manitou, or Spirit, who kept about the wildest recesses of the Catskill mountains, and took a mischievous pleasure in wreaking all kinds of evils and vexations upon the red men. Sometimes he would assume the form of a bear, a panther, or a deer; lead the bewildered hunter a weary chase through tangled forests and among ragged rocks; and then spring off with a loud ho! ho! leaving him aghast on the brink of a beetling precipice or raging torrent.

The favourite abode of this Manitou is still shown. It is a great rock or cliff on the loneliest part of the mountains, and, from the flowering vines which clamber about it, and the wild flowers which abound in its neighbourhood, is known by the name of the Garden Rock. Near the foot of it is a small lake, the haunt of the solitary bittern, with water-snakes basking in the sun on the leaves of the pond-lilies which lie on the surface. This place was held in great awe by the Indians, insomuch that the boldest hunter would not pursue his game within its precincts. Once upon a time, however, a hunter, who had lost his way, penetrated to the Garden Rock, where he beheld a number of gourds placed in the crotches of trees. One of these he seized and made off with it, but in the hurry of his retreat he let it fall among the rocks, when a great stream gushed forth, which washed him away and swept him down precipices, where he was dashed to pieces, and the stream made its way to the Hudson, and continues to flow to the present day, being the identical stream known by the name of the Kaaterskill.

The Spectre Bridegroom

A TRAVELER'S TALE[1]

HE THAT SUPPER FOR IS DIGHT,
HE LYES FULL COLD, I TROW, THIS NIGHT!
YESTREEN TO CHAMBER I HIM LED,
THIS NIGHT GRAY STEEL HAS MADE HIS BED.
SIR EGER, SIR GRAHAME, AND SIR GRAY STEEL

On the summit of one of the heights of the Odenwald, a wild and romantic tract of Upper Germany, that lies not far from the confluence of the Main and the Rhine, there stood, many, many years since, the Castle of the Baron Von Landshort. It is now quite fallen to decay, and almost buried among beech trees and dark firs; above which, however, its old watchtower may still be seen, struggling, like the former possessor I have mentioned, to carry a high head, and look down upon the neighboring country.

The baron was a dry branch of the great family of Katzenellenbogen,[2] and inherited the relics of the property, and all the pride of his ancestors. Though the warlike disposition of his predecessors had much impaired the family possessions, yet the baron still endeavored to keep up some show of former state. The times were peaceable, and the German nobles, in general, had abandoned their inconvenient old castles, perched like eagles' nests among the mountains, and had built more convenient residences in the valleys. Still the baron remained proudly drawn up in his little fortress, cherishing, with hereditary Pinveteracy, all the old family feuds; so that he was on ill terms with some of his nearest neighbors, on account of disputes that had happened between their great-great-grandfathers.

The baron had but one child, a daughter; but Nature, when she grants but one child, always compensates by making it a prodigy; and so it was with the daughter of the baron. All the nurses, gossips, and country cousins assured her father that she had not her equal for beauty in all Germany; and who should know better than they? She had, moreover, been brought up with great care under the superintendence of two maiden aunts, who had spent some years of their early life at one of the little German courts, and were skilled in all the branches of knowledge necessary to the education of a fine lady. Under their instructions she became a miracle of accomplishments. By the time she was eighteen, she could embroider to admiration, and had

[1] The erudite reader well versed in good-for-nothing lore, will perceive that the above tale must have been suggested by a little French anecdote, a circumstance said to have taken place at Paris.

[2] *I.e.* CAT's ELBOW. The name of a family of those parts very powerful in former times. The appellation, we are told, was given in compliment to a peerless dame of the family, celebrated for her fine arm.

worked whole histories of the saints in tapestry, with such strength of expression in their countenances that they looked like so many souls in purgatory. She could read without great difficulty, and had spelled her way through several church legends, and almost all the chivalric wonders of the Heldenbuch. She had even made considerable proficiency in writing; could sign her own name without missing a letter, and so legibly that her aunts could read it without spectacles. She excelled in making little elegant good-for-nothing ladylike knickknacks of all kinds; was versed in the most abstruse dancing of the day; played a number of airs on the harp and guitar; and knew all the tender ballads of the Minnelieders by heart.

Her aunts, too, having been great flirts and coquettes in their younger days, were admirably calculated to be vigilant guardians and strict censors of the conduct of their niece; for there is no duenna so rigidly prudent, and inexorably decorous, as a superannuated coquette. She was rarely suffered out of their sight; never went beyond the domains of the castle, unless well attended, or rather, well watched; had continual lectures read to her about strict decorum and implicit obedience; and, as to the men—pah!—she was taught to hold them at such a distance, and in such absolute distrust, that, unless properly authorized, she would not have cast a glance upon the handsomest cavalier in the world—no, not if he were even lying at her feet.

The good effects of this system were wonderfully apparent. The young lady was a pattern of docility and correctness. While others were wasting their sweetness in the glare of the world, and liable to be plucked and thrown aside by every hand, she was coyly blooming into fresh and lovely womanhood under the protection of those immaculate spinsters like a rosebud blushing forth among guardian thorns. Her aunts looked upon her with pride and exultation, and vaunted that though all the other young ladies in the world might go astray, yet, thank Heaven, nothing of the kind could happen to the heiress of Katzenellenbogen.

But, however scantily the Baron Von Landshort might be provided with children, his household was by no means a small one; for Providence had enriched him with abundance of poor relations. They, one and all, possessed the affectionate disposition common to humble relatives; were wonderfully attached to the baron, and took every possible occasion to come in swarms and enliven the castle. All family festivals were commemorated by these good people at the baron's expense; and when they were filled with good cheer, they would declare that there was nothing on earth so delightful as these family meetings, these jubilees of the heart.

The baron, though a small man, had a large soul, and it swelled with satisfaction at the consciousness of being the greatest man in the little world about him. He loved to tell long stories about the dark old warriors whose portraits looked grimly down from the walls around, and he found no listeners equal to those who fed at his expense. He was much given to the marvelous, and a firm believer in all those supernatural tales with which every mountain and valley in Germany abounds. The faith of his guests exceeded even his own; they listened to every tale of wonder with open eyes and mouth, and never failed to be astonished, even though repeated for the hundredth time. Thus lived the Baron Von Landshort, the oracle of his table, the absolute monarch of his little territory, and happy, above all things, in the persuasion that he was the wisest man of the age.

At the time of which my story treats, there was a great family gathering at the castle, on an affair of the utmost importance; it was to receive the destined bridegroom of the baron's daughter. A negotiation had been carried on between the father and an old nobleman of Bavaria, to unite the dignity of their houses by the marriage of their children. The preliminaries had been conducted with proper punctilio. The young people were betrothed without seeing each other; and the time was appointed for the marriage ceremony. The young Count Von Altenburg had been recalled from the army for the purpose, and was actually on his way to the baron's to receive his bride. Missives had even been received from him, from Würtzburg, where he was accidentally detained, mentioning the day and hour when he might be expected to arrive.

The castle was in a tumult of preparation to give him a suitable welcome. The fair bride had been decked out with uncommon care. The two aunts had superintended her toilet, and quarreled the whole morning about every article of her dress. The young lady had taken advantage of their contest to follow the bent of her own taste; and fortunately it was a good one. She looked as lovely as youthful bridegroom could desire; and the flutter of expectation heightened the lustre of her charms.

The suffusions that mantled her face and neck, the gentle heaving of the bosom, the eye now and then lost in reverie, all betrayed the soft tumult that was going on in her little heart. The aunts were continually hovering around her; for maiden aunts are apt to take great interest in affairs of this nature. They were giving her a world of staid counsel how to deport herself, what to say, and in what manner to receive the expected lover.

The baron was no less busied in preparations. He had, in truth, nothing exactly to do; but he was naturally a fuming, bustling little man, and could not remain passive when all the world was in a hurry. He worried from top to bottom of the castle with an air of infinite anxiety; he continually called the servants from their work to exhort them to be diligent; and buzzed about every hall and chamber, as idly restless and importunate as a bluebottle fly on a warm summer's day.

In the meantime the fatted calf had been killed; the forests had rung with the clamor of the huntsmen; the kitchen was crowded with good cheer; the cellars had yielded up whole oceans of *Rhein-wein*, and *Ferne-wein*; and even the great Heidelberg tun had been laid under contribution. Everything was ready to receive the distinguished guest with *Saus und Braus* in the true spirit of German hospitality—but the guest delayed to make his appearance. Hour rolled after hour. The sun, that had poured his downward rays upon the rich forest of the Odenwald, now just gleamed along the summits of the mountains. The baron mounted the highest tower and strained his eyes in hope of catching a distant sight of the count and his attendants. Once he thought he beheld them; the sound of horns came floating from the valley, prolonged by the mountain echoes. A number of horsemen were seen far below, slowly advancing along the road; but when they had nearly reached the foot of the mountain, they suddenly struck off in a different direction. The last ray of sunshine departed—the bats began to flit by in the twilight—the road grew dimmer and dimmer to the view, and nothing appeared stirring in it but now and then a peasant lagging homeward from his labor.

While the old castle of Landshort was in this state of perplexity, a very interesting scene was transacting in a different part of the Odenwald.

The young Count Von Altenburg was tranquilly pursuing his route in that sober jog-trot way in which a man travels toward matrimony when his friends have taken all the trouble and uncertainty of courtship off his hands, and a bride is waiting for him, as certainly as a dinner at the end of his journey. He had encountered at Würtzburg a youthful companion in arms, with whom he had seen some service on the frontiers—Herman Von Starkenfaust, one of the stoutest hands and worthiest hearts of German chivalry, who was now returning from the army. His father's castle was not far distant from the old fortress of Landshort, although an hereditary feud rendered the families hostile, and strangers to each other.

In the warm-hearted moment of recognition, the young friends related all their past adventures and fortunes, and the count gave the whole history of his intended nuptials with a young lady whom he had never seen, but of whose charms he had received the most enrapturing descriptions.

As the route of the friends lay in the same direction, they agreed to perform the rest of their journey together; and, that they might do it more leisurely, set off from Würtzburg at an early hour, the count having given directions for his retinue to follow and overtake him.

They beguiled their wayfaring with recollections of their military scenes and adventures; but the count was apt to be a little tedious, now and then, about the reputed charms of his bride, and the felicity that awaited him.

In this way they had entered among the mountains of the Odenwald, and were traversing one of its most lonely and thickly wooded passes. It is well known that the forests of Germany have always been as much infested by robbers as its castles by spectres; and, at this time, the former were particularly numerous, from the hordes of disbanded soldiers wandering about the country. It will not appear extraordinary, therefore, that the cavaliers were attacked by a gang of these stragglers, in the midst of the forest. They defended themselves with bravery, but were nearly overpowered, when the count's retinue arrived to their assistance. At sight of them the robbers fled, but not until the count had received a mortal wound. He was slowly and carefully conveyed back to the city of Würtzburg, and a friar summoned from a neighboring convent, who was famous for his skill in administering to both soul and body; but half of his skill was superfluous; the moments of the unfortunate count were numbered.

With his dying breath he entreated his friend to repair instantly to the castle of Landshort and explain the fatal cause of his not keeping his appointment with his bride. Though not the most ardent of lovers, he was one of the most punctilious of men, and appeared earnestly solicitous that his mission should be speedily and courteously executed. 'Unless this is done,' said he, 'I shall not sleep quietly in my grave!' He repeated these last words with peculiar solemnity. A request, at a moment so impressive, admitted no hesitation. Starkenfaust endeavored to soothe him to calmness; promised faithfully to execute his wish, and gave him his hand in solemn pledge. The dying man pressed it in acknowledgment, but soon lapsed into delirium— raved about his bride—his engagements—his plighted word; ordered his horse, that he might ride to the castle of Landshort; and expired in the fancied act of vaulting into the saddle.

Starkenfaust bestowed a sigh and a soldier's tear on the untimely fate of his comrade; and then pondered on the awkward mission he had undertaken. His heart was heavy, and his head perplexed; for he was to present himself an unbidden guest among hostile people, and to damp their festivity with tidings fatal to their hopes. Still there were certain whisperings of curiosity in his bosom to see this far-famed beauty of Katzenellenbogen so cautiously shut up from the world; for he was a passionate admirer of the sex, and there was a dash of eccentricity and enterprise in his character that made him fond of all singular adventure.

Previous to his departure he made all due arrangements with the holy fraternity of the convent for the funeral solemnities of his friend, who was to be buried in the cathedral of Würtzburg, near some of his illustrious relatives; and the mourning retinue of the count took charge of his remains.

It is now high time that we should return to the ancient family of Katzenellenbogen, who were impatient for their guest, and still more for their dinner; and to the worthy little baron, whom we left airing himself on the watchtower.

Night closed in, but still no guest arrived. The baron descended from the tower in despair. The banquet, which had been delayed from hour to hour, could no longer be postponed. The meats were already overdone; the cook in an agony; and the whole household had the look of a garrison that had been reduced by famine. The baron was obliged reluctantly to give orders for the feast without the presence of the guest. All were seated at the table, and just on the point of commencing, when the sound of a horn from without the gate gave notice of the approach of a stranger. Another long blast filled the old courts of the castle with its echoes, and was answered by the warder from the walls. The baron hastened to receive his future son-in-law.

The drawbridge had been let down, and the stranger was before the gate. He was a tall, gallant cavalier, mounted on a black steed. His countenance was pale, but he had a beaming, romantic eye, and an air of stately melancholy. The baron was a little mortified that he should have come in this simple, solitary style. His dignity for a moment was ruffled, and he felt disposed to consider it a want of proper respect for the important occasion, and the important family with which he was to be connected. He pacified himself, however, with the conclusion, that it must have been youthful impatience which had induced him thus to spur on sooner than his attendants.

'I am sorry,' said the stranger, 'to break in upon you thus unseasonably——'

Here the baron interrupted him with a world of compliments and greetings; for, to tell the truth, he prided himself upon his courtesy and eloquence. The stranger attempted, once or twice, to stem the torrent of words, but in vain, so he bowed his head and suffered it to flow on. By the time the baron had come to a pause, they had reached the inner court of the castle; and the stranger was again about to speak, when he was once more interrupted by the appearance of the female part of the family, leading forth the shrinking and blushing bride. He gazed on her for a moment as one entranced. It seemed as if his whole soul beamed forth in the gaze, and rested upon that lovely form. One of the maiden aunts whispered something in her ear; she made an effort to speak; her moist blue eye was timidly raised; gave a shy glance of inquiry on the stranger; and was cast again to the ground. The words died away; but there was a sweet smile playing about her lips, and a soft dimpling of the cheek that showed her glance had not been unsatisfactory. It was impossible for a girl of the fond age of eighteen, highly predisposed for love and matrimony, not to be pleased with so gallant a cavalier.

The late hour at which the guest had arrived left no time for parley. The baron was peremptory, and deferred all particular conversation until the morning, and led the way to the untasted banquet.

It was served up in the great hall of the castle. Around the walls hung the hard-favored portraits of the heroes of the house of Katzenellenbogen, and the trophies which they had gained in the field and in the chase. Hacked corselets, splintered jousting spears, and tattered banners were mingled with the spoils of sylvan warfare; the jaws of the wolf and the tusks of the boar grinned horribly among crossbows and battle-axes, and a huge pair of antlers branched immediately over the head of the youthful bridegroom.

The cavalier took but little notice of the company or the entertainment. He scarcely tasted the banquet, but seemed absorbed in admiration of his bride. He conversed in a low tone that could not be overheard—for the language of love is never loud; but where is the female ear so dull that it cannot catch the softest whisper of the lover? There was a mingled tenderness and gravity in his manner, that appeared to have a powerful effect upon the young lady. Her color came and went as she listened with deep attention. Now and then she made some blushing reply, and when his eye was turned away, she would steal a sidelong glance at his romantic countenance, and heave a gentle sigh of tender happiness. It was evident that the young couple were completely enamored. The aunts, who were deeply versed in the mysteries of the heart, declared that they had fallen in love with each other at first sight.

The feast went on merrily, or at least noisily, for the guests were all blessed with those keen appetites that attend upon light purses and mountain air. The baron told his best and longest stories, and never had he told them so well, or with such great effect. If there was anything marvelous, his auditors were lost in astonishment; and if anything facetious, they were sure to laugh exactly in the right place. The baron, it is true, like most great men, was too dignified to utter any joke but a dull one; it was always enforced, however, by a bumper of excellent Hockheimer; and even a dull joke, at one's own table, served up with jolly old wine, is irresistible. Many good things were said by poorer and keener wits, that would not bear repeating, except on similar occasions; many sly speeches whispered in ladies' ears, that almost convulsed them with suppressed laughter; and a song or two roared out by a poor, but merry and broad-faced cousin of the baron, that absolutely made the maiden aunts hold up their fans.

Amidst all this revelry, the stranger guest maintained a most singular and unseasonable gravity. His countenance assumed a deeper cast of dejection as the evening advanced; and, strange as it may appear, even the baron's jokes seemed only to render him the more melancholy. At times he was lost in thought, and at times there was a perturbed and restless wandering of the eye that bespoke a mind but ill at ease. His conversations with the bride became more and more earnest and mysterious. Lowering clouds began to steal over the fair serenity of her brow, and tremors to run through her tender frame.

All this could not escape the notice of the company. Their gaiety was chilled by the unaccountable gloom of the bridegroom; their spirits were infected; whispers and glances were interchanged, accompanied by shrugs and dubious shakes of the head. The song and the laugh grew less and less frequent; there were dreary pauses in the conversation, which were at length succeeded by wild tales and supernatural legends. One dismal story produced another still more dismal, and the baron nearly frightened some of the ladies into hysterics with the history of the goblin horseman that carried away the fair Leonora; a dreadful story, which has since been put into excellent verse, and is read and believed by all the world.

The bridegroom listened to this tale with profound attention. He kept his eyes steadily fixed on the baron, and, as the story drew to a close, began gradually to rise from his seat, growing taller and taller, until, in the baron's entranced eye, he seemed almost to tower into a giant. The moment the tale was finished, he heaved a deep sigh, and took a solemn farewell of the company. They were all amazement. The baron was perfectly thunderstruck.

What! Going to leave the castle at midnight? Why, everything was prepared for his reception. A chamber was ready for him if he wished to retire.

The stranger shook his head mournfully and mysteriously. 'I must lay my head in a different chamber tonight!'

There was something in this reply, and the tone in which it was uttered, that made the baron's heart misgive him; but he rallied his forces, and repeated his hospitable entreaties.

The stranger shook his head silently, but positively, at every offer; and, waving his farewell to the company, stalked slowly out of the hall. The maiden aunts were absolutely petrified; the bride hung her head, and a tear stole to her eye.

The baron followed the stranger to the great court of the castle, where the black charger stood pawing the earth and snorting with impatience. When they had reached the portal, whose deep archway was dimly lighted by a cresset, the stranger paused, and addressed the baron in a hollow tone of voice, which the vaulted roof rendered still more sepulchral.

'Now that we are alone,' said he, 'I will impart to you the reason at my going. I have a solemn, an indispensable engagement—'

'Why,' said the baron, 'cannot you send someone in your place?'

'It admits of no substitute—I must attend it in person—I must away to Würtzburg Cathedral.'

'Ay,' said the baron, plucking up spirit, 'but not until tomorrow— tomorrow you shall take your bride there.'

'No! no!' replied the stranger, with tenfold solemnity, 'my engagement is with no bride—the worms! the worms expect me! I am a dead man—I have been slain by robbers—my body lies at Würtzburg—at midnight I am to be buried—the grave is waiting for me—I must keep my appointment!'

He sprang on his black charger, dashed over the drawbridge, and the clattering of his horse's hoofs was lost in the whistling of the night-blast.

The baron returned to the hall in the utmost consternation, and related what had passed. Two ladies fainted outright, others sickened at the idea of having banqueted with a spectre. It was the opinion of some that this might be the wild huntsman, famous in German legend. Some talked of mountain sprites, of wood-demons, and of other supernatural beings, with which the good people of Germany have been so grievously harassed since time immemorial. One of the poor relations ventured to suggest that it might be some sportive evasion of the young cavalier, and that the very gloominess of the caprice seemed to accord with so melancholy a personage. This, however, drew on him the indignation of the whole company, and especially the baron, who looked upon him as little better than an infidel; so that he was fain to abjure his heresy as speedily as possible, and come into the faith of the true believers.

But whatever may have been the doubts entertained, they were completely put to an end by the arrival, next day, of regular missives, confirming the intelligence of the young count's murder, and his interment in Würtzburg Cathedral.

The dismay at the castle may well be imagined. The baron shut himself up in his chamber. The guests, who had come to rejoice with him, could not think of abandoning him in his distress. They wandered about the courts, or collected in groups in the hall, shaking their heads and shrugging their shoulders, at the troubles of so good a man; and sat longer than ever at table, and ate and drank more stoutly than ever, by way of keeping up their spirits. But the situation of the widowed bride was the most pitiable. To have lost a husband before she had even embraced him—and such a husband! If the very spectre could be so gracious and noble, what must have been the living man! She filled the house with lamentations.

On the night of the second day of her widowhood, she had retired to her chamber, accompanied by one of her aunts, who insisted on sleeping with her. The aunt, who was one of the best tellers of ghost stories in all Germany, had just been recounting one of her longest, and had fallen asleep in the very midst of it. The chamber was remote and overlooked a small garden. The niece lay pensively gazing at the beams of the rising moon, as they trembled on the leaves of an aspen tree before the lattice. The castle clock had just tolled midnight, when a soft strain of music stole up from the garden. She rose hastily from her bed, and stepped lightly to the window. A tall figure stood among the shadows of the trees. As it raised its head, a beam of moonlight fell upon the countenance. Heaven and earth! She beheld the Spectre Bridegroom! A loud shriek at that moment burst upon her ear, and her aunt, who had been awakened by the music, and had followed her silently to the window, fell into her arms. When she looked again, the spectre had disappeared.

Of the two females, the aunt now required the most soothing, for she was perfectly beside herself with terror. As to the young lady, there was something, even in the spectre of her lover, that seemed endearing. There was still the semblance of manly beauty; and though the shadow of a man is but little calculated to satisfy the affections of a lovesick girl, yet, where the substance is not to be had, even that is consoling. The aunt declared she would never sleep in that chamber again. The niece, for once, was refractory and declared as strongly that she would sleep in no other in the castle: the consequence was, that she had to sleep in it alone; but she drew a promise from her aunt not to relate the story of the spectre, lest she should be denied the only melancholy pleasure left her on earth—that of inhabiting the chamber over which the guardian shade of her lover kept its nightly vigils.

How long the good old lady would have observed this promise is uncertain, for she dearly loved to talk of the marvelous, and there is a triumph in being the first to tell a frightful story; it is, however, still quoted in the neighborhood, as a memorable instance of female secrecy, that she kept it to herself for a whole week; when she was suddenly absolved from all further restraint, by intelligence brought to the breakfast table one morning that the young lady was not to be found. Her room was empty—the bed had not been slept in—the window was open, and the bird had flown!

The astonishment and concern with which the intelligence was received can only be imagined by those who have witnessed the agitation which the mishaps of a great man cause among his friends. Even the poor relations paused for a moment from the indefatigable labors of the trencher; when the aunt, who had at first been struck speechless, wrung her hands and shrieked out, 'The goblin! The goblin! She's carried away by the goblin!'

In a few words she related the fearful scene of the garden, and concluded that the spectre must have carried off his bride. Two of the domestics corroborated the opinion, for they had heard the clattering of a horse's hoofs down the mountain about midnight, and had no doubt that it was the spectre on his black charger, bearing her away to the tomb. All present were struck with the direful probability; for events of the kind are extremely common in Germany, as many well-authenticated histories bear witness.

What a lamentable situation was that of the poor baron! What a heart-rending dilemma for a fond father, and a member of the great family of Katzenellenbogen! His only daughter had either been rapt away to the grave, or he was to have some wood-demon for a son-in-law, and, perchance, a troop of goblin grandchildren. As usual, he was completely bewildered, and all the castle in an uproar. The men were ordered to take horse, and scour every road and path and glen of the Odenwald. The baron himself had just drawn on his jack-boots, girded on his sword, and was about to mount his steed to sally forth on the doubtful quest, when he was brought to a pause by a new apparition. A lady was seen approaching the castle, mounted on a palfrey, attended by a cavalier on horseback. She galloped up to the gate, sprang from her horse, and falling at the baron's feet, embraced his knees. It was his lost daughter, and her companion—the Spectre Bridegroom! The baron was astounded. He looked at his daughter, then at the spectre, and almost doubted the evidence of his senses. The latter, too, was wonderfully improved in his appearance since his visit to the world of spirits. His dress was splendid, and set off a noble figure of manly symmetry. He was no longer pale and melancholy. His fine countenance was flushed with the glow of youth, and joy rioted in his large dark eye.

The mystery was soon cleared up. The cavalier (for, in truth, as you must have known all the while, he was no goblin) announced himself as Sir Herman Von Starkenfaust. He related his adventure with the young count. He told how he had hastened to the castle to deliver the unwelcome tidings, but that the eloquence of the baron had interrupted him in every attempt to tell his tale. How the sight of the bride had completely captivated him, and that to pass a few hours near her, he had tacitly suffered the mistake to continue. How he had been sorely perplexed in what way to make a decent retreat, until the baron's goblin stories had suggested his eccentric exit. How, fearing the feudal hostility of the family, he had repeated his visits by stealth—had haunted the garden beneath the young lady's window—had wooed—had won—had borne away in triumph—and, in a word, had wedded the fair.

Under any other circumstances the baron would have been inflexible, for he was tenacious of paternal authority, and devoutly obstinate in all family feuds. But he loved his daughter; he had lamented her as lost; he rejoiced to find her still alive; and, though her husband was of a hostile house, yet, thank Heaven, he was not a goblin. There was something, it must be acknowledged, that did not exactly accord with his notions of strict veracity, in the joke the knight had passed upon him of his being a dead man. But several old friends present, who had served in the wars, assured him that every stratagem was excusable in love, and that the cavalier was entitled to especial privilege, having lately served as a trooper.

Matters, therefore, were happily arranged. The baron pardoned the young couple on the spot. The revels at the castle were resumed. The poor relations overwhelmed this new member of the family with loving kindness. He was so gallant, so generous—and so rich. The aunts, it is true, were somewhat scandalized that their system of strict seclusion and passive obedience should be so badly exemplified, but attributed it all to their negligence in not having the windows grated. One of them was particularly mortified at having her marvelous story marred, and that the only spectre she had ever seen should turn out a counterfeit. But the niece seemed perfectly happy at having found him substantial flesh and blood—and so the story ends.

NATHANIEL HAWTHORNE
1804-1864

Nathaniel Hawthorne was born in 1804 in Salem, Massachusetts. After a lonely and unhappy childhood, Hawthorne determined to make his way in the world as a writer. However, it was not until his short stories began to be published in an annual magazine and were reprinted in a collection called *Twice-Told Tales* in 1837 that his writing attracted any public acclaim. All of Hawthorne's writing is preoccupied with the influence of Puritanism on American morality and character, perhaps due to the fact that his own great-grandson had been one of those judges who passed the death sentence on men and women in the Salem witchcraft trials. This preoccupation culminated in Hawthorne's masterpiece, *The Scarlet Letter*, and he is widely regarded as one of the most influential American writers of the nineteenth century.

Both of the following stories were first published in 1846 when Hawthorne was at the height of his imaginative powers, in a collection entitled *Mosses from an Old Manse*.

Young Goodman Brown

YOUNG GOODMAN BROWN came forth, at sunset, into the street of Salem village, but put his head back, after crossing the threshold, to exchange a parting kiss with his young wife. And Faith, as the wife was aptly named, thrust her own pretty head into the street, letting the wind play with the pink ribbons of her cap, while she called to Goodman Brown.

'Dearest heart,' whispered she, softly and rather sadly, when her lips were close to his ear, 'pr'y thee, put off your journey until sunrise, and sleep in your own bed tonight. A lone woman is troubled with such dreams and such thoughts, that she's afeared of herself, sometimes. Pray, tarry with me this night, dear husband, of all nights in the year!'

'My love and my Faith,' replied young Goodman Brown, 'of all nights in the year, this one night must I tarry away from thee. My journey, as thou callest it, forth and back again, must needs be done 'twixt now and sunrise. What, my sweet, pretty wife, dost thou doubt me already, and we but three months married!'

'Then, God bless you!' said Faith, with the pink ribbons, 'and may you find all well, when you come back.'

'Amen!' cried Goodman Brown. 'Say thy prayers, dear Faith, and go to bed at dusk, and no harm will come to thee.'

So they parted; and the young man pursued his way, until, being about to turn the corner by the meeting-house, he looked back, and saw the head of Faith still peeping after him, with a melancholy air, in spite of her pink ribbons.

'Poor little Faith!' thought he, for his heart smote him. 'What a wretch am I, to leave her on such an errand! She talks of dreams, too. Methought, as she spoke there was trouble in her face, as if a dream had warned her what work is to be done tonight. But, no, no! 'twould kill her to think it. Well; she's a blessed angel on earth; and after this one night, I'll cling to her skirts and follow her to Heaven.'

With this excellent resolve for the future, Goodman Brown felt himself justified in making more haste on his present evil purpose. He had taken a dreary road, darkened by all the gloomiest trees of the forest, which barely stood aside to let the narrow path creep through, and closed immediately behind. It was all as lonely as could be; and there is this peculiarity in such a solitude, that the traveller knows not who may be concealed by the innumerable trunks and the thick boughs overhead; so that, with lonely footsteps, he may yet be passing through an unseen multitude.

'There may be a devilish Indian behind every tree,' said Goodman Brown, to himself; and he glanced fearfully behind him, as he added, 'What if the devil himself should be at my very elbow!'

His head being turned back, he passed a crook of the road, and looking forward again, beheld the figure of a man, in grave and decent attire, seated at the foot of an old tree. He arose, at Goodman Brown's approach, and walked onward, side by side with him.

'You are late, Goodman Brown,' said he. 'The clock of the Old South was striking as I came through Boston; and that is full fifteen minutes agone.'

'Faith kept me back awhile,' replied the young man, with a tremor in his voice, caused by the sudden appearance of his companion, though not wholly unexpected.

It was now deep dusk in the forest, and deepest in that part of it where these two were journeying. As nearly as could be discerned, the second traveller was about fifty years old, apparently in the same rank of life as Goodman Brown, and bearing a considerable resemblance to him, though perhaps more in expression than features. Still, they might have been taken for father and son. And yet, though the elder person was as simply clad as the younger, and as simple in manner too, he had an indescribable air of one who knew the world, and would not have felt abashed at the governor's dinner table, or in King William's court, were it possible that his affairs should call him thither. But the only thing about him, that could be fixed upon as remarkable, was his staff, which bore the likeness of a great black snake, so curiously wrought, that it might almost be seen to twist and wriggle itself, like a living serpent. This, of course, must have been an ocular deception, assisted by the uncertain light.

'Come, Goodman Brown!' cried his fellow-traveller, 'this is a dull pace for the beginning of a journey. Take my staff, if you are so soon weary.'

'Friend,' said the other, exchanging his slow pace for a full stop, 'having kept covenant by meeting thee here, it is my purpose now to return whence I came. I have scruples, touching the matter thou wot'st of.'

'Sayest thou so?' replied he of the serpent, smiling apart. 'Let us walk on, nevertheless, reasoning as we go, and if I convince thee not, thou shalt turn back. We are but a little way in the forest, yet.'

'Too far, too far!' exclaimed the goodman, unconsciously resuming his walk. 'My father never went into the woods on such an errand, nor his father before him. We have been a race of honest men and good Christians, since the days of the martyrs. And shall I be the first of the name of Brown, that ever took this path, and kept—'

'Such company, thou wouldst say,' observed the elder person, interpreting his pause. 'Well said, Goodman Brown! I have been as well acquainted with your family as with ever a one among the Puritans; and that's no trifle to say. I helped your grandfather, the constable, when he lashed the Quaker woman so smartly through the streets of Salem. And it was I that brought your father a pitch-pine knot, kindled at my own hearth, to set fire to an Indian village, in King Philip's war. They were my good friends, both; and many a pleasant walk have we had along this path, and returned merrily after midnight. I would fain be friends with you, for their sake.'

'If it be as thou sayest,' replied Goodman Brown, 'I marvel they never spoke of these matters. Or, verily, I marvel not, seeing that the least rumor of the sort would have driven them from New-England. We are a people of prayer, and good works, to boot, and abide no such wickedness.'

'Wickedness or not,' said the traveller with the twisted staff, 'I have a very general acquaintance here in New-England. The deacons of many a church have drunk the communion wine with me; the selectmen, of divers towns, make me their chairman; and a majority of the Great and General Court are firm supporters of my interest. The governor and I, too – but these are state-secrets.'

'Can this be so!' cried Goodman Brown, with a stare of amazement at his undisturbed companion. 'Howbeit, I have nothing to do with the governor and council; they have their own ways, and are no rule for a simple husbandman, like me. But, were I to go on with thee, how should I meet the eye of that good old man, our minister, at Salem village? Oh, his voice would make me tremble, both Sabbath-day and lecture-day!'

Thus far, the elder traveller had listened with due gravity, but now burst into a fit of irrepressible mirth, shaking himself so violently, that his snake-like staff actually seemed to wriggle in sympathy.

'Ha! ha! ha!' shouted he, again and again; then composing himself, 'Well, go on, Goodman Brown, go on; but pr'y thee, don't kill me with laughing!'

'Well, then, to end the matter at once,' said Goodman Brown, con-siderably nettled, 'there is my wife, Faith. It would break her dear little heart; and I'd rather break my own!'

'Nay, if that be the case,' answered the other, 'e'en go thy ways, Goodman Brown. I would not, for twenty old women like the one hobbling before us, that Faith should come to any harm.'

As he spoke, he pointed his staff at a female figure on the path, in whom Goodman Brown recognized a very pious and exemplary dame, who had taught him his catechism, in youth, and was still his moral and spiritual adviser, jointly with the minister and Deacon Gookin.

'A marvel, truly, that Goody Cloyse should be so far in the wilderness, at night-fall!' said he. 'But, with your leave, friend, I shall take a cut through the woods, until we have left this Christian woman behind. Being a stranger to you, she might ask whom I was consorting with, and whither I was going.'

'Be it so,' said his fellow-traveller. 'Betake you to the woods, and let me keep the path.'

Accordingly, the young man turned aside, but took care to watch his companion, who advanced softly along the road, until he had come within a staff's length of the old dame. She, meanwhile, was making the best of her way, with singular speed for so aged a woman, and mumbling some indistinct words, a prayer, doubtless, as she went. The traveller put forth his staff, and touched her withered neck with what seemed the serpent's tail.

'The devil!' screamed the pious old lady.

'Then Goody Cloyse knows her old friend?' observed the traveller, confronting her, and leaning on his writhing stick.

'Oh, forsooth, and is it your worship, indeed?' cried the good dame. 'Yea, truly is it, and in the very image of my old gossip, Goodman Brown, the grandfather of the silly fellow that now is. But – would your worship believe it? – by broomstick hath strangely disappeared, stolen, as I suspect, by that unhanged witch, Goody Cory, and that, too, when I was all anointed with the juice of smallage and cinque-foil and wolf's-bane –'

'Mingled with fine wheat and the fat of a new-born babe,' said the shape of old Goodman Brown.

'Ah, your worship knows the receipt,' cried the old lady, cackling aloud.

'So, as I was saying, being all ready for the meeting, and no horse to ride on, I made up my mind to foot it; for they tell me, there is a nice young man to be taken into communion tonight. But now your good worship will lend me your arm, and we shall be there in a twinkling.'

'That can hardly be,' answered her friend. 'I may not spare you my arm, Goody Cloyse, but here is my staff, if you will.'

So saying, he threw it down at her feet, where, perhaps, it assumed life, being one of the rods which its owner had formerly lent to the Egyptian Magi. Of this fact, however, Goodman Brown could not take cognizance. He had cast up his eyes in astonishment, and looking down again, beheld neither Goody Cloyse nor the serpentine staff, but his fellow-traveller alone, who waited for him as calmly as if nothing had happened.

'That old woman taught me my catechism!' said the young man; and there was a world of meaning in this simple comment.

They continued to walk onward, while the elder traveller exhorted his companion to make good speed and persevere in the path, discoursing so aptly, that his arguments seemed rather to spring up in the bosom of his auditor, than to be suggested by himself. As they went, he plucked a branch of maple, to serve for a walking-stick, and began to strip it of the twigs and little boughs, which were wet with evening dew. The moment his fingers touched them, they became strangely withered and dried up, as with a week's sunshine. Thus the pair proceeded, at a good free pace, until suddenly, in a gloomy hollow of the road, Goodman Brown sat himself down on the stump of a tree and refused to go any farther.

'Friend,' said he, stubbornly, 'my mind is made up. Not another step will I budge on this errand. What if a wretched old woman do choose to go to the devil, when I thought she was going to Heaven! Is that any reason why I should quit my dear Faith, and go after her?'

'You will think better of this, by-and-by,' said his acquaintance, composedly. 'Sit here and rest yourself awhile; and when you feel like moving again, there is my staff to help you along.'

Without more words, he threw his companion the maple stick, and was speedily out of sight, as if he had vanished into the deepening gloom. The young man sat a few moments, by the road-side, applauding himself greatly, and thinking with how clear a conscience he should meet the minister, in his morning-walk, nor shrink from the eye of good old Deacon Gookin. And what calm sleep would be his, that very night, which was to have been spent so wickedly, but purely and sweetly now, in the arms of Faith! Amidst these pleasant and praiseworthy meditations, Goodman Brown heard the tramp of horses along the road, and deemed it advisable to conceal himself within the verge of the forest, conscious of the guilty purpose that had brought him thither; though now so happily turned from it.

On came the hoof-tramps and the voices of the riders, two grave old voices, conversing soberly as they drew near. These mingled sounds appeared to pass along the road, within a few yards of the young man's hiding-place; but owing, doubtless, to the depth of the gloom, at that particular spot, neither the travellers nor their steeds were visible. Though their figures brushed the small boughs by the way-side, it could not be seen that they intercepted, even for a moment, the faint gleam from the strip of bright sky, athwart which they must have passed. Goodman Brown alternately crouched and stood on tip-toe, pulling aside the branches, and thrusting forth his head as far as he durst, without discerning so much as a shadow. It vexed him more, because he could have sworn, were such a thing possible, that he recognized the voices of the minister and Deacon Gookin, jogging along quietly, as they were wont to do, when bound to some ordination or ecclesiastical council. While yet within hearing, one of the riders stopped to pluck a switch.

'Of the two, reverend Sir,' said the voice like the deacon's, 'I had rather miss an ordination-dinner than tonight's meeting. They tell me that some of our community are to be here from Falmouth and beyond, and others from Connecticut and Rhode-Island; besides several of the Indian powows, who, after their fashion, know almost as much deviltry as the best of us. Moreover, there is a goodly young woman to be taken into communion.'

'Mighty well, Deacon Gookin!' replied the solemn old tones of the minister. 'Spur up, or we shall be late. Nothing can be done you know, until I get on the ground.'

The hoofs clattered again, and the voices, talking so strangely in the empty air, passed on through the forest, where no church had ever been gathered, nor solitary Christian prayed. Whither, then, could these holy men be journeying, so deep into the heathen wilderness? Young Goodman Brown caught hold of a tree, for support, being ready to sink down on the ground, faint and overburthened with the heavy sickness of his heart. He looked up to the sky, doubting whether there really was a Heaven above him. Yet, there was the blue arch, and the stars brightening in it.

'With Heaven above, and Faith below, I will yet stand firm against the devil!' cried Goodman Brown.

While he still gazed upward, into the deep arch of the firmament, and had lifted his hands to pray, a cloud, though no wind was stirring, hurried across the zenith, and hid the brightening stars. The blue sky was still visible, except directly overhead, where this black mass of cloud was sweeping swiftly northward. Aloft in the air, as if from the depths of the cloud, came a confused and doubtful sound of voices. Once, the listener fancied that he could distinguish the accents of town's-people of his own, men and women, both pious and ungodly, many of whom he had met at the communion-table, and had seen others rioting at the tavern. The next moment, so indistinct were the sounds, he doubted whether he had heard aught but the murmur of the old forest, whispering without a wind. Then came a stronger swell of those familiar tones, heard daily in the sunshine, at Salem village, but never, until now, from a cloud of night. There was one voice, of a young woman, uttering lamentations, yet with an uncertain sorrow, and entreating for some favor, which, perhaps, it would grieve her to obtain. And all the unseen multitude, both saints and sinners, seemed to encourage her onward.

'Faith!' shouted Goodman Brown, in a voice of agony and desperation; and the echoes of the forest mocked him, crying – 'Faith! Faith!' as if bewildered wretches were seeking her, all through the wilderness.

The cry of grief, rage, and terror, was yet piercing the night, when the unhappy husband held his breath for a response. There was a scream, drowned immediately in a louder murmur of voices, fading into far-off laughter, as the dark cloud swept away, leaving the clear and silent sky above Goodman Brown. But something fluttered lightly down through the air, and caught on the branch of a tree. The young man seized it, and beheld a pink ribbon.

'My Faith is gone!' cried he, after one stupefied moment. 'There is no good on earth; and sin is but a name. Come, devil! for to thee is this world given.'

And maddened with despair, so that he laughed loud and long, did Goodman Brown grasp his staff and set forth again, at such a rate, that he seemed to fly along the forest-path, rather than to walk or run. The road grew wilder and drearier, and more faintly traced, and vanished at length, leaving him in the heart of the dark wilderness, still rushing onward, with the instinct that guides mortal man to evil. The whole forest was peopled with frightful sounds; the creaking of trees, the howling of wild beasts, and the yell of Indians; while, sometimes, the wind tolled like a distant church-bell, and sometimes gave a broad roar around the traveller, as if all Nature were laughing him to scorn. But he was himself the chief horror of the scene, and shrank not from its other horrors.

'Ha! ha! ha!' roared Goodman Brown, when the wind laughed at him. 'Let us hear which will laugh loudest! Think not to frighten me with your deviltry! Come witch, come wizard, come Indian powow, come devil himself! and here comes Goodman Brown. You may as well fear him as he fear you!'

In truth, all through the haunted forest, there could be nothing more frightful than the figure of Goodman Brown. On he flew, among the black pines, brandishing his staff with frenzied gestures, now giving vent to an inspiration of horrid blasphemy, and shouting forth such laughter, as set all the echoes of the forest laughing like demons around him. The fiend in his own shape is less hideous, than when he rages in the breast of man. Thus sped the demoniac on his course until, quivering among the trees, he saw a red light before him, as when the felled trunks and branches of a clearing have been set on fire, and throw up their lurid blaze against the sky, at the hour of midnight. He paused, in a lull of the tempest that had driven him onward, and heard the swell of what seemed a hymn, rolling solemnly from a distance, with the weight of many voices. He knew the tune; it was a familiar one in the choir of the village meeting-house. The verse died heavily away, and was lengthened by a chorus, not of human voices, but of all the sounds of the benighted wilderness, pealing in awful harmony together. Goodman Brown cried out; and his cry was lost to his own ear, by its unison with the cry of the desert.

In the interval of silence, he stole forward, until the light glared full upon his eyes. At one extremity of an open space, hemmed in by the dark wall of the forest, arose a rock, bearing some rude, natural resemblance either to an altar or a pulpit, and surrounded by four blazing pines, their tops aflame, their stems untouched, like candles at an evening meeting. The mass of foliage, that had overgrown the summit of the rock, was all on fire, blazing high into the night, and fitfully illuminating the whole field. Each pendent twig and leafy festoon was in a blaze. As the red light arose and fell, a numerous congregation alternately shone forth, then disappeared in shadow, and again grew, as it were, out of the darkness, peopling the heart of the solitary woods at once.

'A grave and dark-clad company!' quoth Goodman Brown.

In truth, they were such. Among them, quivering to-and-fro, between gloom and spendor, appeared faces that would be seen, next day, at the council-board of the province, and others which, Sabbath after Sabbath, looked devoutly heavenward, and benignantly over the crowded pews, from the holiest pulpits in the land. Some affirm, that the lady of the governor was there. At least, there were high dames well known to her, and wives of honored husbands, and widows, a great multitude, and ancient maidens, all of excellent repute, and fair young girls, who trembled, lest their mothers should espy them. Either the sudden gleams of light, flashing over the obscure field, bedazzled Goodman Brown, or he recognized a score of the church-members of Salem village, famous for their special sanctity. Good old Deacon Gookin had arrived, and waited at the skirts of that venerable saint, the revered pastor. But, irreverently consorting with these grave, reputable, and pious people, these elders of the church, these chaste dames and dewy virgins, there were men of dissolute lives and women of spotted fame, wretches given over to all mean and filthy vice, and suspected even of horrid crimes. It was strange to see, that the good shrank not from the wicked, nor were the sinners abashed by the saints. Scattered, also, among their pale-faced enemies, were the Indian priests, or powows, who had often scared their native forest with more hideous incantations than any known to English witchcraft.

'But, where is Faith?' thought Goodman Brown; and, as hope came into his heart, he trembled.

Another verse of the hymn arose, a slow and mournful strain, such as the pious love, but joined to words which expressed all that our nature can conceive of sin, and darkly hinted at far more. Unfathomable to mere mortals is the lore of fiends. Verse after verse was sung, and still the chorus of the desert swelled between, like the deepest tone of a mighty organ. And, with the final peal of that dreadful anthem, there came a sound, as if the roaring wind, the rushing streams, the howling beasts, and every other voice of the unconverted wilderness, were mingling and according with the voice of guilty man, in homage to the prince of all. The four blazing pines threw up a loftier flame, and obscurely discovered shapes and visages of horror on the smoke-wreaths, above the impious assembly. At the same moment, the fire on the rock shot redly forth, and formed a glowing arch above its base, where now appeared a figure. With reverence be it spoken, the figure bore no slight similitude, both in garb and manner, to some grave divine of the New-England churches.

'Bring forth the converts!' cried a voice, that echoed through the field and rolled into the forest.

At the word, Goodman Brown stept forth from the shadow of the trees, and approached the congregation, with whom he felt a loathful brotherhood, by the sympathy of all that was wicked in his heart. He could have well nigh sworn, that the shape of his own dead father beckoned him to advance, looking downward from a smoke-wreath, while a woman, with dim features of despair, threw out her hand to warn him back. Was it his mother? But he had no power to retreat one step, nor to resist, even in thought, when the minister and good old Deacon Gookin seized his arms, and led him to the blazing rock. Thither came also the slender form of a veiled female, led between Goody Cloyse, that pious teacher of the catechism, and Martha Carrier, who had received the devil's promise to be queen of hell. A rampant hag was she! And there stood the proselytes, beneath the canopy of fire.

'Welcome, my children,' said the dark figure, 'to the communion of your race! Ye have found, thus young, your nature and your destiny. My children, look behind you!'

They turned; and flashing forth, as it were, in a sheet of flame, the fiend-worshippers were seen; the smile of welcome gleamed darkly on every visage.

'There,' resumed the sable form, 'are all whom ye have reverenced from youth. Ye deemed them holier than yourselves, and shrank from your own sin, contrasting it with their lives of righteousness, and prayerful aspirations heavenward. Yet, here are they all, in my worshipping assembly! This night it shall be granted you to know their secret deeds; how hoary-bearded elders of the church have whispered wanton words to the young maids of their households; how many a woman, eager for widow's weeds, has given her husband a drink at bed-time, and let him sleep his last sleep in her bosom; how beardless youths have made haste to inherit their fathers' wealth; and how fair damsels – blush not, sweet ones! – have dug little graves in the garden, and bidden me, the sole guest, to an infant's funeral. By the sympathy of your human hearts for sin, ye shall scent out all the places – whether in church, bed-chamber, street, field, or forest – where crime has been committed, and shall exult to behold the whole earth one stain of guilt, one mighty blood-spot. Far more than this! It shall be yours to penetrate, in every bosom, the deep mystery of sin, the fountain of all wicked arts, and which inexhaustibly supplies more evil impulses than human power – than my power, at its utmost! – can make manifest in deeds. And now, my children, look upon each other.'

They did so; and, by the blaze of the hell-kindled torches, the wretched man beheld his Faith, and the wife her husband, trembling before that unhallowed altar.

'Lo! there ye stand, my children,' said the figure, in a deep and solemn tone, almost sad, with its despairing awfulness, as if his once angelic nature could yet mourn for our miserable race. 'Depending upon one another's hearts, ye had still hoped, that virtue were not all a dream. Now are ye undeceived! Evil is the nature of mankind. Evil must be your only happiness. Welcome, again, my children, to the communion of your race!'

'Welcome!' repeated the fiend-worshippers, in one cry of despair and triumph.

And there they stood, the only pair, as it seemed, who were yet hesitating on the verge of wickedness, in this dark world. A basin was hollowed, naturally, in the rock. Did it contain water, reddened by the lurid light? or was it blood? or, perchance, a liquid flame? Herein did the Shape of Evil dip his hand, and prepare to lay the mark of baptism upon their foreheads, that they might be partakers of the mystery of sin, more conscious of the secret guilt of others, both in deed and thought, than they could now be of their own. The husband cast one look at his pale wife, and Faith at him. What polluted wretches would the next glance shew them to each other, shuddering alike at what they disclosed and what they saw!

'Faith! Faith!' cried the husband. 'Look up to Heaven, and resist the Wicked One!'

Whether Faith obeyed, he knew not. Hardly had he spoken, when he found himself amid calm night and solitude, listening to a roar of the wind, which died heavily away through the forest. He staggered against the rock and felt it chill and damp, while a hanging twig, that had been all on fire, besprinkled his cheek with the coldest dew.

The next morning, young Goodman Brown came slowly into the street of Salem village, staring around him like a bewildered man. The good old minister was taking a walk along the grave-yard, to get an appetite for breakfast and meditate his sermon, and bestowed a blessing, as he passed, on Goodman Brown. He shank from the venerable saint, as if to avoid an anathema. Old Deacon Gookin was at domestic worship, and the holy words of his prayer were heard through the open window. 'What God doth the wizard pray to?' quoth Goodman Brown. Goody Cloyse, that excellent old Christian, stood in the early sunshine, at her own lattice, catechizing a little girl, who had brought her a pint of morning's milk. Goodman Brown snatched away the child, as from the grasp of the fiend himself. Turning the corner by the meeting-house, he spied the head of Faith, with the pink ribbons, gazing anxiously forth, and bursting into such joy at sight of him, that she skipt along the street, and almost kissed her husband before the whole village. But, Goodman Brown looked sternly and sadly into her face, and passed on without a greeting.

Had Goodman Brown fallen asleep in the forest, and only dreamed a wild dream of a witch-meeting?

Be it so, if you will. But, alas! it was a dream of evil omen for young Goodman Brown. A stern, a sad, a darkly meditative, a distrustful, if not a desperate man, did he become, from the night of that fearful dream. On the Sabbath-day, when the congregation were singing a holy psalm, he could not listen, because an anthem of sin rushed loudly upon his ear, and drowned all the blessed strain. When the minister spoke from the pulpit, with power and fervid eloquence, and, with his hand on the open Bible, of the sacred truths of our religion, and of saint-like lives and triumphant deaths, and of future bliss or misery unutterable, then did Goodman Brown turn pale, dreading, lest the roof should thunder down upon the gray blasphemer and his hearers. Often, awakening suddenly at midnight, he shrank from the bosom of Faith, and at morning or eventide, when the family knelt down at prayer, he scowled, and muttered to himself, and gazed sternly at his wife, and turned away. And when he had lived long, and was borne to his grave, a hoary corpse, followed by Faith, an aged woman, and children and grandchildren, a goodly procession, besides neighbors, not a few, they carved no hopeful verse upon his tomb-stone, for his dying hour was gloom.

Rappaccini's Daughter

FROM THE WRITINGS OF AUBÉPINE

WE DO NOT REMEMBER to have seen any translated specimens of the productions of M. de l'Aubépine; a fact the less to be wondered at, as his very name is unknown to many of his own countrymen, as well as to the student of foreign literature. As a writer, he seems to occupy an unfortunate position between the Transcendentalists (who, under one name or another; have their share in all the current literature of the world), and the great body of pen-and-ink men who address the intellect and sympathies of the multitude. If not too refined, at all events too remote, too shadowy and unsubstantial in his modes of development, to suit the taste of the latter class, and yet too popular to satisfy the spiritual or metaphysical requisitions of the former, he must necessarily find himself without an audience; except here and there an individual, or possibly an isolated clique. His writings, to do them justice, are not altogether destitute of fancy and originality; they might have won him greater reputation but for an inveterate love of allegory, which is apt to invest his plots and characters with the aspect of scenery and people in the clouds, and to steal away the human warmth out of his conceptions. His fictions are sometimes historical, sometimes of the present day, and sometimes, so far as can be discovered, have little or no reference either to time or space. In any case, he generally contents himself with a very slight embroidery of outward manners, – the faintest possible counterfeit of real life, – and endeavors to create an interest by some less obvious peculiarity of the subject. Occasionally, a breath of nature, a rain-drop of pathos and tenderness, or a gleam of humor will find its way into the midst of his fantastic imagery, and make us feel as if, after all, we were yet within the limits of our native earth. We will only add to this very cursory notice, that M. de l'Aubépine's productions, if the reader chance to take them in precisely the proper point of view, may amuse a leisure hour as well as those of a brighter man; if otherwise, they can hardly fail to look excessively like nonsense.

Our author is voluminous; he continues to write and publish with as much praiseworthy and indefatigable prolixity, as if his efforts were crowned with the brilliant success that so justly attends those of Eugene Sue. His first appearance was by a collection of stories, in a long series of volumes, entitled *Contes deux fois racontées.*' The titles of some of his more recent works (we quote from memory) are as follows:– '*Le Voyage Céleste à Chemin de Fer,*' 3 tom. 1838. '*Le nouveau Père Adam et la nouvelle Mère Eve,*' 2 tom. 1839. '*Roderic; ou le Serpent à l'estomac,*' 2 tom. 1840. '*Le Culte du Feu,*' a folio volume of ponderous research into the religion and ritual of the old Persian Ghebers, published in 1841. '*La Soirée du Château en Espagne,*' 1 tom. 8vo. 1842; and '*L'Artiste du Beau; ou le Papillon Mécanique,*' 5 tom. 4to. 1843. Our somewhat wearisome perusal of this startling catalogue of volumes has left behind it a certain personal affection and sympathy, though by no means admiration, for M. de l'Aubépine; and we would fain do the little in our power towards introducing him favorably to the American public. The ensuing tale is a translation of his *'Beatrice; ou la Belle Empoisonneuse,'* recently published in *'La Revue Anti-Aristocratique.'* This journal, edited by the Comte de Bearhaven, has, for some years past, led the defence of liberal principles and popular rights, with a faithfulness and ability worthy of all praise.

A YOUNG MAN, named Giovanni Guasconti, came, very long ago, from the more southern region of Italy, to pursue his studies at the University of Padua. Giovanni, who had but a scanty supply of gold ducats in his pocket, took lodgings in a high and gloomy chamber of an old edifice, which looked not unworthy to have been the palace of a Paduan noble, and which, in fact, exhibited over its entrance the armorial bearings of a family long since extinct. The young stranger, who was not unstudied in the great poem of his country, recollected that one of the ancestors of his family, and perhaps an occupant of this very mansion, had been pictured by Dante as a partaker of the immortal agonies of his Inferno. These reminiscences and associations, together with the tendency to heart-break natural to a young man for the first time out of his native sphere, caused Giovanni to sigh heavily, as he looked around the desolate and ill-furnished apartment.

'Holy Virgin, Signor,' cried old dame Lisabetta, who, won by the youth's remarkable beauty of person, was kindly endeavoring to give the chamber a habitable air, 'what a sigh was that to come out of a young man's heart! Do you find this old mansion gloomy? For the love of heaven, then put your head out of the window, and you will see as bright sunshine as you have left in Naples.'

Guasconti mechanically did as the old woman advised, but could not quite agree with her that the Paduan sunshine was as cheerful as that of southern Italy. Such as it was, however, it fell upon a garden beneath the window, and expended its fostering influences on a variety of plants, which seemed to have been cultivated with exceeding care.

'Does this garden belong to the house?' asked Giovanni.

'Heaven forbid, Signor! – unless it were fruitful of better pot-herbs than any that grow there now,' answered old Lisabetta. 'No; that garden is cultivated by the own hands of Signor Giacomo Rappaccini, the famous Doctor, who, I warrant him, has been heard of as far as Naples. It is said that he distils these plants into medicines that are as potent as a charm. Oftentimes you may see the Signor Doctor at work, and perchance the Signora his daughter, too, gathering the strange flowers that grow in the garden.'

The old woman had now done what she could for the aspect of the chamber, and, commending the young man to the protection of the saints, took her departure.

Giovanni still found no better occupation than to look down into the garden beneath his window. From its appearance, he judged it to be one of those botanic gardens, which were of earlier date in Padua than elswhere in Italy, or in the world. Or, not improbably, it might once have been the pleasure-place of an opulent family; for there was the ruin of a marble fountain in the centre, sculptured with rare art, but so wofully shattered that it was impossible to trace the original design from the chaos of remaining fragments. The water, however, continued to gush and sparkle into the sunbeams as cheerfully as ever. A little gurgling sound ascended to the young man's window, and made him feel as if the fountain were an immortal spirit, that sung its song unceasingly, and without heeding the vicissitudes around it; while one century embodied it in marble, and another scattered the perishable garniture on the soil. All about the pool into which the water subsided, grew various plants, that seemed to require a plentiful supply of moisture for the nourishment of gigantic leaves, and, in some instances, flowers gorgeously magnificent. There was one shrub in particular, set in a marble vase in the midst of the pool, that bore a profusion of purple blossoms, each of which had the lustre and richness of a gem; and the whole together made a show so resplendent that it seemed enough to illuminate the garden, even had there been no sunshine. Every portion of the soil was peopled with plants and herbs, which, if less beautiful, still bore tokens of assiduous care; as if all had their individual virtues, known to the scientific mind that fostered them. Some were placed in urns, rich with old carving, and others in common garden-pots; some crept serpent-like along the ground, or climbed on high, using whatever means of ascent was offered them. One plant had wreathed itself round a statue of Vertumnus, which was thus quite veiled and shrouded in a drapery of hanging foliage, so happily arranged that it might have served a sculptor for a study.

While Giovanni stood at the window, he heard a rustling behind a screen of leaves, and became aware that a person was at work in the garden. His figure soon emerged into view, and showed itself to be that of no common laborer, but a tall, emaciated, sallow, and sickly-looking man, dressed in a scholar's garb of black. He was beyond the middle term of life, with grey hair, a thin grey beard, and a face singularly marked with intellect and cultivation, but which could never, even in his more youthful days, have expressed much warmth of heart.

Nothing could exceed the intentness with which this scientific gardener examined every shrub which grew in his path; it seemed as if he was looking into their inmost nature, making observations in regard to their creative essence, and discovering why one leaf grew in this shape, and another in that, and wherefore such and such flowers differed among themselves in hue and perfume. Nevertheless, in spite of this deep intelligence on his part, there was no approach to intimacy between himself and these vegetable existences. On the contrary, he avoided their actual touch, or the direct inhaling of their odors, with a caution that impressed Giovanni most disagreeably; for the man's demeanor was that of one walking among malignant influences, such as savage beasts, or deadly snakes, or evil spirits, which, should he allow them one moment of license, would wreak upon him some terrible fatality. It was strangely frightful to the young man's imagination, to see this air of insecurity in a person cultivating a garden, that most simple and innocent of human toils, and which had been alike the joy and labor of the unfallen parents of the race. Was this garden, then, the Eden of the present world? – and this man, with such a perception of harm in what his own hands caused to grow, was he the Adam?

The distrustful gardener, while plucking away the dead leaves or pruning the too luxuriant growth of the shrubs, defended his hands with a pair of thick gloves. Nor were these his only armor. When, in his walk through the garden, he came to the magnificent plant that hung its purple gems beside the marble fountain, he placed a kind of mask over his mouth and nostrils, as if all this beauty did but conceal a deadlier malice. But finding this task still too dangerous, he drew back, removed the mask, and called loudly, but in the infirm voice of a person affected with inward disease:

'Beatrice! – Beatrice!'

'Here am I, my father! What would you?' cried a rich and youthful voice from the window of the opposite house; a voice as rich as a tropical sunset, and which made Giovanni, though he knew not why, think of deep hues of purple or crimson, and of perfumes heavily delectable. – 'Are you in the garden?'

'Yes, Beatrice,' answered the gardener, 'and I need your help.'

Soon there emerged from under a sculptured portal the figure of a young girl, arrayed with as much richness of taste as the most splendid of the flowers, beautiful as the day, and with a bloom so deep and vivid that one shade more would have been too much. She looked redundant with life, health, and energy; all of which attributes were bound down and compressed, as it were, and girdled tensely, in their luxuriance, by her virgin zone. Yet Giovanni's fancy must have grown morbid, while he looked down into the garden; for the impression which the fair stranger made upon him was as if here were another flower, the human sister of those vegetable ones, as beautiful as they – more beautiful than the riches of them – but still to be touched only with a glove, nor to be approached without a mask. As Beatrice came down the garden path, it was observable that she handled and inhaled the odor of several of the plants, which her father had most sedulously avoided.

'Here, Beatrice,' said the latter, – 'see how many needful offices require to be done to our chief treasure. Yet, shattered as I am, my life might pay the penalty of approaching it so closely as circumstances demand. Henceforth, I fear, this plant must be consigned to your sole charge.'

'And gladly will I undertake it,' cried again the rich tones of the young lady, as she bent towards the magnificent plant, and opened her arms as if to embrace it. 'Yes, my sister, my splendor, it shall be Beatrice's task to nurse and serve thee; and thou shalt reward her with thy kisses and perfumed breath, which to her is as the breath of life!'

Then, with all the tenderness in her manner that was so strikingly expressed in her words, she busied herself with such attentions as the plant seemed to require; and Giovanni, at his lofty window, rubbed his eyes, and almost doubted whether it were a girl tending her favorite flower, or one sister performing the duties of affection to another. The scene soon terminated. Whether Doctor Rappaccini had finished his labors in the garden, or that his watchful eye had caught the stranger's face, he now took his daughter's arm and retired. Night was already closing in; oppressive exhalations seemed to proceed from the plants, and steal upward past the open window; and Giovanni, closing the lattice, went to his couch, and dreamed of a rich flower and beautiful girl. Flower and maiden were different and yet the same, and fraught with some strange peril in either shape.

But there is an influence in the light of morning that tends to rectify whatever errors of fancy, or even of judgment, we may have incurred during the sun's decline, or among the shadows of the night, or in the less wholesome glow of moonshine. Giovanni's first movement on starting from sleep, was to throw open the window, and gaze down into the garden which his dreams had made so fertile of mysteries. He was surprised, and a little ashamed, to find how real and matter-of-fact an affair it proved to be, in the first rays of the sun, which gilded the dew-drops that hung upon leaf and blossom, and, while giving a brighter beauty to each rare flower, brought everything within the limits of ordinary experience. The young man rejoiced, that, in the heart of the barren city, he had the privilege of overlooking this spot of lovely and luxuriant vegetation. It would serve, he said to himself, as a symbolic language, to keep him in communion with Nature. Neither the sickly and thought-worn Doctor Giacomo Rappaccini, it is true, nor his brilliant daughter, were now visible; so that Giovanni could not determine how much of the singularity which he attributed to both, was due to their own qualities, and how much to his wonder-working fancy. But he was inclined to take a most rational view of the whole matter.

In the course of the day, he paid his respects to Signor Pietro Baglioni, professor of medicine in the University, a physician of eminent repute, to whom Giovanni had brought a letter of introduction. The Professor was an elderly personage, apparently of genial nature, and habits that might almost be called jovial; he kept the young man to dinner, and made himself very agreeable by the freedom and liveliness of his conversation, especially when warmed by a flask or two of Tuscan wine. Giovanni, conceiving that men of science, inhabitants of the same city, must needs be on familiar terms with one another, took an opportunity to mention the name of Doctor Rappaccini. But the Professor did not respond with so much cordiality as he had anticipated.

'Ill would it become a teacher of the divine art of medicine,' said Professor Pietro Baglioni, in answer to a question of Giovanni, 'to withhold due and well-considered praise of a physician so eminently skilled as Rappaccini. But, on the other hand, I should answer it but scantily to my conscience, were I to permit a worthy youth like yourself, Signor Giovanni, the son of an ancient friend, to imbibe erroneous ideas respecting a man who might hereafter chance to hold your life and death in his hands. The truth is, our worshipful Doctor Rappaccini has as much science as any member of the faculty – with perhaps one single exception – in Padua, or all Italy. But there are certain grave objections to his professional character.'

'And what are they?' asked the young man.

'Has my friend Giovanni any disease of body or heart that he is so inquisitive about physicians?' said the Professor, with a smile. 'But as for Rappaccini, it is said of him – and I, who know the man well, can answer for its truth – that he cares infinitely more for science than for mankind. His patients are interesting to him only as subjects for some new experiment. He would sacrifice human life, his own among the rest, or whatever else was dearest to him, for the sake of adding so much as a grain of mustard-seed to the great heap of his accumulated knowledge.'

'Methinks he is an awful man, indeed,' remarked Guasconti, mentally recalling the cold and purely intellectual aspect of Rappaccini. 'And yet, worshipful Professor, is it not a noble spirit? Are there many men capable of so spiritual a love of science?'

'God forbid,' answered the Professor, somewhat testily – 'at least, unless they take sounder views of the healing art than those adopted by Rappaccini. It is his theory, that all medicinal virtues are comprised within those substances which we term vegetable poisons. These he cultivates with his own hands, and is said even to have produced new varieties of poison, more horribly deleterious than Nature, without the assistance of this learned person, would ever have plagued the world withal. That the Signor Doctor does less mischief than might be expected, with such dangerous substances, is undeniable. Now and then, it must be owned, he has effected – or seemed to effect – a marvellous cure. But, to tell you my private mind, Signor Giovanni, he should receive little credit for such instances of success – they being probably the work of chance – but should be held strictly accountable for his failures, which may justly be considered his own work.'

The youth might have taken Baglioni's opinions with many grains of allowance, had he known that there was a professional warfare of long continuance between him and Doctor Rappaccini, in which the latter was generally thought to have gained the advantage. If the reader be inclined to judge for himself, we refer him to certain black-letter tracts on both sides, preserved in the medical department of the University of Padua.

'I know not, most learned Professor,' returned Giovanni, after musing on what had been said of Rappaccini's exclusive zeal for science – 'I know not how dearly this physician may love his art; but surely there is one object more dear to him. He has a daughter.'

'Aha!' cried the Professor with a laugh. 'So now our friend Giovanni's secret is out. You have heard of this daughter, whom all the young men in Padua are wild about, though not half a dozen have ever had the good hap to see her face. I know little of the Signora Beatrice, save that Rappaccini is said to have instructed her deeply in his science, and that, young and beautiful as fame reports her, she is already qualified to fill a professor's chair. Perchance her father destines her for mine! Other absurd rumors there be, not worth talking about, or listening to. So now, Signor Giovanni, drink off your glass of Lacryma.'

Guasconti returned to his lodgings somewhat heated with the wine he had quaffed, and which caused his brain to swim with strange fantasies in reference to Doctor Rappaccini and the beautiful Beatrice. On his way, happening to pass by a florist's, he bought a fresh bouquet of flowers.

Ascending to his chamber, he seated himself near the window, but within the shadow thrown by the depth of the wall, so that he could look down into the garden with little risk of being discovered. All beneath his eye was a solitude. The strange plants were basking in the sunshine, and now and then nodding gently to one another, as if in acknowledgment of sympathy and kindred. In the midst, by the shattered fountain, grew the magnificent shrub, with its purple gems clustering all over it; they glowed in the air, and gleamed back again out of the depths of the pool, which thus seemed to overflow with colored radiance from the rich reflection that was steeped in it. At first, as we have said, the garden was a solitude. Soon, however, – as Giovanni had half-hoped, half-feared, would be the case, – a figure appeared beneath the antique sculptured portal, and came down between the rows of plants, inhaling their various perfumes, as if she were one of those beings of old classic fable, that lived upon sweet odors. On again beholding Beatrice, the young man was even startled to perceive how much her beauty exceeded his recollection of it; so brilliant, so vivid was its character, that she glowed amid the sunlight, and, as Giovanni whispered to himself, positively illuminated the more shadowy intervals of the garden path. Her face being now more revealed than on the former occasion, he was struck by its expression of simplicity and sweetness; qualities that had not entered into his idea of her character, and which made him ask anew, what manner of mortal she might be. Nor did he fail again to observe, or imagine, an analogy between the beautiful girl and the gorgeous shrub that hung its gem-like flowers over the fountain; a resemblance which Beatrice seemed to have indulged a fantastic humor in heightening, both by the arrangement of her dress and the selection of its hues.

Approaching the shrub, she threw open her arms, as with a passionate ardor, and drew its branches into an intimate embrace; so intimate, that her features were hidden in its leafy bosom, and her glistening ringlets all intermingled with the flowers.

'Give me thy breath, my sister,' exclaimed Beatrice; 'for I am faint with common air! And give me this flower of thine, which I separate with gentlest fingers from the stem, and place it close beside my heart.'

With these words, the beautiful daughter of Rappaccini plucked one of the richest blossoms of the shrub, and was about to fasten it in her bosom. But now, unless Giovanni's draughts of wine had bewildered his senses, a singular incident occurred. A small orange-colored reptile, of the lizard or chameleon species, chanced to be creeping along the path, just at the feet of Beatrice. It appeared to Giovanni – but, at the distance from which he gazed, he could scarcely have seen anything so minute – it appeared to him, however, that a drop or two of moisture from the broken stem of the flower descended upon the lizard's head. For an instant, the reptile contorted itself violently, and then lay motionless in the sunshine. Beatrice observed this remarkable phenomenon, and crossed herself, sadly, but without surprise; nor did she therefore hesitate to arrange the fatal flower in her bosom. There it blushed, and almost glimmered with the dazzling effect of a precious stone, adding to her dress and aspect the one appropriate charm, which nothing else in the world could have supplied. But Giovanni, out of the shadow of his window, bent forward and shrank back, and murmured and trembled.

'Am I awake? Have I my senses?' said he to himself. 'What is this being? – beautiful, shall I call her? – or inexpressibly terrible?'

Beatrice now strayed carelessly through the garden, approaching closer beneath Giovanni's window, so that he was compelled to thrust his head quite out of its concealment in order to gratify the intense and painful curiosity which she excited. At this moment, there came a beautiful insect over the garden wall; it had perhaps wandered through the city and found no flowers nor verdure among those antique haunts of men, until the heavy perfumes of Doctor Rappaccini's shrubs had lured it from afar. Without alighting on the flowers, this winged brightness seemed to be attracted by Beatrice, and lingered in the air and fluttered about her head. Now, here it could not but be that Giovanni Guasconti's eyes deceived him. Be that as it might, he fancied that while Beatrice was gazing at the insect with childish delight, it grew faint and fell at her feet; – its bright wings shivered; it was dead – from no cause that he could discern, unless it were the atmosphere of her breath. Again Beatrice crossed herself and sighed heavily, as she bent over the dead insect.

An impulsive movement of Giovanni drew her eyes to the window. There she beheld the beautiful head of the young man – rather a Grecian than an Italian head, with fair, regular features, and a glistening of gold among his ringlets – gazing down upon her like a being that hovered in mid-air. Scarcely knowing what he did, Giovanni threw down the bouquet which he had hitherto held in his hand.

'Signora,' said he, 'there are pure and healthful flowers. Wear them for the sake of Giovanni Guasconti!'

'Thanks, Signor,' replied Beatrice, with her rich voice, that came forth as it were like a gush of music; and with a mirthful expression half childish and half woman-like. 'I accept your gift, and would fain recompense it with this precious purple flower; but if I toss it into the air, it will not reach you. So Signor Guasconti must even content himself with my thanks.'

She lifted the bouquet from the ground, and then as if inwardly ashamed at having stepped aside from her maidenly reserve to respond to a stranger's greeting, passed swiftly homeward through the garden. But, few as the moments were, it seemed to Giovanni when she was on the point of vanishing beneath the sculptured portal, that his beautiful bouquet was already beginning to wither in her grasp. It was an idle thought; there could be no possibility of distinguishing a faded flower from a fresh one at so great a distance.

For many days after this incident, the young man avoided the window that looked into Doctor Rappaccini's garden, as if something ugly and monstrous would have blasted his eye-sight, had he been betrayed into a glance. He felt conscious of having put himself, to a certain extent, within the influence of an unintelligible power, by the communication which he had opened with Beatrice. The wisest course would have been, if his heart were in any real danger, to quit his lodgings and Padua itself, at once; the next wiser, to have accustomed himself, as far as possible, to the familiar and day-light view of Beatrice; thus bringing her rigidly and systematically within the limits of ordinary experience. Least of all, while avoiding her sight, ought Giovanni to have remained so near this extraordinary being, that the proximity and possibility even of intercourse, should give a kind of substance and reality to the wild vagaries which his imagination ran riot continually in producing. Guasconti had not a deep heart – or at all events, its depths were not sounded now – but he had a quick fancy, and an ardent southern temperament, which rose every instant to a higher fever-pitch. Whether or no Beatrice possessed those terrible attributes – that fatal breath – the affinity with those so beautiful and deadly flowers – which were indicated by what Giovanni had witnessed, she had at least instilled a fierce and subtle poison into his system. It was not love, although her rich beauty was a madness to him; nor horror, even while he fancied her spirit to be imbued with the same baneful essence that seemed to pervade her physical frame; but a wild offspring of both love and horror that had each parent in it, and burned like one and shivered like the other. Giovanni knew not what to dread; still less did he know what to hope; yet hope and dread kept a continual warfare in his breast, alternately vanquishing one another and starting up afresh to renew the contest. Blessed are all simple emotions, be they dark or bright! It is the lurid intermixture of the two that produces the illuminating blaze of the infernal regions.

Sometimes he endeavored to assuage the fever of his spirit by a rapid walk through the streets of Padua, or beyond its gates; his footsteps kept time with the throbbings of his brain, so that the walk was apt to accelerate itself to a race. One day, he found himself arrested; his arm was seized by a portly personage who had turned back on recognizing the young man, and expended much breath in overtaking him.

'Signor Giovanni! – stay, my young friend!' cried he. 'Have you forgotten me? That might well be the case, if I were as much altered as yourself.'

It was Baglioni, whom Giovanni had avoided, ever since their first meeting, from a doubt that the Professor's sagacity would look too deeply into his secrets. Endeavoring to recover himself, he stared forth wildly from his inner world into the outer one, and spoke like a man in a dream:

'Yes; I am Giovanni Guasconti. You are Professor Pietro Baglioni. Now let me pass!'

'Not yet – not yet, Signor Giovanni Guasconti,' said the Professor, smiling, but at the same time scrutinizing the youth with an earnest glance. – 'What; did I grow up side by side with your father, and shall his son pass me like a stranger, in these old streets of Padua? Stand still, Signor Giovanni; for we must have a word or two, before we part.'

'Speedily, then, most worshipful Professor, speedily!' said Giovanni with feverish impatience. 'Does not your worship see that I am in haste?'

Now, while he was speaking, there came a man in black along the street, stooping and moving feebly, like a person in inferior health. His face was all overspread with a most sickly and sallow hue, but yet so pervaded with an expression of piercing and active intellect, that an observer might easily have overlooked the merely physical attributes, and have seen only his wonderful energy. As he passed, this person exchanged a cold and distant salutation with Baglioni, but fixed his eyes upon Giovanni with an intentness that seemed to bring out whatever was within him worthy of notice. Nevertheless, there was a peculiar quietness in the look, as if taking merely a speculative, not a human, interest in the young man.

'It is Doctor Rappaccini!' whispered the Professor, when the stranger had passed. – 'Has he ever seen your face before?'

'Not that I know,' answered Giovanni, starting at the name.

'He *has* seen you! – he must have seen you!' said Baglioni, hastily. 'For some purpose or other, this man of science is making a study of you. I know that look of his! It is the same that coldly illuminates his face, as he bends over a bird, a mouse, or a butterfly, which, in pursuance of some experiment, he has killed by the perfume of a flower; – a look as deep as Nature itself, but without Nature's warmth of love. Signor Giovanni, I will stake my life upon it, you are the subject of one of Rappaccini's experiments!'

'Will you make a fool of me?' cried Giovanni, passionately. '*That*, Signor Professor, were an untoward experiment.'

'Patience, patience!' replied the imperturbable Professor. – 'I tell thee, my poor Giovanni, that Rappaccini has a scientific interest in thee. Thou has fallen into fearful hands! And the Signora Beatrice? What part does she act in this mystery?'

But Guasconti, finding Baglioni's pertinacity intolerable, here broke away, and was gone before the Professor could again seize his arm. He looked after the young man intently, and shook his head.

'This must not be,' said Baglioni to himself. 'The youth is the son of my old friend, and shall not come to any harm from which the arcana of medical science can preserve him. Besides, it is too insufferable an impertinence in Rappaccini, thus to snatch the lad out of my own hands, as I may say, and make use of him for his infernal experiments. This daughter of his! It shall be looked to. Perchance, most learned Rappaccini, I may foil you where you little dream of it!'

Meanwhile, Giovanni had pursued a circuitous route, and at length found himself at the door of his lodgings. As he crossed the threshold, he was met by old Lisabetta, who smirked and smiled, and was evidently desirous to attract his attention; vainly, however, as the ebullition of his feelings had momentarily subsided into a cold and dull vacuity. He turned his eyes full upon the withered face that was puckering itself into a smile, but seemed to behold it not. The old dame, therefore, laid her grasp upon his cloak.

'Signor! – Signor!' whispered she, still with a smile over the whole breadth of her visage, so that it looked not unlike a grotesque carving in wood, darkened by centuries – 'Listen, Signor! There is a private entrance into the garden!'

'What do you say?' exclaimed Giovanni, turning quickly about, as if an inanimate thing should start into feverish life. – 'A private entrance into Doctor Rappaccini's garden!'

'Hush! hush! – not so loud!' whispered Lisabetta, putting her hand over his mouth. 'Yes; into the worshipful Doctor's garden, where you may see all his fine shrubbery. Many a young man in Padua would give gold to be admitted among those flowers.'

Giovanni put a piece of gold into her hand.

'Show me the way,' said he.

A surmise, probably excited by his conversation with Baglioni, crossed his mind, that this interposition of old Lisabetta might perchance be connected with the intrigue, whatever were its nature, in which the Professor seemed to suppose that Doctor Rappaccini was involving him. But such a suspicion, though it disturbed Giovanni, was inadequate to restrain him. The instant that he was aware of the possibility of approaching Beatrice, it seemed an absolute necessity of his existence to do so. It mattered not whether she were angel or demon; he was irrevocably within her sphere, and must obey the law that whirled him onward, in ever lessening circles, towards a result which he did not attempt to foreshadow. And yet, strange to say, there came across him a sudden doubt, whether this intense interest on his part were not delusory – whether it were really of so deep and positive a nature as to justify him in now thrusting himself into an incalculable position – whether it were not merely the fantasy of a young man's brain, only slightly, or not at all connected with his heart!

He paused – hesitated – turned half about – but again went on. His withered guide led him along several obscure passages, and finally undid a door, through which, as it was opened, there came the sight and sound of rustling leaves, with the broken sunshine glimmering among them. Giovanni stepped forth, and forcing himself throught the entanglement of a shrub that wreathed its tendrils over the hidden entrance, he stood beneath his own window, in the open area of Doctor Rappaccini's garden.

How often is it the case, that, when impossibilities have come to pass, and dreams have condensed their misty substance into tangible realities, we find ourselves calm, and even coldly self-possessed, amid circumstances which it would have been a delirium of joy or agony to anticipate! Fate delights to thwart us thus. Passion will choose its own time to rush upon the scene, and lingers sluggishly behind, when an appropriate adjustment of events would seem to summon his appearance. So was it now with Giovanni. Day after day, his pulses had throbbed with feverish blood, at the improbable idea of an interview with Beatrice, and of standing with her, face to face, in this very garden, basking in the Oriental sunshine of her beauty, and snatching from her full gaze the mystery which he deemed the riddle of his own existence. But now there was a singular and untimely equanimity within his breast. He threw a glance around the garden to discover if Beatrice or her father were present, and perceiving that he was alone, began a critical observation of the plants.

The aspect of one and all of them dissatisfied him; their gorgeousness seemed fierce, passionate, and even unnatural. There was hardly an individual shrub which a wanderer, straying by himself through a forest, would not have been startled to find growing wild, as if an unearthly face had glared at him out of the thicket. Several, also, would have shocked a delicate instinct by an appearance of artificialness, indicating that there had been such commixture, and, as it were, adultery of various vegetable species, that the production was no longer of God's making, but the monstrous offspring of man's depraved fancy, glowing with only an evil mockery of beauty. They were probably the result of experiment, which, in one or two cases, had succeeded in mingling plants individually lovely into a compound possessing the questionable and ominous character that distinguished the whole growth of the garden. In fine, Giovanni recognized but two or three plants in the collection, and those of a kind that he well knew to be poisonous. While busy with these contemplations, he heard the rustling of a silken garment, and turning, beheld Beatrice emerging from beneath the sculptured portal.

Giovanni had not considered with himself what should be his deportment; whether he should apologize for his intrusion into the garden, or assume that he was there with the privity, at least, if not by the desire, of Doctor Rappaccini or his daughter. But Beatrice's manner placed him at his ease, though leaving him still in doubt by what agency he had gained admittance. She came lightly along the path, and met him near the broken fountain. There was surprise in her face, but brightened by a simple and kind expression of pleasure.

'You are a connoisseur in flowers, Signor,' said Beatrice with a smile, alluding to the bouquet which he had flung her from the window. 'It is no marvel, therefore, if the sight of my father's rare collection has tempted you to take a nearer view. If he were here, he could tell you many strange and interesting facts as to the nature and habits of these shrubs, for he has spent a life-time in such studies, and this garden is his world.'

'And yourself, lady,' – observed Giovanni – 'if fame says true – you, likewise, are deeply skilled in the virtues indicated by these rich blossoms, and these spicy perfumes. Would you deign to be my instructress, I should prove an apter scholar than if taught by Signor Rappaccini himself.'

'Are there such idle rumors?' asked Beatrice, with the music of a pleasant laugh. 'Do people say that I am skilled in my father's science of plants? What a jest is there! No; though I have grown up among these flowers, I know no more of them than their hues and perfume; and sometimes, methinks I would fain rid myself of even that small knowledge. There are many flowers here, and those not the least brilliant, that shock and offend me, when they meet my eye. But, pray, Signor, do not believe these stories about my science. Believe nothing of me save what you see with your own eyes.'

'And must I believe all that I have seen with my own eyes?' asked Giovanni pointedly, while the recollection of former scenes made him shrink. 'No, Signora, you demand too little of me. Bid me believe nothing, save what comes from your own lips.'

It would appear that Beatrice understood him. There came a deep flush to her cheek; but she looked full into Giovanni's eyes, and responded to his gaze of uneasy suspicion with a queen-like haughtiness.

'I do so bid you, Signor!' she replied. 'Forget whatever you may have fancied in regard to me. If true to the outward senses, still it may be false in its essence. But the words of Beatrice Rappaccini's lips are true from the depths of the heart outward. Those you may believe!'

A fervor glowed in her whole aspect, and beamed upon Giovanni's consciousness like the light of truth itself. But while she spoke, there was a fragrance in the atmosphere around her, rich and delightful, though evanescent, yet which the young man, from an indefinable reluctance, scarcely dared to draw into his lungs. It might be the odor of the flowers. Could it be Beatrice's breath, which thus embalmed her words with a strange richness, as if by steeping them in her heart? A faintness passed like a shadow over Giovanni, and flitted away; he seemed to gaze through the beautiful girl's eyes into her transparent soul, and felt no more doubt or fear.

The tinge of passion that had colored Beatrice's manner vanished; she became gay, and appeared to derive a pure delight from her communion with the youth, not unlike what the maiden of a lonely island might have felt, conversing with a voyager from the civilized world. Evidently her experience of life had been confined within the limits of that garden. She talked now about matters as simple as the daylight or summer-clouds, and now asked questions in reference to the city, or Giovanni's distant home, his friends, his mother, and his sisters; questions indicating such seclusion, and such lack of familiarity with modes and forms, that Giovanni responded as if to an infant. Her spirit gushed out before him like a fresh rill, that was just catching its first glimpse of the sunlight, and wondering at the reflections of earth and sky which were flung into its bosom. There came thoughts, too, from a deep source, and fantasies of a gem-like brilliancy, as if diamonds and rubies sparkled upward among the bubbles of the fountain. Ever and anon, there gleamed across the young man's mind a sense of wonder, that he should be walking side by side with the being who had so wrought upon his imagination – whom he had idealized in such hues of terror – in whom he had positively witnessed such manifestations of dreadful attributes – that he should be conversing with Beatrice like a brother, and should find her so human and so maiden-like. But such reflections were only momentary; the effect of her character was too real, not to make itself familiar at once.

In this free intercourse, they had strayed through the garden, and now, after many turns among its avenues, were come to the shattered fountain, beside which grew the magnificent shrub with its treasury of glowing blossoms. A fragrance was diffused from it, which Giovanni recognized as identical with that which he had attributed to Beatrice's breath, but incomparably more powerful. As her eyes fell upon it, Giovanni beheld her press her hand to her bosom, as if her heart were throbbing suddenly and painfully.

'For the first time in my life,' murmured she, addressing the shrub, 'I had forgotten thee!'

'I remember, Signora,' said Giovanni, 'that you once promised to reward me with one of these living gems for the bouquet, which I had the happy boldness to fling to your feet. Permit me now to pluck it as a memorial of this interview.'

He made a step towards the shrub, with extended hand. But Beatrice darted forward, uttering a shriek that went through his heart like a dagger. She caught his hand, and drew it back with the whole force of her slender figure. Giovanni felt her touch thrilling through his fibres.

'Touch it not!' exclaimed she, in a voice of agony. 'Not for thy life! It is fatal!'

Then, hiding her face, she fled from him, and vanished beneath the sculptured portal. As Giovanni followed her with his eyes, he beheld the emaciated figure and pale intelligence of Doctor Rappaccini, who had been watching the scene, he knew not how long, within the shadow of the entrance.

No sooner was Guasconti alone in his chamber, than the image of Beatrice came back to his passionate musings, invested with all the witchery that had been gathering around it ever since his first glimpse of her, and now likewise imbued with a tender warmth of girlish womanhood. She was human: her nature was endowed with all gentle and feminine qualities; she was worthiest to be worshipped; she was capable, surely, on her part, of the height and heroism of love. Those tokens, which he had hitherto considered as proofs of a frightful peculiarity in her physical and moral system, were now either forgotten, or, by the subtle sophistry of passion, transmuted into a golden crown of enchantment, rendering Beatrice the more admirable, by so much as she was the more unique. Whatever had looked ugly, was now beautiful; or, if incapable of such a change, it stole away and hid itself among those shapeless half-ideas, which throng the dim region beyond the daylight of our perfect consciousness. Thus did he spend the night, nor fell asleep, until the dawn had begun to awake the slumbering flowers in Doctor Rappaccini's garden, whither Giovanni's dreams doubtless led him. Up rose the sun in his due season, and flinging his beams upon the young man's eyelids, awoke him to a sense of pain. When thoroughly aroused, he became sensible of a burning and tingling agony in his hand – in his right hand – the very hand which Beatrice had grasped in her own, when he was on the point of plucking one of the gem-like flowers. On the back of that hand there was now a purple print, like that of four small fingers, and the likeness of a slender thumb upon his wrist.

Oh, how stubbornly does love – or even that cunning semblance of love which flourishes in the imagination, but strikes no depth of root into the heart – how stubbornly does it hold its faith, until the moment come, when it is doomed to vanish into thin mist! Giovanni wrapt a handkerchief about his hand, and wondered what evil thing had stung him, and soon forgot his pain in a reverie of Beatrice.

After the first interview, a second was in the inevitable course of what we call fate. A third; a fourth; and a meeting with Beatrice in the garden was no longer an incident in Giovanni's daily life, but the whole space in which he might be said to live; for the anticipation and memory of that ecstatic hour made up the remainder. Nor was it otherwise with the daughter of Rappaccini. She watched for the youth's appearance, and flew to his side with confidence as unreserved as if they had been playmates from early infancy – as if they were such playmates still. If, by any unwonted chance, he failed to come at the appointed moment, she stood beneath the window, and sent up the rich sweetness of her tones to float around him in his chamber, and echo and reverberate throughout his heart – 'Giovanni! Giovanni! Why tarriest thou? Come down!' – And down he hastened into that Eden of poisonous flowers.

But, with all this intimate familiarity, there was still a reserve in Beatrice's demeanor, so rigidly and invariably sustained, that the idea of infringing it scarcely occurred to his imagination. By all appreciable signs, they loved; they had looked love, with eyes that conveyed the holy secret from the depths of one soul into the depths of the other, as if it were too sacred to be whispered by the way; they had even spoken love, in those gushes of passion when their spirits darted forth in articulated breath, like tongues of long-hidden flame; and yet there had been no seal of lips, no clasp of hands, nor any slightest caress, such as love claims and hallows. He had never touched one of the gleaming ringlets of her hair; her garment – so marked was the physical barrier between them – had never been waved against him by a breeze. On the few occasions when Giovanni had seemed tempted to overstep the limit, Beatrice grew so sad, so stern, and withal wore such a look of desolate separation, shuddering at itself, that not a spoken word was requisite to repel him. At such times, he was startled at the horrible suspicions that rose, monster-like, out of the caverns of his heart, and stared him in the face; his love grew thin and faint as the morning-mist; his doubts alone had substance. But when Beatrice's face brightened again, after the momentary shadow, she was transformed at once from the mysterious, questionable being, whom he had watched with so much awe and horror; she was now the beautiful and unsophisticated girl, whom he felt that his spirit knew with a certainty beyond all other knowledge.

A considerable time had now passed since Giovanni's last meeting with Baglioni. One morning, however, he was disagreeably surprised by a visit from the Professor, whom he had scarcely thought of for whole weeks, and would willingly have forgotten still longer. Given up, as he had long been, to a pervading excitement, he could tolerate no companions, except upon condition of their perfect sympathy with his present state of feeling. Such sympathy was not to be expected from Professor Baglioni.

The visitor chatted carelessly, for a few moments, about the gossip of the city and the University, and then took up another topic.

'I have been reading an old classic author lately,' said he, 'and met with a story that strangely interested me. Possibly you may remember it. It is of an Indian prince, who sent a beautiful woman as a present to Alexander the Great. She was as lovely as the dawn, and gorgeous as the sunset: but what especially distinguished her was a certain rich perfume in her breath – richer than a garden of Persian roses. Alexander, as was natural to a youthful conqueror, fell in love at first sight with this magnificent stranger. But a certain sage physician, happening to be present, discovered a terrible secret in regard to her.'

'And what was that?' asked Giovanni, turning his eyes downward to avoid those of the Professor.

'That this lovely woman,' continued Baglioni, with emphasis, 'had been nourished with poisons from her birth upward, until her whole nature was so imbued with them, that she herself had become the deadliest poison in existence. Poison was her element of life. With that rich perfume of her breath, she blasted the very air. Her love would have been poison! – her embrace death! Is not this a marvellous tale?'

'A childish fable,' answered Giovanni, nervously starting from his chair. 'I marvel how your worship finds time to read such nonsense, among your graver studies.'

'By the bye,' said the Professor, looking uneasily about him, 'what singular fragrance is this in your apartment? Is it the perfume of your gloves? It is faint, but delicious, and yet after all, by no means agreeable. Were I to breathe it long, methinks it would make me ill. It is like the breath of a flower – but I see no flowers in the chamber.'

'Nor are there any,' replied Giovanni, who had turned pale as the Professor spoke; 'nor, I think, is there any fragrance, except in your worship's imagination. Odors, being a sort of element combined of the sensual and the spiritual, are apt to deceive us in this manner. The recollection of a perfume – the bare idea of it – may easily be mistaken for a present reality.'

'Aye; but my sober imagination does not often play such tricks,' said Baglioni; 'and were I to fancy any kind of odor, it would be that of some vile apothecary drug, wherewith my fingers are likely enough to be imbued. Our worshipful friend Rappaccini, as I have heard, tinctures his medicaments with odors richer than those of Araby. Doubtless, likewise, the fair and learned Signora Beatrice would minister to her patients with draughts as sweet as a maiden's breath. But woe to him that sips them!'

Giovanni's face evinced many contending emotions. The tone in which the Professor alluded to the pure and lovely daughter of Rappaccini was a torture to his soul; and yet, the intimation of a view of her character, opposite to his own, gave instantaneous distinctness to a thousand dim suspicions, which now grinned at him like so many demons. But he strove hard to quell them, and to respond to Baglioni with a true lover's perfect faith.

'Signor Professor,' said he, 'you were my father's friend – perchance, too, it is your purpose to act a friendly part towards his son. I would fain feel nothing towards you, save respect and deference. But I pray you to observe, Signor, that there is one subject on which we must not speak. You know not the Signora Beatrice. You cannot, therefore, estimate the wrong – the blasphemy, I may even say – that is offered to her character by a light or injurious word.'

'Giovanni! – my poor Giovanni!' answered the Professor, with a calm expression of pity, 'I know this wretched girl far better than yourself. You shall hear the truth in respect to the poisoner Rappaccini, and his poisonous daughter. Yes; poisonous as she is beautiful! Listen; for even should you do violence to my grey hairs, it shall not silence me. That old fable of the Indian woman has become a truth, by the deep and deadly science of Rappaccini, and in the person of the lovely Beatrice!'

Giovanni groaned and hid his face.

'Her father,' continued Baglioni, 'was not restrained by natural affection from offering up his child, in this horrible manner, as the victim of his insane zeal for science. For – let us do him justice – he is a true man of science as ever distilled his own heart in an alembic. What, then, will be your fate? Beyond a doubt, you are selected as the material of some new experiment. Perhaps the result is to be death – perhaps a fate more awful still! Rappaccini, with what he calls the interest of science before his eyes, will hesitate at nothing.'

'It is a dream!' muttered Giovanni to himself, 'surely it is a dream!'

'But,' resumed the Professor, 'be of good cheer, son of my friend! It is not yet too late for the rescue. Possibly, we may even succeed in bringing back this miserable child within the limits of ordinary nature, from which her father's madness has estranged her. Behold this little silver vase! It was wrought by the hands of the renowned Benvenuto Cellini, and is well worthy to be a love-gift to the fairest dame in Italy. But its contents are invaluable. One little sip of this antidote would have rendered the most virulent poisons of the Borgias innocuous. Doubt not that it will be as efficacious against those of Rappaccini. Bestow the vase, and the precious liquid within it, on your Beatrice, and hopefully await the result.'

Baglioni laid a small, exquisitely wrought silver phial on the table, and withdrew, leaving what he had said to produce its effect upon the young man's mind.

'We will thwart Rappaccini yet!' thought he, chuckling to himself, as he descended the stairs. 'But, let us confess the truth of him, he is a wonderful man! – a wonderful man indeed! A vile empiric, however, in his practice, and therefore not to be tolerated by those who respect the good old rules of the medical profession!'

Throughout Giovanni's whole acquaintance with Beatrice, he had occasionally, as we have said, been haunted by dark surmises as to her character. Yet, so thoroughly had she made herself felt by him as a simple, natural, most affectionate and guileless creature, that the image now held up by Professor Baglioni, looked as strange and incredible, as if it were not in accordance with his own original conception. True, there were ugly recollections connected with his first glimpses of the beautiful girl; he could not quite forget the bouquet that withered in her grasp, and the insect that perished amid the sunny air, by no ostensible agency, save the fragrance of her breath. These incidents, however, dissolving in the pure light of her character, had no longer the efficacy of facts, but were acknowledged as mistaken fantasies, by whatever testimony of the senses they might appear to be substantiated. There is something truer and more real, than what we can see with the eyes, and touch with the finger. On such better evidence, had Giovanni founded his confidence in Beatrice, though rather by the necessary force of her high attributes, than by any deep and generous faith, on his part. But, now, his spirit was incapable of sustaining itself at the height to which the early enthusiasm of passion had exalted it; he fell down, grovelling among earthly doubts, and defiled therewith the pure whiteness of Beatrice's image. Not that he gave her up; he did but distrust. He resolved to institute some decisive test that should satisfy him, once for all, whether there were those dreadful peculiarities in her physical nature, which could not be supposed to exist without some corresponding monstrosity of soul. His eyes, gazing down afar, might have deceived him as to the lizard, the insect, and the flowers. But if he could witness, at the distance of a few paces, the sudden blight of one fresh and healthful flower in Beatrice's hand, there would be room for no further question. With this idea, he hastened to the florist's and purchased a bouquet that was still gemmed with the morning dew-drops.

It was now the customary hour of his daily interview with Beatrice. Before descending into the garden, Giovanni failed not to look at his figure in the mirror; a vanity to be expected in a beautiful young man, yet, as displaying itself at that troubled and feverish moment, the token of a certain shallowness of feeling and insincerity of character. He did gaze, however, and said to himself, that his features had never before possessed so rich a grace, nor his eyes such vivacity, nor his cheeks so warm a hue of superabundant life.

'At least,' thought he, 'her poison has not yet insinuated itself into my system. I am no flower to perish in her grasp!'

With that thought, he turned his eyes on the bouquet, which he had never once laid aside from his hand. A thrill of indefinable horror shot through his frame, on perceiving that those dewy flowers were already beginning to droop; they wore the aspect of things that had been fresh and lovely, yesterday. Giovanni grew white as marble, and stood motionless before the mirror, staring at his own reflection there, as at the likeness of something frightful. He remembered Baglioni's remark about the fragrance that seemed to pervade the chamber. It must have been the poison in his breath! Then he shuddered – shuddered at himself! Recovering from his stupor, be began to watch, with curious eye, a spider that was busily at work, hanging its web from the antique cornice of the apartment, crossing and recrossing the artful system of interwoven lines, as vigorous and active a spider as ever dangled from an old ceiling. Giovanni bent towards the insect, and emitted a deep, long breath. The spider suddenly ceased its toil; the web vibrated with a tremor originating in the body of the small artizan. Again Giovanni sent forth a breath, deeper, longer, and imbued with a venomous feeling out of his heart; he knew not whether he were wicked or only desperate. The spider made a convulsive gripe with his limbs, and hung dead across the window.

'Accursed! Accursed!' muttered Giovanni, addressing himself. 'Hast thou grown so poisonous, that this deadly insect perishes by thy breath?'

At that moment, a rich, sweet voice came floating up from the garden: –

'Giovanni! Giovanni! It is past the hour! Why tarriest thou! Come down!'

'Yes,' muttered Giovanni again. 'She is the only being whom my breath may not slay! Would that it might!'

He rushed down, and in an instant, was standing before the bright and loving eyes of Beatrice. A moment ago, his wrath and despair had been so fierce that he could have desired nothing so much as to wither her by a glance. But, with her actual presence, there came influences which had too real an existence to be at once shaken off; recollections of the delicate and benign power of her feminine nature, which had so often enveloped him in a religious calm; recollections of many a holy and passionate outgush of her heart, when the pure fountain had been unsealed from its depths, and made visible in its transparency to his mental eye; recollections which, had Giovanni known how to estimate them, would have assured him that all this ugly mystery was but an earthly illusion, and that, whatever mist of evil might seem to have gathered over her, the real Beatrice was a heavenly angel. Incapable as he was of such high faith, still her presence had not utterly lost its magic. Giovanni's rage was quelled into an aspect of sullen insensibility. Beatrice, with a quick spiritual sense, immediately felt that there was a gulf of blackness between them, which neither he nor she could pass. They walked on together, sad and silent, and came thus to the marble fountain, and to its pool of water on the ground, in the midst of which grew the shrub that bore gem-like blossoms. Giovanni was affrighted at the eager enjoyment – the appetite, as it were – with which he found himself inhaling the fragrance of the flowers.

'Beatrice,' asked he abruptly, 'whence came this shrub?'

'My father created it,' answered she, with simplicity.

'Created it! created it!' repeated Giovanni. 'What mean you, Beatrice?'

'He is a man fearfully acquainted with the secrets of nature,' replied Beatrice; 'and, at the hour when I first drew breath, this plant sprang from the soil, the offspring of his science, of his intellect, while I was but his earthly child. Approach it not!' continued she, observing with terror that Giovanni was drawing nearer to the shrub. 'It has qualities that you little dream of. But I, dearest Giovanni, – I grew up and blossomed with the plant, and was nourished with its breath. It was my sister, and I loved it with a human affection: for – alas! hast thou not suspected it? there was an awful doom.'

Here Giovanni frowned so darkly upon her that Beatrice paused and trembled. But her faith in his tenderness reassured her, and made her blush that she had doubted for an instant.

'There was an awful doom,' she continued, – 'the effect of my father's fatal love of science – which estranged me from all society of my kind. Until Heaven sent thee, dearest Giovanni, Oh! how lonely was thy poor Beatrice!'

'Was it a hard doom?' asked Giovanni, fixing his eyes upon her.

'Only of late have I known how hard it was,' answered she tenderly. 'Oh, yes; but my heart was torpid, and therefore quiet.'

Giovanni's rage broke forth from his sullen gloom like a lightning-flash out of a dark cloud.

'Accursed one!' cried he, with venomous scorn and anger. 'And finding thy solitude wearisome, thou hast severed me, likewise, from all the warmth of life, and enticed me into thy region of unspeakable horror!'

'Giovanni!' exclaimed Beatrice, turning her large bright eyes upon his face. The force of his words had not found its way into her mind; she was merely thunder-struck.

'Yes, poisonous thing!' repeated Giovanni, beside himself with passion. 'Thou hast done it! Thou hast blasted me! Thou hast filled my veins with poison! Thou hast made me as hateful, as ugly, as loathsome and deadly a creature as thyself, – a world's wonder of hideous monstrosity! Now – if our breath be happily as fatal to ourselves as to all others – let us join our lips in one kiss on unutterable hatred, and so die!'

'What has befallen me?' murmured Beatrice, with a low moan out of her heart. 'Holy Virgin pity me, a poor heart-broken child!'

'Thou! Dost thou pray?' cried Giovanni, still with the same fiendish scorn.

'Thy very prayers, as they come from thy lips, taint the atmosphere with death. Yes, yes; let us pray! Let us to church, and dip our fingers in the holy water at the portal! They that come after us will perish as by a pestilence. Let us sign crosses in the air! It will be scattering curses abroad in the likeness of holy symbols!'

'Giovanni,' said Beatrice calmly, for her grief was beyond passion, 'why dost thou join thyself with me thus in those terrible words? I, it is true, am the horrible thing thou namest me. But thou! – what hast thou to do, save with one other shudder at my hideous misery, to go forth out of the garden and mingle with thy race, and forget that there ever crawled on earth such a monster as poor Beatrice?'

'Dost thou pretend ignorance?' asked Giovanni, scowling upon her. 'Behold! This power have I gained from the pure daughter of Rappaccini!'

There was a swarm of summer-insects flitting through the air, in search of the food promised by the flower-odors of the fatal garden. They circled round Giovanni's head, and were evidently attracted towards him by the same influence which had drawn them, for an instant, within the sphere of several of the shrubs. He sent forth a breath among them, and smiled bitterly at Beatrice, as at least a score of the insects fell dead upon the ground.

'I see it! I see it!' shrieked Beatrice. 'It is my father's fatal science! No, no, Giovanni; it was not I! Never, never! I dreamed only to love thee, and be with thee a little time, and so to let thee pass away, leaving but thine image in mine heart. For, Giovanni – believe it – though my body be nourished with poison, my spirit is God's creature, and craves love as its daily food. But my father! – he has united us in this fearful sympathy. Yes; spurn me! – tread upon me! – kill me! Oh, what is death, after such words as thine? But it was not I! Not for a world of bliss would I have done it!'

Giovanni's passion had exhausted itself in its outburst from his lips. There now came across him a sense, mournful, and not without tenderness, of the intimate and peculiar relationship between Beatrice and himself. They stood, as it were, in an utter solitude, which would be made none the less solitary by the densest throng of human life. Ought not, then, the desert of humanity around them to press this insulated pair closer together? If they should be cruel to one another, who was there to be kind to them? Besides, thought Giovanni, might there not still be a hope of his returning within the limits of ordinary nature, and leading Beatrice – the redeemed Beatrice – by the hand? Oh, weak, and selfish, and unworthy spirit, that could dream of an earthly union and earthly happiness as possible, after such deep love had been so bitterly wronged as was Beatrice's love by Giovanni's blighting words! No, no; there could be no such hope. She must pass heavily, with that broken heart, across the borders of Time – she must bathe her hurts in some fount of Paradise, and forget her grief in the light of immortality – and *there* be well!

But Giovanni did not know it.

'Dear Beatrice,' said he, approaching her, while she shrank away, as always at his approach, but now with a different impulse – 'dearest Beatrice, our fate is not yet so desperate. Behold! There is a medicine, potent, as a wise physician has assured me, and almost divine in its efficacy. It is composed of ingredients the most opposite to those by which thy awful father has brought this calamity upon thee and me. It is distilled of blessed herbs. Shall we not quaff it together, and thus be purified from evil?'

'Give it me!' said Beatrice, extending her hand to receive the little silver phial which Giovanni took from his bosom. She added, with a peculiar emphasis: 'I will drink – but do thou await the result.'

She put Baglioni's antidote to her lips; and, at the same moment, the figure of Rappaccini emerged from the portal, and came slowly towards the marble fountain. As he drew near, the pale man of science seemed to gaze with a triumphant expression at the beautiful youth and maiden, as might an artist who should spend his life achieving a picture or a group of statuary, and finally be satisfied with his success. He paused – his bent form grew erect with conscious power, he spread out his hands over them, in the attitude of a father imploring a blessing upon his children. But those were the same hands that had thrown poison into the stream of their lives! Giovanni trembled. Beatrice shuddered nervously, and pressed her hand upon her heart.

'My daughter,' said Rappaccini, 'thou art no longer lonely in the world! Pluck one of those precious gems from thy sister shrub, and bid thy bridegroom wear it in his bosom. It will not harm him now! My science, and the sympathy between thee and him, have so wrought within his system, that he now stands apart from common men, as thou dost, daughter of my pride and triumph, from ordinary women. Pass on, then, through the world, most dear to one another, and dreadful to all besides!'

'My father,' said Beatrice, feebly – and still, as she spoke, she kept her hand upon her heart – 'wherefore didst thou inflict this miserable doom upon thy child?'

'Miserable!' exclaimed Rappaccini. 'What mean you, foolish girl? Dost thou deem it misery to be endowed with marvellous gifts, against which no power nor strength could avail an enemy? Misery, to be able to quell the mightiest with a breath? Misery, to be as terrible as thou art beautiful? Wouldst thou, then, have preferred the condition of a weak woman, exposed to all evil, and capable of none?'

'I would fain have been loved, not feared,' murmured Beatrice, sinking down upon the ground. – 'But now it matters not; I am going, father, where the evil, which thou hast striven to mingle with my being, will pass away like a dream – like the fragrance of these poisonous flowers, which will no longer taint my breath among the flowers of Eden. Farewell, Giovanni! Thy words of hatred are like lead within my heart – but they, too, will fall away as I ascend. Oh, was there not, from the first, more poison in thy nature than in mine?'

To Beatrice – so radically had her earthly part been wrought upon by Rappaccini's skill – as poison had been life, so the powerful antidote was death. And thus the poor victim of man's ingenuity and of thwarted nature, and of the fatality that attends all such efforts of perverted wisdom, perished there, at the feet of her father and Giovanni. Just at that moment, Professor Pietro Baglioni looked forth from the window, and called loudly, in a tone of triumph mixed with horror, to the thunder-stricken man of science:

'Rappaccini! Rappaccini! And is *this* the upshot of your experiment?'

EDGAR ALLAN POE
1809-1849

Edgar Allan Poe was born in 1809 in Boston, Massachusetts. Orphaned at the age of three, he was brought up by a rich but unsympathetic foster father in Richmond, Virginia. After attending the University of Virginia, Poe went on to the military academy at West Point, but was expelled because he neglected his studies in favor of poetry and short story writing. Fame came early to Poe with his first published tale, 'Ms Found in a Bottle', but tragedy also struck as his foster father disowned him and his young wife died only a short time after their marriage. In spite of the superb quality and remarkable quantity of work Poe produced in his short lifetime, his undoubted literary genius was only recognized in the latter half of the nineteenth century and his reputation has, if anything, grown over the 135 years since his death.

The following stories represent Poe's creative power at its very best, reaching the heights of mystery, suspense and subtle horror. 'The Fall of the House of Usher' first appeared in *Burton's Gentleman's Magazine* in 1839; 'The Gold Bug' was first published in a Philadelphia magazine in 1843 and won a prize of $100 from a literary foundation. 'The Pit and the Pendulum' and 'The Cask of Amontillado' were first published in 1845 and 1846 respectively.

The Fall of
the House of Usher

Son cœur est un luth suspendu;
Sitôt qu'on le touche il résonne.

—*De Béranger*

DURING THE WHOLE OF A dull, dark, and soundless day in the autumn of the year, when the clouds hung oppressively low in the heavens, I had been passing alone, on horseback, through a singularly dreary tract of country, and at length found myself, as the shades of the evening drew on, within view of the melancholy House of Usher. I know not how it was—but, with the first glimpse of the building, a sense of insufferable gloom pervaded my spirit. I say insufferable; for the feeling was unrelieved by any of that half-pleasurable, because poetic, sentiment with which the mind usually receives even the sternest natural images of the desolate or terrible. I looked upon the scene before me—upon the mere house, and the simple landscape features of the domain—upon the bleak walls—upon the vacant eye-like windows—upon a few rank sedges—and upon a few white trunks of decayed trees—with an utter depression of soul which I can compare to no earthly sensation more properly than to the after-dream of the reveller upon opium—the bitter lapse into every-day life—the hideous dropping off of the veil. There was an iciness, a sinking, a sickening of the heart—an unredeemed dreariness of thought which no goading of the imagination could torture into aught of the sublime. What was it—I paused to think—what was it that so unnerved me in the contemplation of the House of Usher? It was a mystery all insoluble; nor could I grapple with the shadowy fancies that crowded upon me as I pondered. I was forced to fall back upon the unsatisfactory conclusion, that while, beyond doubt, there *are* combinations of very simple natural objects which have the power of thus affecting us, still the analysis of this power lies among considerations beyond our depth. It was possible, I reflected, that a mere different arrangement of the particulars of the scene, of the details of the picture, would be sufficient to modify, or perhaps to annihilate its capacity for sorrowful impression; and, acting upon this idea, I reined my horse to the precipitous brink of a black and lurid tarn that lay in unruffled lustre by the dwelling, and gazed down—but with a shudder even more thrilling than before—upon the remodelled and inverted images of the gray sedge, and the ghastly tree-stems, and the vacant and eye-like windows.

Nevertheless, in this mansion of gloom I now proposed to myself a sojourn of some weeks. Its proprietor, Roderick Usher, had been one of my boon companions in boyhood; but many years had elapsed since our last meeting. A letter, however, had lately reached me in a distant part of the country—a letter from him—which, in its wildly importunate nature, had admitted of no other than a personal reply. The MS. gave evidence of nervous agitation. The writer spoke of acute bodily illness—of a mental disorder which oppressed him—and of an earnest desire to see me, as his best and indeed his only personal friend, with a view of attempting, by the cheerfulness of my society, some alleviation of his malady. It was the manner in which all this, and much more, was said—it was the apparent *heart* that went with his request—which allowed me no room for hesitation; and I accordingly obeyed forthwith what I still considered a very singular summons.

Although, as boys, we had been even intimate associates, yet I really knew little of my friend. His reserve had been always excessive and habitual. I was aware, however, that his very ancient family had been noted, time out of mind, for a peculiar sensibility of temperament, displaying itself, through long ages, in many works of exalted art, and manifested, of late, in repeated deeds of munificent yet unobtrusive charity, as well as in a passionate devotion to the intricacies, perhaps even more than to the orthodox and easily recognizable beauties, of musical science. I had learned, too, the very remarkable fact, that the stem of the Usher race, all time-honored as it was, had put forth, at no period, any enduring branch; in other words, that the entire family lay in the direct line of descent, and had always, with very trifling and very temporary variation, so lain. It was this deficiency, I considered, while running over in thought the perfect keeping of the character of the premises with the accredited character of the people, and while speculating upon the possible influence which the one, in the long lapse of centuries, might have exercised upon the other—it was this deficiency, perhaps, of collateral issue, and the consequent undeviating transmission, from sire to son, of the patrimony with the name, which had, at length, so identified the two as to merge the original title of the estate in the quaint and equivocal appellation of the 'House of Usher'—an appellation which seemed to include, in the minds of the peasantry who used it, both the family and the family mansion.

I have said that the sole effect of my somewhat childish experiment—that of looking down within the tarn—had been to deepen the first singular impression. There can be no doubt that the consciousness of the rapid increase of my superstition—for why should I not so term it?—served mainly to accelerate the increase itself. Such, I have long known, is the paradoxical law of all sentiments having terror as a basis. And it might have been for this reason only, that, when I again uplifted my eyes to the house itself, from its image in the pool, there grew in my mind a strange fancy—a fancy so ridiculous, indeed, that I but mention it to show the vivid force of the sensations which oppressed me. I had so worked upon my imagination as really to believe that about the whole mansion and domain there hung an atmosphere peculiar to themselves and their immediate vicinity—an atmosphere which had no affinity with the air of heaven, but which had reeked up from the decayed trees, and the gray wall, and the silent tarn—a pestilent and mystic vapor, dull, sluggish, faintly discernible, and leaden-hued.

Shaking off from my spirit what *must* have been a dream, I scanned more narrowly the real aspect of the building. Its principal feature seemed to be that of an excessive antiquity. The discoloration of ages had been great. Minute fungi overspread the whole exterior, hanging in a fine tangled web-work from the eaves. Yet all this was apart from any extraordinary dilapidation. No portion of the masonry had fallen; and there appeared to be a wild inconsistency between its still perfect adaptation of parts, and the crumbling condition of the individual stones. In this there was much that reminded me of the specious totality of old wood-work which has rotted for long years in some neglected vault, with no disturbance from the breath of the external air. Beyond this indication of extensive decay, however, the fabric gave little token of instability. Perhaps the eye of a scrutinizing observer might have discovered a barely perceptible fissure, which, extending from the roof of the building in front, made its way down the wall in a zigzag direction, until it became lost in the sullen waters of the tarn.

Noticing these things, I rode over a short causeway to the house. A servant in waiting took my horse, and I entered the Gothic archway of the hall. A valet, of stealthy step, thence conducted me, in silence, through many dark and intricate passages in my progress to the *studio* of his master. Much that I encountered on the way contributed, I know not how, to heighten the vague sentiments of which I have already spoken. While the objects around me— while the carvings of the ceilings, the sombre tapestries of the walls, the ebon blackness of the floors, and the phantasmagoric armorial trophies which rattled as I strode, were but matters to which, or to such as which, I had been accustomed from my infancy—while I hesitated not to acknowledge how familiar was all this—I still wondered to find how unfamiliar were the fancies which ordinary images were stirring up. On one of the staircases, I met the physician of the family. His countenance, I thought, wore a mingled expression of low cunning and perplexity. He accosted me with trepidation and passed on. The valet now threw open a door and ushered me into the presence of his master.

The room in which I found myself was very large and lofty. The windows were long, narrow, and pointed, and at so vast a distance from the black oaken floor as to be altogether inaccessible from within. Feeble gleams of encrimsoned light made their way through the trellissed panes, and served to render sufficiently distinct the more prominent objects around; the eye, however, struggled in vain to reach the remoter angles of the chamber, or the recesses of the vaulted and fretted ceiling. Dark draperies hung upon the walls. The general furniture was profuse, comfortless, antique, and tattered. Many books and musical instruments lay scattered about, but failed to give any vitality to the scene. I felt that I breathed an atmosphere of sorrow. An air of stern, deep, and irredeemable gloom hung over and pervaded all.

Upon my entrance, Usher arose from a sofa on which he had been lying at full length, and greeted me with a vivacious warmth which had much in it, I at first thought, of an overdone cordiality—of the constrained effort of the *ennuyé* man of the world. A glance, however, at his countenance convinced me of his perfect sincerity. We sat down; and for some moments, while he spoke not, I gazed upon him with a feeling half of pity, half of awe. Surely, man had never before so terribly altered, in so brief a period, as had Roderick Usher! It was with difficulty that I could bring myself to admit the identity of the wan being before me with the companion of my early boyhood. Yet the character of his face had been at all times remarkable. A cadaverousness of complexion; an eye large, liquid, and luminous beyond comparison; lips somewhat thin and very pallid but of a surpassingly beautiful curve; a nose of a delicate Hebrew model, but with a breadth of nostril unusual in similar formations; a finely moulded chin, speaking, in its want of prominence, of a want of moral energy; hair of a more than web-like softness and tenuity;—these features, with an inordinate expansion above the regions of the temple, made up altogether a countenance not easily to be forgotten. And now in the mere exaggeration of the prevailing character of these features, and of the expression they were wont to convey, lay so much of change that I doubted to whom I spoke. The now ghastly pallor of the skin, and the now miraculous lustre of the eye, above all things startled and even awed me. The silken hair, too, had been suffered to grow all unheeded, and as, in its wild gossamer texture, it floated rather than fell about the face, I could not, even with effort, connect its Arabesque expression with any idea of simple humanity.

In the manner of my friend I was at once struck with an incoherence—an inconsistency; and I soon found this to arise from a series of feeble and futile struggles to overcome an habitual trepidancy—an excessive nervous agitation. For something of this nature I had indeed been prepared, no less by his letter, than by reminiscences of certain boyish traits, and by conclusions deduced from his peculiar physical confirmation and temperament. His action was alternately vivacious and sullen. His voice varied rapidly from a tremulous indecision (when the animal spirits seemed utterly in abeyance) to that species of energetic concision—that abrupt, weighty, unhurried, and hollow-sounding enunciation—that leaden, self-balanced, and perfectly modulated guttural utterance, which may be observed in the lost drunkard, or the irreclaimable eater of opium, during the periods of his most intense excitement.

It was thus that he spoke of the object of my visit, of his earnest desire to see me, and of the solace he expected me to afford him. He entered, at some length, into what he conceived to be the nature of his malady. It was, he said, a constitutional and a family evil, and one for which he despaired to find a remedy—a mere nervous affection, he immediately added, which would undoubtedly soon pass off. It displayed itself in a host of unnatural sensations. Some of these, as he detailed them, interested and bewildered me; although, perhaps, the terms and the general manner of their narration had their weight. He suffered much from a morbid acuteness of the senses; the most insipid food was alone endurable; he could wear only garments of certain texture; the odors of all flowers were oppressive; his eyes were tortured by even a faint light; and there were but peculiar sounds, and these from stringed instruments, which did not inspire him with horror.

To an anomalous species of terror I found him a bounden slave. 'I shall perish,' said he, 'I *must* perish in this deplorable folly. Thus, thus, and not otherwise, shall I be lost. I dread the events of the future, not in themselves, but in their results. I shudder at the thought of any, even the most trivial, incident, which may operate upon this intolerable agitation of soul. I have, indeed, no abhorrence of danger, except in its absolute effect—in terror. In this unnerved, in this pitiable, condition I feel that the period will sooner or later arrive when I must abandon life and reason together, in some struggle with the grim phantasm, FEAR.'

I learned, moreover, at intervals, and through broken and equivocal hints, another singular feature of his mental condition. He was enchained by certain superstitious impressions in regard to the dwelling which he tenanted, and whence, for many years, he had never ventured forth—in regard to an influence whose supposititious force was conveyed in terms too shadowy here to be re-stated—an influence which some peculiarities in the mere form and substance of his family mansion had, by dint of long sufferance, he said, obtained over his spirit—an effect which the *physique* of the gray walls and turrets, and of the dim tarn into which they all looked down, had, at length, brought about upon the *morale* of his existence.

He admitted, however, although with hesitation, that much of the peculiar gloom which thus afflicted him could be traced to a more natural and far more palpable origin—to the severe and long-continued illness—indeed to the evidently approaching dissolution—of a tenderly beloved sister, his sole companion for long years, his last and only relative on earth. 'Her decease,' he said, with a bitterness which I can never forget, 'would leave him (him, the hopeless and the frail) the last of the ancient race of the Ushers.' While he spoke, the lady Madeline (for so was she called) passed through a remote portion of the apartment, and, without having noticed my presence, disappeared. I regarded her with an utter astonishment not unmingled with dread; and yet I found it impossible to account for such feelings. A sensation of stupor oppressed me as my eyes followed her retreating steps. When a door, at length, closed upon her, my glance sought instinctively and eagerly the countenance of the brother; but he had buried his face in his hands, and I could only perceive that a far more than ordinary wanness had overspread the emaciated fingers through which trickled many passionate tears.

The disease of the lady Madeline had long baffled the skill of her physicians. A settled apathy, a gradual wasting away of the person, and frequent although transient affections of a partially cataleptical character were the unusual diagnosis. Hitherto she had steadily borne up against the pressure of her malady, and had not betaken herself finally to bed; but on the closing in of the evening of my arrival at the house, she succumbed (as her brother told me at night with inexpressible agitation) to the prostrating power of the destroyer; and I learned that the glimpse I had obtained of her person would thus probably be the last I should obtain—that the lady, at least while living, would be seen by me no more.

For several days ensuing, her name was unmentioned by either Usher or myself; and during this period I was busied in earnest endeavors to alleviate the melancholy of my friend. We painted and read together, or I listened, as if in a dream, to the wild improvisations of his speaking guitar. And thus, as a closer and still closer intimacy admitted me more unreservedly into the recesses of his spirit, the more bitterly did I perceive the futility of all attempt at cheering a mind from which darkness, as if an inherent positive quality, poured forth upon all objects of the moral and physical universe in one unceasing radiation of gloom.

I shall ever bear about me a memory of the many solemn hours I thus spent alone with the master of the House of Usher. Yet I should fail in any attempt to convey an idea of the exact character of the studies, or of the occupations, in which he involved me, or led me the way. An excited and highly distempered ideality threw a sulphureous lustre over all. His long improvised dirges will ring forever in my ears. Among other things, I hold painfully in mind a certain singular perversion and amplification of the wild air of the last waltz of Von

Weber. From the paintings over which his elaborate fancy brooded, and which grew, touch by touch, into vaguenesses at which I shuddered the more thrillingly, because I shuddered knowing not why—from these paintings (vivid as their images now are before me) I would in vain endeavor to educe more than a small portion which should lie within the compass of merely written words. By the utter simplicity, by the nakedness of his designs, he arrested and overawed attention. If ever mortal painted an idea, that mortal was Roderick Usher. For me at least, in the circumstances then surrounding me, there arose out of the pure abstractions which the hypochondriac contrived to throw upon his canvas, an intensity of intolerable awe, no shadow of which felt I ever yet in the contemplation of the certainly glowing yet too concrete reveries of Fuseli.

One of the phantasmagoric conceptions of my friend, partaking not so rigidly of the spirit of abstraction, may be shadowed forth, although feebly, in words. A small picture presented the interior of an immensely long and rectangular vault or tunnel, with low walls, smooth, white, and without interruption or device. Certain accessory points of the design served well to convey the idea that this excavation lay at an exceeding depth below the surface of the earth. No outlet was observed in any portion of its vast extent, and no torch or other artificial source of light was discernible; yet a flood of intense rays rolled throughout, and bathed the whole in a ghastly and inappropriate splendor.

I have just spoken of that morbid condition of the auditory nerve which rendered all music intolerable to the sufferer, with the exception of certain effects of stringed instruments. It was, perhaps, the narrow limits to which he thus confined himself upon the guitar which gave birth, in great measure, to the fantastic character of his performances. But the fervid *facility* of his *impromptus* could not be so accounted for. They must have been, and were, in the notes, as well as in the words of his wild fantasias (for he not unfrequently accompanied himself with rhymed verbal improvisations), the result of that intense mental collectedness and concentration to which I have previously alluded as observable only in particular moments of the highest artificial excitement. The words of one of these rhapsodies I have easily remembered. I was, perhaps, the more forcibly impressed with it as he gave it, because, in the under or mystic current of its meaning, I fancied that I perceived, and for the first time, a full consciousness on the part of Usher of the tottering of his lofty reason upon her throne. The verses, which were entitled 'The Haunted Palace,' ran very nearly, if not accurately, thus:—

I

In the greenest of our valleys,
    By good angels tenanted,
Once a fair and stately palace—
    Radiant palace—reared its head.
In the monarch Thought's dominion!
    It stood there!
Never seraph spread a pinion
    Over fabric half so fair.

II

Banners yellow, glorious, golden,
   On its roof did float and flow
(This—all this—was in the olden
   Time long ago);
And every gentle air that dallied,
   In that sweet day,
Along the ramparts plumed and pallid,
   A winged odor went away.

III

Wanderers in that happy valley
   Through two luminous windows saw
Spirits moving musically
   to a lute's well-tuned law;
Round about a throne, where sitting
   (Porphyrogene!)
In state his glory well befitting,
   The ruler of the realm was seen.

IV

And all with pearl and ruby glowing
   Was the fair palace door,
Through which came flowing, flowing, flowing
   And sparkling evermore,
A troop of Echoes whose sweet duty
   Was but to sing,
In voices of surpassing beauty,
   The wit and wisdom of their king.

V

But evil things, in robes of sorrow,
   Assailed the monarch's high estate;
(Ah, let us mourn, for never morrow
   Shall dawn upon him, desolate!)
And, round about his home, the glory
   That blushed and bloomed
Is but a dim-remembered story
   Of the old time entombed.

VI

And travellers now within that valley,
   Through the red-litten windows see
Vast forms that move fantastically
   To a discordant melody;
While, like a rapid ghastly river,
   Through the pale door;
A hideous throng rush out forever,
   And laugh—but smile no more.

I well remember that suggestions arising from this ballad led us into a train of thought wherein there became manifest an opinion of Usher's which I mention not so much on account of its novelty (for other men[1] have thought thus), as on account of the pertinacity with which he maintained it. This opinion, in its general form, was that of the sentience of all vegetable things. But, in his disordered fancy, the idea had assumed a more daring character, and trespassed, under certain conditions, upon the kingdom of inorganization. I lack words to express the full extent, or the earnest *abandon* of his persuasion. The belief, however, was connected (as I have previously hinted) with the gray stones of the home of his forefathers. The conditions of the sentence had been here, he imagined, fulfilled in the method of collocation of these stones—in the order of their arrangement, as well as in that of the many *fungi* which overspread them, and of the decayed trees which stood around— above all, in the long undisturbed endurance of this arrangement, and in its reduplication in the still waters of the tarn. Its evidence—the evidence of the sentience—was to be seen, he said (and I here started as he spoke), in the gradual yet certain condensation of an atmosphere of their own about the waters and the walls. The result was discoverable, he added, in that silent yet importunate and terrible influence which for centuries had moulded the destinies of his family, and which made *him* what I now saw him—what he was. Such opinions need no comment, and I will make none.

Our books—the books which, for years, had formed no small portion of the mental existence of the invalid—were, as might be supposed, in strict keeping with this character of phantasm. We pored together over such works as the 'Ververt et Chartreuse' of Gresset; the 'Belphegor' of Machiavelli; the 'Heaven and Hell' of Swedenborg; the 'Subterranean Voyage of Nicholas Klimm' of Holberg; the 'Chiromancy' of Robert Flud, of Jean D'Indaginé, and of Dela Chambre; the 'Journey into the Blue Distance of Tieck'; and the 'City of the Sun of Campanella.' One favorite volume was a small octavo edition of the 'Directorium Inquisitorium,' by the Dominican Eymeric de Gironne; and there were passages in Pomponius Mela, about the old African Satyrs and Œgipans, over which Usher would sit dreaming for hours. His chief delight, however, was found in the perusal of an exceedingly rare and curious book in quarto Gothic—the manual of a forgotten church—the *Vigiliœ Mortuorum secundum Chorum Ecclesiœ Maguntinœ.*

I could not help thinking of the wild ritual of this work, and of its probable influence upon the hypochondriac, when, one evening, having informed me abruptly that the lady Madeline was no more, he stated his intention of preserving her corpse for a fortnight (previously to its final interment), in one of the numerous vaults within the main walls of the building. The worldly reason, however, assigned for this singular proceeding, was one which I did not feel at liberty to dispute. The brother had been led to his resolution (so he told me) by consideration of the unusual character of the malady of the deceased, of certain obtrusive and eager inquiries on the part of her medical men, and of the remote and exposed situation of the burial-ground of the family. I will not deny that when I called to mind the sinister countenance of the person whom I met upon the staircase, on the day of my arrival at the

[1]Watson, Dr. Percival, Spallanzani, and especially the Bishop of Landaff.—See 'Chemical Essays,' vol. v.

house, I had no desire to oppose what I regarded as at best but a harmless, and by no means an unnatural, precaution.

At the request of Usher, I personally aided him in the arrangements for the temporary entombment. The body having been encoffined, we two alone bore it to its rest. The vault in which we placed it (and which had been so long unopened that our torches, half smothered in its oppressive atmosphere, gave us little opportunity for investigation) was small, damp, and entirely without means of admission for light; lying, at great depth, immediately beneath that portion of the building in which was my own sleeping apartment. It had been used, apparently, in remote feudal times, for the worst purposes of a donjon-keep, and, in later days, as a place of deposit for powder, or some other highly combustible substance, as a portion of its floor, and the whole interior of a long archway through which we reached it, were carefully sheathed with copper. The door, of massive iron, had been, also, similarly protected. Its immense weight caused an unusually sharp, grating sound, as it moved upon its hinges.

Having deposited our mournful burden upon tressels within this region of horror, we partially turned aside the yet unscrewed lid of the coffin, and looked upon the face of the tenant. A striking similitude between the brother and sister now first arrested my attention; and Usher, divining, perhaps, my thoughts, murmured out some few words from which I learned that the deceased and himself had been twins, and that sympathies of a scarcely intelligible nature had always existed between them. Our glances, however, rested not long upon the dead—for we could not regard her unawed. The disease which had thus entombed the lady in the maturity of youth, had left, as usual in all maladies of a strictly cataleptical character, the mockery of a faint blush upon the bosom and the face, and that suspiciously lingering smile upon the lip which is so terrible in death. We replaced and screwed down the lid, and, having secured the door of iron, made our way, with toil, into the scarcely less gloomy apartments of the upper portion of the house.

And now, some days of bitter grief having elapsed, an observable change came over the features of the mental disorder of my friend. His ordinary manner had vanished. His ordinary occupations were neglected or forgotten. He roamed from chamber to chamber with hurried, unequal, and objectless step. The pallor of his countenance had assumed, if possible, a more ghastly hue—but the luminousness of his eye had utterly gone out. The once occasional huskiness of his tone was heard no more; and a tremulous quaver, as if of extreme terror, habitually characterized his utterance. There were times, indeed, when I thought his unceasingly agitated mind was laboring with some oppressive secret, to divulge which he struggled for the necessary courage. At times, again, I was obliged to resolve all into the mere inexplicable vagaries of madness, for I beheld him gazing upon vacancy for long hours, in an attitude of the profoundest attention, as if listening to some imaginary sound. It was no wonder that his condition terrified—that it infected me. I felt creeping upon me, by slow yet certain degrees, the wild influences of his own fantastic yet impressive superstitions.

It was, especially, upon retiring to bed late in the night of the seventh or eighth day after the placing of the lady Madeline within the donjon, that I experienced the full power of such feelings. Sleep came not near my couch—while the hours waned and waned away. I struggled to reason off the nervousness which had dominion over me. I endeavored to believe that much, if not all of what I felt, was due to the bewildering influence of the gloomy furniture of the room—of the dark and tattered draperies, which, tortured into motion by the breath of a rising tempest, swayed fitfully to and fro upon the walls, and rustled uneasily about the decorations of the bed. But my efforts were fruitless. An irrepressible tremor gradually pervaded my frame; and, at length, there sat upon my very heart an incubus of utterly causeless alarm. Shaking this off with a gasp and a struggle, I uplifted myself upon the pillows, and, peering earnestly within the intense darkness of the chamber, hearkened —I know not why, except that an instinctive spirit prompted me—to certain low and indefinite sounds which came, through the pauses of the storm, at long intervals, I knew not whence. Overpowered by an intense sentiment of horror, unaccountable yet unendurable, I threw on my clothes with haste (for I felt that I should sleep no more during the night), and endeavored into arouse myself from the pitiable condition into which I had fallen, by pacing rapidly to and fro through the apartment.

I had taken but few turns in this manner, when a light step on an adjoining staircase arrested my attention. I presently recognized it as that of Usher. In an instant afterward he rapped, with a gentle touch, at my door, and entered, bearing a lamp. His countenance was, as usual, cadaverously wan—but, moreover, there was a species of mad hilarity in his eyes—an evidently restrained *hysteria* in his whole demeanor. His air appalled me—but any thing was preferable to the solitude which I had so long endured, and I even welcomed his presence as a relief.

'And you have not seen it?' he said abruptly, after having stared about him for some moments in silence—'you have not then seen it?—but, stay! you shall.' Thus speaking, and having carefully shaded his lamp, he hurried to one of the casements, and threw it freely open to the storm.

The impetuous fury of the entering gust nearly lifted us from our feet. It was, indeed, a tempestuous yet sternly beautiful night, and one wildly singular in its terror and its beauty. A whirlwind had apparently collected its force in our vicinity; for there were frequent and violent alterations in the direction of the wind; and the exceeding density of the clouds (which hung so low as to press upon the turrets of the house) did not prevent our perceiving the life-like velocity with which they flew careering from all points against each other, without passing away into the distance. I say that even their exceeding density did not prevent our perceiving this—yet we had no glimpse of the moon or stars, nor was there any flashing forth of the lightning. But the under surfaces of the huge masses of agitated vapor, as well as all terrestrial objects immediately around us, were glowing in the unnatural light of a faintly luminous and distinctly visible gaseous exhalation which hung about and enshrouded the mansion.

'You must not—you shall not behold this!' said I, shuddering, to Usher, as I led him, with a gentle violence, from the window to a seat. 'These appearances, which bewilder you, are merely electrical phenomena not uncommon—or it may be that they have their ghastly origin in the rank miasma of the tarn. Let us close this casement;—the air is chilling and dangerous to your frame. Here is one of your favorite romances. I will read, and you shall listen:—and so we will pass away this terrible night together.'

The antique volume which I had taken up was the 'Mad Trist' of Sir Launcelot Canning; but I had called it a favorite of Usher's more in sad jest than in earnest; for, in truth, there is little in its uncouth and unimaginative prolixity which could have had interest for the lofty and spiritual ideality of my friend. It was, however, the only book immediately at hand; and I indulged a vague hope that the excitement which now agitated the hypochondriac, might find relief (for the history of mental disorder is full of similar anomalies) even in the extremeness of the folly which I should read. Could I have judged, indeed, by the wild overstrained air of vivacity with which he hearkened, or apparently hearkened, to the words of the tale, I might well have congratulated myself upon the success of my design.

I had arrived at that well-known portion of the story where Ethelred, the hero of the Trist, having sought in vain for peaceable admission into the dwelling of the hermit, proceeds to make good an entrance by force. Here, it will be remembered, the words of the narrative run thus:

'And Ethelred, who was by nature of a doughty heart, and who was now mighty withal, on account of the powerfulness of the wine which he had drunken, waited no longer to hold parley with the hermit, who, in sooth, was of an obstinate and maliceful turn, but, feeling the rain upon his shoulders, and fearing the rising of the tempest, uplifted his mace outright, and, with blows, made quickly room in the plankings of the door for his gauntleted hand; and now pulling therewith sturdily, he so cracked, and ripped, and tore all asunder, that the noise of the dry and hollow-sounding wood alarumed and reverberated throughout the forest.'

At the termination of this sentence I started and, for a moment, paused; for it appeared to me (although I at once concluded that my excited fancy had deceived me)—it appeared to me that, from some very remote portion of the mansion, there came, indistinctly to my ears, what might have been, in its exact similarity of character, the echo (but a stifled and dull one certainly) of the very cracking and ripping sound which Sir Launcelot had so particularly described. It was, beyond doubt, the coincidence alone which had arrested my attention; for, amid the rattling of the sashes of the casements, and the ordinary commingled noises of the still increasing storm, the sound, in itself, had nothing, surely, which should have interested or disturbed me. I continued the story:

'But the good champion Ethelred, now entering within the door, was sore enraged and amazed to perceive no signal of the maliceful hermit; but, in the stead thereof, a dragon of a scaly and prodigious demeanor, and of a fiery tongue, which sate in guard before a palace of gold, with a floor of silver; and upon the wall there hung a shield of shining brass with this legend enwritten—

> Who entereth herein, a conqueror hath bin;
> Who slayeth the dragon, the shield he shall win.

And Ethelred uplifted his mace, and struck upon the head of the dragon, which fell before him, and gave up his pesty breath, with a shriek so horrid and harsh, and withal so piercing, that Ethelred had fain to close his ears with his hands against the dreadful noise of it, the like whereof was never before heard.'

Here again I paused abruptly, and now with a feeling of wild amazement—

for there could be no doubt whatever that, in this instance, I did actually hear (although from what direction it proceeded I found it impossible to say) a low and apparently distant, but harsh, protracted, and most unusual screaming or grating sound—the exact counterpart of what my fancy had already conjured up for the dragon's unnatural shriek as described by the romancer.

Oppressed, as I certainly was, upon the occurrence of this second and most extraordinary coincidence, by a thousand conflicting sensations, in which wonder and extreme terror were predominant, I still retained sufficient presence of mind to avoid exciting, by any observation, the sensitive nervousness of my companion. I was by no means certain that he had noticed the sounds in question; although, assuredly, a strange alteration had, during the last few minutes, taken place in his demeanor. From a position fronting my own, he had gradually brought round his chair, so as to sit with his face to the door of the chamber; and thus I could but partially perceive his features, although I saw that his lips trembled as if he were murmuring inaudibly. His head had dropped upon his breast—yet I knew that he was not asleep, from the wide and rigid opening of the eye as I caught a glance of it in profile. The motion of his body, too, was at variance with this idea—for he rocked from side to side with a gentle yet constant and uniform sway. Having rapidly taken notice of all this, I resumed the narrative of Sir Launcelot, which thus proceeded:

'And now, the champion, having escaped from the terrible fury of the dragon, bethinking himself of the brazen shield, and of the breaking up of the enchantment which was upon it, removed the carcass from out of the way before him, and approached valorously over the silver pavement of the castle to where the shield was upon the wall; which in sooth tarried not for his full coming, but fell down at his feet upon the silver floor, with a mighty great and terrible ringing sound.'

No sooner had these syllables passed my lips, than—as if a shield of brass had indeed, at the moment, fallen heavily upon a floor of silver—I became aware of a distinct, hollow, metallic, and clangorous, yet apparently muffled, reverberation. Completely unnerved, I leaped to my feet; but the measured rocking movement of Usher was undisturbed. I rushed to the chair in which he sat. His eyes were bent fixedly before him, and throughout his whole countenance there reigned a stony rigidity. But, as I placed my hand upon his shoulder, there came a strong shudder over his whole person; a sickly smile quivered about his lips; and I saw that he spoke in a low, hurried, and gibbering murmur, as if unconscious of my presence. Bending closely over him, I at length drank in the hideous import of his words.

'Now hear it?—yes, I hear it, and *have* heard it. Long—long—long—many minutes, many hours, many days, have I heard it—yet I dared not—oh, pity me, miserable wretch that I am!—I dared not—I *dared* not speak! *We have put her living in the tomb!* Said I not that my senses were acute? I *now* tell you that I heard her first feeble movements in the hollow coffin. I heard them—many, many days ago—yet I dared not—*I dared not speak!* And now—to-night— Ethelred—ha! ha!—the breaking of the hermit's door, and the death-cry of the dragon, and the clangor of the shield—say, rather, the rending of her coffin, and the grating of the iron hinges of her prison, and her struggles within the coppered archway of the vault! Oh! whither shall I fly? Will she not be here anon? Is she not hurrying to upbraid me for my haste? Have I not heard her footstep on the stair? Do I not distinguish that heavy and horrible beating of her heart? Madman!'—here he sprang furiously to his feet, and shrieked out his syllables, as if in the effort he were giving up his soul— *'Madman! I tell you that she now stands without the door!'*

As if in the superhuman energy of his utterance there had been found the potency of a spell, the huge antique panels to which the speaker pointed threw slowly back, upon the instant, their ponderous and ebony jaws. It was the work of the rushing gust—but then without those doors there *did* stand the lofty and enshrouded figure of the lady Madeline of Usher. There was blood upon her white robes, and the evidence of some bitter struggle upon every portion of her emaciated frame. For a moment she remained trembling and reeling to and fro upon the threshold—then, with a low moaning cry, fell heavily inward upon the person of her brother, and in her violent and now final death-agonies, bore him to the floor a corpse, and a victim to the terrors he had anticipated.

From that chamber, and from that mansion, I fled aghast. The storm was still abroad in all its wrath as I found myself crossing the old causeway. Suddenly there shot along the path a wild light, and I turned to see whence a gleam so unusual could have issued; for the vast house and its shadows were alone behind me. The radiance was that of the full, setting, and blood-red moon, which now shone vividly through that once barely discernible fissure, of which I have before spoken as extending from the roof of the building, in a zigzag direction, to the base. While I gazed, this entire orb of the satellite burst at once upon my sight—my brain reeled as I saw the mighty walls rushing asunder—there was a long tumultuous shouting sound like the voice of a thousand waters—and the deep and dank tarn at my feet closed sullenly and silently over the fragments of the *'House of Usher.'*

The Gold Bug

What ho! what ho! this fellow is dancing mad!
He hath been bitten by the Tarantula.

—*All in the Wrong*

MANY YEARS AGO, I CONTRACTED an intimacy with a Mr. William Legrand. He was of an ancient Huguenot family, and had once been wealthy; but a series of misfortunes had reduced him to want. To avoid the mortification consequent upon his disasters, he left New Orleans, the city of his forefathers, and took up his residence at Sullivan's Island, near Charleston, South Carolina.

This island is a very singular one. It consists of little else than the sea sand, and is about three miles long. Its breadth at no point exceeds a quarter of a mile. It is separated from the mainland by a scarcely perceptible creek, oozing its way through a wilderness of reeds and slime, a favorite resort of the marsh-hen. The vegetation, as might be supposed, is scant, or at least dwarfish. No trees of any magnitude are to be seen. Near the western extremity, where Fort Moultrie stands, and where are some miserable frame buildings, tenanted, during summer, by the fugitives from Charleston dust and fever, may be found, indeed, the bristly palmetto; but the whole island, with the exception of this western point, and a line of hard, white beach on the sea-coast, is covered with a dense undergrowth of the sweet myrtle so much prized by the horticulturists of England. The shrub here often attains the height of fifteen or twenty feet, and forms an almost impenetrable coppice, burthening the air with its fragrance.

In the inmost recesses of this coppice, not far from the eastern or more remote end of the island, Legrand had built himself a small hut, which he occupied when I first, by mere accident, made his acquaintance. This soon ripened into friendship—for there was much in the recluse to excite interest and esteem. I found him well educated, with unusual powers of mind, but infected with misanthropy, and subject to perverse moods of alternate enthusiasm and melancholy. He had with him many books, but rarely employed them. His chief amusements were gunning and fishing, or saunter-ing along the beach and through the myrtles, in quest of shells or entomologi-cal specimens—his collection of the latter might have been envied by a Swammerdamm. In these excursions he was usually accompanied by an old negro, called Jupiter, who had been manumitted before the reverses of the family, but who could be induced, neither by threats nor by promises, to abandon what he considered his right of attendance upon the footsteps of his young 'Massa Will.' It is not improbable that the relatives of Legrand, conceiving him to be somewhat unsettled in intellect, had contrived to instill this obstinacy into Jupiter, with a view to the supervision and guardianship of the wanderer.

The winters in the latitude of Sullivan's Island are seldom very severe, and in the fall of the year it is a rare event indeed when a fire is considered necessary. About the middle of October, 18—, there occurred, however, a day of remarkable chilliness. Just before sunset I scrambled my way through the evergreens to the hut of my friend, whom I had not visited for several weeks—my residence being, at that time, in Charleston, a distance of nine miles from the island, while the facilities of passage and re-passage were very far behind those of the present day. Upon reaching the hut I rapped, as was my custom, and getting no reply, sought for the key where I knew it was secreted, unlocked the door, and went in. A fine fire was blazing upon the hearth. It was a novelty, and by no means an ungrateful one. I threw off an overcoat, took an arm-chair by the crackling logs, and awaited patiently the arrival of my hosts.

Soon after dark they arrived, and gave me a most cordial welcome. Jupiter, grinning from ear to ear, bustled about to prepare some marsh-hens for supper. Legrand was in one of his fits—how else shall I term them?—of enthusiasm. He had found an unknown bivalve, forming a new genus, and, more than this, he had hunted down and secured, with Jupiter's assistance, a *scarabœus* which he believed to be totally new, but in respect to which he wished to have my opinion on the morrow.

'And why not to-night?' I asked, rubbing my hands over the blaze, and wishing the whole tribe of *scarabœi* at the devil.

'Ah, if I had only known you were here!' said Legrand, 'but it's so long since I saw you; and how could I foresee that you would pay me a visit this very night of all others? As I was coming home I met Lieutenant G——, from the fort, and, very foolishly, I lent him the bug; so it will be impossible for you to see it until the morning. Stay here to-night, and I will send Jup down for it at sunrise. It is the loveliest thing in creation!'

'What?—sunrise?'

'Nonsense! no!—the bug. It is of a brilliant gold color—about the size of a large hickory-nut—with two jet black spots near one extremity of the back, and another, somewhat longer, at the other. The *antennœ* are—'

'Dey aint *no* tin in him, Massa Will, I keep a tellin' on you,' here interrupted Jupiter; 'de bug is a goole bug, solid, ebery bit of him, inside and all, sep him wing—neber feel half so hebby a bug in my life.'

'Well, suppose it is, Jup,' replied Legrand, somewhat more earnestly, it seemed to me, than the case demanded; 'is that any reason for your letting the birds burn? The color'—here he turned to me—'is really almost enough to warrant Jupiter's idea. You never saw a more brilliant metallic lustre than the scales emit—but of this you cannot judge till tomorrow. In the meantime I can give you some idea of the shape.' Saying this, he seated himself at a small table, on which were a pen and ink, but no paper. He looked for some in a drawer, but found none.

'Never mind,' he said at length, 'this will answer'; and he drew from his waistcoat pocket a scrap of what I took to be very dirty foolscap, and made upon it a rough drawing with the pen. While he did this, I retained my seat by the fire, for I was still chilly. When the design was complete, he handed it to me without rising. As I received it, a loud growl was heard, succeeded by a scratching at the door. Jupiter opened it, and a large Newfoundland, belonging to Legrand, rushed in, leaped upon my shoulders, and loaded me with caresses; for I had shown him much attention during previous visits. When his gambols were over, I looked at the paper, and, to speak the truth, found myself not a little puzzled at what my friend had depicted.

'Well!' I said, after contemplating it for some minutes, 'this *is* a strange *scarabæus*, I must confess; new to me; never saw any thing like it before—unless it was a skull, or a death's-head, which it more nearly resembles than any thing else that has come under *my* observation.'

'A death's-head!' echoed Legrand. 'Oh—yes—well, it has something of that appearance upon paper, no doubt. The two upper black spots look like eyes, eh? and the longer one at the bottom like a mouth—and then the shape of the whole is oval.'

'Perhaps so,' said I; 'but, Legrand, I fear you are no artist. I must wait until I see the beetle itself, if I am to form any idea of its personal appearance.'

'Well, I don't know,' said he, a little nettled, 'I draw tolerably—*should* do it at least—have had good masters, and flatter myself that I am not quite a blockhead.'

'But, my dear fellow, you are joking then,' said I, 'this is a very passable *skull*—indeed, I may say that it is a very *excellent* skull, according to the vulgar notions about such specimens of physiology—and your *scarabæus* must be the queerest *scarabæus* in the world if it resembles it. Why, we may get up a very thrilling bit of superstition upon this hint. I presume you will call the bug *scarabæus caput hominis*, or something of that kind—there are many similar titles in the Natural Histories. But where are the *antennæ* you spoke of?'

'The *antennæ!*' said Legrand, who seemed to be getting unaccountably warm upon the subject; 'I am sure you must see the *antennæ*. I made them as distinct as they are in the original insect, and I presume that is sufficient.'

'Well, well,' I said, 'perhaps you have—still I don't see them'; and I handed him the paper without additional remark, not wishing to ruffle his temper; but I was much surprised at the turn affairs had taken; his ill humor puzzled me—and, as for the drawing of the beetle, there were positively *no antennæ* visible, and the whole *did* bear a very close resemblance to the ordinary cuts of a death's-head.

He received the paper very peevishly, and was about to crumple it, apparently to throw it in the fire, when a casual glance at the design seemed suddenly to rivet his attention. In an instant his face grew violently red—in another as excessively pale. For some minutes he continued to scrutinize the drawing minutely where he sat. At length he arose, took a candle from the table, and proceeded to seat himself upon a sea-chest in the farthest corner of the room. Here again he made an anxious examination of the paper; turning it in all directions. He said nothing, however, and his conduct greatly astonished me; yet I thought it prudent not to exacerbate the growing moodiness of his temper by any comment. Presently he took from his coat-pocket a wallet, placed the paper carefully in it, and deposited both in a writing-desk, which he locked. He now grew more composed in his demeanor; but his original air of enthusiasm had quite disappeared. Yet he seemed not so much sulky as abstracted. As the evening wore away he became more and more absorbed in revery, from which no sallies of mine could arouse him. It had been my intention to pass the night at the hut, as I had frequently done before, but seeing my host in this mood, I deemed it proper to take leave. He did not press me to remain, but, as I departed, he shook my hand with even more than his usual cordiality.

It was about a month after this (and during the interval I had seen nothing of Legrand) when I received a visit, at Charleston, from his man, Jupiter. I had never seen the good old negro look so dispirited, and I feared that some serious disaster had befallen my friend.

'Well, Jup,' said I, 'what is the matter now?—how is your master?'

'Why, to speak de troof, massa, him not so berry well as mought be.'

'Not well! I am truly sorry to hear it. What does he complain of?'

'Dar! dat's it!—him neber 'plain of notin'—but him berry sick for all dat.'

'*Very* sick, Jupiter!—why didn't you say so at once? Is he confined to bed?'

'No, dat he aint!—he aint 'fin'd nowhar—dat's just whar de shoe pinch—my mind is got to be berry hebby 'bout poor Massa Will.'

'Jupiter, I should like to understand what it is you are talking about. You say your master is sick. Hasn't he told you what ails him?'

'Why, massa, 'taint worf while for to git mad about de matter—Massa Will say noffin at all aint de matter wid him—but den what make him go about looking dis here way, wid he head down and he soldiers up, and as white as a goose? And den he keep a syphon all de time—'

'Keeps a what, Jupiter?'

'Keeps a syphon wid de figgurs on de slate—de queerest figgurs I ebber did see. Ise gittin' to be skeered, I tell you. Hab for to keep mighty tight eye 'pon him 'noovers. Todder day he gib me slip 'fore de sun up and was gone de whole ob de blessed day. I had a big stick ready cut for to gib him deuced good beating when he did come—but Ise sich a fool dat I hadn't de heart arter all—he looked so berry poorly.'

'Eh?—what?—ah yes!—upon the whole I think you had better not be too severe with the poor fellow—don't flog him, Jupiter—he can't very well stand it—but can you form no idea of what has occasioned this illness or rather this change of conduct? Has any thing unpleasant happened since I saw you?'

'No, massa, dey aint bin noffin onpleasant *since* den—'twas 'fore den I'm feared—'twas de berry day you was dare.'

'How? what do you mean?'

'Why, massa, I mean de bug—dare now.'

'The what?'

'De bug—I'm berry sartain dat Massa Will bin bit somewhere 'bout de head by dat goole bug.'

'And what cause have you, Jupiter, for such a supposition?'

'Claws enuff, massa, and mouff too. I nebber did see sich a deuced bug—he kick and he bite ebery ting what cum near him. Massa Will cotch him fuss, but had for to let him go 'gin mighty quick, I tell you—den was de time he must ha' got de bite. I didn't like de look ob de bug mouff, myself, nohow, so I wouldn't take hold ob him wid my finger, but I cotch him wid a piece ob paper dat I found. I rap him up in de paper and stuff a piece of it in he mouff—dat was de way.'

'And you think, then, that your master was really bitten by the beetle, and that the bite made him sick?'

'I don't think noffin' about it—I nose it. What make him dream 'bout de goole so much, if 'taint cause he bit by de goole bug? Ise heerd 'bout dem goole bugs 'fore dis.'

'But how do you know he dreams about gold?'

'How I know? why, 'cause he talk about it in he sleep—dat's how I nose.'

'Well, Jup, perhaps you are right; but to what fortunate circumstance am I to attribute the honor of a visit from you to-day?'

'What de matter, massa?'

'Did you bring any message from Mr. Legrand?'

'No, massa, I bring dis her pissel'; and here Jupiter handed me a note which ran thus:

'My Dear——

'Why have I not seen you for so long a time? I hope you have not been so foolish as to take offence at any little *brusquerie* of mine; but no, that is improbable.

'Since I saw you I have had great cause for anxiety. I have something to tell you, yet scarcely know how to tell it, or whether I should tell it at all.

'I have not been quite well for some days past, and poor old Jup annoys me, almost beyond endurance, by his well-meant attentions. Would you believe it?—he had prepared a huge stick, the other day, with which to chastise me for giving him the slip, and spending the day, *solus,* among the hills on the main land. I verily believe that my ill looks alone saved me a flogging.

'I have made no addition to my cabinet since we met.

'If you can, in any way, make it convenient, come over with Jupiter. *Do* come. I wish to see you *to-night,* upon business of importance. I assure you that it is of the *highest* importance.

'Ever yours,
'William Legrand'

There was something in the tone of this note which gave me great uneasiness. Its whole style differed materially from that of Legrand. What could he be dreaming of? What new crotchet possessed his excitable brain? What 'business of the highest importance' could *he* possibly have to transact? Jupiter's account of him boded no good. I dreaded lest the continued pressure of misfortune had, at length, fairly unsettled the reason of my friend. Without a moment's hesitation, therefore, I prepared to accompany the negro.

Upon reaching the wharf, I noticed a scythe and three spades, all apparently new, lying in the bottom of the boat in which we were to embark.

'What is the meaning of all this, Jup?' I inquired.

'Him syfe, massa, and spade.'

'Very true; but what are they doing here?'

'Him de syfe and de spade what Massa Will sis 'pon my buying for him in de town, and de debbil's own lot of money I had to gib for 'em.'

'But what, in the name of all that is mysterious, is your "Massa Will" going to do with scythes and spades?'

'Dat's more dan *I* know, and debbil take me if I don't b'lieve 'tis more dan he know too. But it's all cum ob de bug.'

Finding that no satisfaction was to be obtained of Jupiter, whose whole intellect seemed to be absorbed by 'de bug,' I now stepped into the boat, and made sail. With a fair and strong breeze we soon ran into the little cove to the northward of Fort Moultrie and a walk of some two miles brought us to the hut. It was about three in the afternoon when we arrived. Legrand had been awaiting us in eager expectation. He grasped my hand with a nervous *empressement* which alarmed me and strengthened the suspicions already entertained. His countenance was pale even to ghastliness, and his deep-set eyes glared with unnatural lustre. After some inquiries respecting his health, I asked him, not knowing what better to say, if he had yet obtained the *scarabœus* from Lieutenant G——.

'Oh, yes,' he replied, coloring violently, 'I got it from him the next morning. Nothing should tempt me to part with that *scarabœus*. Do you know that Jupiter is quite right about it?'

'In what way?' I asked, with a sad foreboding at heart.

'In supposing it to be a bug of *real gold*." He said this with an air of profound seriousness, and I felt inexpressibly shocked.

'This bug is to make my fortune,' he continued, with a triumphant smile; 'to reinstate me in my family possessions. Is it any wonder, then, that I prize it? Since Fortune has thought fit to bestow it upon me, I have only to use it properly, and I shall arrive at the gold of which it is the index. Jupiter, bring me that *scarabœus!*'

'What! de bug, massa? I'd rudder not go fer trubble dat bug; you mus' git him for your own self.' Hereupon Legrand arose, with a grave and stately air, and brought me the beetle from a glass case in which it was enclosed. It was a beautiful *scarabœus*, and, at that time, unknown to naturalists—of course a great prize in a scientific point of view. There were two round black spots near one extremity of the back, and a long one near the other. The scales were exceedingly hard and glossy, with all the appearance of burnished gold. The weight of the insect was very remarkable, and, taking all things into considera- tion, I could hardly blame Jupiter for his opinion respecting it; but what to make of Legrand's concordance with that opinion, I could not, for the life of me, tell.

'I sent for you,' said he, in a grandiloquent tone, when I had completed my examination of the beetle, 'I sent for you that I might have your counsel and assistance in furthering the views of Fate and of the bug—'

'My dear Legrand,' I cried, interrupting him, 'you are certainly unwell, and had better use some little precautions. You shall go to bed, and I will remain with you a few days, until you get over this. You are feverish and—'

'Feel my pulse,' said he.

I felt it, and, to say the truth, found not the slightest indication of fever.

'But you may be ill and yet have no fever. Allow me this once to prescribe for you. In the first place go to bed. In the next—'

'You are mistaken,' he interposed, 'I am as well as I can expect to be under the excitement which I suffer. If you really wish me well, you will relieve this excitement.'

'And how is this to be done?'

'Very easily. Jupiter and myself are going upon an expedition into the hills, upon the main land, and, in this expedition, we shall need the aid of some person in whom we can confide. You are the only one we can trust. Whether we succeed or fail, the excitement which you now perceive in me will be equally allayed.'

'I am anxious to oblige you in any way,' I replied; 'but do you mean to say that this infernal beetle has any connection with your expedition into the hills?'

'It has.'

'Then, Legrand, I can become a party to no such absurd proceeding.'

'I am sorry—very sorry—for we shall have to try it by ourselves.'

'Try it by yourselves! The man is surely mad!—but stay!—how long do you propose to be absent?'

'Probably all night. We shall start immediately, and be back, at all events, by sunrise.'

'And will you promise me, upon your honor, that when this freak of yours is over, and the bug business (good God!) settled to your satisfaction, you will then return home and follow my advice implicitly, as that of your physician.'

'Yes; I promise; and now let us be off, for we have no time to lose.'

With a heavy heart I accompanied my friend. We started about four o'clock—Legrand, Jupiter, the dog, and myself. Jupiter had with him the scythe and spades—the whole of which he insisted upon carrying—more through fear, it seemed to me, of trusting either of the implements within reach of his master, than from any excess of industry or complaisance. His demeanor was dogged in the extreme, and 'dat deuced bug' were the sole words which escaped his lips during the journey. For my own part, I had charge of a couple of dark lanterns, while Legrand contented himself with the *scarabœus*, which he carried attached to the end of a bit of whip-cord; twirling it to and fro, with the air of a conjuror, as he went. When I observed this last, plain evidence of my friend's aberration of mind, I could scarcely refrain from tears. I thought it best, however, to humor his fancy, at least for the present, or until I could adopt some more energetic measures with a chance of success. In the meantime I endeavored, but all in vain, to sound him in regard to the object of the expedition. Having succeeded in inducing me to accompany him, he seemed unwilling to hold conversation upon any topic of minor impor-tance, and to all my questions vouchsafed no other reply than 'we shall see!'

We crossed the creek at the head of the island by means of a skiff, and, ascending the high grounds on the shore of the main land, proceeded in a northwesterly direction, through a tract of country excessively wild and desolate, where no trace of a human footstep was to be seen. Legrand led the way with decision; pausing only for an instant, here and there, to consult what appeared to be certain landmarks of his own contrivance upon a former occasion.

In this manner we journeyed for about two hours, and the sun was just setting when we entered a region infinitely more dreary than any yet seen. It was a species of table-land, near the summit of an almost inaccessible hill, densely wooded from base to pinnacle, and interspersed with huge crags that appeared to lie loosely upon the soil, and in many cases were prevented from precipitating themselves into the valleys below, merely by the support of the trees against which they reclined. Deep ravines, in various directions, gave an air of still sterner solemnity to the scene.

The natural platform to which we had clambered was thickly overgrown with brambles, through which we soon discovered that it would have been impossible to force our way but for the scythe; and Jupiter, by direction of his master, proceeded to clear for us a path to the foot of an enormously tall tulip-tree, which stood, with some eight or ten oaks, upon the level, and far surpassed them all, and all other trees which I had then ever seen, in the beauty of its foliage and form, in the wide spread of its branches, and in the general majesty of its appearance. When we reached this tree, Legrand turned to Jupiter, and asked him if he thought he could climb it. The old man seemed a little staggered by the question, and for some moments made no reply. At length he approached the huge trunk, walked slowly around it, and examined it with minute attention. When he had completed his scrutiny, he merely said:

'Yes, massa, Jup climb any tree he ebber see in he life.'

'Then up with you as soon as possible, for it will soon be too dark to see what we are about.'

'How far mus' go up, massa?' inquired Jupiter.

'Get up the main trunk first, and then I will tell you which way to go—and here—stop! take this beetle with you.'

'De bug, Massa Will!—de goole bug!' cried the negro, drawing back in dismay— 'what for mus' tote de bug way up de tree?—d—n if I do!'

'If you are afraid, Jup, a great big negro like you, to take hold of a harmless little dead beetle, why you can carry it up by this string—but, if you do not take it up with you in some way, I shall be under the necessity of breaking your head with this shovel.'

'What de matter now, massa?' said Jup, evidently shamed into compliance; 'always want for to raise full wid old nigger. Was only funnin anyhow. *Me* feered de bug! what I keer for de bug?' Here he took cautiously hold of the extreme end of the string, and, maintaining the insect as far from his person as circumstances would permit, prepared to ascend the tree.

In youth, the tulip-tree, or *Liriodendron Tulipiferum*, the most magnificent of American foresters, has a trunk peculiarly smooth, and often rises to a great height without lateral branches; but, in its riper age, the bark becomes gnarled and uneven, while many short limbs make their appearance on the stem. Thus the difficulty of ascension, in the present case, lay more in semblance than in reality. Embracing the huge cylinder, as closely as possible, with his arms and knees, seizing with his hands some projections, and resting his naked toes upon others, Jupiter, after one or two narrow escapes from falling, at length wriggled himself into the first great fork, and seemed to consider the whole business as virtually accomplished. The *risk* of the achievement was, in fact, now over, although the climber was some sixty or seventy feet from the ground.

'Which way mus' go now, Massa Will?' he asked.

'Keep up the largest branch—the one on this side,' said Legrand. The negro obeyed him promptly, and apparently with but little trouble; ascending higher and higher, until no glimpse of his squat figure could be obtained through the dense foliage which enveloped it. Presently his voice was heard in a sort of halloo.

'How much fudder is got for go?'

'How high up are you?' asked Legrand.

'Ebber so fur,' replied the negro; 'can see de sky fru de top ob de tree.'

'Never mind the sky, but attend to what I say. Look down the trunk and count the limbs below you on this side. How many limbs have you passed?'

'One, two, tree, four, fibe—I done pass fibe big limb, massa 'pon dis side.'

'Then go one limb higher.'

In a few minutes the voice was heard again, announcing that the seventh limb was attained.

'Now, Jup,' cried Legrand, evidently much excited, 'I want you to work your way out upon that limb as far as you can. If you see any thing strange let me know.'

By this time what little doubt I might have entertained of my poor friend's insanity was put finally at rest. I had no alternative but to conclude him stricken with lunacy, and I became seriously anxious about getting him home. While I was pondering upon what was best to be done, Jupiter's voice was again heard.

'Mos' feerd for to venture 'pon dis limb berry far—'tis dead limb putty much all de way.'

'Did you say it was a *dead* limb, Jupiter?' cried Legrand in a quavering voice.

'Yes, massa, him dead as de door-nail—done up for sartain—done departed dis here life.'

'What in the name of heaven shall I do?' asked Legrand, seemingly in the greatest distress.

'Do!' said I, glad of an opportunity to interpose a word, 'why come home and go to bed. Come now!—that's a fine fellow. It's getting late, and, besides, you remember your promise.'

'Jupiter,' cried he, without heeding me in the least, 'do you hear me?'

'Yes, Massa Will, hear you ebber so plain.'

'Try the wood well, then, with your knife, and see if you think it *very* rotten.'

'Him rotten, massa, sure nuff,' replied the negro in a few moments, 'but not so berry rotten as mought be. Mought venture out lettle way 'pon de limb by myself, dat's true.'

'By yourself!—what do you mean?'

'Why, I mean de bug. 'Tis *berry* hebby bug. Spose I drop him down fuss, and den de limb won't break wid just de weight ob one nigger.'

'You infernal scoundrel!' cried Legrand, apparently much relieved, 'what do you mean by telling me such nonsense as that? As sure as you drop that beetle I'll break your neck. Look here, Jupiter, do you hear me?'

'Yes, massa, needn't hollo at poor nigger dat style.'

'Well! now listen!—if you will venture out on the limb as far as you think safe, and not let go the beetle, I'll make you a present of a silver dollar as soon as you get down.'

'I'm gwine, Massa Will—deed I is,' replied the negro very promptly—'mos' out to the eend now.'

'*Out to the end!*' here fairly screamed Legrand; 'do you say you are out to the end of that limb?'

'Soon be to de eend, massa—o-o-o-o-oh! Lor-gol-a-marcy! what *is* dis here pon de tree?'

'Well!' cried Legrand, highly delighted, 'what is it?'

'Why taint noffin but a skull—somebody bin left him dead up de tree, and de crows done gobble ebery bit ob de meat off.'

'A skull, you say!—very well,—how is it fastened to the limb?—what holds it on?'

'Sure nuff, massa; mus' look. Why dis berry curous sarcumstance, 'pon my word—dare's a great big nail in de skull, what fastens ob it on to de tree.'

'Well now, Jupiter, do exactly as I tell you—do you hear?'

'Yes, massa.'

'Pay attention, then—find the left eye of the skull.'

'Hum! hoo! dat's good! why dey aint no eye lef' at all.'

'Curse your stupidity! do you know your right hand from your left?'

'Yes, I knows dat—know all bout dat—'tis my lef' hand what I chops de wood wid.'

'To be sure! you are left-handed; and your left eye is on the same side as your left hand. Now, I suppose, you can find the left eye of the skull, or the place where the left eye has been. Have you found it?'

Here was a long pause. At length the negro asked:

'Is de lef' eye ob de skull 'pon de same side as de lef' hand ob de skull too?—cause de skull ain't got not a bit ob a hand at all—nebber mind! I got de lef' eye now—here de lef' eye! what mus' do wid it?'

'Let the beetle drop through it, as far as the string will reach—but be careful and not let go your hold of the string.'

'All dat done, Massa Will; mighty easy ting for to put the bug fru de hole—look out for him dare below!'

During this colloquy no portion of Jupiter's person could be seen; but the beetle, which he had suffered to descend, was now visible at the end of the string, and glistened, like a globe of burnished gold, in the last rays of the setting sun, some of which still faintly illumined the eminence upon which we stood. The *scarabæus* hung quite clear of any branches, and, if allowed to fall, would have fallen at our feet. Legrand immediately took the scythe, and cleared with it a circular space, three or four yards in diameter, just beneath the insect, and, having accomplished this, ordered Jupiter to let go the string and come down from the tree.

Driving a peg, with great nicety, into the ground, at the precise spot where the beetle fell, my friend now produced from his pocket a tape measure. Fastening one end of this at that point of the trunk of the tree which was nearest the peg, he unrolled it till it reached the peg and thence further unrolled it, in the direction already established by the two points of the tree and the peg, for the distance of fifty feet—Jupiter clearing away the brambles with the scythe. At the spot thus attained a second peg was driven, and about this, as a center, a rude circle, about four feet in diameter, described. Taking now a spade himself, and giving one to Jupiter and one to me, Legrand begged us to set about digging as quickly as possible.

To speak the truth, I had no especial relish for such amusement at any time, and, at that particular moment, would most willingly have declined it; for the night was coming on, and I felt much fatigued with the exercise already taken; but I saw no mode of escape, and was fearful of disturbing my poor friend's equanimity by a refusal. Could I have depended, indeed upon Jupiter's aid, I would have had no hesitation in attempting to get the lunatic home by force; but I was too well assured of the old negro's disposition, to hope that he would assist me, under any circumstances, in a personal contest with his master. I made no doubt that the latter had been infected with some of the innumerable Southern superstitions about money buried, and that his phantasy had received confirmation by the finding of the *scarabæus,* or, perhaps, by Jupiter's obstinacy in maintaining it to be 'a bug of real gold.' A mind disposed to lunacy would readily be led away by such suggestions—especially if chiming in with favorite preconceived ideas—and then I called to mind the poor fellow's speech about the beetle's being 'the index of his fortune.' Upon the whole, I was sadly vexed and puzzled, but at length, I concluded to make a virtue of necessity—to dig with a good will, and thus the sooner to convince the visionary, by ocular demonstration, of the fallacy of the opinions he entertained.

The lanterns having been lit, we all fell to work with a zeal worthy a more rational cause; and, as the glare fell upon our persons and implements, I could not help thinking how picturesque a group we composed, and how strange and suspicious our labors must have appeared to any interloper who, by chance, might have stumbled upon our whereabouts.

We dug very steadily for two hours. Little was said; and our chief embarrassment lay in the yelpings of the dog, who took exceeding interest in our proceedings. He, at length, became so obstreperous that we grew fearful of his giving alarm to some stragglers in the vicinity,—or, rather, this was the apprehension of Legrand;—for myself, I should have rejoiced at any interruption which might have enabled me to get the wanderer home. The noise was, at length, very effectually silenced by Jupiter, who, getting out of the hole with a dogged air of deliberation, tied the brute's mouth up with one of his suspenders, and then returned, with a grave chuckle, to his task.

When the time mentioned had expired, we had reached a depth of five feet, and yet no signs of any treasure became manifest. A general pause ensued, and I began to hope that the farce was at an end. Legrand, however, although evidently much disconcerted, wiped his brow thoughtfully and recommenced. We had excavated the entire circle of four feet diameter, and now we slightly enlarged the limit, and went to the farther depth of two feet. Still nothing appeared. The gold seeker, whom I sincerely pitied, at length clambered from the pit, with the bitterest disappointment imprinted upon every feature, and proceeded, slowly and reluctantly, to put on his coat, which he had thrown off at the beginning of his labor. In the meantime I made no remark. Jupiter, at a signal from his master, began to gather up his tools. This done, and the dog having been unmuzzled, we turned in profound silence toward home.

We had taken, perhaps, a dozen steps in this direction, when with a loud oath, Legrand strode up to Jupiter, and seized him by the collar. The astonished negro opened his eyes and mouth to the fullest extent, let fall the spades, and fell upon his knees.

'You scoundrel!' said Legrand, hissing out the syllables from between his clenched teeth—'you infernal black villain!—speak, I tell you!—answer me this instant, without prevarication!—which—which is your left eye?'

'Oh, my golly, Massa Will! aint dis here my lef' eye for sartain?' roared the terrified Jupiter, placing his hand upon his *right* organ of vision, and holding it there with a desperate pertinacity, as if in immediate dread of his master's attempt at a gouge.

'I thought so!—I knew it! hurrah!' vociferated Legrand, letting the negro go and executing a series of curvets and caracols, much to the astonishment of his valet, who, arising from his knees, looked, mutely, from his master to myself, and then from myself to his master.

'Come! we must go back,' said the latter, 'the game's not up yet'; and he again led the way to the tulip-tree.

'Jupiter,' said he, when we reached its foot, 'come here! was the skull nailed to the limb with the face outward, or with the face to the limb?'

'De face was out, massa, so dat de crows could get at de eyes good, widout any trouble.'

'Well, then, was it this eye or that through which you dropped the beetle?'—here Legrand touched each of Jupiter's eyes.

"Twas dis eye, massa—de lef'eye—jis as you tell me,' and here it was his right eye that the negro indicated.

'That will do—we must try it again.'

Here my friend, about whose madness I now saw, or fancied that I saw, certain indications of method, removed the peg which marked the spot where the beetle fell, to a spot about three inches to the westward of its former position. Taking, now, the tape measure from the nearest point of the trunk to the peg, as before, and continuing the extension in a straight line to the distance of fifty feet, a spot was indicated, removed, by several yards, from the point at which we had been digging.

Around the new position a circle, somewhat larger than in the former instance, was now described, and we again set to work with the spade. I was dreadfully weary, but scarcely understanding what had occasioned the change in my thoughts, I felt no longer any great aversion from the labor imposed. I had become most unaccountably interested—nay, even excited. Perhaps there was something, amid all the extravagant demeanor of Legrand—some air of forethought, or of deliberation, which impressed me. I dug eagerly, and now and then caught myself actually looking, with something that very much resembled expectation, for the fancied treasure, the vision of which had demented my unfortunate companion. At a period when such vagaries of thought most fully possessed me, and when we had been at work perhaps an hour and a half, we were again interrupted by the violent howlings of the dog. His uneasiness, in the first instance, had been, evidently, but the result of playfulness or caprice, but he now assumed a bitter and serious tone. Upon Jupiter's again attempting to muzzle him, he made furious resistance, and, leaping into the hole, tore up the mould frantically with his claws. In a few seconds he had uncovered a mass of human bones, forming two complete skeletons, intermingled with several buttons of metal, and what appeared to be the dust of decayed woollen. One or two strokes of a spade up-turned the blade of a large Spanish knife, and, as we dug farther, three or four loose pieces of gold and silver coin came to light.

At sight of these the joy of Jupiter could scarcely be restrained, but the countenance of his master wore an air of extreme disappointment. He urged us, however, to continue our exertions, and the words were hardly uttered when I stumbled and fell forward, having caught the toe of my boot in a large ring of iron that lay half buried in the loose earth.

We now worked in earnest, and never did I pass ten minutes of more intense excitement. During this interval we had fairly unearthed an oblong chest of wood, which, from its perfect preservation and wonderful hardness, had plainly been subjected to some mineralizing process—perhaps that of the bi-chloride of mercury. This box was three feet and a half long, three feet broad, and two and a half feet deep. It was firmly secured by bands of wrought iron, riveted, and forming a kind of open trellis-work over the whole. On each

side of the chest, near the top, were three rings of iron—six in all—by means
of which a firm hold could be obtained by six persons. Our utmost united
endeavors served only to disturb the coffer very slightly in its bed. We at once
saw the impossibility of removing so great a weight. Luckily, the sole
fastenings of the lid consisted of two sliding bolts. These we drew back—
trembling and panting with anxiety. In an instant, a treasure of incalculable
value lay gleaming before us. As the rays of the lanterns fell within the pit,
there flashed upward a glow and a glare, from a confused heap of gold and
jewels, that absolutely dazzled our eyes.

I shall not pretend to describe the feelings with which I gazed. Amazement
was, of course, predominant. Legrand appeared exhausted with excitement,
and spoke very few words. Jupiter's countenance wore, for some minutes, as
deadly a pallor as it is possible, in the nature of things, for any negro's visage to
assume. He seemed stupefied—thunderstricken. Presently he fell upon his
knees in the pit, and burying his naked arms up to the elbows in gold, let them
there remain, as if enjoying the luxury of a bath. At length, with a deep sigh,
he exclaimed, as if in a soliloquy:

'And dis all cum ob de goole bug! de putty goole bug! the poor little goole
bug, what I boosed in dat sabage kind ob style! Aint you shamed ob yourself,
nigger?—answer me dat!'

It became necessary, at last, that I should arouse both master and valet to
the expediency of removing the treasure. It was growing late, and it behooved
us to make exertion, that we might get every thing housed before daylight. It
was difficult to say what should be done, and much time was spent in
deliberation—so confused were the ideas of all. We, finally, lightened the box
by removing two thirds of its contents, when we were enabled, with some
trouble, to raise it from the hole. The articles taken out were deposited among
the brambles, and the dog left to guard them, with strict orders from Jupiter
neither, upon any pretence, to stir from the spot, nor to open his mouth until
our return. We then hurriedly made for home with the chest; reaching the hut
in safety, but after excessive toil, at one o'clock in the morning. Worn out as we
were, it was not in human nature to do more immediately. We rested until two,
and had supper; starting for the hills immediately afterward, armed with
three stout sacks, which, by good luck, were upon the premises. A little before
four we arrived at the pit, divided the remainder of the booty, as equally as
might be, among us, and, leaving the holes unfilled, again set out for the hut,
at which, for the second time, we deposited our golden burthens, just as the
first faint streaks of the dawn gleamed from over the tree tops in the East.

We were now thoroughly broken down; but the intense excitement of the
time denied us repose. After an unquiet slumber of some three or four hours'
duration, we arose, as if by preconcert, to make examination of our treasure.

The chest had been full to the brim, and we spent the whole day, and the
greater part of the next night, in a scrutiny of its contents. There had been
nothing like order or arrangement. Every thing had been heaped in promiscuously. Having assorted all with care, we found ourselves possessed of even
vaster wealth than we had at first supposed. In coin there was rather more
than four hundred and fifty thousand dollars—estimating the value of the
pieces, as accurately as we could, by the tables of the period. There was not a
particle of silver. All was gold of antique date and of great variety—French,
Spanish, and German money, with a few English guineas, and some counters,

of which we had never seen specimens before. There were several very large and heavy coins, so worn that we could make nothing of their inscriptions. There was no American money. The value of the jewels we found more difficulty in estimating. There were diamonds—some of them exceedingly large and fine—a hundred and ten in all, and not one of them small; eighteen rubies of remarkable brilliancy;—three hundred and ten emeralds, all very beautiful; and twenty-one sapphires, with an opal. These stones had all been broken from their settings and thrown loose in the chest. The settings themselves which we picked out from among the other gold, appeared to have been beaten up with hammers, as if to prevent identification. Besides all this, there was a vast quantity of solid gold ornaments: nearly two hundred massive finger and ear-rings: rich chains—thirty of these, if I remember; eighty-three very large and heavy crucifixes; five gold censers of great value; a prodigious golden punch bowl, ornamented with richly chased vine-leaves and Bacchanalian figures; with two sword handles exquisitely embossed, and many other smaller articles which I cannot recollect. The weight of these valuables exceeded three hundred and fifty pounds avoirdupois; and in this estimate I have not included one hundred and ninety-seven superb gold watches; three of the number being worth each five hundred dollars, if one. Many of them were very old, and as timekeepers valueless; the works having suffered, more or less, from corrosion—but all were richly jewelled and in cases of great worth. We estimated the entire contents of the chest, that night, at a million and a half dollars; and upon the subsequent disposal of the trinkets and jewels (a few being retained for our own use), it was found that we had greatly undervalued the treasure.

When at length, we had concluded our examination, and the intense excitement of the time had, in some measure, subsided, Legrand, who saw that I was dying with impatience for a solution of this most extraordinary riddle, entered into a full detail of all the circumstances connected with it.

'You remember,' said he, 'the night when I handed you the rough sketch I had made of the *scarabœus*. You recollect also, that I became quite vexed at you for insisting that my drawing resembled a death's-head. When you first made this assertion I thought you were jesting; but afterward I called to mind the peculiar spots on the back of the insect, and admitted to myself that your remark had some little foundation in fact. Still, the sneer at my graphic powers irritated me—for I am considered a good artist—and, therefore, when you handed me the scrap of parchment, I was about to crumple it up and throw it angrily into the fire.'

'The scrap of paper, you mean,' said I.

'No; it had much of the appearance of paper, and at first I supposed it to be such, but when I came to draw upon it, I discovered it at once to be a piece of very thin parchment. It was quite dirty, you remember. Well, as I was in the very act of crumpling it up, my glance fell upon the sketch at which you had been looking, and you may imagine my astonishment when I perceived, in fact, the figure of a death's-head just where, it seemed to me, I had made the drawing of the beetle. For a moment I was too much amazed to think with accuracy. I knew that my design was very different in detail from this— although there was a certain similarity in general outline. Presently I took a candle, and seating myself at the other end of the room, proceeded to scrutinize the parchment more closely. Upon turning it over, I saw my own sketch upon the reverse, just as I had made it. My first idea, now, was mere surprise at the really remarkable similarity of outline—at the singular coincidence involved in the fact that, unknown to me, there should have been a skull upon the other side of the parchment, immediately beneath my figure of the *scarabæus,* and that this skull, not only in outline, but in size, should so closely resemble my drawing. I say the singularity of this coincidence absolutely stupefied me for a time. This is the usual effect of such coincidences. The mind struggles to establish a connection—a sequence of cause and effect— and, being unable to do so, suffers a species of temporary paralysis. But, when I recovered from this stupor, there dawned upon me gradually a conviction which startled me even far more than the coincidence. I began distinctly, positively, to remember that there had been *no* drawing upon the parchment when I made my sketch of the *scarabæus.* I became perfectly certain of this; for I recollected turning up first one side and then the other, in search of the cleanest spot. Had the skull been then there, of course I could not have failed to notice it. Here was indeed a mystery which I felt it impossible to explain; but even at that early moment, there seemed to glimmer, faintly, within the most remote and secret chambers of my intellect, a glow-worm-like conception of that truth which last night's adventure brought to so magnificent a demonstration. I arose at once, and putting the parchment securely away, dismissed all further reflection until I should be alone.

'When you had gone, and when Jupiter was fast asleep, I betook myself to a more methodical investigation of the affair. In the first place I considered the manner in which the parchment had come into my possession. The spot where we discovered the *scarabæus* was on the coast of the main land, about a mile eastward of the island, and but a short distance above high water mark. Upon my taking hold of it, it gave me a sharp bite, which caused me to let it drop. Jupiter, with his accustomed caution, before seizing the insect, which had flown toward him, looked about him for a leaf, or something of that nature, by which to take hold of it. It was at this moment that his eyes, and mine also, fell upon the scrap of parchment, which I then supposed to be paper. It was lying half buried in the sand, a corner sticking up. Near the spot where we found it, I observed the remnants of the hull of what appeared to have been a ship's long boat. The wreck seemed to have been there for a very great while; for the resemblance to boat timbers could scarcely be traced.

'Well, Jupiter picked up the parchment, wrapped the beetle in it, and gave it to me. Soon afterward we turned to go home, and on the way met Lieutenant G——. I showed him the insect, and he begged me to let him take it to the fort. Upon my consenting, he thrust it forthwith into his waistcoat pocket, without the parchment in which it had been wrapped, and which I had continued to hold in my hand during his inspection. Perhaps he dreaded my changing my mind, and thought it best to make sure of the prize at once—you know how enthusiastic he is on all subjects connected with Natural History. At the same time, without being conscious of it, I must have deposited the parchment in my own pocket.

'You remember that when I went to the table, for the purpose of making a sketch of the beetle, I found no paper where it was usually kept. I looked in the drawer, and found none there. I searched my pockets, hoping to find an old letter, when my hand fell upon the parchment. I thus detail the precise mode in which it came into my possession; for the circumstances impressed me with peculiar force.

'No doubt you will think me fanciful—but I had already established a kind of *connection*. I had put together two links of a great chain. There was a boat lying upon the sea coast, and not far from the boat was a parchment—*not a paper*—with a skull depicted upon it. You will, of course, ask "where is the connection?" I reply that the skull, or death's-head, is the well-known emblem of the pirate. The flag of the death's-head is hoisted in all engagements.

'I have said that the scrap was parchment, and not paper. Parchment is durable—almost imperishable. Matters of little moment are rarely consigned to parchment; since, for the mere ordinary purposes of drawing or writing, it is not nearly so well adapted as paper. This reflection suggested some meaning—some relevancy—in the death's-head. I did not fail to observe, also, the *form* of the parchment. Although one of its corners had been, by some accident, destroyed, it could be seen that the original form was oblong. It was just such a slip, indeed, as might have been chosen for a memorandum—for a record of something to be long remembered and carefully preserved.'

'But,' I interposed, 'you say that the skull was *not* upon the parchment when you made the drawing of the beetle. How then do you trace any connection between the boat and the skull—since this latter, according to your own admission, must have been designed (God only knows how or by whom) at some period subsequent to your sketching the *scarabœus?*'

'Ah, hereupon turns the whole mystery; although the secret, at this point, I had comparatively little difficulty in solving. My steps were sure, and could afford a single result. I reasoned, for example, thus: When I drew the *scarabœus*, there was no skull apparent upon the parchment. When I had completed the drawing I gave it to you, and observed you narrowly until you returned it. *You*, therefore, did not design the skull, and no one else was present to do it. Then it was not done by human agency. And nevertheless it was done.

'At this stage of my reflections I endeavored to remember, and *did* remember, with entire distinctness, every incident which occurred about the period in question. The weather was chilly (oh, rare and happy accident!), and a fire was blazing upon the hearth. I was heated with exercise and sat near the table. You, however, had drawn a chair close to the chimney. Just as I placed the parchment in your hand, and as you were in the act of inspecting it, Wolf, the Newfoundland, entered, and leaped upon your shoulders. With your left hand you caressed him and kept him off, while your right, holding the parchment, was permitted to fall listlessly between your knees, and in close proximity to the fire. At one moment I thought the blaze had caught it, and was about to caution you, but, before I could speak, you had withdrawn it, and were engaged in its examination. When I considered all these particulars, I doubted not for a moment that *heat* had been the agent in bringing to light, upon the parchment, the skull which I saw designed upon it. You are well aware that chemical preparations exist, and have existed time out of mind, by means of which it is possible to write upon either paper or vellum, so that the characters shall become visible only when subjected to the action of fire. Zaffre, digested in *aqua regia,* and diluted with four times its weight of water, is sometimes employed; a green tint results. The regulus of cobalt, dissolved in spirit of nitre, gives a red. These colors disappear at longer or shorter intervals after the material written upon cools, but again become apparent upon the re-application of heat.

'I now scrutinized the death's-head with care. Its outer edges—the edges of the drawing nearest the edge of the vellum—were far more *distinct* than the others. It was clear that the action of the caloric had been imperfect or unequal. I immediately kindled a fire, and subjected every portion of the parchment to a glowing heat. At first, the only effect was the strengthening of the faint lines in the skull; but, upon persevering in the experiment, there became visible, at the corner of the slip, diagonally opposite to the spot in which the death's-head was delineated, the figure of what I at first supposed to be a goat. A closer scrutiny, however, satisfied me that it was intended for a kid.'

'Ha! ha!' said I, 'to be sure I have no right to laugh at you—a million and a half of money is too serious a matter for mirth—but you are not about to establish a third link in your chain—you will not find any especial connection between your pirates and a goat—pirates, you know, have nothing to do with goats; they appertain to the farming interest.'

'But I have just said that the figure was *not* that of a goat.'

'Well, a kid then—pretty much the same thing.'

'Pretty much, but not altogether,' said Legrand. 'You may have heard of one *Captain* Kidd. I at once looked upon the figure of the animal as a kind of punning or hieroglyphical signature. I say signature; because its position upon the vellum suggested this idea. The death's-head at the corner diagonally opposite, had, in the same manner, the air of a stamp, or seal. But I was sorely put out by the absence of all else—of the body to my imagined instrument—of the text for my context.'

'I presume you expected to find a letter between the stamp and the signature.'

'Something of that kind. The fact is, I felt irresistibly impressed with a presentiment of some vast good fortune impending. I can scarcely say why. Perhaps, after all, it was rather a desire than an actual belief;—but do you know that Jupiter's silly words, about the bug being of solid gold, had a remarkable effect upon my fancy? And then the series of accidents and coincidences—these were so *very* extraordinary. Do you observe how mere an accident it was that these events should have occurred upon the *sole* day of all the year in which it has been, or may be sufficiently cool for fire, and that without the fire, or without the intervention of the dog at the precise moment in which he appeared, I should never have become aware of the death's-head, and so never the possessor of the treasure?'

'But proceed—I am all impatience.'

'Well; you have heard, of course, the many stories current—the thousand vague rumors afloat about money buried, somewhere upon the Atlantic coast, by Kidd and his associates. These rumors must have had some foundation in fact. And that the rumors have existed so long and so continuous, could have resulted, it appeared to me, only from the circumstance of the buried treasure still *remaining* entombed. Had Kidd concealed his plunder for a time, and afterward reclaimed it, the rumors would scarcely have reached us in their present unvarying form. You will observe that the stories told are all about money seekers, not about money finders. Had the pirate recovered his money, there the affair would have dropped. It seemed to me that some accident—say the los f a memorandum indicating its locality—had deprived him of the means of recovering it, and that this accident had become known to his followers, who otherwise might never have heard that treasure had been concealed at all, and who, busying themselves in vain, because unguided, attempts to regain it, had given first birth, and then universal currency, to the reports which are now so common. Have you ever heard of any important treasure being unearthed along the coast?'

'Never.'

'But that Kidd's accumulations were immense, is well known. I took it for granted, therefore, that the earth still held them; and you will scarcely be surprised when I tell you that I felt a hope, nearly amounting to certainty, that the parchment so strangely found involved a lost record of the place of deposit.'

'But how did you proceed?'

'I held the vellum again to the fire, after increasing the heat, but nothing appeared. I now thought it possible that the coating of dirt might have something to do with the failure: so I carefully rinsed the parchment by pouring warm water over it, and, having done this, I placed it in a tin pan, with the skull downward, and put the pan upon a furnace of lighted charcoal. In a few minutes, the pan having become thoroughly heated, I removed the slip, and, to my inexpressible joy, found it spotted, in several places, with what appeared to be figures arranged in lines. Again I placed it in the pan, and suffered it to remain another minute. Upon taking it off, the whole was just as you see it now.'

Here Legrand, having re-heated the parchment, submitted it to my inspection. The following characters were rudely traced, in a red tint, between the death's-head and the goat:

53‡‡†305))6*;4826)4‡.)4‡);806*;48†8¶60))85;1‡(;:‡*8†83(88)5*†;46
(;88*96*?;8)*‡(;485);5*†2:*‡(;4956*2(5*—4)8¶8*;4069285);)6†8)4‡‡;
1(‡9;48081;8:8‡1;48†85;4)485†528806*81(‡9;48;(88;4(‡?34;48)4‡;161;
:188;‡?;'

'But,' said I, returning him the slip, 'I am as much in the dark as ever. Were all the jewels of Golconda awaiting me upon my solution of this enigma, I am quite sure that I should be unable to earn them.'

'And yet,' said Legrand, 'the solution is by no means so difficult as you might be led to imagine from the first hasty inspection of the characters. These characters, as any one might readily guess, form a cipher—that is to say, they convey a meaning; but then from what is known of Kidd, I could not suppose him capable of constructing any of the more abstruse cryptographs. I made up my mind, at once, that this was of a simple species—such, however, as would appear, to the crude intellect of the sailor, absolutely insoluble without the key.'

'And you really solved it?'

'Readily; I have solved others of an abstruseness ten thousand times greater. Circumstances, and a certain bias of mind, have led me to take interest in such riddles, and it may well be doubted whether human ingenuity can construct an enigma of the kind which human ingenuity may not, by proper application, resolve. In fact, having once established connected and legible characters, I scarcely gave a thought to the mere difficulty of developing their import.

'In the present case—indeed in all cases of secret writing—the first question regards the *language* of the cipher; for the principles of solution, so far, especially, as the more simple ciphers are concerned, depend upon, and are varied by, the genius of the particular idiom. In general, there is no alternative but experiment (directed by probabilities) of every tongue known to him who attempts the solution, until the true one be attained. But, with the cipher now before us all difficulty was removed by the signature. The pun upon the word 'Kidd' is appreciable in no other language than the English. But for this consideration I should have begun my attempts with the Spanish and French, as the tongues in which a secret of this kind would most naturally have been written by a pirate of the Spanish main. As it was, I assumed the cryptograph to be English.

'You observe there are no divisions between the words. Had there been divisions the task would have been comparatively easy. In such cases I should have commenced with a collation and analysis of the shorter words, and, had a word of a single letter occurred, as is most likely (*a* or *I*, for example), I should have considered the solution as assured. But, there being no division, my first step was to ascertain the predominant letters, as well as the least frequent. Counting all, I constructed a table thus:

Of the character 8 there are		33.
;	"	26.
4	"	19.
‡)	"	16.
*	"	13.
5	"	12.
6	"	11.
†1	"	8.
0	"	6.
92	"	5.
:3	"	4.
?	"	3.
¶	"	2.
—.	"	1.

'Now, in English, the letter which most frequently occurs is *e*. Afterward, the succession runs thus: *a o i d h n r s t u y c f g l m w b k p q x z*. *E* predominates so remarkably, that an individual sentence of any length is rarely seen, in which it is not the prevailing character.

'Here, then, we have, in the very beginning, the groundwork for something more than a mere guess. The general use which may be made of the table is obvious—but, in this particular cipher, we shall only very partially require its aid. As our predominant character is 8, we will commence by assuming it as the *e* of the natural alphabet. To verify the supposition, let us observe if the 8 be seen often in couples—for *e* is doubled with great frequency in English—in such words, for example, as 'meet' 'fleet,' 'speed,' 'seen,' 'been,' 'agree,' etc. In the present instance we see it doubled no less than five times, although the cryptograph is brief.

'Let us assume 8, then, as *e*. Now, of all *words* in the language, 'the' is most usual; let us see, therefore, whether there are not repetitions of any three characters, in the same order of collocation, the last of them being 8. If we discover repetitions of such letters, so arranged, they will most probably represent the word 'the.' Upon inspection, we find no less than seven such arrangements, the characters being ;48. We may, therefore, assume that ; represents *t*, 4 represents *h*, and 8 represents *e*—the last being now well confirmed. Thus a great step has been taken.

'But, having established a single word, we are enabled to establish a vastly important point; that is to say, several commencements and terminations of other words. Let us refer, for example, to the last instance but one, in which the combination; 48 occurs—not far from the end of the cipher. We know that the ; immediately ensuing is the commencement of a word, and, of the six characters succeeding this 'the,' we are cognizant of no less than five. Let us set these characters down, thus, by the letters we know them to represent, leaving a space for the unknown—

> t eeth.

'Here we are enabled, at once, to discard the '*th*,' as forming no portion of the word commencing with the first *t;* since, by experiment of the entire alphabet for a letter adapted to the vacancy, we perceive that no word can be formed of which this *th* can be a part. We are thus narrowed into

> t ee,

and going through the alphabet, if necessary, as before, we arrive at the word 'tree,' as the sole possible reading. We thus gain another letter, *r,* represented by (, with the words 'the tree' in juxtaposition.

'Looking beyond these words, for a short distance, we again see the combination ;48, and employ it by way of *termination* to what immediately precedes. We have thus this arrangement:

> the tree;4(‡?34 the,

or, substituting the natural letters, where known, it reads thus:

> the tree thr‡?3h the.

'Now, if, in place of the unknown characters, we leave blank spaces, or substitute dots, we read thus:

> the tree thr . . . h the,

when the word '*through*' makes itself evident at once. But this discovery gives us three new letters, *o, u,* and *g,* represented by ‡,?, and 3.

'Looking now, narrowly, through the cipher for combinations of known characters, we find, not very far from the beginning, this arrangement,

83(88, or egree,

which, plainly, is the conclusion of the word 'degree,' and gives us another letter, *d*, represented by †.

'Four letters beyond the word 'degree,' we perceive the combination

;46(;88.

'Translating the known characters, and representing the unknown by dots, as before, we read thus:

th.rtee,

an arrangement immediately suggestive of the word 'thirteen,' and again furnishing us with two new characters, *i* and *n*, represented by 6 and *.

'Referring, now, to the beginning of the cryptograph, we find the combination,

53‡‡†

'Translating as before, we obtain

.good,

which assures us that the first letter is *A*, and that the first two words are 'A good.'

'It is now time that we arrange our key, as far as discovered, in a tabular form, to avoid confusion. It will stand thus:

5	represents	a
†	"	d
8	"	e
3	"	g
4	"	h
6	"	i
*	"	n
‡	"	o
(	"	r
;	"	t
?	"	u

'We have, therefore, no less than eleven of the most important letters represented, and it will be unnecessary to proceed with the details of the solution. I have said enough to convince you that ciphers of this nature are readily soluble, and to give you some insight into the *rationale* of their development. But be assured that the specimen before us appertains to the very simplest species of cryptograph. It now only remains to give you the full translation of the characters upon the parchment, as unriddled. Here it is:

'"*A good glass in the bishop's hostel in the devil's seat forty-one degrees and thirteen minutes northeast and by north main branch seventh limb east side shoot from the left eye of the death's-head a bee-line from the tree through the shot fifty feet out.'"*

'But,' said I, 'the enigma seems still in as bad a condition as ever. How is it possible to extort a meaning from all this jargon about "devil's seats," "death's-heads," and "bishop's hostels"?'

'I confess,' replied Legrand, 'that the matter still wears a serious aspect, when regarded with a casual glance. My first endeavor was to divide the sentence into the natural division intended by the cryptographist.'

'You mean, to punctuate it?'

'Something of that kind.'

'But how was it possible to effect this?'

'I reflected that it had been a *point* with the writer to run his words together without division, so as to increase the difficulty of solution. Now, a not over-acute man, in pursuing such an object, would be nearly certain to overdo the matter. When, in the course of his composition, he arrived at a break in his subject which would naturally require a pause, or a point, he would be exceedingly apt to run his characters, at this place, more than usually close together. If you will observe the Ms., in the present instance, you will easily detect five such cases of unusual crowding. Acting upon this hint, I made the division thus:

' *"A good glass in the bishop's hostel in the devil's seat—forty one degrees and thirteen minutes—northeast and by north—main branch seventh limb east side—shoot from the left eye of the death's-head—a bee-line from the tree through the shot fifty feet out."* '

'Even this division,' said I, 'leaves me still in the dark.'

'It left me also in the dark,' replied Legrand, 'for a few days; during which I made diligent inquiry, in the neighborhood of Sullivan's Island, for any building which went by the name of the "Bishop's Hotel"; for, of course, I dropped the obsolete word "hostel." Gaining no information on the subject, I was on the point of extending my sphere of search, and proceeding in a more systematic manner, when, one morning, it entered into my head, quite suddenly, that this "Bishop's Hostel" might have some reference to an old family, of the name of Bessop, which, time out of mind, had held possession of an ancient manor-house, about four miles to the northward of the island. I accordingly went over to the plantation, and re-instituted my inquires among the older negroes of the place. At length one of the most aged of the women said that she had heard of such a place as *Bessop's Castle*, and thought that she could guide me to it, but that it was not a castle, nor a tavern, but a high rock.

'I offered to pay her well for her trouble, and, after some demur, she consented to accompany me to the spot. We found it without much difficulty, when, dismissing her, I proceeded to examine the place. The "castle" consisted of an irregular assemblage of cliffs and rocks—one of the latter being quite remarkable for its height as well as for its insulated and artificial appearance. I clambered to its apex, and then felt much at a loss as to what should be next done.

'While I was busied in reflection, my eyes fell upon a narrow ledge in the eastern face of the rock, perhaps a yard below the summit upon which I stood. This ledge projected about eighteen inches, and was not more than a foot wide, while a niche in the cliff just above it gave it a rude resemblance to one of the hollow-backed chairs used by our ancestors. I made no doubt that here was the "devil's-seat" alluded to in the MS., and now I seemed to grasp the full secret of the riddle.

'The "good glass," I knew, could have reference to nothing but a telescope; for the word "glass" is rarely employed in any other sense by seamen. Now here, I at once saw, was a telescope to be used, and a definite point of view, *admitting no variation,* from which to use it. Nor did I hesitate to believe that the phrases, "forty-one degrees and thirteen minutes," and "northeast and by north," were intended as directions for the levelling of the glass. Greatly excited by these discoveries, I hurried home, procured a telescope, and returned to the rock.

'I let myself down to the ledge, and found that it was impossible to retain a seat upon it except in one particular position. This fact confirmed my preconceived idea. I proceeded to use the glass. Of course, the "forty-one degrees and thirteen minutes" could allude to nothing but elevation above the visible horizon, since the horizontal direction was clearly indicated by the words, "northeast and by north." This latter direction I at once established by means of a pocket compass; then, pointing the glass as nearly at an angle of forty-one degrees of elevation as I could do it by guess, I moved it cautiously up or down, until my attention was arrested by a circular rift or opening in the foliage of a large tree that overtopped its fellows in the distance. In the centre of this rift I perceived a white spot, but could not, at first, distinguish what it was. Adjusting the focus of the telescope, I again looked, and now made it out to be a human skull.

'Upon this discovery I was so sanguine as to consider the enigma solved; for the phrase "main branch, seventh limb, east side," could refer only to the position of the skull upon the tree, while "shoot from the left eye of the death's-head" admitted, also, of but one interpretation, in regard to a search for buried treasure. I perceived that the design was to drop a bullet from the left eye of the skull, and that a bee-line, or, in other words, a straight line, drawn from the nearest point of the trunk through "the shot" (or the spot where the bullet fell), and thence extended to a distance of fifty feet, would indicate a definite point—and beneath this point I thought it at least *possible* that a deposit of value lay concealed.'

'All this,' I said, 'is exceedingly clear, and, although ingenious, still simple and explicit. When you left the "Bishop's Hotel," what then?'

'Why, having carefully taken the bearings of the tree, I turned homeward. The instant that I left "the devil's-seat," however, the circular rift vanished; nor could I get a glimpse of it afterward, turn as I would. What seems to me the chief ingenuity in this whole business, is the fact (for repeated experiment has convinced me it *is* a fact) that the circular opening in question is visible from no other attainable point of view than that afforded by the narrow ledge upon the face of the rock.

'In this expedition to the "Bishop's Hotel" I had been attended by Jupiter, who had, no doubt, observed, for some weeks past, the abstraction of my demeanor, and took especial care not to leave me alone. But, on the next day, getting up very early, I contrived to give him the slip, and went into the hills in search of the tree. After much toil I found it. When I came home at night my valet proposed to give me a flogging. With the rest of the adventure I believe you are as well acquainted as myself.'

'I suppose,' said I, 'you missed the spot, in the first attempt at digging, through Jupiter's stupidity in letting the bug fall through the right instead of through the left eye of the skull.'

'Precisely. This mistake made a difference of about two inches and a half in the "shot"—that is to say, in the position of the peg nearest the tree; and had the treasure been *beneath* the "shot," the error would have been of little moment; but "the shot," together with the nearest point of the tree, were merely two points for the establishment of a line of direction; of course the error, however trivial in the beginning, increased as we proceeded with the line, and by the time we had gone fifty feet threw us quite off the scent. But for my deep seated impressions that treasure was here somewhere actually buried, we might have had all our labor in vain.'

'But your grandiloquence, and your conduct in swinging the beetle—how excessively odd! I was sure you were mad. And why did you insist upon letting fall the bug, instead of a bullet, from the skull?'

'Why, to be frank, I felt somewhat annoyed by your evident suspicions touching my sanity, and so resolved to punish you quietly, in my own way, by a little bit of sober mystification. For this reason I swung the beetle, and for this reason I let it fall from the tree. An observation of yours about its great weight suggested the latter idea.'

'Yes, I perceive; and now there is only one point which puzzles me. What are we to make of the skeletons found in the hole?'

'That is a question I am no more able to answer than yourself. There seems, however, only one plausible way of accounting for them—and yet it is dreadful to believe in such atrocity as my suggestion would imply. It is clear that Kidd—if Kidd indeed secreted this treasure, which I doubt not—it is clear that he must have had assistance in the labor. But this labor concluded, he may have thought it expedient to remove all participants in his secret. Perhaps a couple of blows with a mattock were sufficient, while his coadjutors were busy in the pit; perhaps it required a dozen—who shall tell?'

The Pit and the Pendulum

Impia tortorum longas hic turba furores
Sanguinis innocui, non satiata, aluit.
Sospite nunc patria, fracto nunc funeris antro,
Mors ubi dira fuit vita salusque patent.
[Quatrain composed for the gates of a market to be erected upon the site of the
Jacobin Club House at Paris.]

I WAS SICK——SICK UNTO death with that long agony; and when they at length unbound me, and I was permitted to sit, I felt that my senses were leaving me. The sentence—the dread sentence of death—was the last of distinct accentuation which reached my ears. After that, the sound of the inquisitorial voices seemed merged in one dreamy indeterminate hum. It conveyed to my soul the idea of *revolution*—perhaps from its association in fancy with the burr of a millwheel. This only for a brief period, for presently I heard no more. Yet, for a while, I saw—but with how terrible an exaggeration! I saw the lips of the blackrobed judges. They appeared to me white—whiter than the sheet upon which I trace these words—and thin even to grotesqueness; thin with the intensity of their expression of firmness—of immovable resolution—of stern contempt of human torture. I saw that the decrees of what to me was Fate were still issuing from those lips. I saw them writhe with a deadly locution. I saw them fashion the syllables of my name; and I shuddered because no sound succeeded. I saw, too, for a few moments of delirious horror, the soft and nearly imperceptible waving of the sable draperies which enwrapped the walls of the apartment. And then my vision fell upon the seven tall candles upon the table. At first they wore the aspect of charity, and seemed white slender angels who would save me; but then, all at once, there came a most deadly nausea over my spirit, and I felt every fibre in my frame thrill as if I had touched the wire of a galvanic battery, while the angel forms became meaningless spectres, with heads of flame, and I saw that from them there would be no help. And then there stole into my fancy, like a rich musical note, the thought of what sweet rest there must be in the grave. The thought came gently and stealthily, and it seemed long before it attained full appreciation; but just as my spirit came at length properly to feel and entertain it, the figures of the judges vanished, as if magically, from before me; the tall candles sank into nothingness; their flames went out utterly; the blackness of darkness supervened; all sensations appeared swallowed up in a mad rushing descent as of the soul into Hades. Then silence, and stillness, and night were the universe.

I had swooned; but still will not say that all of consciousness was lost. What of it there remained I will not attempt to define, or even to describe; yet all was not lost. In the deepest slumber—no! In delirium—no! In a swoon—no! In death—no! even in the grave all *is not* lost. Else there is no immortality for man. Arousing from the most profound of slumbers, we break the gossamer web of *some* dream. Yet in a second afterward (so frail may that web have been) we remember not that we have dreamed. In the return to life from the swoon there are two stages: first, that of the sense of mental or spiritual; secondly, that of the sense of physical, existence. It seems probable that if, upon reaching the second stage, we could recall the impressions of the first, we should find these impressions eloquent in memories of the gulf beyond. And that gulf is—what? How at least shall we distinguish its shadows from those of the tomb? But if the impressions of what I have termed the first stage are not, at will, recalled, yet, after long interval, do they not come unbidden, while we marvel whence they come? He who has never swooned, is not he who finds strange palaces and wildly familiar faces in coals that glow; is not he who beholds floating in mid-air the sad visions that the many may not view; is not he who ponders over the perfume of some novel flower; is not he whose brain grows bewildered with the meaning of some musical cadence which has never before arrested his attention.

Amid frequent and thoughtful endeavors to remember, amid earnest struggles to regather some token of the state of seeming nothingness into which my soul had lapsed, there have been moments when I have dreamed of success; there have been brief, very brief periods when I have conjured up remembrances which the lucid reason of a later epoch assures me could have had reference only to that condition of seeming unconsciousness. These shadows of memory tell, indistinctly, of tall figures that lifted and bore me in silence down—down—still down—till a hideous dizziness oppressed me at the mere idea of the interminableness of the descent. They tell also of a vague horror at my heart, on account of that heart's unnatural stillness. Then comes a sense of sudden motionlessness throughout all things; as if those who bore me (a ghastly train!) had outrun, in their descent, the limits of the limitless, and paused from the wearisomeness of their toil. After this I call to mind flatness and dampness; and then all is *madness*—the madness of a memory which busies itself among forbidden things.

Very suddenly there came back to my soul motion and sound—the tumultuous motion of the heart, and, in my ears, the sound of its beating. Then a pause in which all is blank. Then again sound, and motion, and touch—a tingling sensation pervading my frame. Then the mere consciousness of existence, without thought—a condition which lasted long. Then, very suddenly, *thought*, and shuddering terror, and earnest endeavor to comprehend my true state. Then a strong desire to lapse into insensibility. Then a rushing revival of soul and a successful effort to move. And now a full memory of the trial, of the judges, of the sable draperies, of the sentence, of the sickness, of the swoon. Then entire forgetfulness of all that followed; of all that a later day and much earnestness of endeavor have enabled me vaguely to recall.

So far, I had not opened my eyes. I felt that I lay upon my back, unbound. I reached out my hand, and it fell heavily upon something damp and hard. There I suffered it to remain for many minutes, while I strove to imagine where and *what* I could be. I longed, yet dared not, to employ my vision. I dreaded the first glance at objects around me. It was not that I feared to look upon things horrible, but that I grew aghast lest there should be *nothing* to see. At length, with a wild desperation at heart, I quickly unclosed my eyes. My worst thoughts, then, were confirmed. The blackness of eternal night encompassed me. I struggled for breath. The intensity of the darkness seemed to oppress and stifle me. The atmosphere was intolerably close. I still lay quietly, and made effort to exercise my reason. I brought to mind the inquisitorial proceedings, and attempted from that point to deduce my real condition. The sentence had passed; and it appeared to me that a very long interval of time had since elapsed. Yet not for a moment did I suppose my self actually dead. Such a supposition, notwithstanding what we read in fiction, is altogether inconsistent with real existence;—but where and in what state was I? The condemned to death, I knew, perished usually at the *auto-da-fés*, and one of these had been held on the very night of the day of my trial. Had I been remanded to my dungeon, to await the next sacrifice, which would not take place for many months? This I at once saw could not be. Victims had been in immediate demand. Moreover, my dungeon, as well as all the condemned cells at Toledo, had stone floors, and light was not altogether excluded.

A fearful idea now suddenly drove the blood in torrents upon my heart, and for a brief period I once more relapsed into insensibility. Upon recovering, I at once started to my feet, trembling convulsively in every fibre. I thrust my arms wildly above and around me in all directions. I felt nothing; yet dreaded to move a step, lest I should be impeded by the walls of a *tomb*. Perspiration burst from every pore, and stood in cold big beads upon my forehead. The agony of suspense grew at length intolerable, and I cautiously moved forward, with my arms extended, and my eyes straining from their sockets in the hope of catching some faint ray of light. I proceeded for many paces; but still all was blackness and vacancy. I breathed more freely. It seemed evident that mine was not, at least, the most hideous of fates.

And now, as I still continued to step cautiously onward, there came thronging upon my recollection a thousand vague rumors of the horrors of Toledo. Of the dungeons there had been strange things narrated—fables I had always deemed them—but yet strange, and too ghastly to repeat, save in a whisper. Was I left to perish of starvation in this subterranean world of darkness; or what fate, perhaps even more fearful, awaited me? That the result would be death, and a death of more than customary bitterness, I knew too well the character of my judges to doubt. The mode and the hour were all that occupied or distracted me.

My outstretched hands at length encountered some solid obstruction. It was a wall, seemingly of stone masonry—very smooth, slimy, and cold. I followed it up; stepping with all the careful distrust with which certain antique narratives had inspired me. This process, however, afforded me no means of ascertaining the dimensions of my dungeon, as I might make its circuit and return to the point whence I set out without being aware of the fact, so perfectly uniform seemed the wall. I therefore sought the knife which had been in my pocket when led into the inquisitorial chamber; but it was gone; my clothes had been exchanged for a wrapper of coarse serge. I had thought of forcing the blade in some minute crevice of the masonry, so as to identify my point of departure. The difficulty, nevertheless, was but trivial; although, in the disorder of my fancy, it seemed at first insuperable. I tore a part of the hem from the robe and placed the fragment at full length, and at right angles to the wall. In groping my way around the prison, I could not fail to encounter this rag upon completing the circuit. So, at least, I thought; but I had not counted upon the extent of the dungeon, or upon my own weakness. The ground was moist and slippery. I staggered onward for some time, when I stumbled and fell. My excessive fatigue induced me to remain prostrate; and sleep soon overtook me as I lay.

Upon awaking, and stretching forth an arm, I found beside me a loaf and a pitcher with water. I was too much exhausted to reflect upon this circumstance, but ate and drank with avidity. Shortly afterward, I resumed my tour around the prison, and with much toil, came at last upon the fragment of the serge. Up to the period when I fell, I had counted fifty-two paces, and, upon resuming my walk, I had counted forty-eight more—when I arrived at the rag. There were in all, then, a hundred paces; and, admitting two paces to the yard, I presumed the dungeon to be fifty yards in circuit. I had met, however, with many angles in the wall, and thus I could form no guess at the shape of the vault, for vault I could not help supposing it to be.

I had little object—certainly no hope—in these researches; but a vague curiosity prompted me to continue them. Quitting the wall, I resolved to cross the area of the enclosure. At first, I proceeded with extreme caution, for the floor, although seemingly of solid material, was treacherous with slime. At length, however, I took courage, and did not hesitate to step firmly— endeavoring to cross in as direct a line as possible. I had advanced some ten or twelve paces in this manner, when the remnant of the torn hem of my robe became entangled between my legs. I stepped on it, and fell violently on my face.

In the confusion attending my fall, I did not immediately apprehend a somewhat startling circumstance, which yet, in a few seconds afterward, and while I still lay prostrate, arrested my attention. It was this: my chin rested upon the floor of the prison, but my lips, and the upper portion of my head, although seemingly at a less elevation than the chin, touched nothing. At the same time, my forehead seemed bathed in a clammy vapor, and the peculiar smell of decayed fungus arose to my nostrils. I put forward my arm, and shuddered to find that I had fallen at the very brink of a circular pit, whose extent, of course, I had no means of ascertaining at the moment. Groping about the masonry just below the margin, I succeeded in dislodging a small fragment, and let it fall into the abyss. For many seconds I hearkened to its reverberations as it dashed against the sides of the chasm in its descent; at length, there was a sullen plunge into water, succeeded by loud echoes. At the same moment, there came a sound resembling the quick opening and as rapid closing of a door overhead, while a faint gleam of light flashed suddenly through the gloom, and as suddenly faded away.

I saw clearly the doom which had been prepared for me, and congratulated myself upon the timely accident by which I had escaped. Another step before my fall, and the world had seen me no more. And the death just avoided was of that very character which I had regarded as fabulous and frivolous in the tales respecting the Inquisition. To the victims of its tyranny, there was the choice of death with its direst physical agonies, or death with its most hideous moral horrors. I had been reserved for the latter. By long suffering my nerves had been unstrung, until I trembled at the sound of my own voice, and had become in every respect a fitting subject for the species of torture which awaited me.

Shaking in every limb, I groped my way back to the wall—resolving there to

perish rather than risk the terrors of the wells, of which my imagination now
pictured many in various positions about the dungeon. In other conditions of
mind, I might have had courage to end my misery at once, by a plunge into
one of these abysses; but now I was the veriest of cowards. Neither could I
forget what I had read of these pits—that the *sudden* extinction of life formed
no part of their most horrible plan.

Agitation of spirit kept me awake for many long hours, but at length I again
slumbered. Upon arousing, I found by my side, as before, a loaf and a pitcher
of water. A burning thirst consumed me, and I emptied the vessel at a
draught. It must have been drugged—for scarcely had I drunk, before I
became irresistibly drowsy. A deep sleep fell upon me—a sleep like that of
death. How long it lasted, of course I know not; but when, once again, I
unclosed my eyes, the objects around me were visible. By a wild, sulphurous
lustre, the origin of which I could not at first determine, I was enabled to see
the extent and aspect of the prison.

In its size I had been greatly mistaken. The whole circuit of its walls did not
exceed twenty-five yards. For some minutes this fact occasioned me a world of
vain trouble; vain indeed—for what could be of less importance, under the
terrible circumstances which environed me, than the mere dimensions of my
dungeon? But my soul took a wild interest in trifles, and I busied myself in
endeavors to account for the error I had committed in my measurement. The
truth at length flashed upon me. In my first attempt at exploration I had
counted fifty-two paces, up to the period when I fell: I must then have been
within a pace or two of the fragment of serge; in fact, I had nearly performed
the circuit of the vault. I then slept—and, upon awaking, I must have returned
upon my steps—thus supposing the circuit nearly double what it actually was.
My confusion of mind prevented me from observing that I began my tour with
the wall to the left, and ended it with the wall to the right.

I had been deceived, too, in respect to the shape of the enclosure. In feeling
my way I had found many angles, and thus deduced an idea of great
irregularity; so potent is the effect of total darkness upon one arousing from
lethargy or sleep! The angles were simply those of a few slight depressions, or
niches, at odd intervals. The general shape of the prison was square. What I
had taken for masonry seemed now to be iron, or some other metal, in huge
plates, whose sutures or joints occasioned the depression. The entire surface
of this metallic enclosure was rudely daubed in all the hideous and repulsive
devices to which the charnel superstition of the monks has given rise. The
figures of fiends in aspects of menace, with skeleton forms, and other more
really fearful images, overspread and disfigured the walls. I observed that the
outlines of these monstrosities were sufficiently distinct, but that the colors
seemed faded and blurred, as if from the effects of a damp atmosphere. I now
noticed the floor, too, which was of stone. In the centre yawned the circular pit
from whose jaws I had escaped; but it was the only one in the dungeon.

All this I saw indistinctly and by much effort—for my personal condition
had been greatly changed during slumber. I now lay upon my back, and at full
length, on a species of low framework of wood. To this I was securely bound
by a long strap resembling a surcingle. It passed in many convolutions about
my limbs and body, leaving at liberty only my head, and my left arm to such
extent, that I could, by dint of much exertion, supply myself with food from
an earthen dish which lay by my side on the floor. I saw, to my horror, that the

pitcher had been removed. I say to my horror—for I was consumed with intolerable thirst. This thirst it appeared to be the design of my persecutors to stimulate—for the food in the dish was meat pungently seasoned.

Looking upward, I surveyed the ceiling of my prison. It was some thirty or forty feet overhead, and constructed much as the side walls. In one of its panels a very singular figure riveted my whole attention. It was the painted figure of Time as he is commonly represented, save that, in lieu of a scythe, he held what, at a casual glance, I supposed to be the pictured image of a huge pendulum, such as we see on antique clocks. There was something, however, in the appearance of this machine which caused me to regard it more attentively. While I gazed directly upward at it (for its position was immediately over my own) I fancied that I saw it in motion. In an instant afterward the fancy was confirmed. Its sweep was brief, and of course slow. I watched it for some minutes somewhat in fear, but more in wonder. Wearied at length with observing its dull movement, I turned my eyes upon the other objects in the cell.

A slight noise attracted my notice, and looking to the floor, I saw several enormous rats traversing it. They had issued from the well which lay just within view to my right. Even then, while I gazed, they came up in troops, hurriedly, with ravenous eyes, allured by the scent of the meat. From this it required much effort and attention to scare them away.

It might have been half an hour, perhaps even an hour (for I could take but imperfect note of time), before I again cast my eyes upward. What I then saw confounded and amazed me. The sweep of the pendulum had increased in extent by nearly a yard. As a natural consequence its velocity was also much greater. But what mainly disturbed me was the idea that it had perceptibly *descended*. I now observed—with what horror it is needless to say—that its nether extremity was formed of a crescent of glittering steel, about a foot in length from horn to horn; the horns upward, and the under edge evidently as keen as that of a razor. Like a razor also, it seemed massy and heavy, tapering from the edge into a solid and broad structure above. It was appended to a weighty rod of brass, and the whole *hissed* as it swung through the air.

I could no longer doubt the doom prepared for me by monkish ingenuity in torture. My cognizance of the pit had become known to the inquisitorial agents—*the pit*, whose horrors had been destined for so bold a recusant as myself—*the pit*, typical of hell and regarded by rumor as the Ultima Thule of all their punishments. The plunge into this pit I had avoided by the merest of accidents, and I knew that surprise, or entrapment into torment, formed an important portion of all the grotesquerie of these dungeon deaths. Having failed to fall, it was no part of the demon plan to hurl me into the abyss, and thus (there being no alternative) a different and a milder destruction awaited me. Milder! I half smiled in my agony as I thought of such application of such a term.

What boots it to tell of the long, long hours of horror more than mortal, during which I counted the rushing oscillations of the steel! Inch by inch—line by line—with a descent only appreciable at intervals that seemed ages—down and still down it came! Days passed—it might have been that many days passed—ere it swept so closely over me as to fan me with its acrid breath. The odor of the sharp steel forced itself into my nostrils. I prayed—I wearied heaven with my prayer for its more speedy descent. I grew frantically mad, and struggled to force myself upward against the sweep of the fearful scimitar. And then I fell suddenly calm, and lay smiling at the glittering death, as a child at some rare bauble.

There was another interval of utter insensibility; it was brief; for, upon again lapsing into life, there had been no perceptible descent in the pendulum. But it might have been long—for I knew there were demons who took note of my swoon, and who could have arrested the vibration at pleasure. Upon my recovery, too, I felt very—oh! inexpressibly—sick and weak, as if through long inanition. Even amid the agonies of that period, the human nature craved food. With painful effort I outstretched my left arm as far as my bonds permitted, and took possession of the small remnant which had been spared me by the rats. As I put a portion of it within my lips, there rushed to my mind a half-formed thought of joy—of hope. Yet what business had I with hope? It was, as I say, a half-formed thought—man has many such, which are never completed. I felt that it was of joy—of hope; but I felt also that it had perished in its formation. In vain I struggled to perfect—to regain it. Long suffering had nearly annihilated all my ordinary powers of mind. I was an imbecile—an idiot.

The vibration of the pendulum was at right angles to my length. I saw that the crescent was designed to cross the region of the heart. It would fray the serge of my robe—it would return and repeat its operations—again—and again. Notwithstanding its terrifically wide sweep (some thirty feet or more), and the hissing vigor of its descent, sufficient to sunder these very walls of iron, still the fraying of my robe would be all that, for several minutes, it would accomplish. And at this thought I paused. I dared not go further than this reflection. I dwelt upon it with a pertinacity of attention—as if, in so dwelling, I could arrest *here* the descent of the steel. I forced myself to ponder upon the sound of the crescent as it should pass across the garment—upon the peculiar thrilling sensation which the friction of cloth produces on the nerves. I pondered upon all this frivolity until my teeth were on edge.

Down—steadily down it crept. I took a frenzied pleasure in contrasting its downward with its lateral velocity. To the right—to the left—far and wide— with the shriek of a damned spirit! to my heart, with the stealthy pace of the tiger! I alternately laughed and howled, as the one or the other idea grew predominant.

Down—certainly, relentlessly down! It vibrated within three inches of my bosom! I struggled violently—furiously—to free my left arm. This was free only from the elbow to the hand. I could reach the latter, from the platter beside me, to my mouth, with great effort, but no farther. Could I have broken the fastenings above the elbow, I would have seized and attempted to arrest the pendulum. I might as well have attempted to arrest an avalanche!

Down—still unceasingly—still inevitably down! I gasped and struggled at each vibration. I shrunk convulsively at its every sweep. My eyes followed its outward or upward whirls with the eagerness of the most unmeaning despair; they closed themselves spasmodically at the descent, although death would have been a relief, oh, how unspeakable! Still I quivered in every nerve to think how slight a sinking of the machinery would precipitate that keen, glistening axe upon my bosom. It was *hope* that prompted the nerve to quiver—the frame to shrink. It was *hope*—the hope that triumphs on the rack—that whispers to the death-condemned even in the dungeons of the Inquisition.

I saw that some ten or twelve vibrations would bring the steel in actual contact with my robe—and with this observation there suddenly came over my spirit all the keen, collected calmness of despair. For the first time during many hours—or perhaps days—I *thought*. It now occurred to me, that the bandage, or surcingle, which enveloped me, was *unique*. I was tied by no separate cord. The first stroke of the razor-like crescent athwart any portion of the band would so detach it that it might be unwound from my person by means of my left hand. But how fearful, in that case, the proximity of the steel! The result of the slightest struggle, how deadly! Was it likely, moreover, that the minions of the torturer had not foreseen and provided for this possibilty? Was it probable that the bandage crossed my bosom in the track of the pendulum? Dreading to find my faint and, as it seemed, my last hope frustrated, I so far elevated my head as to obtain a distinct view of my breast. The surcingle enveloped my limbs and body close in all directions—*save in the path of the destroying crescent*.

Scarcely had I dropped my head back into its original position, when there flashed upon my mind what I cannot better describe than as the unformed half of that idea of deliverance to which I have previously alluded, and of which a moiety only floated indeterminately through my brain when I raised food to my burning lips. The whole thought was now present—feeble, scarcely sane, scarcely definite—but still entire. I proceeded at once, with the nervous energy of despair, to attempt its execution.

For many hours the immediate vicinity of the low framework upon which I lay had been literally swarming with rats. They were wild, bold, ravenous—their red eyes glaring upon me as if they waited but for motionlessness on my part to make me their prey. 'To what food,' I thought, 'have they been accustomed in the well?'

They had devoured, in spite of all my efforts to prevent them, all but a small remnant of the contents of the dish. I had fallen into an habitual see-saw or wave of the hand about the platter; and, at length, the unconscious uniformity of the movement deprived it of effect. In their voracity, the vermin frequently fastened their sharp fangs in my fingers. With the particles of the oily and spicy viand which now remained, I thoroughly rubbed the bandage wherever I could reach it; then, raising my hand from the floor, I lay breathlessly still.

At first, the ravenous animals were startled and terrified at the change—at the cessation of movement. They shrank alarmedly back; many sought the well. But this was only for a moment. I had not counted in vain upon their voracity. Observing that I remained without motion, one or two of the boldest leaped upon the framework, and smelt at the surcingle. This seemed the signal for a general rush. Forth from the well they hurried in fresh troops. They clung to the wood—they overran it, and leaped in hundreds upon my person. The measured movement of the pendulum disturbed them not at all. Avoiding its strokes, they busied themselves with the anointed bandage. They pressed—they swarmed upon me in ever accumulating heaps. They writhed upon my throat; their cold lips sought my own; I was half stifled by their thronging pressure; disgust, for which the world has no name, swelled my bosom, and chilled, with a heavy clamminess, my heart. Yet one minute, and I felt that the struggle would be over. Plainly I perceived the loosening of the bandage. I knew that in more than one place it must be already severed. With a more than human resolution I lay *still*.

Nor had I erred in my calculations—nor had I endured in vain. I at length felt that I was *free*. The surcingle hung in ribands from my body. But the stroke of the pendulum already pressed upon my bosom. It had divided the serge of the robe. It had cut through the linen beneath. Twice again it swung, and a sharp sense of pain shot through every nerve. But the moment of escape had arrived. At a wave of my hand my deliverers hurried tumultuously away. With a steady movement—cautious, sidelong, shrinking, and slow—I slid from the embrace of the bandage and beyond the reach of the scimitar. For the moment, at least, *I was free*.

Free!—and in the grasp of the Inquisition! I had scarcely stepped from my wooden bed of horror upon the stone floor of the prison, when the motion of the hellish machine ceased, and I beheld it drawn up, by some invisible force, through the ceiling. This was a lesson which I took desperately to heart. My every motion was undoubtedly watched. Free!—I had but escaped death in one form of agony, to be delivered unto worse than death in some other. With that thought I rolled my eyes nervously around on the barriers of iron that hemmed me in. Something unusual—some change which, at first, I could not appreciate distinctly—it was obvious, had taken place in the apartment. For many minutes of a dreamy and trembling abstraction, I busied myself in vain, unconnected conjecture. During this period, I became aware, for the first time, of the origin of the sulphurous light which illumined the cell. It proceeded from a fissure, about half an inch in width, extending entirely around the prison at the base of the walls, which thus appeared, and were completely separated from the floor. I endeavored, but of course in vain, to look through the aperture.

As I arose from the attempt, the mystery of the alteration in the chamber broke at once upon my understanding. I have observed that, although the outlines of the figures upon the walls were sufficiently distinct, yet the colors seemed blurred and indefinite. These colors had now assumed, and were momentarily assuming, a startling and most intense brilliancy, that gave to the spectral and fiendish portraitures an aspect that might have thrilled even firmer nerves than my own. Demon eyes, of a wild and ghastly vivacity, glared upon me in a thousand directions, where none had been visible before, and gleamed with the lurid lustre of a fire that I could not force my imagination to regard as unreal.

Unreal!—Even while I breathed there came to my nostrils the breath of the vapor of heated iron! A suffocating odor pervaded the prison! A deeper glow settled each moment in the eyes that glared at my agonies! A richer tint of crimson diffused itself over the pictured horrors of blood. I panted! I gasped for breath! There could be no doubt of the design of my tormentors—oh! most unrelenting! oh! most demoniac of men! I shrank from the glowing metal to the centre of the cell. Amid the thought of the fiery destruction that impended, the idea of the coolness of the well came over my soul like balm. I rushed to its deadly brink. I threw my straining vision below. The glare from the enkindled roof illumined its inmost recesses. Yet, for a wild moment, did my spirit refuse to comprehend the meaning of what I saw. At length it forced—it wrestled its way into my soul—it burned itself in upon my shuddering reason. Oh! for a voice to speak!—oh! horror!—oh! any horror but this! With a shriek, I rushed from the margin, and buried my face in my hands—weeping bitterly.

The heat rapidly increased, and once again I looked up, shuddering as with a fit of the ague. There had been a second change in the cell—and now the change was obviously in the *form*. As before, it was in vain that I at first endeavored to appreciate or understand what was taking place. But not long was I left in doubt. The Inquisitorial vengeance had been hurried by my two-fold escape, and there was to be no more dallying with the King of Terrors. The room had been square. I saw that two of its iron angles were now acute—two, consequently, obtuse. The fearful difference quickly increased with a low rumbling or moaning sound. In an instant the apartment had shifted its form into that of a lozenge. But the alteration stopped not here—I neither hoped nor desired it to stop. I could have clasped the red walls to my bosom as a garment of eternal peace. 'Death,' I said, 'any death but that of the pit!' Fool! might I not have known that *into the pit* it was the object of the burning iron to urge me? Could I resist its glow? or if even that, could I withstand its pressure? And now, flatter and flatter grew the lozenge, with a rapidity that left me no time for contemplation. Its centre, and of course its greatest width, came just over the yawning gulf. I shrank back—but the closing walls pressed me resistlessly onward. At length for my seared and writhing body there was no longer an inch of foothold on the firm floor of the prison. I struggled no more, but the agony of my soul found vent in one loud, long, and final scream of despair. I felt that I tottered upon the brink—I averted my eyes—

There was a discordant hum of human voices! There was a loud blast as of many trumpets! There was a harsh grating as of a thousand thunders! The fiery walls rushed back! An outstretched arm caught my own as I fell, fainting, into the abyss. It was that of General Lasalle. The French army had entered Toledo. The Inquisition was in the hands of its enemies.

The Cask of Amontillado

THE THOUSAND INJURIES OF Fortunato I had borne as I best could; but when he ventured upon insult, I vowed revenge. You, who so well know the nature of my soul, will not suppose, however, that I gave utterance to a threat. *At length* I would be avenged; this was a point definitively settled—but the very definitiveness with which it was resolved, precluded the idea of risk. I must not only punish, but punish with impunity. A wrong is unredressed when retribution overtakes its redresser. It is equally unredressed when the avenger fails to make himself felt as such to him who has done the wrong.

It must be understood, that neither by word nor deed had I given Fortunato cause to doubt my good-will. I continued, as was my wont, to smile in his face, and he did not perceive that my smile *now* was at the thought of his immolation.

He had a weak point—this Fortunato—although in other regards he was a man to be respected and even feared. He prided himself on his connoisseurship in wine. Few Italians have the true virtuoso spirit. For the most part their enthusiasm is adopted to suit the time and opportunity—to practise imposture upon the British and Austrian *millionnaires.* In painting and gemmary Fortunato, like his countrymen, was a quack—but in the matter of old wines he was sincere. In this respect I did not differ from him materially: I was skilful in the Italian vintages myself, and bought largely whenever I could.

It was about dusk, one evening during the supreme madness of the carnival season, that I encountered my friend. He accosted me with excessive warmth, for he had been drinking much. The man wore motley. He had on a tight-fitting parti-striped dress, and his head was surmounted by the conical cap and bells. I was so pleased to see him, that I thought I should never have done wringing his hand.

I said to him: 'My dear Fortunato, you are luckily met. How remarkably well you are looking to-day! But I have received a pipe of what passes for Amontillado, and I have my doubts.'

'How?' said he. 'Amontillado? A pipe? Impossible! And in the middle of the carnival!'

'I have my doubts,' I replied; 'and I was silly enough to pay the full Amontillado price without consulting you in the matter. You were not to be found, and I was fearful of losing a bargain.'

'Amontillado!'

'I have my doubts.'

'Amontillado!'

'And I must satisfy them.'

'Amontillado!'

'As you are engaged, I am on my way to Luchesi. If any one has a critical turn, it is he. He will tell me——'

'Luchesi cannot tell Amontillado from Sherry.'

'And yet some fools will have it that his taste is a match for your own.'

'Come, let us go.'

'Whither?'

'To your vaults.'

'My friend, no; I will not impose upon your good nature. I perceive you have an engagement. Luchesi——'

'I have no engagement;—come.'

'My friend, no. It is not the engagement, but the severe cold with which I perceive you are afflicted. The vaults are insufferably damp. They are encrusted with nitre.'

'Let us go, nevertheless. The cold is merely nothing. Amontillado! You have been imposed upon. And as for Luchesi, he cannot distinguish Sherry from Amontillado.'

Thus speaking, Fortunato possessed himself of my arm. Putting on a mask of black silk, and drawing a *roquelaire* closely about my person, I suffered him to hurry me to my palazzo.

There were no attendants at home; they had absconded to make merry in honor of the time. I had told them that I should not return until the morning, and had given them explicit orders not to stir from the house. These orders were sufficient, I well knew, to insure their immediate disappearance, one and all, as soon as my back was turned.

I took from their sconces two flambeaux, and giving one to Fortunato, bowed him through several suites of rooms to the archway that led into the vaults. I passed down a long and winding staircase, requesting him to be cautious as he followed. We came at length to the foot of the descent, and stood together on the damp ground of the catacombs of the Montresors.

The gait of my friend was unsteady, and the bells upon his cap jingled as he strode.

'The pipe?' said he.

'It is farther on,' said I; 'but observe the white web-work which gleams from these cavern walls.'

He turned toward me, and looked into my eyes with two filmy orbs that distilled the rheum of intoxication.

'Nitre?' he asked, at length.

'Nitre,' I replied. 'How long have you had that cough?'

'Ugh! ugh! ugh!—ugh! ugh! ugh!—ugh! ugh! ugh!—ugh! ugh! ugh!—ugh! ugh! ugh!'

My poor friend found it impossible to reply for many minutes.

'It is nothing,' he said, at last.

'Come,' I said, with decision, 'we will go back; your health is precious. You are rich, respected, admired, beloved; you are happy, as once I was. You are a man to be missed. For me it is no matter. We will go back; you will be ill, and I cannot be responsible. Besides, there is Luchesi——'

'Enough,' he said; 'the cough is a mere nothing; it will not kill me. I shall not die of a cough.'

'True—true,' I replied; 'and, indeed, I had no intention of alarming you unnecessarily; but you should use all proper caution. A draught of this Medoc will defend us from the damps.'

Here I knocked off the neck a bottle which I drew from a long row of its fellows that lay upon the mould.

'Drink,' I said, presenting him the wine.

He raised it to his lips with a leer. He paused and nodded to me familiarly, while his bells jingled.

'I drink,' he said, 'to the buried that repose around us.'

'And I to your long life.'

He again took my arm, and we proceeded.

'These vaults,' he said, 'are extensive.'

'The Montresors,' I replied, 'were a great and numerous family.'

'I forget your arms.'

'A huge human foot d'or, in a field azure; the foot crushes a serpent rampant whose fangs are imbedded in the heel.'

'And the motto?'

'*Nemo me impune lacessit.*'

'Good!' he said.

The wine sparkled in his eyes and the bells jingled. My own fancy grew warm with the Medoc. We had passed through walls of piled bones, with casks and puncheons intermingling, into the inmost recesses of the catacombs. I paused again, and this time I made bold to seize Fortunato by an arm above the elbow.

'The nitre!' I said; 'see, it increases. It hangs like moss upon the vaults. We are below the river's bed. The drops of moisture trickle among the bones. Come, we will go back ere it is too late. Your cough——'

'It is nothing,' he said; 'let us go on. But first, another draught of the Medoc.'

I broke and reached him a flagon of De Grâve. He emptied it at a breath. His eyes flashed with a fierce light. He laughed and threw the bottle upward with a gesticulation I did not understand.

I looked at him in surprise. He repeated the movement—a grotesque one.

'You do not comprehend?' he said.

'Not I,' I replied.

'Then you are not of the brotherhood.'

'How?'

'You are not of the masons.'

'Yes, yes,' I said; 'yes, yes.'

'You? Impossible! A mason?'

'A mason,' I replied.

'A sign,' he said.

'It is this,' I answered, producing a trowel from beneath the folds of my *roquelaire.*

'You jest,' he exclaimed, recoiling a few paces. 'But let us proceed to the Amontillado.'

'Be it so,' I said, replacing the tool beneath the cloak, and again offering him my arm. He leaned upon it heavily. We continued our route in search of the Amontillado. We passed through a range of low arches, descended, passed on, and descending again, arrived at a deep crypt, in which the foulness of the air caused our flambeaux rather to glow than flame.

At the most remote end of the crypt there appeared another less spacious. Its walls had been lined with human remains, piled to the vault overhead, in the fashion of the great catacombs of Paris. Three sides of this interior crypt were still ornamented in this manner. From the fourth the bones had been thrown down, and lay promiscuously upon the earth, forming at one point a mound of some size. Within the wall thus exposed by the displacing of the bones, we perceived a still interior recess, in depth about four feet, in width three, in height six or seven. It seemed to have been constructed for no especial use within itself, but formed merely the interval between two of the colossal supports of the roof of the catacombs, and was backed by one of their circumscribing walls of solid granite.

It was in vain that Fortunato, uplifting his dull torch, endeavored to pry into the depth of the recess. Its termination the feeble light did not enable us to see.

'Proceed,' I said; 'herein is the Amontillado. As for Luchesi——'

'He is an ignoramus,' interrupted my friend, as he stepped unsteadily forward, while I followed immediately at his heels. In an instant he had reached the extremity of the niche, and finding his progress arrested by the rock, stood stupidly bewildered. A moment more and I had fettered him to the granite. In its surface were two iron staples, distant from each other about two feet, horizontally. From one of these depended a short chain, from the other a padlock. Throwing the links about his waist, it was but the work of a few seconds to secure it. He was too much astounded to resist. Withdrawing the key I stepped back from the recess.

'Pass your hand,' I said, 'over the wall; you cannot help feeling the nitre. Indeed it is *very* damp. Once more let me *implore* you to return. No? Then I must positively leave you. But I must first render you all the little attentions in my power.'

'The Amontillado!' ejaculated my friend, not yet recovered from his astonishment.

'True,' I replied; 'the Amontillado.'

As I said these words I busied myself among the pile of bones of which I have before spoken. Throwing them aside, I soon uncovered a quantity of building stone and mortar. With these materials and with the aid of my trowel, I began vigorously to wall up the entrance of the niche.

I had scarcely laid the first tier of the masonry when I discovered that the intoxication of Fortunato had in a great measure worn off. The earliest indication I had of this was a low moaning cry from the depth of the recess. It was *not* the cry of a drunken man. There was then a long and obstinate silence. I laid the second tier, and the third, and the fourth; and then I heard the furious vibrations of the chain. The noise lasted for several minutes, during which, that I might hearken to it with the more satisfaction, I ceased my labors and sat down upon the bones. When at last the clanking subsided, I resumed the trowel, and finished without interruption the fifth, the sixth, and the seventh tier. The wall was now nearly upon a level with my breast. I again paused, and holding the flambeaux over the mason-work, threw a few feeble rays upon the figure within.

A succession of loud and shrill screams, bursting suddenly from the throat of the chained form, seemed to thrust me violently back. For a brief moment I hesitated—I trembled. Unsheathing my rapier, I began to grope with it about the recess; but the thought of an instant reassured me. I placed my hand upon the solid fabric of the catacombs, and felt satisfied. I reapproached the wall. I replied to the yells of him who clamored. I re-echoed—I aided—I surpassed them in volume and in strength. I did this, and the clamorer grew still.

It was now midnight, and my task was drawing to a close. I had completed the eighth, the ninth, and the tenth tier. I had finished a portion of the last and the eleventh; there remained but a single stone to be fitted and plastered in. I struggled with its weight; I placed it partially in its destined position. But now there came from out the niche a low laugh that erected the hairs upon my head. It was succeeded by a sad voice, which I had difficulty in recognizing as that of the noble Fortunato. The voice said—

'Ha! ha! ha!—he! he!—a very good joke indeed—an excellent jest. We will have many a rich laugh about it at the palazzo—he! he! he!—over our wine—he! he! he!'

'The Amontillado!' I said.

'He! he! he!—he! he! he!—yes, the Amontillado. But is it not getting late? Will not they be awaiting us at the palazzo, the Lady Fortunato and the rest? Let us be gone.'

'Yes,' I said, 'let us be gone.'

'For the love of God, Montresor!'

'Yes,' I said, 'for the love of God!'

But to these words I hearkened in vain for a reply. I grew impatient. I called aloud:

'Fortunato!'

No answer. I called again:

'Fortunato!'

No answer still. I thrust a torch through the remaining aperture and let it fall within. There came forth in return only a jingling of the bells. My heart grew sick—on account of the dampness of the catacombs. I hastened to make an end of my labor. I forced the last stone into its position; I plastered it up. Against the new masonry I re-erected the old rampart of bones. For the half of a century no mortal has disturbed them. *In pace requiescat!*

HARRIET
BEECHER STOWE
1811-1896

The first important American woman writer, Harriet Beecher Stowe was born in Connecticut in 1811. Although her strict Calvinist upbringing inevitably influenced the moral tone of her writing, her most famous work *Uncle Tom's Cabin* remains today one of the most popular books ever published in the United States. In spite of the somewhat limited scope of her imaginative world Harriet Beecher Stowe's undeniable gifts of narrative technique and characterization have earned her an important place in the evolutionary development of American fiction.

Although less well-known for her shorter writings, Harriet Beecher Stowe produced, in fact, several collections of 'fireside tales', stories of domestic and rural life. 'Captain Kidd's Money' (1872) is one of the best of these humorous tales, based on the favorite belief that there is a pot of gold, especially pirate gold, at the end of the rainbow for him who deserves it.

Captain Kidd's Money

ONE OF OUR MOST FAVORITE legendary resorts was the old barn.

Sam Lawson preferred it on many accounts. It was quiet and retired, that is to say, at such distance from his own house, that he could not hear if Hepsy called ever so loudly, and farther off than it would be convenient for that industrious and painstaking woman to follow him. Then there was the soft fragrant cushion of hay, on which his length of limb could be easily bestowed.

Our barn had an upper loft with a swinging outer door that commanded a view of the old mill, the waterfall, and the distant windings of the river, with its grassy green banks, its graceful elm draperies, and its white flocks of water-lilies; and then on this Saturday afternoon we had Sam all to ourselves. It was a drowsy, dreamy October day, when the hens were lazily 'craw, crawing,' in a soft, conversational undertone with each other, as they scratched and picked the hay-seed under the barn windows. Below in the barn black Caesar sat quietly hatchelling flax, sometimes gurgling and giggling to himself with an overflow of that interior jollity with which he seemed to be always full. The African in New England was a curious contrast to everybody around him in the joy and satisfaction that he seemed to feel in the mere fact of being alive. Every white person was glad or sorry for some appreciable cause in the past, present, or future, which was capable of being definitely stated: but black Caesar was in an eternal giggle and frizzle and simmer of enjoyment for which he could give no earthly reason: he was an 'embodied joy,' like Shelley's skylark.

'Jest hear him,' said Sam Lawson, looking pensively over the haymow, and strewing hayseed down on his wool. 'How that 'are critter seems to tickle and laugh all the while 'bout nothin'. Lordy massy he don't seem never to consider that "this life's a dream, an empty show."'

'Look here, Sam,' we broke in, anxious to cut short a threatened stream of morality, 'you promised to tell us about Capt. Kidd, and how you dug for his money.'

'Did I, now? Wal, boys, that 'are history o' Kidd's is a warnin' to fellers. Why, Kidd had pious parents and Bible and sanctuary privileges when he was a boy, and yet come to be hanged. It's all in this 'ere song I'm goin' to sing ye. Lordy massy! I wish I had my bass-viol now. – Caesar,' he said, calling down from his perch, 'can't you strike the pitch o' "Cap'n Kidd," on your fiddle?'

Caesar's fiddle was never far from him. It was, in fact, tucked away in a nice little nook just over the manger; and he often caught an interval from his work to scrape a dancing-tune on it, keeping time with his heels, to our great delight.

A most wailing minor-keyed tune was doled forth, which seemed quite refreshing to Sam's pathetic vein, as he sang in his most lugubrious tones, –

> ‘"My name was Robert Kidd
>   As I sailed, as I sailed,
> My name was Robert Kidd;
> God's laws I did forbid,
> And so wickedly I did,
>   As I sailed, as I sailed."

'Now ye see, boys, he's goin' to tell how he abused his religious privileges; just here now: –

> ‘"My father taught me well,
>   As I sailed, as I sailed;
> My father taught me well
> To shun the gates of hell,
> But yet I did rebel,
>   As I sailed, as I sailed.

> ‘"He put a Bible in my hand,
>   As I sailed, as I sailed;
> He put a Bible in my hand,
> And I sunk it in the sand
> Before I left the strand,
>   As I sailed, as I sailed."

'Did ye ever hear o' such a hardened, contrary critter, boys? It's awful to think on. Wal, ye see that 'are's the way fellers allers begin the ways of sin, by turnin' their backs on the Bible and the advice o' pious parents. Now hear what he come to: –

> ‘"Then I murdered William More,
>   As I sailed, as I sailed;
> I murdered William More,
> And left him in his gore,
> Not many leagues from shore,
>   As I sailed, as I sailed.

> ‘"To execution dock
>   I must go, I must go.
> To execution dock,
> While thousands round me flock,
> To see me on the block,
>   I must go, I must go."

'There was a good deal more on't,' said Sam, pausing, 'but I don't seem to remember it; but it's real solemn and affectin'.'

'Who was Capt. Kidd, Sam?' said I.

'Wal, he was an officer in the British navy, and he got to bein' a pirate: used to take ships and sink 'em, and murder the folks; and so they say he got no end o' money, – gold and silver and precious stones, as many as the wise men in the East. But ye see, what good did it all do him? He couldn't use it, and dar'sn't keep it; so he used to bury it in spots round here and there in the awfullest heathen way ye ever heard of. Why, they say he allers used to kill one or two men or women or children of his prisoners, and bury with it, so that their sperits might keep watch on it ef anybody was to dig arter it. That 'are thing has been tried and tried and tried, but no man nor mother's son on 'em ever got a cent that dug. 'Twas tried here'n Oldtown; and they come pretty nigh gettin' on't, but it gin 'em the slip. Ye see, boys, *it's the Devil's money*, and he holds a pretty tight grip on't.'

'Well, how was it about digging for it? Tell us, did *you* do it? Were *you* there? Did you see it? and why couldn't they get it?' we both asked eagerly and in one breath.

'Why, Lordy massy! boys, your questions tumbles over each other thick as martins out o' a martin-box. Now, you jest be moderate and let alone, and I'll tell you all about it from the beginnin' to the end. I didn't railly have no hand in't, though I was knowin' to 't, as I be to most things that goes on round here; but my conscience wouldn't railly a let me start on no sich undertakin'.

'Wal, the one that fust sot the thing a goin' was old Mother Hokum, that used to live up in that little tumble-down shed by the cranberry-pond up beyond the spring pastur'. They had a putty bad name, them Hokums. How they got a livin' nobody knew; for they didn't seem to pay no attention to raisin' nothin' but childun, but the duce knows, there was plenty o' them. Their old hut was like a rabbit-pen: there was a tow-head to every crack and cranny. 'Member what old Caesar said once when the word come to the store that old Hokum had got twins. "S'pose de Lord knows best," says Caesar, "but *I* thought dere was Hokums enough afore." Wal, even poor workin' industrious folks like me finds it's hard gettin' along when there's so many mouths to feed. Lordy massy! there don't never seem to be no end on't, and so it ain't wonderful, come to thing on't, ef folks like them Hokums gets tempted to help along in ways that ain't quite right. Anyhow, folks did use to think that old Hokum was too sort o' familiar with their wood-piles 'long in the night, though they couldn't never prove it on him; and when Mother Hokum come to houses round to wash, folks use sometimes to miss pieces, here and there, though they never could find 'em on her; then they was allers a gettin' in debt here and a gettin' in debt there. Why, they got to owin' two dollars to Joe Gidger for butcher's meat. Joe was sort o' good-natured and let 'em have meat, 'cause Hokum he promised so fair to pay; but he couldn't never get it out o' him. 'Member once Joe walked clear up to the cranberry-pond arter that 'are two dollars; but Mother Hokum she see him a comin' jest as he comes past the juniper-bush on the corner. She says to Hokum, "Get into bed, old man, quick, and let me tell the story," says she. So she covered him up; and when Gidger come in she come up to him, and says she, "Why, Mr Gidger, I'm jest ashamed to see ye: why, Mr Hokum was jest a comin' down to pay ye that 'are money last week, but ye see he was took down with the small-pox" – Joe didn't hear no more: he just turned round, and he streaked it out that 'are door with his coat-tails flyin' out straight ahind him; and old Mother Hokum she jest stood at the window holdin' her sides and laughin' fit to split, to see him run. That 'are's jest a sample of the ways them Hokums cut up.

'Wal, you see, boys, there's a queer kind o' rock down on the bank o' the river, that looks sort o' like a grave-stone. The biggest part on't is sunk down under ground, and it's pretty well growed over with blackberry-vines; but, when you scratch the bushes away, they used to make out some queer marks on that 'are rock. They was sort o' lines and crosses; and folks would have it that them was Kidd's private marks, and that there was one o' the places where he hid his money.

'Wal, there's no sayin' fairly how it come to be thought so; but fellers used to say so, and they used sometimes to talk it over to the tahvern; and kind o' wonder whether or no, if they should dig, they wouldn't come to suthin'.

'Wal, old Mother Hokum she heard on't, and she was a sort o' enterprisin' old crittur: fact was, she had to be, 'cause the young Hokums was jest like bag-worms, the more they growed the more they eat, and I expect she found it pretty hard to fill their mouths; and so she said ef there *was* any thing under that 'are rock, they'd as good's have it as the Devil; and so she didn't give old Hokum no peace o' his life, but he must see what there was there.

'Wal, I was with 'em the night they was a talkin' on't up. Ye see, Hokum he got thirty-seven cents' worth o' lemons and sperit. I see him goin' by as I was out a splittin' kindlin's; and says he, "Sam, you jest go 'long up to our house tonight," says he: "Toddy Whitney and Harry Wiggin's comin' up, and we're goin' to have a little suthin' hot," says he; and he kind o' showed me the lemons and sperit. And I told him I guessed I would go 'long. Wal, I kind o' wanted to see what they'd be up to, ye know.

'Wal, come to find out, they was a talkin' about Cap'n Kidd's treasures, and layin' out how they should get it, and a settin' one another on with gret stories about it.

'"I've heard that there was whole chists full o' gold guineas," says one.

'"And I've heard o' gold bracelets and ear-rings and finger-rings all sparklin' with diamonds," says another.

'"Maybe it's old silver plate from some o' them old West Indian grandees," says another.

'"Wal, whatever it is," says Mother Hokum, "I want to be into it," says she.

'"Wal, Sam, won't you jine?" says they.

'"Wal, boys," says I, "I kind o' don't feel jest like j'inin'. I sort o' ain't clear about the rights on't: seems to me it's mighty nigh like goin' to the Devil for money."

'"Wal," says Mother Hokum, "what if 'tis? Money's money, get it how ye will; and the Devil's money 'll buy as much meat as any. I'd go to the Devil, if he gave good money."

'"Wal, I guess I wouldn't," says I. "Don't you 'member the sermon Parson Lothrop preached about hastin' to be rich, last Sabba' day?"

'"Parson Lothrop be hanged!" says she. "Wal, now," says she, "I like to see a parson with his silk stockin's and great gold-headed cane, a lollopin' on his carriage behind his fat, prancin' hosses, comin' to meetin' to preach to us poor folks not to want to be rich! How'd he like to have forty-'leven children, and nothin' to put onto 'em or into 'em, I wonder? Guess if lady Lothrop had to rub and scrub, and wear her fingers to the bone as I do, she'd want to be rich; and I guess the parson, if he couldn't get a bellyful for a week, would be for diggin' up Kidd's money, or doing 'most any thing else to make the pot bile."

"'Wal," says I, "I'll kind o' go with ye, boys, and sort o' see how things turn out; but I guess I won't take no shere in't," says I.

'Wal, they got it all planned out. They was to wait till the full moon, and then they was to get Primus King to go with 'em and help do the diggin'. Ye see, Hokum and Toddy Whitney and Wiggin are all putty softly fellers, and hate dreffully to work; and I tell you the Kidd money ain't to be got without a pretty tough piece o' diggin'. Why, it's jest like diggin' a well to get at it. Now, Primus King was the master hand for diggin' wells, and so they said they'd get him by givin' on him a shere.

'Harry Wiggin he didn't want no nigger a sherin' in it, he said; but Toddy and Hokum they said that when there was such stiff diggin' to be done, they didn't care if they did go in with a nigger.

'Wal, Wiggin he said he hadn't no objection to havin' the nigger do the diggin',' it was *sherin' the profits* he objected to.

"'Wal," says Hokum, "you can't get him without," says he. "Primus knows too much," says he: "you can't fool him." Finally they 'greed that they was to give Primus twenty dollars, and shere the treasure 'mong themselves.

'Come to talk with Primus, he wouldn't stick in a spade, unless they'd pay him aforehand. Ye see, Primus was up to 'em; he knowed about Gidger and there wa'n't none on 'em that was particular good pay; and so they all jest hed to rake and scrape, and pay him down the twenty dollars among 'em; and they 'greed for the fust full moon, at twelve o'clock at night, the 9th of October.

'Wal, ye see I had to tell Hepsy I was goin' out to watch. Wal, so I was; but not jest in the way she took it: but, Lordy massy! a feller has to tell his wife suthin' to keep her quiet, ye know, 'specially Hepsy.

'Wal, wal, of all the moonlight nights that ever I did see, I never did see one equal to that. Why, you could see the color o' every thing. I 'member I could see how the huckleberry-bushes on the rock was red as blood when the moonlight shone through 'em; 'cause the leaves, you see, had begun to turn.

'Goin' on our way we got to talkin' about the sperits.

"'I ain't afraid on 'em," says Hokum. "What harm can a sperit do me?" says he. "I don't care ef there's a dozen on 'em;" and he took a swig at his bottle.

"'Oh! there ain't no sperits," says Harry Wiggin. "That 'are talk's all nonsense;" and he took a swig at *his* bottle.

"'Wal," says Toddy, "I don't know 'bout that 'are. Me and Ike Sanders has seen the sperits in the Cap'n Brown house. We thought we'd jest have a peek into the window one night; and there was a whole flock o' black colts without no heads on come rushin' on us and knocked us flat."

"'I expect you'd been at the tahvern," said Hokum.

"'Wal, yes, we had; but them was sperits: we wa'n't drunk, now; we was jest as sober as ever we was."

"'Wal, they won't get away my money," says Primus, "for I put it safe away in Dinah's teapot afore I come out;" and then he showed all his ivories from ear to ear. "I think all this 'are's sort o' foolishness," says Primus.

"'Wal," says I, "boys, I ain't a goin' to have no part or lot in this 'ere matter, but I'll jest lay it off to you how it's to be done. Ef Kidd's money is under this rock, there's *sperits* that watch it, and you mustn't give 'em no advantage. There mustn't be a word spoke from the time ye get sight o' the treasure till ye get it safe up on to firm ground," says I. "Ef ye do, it'll vanish right out o' sight. I've talked with them that has dug down to it and seen it; but they allers lost it, 'cause they'd call out and say suthin'; and the minute they spoke, away it went."

'Wal, so they marked off the ground; and Primus he begun to dig, and the rest kind o' sot round. It was so still it was kind o' solemn. Ye see, it was past twelve o'clock, and every critter in Oldtown was asleep; and there was two whippoorwills on the great Cap'n Brown elm-trees, that kep' a answerin' each other back and forward sort o' solitary like; and then every once in a while there'd come a sort o' strange whisper up among the elm-tree leaves, jest as if there was talkin' goin' on; and every time Primus struck his spade into the ground it sounded sort o' holler, jest as if he'd been a diggin' a grave. "It's kind o' melancholy," says I, "to think o' them poor critters that had to be killed and buried jest to keep this 'ere treasure. What awful things 'll be brought to light in the judgment day! Them poor critters they loved to live and hated to die as much as any on us; but no, they had to die jest to satisfy that critter's wicked will. I've heard them as though they could tell the Cap'n Kidd places by layin' their ear to the ground at midnight, and they'd hear groans and wailin's."'

'Why, Sam! were there really people who could tell where Kidd's money was?' I here interposed.

'Oh, sartin! why, yis. There was Shebna Bascom, he was one. Shebna could always tell what was under the earth. He'd cut a hazel-stick and hold it in his hand when folks was wantin' to know where to dig wells; and that 'are stick would jest turn in his hand, and p'int down till it would fairly grind the bark off; and ef you dug in that place you was sure to find a spring. Oh, yis! Shebna he's told many where the Kidd money was, and been with 'em when they dug for it; but the pester on't was they allers lost it, 'cause they would some on 'em speak afore they thought.'

'But, Sam, what about this digging? Let's know what come of it,' said we, as Sam appeared to lose his way in his story.

'Wal, ye see, they dug down about five feet, when Primus he struck his spade smack on something that chinked like iron.

'Wal, then Hokum and Toddy Whitney was into the hole in a minute: they made Primus get out, and they took the spade, 'cause they wanted to be sure to come on it themselves.

'Wal, they begun, and they dug and he scraped, and sure enough they came to a gret iron pot as big as your granny's dinner-pot, with an iron bale to it.

'Wal, then they put down a rope, and he put the rope through the handle; then Hokum and Toddy they clambered upon the bank, and all on 'em began to draw up jest as still and silent as could be. They drawed and they drawed, till they jest got it even with the ground, when Toddy spoke out all in a tremble, "There," says he, "*we've got it!*" And the minit he spoke they was both struck by *suthin'* that knocked 'em clean over; and the rope give a crack like a pistol-shot, and broke short off; and the pot went down, down, down, and they heard it goin', jink, jink, jink; and it went way down into the earth, and the ground closed over it; and then they heard the screechin'est laugh ye ever did hear.'

'I want to know, Sam, did you see the pot?' I exclaimed at this part of the story.

'Wal, no, I didn't. Ye see, I jest happened to drop asleep while they was diggin', I was so kind o' tired, and I didn't wake up till it was all over.

'I was waked up, 'cause there was consid'able of a scuffle; for Hokum was so mad at Toddy for speakin', that he was a fistin' on him; and old Primus he jest haw-hawed and laughed. "Wal, I got *my* money safe, anyhow," says he.

'"Wal, come to," say I. "'Tain't no use cryin' for spilt milk: You've jest got to turn in now and fill up this 'ere hole, else the selectmen 'll be down on ye."

'"Wal," says Primus, "I didn't engage to fill up no holes;" and he put his spade on his shoulder and trudged off.

'Wal, it was putty hard work, fillin' in that hole; but Hokum and Toddy and Wiggin had to do it, 'cause they didn't want to have everybody a laughin' at 'em; and I kind o' tried to set it home to 'em, showin' on 'em that 'twas all for the best.

'"Ef you'd a been left to get that 'are money, there'd a come a cuss with it," says I. "It shows the vanity o' hastin' to be rich."

'"Oh, you shet up!" says Hokum, says he. "You never hasted to any thing," says he. Ye see, he was riled, that's why he spoke so.'

'Sam,' said we, after maturely reflecting over the story, 'what do you suppose was in that pot?'

'Lordy massy! boys: ye never will be done askin' questions. Why, how should I know?'

HERMAN MELVILLE
1818-1891

The eventful life of Herman Melville began in New York
City in 1818. At fifteen he set to sea as a cabin boy and two
years later embarked on the eighteen-month voyage on a
whaler, which was to form the basis of Melville's
masterpiece, *Moby Dick*. On his return to the United States
in 1843, Melville wrote five books relating his experiences
on board ship and among the islands of the South Seas,
which immediately established his literary reputation and
acclaim. Extraordinarily, the publication in 1851 of his epic
whaling novel, *Moby Dick*, threw Melville back into
obscurity. All his later work, including the remarkable
Piazza Tales (1856), was scorned or went unnoticed and it
was not until the 1920s, thirty years after his death in
poverty, that this extraordinary genius received the
worldwide acclaim he so richly deserved.

The stories that follow were first published in *The
Piazza Tales* and reveal to the full Melville's striking natural
gifts as a story-teller of infinite ingenuity.

Benito Cereno

IN THE YEAR 1799, CAPTAIN AMASA DELANO, of Duxbury in Massachusetts, commanding a large sealer and general trader, lay at anchor with a valuable cargo in the harbor of St Maria – a small, desert, uninhabited island toward the southern extremity of the long coast of Chile. There he had touched for water.

On the second day, not long after dawn, while lying in his berth, his mate came below, informing him that a strange sail was coming into the bay. Ships were then not so plenty in those waters as now. He rose, dressed, and went on deck.

The morning was one peculiar to that coast. Everything was mute and calm; everything gray. The sea, though undulated into long roods of swells, seemed fixed, and was sleeked at the surface like waved lead that has cooled and set in the smelter's mold. The sky seemed a gray surtout. Flights of troubled gray fowl, kith and kin with flights of troubled gray vapors among which they were mixed, skimmed low and fitfully over the waters, as swallows over meadows before storms. Shadows present, foreshadowing deeper shadows to come.

To Captain Delano's surprise, the stranger, viewed through the glass, showed no colors, though to do so upon entering a haven, however uninhabited in its shores, where but a single other ship might be lying, was the custom among peaceful seamen of all nations. Considering the lawlessness and loneliness of the spot, and the sort of stories at that day associated with those seas, Captain Delano's surprise might have deepened into some uneasiness had he not been a person of a singularly undistrustful good nature, not liable except on extraordinary and repeated incentives, and hardly then, to indulge in personal alarms any way involving the imputation of malign evil in man. Whether, in view of what humanity is capable, such trait implies, along with a benevolent heart, more than ordinary quickness and accuracy of intellectual perception, may be left to the wise to determine.

But whatever misgivings might have obtruded on first seeing the stranger would almost, in any seaman's mind, have been dissipated by observing that the ship, in navigating into the harbor, was drawing too near the land, a sunken reef making out off her bow. This seemed to prove her a stranger, indeed, not only to the sealer, but the island; consequently she could be no wonted freebooter on that ocean. With no small interest Captain Delano continued to watch her – a proceeding not much facilitated by the vapors partly mantling the hull, through which the far matin light from her cabin streamed equivocally enough; much like the sun – by this time hemisphered on the rim of the horizon, and, apparently, in company with the strange ship entering the harbor – which, wimpled by the same low, creeping clouds,

157

showed not unlike a Lima intrigante's one sinister eye peering across the Plaza from the Indian loophole of her dusk *saya-y-manta*.

It might have been but a deception of the vapors, but the longer the stranger was watched the more singular appeared her maneuvers. Erelong it seemed hard to decide whether she meant to come in or no – what she wanted, or what she was about. The wind, which had breezed up a little during the night, was now extremely light and baffling, which the more increased the apparent uncertainty of her movements.

Surmising at last that it might be a ship in distress, Captain Delano ordered his whaleboat to be dropped, and, much to the wary opposition of his mate, prepared to board her, and, at the least, pilot her in. On the night previous, a fishing party of the seamen had gone a long distance to some detached rocks out of sight from the sealer, and, an hour or two before daybreak, had returned, having set with no small success. Presuming that the stranger might have been long off soundings, the good captain put several baskets of the fish, for presents, into his boat, and so pulled away. From her continuing too near the sunken reef deeming her in danger, calling to his men he made all haste to apprise those on board of their situation. But, some time ere the boat came up, the wind, light though it was, having shifted, had headed the vessel off, as well as partly broken the vapors from about her.

Upon gaining a less remote view, the ship, when made signally visible on the verge of the leaden-hued swells, with the shreds of fog here and there raggedly furring her, appeared like a whitewashed monastery after a thunderstorm, seen perched upon some dun cliff among the Pyrenees. But it was no purely fanciful resemblance which now, for a moment, almost led Captain Delano to think that nothing less than a shipload of monks was before him. Peering over the bulwarks were what really seemed, in the hazy distance, throngs of dark cowls; while, fitfully revealed through the open portholes, other dark moving figures were dimly descried, as of Black Friars pacing the cloisters.

Upon a still nigher approach, this appearance was modified, and the true character of the vessel was plain – a Spanish merchantman of the first class, carrying Negro slaves, amongst other valuable freight, from one colonial port to another. A very large, and in its time, a very fine vessel, such as in those days were at intervals encountered along that main; sometimes superseded Acapulco treasure ships, or retired frigates of the Spanish king's navy, which, like superannuated Italian palaces, still, under a decline of masters, preserved signs of former state.

As the whaleboat drew more and more nigh, the cause of the peculiar pipe-clayed aspect of the stranger was seen in the slovenly neglect pervading her. The spars, ropes, and great part of the bulwarks looked woolly from long unacquaintance with the scraper, tar, and the brush. Her keel seemed laid, her ribs put together, and she launched, from Ezekiel's Valley of Dry Bones.

In the present business in which she was engaged, the ship's general model and rig appeared to have undergone no material change from their original warlike and Froissart pattern. However, no guns were seen.

The tops were large, and were railed about with what had once been octagonal network, all now in sad disrepair. These tops hung overhead like three ruinous aviaries, in one of which was seen perched, on a ratline, a white noddy, a strange fowl so called from its lethargic, somnambulistic character, being frequently caught by hand at sea. Battered and moldy, the castellated forecastle seemed some ancient turret long ago taken by assault, and then left to decay. Toward the stern, two high-raised quarter galleries – the balustrades here and there covered with dry tindery sea moss – opening out from the unoccupied state cabin, whose deadlights, for all the mild weather, were hermetically closed and calked – these tenantless balconies hung over the sea as if it were the grand Venetian canal. But the principal relic of faded grandeur was the ample oval of the shieldlike sternpiece, intricately carved with the arms of Castile and Leon, medallioned about by groups of mythological or symbolical devices, uppermost and central of which was a dark satyr in a mask holding his foot on the prostrate neck of a writhing figure, likewise masked.

Whether the ship had a figurehead, or only a plain beak, was not quite certain, owing to canvas wrapped about that part, either to protect it while undergoing a refurbishing, or else decently to hide its decay. Rudely painted or chalked, as in a sailor freak, along the forward side of a sort of pedestal below the canvas, was the sentence, SEGUID VUESTRO JEFE ('follow your leader'); while upon the tarnished headboards near by appeared, in stately capitals, once gilt, the ship's name *SAN DOMINICK*, each letter streakingly corroded with tricklings of copper-spike rust; while, like mourning weeds, dark festoons of sea grass slimily swept to and fro over the name with every hearselike role of the hull.

As, at last, the boat was hooked from the bow along toward the gangway amidship, its keel, while yet some inches separated from the hull, harshly grated as on a sunken coral reef. It proved a huge bunch of conglobated barnacles adhering below the water to the side like a wen – a token of baffling airs and long calms passed somewhere in those seas.

Climbing the side, the visitor was at once surrounded by a clamorous throng of whites and blacks, but the latter outnumbering the former more than could have been expected, Negro transportation ship as the stranger in port was. But, in one language, and as with one voice, all poured out a common tale of suffering; in which the Negresses, of whom there were not a few, exceeded the others in their dolorous vehemence. The scurvy, together with the fever, had swept off a great part of their number, more especially the Spaniards. Off Cape Horn they had narrowly escaped shipwreck; then, for days together, they had lain tranced without wind; their provisions were low; their water next to none; their lips that moment were baked.

While Captain Delano was thus made the mark of all eager tongues, his one eager glance took in all faces, with every other object about him.

Always upon first boarding a large and populous ship at sea, especially a foreign one, with a nondescript crew such as Lascars or Manila men, the impression varies in a peculiar way from that produced by first entering a strange house with strange inmates in a strange land. Both house and ship – the one by its walls and blinds, the other by its high bulwarks like ramparts – hoard from view their interiors till the last moment, but in the case of the ship there is this addition: that the living spectacle it contains, upon its sudden and complete disclosure, has, in contrast with the blank ocean which zones it, something of the effect of enchantment. The ship seems unreal; these strange costumes, gestures, and faces but a shadowy tableau just emerged from the deep, which directly must receive back what it gave.

Perhaps it was some such influence, as above is attempted to be described, which, in Captain Delano's mind, heightened whatever, upon a staid scrutiny, might have seemed unusual, especially the conspicuous figures of four elderly grizzled Negroes, their heads like black, doddered willow tops, who, in venerable contrast to the tumult below them, were crouched, sphinxlike, one on the starboard cathead, another on the larboard, and the remaining pair face to face on the opposite bulwarks above the mainchains. They each had bits of unstranded old junk in their hands, and, with a sort of stoical self-content, were picking the junk into oakum, a small heap of which lay by their sides. They accompanied the task with a continuous, low monotonous chant, droning and druling away like so many gray-headed bagpipers playing a funeral march.

The quarter-deck rose into an ample elevated poop, upon the forward verge of which, lifted, like the oakum-pickers, some eight feet above the general throng, sat along in a row, separated by regular spaces, the cross-legged figures of six other blacks, each with a rusty hatchet in his hand, which, with a bit of brick and a rag, he was engaged like a scullion in scouring, while between each two was a small stack of hatchets, their rusted edges turned forward awaiting a like operation. Though occasionally the four oakum-pickers would briefly address some person or persons in the crowd below, yet the six hatchet-polishers neither spoke to others nor breathed a whisper among themselves, but sat intent upon their task, except at intervals, when, with the peculiar love in Negroes of uniting industry with pastime, two and two they sideways clashed their hatchets together, like cymbals, with a barbarous din. All six, unlike the generality, had the raw aspect of unsophisticated Africans.

But that first comprehensive glance which took in those ten figures, with scores less conspicuous, rested but an instant upon them, as, impatient of the hubbub of voices, the visitor turned in quest of whomsoever it might be that commanded the ship.

But as if not unwilling to let nature make known her own case among his suffering charge, or else in despair of restraining it for the time, the Spanish captain, a gentlemanly, reserved-looking, and rather young man to a stranger's eye, dressed with singular richness but bearing plain traces of recent sleepless cares and disquietudes, stood passively by, leaning against the mainmast, at one moment casting a dreary, spiritless look upon his excited people, at the next an unhappy glance toward his visitor. By his side stood a black of small stature, in whose rude face, as occasionally, like a shepherd's dog, he mutely turned it up into the Spaniard's, sorrow and affection were equally blended.

Struggling through the throng, the American advanced to the Spaniard, assuring him of his sympathies, and offering to render whatever assistance might be in his power. To which the Spaniard returned for the present but grave and ceremonious acknowledgments, his national formality dusked by the saturnine mood of ill-health.

But losing no time in mere compliments, Captain Delano, returning to the gangway, had his basket of fish brought up, and as the wind still continued light, so that some hours at least must elapse ere the ship could be brought to the anchorage, he bade his men return to the sealer and fetch back as much water as the whaleboat could carry, with whatever soft bread the steward might have, all the remaining pumpkins on board, with a box of sugar and a dozen of his private bottles of cider.

Not many minutes after the boat's pushing off, to the vexation of all, the wind entirely died away, and, the tide turning, began drifting back the ship helplessly seaward. But trusting this would not long last, Captain Delano sought, with good hopes, to cheer up the strangers, feeling no small satisfaction that, with persons in their condition, he could – thanks to his frequent voyages along the Spanish Main – converse with some freedom in their native tongue.

While left alone with them, he was not long in observing some things tending to heighten his first impressions; but surprise was lost in pity, both for the Spaniards and blacks, alike evidently reduced from scarcity of water and provisions, while long-continued suffering seemed to have brought out the less good-natured qualities of the Negroes, besides at the same time impairing the Spaniard's authority over them. But, under the circumstances, precisely this condition of things was to have been anticipated. In armies, navies, cities, or families, in nature herself, nothing more relaxes good order than misery. Still, Captain Delano was not without the idea that had Benito Cereno been a man of greater energy, misrule would hardly have come to the present pass. But the debility, constitutional or induced by hardships bodily and mental, of the Spanish captain was too obvious to be overlooked. A prey to settled dejection, as if long mocked with hope he would not now indulge it even when it had ceased to be a mock, the prospect of that day, or evening at furthest, lying at anchor, with plenty of water for his people, and a brother captain to counsel and befriend, seemed in no perceptible degree to encourage him. His mind appeared unstrung, if not still more seriously affected. Shut up in these oaken walls, chained to one dull round of command whose unconditionality cloyed him, like some hypochondriac abbott he moved slowly about, at times suddenly pausing, starting, or staring, biting his lip, biting his fingernail, flushing, paling, twitching his beard, with other symptoms of an absent or moody mind. This distempered spirit was lodged, as before hinted, in as distempered a frame. He was rather tall, but seemed never to have been robust, and now with nervous suffering was almost worn to a skeleton. A tendency to some pulmonary complaint appeared to have been lately confirmed. His voice was like that of one with lungs half gone—hoarsely suppressed, a husky whisper. No wonder that, as in this state he tottered about, his private servant apprehensively followed him. Sometimes the Negro gave his master his arm, or took his handkerchief out of his pocket for him; performing these and similar offices with that affectionate zeal which transmutes into something filial or fraternal acts in themselves but menial, and which has gained for the Negro the repute of making the most pleasing body servant in the world; one, too, whom a master need be on no stiffly superior terms with, but may treat with familiar trust – less a servant than a devoted companion.

Marking the noisy indocility of the blacks in general, as well as what seemed the sullen inefficiency of the whites, it was not without humane satisfaction that Captain Delano witnessed the steady good conduct of Babo.

But the good conduct of Babo, hardly more than the ill-behavior of others, seemed to withdraw the half-lunatic Don Benito from his cloudy languor. Not that such precisely was the impression made by the Spaniard on the mind of his visitor. The Spaniard's individual unrest was, for the present, but noted as a conspicuous feature in the ship's general affliction. Still, Captain Delano was not a little concerned at what he could not help taking for the time to be Don Benito's unfriendly indifference towards himself. The Spaniard's manner, too, conveyed a sort of sour and gloomy disdain, which he seemed at no pains to disguise. But this the American in charity ascribed to the harassing effects of sickness, since, in former instances, he had noted that there are peculiar natures on whom prolonged physical suffering seems to cancel every social instinct of kindness, as if, forced to black bread themselves, they deemed it but equity that each person coming nigh them should, indirectly, by some slight or affront, be made to partake of their fare.

But erelong Captain Delano bethought him that, indulgent as he was at the first in judging the Spaniard, he might not after all have exercised charity enough. At bottom it was Don Benito's reserve which displeased him, but the same reserve was shown towards all but his faithful personal attendant. Even the formal reports which, according to sea usage, were, at stated times, made to him by some petty underling, either a white, mulatto, or black, he hardly had patience enough to listen to without betraying contemptuous aversion. His manner upon such occasions was, in its degree, not unlike that which might be supposed to have been his imperial countryman's, Charles V, just previous to the anchoritish retirement of that monarch from the throne.

This splenetic disrelish of his place was evinced in almost every function pertaining to it. Proud as he was moody, he condescended to no personal mandate. Whatever special orders were necessary, their delivery was delegated to his body servant, who in turn transferred them to their ultimate destination, through runners, alert Spanish boys or slave boys, like pages or pilot fish within easy call continually hovering round Don Benito. So that to have beheld this undemonstrative invalid gliding about, apathetic and mute, no landsman could have dreamed that in him was lodged a dictatorship beyond which, while at sea, there was no earthly appeal.

Thus the Spaniard, regarded in his reserve, seemed the involuntary victim of mental disorder. But, in fact, his reserve might, in some degree, have proceeded from design. If so, then here was evinced the unhealthy climax of that icy though conscientious policy more or less adopted by all commanders of large ships, which, except in signal emergencies, obliterates alike the manifestation of sway with every trace of sociality, transforming the man into a block or rather into a loaded cannon, which, until there is call for thunder, has nothing to say.

Viewing him in this light, it seemed but a natural token of the perverse habit induced by a long course of such hard self-restraint that, notwithstanding the present condition of his ship, the Spaniard should still persist in a demeanor which, however harmless or, it may be, appropriate, in a well-appointed vessel such as the *San Dominick* might have been at the outset of the voyage, was anything but judicious now. But the Spaniard, perhaps, thought that it was with captains as with gods: reserve, under all events, must still be their cue. But probably this appearance of slumbering dominion might have been but an attempted disguise to conscious imbecility—not deep policy, but shallow device. But be all this as it might, whether Don Benito's manner was designed or not, the more Captain Delano noted its pervading reserve, the less he felt uneasiness at any particular manifestation of that reserve towards himself.

Neither were his thoughts taken up by the captain alone. Wonted to the quiet orderliness of the sealer's comfortable family of a crew, the noisy confusion of the *San Dominick*'s suffering host repeatedly challenged his eye. Some prominent breaches, not only of discipline but of decency, were observed. These Captain Delano could not but ascribe, in the main, to the absence of those subordinate deck officers to whom, along with higher duties, is intrusted what may be styled the police department of a populous ship. True, the old oakum-pickers appeared at times to act the part of monitorial constables to their countrymen, the blacks, but though occasionally succeeding in allaying trifling outbreaks now and then between man and man, they could do little or nothing toward establishing general quiet. The *San Dominick* was in the condition of a transatlantic emigrant ship, among whose multitude of living freight are some individuals, doubtless, as little troublesome as crates and bales, but the friendly remonstrances of such with their ruder companions are of not so much avail as the unfriendly arm of the mate. What the *San Dominick* wanted was, what the emigrant ship has, stern superior officers. But on these decks not so much as a fourth mate was to be seen.

The visitor's curiosity was roused to learn the particulars of those mishaps which had brought about such absenteeism, with its consequences, because, though deriving some inkling of the voyage from the wails which at the first moment had greeted him, yet of the details no clear understanding had been had. The best account would, doubtless, be given by the captain. Yet at first the visitor was loath to ask it, unwilling to provoke some distant rebuff. But, plucking up courage, he at last accosted Don Benito, renewing the expression of his benevolent interest, adding that, did he (Captain Delano) but know the particulars of the ship's misfortunes, he would, perhaps be better able in the end to relieve them. Would Don Benito favor him with the whole story.

Don Benito faltered, then, like some somnambulist suddenly interfered with, vacantly stared at his visitor, and ended by looking down on the deck. He maintained this posture so long that Captain Delano, almost equally disconcerted, and involuntarily almost as rude, turned suddenly from him, walking forward to accost one of the Spanish seamen for the desired information. But he had hardly gone five paces, when, with a sort of eagerness, Don Benito invited him back, regretting his momentary absence of mind, and professing readiness to gratify him.

While most part of the story was being given, the two captains stood on the after part of the main deck, a priviliged spot, no one being near but the servant.

'It is now a hundred and ninety days,' began the Spaniard, in his husky whisper, 'that this ship, well officered and well manned, with several cabin passengers – some fifty Spaniards in all – sailed from Buenos Ayres bound to Lima, with a general cargo, hardware, Paraguay tea and the like – and,' pointing forward, 'that parcel of Negroes, now not more than a hundred and fifty, as you see, but then numbering over three hundred souls. Off Cape Horn we had heavy gales. In one moment, by night, three of my best officers, with fifteen sailors, were lost, with the mainyard, the spar snapping under them in the slings as they sought, with heavers, to beat down the icy sail. To lighten the hull, the heavier sacks of maté were thrown into the sea, with most of the water pipes lashed on deck at the time. And this last necessity it was, combined with the prolonged detentions afterwards experienced, which eventually brought about our chief causes of suffering. When—'

Here there was a sudden fainting attack of his cough, brought on, no doubt, by his mental distress. His servant sustained him, and, drawing a cordial from his pocket, placed it to his lips. He a little revived. But, unwilling to leave him unsupported while yet imperfectly restored, the black with one arm still encircled his master, as the same time keeping his eye fixed on his face, as if to watch for the first sign of complete restoration, or relapse, as the event might prove.

The Spaniard proceeded, but brokenly and obscurely, as one in a dream.

– 'Oh, my God! rather than pass through what I have, with joy I would have hailed the most terrible gales; but—'

His cough returned and with increased violence; this subsiding, with reddened lips and closed eyes he fell heavily against his supporter.

'His mind wanders. He was thinking of the plague that followed the gales,' plaintively sighed the servant; 'my poor, poor master!' wringing one hand, and with the other wiping the mouth. 'But be patient, *señor*,' again turning to Captain Delano, 'these fits do not last long; master will soon be himself.'

Don Benito reviving, went on; but, as this portion of the story was very brokenly delivered, the substance only will be set down.

It appeared that after the ship had been many days tossed in storms off the Cape, the scurvy broke out, carrying off numbers of the whites and blacks. When at last they had worked round into the Pacific, their spars and sails were so damaged, and so inadequately handled by the surviving mariners, most of whom were become invalids, that, unable to lay her northerly course by the wind, which was powerful, the unmanageable ship for successive days and nights was blown northwestward, where the breeze suddenly deserted her, in unknown waters to sultry calms. The absence of the water pipes now proved as fatal to life as before their presence had menaced it. Induced, or at least aggravated, by the more than scanty allowance of water, a malignant fever followed the scurvy, with the excessive heat of the lengthened calm making such short work of it as to sweep away, as by billows, whole families of the Africans, and a yet larger number, proportionally, of the Spaniards, including, by a luckless fatality, every remaining officer on board. Consequently, in the smart west winds eventually following the calm, the already rent sails, having to be simply dropped, not furled, at need, had been gradually reduced to the beggars' rags they were now. To procure substitutes for his lost sailors, as well as supplies of water and sails, the captain, at the earliest opportunity, had made for Baldivia, the southernmost civilized port of Chile and South America, but upon nearing the coast the thick weather had prevented him from so much as sighting that harbor. Since which period, almost without a crew, and almost without canvas and almost without water, and at intervals giving its added dead to the sea, the *San Dominick* had been battledored about by contrary winds, inveigled by currents, or grown weedy in calms. Like a man lost in woods, more than once she had doubled upon her own track.

'But throughout these calamities,' huskily continued Don Benito, painfully turning in the half-embrace of his servant, 'I have to thank those Negroes you see, who, though to your inexperienced eyes appearing unruly, have, indeed, conducted themselves with less of restlessness than even their owner could have thought possible under such circumstances.'

Here he again fell faintly back. Again his mind wandered, but he rallied, and less obscurely proceeded.

'Yes, their owner was quite right in assuring me that no fetters would be needed with his blacks; so that while, as is wont in his transportation, those Negroes have always remained upon deck – not thrust below, as in the Guineamen – they have, also, from the beginning, been freely permitted to range within given bounds at their pleasure.'

Once more the faintness returned – his mind roved – but, recovering, he resumed:

'But it is Babo here to whom, under God, I owe not only my own preservation, but likewise to him, chiefly, the merit is due of pacifying his more ignorant brethren, when at intervals tempted to murmurings.'

'Ah, master,' sighed the black, bowing his face, 'don't speak of me; Babo is nothing; what Babo has done was but duty.'

'Faithful fellow!' cried Captain Delano. 'Don Benito, I envy you such a friend; slave I cannot call him.'

As master and man stood before him, the black upholding the white, Captain Delano could not but bethink him of the beauty of that relationship which could present such a spectacle of fidelity on the one hand and confidence on the other. The scene was heightened by the contrast in dress, denoting their relative positions. The Spaniard wore a loose Chile jacket of dark velvet; white smallclothes and stockings, with silver buckles at the knee and instep; a high-crowned sombrero of fine grass; a slender sword, silver mounted, hung from a knot in his sash – the last being an almost invariable adjunct, more for utility than ornament, of a South American gentleman's dress to this hour. Excepting when his occasional nervous contortions brought about disarray, there was a certain precision in his attire curiously at variance with the unsightly disorder around, especially in the belittered ghetto, forward of the mainmast, wholly occupied by the blacks.

The servant wore nothing but wide trousers, apparently, from their coarseness and patches, made out of some old topsail; they were clean, and confined at the waist by a bit of unstranded rope, which, with his composed, deprecatory air at times, made him look something like a begging friar of St Francis.

However unsuitable for the time and place, at least in the blunt-thinking American's eyes, and however strangely surviving in the midst of all his afflictions, the toilette of Don Benito might not, in fashion at least, have gone beyond the style of the day among South Americans of his class. Though on the present voyage sailing from Buenos Ayres, he had avowed himself a native and resident of Chile, whose inhabitants had not so generally adopted the plain coat and once plebeian pantaloons, but, with a becoming modification, adhered to their provincial costume, picturesque as any in the world. Still, relatively to the pale history of the voyage, and his own pale face, there seemed something so incongruous in the Spaniard's apparel as almost to suggest the image of an invalid courtier tottering about London streets in the time of the plague.

The portion of the narrative which perhaps most excited interest, as well as some surprise, considering the latitudes in question, was the long calms spoken of, and more particularly the ship's so long drifting about. Without communicating the opinion, of course, the American could not but impute at least part of the detentions both to clumsy seamanship and faulty navigation. Eying Don Benito's small, yellow hands, he easily inferred that the young captain had not got into command at the hawsehole, but the cabin window; and if so, why wonder at incompetence, in youth, sickness, and gentility united?

But, drowning criticism in compassion, after a fresh repetition of his sympathies, Captain Delano, having heard out his story, not only engaged, as in the first place, to see Don Benito and his people supplied in their immediate bodily needs, but, also now further promised to assist him in procuring a large permanent supply of water, as well as some sails and rigging; and, though it would involve no small embarrassment to himself, yet he would spare three of his best seamen for temporary deck officers, so that without delay the ship might proceed to Conception, there fully to refit for Lima, her destined port.

Such generosity was not without its effect, even upon the invalid. His face lighted up; eager and hectic, he met the honest glance of his visitor. With gratitude he seemed overcome.

'This excitement is bad for master,' whispered the servant, taking his arm, and with soothing words gently drawing him aside.

When Don Benito returned, the American was pained to observe that his hopefulness, like the sudden kindling in his cheek, was but febrile and transient.

Erelong, with a joyless mien, looking up towards the poop, the host invited his guest to accompany him there, for the benefit of what little breath of wind might be stirring.

As, during the telling of the story, Captain Delano had once or twice started at the occasional cymbaling of the hatchet-polishers, wondering why such an interruption should be allowed, especially in that part of the ship, and in the ears of an invalid; and moreover, as the hatchets had anything but an attractive look, and the handlers of them still less so, it was, therefore, to tell the truth, not without some lurking reluctance, or even shrinking, it may be, that Captain Delano, with apparent complaisance, acquiesced in his host's invitation. The more so since, with an untimely caprice of punctilio, rendered distressing by his cadaverous aspect, Don Benito, with Castilian bows, solemnly insisted upon his guest's preceding him up the ladder leading to the elevation, where, one on each side of the last step, sat for armorial supporters and sentries two of the ominous file. Gingerly enough stepped good Captain Delano between them, and in the instant of leaving them behind, like one running the gantlet, he felt an apprehensive twitch in the calves of his legs.

But when, facing about, he saw the whole file, like so many organ-grinders, still stupidly intent on their work, unmindful of everything beside, he could not but smile at his late fidgety panic.

Presently, while standing with his host looking forward upon the decks below, he was struck by one of those instances of insubordination previously alluded to. Three black boys, with two Spanish boys, were sitting together on the hatches, scraping a rude wooden platter in which some scanty mess had recently been cooked. Suddenly one of the black boys, enraged at a word dropped by one of his white companions, seized a knife, and, though called to forbear by one of the oakum-pickers, struck the lad over the head, inflicting a gash from which blood flowed.

In amazement, Captain Delano inquired what this meant. To which the pale Don Benito dully muttered that it was merely the sport of the lad.

'Pretty serious sport, truly,' rejoined Captain Delano. 'Had such a thing happened on board the *Bachelor's Delight,* instant punishment would have followed.'

At these words the Spaniard turned upon the American one of his sudden, staring, half-lunatic looks, then, relapsing into his torpor, answered, 'Doubtless, doubtless, *senõr.*'

Is it, thought Captain Delano, that this hapless man is one of those paper captains I've known, who by policy wink at what by power they cannot put down? I know no sadder sight than a commander who has little of command but the name.

'I should think, Don Benito,' he now said, glancing toward the oakum-picker who had sought to interfere with the boys, 'that you would find it advantageous to keep all your blacks employed, especially the younger ones, no matter at what useless task, and no matter what happens to the ship. Why, even with my little band, I find such a course indispensable. I once kept a crew on my quarter-deck thrumming mats for my cabin, when, for three days, I had given up my ship – mats, men, and all – for a speedy loss, owing to the violence of a gale, in which we could do nothing, but helplessly drive before it.'

'Doubtless, doubtless,' muttered Don Benito.

'But,' continued Captain Delano, again glancing upon the oakum-pickers and then at the hatchet-polishers, near by, 'I see you keep some, at least, of your host employed.'

'Yes,' was again the vacant response.

'Those old men there, shaking their pows from their pulpits,' continued Captain Delano, pointing to the oakum-pickers, 'seem to act the part of old dominies to the rest, little heeded as their admonitions are at times. Is this voluntary on their part, Don Benito, or have you appointed them shepherds to your flock of black sheep?'

'What posts they fill, I appointed them,' rejoined the Spaniard, in an acrid tone, as if resenting some supposed satiric reflection.

'And these others, these Ashantee conjurers here,' continued Captain Delano, rather uneasily eying the brandished steel of the hatchet-polishers, where in spots, it had been brought to a shine, 'this seems a curious business they are at, Don Benito?'

'In the gales we met,' answered the Spaniard, 'what of our general cargo was not thrown overboard was much damaged by the brine. Since coming into calm weather, I have had several cases of knives and hatchets daily brought up for overhauling and cleaning.'

'A prudent idea, Don Benito. You are part owner of ship and cargo, I presume; but none of the slaves, perhaps?'

'I am owner of all you see,' impatiently returned Don Benito, 'except the main company of blacks, who belonged to my late friend, Alexandro Aranda.'

As he mentioned this name, his air was heartbroken; his knees shook; his servant supported him.

Thinking he divined the cause of such unusual emotion, to confirm his surmise Captain Delano after a pause said: 'And may I ask, Don Benito, whether – since awhile ago you spoke of some cabin passengers – the friend, whose loss so afflicts you, at the outset of the voyage accompanied his blacks?'

'Yes.'

'But died of the fever?'

'Died of the fever. Oh, could I but—'

Again quivering, the Spaniard paused.

'Pardon me,' said Captain Delano, lowly, 'but I think that, by a sympathetic experience, I conjecture, Don Benito, what it is that gives the keener edge to your grief. It was once my hard fortune to lose, at sea, a dear friend, my own brother, then supercargo. Assured of the welfare of his spirit, its departure I could have borne like a man, but that honest eye, that honest hand – both of which had so often met mine – and that warm heart – all, all – like scraps to the dogs – to throw it all to the sharks! It was then I vowed never to have for fellow voyager a man I loved, unless, unbeknown to him, I had provided requisite in case of a fatality, for embalming his mortal part for interment on shore. Were your friend's remains now on board this ship, Don Benito, not thus strangely would the mention of his name affect you.'

'On board this ship?' echoed the Spaniard. Then with horrified gestures, as directed against some specter, he unconsciously fell into the ready arms of his attendant, who, with a silent appeal toward Captain Delano, seemed beseeching him not again to broach a theme so unspeakably distressing to his master.

This poor fellow now, thought the pained American, is the victim of that sad superstition which associates goblins with the deserted body of man, as ghosts with an abandoned house. How unlike are we made! What to me, in like case, would have been a solemn satisfaction, the bare suggestion, even, terrifies the Spaniard into his trance. Poor Alexandro Aranda! what would you say could you here see your friend – who on former voyages, when you for months were left behind, has, I dare say, often longed and longed for one peep at you – not transported with terror at the least thought of having you anyway nigh him.

At this moment, with a dreary graveyard toll betokening a flaw, the ship's forecastle bell, smote by one of the grizzled oakum-pickers, proclaimed ten o'clock through the leaden calm, when Captain Delano's attention was caught by the moving figure of a gigantic black emerging from the general crowd below and slowly advancing towards the elevated poop. An iron collar was about his neck, from which depended a chain thrice wound round his body, the terminating links padlocked together at a broad band of iron, his girdle.

'How like a mute Atufal moves,' murmured the servant.

The black mounted the steps of the poop, and, like a brave prisoner brought up to receive sentence, stood in unquailing muteness before Don Benito, now recovered from his attack.

At the first glimpse of his approach, Don Benito had started; a resentful shadow swept over his face, and, as with the sudden memory of bootless rage, his white lips glued together.

This is some mulish mutineer, thought Captain Delano, surveying, not without a mixture of admiration, the colossal form of the Negro.

'See, he waits your question, master,' said the servant.

Thus reminded, Don Benito, nervously averting his glance as if shunning, by anticipation, some rebellious response, in a disconcerted voice, thus spoke:

'Atufal, will you ask my pardon now?'

The black was silent.

'Again, master,' murmured the servant, with bitter upbraiding eying his countryman; 'Again, master; he will bend to master yet.'

'Answer,' said Don Benito, still averting his glance, 'say but the one word, *pardon*, and your chains shall be off.'

Upon this, the black, slowly raising both arms, let them lifelessly fall, his links clanking, his head bowed; as much as to say, 'No, I am content.'

'Go,' said Don Benito, with inkept and unknown emotion.

Deliberately as he had come, the black obeyed.

'Excuse me, Don Benito,' said Capatin Delano, 'but this scene surprises me; what means it, pray?'

'It means that that Negro alone, of all the band, has given me peculiar cause of offense. I have put him in chains; I—'

Here he paused; his hand to his head, as if there were a swimming there, or a sudden bewilderment of memory had come over him; but meeting his servant's kindly glance seemed reassured, and proceeded:

'I could not scourge such a form. But I told him he must ask my pardon. As yet he has not. At my command, every two hours he stands before me.'

'And how long has this been?'

'Some sixty days.'

'And obedient in all else? And respectful?'

'Yes.'

'Upon my conscience, then,' exclaimed Captain Delano, impulsively, 'he has a royal spirit in him, this fellow.'

'He may have some right to it,' bitterly returned Don Benito, 'he says he was king in his own land.'

'Yes,' said the servant, entering a word, 'those slits in Atufal's ears once held wedges of gold; but poor Babo here, in his own land, was only a poor slave; a black man's slave was Babo, who now is the white's.'

Somewhat annoyed by these conversational familiarities, Captain Delano turned curiously upon the attendant, then glanced inquiringly at his master; but, as if long wonted to these little informalities, neither master nor man seemed to understand him.

'What, pray, was Atufal's offense, Don Benito?' asked Captain Delano; 'if it was not something very serious, take a fool's advice, and, in view of his general docility, as well as in some natural respect for his spirit, remit him his penalty.'

'No, no, master never will do that,' here murmured the servant to himself, 'proud Atufal must first ask master's pardon. The slave there carries the padlock, but master here carries the key.'

His attention thus directed, Captain Delano now noticed for the first time that, suspended by a slender silken cord from Don Benito's neck, hung a key. At once, from the servant's muttered syllables, divining the key's purpose, he smiled and said: 'So, Don Benito – padlock and key – significant symbols, truly.'

Biting his lip, Don Benito faltered.

Though the remark of Captain Delano, a man of such native simplicity as to be incapable of satire or irony, had been dropped in playful allusion to the Spaniard's singularly evidenced lordship over the black, yet the hypochondriac seemed some way to have taken it as a malicious reflection upon his confessed inability thus far to break down, at least on a verbal summons, the entrenched will of the slave. Deploring this supposed misconception, yet despairing of correcting it, Captain Delano shifted the subject; but finding his companion more than ever withdrawn, as if still sourly digesting the lees of the presumed affront above mentioned, by and by Captain Delano likewise became less talkative, oppressed, against his own will, by what seemed the secretive vindictiveness of the morbidly sensitive Spaniard. But the good sailor, himself of a quite contrary disposition, refrained on his part alike from the appearance as from the feeling of resentment, and if silent, was only so from contagion.

Presently the Spaniard, assisted by his servant, somewhat discourteously crossed over from his guest, a procedure which, sensibly enough, might have been allowed to pass for idle caprice of ill-humor had not master and man, lingering round the corner of the elevated skylight, begun whispering together in low voices. This was unpleasing. And more: the moody air of the Spaniard, which at times had not been without a sort of valetudinarian stateliness, now seemed anything but dignified, while the menial familiarity of the servant lost its original charm of simple-hearted attachment.

In his embarrassment, the visitor turned his face to the other side of the ship. By so doing, his glance accidentally fell on a young Spanish sailor, a coil of rope in his hand, just stepped from the deck to the first round of the mizzen rigging. Perhaps the man would not have been particularly noticed were it not that, during his ascent to one of the yards, he, with a sort of covert intentness, kept his eye fixed on Captain Delano, from whom, presently, it passed, as if by a natural sequence, to the two whisperers.

His own attention thus redirected to that quarter, Captain Delano gave a slight start. From something in Don Benito's manner just then, it seemed as if the visitor had, at least partly, been the subject of the withdrawn consultation going on – a conjecture as little agreeable to the guest as it was flattering to the host.

The singular alternations of courtesy and ill-breeding in the Spanish captain were unaccountable, except on one of two suppositions – innocent lunacy, or wicked imposture.

But the first idea, though it might naturally have occurred to an indifferent observer, and, in some respect, had not hitherto been wholly a stranger to Captain Delano's mind, yet, now that, in an incipient way, he began to regard the stranger's conduct something in the light of an intentional affront, of course the idea of lunacy was virtually vacated. But if not a lunatic, what then? Under the circumstances, would a gentleman, nay, any honest boor, act the part now acted by his host? The man was an imposter. Some low-born adventurer, masquerading as an oceanic grandee, yet so ignorant of the first requisites of mere gentlemanhood as to be betrayed into the present remarkable indecorum. That strange ceremoniousness, too, at other times evinced, seemed not uncharacteristic of one playing a part above his real level. Benito Cereno – Don Benito Cereno – a sounding name. One, too, at that period not unknown, in the surname, to supercargoes and sea captains trading along the Spanish Main, as belonging to one of the most enterprising and extensive mercantile families in all those provinces, several members of it having titles; a sort of Castilian Rothschild, with a noble brother, or cousin, in every great trading town of South America. The alleged Don Benito was in early manhood, about twenty-nine or thirty. To assume a sort of roving cadetship in the maritime affairs of such a house, what more likely scheme for a young knave of talent and spirit? But the Spaniard was a pale invalid. Never mind. For even to the degree of simulating mortal disease, the craft of some tricksters has been known to attain. To think that, under the aspect of infantile weakness, the most savage energies might be couched – those velvets of the Spaniard but the silky paw to his fangs.

From no train of thought did these fancies come; not from within, but from without; suddenly, too, and in one throng, like hoarfrost, yet as soon to vanish, as the mild sun of Captain Delano's good nature regained its meridian.

Glancing over once more towards his host – whose side face, revealed above the skylight, was now turned towards him – he was struck by the profile, whose clearness of cut was refined by the thinness incident to ill-health, as well as ennobled about the chin by the beard. Away with suspicion. He was a true offshoot of a true hidalgo Cereno.

Relieved by these and other better thoughts, the visitor, lightly humming a tune, now began indifferently pacing the poop, so as not to betray to Don Benito that he had at all mistrusted incivility, much less duplicity; for such mistrust would yet be proved illusory, and by the event, though, for the present, the circumstance which had provoked that distrust remained unexplained. But when that little mystery should have been cleared up, Captain Delano thought he might extremely regret it did he allow Don Benito to become aware that he had indulged in ungenerous surmises. In short, to the Spaniard's black-letter text, it was best, for a while, to leave open margin.

Presently, his pale face twitching and overcast, the Spaniard still supported by his attendant, moved over towards his guest, when, with even more than his usual embarrassment, and a strange sort of intriguing intonation in his whisper, the following conversation began:

'*Señor*, may I ask how long you have lain at this isle?'

'Oh, but a day or two, Don Benito.'

'And from what port are you last?'

'Canton.'

'And there, *señor*, you exchanged your sealskins for teas and silks, I think you said?'

'Yes. Silks, mostly.'

'And the balance you took in specie, perhaps?'

Captain Delano, fidgeting a little, answered, 'Yes; some silver; not a very great deal, though.'

'Ah – well. May I ask how many men have you, *señor*?'

Captain Delano slightly started, but answered, 'About five-and-twenty, all told.'

'And at present, *señor*, all on board, I suppose?'

'All on board, Don Benito,' replied the Captain, now with satisfaction.

'And will be tonight, *señor*?'

At this last question, following so many pertinacious ones, for the soul of him Captain Delano could not but look very earnestly at the questioner, who, instead of meeting the glance, with every token of craven discomposure dropped his eyes to the deck; presenting an unworthy contrast to his servant, who, just then, was kneeling at his feet, adjusting a loose shoe buckle, his disengaged face meantime, with humble curiosity, turned openly up into his master's downcast one.

The Spaniard, still with a guilty shuffle, repeated his question:

'And – will be tonight, *señor*?'

'Yes, for aught I know,' returned Captain Delano – 'But nay,' rallying himself into fearless truth, 'some of them talked of going off on another fishing party about midnight.'

'Your ships generally go – go more or less armed, I believe, *señor*?'

'Oh, a six-pounder or two, in case of emergency,' was the intrepidly indifferent reply, 'with a small stock of muskets, sealing spears, and cutlasses, you know.'

As he thus responded, Captain Delano again glanced at Don Benito, but the latter's eyes were averted, while, abruptly and awkwardly shifting the subject, he made some peevish allusion to the calm, and then, without apology, once more, with his attendant, withdrew to the opposite bulwarks, where the whispering was resumed.

At this moment, and ere Captain Delano could cast a cool thought upon what had just passed, the young Spanish sailor before mentioned was seen descending from the rigging. In act of stooping over to spring inboard to the deck, his voluminous, unconfined frock, or shirt, of coarse woolen, much spotted with tar, opened out far down the chest, revealing a soiled undergarment of what seemed the finest linen, edged, about the neck, with a narrow blue ribbon, sadly faded and worn. At this moment the young sailor's eye was again fixed on the whisperers, and Captain Delano thought he observed a lurking significance in it, as if silent signs, of some Freemason sort, had that instant been interchanged.

This once more impelled his own glance in the direction of Don Benito, and, as before, he could not but infer that himself formed the subject of the conference. He paused. The sound of the hatchet polishing fell on his ears. He cast another swift side look at the two. They had the air of conspirators. In connection with the late questionings, and the incident of the young sailor, these things now begat such return of involuntary suspicion that the singular guilelessness of the American could not endure it. Plucking up a gay and humorous expression, he crossed over to the two rapidly, saying: 'Ha, Don Benito, your black here seems high in your trust, a sort of privy councilor, in fact.'

Upon this, the servant looked up with a good-natured grin, but the master started as from a venomous bite. It was a moment or two before the Spaniard sufficiently recovered himself to reply; which he did, at last, with cold constraint: 'Yes, *señor*, I have trust in Babo.'

Here Babo, changing his previous grin of mere animal humor into an intelligent smile, not ungratefully eyed his master.

Finding that the Spaniard now stood silent and reserved, as if involuntarily, or purposely giving hint that his guest's proximity was inconvenient just then, Captain Delano, unwilling to appear uncivil even to incivility itself, made some trivial remark and moved off, again and again turning over in his mind the mysterious demeanor of Don Benito Cereno.

He had descended from the poop, and, wrapped in thought, was passing near a dark hatchway leading down into the steerage, when, perceiving motion there, he looked to see what moved. The same instant there was a sparkle in the shadowy hatchway and he saw one of the Spanish sailors, prowling there, hurriedly placing his hand in the bosom of his frock, as if hiding something. Before the man could have been certain who it was that was passing, he slunk below out of sight. But enough was seen of him to make it sure that he was the same young sailor before noticed in the rigging.

What was that which so sparkled? thought Captain Delano. It was no lamp – no match – no live coal. Could it have been a jewel? But how come sailors with jewels? – or with silk-trimmed undershirts either? Has he been robbing the trunks of the dead cabin passengers? But if so he would hardly wear one of the stolen articles on board ship here. Ah, ah – if, now, that was indeed, a secret sign I saw passing between this suspicious fellow and his captain awhile since; if I could only be certain that, in my uneasiness, my senses did not deceive me, then—

Here, passing from one suspicious thing to another, his mind revolved the strange questions put to him concerning his ship.

By a curious coincidence, as each point was recalled, the black wizards of Ashantee would strike up with their hatchets, as in ominous comment on the white stranger's thoughts. Pressed by such enigmas and portents, it would have been almost against nature had not, even into the least distrustful heart, some ugly misgivings obtruded.

Observing the ship, now helplessly fallen into a current, with enchanted sails drifting with increased rapidity seaward, and noting that, from a lately intercepted projection of the land, the sealer was hidden, the stout mariner began to quake at thoughts which he barely durst confess to himself. Above all, he began to feel a ghostly dread of Don Benito. And yet, when he roused himself, dilated his chest, felt himself strong on his legs, and coolly considered it – what did all these phantoms amount to?

Had the Spaniard any sinister scheme, it must have reference not so much to him (Captain Delano) as to his ship (the *Bachelor's Delight*). Hence the present drifting away of the one ship from the other, instead of favoring any such possible scheme, was, for the time at least, opposed to it. Clearly any suspicion combining such contradictions must need be delusive. Beside, was it not absurd to think of a vessel in distress – a vessel by sickness almost dismanned of her crew – a vessel whose inmates were parched for water – was it not a thousand times absurd that such a craft should, at present, be of a piratical character; or her commander, either for himself or those under him, cherish any desire but for speedy relief and refreshment? But, then, might not general distress, and thirst in particular, be affected? And might not that same undiminished Spanish crew, alleged to have perished off to a remnant, be at that very moment lurking in the hold? On heartbroken pretense of entreating a cup of cold water, fiends in human form had got into lonely dwellings, nor retired until a dark deed had been done. And among

the Malay pirates it was no unusual thing to lure ships after them into their
treacherous harbors, or entice boarders from a declared enemy at sea, by the
spectacle of thinly manned or vacant decks, beneath which prowled a
hundred spears with yellow arms ready to upthrust them through the mats.
Not that Captain Delano had entirely credited such things. He had heard of
them – and now, as stories, they recurred. The present destination of the ship
was the anchorage. There she would be near his own vessel. Upon gaining
that vicinity, might not the *San Dominick*, like a slumbering volcano, suddenly
let loose energies now hid?

He recalled the Spaniard's manner while telling his story. There was a
gloomy hesitancy and subterfuge about it. It was just the manner of one
making up his tale for evil purposes, as he goes. But if that story was not true,
what was the truth? That the ship had unlawfully come into the Spaniard's
possession? But in many of its details, especially in reference to the more
calamitous parts, such as the fatalities among the seamen, the consequent
prolonged beating about, the past sufferings from obstinate calms and still
continued suffering from thirst; in all these points, as well as others, Don
Benito's story had corroborated not only the wailing ejaculations of the
indiscriminate multitude, white and black, but likewise – what seemed
impossible to be counterfeit – by the very expression and play of every
human feature which Captain Delano saw. If Don Benito's story was
throughout an invention, then every soul on board, down to the youngest
Negress, was his carefully drilled recruit in the plot: an incredible inference.
And yet, if there was ground for mistrusting his veracity, that inference was a
legitimate one.

But those questions of the Spaniard. There, indeed, one might pause. Did
they not seem put with much the same object with which the burglar or
assassin, by daytime, reconnoiters the walls of a house? But, with ill purposes
to solicit such information openly of the chief person endangered, and so, in
effect, setting him on his guard – how unlikely a procedure was that? Absurd,
then, to suppose that those questions had been prompted by evil designs.
Thus, the same conduct which in this instance had raised the alarm, served
to dispel it. In short, scarce any suspicion or uneasiness, however apparently
reasonable at the time, which was not now with equal apparent reason
dismissed.

At last he began to laugh at his former forebodings, and laugh at the
strange ship for, in its aspect, someway siding with them, as it were; and
laugh, too, at the odd-looking blacks, particularly those old scissors-grinders,
the Ashantees; and those bed-ridden old knitting women, the oakum-pickers;
and almost at the dark Spaniard himself, the central hobgoblin of all.

For the rest, whatever in a serious way seemed enigmatical was now good-
naturedly explained away by the thought that, for the most part, the poor
invalid scarcely knew what he was about; either sulking in black vapors, or
putting idle questions without sense or object. Evidently, for the present the
man was not fit to be intrusted with the ship. On some benevolent plea
withdrawing the command from him, Captain Delano would yet have to
send her to Conception, in charge of his second mate, a worthy person and
good navigator – a plan not more convenient for the *San Dominick* than for
Don Benito; for, relieved from all anxiety, keeping wholly to his cabin, the
sick man, under the good nursing of his servant, would, probably, by the end

of the passage, be in a measure restored to health, and with that he should also be restored to authority.

Such were the American's thoughts. They were tranquilizing. There was a difference between the idea of Don Benito's darkly preordaining Captain Delano's fate and Captain Delano's lightly arranging Don Benito's. Nevertheless, it was not without something of relief that the good seaman presently perceived his whaleboat in the distance. Its absence had been prolonged by unexpected detention at the sealer's side, as well as its returning trip lengthened by the continual recession of the goal.

The advancing speck was observed by the blacks. Their shouts attracted the attention of Don Benito, who, with a return of courtesy approaching Captain Delano, expressed satisfaction at the coming of some supplies, slight and temporary as they must necessarily prove.

Captain Delano responded, but while doing so, his attention was drawn to something passing on the deck below: among the crowd climbing the landward bulwarks, anxiously watching the coming boat, two blacks, to all appearances accidentally incommoded by one of the sailors, violently pushed him aside, which the sailor someway resenting, they dashed him to the deck, despite the earnest cries of the oakum-pickers.

'Don Benito,' said Captain Delano quickly, 'do you see what is going on here? Look!'

But, seized by his cough, the Spaniard staggered, with both hands to his face, on the point of falling. Captain Delano would have supported him, but the servant was more alert, who, with one hand sustaining his master, with the other applied the cordial. Don Benito restored, the black withdrew his support, slipping aside a little, but dutifully remaining within call of a whisper. Such discretion was here evinced as quite wiped away, in the visitor's eyes, any blemish of impropriety which might have attached to the attendant from the indecorous conferences before mentioned, showing, too, that if the servant were to blame it might be more the master's fault than his own, since, when left to himself, he could conduct thus well.

His glance called away from the spectacle of disorder to the more pleasing one before him, Captain Delano could not avoid again congratulating his host upon possessing such a servant, who, though perhaps a little too forward now and then, must upon the whole be invaluable to one in the invalid's situation.

'Tell me, Don Benito,' he added, with a smile – 'I should like to have your man here myself – what will you take for him? Would fifty doubloons be any object?'

'Master wouldn't part with Babo for a thousand doubloons,' murmured the black, overhearing the offer and taking it in earnest, and, with the strange vanity of a faithful slave appreciated by his master, scorning to hear so paltry a valuation put upon him by a stranger. But Don Benito, apparently hardly yet completely restored, and again interrupted by his cough, made but some broken reply.

Soon his physical distress became so great, affecting his mind, too, apparently, that, as if to screen the sad spectacle, the servant gently conducted his master below.

Left to himself, the American, to while away the time till his boat should arrive, would have pleasantly accosted some one of the few Spanish seamen he saw, but recalling something that Don Benito had said touching their ill conduct, he refrained, as a shipmaster indisposed to countenance cowardice or unfaithfulness in seamen.

While, with these thoughts, standing with eye directed forward towards that handful of sailors, suddenly he thought that one or two of them returned the glance and with a sort of meaning. He rubbed his eyes and looked again, but again seemed to see the same thing. Under a new form, but more obscure than any previous one, the old suspicions recurred, but, in the absence of Don Benito, with less of panic than before. Despite the bad account given of the sailors, Captain Delano resolved forthwith to accost one of them. Descending the poop, he made his way through the blacks, his movement drawing a queer cry from the oakum-pickers, prompted by whom, the Negroes, twitching each other aside, divided before him, but, as if curious to see what was the object of his deliberate visit to their ghetto, closing in behind in tolerable order, followed the white stranger up. His progress thus proclaimed as by mounted kings-at-arms, and escorted as by a Kaffir guard of honor, Captain Delano, assuming a good-humored, off-handed air, continued to advance; now and then saying a blithe word to the Negroes, and his eye curiously surveying the white faces, here and there sparsely mixed in with the blacks, like stray white pawns venturously involved in the ranks of the chessmen opposed.

While thinking which of them to select for his purpose, he chanced to observe a sailor seated on the deck engaged in tarring the strap of a large block, a circle of blacks squatted round him inquisitively eying the process.

The mean employment of the man was in contrast with something superior in his figure. His hand, black with continually thrusting it into the tarpot held for him by a Negro, seemed not naturally allied to his face, a face which would have been a very fine one but for its haggardness. Whether this haggardness had aught to do with criminality could not be determined, since, as intense heat and cold, though unlike, produce like sensations, so innocence and guilt, when, through casual association with mental pain stamping any visible impress, use one seal – a hacked one.

Not again that this reflection occurred to Captain Delano at the time, charitable man as he was. Rather another idea. Because observing so singular a haggardness combined with a dark eye, averted as in trouble and shame, and then again recalling Don Benito's confessed ill opinion of his crew, insensible, he was operated upon by certain general notions which, while disconnecting pain and abashment from virtue, invariably link them with vice.

If, indeed, there be any wickedness on board this ship, thought Captain Delano, be sure that man there has fouled his hand in it, even as now he fouls it in the pitch. I don't like to accost him. I will speak to this other, this old Jack here on the windlass.

He advanced to an old Barcelona tar, in ragged red breeches and dirty nightcap, cheeks trenched and bronzed, whiskers dense as thorn hedges. Seated between two sleepy-looking Africans, this mariner, like his younger shipmate, was employed upon some rigging – splicing a cable – the sleepy-looking blacks performing the inferior function of holding the outer parts of the ropes for him.

Upon Captain Delano's approach, the man at once hung his head below its previous level; the one necessary for business. It appeared as if he desired to be thought absorbed with more than common fidelity in his task. Being addressed, he glanced up, but with what seemed a furtive, diffident air, which sat strangely enough on his weather-beaten visage, much as if a grizzly bear, instead of growling and biting, should simper and cast sheep's eyes. He was asked several questions concerning the voyage – questions purposely referring to several particulars in Don Benito's narrative, not previously corroborated by those impulsive cries greeting the visitor on first coming on board. The questions were briefly answered, confirming all that remained to be confirmed of the story. The Negroes about the windlass joined in with the old sailor, but, as they became talkative, he by degrees became mute, and at length quite glum, seemed morosely unwilling to answer more questions, and yet, all the while, this ursine air was somehow mixed with his sheepish one.

Despairing of getting into unembarrassed talk with such a centaur, Captain Delano, after glancing round for a more promising countenance but seeing none, spoke pleasantly to the blacks to make way for him, and so, amid various grins and grimaces, returned to the poop, feeling a little strange at first, he could hardly tell why, but upon the whole with regained confidence in Benito Cereno.

How plainly, thought he, did that old whiskerando yonder betray a consciousness of ill desert. No doubt when he saw me coming he dreaded lest I, apprised by his captain of the crew's general misbehavior, came with sharp words for him, and so down with his head. And yet – and yet, now that I think of it, that very old fellow, if I err not, was one of those who seemed so earnestly eying me here awhile since. Ah, these currents spin one's head round almost as much as they do the ship. Ha, there now's a pleasant sort of sunny sight; quite sociable, too.

His attention had been drawn to a slumbering Negress, partly disclosed through the lacework of some rigging, lying, with youthful limbs carelessly disposed, under the lee of the bulwarks, like a doe in the shade of a woodland rock. Sprawling at her lapped breasts was her wide-awake fawn, stark naked, its black little body half lifted from the deck, crosswise with its dam's; its hands, like two paws, clambering upon her; its mouth and nose ineffectually rooting to get at the mark; and meantime giving a vexatious half-grunt, blending with the composed snore of the Negress.

The uncommon vigor of the child at length roused the mother. She started up, at a distance facing Captain Delano. But as if not at all concerned at the attitude in which she had been caught, delightedly she caught the child up, with maternal transports, covering it with kisses.

There's naked nature, now, pure tenderness and love, thought Captain Delano, well pleased.

This incident prompted him to remark the other Negresses more particularly than before. He was gratified with their manners: like most uncivilized women, they seemed at once tender of heart and tough of constitution, equally ready to die for their infants or fight for them. Unsophisticated as leopardesses, loving as doves. Ah! thought Captain Delano, these, perhaps, are some of the very women whom Ledyard saw in Africa, and gave such a noble account of.

These natural sights somehow insensibly deepened his confidence and ease. At last he looked to see how his boat was getting on, but it was still pretty remote. He turned to see if Don Benito had returned, but he had not.

To change the scene, as well as to please himself with a leisurely observation of the coming boat, stepping over into the mizzen-chains, he clambered his way into the starboard quarter-gallery – one of those abandoned Venetian-looking water balconies previously mentioned – retreats cut off from the deck. As his foot pressed the half-damp, half-dry sea mosses matting the place, and a chance phantom cat's-paw – an islet of breeze, unheralded, unfollowed – as this ghostly cat's-paw came fanning his cheek; as his glance fell upon the row of small, round deadlights – all closed liked coppered eyes of the coffined – and the state-cabin door, one connecting with the gallery, even as the deadlights had once looked out upon it, but now calked fast like a sarcophagus lid; and to a purple-black, tarred-over, panel, threshold, and post; and he bethought him of the time when that state cabin and this state balcony had heard the voices of the Spanish king's officers, and the forms of the Lima viceroy's daughters had perhaps leaned where he stood – as these and other images flitted through his mind as the cat's-paw through the calm, gradually he felt rising a dreamy inquietude, like that of one who alone on the prairie feels unrest from the repose of the noon.

He leaned against the carved balustrade, again looking off toward his boat, but found his eye falling upon the ribbon grass, trailing along the ship's water line, straight as a border of green box, and parterres of seaweed, broad ovals and crescents, floating nigh and far, with what seemed long formal alleys between, crossing the terraces of swells, and sweeping round as if leading to the grottoes below. And overhanging all was the balustrade by his arm, which, partly stained with pitch and partly embossed with moss, seemed the charred ruin of some summerhouse in a grand garden long running to waste.

Trying to break one charm, he was but becharmed anew. Though upon the wide sea, he seemed in some far inland country, prisoner in some deserted château, left to stare at empty grounds and peer out at vague roads where never wagon or wayfarer passed.

But these enchantments were a little disenchanted as his eye fell on the corroded mainchains. Of an ancient style, massy and rusty in link, shackle and bolt, they seemed even more fit for the ship's present business than the one for which she had been built.

Presently he thought something moved nigh the chains. He rubbed his eyes, and looked hard. Groves of rigging were about the chains; and there, peering from behind a great stay, like an Indian from behind a hemlock, a Spanish sailor, a marlinespike in his hand, was seen, who made what seemed an imperfect gesture towards the balcony, but immediately, as if alarmed by some advancing step along the deck within, vanished into the recesses of the hempen forest like a poacher.

What meant this? Something the man had sought to communicate, unbeknown to anyone, even to his captain. Did the secret involve aught unfavorable to his captain? Were those previous misgivings of Captain Delano's about to be verified? Or, in his haunted mood at the moment, had some random, unintentional motion of the man, while busy with the stay as if repairing it, been mistaken for a significant beckoning?

Not unbewildered, again he gazed off for his boat. But it was temporarily hidden by a rocky spur of the isle. As with some eagerness he bent forward, watching for the first shooting view of its beak, the balustrade gave way before him like charcoal. Had he not clutched an outreaching rope he would have fallen into the sea. The crash, though feeble, and the fall, though hollow, of rotten fragments, must have been overheard. He glanced up. With sober curiosity peering down upon him was one of the old oakum-pickers, slipped from his perch to an outside boom, while below the old Negro, and, invisible to him, reconnoitering from a porthole like a fox from the mouth of its den, crouched the Spanish sailor again. From something suddenly suggested by the man's air, the mad idea now darted into Captain Delano's mind that Don Benito's plea of indisposition, in withdrawing below, was but a pretense: that he was engaged there maturing his plot, of which the sailor, by some means gaining an inkling had a mind to warn the stranger against, incited, it may be, by gratitude for a kind word on first boarding the ship. Was it from foreseeing some possible interference like this that Don Benito had, beforehand, given such a bad character of his sailors, while praising the Negroes, though, indeed, the former seemed as docile as the latter the contrary? The whites, too, by nature, were the shrewder race. A man with some evil design, would he not be likely to speak well of that stupidity which was blind to his depravity, and malign that intelligence from which it might not be hidden? Not unlikely, perhaps. But if the whites had dark secrets concerning Don Benito, could then Don Benito be any way in complicity with the blacks? But they were too stupid. Besides, who ever heard of a white so far a renegade as to apostatize from his very species almost, by leaguing in against it with Negroes? These difficulties recalled former ones. Lost in their mazes, Captain Delano, who had now regained the deck, was uneasily advancing along it when he observed a new face; an aged sailor seated cross-legged near the main hatchway. His skin was shrunk up with wrinkles like a pelican's empty pouch, his hair frosted, his countenance grave and composed. His hands were full of ropes, which he was working into a large knot. Some blacks were about him obligingly dipping the strands for him, here and there, as the exigencies of the operation demanded.

Captain Delano crossed over to him and stood in silence surveying the knot, his mind, by a not uncongenial transition, passing from its own entanglements to those of the hemp. For intricacy, such a knot he had never seen in an American ship, nor indeed any other. The old man looked like an Egyptian priest making Gordian knots for the temple of Ammon. The knot seemed a combination of double-bowline-knot, treble-crown-knot, back-handed-well-knot, knot-in-and-out-knot and jamming knot.

At last, puzzled to comprehend the meaning of such a knot, Captain Delano addressed the knotter: 'What are you knotting there, my man?'

'The knot,' was the brief reply, without looking up.

'So it seems; but what is it for?'

'For someone else to undo,' muttered back the old man, plying his fingers harder than ever, the knot being now nearly completed.

While Captain Delano stood watching him, suddenly the old man threw the knot towards him, saying in broken English – the first heard in the ship – something to this effect: 'Undo it, cut it, quick.' It was said lowly, but with such condensation of rapidity, that the long, slow words in Spanish, which had preceded and followed, almost operated as covers to the brief English between.

For a moment, knot in hand, and knot in head, Captain Delano stood mute, while, without further heeding him, the old man was now intent upon other ropes. Presently there was a slight stir behind Captain Delano. Turning, he saw the chained Negro, Atufal, standing quietly there. The next moment the old sailor rose, muttering, and, followed by his subordinate Negroes, removed to the forward part of the ship, where in the crowd he disappeared.

An elderly Negro, in a clout like an infant's, and with a pepper-and-salt head and a kind of attorney air, now approached Captain Delano. In tolerable Spanish, and with a good-natured, knowing wink, he informed him that the old knotter was simple-witted, but harmless, often playing his odd tricks. The Negro concluded by begging the knot, for of course the stranger would not care to be troubled with it. Unconsciously, it was handed to him. With a sort of congé, the Negro received it, and, turning his back, ferreted into it like a detective custom-house officer after smuggled laces. Soon, with some African words equivalent to pshaw, he tossed the knot overboard.

All this is very queer, thought Captain Delano, with a qualmish sort of emotion; but, as one feeling incipient seasickness, he strove, by ignoring the symptoms, to get rid of the malady. Once more he looked off for his boat. To his delight, it was now again in view, leaving the rocky spur astern.

The sensation here experienced, after at first relieving his uneasiness, with unforeseen efficacy soon began to remove it. The less distant sight of that well-known boat – showing it, not as before, half blended with the haze but with outline defined, so that its individuality, like a man's, was manifest; that boat, *Rover* by name, which, though now in strange seas, had often pressed the beach of Captain Delano's home, and, brought to its threshold for repairs, had familiarly lain there, as a Newfoundland dog; the sight of that household boat evoked a thousand trustful associations, which, contrasted with previous suspicions, filled him not only with lightsome confidence, but somehow with half humorous self-reproaches at his former lack of it.

'What, I, Amasa Delano – Jack of the Beach, as they called me when a lad – I, Amasa, the same that, duck-satchel in hand, used to paddle along the waterside to the schoolhouse made from the old hulk – I, little Jack of the Beach, that used to go berrying with cousin Nat and the rest – I to be murdered here at the ends of the earth on board a haunted pirate ship by a horrible Spaniard? Too nonsensical to think of! Who would murder Amasa Delano? His conscience is clean. There is someone above. Fie, fie, Jack of the Beach! you are a child indeed; a child of the second childhood, old boy; you are beginning to dote and drool, I'm afraid.'

Light of heart and foot, he stepped aft, and there was met by Don Benito's servant, who, with a pleasing expression responsive to his own present feelings, informed him that his master had recovered from the effects of his coughing fit, and had just ordered him to go present his compliments to his good guest, Don Amasa, and say that he (Don Benito) would soon have the happiness to rejoin him.

There now, do you mark that? again thought Captain Delano, walking the poop. What a donkey I was. This kind gentleman who here sends me his kind compliments, he, but ten minutes ago, dark-lantern in hand, was dodging round some old grindstone in the hold, sharpening a hatchet for me, I thought. Well, well; these long calms have a morbid effect on the mind, I've often heard, though I never believed it before. Ha! glancing towards the boat, there's *Rover*, a good dog, a white bone in her mouth. A pretty big bone though, seems to me. – What? Yes, she has fallen afoul of the bubbling tide rip there. It sets her the other way, too, for the time. Patience.

It was now about noon, though, from the grayness of everything, it seemed to be getting towards dusk.

The calm was confirmed. In the far distance, away from the influence of land, the leaden ocean seemed laid out and leaded up, its course finished, soul gone, defunct. But the current from landward, where the ship was, increased, silently sweeping her further and further towards the tranced waters beyond.

Still, from his knowledge of those latitudes, cherishing hopes of a breeze, and a fair and fresh one, at any moment, Captain Delano, despite present prospects, buoyantly counted upon bringing the *San Dominick* safely to anchor ere night. The distance swept over was nothing, since, with a good wind, ten minutes' sailing would retrace more than sixty minutes' drifting. Meantime, one moment turning to mark *Rover* fighting the tide rip and the next to see Don Benito approaching, he continued walking the poop.

Gradually he felt a vexation arising from the delay of his boat; this soon merged into uneasiness, and at last – his eye falling continually, as from a stage box into the pit, upon the strange crowd before and below him, and by and by recognizing there the face, now composed to indifference, of the Spanish sailor who had seemed to beckon from the mainchains – something of his old trepidations returned.

Ah, thought he, gravely enough, this is like the ague: because it went off, it follows not that it won't come back.

Though ashamed of the relapse, he could not altogether subdue it; and so, exerting his good nature to the utmost, insensibly he came to a compromise.

Yes, this is a strange craft, a strange history, too, and strange folks on board. But – nothing more.

By way of keeping his mind out of mischief till the boat should arrive, he tried to occupy it with turning over and over, in a purely speculative sort of way, some lesser peculiarities of the captain and crew. Among others, four curious points recurred:

First, the affair of the Spanish lad assailed with a knife by the slave boy; an act winked at by Don Benito. Second the tyranny in Don Benito's treatment of Atufal, the black, as if a child should lead a bull of the Nile by the ring in his nose. Third, the trampling of the sailor by the two Negroes, a piece of insolence passed over without so much as a reprimand. Fourth, the cringing submission to their master of all the ship's underlings, mostly blacks, as if by the least inadvertence they feared to draw down his despotic displeasure.

Coupling these points, they seemed somewhat contradictory. But what then, thought Captain Delano, glancing towards his now nearing boat – what then? Why, Don Benito is a very capricious commander. But he is not the first of the sort I have seen, though it's true he rather exceeds any other. But as a nation – continued he in his reveries – these Spaniards are all an odd set; the very word Spaniard has a curious, conspirator, Guy-Fawkish twang to it. And yet I dare say Spaniards in the main are as good folks as any in Duxbury, Massachusetts. Ah good! At last *Rover* has come.

As, with its welcome freight, the boat touched the side, the oakum-pickers, with venerable gestures, sought to restrain the blacks, who, at the sight of three gurried water casks in its bottom and a pile of wilted pumpkins in its bow, hung over the bulwarks in disorderly raptures.

Don Benito, with his servant, now appeared, his coming, perhaps, hastened by hearing the noise. Of him Captain Delano sought permission to serve out the water, so that all might share alike, and none injure themselves by unfair excess. But sensible, and, on Don Benito's account, kind as this offer was, it was received with what seemed impatience; as if aware that he lacked energy as a commander, Don Benito, with the true jealousy of weakness, resented as an affront any interference. So, at least, Captain Delano inferred.

In another moment the casks were being hoisted in, when some of the eager Negroes accidentally jostled Captain Delano where he stood by the gangway, so that, unmindful of Don Benito, yielding to the impulse of the moment, with good-natured authority he bade the black stand back, to enforce his words making use of a half-mirthful, half-menacing gesture. Instantly the blacks paused, just where they were, each Negro and Negress suspended in his or her posture, exactly as the word had found them – for a few seconds continuing so – while, as between the responsive posts of a telegraph, an unknown syllable ran from man to man among the perched oakum-pickers. While the visitor's attention was fixed by this scene, suddenly the hatchet-polishers half rose, and a rapid cry came from Don Benito.

Thinking that at the signal of the Spaniard he was about to be massacred, Captain Delano would have sprung for his boat, but paused, as the oakum-pickers, dropping down into the crowd with earnest exclamations, forced every white and every Negro back, at the same moment, with gestures friendly and familiar, almost jocose, bidding him, in substance, not be a fool. Simultaneously the hatchet-polishers resumed their seats, quietly as so many tailors, and at once, as if nothing had happened, the work of hoisting the casks was resumed, white and blacks singing at the tackle.

Captain Delano glanced towards Don Benito. As he saw his meager form in the act of recovering itself from reclining in the servant's arms, into which the agitated invalid had fallen, he could not but marvel at the panic by which himself had been surprised, on the darting supposition that such a commander, who, upon a legitimate occasion, so trivial too, as it now appeared, could lose all self-command, was, with energetic iniquity, going to bring about his murder.

The casks being on deck, Captain Delano was handed a number of jars and cups by one of the steward's aids, who, in the name of his captain, entreated him to do as he had proposed – dole out the water. He complied, with republican impartiality as to this republican element, which always seeks one level, serving the oldest white no better than the youngest black, excepting, indeed, poor Don Benito, whose condition, if not rank, demanded an extra allowance. To him, in the first place, Captain Delano presented a fair pitcher of the fluid, but, thirsting as he was for it, the Spaniard quaffed not a drop until after several grave bows and salutes, a reciprocation of courtesies which the sight-loving Africans hailed with clapping of hands.

Two of the less wilted pumpkins being reserved for the cabin table, the residue were minced up on the spot for the general regalement. But the soft bread, sugar, and bottled cider Captain Delano would have given the whites alone, and in chief Don Benito, but the latter objected; which disinterestedness not a little pleased the American; and so mouthfuls all around were given alike to whites and blacks, excepting one bottle of cider, which Babo insisted upon setting aside for his master.

Here it may be observed that as, on the first visit of the boat, the American had not permitted his men to board the ship, neither did he now, being unwilling to add to the confusion of the decks.

Not uninfluenced by the peculiar good humor at present prevailing, and for the time oblivious of any but benevolent thought, Captain Delano, who from recent indications counted upon a breeze within an hour or two at furthest, dispatched the boat back to the sealer, with orders for all the hands that could be spared immediately to set about rafting casks to the watering place and filling them. Likewise he bade word be carried to his chief officer that if against present expectation, the ship was not brought to anchor by sunset, he need be under no concern; for as there was to be a full moon that night, he (Captain Delano) would remain on board ready to play the pilot, come the wind soon or late.

As the two Captains stood together observing the departing boat – the servant, as it happened, having just spied a spot on his master's velvet sleeve, and silently engaged rubbing it out – the American expressed his regrets that the *San Dominick* had no boats, none, at least, but the unseaworthy old hulk of the longboat, which, warped as a camel's skeleton in the desert and almost as bleached, lay pot-wise inverted amidships, one side a little tipped, furnishing a subterraneous sort of den for family groups of the blacks, mostly women and small children, who, squatting on old mats below, or perched above in the dark dome on the elevated seats, were descried, some distance within, like a social circle of bats sheltering in some friendly cave, at intervals, ebon flights of naked boys and girls three or four years old darting in and out of the den's mouth.

'Had you three or four boats now, Don Benito,' said Captain Delano, 'I think that, by tugging at the oars, your Negroes here might help along matters some. Did you sail from port without boats, Don Benito?'

'They were stove in the gales, *señor*.'

'That was bad. Many men, too, you lost then. Boats and men. Those must have been hard gales, Don Benito.'

'Past all speech,' cringed the Spaniard.

'Tell me, Don Benito,' continued his companion with increased interest, 'tell me, were these gales immediately off the pitch of Cape Horn?'

'Cape Horn? – who spoke of Cape Horn?'

'Yourself did, when giving me an account of your voyage,' answered Captain Delano, with almost equal astonishment at this eating of his own words, even as he ever seemed eating his own heart, on the part of the Spaniard. 'You yourself, Don Benito, spoke of Cape Horn,' he emphatically repeated.

The Spaniard turned, in a sort of stooping posture, pausing an instant as one about to make a plunging exchange of elements, as from air to water.

At this moment a messenger boy, a white, hurried by, in the regular performance of his function carrying the last expired half-hour forward to the forecastle from the cabin timepiece, to have it struck at the ship's large bell.

'Master,' said the servant, discontinuing his work on the coat sleeve and addressing the rapt Spaniard with a sort of timid apprehensiveness, as one charged with a duty the discharge of which, it was foreseen, would prove irksome to the very person who had imposed it and for whose benefit it was intended, 'master told me never mind where he was, or how engaged, always to remind him, to a minute, when shaving-time comes. Miguel has gone to strike the half-hour afternoon. It is *now*, master. Will master go into the cuddy?'

'Ah – yes,' answered the Spaniard, starting, as from dreams into realities, then, turning upon Captain Delano, he said that erelong he would resume the conversation.

'Then if master means to talk more to Don Amasa,' said the servant, 'why not let Don Amasa sit by master in the cuddy, and master can talk, and Don Amasa can listen, while Babo here lathers and strops.'

'Yes,' said Captain Delano, not unpleased with this sociable plan, 'yes, Don Benito, unless you had rather not, I will go with you.'

'Be it so, *señor*.'

As the three passed aft, the American could not but think it another strange instance of his host's capriciousness, this being shaved with such uncommon punctuality in the middle of the day. But he deemed it more than likely that the servant's anxious fidelity had something to do with the matter, inasmuch as the timely interruption served to rally his master from the mood which had evidently been coming upon him.

The place called the cuddy was a light deck cabin formed by the poop, a sort of attic to the large cabin below. Part of it had formerly been the quarters of the officers, but since their death all the partitionings had been thrown down and the whole interior converted into one spacious and airy marine hall; for absence of fine furniture and picturesque disarray of odd appurtenances, somewhat answering to the wide, cluttered hall of some eccentric bachelor squire in the country, who hangs his shooting jacket and tobacco pouch on deer antlers, and keeps his fishing rod, tongs, and walking stick in the same corner.

The similitude was heightened, if not originally suggested, by glimpses of the surrounding sea, since, in one aspect, the country and the ocean seem cousins-german.

The floor of the cuddy was matted. Overhead, four or five old muskets were stuck into horizontal holes along the beams. On one side was a claw-footed old table lashed to the deck, a thumbed missal on it, and over it, a small, meager crucifix attached to the bulkhead. Under the table lay a dented cutlass or two with a hacked harpoon, among some melancholy old rigging, like a heap of poor friars' girdles. There were also two long, sharp-ribbed settees of Malacca cane, black with age, and uncomfortable to look at as inquisitors' racks, with a large, misshapen armchair, which, furnished with a rude barber's crotch at the back, working with a screw, seemed some grotesque engine of torment. A flag locker was in one corner, open, exposing various colored buntings, some rolled up, others half unrolled, still others tumbled. Opposite was a cumbrous washstand of black mahogany, all of one block, with a pedestal like a font, and over it a railed shelf, containing combs, brushes, and other implements of the toilet. A torn hammock of stained grass swung near, the sheets tossed, and the pillow wrinkled up like a brow, as if whoever slept here slept but illy, with alternate visitations of sad thoughts and bad dreams.

The further extremity of the cuddy, overhanging the ship's stern, was pierced with three openings, windows or portholes, according as men or cannon might peer, socially or unsocially, out of them. At present neither men nor cannon were seen, though huge ringbolts and other rusty iron fixtures of the woodwork hinted of twenty-four-pounders.

Glancing towards the hammock as he entered, Captain Delano said, 'You sleep here, Don Benito?'

'Yes, *señor*, since we got into mild weather.'

'This seems a sort of dormitory, sitting room, sail loft, chapel, armory, and private closet all together, Don Benito,' added Captain Delano, looking round.

'Yes, *señor*; events have not been favorable to much order in my arrangements.'

Here the servant, napkin on arm, made a motion as if waiting his master's good pleasure. Don Benito signified his readiness, when, seating him at the Malacca armchair, and for the guest's convenience drawing opposite one of the settees, the servant commenced operations by throwing back his master's collar and loosening his cravat.

There is something in the Negro which, in a peculiar way, fits him for avocations about one's person. Most Negroes are natural valets and hairdressers, taking to the comb and brush congenially as to the castinets, and flourishing them apparently with almost equal satisfaction. There is, too, a smooth tact about them in this employment with a marvelous, noiseless, gliding briskness, not ungraceful in its way, singularly pleasing to behold, and still more so to be the manipulated subject of. And above all is the great gift of good humor. Not the mere grin or laugh is here meant. Those were unsuitable. But a certain easy cheerfulness, harmonious in every glance and gesture, as though God had set the whole Negro to some pleasant tune.

When to this is added the docility arising from the unaspiring contentment of a limited mind, and that susceptibility of blind attachment sometimes inhering in indisputable inferiors, one readily perceives why those hypochondriacs, Johnson and Byron – it may be, something like the hypochondriac Benito Cereno – took to their hearts, almost to the exclusion of the entire white race, their servingmen, the Negroes, Barber and Fletcher. But if there be that in the Negro which exempts him from the inflicted sourness of the morbid or cynical mind, how, in his most prepossessing aspects, must he appear to a benevolent one? When at ease with respect to exterior things, Captain Delano's nature was not only benign, but familiarly and humorously so. At home, he had often taken rare satisfaction in sitting in his door, watching some free man of color at his work or play. If on a voyage he chanced to have a black sailor, invariably he was on chatty and half-gamesome terms with him. In fact, like most men of a good, blithe heart, Captain Delano took to Negroes, not philanthropically, but genially, just as other men to Newfoundland dogs.

Hitherto, the circumstances in which he found the *San Dominick* had repressed the tendency. But in the cuddy, relieved from his former uneasiness, and, for various reasons, more sociably inclined than at any previous period of the day, and seeing the colored servant, napkin on arm, so debonair about his master, in a business so familiar as that of shaving too, all his old weakness for Negroes returned.

Among other things, he was amused with an odd instance of the African love of bright colors and fine shows, in the black's informally taking from the flag locker a great piece of bunting of all hues and lavishly tucking it under his master's chin for an apron.

The mode of shaving among the Spaniards is a little different from what it is with other nations. They have a basin, specifically called a barber's basin, which on one side is scooped out, so as accurately to receive the chin, against which it is closely held in lathering, which is done, not with a brush, but with soap dipped in the water of the basin and rubbed on the face.

In the present instance salt water was used for lack of better, and the parts lathered were only the upper lip and low down under the throat, all the rest being cultivated beard.

The preliminaries being somewhat novel to Captain Delano, he sat curiously eying them, so that no conversation took place, nor, for the present, did Don Benito appear disposed to renew any.

Setting down his basin, the Negro searched among the razors, as for the sharpest, and having found it, gave it an additional edge by expertly stropping it on the firm smooth, oily skin of his open palm; he then made a gesture as if to begin, but midway stood suspended for an instant, one hand elevating the razor, the other professionally dabbling among the bubbling suds on the Spaniard's lank neck. Not unaffected by the close sight of the gleaming steel, Don Benito nervously shuddered; his usual ghastliness was heightened by the lather, which lather, again, was intensified in its hue by the contrasting sootiness of the Negro's body. Altogether the scene was somewhat peculiar, at least to Captain Delano, nor, as he saw the two thus postured, could he resist the vagary that in the black he saw a headsman, and in the white a man at the block. But this was one of those antic conceits, appearing and vanishing in a breath, from which, perhaps, the best-regulated mind is not always free.

Meantime the agitation of the Spaniard had a little loosened the bunting from around him, so that one broad fold swept curtainlike over the chair arm to the floor, revealing, amid a profusion of armorial bars and ground color – black, blue, and yellow – a closed castle in a blood-red field diagonal with a lion rampant in a white.

'The castle and the lion,' exclaimed Captain Delano – 'why, Don Benito, this is the flag of Spain you use here. It's well it's only I, and not the King, that sees this,' he added, with a smile, 'but' – turning towards the black – 'it's all one, I suppose, so the colors be gay'; which playful remark did not fail somewhat to tickle the Negro.

'Now, master,' he said, readjusting the flag, and pressing the head gently further back into the crotch of the chair, 'now, master,' and the steel glanced nigh the throat.

Again Don Benito faintly shuddered.

'You must not shake so, master. See, Don Amasa, master always shakes when I shave him. And yet master knows I never yet have drawn blood, though it's true if master will shake so I may some of these times. Now master,' he continued. 'And now, Don Amasa, please go on with your talk about the gale, and all that; master can hear, and, between times, master can answer.'

'Ah yes, these gales,' said Captain Delano; 'but the more I think of your voyage, Don Benito, the more I wonder, not at the gales, terrible as they must have been, but at the disastrous interval following them. For here, by your account, have you been these two months and more getting from Cape Horn to St Maria, a distance which I myself with a good wind, have sailed in a few days. True, you had calms, and long ones, but to be becalmed for two months, that is, at least, unusual. Why, Don Benito, had almost any other gentleman told me such a story, I should have been half disposed to a little incredulity.'

Here an involuntary expression came over the Spaniard, similar to that just before on the deck, and whether it was the start he gave, or a sudden gawky roll of the hull in the calm, or a momentary unsteadiness of the servant's hand, however it was, just then the razor drew blood, spots of which stained the creamy lather under the throat; immediately the black barber drew back his steel, and, remaining in his professional attitude, back to Captain Delano, and face to Don Benito, held up the trickling razor, saying, with a sort of half humorous sorrow, 'See, master – you shook so – here's Babo's first blood.'

No sword drawn before James the First of England, no assassination in that timid king's presence, could have produced a more terrified aspect than was now presented by Don Benito.

Poor fellow, thought Captain Delano, so nervous he can't even bear the sight of barber's blood; and this unstrung, sick man, is it credible that I should have imagined he meant to spill all my blood, who can't endure the sight of one little drop of his own? Surely, Amasa Delano, you have been beside youself this day. Tell it not when you get home, sappy Amasa. Well, well, he looks like a murderer, doesn't he? More like as if himself were to be done for. Well, well, this day's experience shall be a good lesson.

Meantime, while these things were running through the honest seaman's mind, the servant had taken the napkin from his arm, and to Don Benito had said - 'But anwer Don Amasa, please, master, while I wipe this ugly stuff off the razor, and strop it again.'

As he said the words, his face was turned half round, so as to be alike visible to the Spaniard and the American, and seemed, by its expression, to hint that he was desirous, by getting his master to go on with the conversation, considerately to withdraw his attention from the recent annoying accident. As if glad to snatch the offered relief, Don Benito resumed, rehearsing to Captain Delano that, not only were the calms of unusual duration, but the ship had fallen in with obstinate currents, and other things he added, some of which were but repetitions of former statements, to explain how it came to pass that the passage from Cape Horn to St Maria had been so exceedingly long, now and then mingling with his words incidental praises, less qualified than before, to the blacks, for their general good conduct. These particulars were not given consecutively, the servant, at convenient times, using his razor, and so, between the intervals of shaving, the story and panegyric went on with more than usual huskiness.

To Captain Delano's imagination, now again not wholly at rest, there was something so hollow in the Spaniard's manner, with apparently some reciprocal hollowness in the servant's dusky comment of silence, that the idea flashed across him that possibly master and man, for some unknown purpose were acting out, both in word and deed, nay, to the very tremor of Don Benito's limbs, some juggling play before him. Neither did the suspicion of collusion lack apparent support, from the fact of those whispered conferences before mentioned. But then, what could be the object of enacting this play of the barber before him? At last, regarding the notion as a whimsey, insensibly suggested, perhaps, by the theatrical aspect of Don Benito in his harlequin ensign, Captain Delano speedily banished it.

The shaving over, the servant bestirred himself with a small bottle of scented waters, pouring a few drops on the head, and then diligently rubbing, the vehemence of the exercise causing the muscles of his face to twitch rather strangely.

His next operation was with comb, scissors, and brush, going round and round, smoothing a curl here, clipping an unruly whisker hair there, giving a graceful sweep to the temple lock, with other impromptu touches evincing the hand of a master, while, like any resigned gentleman in barber's hands, Don Benito bore all much less uneasily, at least, than he had done the razoring; indeed, he sat so pale and rigid now that the Negro seemed a Nubian sculptor finishing off a white statue head.

All being over at last, the standard of Spain removed, tumbled up, and tossed back into the flag locker, the Negro's warm breath blowing away any stray hair which might have lodged down his master's neck, collar and cravat readjusted, a speck of lint whisked off the velvet lapel – all this being done, backing off a little space, and pausing with an expression of subdued self-complacency, the servant for a moment surveyed his master, as, in toilette at least, the creature of his own tasteful hands.

Captain Delano playfully complimented him upon his achievement, at the same time congratulating Don Benito.

But neither sweet waters, nor shampooing, nor fidelity, nor sociality, delighted the Spaniard. Seeing him relapsing into forbidding gloom, and still remaining seated, Captain Delano, thinking that his presence was undesired just then, withdrew, on pretense of seeing whether, as he had prophesied, any signs of a breeze were visible.

Walking forward to the mainmast, he stood awhile thinking over the scene, and not without some undefined misgivings, when he heard a noise near the cuddy, and turning, saw the Negro, his hand to his cheek. Advancing, Captain Delano perceived that the cheek was bleeding. He was about to ask the cause, when the Negro's wailing soliloquy enlightened him.

'Ah, when will master get better from his sickness; only the sour heart that sour sickness breeds made him serve Babo so, cutting Babo with the razor because, only by accident, Babo had given master one little scratch, and for the first time in so many a day, too. Ah, ah, ah,' holding his hand to his face.

Is it possible, thought Captain Delano; was it to wreak in private his Spanish spite against this poor friend of his that Don Benito, by his sullen manner, impelled me to withdraw? Ah this slavery breeds ugly passions in man. – Poor fellow!

He was about to speak in sympathy to the Negro, but with a timid reluctance he now re-entered the cuddy.

Presently master and man came forth, Don Benito leaning on his servant as if nothing had happened.

But a sort of love quarrel, after all, thought Captain Delano.

He accosted Don Benito, and they slowly walked together. They had gone but a few paces, when the steward – a tall, rajah-looking mulatto, Orientally set off with a pagoda turban formed by three or four Madras handkerchiefs wound about his head, tier on tier – approaching with a salaam, announced lunch in the cabin.

On their way thither, the two captains were preceded by the mulatto, who, turning round as he advanced, with continual smiles and bows, ushered them on, a display of elegance which quite completed the insignificance of the small bareheaded Babo, who, as if not unconscious of inferiority, eyed askance the graceful steward. But, in part, Captain Delano imputed his jealous watchfulness to that peculiar feeling which the full-blooded African entertains for the adulterated one. As for the steward, his manner, if not bespeaking much dignity of self-respect, yet evidenced his extreme desire to please, which is doubly meritorious, as at once Christian and Chester-fieldian.

Captain Delano observed with interest that while the complexion of the mulatto was hybrid, his physiognomy was European – classically so.

'Don Benito,' whispered he, 'I am glad to see this usher-of-the-golden-rod of yours; the sight refutes an ugly remark once made to me by a Barbados planter, that when a mulatto has a regular European face, look out for him; he is a devil. But see, your steward here has features more regular than King George's of England, and yet there he nods, and bows, and smiles, a king, indeed – the king of kind hearts and polite fellows. What a pleasant voice he has, too.'

'He has, *señor*.'

'But tell me, has he not, so far as you have known him, always proved a good, worthy fellow?' said Captain Delano, pausing, while with a final genuflexion the steward disappeared into the cabin; 'come, for the reason just mentioned, I am curious to know.'

'Francesco is a good man,' a sort of sluggishly responded Don Benito, like a phlegmatic appreciator, who would neither find fault nor flatter.

'Ah, I thought so. For it were strange indeed, and not very creditable to us whiteskins, if a little of our blood mixed with the African's should, far from improving the latter's quality, have the sad effect of pouring vitriolic acid into black broth – improving the hue, perhaps, but not the wholesomeness.'

'Doubtless, doubtless, *señor*, but' – glancing at Babo – 'not to speak of Negroes, your planter's remark I have heard applied to the Spanish and Indian intermixtures in our provinces. But I know nothing about the matter,' he listlessly added.

And here they entered the cabin.

The lunch was a frugal one. Some of Captain Delano's fresh fish and pumpkins, biscuit and salt beef, the reserved bottle of cider, and the *San Dominick*'s last bottle of Canary.

As they entered, Francesco, with two or three colored aids, was hovering over the table giving the last adjustments. Upon perceiving their master they withdrew, Francesco making a smiling *congé*, and the Spaniard, without condescending to notice it, fastidiously remarking to his companion that he relished not superfluous attendance.

Without companions, host and guest sat down, like a childless married couple, at opposite ends of the table, Don Benito waving Captain Delano to his place, and, weak as he was, insisting upon that gentleman being seated before himself.

The Negro placed a rug under Don Benito's feet, and a cushion behind his back, and then stood behind, not his master's chair, but Captain Delano's. At first, this a little surprised the latter. But it was soon evident that, in taking his position, the black was still true to his master, since by facing him he could the more readily anticipate his slightest want.

'This is an uncommonly intelligent fellow of yours, Don Benito,' whispered Captain Delano across the table.

'You say true, *señor*.'

During the repast, the guest again reverted to parts of Don Benito's story, begging further particulars here and there. He inquired how it was that the scurvy and fever should have committed such wholesale havoc upon the whites, while destroying less than half of the blacks. As if this question reproduced the whole scene of plague before the Spaniard's eyes, miserably reminding him of his solitude in a cabin where before he had had so many friends and officers round him, his hand shook, his face became hueless, broken words escaped; but directly the same memory of the past seemed replaced by insane terrors of the present. With starting eyes he stared before him at vacancy. For nothing was to be seen but the hand of his servant pushing the Canary over towards him. At length a few sips served partially to restore him. He made random reference to the different constitution of races, enabling one to offer more resistance to certain maladies than another. The thought was new to his companion.

Presently Captain Delano, intending to say something to his host concerning the pecuniary part of the business he had undertaken for him, especially – since he was strictly accountable to his owners – with reference to the new suit of sails, and other things of that sort, and naturally preferring to conduct such affairs in private, was desirous that the servant should withdraw, imagining that Don Benito for a few minutes could dispense with his attendance. He, however, waited awhile, thinking that, as the conversation proceeded, Don Benito, without being prompted, would perceive the propriety of the step,

But it was otherwise. At last catching his host's eye, Captain Delano, with a slight backward gesture of his thumb, whispered, 'Don Benito, pardon me, but there is an interference with the full expression of what I have to say to you.'

Upon this the Spaniard changed countenance, which was imputed to his resenting the hint, as in some way a reflection upon his servant. After a moment's pause, he assured his guest that the black's remaining with them could be of no disservice; because since losing his officers he had made Babo (whose original office, it now appeared, had been captain of the slaves) not only his constant attendant and companion, but in all things his confidant.

After this, nothing more could be said; though indeed Captain Delano could hardly avoid some little tinge of irritation upon being left ungratified in so inconsiderable a wish, by one, too, for whom he intended such solid services. But it is only his querulousness, thought he, and so, filling his glass, he proceeded to business.

The price of the sails and other matters was fixed upon. But while this was being done, the American observed that, though his original offer of assistance had been hailed with hectic animation, yet now when it was reduced to a business transaction, indifference and apathy were betrayed. Don Benito, in fact, appeared to submit to hearing the details more out of regard to common propriety than from any impression that weighty benefit to himself and his voyage was involved.

Soon his manner became still more reserved. The effort was vain to seek to draw him into social talk. Gnawed by his splenetic mood, he sat twitching his beard, while to little purpose the hand of his servant, mute as that on the wall, slowly pushed over the Canary.

Lunch being over, they sat down on the cushioned transom, the servant placing a pillow behind his master. The long continuance of the calm had now affected the atmosphere. Don Benito sighed heavily, as if for breath.

'Why not adjourn to the cuddy,' said Captain Delano; 'there is more air there.' But the host sat silent and motionless.

Meantime his servant knelt before him with a large fan of feathers. And Francesco, coming in on tiptoes, handed the Negro a little cup of aromatic waters, with which at intervals he chafed his master's brow, smoothing the hair along the temples as a nurse does a child's. He spoke no word. He only rested his eye on his master's as if, amid all Don Benito's distress, a little to refresh his spirit by the silent sight of fidelity.

Presently the ship's bell sounded two o'clock, and through the cabin windows a slight rippling of the sea was discerned, and from the desired direction.

'There,' exclaimed Captain Delano, 'I told you so, Don Benito, look!'

He had risen to his feet, speaking in a very animated tone, with a view the more to rouse his companion. But though the crimson curtain of the stern window near him that moment fluttered against his pale cheek, Don Benito seemed to have even less welcome for the breeze than the calm.

Poor fellow, thought Captain Delano, bitter experience has taught him that one ripple does not make a wind, any more than one swallow a summer. But he is mistaken for once. I will get his ship in for him, and prove it.

Briefly alluding to his weak condition, he urged his host to remain quietly where he was, since he (Captain Delano) would with pleasure take upon himself the responsibility of making the best use of the wind.

Upon gaining the deck, Captain Delano started at the unexpected figure of Atufal, monumentally fixed at the threshold, like one of those sculptured porters of black marble guarding the porches of Egyptian tombs.

But this time the start was, perhaps, purely physical. Atufal's presence, singularly attesting docility even in sullenness, was contrasted with that of the hatchet-polishers, who in patience evinced their industry; while both spectacles showed that, lax as Don Benito's general authority might be, still, whenever he chose to exert it, no man so savage or colossal but must, more or less, bow.

Snatching a trumpet which hung from the bulwarks, with a free step Captain Delano advanced to the forward edge of the poop, issuing his orders in his best Spanish. The few sailors and many Negroes, all equally pleased, obediently set about heading the ship towards the harbor.

While giving some directions about setting a lower stunsail, suddenly Captain Delano heard a voice faithfully repeating his orders. Turning, he saw Babo, now for the time acting, under the pilot, his original part of captain of the slaves. This assistance proved valuable. Tattered sails and warped yards were soon brought into some trim. And no brace or halyard was pulled but to the blithe songs of the inspirited Negroes.

Good fellows, thought Captain Delano, a little training would make fine sailors of them. Why see, the very women pull and sing too. These must be some of those Ashantee Negresses that make such capital soldiers, I've heard. But who's at the helm? I must have a good hand there.

He went to see.

The *San Dominick* steered with a cumbrous tiller, with large horizontal pulleys attached. At each pulley end stood a subordinate black, and between them, at the tillerhead, the responsible post, a Spanish seaman, whose countenance evinced his due share in the general hopefulness and confidence at the coming of the breeze.

He proved the same man who had behaved with so shamefaced an air on the windlass.

'Ah – it is you, my man,' exclaimed Captain Delano – 'well, no more sheep's-eyes now; look straight forward and keep the ship so. Good hand, I trust? And want to get into the harbor, don't you?'

The man assented with an inward chuckle, grasping the tillerhead firmly. Upon this, unperceived by the American, the two blacks eyed the sailor intently.

Finding all right at the helm, the pilot went forward to the forecastle to see how matters stood there.

The ship now had way enough to breast the current. With the approach of evening, the breeze would be sure to freshen.

Having done all that was needed for the present, Captain Delano, giving his last orders to the sailors, turned aft to report affairs to Don Benito in the cabin, perhaps additionally incited to rejoin him by the hope of snatching a moment's private chat while the servant was engaged upon deck.

From opposite sides, there were, beneath the poop, two approaches to the cabin, one further forward than the other, and consequently communicating with a longer passage. Marking the servant still above, Captain Delano, taking the nighest entrance – the one last named, and at whose porch Atufal still stood – hurried on his way, till, arrived at the cabin threshold, he paused an instant, a little to recover from his eagerness. Then, with the words of his intended business upon his lips, he entered. As he advanced toward the seated Spaniard, he heard another footstep, keeping time with his. From the opposite door, a salver in hand, the servant was likewise advancing.

'Confound the faithful fellow,' thought Captain Delano; 'what a vexatious coincidence.'

Possibly the vexation might have been something different, were it not for the brisk confidence inspired by the breeze. But even as it was he felt a slight twinge, from a sudden indefinite association in his mind of Babo with Atufal.

'Don Benito,' said he, 'I give you joy; the breeze will hold, and will increase. By the way, your tall man and timepiece, Atufal, stands without. By your order, of course?'

Don Benito recoiled, as if at some bland satirical touch delivered with such adroit garnish of apparent good breeding as to present no handle for retort.

He is like one flayed alive, thought Captain Delano; where may one touch him without causing a shrink.

The servant moved before his master, adjusting a cushion; recalled to civility, the Spaniard stiffly replied: 'You are right. The slave appears where you saw him, according to my command, which is that if at the given hour I am below he must take his stand and abide my coming.'

'Ah now, pardon me, but that is treating the poor fellow like an ex-king indeed. Ah, Don Benito,' smiling, 'for all the license you permit in some things, I fear lest, at bottom, you are a bitter hard master.'

Again Don Benito shrank, and this time, as the good sailor thought, from a genuine twinge of his conscience.

Again conversation became constrained. In vain Captain Delano called attention to the now perceptible motion of the keel gently cleaving the sea; with lackluster eye, Don Benito returned words few and reserved.

By and by, the wind having steadily risen, and still blowing right into the harbor, bore the *San Dominick* swiftly on. Rounding a point of land, the sealer at distance came into open view.

Meantime Captain Delano had again repaired to the deck, remaining there some time. Having at last altered the ship's course so as to give the reef a wide berth, he returned for a few moments below.

I will cheer up my poor friend this time, thought he.

'Better and better, Don Benito,' he cried as he blithely re-entered: 'there will soon be an end to your cares, at least for a while. For when, after a long, sad voyage, you know, the anchor drops into the haven, all its vast weight seems lifted from the captain's heart. We are getting on famously, Don Benito. My ship is in sight. Look through this side light here; there she is, all a-taunt-o! The *Bachelor's Delight*, my good friend. Ah, how this wind braces one up. Come, you must take a cup of coffee with me this evening. My old steward will give you as fine a cup as ever any sultan tasted. What say you, Don Benito, will you?'

At first, the Spaniard glanced feverishly up, casting a longing look towards the sealer, while, with mute concern his servant gazed into his face. Suddenly the old ague of coldness returned, and dropping back to his cushions he was silent.

'You do not answer. Come, all day you have been my host; would you have hospitality all on one side?'

'I cannot go,' was the response.

'What? it will not fatigue you. The ships will lie together as near as they can without swinging foul. It will be little more than stepping from deck to deck, which is but as from room to room. Come, come, you must not refuse me.'

'I cannot go,' decisively and repulsively repeated Don Benito.

Renouncing all but the last appearance of courtesy, with a sort of cadaverous sullenness, and biting his thin nails to the quick, he glanced, almost glared, at his guest, as if impatient that a stranger's presence should interfere with the full indulgence of his morbid hour. Meantime the sound of the parted waters came more and more gurglingly and merrily in at the windows; as reproaching him for his dark spleen, as telling him that, sulk as he might, and go mad with it, nature cared not a jot, since whose fault was it, pray?

But the foul mood was now at its depth, as the fair wind at its height.

There was something in the man so far beyond any mere unsociality or sourness previously evinced that even the forbearing good nature of his guest could no longer endure it. Wholly at a loss to account for such demeanor, and deeming sickness with eccentricity, however extreme, no adequate excuse, well satisfied, too, that nothing in his own conduct could justify it, Captain Delano's pride began to be roused. Himself became reserved. But all seemed one to the Spaniard. Quitting him, therefore, Captain Delano once more went to the deck.

The ship was now within less than two miles of the sealer. The whaleboat was seen darting over the interval.

To be brief, the two vessels, thanks to the pilot's skill, erelong in neighborly style lay anchored together.

Before returning to his own vessel, Captain Delano had intended communicating to Don Benito the smaller details of the proposed services to be rendered. But as it was, unwilling anew to subject himself to rebuffs, he resolved, now that he had seen the *San Dominick* safely moored, immediately to quit her, without further allusion to hospitality or business. Indefinitely postponing his ulterior plans, he would regulate his future actions according to future circumstances. His boat was ready to receive him; but his host still tarried below. Well, thought Captain Delano, if he has little breeding, the more need to show mine. He descended to the cabin to bid a ceremonious, and, it may be, tacitly rebukeful adieu. But to his great satisfaction, Don Benito, as if he began to feel the weight of that treatment with which his slighted guest had, not indecorously, retaliated upon him, now, supported by his servant, rose to his feet, and grasping Captain Delano's hand, stood tremulous, too much agitated to speak. But the good augury hence drawn was suddenly dashed by his resuming all his previous reserve with augmented gloom, as, with half-averted eyes, he silently reseated himself on his cushions. With a corresponding return of his own chilled feelings, Captain Delano bowed and withdrew.

He was hardly midway in the narrow corridor, dim as a tunnel, leading from the cabin to the stairs, when a sound, as of the tolling for execution in some jailyard, fell on his ears. It was the echo of the ship's flawed bell striking the hour, drearily reverberated in this subterranean vault. Instantly, by a fatality not to be withstood, his mind, responsive to the portent, swarmed with superstitious suspicions. He paused. In images far swifter than these sentences, the minutest details of all his former distrusts swept through him.

Hitherto, credulous good nature had been too ready to furnish excuses for reasonable fears. Why was the Spaniard, so superfluously punctilious at times, now heedless of common propriety in not accompanying to the side his departing guest? Did indisposition forbid? Indisposition had not forbidden more irksome exertion that day. His last equivocal demeanor recurred. He had risen to his feet, grasped his guest's hand, motioned toward his hat; then, in an instant, all was eclipsed in sinister muteness and gloom. Did this imply one brief repentant relenting at the final moment from some iniquitous plot, followed by remorseless return to it? His last glance seemed to express a calamitous yet acquiescent farewell to Captain Delano forever. Why decline the invitation to visit the sealer that evening? Or was the Spaniard less hardened than the Jew, who refrained not from supping at the board of him whom the same night he meant to betray? What imported all those daylong

enigmas and contradictions, except they were intended to mystify, preliminary to some stealthy blow? Atufal, the pretended rebel but punctual
shadow, that moment lurked by the threshold without. He seemed a sentry,
and more. Who, by his own confession had stationed him there? Was the
Negro now lying in wait?

The Spaniard behind – his creature before: to rush from darkness to light
was the involuntary choice.

The next moment, with clenched jaw and hand, he passed Atufal, and
stood unharmed in the light. As he saw his trim ship lying peacefully at
anchor and almost within ordinary call; as he saw his household boat, with
familiar faces in it, patiently rising and falling on the short waves by the *San
Dominick*'s side; and then, glancing about the decks where he stood, saw the
oakum-pickers still gravely plying their fingers, and heard the low, buzzing
whistle and industrious hum of the hatchet-polishers still bestirring themselves over their endless ocupation; and more than all, as he saw the benign
aspect of nature taking her innocent repose in the evening, the screened sun
in the quiet camp of the west shining out like the mild light from Abraham's
tent – as charmed eye and ear took in all these, with the chained figure of the
black, clenched jaw and hand relaxed. Once again he smiled at the phantoms
which had mocked him, and felt something like a tinge of remorse that, by
harboring them even for a moment, he should by implication have betrayed
an atheist doubt of the ever-watchful Providence above.

There was a few minutes' delay, while, in obedience to his orders, the boat
was being hooked along to the gangway. During this interval, a sort of
saddened satisfaction stole over Captain Delano at thinking of the kindly
offices he had that day discharged for a stranger. Ah, thought he, after good
actions one's conscience is never ungrateful, however much so the benefited
party may be.

Presently his foot, in the first act of descent into the boat, pressed the first
round of the side ladder, his face presented inward upon the deck. In the
same moment he heard his name courteously sounded, and, to his pleased
surprise, saw Don Benito advancing – an unwonted energy in his air, as if, at
the last moment, intent upon making amends for his recent discourtesy. With
instinctive good feeling, Captain Delano, withdrawing his foot, turned and
reciprocally advanced. As he did so, the Spaniard's nervous eagerness
increased, but his vital energy failed, so that, the better to support him, the
servant, placing his master's hand on his naked shoulder, and gently holding
it there, formed himself into a sort of crutch.

When the two captains met, the Spaniard again fervently took the hand of
the American, at the same time casting an earnest glance into his eyes, but,
as before, too much overcome to speak.

I have done him wrong, self-reproachfully thought Captain Delano; his
apparent coldness has deceived me; in no instance has he meant to offend.

Meantime, as if fearful that the continuance of the scene might too much
unstring his master, the servant seemed anxious to terminate it. And so, still
presenting himself as a crutch, and walking between the two captains, he
advanced with them towards the gangway; while still, as if full of kindly
contrition, Don Benito would not let go the hand of Captain Delano but
retained it in his, across the black's body.

Soon they were standing by the side, looking over into the boat, whose crew turned up their curious eyes. Waiting a moment for the Spaniard to relinquish his hold, the now embarrassed Captain Delano lifted his foot to overstep the threshold of the open gangway, but still Don Benito would not let go his hand. And yet, with an agitated tone, he said, 'I can go no further; here I must bid you adieu. Adieu, my dear, dear Don Amasa. Go – go!' suddenly tearing his hand loose, 'go, and God guard you better than me, my best friend.'

Not unaffected, Captain Delano would now have lingered, but, catching the meekly admonitory eye of the servant, with a hasty farewell he descended into his boat, followed by the continual adieus of Don Benito, standing rooted in the gangway.

Seating himself in the stern, Captain Delano, making a last salute, ordered the boat shoved off. The crew had their oars on end. The bowsmen pushed the boat a sufficient distance for the oars to be lengthwise dropped. The instant that was done, Don Benito sprang over the bulwarks, falling at the feet of Captain Delano; at the same time calling towards his ship, but in tones so frenzied that none in the boat could understand him. But, as if not equally obtuse, three sailors, from different and distant parts of the ship, splashed into the sea, swimming after their captain, as if intent upon his rescue.

The dismayed officer of the boat eagerly asked what this meant. To which Captain Delano, turning a disdainful smile upon the unaccountable Spaniard, answered that, for his part, he neither knew nor cared; but it seemed as if Don Benito had taken it into his head to produce the impression among his people that the boat wanted to kidnap him. 'Or else – give way for your lives,' he wildly added, starting at a clattering hubbub in the ship, above which rang the tocsin of the hatchet-polishers, and seizing Don Benito by the throat he added, 'this plotting pirate means murder!' Here, in apparent verification of the words, the servant, a dagger in his hand, was seen on the rail overhead, poised, in the act of leaping, as if the desperate fidelity to befriend his master to the last; while, seemingly to aid the black, the three white sailors were trying to clamber into the hampered bow. Meantime, the whole host of Negroes, as if inflamed at the sight of their jeopardized captain, impended in one sooty avalanche over the bulwarks.

All this, with what preceded and what followed, occurred with such involutions of rapidity that past, present, and future seemed one.

Seeing the Negro coming, Captain Delano had flung the Spaniard aside, almost in the very act of clutching him, and, by the unconscious recoil shifting his place, with arms thrown up so promptly grappled the servant in his descent, that with the dagger presented at Captain Delano's heart, the black seemed of purpose to have leaped there as to his mark. But the weapon was wrenched away, and the assailant dashed down into the bottom of the boat, which now, with disentangled oars, began to speed through the sea.

At this juncture, the left hand of Captain Delano, on one side, again clutched the half-reclined Don Benito, heedless that he was in a speechless faint, while his right foot, on the other side, ground the prostrate Negro, and his right arm pressed for added speed on the after oar, his eye bent forward, encouraging his men to their utmost.

But here the officer of the boat, who had at last succeeded in beating off the towing sailors, and was now, with face turned aft, assisting the bowsman at his oar, suddenly called to Captain Delano to see what the black was about, while a Portuguese oarsman shouted to him to give heed to what the Spaniard was saying.

Glancing down at his feet, Captain Delano saw the free hand of the servant aiming with a second dagger – a small one, before concealed in his wool – with this he was snakishly writhing up from the boat's bottom at the heart of his master, his countenance lividly vindictive, expressing the centered purpose of his soul; while the Spaniard, half-choked, was vainly shrinking away, with husky words, incoherent to all but the Portuguese.

That moment, across the long-benighted mind of Captain Delano, a flash of revelation swept, illuminating, in unanticipated clearness, his host's whole mysterious demeanor, with every enigmatic event of the day, as well as the entire past voyage of the *San Dominick*. He smote Babo's hand down, but his own heart smote him harder. With infinite pity he withdrew his hold from Don Benito. Not Captain Delano, but Don Benito, the black in leaping into the boat, had intended to stab.

Both the black's hands were held, as, glancing up towards the *San Dominick*, Captain Delano, now with scales dropped from his eyes, saw the Negroes, not in misrule, not in tumult, not as if frantically concerned for Don Benito, but, with mask torn away, flourishing hatchets and knives in ferocious piratical revolt. Like delirious black dervishes, the six Ashantees danced on the poop. Prevented by their foes from springing into the water, the Spanish boys were hurrying up to the upmost spars, while such of the few Spanish sailors not already in the sea, less alert, were descried, helplessly mixed in, on deck with the blacks.

Meantime Captain Delano hailed his own vessel, ordering the ports up, and the guns run out. But by this time the cable of the *San Dominick* had been cut, and the fag end, in lashing out, whipped away the canvas shroud about the beak, suddenly revealing, as the bleached hull swung round towards the open ocean, death for the figurehead, in a human skeleton, chalky comment on the chalked words below, FOLLOW YOUR LEADER.

At the sight, Don Benito, covering his face, wailed out: ''Tis he, Aranda! my murdered, unburied friend!'

Upon reaching the sealer, calling for ropes, Captain Delano bound the Negro who made no resistance, and had him hoisted to the deck. He would then have assisted the now almost helpless Don Benito up the side; but Don Benito, wan as he was, refused to move, or be moved, until the Negro should have been first put below out of view. When, presently assured that it was done, he no more shrank from the ascent.

The boat was immediately dispatched back to pick up the three swimming sailors. Meantime, the guns were in readiness, though, owing to the *San Dominick* having glided somewhat astern of the sealer, only the aftermost one could be brought to bear. With this, they fired six times, thinking to cripple the fugitive ship by bringing down her spars, but only a few inconsiderable ropes were shot away. Soon the ship was beyond the gun's range, steering broad out of the bay, the blacks thickly clustering round the bowsprit, one moment with taunting cries towards the whites, the next with upthrown gestures hailing the now dusky moors of the ocean – cawing crows escaped from the hand of the fowler.

The first impulse was to slip the cables and give chase. But, upon second thoughts, to pursue with whaleboat and yawl seemed more promising.

Upon inquiring of Don Benito what firearms they had on board the *San Dominick*, Captain Delano was answered that they had none that could be used, because, in the earlier stages of the mutiny, a cabin passenger, since dead, had secretly put out of order the locks of what few muskets there were. But with all his remaining strength Don Benito entreated the Americans not to give chase, either with ship or boat, for the Negroes had already proved themselves such desperadoes that, in case of a present assault, nothing but a total massacre of the whites could be looked for. But, regarding this warning as coming from one whose spirit had been crushed by misery, the American did not give up his design.

The boats were got ready and armed. Captain Delano ordered his men into them. He was going himself when Don Benito grasped his arm.

'What! have you saved my life, *señor*, and are you now going to throw away your own?'

The officers also, for reasons connected with their interests and those of the voyage, and a duty owing to the owners, strongly objected against their commander's going. Weighing their remonstrances a moment, Captain Delano felt bound to remain; appointing his chief mate – an athletic and resolute man, who had been a privateer's-man – to head the party. The more to encourage the sailors, they were told that the Spanish captain considered his ship good as lost; that she and her cargo, including some gold and silver, were worth more than a thousand doubloons. Take her, and no small part should be theirs. The sailors replied with a shout.

The fugitives had now almost gained an offing. It was nearly night, but the moon was rising. After hard, prolonged pulling, the boats came up on the ship's quarters, at a suitable distance laying upon their oars to discharge their muskets. Having no bullets to return, the Negroes sent their yells. But upon the second volley, Indianlike, they hurtled their hatchets. One took off a sailor's fingers. Another struck the whaleboat's bow, cutting off the rope there, and remaining stuck in the gunwale like a woodman's ax. Snatching it, quivering, from its lodgment, the mate hurled it back. The returned gauntlet now stuck in the ship's broken quarter-gallery, and so remained.

The Negroes giving too hot a reception, the whites kept a more respectful distance. Hovering now just out of reach of the hurtling hatchets, they, with a view to the close encounter which must soon come, sought to decoy the blacks into entirely disarming themselves of their most murderous weapons in a hand-to-hand fight, by foolishly flinging them, as missiles, short of the mark, into the sea. But, erelong perceiving the stratagem, the Negroes desisted, though not before many of them had to replace their lost hatchets with handspikes, an exchange which, as counted upon, proved, in the end, favorable to the assailants.

Meantime, with a strong wind the ship still clove the water, the boats alternately falling behind and pulling up to discharge fresh volleys.

The fire was mostly directed towards the stern, since there, chiefly, the Negroes at present were clustering. But to kill or maim the Negroes was not the object. To take them, with the ship, was the object. To do it, the ship must be boarded, which could not be done by boats while she was sailing so fast.

A thought now struck the mate. Observing the Spanish boys still aloft, high as they could get, he called to them to descend to the yards, and cut adrift the sails. It was done. About this time, owing to causes hereafter to be shown, two Spaniards, in the dress of sailors and conspicuously showing themselves, were killed, not by volleys, but by deliberate marksman's shots; while, as it afterwards appeared, by one of the general discharges Atufal, the black, and the Spaniard at the helm likewise were killed. What, now, with the loss of the sails and loss of leaders, the ship became unmanageable to the Negroes.

With creaking masts, she came heavily round to the wind, the prow slowly swinging into view of the boats, its skeleton gleaming in the horizontal moonlight and casting a gigantic ribbed shadow upon the water. One extended arm of the ghost seemed beckoning the whites to avenge it.

'Follow your leader!' cried the mate; and, one on each bow, the boats boarded. Sealing-spears and cutlasses crossed hatchets and handpikes. Huddled upon the longboat amidships, the Negresses raised a wailing chant, whose chorus was the clash of the steel.

For a time, the attack wavered, the Negroes wedging themselves to beat it back, the half-repelled sailors, as yet unable to gain a footing, fighting as troopers in the saddle, one leg sideways flung over the bulwark and one without, plying their cutlasses like carters' whips. But in vain. They were almost overborne, when, rallying themselves into a squad as one man, with a huzzah they sprang inboard, where, entangled, they involuntarily separated again. For a few breaths' space there was a vague, muffled, inner sound, as of submerged swordfish rushing hither and thither through shoals of blackfish. Soon, in a reunited band, and joined by the Spanish seamen, the whites came to the surface, irresistibly driving the Negroes towards the stern. But a barricade of casks and sacks, from side to side, had been thrown up by the mainmast. Here the Negroes faced about, and though scorning peace or truce, yet fain would have had respite. But, without pause overleaping the barrier, the unflagging sailors again closed. Exhausted, the blacks now fought in despair. Their red tongues lolled, wolflike, from their black mouths. But the pale sailors' teeth were set; not a word was spoken, and, in five minutes more, the ship was won.

Nearly a score of the Negroes were killed. Exclusive of those by the balls, many were mangled; their wounds – mostly inflicted by the long-edged sealing-spears, resembling those shaven ones of the English at Preston Pans, made by the poled scythes of the Highlanders. On the other side, none were killed, though several were wounded, some severely, including the mate. The surviving Negroes were temporarily secured, and the ship, towed back into the harbor at midnight, once more lay anchored.

Omitting the incidents and arrangements ensuing, suffice it that, after two days spent in refitting, the ships sailed in company for Conception, in Chile, and thence for Lima, in Peru; where, before the viceregal courts, the whole affair, from the beginning, underwent investigation.

Though, midway on the passage, the ill-fated Spaniard, relaxed from constraint, showed some signs of regaining health with free-will, yet, agreeably to his own foreboding, shortly before arriving at Lima, he relapsed, finally becoming so reduced as to be carried ashore in arms. Hearing of his story and plight, one of the many religious institutions of the City of Kings opened an hospitable refuge to him, where both physician and priest were his nurses, and a member of the order volunteered to be his one special guardian and consoler, by night and by day.

The following extracts, translated from one of the official Spanish documents, will, it is hoped, shed light on the preceding narrative, as well as, in the first place, reveal the true port of departure and true history of the *San Dominick*'s voyage down to the time of her touching at the island of St Maria.

But ere the extracts come it may be well to preface them with a remark.

The document selected, from among many others, for partial translation, contains the deposition of Benito Cereno, the first taken in the case. Some disclosures therein were at the time held dubious, for both learned and natural reasons. The tribunal inclined to the opinion that the deponent, not undisturbed in his mind by recent events, raved of some things which could never have happened. But subsequent depositions of the surviving sailors, bearing out the revelations of their captain in several of the strangest particulars, gave credence to the rest. So that the tribunal, in its final decision, rested its capital sentences upon statements which, had they lacked confirmation, it would have deemed it but duty to reject.

———

I, DON JOSÉ DE ABOS AND PADILLA, His Majesty's Notary for the Royal Revenue, and Register of this Province, and Notary Public of the Holy Crusade of this Bishopric, etc.

Do certify and declare, as much as is requisite in law, that, in the criminal cause commenced the twenty-fourth of the month of September, in the year seventeen hundred and ninety-nine, against the Negroes of the ship *San Dominick*, the following declaration before me was made:

Declaration of the first witness, DON BENITO CERENO.

The same day, and month, and year, His Honor, Doctor Juan Martínez de Rozas, Councilor of the Royal Audience of this Kingdom, and learned in the law of this Intendency, ordered the captain of the ship *San Dominick*, Don Benito Cereno, to appear, which he did in his litter, attended by the monk Infelez, of whom he received the oath, which he took by God, our Lord, and a sign of the Cross, under which he promised to tell the truth of whatever he should know and should be asked; and being interrogated agreeably to the tenor of the act commencing the process, he said that, on the twentieth of May last, he set sail with his ship from the port of Valparaiso, bound to that of Callao, loaded with the produce of the country beside thirty cases of hardware and one hundred and sixty blacks of both sexes, mostly belonging to Don Alexandro Aranda, gentleman, of the city of Mendoza; that the crew of the ship consisted of thirty-six men beside the persons who went as passengers; that the Negroes were in part as follows:

[*Here, in the original, follows a list of some fifty names, descriptions, and ages, compiled from certain recovered documents of Aranda's, and also from recollections of the deponent, from which portions only are extracted.*]

– One, from about eighteen to nineteen years, named José, and this was the man that waited upon his master, Don Alexandro, and who speaks well the Spanish, having served him four or five years; ... a mulatto, named Francesco, the cabin steward, of a good person and voice, having sung in the Valparaiso churches, native of the province of Buenos Ayres, aged about thirty-five years. ... A smart Negro, named Dago, who had been for many years a gravedigger among the Spaniards, aged forty-six years. ... Four old Negroes, born in Africa, from sixty to seventy, but sound, calkers by trade, whose names are as follows: the first was named Muri, and he was killed (as was also his son named Diamelo); the second, Nacta; the third, Yola, likewise killed; the fourth, Ghofan; and six full-grown Negroes, aged from thirty to forty-five, all raw, and born among the Ashantees – Matiluqui, Yan, Lecbe, Mapenda, Yambaio, Akim; four of whom were killed; ... a powerful Negro named Atufal, who being supposed to have been a chief in Africa, his owner set great store by him. ... And a small Negro of Senegal, but some years among the Spaniards, aged about thirty, which Negro's name was Babo; ... that he does not remember the names of the others, but that still expecting the residue of Don Alexandro's papers will be found, will then take due account of them all, and remit to the court; ... and thirty-nine women and children of all ages.

[*The catalogue over, the deposition goes on:*]

... That all the Negroes slept upon deck, as is customary in this navigation, and none wore fetters, because the owner, his friend Aranda, told him that they were all tractable; ... that on the seventh day after leaving port, at three o'clock in the morning, all the Spaniards being asleep except the two officers on the watch, who were the boatswain, Juan Robles, and the carpenter, Juan Bautista Gayete, and the helmsman and his boy, the Negroes revolted suddenly, wounded dangerously the boatswain and the carpenter, and successively killed eighteen men of those who were sleeping upon deck, some with handspikes and hatchets, and others by throwing them alive overboard, after tying them; that of the Spaniards upon deck they left about seven, as he thinks, alive and tied, to maneuver the ship, and three or four more, who hid themselves, remained also alive. Although in the act of revolt the Negroes made themselves masters of the hatchway, six or seven wounded went through it to the cockpit, without any hindrance on their part; that during the act of revolt the mate and another person, whose name he does not recollect, attempted to come up through the hatchway, but, being quickly wounded, were obliged to return to the cabin; that the deponent resolved at break of day to come up the companionway, where the Negro Babo was, being the ringleader, and Atufal, who assisted him, and having spoken to them, exhorted them to cease committing such atrocities, asking them, at the same time what they wanted and intended to do, offering, himself, to obey their commands; that notwithstanding this, they threw, in his presence, three men, alive and tied, overboard; that they told the deponent to come up and that they would not kill him; which having done, the Negro Babo asked him whether there were in those seas any Negro countries where they might be carried, and he answered them, No; that the Negro Babo afterwards told him to carry them to Senegal, or to the neighboring islands of St Nicholas, and he answered that this was impossible on account of the great distance, the necessity involved of rounding Cape Horn, the bad condition of the vessel, the want of provisions, sails, and water; but that the Negro Babo replied to him he must carry them in anyway, that they would do and conform themselves to everything the deponent should require as to eating and drinking; that after a long conference, being absolutely compelled to please them, for they threatened to kill all the whites if they were not, at all events, carried to Senegal, he told them that what was most wanting for the voyage was water, that they would go near the coast to take it, and thence they would proceed on their course; that the Negro Babo agreed to it, and the deponent steered towards the intermediate ports, hoping to meet some Spanish or foreign vessel that would save them; that within ten or eleven days they saw the land, and continued their course by it in the vicinity of Nasca; that the deponent observed that the Negroes were now restless and mutinous because he did not effect the taking in of water, the Negro Babo having required, with threats, that it should be done, without fail, the following day; he told him he saw plainly that the coast was steep, and the rivers designated in the maps were not to be found, with other reasons suitable to the circumstances, that the best way would be to go to the island of Santa Maria, where they might water easily, it being a solitary island, as the foreigners did; that the deponent did not go to Pisco, that was near, nor make any other port of the coast, because the Negro Babo had intimated to him several times that he would kill all the whites the very moment he should perceive any city, town, or settlement of any kind on the shores to which they should be carried; that having determined to go to the island of Santa Maria, as the deponent had planned, for the purpose of trying whether, on the passage or near the island itself, they could find any vessel that should favor them, or whether he could escape from it in a boat to the neighboring coast of Arruco, to adopt the necessary means he immediately changed his course, steering for the island; that the Negroes Babo and Atufal held daily conferences, in which they discussed what was necessary for their design of returning to Senegal, whether they were to kill all the Spaniards, and particularly the deponent; that eight days after parting from the coast of Nasca, the deponent being on the watch a little after daybreak, and soon after the Negroes had their meeting, the Negro Babo came to the place where the deponent was and told him that he had determined to kill his master, Don Alexandro Aranda, both because he and his companions could not otherwise be sure of their liberty, and that, to keep the seamen in subjection, he wanted to prepare a warning of what road they should be made to take did they or any of them oppose him, and that, by means of the death of Don Alexandro, that warning would best be given, but that what this last meant the deponent did not at the time comprehend, nor could not, further than that the death of Don

Alexandro was intended; and moreover the Negro Babo proposed to the deponent to call the mate Raneds, who was sleeping in the cabin, before the thing was done, for fear, as the deponent understood it, that the mate, who was a good navigator, should be killed with Don Alexandro and the rest; that the deponent, who was a friend from youth of Don Alexandro, prayed and conjured, but all was useless, for the Negro Babo answered him that the thing could not be prevented, and that all the Spaniards risked their death if they should attempt to frustrate his will in this matter or any other; that, in this conflict, the deponent called the mate, Raneds, who was forced to go apart, and immediately the Negro Babo commanded the Ashantee Martinqui and the Ashantee Lecbe to go and commit the murder; that those two went down with hatchets to the berth of Don Alexandro, that, yet half alive and mangled, they dragged him on deck; that they were going to throw him overboard in that state, but the Negro Babo stopped them, bidding the murder be completed on the deck before him, which was done, when, by his orders, the body was carried below, forward; that nothing more was seen of it by the deponent for three days; ... that Don Alonzo Sidonia, an old man, long resident at Valparaiso, and lately appointed to a civil office in Peru, whither he had taken passage, was at the time sleeping in the berth opposite Don Alexandro's; that awakening at his cries, surprised them, and at the sight of the Negroes with their bloody hatchets in their hands, he threw himself into the sea through a window which was near him, and was drowned, without it being in the power of the deponent to assist or take him up; ... that a short time after killing Aranda, they brought upon deck his german-cousin, of middle-age, Don Francisco Masa, of Mendoza and the young Don Joaquín, Marqués de Aramboalaza, then lately from Spain, with his Spanish servant Ponce, and the three young clerks of Aranda, José Mozairi, Lorenzo Bargas, and Hermenegildo Gandix, all of Cádiz; that Don Joaquín and Hermenegildo Gandix, the Negro Babo, for purposes hereafter to appear, preserved alive, but Don Francisco Masa, José Mozairi, and Lorenzo Bargas, with Ponce the servant, beside the boatswain, Juan Robles, the boatswain's mates, Manuel Viscaya and Roderigo Hurta, and four of the sailors the Negro Babo ordered to be thrown alive into the sea, although they made no resistance nor begged for anything else but mercy; that the boatswain, Juan Robles, who knew how to swim, kept the longest above water, making acts of contrition, and, in the last words he uttered, charged this deponent to cause mass to be said for his soul to our Lady of Succor; ... that, during the three days which followed, the deponent, uncertain what fate had befallen the remains of Don Alexandro, frequently asked the Negro Babo where they were, and, if still on board, whether they were to be preserved for interment ashore, entreating him so to order it; that the Negro Babo answered nothing till the fourth day, when, at sunrise, the deponent coming on deck, the Negro Babo showed him a skeleton, which had been substituted for the ship's proper figurehead – the image of Christopher Colón, the discoverer of the New World; that the Negro Babo asked him whose skeleton that was, and whether, from its whiteness, he should not think it a white's, that, upon discovering his face, the Negro Babo, coming close, said words to this effect: 'Keep faith with the blacks from here to Senegal, or you shall in spirit, as now in body, follow your leader,' pointing to the prow; ... that the same morning the Negro Babo took by succession each Spaniard forward, and asked him whose skeleton that was, and whether, from its whiteness, he should not think it a white's; that each Spaniard covered his face; that then to each the Negro Babo repeated the words in the first place said to the deponent; ... that they (the Spaniards), being then assembled aft, the Negro Babo harangued them, saying that he had now done all; that the deponent (as navigator for the Negroes) might pursue his course, warning him and all of them that they should, soul and body, go the way of Don Alexandro if he saw them (the Spaniards) speak or plot anything against them (the Negroes) – a threat which was repeated every day; that, before the events last mentioned, they had tied the cook to throw him overboard, for it is not known what thing they heard him speak, but finally the Negro Babo spared his life, at the request of the deponent; that a few days after, the deponent, endeavoring not to omit any means to preserve the lives of the remaining whites, spoke to the Negroes of peace and tranquillity, and agreed to draw up a paper, signed by the deponent and the sailors who could write, as also by the Negro Babo, for himself and all the blacks, in which the deponent obliged himself to carry them to Senegal, and they not to kill any more, and he formally to make over to them the ship, with the cargo, with which they were for that time satisfied and quieted. ... But the next day, the more surely to guard against the sailors' escape, the Negro Babo commanded all the boats to be destroyed but the longboat, which was unseaworthy, and another, a cutter in good condition, which, knowing it would yet be wanted for towing the water casks, he had it lowered down into the hold.

[*Various particulars of the prolonged and perplexed navigation ensuing here follow, with incidents of a calamitous calm, from which portion one passage is extracted, to wit:*]

– That on the fifth day of the calm, all on board suffering much from the heat and want of water, and five having died in fits, and mad, the Negroes became irritable, and for a chance gesture, which they deemed suspicious – though it was harmless – made by the mate, Raneds, to the deponent in the act of handing a quadrant, they killed him; but that for this they afterwards were sorry, the mate being the only remaining navigator on board, except the deponent.

– That omitting other events which daily happened, and which can only serve uselessly to recall past misfortunes and conflicts, after seventy-three day's navigation, reckoned from the time they sailed from Nasca, during which they navigated under a scanty allowance of water, and were afflicted with the calms before mentioned, they at last arrived at the island of Santa Maria, on the seventeenth of the month of August, at about six o'clock in the afternoon, at which hour they cast anchor very near the American ship *Bachelor's Delight*, which lay in the same bay, commanded by the generous Captain Amasa Delano; but at six o'clock in the morning they had already descried the port, and the Negroes became uneasy, as soon as at distance they saw the ship, not having expected to see one there; that the Negro Babo pacified them, assuring them that no fear need be had; that straightway he ordered the figure on the bow to be covered with canvas, as for repairs, and had the decks a little set in order; that for a time the Negro Babo and the Negro Atufal conferred; that the Negro Atufal was for sailing away but the Negro Babo would not, and, by himself, cast about what to do; that at last he came to the deponent proposing to him to say and do all that the deponent declares to have said and done to the American captain; ... that the Negro Babo warned him that if he varied in the least, or uttered any word, or gave any look that should give the least intimation of the past events or present state, he would instantly kill him, with all his companions, showing a dagger which he carried hid, saying something which, as he understood it, meant that the dagger would be alert as his eye; that the Negro Babo then announced the plan to all his companions, which pleased them; that he then, the better to disguise the truth, devised many expedients, in some of them uniting deceit and defense; that of this sort was the device of the six Ashantees before named, who were his bravoes; that them he stationed on the break of the poop, as if to clean certain hatchets (in cases, which were part of the cargo), but in reality to use them, and distribute them at need, and at a given word he told them; that, among other devices, was the device of presenting Atufal, his right-hand man, as chained, though in a moment the chains could be dropped; that in every particular he informed the deponent what part he was expected to enact in every device, and what story he was to tell on every occasion, always threatening him with instant death if he varied in the least; that, conscious that many of the Negroes would be turbulent, the Negro Babo appointed the four aged Negroes, who were calkers, to keep what domestic order they could on the decks; that again and again he harangued the Spaniards and his companions, informing them of his intent and of his devices, and of the invented story that this deponent was to tell, charging them lest any of them varied from the story; that these arrangements were made and matured during the interval of two or three hours between their first sighting the ship and the arrival on board of Captain Amasa Delano; that this happened about half-past seven o'clock in the morning, Captain Amasa Delano coming in his boat, and all gladly receiving him; that the deponent, as well as he could force himself, acting then the part of principal owner and a free captain of the ship, told Captain Amasa Delano, when called upon, that he came from Buenos Ayres, bound to Lima, with three hundred Negroes; that off Cape Horn, and in a subsequent fever, many Negroes had died; that also, by similar casualties, all the sea officers and the greatest part of the crew had died.

[*And so the deposition goes on, circumstantially recounting the fictitious story dictated to the deponent by Babo, and through the deponent imposed upon Captain Delano, and also recounting the friendly offers of Captain Delano, with other things, but all of which is here omitted. After the fictitious story, etc., the deposition proceeds:*]

– that the generous Captain Amasa Delano remained on board all the day, till he left the ship anchored at six o'clock in the evening, deponent speaking to him always of his pretended misfortunes, under the fore-mentioned principles, without having had it in his power to tell a single word or give him the least hint, that he might know the truth and state of things, because the Negro Babo, performing the office of an officious servant with all the appearance of submission of the humble slave, did not leave the deponent one moment; that this was in order to observe the deponent's actions and words, for the Negro Babo understands well the Spanish, and besides, there were thereabout some others who were constantly on the watch, and likewise understood the Spanish; ... that upon one occasion, while deponent was standing on the deck convers-ing with Amasa Delano, by a secret sign the Negro Babo drew him (the deponent) aside, the act appearing as if originating with the deponent; that then, he being drawn aside, the Negro Babo proposed to him to gain from Amasa Delano full particulars about his ship, and crew, and arms; that the deponent asked 'For what?' that, the Negro Babo answered he might conceive; that, grieved at the prospect of what might overtake the generous Captain Amasa Delano, the deponent at first refused to ask the desired questions, and used every argument to induce the Negro Babo to give up this new design; that the Negro Babo showed the point of his dagger, that after the information had been obtained the Negro Babo again drew him aside, telling him that that very night he (the deponent) would be captain of two ships, instead of one, for that, great part of the American's ship's crew being to be absent fishing, the six Ashantees, without anyone else, would easily take it; that at this time he said other things to the same purpose; that no entreaties availed; that, before Amasa Delano's coming on board, no hint had been given touching the capture of the American ship; that to prevent this project the deponent was powerless; ... – that in some things his memory is confused, he cannot distinctly recall every event; ... – that as soon as they had cast anchor at six of the clock in the evening, as has before been stated, the American captain took leave, to return to his vessel; that upon a sudden impulse, which the deponent believes to have come from God and his angels, he after the farewell had been said, followed the generous Captain Amasa Delano as far as the gunwale, where he stayed, under pretense of taking leave, until Amasa Delano should have been seated in his boat; that, on shoving off, the deponent sprang from the gunwale into the boat, and fell into it, he knows not how, God guarding him; that—

[*Here, in the original, follows the account of what further happened at the escape, and how the* San Dominick *was retaken, and of the passage to the coast; including in the recital many expressions of 'eternal gratitude' to the 'generous Captain Amasa Delano.' The deposition then proceeds with recapitulatory remarks, and a partial renumeration of the Negroes, making record of their individual part in the past events, with a view to furnishing, according to command of the court, the data whereon to found the criminal sentences to be pronounced.*

From this portion is the following;]

– That he believes that all the Negroes, though not in the first place knowing to the design of revolt, when it was accomplished, approved it. . . . That the Negro José, eighteen years old, and in the personal service of Don Alexandro, was the one who communicated the information to the Negro Babo about the state of things in the cabin, before the revolt; that this is known, because, in the preceding midnight, he used to come from his berth, which was under his master's, in the cabin, to the deck where the ringleader and his associates were, and had secret conversations with the Negro Babo, in which he was several times seen by the mate; that, one night, the mate drove him away twice; . . . that this same Negro José was the one who, without being commanded to do so by the Negro Babo, as Lecbe and Martinqui were, stabbed his master, Don Alexandro, after he had been dragged half-lifeless to the deck; . . . that the mulatto steward, Francesco, was of the first band of revolters, that he was, in all things, the creature and tool of the Negro Babo; that, to make his court, he, just before a repast in the cabin, proposed to the Negro Babo poisoning a dish for the generous Captain Amasa Delano; this is known and believed, because the Negroes have said it; but that the Negro Babo, having another design, forbade Francesco; . . . that the Ashantee Lecbe was one of the worst of them, for that, on the day the ship was retaken, he assisted in the defense of her with a hatchet in each hand, with one of which he wounded in the breast the chief mate of Amasa Delano, in the first act of boarding; this all knew; that, in sight of the deponent, Lecbe struck with a hatchet, Don Francisco Masa, when, by the Negro Babo's orders, he was carrying him to throw him overboard alive, beside participating in the murder, before mentioned, of Don Alexandro Aranda and others of the cabin passengers; that, owing to the fury with which the Ashantees fought in the engagement with the boats, but this Lecbe and Yan survived; that Yan was bad as Lecbe; that Yan was the man who, by Babo's command, willingly prepared the skeleton of Don Alexandro, in a way the Negroes afterwards told the deponent, but which he, so long as reason is left him, can never divulge; that Yan and Lecbe were the two who, in a calm by night, riveted the skeleton to the bow; this also the Negroes told him; that the Negro Babo was he who traced the inscription below it; that the Negro Babo was the plotter from first to last; he ordered every murder, and was the helm and keel of the revolt; that Atufal was his lieutenant in all, but Atufal with his own hand committed no murder, nor did the Negro Babo; . . . that Atufal was shot, being killed in the fight with the boats, ere boarding; . . . that the Negresses, of age, were knowing to the revolt, and testified themselves satisfied at the death of their master, Don Alexandro; that, had the Negroes not restrained them, they would have tortured to death, instead of simply killing, the Spaniards slain by command of the Negro Babo; that the Negresses used their utmost influence to have the deponent made away with; that, in the various acts of murder, they sang songs and danced – not gaily, but solemnly, and before the engagement with the boats, as well as during the action, they sang melancholy songs to the Negroes, and that this melancholy tone was more inflaming than a different one would have been, and was so intended; that all this is believed, because the Negroes have said it. ... – that of the thirty-six men of the crew, exclusive of the passengers (all of whom are now dead), which the deponent had knowledge of, six only remained alive, with four cabin boys and ship boys, not included with the crew; ... – that the Negroes broke an arm of one of the cabin boys and gave him strokes with hatchets.

[*Then follow various random disclosures referring to various periods of time. The following are extracted;*]

– That during the presence of Captain Amasa Delano on board, some attempts were made by the sailors, and one by Hermenegildo Gandix, to convey hints to him of the true state of affairs, but that these attempts were ineffectual, owing to fear of incurring death, and, further-more, owing to the devices which offered contradictions to the true state of affairs, as well as owing to the generosity and piety of Amasa Delano incapable of sounding such wickedness; ... that Luys Galgo, a sailor about sixty years of age, and formerly of the king's navy, was one of those who sought to convey tokens to Captain Amasa Delano; but his intent, though undiscovered, being suspected, he was, on a pretense, made to retire out of sight, and at last into the hold, and there was made away with. This the Negroes have since said; ... that one of the ship boys feeling, from Captain Amasa Delano's presence, some hopes of release, and not having enough prudence, dropped some chance word respecting his expectations, which being overheard and under-stood by a slave boy with whom he was eating at the time, the latter struck him on the head with a knife, inflicting a bad wound, but of which the boy is now healing; that likewise, not long before the ship was brought to anchor, one of the seamen steering at the time endangered himself by letting the blacks remark some expression in his countenance, arising from a cause similar to the above, but this sailor, by his heedful after conduct, escaped; ... that these statements are made to show the court that from the beginning to the end of the revolt it was impossible for the deponent and his men to act otherwise than they did; ... – that the third clerk, Hermenegildo Gandix, who before had been forced to live among the seamen, wearing a seaman's habit, and in all respects appearing to be one for the time, he, Gandix, was killed by a musket ball fired through mistake from the boats before boarding; having in his fright run up the mizzen rigging, calling to the boats – 'don't board,' lest upon their boarding the Negroes should kill him; that this inducing the Americans to believe he some way favored the cause of the Negroes, they fired two balls at him, so that he fell wounded from the rigging, and was drowned in the sea; ... – that the young Don Joaquín, Marqués de Aramboalaza, like Hermenegildo Gandix, the third clerk, was degraded to the office and appearance of a common seaman; that upon one occasion when Don Joaquín shrank, the Negro Babo commanded the Ashantee Lecbe to take tar and heat it, and pour it upon Don Joaquín's hands; ... – that Don Joaquín was killed owing to another mistake of the Americans, but one impossible to be avoided, as, upon the approach of the boats, Don Joaquín, with a hatchet tied edge out and upright to his hand, was made by the Negroes to appear on the bulwarks; whereupon, seen with arms in his hands and in a questionable attitude, he was shot for a renegade seaman; ... – that on the person of Don Joaquín was found secreted a jewel, which, by papers that were discovered, proved to have been meant for the shrine of our Lady of Mercy in Lima, a votive offering, beforehand prepared and guarded, to attest his gratitude when he should have landed in Peru, his last destination, for the safe conclusion of his entire voyage from Spain; ... – that the jewel, with the other effects of the late Don Joaquín, is in the custody of the brethren of the Hospital de Sacerdotes, awaiting the disposition of the honorable court; ... – that, owing to the condition of the deponent, as well as the haste in which the boats departed for the attack, the Americans were not forewarned that there were, among the apparent crew, a passenger and one of the clerks disguised by the Negro Babo; ... – that, beside the Negroes killed in action, some were killed after the capture and reanchoring at night, when shackled to the ringbolts on deck; that these deaths were committed by the sailors, ere they could be prevented. That as soon as informed of it, Captain Amasa Delano used all his authority, and in particular with his own hand struck down Martínez Gola, who having found a razor in the pocket of an old jacket of his which one of the shackled Negroes had on, was aiming it at the Negro's throat; that the noble Captain Amasa Delano also wrenched from the hand of Bartholomew Barlo a dagger, secreted at the time of the massacre of the whites, with which he was in the act of stabbing a shackled Negro, who, the same day, with another Negro, had thrown him down and jumped upon him; ... – that, for all events, befalling through so long a time, during which the ship was in the hands of the Negro Babo, he cannot here give account, but that what he has said is the most substantial of what occurs to him at present, and is the truth under the oath which he has taken; which declaration he affirmed and ratified, after hearing it read to him.

He said that he is twenty-nine years of age, and broken in body and mind; that when finally dismissed by the court, he shall not return home to Chile but betake himself to the monastery on Mount Agonia without; and signed with his honor, and crossed himself, and, for the time, departed as he came, in his litter, with the monk Infelez, to the Hospital de Sacerdotes.

Benito Cereno.

Doctor Rozas.

If the deposition have served as the key to fit into the lock of the complications which precede it, then, as a vault whose door has been flung back, the San Dominick's hull lies open today.

Hitherto the nature of this narrative, besides rendering the intricacies in the beginning unavoidable, has more or less required that many things, instead of being set down in the order of occurrence, should be retrospectively or irregularly given; this last is the case with the following passages, which will conclude the account:

During the long, mild voyage to Lima, there was, as before hinted, a period during which the sufferer a little recovered his health, or, at least in some degree, his tranquillity. Ere the decided relapse which came, the two captains had many cordial conversations – their fraternal unreserve in singular contrast with former withdrawments.

Again and again it was repeated how hard it had been to enact the part forced on the Spaniard by Babo.

'Ah, my dear friend,' Don Benito once said, 'at those very times when you thought me so morose and ungrateful, nay, when, as you now admit, you half thought me plotting your murder, at those very times my heart was frozen; I could not look at you, thinking of what, both on board this ship and your own, hung, from other hands, over my kind benefactor. And as God lives, Don Amasa, I know not whether desire for my own safety alone could have nerved me to that leap into your boat, had it not been for the thought that, did you, unenlightened, return to your ship, you, my best friend, with all who might be with you, stolen upon that night in your hammocks, would never in this world have wakened again. Do but think how you walked this deck, how you sat in this cabin, every inch of ground mined into honeycombs under you. Had I dropped the least hint, made the least advance towards an understanding between us, death, explosive death – yours as mine – would have ended the scene.'

'True, true,' cried Captain Delano, starting, 'you have saved my life, Don Benito, more than I yours; saved it, too, against my knowledge and will.'

'Nay, my friend,' rejoined the Spaniard, courteous even to the point of religion, 'God charmed your life, but you saved mine. To think of some things you did – those smilings and chattings, rash pointings and gesturings. For less than these, they slew my mate, Raneds; but you had the Prince of Heaven's safe conduct through all ambuscades.'

'Yes, all is owing to Providence, I know: but the temper of my mind that morning was more than commonly pleasant, while the sight of so much suffering, more apparent than real, added to my good-nature, compassion, and charity, happily interweaving the three. Had it been otherwise, doubtless, as you hint, some of my interferences might have ended, unhappily enough. Besides, those feelings I spoke of enabled me to get the better of momentary distrust, at times when acuteness might have cost me my life, without saving another's. Only at the end did my suspicions get the better of me, and you know how wide of the mark they then proved.'

'Wide, indeed,' said Don Benito, sadly; 'you were with me all day; stood with me, sat with me, talked with me, looked at me, ate with me, drank with me; and yet, your last act was to clutch for a monster, not only an innocent man, but the most pitiable of all men. To such degree may malign machinations and deceptions impose. So far may even the best man err in judging the conduct of one with the recesses of whose condition he is not acquainted. But you were forced to it, and you were in time undeceived. Would that, in both respects, it was so ever, and with all men.'

'You generalize, Don Benito; and mournfully enough. But the past is passed; why moralize upon it? Forget it. See, yon bright sun has forgotten it all, and the blue sea, and the blue sky; these have turned over new leaves.'

'Because they have no memory,' he dejectedly replied; 'because they are not human.'

'But these mild trades that now fan your cheek, do they not come with a human-like healing to you? Warm friends, steadfast friends are the trades.'

'With their steadfastness they but waft me to my tomb, *señor*,' was the foreboding response.

'You are saved,' cried Captain Delano, more and more astonished and pained; 'you are saved: what has cast such a shadow upon you?'

'The Negro.'

There was silence, while the moody man sat, slowly and unconsciously gathering his mantle about him, as if it were a pall.

There was no more conversation that day.

But if the Spaniard's melancholy sometimes ended in muteness upon topics like the above, there were others upon which he never spoke at all; on which, indeed, all his old reserves were piled. Pass over the worst, and, only to elucidate, let an item or two of these be cited. The dress, so precise and costly, worn by him on the day whose events have been narrated, had not willingly been put on. And that silver-mounted sword, apparent symbol of despotic command, was not, indeed, a sword, but the ghost of one. The scabbard, artificially stiffened, was empty.

As for the black – whose brain, not body, had schemed and led the revolt, with the plot – his slight frame, inadequate to that which it held, had at once yielded to the superior muscular strength of his captor, in the boat. Seeing all was over, he uttered no sound, and could not be forced to. His aspect seemed to say: since I cannot do deeds, I will not speak words. Put in irons in the hold with the rest, he was carried to Lima. During the passage, Don Benito did not visit him. Nor then, nor at any time after, would he look at him. Before the tribunal he refused. When pressed by the judges he fainted. On the testimony of the sailors alone rested the legal identity of Babo.

Some months after, dragged to the gibbet at the tail of a mule, the black met his voiceless end. The body was burned to ashes; but for many days, the head, that hive of subtlety, fixed on a pole in the plaza, met, unabashed, the gazes of the whites, and across the Plaza looked towards St Bartholomew's church, in whose vaults slept then, as now, the recovered bones of Aranda, and across the Rimac bridge looked towards the monastery, on Mount Agonia without; where, three months after being dismissed by the court, Benito Cereno, borne on the bier, did, indeed, follow his leader.

The Lightning-rod Man

WHAT GRAND IRREGULAR thunder, thought I, standing on my hearthstone among the Acroceraunian hills, as the scattered bolts boomed overhead, and crashed down among the valleys, every bolt followed by zigzag irradiations and swift slants of sharp rain, which audibly rang, like a charge of spear points, on my low shingled roof. I suppose, though, that the mountains hereabouts break and churn up the thunder, so that it is far more glorious here than on the plain. Hark! – someone at the door. Who is this that chooses a time of thunder for making calls? And why don't he, man-fashion, use the knocker, instead of making that doleful undertaker's clatter with his fist against the hollow panel? But let him in. Ah, here he comes. 'Good day, sir' – an entire stranger. 'Pray be seated.' What is that strange-looking walking stick he carries: 'A fine thunderstorm, sir.'

'Fine? – Awful!'

'You are wet. Stand here on the hearth before the fire.'

'Not for worlds!'

The stranger still stood in the exact middle of the cottage, where he had first planted himself. His singularity impelled a closer scrutiny. A lean, gloomy figure. Hair dark and lank, mattedly streaked over his brow. His sunken pitfalls of eyes were ringed by indigo halos, and played with an innocuous sort of lightning: the gleam without the bolt. The whole man was dripping. He stood in a puddle on the bare oak floor; his strange walking stick vertically resting at his side.

It was a polished copper rod, four feet long, lengthwise attached to a neat wooden staff, by insertion into two balls of greenish glass, ringed with copper bands. The metal rod terminated at the top, tripodwise, in three keen tines, brightly gilt. He held the thing by the wooden part alone.

'Sir,' said I, bowing politely, 'have I the honor of a visit from that illustrious god, Jupiter Tonans? So stood he in the Greek statue of old, grasping the lightning bolt. If you be he, or his viceroy, I have to thank you for this noble storm you have brewed among our mountains. Listen: That was a glorious peal. Ah, to a lover of the majestic, it is a good thing to have the Thunderer himself in one's cottage. The thunder grows finer for that. But pray be seated. This old rush-bottomed armchair, I grant, is a poor substitute for your evergreen throne on Olympus, but condescend to be seated.'

While I thus pleasantly spoke, the stranger eyed me, half in wonder, and half in a strange sort of horror, but did not move a foot.

'Do, sir, be seated; you need to be dried ere going forth again.'

I planted the chair invitingly on the broad hearth, where a little fire had been kindled that afternoon to dissipate the dampness, not the cold, for it was early in the month of September.

But without heeding my solicitation, and still standing in the middle of the floor, the stranger gazed at me portentously and spoke.

'Sir,' said he, 'excuse me; but instead of my accepting your invitation to be seated on the hearth there, I solemnly warn *you* that you had best accept *mine*, and stand with me in the middle of the room. Good heavens!' he cried, starting – 'there is another of those awful crashes. I warn you, sir, quit the hearth.'

'Mr Jupiter Tonans,' said I, quietly rolling my body on the stone, 'I stand very well here.'

'Are you so horridly ignorant, then,' he cried, 'as not to know that by far the most dangerous part of a house during such a terrific tempest as this is the fireplace?'

'Nay, I did not know that,' involuntarily stepping upon the first board next to the stone.

The stranger now assumed such an unpleasant air of successful admonition, that – quite involuntarily again – I stepped back upon the hearth, and threw myself into the erectest, proudest posture I could command. But I said nothing.

'For Heaven's sake,' he cried, with a strange mixture of alarm and intimidation – 'for Heaven's sake, get off the hearth! Know you not that the heated air and soot are conductors – to say nothing of those immense iron firedogs? Quit the spot – I conjure – I command you.'

'Mr Jupiter Tonans, I am not accustomed to be commanded in my own house.'

'Call me not by that pagan name. You are profane in this time of terror.'

'Sir, will you be so good as to tell me your business? If you seek shelter from the storm, you are welcome, so long as you be civil, but if you come on business, open it forthwith. Who are you?'

'I am a dealer in lightning rods,' said the stranger, softening his tone; 'my special business is— Merciful heaven! what a crash! – Have you ever been struck – your premises, I mean? No? It's best to be provided' – significantly rattling his metallic staff on the floor; – 'by nature, there are no castles in thunderstorms; yet, say but the word, and of this cottage I can make a Gibraltar by a few waves of this wand. Hark, what Himalayas of concussions!'

'You interrupted yourself; your special business you were about to speak of.'

'My special business is to travel the country for orders for lightning rods. This is my specimen rod' – tapping his staff; 'I have the best of references' – fumbling in his pockets. 'In Criggan last month I put up three-and-twenty rods on only five buildings.'

'Let me see. Was it not at Criggan last week, about midnight on Saturday, that the steeple, the big elm, and the assembly-room cupola were struck? Any of your rods there?'

'Not on the tree and cupola, but the steeple.'

'Of what use is your rod, then?'

'Of life-and-death use. But my workman was heedless. In fitting the rod at top to the steeple, he allowed a part of the metal to graze the tin sheeting. Hence the accident. Not my fault, but his. Hark!'

'Never mind. That clap burst quite loud enough to be heard without finger-pointing. Did you hear of the event at Montreal last year? A servant girl struck at her bedside with a rosary in her hand, the beads being metal. Did your beat extend into the Canadas?'

'No. And I hear that there iron rods only are in use. They should have *mine*, which are copper. Iron is easily fused. Then they draw out the rod so slender that it has not body enough to conduct the full electric current. The metal melts; the building is destroyed. My copper rods never act so. Those Canadians are fools. Some of them knob the rod at the top, which risks a deadly explosion, instead of imperceptibly carrying down the current into the earth, as this sort of rod does. *Mine* is the only true rod. Look at it. Only one dollar a foot.'

'This abuse of your own calling in another might make one distrustful with respect to yourself.'

'Hark! The thunder becomes less muttering. It is nearing us, and nearing the earth, too. Hark! One crammed crash! All the vibrations made one by nearness. Another flash. Hold!'

'What do you?' I said, seeing him now, instantaneously relinquishing his staff, lean intently forward towards the window, with his right fore and middle fingers on his left wrist.

But ere the words had well escaped me, another exclamation escaped him.

'Crash! only three pulses – less than a third of a mile off – yonder, somewhere in that wood. I passed three stricken oaks there, ripped out new and glittering. The oak draws lightning more than other timber, having iron in solution in its sap. Your floor here seems oak.'

'Heart-of-oak. From the peculiar time of your call upon me, I suppose you purposely select stormy weather for your journeys. When the thunder is roaring you deem it an hour peculiarly favorable for producing impressions favorable to your trade.'

'Hark – Awful!'

'For one who would arm others with fearlessness, you seem unbeseemingly timorous yourself. Common men choose fair weather for their travels: you choose thunderstorms; and yet—'

'That I travel in thunderstorms, I grant, but not without particular precautions, such as only a lightning-rod man may know. Hark! Quick – look at my specimen rod. Only one dollar a foot.'

'A very fine rod, I dare say. But what are these particular precautions of yours? Yet first let me close yonder shutters; the slanting rain is beating through the sash. I will bar up.'

'Are you mad? Know you not that yon iron bar is a swift conductor? Desist.'

'I will simply close the shutters, then, and call my boy to bring me a wooden bar. Pray, touch the bellpull there.'

'Are you frantic? That bell wire might blast you. Never touch bell wire in a thunderstorm, nor ring a bell of any sort.'

'Nor those in belfries? Pray, will you tell me where and how one may be safe in a time like this? Is there any part of my house I may touch with hopes of my life?'

'There is; but not where you now stand. Come away from the wall. The current will sometimes run down a wall, and – a man being a better conductor than a wall – it would leave the wall and run into him. Swoop! *That* must have fallen very nigh. That must have been globular lightning.'

'Very probably. Tell me at once, which is, in your opinion, the safest part of this house?'

'This room, and this one spot in it where I stand. Come hither.'

'The reasons first.'

'Hark! – after the flash the gust – the sashes shiver – the house, the house! Come hither to me!'

'The reasons, if you please.'

'Come hither to me!'

'Thank you again, I think I will try my old stand – the hearth. And now. Mr Lightning-rod Man, in the pauses of the thunder, be so good as to tell me your reasons for esteeming this one room of the house the safest, and your own one standpoint there the safest spot in it.'

There was now a little cessation of the storm for a while. The lightning-rod man seemed relieved, and replied:

'Your house is a one-storied house, with an attic and a cellar; this room is between. Hence its comparative safety. Because lightning sometimes passes from the clouds to the earth, and sometimes from the earth to the clouds. Do you comprehend? – and I choose the middle of the room, because, if the lightning should strike the house at all, it would come down the chimney or walls; so, obviously, the further you are from them, the better. Come hither to me, now.'

'Presently. Something you just said, instead of alarming me, has strangely inspired confidence.'

'What have I said?'

'You said that sometimes lightning flashes from the earth to the clouds.'

'Aye, the returning stroke, as it is called; when the earth, being overcharged with the fluid, flashes its surplus upward.'

'The returning stroke; that is, from earth to sky. Better and better. But come here on the hearth and dry yourself.'

'I am better here, and better wet.'

'How?'

'It is the safest thing you can do – hark, again! – to get yourself thoroughly drenched in a thunderstorm. Wet clothes are better conductors than the body, and so, if the lightning strike, it might pass down the wet clothes without touching the body. The storm deepens again. Have you a rug in the house? Rugs are nonconductors. Get one, that I may stand on it here, and you, too. The skies blacken – it is dusk at noon. Hark! – the rug, the rug!'

I gave him one, while the hooded mountains seemed closing and tumbling into the cottage.

'And now, since our being dumb will not help us,' said I, resuming my place, 'let me hear your precautions in traveling during thunderstorms.'

'Wait till this one is passed.'

'Nay, proceed with the precautions. You stand in the safest possible place according to your own account. Go on.'

'Briefly, then. I avoid pine trees, high houses, lonely barns, upland pastures, running water, flocks of cattle and sheep, a crowd of men. If I travel on foot – as today – I do not walk fast; if in my buggy, I touch not its back or sides; if on horseback, I dismount and lead the horse. But of all things, I avoid tall men.'

'Do I dream? Man avoid man? and in danger-time, too.'

'Tall men in a thunderstorm I avoid. Are you so grossly ignorant as not to know that the height of a six-footer is sufficient to discharge an electric cloud upon him? Are not lonely Kentuckians, plowing, smit in the unfinished furrow? Nay, if the six-footer stand by running water, the cloud will sometimes *select* him as its conductor to that running water. Hark! Sure, yon black pinnacle is split. Yes, a man is a good conductor. The lightning goes through and through a man, but only peels a tree. But sir, you have kept me so long answering your questions that I have not yet come to business. Will you order one of my rods? Look at this specimen one. See: it is of the best of copper. Copper's the best conductor. Your house is low, but, being upon the mountains, that lowness does not one whit depress it. You mountaineers are most exposed. In mountainous countries the lightning-rod man should have most business. Look at the specimen, sir. One rod will answer for a house so small as this. Look over these recommendations. Only one rod, sir; cost, only twenty dollars. Hark! There go all the granite Taconics and Hoosics dashed together like pebbles. By the sound, that must have struck something. An elevation of five feet above the house will protect twenty feet radius all about the rod. Only twenty dollars, sir – a dollar a foot. Hark! – Dreadful! – Will you order? Will you buy? Shall I put down your name? Think of being a heap of charred offal, like a haltered horse burnt in his stall – and all in one flash!'

'You pretended envoy extraordinary and minister plenipotentiary to and from Jupiter Tonans,' laughed I; 'you mere man who come here to put you and your pipestem between clay and sky, do you think that because you can strike a bit of green light from the Leyden jar that you can thoroughly avert the supernal bolt? Your rod rusts, or breaks, and where are you? Who has empowered you, you Tetzel, to peddle round your indulgences from divine ordinations? The hairs of our heads are numbered, and the days of our lives. In thunder as in sunshine, I stand at ease in the hands of my God. False negotiator, away! See, the scroll of the storm is rolled back; the house is unharmed; and in the blue heavens I read in the rainbow that the Deity will not, of purpose, make war on man's earth.'

'Impious wretch!' foamed the stranger, blackening in the face as the rainbow beamed, 'I will publish your infidel notions.'

The scowl grew blacker on his face; the indigo circles enlarged round his eyes as the storm rings round the midnight moon. He sprang upon me, his tri-forked thing at my heart.

I seized it; I snapped it; I dashed it; I trod it; and, dragging the dark lightning-king out of my door, flung his elbowed, copper scepter after him.

But spite of my treatment, and spite of my dissuasive talk of him to my neighbors, the lightning-rod man still dwells in the land; still travels in storm-time, and drives a brave trade with the fears of man.

FITZ-JAMES O'BRIEN
1828-1862

An immigrant to the United States from Ireland, Fitz-James O'Brien yet claims a place among the great short story writing history of America as a continuer of the tradition of horror and suspense fiction begun by Edgar Allan Poe.

Although time has not been kind to much of O'Brien's work, he will undoubtedly be remembered for one story, 'The Diamond Lens' (1858). This work of suspense stands as a masterpiece of the genre, betraying an originality and versatility of concise invention which mark it out as a world-class short story on a theme which owes its life to native American genius.

The Diamond Lens

1 THE BENDING OF THE TWIG

FROM A VERY EARLY PERIOD of my life the entire bent of my inclinations has been towards microscopic investigations. When I was not more than ten years old a distant relative of our family, hoping to astonish my inexperience, constructed a simple microscope for me, by drilling in a disk of copper a small hole, in which a drop of pure water was sustained by capillary attraction. This very primitive apparatus, magnifying some fifty diameters, presented, it is true, only indistinct and imperfect forms, but still sufficiently wonderful to work up my imagination to a preternatural state of excitement.

Seeing me so interested in this rude instrument, my cousin explained to me all that he knew about the principles of the microscope, related to me a few of the wonders which had been accomplished through its agency, and ended by promising to send me one regularly constructed, immediately on his return to the city. I counted the days, the hours, the minutes, that intervened between that promise and his departure.

Meantime I was not idle. Every transparent substance that bore the remotest semblance to a lens I eagerly seized upon and employed in vain attempts to realize that instrument, the theory of whose construction I as yet only vaguely comprehended. All panes of glass containing those oblate spheroidal knots familiarly known as 'bull's-eyes' were ruthlessly destroyed, in the hope of obtaining lenses of marvellous power. I even went so far as to extract the crystalline humour from the eyes of fishes and animals, and endeavoured to press it into the microscopic service. I plead guilty to having stolen the glasses from my Aunt Agatha's spectacles, with a dim idea of grinding them into lenses of wondrous magnifying properties – in which attempt it is scarcely necessary to say that I totally failed.

At last the promised instrument came. It was of that order known as Field's simple microscope, and had cost perhaps about fifteen dollars. As far as educational purposes went, a better apparatus could not have been selected. Accompanying it was a small treatise on the microscope – its history, uses, and discoveries. I comprehended then for the first time the *Arabian Nights' Entertainments*. The dull veil of ordinary existence that hung across the world seemed suddenly to roll away, and to lay bare a land of enchantments. I felt towards my companions as the seer might feel towards the ordinary masses of men. I held conversations with Nature in a tongue which they could not understand. I was in daily communication with living wonders, such as they never imagined in their wildest visions. I penetrated beyond the external portal of things, and roamed through the sanctuaries. Where they beheld only a drop of rain slowly rolling down the window-glass,

I saw a universe of beings animated with all the passions common to physical life, and convulsing their minute sphere with struggles as fierce and protracted as those of men. In the common spots of mould, which my mother, good housekeeper that she was, fiercely scooped away from her jam-pots, there abode for me, under the name of mildew, enchanted gardens, filled with dells and avenues of the densest foliage and most astonishing verdure, while from the fantastic boughs of these microscopic forests hung stange fruits glittering with green and silver and gold.

It was no scientific thirst that at this time filled my mind. It was the pure enjoyment of a poet to whom a world of wonders has been disclosed. I talked of my solitary pleasures to none. Alone with my microscope, I dimmed my sight, day after day and night after night poring over the marvels which it unfolded to me. I was like one who, having discovered the ancient Eden still existing in all its primitive glory, should resolve to enjoy it in solitude, and never betray to mortal the secret of its locality. The rod of my life was bent at this moment. I destined myself to be a microscopist.

Of course, like every novice, I fancied myself a discoverer. I was ignorant at the time of the thousands of acute intellects engaged in the same pursuit as myself, and with the advantages of instruments a thousand times more powerful than mine. The names of Leeuwenhoek, Williamson, Spencer, Ehrenberg, Schultz, Dujardin, Schacht, and Schleiden were then entirely unknown to me, or if known, I was ignorant of their patient and wonderful researches. In every fresh specimen of cryptogamia which I placed beneath my instrument I believed that I discovered wonders of which the world was as yet ignorant. I remember well the thrill of delight and admiration that shot through me the first time that I discovered the common wheel animalcule (*Rotifera vulgaris*) expanding and contracting its flexible spokes, and seemingly rotating through the water. Alas! as I grew older, and obtained some works treating of my favourite study, I found that I was only on the threshold of a science to the investigation of which some of the greatest men of the age were devoting their lives and intellects.

As I grew up, my parents, who saw but little likelihood of anything practical resulting from the examination of bits of moss and drops of water through a brass tube and a piece of glass, were anxious that I should choose a profession. It was their desire that I should enter the counting-house of my uncle, Ethan Blake, a prosperous merchant, who carried on business in New York. This suggestion I decisively combated. I had no taste for trade; I should only make a failure; in short, I refused to become a merchant.

But it was necessary for me to select some pursuit. My parents were staid New England people, who insisted on the necessity of labour; and therefore, although, thanks to the bequest of my poor Aunt Agatha, I should, on coming of age, inherit a small fortune sufficient to place me above want, it was decided that, instead of waiting for this, I should act the nobler part, and employ the intervening years in rendering myself independent.

After much cogitation I complied with the wishes of my family, and selected a profession. I determined to study medicine at the New York Academy. This disposition of my future suited me. A removal from my relatives would enable me to dispose of my time as I pleased, without fear of detection. As long as I paid my academy fees, I might shirk attending the lectures, if I chose; and as I never had the remotest intention of standing an examination, there was no danger of my being 'plucked.' Besides, a metropolis was the place for me. There I could obtain excellent instruments, the newest publications, intimacy with men of pursuits kindred to my own – in short, all things necessary to ensure a profitable devotion of my life to my beloved science. I had an abundance of money, few desires that were not bounded by my illuminating mirror on one side and my object-glass on the other; what, therefore, was to prevent my becoming an illustrious investigator of the veiled worlds? It was with the most buoyant hopes that I left my New England home and established myself in New York.

2 THE LONGING OF A MAN OF SCIENCE

My first step, of course, was to find suitable apartments. These I obtained, after a couple of days' search, in Fourth Avenue; a very pretty second-floor unfurnished, containing sitting-room, bedroom, and a smaller apartment which I intended to fit up as a laboratory. I furnished my lodgings simply, but rather elegantly, and then devoted all my energies to the adornment of the temple of my worship. I visited Pike, the celebrated optician, and passed in review his splendid collection of microscopes – Field's Compound, Higham's, Spencer's, Nachet's Binocular (that founded on the principles of the stereoscope), and at length fixed upon that form known as Spencer's Trunnion Microscope, as combining the greatest number of improvements with an almost perfect freedom from tremor. Along with this I purchased every possible accessory – draw-tubes, micrometers, a camera-lucida, lever-stage, achromatic condensers, white cloud illuminators, prisms, parabolic condensers, polarizing apparatus, forceps, aquatic boxes, fishing-tubes, with a host of other articles, all of which would have been useful in the hands of an experienced microscopist, but, as I afterwards discovered, were not of the slightest present value to me. It takes years of practice to know how to use a complicated microscope. The optician looked suspiciously at me as I made these wholesale purchases. He evidently was uncertain whether to set me down as some scientific celebrity or a madman. I think he inclined to the latter belief. I suppose I was mad. Every great genius is mad upon the subject in which he is greatest. The unsuccessful madman is disgraced, and called a lunatic.

Mad or not, I set myself to work with a zeal which few scientific students have ever equalled. I had everything to learn relative to the delicate study upon which I had embarked – a study involving the most earnest patience, the most rigid analytic powers, the steadiest hand, the most untiring eye, the most refined and subtle manipulation.

For a long time half my apparatus lay inactively on the shelves of my laboratory, which was now most amply furnished with every possible contrivance for facilitating my investigations. The fact was that I did not know how to use some of my scientific accessories – never having been taught microscopics – and those whose use I understood theoretically were of little avail, until by practice I could attain the necessary delicacy of handling. Still, such was the fury of my ambition, such the untiring perseverance of my experiments, that, difficult of credit as it may be, in the course of one year I became theoretically and practically an accomplished microscopist.

During this period of my labours, in which I submitted specimens of every substance that came under my observation to the action of my lenses, I became a discoverer – in a small way, it is true, for I was very young, but still a discoverer. It was I who destroyed Ehrenberg's theory that the *Volvox globator* was an animal, and proved that his 'monads' with stomachs and eyes were merely phases of the formation of a vegetable cell, and were, when they reached their mature state, incapable of the act of conjugation, or any true generative act, without which no organism rising to any stage of life higher than vegetable can be said to be complete. It was I who resolved the singular problem of rotation in cells and hairs of plants into ciliary attraction, in spite of the assertions of Mr Wenham and others that my explanation was the result of an optical illusion.

But notwithstanding these discoveries, laboriously and painfully made as they were, I felt horribly dissatisfied. At every step I found myself stopped by the imperfections of my instruments. Like all active microscopists, I gave my imagination full play. Indeed, it is a common complaint against many such, that they supply the defects of their instruments with the creations of their brains. I imagined depths beyond depths in nature which the limited power of my lenses prohibited me from exploring. I lay awake at night constructing imaginary microscopes of immeasurable power, with which I seemed to pierce through all the envelopes of matter down to its original atom. How I cursed those imperfect mediums which necessity through ignorance compelled me to use! How I longed to discover the secret of some perfect lens whose magnifying power should be limited only by the resolvability of the object, and which at the same time should be free from spherical and chromatic aberrations, in short from all the obstacles over which the poor microscopist finds himself continually stumbling! I felt convinced that the simple microscope, composed of a single lens of such vast yet perfect power, was possible of construction. To attempt to bring the compound microscope up to such a pitch would have been commencing at the wrong end; this latter being simply a partially successful endeavour to remedy those very defects of the simple instrument which, if conquered, would leave nothing to be desired.

It was in this mood of mind that I became a constructive microscopist. After another year passed in this new pursuit, experimenting on every imaginable substance – glass, gems, flints, crystals, artificial crystals formed of the alloy of various vitreous materials – in short, having constructed as many varieties of lenses as Argus had eyes, I found myself precisely where I started, with nothing gained save an extensive knowledge of glass-making. I was almost dead with despair. My parents were surprised at my apparent want of progress in my medical studies (I had not attended one lecture since my arrival in the city), and the expenses of my mad pursuit had been so great as to embarrass me very seriously.

I was in this frame of mind one day, experimenting in my laboratory on a small diamond – that stone, from its great refracting power, having always occupied my attention more than any other – when a young Frenchman, who lived on the floor above me, and who was in the habit of occasionally visiting me, entered the room.

I think that Jules Simon was a Jew. He had many traits of the Hebrew character: a love of jewellery, of dress, and of good living. There was something mysterious about him. He always had something to sell, and yet went into excellent society. When I say sell, I should perhaps have said peddle; for his operations were generally confined to the disposal of single articles – a picture, for instance, or a rare carving in ivory, or a pair of duelling-pistols, or the dress of a Mexican caballero. When I was first furnishing my rooms he paid me a visit, which ended in my purchasing an antique silver lamp, which he assured me was a Cellini – it was handsome enough even for that – and some other knick-knacks for my sitting-room. Why Simon should pursue this petty trade I never could imagine. He apparently had plenty of money, and had the entrée of the best houses in the city – taking care, however, I suppose, to drive no bargains within the enchanted circle of the Upper Ten. I came at length to the conclusion that this peddling was but a mask to cover some greater object, and even went so far as to believe my young acquaintance to be implicated in the slave-trade. That, however, was none of my affair.

On the present occasion Simon entered my room in a state of considerable excitement.

'Ah! *mon ami!*' he cried, before I could even offer him the ordinary salutation, 'it has occurred to me to be the witness of the most astonishing thing in the world. I promenade myself to the house of Madame – How does the little animal – *le renard* – name himself in the Latin?'

'Vulpes,' I answered.

'Ah! yes – Vulpes. I promenade myself to the house of Madame Vulpes.'

'The spirit medium?'

'Yes, the great medium. Great heavens! what a woman! I write on a slip of paper many of questions concerning the affairs the most secret – affairs that conceal themselves in the abysses of my heart the most profound; and behold! by example! what occurs? This devil of a woman makes me replies the most truthful to all of them. She talks to me of things that I do not love to talk of to myself. What am I to think? I am fixed to the earth!'

'Am I to understand you, Monsieur Simon, that this Mrs Vulpes replied to questions secretly written by you, which questions related to events known only to yourself?'

'Ah! more than that, more than that,' he answered, with an air of some alarm. 'She related to me things – But,' he added, after a pause, and suddenly changing his manner, 'why occupy ourselves with these follies? It was all the biology, without doubt. It goes without saying that it has not my credence. But why are we here, *mon ami*? It has occurred to me to discover the most beautiful thing as you can imagine – a vase with green lizards on it, composed by the great Bernard Palissy. It is in my apartment; let us mount. I go to show it to you.'

I followed Simon mechanically; but my thoughts were far from Palissy and his enamelled ware, although I, like him, was seeking in the dark after a great discovery. This casual mention of the spiritualist, Madame Vulpes, set me on a new track. What if this spiritualism should be really a great fact? What if, through communication with subtiler organisms than my own, I could reach at a single bound the goal which perhaps a life of agonizing mental toil would never enable me to attain?

While purchasing the Palissy vase from my friend Simon I was mentally arranging a visit to Madame Vulpes.

3 THE SPIRIT OF LEEUWENHOEK

Two evenings after this, thanks to an arrangement by letter and the promise of an ample fee, I found Madame Vulpes awaiting me at her residence alone. She was a coarse-featured woman, with a keen and rather cruel dark eye, and an exceedingly sensual expression about her mouth and under-jaw. She received me in perfect silence, in an apartment on the ground floor, very sparely furnished. In the centre of the room, close to where Mrs Vulpes sat, there was a common round mahogany table. If I had come for the purpose of sweeping her chimney, the woman could not have looked more indifferent to my appearance. There was no attempt to inspire the visitor with any awe. Everything bore a simple and practical aspect. The intercourse with the spiritual world was evidently as familiar an occupation with Mrs Vulpes as eating her dinner or riding in an omnibus.

'You come for a communication, Mr Linley?' said the medium, in a dry, businesslike tone of voice.

'By appointment – yes.'

'What sort of communication do you want? A written one?'

'Yes – I wish for a written one.'

'From any particular spirit?'

'Yes.'

'Have you ever known this spirit on this earth?'

'Never. He died long before I was born. I wish merely to obtain from him some information which he ought to be able to give better than any other.'

'Will you seat yourself at the table, Mr Linley,' said the medium, 'and place your hands upon it?'

I obeyed – Mrs Vulpes being seated opposite me, with her hands also on the table. We remained thus for about a minute and a half, when a violent succession of raps came on the table, on the back of my chair, on the floor immediately under my feet, and even on the window-panes. Mrs Vulpes smiled composedly.

'They are very strong tonight,' she remarked. 'You are fortunate.' She then continued, 'Will the spirits communicate with this gentleman?'

Vigorous affirmative.

'Will the particular spirit he desires to speak with communicate?'

A very confused rapping followed this question.

'I know what they mean,' said Mrs Vulpes, addressing herself to me; 'they wish you to write down the name of the particular spirit that you desire to converse with. Is that so?' she added, speaking to her invisible guests.

That it was so was evident from the numerous affirmatory responses. While this was going on, I tore a slip from my pocket-book, and scribbled a name under the table.

'Will this spirit communicate in writing with this gentleman?' asked the medium once more.

After a moment's pause her hand seemed to be seized with a violent tremor, shaking so forcibly that the table vibrated. She said that a spirit had seized her hand and would write. I handed her some sheets of paper that were on the table, and a pencil. The latter she held loosely in her hand, which presently began to move over the paper with a singular and seemingly involuntary motion. After a few moments had elapsed she handed me the paper, on which I found written, in a large, uncultivated hand, the words, 'He is not here, but has been sent for.' A pause of a minute or so now ensued, during which Mrs Vulpes remained perfectly silent, but the raps continued at regular intervals. When the short period I mentioned had elapsed, the hand of the medium was again seized with its convulsive tremor, and she wrote, under this strange influence, a few words on the paper, which she handed to me. They were as follows:

I am here. Question me.
LEEUWENHOEK.

I was astounded. The name was identical with that I had written beneath the table, and carefully kept concealed. Neither was it at all probable that an uncultivated woman like Mrs Vulpes should know even the name of the great father of microscopics. It may have been biology; but this theory was soon doomed to be destroyed. I wrote on my slip – still concealing it from Mrs Vulpes – a series of questions, which, to avoid tediousness, I shall place with the reponses in the order in which they occurred.

I. Can the microscope be brought to perfection?

Spirit. Yes.

I. Am I destined to accomplish this great task?

Spirit. You are.

I. I wish to know how to proceed to attain this end. For the love which you bear to science, help me!

Spirit. A diamond of one hundred and forty carats, submitted to electromagnetic currents for a long period will experience a rearrangement of its atoms *inter se*, and from that stone you will form the universal lens.

I. Will great discoveries result from the use of such a lens?

Spirit. So great, that all that has gone before is as nothing.

I. But the refractive power of the diamond is so immense that the image will be formed within the lens. How is that difficulty to be surmounted?

Spirit. Pierce the lens through its axis, and the difficulty is obviated. The image will be formed in the pierced space, which will itself serve as a tube to look through. Now I am called. Good night!

I cannot at all describe the effect that these extraordinary communications had upon me. I felt completely bewildered. No biological theory could account for the *discovery* of the lens. The medium might, by means of biological *rapport* with my mind, have gone so far as to read my questions, and reply to them coherently. But biology could not enable her to discover that magnetic currents would so alter the crystals of the diamond as to remedy its previous defects, and admit of its being polished into a perfect lens. Some such theory may have passed through my head, it is true; but if so, I had forgotten it. In my excited condition of mind there was no course left but to become a convert, and it was in a state of the most painful nervous exaltation that I left the medium's house that evening. She accompanied me to the door, hoping that I was satisfied. The raps followed us as we went through the hall, sounding on the balusters, the flooring, and even the lintels of the door. I hastily expressed my satisfaction, and escaped hurriedly into the cool night air. I walked home with but one thought possessing me – how to obtain a diamond of the immense size required. My entire means multiplied a hundred times over would have been inadequate to its purchase. Besides, such stones are rare, and become historical. I could find such only in the regalia of Eastern or European monarchs.

4 THE EYE OF MORNING

There was a light in Simon's room as I entered my house. A vague impulse urged me to visit him. As I opened the door of his sitting-room unannounced he was bending, with his back toward me, over a Carcel lamp, apparently engaged in minutely examining some object which he held in his hands. As I entered he started suddenly, thrust his hand into his breast pocket, and turned to me with a face crimson with confusion.

'What!' I cried, 'poring over the miniature of some fair lady? Well, don't blush so much; I won't ask to see it.'

Simon laughed awkwardly enough, but made none of the negative protestations usual on such occasions. He asked me to take a seat.

'Simon,' said I, 'I have just come from Madame Vulpes.'

This time Simon turned as white as a sheet, and seemed stupefied, as if a sudden electric shock had smitten him. He babbled some incoherent words, and went hastily to a small closet where he usually kept his liquors. Although astonished at his emotion, I was too preoccupied with my own idea to pay much attention to anything else.

'You say truly when you call Madame Vulpes a devil of a woman,' I continued. 'Simon, she told me wonderful things tonight, or rather was the means of telling me wonderful things. Ah! if I could only get a diamond that weighed one hundred and forty carats!'

Scarcely had the sigh with which I uttered this desire died upon my lips, when Simon, with the aspect of a wild beast, glared at me savagely, and rushing to the mantelpiece, where some foreign weapons hung on the wall, caught up a Malay creese, and brandished it furiously before him.

'No!' he cried in French, into which he always broke when excited. 'No! you shall not have it! You are perfidious! You have consulted with that demon, and desire my treasure! But I will die first! Me! I am brave! You cannot make me fear!'

All this, uttered in a loud voice trembling with excitement, astounded me. I saw at a glance that I had accidentally trodden upon the edges of Simon's secret, whatever it was. It was necessary to reassure him.

'My dear Simon,' I said, 'I am entirely at a loss to know what you mean. I went to Madame Vulpes to consult with her on a scientific problem, to the solution of which I discovered that a diamond of the size I just mentioned was necessary. You were never alluded to during the evening, nor, so far as I was concerned, even thought of. What can be the meaning of this outburst? If you happen to have a set of valuable diamonds in your possession, you need fear nothing from me. The diamond which I require you could not possess; or if you did possess it, you would not be living here.'

Something in my tone must have completely reassured him; for his expression immediately changed to a sort of constrained merriment, combined, however, with a certain suspicious attention to my movements. He laughed, and said that I must bear with him; that he was at certain moments subject to a species of vertigo, which betrayed itself in incoherent speeches, and that the attacks passed off as rapidly as they came. He put his weapon aside while making this explanation, and endeavoured, with some success, to assume a more cheerful air.

All this did not impose on me in the least. I was too much accustomed to analytical labours to be baffled by so flimsy a veil. I determined to probe the mystery to the bottom.

'Simon,' I said gaily, 'let us forget all this over a bottle of Burgundy. I have a case of Lausseure's Clos Vougeot downstairs, fragrant with the odours and ruddy with the sunlight of the Côte d'Or. Let us have up a couple of bottles. What say you?'

'With all my heart,' answered Simon smilingly.

I produced the wine and we seated ourselves to drink. It was of a famous vintage, that of 1848, a year when war and wine throve together – and its pure but powerful juice seemed to impart renewed vitality to the system. By the time we had half finished the second bottle Simon's head, which I knew was a weak one, had begun to yield, while I remained calm as ever, only that every draught seemed to send a flush of vigour through my limbs. Simon's utterance became more and more indistinct. He took to singing French chansons of a not very moral tendency. I rose suddenly from the table just at the conclusion of one of those incoherent verses, and fixing my eyes on him with a quiet smile, said:

'Simon, I have deceived you. I learned your secret this evening. You may as well be frank with me. Mrs Vulpes, or rather, one of her spirits, told me all.'

He started with horror. His intoxication seemed for the moment to fade away, and he made a movement towards the weapon that he had a short time before laid down. I stopped him with my hand.

'Monster!' he cried passionately, 'I am ruined! What shall I do? You shall never have it! I swear by my mother!'

'I don't want it,' I said; 'rest secure, but be frank with me. Tell me all about it.'

The drunkenness began to return. He protested with maudlin earnestness that I was entirely mistaken – that I was intoxicated; then asked me to swear eternal secrecy, and promised to disclose the mystery to me. I pledged myself, of course, to all. With an uneasy look in his eyes, and hands unsteady with drink and nervousness, he drew a small case from his breast and opened it. Heavens! How the mild lamp-light was shivered into a thousand prismatic arrows, as it fell upon a vast rose-diamond that glittered in the case! I was no judge of diamonds, but I saw at a glance that this was a gem of rare size and purity. I looked at Simon with wonder, and – must I confess it? – with envy. How could he have obtained this treasure? In reply to my questions, I could just gather from his drunken statements (of which, I fancy, half the incoherence was affected) that he had been superintending a gang of slaves engaged in diamond-washing in Brazil; that he had seen one of them secrete a diamond, but, instead of informing his employers, had quietly watched the negro until he saw him bury his treasure; that he had dug it up, and fled with it, but that as yet he was afraid to attempt to dispose of it publicly – so valuable a gem being almost certain to attract too much attention to its owner's antecedents – and he had not been able to discover any of those obscure channels by which such matters are conveyed away safely. He added that, in accordance with Oriental practice, he had named his diamond by the fanciful title of The Eye of Morning.

While Simon was relating this to me, I regarded the great diamond attentively. Never had I beheld anything so beautiful. All the glories of light, ever imagined or described, seemed to pulsate in its crystalline chambers. Its weight, as I learned from Simon, was exactly one hundred and forty carats. Here was an amazing coincidence. The hand of Destiny seemed in it. On the very evening when the spirit of Leeuwenhoek communicates to me the great secret of the microscope, the priceless means which he directs me to employ start up within my easy reach! I determined, with the most perfect deliberation, to possess myself of Simon's diamond.

I sat opposite him while he nodded over his glass, and calmly revolved the whole affair. I did not for an instant contemplate so foolish an act as a common theft, which would of course be discovered, or at least necessitate flight and concealment, all of which must interfere with my scientific plans. There was but one step to be taken – to kill Simon. After all, what was the life of a little peddling Jew in comparison with the interests of science? Human beings are taken every day from the condemned prisons to be experimented on by surgeons. This man, Simon, was by his own confession a criminal, a robber, and I believed on my soul a murderer. He deserved death quite as much as any felon condemned by the laws; why should I not, like government, contrive that his punishment should contribute to the progress of human knowledge?

The means for accomplishing everything I desired lay within my reach. There stood upon the mantelpiece a bottle half full of French laudanum. Simon was so occupied with his diamond, which I had just restored to him, that it was an affair of no difficulty to drug his glass. In a quarter of an hour he was in a profound sleep.

I now opened his waistcoat, took the diamond from the inner pocket in which he had placed it, and removed him to the bed, on which I laid him so that his feet hung down over the edge. I had possessed myself of the Malay creese, which I held in my right hand, while with the other I discovered as accurately as I could by pulsation the exact locality of the heart. It was essential that all the aspects of his death should lead to the surmise of self-murder. I calculated the exact angle at which it was probable that the weapon, if levelled by Simon's own hand, would enter his breast; then with one powerful blow I thrust it up to the hilt in the very spot which I desired to penetrate. A convulsive thrill ran through Simon's limbs. I heard a smothered sound issue from his throat, precisely like the bursting of a large air-bubble, sent up by a diver, when it reaches the surface of the water; he turned half round on his side, and as if to assist my plans more effectually, his right hand, moved by some mere spasmodic impulse, clasped the handle of the creese, which it remained holding with extraordinary muscular tenacity. Beyond this there was no apparent struggle. The laudanum, I presume, paralyzed the usual nervous action. He must have died instantaneously.

There was yet something to be done. To make it certain that all suspicion of the act should be diverted from any inhabitant of the house to Simon himself, it was necessary that the door should be found in the morning *locked on the inside*. How to do this, and afterwards escape myself? Not by the window; that was a physical impossibility. Besides, I was determined that the windows *also* should be found bolted. The solution was simple enough. I descended softly to my own room for a peculiar instrument which I had used for holding small slippery substances, such as minute spheres of glass, etc. This instrument was nothing more than a long slender hand-vice, with a very powerful grip and a considerable leverage, which last was accidentally owing to the shape of the handle. Nothing was simpler than, when the key was in the lock, to seize the end of its stem in this vice, through the keyhole, from the outside, and so lock the door. Previously, however, to doing this, I burned a number of papers on Simon's hearth. Suicides almost always burn papers before they destroy themselves. I also emptied some more laudanum into Simon's glass – having first removed from it all traces of wine – cleaned the other wine-glass and brought the bottles away with me. If traces of two persons drinking had been found in the room, the question naturally would have arisen, Who was the second? Besides, the wine-bottles might have been identified as belonging to me. The laudanum I poured out to account for its presence in his stomach, in case of a post-mortem examination. The theory naturally would be that he first intended to poison himself, but, after swallowing a little of the drug, was either disgusted with its taste, or changed his mind from other motives, and chose the dagger. These arrangements made, I walked out, leaving the gas burning, locked the door with my vice, and went to bed.

Simon's death was not discovered until nearly three in the afternoon. The servant, astonished at seeing the gas burning – the light streaming on the dark landing from under the door – peeped through the keyhole and saw Simon on the bed. She gave the alarm. The door was burst open, and the neighbourhood was in a fever of excitement.

Everyone in the house was arrested, myself included. There was an inquest; but no clue to his death, beyond that of suicide, could be obtained. Curiously enough, he had made several speeches to his friends the preceding week that seemed to point to self-destruction. One gentleman swore that Simon had said in his presence that 'he was tired of life.' His landlord affirmed that Simon, when paying him his last month's rent, remarked that 'he would not pay him rent much longer.' All the other evidence corresponded – the door locked inside, the position of the corpse, the burnt papers. As I anticipated, no one knew of the possession of the diamond by Simon, so that no motive was suggested for his murder. The jury, after a prolonged examination, brought in the usual verdict, and the neighbourhood once more settled down into its accustomed quiet.

5 ANIMULA

The three months succeeding Simon's catastrophe I devoted night and day to my diamond lens. I had constructed a vast galvanic battery, composed of nearly two thousand pairs of plates – a higher power I dared not use, lest the diamond should be calcined. By means of this enormous engine I was enabled to send a powerful current of electricity continually through my great diamond, which it seemed to me gained in lustre every day. At the expiration of a month I commenced the grinding and polishing of the lens, a work of intense toil and exquisite delicacy. The great density of the stone, and the care required to be taken with the curvatures of the surfaces of the lens, rendered the labour the severest and most harassing that I had yet undergone.

At last the eventful moment came; the lens was completed. I stood trembling on the threshold of new worlds. I had the realization of Alexander's famous wish before me. The lens lay on the table, ready to be placed upon its platform. My hand fairly shook as I enveloped a drop of water with a thin coating of oil of turpentine, preparatory to its examination – a process necessary in order to prevent the rapid evaporation of the water. I now placed the drop on a thin slip of glass under the lens and, throwing upon it, by the combined aid of a prism and a mirror, a powerful stream of light, I approached my eye to the minute hole drilled through the axis of the lens. For an instant I saw nothing save what seemed to be an illuminated chaos, a vast luminous abyss. A pure white light, cloudless and serene, and seemingly limitless as space itself, was my first impression. Gently, and with the greatest care, I depressed the lens a few hairs' breadths. The wondrous illumination still continued, but as the lens approached the object a scene of indescribable beauty was unfolded to my view.

I seemed to gaze upon a vast space, the limits of which extended far beyond my vision. An atmosphere of magical luminousness permeated the entire field of view. I was amazed to see no trace of animalculous life. Not a living thing, apparently, inhabited that dazzling expanse. I comprehended instantly that, by the wondrous power of my lens, I had penetrated beyond the grosser particles of aqueous matter, beyond the realms of Infusoria and Protozoa, down to the original gaseous globule, into whose luminous interior I was gazing, as into an almost boundless dome filled with a supernatural radiance.

It was, however, no brilliant void into which I looked. On every side I beheld beautiful inorganic forms, of unknown texture, and coloured with the most enchanting hues. These forms presented the appearance of what might be called, for want of a more specific definition, foliated clouds of the highest rarity; that is, they undulated and broke into vegetable formations, and were tinged with splendours compared with which the gilding of our autumn woodlands is as dross compared with gold. Far away into the illimitable distance stretched long avenues of these gaseous forests dimly transparent, and painted with prismatic hues of unimaginable brilliancy. The pendent branches waved along the fluid glades until every vista seemed to break through half-lucent ranks of many-coloured, drooping silken pennons. What seemed to be either fruits or flowers, pied with a thousand hues lustrous and ever varying, bubbled from the crowns of this fairy foliage. No hills, no lakes, no rivers, no forms animate or inanimate were to be seen, save those vast auroral copses that floated serenely in the luminous stillness, with leaves and fruits and flowers gleaming with unknown fires, unrealizable by mere imagination.

How strange, I thought, that this sphere should be thus condemned to solitude! I had hoped, at least, to discover some new form of animal life – perhaps of a lower class than any with which we are at present acquainted – but still, some living organism. I find my newly discovered world, if I may so speak, a beautiful chromatic desert.

While I was speculating on the singular arrangements of the internal economy of nature, with which she so frequently splinters into atoms our most compact theories, I thought I beheld a form moving slowly through the glades of one of the prismatic forests. I looked more attentively, and found that I was not mistaken. Words cannot depict the anxiety with which I awaited the nearer approach of this mysterious object. Was it merely some inanimate substance, held in suspense in the attenuated atmosphere of the globule? Or was it an animal endowed with vitality and motion? It approached, flitting beyond the gauzy, coloured veils of cloud foliage, for seconds dimly revealed, then vanishing. At last the violet pennons that trailed nearest to me vibrated; they were gently pushed aside, and the form floated out into the broad light.

It was a female human shape. When I say 'human,' I mean it possessed the outlines of humanity – but there the analogy ends. Its adorable beauty lifted it illimitable heights beyond the loveliest daughter of Adam.

I cannot, I dare not, attempt to inventory the charms of this divine revelation of perfect beauty. Those eyes of mystic violet, dewy and serene, evade my words. Her long lustrous hair following her glorious head in a golden wake, like the track sown in heaven by a falling star, seems to quench my most burning phrases with its splendours. If all the bees of Hybla nestled upon my lips, they would still sing but hoarsely the wondrous harmonies of outline that enclosed her form.

She swept out from between the rainbow-curtains of the cloud-trees into the broad sea of light that lay beyond. Her motions were those of some graceful naiad, cleaving, by a mere effort of her will, the clear, unruffled waters that fill the chambers of the sea. She floated forth with the serene grace of a frail bubble ascending through the still atmosphere of a June day. The perfect roundness of her limbs formed suave and enchanting curves. It was like listening to the most spiritual symphony of Beethoven, the divine, to watch the harmonious flow of lines. This, indeed, was a pleasure cheaply purchased at any price. What cared I, if I had waded to the portal of this wonder through another's blood? I would have given my own to enjoy one such moment of intoxication and delight.

Breathless with gazing on this lovely wonder, and forgetful for an instant of everything save her presence, I withdrew my eye from the microscope eagerly – alas! As my gaze fell on the thin slide that lay beneath my instrument, the bright light from mirror and from prism sparkled on a colourless drop of water! There, in that tiny bead of dew, this beautiful being was forever imprisoned. The planet Neptune was not more distant from me than she. I hastened once more to apply my eye to the microscope.

Animula (let me now call her by that dear name which I subsequently bestowed on her) had changed her position. She had again approached the wondrous forest, and was gazing earnestly upwards. Presently one of the trees – as I must call them – unfolded a long ciliary process, with which it seized one of the gleaming fruits that glittered on its summit, and sweeping slowly down, held it within reach of Animula. The sylph took it in her delicate hand, and began to eat. My attention was so entirely absorbed by her that I could not apply myself to the task of determining whether this singular plant was or was not instinct with volition.

I watched her, as she made her repast, with the most profound attention.

The suppleness of her motions sent a thrill of delight through my frame; my heart beat madly as she turned her beautiful eyes in the direction of the spot in which I stood. What would I not have given to have had the power to precipitate myself into that luminous ocean, and float with her through those groves of purple and gold! While I was thus breathlessly following her every movement, she suddenly started, seemed to listen for a moment, and then cleaving the brilliant ether in which she was floating, like a flash of light, pierced through the opaline forest, and disappeared.

Instantly a series of the most singular sensations attacked me. It seemed as if I had suddenly gone blind. The luminous sphere was still before me, but my daylight had vanished. What caused this sudden disappearance? Had she a lover, or a husband? Yes, that was the solution! Some signal from a happy fellow-being had vibrated through the avenues of the forest, and she had obeyed the summons.

The agony of my sensations, as I arrived at this conclusion, startled me. I tried to reject the conviction that my reason forced upon me. I battled against the fatal conclusion – but in vain. It was so. I had no escape from it. I loved an animalcule!

It is true, that, thanks to the marvellous power of my microscope, she appeared of human proportions. Instead of presenting the revolting aspect of the coarser creatures, that live and struggle and die in the more easily resolvable portions of the water-drop, she was fair and delicate and of surpassing beauty. But of what account was all that? Every time that my eye was withdrawn from the instrument, it fell on a miserable drop of water, within which, I must be content to know, dwelt all that could make my life lovely.

Could she but see me once! Could I for one moment pierce the mystical walls that so inexorably rose to separate us, and whisper all that filled my soul, I might consent to be satisfied for the rest of my life with the knowledge of her remote sympathy. It would be something to have established even the faintest personal link to bind us together – to know that at times, when roaming through those enchanted glades, she might think of the wonderful stranger who had broken the monotony of her life with his presence, and left a gentle memory in her heart!

But it could not be. No invention of which human intellect was capable could break down the barriers that nature had erected. I might feast my soul upon her wondrous beauty, yet she must always remain ignorant of the adoring eyes that day and night gazed upon her, and, even when closed, beheld her in dreams. With a bitter cry of anguish I fled from the room, and, flinging myself on my bed, sobbed myself to sleep like a child.

6 THE SPILLING OF THE CUP

I arose the next morning almost at daybreak, and rushed to my microscope. I trembled as I sought the luminous world in miniature that contained my all. Animula was there. I had left the gas-lamp, surrounded by its moderators, burning, when I went to bed the night before. I found the sylph bathing, as it were, with an expression of pleasure animating her features, in the brilliant light which surrounded her. She tossed her lustrous golden hair over her shoulders with innocent coquetry. She lay at full length in the transparent medium, in which she supported herself with ease, and gambolled with the enchanting grace that the Nymph Salmacis might have exhibited when she sought to conquer the modest Hermaphroditus. I tried an experiment to satisfy myself if her powers of reflection were developed. I lessened the lamp-light considerably. By the dim light that remained I could see an expression of pain flit across her face. She looked upward suddenly, and her brows contracted. I flooded the stage of the microscope again with a full stream of light, and her whole expression changed. She sprang forward like some substance deprived of all weight. Her eyes sparkled, and her lips moved. Ah! if science had only the means of conducting and reduplicating sounds, as it does the rays of light, what carols of happiness would then have entranced my ears! What jubilant hymns to Adonais would have thrilled the illumined air!

I now comprehended how it was that the Count de Gabalis peopled his mystic world with sylphs – beautiful beings whose breath of life was lambent fire, and who sported forever in regions of purest ether and purest light. The Rosicrucian had anticipated the wonder that I had practically realized.

How long this worship of my strange divinity went on thus I scarcely know. I lost all note of time. All day from early dawn, and far into the night, I was to be found peering through that wonderful lens. I saw no one, went nowhere, and scarce allowed myself sufficient time for my meals. My whole life was absorbed in contemplation as rapt as that of any of the Romish saints. Every hour that I gazed upon the divine form strengthened my passion – a passion that was always overshadowed by the maddening conviction that, although I could gaze on her at will, she never, never could behold me!

At length I grew so pale and emaciated, from want of rest, and continual brooding over my insane love and its cruel conditions, that I determined to make some effort to wean myself from it. 'Come,' I said, 'this is at best but a fantasy. Your imagination has bestowed on Animula charms which in reality she does not possess. Seclusion from female society has produced this morbid condition of mind. Compare her with the beautiful women of your own world, and this false enchantment will vanish.'

I looked over the newspapers by chance. There I beheld the advertisement of a celebrated danseuse who appeared nightly at Niblo's. The Signorina Caradolce had the reputation of being the most beautiful as well as the most graceful woman in the world. I instantly dressed and went to the theatre.

The curtain drew up. The usual semicircle of fairies in white muslin were standing on the right toe around the enamelled flower-bank, of green canvas, on which the belated prince was sleeping. Suddenly a flute is heard. The fairies start. The trees open, the fairies all stand on the left toe, and the queen enters. It was the signorina. She bounded forward amid thunders of applause, and lighting on one foot remained poised in air. Heavens! Was this the great enchantress that had drawn monarchs at her chariot-wheels? Those heavy muscular limbs, those thick ankles, those cavernous eyes, that stereotyped smile, those crudely-painted cheeks! Where were the vermeil blooms, the liquid, expressive eyes, the harmonious limbs of Animula?

The signorina danced. What gross, discordant movements! The play of her limbs was all false and artificial. Her bounds were painful athletic efforts; her poses were angular and distressed the eye. I could bear it no longer; with an exclamation of disgust that drew every eye upon me, I rose from my seat in the very middle of the signorina's *pas de fascination*, and abruptly quitted the house.

I hastened home to feast my eyes once more on the lovely form of my sylph. I felt that henceforth to combat this passion would be impossible. I applied my eyes to the lens. Animula was there – but what could have happened? Some terrible change seemed to have taken place during my absence. Some secret grief seemed to cloud the lovely features of her I gazed upon. Her face had grown thin and haggard; her limbs trailed heavily; the wondrous lustre of her golden hair had faded. She was ill! ill, and I could not assist her! I believe at that moment I would have gladly forfeited all claims to my human birthright, if I could only have been dwarfed to the size of an animalcule, and permitted to console her from whom fate had forever divided me.

I racked my brain for the solution of this mystery. What was it that afflicted the sylph? She seemed to suffer intense pain. Her features contracted, and she even writhed, as if with some internal agony. The wondrous forests appeared also to have lost half their beauty. Their hues were dim and in some places faded away altogether. I watched Animula for hours with a breaking heart, and she seemed absolutely to wither away under my very eye. Suddenly I remembered that I had not looked at the water-drop for several days. In fact, I hated to see it; for it reminded me of the natural barrier between Animula and myself. I hurriedly looked down on the stage of the microscope. The slide was still there – but, great heavens! the water-drop had vanished! The awful truth burst upon me; it had evaporated, until it had become so minute as to be invisible to the naked eye; I had been gazing on its last atom, the one that contained Animula – and she was dying!

I rushed again to the front of the lens, and looked through. Alas! the last agony had seized her. The rainbow-hued forests had all melted away, and Animula lay struggling feebly in what seemed to be a spot of dim light. Ah! the sight was horrible: the limbs once so round and lovely shrivelling up into nothings; the eyes – those eyes that shone like heaven – being quenched into black dust; the lustrous golden hair now lank and discoloured. The last throe came. I beheld that final struggle of the blackening form – and I fainted.

When I awoke out of a trance of many hours, I found myself lying amid the wreck of my instrument, myself as shattered in mind and body as it. I crawled feebly to my bed, from which I did not rise for months.

They say now that I am mad: but they are mistaken. I am poor, for I have neither the heart nor the will to work; all my money is spent, and I live on charity. Young men's associations that love a joke invite me to lecture on optics before them, for which they pay me, and laugh at me while I lecture. 'Linley, the mad microscopist,' is the name I go by. I suppose that I talk incoherently while I lecture. Who could talk sense when his brain is haunted by such ghastly memories, while ever and anon among the shapes of death I behold the radiant form of my lost Animula!

MARK TWAIN
1835-1910

Mark Twain (or Samuel Langhorne Clemens as was his given name) was born in Florida in 1835. Dropping out of school at the age of twelve, Twain became apprenticed to a journeyman printer and passed thence into occasional journalism. For a time he was a steamship pilot on the Mississippi river before serving briefly in the Confederate Army and then heading West. His double career as a miner and newspaperman provided much of the material for his earlier stories. From the publication of his first collection of tales and sketches in 1867, Twain was a hugely popular writer. Mark Twain's two most important works, *The Adventures of Tom Sawyer* (1876) and *The Adventures of Huckleberry Finn* have formed the bases of many films and dramatizations and have lost none of their immediate appeal to adults and children alike.

The four stories included here, from the tale which first established his reputation 'The Celebrated Jumping Frog of Calaveras County' (1867), to perhaps his finest work of cynicism and social comedy 'The Man Tha Corrupted Hadleyburg' (1900) amply reveal the grounds for regarding Twain as the first pioneer of what has become a world-renowned tradition of American humorous writing.

The Celebrated Jumping Frog of Calaveras County

IN COMPLIANCE WITH THE REQUEST of a friend of mine, who wrote me from the East, I called on good-natured, garrulous old Simon Wheeler, and inquired after my friend's friend, *Leonidas W.* Smiley, as requested to do, and I hereunto append the result. I have a lurking suspicion that *Leonidas W.* Smiley is a myth; that my friend never knew such a personage; and that he only conjectured that, if I asked old Wheeler about him, it would remind him of his infamous *Jim* Smiley, and he would go to work and bore me nearly to death with some infernal reminiscence of him as long and tedious as it should be useless to me. If that was the design, it certainly succeeded.

I found Simon Wheeler dozing comfortably by the bar-room stove of the old, dilapidated tavern in the ancient mining camp of Angel's, and I noticed that he was fat and bald-headed, and had an expression of winning gentleness and simplicity upon his tranquil countenance. He roused up and gave me good-day. I told him a friend of mine had commissioned me to make some inquiries about a cherished companion of his boyhood named *Leonidas* W. Smiley—*Rev. Leonidas W.* Smiley—a young minister of the Gospel, who he had heard was at one time a resident of Angel's Camp. I added that, if Mr. Wheeler could tell me anything about this Rev. Leonidas W. Smiley, I would feel under many obligations to him.

Simon Wheeler backed me into a corner and blockaded me there with his chair, and then sat me down and reeled off the monotonous narrative which follows this paragraph. He never smiled, he never frowned, he never changed his voice from the gentle-flowing key to which he tuned the initial sentence, he never betrayed the slightest suspicion of enthusiasm; but all through the interminable narrative there ran a vein of impressive earnestness and sincerity, which showed me plainly that, so far from his imagining that there was anything ridiculous or funny about this story, he regarded it as a really important matter, and admired its two heroes as men of transcendent genius in finesse. To me, the spectacle of a man drifting serenely along through such a queer yarn without ever smiling, was exquisitely absurd. As I said before, I asked him to tell me what he knew of Rev. Leonidas W. Smiley, and he replied as follows. I let him go on in his own way, and never interrupted him once:

There was a feller here once by the name of *Jim* Smiley, in the winter of '49—or maybe it was the spring of '50—I don't recollect exactly, somehow, though what makes me think it was one or the other is because I remember the big flume wasn't finished when he first came to the camp; but anyway, he was the curiousest man about always betting on anything that turned up you ever see, if he could get anybody to bet on the other side; and if he couldn't he'd change sides. Any way what suited the other man would suit him—any way just so's he got a bet, *he* was satisfied. But still he was lucky, uncommon lucky; he most always come out winner. He was always ready and laying for a chance; there couldn't be no solit'ry thing mentioned but that feller'd offer to bet on it, and take any side you please, as I was just telling you. If there was a horse race, you'd find him flush, or you'd find him busted at the end of it; if there was a dog-fight, he'd bet on it; if there was a cat-fight, he'd bet on it; if there was a chicken-fight, he'd bet on it; why, if there was two birds setting on a fence, he would bet you which one would fly first; or if there was a camp meeting, he would be there reg'lar, to bet on Parson Walker, which he judged to be the best exhorter about here, and so he was, too, and a good man. If he even seen a straddlebug start to go anywheres, he would bet you how long it would take him to get wherever he was going to, and if you took him up, he would foller that straddlebug to Mexico but what he would find out where he was bound for and how long he was on the road. Lots of the boys here has seen that Smiley, and can tell you about him. Why, it never made no difference to *him*—he would bet on *anything*—the dangdest feller. Parson Walker's wife laid very sick once, for a good while, and it seemed as if they warn't going to save her; but one morning he come in, and Smiley asked how she was, and he said she was considerable better—thank the Lord for his inf'nit mercy—and coming on so smart that, with the blessing of Prov'dence, she'd get well yet; and Smiley, before he thought, says, 'Well, I'll risk two-and-a-half that she don't, anyway.'

Thish-yer Smiley had a mare—the boys called her the fifteen-minute nag, but that was only in fun, you know, because, of course, she was faster than that—and he used to win money on that horse, for all she was so slow and always had the asthma, or the distemper, or the consumption, or something of that kind. They used to give her two or three hundred yards start, and then pass her under way; but always at the fag end of the race she'd get excited and desperate-like, and come cavorting and straddling up, and scattering her legs around limber, sometimes in the air, and sometimes out to one side amongst the fences, and kicking up m-o-r-e dust, and raising m-o-r-e racket with her coughing and sneezing and blowing her nose—and always fetch up at the stand just about a neck ahead, as near as you could cipher it down.

And he had a little small bull pup, that to look at him you'd think he wan't worth a cent, but to set around and look ornery, and lay for a chance to steal something. But as soon as money was up on him, he was a different dog; his underjaw'd begin to stick out like the fo-castle of a steamboat, and his teeth would uncover, and shine savage like the furnaces. And a dog might tackle him, and bullyrag him, and bite him, and throw him over his shoulder two or three times, and Andrew Jackson—which was the name of the pup—Andrew Jackson would never let on but what *he* was satisfied, and hadn't expected nothing else—and the bets being doubled and doubled on the other side all the time, till the money was all up; and then all of a sudden he would grab that other dog jest by the j'int of his hand leg and freeze to it—not chaw, you understand, but only jest grip and hang on till they throwed up the sponge, if it was a year. Smiley always come out winner on that pup, till he harnessed a dog once that didn't have no hind legs, because they'd been sawed off by a circular saw, and when the thing had gone along far enough, and the money was all up, and he come to make a snatch for his pet holt, he saw in a minute how he'd been imposed on, and how the other dog had him in the door, so to speak, and he 'peared surprised, and then he looked sorter discouraged-like, and didn't try no more to win the fight, and so he got shucked out bad. He give Smiley a look, as much as to say his heart was broke, and it was *his* fault for putting up a dog that hadn't no hind legs for him to take holt of, which was his main dependence in a fight, and then he limped off a piece and laid down and died. It was a good pup, was that Andrew Jackson, and would have made a name for hisself if he'd lived, for the stuff was in him, and he had genius—I know it, because he hadn't had no opportunities to speak of, and it don't stand to reason that a dog could make such a fight as he could under them circumstances if he hadn't no talent. It always makes me feel sorry when I think of that last fight of his'n, and the way it turned out.

Well, thish-yer Smiley had rat-tarriers, and chicken cocks, and tomcats, and all them kind of things, till you couldn't rest, and you couldn't fetch nothing for him to bet on but he'd match you. He ketched a frog one day, and took him home, and said he cal'klated to edercute him; and so he never done nothing for three months but set in his back yard and learn that frog to jump. And you bet you he *did* learn him, too. He'd give him a little punch behind, and the next minute you'd see that frog whirling in the air like a doughnut—see him turn one summerset, or may be a couple, if he got a good start, and come down flatfooted and all right, like a cat. He got him up so in the matter of catching flies, and kept him in practice so constant, that he'd nail a fly every time as far as he could see him. Smiley said all a frog wanted was education, and he could do most anything—and I believe him. Why, I've seen him set Dan'l Webster down here on this floor—Dan'l Webster was the name of the frog—and sing out, 'Flies, Dan'l, flies!' and quicker'n you could wink, he'd spring straight up, and snake a fly off'n the counter there, and flop down on the floor again as solid as a gob of mud, and fall to scratching the side of his head with his hind foot as indifferent as if he hadn't no idea he'd been doin' any more'n any frog might do. You never see a frog so modest and straightfor'ard as he was, for all he was so gifted. And when it come to fair and square jumping on a dead level, he could get over more ground at one straddle than any animal of his breed you ever see. Jumping on a dead level was his strong suit, you understand; and when it come to that, Smiley would ante up money on him as long as he had a red. Smiley was monstrous proud of his frog, and well he might be, for fellers that had traveled and been everywheres, all said he laid over any frog that ever *they* see.

Well, Smiley kept the beast in a little lattice box, and he used to fetch him downtown sometimes and lay for a bet. One day a feller—a stranger in the camp, he was—come across him with his box, and says:

'What might it be that you've got in the box?'

And Smiley says, sorter indifferent like, 'It might be a parrot, or it might be a canary, maybe, but it ain't—it's only just a frog.'

And the feller took it, and looked at it careful, and turned it round this way and that, and says, 'H'm—so 'tis. Well, what's *he* good for?'

'Well,' Smiley says, easy and careless, 'he's good enough for *one* thing, I should judge—he can outjump any frog in Calaveras county.'

The feller took the box again, and took another long, particular look, and give it back to Smiley, and says, very deliberate, 'Well, I don't see no p'ints about that frog that's any better'n any other frog.'

'Maybe you don't,' Smiley says. 'Maybe you understand frogs, and maybe you don't understand 'em; maybe you've had experience, and maybe you an't only a amature, as it were. Anyways, I've got *my* opinion, and I'll risk forty dollars that he can outjump any frog in Calaveras county.'

And the feller studied a minute, and then says, kinder sad like, 'Well, I'm only a stranger here, and I an't got no frog; but if I had a frog, I'd bet you.'

And then Smiley says, 'That's all right—that's all right—if you'll hold my box a minute, I'll go and get you a frog.' And so the feller took the box, and put up his forty dollars along with Smiley's, and set down to wait.

So he set there a good while thinking and thinking to hisself, and then he got the frog out and prized his mouth open and took a teaspoon and filled him full of quail shot—filled him pretty near up to his chin—and set him on the floor. Smiley he went to the swamp and slopped around in the mud for a long time, and finally he ketched a frog, and fetched him in, and give him to this feller, and says:

'Now, if you're ready, set him alongside of Dan'l, with his fore-paws just even with Dan'l, and I'll give the word.' Then he says, 'One—two—three—jump!' and him and the feller touched up the frogs from behind, and the new frog hopped off, but Dan'l give a heave, and hysted up his shoulders—so—like a Frenchman, but it wan't no use—he couldn't budge; he was planted as solid as an anvil, and he couldn't no more stir than if he was anchored out. Smiley was a good deal surprised, and he was disgusted too, but he didn't have no idea what the matter was, of course.

The feller took the money and started away; and when he was going out at the door, he sorter jerked his thumb over his shoulders—this way—at Dan'l, and says again, very deliberate, 'Well, *I* don't see no p'ints about that frog that's any better'n any other frog.'

Smiley he stood scratching his head and looking down at Dan'l a long time, and at last he says, 'I do wonder what in the nation that frog throw'd off for—I wonder if there an't something the matter with him—he 'pears to look might baggy, somehow.' And he ketched Dan'l by the nap of the neck, and lifted him and says, 'Why, blame my cats, if he don't weigh five pound!' and turned him upside down, and he belched out a double handful of shot. And then he see how it was, and he was the maddest man—he set the frog down and took out after that feller, but he never ketched him. And—

[Here Simon Wheeler heard his name called from the front yard, and got up to see what was wanted.] And turning to me as he moved away, he said: 'Just set where you are, stranger, and rest easy—I an't going to be gone a second.'

But, by your leave, I did not think that a continuation of the history of the enterprising vagabond *Jim* Smiley would be likely to afford me much information concerning the Rev. *Leonidas W.* Smiley, and so I started away.

At the door I met the sociable Wheeler returning, and he buttonholed me and recommenced:

'Well, thish-yer Smiley had a yaller one-eyed cow that didn't have no tail, only jest a short stump like a bannanner, and—'

'Oh! hang Smiley and his afflicted cow!' I muttered, good-naturedly, and bidding the old gentleman good-day, I departed.

The £1,000,000 Bank-Note

WHEN I WAS TWENTY-SEVEN years old, I was a mining broker's clerk in San Francisco, and an expert in all the details of stock traffic. I was alone in the world, and had nothing to depend upon but my wits and a clean reputation; but these were setting my feet in the road to eventual fortune, and I was content with the prospect.

My time was my own after the afternoon board, Saturdays, and I was accustomed to put it in on a little sailboat on the bay. One day I ventured too far, and was carried out to sea. Just at nightfall, when hope was about gone, I was picked up by a small brig which was bound for London. It was a long and stormy voyage, and they made me work my passage without pay, as a common sailor. When I stepped ashore in London my clothes were ragged and shabby, and I had only a dollar in my pocket. This money fed and sheltered me twenty-four hours. During, the next twenty-four I went without food and shelter.

About ten o'clock on the following morning, seedy and hungry, I was dragging myself along Portland Place, when a child that was passing, towed by a nursemaid, tossed a luscious big pear—minus one bite—into the gutter. I stopped, of course, and fastened my desiring eye on the muddy treasure. My mouth watered for it, my stomach craved it, my whole being begged for it. But every time I made a move to get it some passing eye detected my purpose, and of course I straightened up, then, and looked indifferent, and pretended that I hadn't been thinking about the pear at all. This same thing kept happening and happening, and I couldn't get the pear. I was just getting desperate enough to brave all the shame, and to seize it, when a window behind me was raised, and a gentleman spoke out of it, saying:

'Step in here, please.'

I was admitted by a gorgeous flunky, and shown into a sumptuous room where a couple of elderly gentlemen were sitting. They sent away the servant, and made me sit down. They had just finished their breakfast, and the sight of the remains of it almost overpowered me. I could hardly keep my wits together in the presence of that food, but as I was not asked to sample it, I had to bear my trouble as best I could.

Now, something had been happening there a little before, which I did not know anything about until a good many days afterward, but I will tell you about it now. Those two old brothers had been having a pretty hot argument a couple of days before, and had ended by agreeing to decide it by a bet, which is the English way of settling everything.

You will remember that the Bank of England once issued two notes of a million pounds each, to be used for a special purpose connected with some public transaction with a foreign country. For some reason or other only one of these had been used and canceled; the other still lay in the vaults of the Bank. Well, the brothers, chatting along, happened to get to wondering what might be the fate of a perfectly honest and intelligent stranger who should be turned adrift in London without a friend, and with no money but that million-pound bank-note, and no way to account for his being in possession of it. Brother A said he would starve to death; Brother B said he wouldn't. Brother A said he couldn't offer it at a bank or anywhere else, because he would be arrested on the spot. So they went on disputing till Brother B said he would bet twenty thousand pounds that the man would live thirty days, *anyway*, on that million, and keep out of jail, too. Brother A took him up. Brother B went down to the Bank and bought that note. Just like an Englishman, you see; pluck to the backbone. Then he dictated a letter, which one of his clerks wrote out in a beautiful round hand, and then the two brothers sat at the window a whole day watching for the right man to give it to.

They saw many honest faces go by that were not intelligent enough; many that were intelligent, but not honest enough; many that were both, but the possessors were not poor enough, or, if poor enough, were not strangers. There was always a defect, until I came along; but they agreed that I filled the bill all around; so they elected me unanimously, and there I was, now, waiting to know why I was called in. They began to ask me questions about myself, and pretty soon they had my story. Finally they told me I would answer their purpose. I said I was sincerely glad, and asked what it was. Then one of them handed me an envelope, and said I would find the explanation inside. I was going to open it, but he said no; take it to my lodgings, and look it over carefully, and not be hasty or rash. I was puzzled, and wanted to discuss the matter a little further, but they didn't; so I took my leave, feeling hurt and insulted to be made the butt of what was apparently some kind of a practical joke, and yet obliged to put up with it, not being in circumstances to resent affronts from rich and strong folk.

I would have picked up the pear, now, and eaten it before all the world, but it was gone; so I had lost that by this unlucky business, and the thought of it did not soften my feeling toward those men. As soon as I was out of sight of that house I opened my envelope, and saw that it contained money! My opinion of those people changed, I can tell you! I lost not a moment, but shoved note and money into my vest-pocket,and broke for the nearest cheap eating house. Well, how I did eat! When at last I couldn't hold any more, I took out my money and unfolded it, took one glimpse and nearly fainted. Five millions of dollars! Why, it made my head swim.

I must have sat there stunned and blinking at the note as much as a minute before I came rightly to myself again. The first thing I noticed, then, was the landlord. His eye was on the note, and he was petrified. He was worshiping, with all his body and soul, but he looked as if he couldn't stir hand or foot. I took my cue in a moment, and did the only rational thing there was to do. I reached the note toward him, and said carelessly:

'Give me the change, please.'

Then he was restored to his normal condition, and made a thousand apologies for not being able to break the bill, and I couldn't get him to touch it. He wanted to look at it, and keep on looking at it; he couldn't seem to get enough of it to quench the thirst of his eye, but he shrank from touching it as if it had been something too sacred for poor common clay to handle. I said:

'I am sorry if it is an inconvenience, but I must insist. Please change it; I haven't anything else.'

But he said that wasn't any matter; he was quite willing to let the trifle stand over till another time. I said I might not be in his neighborhood again for a good while; but he said it was of no consequence, he could wait, and, moreover, I could have anything I wanted, any time I chose, and let the account run as long as I pleased. He said he hoped he wasn't afraid to trust as rich a gentleman as I was, merely because I was of a merry disposition, and chose to play larks on the public in the matter of dress. By this time another customer was entering, and the landlord hinted to me to put the monster out of sight; then he bowed me all the way to the door, and I started straight for that house and those brothers, to correct the mistake which had been made before the police should hunt me up, and help me do it. I was pretty nervous, in fact pretty badly frightened, though, of course, I was no way in fault; but I knew men well enough to know that when they find they've given a tramp a million-pound bill when they thought it was a one-pounder, they are in a frantic rage against *him* instead of quarreling with their own nearsightedness, as they ought. As I approached the house my excitement began to abate, for all was quiet there, which made me feel pretty sure the blunder was not discovered yet. I rang. The same servant appeared. I asked for those gentlemen.

'They are gone.' This in the lofty, cold way of that fellow's tribe.

'Gone? Gone where?'

'On a journey.'

'But whereabouts?'

'To the Continent, I think.'

'The Continent?'

'Yes, sir.'

'Which way—by what route?'

'I can't say, sir.'

'When will they be back?'

'In a month, they said.'

'A month! Oh, this is awful! Give me *some* sort of idea of how to get a word to them. It's of the last importance.'

'I can't, indeed. I've no idea where they've gone, sir.'

'Then I must see some member of the family.'

'Family's away too; been abroad months—in Egypt and India, I think.'

'Man, there's been an immense mistake made. They'll be back before night. Will you tell them I've been here, and that I will keep coming till it's all made right, and they needn't be afraid?'

'I'll tell them, if they come back, but I am not expecting them. They said you would be here in an hour to make inquiries, but I must tell you it's all right, they'll be here on time and expect you.'

So I had to give it up and go away. What a riddle it all was! I was like to lose my mind. They would be here 'on time.' What could that mean? Oh, the letter would explain, maybe. I had forgotten the letter; I got it out and read it. This is what it said:

You are an intelligent and honest man, as one may see by your face. We conceive you to be poor and a stranger. Enclosed you will find a sum of

money. It is lent to you for thirty days, without interest. Report at this
house at the end of that time. I have a bet on you. If I win it you shall have
any situation that is in my gift—any, that is, that you shall be able to prove
yourself familiar with and competent to fill.

No signature, no address, no date.

Well, here was a coil to be in! You are posted on what had preceded all this,
but I was not. It was just a deep, dark puzzle to me. I hadn't the least idea what
the game was, nor whether harm was meant me or a kindness. I went into a
park, and sat down to try to think it out, and to consider what I had best do.

At the end of an hour, my reasonings had crystallized into this verdict.

Maybe those men mean me well, maybe they mean me ill; no way to decide
that—let it go. They've got a game, or a scheme, or an experiment, of some
kind on hand; no way to determine what it is—let it go. There's a bet on me;
no way to find out what it is—let it go. That disposes of the indeterminable
quantities; the remainder of the matter is tangible, solid, and may be classed
and labeled with certainty. If I ask the Bank of England to place this bill to the
credit of the man it belongs to, they'll do it, for they know him, although I
don't; but they will ask me how I came in possession of it, and if I tell the truth,
they'll put me in the asylum, naturally, and a lie will land me in jail. The same
result would follow if I tried to bank the bill anywhere or to borrow money on
it. I have got to carry this immense burden around until those men come back,
whether I want to or not. It is useless to me, as useless as a handful of ashes,
and yet I must take care of it, and watch over it, while I beg my living. I
couldn't *give* it away, if I should try, for neither honest citizen nor highwayman
would accept it or meddle with it for anything. Those brothers are safe. Even
if I lose their bill, or burn it, they are still safe, because they can stop payment,
and the Bank will make them whole; but meantime, I've got to do a month's
suffering without wages or profit—unless I help win that bet, whatever it may
be, and get that situation that I am promised. I *should* like to get that; men of
their sort have situations in their gift that are worth having.

I got to thinking a good deal about that situation. My hopes began to rise
high. Without doubt the salary would be large. It would begin in a month;
after that I should be all right. Pretty soon I was feeling first rate. By this time I
was tramping the streets again. The sight of a tailor shop gave me a sharp
longing to shed my rags, and to clothe myself decently once more. Could I
afford it? No; I had nothing in the world but a million pounds. So I forced
myself to go on by. But soon I was drifting back again. The temptation
persecuted me cruelly. I must have passed that shop back and forth six times
during that manful struggle. At last I gave in; I had to. I asked if they had a
misfit suit that had been thrown on their hands. The fellow I spoke to nodded
his head toward another fellow, and gave me no answer. I went to the
indicated fellow, and he indicated another fellow with *his* head, and no words I
went to him, and he said:

"Tend to you presently.'

I waited till he was done with what he was at, then he took me into a back
room, and overhauled a pile of rejected suits, and selected the rattiest one for
me. I put it on. It didn't fit, and wasn't in any way attractive, but it was new,
and I was anxious to have it; so I didn't find any fault, but said with some
diffidence:

'It would be an accommodation to me if you could wait some days for the money. I haven't any small change about me.'

The fellow worked up a most sarcastic expression of countenance, and said:

'Oh, you haven't? Well, of course, I didn't expect it. I'd only expect gentlemen like you to carry large change.'

I was nettled, and said:

'My friend, you shouldn't judge a stranger always by the clothes he wears. I am quite able to pay for this suit; I simply didn't wish to put you to the trouble of changing a large note.'

He modified his style a little at that, and said, though still with something of an air:

'I didn't mean any particular harm, but as long as rebukes are going, I might say it wasn't quite your affair to jump to the conclusion that we couldn't change any note that you might happen to be carrying around. On the contrary, we *can*."

I handed the note to him, and said:

'Oh, very well; I apologize.'

He received it with a smile, one of those large smiles which goes all around over, and has folds in it, and wrinkles, and spirals, and looks like the place where you have thrown a brick in a pond; and then in the act of his taking a glimpse of the bill this smile froze solid, and turned yellow, and looked like those wavy, wormy spreads of lava which you find hardened on little levels on the side of Vesuvius. I never before saw a smile caught like that, and perpetuated. The man stood there holding the bill, and looking like that, and the proprietor hustled up to see what was the matter, and said briskly:

'Well, what's up? what's the trouble? what's wanting?'

I said: 'There isn't any trouble. I'm waiting for my change.'

'Come, come; get him his change, Tod; get him his change.'

Tod retorted: 'Get him his change! It's easy to say, sir; but look at the bill yourself.'

The proprietor took a look, gave a low, eloquent whistle, then made a dive for the pile of rejected clothing, and began to snatch it this way and that, talking all the time excitedly, and as if to himself:

'Sell an eccentric millionaire such an unspeakable suit as that—Tod's a fool—a born fool. Always doing something like this. Drives every millionaire away from this place, because he can't tell a millionaire from a tramp, and never could. Ah, here's the thing I'm after. Please get those things off, sir, and throw them in the fire. Do me the favor to put on this shirt and this suit; it's just the thing, the very thing—plain, rich, modest, and just ducally nobby; made to order for a foreign prince—you may know him, sir, his Serene Highness the Hospodar of Halifax; had to leave it with us and take a mourning suit because his mother was going to die—which she didn't. But that's all right; we can't always have the things the way we—that is, the way they—there! trousers all right, they fit you to a charm, sir; now the waistcoat; aha, right again! now the coat—Lord! look at that, now—Perfect—the whole thing! I never saw such a triumph in all my experience.'

I expressed my satisfaction.

'Quite right, sir, quite right; it'll do for a makeshift, I'm bound to say. But wait till you see what we'll get up for you on your own measure. Come, Tod, book and pen; get at it. Length of leg, 32"—and so on. Before I could get in a word he had measured me, and was giving orders for dress suits, morning suits, shirts, and all sorts of things. When I got a chance I said:

'But, my dear sir, I *can't* give these orders, unless you can wait indefinitely, or change the bill.'

'Indefinitely! It's a weak word, sir, a weak word. Eternally—*that's* the word, sir. Tod, rush these things through, and send them to the gentleman's address without any waste of time. Let the minor customers wait. Set down the gentleman's address and—'

'I'm changing my quarters. I will drop in and leave the new address.'

'Quite right, sir, quite right. One moment—let me show you out, sir. There—good day, sir, good day.'

Well, don't you see what was bound to happen? I drifted naturally into buying whatever I wanted, and asking for change. Within a week I was sumptuously equipped with all needful comforts and luxuries, and was housed in an expensive private hotel in Hanover Square. I took my dinners there, but for breakfast I stuck by Harris's humble feeding house, where I had got my first meal on my million-pound bill. I was the making of Harris. The fact had gone all abroad that the foreign crank who carried million-pound bills in his vest-pocket was the patron saint of the place. That was enough. From being a poor, struggling, little hand-to-mouth enterprise, it had become celebrated, and overcrowded with customers. Harris was so grateful that he forced loans upon me, and would not be denied; and so, pauper as I was, I had money to spend, and was living like the rich and the great. I judged that there was going to be a crash by and by, but I was in, now, and must swim across or drown. You see there was just that element of impending disaster to give a serious side, a sober side, yes, a tragic side, to a state of things which would otherwise have been purely ridiculous. In the night, in the dark, the tragedy part was always to the front, and always warning, always threatening; and so I moaned and tossed, and sleep was hard to find. But in the cheerful daylight the tragedy element faded out and disappeared, and I walked on air, and was happy to giddiness, to intoxication, you may say.

And it was natural; for I had become one of the notorieties of the metropolis of the world, and it turned my head, not just a little, but a good deal. You could not take up a newspaper, English, Scotch, or Irish, without finding in it one or more references to the 'vest-pocket million-pounder' and his latest doings and sayings. At first, in these mentions, I was at the bottom of the personal gossip column; next, I was listed above the knights; next, above the baronets; next, above the barons, and so on; and so on, climbing steadily as my notoriety augmented, until I reached the highest altitude possible, and there I remained, taking precedence of all dukes not royal, and of all ecclesiastics except the primate of all England. But mind, this was not fame; as yet I had achieved only notoriety. Then came the climaxing stroke—the accolade, so to speak—which in a single instant transmuted the perishable dross of notoriety into the enduring gold of fame: *Punch* caricatured me! Yes, I was a made man, now; my place was established. I might be joked about still, but reverently, not hilariously, not rudely; I could be smiled at, but not laughed at. The time for that had gone by. *Punch* pictured me all a-flutter with rags, dickering with a beefeater for the Tower of London. Well, you can imagine how it was with a young fellow who had never been taken notice of before, and now all of a sudden couldn't say a thing that wasn't taken up and repeated everywhere; couldn't stir abroad without constantly overhearing the remark flying from lip to lip, 'There he goes; that's him!' couldn't take his breakfast without a crowd to look on; couldn't appear in an opera box without concentrating there the fire of a thousand lorgnettes. Why, I just swam in glory all day long—that is the amount of it.

You know, I even kept my old suit of rags, and every now and then appeared in them, so as to have the old pleasure of buying trifles, and being insulted, and then shooting the scoffer dead with the million-pound bill. But I couldn't keep that up. The illustrated papers made the outfit so familiar that when I went out in it I was at once recognized and followed by a crowd, and if I attempted to purchase the man would offer me his whole shop on credit before I could pull my note to him.

About the tenth day of my fame I went to fulfill my duty to my flag by paying my respects to the American minister. He received me with the enthusiasm proper in my case, upbraided me for being so tardy in my duty, and said that there was only one way to get his forgiveness, and that was to take the seat at his dinner party that night made vacant by the illness of one of his guests. I said I would, and we got to talking. It turned out that he and my father had been schoolmates in boyhood, Yale students together later, and always warm friends up to my father's death. So then he required me to put in at his house all the odd time I might have to spare, and I was very willing, of course.

In fact I was more than willing; I was glad. When the crash should come, he might somehow be able to save me from total destruction; I didn't know how, but he might think of a way, maybe. I couldn't venture to unbosom myself to him at this late date, a thing which I would have been quick to do in the beginning of this awful career of mine in London. No, I couldn't venture it now; I was in too deep; that is, too deep for me to be risking revelations to so new a friend, though not yet clear beyond my depth, as *I* looked at it. Because, you see, with all my borrowing, I was carefully keeping within my means—I mean within my salary. Of course I couldn't *know* what my salary was going to be, but I had a good enough basis for an estimate in the fact that, if I won the bet, I was to have *choice* of any situation in that rich old gentleman's gift provided I was competent—and I should certainly prove competent; I hadn't any doubt about that. And as to the bet, I wasn't worrying about that; I had always been lucky. Now my estimate of the salary was six hundred to a thousand a year; say, six hundred for the first year, and so on up year by year, till I struck the upper figure by proved merit. At present I was only in debt for my first year's salary. Everybody had been trying to lend me money, but I had fought off the most of them on one pretext or another; so this indebtedness represented only £300 borrowed money, the other £300 represented my keep and my purchases. I believed my second year's salary would carry me through the rest of the month if I went on being cautious and economical, and I intended to look sharply out for that. My month ended, my employer back from his journey, I should be all right once more, for I should at once divide the two years' salary among my creditors by assignment, and get right down to my work.

It was a lovely dinner party of fourteen. The Duke and Duchess of Shoreditch, and their daughter the Lady Anne-Grace-Eleanor-Celeste-and-so-forth-and-so-forth-de-Bohun, the Earl and Countess of Newgate, Viscount Cheapside, Lord and Lady Blatherskite, some untitled people of both sexes, the minister and his wife and daughter, and this daughter's visiting friend, an English girl of twenty-two, named Portia Langham, whom I fell in love with in two minutes, and she with me—I could see it without glasses. There was still another guest, an American—but I am a little ahead of my story. While the people were still in the drawing room, whetting up for dinner, and coldly inspecting the late-comers, the servant announced:

'Mr. Lloyd Hastings.'

The moment the usual civilities were over, Hastings caught sight of me, and came straight with cordially outstretched hand; then stopped short when about to shake; and said with an embarrassed look:

'I beg your pardon, sir, I thought I knew you.'

'Why, you do know me, old fellow.'

'No! Are *you* the—the—'

'Vest-pocket monster? I am, indeed. Don't be afraid to call me by my nickname; I'm used to it.'

'Well, well, well, this is a surprise. Once or twice I've seen your own name coupled with the nickname, but it never occurred to me that *you* could be the Henry Adams referred to. Why, it isn't six months since you were clerking for Blake Hopkins in Frisco on a salary, and sitting up nights on an extra allowance, helping me arrange and verify the Gould and Curry Extension papers and statistics. The idea of your being in London, and a vast millionaire, and a colossal celebrity! Why, it's the Arabian Nights come again. Man, I can't take it in at all; can't realize it; give me time to settle the whirl in my head.'

'The fact is, Lloyd, you are no worse off than I am. I can't realize it myself.'

'Dear me, it *is* stunning, now isn't it? Why, it's just three months today since we went to the Miners' restaurant—'

'No; the What Cheer.'

'Right, it *was* the What Cheer; went there at two in the morning, and had a chop and coffee after a hard six hours' grind over those Extension papers, and I tried to persuade you to come to London with me, and offered to get leave of absence for you and pay all your expenses, and give you something over if I succeeded in making the sale; and you would not listen to me, said I wouldn't succeed, and you couldn't afford to lose the run of business and be no end of time getting the hang of things again when you got back home. And yet here you are. How odd it all is! How did you happen to come, and whatever *did* give you this incredible start?'

'Oh, just an accident. It's a long story—a romance, a body may say. I'll tell you all about it, but not now.'

'When?'

'The end of this month.'

'That's more than a fortnight yet. It's too much of a strain on a person's curiosity. Make it a week.'

'I can't. You'll know why, by and by. But how's the trade getting along?'

His cheerfulness vanished like a breath, and he said with a sigh:

'You were a true prophet, Hal, a true prophet. I wish I hadn't come. I don't want to talk about it.'

'But you must. You must come and stop with me tonight, when we leave here, and tell me all about it.'

'Oh, may I? Are you in earnest?' and the water showed in his eyes.

'Yes; I want to hear the whole story, every word.'

'I'm so grateful! Just to find a human interest once more, in some voice and in some eye, in me and affairs of mine, after what I've been through here—Lord! I could go down on my knees for it!'

He gripped my hand hard, and braced up, and was all right and lively after that for the dinner—which didn't come off. No; the usual thing happened, the thing that is always happening under that vicious and aggravating English system—the matter of precedence couldn't be settled, and so there was no dinner. Englishmen always eat dinner before they go out to dinner, because *they* know the risks they are running; but nobody ever warns the stranger, and so he walks placidly into the trap. Of course nobody was hurt this time, because we had all been to dinner, none of us being novices except Hastings, and he having been informed by the minister at the time that he invited him that in deference to the English custom he had not provided any dinner. Everybody took a lady and processioned down to the dining room, because it is usual to go through the motions; but there the dispute began. The Duke of Shoreditch wanted to take precedence, and sit at the head of the table, holding that he outranked a minister who represented merely a nation and not a monarch; but I stood for my rights, and refused to yield. In the gossip column I ranked all dukes not royal, and said so, and claimed precedence of this one. It couldn't be settled, of course, struggle as we might and did, he finally (and injudiciously) trying to play birth and antiquity, and I 'seeing' his Conqueror and 'raising' him with Adam, whose direct posterity I was, as shown by my name, while *he* was of a collateral branch, as shown by *his*, and by his recent Norman origin; so we all processioned back to the drawing room again and had a perpendicular lunch—plate of sardines and a strawberry, and you group yourself and stand up and eat it. Here the religion of precedence is not so strenuous; the two persons of highest rank chuck up a shilling, the one the wins has first go at his strawberry, and the loser gets the shilling. The next two chuck up, then the next two, and so on. After refreshment, tables were brought, and we all played cribbage, sixpence a game. The English never play any game for amusement. If they can't make something or lose something— they don't care which—they won't play.

We had a lovely time; certainly two of us had, Miss Langham and I. I was so bewitched with her that I couldn't count my hands if they went above a double sequence; and when I struck home I never discovered it, and started up the outside row again, and would have lost the game every time, only the girl did the same, she being in just my condition, you see; and consequently neither of us ever got out, or cared to wonder why we didn't; we only just knew we were happy, and didn't wish to know anything else, and didn't want to be interrupted. And I *told* her—I did indeed—told her I loved her; and she—well, she blushed till her hair turned red, but she liked it; she *said* she did. Oh, there was never such an evening! Every time I pegged I put on a postscript; every time she pegged she acknowledged receipt of it, counting the hands the same. Why, I couldn't even say 'Two for his heels' without adding, 'My, how sweet you do look!' and she would say, 'Fifteen two, fifteen four, fifteen six, and a pair are eight, and eight are sixteen—*do* you think so?'—peeping out aslant from under her lashes, you know, so sweet and cunning. Oh, it was just *too*-too!

Well, I was perfectly honest and square with her; told her I hadn't a cent in the world but just the million-pound note she'd heard so much talk about, and *it* didn't belong to me; and that started her curiosity, and then I talked low, and told her the whole history right from the start, and it nearly killed her, laughing. What in the nation she could find to laugh about, I couldn't see, but there it was; every half minute some new detail would fetch her, and I would have to stop as much as a minute and a half to give her a chance to settle down again. Why, she laughed herself lame, she did indeed; I never saw anything like it. I mean I never saw a painful story—a story of a person's troubles and worries and fears—produce just *that* kind of effect before. So I loved her all the more, seeing she could be so cheerful when there wasn't anything to be cheerful about; for I might soon need that kind of wife, you know, the way things looked. Of course I told her we should have to wait a couple of years, till I could catch up on my salary; but she didn't mind that, only she hoped I would be as careful as possible in the matter of expenses, and not let them run the least risk of trenching on our third year's pay. Then she began to get a little worried, and wondered if we were making any mistake, and starting the salary on a higher figure for the first year than I would get. This was good sense, and it made me feel a little less confident than I had been feeling before; but it gave me a good business idea, and I brought it frankly out.

'Portia, dear, would you mind going with me that day, when I confront those old gentlemen?'

She shrank a little, but said:

'N-o; if my being with you would help hearten you. But—would it be quite proper, do you think?'

'No, I don't know that it would; in fact I'm afraid it wouldn't: but you see, there's so *much* dependent upon it that—'

'Then I'll go anyway, proper or improper,' she said, with a beautiful and generous enthusiasm. 'Oh, I shall be so happy to think I'm helping.'

'Helping, dear? Why, you'll be doing it all. You're so beautiful and so lovely and so winning, that with you there I can pile our salary up till I break those good old fellows, and they'll never have the heart to struggle.'

Sho! you should have seen the rich blood mount, and her happy eyes shine!

'You wicked flatterer! There isn't a word of truth in what you say, but still I'll go with you. Maybe it will teach you not to expect other people to look with your eyes.'

Were my doubts dissipated? Was my confidence restored? You may judge by this fact: privately I raised my salary to twelve hundred the first year on the spot. But I didn't tell her; I saved it for a surprise.

All the way home I was in the clouds, Hastings talking, I not hearing a word. When he and I entered my parlor, he brought me to myself with his fervent appreciations of my manifold comforts and luxuries.

'Let me just stand here a little and look my fill! Dear me, it's a palace; it's just a palace! And in it everything a body *could* desire, including cozy coal fire and supper standing ready. Henry, it doesn't merely make me realize how rich you are; it makes me realize, to the bone, to the marrow, how poor I am—how poor I am, and how miserable, how defeated, routed, annihilated!'

Plague take it! this language gave me the cold shudders. It scared me broad awake, and made me comprehend that I was standing on a half-inch crust, with a crater underneath. *I* didn't know I had been dreaming—that is, I hadn't been allowing myself to know it for a while back; but *now*—oh, dear! Deep in debt, not a cent in the world, a lovely girl's happiness or woe in my hands, and nothing in front of me but a salary which might never—oh, *would* never—materialize! Oh, oh, oh, I am ruined past hope; nothing can save me!'

'Henry, the mere unconsidered drippings of your daily income would—'

'Oh, my daily income! Here, down with this hot Scotch, and cheer up your soul. Here's with you! Or, no—you're hungry; sit down and—'

'Not a bite for me; I'm past it. I can't eat, these days; but I'll drink with you till I drop. Come!'

'Barrel for barrel, I'm with you! Ready? Here we go! Now, then, Lloyd, unreel your story while I brew.'

'Unreel it? What, again?'

'Again? What do you mean by that?'

'Why, I mean do you want to hear it *over* again?'

'Do I want to hear it *over* again? This *is* a puzzler. Wait; don't take any more of that liquid. You don't need it.'

'Look here, Henry, you alarm me. Didn't I tell you the whole story on the way here?'

'You?'

'Yes, I.'

'I'll be hanged if I heard a word of it.'

'Henry, this is a serious thing. It troubles me. What did you take up yonder at the minister's?'

Then it all flashed on me, and I owned up, like a man.

'I took the dearest girl in this world—prisoner!'

So then he came with a rush, and we shook, and shook, and shook till our hands ached; and he didn't blame me for not having heard a word of a story which had lasted while we walked three miles. He just sat down then, like the patient, good fellow he was, and told it all over again. Synopsized, it amounted to this: He had come to England with what he thought was a grand opportunity; he had an 'option' to sell the Gould and Curry Extension for the 'locators' of it, and keep all he could get over a million dollars. He had worked hard, had pulled every wire he knew of, had left no honest expedient untried, had spent nearly all the money he had in the world, had not been able to get a solitary capitalist to listen to him, and his option would run out at the end of the month. In a word, he was ruined. Then he jumped up and cried out:

'Henry, you can save me! You can save me, and you're the only man in the universe that can. Will you do it? *Won't* you do it?'

'Tell me how. Speak out, my boy.'

'Give me a million and my passage home for my 'option'! Don't, *don't* refuse!'

I was in a kind of agony. I was right on the point of coming out with the words, 'Lloyd, I'm a pauper myself—absolutely penniless, and in *debt!*' But a white-hot idea came flaming through my head, and I gripped my jaws together, and calmed myself down till I was as cold as capitalist. Then I said, in a commercial and self-possessed way:

'I will save you, Lloyd—'

'Then I'm already saved! God be merciful to you forever! If ever I—'

'Let me finish, Lloyd. I will save you, but not in that way; for that would not be fair to you, after your hard work, and the risks you've run. I don't need to buy mines; I can keep my capital moving, in a commercial center like London without that; it's what I'm at, all the time; but here is what I'll do. I know all about that mine, of course; I know its immense value, and can swear to it if anybody wishes it. You shall sell out inside of the fortnight for three millions cash, using my name freely, and we'll divide, share and share alike.'

Do you know, he would have danced the furniture to kindling wood in his insane joy, and broken everything on the place, if I hadn't tripped him up and tied him.

Then he lay there, perfectly happy, saying:

'I may use your name! Your name—think of it! Man, they'll flock in droves, these rich Londoners; they'll *fight* for that stock! I'm a made man, I'm a made man forever, and I'll never forget you as long as I live!'

In less than twenty-four hours London was abuzz! I hadn't anything to do, day after day, but sit at home, and say to all comers:

'Yes, I told him to refer to me. I know the man, and I know the mine. His character is above reproach, and the mine is worth far more than he asks for it.'

Meantime I spent all my evenings at the minister's with Portia. I didn't say a word to her about the mine; I saved it for a surprise. We talked salary; never anything but salary and love; sometimes love, sometimes salary, sometimes love and salary together. And my! the interest the minister's wife and daughter took in our little affair, and the endless ingenuities they invented to save us from interruption, and to keep the minister in the dark and unsuspicious—well, it was just lovely of them!

When my month was up, at last, I had a million dollars to my credit in the London and County Bank, and Hastings was fixed in the same way. Dressed at my level best, I drove by the house in Portland Place, judged by the look of things that my birds were home again, went on toward the minister's and got my precious, and we started back, talking salary with all our might. She was so excited and anxious that it made her just intolerably beautiful. I said:

'Dearie, the way you're looking it's a crime to strike for a salary a single penny under three thousand a year.'

'Henry, Henry, you'll ruin us!'

'Don't you be afraid. Just keep up those looks, and trust to me. It'll come out right.'

So as it turned out, I had to keep bolstering up *her* courage all the way. She kept pleading with me, and saying:

'Oh, please remember that if we ask for too much we may get no salary at all; and then what will become of us, with no way in the world to earn our living?'

We were ushered in by that same servant, and there they were, the two old gentlemen. Of course they were surprised to see that wonderful creature with me, but I said:

'It's all right, gentlemen; she is my future stay and helpmate.'

And I introduced them to her, and called them by name. It didn't surprise them; they knew I would know enough to consult the directory. They seated us, and were very polite to me, and very solicitous to relieve her from embarrassment, and put her as much at her ease as they could. Then I said:

'Gentlemen, I am ready to report.'

'We are glad to hear it,' said *my* man, 'for now we can decide the bet which my brother Abel and I made. If you have won for me, you shall have any situation in my gift. Have you the million-pound note?'

'Here it is, sir,' and I handed it to him.

'I've won!' he shouted, and slapped Abel on the back. '*Now* what do you say, brother?'

'I say he *did* survive, and I've lost twenty thousand pounds. I never would have believed it.'

'I've a further report to make,' I said, 'and a pretty long one. I want you to let me come soon, and detail my whole month's history; and I promise you it's worth hearing. Meantime, take a look at that.'

'What, man! Certificate of deposit for £200,000? Is it yours?'

'Mine. I earned it by thirty days' judicious use of that little loan you let me have. And the only use I made of it was to buy trifles and offer the bill in change.'

'Come, this is astonishing! It's incredible, man!'

'Never mind, I'll prove it. Don't take my word unsupported.'

But now Portia's turn was come to be surprised. Her eyes were spread wide, and she said:

'Henry, is that really your money? Have you been fibbing to me?'

'I have indeed, dearie. But you'll forgive me, *I* know.'

She put up an arch pout, and said:

'Don't you be so sure. You are a naughty thing to deceive me so!'

'Oh, you'll get over it, sweetheart, you'll get over it; it was only fun, you know. Come, let's be going.'

'But wait, wait! The situation, you know. I want to give you the situation,' said one man.

'Well,' I said, 'I'm just as grateful as I can be, but really I don't want one.'

'But you can have the very choicest one in my gift.'

'Thanks again, with all my heart; but I don't even want *that* one.'

'Henry, I'm ashamed of you. You don't half thank the good gentleman. May I do it for you?'

'Indeed you shall, dear, if you can improve it. Let us see you try.'

She walked to my man, got up in his lap, put her arm round his neck, and kissed him right on the mouth. Then the two old gentlemen shouted with laughter, but I was dumfounded, just petrified, as you may say. Portia said:

'Papa, he has said you haven't a situation in your gift that he'd take; and I feel just as hurt as—'

'My darling!—Is that your papa?'

'Yes; he's my step-papa, and the dearest one that ever was. You understand now, don't you, why I was able to laugh when you told me at the minister's, not knowing my relationships, what trouble and worry papa's and Uncle Abel's scheme was giving you?'

Of course I spoke right up, now, without any fooling, and went straight to the point.

'Oh, my dearest dear sir, I want to take back what I said. You *have* got a situation open that I want.'

'Name it.'

'Son-in-law.'

'Well, well, well! But you know, if you haven't ever served in that capacity, you of course can't furnish recommendations of a sort to satisfy the conditions of the contract, and so—'

'Try me—oh, do, I beg of you! Only just try me thirty or forty years, and if—'

'Oh, well, all right; it's but a little thing to ask. Take her along.'

Happy, we two? There're not words enough in the unabridged to describe it. And when London got the whole history, a day or two later, of my month's adventures with that bank-note, and how they ended, did London talk, and have a good time? Yes.

My Portia's papa took that friendly and hospitable bill back to the Bank of England and cashed it; then the Bank canceled it and made him a present of it, and he gave it to us at our wedding, and it has always hung in its frame in the sacredest place in our home, ever since. For it gave me my Portia. But for it I could not have remained in London, would not have appeared at the minister's, never should have met her. And so I always say, 'Yes, it's a million-pounder, as you see; but it never made but one purchase in its life, and *then* got the article for only about a tenth part of its value.'

The Man That Corrupted Hadleyburg

1

IT WAS MANY YEARS AGO. Hadleyburg was the most honest and upright town in all the region round about. It had kept that reputation unsmirched during three generations, and was prouder of it than of any other of its possessions. It was so proud of it, and so anxious to insure its perpetuation, that it began to teach the principles of honest dealing to its babies in the cradle, and made the like teachings the staple of their culture thenceforward through all the years devoted to their education. Also, throughout the formative years temptations were kept out of the way of the young people, so that their honesty could have every chance to harden and solidify, and become a part of their very bone. The neighboring towns were jealous of this honorable supremacy, and affected to sneer at Hadleyburg's pride in it and call it vanity; but all the same they were obliged to acknowledge that Hadleyburg was in reality an incorruptible town; and if pressed they would also acknowledge that the mere fact that a young man hailed from Hadleyburg was all the recommendation he needed when he went forth from his natal town to seek for responsible employment.

But at last, in the drift of time, Hadleyburg had the ill luck to offend a passing stranger—possibly without knowing it, certainly without caring, for Hadleyburg was sufficient unto itself, and cared not a rap for strangers or their opinions. Still, it would have been well to make an exception in this one's case, for he was a bitter man and revengeful. All through his wanderings during a whole year he kept his injury in mind, and gave all his leisure moments to trying to invent a compensating satisfaction for it. He contrived many plans, and all of them were good, but none of them was quite sweeping enough; the poorest of them would hurt a great many individuals, but what he wanted was a plan which would comprehend the entire town, and not let so much as one person escape unhurt. At last he had a fortunate idea, and when it fell into his brain it lit up his whole head with an evil joy. He began to form a plan at once, saying to himself, 'That is the thing to do—I will corrupt the town.'

Six months later he went to Hadleyburg, and arrived in a buggy at the house of the old cashier of the bank about ten at night. He got a sack out of the buggy, shouldered it, and staggered with it through the cottage yard, and knocked at the door. A woman's voice said 'Come in,' and he entered, and set his sack behind the stove in the parlor, saying politely to the old lady who sat reading the *Missionary Herald* by the lamp:

'Pray keep your seat, madam, I will not disturb you. There—now it is pretty well concealed; one would hardly know it was there. Can I see your husband a moment, madam?'

255

No, he was gone to Brixton, and might not return before morning.

'Very well, madam, it is no matter. I merely wanted to leave that sack in his care, to be delivered to the rightful owner when he shall be found. I am a stranger; he does not know me; I am merely passing through the town tonight to discharge a matter which has been long in my mind. My errand is now completed, and I go pleased and a little proud, and you will never see me again. There is a paper attached to the sack which will explain everything. Good night, madam.'

The old lady was afraid of the mysterious big stranger, and was glad to see him go. But her curiosity was roused, and she went straight to the sack and brought away the paper. It began as follows:

TO BE PUBLISHED: or, the right man sought out by private inquiry—either will answer. This sack contains gold coin weighing a hundred and sixty pounds four ounces—

'Mercy on us, and the door not locked!'

Mrs. Richards flew to it all in a tremble and locked it, then pulled down the window shades and stood frightened, worried, and wondering if there was anything else she could do toward making herself and the money more safe. She listened awhile for burglars, then surrendered to curiosity and went back to the lamp and finished reading the paper:

I am a foreigner, and am presently going back to my own country, to remain there permanently. I am grateful to America for what I have received at her hands during my long stay under her flag; and to one of her citizens—a citizen of Hadleyburg—I am especially grateful for a great kindness done me a year or two ago. Two great kindnesses, in fact. I will explain. I was a gambler. I say I WAS. I was a ruined gambler. I arrived in this village at night, hungry and without a penny. I asked for help—in the dark; I was ashamed to beg in the light. I begged of the right man. He gave me twenty dollars—that is to say, he gave me life, as I considered it. He also gave me fortune; for out of that money I have made myself rich at the gaming table. And finally, a remark which he made to me has remained with me to this day, and has at last conquered me; and in conquering has saved the remnant of my morals: I shall gamble no more. Now I have no idea who that man was, but I want him found, and I want him to have this money, to give away, throw away, or keep, as he pleases. It is merely my way of testifying my gratitude to him. If I could stay, I would find him myself; but no matter, he will be found. This is an honest town, an incorruptible town, and I know I can trust it without fear. This man can be identified by the remark which he made to me; I feel persuaded that he will remember it.

And now my plan is this: If you prefer to conduct the inquiry privately, do so. Tell the contents of this present writing to anyone who is likely to be the right man. If he shall answer, 'I am the man; the remark I made was so-and-so,' apply the test—to wit: open the sack, and in it you will find a sealed envelope containing that remark. If the remark mentioned by the candidate tallies with it, give him the money, and ask no further questions, for he is certainly the right man.

But if you shall prefer a public inquiry, then publish this present writing in the local paper—with these instructions added, to wit: Thirty days from now, let the candidate appear at the town hall at eight in the evening (Friday), and hand his remark, in a sealed envelope, to the Rev. Mr. Burgess (if he will be kind enough to act); and let Mr. Burgess there and then destroy the seals of the sack, open it, and see if the remark is correct: if correct, let the money be delivered, with my sincere gratitude, to my benefactor thus identified.

Mrs. Richards sat down, gently quivering with excitement, and was soon lost in thinkings—after this pattern: 'What a strange thing it is! . . . And what a fortune for that kind man who set his bread afloat upon the waters! . . . If it had only been my husband that did it!—for we are so poor, so old and poor! . . . ' Then, with a sigh—'But it was not my Edward; no, it was not he that gave a stranger twenty dollars. It is a pity, too; I see it now . . .' Then, with a shudder—'But it is *gambler's* money! the wages of sin: we couldn't take it; we couldn't touch it. I don't like to be near it; it seems a defilement.' She moved to a farther chair . . . 'I wish Edward would come, and take it to the bank; a burglar might come at any moment; it is dreadful to be here all alone with it.'

At eleven Mr. Richards arrived, and while his wife was saying, 'I am *so* glad you've come!' he was saying, 'I'm so tired—tired clear out; it is dreadful to be poor, and have to make these dismal journeys at my time of life. Always at the grind, grind, grind, on a salary—another man's slave, and he sitting at home in his slippers, rich and comfortable.'

'I am so sorry for you, Edward, you know that; but be comforted: we have our livelihood; we have our good name—'

'Yes, Mary, and that is everything. Don't mind my talk—it's just a moment's irritation and doesn't mean anything. Kiss me—there, it's all gone now, and I am not complaining any more. What have you been getting? What's in the sack?'

Then his wife told him the great secret. It dazed him for a moment; then he said:

'It weighs a hundred and sixty pounds? Why, Mary, it's for-ty thou-sand dollars—think of it—a whole fortune! Not ten men in this village are worth that much. Give me the paper.'

He skimmed through it and said:

'Isn't it an adventure! Why, it's a romance; it's like the impossible things one reads about in books, and never sees in life.' He was well stirred up now; cheerful, even gleeful. He tapped his old wife on the cheek, and said, humorously, 'Why, we're rich, Mary, rich; all we've got to do is to bury the money and burn the papers. If the gambler ever comes to inquire, we'll merely look coldly upon him and say: "What is this nonsense you are talking? We have never heard of you and your sack of gold before"; and then he would look foolish, and—'

'And in the meantime, while you are running on with your jokes, the money is still here, and it is fast getting along toward burglar-time.'

'True. Very well, what shall we do—make the inquiry private? No, not that; it would spoil the romance. The public method is better. Think what a noise it will make! And it will make all the other towns jealous; for no stranger would trust such a thing to any town but Hadleyburg, and they know it. It's a great card for us. I must get to the printing office now, or I shall be too late.'

'But—stop—stop—don't leave me here alone with it, Edward!'

But he was gone. For only a little while, however. Not far from his own house he met the editor-proprietor of the paper, and gave him the document, and said, 'Here is a good thing for you, Cox—put it in.'

'It may be too late, Mr. Richards, but I'll see.'

At home again he and his wife sat down to talk the charming mystery over; they were in no condition for sleep. The first question was, Who could the citizen have been who gave the stranger the twenty dollars? It seemed a simple one; both answered it in the same breath.

'Barclay Goodson.'

'Yes,' said Richards, 'he could have done it, and it would have been like him, but there's not another in the town.'

'Everybody will grant that, Edward—grant it privately, anyway. For six months, now, the village has been its own proper self once more—honest, narrow, self-righteous, and stingy.'

'It is what he always called it, to the day of his death—said it right out publicly, too.'

'Yes, and he was hated for it.'

'Oh, of course; but he didn't care. I reckon he was the best-hated man among us, except the Reverend Burgess.'

'Well, Burgess deserves it—he will never get another congregation here. Mean as the town is, it knows how to estimate *him*. Edward, doesn't it seem odd that the stranger should appoint Burgess to deliver the money?'

'Well, yes—it does. That is—that is—'

'Why so much that-*is*-ing? Would *you* select him?'

'Mary, maybe the stranger knows him better than this village does.'

'Much *that* would help Burgess!'

The husband seemed perplexed for an answer; the wife kept a steady eye upon him, and waited. Finally Richards said, with the hesitancy of one who is making a statement which is likely to encounter doubt:

'Mary, Burgess is not a bad man.'

His wife was certainly surprised.

'Nonsense!' she exclaimed.

'He is not a bad man. I know. The whole of his unpopularity had its foundation in that one thing—the thing that made so much noise.'

'That "one thing," indeed! As if that "one thing" wasn't enough, all by itself.'

'Plenty. Plenty. Only he wasn't guilty of it.'

'How you talk! Not guilty of it! Everybody knows he *was* guilty.'

'Mary, I give you my word—he was innocent.'

'I can't believe it, and I don't. How do you know?'

'It is a confession. I am ashamed, but I will make it. I was the only man who knew he was innocent. I could have saved him, and—and—well, you know how the town was wrought up—I hadn't the pluck to do it. It would have turned everybody against me. I felt mean, ever so mean; but I didn't dare; I hadn't the manliness to face that.'

Mary looked troubled, and for a while was silent. Then she said, stammeringly:

'I—I don't think it would have done for you to—to—One mustn't—er—public opinion—one has to be so careful—so—' It was a difficult road, and she got mired; but after a little she got started again. 'It was a great pity, but—Why, we couldn't afford it, Edward—we couldn't indeed. Oh, I wouldn't have had you do it for anything!'

'It would have lost us the good will of so many people, Mary; and then—and then—'

'What troubles me now is, what *he* thinks of us, Edward.'

'He? *He* doesn't suspect that I could have saved him.'

'Oh,' exclaimed the wife, in a tone of relief, 'I am glad of that. As long as he doesn't know that you could have saved him, he—he—well, that makes it a great deal better. Why, I might have known he didn't know, because he is always trying to be friendly with us, as little encouragement as we give him. More than once people have twitted me with it. There's the Wilsons, and the Wilcoxes, and the Harknesses, they take a mean pleasure in saying, '*Your friend* Burgess,' because they know it pesters me. I wish he wouldn't persist in liking us so; I can't think why he keeps it up.'

'I can explain it. It's another confession. When the thing was new and hot, and the town made a plan to ride him on a rail, my conscience hurt me so that I couldn't stand it, and I went privately and gave him notice, and he got out of the town and stayed out till it was safe to come back.'

'Edward! If the town had found it out—'

'*Don't*! It scares me yet, to think of it. I repented of it the minute it was done; and I was even afraid to tell you, lest your face might betray it to somebody. I didn't sleep any that night, for worrying. But after a few days I saw that no one was going to suspect me, and after that I got to feeling glad I did it. And I feel glad yet, Mary—glad through and through.'

'So do I, now, for it would have been a dreadful way to treat him. Yes, I'm glad; for really you did owe him that, you know. But, Edward, suppose it should come out yet, some day!'

'It won't.'

'Why?'

'Because everybody thinks it was Goodson.'

'Of course they would!'

'Certainly. And of course *he* didn't care. They persuaded poor old Sawlsberry to go and charge it on him, and he went blustering over there and did it. Goodson looked him over, like as if he was hunting for a place on him that he could despise the most, then he says, "So you are the Committee of Inquiry, are you?" Sawlsberry said that was about what he was. "Hm. Do they require particulars, or do you reckon a kind of a *general* answer will do?" "If they require particulars, I will come back. Mr. Goodson; I will take the general answer first." "Very well, then, tell them to go to hell—I reckon that's general enough. And I'll give you some advice, Sawlsberry; when you come back for the particulars, fetch a basket to carry the relics of yourself home in."'

'Just like Goodson; it's got all the marks. He had only one vanity: he thought he could give advice better than any other person.'

'It settled the business, and saved us, Mary. The subject was dropped.'

'Bless you, I'm not doubting *that*.'

Then they took up the gold-sack mystery again, with strong interest. Soon the conversation began to suffer breaks—interruptions caused by absorbed thinkings. The breaks grew more and more frequent. At last Richards lost himself wholly in thought. He sat long, gazing vacantly at the floor, and by and by he began to punctuate his thoughts with little nervous movements of his hands that seemed to indicate vexation. Meantime his wife too had relapsed into a thoughtful silence, and her movements were beginning to show a troubled discomfort. Finally Richards got up and strode aimlessly about the room, plowing his hands through his hair, much as a somnambulist might do who was having a bad dream. Then he seemed to arrive at a definite purpose; and without a word he put on his hat and passed quickly out of the house. His wife sat brooding, with a drawn face, and did not seem to be aware that she was alone. Now and then she murmured, 'Lead us not into t—... but—but—we are so poor, so poor! ... Lead us not into. ... Ah, who would be hurt by it?—and no one would ever know. ... Lead us. ...' The voice died out in mumblings. After a little she glanced up and muttered in a half-frightened, half-glad way:

'He is gone! But, oh dear, he may be too late—too late .... Maybe not—maybe there is still time.' She rose and stood thinking, nervously clasping and unclasping her hands. A slight shudder shook her frame, and she said, out of a dry throat, 'God forgive me—it's awful to think such things—but ... Lord, how we are made—how strangely we are made!'

She turned the light low, and slipped stealthily over and kneeled down by the sack and felt of its ridgy sides with her hands, and fondled them lovingly; and there was a gloating light in her poor old eyes. She fell into fits of absence; and came half out of them at times to mutter, 'If we had only waited!—oh, if we had only waited a little, and not been in such a hurry!'

Meantime Cox had gone home from his office and told his wife all about the strange thing that had happened, and they had talked it over eagerly, and guessed that the late Goodson was the only man in the town who could have helped a suffering stranger with so noble a sum as twenty dollars. Then there was a pause, and the two became thoughtful and silent. And by and by nervous and fidgety. At last the wife said, as if to herself:

'Nobody knows this secret but the Richardses ... and us ... nobody.'

The husband came out of his thinkings with a slight start, and gazed wistfully at his wife, whose face was become very pale; then he hesitatingly rose, and glanced furtively at his hat, then at his wife—a sort of mute inquiry. Mrs. Cox swallowed once or twice, with her hand at her throat, then in place of speech she nodded her head. In a moment she was alone, and mumbling to herself.

And now Richards and Cox were hurrying through the deserted streets, from opposite directions. They met, panting, at the foot of the printing office stairs; by the night light there they read each other's face. Cox whispered:

'Nobody knows about this but us?'

The whispered answer was:

'Not a soul—on honor, not a soul!'

'If it isn't too late to—'

The men were starting upstairs; at this moment they were overtaken by a boy, and Cox asked:

'Is that you, Johnny?'

'Yes, sir.'

'You needn't ship the early mail—nor *any* mail; wait till I tell you.'

'It's already gone, sir.'

'*Gone*? It had the sound of an unspeakable disappointment in it.

'Yes, sir. Timetable for Brixton and all the towns beyond changed today, sir—had to get the papers in twenty minutes earlier than common. I had to rush; if I had been two minutes later—'

The men turned and walked slowly away, not waiting to hear the rest. Neither of them spoke during ten minutes; then Cox said, in a vexed tone:

'What possessed you to be in such a hurry, *I* can't make out.'

The answer was humble enough:

'I see it now, but somehow I never thought, you know, until it was too late. But the next time—'

'Next time be hanged! It won't come in a thousand years.'

Then the friends separated without a good night, and dragged themselves home with the gait of mortally stricken men. At their homes their wives sprang up with an eager 'Well?'—then saw the answer with their eyes and sank down sorrowing, without waiting for it to come in words. In both houses a discussion followed of a heated sort—a new thing; there had been discussions before, but not heated ones, not ungentle ones. The discussions tonight were a sort of seeming plagiarisms of each other. Mrs. Richards said:

'If you had only waited, Edward—if you had only stopped to think; but no, you must run straight to the printing office and spread it all over the world.'

'It *said* publish it.'

'That is nothing; it also said do it privately, if you liked. There, now—is that true, or not?'

'Why, yes—yes, it is true; but when I thought what a stir it would make, and what a compliment it was to Hadleyburg that a stranger should trust it so—'

'Oh, certainly, I know all that; but if you had only stopped to think, you would have seen that you *couldn't* find the right man, because he is in his grave, and hasn't left chick nor child nor relation behind him; and as long as the money went to somebody that awfully needed it, and nobody would be hurt by it, and—and—'

She broke down, crying. Her husband tried to think of some comforting thing to say, and presently came out with this:

'But after all, Mary, it must be for the best—it *must* be; we know that. And we must remember that it was so ordered—'

'Ordered! Oh, everything's *ordered*, when a person has to find some way out when he has been stupid. Just the same, it was *ordered* that the money should come to us in this special way, and it was you that must take it on yourself to go meddling with the designs of Providence—and who gave you the right? It was wicked, that is what it was—just blaspemous presumption, and no more becoming to a meek and humble professor of—'

'But, Mary, you know how we have been trained all our lives long, like the whole village, till it is absolutely second nature to us to stop not a single moment to think when there's an honest thing to be done—'

'Oh, I know it, I know it—it's been one everlasting training and training and training in honesty—honesty shielded, from the very cradle, against every possible temptation, and so it's *artificial* honesty, and weak as water when temptation comes, as we have seen this night. God knows I never had shade nor shadow of a doubt of my petrified and indestructible honesty until now—and now, under the very first big and real temptation, I—Edward, it is my belief that this town's honesty is as rotten as mine is; as rotten as yours is. It is a mean town, a hard, stingy town, and hasn't a virtue in the world but this honesty it is so celebrated for and so conceited about; and so help me, I do believe that if ever the day comes that its honesty falls under great temptation, its grand reputation will go to ruin like a house of cards. There, now, I've made confession, and I feel better; I am a humbug, and I've been one all my life, without knowing it. Let no man call me honest again—I will not have it.'

'I—well, Mary, I feel a good deal as you do; I certainly do. It seems strange, too, so strange. I never could have believed it—never.'

A long silence followed; both were sunk in thought. At last the wife looked up and said:

'I know what you are thinking, Edward.'

Richards had the embarrassed look of a person who is caught.

'I am ashamed to confess it, Mary, but—'

'It's no matter, Edward, I was thinking the same question myself.'

'I hope so. State it.'

'You were thinking, if a body could only guess out *what the remark was* that Goodson made to the stranger.'

'It's perfectly true. I feel guilty and ashamed. And you?'

'I'm past it. Let us make a pallet here; we've got to stand watch till the bank vault opens in the morning and admits the sack . . . . Oh dear, oh dear—if we hadn't made the mistake!'

The pallet was made, and Mary said:

'The open sesame—what could it have been? I do wonder what that remark could have been? But come; we will get to bed now.'

'And sleep?'

'No: think.'

'Yes, think.'

By this time the Coxes too had completed their spat and their reconciliation, and were turning in—to think, to think, and toss, and fret, and worry over what the remark could possibly have been which Goodson made to the stranded derelict; that golden remark; that remark worth forty thousand dollars, cash.

The reason that the village telegraph office was open later than usual that night was this: The foreman of Cox's paper was the local representative of the Associated Press. One might say its honorary representative, for it wasn't four times a year that he could furnish thirty words that would be accepted. But this time it was different. His dispatch stating what he had caught got an instant answer:

Send the whole thing—all the details—twelve hundred words.

A colossal order! The foreman filled the bill; and he was the proudest man in the state. By breakfast time the next morning the name of Hadleyburg the Incorruptible was on every lip in America, from Montreal to the Gulf, from the glaciers of Alaska to the orange groves of Florida; and millions and millions of people were discussing the stranger and his money sack, and wondering if the right man would be found, and hoping some more news about the matter would come soon—right away.

2

HADLEYBURG VILLAGE woke up world-celebrated—astonished—happy—vain. Vain beyond imagination. Its nineteen principal citizens and their wives went about shaking hands with each other, and beaming, and smiling, and congratulating, and saying *this* thing adds a new word to the dictionary— *Hadleyburg*, synonym for *incorruptible*—destined to live in dictionaries forever! And the minor and unimportant citizens and their wives went around acting in much the same way. Everybody ran to the bank to see the gold sack; and before noon grieved and envious crowds began to flock in from Brixton and all neighboring towns; and that afternoon and next day reporters began to arrive from everywhere to verify the sack and its history and write the whole thing up anew, and make dashing freehand pictures of the sack, and of Richard's house, and the bank, and the Presbyterian church, and the Baptist church, and the public square, and the town hall where the test would be applied and the money delivered; and damnable portraits of the Richardses, and Pinkerton the banker, and Cox, and the foreman, and Reverand Burgess, and the postmaster—and even of Jack Halliday, who was the loafing, good-natured, no-account, irreverent fisherman, hunter, boys' friend, stray-dogs' friend, typical 'Sam Lawson' of the town. The little mean, smirking, oily Pinkerton showed the sack to all comers, and rubbed his sleek palms together pleasantly, and enlarged upon the town's fine old reputation for honesty and upon this wonderful endorsement of it, and hoped and believed that the example would now spread far and wide over the American world, and be epoch-making in the matter of moral regeneration. And so on, and so on.

By the end of a week things had quieted down again; the wild intoxication of pride and joy had sobered to a soft, sweet, silent delight—a sort of deep, nameless, unutterable content. All faces bore a look of peaceful, holy happiness.

Then a change came. It was a gradual change: so gradual that its beginnings were hardly noticed; maybe were not noticed at all, except by Jack Halliday, who always noticed everything; and always made fun of it, too, no matter what it was. He began to throw out chaffing remarks about people not looking quite so happy as they did a day or two ago; and next he claimed that the new aspect was deepening to positive sadness; next, that it was taking on a sick look; and finally he said that everybody was become so moody, thoughtful, and absent-minded that he could rob the meanest man in town of a cent out of the bottom of his breeches pocket and not disturb his revery.

At this stage—or at about this stage—a saying like this was dropped at bedtime—with a sigh, usually—by the head of each of the nineteen principal households: 'Ah, what *could* have been the remark that Goodson made?'

And straightway—with a shudder—came this, from the man's wife:

'Oh, *don't*! What horrible thing are you mulling in your mind? Put it away from you, for God's sake!'

But that question was wrung from those men again the next night—and got the same retort. But weaker.

And the third night the men uttered the question yet again—with anguish, and absently. This time—and the following night—the wives fidgeted feebly, and tried to say something. But didn't.

And the night after that they found their tongues and responded—longingly:

'Oh, if we *could* only guess!'

Halliday's comments grew daily more and more sparklingly disagreeable and disparaging. He went diligently about, laughing at the town, individually and in mass. But his laugh was the only one left in the village: it fell upon a hollow and mournful vacancy and emptiness. Not even a smile was findable anywhere. Halliday carried a cigar box around on a tripod, saying that it was a camera, and halted all passers and aimed the thing and said, 'Ready!—now look pleasant, please,' but not even this capital joke could surprise the dreary faces into any softening.

So three weeks passed—one week was left. It was Saturday evening—after supper. Instead of the aforetime Saturday evening flutter and bustle and shopping and larking, the streets were empty and desolate. Richards and his old wife sat apart in their little parlor—miserable and thinking. This was become their evening habit now: the lifelong habit which had preceded it, of reading, knitting, and contented chat, or receiving or paying neighborly calls, was dead and gone and forgotten, ages ago—two or three weeks ago; nobody talked now, nobody read, nobody visited—the whole village sat at home, sighing, worrying, silent. Trying to guess out that remark.

The postman left a letter. Richards glanced listlessly at the superscription and the postmark—unfamiliar, both—and tossed the letter on the table and resumed his might-have-beens and his hopeless dull miseries where he had left them off. Two or three hours later his wife got wearily up and was going away to bed without a good-night—custom now—but she stopped near the letter and eyed it awhile with a dead interest, then broke it open, and began to skim it over. Richards, sitting there with his chair tilted back against the wall and his chin between his knees, heard something fall. It was his wife. He sprang to her side, but she cried out:

'Leave me alone, I am too happy. Read the letter—read it!'

He did. He devoured it, his brain reeling. The letter was from a distant state, and it said:

I am a stranger to you, but no matter: I have something to tell. I have just arrived home from Mexico, and learned about that episode. Of course you do not know who made that remark, but I know, and I am the only person living that does know. It was GOODSON. I knew him well, many years ago. I passed through your village that very night, and was his guest till the midnight train came along. I overheard him make that remark to the stranger in the dark—it was in Hale Alley. He and I talked of it the rest of the way home, and while smoking in his house. He mentioned many of your villagers in the course of his talk—most of them in a very uncomplimentary way, but two or three favorably; among these latter yourself. I say 'favorably'—nothing stronger. I remember his saying he did not actually LIKE any person in the town—not one; but that you—I THINK he said you—am almost sure—had done him a very great service once, possibly without knowing the full value of it, and he wished he had a fortune, he would leave it to you when he died, and a curse apiece for the rest of the citizens. Now, then, if it was you that did him that service, you are his legitimate heir, and entitled to the sack of gold. I know that I can trust to your honor and honesty, for in a citizen of Hadleyburg these virtues are an unfailing inheritance, and so I am going to reveal to you the remark, well satisfied that if you are not the right man you will seek and find the right one and see that poor Goodson's debt of gratitude for the service referred to is paid. This is the remark: 'YOU ARE FAR FROM BEING A BAD MAN: GO, AND REFORM.'

HOWARD L. STEPHENSON.

'Oh, Edward, the money is ours, and I am so grateful, *oh*, so grateful—kiss me, dear, it's forever since we kissed—and we needed it so—the money—and now you are free of Pinkerton and his bank, and nobody's slave any more; it seems to me I could fly for joy.'

It was a happy half-hour that the couple spent there on the settee caressing each other; it was the old days come again—days that had begun with their courtship and lasted without a break till the stranger brought the deadly money. By and by the wife said:

'Oh, Edward, how lucky it was you did him that grand service, poor Goodson! I never liked him, but I love him now. And it was fine and beautiful of you never to mention it or brag about it.' Then, with a touch of reproach, 'But you ought to have told *me*, Edward, you ought to have told your wife, you know.'

'Well, I—er,—well, Mary, you see—'

'Now stop hemming and hawing, and tell me about it, Edward. I always loved you, and now I'm proud of you. Everybody believes there was only one good generous soul in this village, and now it turns out that you—Edward, why don't you tell me?'

'Well—er—er—Why, Mary, I can't!'

'You *can't*? *Why* can't you?'

'You see, he—well, he—he made me promise I wouldn't.'

The wife looked him over, and said, very slowly.

'Made—you—promise? Edward, what do you tell me that for?'

'Mary, do you think I would lie?'

She was troubled and silent for a moment, then she laid her hand within his and said:

'No . . . no. We have wandered far enough from our bearings—God spare us that! In all your life you have never uttered a lie. But now—now that the foundations of things seem to be crumbling from under us, we—we—' She lost her voice for a moment, then said, brokenly, 'Lead us not into temptation . . . . I think you made the promise, Edward. Let it rest so. Let us keep away from that ground. Now—that is all gone by; let us be happy again; it is no time for clouds.'

Edward found it something of an effort to comply, for his mind kept wandering—trying to remember what the service was that he had done Goodson.

The couple lay awake the most of the night, Mary happy and busy, Edward busy but not so happy. Mary was planning what she would do with the money. Edward was trying to recall that service. At first his conscience was sore on account of the lie he had told Mary—if it was a lie. After much reflection—suppose it *was* a lie? What then? Was it such a great matter? Aren't we always *acting* lies? Then why not *tell* them? Look at Mary—look what she had done. While he was hurrying off on his honest errand, what was she doing? Lamenting because the papers hadn't been destroyed and the money kept! Is theft better than lying?

That point lost its sting—the lie dropped into the background and left comfort behind it. The next point came to the front: *Had* he rendered that service? Well, here was Goodson's own evidence as reported in Stephenson's letter; there could be no better evidence than that—it was even *proof* that he had rendered it. Of course. So that point was settled. . . . No, not quite. He recalled with a wince that this unknown Mr. Stephenson was just a trifle unsure as to whether the performer of it was Richards or some other—and, oh dear, he had put Richards on his honor! He must himself decide whither that money must go—and Mr. Stephenson was not doubting that if he was the wrong man he would go honorably and find the right one. Oh, it was odious to put a man in such a situation—ah, why couldn't Stephenson have left out that doubt! What did he want to intrude that for?

Further reflection. How did it happen that *Richards'* name remained in Stephenson's mind as indicating the right man, and not some other man's name? That looked good. Yes, that looked very good. In fact, it went on looking better and better, straight along—until by and by it grew into positive *proof*. And then Richards put the matter at once out of his mind, for he had a private instinct that a proof once established is better left so.

He was feeling reasonably comfortable now, but there was still one other detail that kept pushing itself on his notice: of course he had done that service—that was settled; but what *was* that service? He must recall it—he would not go to sleep till he had recalled it; it would make his peace of mind perfect. And so he thought and thought. He thought of a dozen things— possible services, even probable services—but none of them seemed adequate, none of them seemed large enough, none of them seemed worth the money—worth the fortune Goodson had wished he could leave in his will. And besides, he couldn't remember having done them, anyway. Now, then— now, then—what *kind* of a service would it be that would make a man so inordinately grateful? Ah—the saving of his soul! That must be it. Yes, he could remember, now, how he once set himself the task of converting Goodson, and labored at it as much as—he was going to say three months; but upon closer examination it shrunk to a month, then to a week, then to a day, then to nothing. Yes, he remembered now, and with unwelcome vividness, that Goodson had told him to go to thunder and mind his own business—*he* wasn't hankering to follow Hadleyburg to heaven!

So that solution was a failure—he hadn't saved Goodson's soul. Richards was discouraged. Then after a little came another idea: had he saved Goodson's property? No, that wouldn't do—he hadn't any. His life? That is it! Of course. Why, he might have thought of it before. This time he was on the right track, sure. His imagination mill was hard at work in a minute, now.

Thereafter during a stretch of two exhausting hours he was busy saving Goodson's life. He saved it in all kinds of difficult and perilous ways. In every case he got it saved satisfactorily up to a certain point; then, just as he was beginning to get well persuaded that it had really happened, a troublesome detail would turn up which made the whole thing impossible. As in the matter of drowning, for instance. In that case he had swum out and tugged Goodson ashore in an unconscious state with a great crowd looking on and applauding, but when he had got it all thought out and was just beginning to remember all about it, a whole swarm of disqualifying details arrived on the ground: the town would have known of the circumstance, Mary would have known it, it would glare like a limelight in his own memory instead of being an inconspicuous service which he had possibly rendered 'without knowing its full value.' And at this point he remembered that he couldn't swim, anyway.

Ah—*there* was a point which he had been overlooking from the start: it had to be a service which he had rendered 'possibly without knowing the full value of it.' Why, really, that ought to be an easy hunt—much easier than those others. And sure enough, by and by he found it. Goodson, years and years go, came near marrying a very sweet and pretty girl, named Nancy Hewitt, but in some way or other the match had been broken off; the girl died, Goodson remained a bachelor, and by and by became a soured one and a frank despiser of the human species. Soon after the girl's death the village found out, or thought it had found out, that she carried a spoonful of Negro blood in her veins. Richards worked at these details a good while, and in the end he thought he remembered things concerning them which must have gotten mislaid in his memory through long neglect. He seemed to dimly remember that it was *he* that found out about the Negro blood; that it was he that told the village; that the village told Goodson where they got it; that he thus saved Goodson from marrying the tainted girl; that he had done him this great service 'without knowing the full value of it,' in fact without knowing that he *was* doing it; but that Goodson knew the value of it, and what a narrow escape he had had, and so went to his grave grateful to his benefactor and wishing he had a fortune to leave him. It was all clear and simple now, and the more he went over it the more luminous and certain it grew; and at last, when he nestled to sleep satisfied and happy, he remembered the whole thing just as if it had been yesterday. In fact, he dimly remembered Goodson's *telling* him his gratitude once. Meantime Mary had spent six thousand dollars on a new house for herself and a pair of slippers for her pastor, and then had fallen peacefully to rest.

That same Saturday evening the postman had delivered a letter to each of the other principal citizens—nineteen letters in all. No two of the envelopes were alike, and no two of the superscriptions were in the same hand, but the letters inside were just like each other in every detail but one. They were exact copies of the letter received by Richards—handwriting and all—and were all signed by Stephenson, but in place of Richards' name each receiver's own name appeared.

All night long eighteen principal citizens did what their caste-brother Richards was doing at the same time—they put in their energies trying to remember what notable service it was that they had unconsciously done Barclay Goodson. In no case was it a holiday job; still they succeeded.

And while they were at this work, which was difficult, their wives put in the night spending the money, which was easy. During that one night the nineteen wives spent an average of seven thousand dollars each out of the forty thousand in the sack—a hundred and thirty-three thousand altogether.

Next day there was a surprise for Jack Halliday. He noticed that the faces of the nineteen chief citizens and their wives bore that expression of peaceful and holy happiness again. He could not understand it, neither was he able to invent any remarks about it that could damage it or disturb it. And so it was his turn to be dissatisfied with life. His private guesses at the reasons for the happiness failed in all instances, upon examination. When he met Mrs. Wilcox and noticed the placid ecstacy in her face, he said to himself, 'Her cat has had kittens'—and went and asked the cook: it was not so; the cook had detected the happiness, but did not know the cause. When Halliday found the duplicate ecstacy in the face of 'Shadbelly' Billson (village nickname), he was sure some neighbor of Billison's had broken his leg, but inquiry showed that this had not happened. The subdued ecstacy in Gregory Yate's face could mean but one thing—he was a mother-in-law short: it was another mistake. 'And Pinkerton— Pinkerton—he has collected ten cents that he thought he was going to lose.' And so on, and so on. In some cases the guesses had to remain in doubt, in the others they proved distinct errors. In the end Halliday said to himself, 'Anyway it foots up that there's nineteen Hadleyburg families temporarily in heaven: I don't know how it happened; I only know Providence is off duty today.'

An architect and builder from the next state had lately ventured to set up a small business in this unpromising village, and his sign had now been hanging out a week. Not a customer yet; he was a discouraged man, and sorry he had come. But his weather changed suddenly now. First one and then another chief citizen's wife said to him privately:

'Come to my house Monday week—but say nothing about it for the present. We think of building.'

He got eleven invitations that day. That night he wrote his daughter and broke off her match with her student. He said she could marry a mile higher than that.

Pinkerton the banker and two or three other well-to-do men planned country-seats—but waited. That kind don't count their chickens until they are hatched.

The Wilsons devised a grand new thing—a fancy-dress ball. They made no actual promises, but told all their acquaintanceship in confidence that they were thinking the matter over and thought they should give it—'and if we do, you will be invited, of course.' People were surprised, and said, one to another, 'Why, they are crazy, those poor Wilsons, they can't afford it.' Several among the nineteen said privately to their husbands, 'It is a good idea: we will keep still till their cheap thing is over, then *we* will give one that will make it sick.'

The days drifted along, and the bill of future squanderings rose higher and higher, wider and wider, more and more foolish and reckless. It began to look as if every member of the nineteen would not only spend his whole forty thousand dollars before receiving day, but be actually in debt by the time he got the money. In some cases lightheaded people did not stop with planning to spend, they really spent—on credit. They bought land, mortgages, farms, speculative stocks, fine clothes, horses, and various other things, paid down the bonus, and made themselves liable for the rest—at ten days. Presently the sober second thought came, and Halliday noticed that a ghastly anxiety was beginning to show up in a good many faces. Again he was puzzled, and didn't know what to make of it. 'The Wilcox kittens aren't dead, for they weren't born; nobody's broken a leg; there's no shrinkage in mother-in-laws; *nothing* has happened—it is an unsolvable mystery.'

There was another puzzled man, too—the Rev. Mr. Burgess. For days, wherever he went, people seemed to follow him or to be watching out for him; and if he ever found himself in a retired spot, a member of the nineteen would be sure to appear, thrust an envelope privately into his hand, whisper 'To be opened at the town hall Friday evening,' then vanish away like a guilty thing. He was expecting that there might be one claimant for the sack,—doubtful, however, Goodson being dead—but it never occurred to him that all this crowd might be claimants. When the great Friday came at last, he found that he had nineteen envelopes.

3

THE TOWN HALL had never looked finer. The platform at the end of it was backed by a showy draping of flags; at intervals along the walls were festoons of flags; the gallery fronts were clothed in flags; the supporting columns were swathed in flags; all this was to impress the stranger, for he would be there in considerable force, and in a large degree he would be connected with the press. The house was full. The 412 fixed seats were occupied; also the 68 extra chairs which had been packed into the aisles; the steps of the platform were occupied; some distinguished strangers were given seats on the platform; at the horseshoe of tables which fenced the front and sides of the platform sat a strong force of special correspondents who had come from everywhere. It was the best-dressed house the town had ever produced. There were some tolerably expensive toilets there, and in several cases the ladies who wore them had the look of being unfamiliar with that kind of clothes. At least the town thought they had that look, but the notion could have arisen from the town's knowledge of the fact that these ladies had never inhabited such clothes before.

The gold sack stood on a little table at the front of the platform where all the house could see it. The bulk of the house gazed at it with a burning interest, a mouth-watering interest, a wistful and pathetic interest; a minority of nineteen couples gazed at it tenderly, lovingly, proprietarily, and the male half of this minority kept saying over to themselves the moving little impromptu speeches of thankfulness for the audience's applause and congratulations which they were presently going to get up and deliver. Every now and then one of these got a piece of paper out of his vest-pocket and privately glanced at it to refresh his memory.

Of course there was a buzz of conversation going on—there always is; but at last when the Rev. Mr. Burgess rose and laid his hand on the sack he could hear the microbes gnaw, the place was so still. He related the curious history of the sack, then went on to speak in warm tones of Hadleyburg's old and well-earned reputation for spotless honesty, and of the town's just pride in this reputation. He said that this reputation was a treasure of priceless value; that under Providence its value had now become inestimably enhanced, for the recent episode had spread this fame far and wide, and thus had focused the eyes of the American world upon this village, and made its name for all time, as he hoped and believed, a synonym for commercial incorruptibility. [*Applause.*] 'And who is to be the guardian of this noble treasure—the community as a whole? No! The responsibility is individual, not communal. From this day forth each and every one of you is in his own person its special guardian, and individually responsible that no harm shall come to it. Do you—does each of you—accept this great trust? [*Tumultuous assent.*] Then all is well. Transmit it to your children and to your children's children. Today your purity is beyond reproach—see to it that it shall remain so. Today there is not a person in your community who could be beguiled to touch a penny not his own—see to it that you abide in this grace. ['*We will! we will!*'] This is not the place to make comparisons between ourselves and other communities—some of them ungracious toward us; they have their ways, we have ours; let us be content. [*Applause.*] I am done. Under my hand, my friends, rests a stranger's eloquent recognition of what we are; through him the world will always henceforth know what we are. We do not know who he is, but in your name I utter your gratitude, and ask you to raise your voices in endorsement.'

The house rose in a body and made the walls quake with the thunders of its thankfulness for the space of a long minute. Then it sat down, and Mr. Burgess took an envelope out of his pocket. The house held its breath when he slit the envelope open and took from it a slip of paper. He read its contents—slowly and impressively—the audience listening with tranced attention to this magic document, each of whose words stood for an ingot of gold.

' "*The remark which I made to the distressed stranger was this: 'You are very far from being a bad man: go, and reform.'* " ' Then he continued:

'We shall know in a moment now whether the remark here quoted corresponds with the one concealed in the sack; and if that shall prove to be so—and it undoubtedly will—this sack of gold belongs to a fellow citizen who will henceforth stand before the nation as the symbol of the special virtue which has made our town famous throughout the land—Mr. Billson!'

The house had gotten itself all ready to burst into the proper tornado of applause; but instead of doing it, it seemed stricken with a paralysis; there was a deep hush for a moment or two, then a wave of whispered murmurs swept the place—of about this tenor: '*Billson!* oh, come, this is *too* thin! Twenty dollars to a stranger—or *anybody*—*Billson!* Tell it to the marines!' And now at this point the house caught its breath all of a sudden in a new access of astnoishment, for it discovered that whereas in one part of the hall Deacon Billson was standing up with his head meekly bowed, in another part of it Lawyer Wilson was doing the same. There was a wondering silence now for a while.

Everybody was puzzled, and nineteen couples were surprised and indignant.

Billson and Wilson turned and stared at each other. Billson asked, bitingly:

'Why do *you* rise, Mr. Wilson?'

'Because I have a right to. Perhaps you will be good enough to explain to the house why *you* rise?'

'With great pleasure. Because I wrote that paper.'

'It is an impudent falsity! I wrote it myself.'

It was Burgess's turn to be paralyzed. He stood looking vacantly at first one of the men and then the other, and did not seem to know what to do. The house was stupefied. Lawyer Wilson spoke up, now, and said:

'I ask the Chair to read the name signed to that paper.'

That brought the Chair to itself, and it read out the name:

' "John Wharton *Billson*." '

'There!' shouted Billson. 'What have you got to say for yourself, now? And

what kind of apology are you going to make to me and to this insulted house
for the imposture which you have attempted to play here?'

'No apologies are due, sir; and as for the rest of it, I publicly charge you with
pilfering my note from Mr. Burgess and substituting a copy of it signed with
your own name. There is no other way by which you could have gotten hold of
the test-remark; I alone, of living men, possessed the secret of its wording.'

There was likely to be a scandalous state of things if this went on; everybody
noticed with distress that the shorthand scribes were scribbling like mad; many
people were crying 'Chair, Chair! Order! Order!' Burgess rapped with his
gavel, and said:

'Let us not forget the proprieties due. There has evidently been a mistake
somewhere, but surely that is all. If Mr. Wilson gave me an envelope—and I
remember now that he did—I still have it.'

He took one out of his pocket, opened it, glanced at it, looked surprised and
worried, and stood silent a few moments. Then he waved his hand in a
wandering and mechanical way, and made an effort or two to say something,
then gave it up, despondently. Several voices cried out:

'Read it! Read it! What is it?'

So he began in a dazed and sleepwalker fashion:

'*"The remark which I made to the unhappy stranger was this: 'You are far from being
a bad man.* [The house gazed at him, marveling.] *Go, and reform.'"* [*Murmurs:*
'Amazing! what can this mean?'] This one,' said the Chair, 'is signed Thurlow
G. Wilson.'

'There!' cried Wilson, 'I reckon that settles it! I knew perfectly well my note
was purloined.'

'Purloined!' retorted Billson. 'I'll let you know that neither you nor any man
of your kidney must venture to—'

The Chair. 'Order, gentlemen, order! Take your seats, both of you, please.'

They obeyed, shaking their heads and grumbling angrily. The house was
profoundly puzzled; it did not know what to do with this curious emergency.
Presently Thompson got up. Thompson was the hatter. He would have liked
to be a Nineteener; but such was not for him: his stock of hats was not
considerable enough for the position. He said:

'Mr. Chairman, if I may be permitted to make a suggestion, can both of
these gentlemen be right? I put it to you, sir, can both have happened to say
the very same words to the stranger? It seems to me—'

The tanner got up and interrupted him. The tanner was a disgruntled man;
he believed himself entitled to be a Nineteener, but he couldn't get recognition. It made him a little unpleasant in his ways and speech. Said he:

'Sho, *that's* not the point! *That* could happen—twice in a hundred years—but
not the other thing. *Neither* of them gave the twenty dollars!'

[*A ripple of applause.*]

Billson. 'I did!'

Wilson. 'I did!'

Then each accused the other of pilfering.

The Chair. 'Order! Sit down, if you please—both of you. Neither of the notes
has been out of my possession at any moment.'

A Voice. 'Good—that settles *that*!'

The Tanner. 'Mr. Chairman, one thing is now plain: one of these men has
been eavesdropping under the other one's bed, and filching family secrets. If

it is not unparliamentary to suggest it, I will remark that both are equal to it. [*The Chair.* 'Order! Order!'] I withdraw the remark, sir, and will confine myself to suggesting that *if* one of them has overheard the other reveal the test-remark to his wife, we shall catch him now.'

A Voice. 'How?'

The Tanner. 'Easily. The two have not quoted the remark in exactly the same words. You would have noticed that, if there hadn't been a considerable stretch of time and an exciting quarrel inserted between the two readings.'

A Voice. 'Name the difference.'

The Tanner. 'The word *very* is in Billson's note, and not in the other.'

Many Voices. 'That's so—he's right!'

The Tanner. 'And so, if the Chair will examine the test-remark in the sack, we shall know which of these two frauds— [*The Chair.* 'Order!']—which of these two adventurers— [*The Chair.* 'Order! Order!']—which of these two gentle-men—[*Laughter and applause*]—is entitled to wear the belt as being the first dishonest blatherskite ever bred in this town—which he has dishonored, and which will be a sultry place for him from now out!' [*Vigorous applause.*]

Many Voices. 'Open it—open the sack!'

Mr. Burgess made a slit in the sack, slid his hand in and brought out an envelope. In it were a couple of folded notes. He said:

'One of these is marked, "Not to be examined until all written communications which have been addressed to the Chair—if any—shall have been read." The other is marked "*The Test.*" Allow me. It is worded—to wit:

'"I do not require that the first half of the remark which was made to me by my benefactor shall be quoted with exactness, for it was not striking, and could be forgotten; but its closing fifteen words are quite striking, and I think easily rememberable; unless *these* shall be accurately reproduced, let the applicant be regarded as an impostor. My benefactor began by saying he seldom gave advice to anyone, but that it always bore the hallmark of high value when he did give it. Then he said this—and it has never faded from my memory: '*You are far from being a bad man—*'"'

Fifty Voices. 'That settles it—the money's Wilson's! Wilson! Wilson! Speech! Speech!'

People jumped up and crowded around Wilson, wringing his hand and congratulating feverently—meantime the Chair was hammering with the gavel and shouting:

'Order, gentlemen! Order! Order! Let me finish reading, please.' When quiet was restored, the reading was resumed, as follows:

'"*Go, and reform—or, mark my words—some day, for your sins, you will die and go to hell or Hadleyburg—TRY AND MAKE IT THE FORMER.*"'

A ghastly silence followed. First an angry cloud began to settle darkly upon the faces of the citizenship; after a pause the cloud began to rise, and a tickled expression tried to take its place; tried so hard that it was only kept under with great and painful difficulty; the reporters, the Brixtonites, and other strangers bent their heads down and shielded their faces with their hands, and managed to hold in by main strength and heroic courtesy. At this most inopportune time burst upon the stillness the roar of a solitary voice—Jack Halliday's:

'*That's* got the hallmark on it!'

Then the house let go, strangers and all. Even Mr. Burgess' gravity broke down presently, then the audience considered itself officially absolved from all restraint, and it made the most of its privilege. It was a good long laugh, and a tempestuously wholehearted one, but it ceased at last—long enough for Mr. Burgess to try to resume, and for the people to get their eyes partially wiped; then it broke out again; and afterward yet again; then at last Burgess was able to get out these serious words:

'It is useless to try to disguise the fact—we find ourselves in the presence of a matter of grave import. It involves the honor of your town, it strikes at the town's good name. The difference of a single word between the test-remarks offered by Mr. Wilson and Mr. Billson was itself a serious thing, since it indicated that one or the other of these gentlemen had committed a theft—'

The two men were sitting limp, nerveless, crushed; but at these words both were electrified into movement, and started to get up.

'Sit down!' said the Chair, sharply, and they obeyed. 'That, as I have said, was a serious thing. And it was—but for only one of them. But the matter has become graver; for the honor of *both* is now in formidable peril. Shall I go even further, and say in inextricable peril? *Both* left out the crucial fifteen words.' He paused. During several moments he allowed the pervading stillness to gather and deepen its impressive effects, then added: 'There would seem to be but one way whereby this could happen. I ask these gentlemen—Was there *collusion?—agreement?*'

A low murmur sifted through the house; its import was, 'He's got them both.'

Billson was not used to emergencies; he sat in a helpless collapse. But Wilson was a lawyer. He struggled to his feet, pale and worried, and said:

'I ask the indulgence of the house while I explain this most painful matter. I am sorry to say what I am about to say, since it must inflict irreparable injury upon Mr. Billson, whom I have always esteemed and respected until now, and in whose invulnerability to temptation I entirely believed—as did you all. But for the preservation of my own honor I must speak—and with frankness. I confess with shame—and I now beseech your pardon for it—that I said to the ruined stranger all of the words contained in the test-remark, including the disparaging fifteen. [*Sensation.*] When the late publication was made I recalled them, and I resolved to claim the sack of coin, for by every right I was entitled to it. Now I will ask you to consider this point, and weigh it well: that stranger's gratitude to me that night knew no bounds; he said himself that he could find no words for it that were adequate, and that if he should ever be able he would repay me a thousandfold. Now, then, I ask you this: Could I expect—could I believe—could I even remotely imagine—that, feeling as he did, he would do so ungrateful a thing as to add those quite unnecessary fifteen words to his test?—set a trap for me?—expose me as a slanderer of my own town before my own people assembled in a public hall? It was preposterous; it was impossible. His test would contain only the kindly opening clause of my remark. Of that I had no shadow of doubt. You would have thought as I did. You would not have expected a base betrayal from one whom you had befriended and against whom you had committed no offense. And so, with perfect confidence, perfect trust, I wrote on a piece of paper the opening words—ending with "Go, and reform"—and signed it. When I was about to put it in an envelope I was called into my back office, and without thinking I left the paper lying open on my desk.' He stopped, turned his head slowly toward Billson, waited a moment, then added: 'I ask you to note this: when I returned, a little later, Mr. Billson was retiring by my street door.' [*Sensation.*]

In a moment Billson was on his feet and shouting:

'It's a lie! It's an infamous lie!'

The Chair: 'Be seated, sir! Mr. Wilson has the floor.'

Billson's friends pulled him into his seat and quieted him, and Wilson went on:

'Those are the simple facts. My note was now lying in a different place on the table from where I had left it. I noticed that, but attached no importance to it, thinking a draft had blown it there. That Mr. Billson would read a private paper was a thing which could not occur to me; he was an honorable man, and he would be above that. If you will allow me to say it, I think his extra word 'very' stands explained; it is attributable to a defect of memory. I was the only man in the world who could furnish here any detail of the test-remark—by *honorable* means. I have finished.'

There is nothing in the world like a persuasive speech to fuddle the mental apparatus and upset the convictions and debauch the emotions of an audience not practiced in the tricks and delusions of oratory. Wilson sat down victorious. The house submerged him in tides of approving applause; friends swarmed to him and shook him by the hand and congratulated him, and Billson was shouted down and not allowed to say a word. The Chair hammered and hammered with its gavel, and kept shouting:

'But let us proceed, gentlemen, let us proceed!'

At last there was a measurable degree of quiet, and the hatter said:

'But what is there to proceed with, sir, but to deliver the money?'

Voices. 'That's it! That's it! Come forward, Wilson!'

The Hatter. 'I move three cheers for Mr. Wilson, Symbol of the special virtue which—'

The cheers bust forth before he could finish; and in the midst of them—and in the midst of the clamor of the gavel also—some enthusiasts mounted Wilson on a big friend's shoulder and were going to fetch him in triumph to the platform. The Chair's voice now rose above the noise.

'Order! To your places! You forget that there is still a document to be read.' When quiet had been restored he took up the document, and was going to read it, but laid it down again, saying, 'I forgot; this is not to be read until all written communications received by me have first been read.' He took an envelope out of his pocket, removed its enclosure, glanced at it—seemed astonished—held it out and gazed at it—stared at it.

Twenty or thirty voices cried out:

'What is it? Read it! Read it!'

And he did—slowly, and wondering:

'"The remark which I made to the stranger—[*Voices.* 'Hello! how's this?']—was this: 'You are far from being a bad man. [*Voices.* 'Great Scott!'] Go, and reform.'" [*Voice.* 'Oh, saw my leg off!'] Signed by Mr. Pinkerton the banker.'

The pandemonium of delight which turned itself loose now was of a sort to make the judicious weep. Those whose withers were unwrung laughed till the tears ran down; the reporters, in throes of laughter, set down disordered pothooks which would never in the world be decipherable; and a sleeping dog jumped up, scared out of its wits, and barked itself crazy at the turmoil. All manner of cries were scattered through the din: 'We're getting rich—*two* Symbols of Incorruptibility!—without counting Billson!' '*Three*!—count Shadbelly in—we can't have too many!' 'All right—Billson's elected!' 'Alas, poor Wilson—victim of *two* thieves!'

A Powerful Voice. 'Silence! The Chair's fished up something more out of its pocket.'

Voices. 'Hurrah! Is it something fresh? Read it! Read! Read!'

The Chair [reading.] ' "The remark which I made," etc.': 'You are far from being a bad man. Go,' etc. Signed, Gregory Yates." '

Tornado of Voices. 'Four Symbols!' 'Rah for Yates!' 'Fish again!'

The house was in a roaring humor now, and ready to get all the fun out of the occasion that might be in it. Several Nineteeners, looking pale and distressed, got up and began to work their way toward the aisles, but a score of shouts went up:

'The doors, the doors—close the doors; no Incorruptible shall leave this place! Sit down, everybody!'

The mandate was obeyed.

'Fish again! Read! Read!'

The Chair fished again, and once more the familiar words began to fall from its lips— ' "You are far from being a bad man—" '

'Name! name! What's his name?'

'L. Ingoldsby Sargent.'

'Five elected! Pile up the Symbols! Go on, go on!'

' "You are far from being a bad—" '

'Name! name!'

'Nicholas Whitworth.'

'Hooray! hooray! It's a symbolical day!'

Somebody wailed in, and began to sing this rhyme (leaving out 'it's') to the lovely 'Mikado' tune of 'When a man's afraid, a beautiful maid—'; the audience joined in, with joy; then, just in time, somebody contributed another line:

'And don't you this forget—'

The house roared it out. A third line was at once furnished:

'Corruptibles far from Hadleyburg are—'

The house roared that one too. As the last note died, Jack Halliday's voice rose high and clear, freighted with a final line:

'But the Symbols are here, you bet!'

That was sung, with booming enthusiasm. Then the happy house started in at the beginning and sang the four lines through twice, with immense swing and dash, and finished up with a crashing three-times-three and a tiger for 'Hadleyburg the Incorruptible and all Symbols of it which we shall find worthy to receive the hallmark tonight.'

Then the shoutings at the Chair began again, all over the place:

'Go on! Go on! Read! Read some more! Read all you've got!'

'That's it—go on! We are winning eternal celebrity!'

A dozen men got up now and began to protest. They said that this farce was the work of some abandoned joker, and was an insult to the whole community. Without a doubt these signatures were all forgeries—

'Sit down! Sit down! Shut up! You are confessing. We'll find *your* names in the lot.'

'Mr. Chairman, how many of those envelopes have you got?'

The Chair counted.

'Together with those that have been already examined, there are nineteen.'

A storm of derisive applause broke out.

'Perhaps they all contain the secret. I move that you open them all and read every signature that is attached to a note of that sort—and read also the first eight words of the note.'

'Second the motion!'

It was put and carried—uproariously. Then poor old Richards got up, and his wife rose and stood at his side. Her head was bent down, so that none might see that she was crying. Her husband gave her his arm, and so supporting her, he began to speak in a quavering voice:

'My friends, you have known us two—Mary and me—all our lives, and I think you have liked us and respected us—'

The Chair interrupted him:

'Allow me. It is quite true—that which you are saying, Mr. Richards: this town *does* know you two; it *does* like you; it *does* respect you; more—it honors you and *loves* you—'

Halliday's voice rang out:

'That's the hallmarked truth, too! If the Chair is right, let the house speak up and say it. Rise! Now, then—hip! hip! hip!—all together!'

The house rose in mass, faced toward the old couple eagerly, filled the air with a snowstorm of waving handkerchiefs, and delivered the cheers with all its affectionate heart.

The Chair then continued:

'What I was going to say is this: We know your good heart, Mr. Richards, but this is not a time for the exercise of charity toward offenders. [*Shouts of 'Right! right!'*] I see your generous purpose in your face, but I cannot allow you to plead for these men—'

'But I was going to—'

'Please take your seat, Mr. Richards. We must examine the rest of these notes—simple fairness to the men who have already been exposed requires this. As soon as that has been done—I give you my word for this—you shall be heard.'

Many Voices. 'Right—the Chair is right—no interruption can be permitted at this stage! Go on!—the names! the names!—according to the terms of the motion!'

The old couple sat reluctantly down, and the husband whispered to the wife, 'It is pitifully hard to have to wait; the shame will be greater than ever when they find we were only going to plead for *ourselves*.'

Straightway the jollity broke loose again with the reading of the names.

'"You are far from being a bad man—" Signature, Robert J. Titmarsh.

'"You are far from being a bad man—" Signature, Eliphalet Weeks.

'"You are far from being a bad man—" Signature, Oscar B. Wilder.'

At this point the house lit upon the idea of taking the eight words out of the Chairman's hands. He was not unthankful for that. Thenceforward he held up each note in its turn, and waited. The house droned out the eight words in a massed and measured and musical deep volume of sound (with a daringly close resemblance to a well-known church chant)— ' "You are f-a-r from being a b-a-a-a-d man." ' Then the Chair said, 'Signature, Archibald Wilcox.' And so on, and so on, name after name, and everybody had an increasingly and gloriously good time except the wretched Nineteen. Now and then, when a particularly shining name was called, the house made the Chair wait while it chanted the whole of the test-remark from the beginning to the closing words, "And go to hell or Hadleyburg—try and make it the for-or-m-e-r!" and in these special cases they added a grand and agonizing and imposing 'A-a-a-a-men!'

The list dwindled, dwindled, dwindled, poor old Richards keeping tally of the count, wincing when a name resembling his own was pronounced, and waiting in miserable suspense for the time to come when it would be his humiliating privilege to rise with Mary and finish his plea, which he was intending to word thus: '. . . for until now we have never done any wrong thing, but have gone our humble way unreproached. We are very poor, we are old, and have no chick nor child to help us; we were sorely tempted, and we fell. It was my purpose when I got up before to make confession and beg that my name might not be read out in this public place, for it seemed to us that we could not bear it; but I was prevented. It was just; it was our place to suffer with the rest. It has been hard for us. It is the first time we have ever heard our name fall from anyone's lips—sullied. Be merciful—for the sake of the better days; make our shame as light to bear as in your charity you can.' At this point in his reverie Mary nudged him, perceiving that his mind was absent. The house was chanting. 'You are f-a-r,' etc.

'Be ready,' Mary whispered. 'Your name comes now; he has read eighteen.'

The chant ended.

'Next! next! next!' came volleying from all over the house.

Burgess put his hand into his pocket. The old couple, trembling, began to rise. Burgess fumbled a moment, then said:

'I find I have read them all.'

Faint with joy and surprise, the couple sank into their seats, and Mary whispered:

'Oh, bless God, we are saved! He has lost ours—I wouldn't give this for a hundred of those sacks!'

The house burst out with its 'Mikado' travesty, and sang it three times with ever-increasing enthusiasm, rising to its feet when it reached for the third time the closing line:

'But the Symbols are here, you bet!'

and finishing up with cheers and a tiger for 'Hadleyburg purity and our eighteen immortal representatives of it.'

Then Wingate, the saddler, got up and proposed cheers 'for the cleanest man in town, the one solitary important citizen in it who didn't try to steal that money—Edward Richards.'

They were given with great and moving heartiness; then somebody proposed that Richards be elected sole guardian and Symbol of the now Sacred Hadleyburg Tradition, with power and right to stand up and look the whole sarcastic world in the face.

Passed, by acclamation. Then they sang the 'Mikado' again, and ended it with:

'And there's *one* Symbol left, you bet!'

There was a pause; then:

A Voice. 'Now, then, who's to get the sack?'

The Tanner (with bitter sarcasm.) 'That's easy. The money has to be divided among the eighteen Incorruptibles. They gave the suffering stranger twenty dollars apiece—and that remark—each in his turn—it took twenty-two minutes for the procession to move past. Staked the stranger—total contribution, $360. All they want is just the loan back—and interest—forty thousand dollars altogether.'

Many Voices [derisively.] 'That's it! Divvy! Divvy! Be kind to the poor—don't keep them waiting!'

The Chair. 'Order! I now offer the stranger's remaining document. It says: "If no claimant shall appear [*grand chorus of groans*], I desire that you open the sack and count out the money to the principal citizens of your town, they to take it in trust [*cries of 'Oh! Oh! Oh!'*], and use it in such ways as to them shall seem best for the propagation and preservation of your community's noble reputation for incorruptible honesty [*more cries*]—a reputation to which their names and their efforts will add a new and far-fetching luster." [*Enthusiastic outburst of sarcastic applause.*] That seems to be all. No—here is a postscript:

' "P. S.—CITIZENS OF HADLEYBURG: There *is* no test-remark—nobody made one. [*Great sensation.*] There wasn't any pauper stranger, nor any twenty-dollar contribution, nor any accompanying benediction and compliment—these are all inventions. [*General buzz and hum of astonishment and delight.*] Allow me to tell my story—it will take but a word or two. I passed through your town at a certain time, and received a deep offense which I had not earned. Any other man would have been content to kill one or two of you and call it square, but to me that would have been a trivial revenge, and inadequate; for the dead do not *suffer*. Besides, I could not kill you all—and, anyway, made as I am, even that would not have satisfied me. I wanted to damage every man in the place, and every woman—and not in their bodies or in their estate, but in their vanity—the place where feeble and foolish people are most vulnerable. So I disguised myself and came back and studied you. You were easy game. You had an old and lofty reputation for honesty, and naturally you were proud of it—it was your treasure of treasures, the very apple of your eye. As soon as I found out that you carefully and vigilantly kept yourselves and your children *out of temptation*, I knew how to proceed. Why, you simple creatures, the weakest of all weak things is a virtue which has not been tested in the fire. I laid a plan, and gathered a list of names. My project was to corrupt Hadleyburg the Incorruptible. My idea was to make liars and thieves of nearly half a hundred smirchless men and women who had never in their lives uttered a lie or stolen a penny. I was afraid of Goodson. He was neither born nor reared in Hadleyburg. I was afraid that if I started to operate my scheme by getting my letter laid before you, you would say to yourselves, 'Goodson is the only man among us who would give away twenty dollars to a poor devil'—and then you might not bite at my bait. But Heaven took Goodson; then I knew I was safe, and I set my trap and baited it. It may be that I shall not catch all the men to whom I mailed the pretended test secret, but I shall catch the most of them, if I know Hadleyburg nature. [*Voices.* 'Right—he got every last one of them.'] I believe they will even steal ostensible *gamble*-money, rather than miss, poor, tempted, and mistrained fellows. I am hoping to eternally and everlastingly squelch your vanity and give Hadleyburg a new renown—one that will *stick*—and spread far. If I have succeeded, open the sack and summon the Committee on Propagation and Preservation of the Hadleyburg Reputation."'

A Cyclone of Voices. 'Open it! Open it! The Eighteen to the front! Committee on Propagation of the Tradition! Forward—the Incorruptibles!'

The Chair ripped the sack wide, and gathered up a handful of bright, broad, yellow coins, shook them together, then examined them.

'Friends, they are only gilded disks of lead!'

There was a crashing outbreak of delight over this news, and when the noise had subsided, the tanner called out:

'By right of apparent seniority in this business, Mr. Wilson is Chairman of the Committee on Propagation of the Tradition. I suggest that he step forward on behalf of his pals, and receive in trust the money.'

A Hundred Voices. 'Wilson! Wilson! Wilson! Speech! Speech!'

Wilson [in a voice trembling with anger.] 'You will allow me to say, and without apologies for my language, *damn* the money!'

A Voice. 'Oh, and him a Baptist!'

A Voice. 'Seventeen Symbols left! Step up, gentlemen, and assume your trust!'

There was a pause—no response.

The Saddler. 'Mr. Chairman, we've got *one* clean man left, anyway, out of the late aristocracy; and he needs money, and deserves it. I move that you appoint Jack Halliday to get up there and auction off that sack of gilt twenty-dollar pieces, and give the result to the right man—the man whom Hadleyburg delights to honor—Edward Richards.'

This was received with great enthusiasm, the dog taking a hand again; the saddler started the bids at a dollar, the Brixton folk and Barnum's representative fought hard for it, the people cheered every jump that the bids made, the excitement climbed moment by moment higher and higher, the bidders got on their mettle and grew steadily more and more daring, more and more determined, the jumps went from a dollar up to five, then to ten, then to twenty, then fifty, then to a hundred, then—

At the beginning of the auction Richards whispered in distress to his wife: 'O Mary, can we allow it? It—it—you see, it is an honor reward, a testimonial to purity of character, and—and—can we allow it? Hadn't I better get up and—O Mary, what ought we to do?—what do you think we—' [*Halliday's voice. 'Fifteen I'm bid!—fifteen for the sack!—twenty!—ah, thanks!—thirty—thanks again! Thirty, thirty, thirty!—do I hear forty?—forty it is! Keep the ball rolling, gentlemen, keep it rolling!—fifty!—thanks, noble Roman! going at fifty, fifty, fifty!—seventy!—ninety!— splendid—a hundred!—pile it up, pile it up!—hundred and twenty—forty!—just in time!—hundred and fifty!—TWO hundred!—superb! Do I hear two h—thanks!—two hundred and fifty!—'*]

'It is another temptation, Edward—I'm all in a tremble—but, oh, we've escaped *one* temptation, and that ought to warn us to— [*'Six did I hear?—thanks!—six fifty, six f*—SEVEN *hundred!'*] And yet, Edward, when you think—nobody susp— [*'Eight hundred dollars!—hurrah!—make it nine!—Mr. Parsons, did I hear you say—thanks—nine!—this noble sack of virgin lead going at only nine hundred dollars, gilding and all—come! do I hear—a thousand!—gratefully yours!—did someone say eleven?—a sack which is going to be the most celebrated in the whole Uni—'*] O Edward' (beginning to sob), 'we are *so* poor!—but—but—do as you think best—do as you think best.'

Edward fell—that is, he sat still; sat with a conscience which was not satisfied, but which was overpowered by circumstances.

Meantime a stranger, who looked like an amateur detective gotten up as an impossible English earl, had been watching the evening's proceedings with manifest interest, and with a contented expression in his face; and he had been privately commenting to himself. He was now soliloquizing somewhat like this: 'None of the Eighteen are bidding; that is not satisfactory; I must change that—the dramatic unities require it; they must buy the sack they tried to steal; they must pay a heavy price, too—some of them are rich. And another thing, when I make a mistake in Hadleyburg nature the man that puts that error upon me is entitled to a high honorarium, and someone must pay it. This poor old Richards has brought my judgment to shame; he is an honest man. I don't understand it, but I acknowledge it. Yes, he saw my deuces *and* with a straight flush, and by rights the pot is his. And it shall be a jackpot, too, if I can manage it. He disappointed me, but let that pass.'

He was watching the bidding. At a thousand, the market broke; the prices tumbled swiftly. He waited—and still watched. One competitor dropped out; then another, and another. He put in a bid or two, now. When the bids had sunk to ten dollars, he added a five; someone raised him a three; he waited a moment, then flung in a fifty dollar jump, and the sack was his—at $1,282. The house broke out in cheers—then stopped; for he was on his feet, and had lifted his hand. He began to speak.

'I desire to say a word, and ask a favor. I am a speculator in rarities, and I have dealings with persons interested in numismatics all over the world. I can make a profit on this purchase, just as it stands; but there is a way, if I can get your approval, whereby I can make every one of these leaden twenty-dollar pieces worth its face in gold, and perhaps more. Grant me that approval, and I will give part of my gains to your Mr. Richards, whose invulnerable probity you have so justly and so cordially recognized to-night; his share shall be ten thousand dollars, and I will hand him the money to-morrow. [*Great applause from the house.* But the 'invulnerable probity' made the Richardses blush prettily; however, it went for modesty, and did no harm.] If you will pass my proposition by a good majority—I would like a two-thirds vote—I will regard that as the town's consent, and that is all I ask. Rarities are always helped by any device which will rouse curiosity and compel remark. Now if I may have your permission to stamp upon the faces of each of these ostensible coins the names of the eighteen gentlemen who—'

Nine-tenths of the audience were on their feet in a moment—dog and all—and the proposition was carried with a whirlwind of approving applause and laughter.

They sat down, and all the Symbols except 'Dr.' Clay Harkness got up, violently protesting against the proposed outrage, and threatening to—

'I beg you not to threaten me,' said the stranger, calmly. 'I know my legal rights, and am not accustomed to be frightened at bluster.' [*Applause.*] He sat down. 'Dr.' Harkness saw an opportunity here. He was one of the two very rich men of the place, and Pinkerton was the other. Harkness was proprietor of a mint; that is to say, a popular patent medicine. He was running for the Legislature on one ticket, and Pinkerton on the other. It was a close race and a hot one, and getting hotter every day. Both had strong appetites for money; each had bought a great tract of land, with a purpose; there was going to be a new railway, and each wanted to be in the Legislature and help locate the route to his own advantage; a single vote might make the decision, and with it two or three fortunes. The stake was large, and Harkness was a daring speculator. He was sitting close to the stranger. He leaned over while one or another of the other Symbols was entertaining the house with protests and appeals, and asked, in a whisper:

'What is your price for the sack?'

'Forty thousand dollars.'

'I'll give you twenty.'

'No.'

'Twenty-five.'

'No.'

'Say thirty.'

'The price is forty thousand dollars; not a penny less.'

'All right, I'll give it. I will come to the hotel at ten in the morning. I don't want it known; will see you privately.'

'Very good.' Then the stranger got up and said to the house:

'I find it late. The speeches of these gentlemen are not without merit, not without interest, not without grace; yet if I may be excused I will take my leave. I thank you for the great favor which you have shown me in granting my petition. I ask the Chair to keep the sack for me until tomorrow, and to hand these three five-hundred-dollar notes to Mr. Richards.' They were passed up to the Chair. 'At nine I will call for the sack, and at eleven will deliver the rest of the ten thousand to Mr. Richards in person, at his home. Good night.'

Then he slipped out, and left the audience making a vast noise, which was composed of a mixture of cheers, the 'Mikado' song, dog-disapproval, and the chant, 'You are f-a-r from being a b-a-a-d man—a-a-a a-men!'

4

AT HOME THE RICHARDSES had to endure congratulations and compliments until midnight. Then they were left to themselves. They look a little sad, and they sat silent and thinking. Finally Mary sighed and said:

'Do you think we are to blame, Edward—*much* to blame?' And her eyes wandered to the accusing triplet of big banknotes lying on the table, where the congratulators had been gloating over them and reverently fingering them. Edward did not answer at once; then he brought out a sigh and said, hesitatingly:

'We—we couldn't help it, Mary. It—well, it was ordered. *All* things are.'

Mary glanced up and looked at him steadily, but he didn't return the look. Presently she said:

'I thought congratulations and praises always tasted good. But—it seems to me, now—Edward?'

'Well?'

'Are you going to stay in the bank?'

'N-no.'

'Resign?'

'In the morning—by note.'

'It does seem best.'

Richards bowed his head in his hands and muttered:

'Before, I was not afraid to let oceans of people's money pour through my hands, but—Mary, I am so tired, so tired—'

'We will go to bed.'

At nine in the morning the stranger called for the sack and took it to the hotel in a cab. At ten Harkness had a talk with him privately. The stranger asked for and got five checks on a metropolitan bank—drawn to 'Bearer' —four for $1,500 each, and one for $34,000. He put one of the former in his pocketbook, and the remainder, representing $38,500, he put in an envelope, and with these he added a note, which he wrote after Harkness was gone. At eleven he called at the Richards house and knocked. Mrs. Richards peeped through the shutters, then went and received the envelope, and the stranger disappeared without a word. She came back flushed and a little unsteady on her legs, and gasped out:

'I am sure I recognized him! Last night it seemed to me that maybe I had seen him somewhere before.'

'He is the man that brought the sack here?'

'I am almost sure of it.'

'Then he is the ostensible Stephenson, too, and sold every important citizen in this town with his bogus secret. Now if he has sent checks instead of money, we are sold, too, after we thought we had escaped. I was beginning to feel fairly comfortable once more, after my night's rest, but the look of that envelope makes me sick. It isn't fat enough; $8,500 in even the largest banknotes makes more bulk than that.'

'Edward, why do you object to checks?'

'Checks signed by Stephenson! I am resigned to take the $8,500 if it could come in banknotes—for it does seem that it was so ordered, Mary—but I have never had much courage, and I have not the pluck to try to market a check signed with that disastrous name. It would be a trap. That man tried to catch me; we escaped somehow or other; and now he is trying a new way. If it is checks—'

'Oh, Edward, it is *too* bad!' And she held up the checks and began to cry.

'Put them in the fire! Quick! We mustn't be tempted. It is a trick to make the world laugh at *us*, along with the rest, and—Give them to *me*, since you can't do it!' He snatched them and tried to hold his grip till he could get to the stove; but he was human, he was a cashier, and he stopped a moment to make sure of the signature. Then he came near to fainting.

'Fan me, Mary, fan me! They are the same as gold!'

'Oh, how lovely, Edward! Why?'

'Signed by Harkness. What can the mystery of that be, Mary?'

'Edward, do you think—'

'Look here—look at this! Fifteen—fifteen—fifteen—thirty-four. Thirty-eight thousand five hundred! Mary, the sack isn't worth twelve dollars, and Harkness—apparently—has paid about par for it.'

'And does it all come to us, do you think—instead of the ten thousand?'

'Why, it looks like it. And the checks are made to 'Bearer,' too.'

'Is that good, Edward? What is it for?'

'A hint to collect them at some distant bank, I reckon. Perhaps Harkness doesn't want the matter known. What is that—a note?'

'Yes. It was with the checks.'

It was in the 'Stephenson' handwriting, but there was no signature. It said:

I am a disappointed man. Your honesty is beyond the reach of temptation. I had a different idea about it, but I wronged you in that, and I beg pardon, and do it sincerely. I honor you—and that is sincere too. This town is not worthy to kiss the hem of your garment. Dear sir, I made a square bet with myself that there were nineteen debauchable men in your self-righteous community. I have lost. Take the whole pot, you are entitled to it.

Richards drew a deep sigh, and said:

'It seems written with fire—it burns so. Mary—I am miserable again.'

'I, too. Ah, dear, I wish—'

'To think, Mary—he *believes* in me.'

'Oh, don't, Edward—I can't bear it.'

'If those beautiful words were deserved, Mary—and God knows I believed I deserved them once—I think I could give the forty thousand dollars for them. And I would put that paper away, as representing more than gold and jewels, and keep it always. But now— We could not live in the shadow of its accusing presence, Mary.'

He put it in the fire.

A messenger arrived and delivered an envelope.

Richards took from it a note and read it; it was from Burgess.

You saved me, in a difficult time. I saved you last night. It was at cost of a lie, but I made the sacrifice freely, and out of a grateful heart. None in this village knows so well as I know how brave and good and noble you are. At bottom you cannot respect me, knowing as you do of that matter of which I am accused, and by the general voice comdemned; but I beg that you will at least believe that I am a grateful man; it will help me to bear my burden.

[Signed]   *Burgess.*

'Saved, once more. And on such terms!' He put the note in the fire. 'I—I wish I were dead, Mary, I wish I were out of it all.'

'Oh, these are bitter, bitter days, Edward. The stabs, through their very generosity, are so deep—and they come so fast!'

Three days before the election each of two thousand voters suddenly found himself in possession of a prized memento—one of the renowned bogus double eagles. Around one of its faces was stamped these words: 'THE REMARK I MADE TO THE POOR STRANGER WAS—' Around the other face was stamped these: 'GO, AND REFORM. [SIGNED] PINKERTON.'

Thus the entire remaining refuse of the renowned joke was emptied upon a single head, and with calamitous effect. It revived the recent vast laugh and concentrated it upon Pinkerton; and Harkness's election was a walkover.

Within twenty-four hours after the Richardses had received their checks their consciences were quieting down, discouraged; the old couple were learning to reconcile themselves to the sin which they had committed. But they were to learn, now, that a sin takes on new and real terrors when there seems a chance that it is going to be found out. This gives it a fresh and most substantial and important aspect. At church the morning sermon was of the usual pattern; it was the same old things said in the same old way; they had heard them a thousand times and found them innocuous, next to meaningless, and easy to sleep under; but now it was different: the sermon seemed to bristle with accusations; it seemed aimed straight and specially at people who were concealing deadly sins. After church they got away from the mob of congratulators as soon as they could, and hurried homeward, chilled to the bone at they did not know what—vague, shadowy, indefinite fears. And by chance they caught a glimpse of Mr. Burgess as he turned a corner. He paid no attention to their nod of recognition! He hadn't seen it; but they did not know that. What could his conduct mean? It might mean—it might mean—oh, a dozen dreadful things. Was it possible that he knew that Richards could have cleared him of guilt in that bygone time, and had been silently waiting for a chance to even up accounts? At home, in their distress they got to imagining that their servant might have been in the next room listening when Richards revealed the secret to his wife that he knew of Burgess's innocence; next, Richards began to imagine that he had heard the swish of a gown in there at that time; next, he was sure he *had* heard it. They would call Sarah in, on a pretext, and watch her face: if she had been betraying them to Mr. Burgess, it would show in her manner. They asked her some questions—questions which were so random and incoherent and seemingly purposeless that the girl felt sure that the old people's minds had been affected by their sudden good fortune; the sharp and watchful gaze which they bent upon her frightened her, and that completed the business. She blushed, she became nervous and confused, and to the old people these were plain signs of guilt—guilt of some fearful sort or other—without doubt she was a spy and a traitor. When they were alone again they began to piece many unrelated things together and get horrible results out of the combination. When things had got about to the worst, Richards was delivered of a sudden gasp, and his wife asked:

'Oh what is it?—What is it?'

'The note—Burgess's note! Its language was sarcastic, I see it now.' He quoted: '"At bottom you cannot respect me, *knowing*, as you do, of *that matter* of which I am accused"—oh, it is perfectly plain, now, God help me! He knows that I know! You see the ingenuity of the phrasing. It was a trap—and like a fool, I walked into it. And Mary—?'

'Oh, it is dreadful—I know what you are going to say—he didn't return your transcript of the pretended test-remark.'

'No—kept it to destroy us with. Mary, he has exposed us to some already. I know it—I know it well. I saw it in a dozen faces after church. Ah, he wouldn't answer our nod of recognition—*he* knew what he had been doing!'

In the night the doctor was called. The news went around in the morning that the old couple were rather seriously ill—prostrated by the exhausting excitement growing out of their great windfall, the congratulations, and the late hours, the doctor said. The town was sincerely distressed; for these old people were about all it had left to be proud of, now.

Two days later the news was worse. The old couple were delirious, and were doing strange things. By witness of the nurses, Richards had exhibited checks—for $8,500? No—for an amazing sum—$38,500! What could be the explanation of this gigantic piece of luck?

The following day the nurses had more news—and wonderful. They had concluded to hide the checks, lest harm come to them; but when they searched they were gone from under the patient's pillow—vanished away. The patient said:

'Let the pillow alone; what do you want?'

'We thought it best that the checks—'

'You will never see them again—they are destroyed. They came from Satan. I saw the hell-brand on them, and I knew they were sent to betray me to sin.' Then he fell to gabbling strange and dreadful things which were not clearly understandable, and which the doctor admonished them to keep to themselves.

Richards was right; the checks were never seen again.

A nurse must have talked in her sleep, for within two days the forbidden gabblings were the property of the town; and they were of a surprising sort. They seemed to indicate that Richards had been a claimant for the sack himself, and that Burgess had concealed that fact and then maliciously betrayed it.

Burgess was taxed with this and stoutly denied it. And he said it was not fair to attach weight to the chatter of a sick old man who was out of his mind. Still, suspicion was in the air, and there was much talk.

After a day or two it was reported that Mrs. Richards' delirious deliveries were getting to be duplicates of her husband's. Suspicion flamed up into conviction, now, and the town's pride in the purity of its one undiscredited important citizen began to dim down and flicker toward extinction.

Six days passed, then came more news. The old couple were dying. Richards' mind cleared in his latest hour, and he sent for Burgess. Burgess said:

'Let the room be cleared. I think he wishes to say something in privacy.'

'No!' said Richards: 'I want witnesses. I want you all to hear my confession, so that I may die a man, and not a dog. I was clean—artificially—like the rest; and like the rest I fell when temptation came. I signed a lie, and claimed the miserable sack. Mr. Burgess remembered that I had done him a service, and in gratitude (and ignorance) he suppressed my claim and saved me. You know the thing that was charged against Burgess years ago. My testimony, and mine alone, could have cleared him, and I was a coward, and left him to suffer disgrace—'

'No—no—Mr. Richards, you—'

'My servant betrayed my secret to him—'

'No one has betrayed anything to me—'

'—and then he did a natural and justifiable thing, he repented of the saving kindness which he had done me, and he *exposed* me—as I deserved—'

'Never!—I make oath—'

'Out of my heart I forgive him.'

Burgess's impassioned protestations fell upon deaf ears; the dying man passed away without knowing that once more he had done poor Burgess a wrong. The old wife died that night.

The last of the sacred Nineteen had fallen a prey to the fiendish sack; the town was stripped of the last rag of its ancient glory. Its mourning was not showy, but it was deep.

By act of the Legislature—upon prayer and petition—Hadleyburg was allowed to change its name to (never mind what—I will not give it away), and leave one word out of the motto that for many generations had graced the town's official seal.

It is an honest town once more, and the man will have to rise early that catches it napping again.

BRET HARTE 1836-1902

Born Francis Bret Harte in Albany, New York in 1836, Bret Harte assumed this shortened form of his name when embarking on a career as a journalist, following an unsuccessful attempt to make his fortune in the California Gold Rush in the 1840s and 1850s. In 1870 he published a collection of short stories entitled *The Luck of Roaring Camp and Other Sketches* which became, almost overnight, a runaway national success.

Although retained by the *Atlantic Monthly* magazine and besieged with offers from New York publishers, Bret Harte never again achieved, in a long and prolific career, the success of his early tales of miners and prospectors. The three stories which follow are all taken from his first collection and serve to illustrate the freshness and immediate appeal which made Bret Harte an important figure in the development of the American short story.

The Luck of Roaring Camp

THERE WAS COMMOTION IN Roaring Camp. It could not have been a fight, for in 1850 that was not novel enough to have called together the entire settlement. The ditches and claims were not only deserted, but 'Tuttle's grocery' had contributed its gamblers, who, it will be remembered, calmly continued their game the day that French Pete and Kanaka Joe shot each other to death over the bar in the front room. The whole camp was collected before a rude cabin on the outer edge of the clearing. Conversation was carried on in a low tone, but the name of a woman was frequently repeated. It was a name familiar enough to the camp – 'Cherokee Sal.'

Perhaps the less said of her the better. She was a coarse and, it is to be feared, a very sinful woman. But at that time she was the only woman in Roaring Camp, and was just then lying in sore extremity, when she most needed the ministration of her own sex. Dissolute, abandoned, and irreclaimable, she was yet suffering a martyrdom hard enough to bear even when veiled by sympathizing womanhood, but now terrible in her loneliness. The primal curse had come to her in that original isolation which must have made the punishment of the first transgression so dreadful. It was, perhaps, part of the expiation of her sin that, at a moment when she most lacked her sex's intuitive tenderness and care, she met only the half-contemptuous faces of her masculine associates. Yet a few of the spectators were, I think, touched by her sufferings. Sandy Tipton thought it was 'rough on Sal,' and in the contemplation of her condition, for a moment rose superior to the fact that he had an ace and two bowers in his sleeve.

It will be seen also that the situation was novel. Deaths were by no means uncommon in Roaring Camp, but a birth was a new thing. People had been dismissed the camp effectively, finally, and with no possibility of return; but this was the first time that anybody had been introduced *ab initio*. Hence the excitement.

'You go in there, Stumpy,' said a prominent citizen known as 'Kentuck,' addressing one of the loungers. 'Go in there, and see what you kin do. You've had experience in them things.'

Perhaps there was a fitness in the selection. Stumpy, in other climes, had been the putative head of two families; in fact, it was owing to some legal informality in these proceedings that Roaring Camp – a city of refuge – was indebted to his company. The crowd approved the choice, and Stumpy was wise enough to bow to the majority. The door closed on the extempore surgeon and midwife, and Roaring Camp sat down outside, smoked its pipe, and awaited the issue.

The assemblage numbered about a hundred men. One or two of these were actual fugitives from justice, some were criminal, and all were reckless.

Physically they exhibited no indication of their past lives and character. The greatest scamp had a Raphael face, with a profusion of blond hair; Oakhurst, a gambler, had the melancholy air and intellectual abstraction of a Hamlet; the coolest and most courageous man was scarcely over five feet in height, with a soft voice and an embarrassed, timid manner. The term 'roughs' applied to them was a distinction rather than a definition. Perhaps in the minor details of fingers, toes, ears, etc., the camp may have been deficient, but these slight omissions did not detract from their aggregate force. The strongest man had but three fingers on his right hand; the best shot had but one eye.

Such was the physical aspect of the men that were dispersed around the cabin. The camp lay in a triangular valley between two hills and a river. The only outlet was a steep trail over the summit of a hill that faced the cabin, now illuminated by the rising moon. The suffering woman might have seen it from the rude bunk whereon she lay – seen it winding like a silver thread until it was lost in the stars above.

A fire of withered pine boughs added sociability to the gathering. By degrees the natural levity of Roaring Camp returned. Bets were freely offered and taken regarding the result. Three to five that 'Sal would get through with it'; even that the child would survive; side bets as to the sex and complexion of the coming stranger. In the midst of an excited discussion an exclamation came from those nearest the door, and the camp stopped to listen. Above the swaying and moaning of the pines, the swift rush of the river, and the crackling of the fire rose a sharp, querulous cry – a cry unlike anything heard before in the camp. The pines stopped moaning, the river ceased to rush, and the fire to crackle. It seemed as if Nature had stopped to listen too.

The camp rose to its feet as one man! It was proposed to explode a barrel of gunpowder; but in consideration of the situation of the mother, better counsels prevailed, and only a few revolvers were discharged; for whether owing to the rude surgery of the camp, or some other reason, Cherokee Sal was sinking fast. Within an hour she had climbed, as it were, that rugged road that led to the stars, and so passed out of Roaring Camp, its sin and shame, forever. I do not think that the announcement disturbed them much, except in speculation as to the fate of the child. 'Can he live now?' was asked of Stumpy. The answer was doubtful. The only other being of Cherokee Sal's sex and maternal condition in the settlement was an ass. There was some conjecture as to fitness, but the experiment was tried. It was less problematical than the ancient treatment of Romulus and Remus, and apparently as successful.

When these details were completed, which exhausted another hour, the door was opened, and the anxious crowd of men, who had already formed themselves into a queue, entered in single file. Beside the low bunk or shelf, on which the figure of the mother was starkly outlined below the blankets, stood a pine table. On this a candlebox was placed, and within it, swathed in staring red flannel, lay the last arrival at Roaring Camp. Beside the candlebox was placed a hat. Its use was soon indicated. 'Gentlemen,' said Stumpy, with a singular mixture of authority and *ex officio* complacency – 'gentlemen will please pass in at the front door, round the table, and out at the back door. Them as wishes to contribute anything toward the orphan will find a hat handy.' The first man entered with his hat on; he uncovered, however, as he looked about him, and so unconsciously set an example to the next. In such communities good and bad actions are catching. As the procession filed in comments were audible – criticisms addressed perhaps rather to Stumpy in the character of showman: 'Is that him?' 'Mighty small specimen;' 'Hasn't more'n got the color;' 'Ain't bigger nor a derringer.' The contributions were as characteristic: A silver tobacco box; a doubloon; a navy revolver, silver mounted; a gold specimen; a very beautifully embroidered lady's handkerchief (from Oakhurst the gambler); a diamond breastpin; a diamond ring (suggested by the pin, with the remark from the giver that he 'saw that pin and went two diamonds better'); a slung shot; a Bible (contributor not detected); a golden spur; a silver teaspoon (the initials, I regret to say, were not the giver's); a pair of surgeon's shears; a lancet; a Bank of England note for £5; and about $200 in loose gold and silver coin. During these proceedings Stumpy maintained a silence as impassive as the dead on his left, a gravity as inscrutable as that of the newly born on his right. Only one incident occurred to break the monotony of the curious procession. As Kentuck bent over the candlebox half curiously, the child turned, and, in a spasm of pain, caught at his groping finger and held it fast for a moment. Kentuck looked foolish and embarrassed. Something like a blush tried to assert itself in his weather-beaten cheek. 'The d – d little cuss!' he said, as he extricated his finger, with perhaps more tenderness and care than he might have been deemed capable of showing. He held that finger a little apart from its fellows as he went out, and examined it curiously. The examination provoked the same original remark in regard to the child. In fact, he seemed to enjoy repeating it. 'He rastled with my finger,' he remarked to Tipton, holding up the member, 'the d – d little cuss!'

It was four o'clock before the camp sought repose. A light burnt in the cabin where the watchers sat, for Stumpy did not go to bed that night. Nor did Kentuck. He drank quite freely, and related with great gusto his experience, invariably ending with his characteristic condemnation of the newcomer. It seemed to relieve him of any unjust implication of sentiment, and Kentuck had the weaknesses of the nobler sex. When everybody else had gone to bed, he walked down to the river and whistled reflectingly. Then he walked up the gulch past the cabin, still whistling with demonstrative unconcern. At a large redwood tree he paused and retraced his steps, and again passed the cabin. Halfway down to the river's bank he again paused, and then returned and knocked at the door. It was opened by Stumpy. 'How goes it?' said Kentuck, looking past Stumpy toward the candlebox. 'All serene!' replied Stumpy. 'Anything up?' 'Nothing.' There was a pause – an embarrassing one – Stumpy still holding the door. Then Kentuck had recourse to his finger, which he held up to Stumpy. 'Rastled with it – the d – d little cuss,' he said, and retired.

The next day Cherokee Sal had such rude sepulture as Roaring Camp afforded. After her body had been committed to the hillside, there was a formal meeting of the camp to discuss what should be done with her infant. A resolution to adopt it was unanimous and enthusiastic. But an animated discussion in regard to the manner and feasibility of providing for its wants at once sprang up. It was remarkable that the argument partook of none of those fierce personalities with which discussions were usually conducted at Roaring Camp. Tipton proposed that they should send the child to Red Dog

– a distance of forty miles – where female attention could be procured. But the unlucky suggestion met with fierce and unanimous opposition. It was evident that no plan which entailed parting from their new acquisition would for a moment be entertained. 'Besides,' said Tom Ryder, 'them fellows at Red Dog would swap it, and ring in somebody else on us.' A disbelief in the honesty of other camps prevailed at Roaring Camp, as in other places.

The introduction of a female nurse in the camp also met with objection. It was argued that no decent woman could be prevailed to accept Roaring Camp as her home, and the speaker urged that 'they didn't want any more of the other kind.' This unkind allusion to the defunct mother, harsh as it may seem, was the first spasm of propriety – the first symptom of the camp's regeneration. Stumpy advanced nothing. Perhaps he felt a certain delicacy in interfering with the selection of a possible successor in office. But when questioned, he averred stoutly that he and 'Jinny' – the mammal before alluded to – could manage to rear the child. There was something original, independent, and heroic about the plan that pleased the camp. Stumpy was retained. Certain articles were sent for to Sacramento. 'Mind,' said the treasurer, as he pressed a bag of gold dust into the expressman's hand, 'the best that can be got – lace, you know, and filigree work and frills – d – n the cost!'

Strange to say, the child thrived. Perhaps the invigorating climate of the mountain camp was compensation for material deficiencies. Nature took the foundling to her broader breast. In that rare atmosphere of the Sierra foothills – that air pungent with balsamic odor, that ethereal cordial at once bracing and exhilarating – he may have found food and nourishment, or a subtle chemistry that transmuted ass's milk to lime and phosphorus. Stumpy inclined to the belief that it was the latter and good nursing. 'Me and that ass,' he would say, 'has been father and mother to him! Don't you,' he would add, apostrophizing the helpless bundle before him, 'never go back on us.'

By the time he was a month old the necessity of giving him a name became apparent. He had generally been known as 'The Kid,' 'Stumpy's Boy,' 'The Coyote' (an allusion of his vocal powers), and even by Kentuck's endearing diminutive of 'The d – d little cuss.' But these were felt to be vague and unsatisfactory, and were at last dismissed under another influence. Gamblers and adventurers are generally superstitious, and Oakhurst one day declared that the baby had brought 'the luck' to Roaring Camp. It was certain that of late they had been successful. 'Luck' was the name agreed upon, with the prefix of Tommy for greater convenience. No allusion was made to the mother, and the father was unknown. 'It's better,' said the philosophical Oakhurst, 'to take a fresh deal all round. Call him Luck, and start him fair.' A day was accordingly set apart for the christening. What was meant by this ceremony the reader may imagine who has already gathered some idea of the reckless irreverence of Roaring Camp. The master of ceremonies was one 'Boston,' a noted wag, and the occasion seemed to promise the greatest facetiousness. This ingenious satirist had spent two days in preparing a burlesque of the Church service, with pointed local allusions. The choir was properly trained, and Sandy Tipton was to stand godfather. But after the procession had marched to the grove with music and banners, and the child had been deposited before a mock altar, Stumpy stepped before the expectant crowd. 'It ain't my style to spoil fun, boys,' said the little man, stoutly eying the faces around him, 'but it strikes me that this thing ain't exactly on the squar. It's playing it pretty low down on this yer baby to ring in fun on him that he ain't goin' to understand. And ef there's goin' to be any godfathers round, I'd like to see who's got any better rights than me.' A silence followed Stumpy's speech. To the credit of all humorists be it said that the first man to acknowledge its justice was the satirist thus stopped of his fun. 'But,' said Stumpy, quickly following up his advantage, 'we're here for a christening, and we'll have it. I proclaim you Thomas Luck, according to the laws of the United States and the State of California, so help me God.' It was the first time that the name of the Deity had been otherwise uttered than profanely in the camp. The form of christening was perhaps ever more ludicrous than the satirist had conceived; but strangely enough, nobody saw it and nobody laughed. 'Tommy' was christened as seriously as he would have been under a Christian roof, and cried and was comforted in as orthodox fashion.

And so the work of regeneration began in Roaring Camp. Almost imperceptibly a change came over the settlement. The cabin assigned to 'Tommy Luck' – or 'The Luck,' as he was more frequently called – first showed signs of improvement. It was kept scrupulously clean and whitewashed. Then it was boarded, clothed, and papered. The rosewood cradle, packed eighty miles by mule, had, in Stumpy's way of putting it, 'sorter killed the rest of the furniture.' So the rehabilitation of the camp became a necessity. The men who were in the habit of lounging in at Stumpy's to see 'how "The Luck" got on' seemed to appreciate the change, and in self-defense the rival establishment of 'Tuttle's grocery' bestirred itself and imported a carpet and mirrors. The reflections of the latter on the appearance of Roaring Camp tended to produce stricter habits of personal cleanliness. Again Stumpy imposed a kind of quarantine upon those who aspired to the honor and privilege of holding The Luck. It was a cruel mortification to Kentuck – who, in the carelessness of a large nature and the habits of frontier life, had begun to regard all garments as a second cuticle, which, like a snake's, only sloughed off through decay – to be debarred this privilege from certain prudential reasons. Yet such was the subtle influence of innovation that he thereafter appeared regularly every afternoon in a clean shirt and face still shining from his ablutions. Nor were moral and social sanitary laws neglected. 'Tommy,' who was supposed to spend his whole existence in a persistent attempt to repose, must not be disturbed by noise. The shouting and yelling, which had gained the camp its infelicitous title, were not permitted within hearing distance of Stumpy's. The men conversed in whispers or smoked with Indian gravity. Profanity was tacitly given up in these sacred precincts, and throughout the camp a popular form of expletive, known as 'D – n the luck!' and 'Curse the luck!' was abandoned, as having a new personal bearing. Vocal music was not interdicted, being supposed to have a soothing, tranquilizing quality; and one song, sung by 'Man-o'-War Jack,' an English sailor from her Majesty's Australian colonies, was quite popular as a lullaby. It was a lugubrious recital of the exploits of 'the Arethusa, Seventy-four,' in a muffled minor, ending with a prolonged dying fall at the burden of each verse, 'On b-oo-o-ard of the Arethusa.' It was a fine sight to see Jack holding The Luck, rocking from side to side as if with the motion of a ship, and crooning forth this naval ditty. Either through the peculiar rocking of Jack or the length of his song – it contained ninety stanzas, and was continued with conscientious deliberation to the bitter end – the lullaby generally had the desired effect. At such times the men would lie at full length under the trees in the soft summer twilight, smoking their pipes and drinking in the melodious utterances. An indistinct idea that this was pastoral happiness pervaded the camp. 'This 'ere kind o' think,' said the Cockney Simmons, meditatively reclining on his elbow, 'is 'evingly.' It reminded him of Greenwich.

On the long summer days The Luck was usually carried to the gulch from whence the golden store of Roaring Camp was taken. There, on a blanket spread over pine boughs, he would lie while the men were working in the ditches below. Latterly there was a rude attempt to decorate this bower with flowers and sweet-smelling shrubs, and generally some one would bring him a cluster of wild honeysuckles, azaleas, or the painted blossoms of Las Mariposas. The men had suddenly awakened to the fact that there were beauty and significance in these trifles, which they had so long trodden carelessly beneath their feet. A flake of glittering mica, a fragment of variegated quartz, a bright pebble from the bed of the creek, became beautiful to eyes thus cleared and strengthened, and were invariably put aside for The Luck. It was wonderful how many treasures the woods and hillsides yielded that 'would do for Tommy.' Surrounded by playthings such as never child out of fairyland had before, it is to be hoped that Tommy was content. He appeared to be serenely happy, albeit there was an infantine gravity about him, a contemplative light in his round gray eyes, that sometimes worried Stumpy. He was always tractable and quiet, and it is recorded that once, having crept beyond his 'corral' – a hedge of tessellated pine boughs, which surrounded his bed – he dropped over the bank on his head in the soft earth, and remained with his mottled legs in the air in that position for at least five minutes with unflinching gravity. He was extricated without a murmur. I hesitate to record the many other instances of his sagacity, which rest, unfortunately, upon the statements of prejudiced friends. Some of them were not without a tinge of superstition. 'I crep' up the bank just now,' said Kentuck one day, in a breathless state of excitement, 'and dern my skin if he wasn't a-talking to a jay bird as was a-sittin' on his lap. There they was, just as free and sociable as anything you please, a-jawin' at each other just like two cherrybums.' Howbeit, whether creeping over the pine boughs or lying lazily on his back blinking at the leaves above him, to him the birds sang, the squirrels chattered, and the flowers bloomed. Nature was his nurse and playfellow. For him she would let slip between the leaves golden shafts of sunlight that fell just within his grasp; she would send wandering breezes to visit him with the balm of bay and resinous gum; to him the tall redwoods nodded familiarly and sleepily, the bumblebees buzzed, and the rooks cawed a slumbrous accompaniment.

Such was the golden summer of Roaring Camp. They were 'flush times,' and the luck was with them. The claims had yielded enormously. The camp was jealous of its privileges and looked suspiciously on strangers. No encouragement was given to immigration, and, to make their seclusion more perfect, the land on either side of the mountain wall that surrounded the camp they duly pre-empted. This, and a reputation for singular proficiency with the revolver, kept the reserve of Roaring Camp inviolate. The expressman – their only connecting link with the surrounding world – sometimes told wonderful stories of the camp. He would say, 'They've a street up there in "Roaring" that would lay over any street in Red Dog. They've got vines and flowers round their houses, and they wash themselves twice a day. But they're mighty rough on strangers, and they worship an Ingin baby.'

With the prosperity of the camp came a desire for further improvement. It was proposed to build a hotel in the following spring, and to invite one or two decent families to reside there for the sake of The Luck, who might perhaps profit by female companionship. The sacrifice that this concession to the sex cost these men, who were fiercely skeptical in regard to its general virtue and usefulness, can only be accounted for by their affection for Tommy. A few still held out. But the resolve could not be carried into effect for three months, and the minority meekly yielded in the hope that something might turn up to prevent it. And it did.

The winter of 1851 will long be remembered in the foothills. The snow lay deep on the Sierras, and every mountain creek became a river, and every river a lake. Each gorge and gulch was transformed into a tumultuous watercourse that descended the hillsides, tearing down giant trees and scattering its drift and debris along the plain. Red Dog had been twice under water, and Roaring Camp had been forewarned. 'Water put the gold into them gulches,' said Stumpy. 'It's been here once and will be here again!' And that night the North Fork suddenly leaped over its banks and swept up the triangular valley of Roaring Camp.

In the confusion of rushing water, crashing trees, and crackling timber, and the darkness which seemed to flow with the water and blot out the fair valley, but little could be done to collect the scattered camp. When the morning broke, the cabin of Stumpy, nearest the river-bank, was gone. Higher up the gulch they found the body of its unlucky owner; but the pride, the hope, the joy, The Luck, of Roaring Camp had disappeared. They were returning with sad hearts when a shout from the bank recalled them.

It was a relief-boat from down the river. They had picked up, they said, a man and an infant, nearly exhausted, about two miles below. Did anybody know them, and did they belong here?

It needed but a glance to show them Kentuck lying there, cruelly crushed and bruised, but still holding The Luck of Roaring Camp in his arms. As they bent over the strangely assorted pair, they saw that the child was cold and pulseless. 'He is dead,' said one. Kentuck opened his eyes. 'Dead?' he repeated feebly. 'Yes, my man, and you are dying too.' A smile lit the eyes of the expiring Kentuck. 'Dying!' he repeated; 'he's a-taking me with him. Tell the boys I've got The Luck with me now;' and the strong man, clinging to the frail babe as a drowning man is said to cling to a straw, drifted away into the shadowy river that flows forever to the unknown sea.

The Outcasts of Poker Flat

AS MR JOHN OAKHURST, gambler, stepped into the main street of Poker Flat on the morning of the 23d of November, 1850, he was conscious of a change in its moral atmosphere since the preceding night. Two or three men, conversing earnestly together, ceased as he approached, and exchanged significant glances. There was a Sabbath lull in the air, which, in a settlement unused to Sabbath influences, looked ominous.

Mr Oakhurst's calm, handsome face betrayed small concern in these indications. Whether he was conscious of any predisposing cause was another question. 'I reckon they're after somebody,' he reflected; 'likely it's me.' He returned to his pocket the handkerchief with which he had been whipping away the red dust of Poker Flat from his neat boots, and quietly discharged his mind of any further conjecture.

In point of fact, Poker Flat was 'after somebody.' It had lately suffered the loss of several thousand dollars, two valuable horses, and a prominent citizen. It was experiencing a spasm of virtuous reaction, quite as lawless and ungovernable as any of the acts that had provoked it. A secret committee had determined to rid the town of all improper persons. This was done permanently in regard of two men who were then hanging from the boughs of a sycamore in the gulch, and temporarily in the banishment of certain other objectionable characters. I regret to say that some of these were ladies. It is but due to the sex, however, to state that their impropriety was professional, and it was only in such easily established standards of evil that Poker Flat ventured to sit in judgment.

Mr Oakhurst was right in supposing that he was included in this category. A few of the committee had urged hanging him as a possible example and a sure method of reimbursing themselves from his pockets of the sums he had won from them. 'It's agin justice,' said Jim Wheeler, 'to let this yer young man from Roaring Camp – an entire stranger – carry away our money.' But a crude sentiment of equity residing in the breasts of those who had been fortunate enough to win from Mr Oakhurst overruled this narrower local prejudice.

Mr Oakhurst received his sentence with philosophic calmness, none the less coolly that he was aware of the hesitation of his judges. He was too much of a gambler not to accept fate. With him life was at best an uncertain game, and he recognized the usual percentage in favor of the dealer.

A body of armed men accompanied the deported wickedness of Poker Flat to the outskirts of the settlement. Besides Mr Oakhurst, who was known to be a coolly desperate man, and for whose intimidation the armed escort was intended, the expatriated party consisted of a young woman familiarly known as 'The Duchess'; another who had won the title of 'Mother Shipton';

and 'Uncle Billy,' a suspected sluice-robber and confirmed drunkard. The cavalcade provoked no comments from the spectators, nor was any word uttered by the escort. Only when the gulch which marked the uttermost limit of Poker Flat was reached, the leader spoke briefly and to the point. The exiles were forbidden to return at the peril of their lives.

As the escort disappeared, their pent-up feelings found vent in a few hysterical tears from the Duchess, some bad language from Mother Shipton, and a Parthian volley of expletives from Uncle Billy. The philosophic Oakhurst alone remained silent. He listened calmly to Mother Shipton's desire to cut somebody's heart out, to the repeated statements of the Duchess that she would die in the road, and to the alarming oaths that seemed to be bumped out of Uncle Billy as he rode forward. With the easy good humor characteristic of his class, he insisted upon exchanging his own riding-horse, 'Five-Spot,' for the sorry mule which the Duchess rode. But even this act did not draw the party into any closer sympathy. The young woman readjusted her somewhat draggled plumes with a feeble, faded coquetry; Mother Shipton eyed the possessor of 'Five-Spot' with malevolence, and Uncle Billy included the whole party in one sweeping anathema.

The road to Sandy Bar – a camp that, not having as yet experienced the regenerating influences of Poker Flat, consequently seemed to offer some invitation to the emigrants – lay over a steep mountain range. It was distant a day's severe travel. In that advanced season the party soon passed out of the moist, temperate regions of the foothills into the dry, cold, bracing air of the Sierras. The trail was narrow and difficult. At noon the Duchess, rolling out of her saddle upon the ground, declared her intention of going no farther, and the party halted.

The spot was singularly wild and impressive. A wooded amphitheatre, surrounded on three sides by precipitous cliffs of naked granite, sloped gently toward the crest of another precipice that overlooked the valley. It was, undoubtedly, the most suitable spot for a camp, had camping been advisable. But Mr Oakhurst knew that scarcely half the journey to Sandy Bar was accomplished, and the party were not equipped or provisioned for delay. This fact he pointed out to his companions curtly, with a philosophic commentary on the folly of 'throwing up their hand before the game was played out.' But they were furnished with liquor, which in this emergency stood them in place of food, fuel, rest, and prescience. In spite of his remonstrances, it was not long before they were more or less under its influence. Uncle Billy passed rapidly from a bellicose state into one of stupor, the Duchess became maudlin, and Mother Shipton snored. Mr Oakhurst alone remained erect, leaning against a rock, calmly surveying them.

Mr Oakhurst did not drink. It interfered with a profession which required coolness, impassiveness, and presence of mind, and in his own language, he 'couldn't afford it.' As he gazed at his recumbent fellow exiles, the loneliness begotten of his pariah trade, his habits of life, his very vices, for the first time seriously oppressed him. He bestirred himself in dusting his black clothes, washing his hands and face, and other acts characteristic of his studiously neat habits, and for a moment forgot his annoyance. The thought of deserting his weaker and more pitiable companions never perhaps occurred to him. Yet he could not help feeling the want of that excitement which, singularly enough, was most conducive to that calm equanimity for which he was notorious. He looked at the gloomy walls that rose a thousand feet sheer above the circling pines around him, at the sky ominously clouded, at the valley below, already deepening into shadow; and doing so, suddenly he heard his own name called.

A horseman slowly ascended the trail. In the fresh, open face of the newcomer Mr Oakhurst recognized Tom Simson, otherwise known as 'The Innocent,' of Sandy Bar. He had met him some months before over a 'little game,' and had, with perfect equanimity, won the entire fortune – amounting to some forty dollars – of that guileless youth. After the game was finished, Mr Oakhurst drew the youthful speculator behind the door and thus addressed him: 'Tommy, you're a good little man, but you can't gamble worth a cent. Don't try it over again.' He then handed him his money back, pushed him gently from the room, and so made a devoted slave of Tom Simson.

There was a remembrance of this in his boyish and enthusiastic greeting of Mr Oakhurst. He had started, he said, to go to Poker Flat, to seek his fortune. 'Alone?' No, not exactly alone; in fact (a giggle), he had run away with Piney Woods. Didn't Mr Oakhurst remember Piney? She that used to wait on the table at the Temperance House? They had been engaged a long time, but old Jake Woods had objected, and so they had run away, and were going to Poker Flat to be married, and here they were. And they were tired out, and how lucky it was they had found a place to camp, and company. All this the Innocent delivered rapidly, while Piney, a stout, comely damsel of fifteen, emerged from behind the pine tree, where she had been blushing unseen, and rode to the side of her lover.

Mr Oakhurst seldom troubled himself with sentiment, still less with propriety; but he had a vague idea that the situation was not fortunate. He retained, however, his presence of mind sufficiently to kick Uncle Billy, who was about to say something, and Uncle Billy was sober enough to recognize in Mr Oakhurst's kick a superior power that would not bear trifling. He then endeavored to dissuade Tom Simson from delaying further, but in vain. He even pointed out the fact that there was no provision, nor means of making a camp. But, unluckily, the Innocent met this objection by assuring the party that he was provided with an extra mule loaded with provisions, and by the discovery of a rude attempt at a log house near the trail. 'Piney can stay with Mrs Oakhurst,' said the Innocent, pointing to the Duchess, 'and I can shift for myself.'

Nothing but Mr Oakhurst's admonishing foot saved Uncle Billy from bursting into a roar of laughter. As it was, he felt compelled to retire up the canyon until he could recover his gravity. There he confided the joke to the tall pine trees, with many slaps of his leg, contortions of his face, and the usual profanity. But when he returned to the party, he found them seated by a fire – for the air had grown strangely chill and the sky overcast – in apparently amicable conversation. Piney was actually talking in an impulsive girlish fashion to the Duchess, who was listening with an interest and animation she had not shown for many days. The Innocent was holding forth, apparently with equal effect, to Mr Oakhurst and Mother Shipton, who was actually relaxing into amiability. 'Is this yer a d – d picnic?' said

Uncle Billy, with inward scorn, as he surveyed the sylvan group, the glancing firelight, and the tethered animals in the foreground. Suddenly an idea mingled with the alcoholic fumes that disturbed his brain. It was apparently of a jocular nature, for he felt impelled to slap his leg again and cram his fist into his mouth.

As the shadows crept slowly up the mountains, a slight breeze rocked the tops of the pine trees and moaned through their long and gloomy aisles. The ruined cabin, patched and covered with pine boughs, was set apart for the ladies. As the lovers parted, they unaffectedly exchanged a kiss, so honest and sincere that it might have been heard above the swaying pines. The frail Duchess and the malevolent Mother Shipton were probably too stunned to remark upon this last evidence of simplicity, and so turned without a word to the hut. The fire was replenished, the men lay down before the door, and in a few minutes were asleep.

Mr Oakhurst was a light sleeper. Toward morning he awoke benumbed and cold. As he stirred the dying fire, the wind, which was now blowing strongly, brought to his cheek that which caused the blood to leave it – snow!

He started to his feet with the intention of awakening the sleepers, for there was no time to lose. But turning to where Uncle Billy had been lying, he found him gone. A suspicion leaped to his brain, and a curse to his lips. He ran to the spot where the mules had been tethered – they were no longer there. The tracks were already rapidly disappearing in the snow.

The momentary excitement brought Mr Oakhurst back to the fire with his usual calm. He did not waken the sleepers. The Innocent slumbered peacefully, with a smile on his good-humored, freckled face; the virgin Piney slept beside her frailer sisters as sweetly as though attended by celestial guardians; and Mr Oakhurst, drawing his blanket over his shoulders, stroked his mustaches and waited for the dawn. It came slowly in a whirling mist of snowflakes that dazzled and confused the eye. What could be seen of the landscape appeared magically changed. He looked over the valley, and summed up the present and future in two words, 'Snowed in!'

A careful inventory of the provisions, which, fortunately for the party, had been stored within the hut, and so escaped the felonious fingers of Uncle Billy, disclosed the fact that with care and prudence they might last ten days longer. 'That is,' said Mr Oakhurst *sotto voce* to the Innocent, 'if you're willing to board us. If you ain't – and perhaps you'd better not – you can wait till Uncle Billy gets back with provisions.' For some occult reason, Mr Oakhurst could not bring himself to disclose Uncle Billy's rascality, and so offered the hypothesis that he had wandered from the camp and had accidentally stampeded the animals. He dropped a warning to the Duchess and Mother Shipton, who of course knew the facts of their associate's defection. 'They'll find out the truth about us *all* when they find out anything,' he added significantly, 'and there's no good frightening them now.'

Tom Simson not only put all his worldly store at the disposal of Mr Oakhurst, but seemed to enjoy the prospect of their enforced seclusion. 'We'll have a good camp for a week, and then the snow'll melt, and we'll all go back together.' The cheerful gayety of the young man and Mr Oakhurst's calm infected the others. The Innocent, with the aid of pine boughs, extemporized a thatch for the roofless cabin, and the Duchess directed Piney in the rearrangement of the interior with a taste and tact that opened the blue eyes of that provincial maiden to their fullest extent. 'I reckon now you're used to fine things at Poker Flat,' said Piney. The Duchess turned away sharply to conceal something that reddened her cheeks through their professional tint, and Mother Shipton requested Piney not to 'chatter.' But when Mr Oakhurst returned from a weary search for the trail, he heard the sound of happy laughter echoed from the rocks. He stopped in some alarm, and his thoughts first naturally reverted to the whiskey, which he had prudently cached. 'And yet it don't somehow sound like whiskey,' said the gambler. It was not until he caught sight of the blazing fire through the still blinding storm, and the group around it, that he settled to the conviction that it was 'square fun.'

Whether Mr Oakhurst had cached his cards with the whiskey as something debarred the free access of the community, I cannot say. It was certain that, in Mother Shipton's words, he 'didn't say "cards" once' during that evening. Haply the time was beguiled by an accordion, produced somewhat ostentatiously by Tom Simson from his pack. Notwithstanding some difficulties attending the manipulation of this instrument, Piney Woods managed to pluck several reluctant melodies from its keys to an accompaniment by the Innocent on a pair of bone castanets. But the crowning festivity of the evening was reached in a rude camp-meeting hymn, which the lovers, joining hands, sang with great earnestness and vociferation. I fear that a certain defiant tone and convenanter's swing to its chorus, rather than any devotional quality, caused it speedily to infect the others, who at last joined in the refrain:

> *'I'm proud to live in the service of the Lord,*
> *And I'm bound to die in His army.'*

The pines rocked, the storm eddied and whirled above the miserable group, and the flames of their altar leaped heavenward, as if in token of the vow.

At midnight the storm abated, the rolling clouds parted, and the stars glittered keenly above the sleeping camp. Mr Oakhurst, whose professional habits had enabled him to live on the smallest possible amount of sleep, in dividing the watch with Tom Simson somehow managed to take upon himself the greater part of that duty. He excused himself to the Innocent by saying that he had 'often been a week without sleep.' 'Doing what?' asked Tom. 'Poker!' replied Oakhurst sententiously. 'When a man gets a streak of luck – nigger-luck – he don't get tired. The luck gives in first. Luck,' continued the gambler reflectively, 'is a mighty queer thing. All you know about it for certain is that it's bound to change. And it's finding out when it's going to change that makes you. We've had a streak of bad luck since we left Poker Flat – you come along, and slap you get into it, too. If you can hold your cards right along you're all right. For,' added the gambler, with cheerful irrelevance –

> *'"I'm proud to live in the service of the Lord,*
> *And I'm bound to die in His army."'*

The third day came, and the sun, looking through the white-curtained valley, saw the outcasts divide their slowly decreasing store of provisions for the morning meal. It was one of the peculiarities of that mountain climate that its rays diffused a kindly warmth over the wintry landscape, as if in regretful commiseration of the past. But it revealed drift on drift of snow piled high around the hut – a hopeless, uncharted, trackless sea of white lying below the rocky shores to which the castaways still clung. Through the marvelously clear air the smoke of the pastoral village of Poker Flat rose miles away. Mother Shipton saw it, and from a remote pinnacle of her rocky fastness, hurled in that direction a final malediction. It was her last vituperative attempt, and perhaps for that reason was invested with a certain degree of sublimity. It did her good, she privately informed the Duchess. 'Just you go out there and cuss, and see.' She then set herself to the task of amusing 'the child,' as she and the Duchess were pleased to call Piney. Piney was no chicken, but it was a soothing and original theory of the pair thus to account for the fact that she didn't swear and wasn't improper.

When night crept up again through the gorges, the reedy notes of the accordion rose and fell in fitful spasms and long-drawn gasps by the flickering campfire. But music failed to fill entirely the aching void left by insufficient food, and a new diversion was proposed by Piney – storytelling. Neither Mr Oakhurst nor his female companions caring to relate their personal experiences, this plan would have failed too, but for the Innocent. Some months before he had chanced upon a stray copy of Mr Pope's ingenious translation of the Iliad. He now proposed to narrate the principal incidents of that poem – having thoroughly mastered the argument and fairly forgotten the words – in the current vernacular of Sandy Bar. And so for the rest of that night the Homeric demigods again walked the earth. Trojan bully and wily Greek wrestled in the winds, and the great pines in the canyon seemed to bow to the wrath of the son of Peleus. Mr Oakhurst listened with quiet satisfaction. Most especially was he interested in the fate of 'Ash-heels,' as the Innocent persisted in denominating the 'swift-footed Achilles.'

So, with small food and much of Homer and the accordion, a week passed over the heads of the outcasts. The sun again forsook them, and again from leaden skies the snowflakes were sifted over the land. Day by day closer around them drew the snowy circle, until at last they looked from their prison over drifted walls of dazzling white that towered twenty feet above their heads. It became more and more difficult to replenish their fires, even from the fallen trees beside them, now half hidden in the drifts. And yet no one complained. The lovers turned from the dreary prospect and looked into each other's eyes, and were happy. Mr Oakhurst settled himself coolly to the losing game before him. The Duchess, more cheerful than she had been, assumed the care of Piney. Only Mother Shipton – once the strongest of the party – seemed to sicken and fade. At midnight on the tenth day she called Oakhurst to her side. 'I'm going,' she said, in a voice of querulous weakness, 'but don't say anything about it. Don't waken the kids. Take the bundle from under my head, and open it.' Mr Oakhurst did so. It contained Mother Shipton's rations for the last week, untouched. 'Give 'em to the child,' she said, pointing to the sleeping Piney. 'You've starved yourself,' said the gambler. 'That's what they call it,' said the woman querulously, as she lay down again, and turning her face to the wall, passed quietly away.

The accordion and the bones were put aside that day, and Homer was forgotten. When the body of Mother Shipton had been committed to the snow, Mr Oakhurst took the Innocent aside, and showed him a pair of snowshoes, which he had fashioned from the old pack-saddle. 'There's one chance in a hundred to save her yet,' he said, pointing to Piney; 'but it's there,' he added, pointing toward Poker Flat. 'If you can reach there in two days she's safe.' 'And you?' asked Tom Simson. 'I'll stay here,' was the curt reply.

The lovers parted with a long embrace. 'You are not going, too?' said the Duchess, as she saw Mr Oakhurst apparently waiting to accompany him. 'As far as the canyon,' he replied. He turned suddenly and kissed the Duchess, leaving her pallid face aflame, and her trembling limbs rigid with amazement.

Night came, but not Mr Oakhurst. It brought the storm again and the whirling snow. Then the Duchess, feeding the fire, found that someone had quietly piled beside the hut enough fuel to last a few days longer. The tears rose to her eyes, but she hid them from Piney.

The women slept but little. In the morning, looking into each other's faces, they read their fate. Neither spoke, but Piney, accepting the position of the stronger, drew near and placed her arm around the Duchess's waist. They kept this attitude for the rest of the day. That night the storm reached its greatest fury, and rending asunder the protecting vines, invaded the very hut.

Toward morning they found themselves unable to feed the fire, which gradually died away. As the embers slowly blackened, the Duchess crept closer to Piney, and broke the silence of many hours: 'Piney, can you pray?' 'No, dear,' said Piney simply. The Duchess, without knowing exactly why, felt relieved, and putting her head upon Piney's shoulder, spoke no more. And so reclining, the younger and purer pillowing the head of her soiled sister upon her virgin breast, they fell asleep.

The wind lulled as if it feared to waken them. Feathery drifts of snow, shaken from the long pine boughs, flew like white winged birds, and settled about them as they slept. The moon through the rifted clouds looked down upon what had been the camp. But all human stain, all trace of earthly travail, was hidden beneath the spotless mantle mercifully flung from above.

They slept all that day and the next, nor did they waken when voices and footsteps broke the silence of the camp. And when pitying fingers brushed the snow from their wan faces, you could scarcely have told from the equal peace that dwelt upon them which was she that had sinned. Even the law of Poker Flat recognized this, and turned away, leaving them still locked in each other's arms.

But at the head of the gulch, on one of the largest pine trees, they found the deuce of clubs pinned to the bark with a bowie knife. It bore the following, written in pencil in a firm hand:

BENEATH THIS TREE

LIES THE BODY

OF

JOHN OAKHURST,

WHO STRUCK A STREAK OF BAD LUCK

ON THE 23D OF NOVEMBER, 1850,

AND

HANDED IN HIS CHECKS

ON THE 7TH DECEMBER, 1850.

And pulseless and cold, with a derringer by his side and a bullet in his heart, though still calm as in life, beneath the snow lay he who was at once the strongest and yet the weakest of the outcasts of Poker Flat.

Tennessee's Partner

I DO NOT THINK THAT we ever knew his real name. Our ignorance of it certainly never gave us any social inconvenience, for at Sandy Bar in 1854 most men were christened anew. Sometimes these appellatives were derived from some distinctiveness of dress, as in the case of 'Dungaree Jack'; or from some peculiarity of habit, as shown in 'Saleratus Bill,' so called from an undue proportion of that chemical in his daily bread; or from some unlucky slip, as exhibited in 'The Iron Pirate,' a mild, inoffensive man, who earned that baleful title by his unfortunate mispronunciation of the term 'iron pyrites.' Perhaps this may have been the beginning of a rude heraldry; but I am constrained to think that it was because a man's real name in that day rested solely upon his own unsupported statement. 'Call yourself Clifford, do you?' said Boston, addressing a timid newcomer with infinite scorn; 'hell is full of such Cliffords!' He then introduced the unfortunate man, whose name happened to be really Clifford, as 'Jaybird Charley' – an unhallowed inspiration of the moment that clung to him ever after.

But to return to Tennessee's Partner, whom we never knew by any other than this relative title. That he had ever existed as a separate and distinct individuality we only learned later. It seems that in 1853 he left Poker Flat to go to San Francisco, ostensibly to procure a wife. He never got any farther than Stockton. At that place he was attracted by a young person who waited upon the table at the hotel where he took his meals. One morning he said something to her which caused her to smile not unkindly, to somewhat coquettishly break a plate of toast over his upturned, serious, simple face, and to retreat to the kitchen. He followed her, and emerged a few moments later, covered with more toast and victory. That day week they were married by a justice of the peace, and returned to Poker Flat. I am aware that something more might be made of this episode, but I prefer to tell it as it was current at Sandy Bar – in the gulches and bar-rooms – where all sentiment was modified by a strong sense of humor.

Of their married felicity but little is known, perhaps for the reason that Tennessee, then living with his partner, one day took occasion to say something to the bride on his own account, at which, it is said, she smiled not unkindly and chastely retreated – this time as far as Marysville, where Tennessee followed her, and where they went to housekeeping without the aid of a justice of the peace. Tennessee's Partner took the loss of his wife simply and seriously, as was his fashion. But to everybody's surprise, when Tennessee one day returned from Marysville, without his partner's wife – she having smiled and retreated with somebody else – Tennessee's Partner was the first man to shake his hand and greet him with affection. The boys who had gathered in the canyon to see the shooting were naturally indignant.

Their indignation might have found vent in sarcasm but for a certain look in Tennessee's Partner's eye that indicated a lack of humorous appreciation. In fact, he was a grave man, with a steady application to practical detail which was unpleasant in a difficulty.

Meanwhile a popular feeling against Tennessee had grown up on the Bar. He was known to be a gambler; he was suspected to be a thief. In these suspicions Tennessee's Partner was equally compromised; his continued intimacy with Tennessee after the affair above quoted could only be accounted for on the hypothesis of a copartnership of crime. At last Tennessee's guilt became flagrant. One day he overtook a stranger on his way to Red Dog. The stranger afterward related that Tennessee beguiled the time with interesting anecdote and reminiscence, but illogically concluded the interview in the following words: 'And now, young man, I'll trouble you for your knife, your pistols, and your money. You see your weppings might get you into trouble at Red Dog, and your money's a temptation to the evilly disposed. I think you said your address was San Francisco. I shall endeavor to call.' It may be stated here that Tennessee had a fine flow of humor, which no business preoccupation could wholly subdue.

This exploit was his last. Red Dog and Sandy Bar made common cause against the highwayman. Tennessee was hunted in very much the same fashion as his prototype, the grizzly. As the toils closed around him, he made a desperate dash through the Bar, emptying his revolver at the crowd before the Arcade Saloon, and so on up Grizzly Canyon; but at its farther extremity he was stopped by a small man on a gray horse. The men looked at each other a moment in silence. Both were fearless, both self-possessed and independent, and both types of a civilization that in the seventeenth century would have been called heroic, but in the nineteenth simply 'reckless.'

'What have you got there? – I call,' said Tennessee quietly.

'Two bowers and an ace,' said the stranger as quietly, showing two revolvers and a bowie knife.

'That takes me,' returned Tennessee; and with this gambler's epigram, he threw away his useless pistol and rode back with his captor.

It was a warm night. The cool breeze which usually sprang up with the going down of the sun behind the chaparral-crested mountain was that evening withheld from Sandy Bar. The little canyon was stifling with heated resinous odors, and the decaying driftwood on the Bar sent forth faint sickening exhalations. The feverishness of day and its fierce passions still filled the camp. Lights moved restlessly along the bank of the river, striking no answering reflection from its tawny current. Against the blackness of the pines the windows of the old loft above the express office stood out staringly bright; and through their curtainless panes the loungers below could see the forms of those who were even then deciding the fate of Tennessee. And above all this, etched on the dark firmament, rose the Sierra, remote and passionless, crowned with remoter passionless stars.

The trial of Tennessee was conducted as fairly as was consistent with a judge and jury who felt themselves to some extent obliged to justify, in their verdict, the previous irregularities of arrest and indictment. The law of Sandy Bar was implacable, but not vengeful. The excitement and personal feeling of the chase were over; with Tennessee safe in their hands, they were ready to listen patiently to any defense, which they were already satisfied was insufficient. There being no doubt in their own minds, they were willing to give the prisoner the benefit of any that might exist. Secure in the hypothesis that he ought to be hanged on general principles, they indulged him with more latitude of defense than his reckless hardihood seemed to ask. The Judge appeared to be more anxious than the prisoner, who, otherwise unconcerned, evidently took a grim pleasure in the responsibility he had created. 'I don't take any hand in this yer game,' had been his invariable but good-humored reply to all questions. The Judge – who was also his captor – for a moment vaguely regretted that he had not shot him 'on sight' that morning, but presently dismissed this human weakness as unworthy of the judicial mind. Nevertheless, when there was a tap at the door, and it was said that Tennessee's Partner was there on behalf of the prisoner, he was admitted at once without question. Perhaps the younger members of the jury, to whom the proceedings were becoming irksomely thoughtful, hailed him as a relief.

For he was not, certainly, an imposing figure. Short and stout, with a square face, sunburned into a preternatural redness, clad in a loose duck 'jumper' and trousers streaked and splashed with red soil, his aspect under any circumstances would have been quaint, and was now even ridiculous. As he stooped to deposit at his feet a heavy carpetbag he was carrying, it became obvious, from partially developed legends and inscriptions, that the material with which his trousers had been patched had been originally intended for a less ambitious covering. Yet he advanced with great gravity, and after shaking the hand of each person in the room with labored cordiality, he wiped his serious perplexed face on a red bandana handkerchief, a shade lighter than his complexion, laid his powerful hand upon the table to steady himself, and thus addressed the Judge:

'I was passin' by,' he began, by way of apology, 'and I thought I'd just step in and see how things was gittin' on with Tennessee thar – my pardner. It's a hot night. I disremember any sich weather before on the Bar.'

He paused a moment, but nobody volunteering any other meteorological recollection, he again had recourse to his pocket handkerchief, and for some moments mopped his face diligently.

'Have you anything to say on behalf of the prisoner?' said the Judge finally.

'Thet's it,' said Tennessee's Partner, in a tone of relief. 'I come yar as Tennessee's pardner – knowing him nigh on four year, off and on, wet and dry, in luck and out o' luck. His ways ain't aller my ways, but thar ain't any p'ints in that young man, thar ain't any liveliness as he's been up to, as I don't know. And you sez to me, sez you – confidential-like, and between man and man – sez you, "Do you know anything in his behalf?" and I sez to you, sez I – confidential-like, as between man and man – "What should a man know of his pardner?"'

'Is this all you have to say?' asked the Judge impatiently, feeling, perhaps, that a dangerous sympathy of humor was beginning to humanize the court.

'Thet's so,' continued Tennessee's Partner. 'It ain't for me to say anything agin' him. And now, what's the case? Here's Tennessee wants money, wants it bad, and doesn't like to ask it of his old pardner. Well, what does Tennessee do? He lays for a stranger, and he fetches that stranger; and you lays for *him*, and you fetches *him*; and the honors is easy. And I put it to you, bein' a fa'r-minded man, and to you, gentlemen all, as fa'r-minded men, ef this isn't so.'

'Prisoner,' said the Judge, interrupting, 'have you any questions to ask this man?'

'No! no!' continued Tennessee's Partner hastily. 'I play this yer hand alone. To come down to the bedrock, it's just this: Tennessee thar has played it pretty rough and expensivelike on a stranger, and on this yer camp. And now, what's the fair thing? Some would say more, some would say less. Here's seventeen hundred dollars in coarse gold and a watch – it's about all my pile – and call it square!' And before a hand could be raised to prevent him, he had emptied the contents of the carpetbag upon the table.

For a moment his life was in jeopardy. One or two men sprang to their feet, several hands groped for hidden weapons, and a suggestion to 'throw him from the window' was only overridden by a gesture from the Judge. Tennessee laughed. And apparently oblivious of the excitement, Tennessee's Partner improved the opportunity to mop his face again with his handkerchief.

When order was restored, and the man was made to understand by the use of forcible figures and rhetoric that Tennessee's offense could not be condoned by money, his face took a more serious and sanguinary hue, and those who were nearest to him noticed that his rough hand trembled slightly on the table. He hesitated a moment as he slowly returned the gold to the carpetbag, as if he had not yet entirely caught the elevated sense of justice which swayed the tribunal, and was perplexed with the belief that he had not offered enough. Then he turned to the Judge, and saying, 'This yer is a lone hand, played alone, and without any pardner,' he bowed to the jury and was about to withdraw, when the Judge called him back:

'If you have anything to say to Tennessee, you had better say it now.'

For the first time that evening the eyes of the prisoner and his strange advocate met. Tennessee smiled, showed his white teeth, and saying, 'Euchred, old man!' held out his hand. Tennessee's Partner took it in his own, and saying, 'I just dropped in as I was passin' to see how things was gettin' on,' let the hand passively fall, and adding that 'it was a warm night,' again mopped his face with his handkerchief, and without another word withdrew.

The two men never again met each other alive. For the unparalleled insult of a bribe offered to Judge Lynch – who, whether bigoted, weak, or narrow, was at least incorruptible – firmly fixed in the mind of that mythical personage any wavering determination of Tennessee's fate; and at the break of day he was marched, closely guarded, to meet it at the top of Marley's Hill.

How he met it, how cool he was, how he refused to say anything, how perfect were the arrangements of the committee, were all duly reported, with the addition of a warning moral and example to all future evildoers, in the *Red Dog Clarion* by its editor, who was present, and to whose vigorous English I cheerfully refer the reader. But the beauty of that midsummer morning, the blessed amity of earth and air and sky, the awakened life of the free woods and hills, the joyous renewal and promise of Nature, and above all, the infinite serenity that thrilled through each, was not reported, as not being a part of the social lesson. And yet, when the weak and foolish deed was done, and a life, with its possibilities and responsibilities, had passed out of the misshapen thing that dangled between earth and sky, the birds sang, the flowers bloomed, the sun shone, as cheerily as before; and possibly the *Red Dog Clarion* was right.

Tennessee's Partner was not in the group that surrounded the ominous tree. But as they turned to disperse, attention was drawn to the singular appearance of a motionless donkey cart halted at the side of the road. As they approached, they at once recognized the venerable Jenny and the two-wheeled cart as the property of Tennessee's Partner, used by him in carrying dirt from his claim; and a few paces distant the owner of the equipage himself, sitting under a buckeye tree, wiping the perspiration from his glowing face. In answer to an enquiry, he said he had come for the body of the 'diseased,' 'if it was all the same to the committee.' He didn't wish to 'hurry anything;' he could 'wait.' He was not working that day; and when the gentlemen were done with the 'diseased,' he would take him. 'Ef thar is any present,' he added in his simple, serious way, 'as would care to jine in the fun'l, they kin come.' Perhaps it was from a sense of humor, which I have already intimated was a feature of Sandy Bar – perhaps it was from something even better than that, but two thirds of the loungers accepted the invitation at once.

It was noon when the body of Tennessee was delivered into the hands of his partner. As the cart drew up to the fatal tree, we noticed that it contained a rough oblong box – apparently made from a section of sluicing – and half filled with bark and the tassels of pine. The cart was further decorated with slips of willow and made fragrant with buckeye blossoms. When the body was deposited in the box, Tennessee's Partner drew over it a piece of tarred canvas, and gravely mounting the narrow seat in front with his feet upon the shafts, urged the little donkey forward. The equipage moved slowly on, at that decorous pace which was habitual with Jenny even under less solemn circumstances. The men – half curiously, half jestingly, but all good-humoredly – strolled along beside the cart, some in advance, some a little in the rear of the homely catalfalque. But whether from the narrowing of the road or some present sense of decorum, as the cart passed on, the company fell to the rear in couples, keeping step, and otherwise assuming the external show of a formal procession. Jack Folinsbee, who had at the outset played a funeral march in dumb show upon an imaginary trombone, desisted from a lack of sympathy and appreciation – not having, perhaps, your true humorist's capacity to be content with the enjoyment of his own fun.

The way led through Grizzly Canyon, by this time clothed in funeral drapery and shadows. The redwoods, burying their moccasined feet in the red soil, stood in Indian file along the track, trailing an uncouth benediction from their bending boughs upon the passing bier. A hare, surprised into helpless inactivity, sat upright and pulsating in the ferns by the roadside as the cortège went by. Squirrels hastened to gain a secure outlook from higher boughs; and the blue jays, spreading their wings, fluttered before them like outriders, until the outskirts of Sandy Bar were reached, and the solitary cabin of Tennessee's Partner.

Viewed under more favorable circumstances, it would not have been a cheerful place. The unpicturesque site, the rude and unlovely outlines, the unsavory details, which distinguish the nest-building of the California miner, were all here with the dreariness of decay superadded. A few paces from the cabin there was a rough enclosure, which, in the brief days of Tennessee's Partner's matrimonial felicity, had been used as a garden, but was now overgrown with fern. As we approached it, we were surprised to find that what we had taken for a recent attempt at cultivation was the broken soil about an open grave.

The cart was halted before the enclosure, and rejecting the offers of assistance with the same air of simple self-reliance he had displayed throughout, Tennessee's Partner lifted the rough coffin on his back, and deposited it unaided within the shallow grave. He then nailed down the board which served as a lid, and mounting the little mound of earth beside it, took off his hat and slowly mopped his face with his handkerchief. This the crowd felt was a preliminary to speech, and they disposed themselves variously on stumps and boulders, and sat expectant.

'When a man,' began Tennessee's Partner slowly, 'has been running free all day, what's the natural thing for him to do? Why, to come home. And if he ain't in a condition to go home, what can his best friend do? Why, bring him home. And here's Tennessee has been running free, and we brings him home from his wandering.' He paused and picked up a fragment of quartz, rubbed it thoughtfully on his sleeve, and went on: 'It ain't the first time that I've packed him on my back, as you see'd me now. It ain't the first time that I brought him to this yer cabin when he couldn't help himself; it ain't the first time that I and Jinny have waited for him on yon hill, and picked him up and so fetched him home, when he couldn't speak and didn't know me. And now that it's the last time, why' – he paused and rubbed the quartz gently on his sleeve – 'you see it's sort of rough on his pardner. And now, gentlemen,' he added abruptly, picking up his long-handled shovel, 'the fun'l's over; and my thanks, and Tennessee's thanks, to you for your trouble.'

Resisting any proffers of assistance, he began to fill in the grave, turning his back upon the crowd, that after a few moments' hesitation gradually withdrew. As they crossed the little ridge that hid Sandy Bar from view, some, looking back, thought they could see Tennessee's Partner, his work done, sitting upon the grave, his shovel between his knees, and his face buried in his red bandana handkerchief. But it was argued by others that you couldn't tell his face from his handkerchief at that distance, and this point remained undecided.

In the reaction that followed the feverish excitement of that day, Tennessee's Partner was not forgotten. A secret investigation had cleared him of any complicity in Tennessee's guilt, and left only a suspicion of his general sanity. Sandy Bar made a point of calling on him, and proffering various uncouth but well-meant kindnesses. But from that day his rude health and great strength seemed visibly to decline; and when the rainy season fairly set in, and the tiny grass blades were beginning to peep from the rocky mound above Tennessee's grave, he took to his bed.

One night, when the pines beside the cabin were swaying in the storm and trailing their slender fingers over the roof, and the roar and rush of the swollen river were heard below, Tennessee's Partner lifted his head from the pillow, saying, 'It is time to go for Tennessee; I must put Jinny in the cart;' and would have risen from his bed but for the restraint of his attendant. Struggling, he still pursued his singular fancy: 'There, now, steady, Jinny, steady, old girl. How dark it is! Look out for the ruts, and look out for him, too, old gal. Sometimes, you know, when he's blind drunk, he drops down right in the trail. Keep on straight up to the pine on the top of the hill. Thar! I told you so! – thar he is – coming this way, too – all by himself, sober, and his face a-shining. Tennessee! Pardner!'

And so they met.

AMBROSE BIERCE 1842-1914

Ambrose Bierce was born in Ohio in 1842. After serving in the Civil War, he became a journalist in California and rapidly achieved a reputation and the nickname 'Bitter' Bierce, for his brilliant but acerbic wit. His first literary collection, *Tales of Soldiers and Civilians*, which was published in 1891, included several macabre stories based on Bierce's experiences in the Civil War and was much praised. His next collection *Can Such Things Be?* (1893) established him as a leading exponent of macabre fiction.

The stories which follow are taken from the two volumes mentioned above and reveal the combination of realism and nightmarish phantasm which typify all of Bierce's remarkable tales.

An Occurrence at Owl Creek Bridge

1

A MAN STOOD UPON A RAILROAD BRIDGE in northern Alabama, looking down into the swift water twenty feet below. The man's hands were behind his back, the wrists bound with a cord. A rope closely encircled his neck. It was attached to a stout cross-timber above his head and the slack fell to the level of his knees. Some loose boards laid upon the sleepers supporting the metals of the railway supplied a footing for him and his executioners – two private soldiers of the Federal army, directed by a sergeant who in civil life may have been a deputy sheriff. At a short remove upon the same temporary platform was an officer in the uniform of his rank, armed. He was a captain. A sentinel at each end of the bridge stood with his rifle in the position known as 'support,' that is to say, vertical in front of the left shoulder, the hammer resting on the forearm thrown straight across the chest – a formal and unnatural position, enforcing an erect carriage of the body. It did not appear to be the duty of these two men to know what was occurring at the center of the bridge; they merely blockaded the two ends of the foot planking that traversed it.

Beyond one of the sentinels nobody was in sight; the railroad ran straight away into a forest for a hundred yards, then, curving, was lost to view. Doubtless there was an outpost farther along. The other bank of the stream was open ground – a gentle acclivity topped with a stockade of vertical tree trunks, loopholed for rifles, with a single embrasure through which protruded the muzzle of a brass cannon commanding the bridge. Midway of the slope between bridge and fort were the spectators – a single company of infantry in line, at 'parade rest,' the butts of the rifles on the ground, the barrels inclining slightly backward against the right shoulder, the hands crossed upon the stock. A lieutenant stood at the right of the line, the point of his sword upon the ground, his left hand resting upon his right. Excepting the group of four at the center of the bridge, not a man moved. The company faced the bridge, staring stonily, motionless. The sentinels, facing the banks of the stream, might have been statues to adorn the bridge. The captain stood with folded arms, silent, observing the work of his subordinates, but making no sign. Death is a dignitary who when he comes announced is to be received with formal manifestations of respect, even by those most familiar with him. In the code of military etiquette silence and fixity are forms of deference.

The man who was engaged in being hanged was apparently about thirty-five years of age. He was a civilian, if one might judge from his habit, which was that of a planter. His features were good – straight nose, firm mouth, broad forehead, from which his long, dark hair was combed straight back, falling behind his ears to the collar of his well-fitting frock coat. He wore a mustache and pointed beard, but no whiskers; his eyes were large and dark gray, and had a kindly expression which one would hardly have expected in one whose neck was in the hemp. Evidently this was no vulgar assassin. The liberal military code makes provision for hanging many kinds of persons, and gentlemen are not excluded.

The preparations being complete, the two private soldiers stepped aside and each drew away the plank upon which he had been standing. The sergeant turned to the captain, saluted, and placed himself immediately behind that officer, who in turn moved apart one pace. These movements left the condemned man and the sergeant standing on the two ends of the same plank, which spanned three of the cross-ties of the bridge. The end upon which the civilian stood almost, but not quite, reached a fourth. This plank had been held in place by the weight of the captain; it was not held by that of the sergeant. At a signal from the former the latter would step aside, the plank would tilt and the condemned man go down between two ties. The arrangement commended itself to his judgment as simple and effective. His face had not been covered nor his eyes bandaged. He looked a moment at his 'unsteadfast footing,' then let his gaze wander to the swirling water of the stream racing madly beneath his feet. A piece of dancing driftwood caught his attention and his eyes followed it down the current. How slowly it appeared to move! What a sluggish stream!

He closed his eyes in order to fix his last thoughts upon his wife and children. The water, touched to gold by the early sun, the brooding mists under the banks at some distance down the stream, the fort, the soldiers, the piece of drift – all had distracted him. And now he became conscious of a new disturbance. Striking through the thought of his dear ones was a sound which he could neither ignore nor understand, a sharp, distinct, metallic percussion like the stroke of a blacksmith's hammer upon the anvil; it had the same ringing quality. He wondered what it was, and whether immeasurably distant or nearby – it seemed both. Its recurrence was regular, but as slow as the tolling of a death knell. He awaited each stroke with impatience and – he knew not why – apprehension. The intervals of silence grew progressively longer; the delays became maddening. With their greater infrequency the sounds increased in strength and sharpness. They hurt his ear like the thrust of a knife; he feared he would shriek. What he heard was the ticking of his watch.

He unclosed his eyes and saw again the water below him. 'If I could free my hands,' he thought, 'I might throw off the noose and spring into the stream. By diving I could evade the bullets and, swimming vigorously, reach the bank, take to the woods and get away home. My home, thank God, is as yet outside their lines; my wife and little ones are still beyond the invader's farthest advance.'

As these thoughts, which have here to be set down in words, were flashed into the doomed man's brain rather than evolved from it the captain nodded to the sergeant. The sergeant stepped aside.

2

Peyton Farquhar was a well-to-do planter, of an old and highly respected

Alabama family. Being a slave owner and like other slave owners a politician he was naturally an original secessionist and ardently devoted to the Southern cause. Circumstances of an imperious nature, which it is unnecessary to relate here, had prevented him from taking service with the gallant army that had fought the disastrous campaigns ending with the fall of Corinth, and he chafed under the inglorious restraint, longing for the release of his energies, the larger life of the soldier, the opportunity for distinction. That opportunity, he felt, would come, as it comes to all in wartime. Meanwhile he did what he could. No service was too humble for him to perform in aid of the South, no adventure too perilous for him to undertake if consistent with the character of a civilian who was at heart a soldier, and who in good faith and without too much qualification assented to at least a part of the frankly villainous dictum that all is fair in love and war.

One evening while Farquhar and his wife were sitting on a rustic bench near the entrance to his grounds, a gray-clad soldier rode up to the gate and asked for a drink of water. Mrs Farquhar was only too happy to serve him with her own white hands. While she was fetching the water her husband approached the dusty horseman and inquired eagerly for news from the front.

'The Yanks are repairing the railroads,' said the man, 'and are getting ready for another advance. They have reached the Owl Creek bridge, put it in order, and built a stockade on the north bank. The commandant has issued an order, which is posted everywhere, declaring that any civilian caught interfering with the railroad, its bridges, tunnels or trains will be summarily hanged. I saw the order.'

'How far is it to the Owl Creek bridge?' Farquhar asked.

'About thirty miles.'

'Is there no force on this side the creek?'

'Only a picket post half a mile out, on the railroad, and a single sentinel at this end of the bridge.'

'Suppose a man – a civilian and student of hanging – should elude the picket post and perhaps get the better of the sentinel,' said Farquhar, smiling, 'what could he accomplish?'

The soldier reflected. 'I was there a month ago,' he replied. 'I observed that the flood of last winter had lodged a great quantity of drift wood against the wooden pier at this end of the bridge. It is now dry and would burn like tow.'

The lady had now brought the water, which the soldier drank. He thanked her ceremoniously, bowed to her husband, and rode away. An hour later, after nightfall, he repassed the plantation, going northward in the direction from which he had come. He was a Federal scout.

3

As Peyton Farquhar fell straight downward through the bridge he lost consciousness and was as one already dead. From this state he was awakened – ages later, it seemed to him – by the pain of a sharp pressure upon his throat, followed by a sense of suffocation. Keen, poignant agonies seemed to shoot from his neck downward through every fiber of his body and limbs.

These pains appeared to flash along well-defined lines of ramification and to beat with an inconceivably rapid periodicity. They seemed like streams of pulsating fire heating him to an intolerable temperature. As to his head, he was conscious of nothing but a feeling of fullness – of congestion. These sensations were unaccompanied by thought. The intellectual part of his nature was already effaced; he had power only to feel, and feeling was torment. He was conscious of motion. Encompassed in a luminous cloud, of which he was now merely the fiery heart, without material substance, he swung through unthinkable arcs of oscillation, like a vast pendulum. Then all at once, with terrible suddenness, the light about him shot upward with the noise of a loud plash; a frightful roaring was in his ears, and all was cold and dark. The power of thought was restored; he knew that the rope had broken and he had fallen into the stream. There was no additional strangulation; the noose about his neck was already suffocating him and kept the water from his lungs. To die of hanging at the bottom of a river! – the idea seemed to him ludicrous. He opened his eyes in the darkness and saw above him a gleam of light, but how distant, how inaccessible! He was still sinking, for the light became fainter and fainter until it was a mere glimmer. Then it began to grow and brighten, and he knew that he was rising toward the surface – knew it with reluctance, for he was now very comfortable. 'To be hanged and drowned,' he thought, 'that is not so bad, but I do not wish to be shot. No, I will not be shot. That is not fair.'

He was not conscious of an effort, but a sharp pain in his wrist apprised him that he was trying to free his hands. He gave the struggle his attention, as an idler might observe the feat of a juggler, without interest in the outcome. What spendid effort! What magnificent, what superhuman strength! Ah, that was a fine endeavor! Bravo! The cord fell away; his arms parted and floated upward, the hands dimly seen on each side in the growing light. He watched them with a new interest as first one and then the other pounced upon the noose at his neck. They tore it away and thrust it fiercely aside, its undulations resembling those of a water snake. 'Put it back, put it back!' He thought he shouted these words to his hands, for the undoing of the noose had been succeeded by the direst pang that he had yet experienced. His neck ached horribly; his brain was on fire; his heart, which had been fluttering faintly, gave a great leap, trying to force itself out at his mouth. His whole body was racked and wrenched with an insupportable anguish! But his disobedient hands gave no heed to the command. They beat the water vigorously with quick, downward strokes, forcing him to the surface. He felt his head emerge; his eyes were blinded by the sunlight; his chest expanded convulsively, and with a supreme and crowning agony his lungs engulfed a great draught of air, which instantly he expelled in a shriek!

He was now in full possession of his physical senses. They were, indeed, preternaturally keen and alert. Something in the awful disturbance of his organic system had so exalted and refined them that they made record of things never before perceived. He felt the ripples upon his face and heard their separate sounds as they struck. He looked at the forest on the bank of the stream, saw the individual trees, the leaves and the veining of each leaf – saw the very insects upon them: the locusts, the brilliant-bodied flies, the gray spiders stretching their webs from twig to twig. He noted the prismatic colors in all the dewdrops upon a million blades of grass. The humming of the gnats that danced above the eddies of the stream, the beating of the dragonflies' wings, the strokes of the water spiders' legs, like oars which had lifted their boat – all these made audible music. A fish slid along beneath his eyes and he heard the rush of its body parting the water.

He had come to the surface facing down the stream; in a moment the visible world seemed to wheel slowly round, himself the pivotal point, and he saw the bridge, the fort, the soldiers upon the bridge, the captain, the sergeant, the two privates, his executioners. They were in silhouette against the blue sky. They shouted and gesticulated, pointing at him. The captain had drawn his pistol, but did not fire; the others were unarmed. Their movements were grotesque and horrible, their forms gigantic.

Suddenly he heard a sharp report and something struck the water smartly within a few inches of his head, spattering his face with spray. He heard a second report, and saw one of the sentinels with his rifle at his shoulder, a light cloud of blue smoke rising from the muzzle. The man in the water saw the eye of the man on the bridge gazing into his own through the sights of the rifle. He observed that it was a gray eye and remembered having read that gray eyes were keenest, and that all famous marksmen had them. Nevertheless, this one had missed.

A counterswirl had caught Farquhar and turned him half round; he was again looking into the forest on the bank opposite the fort. The sound of a clear, high voice in a monotonous singsong now rang out behind him and came across the water with a distinctness that pierced and subdued all other sounds, even the beating of the ripples in his ears. Although no soldier, he had frequented camps enough to know the dread significance of that deliberate, drawling aspirated chant; the lieutenant on shore was taking a part in the morning's work. How coldly and pitilessly – with what an even, calm intonation, presaging, and enforcing tranquillity in the men – with what accurately measured intervals fell those cruel words:

'Attention, company! ... Shoulder arms! ... Ready! ... Aim! ... Fire!'

Farquhar dived – dived as deeply as he could. The water roared in his ears like the voice of Niagara, yet he heard the dulled thunder of the volley and, rising again toward the surface, met shining bits of metal, singularly flattened, oscillating slowly downward. Some of them touched him on the face and hands, then fell away, continuing their descent. One lodged between his collar and neck; it was uncomfortably warm and he snatched it out.

As he rose to the surface, gasping for breath, he saw that he had been a long time under water; he was perceptibly farther downstream – nearer to safety. The soldiers had almost finished reloading; the metal ramrods flashed all at once in the sunshine as they were drawn from the barrels, turned in the air, and thrust into their sockets. The two sentinels fired again, independently and ineffectually.

The hunted man saw all this over his shoulder; he was now swimming vigorously with the current. His brain was as energetic as his arms and legs; he thought with the rapidity of lightning.

'The officer,' he reasoned, 'will not make that martinet's error a second time. It is as easy to dodge a volley as a single shot. He has probably already given the command to fire at will. God help me, I cannot dodge them all!'

An appalling plash within two yards of him was followed by a loud, rushing sound, diminuendo, which seemed to travel back through the air to the fort and died in an explosion which stirred the very river to its deeps! A rising sheet of water curved over him, fell down upon him, blinded him, strangled him! The cannon had taken a hand in the game. As he shook his head free from the commotion of the smitten water he heard the deflected shot humming through the air ahead, and in an instant it was cracking and smashing the branches in the forest beyond.

'They will not do that again,' he thought. 'The next time they will use a charge of grape. I must keep my eye upon the gun. The smoke will apprise me – the report arrives too late; it lags behind the missile. That is a good gun.'

Suddenly he felt himself whirled round and round – spinning like a top. The water, the banks, the forests, the now distant bridge, fort and men – all were commingled and blurred. Objects were represented by their colors only; circular horizontal streaks of color – that was all he saw. He had been caught in a vortex and was being whirled on with a velocity of advance and gyration that made him giddy and sick. In a few moments he was flung upon the gravel at the foot of the left bank of the stream – the southern bank – and behind a projecting point which concealed him from his enemies. The sudden arrest of his motion, the abrasion of one of his hands on the gravel, restored him, and he wept with delight. He dug his fingers into the sand, threw it over himself in handfuls and audibly blessed it. It looked like diamonds, rubies, emeralds; he could think of nothing beautiful which it did not resemble. The trees upon the bank were giant garden plants; he noted a definite order in their arrangement, inhaled the fragrance of their blooms. A strange, roseate light shone through the spaces among their trunks and the wind made in their branches the music of aeolian harps. He had no wish to perfect his escape – was content to remain in that enchanting spot until retaken.

A whiz and rattle of grapeshot among the branches high above his head roused him from his dream. The baffled cannoneer had fired him a random farewell. He sprang to his feet, rushed up the sloping bank and plunged into the forest.

All that day he traveled, laying his course by the rounding sun. The forest seemed interminable; nowhere did he discover a break in it, not even a woodman's road. He had not known that he lived in so wild a region. There was something uncanny in the revelation.

By nightfall he was fatigued, footsore, famishing. The thought of his wife and children urged him on. At last he found a road which led him in what he knew to be the right direction. It was as wide and straight as a city street, yet it seemed untraveled. No fields bordered it, no dwelling anywhere. Not so much as the barking of a dog suggested human habitation. The black bodies of the trees formed a straight wall on both sides, terminating on the horizon in a point, like a diagram in a lesson in perspective. Overhead, as he looked up through this rift in the wood, shone great golden stars looking unfamiliar and grouped in strange constellations. He was sure they were arranged in some order which had a secret and malign significance. The wood on either side was full of singular noises, among which – once, twice, and again – he distinctly heard whispers in an unknown tongue.

His neck was in pain and lifting his hand to it he found it horribly swollen. He knew that it had a circle of black where the rope had bruised it. His eyes felt congested; he could no longer close them. His tongue was swollen with thirst; he relieved its fever by thrusting it forward from between his teeth into the cold air. How softly the turf had carpeted the untraveled avenue – he could no longer feel the roadway beneath his feet!

Doubtless, despite his suffering, he had fallen asleep while walking, for now he sees another scene – perhaps he has merely recovered from a delirium. He stands at the gate of his own home. All is as he left it, and all bright and beautiful in the morning sunshine. He must have traveled the entire night. As he pushes open the gate and passes up the wide white walk, he sees a flutter of female garments; his wife, looking fresh and cool and sweet, steps down from the veranda to meet him. At the bottom of the steps she stands waiting, with a smile of ineffable joy, an attitude of matchless grace and dignity. Ah, how beautiful she is! He springs forward with extended arms. As he is about to clasp her he feels a stunning blow upon the back of the neck; a blinding white light blazes all about him with a sound like the shock of a cannon – then all is darkness and silence!

Peyton Farquhar was dead; his body, with a broken neck, swung gently from side to side beneath the timbers of the Owl Creek bridge.

A Horseman in the Sky

1

ONE SUNNY AFTERNOON in the autumn of the year 1861 a soldier lay in a clump of laurel by the side of a road in western Virginia. He lay at full length upon his stomach, his feet resting upon the toes, his head upon the left forearm. His extended right hand loosely grasped his rifle. But for the somewhat methodical disposition of his limbs and a slight rhythmic movement of the cartridge box at the back of his belt he might have been thought to be dead. He was asleep at his post of duty. But if detected he would be dead shortly afterward, death being the just and legal penalty of his crime.

The clump of laurel in which the criminal lay was in the angle of a road which after ascending southward a steep acclivity to that point turned sharply to the west, running along the summit for perhaps one hundred yards. There it turned southward again and went zigzagging downward through the forest. At the salient of that second angle was a large flat rock, jutting out northward, overlooking the deep valley from which the road ascended. The rock capped a high cliff; a stone dropped from its outer edge would have fallen sheer downward one thousand feet to the tops of the pines. The angle where the soldier lay was on another spur of the same cliff. Had he been awake he would have commanded a view, not only of the short arm of the road and the jutting rock, but of the entire profile of the cliff below it. It might well have made him giddy to look.

The country was wooded everywhere except at the bottom of the valley to the northward, where there was a small natural meadow, through which flowed a stream scarcely visible from the valley's rim. This open ground looked hardly larger than an ordinary dooryard, but was really several acres in extent. Its green was more vivid than that of the enclosing forest. Away beyond it rose a line of giant cliffs similar to those upon which we are supposed to stand in our survey of the savage scene, and through which the road had somehow made its climb to the summit. The configuration of the valley, indeed, was such that from this point of observation it seemed entirely shut in, and one could but have wondered how the road which found a way out of it had found a way into it, and whence came and whither went the waters of the stream that parted the meadow more than a thousand feet below.

No country is so wild and difficult but men will make it a theater of war; concealed in the forest at the bottom of that military rat-trap, in which half a hundred men in possession of the exits might have starved an army into submission, lay five regiments of Federal infantry. They had marched all the previous day and night, and were resting. At nightfall they would take to the road again, climb to the place where their unfaithful sentinel now slept, and

320

descending the other slope of the ridge fall upon a camp of the enemy at about midnight. Their hope was to surprise it, for the road led to the rear of it. In case of failure, their position would be perilous in the extreme; and fail they surely would should accident or vigilance apprise the enemy of the movement.

2

The sleeping sentinel in the clump of laurel was a young Virginian named Carter Druse. He was the son of wealthy parents, an only child, and had known such ease and cultivation and high living as wealth and taste were able to command in the mountain country of western Virginia. His home was but a few miles from where he now lay. One morning he had risen from the breakfast table and said, quietly but gravely, 'Father, a Union regiment has arrived at Grafton. I am going to join it.'

The father lifted his leonine head, looked at the son a moment in silence, and replied, 'Well, go sir, and whatever may occur do what you conceive to be your duty. Virginia, to which you are a traitor, must get on without you. Should we both live to the end of the war, we will speak further of the matter. Your mother, as the physician has informed you, is in a most critical condition; at the best she cannot be with us longer than a few weeks, but that time is precious. It would be better not to disturb her.'

So Carter Druse, bowing reverently to his father, who returned the salute with a stately courtesy that masked a breaking heart, left the home of his childhood to go soldiering. By conscience and courage, by deeds of devotion and daring, he soon commended himself to his fellows and his officers; and it was to these qualities and to some knowledge of the country that he owed his selection for his present perilous duty at the extreme outpost. Nevertheless, fatigue had been stronger than resolution, and he had fallen asleep. What good or bad angel came in a dream to rouse him from his state of crime, who shall say? Without a movement, without a sound, in the profound silence and the languor of the late afternoon, some invisible messenger of fate touched with unsealing finger the eyes of his consciousness – whispered into the ear of his spirit the mysterious awakening work which no human lips ever have spoken, no human memory ever has recalled. He quietly raised his forehead from his arm and looked between the masking stems of the laurels, instinctively closing his right hand about the stock of his rifle.

His first feeling was a keen artistic delight. On a colossal pedestal, the cliff – motionless at the extreme edge of the capping rock and sharply outlined against the sky – was an equestrian statue of impressive dignity. The figure of the man sat the figure of the horse, straight and soldierly, but with the repose of a Grecian god carved in the marble which limits the suggestion of activity. The gray costume harmonized with its aerial background; the metal of accouterment and caparison was softened and subdued by the shadow; the animal's skin had no points of highlight. A carbine strikingly foreshortened lay across the pommel of the saddle, kept in place by the right hand grasping it at the 'grip'; the left hand, holding the bridle rein, was invisible. In silhouette against the sky the profile of the horse was cut with the sharpness of a cameo; it looked across the heights of air to the confronting cliffs beyond.

The face of the rider, turned slightly away, showed only an outline of temple and beard; he was looking downward to the bottom of the valley. Magnified by its lift against the sky and by the soldier's testifying sense of the formidableness of a near enemy, the group appeared of heroic, almost colossal, size.

For an instant Druse had a strange, half-defining feeling that he had slept to the end of the war and was looking upon a noble work of art reared upon that eminence to commemorate the deeds of a heroic past of which he had been an inglorious part. The feeling was dispelled by a slight movement of the group: the horse, without moving its feet, had drawn its body slightly backward from the verge; the man remained immobile as before. Broad awake and keenly alive to the significance of the situation, Druse now brought the butt of his rifle against his cheek by cautiously pushing the barrel forward through the bushes, cocked the piece, and glancing through the sights covered a vital spot of the horseman's breast. A touch upon the trigger and all would have been well with Carter Druse. At that instant the horseman turned his head and looked in the direction of his concealed foeman – seemed to look into his very face, into his eyes, into his brave compassionate heart.

Is it then so terrible to kill an enemy in war – an enemy who has surprised a secret vital to the safety of one's self and comrades – an enemy more formidable for his knowledge than all his army for its numbers? Carter Druse grew pale; he shook in every limb, turned faint, and saw the statuesque group before him as black figures, rising, falling, moving unsteadily in arcs of circles in a fiery sky. His hand fell away from his weapon, his head slowly dropped until his face rested on the leaves in which he lay. This courageous gentleman and hardy soldier was near swooning from intensity of emotion.

It was not for long; in another moment his face was raised from earth, his hands resumed their places on the rifle, his forefinger sought the trigger; mind, heart, and eyes were clear, conscience and reason sound. He could not hope to capture that enemy; to alarm him would but send him dashing to his camp with his fatal news. The duty of the soldier was plain: the man must be shot dead from ambush – without warning, without a moment's spiritual preparation, with never so much as an unspoken prayer, he must be sent to his account. But no – there is a hope; he may have discovered nothing – perhaps he is but admiring the sublimity of the landscape. If permitted, he may turn and ride carelessly away in the direction whence he came. Surely it will be possible to judge at the instant of his withdrawing whether he knows. It may well be that his fixity of attention – Druse turned his head and looked through the deeps of air downward, as from the surface to the bottom of a translucent sea. He saw creeping across the green meadow a sinuous line of figures of men and horses – some foolish commander was permitting the soldiers of his escort to water their beasts in the open, in plain view from a dozen summits!

Druse withdrew his eyes from the valley and fixed them again upon the group of man and horse in the sky, and again it was through the sights of his rifle. But this time his aim was at the horse. In his memory, as if they were a divine mandate, rang the words of his father at their parting: 'Whatever may occur, do what you conceive to be your duty.' He was calm now. His teeth were firmly but not rigidly closed; his nerves were as tranquil as a sleeping babe's – not a tremor affected any muscle of his body; his breathing, until suspended in the act of taking aim, was regular and slow. Duty had conquered; the spirit had said to the body: 'Peace, be still.' He fired.

3

An officer of the Federal force, who in a spirit of adventure or in quest of knowledge had left the hidden bivouac in the valley, and with aimless feet had made his way to the lower edge of a small open space near the foot of the cliff, was considering what he had to gain by pushing his exploration further. At a distance of a quarter-mile before him, but apparently at a stone's throw, rose from its fringe of pines the gigantic face of rock, towering to so great a height above him that it made him giddy to look up to where its edge cut a sharp, rugged line against the sky. It presented a clean, vertical profile against a background of blue sky to a point half the way down, and of distant hills, hardly less blue, thence to the tops of the trees at its base. Lifting his eyes to the dizzy altitude of its summit the officer saw an astonishing sight – a man on horseback riding down into the valley through the air!

Straight upright sat the rider, in military fashion, with a firm seat in the saddle, a strong clutch upon the rein to hold his charger from too impetuous a plunge. From his bare head his long hair streamed upward, waving like a plume. His hands were concealed in the cloud of the horse's lifted mane. The animal's body was as level as if every hoof-stroke encountered the resistant earth. Its motions were those of a wild gallop, but even as the officer looked they ceased, with all the legs thrown sharply forward as in the act of alighting from a leap. But this was a flight!

Filled with amazement and terror by this apparition of a horseman in the sky – half believing himself the chosen scribe of some new Apocalypse, the officer was overcome by the intensity of his emotions; his legs failed him and he fell. Almost at the same instant he heard a crashing sound in the trees – a sound that died without an echo – and all was still.

The officer rose to his feet, trembling. The familiar sensation of an abraded shin recalled his dazed faculties. Pulling himself together he ran rapidly obliquely away from the cliff to a point distant from its foot; thereabout he expected to find his man; and thereabout he naturally failed. In the fleeting instant of his vision his imagination had been so wrought upon by the apparent grace and ease and intention of the marvelous performance that it did not occur to him that the line of march of aerial cavalry is directly downward, and that he could find the objects of his search at the very foot of the cliff. A half-hour later he returned to camp.

This officer was a wise man; he knew better than to tell an incredible truth. He said nothing of what he had seen. But when the commander asked him if in his scout he had learned anything of advantage to the expedition he answered:

'Yes sir. There is no road leading down into this valley from the southward.'

The commander, knowing better, smiled.

4

After firing his shot, Private Carter Druse reloaded his rifle and resumed his watch. Ten minutes had hardly passed when a Federal sergeant crept cautiously to him on hands and knees. Druse neither turned his head nor looked at him, but lay without motion or sign of recognition.

'Did you fire?' the sergeant whispered.

'Yes.'

'At what?'

'A horse. It was standing on yonder rock – pretty far out. You see it is no longer there. It went over the cliff.'

The man's face was white, but he showed no other sign of emotion. Having answered, he turned away his eyes and said no more. The sergeant did not understand.

'See here, Druse,' he said, after a moment's silence, 'It's no use making a mystery. I order you to report. Was there anybody on the horse?'

'Yes.'

'Well?'

'My father.'

The sergeant rose to his feet and walked away. 'Good God!' he said.

The Damned Thing

BY THE LIGHT OF A tallow candle which had been placed on one end of a rough table a man was reading something written in a book. It was an old account book, greatly worn; and the writing was not, apparently, very legible, for the man sometimes held the page close to the flame of the candle to get a stronger light on it. The shadow of the book would then throw into obscurity a half of the room, darkening a number of faces and figures; for besides the reader, eight other men were present. Seven of them sat against the rough log walls, silent, motionless, and the room being small, not very far from the table. By extending an arm any one of them could have touched the eighth man, who lay on the table, face upward, partly covered by a sheet, his arms at his sides. He was dead.

The man with the book was not reading aloud, and no one spoke. All seemed to be waiting for something to occur; the dead man only was without expectation. From the blank darkness outside came in, through the aperture that served for a window, all the ever unfamiliar noises of night in the wilderness – the long nameless note of a distant coyote; the stilly pulsing trill of tireless insects in trees; strange cries of night birds, so different from those of the birds of the day; the drone of great blundering beetles, and all that mysterious chorus of small sounds that seem always to have been but half heard when they have suddenly ceased, as if conscious of an indiscretion. But nothing of all this was noted in that company; its members were not overmuch addicted to idle interest in matters of no practical importance; that was obvious in every line of their rugged faces – obvious even in the dim light of the single candle. They were evidently men of the vicinity – farmers and woodsmen.

The person reading was a trifle different; one would have said of him that he was of the world, worldly, albeit there was that in his attire which attested a certain fellowship with the organisms of his environment. His coat would hardly have passed muster in San Francisco; his footgear was not of urban origin, and the hat that lay by him on the floor (he was the only one uncovered) was such that if one had considered it as an article of mere personal adornment he would have missed its meaning. In countenance the man was rather prepossessing, with just a hint of sternness; though that he may have assumed or cultivated, as appropriate to one in authority. For he was a coroner. It was by virtue of his office that he had possession of the book in which he was reading. It had been found among the dead man's effects – in his cabin, where the inquest was now taking place.

When the coronor had finished reading he put the book into his breast pocket. At that moment the door was pushed open and a young man entered. He, clearly, was not of mountain birth and breeding: he was clad as those

325

who dwell in cities. His clothing was dusty, however, as from travel. He had, in fact, been riding hard to attend the inquest.

The coroner nodded. No one else greeted him.

'We have waited for you,' said the coroner. 'It is necessary to have done with this business tonight.'

The young man smiled. 'I am sorry to have kept you,' he said. 'I went away, not to evade your summons, but to post to my newspaper an account of what I suppose I am called back to relate.'

The coroner smiled.

'The account that you posted to your newspaper,' he said, 'differs, probably, from that which you will give here under oath.'

'That,' replied the other, rather hotly and with a visible flush, 'is as you please. I used manifold paper and have a copy of what I sent. It was not written as news, for it is incredible, but as fiction. It may go as a part of my testimony under oath.'

'But you say it is incredible.'

'That is nothing to you, sir, if I also swear that it is true.'

The coroner was silent for a time, his eyes upon the floor. The men about the sides of the cabin talked in whispers, but seldom withdrew their gaze from the face of the corpse. Presently the coroner lifted his eyes and said, 'We will resume the inquest.'

The men removed their hats. The witness was sworn.

'What is your name?' the coroner asked.

'William Harker.'

'Age?'

'Twenty-seven.'

'You knew the deceased, Hugh Morgan?'

'Yes.'

'You were with him when he died?'

'Near him.'

'How did that happen – your presence, I mean?'

'I was visiting him at this place to shoot and fish. A part of my purpose, however, was to study him and his odd, solitary way of life. He seemed a good model for a character in fiction. I sometimes write stories.'

'I sometimes read them.'

'Thank you.'

'Stories in general – not yours.'

Some of the jurors laughed. Against a somber background humor shows high lights. Soldiers in the intervals of battle laugh easily, and a jest in the death chamber conquers by surprise.

'Relate the circumstances of this man's death,' said the coroner. 'You may use any notes or memoranda that you please.'

The witness understood. Pulling a manuscript from his breast pocket he held it near the candle and turning the leaves until he found the passage that he wanted began to read.

2 WHAT MAY HAPPEN IN A FIELD OF WILD OATS

'... The sun had hardly risen when we left the house. We were looking for quail, each with a shotgun, but we had only one dog. Morgan said our best ground was beyond a certain ridge that he pointed out, and we crossed it by a trail through the chaparral. On the other side was comparatively level ground, thickly covered with wild oats. As we emerged from the chaparral Morgan was but a few yards in advance. Suddenly we heard, at a little distance to our right and partly in front, a noise as of some animal thrashing about in the bushes, which we could see were violently agitated.

'"We've started a deer," I said. "I wish we had brought a rifle."

'Morgan, who had stopped and was intently watching the agitated chaparral, said nothing, but had cocked both barrels of his gun and was holding it in readiness to aim. I thought him a trifle excited, which surprised me, for he had a reputation for exceptional coolness, even in moments of sudden and imminent peril.

'"O, come," I said. "You are not going to fill up a deer with quail-shot, are you?"

'Still he did not reply, but catching a sight of his face as he turned it slightly toward me I was struck by the intensity of his look. Then I understood that we had serious business in hand, and my first conjecture was that we had jumped a grizzly. I advanced to Morgan's side, cocking my piece as I moved.

'The bushes were now quiet and the sounds had ceased, but Morgan was as attentive to the place as before.

'"What is it? What the devil is it?" I asked.

'"That Damned Thing!" he replied, without turning his head. His voice was husky and unnatural. He trembled visibly.

'I was about to speak further, when I observed the wild oats near the place of the disturbance moving in the most inexplicable way. I can hardly describe it. It seemed as if stirred by a streak of wind, which not only bent it, but pressed it down – crushed it so that it did not rise – and this movement was slowly prolonging itself directly toward us.

'Nothing that I had ever seen had affected me so strangely as this unfamiliar and unaccountable phenomenon, yet I am unable to recall any sense of fear. I remember – and tell it here because, singularly enough, I recollected it then – that once in looking carelessly out of an open window I momentarily mistook a small tree close at hand for one of a group of larger trees at a little distance away. It looked the same size as the others, but being more distinctly and sharply defined in mass and detail seemed out of harmony with them. It was a mere falsification of the law of aerial perspective, but it startled, almost terrified me. We so rely upon the orderly operation of familiar natural laws that any seeming suspension of them is noted as a menace to our safety, a warning of unthinkable calamity. So now the apparently causeless movement of the herbage and the slow, undeviating approach of the line of disturbance were distinctly disquieting. My companion appeared actually frightened, and I could hardly credit my senses when I saw him suddenly throw his gun to his shoulder and fire both barrels at the agitated grain! Before the smoke of the discharge had cleared away I heard a loud savage cry – a scream like that of a wild animal – and flinging his gun upon the ground Morgan sprang away and ran swiftly from the spot. At the same instant I was thrown violently to the ground by the impact of something unseen in the smoke – some soft, heavy substance that seemed thrown against me with great force.

'Before I could get upon my feet and recover my gun, which seemed to have been struck from my hands, I heard Morgan crying out as if in mortal agony, and mingling with his cries were such hoarse, savage sounds as one hears from fighting dogs. Inexpressibly terrified, I struggled to my feet and looked in the direction of Morgan's retreat – and may Heaven in mercy spare me from another sight like that! At a distance of less than thirty yards was my friend, down upon one knee, his head thrown back at a frightful angle, hatless, his long hair in disorder and his whole body in violent movement from side to side, backward and forward. His right arm was lifted and seemed to lack the hand – at least, I could see none. The other arm was invisible. At times, as my memory now reports this extraordinary scene, I could discern but a part of his body. It was as if he had been partly blotted out – I cannot otherwise express it – then a shifting of his position would bring it all into view again.

'All this must have occurred within a few seconds, yet in that time Morgan assumed all the postures of a determined wrestler vanquished by superior weight and strength. I saw nothing but him, and him not always distinctly. During the entire incident his shouts and curses were heard, as if through an enveloping uproar of such sounds of rage and fury as I had never heard from the throat of man or brute!

'For a moment only I stood irresolute, then throwing down my gun I ran forward to my friend's assistance. I had a vague belief that he was suffering from a fit, or some form of convulsion. Before I could reach his side he was down and quiet. All sounds had ceased, but with a feeling of such terror as even these awful events had not inspired I now saw again the mysterious movement of the wild oats, prolonging itself from the trampled area about the prostrate man toward the edge of a wood. It was only when it had reached the wood that I was able to withdraw my eyes and look at my companion. He was dead.'

3 A MAN THOUGH NAKED MAY BE IN RAGS

The coroner rose from his seat and stood beside the dead man. Lifting an edge of the sheet he pulled it away, exposing the entire body, altogether naked and showing in the candlelight a claylike yellow. It had, however, broad maculations of bluish black, obviously caused by extravasated blood from contusions. The chest and sides looked as if they had been beaten with a bludgeon. There were dreadful lacerations; the skin was torn in strips and shreds.

The coroner moved round to the end of the table and undid a silk handkerchief which had been passed under the chin and knotted on the top of the head. When the handkerchief was drawn away it exposed what had been the throat. Some of the jurors who had risen to get a better view repented their curiosity and turned away their faces. Witness Harker went to the open window and leaned out across the sill, faint and sick. Dropping the handkerchief upon the dead man's neck the coroner stepped to an angle of the room and from a pile of clothing produced one garment after another, each of which he held up a moment for inspection. All were torn, and stiff with blood. The jurors did not make a closer inspection. They seemed rather uninterested. They had, in truth, seen all this before, the only thing that was new to them being Harker's testimony.

'Gentlemen,' the coroner said, 'we have no more evidence, I think. Your duty has been already explained to you. If there is nothing you wish to ask you may go outside and consider your verdict.'

The foreman rose – a tall, bearded man of sixty, coarsely clad.

'I should like to ask one question, Mr Coroner,' he said. 'What asylum did this yer witness escape from?'

'Mr Harker,' said the coroner, gravely and tranquilly, 'from what asylum did you last escape?'

Harker flushed crimson again, but said nothing, and the seven jurors rose and solemnly filed out of the cabin.

'If you have done insulting me, sir,' said Harker, as soon as he and the officer were left alone with the dead man, 'I suppose I am at liberty to go?'

'Yes.'

Harker started to leave, but paused, with his hand on the door latch. The habit of his profession was strong in him – stronger than his sense of personal dignity. He turned about and said:

'The book that you have there – I recognize it as Morgan's diary. You seemed greatly interested in it; you read in it while I was testifying. May I see it? The public would like –'

'The book will cut no figure in this matter,' replied the official, slipping it into his coat pocket. 'All the entries in it were made before the writer's death.'

As Harker passed out of the house the jury reentered and stood about the table, on which the now covered corpse showed under the sheet with sharp definition. The foreman seated himself near the candle, produced from his breast pocket a pencil and scrap of paper and wrote rather laboriously the following verdict, which with various degrees of effort all signed:

'We, the jury, do find that the remains come to their death at the hands of a mountain lion, but some of us thinks, all the same, they had fits.'

4 AN EXPLANATION FROM THE TOMB

In the diary of the late Hugh Morgan are certain interesting entries having, possibly, a scientific value as suggestions. At the inquest upon his body the book was not put in evidence; possibly the coroner thought it not worthwhile to confuse the jury. The date of the first entries mentioned cannot be ascertained; the upper part of the leaf is torn away. The part of the entry remaining follows:

'... would run in a half-circle, keeping his head turned always toward the center, and again he would stand still, barking furiously. At last he ran away into the brush as fast as he could go. I thought at first that he had gone mad, but on returning to the house found no other alteration in his manner than what was obviously due to fear of punishment.

'Can a dog see with his nose? Do odors impress some cerebral center with images of the thing that emitted them? ...

'Sept. 2 – Looking at the stars last night as they rose above the crest of the ridge east of the house, I observed them successively disappear – from left to right. Each was eclipsed but an instant, and only a few at the same time, but along the entire length of the ridge all that were within a degree or two of the crest were blotted out. It was as if something had passed along between me and them; but I could not see it, and the stars were not thick enough to define its outline. Ugh! I don't like this.'

Several weeks' entries are missing, three leaves being torn from the book.

'Sept. 27 – It has been about here again – I find evidences of its presence every day. I watched again all last night in the same cover, gun in hand, double-charged with buckshot. In the morning the fresh footprints were there, as before. Yet I would have sworn that I did not sleep – indeed, I hardly sleep at all. It is terrible, insupportable! If these amazing experiences are real I shall go mad; if they are fanciful I am mad already.

'Oct. 3 – I shall not go – it shall not drive me away. No, this is *my* house, *my* land. God hates a coward....

'Oct. 5 – I can stand it no longer; I have invited Harker to pass a few weeks with me – he has a level head. I can judge from his manner if he thinks me mad.

'Oct. 7 – I have the solution of the mystery; it came to me last night – suddenly, as by revelation. How simple – how terribly simple!

'There are sounds that we cannot hear. At either end of the scale are notes that stir no chord of that imperfect instrument, the human ear. They are too high or too grave. I have observed a flock of blackbirds occupying an entire treetop – the tops of several trees – and all in full song. Suddenly – in a moment – at absolutely the same instant – all spring into the air and fly away. How? They could not all see one another – whole treetops intervened. At no point could a leader have been visible to all. There must have been a signal of warning or command, high and shrill above the din, but by me unheard. I have observed, too, the same simultaneous flight when all were silent, among not only blackbirds, but other birds – quail, for example, widely separated by bushes – even on opposite sides of a hill.

'It is known to seamen that a school of whales basking or sporting on the surface of the ocean, miles apart, with the convexity of the earth between, will sometimes dive at the same instant – all gone out of sight in a moment. The signal has been sounded – too grave for the ear of the sailor at the masthead and his comrades on the deck – who nevertheless feel its vibrations in the ship as the stones of a cathedral are stirred by the bass of the organ.

'As with sounds, so with colors. At each end of the solar spectrum the chemist can detect the presence of what are known as actinic rays. They represent colors – integral colors in the composition of light – which we are unable to discern. The human eye is an imperfect instrument; its range is but a few octaves of the real chromatic scale. I am not mad; there are colors that we cannot see.

'And, God help me! the Damned Thing is of such a color!'

HENRY JAMES
1843-1916

Born in New York in 1843, Henry James was educated in his home town, in London, Paris and Geneva. Gaining a taste for Europe during his studies abroad, he settled there in 1875. Many of his major novels (among them *The Europeans* and *Portrait of a Lady*) deal with the plight of the American in Europe or vice versa and it is for these longer works of fiction that James is best known. However, from as early as 1865 he contributed short stories and travel sketches to American periodicals and this high level of output was continued almost until the end of his life.

'The Turn of the Screw' is one of the finest and best known of his longer short stories. Since its first publication in 1898 the tale's superb dramatic qualities have inspired many stage, screen and even operatic versions. By contrast, 'The Jolly Corner' (1908) is a shorter tale which admirably illustrates James's ability to achieve his uncanny effect in so disciplined and concise a form as the traditional short story.

The Turn of the Screw

THE STORY HAD HELD US, round the fire, sufficiently breathless, but except the obvious remark that it was gruesome, as, on Christmas eve in an old house, a strange tale should essentially be, I remember no comment uttered till somebody happened to say that it was the only case he had met in which such a visitation had fallen on a child. The case, I may mention, was that of an apparition in just such an old house as had gathered us for the occasion of an appearance, of a dreadful kind, to a little boy sleeping in the room with his mother and waking her up in the terror of it; waking her not to dissipate his dread and soothe him to sleep again, but to encounter also, herself, before she had succeeded in doing so, the same sight that had shaken him. It was this observation that drew from Douglas – not immediately, but later in the evening – a reply that had the interesting consequence to which I call attention. Someone else told a story not particularly effective, which I saw he was not following. This I took for a sign that he had himself something to produce and that we should only have to wait. We waited in fact till two nights later; but that same evening, before we scattered, he brought out what was in his mind.

'I quite agree – in regard to Griffin's ghost, or whatever it was – that its appearing first to the little boy, at so tender an age, adds a particular touch. But it's not the first occurrence of its charming kind that I know to have involved a child. If the child gives the effect another turn of the screw, what do you say to *two* children—?'

'We say, of course,' somebody exclaimed, 'that they give two turns! Also that we want to hear about them.'

I can see Douglas there before the fire, to which he had got up to present his back, looking down at his interlocutor with his hands in his pockets. 'Nobody but me, till now, has ever heard. It's quite too horrible.' This, naturally, was declared by several voices to give the thing the utmost price, and our friend, with quiet art, prepared his triumph by turning his eyes over the rest of us and going on: 'It's beyond everything. Nothing at all that I know touches it.'

'For sheer terror?' I remember asking.

He seemed to say it was not so simple as that; to be really at a loss how to qualify it. He pased his hand over his eyes, made a little wincing grimace. 'For dreadful – dreadfulness!'

'Oh, how delicious!' cried one of the women.

He took no notice of her; he looked at me, but as if, instead of me, he saw what he spoke of. 'For general uncanny ugliness and horror and pain.'

'Well then,' I said, 'just sit right down and begin.'

He turned round to the fire, gave a kick to a log, watched it an instant.

Then as he faced us again: 'I can't begin. I shall have to send to town.' There was a unanimous groan at this, and much reproach; after which, in his preoccupied way, he explained. 'The story's written. It's in a locked drawer – it has not been out for years. I could write to my man and enclose the key; he could send down the packet as he finds it.' It was to me in particular that he appeared to propound this – appeared almost to appeal for aid not to hesitate. He had broken a thickness of ice, the formation of many a winter; had had his reasons for a long silence. The others resented postponement, but it was just his scruples that charmed me. I adjured him to write by the first post and to agree with us for an early hearing; then I asked him if the experience in question had been his own. To this his answer was prompt. 'Oh, thank God, no!'

'And is the record yours? You took the thing down?'

'Nothing but the impression. I took that *here*' – he tapped his heart. 'I've never lost it.'

'Then your manuscript—?'

'Is in old, faded ink, and in the most beautiful hand.' He hung fire again. 'A woman's. She has been dead these twenty years. She sent me the pages in question before she died.' They were all listening now, and of course there was somebody to be arch, or at any rate to draw the inference. But if he put the inference by without a smile it was also without irritation. 'She was a most charming person, but she was ten years older than I. She was my sister's governess,' he quietly said. 'She was the most agreeable woman I've ever known in her position; she would have been worthy of any whatever. It was long ago, and this episode was long before. I was at Trinity, and I found her at home on my coming down the second summer. I was much there that year – it was a beautiful one; and we had, in her off-hours, some strolls and talks in the garden – talks in which she struck me as awfully clever and nice. Oh yes; don't grin: I liked her extremely and am glad to this day to think she liked me too. If she hadn't she wouldn't have told me. She had never told anyone. It wasn't simply that she said so, but that I knew she hadn't. I was sure; I could see. You'll easily judge why when you hear.'

'Because the thing had been such a scare?'

He continued to fix me. 'You'll easily judge,' he repeated: '*you* will.'

I fixed him too. 'I see. She was in love.'

He laughed for the first time. 'You *are* acute. Yes, she was in love. That is she had been. That came out – she couldn't tell her story without it's coming out. I saw it, and she saw I saw it; but neither of us spoke of it. I remember the time and the place – the corner of the lawn, the shade of the great beeches and the long, hot summer afternoon. It wasn't a scene for a shudder; but oh—!' He quitted the fire and dropped back into his chair.

'You'll receive the packet Thursday morning?' I inquired.

'Probably not till the second post.'

'Well then; after dinner—'

'You'll all meet me here?' He looked us round again. 'Isn't anybody going?' It was almost the tone of hope.

'Everybody will stay!'

'*I* will – and *I* will!' cried the ladies whose departure had been fixed. Mrs Griffin, however, expressed the need for a little more light. 'Who was it she was in love with?'

'The story will tell,' I took upon myself to reply.

'Oh, I can't wait for the story!'

'The story *won't* tell,' said Douglas; 'not in any literal, vulgar way.'

'More's the pity then. That's the only way I ever understand.'

'Won't *you* tell, Douglas?' Somebody else inquired.

He sprang to his feet again. 'Yes – tomorrow. Now I must go to bed. Good night.' And, quickly, catching up a candlestick, he left us slightly bewildered. From our end of the great brown hall we heard his step on the stair; whereupon Mrs Griffin spoke. 'Well, if I don't know who she was in love with, I know who *he* was.'

'She was ten years older,' said her husband.

'*Raison de plus* – at that age! But it's rather nice, his long reticence.'

'Forty years!' Griffin put in.

'With this outbreak at last.'

'The outbreak,' I returned, 'will make a tremendous occasion of Thursday night'; and everyone so agreed with me that, in the light of it, we lost all attention for everything else. The last story, however incomplete and like the mere opening of a serial, had been told; we handshook and 'candle-stuck', as somebody said, and went to bed.

I knew the next day that a letter containing the key had, by the first post, gone off to his London apartments; but in spite of – or perhaps just on account of – the eventual diffusion of this knowledge we quite let him alone till after dinner, till such an hour of the evening, in fact, as might best accord with the kind of emotion on which our hopes were fixed. Then he became as communicative as we could desire and indeed gave us his best reason for being so. We had it from him again before the fire in the hall, as we had had our mild wonders of the previous night. It appeared that the narrative he had promised to read us really required for a proper intelligence a few words of prologue. Let me say here distinctly, to have done with it, that this narrative, from an exact transcript of my own made much later, is what I shall presently give. Poor Douglas, before his death – when it was in sight – committed to me the manuscript that reached him on the third of these days and that, on the same spot, with immense effect, he began to read to our hushed little circle on the night of the fourth. The departing ladies who had said they would stay didn't, of course, thank heaven, stay: they departed, in consequence of arrangements made, in a rage of curiosity, as they professed, produced by the touches with which he had already worked us up. But that only made his little final auditory more compact and select, kept it, round the hearth, subject to a common thrill.

The first of these touches conveyed that the written statement took up the tale at a point after it had, in a manner, begun. The fact to be in possession of was therefore that his old friend, the youngest of several daughters of a poor country parson, had, at the age of twenty, on taking service for the first time in the schoolroom, come up to London, in trepidation, to answer in person an advertisement that had already placed her in brief correspondence with the advertiser. This person proved, on her presenting herself, for judgement, at a house, in Harley Street, that impressed her as vast and imposing – this prospective patron proved a gentleman, a bachelor in the prime of life, such a figure as had never risen, save in a dream or an old novel, before a fluttered, anxious girl out of a Hampshire vicarage. One could easily fix his type; it never, happily, dies out. He was handsome and bold and pleasant, off-hand and gay and kind. He struck her, inevitably, as gallant and splendid, but what took her most of all and gave her the courage she afterwards showed was that he put the whole thing to her as a kind of favour, an obligation he should gratefully incur. She conceived him as rich, but as fearfully extravagant – saw him all in a glow of high fashion, of good looks, of expensive habits, of charming ways with women. He had for his town residence a big house filled with the spoils of travel and the trophies of the chase; but it was to his country home, an old family place in Essex, that he wished her immediately to proceed.

He had been left, by the death of their parents in India, guardian to a small nephew and a small niece, children of a younger, a military brother, whom he had lost two years before. These children were, by the strangest of chances for a man in his position – a lone man without the right sort of experience or a grain of patience – very heavily on his hands. It had all been a great worry and, on his own part doubtless, a series of blunders, but he immensely pitied the poor chicks and had done all he could; had in particular sent them down to his other house, the proper place for them being of course the country, and kept them there, from the first, with the best people he could find to look after them, parting even with his own servants to wait on them and going down himself, whenever he might, to see how they were doing. The awkward thing was that they had practically no other relations and that his own affairs took up all his time. He had put them in possession of Bly, which was healthy and secure, and had placed at the head of their little establishment – but below stairs only – an excellent woman, Mrs Grose, whom he was sure his visitor would like and who had formerly been maid to his mother. She was now housekeeper and was also acting for the time as superintendent to the little girl, of whom, without children of her own, she was, by good luck, extremely fond. There were plenty of people to help, but of course the young lady who should go down as governess would be in supreme authority. She would also have, in holidays, to look after the small boy, who had been for a term at school – young as he was to be sent, but what else could be done? – and who, as the holidays were about to begin, would be back from one day to the other. There had been for the two children at first a young lady whom they had had the misfortune to lose. She had done for them quite beautifully – she was a most respectable person – till her death, the great awkwardness of which had, precisely, left no alternative but the school for little Miles. Mrs Grose, since then, in the way of manners and things, had done as she could for Flora; and there were further, a cook, a housemaid, a dairywoman, an old pony, an old groom and an old gardener, all likewise thoroughly respectable.

So far had Douglas presented his picture when someone put a question. 'And what did the former governess die of? – of so much respectability.'

Our friend's answer was prompt. 'That will come out. I don't anticipate.'

'Excuse me – I thought that was just what you *are* doing.'

'In her successor's place,' I suggested, 'I should have wished to learn that the office brought with it—'

'Necessary danger to life?' Douglas completed my thought. 'She did wish to learn, and she did learn. You shall hear tomorrow what she learnt. Meanwhile, of course, the prospect struck her as slightly grim. She was young, untried, nervous: it was a vision of serious duties and little company, of really great loneliness. She hesitated – took a couple of days to consult and consider. But the salary offered much exceeded her modest measure, and on a second interview she faced the music, she engaged.' And Douglas, with this, made a pause that, for the benefit of the company, moved me to throw in—

'The moral of which was of course the seduction exercised by the spendid young man. She succumbed to it.'

He got up and, as he had done the night before, went to the fire, gave a stir to a log with his foot, then stood a moment with his back to us. 'She saw him only twice.'

'Yes, but that's just the beauty of her passion.'

A little to my surprise, on this, Douglas turned round to me. 'It *was* the beauty of it. There were others,' he went on, 'who hadn't succumbed. He told her frankly all his difficulty – that for several applicants the conditions had been prohibitive. They were, somehow, simply afraid. It sounded dull – it sounded strange; and all the more so because of his main condition.'

'Which was—?'

'That she should never trouble him – but never, never: neither appeal nor complain nor write about anything; only meet all questions herself, receive all moneys from his solicitor, take the whole thing over and let him alone. She promised to do this, and she mentioned to me that when, for a moment, disburdened, delighted, he held her hand, thanking her for the sacrifice, she already felt rewarded.'

'But was that all her reward?' one of the ladies asked.

'She never saw him again.'

'Oh!' said the lady; which, as our friend immediately left us again, was the only other word of importance contributed to the subject till, the next night, by the corner of the hearth, in the best chair, he opened the faded red cover of a thin old-fashioned gilt-edged album. The whole thing took indeed more nights than one, but on the first occasion the same lady put another question. 'What is your title?'

'I haven't one.'

'Oh, *I* have!' I said. But Douglas, without heeding me, had begun to read with a fine clearness that was like a rendering to the ear of the beauty of his author's hand.

1

I remember the whole beginning as a succession of flights and drops, a little see-saw of the right throbs and the wrong. After rising, in town, to meet his appeal, I had at all events a couple of very bad days – found myself doubtful again, felt indeed sure I had made a mistake. In this state of mind I spent the long hours of bumping, swinging coach that carried me to the stopping place at which I was to be met by a vehicle from the house. This convenience I was told, had been ordered, and I found, towards the close of the June afternoon, a commodious fly in waiting for me. Driving at that hour, on a lovely day, through a country to which the summer sweetness seemed to offer me a friendly welcome, my fortitude mounted afresh and, as we turned into the avenue, encountered a reprieve that was probably but a proof of the point to which it had sunk. I suppose I had expected, or had dreaded, something so melancholy that what greeted me was a good surprise. I remember as a most pleasant impression the broad, clear front, its open windows and fresh curtains and the pair of maids looking out; I remember the lawn and the bright flowers and the crunch of my wheels on the gravel and the clustered tree-tops over which the rooks circled and cawed in the golden sky. The scene had a greatness that made it a different affair from my own scant home, and there immediately appeared at the door, with a little girl in her hand, a civil person who dropped me as decent a curtsey as if I had been the mistress or a distinguished visitor. I had received in Harley Street a narrower notion of the place, and that, as I recalled it, made me think the proprietor still more of a gentleman, suggested that what I was to enjoy might be something beyond his promise.

I had no drop again till the next day, for I was carried triumphantly through the following hours by my introduction to the younger of my pupils. The little girl who had accompanied Mrs Grose appeared to me on the spot a creature so charming as to make it a great fortune to have to do with her. She was the most beautiful child I had ever seen, and I afterwards wondered that my employer had not told me more of her. I slept little that night. I was too much excited; and this astonished me too, I recollect, remained with me, adding to my sense of the liberality with which I was treated. The large impressive room, one of the best in the house, the great state bed, as I almost felt it, the full, figured draperies, the long glasses in which, for the first time I could see myself from head to foot, all struck me – like the extraordinary charm of my small charge – as so many things thrown in. It was thrown in as well, from the first moment, that I should get on with Mrs Grose in a relation over which, on my way, in the coach, I fear I had rather brooded. The only thing indeed that in this early outlook might have made me shrink again was the clear circumstance of her being so glad to see me. I perceived within half an hour that she was so glad – stout, simple, plain, clean wholesome woman – as to be positively on her guard against showing it too much. I wondered even then a little why she should wish not to show it and that, with reflection, with suspicion, might of course have made me uneasy.

But it was a comfort that there could be no uneasiness in a connexion with anything so beatific as the radiant image of my little girl, the vision of whose angelic beauty had probably more than anything else to do with the restlessness that, before morning, made me several times rise and wander about my room to take in the whole picture and prospect; to watch, from my open window, the faint summer dawn, to look at such portions of the rear of the house as I could catch, and to listen, while, in the fading dusk, the first birds began to twitter, for the possible recurrence of a sound or two, less natural and not without, but within, that I fancied I heard. There had been a moment when I believed I recognized, faint and far, the cry of a child; there had been another when I found myself just consciously starting up at the passage, before my door, of a light footstep. But these fancies were not marked enough not to be thrown off, and it is only in the light, or the gloom, I should rather say, of other and subsequent matters that they now come back to me. To watch, teach, 'form' little Flora would too evidently be the making of a happy and useful life. It had been agreed between us downstairs that after this first occasion I should have her as a matter of course at night, her small white bed being already arranged, to that end, in my room. What I had undertaken was the whole care of her, and she had remained, just this last time, with Mrs Grose only as an effect of our consideration for my inevitable strangeness and her natural timidity. In spite of this timidity – which the child herself, in the oddest way in the world, had been perfectly frank and brave about, allowing it, without a sign of uncomfortable consciousness, with the deep, sweet serenity indeed of one of Raphael's holy infants, to be discussed, to be imputed to her and to determine us. I felt quite sure she would presently like me. It was part of what I already liked Mrs Grose herself for, the pleasure I could see her feel in my admiration and wonder as I sat at supper with four tall candles and with my pupil, in a high chair and bib, brightly facing me, between them, over bread and milk. There were naturally things that in Flora's presence could pass between us only as prodigious and gratified looks, obscure and roundabout allusions.

'And the little boy – does he look like her? Is he too so very remarkable?'

One wouldn't flatter a child. 'Oh Miss, *most* remarkable. If you think well of this one!' – and she stood there with a plate in her hand, beaming at our companion, who looked from one of us to the other with placid heavenly eyes that contained nothing to check us.

'Yes; if I do—?'

'You *will* be carried away by the little gentleman!'

'Well, that, I think, is what I came for – to be carried away. I'm afraid, however,' I remember feeling the impulse to add, 'I'm rather easily carried away. I was carried away in London!'

I can still see Mrs Grose's broad face as she took this in. 'In Harley Street?'

'In Harley Street.'

'Well, Miss, you're not the first – and you won't be the last.'

'Oh, I've no pretension,' I could laugh, 'to being the only one. My other pupil, at any rate, as I understand, comes back tomorrow?'

'Not tomorrow – Friday, Miss. He arrives, as you did, by the coach, under care of the guard, and is to be met by the same carriage.'

I forthwith expressed that the proper as well as the pleasant and friendly thing would be therefore that on the arrival of the public conveyance I should be waiting for him with his little sister; an idea in which Mrs Grose concurred so heartily that I somehow took her manner as a kind of comforting pledge – never falsified, thank heaven! – that we should on every question be quite at one. Oh, she was glad I was there!

What I felt the next day was, I suppose, nothing that could be fairly called a reaction from the cheer of my arrival; it was probably at the most only a slight oppression produced by a fuller measure of the scale, as I walked round them, gazed up at them, took them in, of my new circumstances. They had, as it were, an extent and mass for which I had not been prepared and in the presence of which I found myself, freshly, a little scared as well as a little proud. Lessons, in this agitation, certainly suffered some delay; I reflected that my first duty was, by the gentlest arts I could contrive, to win the child into the sense of knowing me. I spent the day with her out of doors; I arranged with her, to her great satisfaction, that it should be she, she only, who might show me the place. She showed it step by step and room by room and secret by secret, with droll, delightful, childish talk about it and with the result, in half an hour, of our becoming immense friends. Young as she was, I was struck, throughout our little tour, with her confidence and courage with the way, in empty chambers and dull corridors, on crooked staircases that made me pause and even on the summit of an old machicolated square tower that made me dizzy, her morning music, her disposition to tell me so many more things than she asked, rang out and led me on. I have not seen Bly since the day I left it, and I dare say that to my older and more informed eyes it would now appear sufficiently contracted. But as my little conductress with her hair of gold and her frock of blue, danced before me round corners and pattered down passages, I had the view of a castle of romance inhabited by a rosy sprite, such a place as would somehow, for diversion of the young idea, take all colour out of storybooks and fairy-tales. Wasn't it just a storybook over which I had fallen a-doze and a-dream? No; it was a big ugly, antique, but convenient house, embodying a few features of a building still older, half replaced and half utilized, in which I had the fancy of our being almost as lost as a handful of passengers in a great drifting ship. Well, I was, strangely, at the helm!

2

This came home to me when, two days later, I drove over with Flora to meet, as Mrs Grose said, the little gentleman; and all the more for an incident that, presenting itself the second evening, had deeply disconcerted me. The first day had been, on the whole, as I have expressed, reassuring, but I was to see it wind up in keen apprehension. The postbag, that evening – it came late – contained a letter for me, which, however, in the hand of my employer, I found to be composed but of a few words enclosing another, addressed to himself, with a seal still unbroken. 'This, I recognize, is from the head-master, and the head-master's an awful bore. Read him, please; deal with him; but mind you don't report. Not a word. I'm off!' I broke the seal with a great effort – so great a one that I was a long time coming to it; took the unopened missive at last up to my room and only attacked it just before going to bed. I had better have let it wait till morning, for it gave me a second sleepless night. With no counsel to take, the next day, I was full of distress; and it finally got so the better of me that I determined to open myself at least to Mrs Grose.

'What does it mean? The child's dismissed his school.'

She gave me a look that I remarked at the moment; then, visibly, with a quick blankness, seemed to try to take it back. 'But aren't they all—?'

'Sent home – yes. But only for the holidays. Miles may never go back at all.'

Consciously, under my attention, she reddened. 'They won't take him?'

'They absolutely decline.'

At this she raised her eyes, which she had turned to me; I saw them fill with good tears. 'What has he done?'

I hesitated; then I judged best simply to hand her my letter – which, however, had the effect of making her, without taking it, simply put her hands behind her. She shook her head sadly. 'Such things are not for me, Miss.'

My counsellor couldn't read! I winced at my mistake, which I attenuated as I could, and opened my letter again to repeat it to her; then, faltering in the act and folding it up once more, I put it back in my pocket. 'Is he really *bad*?'

The tears were still in her eyes. 'Do the gentlemen say so?'

'They go into no particulars. They simply express their regret that it should be impossible to keep him. That can have only one meaning.' Mrs Grose listened with dumb emotion; she forbore to ask me what this meaning might be; so that, presently, to put the thing with some coherence and with the mere aid of her presence to my own mind, I went on: 'That he's an injury to the others.'

At this, with one of the quick turns of simple folk, she suddenly flamed up. 'Master Miles! – *him* an injury?'

There was such a flood of good faith in it that, though I had not yet seen the child, my very fears made me jump to the absurdity of the idea. I found myself, to meet my friend the better, offering it, on the spot, sarcastically. 'To his poor little innocent mates!'

'It's too dreadful,' cried Mrs Grose, 'to say such cruel things! Why, he's scarce ten years old.'

'Yes, yes; it would be incredible.'

She was evidently grateful for such a profession. 'See him, Miss, first. *Then* believe it!' I felt forthwith a new impatience to see him; it was the beginning of a curiosity that, for all the next hours, was to deepen almost to pain. Mrs Grose was aware, I could judge, of what she had produced in me, and she followed it up with assurance. 'You might as well believe it of the little lady. Bless her,' she added the next moment – '*look* at her!'

I turned and saw Flora, whom, ten minutes before, I had established in the school room with a sheet of white paper, a pencil and a copy of nice 'round O's', now presented herself to view at the open door. She expressed in her little way an extraordinary detachment from disagreeable duties, looking at me, however, with a great childish light that seemed to offer it as a mere result of the affection she had conceived for my person, which had rendered necessary that she should follow me. I needed nothing more than this to feel the full force of Mrs Grose's comparison, and, catching my pupil in my arms, covered her with kisses in which there was a sob of atonement.

None the less, the rest of the day, I watched for further occasion to approach my colleague, especially as, towards evening, I began to fancy she rather sought to avoid me. I overtook her, I remember, on the staircase, we went down together, and at the bottom I detained her, holding her there with a hand on her arm. 'I take what you said to me at noon as a declaration that *you've* never known him to be bad.'

She threw back her head; she had clearly, by this time, and very honestly adopted an attitude. 'Oh, never known him – I don't pretend *that*!'

I was upset again. 'Then you *have* known him—?'

'Yes indeed, Miss, thank God!'

On reflection I accepted this. 'You mean that a boy who never is—?'

'Is no boy for *me*!'

I held her tighter. 'You like them with the spirit to be naughty?' Then keeping pace with her answer. 'So do I!' I eagerly brought out. 'But not to the degree to contaminate—'

'To contaminate?' – my big word left her at a loss.

I explained it. 'To corrupt.'

She stared, taking my meaning in; but it produced in her an odd laugh. 'Are you afraid he'll corrupt *you*?' She put the question with such a fine bold humour that, with a laugh, a little silly doubtless, to match her own I gave way for the time to the apprehension of ridicule.

But the next day, as the hour for my drive approached, I cropped up in another place. 'What was the lady who was here before?'

'The last governess? She was also young and pretty – almost as young and almost as pretty, Miss, even as you.'

'Ah, then, I hope her youth and her beauty helped her!' I recollect throwing off. 'He seems to like us young and pretty!'

'Oh, he *did*,' Mrs Grose assented: 'it was the way he liked everyone!' She had no sooner spoken indeed than she caught herself up. 'I mean that's *his* way – the master's.'

I was struck. 'But of whom did you speak first?'

She looked blank, but she coloured. 'Why, of *him*.'

'Of the master?'

'Of who else?'

There was so obviously no one else that the next moment I had lost my impression of her having accidentally said more than she meant; and I merely asked what I wanted to know. 'Did *she* see anything in the boy—?'

'That wasn't right? she never told me.'

I had a scruple, but I overcame it. 'Was she careful – particular?'

Mrs Grose appeared to try to be conscientious. 'About some things – yes.'

'But not about all?'

Again she considered. 'Well, Miss – she's gone. I won't tell tales.'

'I quite understand your feeling,' I hastened to reply; but I thought it, after an instant, not opposed to this concession to pursue: 'Did she die here?'

'No – she went off.'

I don't know what there was in this brevity of Mrs Grose's that struck me as ambiguous. 'Went off to die?' Mrs Grose looked straight out of the window, but I felt that, hypothetically, I had a right to know what young persons engaged for Bly were expected to do. 'She was taken ill, you mean, and went home?'

'She was not taken ill, so far as appeared, in this house. She left it, at the end of the year, to go home, as she said, for a short holiday, to which the time she had put in had certainly given her a right. We had then a young woman – a nursemaid who had stayed on and who was a good girl and clever; and *she* took the children altogether for the interval. But our young lady never came back, and at the very moment I was expecting her I heard from the master that she was dead.'

I turned this over. 'But of what?'

'He never told me! But please, Miss,' said Mrs Grose, 'I must get to my work.'

3

Her thus turning her back on me was fortunately not, for my just preoccupations, a snub that could check the growth of our mutual esteem.

We met, after I had brought home little Miles, more intimately than ever on the ground of my stupefaction, my general emotion: so monstrous was I then ready to pronounce it that such a child as had now been revealed to me should be under an interdict. I was a little late on the scene, and I felt, as he stood wistfully looking out for me before the door of the inn at which the coach had put him down, that I had seen him, on the instant, without and within, in the great glow of freshness, the same positive fragrance of purity, in which I had, from the first moment, seen his little sister. He was incredibly beautiful, and Mrs Grose had put her finger on it: everything but a sort of passion of tenderness for him was swept away by his presence. What I then and there took him to my heart for was something divine that I have never found to the same degree in any child – his indescribable little air of knowing nothing in the world but love. It would have been impossible to carry a bad name with a greater sweetness of innocence, and by the time I had got back to Bly with him I remained merely bewildered – so far, that is, as I was not outraged – by the sense of the horrible letter locked up in my room, in a drawer. As soon as I could compass a private word with Mrs Grose I declared to her that it was grotesque.

She promptly understood me. 'You mean the cruel charge—?'

'It doesn't live an instant. My dear woman, *look* at him!'

She smiled at my pretension to have discovered his charm. 'I assure you, Miss, I do nothing else! What will you say, then?' she immediately added.

'In answer to the letter?' I had made up my mind. 'Nothing.'

'And to his uncle?'

I was incisive. 'Nothing.'

'And to the boy himself?'

I was wonderful. 'Nothing.'

She gave with her apron a great wipe to her mouth. 'Then I'll stand by you. We'll see it out.'

'We'll see it out!' I ardently echoed, giving her my hand to make it a vow.

She held me there a moment, then whisked up her apron again with her detached hand. 'Would you mind, Miss, if I used the freedom—'

'To kiss me? No!' I took the good creature in my arms and, after we had embraced like sisters, felt still more fortified and indignant.

This, at all events, was for the time: a time so full that, as I recall the way it went, it reminds me of all the art I now need to make it a little distinct. What I look back at with amazement is the situation I accepted. I had undertaken, with my companion, to see it out, and I was under a charm, apparently, that could smooth away the extent and the far and difficult connexions of such an effort. I was lifted aloft on a great wave of infatuation and pity. I found it simple, in my ignorance, my confusion, and perhaps my conceit, to assume that I could deal with the boy whose education for the world was all on the point of beginning. I am unable even to remember at this day what proposal I framed for the end of his holidays and the resumption of his studies. Lessons with me indeed, that charming summer, we all had a theory that he was to have; but I now feel that, for weeks, the lessons must have been rather my own. I learnt something – at first certainly – that had not been one of the teachings of my small, smothered life; learnt to be amused, and even amusing, and not to think for the morrow. It was the first time, in a manner, that I had known space and air and freedom, all the music of summer and all the mystery of nature. And then there was consideration – and consideration was sweet. Oh, it was a trap – not designed, but deep – to my imagination, to my delicacy, perhaps to my vanity; to whatever, in me, was most excitable. The best way to picture it all is to say that I was off my guard. They gave me so little trouble – they were of a gentleness so extraordinary. I used to speculate – but even this with a dim disconnectedness – as to how the rough future (for all futures are rough!) would handle them and might bruise them. They had the bloom of health and happiness; and yet, as if I had been in charge of a pair of little grandees, of princes of the blood, for whom everything, to be right, would have to be enclosed and protected, the only form that, in my fancy, the after-years could take for them was that of a romantic, a really royal extension of the garden and the park. It may be, of course, above all, that what suddenly broke into this gives the previous time a charm of stillness – that hush in which something gathers or crouches. The change was actually like the spring of a beast.

In the first weeks the days were long; they often, at their finest, gave me what I used to call my own hour, the hour when, for my pupils, tea-time and bed-time having come and gone, I had, before my final retirement, a small interval alone. Much as I liked my companions, this hour was the thing in the day I liked most; and I liked it best of all when, as the light faded – or rather, I should say, the day lingered and the last calls of the last birds sounded, in a flushed sky, from the old trees – I could take a turn into the grounds and enjoy, almost with a sense of property that amused and flattered me, the beauty and dignity of the place. It was a pleasure at these moments to feel myself tranquil and justified; doubtless, perhaps, also to reflect that by my discretion, my quiet good sense and general high propriety, I was giving pleasure – if he ever thought of it! – to the person to whose pressure I had responded. What I was doing was what he had earnestly hoped and directly asked of me, and that I *could*, after all, do it proved even a greater joy than I had expected. I dare say I fancied myself, in short, a remarkable young woman and took comfort in the faith that this would more publicly appear. Well, I needed to be remarkable to offer a front to the remarkable things that presently gave their first sign.

It was plump, one afternoon, in the middle of my very hour: the children were tucked away and I had come out for my stroll. One of the thoughts that, as I don't in the least shrink now from noting, used to be with me in these wanderings was that it would be as charming as a charming story suddenly to meet someone. Someone would appear there at the turn of a path and would stand before me and smile and approve. I didn't ask more than that – I only asked that he should *know*; and the only way to be sure he knew would be to see it, and the kind light of it, in his handsome face. That was exactly present to me – by which I mean the face was – when, on the first of these occasions, at the end of a long June day, I stopped short on emerging from one of the plantations and coming into view of the house. What arrested me on the spot – and with a shock much greater than any vision had allowed for – was the sense that my imagination had, in a flash turned real. He did stand there! – but high up, beyond the lawn and at the very top of the tower to which, on that first morning, little Flora had conducted me. This tower was one of a pair – square, incongruous, crenelated structures – that were distinguished, for some reason, though I could see little difference, as the new and the old. They flanked opposite ends of the house and were probably architectural absurdities, redeemed in a measure indeed by not being wholly disengaged nor of a height too pretentious, dating, in their gingerbread antiquity, from a romantic revival that was already a respectable past. I admired them, had fancies about them, for we could all profit in a degree, especially when they loomed through the dusk, by the grandeur of their actual battlements; yet it was not at such an elevation that the figure I had so often invoked seemed most in place.

It produced in me, this figure, in the clear twilight, I remember, two distinct gasps of emotion, which were, sharply, the shock of my first and that of my second surprise. My second was a violent perception of the mistake of my first: the man who met my eyes was not the person I had precipitately supposed. There came to me thus a bewilderment of vision of which, after these years, there is no living view that I can hope to give. An unknown man in a lonely place is a permitted object of fear to a young woman privately bred; and the figure that faced me was – a few more seconds assured me – as little anyone else I knew as it was the image that had been in my mind. I had not seen it in Harley Street – I had not seen it anywhere. The place, moreover, in the strangest way in the world, had, on the instant, and by the very fact of its appearance, become a solitude. To me at least, making my statement here with a deliberation with which I have never made it, the whole feeling of the moment returns. It was as if, while I took in – what I did take in – all the rest of the scene had been stricken with death. I can hear again, as I write, the intense hush in which the sounds of evening dropped. The rooks stopped cawing in the golden sky and the friendly hour lost, for a minute, all its voice. But there was no other change in nature, unless indeed it were a change that I saw with a stranger sharpness. The gold was still in the sky, the clearness in the air, and the man who looked at me over the battlements was as definite as a picture in a frame. That's how I thought, with extraordinary quickness, of each person that he might have been and that he was not. We were confronted across our distance quite long enough for me to ask myself with intensity who then he was and to feel, as an effect of my inability to say, a wonder that in a few instants more became intense.

The great question, or one of these, is, afterwards, I know, with regard to certain matters, the question of how long they have lasted. Well, this matter of mine, think what you will of it, lasted while I caught at a dozen possibilities, none of which made a difference for the better, that I could see in there having been in the house – and for how long, above all? – a person of whom I was in ignorance. It lasted while I just bridled a little with the sense that my office demanded that there should be no such ignorance and no such person. It lasted while this visitant, at all events – and there was a touch of the strange freedom, as I remember, in the sign of familiarity of his wearing no hat – seemed to fix me, from his position, with just the question, just the scrutiny through the fading light, that his own presence provoked. We were too far apart to call to each other, but there was a moment at which, at shorter range, some challenge between us, breaking the hush, would have been the right result of our straight mutual stare. He was in one of the angles, the one away from the house, very erect, as it struck me, and with both hands on the ledge. So I saw him as I see the letters I form on this page; then, exactly, after a minute, as if to add to the spectacle, he slowly changed his place – passed, looking at me hard all the while, to the opposite corner of the platform. Yes, I had the sharpest sense that during this transit he never took his eyes from me, and I can see at this moment the way his hand, as he went, passed from one of the crenelations to the next. He stopped at the other corner, but less long, and even as he turned away still markedly fixed me. He turned away; that was all I knew.

4

It was not that I didn't wait, on this occasion, for more, for I was rooted as deeply as I was shaken. Was there a 'secret' at Bly – a mystery of Udolpho or an insane, an unmentionable relative kept in unsuspected confinement? I can't say how long I turned it over, or how long, in a confusion of curiosity and dread, I remained where I had had my collision; I only recall that when I re-entered the house darkness had quite closed in. Agitation, in the interval, certainly had held me and driven me, for I must, in circling about the place, have walked three miles; but I was to be, later on, so much more overwhelmed that this mere dawn of alarm was a comparatively human chill. The most singular part of it in fact – singular as the rest had been – was the part I became, in the hall, aware of in meeting Mrs Grose. This picture comes back to me in the general train – the impression, as I received it on my return, of the wide white panelled space, bright in the lamplight and with its portraits and red carpet, and of the good surprised look of my friend, which immediately told me she had missed me. It came to me straightway, under her contact, that, with plain heartiness, mere relieved anxiety at my appearance, she knew nothing whatever that could bear upon the incident I had there ready for her. I had not suspected in advance that her comfortable face would pull me up, and I somehow measured the importance of what I had seen by my thus finding myself hesitate to mention it. Scarce anything in the whole history seems to me so odd as this fact that my real beginning of fear was one, as I may say, with the instinct of sparing my companion. On the spot, accordingly, in the pleasant hall and with her eyes on me, I, for a reason that I couldn't then have phrased, achieved an inward revolution – offered a vague pretext for my lateness and, with the plea of the beauty of the night and of the heavy dew and wet feet, went as soon as possible to my room.

Here it was another affair; here, for many days after, it was a queer affair enough. There were hours, from day to day – or at least there were moments, snatched even from clear duties – when I had to shut myself up to think. It was not so much yet that I was more nervous than I could bear to be as that I was remarkably afraid of becoming so; for the trust I had now to turn over was, simply and clearly, the truth that I could arrive at no account whatever of the visitor with whom I had been so inexplicably and yet, as it seemed to me, so intimately concerned. It took little time to see that I could sound without forms of inquiry and without exciting remark any domestic complication. The shock I had suffered must have sharpened all my senses; I felt sure, at the end of three days and as the result of mere closer attention, that I had not been practised upon by the servants nor made the object of any 'game'. Of whatever it was that I knew nothing was known around me. There was but one sane inference: someone had taken a liberty rather gross.

That was what, repeatedly, I dipped into my room and locked the door to say to myself. We had been, collectively, subject to an intrusion; some unscrupulous traveller, curious in old houses, had made his way in unobserved, enjoyed the prospect from the best point of view and then stolen out as he came. If he had given me such a bold hard stare, that was but a part of his indiscretion. The good thing, after all, was that we should surely see no more of him.

This was not so good a thing, I admit, as not to leave me to judge that what, essentially, made nothing else much signify was simply my charming work. My charming work was just my life with Miles and Flora, and through nothing could I so like it as through feeling that I could throw myself into it in trouble. The attraction of my small charges was a constant joy, leading me to wonder afresh at the vanity of my original fears, the distaste I had begun by entertaining for the probable grey prose of my office. There was to be no grey prose, it appeared, and no long grind; so how could work not be charming that presented itself as daily beauty? It was all the romance of the nursery and the poetry of the schoolroom. I don't mean by this, of course, that we studied only fiction and verse; I mean I can express no otherwise the sort of interest my companions inspired. How can I describe that except by saying that instead of growing used to them – and it's a marvel for a governess: I call the sisterhood to witness! – I made constant fresh discoveries. There was one direction, assuredly, in which these discoveries stopped: deep obscurity continued to cover the region of the boy's conduct at school. It had been promptly given me, I have noted, to face that mystery without a pang. Perhaps even it would be nearer the truth to say that – without a word – he himself had cleared it up. He had made the whole charge absurd. My conclusion bloomed there with the real rose-flush of his innocence: he was only too fine and fair for the little horrid, unclean school world, and he had paid a price for it. I reflected acutely that the sense of such differences, such superiorities of quality, always, on the part of the majority – which could include even stupid, sordid head-masters – turns infallibly to the vindictive.

Both the children had a gentleness (it was their only fault, and it never made Miles a muff) that kept them – how shall I express it? – almost impersonal and certainly quite unpunishable. They were like cherubs of the anecdote, who had – morally at any rate – nothing to whack! I remember feeling with Miles in especial as if he had had, as it were, no history. We expect of a small child a scant one, but there was in this beautiful little boy something extraordinarily sensitive, yet extraordinarily happy, that, more than in any creature of his age I have seen, struck me as beginning anew each day. He had never for a second suffered. I took this as a direct disproof of his having really been chastised. If he had been wicked he would have 'caught' it, and I should have caught it by the rebound – I should have found the trace. I found nothing at all, and he was therefore an angel. He never spoke of his school, never mentioned a comrade or a master; and I, for my part, was quite too much disgusted to allude to them. Of course I was under the spell, and the wonderful part is that, even at the time, I perfectly knew I was. But I gave myself up to it; it was an antidote to any pain, and I had more pains than one. I was in receipt in these days of disturbing letters from home, where things were not going well. But with my children, what things in the world mattered? That was the question I used to put to my scrappy retirements. I was dazzled by their loveliness.

There was a Sunday – to get on – when it rained with such force and for so many hours that there could be no procession to church; in consequence of which, as the day declined, I had arranged with Mrs Grose that, should the evening show improvement, we would attend together the late service. The rain happily stopped, and I prepared for our walk, which, through the park and by the good road to the village, would be a matter of twenty minutes. Coming down stairs to meet my colleague in the hall, I remembered a pair of gloves that had required three stitches and that had received them – with a publicity perhaps not edifying – while I sat with the children at their tea, served on Sundays, by exception, in that cold, clean temple of mahogany and brass, the 'grown-up' dining-room. The gloves had been dropped there, and I turned to recover them. The day was grey enough, but the afternoon light still lingered, and it enabled me, on crossing the threshold, not only to recognize, on a chair near the wide window, then closed, the articles I wanted, but to become aware of a person on the other side of the window and looking straight in. One step into the room had sufficed; my vision was instantaneous; it was all there. The person looking straight in was the person who had already appeared to me. He appeared thus again with I won't say greater distinctness, for that was impossible, but with a nearness that represented a forward stride in our intercourse and made me, as I met him, catch my breath and turn cold. He was the same – he was the same, and seen, this time, as he had been seen before, from the waist up, the window, though the dining-room was on the ground floor, not going down to the terrace on which he stood. His face was close to the glass, yet the effect of this better view was, strangely, only to show me how intense the former had been. He remained but a few seconds – long enough to convince me he also saw and recognized; but it was as if I had been looking at him for years and had known him always. Something, however, happened this time that had not happened before; his stare into my face, through the glass and across the room, was as deep and hard as then, but it quitted me for a moment during which I could still watch it, see it fix successively several other things. On the spot there came to me the added shock of a certitude that it was not for me he had come there. He had come for someone else.

The flash of this knowledge – for it was knowledge in the midst of dread – produced in me the most extraordinary effect, started, as I stood there, a sudden vibration of duty and courage. I say courage because I was beyond all doubt already far gone. I bounded straight out of the door again, reached that of the house, got, in an instant, upon the drive, and, passing along the terrace as fast as I could rush, turned a corner and came full in sight. But it was in sight of nothing now – my visitor had vanished. I stopped, I almost dropped, with the real relief of this; but I took in the whole scene – I gave him time to reappear. I call it time, but how long was it? I can't speak to the purpose today of the duration of these things. That kind of measure must have left me: they couldn't have lasted as they actually appeared to me to last. The terrace and the whole place, the lawn and the garden beyond it, all I could see of the park, were empty with a great emptiness. There were shrubberies and big trees, but I remember the clear assurance I felt that none of them concealed him. He was there or was not there: not there if I didn't see him. I got hold of this; then, instinctively, instead of returning as I had come, went to the window. It was confusedly present to me that I ought to place myself where he had stood. I did so; I applied my face to the pane and looked, as he had looked, into the room. As if, at this moment, to show me exactly what his range had been, Mrs Grose, as I had done for himself just before, came in from the hall. With this I had the full image of a repetition of what had already occurred. She saw me as I had seen my own visitant; she pulled up short as I had done; I gave her something of the shock that I had received. She turned white, and this made me ask myself if I had blanched as much. She stared, in short, and retreated on just *my* lines, and I knew she had then passed out and come round to me and that I should presently meet her. I remained where I was, and while I waited I thought of more things than one. But there's only one I take space to mention. I wondered why *she* should be scared.

5

Oh, she let me know as soon as, round the corner of the house, she loomed again into view. 'What in the name of goodness is the matter—?' She was now flushed and out of breath.

I said nothing till she came quite near. 'With me?' I must have made a wonderful face. 'Do I show it?'

'You're as white as a sheet. You look awful.'

I considered; I could meet on this, without scruple, any innocence. My need to respect the bloom of Mrs Grose's had dropped, without a rustle from my shoulders, and if I wavered for the instant it was not with what I kept back. I put out my hand to her and she took it; I held her hard a little, liking to feel her close to me. There was a kind of support in the shy heave of her surprise. 'You came for me for church, of course, but I can't go.'

'Has anything happened?'

'Yes. You must know now. Did I look very queer?'

'Through this window? Dreadful!'

'Well,' I said, 'I've been frightened.' Mrs Grose's eyes expressed plainly that *she* had no wish to be, yet also that she knew too well her place not to be ready to share with me any marked inconvenience. Oh, it was quite settled that she *must* share! 'Just what you saw from the dining-room a minute ago was the effect of that. What *I* saw – just before – was much worse.'

Her hand tightened. 'What was it?'

'An extraordinary man. Looking in.'

'What extraordinary man?'

'I haven't the least idea.'

Mrs Grose gazed round us in vain. 'Then where is he gone?'

'I know still less.'

'Have you seen him before?'

'Yes – once. On the old tower.'

She could only look at me harder. 'Do you mean he's a stranger?'

'Oh, very much!'

'Yet you didn't tell me?'

'No – for reasons. But now that you've guessed—'

Mrs Grose's round eyes encountered this charge. 'Ah, I haven't guessed!'

she said very simply. 'How can I if *you* don't imagine?'

'I don't in the very least.'

'You've seen him nowhere but on the tower?'

'And on this spot just now.'

Mrs Grose looked round again. 'What was he doing on the tower?'

'Only standing there and looking down at me'.

She thought a minute. 'Was he a gentleman?'

I found I had no need to think. 'No.' She gazed in deeper wonder. 'No.'

'Then nobody about the place? Nobody from the village?'

'Nobody – nobody. I didn't tell you, but I made sure.'

She breathed a vague relief: this was, oddly, so much to the good. It only went indeed a little way. 'But if he isn't a gentleman—'

'What *is* he? He's a horror.'

'A horror?'

'He's – God help me if I know *what* he is!'

Mrs Grose looked round once more; she fixed her eyes on the duskier distance, then, pulling herself together, turned to me with abrupt inconsequence. 'It's time we should be at church.'

'Oh, I'm not fit for church.'

'Won't it do you good?'

'It won't do *them*—!' I nodded at the house.

'The children?'

'I can't leave them now.'

'You're afraid—?'

I spoke boldly, 'I'm afraid of *him*.'

Mrs Grose's large face showed me, at this, for the first time, the far-away faint glimmer of a consciousness more acute: I somehow made out in it the delayed dawn of an idea I myself had not given her and that was as yet quite obscure to me. It comes back to me that I thought instantly of this as something I could get from her; and I felt it to be connected with the desire she presently showed to know more. 'When was it – on the tower?'

'About the middle of the month. At this same hour.'

'Almost at dark,' said Mrs Grose.

'Oh no, not nearly. I saw him as I see you.'

'Then how did he get in?'

'And how did he get out?' I laughed. 'I had no opportunity to ask him! This evening, you see,' I pursued, 'he has not been able to get in.'

'He only peeps?'

'I hope it will be confined to that!' She had now let go my hand; she turned away a little. I waited an instant; then I brought out: 'Go to church. Goodbye. I must watch.'

Slowly she faced me again. 'Do you fear for them?'

We met in another long look. 'Don't *you*?' Instead of answering she came nearer to the window and, for a minute, applied her face to the glass. 'You see how he could see,' I meanwhile went on.

She didn't move. 'How long was he here?'

'Till I came out. I came to meet him.'

Mrs Grose at last turned round, and there was still more in her face. '*I* couldn't have come out.'

'Neither could I!' I laughed again. 'But I did come. I have my duty.'

'So have I mine,' she replied; after, which she added: 'What is he like?'

'I've been dying to tell you. But he's like nobody.'

'Nobody?' she echoed.

'He has no hat.' Then seeing in her face that she already, in this, with a deeper dismay, found a touch of picture, I quickly added stroke to stroke. 'He has red hair, very red, close-curling, and a pale face, long in shape, with straight, good features and little, rather queer whiskers that are as red as his hair. His eyebrows are, somehow, darker; they look particularly arched and as if they might move a good deal. His eyes are sharp, strange – awfully, but I only know clearly that they're rather small and very fixed. His mouth's wide, and his lips are thin, and except for his little whiskers he's quite clean-shaven. He gives me a sort of sense of looking like an actor.'

'An actor!' It was impossible to resemble one less, at least, than Mrs Grose at that moment.

'I've never seen one, but so I suppose them. He's tall, active, erect,' I continued, 'but never – no, never! – a gentleman.'

My companion's face had blanched as I went on; her round eyes started and her mild mouth gaped. 'A gentleman?' she gasped, confounded, stupefied, 'a gentleman *he*?'

'You know him then?'

She visibly tried to hold herself. 'But he *is* handsome?'

I saw the way to help her. 'Remarkably!'

'And dressed—?'

'In somebody's clothes. They're smart, but they're not his own.'

She broke into a breathless affirmative groan. 'They're the master's!'

I caught it up. 'You *do* know him?'

She faltered but a second. 'Quint!' she cried.

'Quint?'

'Peter Quint – his own man, his valet, when he was here!'

'When the master was?'

Gaping still, but meeting me, she pieced it all together. 'He never wore his hat, but he did wear – well, there were waistcoats missed! They were both here – last year. Then the master went, and Quint was alone,'

I followed, but halting a little. 'Alone?'

'Alone with *us*.' Then, as from a deeper depth, 'In charge,' she added.

'And what became of him?'

She hung fire so long that I was still more mystified. 'He went too,' she brought out at last.

'Went where?'

Her expression, at this, became extraordinary. 'God knows where! He died.'

'Died?' I almost shrieked.

She seemed fairly to square herself, plant herself more firmly to utter the wonder of it. 'Yes. Mr Quint is dead.'

6

It took of course more than that particular passage to place us together in presence of what we had now to live with as we could – my dreadful liability to impressions of the order so vividly exemplified, and my companion's knowledge, henceforth – a knowledge half consternation and half compassion – of that liability. There had been, this evening, after the revelation that left me, for an hour, so prostrate – there had been, for either of us, no attendance on any service but a little service of tears and vows, of prayers and promises, a climax to the series of mutual challenges and pledges that had straightway ensued on our retreating together to the schoolroom and shutting ourselves up there to have everything out. The result of our having everything out was simply to reduce our situation to the last rigour of its elements. She herself had seen nothing, not the shadow of a shadow, and nobody in the house but the governess was in the governess's plight; yet she accepted without directly impugning my sanity the truth as I gave it to her, and ended by showing me, on this ground, an awe-stricken tenderness, an expression of the sense of my more than questionable privilege, of which the very breath has remained with me as that of the sweetest of human charities.

What was settled between us, accordingly, that night, was that we thought we might bear things together; and I was not even sure that, in spite of her exemption, it was she who had the best of the burden. I knew at this hour, I think, as well as I knew later what I was capable of meeting to shelter my pupils; but it took me some time to be wholly sure of what my honest ally was prepared for to keep terms with so compromising a contract. I was queer company enough – quite as queer as the company I received; but as I trace over what we went through I see how much common ground we must have found in the one idea that, by good fortune, *could* steady us. It was the idea, the second movement, that led me straight out, as I may say, of the inner chamber of my dread. I could take the air in the court, at least, and there Mrs Grose could join me. Perfectly can I recall now the particular way strength came to me before we separated for the night. We had gone over and over every feature of what I had seen.

'He was looking for someone else, you say – someone who was not you?'

'He was looking for little Miles.' A portentous clearness now possessed me. '*That's* whom he was looking for.'

'But how do you know?'

'I know, I know, I know!' My exaltation grew. 'And *you* know, my dear!'

She didn't deny this, but I required, I felt, not even so much telling as that. She resumed in a moment, at any rate: 'What if *he* should see him?'

'Little Miles? That's what he wants!'

She looked immensely scared again. 'The child?'

'Heaven forbid! The man. He wants to appear to *them*.' That he might was an awful conception, and yet, somehow, I could keep at bay; which, moreover, as we lingered there, was what I succeeded in practically proving. I had an absolute certainty that I should see again what I had already seen, but something within me said that by offering myself bravely as the sole subject of such experience, by accepting, by inviting, by surmounting it all, I should serve as an expiatory victim and guard the tranquillity of my companions. The children, in especial, I should thus fence about and absolutely save. I recall one of the last things I said that night to Mrs Grose.

'It does strike me that my pupils have never mentioned—'

She looked at me hard as I musingly pulled up. 'His having been here and the time they were with him?'

'The time they were with him, and his name, his presence, his history, in any way.'

'Oh, the little lady doesn't remember. She never heard or knew.'

'The circumstances of his death?' I thought with some intensity. 'Perhaps not. But Miles would remember – Miles would know.'

'Ah, don't try him!' broke from Mrs Grose.

I returned her the look she had given me. 'Don't be afraid.' I continued to think. 'It *is* rather odd.'

'That he has never spoken of him?'

'Never by the least allusion. And you tell me they were "great friends"?'

'Oh, it wasn't *him*!' Mrs Grose with emphasis declared. 'It was Quint's own fancy. To play with him, I mean – to spoil him.' She paused a moment, then she added: 'Quint was much too free.'

This gave me, straight from my vision of his face – *such* a face! – a sudden sickness of disgust. 'Too free with *my* boy?'

'Too free with everyone!'

I forebore, for the moment, to analyse this description further than by the reflection that a part of it applied to several of the members of the household, of the half-dozen maids and men who were still of our small colony. But there was everything, for our apprehension, in the lucky fact that no discomfortable legend, no perturbation of scullions, had ever, within anyone's memory, attached to the kind old place. It had neither bad name nor ill fame, and Mrs Grose, most apparently, only desired to cling to me and to quake in silence. I even put her, the very last thing of all, to the test. It was when, at midnight, she had her hand on the schoolroom door to take her leave. 'I have it from you then – for it's of great importance – that he was definitely and admittedly bad?'

'Oh, not admittedly. *I* knew it – but the master didn't.'

'And you never told him?'

'Well, he didn't like tale-bearing – he hated complaints. He was terribly short with anything of that kind, and if people were all right to *him*—'

'He wouldn't be bothered with more?' This squared well enough with my impression of him: he was not a trouble-loving gentleman, nor so very particular perhaps about some of the company *he* kept. All the same, I pressed my interlocutress. 'I promise you *I* would have told!'

She felt my discrimination. 'I dare say I was wrong. But, really, I was afraid.'

'Afraid of what?'

'Of things that man could do. Quint was so clever – he was so deep.'

I took this in still more than, probably, I showed. 'You weren't afraid of anything else? Not of his effect—?'

'His effect?' she repeated with a face of anguish and waiting while I faltered.

'On innocent little precious lives. They were in your charge.'

'No, they were not in mine!' she roundly and distressfully returned. 'The master believed in him and placed him here because he was supposed not to be well and the country air so good for him. So he had everything to say. Yes' – she let me have it – 'even about *them*.'

'Them – that creature?' I had to smother a kind of howl. 'And you could bear it?'

'No. I couldn't – and I can't now!' And the poor woman burst into tears.

A rigid control, from the next day, was, as I have said, to follow them; yet how often and how passionately, for a week, we came back together to the subject! Much as we had discussed it that Sunday night, I was, in the immediate later hours in especial – for it may be imagined whether I slept – still haunted with the shadow of something she had not told me. I myself had kept back nothing, but there was a word Mrs Grose had kept back. I was sure, moreover, by morning, that this was not from a failure of frankness, but because on every side there were fears. It seems to me indeed, in retrospect, that by the time the morrow's sun was high I had restlessly read into the facts before us almost all the meaning they were to receive from subsequent and more cruel occurrences. What they gave me above all was just the sinister figure of the living man – the dead one would keep a while! – and of the months he had continuously passed at Bly, which, added up, made a formidable stretch. The limit of this evil time had arrived only when, on the dawn of a winter's morning, Peter Quint was found, by a labourer going to early work, stone dead on the road from the village: a catastrophe explained – superficially at least – by a visible wound to his head; such a wound as might have been produced – and as, on the final evidence, *had* been – by a fatal slip, in the dark and after leaving the public-house, on the steepish icy slope, a wrong path altogether, at the bottom of which he lay. The icy slope, the turn mistaken at night and in liquor, accounted for much – practically, in the end and after the inquest and boundless chatter, for everything; but there had been matters in his life – strange passages and perils, secret disorders, vices more than suspected – that would have accounted for a good deal more.

I scarce know how to put my story into words that shall be a credible picture of my state of mind; but I was in these days literally able to find a joy in the extraordinary flight of heroism the occasion demanded of me. I now saw that I had been asked for a service admirable and difficult; and there would be a greatness in letting it be seen – oh, in the right quarter! – that I could succeed where many another girl might have failed. It was an immense help to me – I confess I rather applaud myself as I look back! – that I saw my service so strongly and so simply. I was there to protect and defend the little creatures in the world the most bereaved and the most lovable, the appeal of whose helplessness had suddenly become only too explicit. a deep, constant ache of one's own committed heart. We were cut off, really, together; we were united in our danger. They had nothing but me, and I – well, I had *them*. It was in short a magnificent chance. This chance presented itself to me in an image richly material. I was a screen – I was to stand before them. The more I saw, the less they would. I began to watch them in a stifled suspense, a disguised excitement that might well, had it continued too long, have turned to something like madness. What saved me, as I now see, was that it turned to something else altogether. It didn't last as suspense – it was superseded by horrible proofs. Proofs, I say, yes – from the moment I really took hold.

This moment dated from an afternoon hour that I happened to spend in the grounds with the younger of my pupils alone. We had left Miles indoors, on the red cushion of a deep window-seat; he had wished to finish a book, and I had been glad to encourage a purpose so laudable in a young man whose only defect was an occasional excess of the restless. His sister, on the contrary, had been alert to come out, and I strolled with her half an hour, seeking the shade, for the sun was still high and the day exceptionally warm. I was aware afresh, with her, as we went, of how, like her brother, she contrived – it was the charming thing in both children – to let me alone without appearing to drop me and to accompany me without appearing to surround. They were never importunate and yet never listless. My attention to them all really went to seeing them amuse themselves immensely without me: this was a spectacle they seemed actively to prepare and that engaged me as an active admirer. I walked in a world of their invention – they had no occasion whatever to draw upon mine; so that my time was taken only with being, for them, some remarkable person or thing that the game of the moment required and that was merely, thanks to my superior, my exalted stamp, a happy and highly distinguished sinecure. I forget what I was on the present occasion; I only remember that I was something very important and very quiet and that Flora was playing very hard. We were on the edge of the lake, and, as we had lately begun geography, the lake was the Sea of Azof.

Suddenly, in these circumstances, I became aware that, on the other side of the Sea of Azof, we had an interested spectator. The way this knowledge gathered in me was the strangest thing in the world – the strangest, that is, except the very much stranger in which it quickly merged itself. I had sat down with a piece of work – for I was something or other that could sit – on the old stone bench which overlooked the pond; and in this position I began to take in with certitude, and yet without direct vision, the presence, at a distance, of a third person. The old trees, the thick shrubbery, made a great and pleasant shade, but it was all suffused with the brightness of the hot, still hour. There was no ambiguity in anything; none whatever, at least in the conviction I from one moment to another found myself forming as to what I should see straight before me and across the lake as a consequence of raising my eyes. They were attached at this juncture to the stitching in which I was engaged, and I can feel once more the spasm of my effort not to move them till I should so have steadied myself as to be able to make up my mind what to do. There was an alien object in view – a figure whose right of presence I instantly, passionately questioned. I recollect counting over perfectly the possibilities, reminding myself that nothing was more natural, for instance, than the appearance of one of the men about the place, or even of a messenger, a postman or a tradesman's boy, from the village. That reminder had as little effect on my practical certitude as I was conscious – still even without looking – of its having upon the character and attitude of our visitor. Nothing was more natural than that these things should be the other things that they absolutely were not.

Of the positive identity of the apparition I would assure myself as soon as the small clock of my courage should have ticked out the right second; meanwhile, with an effort that was already sharp enough, I transferred my eyes straight to little Flora, who, at the moment, was about ten yards away. My heart had stood still for an instant with the wonder and terror of the question whether she too would see; and I held my breath while I waited for what a cry from her, what some sudden innocent sign either of interest or of alarm, would tell me. I waited, but nothing came; then, in the first place – and there is something more dire in this, I feel, than in anything I have to relate – I was determined by a sense that, within a minute, all sounds from her had previously dropped; and, in the second, by the circumstance that, also within the minute, she had, in her play, turned her back to the water. This was her attitude when I at last looked at her – looked with the confirmed conviction that we were still, together, under direct personal notice. She had picked up a small flat piece of wood, which happened to have in it a little hole that had evidently suggested to her the idea of sticking in another fragment that might figure as a mast and make the thing a boat. This second morsel, as I watched her, she was very markedly and intently attempting to tighten in its place. My apprehension of what she was doing sustained me so that after some seconds I felt I was ready for more. Then I again shifted my eyes – I faced what I had to face.

7

I got hold of Mrs Grose as soon after this as I could; and I can give no intelligible account of how I fought out the interval. Yet I still hear myself cry as I fairly threw myself into her arms: 'They *know* – it's too monstrous: they know, they know!'

'And what on earth—?' I felt her incredulity as she held me.

'Why, all that *we* know – and heaven knows what else besides!' Then, as she released me, I made it out to her, made it out perhaps only now with full coherency even to myself. 'Two hours ago, in the garden' – I could scarce articulate – 'Flora *saw!*'

Mrs Grose took it as she might have taken a blow to the stomach. 'She has told you?' she panted.

'Not a word – that's the horror. She kept it to herself! the child of eight, *that* child!' Unutterable still, for me, was the stupefaction of it.

Mrs Grose, of course, could only gape the wider. 'Then how do you know?'

'I was there – I saw with my eyes: saw that she was perfectly aware.'

'Do you mean aware of *him?*'

'No – of *her.*' I was conscious as I spoke that I looked prodigious things for I got the slow reflection of them in my companion's face. 'Another person – this time; but a figure of quite unmistakable horror and evil: a woman in black, pale and dreadful – with such an air also, and such a face! – on the other side of the lake. I was there with the child – quiet for the hour, and in the midst of it she came.'

'Came how – from where?'

'From where they come from! she just appeared and stood there – but not so near.'

'And without coming nearer?'

'Oh, for the effect and the feeling, she might have been as close as you!'

My friend, with an odd impulse, fell back a step. 'Was she someone you've never seen?'

'Yes. But someone the child has. Someone *you* have.' Then, to show how I had thought it all out: 'My predecessor – the one who died.'

'Miss Jessel?'

'Miss Jessel. You don't believe me?' I pressed.

She turned right and left in her distress. 'How can you be sure?'

This drew from me, in the state of my nerves, a flash of impatience. 'Then ask Flora – *she's* sure!' But I had no sooner spoken than I caught myself up.

'No, for God's sake, *don't*! She'll say she isn't – she'll lie!'

Mrs Grose was not too bewildered instinctively to protest. 'Ah, how *can* you?'

'Because I'm clear. Flora doesn't want me to know.'

'It's only then to spare you.'

'No, no – there are depths, depths! The more I go over it, the more I see in it, and the more I see in it the more I fear. I don't know what I *don't* see – what I *don't* fear!'

Mrs Grose tried to keep up with me. 'You mean you're afraid of seeing her again?'

'Oh no; that's nothing – now!' Then I explained. 'It's of *not* seeing her.'

But my companion only looked wan. 'I don't understand you.'

'Why, it's that the child may keep it up – and that the child assuredly *will* – without my knowing it.'

At the image of this possibility Mrs Grose for a moment collapsed, yet presently to pull herself together again, as if from the positive force of the sense of what, should we yield an inch, there would really be to give way to. 'Dear, dear – we must keep our heads! And after all, if she doesn't mind it—!' She even tried a grim joke. 'Perhaps she likes it!'

'Likes *such* things – a scrap of an infant!'

'Isn't it just a proof of her blessed innocence?' my friend bravely inquired.

She brought me, for the instant, almost round. 'Oh, we must clutch at *that* – we must cling to it! If it isn't a proof of what you say, it's a proof of – God knows what! For the woman's a horror of horrors.'

Mrs Grose, at this, fixed her eyes a minute on the ground; then at last raising them, 'Tell me how you know,' she said.

'Then you admit it's what she was?' I cried.

'Tell me how you know,' my friend simply repeated.

'Know? By seeing her! By the way she looked.'

'At you, do you mean – so wickedly?'

'Dear me, no – I could have borne that. She gave me never a glance. She only fixed the child.'

Mrs Grose tried to see it. 'Fixed her?'

'Ah, with such awful eyes!'

She stared at mine as if they might really have resembled them. 'Do you mean of dislike?'

'God help us, no. Of something much worse.'

'Worse than dislike?' – this left her indeed at a loss.

'With a determination – indescribable. With a kind of fury of intention.' I made her turn pale. 'Intention?'

'To get hold of her.' Mrs Grose – her eyes just lingering on mine - gave a shudder and walked to the window; and while she stood there looking out I completed my statement. '*That's* what Flora knows.'

After a little she turned round. 'The person was in black, you say?'

'In mourning – rather poor, almost shabby. But – yes – with extraordinary beauty.' I now recognized to what I had at last, stroke by stroke, brought the victim of my confidence, for she quite visibly weighed this. 'Oh, handsome – very, very,' I insisted; 'wonderfully handsome. But infamous.'

She slowly came back to me. 'Miss Jessel – *was* infamous.' She once more took my hand in both her own, holding it as tight as if to fortify me against the increase of alarm I might draw from this disclosure. 'They were both infamous,' she finally said.

So, for a little, we faced it once more together; and I found absolutely a degree of help in seeing it now so straight. 'I appreciate,' I said, 'the great decency of your not having hitherto spoken; but the time has certainly come to give me the whole thing.' She appeared to assent to this, but still only in silence; seeing which I went on: 'I must have it now. Of what did she die? Come, there was something between them.'

'There was everything.'

'In spite of the difference—?'

'Oh, of their rank, their condition' – she brought it woefully out. '*She* was a lady.'

I turned it over; I again saw. 'Yes – she was a lady.'

'And he so dreadfully below,' said Mrs Grose.

I felt that I doubtless needn't press too hard, in such company, on the place of a servant in the scale; but there was nothing to prevent an acceptance of my companion's own measure of my predecessor's abasement. There was a way to deal with that, and I dealt; the more readily for my full vision – on the evidence – of our employer's late clever, good-looking 'own' man; impudent, assured, spoiled, depraved. 'The fellow was a hound.'

Mrs Grose considered as if it were perhaps a little a case for a sense of shades. 'I've never seen one like him. He did what he wished.'

'With *her*?'

'With them all.'

It was as if now in my friend's own eyes Miss Jessel had again appeared. I seemed at any rate, for an instant, to see their evocation of her as distinctly as I had seen her by the pond; and I brought out with decision: 'It must have been also what *she* wished!'

Mrs Grose's face signified that it had been indeed, but she said at the same time: 'Poor woman – she paid for it!'

'Then you do know what she died of?' I asked.

'No – I know nothing. I wanted not to know; I was glad enough I didn't and I thanked heaven she was well out of this!'

'Yet you had, then, your idea—'

'Of her real reason for leaving? Oh yes – as to that. She couldn't have stayed. Fancy it here – for a governess! And afterwards I imagined – and I still imagine. And what I imagine is dreadful.'

'Not so dreadful as what I do,' I replied; on which I must have shown her – as I was indeed but too conscious – a front of miserable defeat. It brought out again all her compassion for me, and at the renewed touch of her kindness my power to resist broke down. I burst, as I had, the other time, made her burst, into tears; she took me to her motherly breast, and my lamentation overflowed. 'I don't do it!' I sobbed in despair; 'I don't save or shield them! It's far worse than I dreamed – they're lost!'

8

What I had said to Mrs Grose was true enough: there were in the matter I had put before her depths and possibilities that I lacked resolution to sound; so that when we met once more in the wonder of it we were of a common mind about the duty of resistance to extravagant fancies. We were to keep our heads if we should keep nothing else – difficult indeed as that might be in the face of what, in our prodigious experience, was least to be questioned. Late that night, while the house slept, we had another talk in my room; when she went all the way with me as to its being beyond doubt that I had seen exactly what I had seen. To hold her pefectly in the pinch of that, I found, I had only to ask her how, if I had 'made it up', I came to be able to give, of each of the persons appearing to me, a picture disclosing, to the last detail, their special marks – a portrait on the exhibition of which she had instantly recognized and named them. She wished, of course – small blame to her! – to sink the whole subject; and I was quick to assure her that my own interest in it had now violently taken the form of a search for the way to escape from it. I encountered her on the ground of a probability that with recurrence – for recurrence we took for granted – I should get used to my danger; distinctly professing that my personal exposure had suddenly become the least of my discomforts. It was my new suspicion that was intolerable; and yet even to this complication the later hours of the day had brought a little ease.

On leaving her, after my first outbreak, I had of course returned to my pupils, associating the right remedy for my dismay with the sense of their charm which I had already found to be a thing I could positively cultivate and which had never failed me yet. I had simply, in other words, plunged afresh into Flora's special society and there become aware – it was almost a luxury! – that she could put her little conscious hand straight upon the spot that ached. She had looked at me in sweet speculation and then had accused me to my face of having 'cried'. I had supposed I had brushed away the ugly signs; but I could literally – for the time, at all events – rejoice, under this fathomless charity, that they had not entirely disappeared. To gaze into the depths of blue of the child's eyes and pronounce their loveliness a trick of premature cunning was to be guilty of a cynicism in preference to which I naturally preferred to abjure my judgement and, so far as might be, my agitation. I couldn't abjure for merely wanting to, but I could repeat to Mrs Grose – as I did there, over and over, in the small hours – that with their voices in the air, their pressure on one's heart and their fragrant faces against one's cheek, everything fell to the ground but their incapacity and their beauty. It was a pity that, somehow, to settle this once for all, I had equally to re-enumerate the signs of subtlety that, in the afternoon, by the lake, had made a miracle of my show of self-possession. It was a pity to be obliged to re-investigate the certitude of the moment itself and repeat how it had come to me as a revelation that the inconceivable communion I then surprised was a matter, for either party, of habit. It was a pity that I should have had to quaver out again the reasons for my not having, in my delusion, so much as questioned that the little girl saw our visitant even as I actually saw Mrs Grose herself, and that she wanted, by just so much as she did thus see, to make me suppose she didn't, and at the same time, without showing anything, arrive at a guess as to whether I myself did! It was a pity that I needed once more to describe the portentous little activity by which she sought to divert my attention – the perceptible increase of movement, the greater intensity of play, the singing, the gabbling, of nonsense and the invitation to romp.

Yet if I had not indulged, to prove there was nothing in it, in this review, I should have missed the two or three dim elements of comfort that still remained to me. I should not for instance have been able to asseverate to my friend that I was certain – which was so much to the good – that *I* at least had not betrayed myself. I should not have been prompted, by stress of need, by desperation of mind – I scarce know what to call it – to invoke such further aid to intelligence as might spring from pushing my colleague fairly to the wall. She had told me, bit by bit, under pressure, a great deal; but a small shifty spot on the wrong side of it all still sometimes brushed my brow like the wing of a bat; and I remember how on this occasion – for the sleeping house and the concentration alike of our danger and our watch seemed to help – I felt the importance of giving the last jerk to the curtain. 'I don't believe anything so horrible,' I recollect saying; 'no, let us put it definitely, my dear, that I don't. But if I did, you know, there's a thing I should require now, just without sparing you the least bit more – oh, not a scrap, come! – to get out of you. What was it you had in mind when, in our distress, before Miles came back, over the letter from his school, you said, under my insistence, that you didn't pretend for him that he had not literally *ever* been "bad"? He has *not* literally "ever", in these weeks that I myself have lived with him and so closely watched him; he has been an imperturbable little prodigy of delightful, loveable goodness. Therefore you might perfectly have made the claim for him if you had not, as it happened, seen an exception to take. What was your exception, and to what passage in your personal observation of him did you refer?'

It was a dreadfully austere inquiry, but levity was not our note, and, at any rate, before the grey dawn admonished us to separate I had got my answer. What my friend had had in mind proved to be immensely to the purpose. It was neither more nor less than the circumstance that for a period of several months Quint and the boy had been perpetually together. It was in fact the very appropriate truth that she had ventured to criticize the propriety, to hint at the incongruity, of so close an alliance, and even to go so far on the subject as a frank overture to Miss Jessel. Miss Jessel had, with a most strange manner, requested her to mind her business, and the good woman had, on this, directly approached little Miles. What she had said to him, since I pressed, was that *she* liked to see young gentlemen not forget their station.

I pressed again, of course, at this. 'You reminded him that Quint was only a base menial?'

'As you might say! And it was his answer, for one thing, that was bad.'

'And for another thing?' I waited. 'He repeated your words to Quint?'

'No, not that. It's just that he *wouldn't*!' she could still impress upon me. 'I was sure, at any rate,' she added, 'that he didn't. But he denied certain occasions.'

'What occasions?'

'When they had been about together quite as if Quint were his tutor – and a very grand one – and Miss Jessel only for the little lady. When he had gone off with the fellow, I mean, and spent hours with him.'

'He then prevaricated about it – he said he hadn't?' Her assent was clear enough to cause me to add in a moment: 'I see. He lied.'

'Oh!' Mrs Grose mumbled. This was a suggestion that it didn't matter, which indeed she backed up by a further remark. 'You see, after all, Miss

Jessel didn't mind. She didn't forbid him.'

I considered. 'Did he put that to you as a justification?'

At this she dropped again. 'No, he never spoke of it.'

'Never mentioned her in connexion with Quint?'

She saw, visibly flushing, where I was coming out. 'Well, he didn't show anything. He denied,' she repeated; 'he denied.'

Lord, how I pressed her now! 'So that you could see he knew what was between the two wretches?'

'I don't know – I don't know!' the poor woman groaned.

'You do know, you dear thing,' I replied; 'only you haven't my dreadful boldness of mind, and you keep back, out of timidity and modesty and delicacy, even the impression that, in the past, when you had, without my aid, to flounder about in silence, most of all made you miserable. But I shall get it out of you yet! There was something in the boy that suggested to you,' I continued, 'that he covered and concealed their relation.'

'Oh, he couldn't prevent—'

'Your learning the truth? I dare say! But, heavens,' I fell, with vehemence, a-thinking, 'what it shows that they must, to that extent, have succeeded in making of him!'

'Ah, nothing that's not nice *now*!' Mrs Grose lugubriously pleaded.

'I don't wonder you looked queer,' I persisted, 'when I mentioned to you the letter from his school!'

'I doubt if I looked as queer as you!' she retorted with homely force. 'And if he was so bad then as that comes to, how is he such an angel now?'

'Yes indeed – and if he was a fiend at school! How, how, how? Well,' I said in my torment, 'you must put it to me again, but I shall not be able to tell you for some days. Only, put it to me again!' I cried in a way that made my friend stare. 'There are directions in which I must not for the present let myself go.' Meanwhile I returned to her first example – the one to which she had just previously referred – of the boy's happy capacity for an occasional slip. 'If Quint – on your remonstrance at the time you speak of – was a base menial, one of the things Miles said to you, I find myself guessing, was that you were another.' Again her admission was so adequate that I continued: 'And you forgave him that?'

'Wouldn't *you*?'

'Oh yes!' And we exchanged there, in the stillness, a sound of the oddest amusement. Then I went on: 'At all events, while he was with the man—'

'Miss Flora was with the woman. It suited them all!'

It suited me too, I felt, only too well; by which I mean that it suited exactly the particular deadly view I was in the very act of forbidding myself to entertain. But I so far succeeded in checking the expression of this view that I will throw, just here, no further light on it than may be offered by the mention of my final observation to Mrs Grose. 'His having lied and been impudent are, I confess, less engaging specimens than I had hoped to have from you of the outbreak in him of the little natural man. Still,' I mused, 'they must do, for they make me feel more than ever that I must watch.'

It made me blush, the next minute, to see in my friend's face how much more unreservedly she had forgiven him than her anecdote struck me as presenting to my own tenderness an occasion for doing. This came out when, at the schoolroom door, she quitted me. 'Surely you don't accuse *him*—'

'Of carrying on an intercourse that he conceals from me? Ah, remember that, until further evidence, I now accuse nobody.' Then, before shutting her out to go, by another passage, to her own place, 'I must just wait,' I wound up.

9

I waited and waited, and the days, as they elapsed, took something from my consternation. A very few of them, in fact, passing, in constant sight of my pupils, without a fresh incident, sufficed to give to grievous fancies and even to odious memories a kind of brush of the sponge. I have spoken of the surrender to their extraordinary childish grace as a thing I could actively cultivate, and it may be imagined if I neglected now to address myself to this source for whatever it would yield. Stranger than I can express, certainly, was the effort to struggle against my new lights; it would doubtless have been, however, a greater tension still had it not been so frequently successful. I used to wonder how my little charges could help guessing that I thought strange things about them; and the circumstances that these things only made them more interesting was not by itself a direct aid to keeping them in the dark. I trembled lest they should see that they *were* so immensely more interesting. Putting things at the worst, at all events, as in meditation I so often did, any clouding of their innocence could only be – blameless and foredoomed as they were – a reason the more for taking risks. There were moments when, by an irresistible impulse, I found myself catching them up and pressing them to my heart. As soon as I had done so I used to say to myself: 'What will they think of that? Doesn't it betray too much?' It would have been easy to get into a sad, wild tangle about how much I might betray, but the real account, I feel, of the hours of peace that I could still enjoy was that the immediate charm of my companions was a beguilement still effective even under the shadow of the possibility that it was studied. For if it occurred to me that I might occasionally excite suspicion by the little outbreaks of my sharper passion for them, so too I remember wondering if I mightn't see a queerness in the traceable increase of their own demonstrations.

They were at this period extravagantly and preternaturally fond of me, which, after all, I could reflect, was no more than a graceful response in children perpetually bowed over and hugged. The homage of which they were so lavish succeeded, in truth, for my nerves, quite as well as if I never appeared to myself, as I may say, literally to catch them at a purpose in it. They had never, I think, wanted to do so many things for their poor protectress; I mean – though they got their lessons better and better, which was naturally what would please her most – in the way of diverting, entertaining, surprising her; reading her passages, telling her stories, acting her charades, pouncing out at her, in disguises, as animals and historical characters, and above all astonishing her by the 'pieces' they had secretly got by heart and could interminably recite. I should never get to the bottom – were I to let myself go even now – of the prodigious private commentary, all under still more private correction, with which, in these days, I overscored their full hours. They had shown me from the first a facility for everything, a general faculty which, taking a fresh start, achieved remarkable flights. They got their little tasks as if they loved them, and indulged, from the mere exuberance of the gift, in the most unimposed little miracles of memory. They not only popped out at me as tigers and as Romans, but as Shakespeareans, astronomers and navigators. This was so singularly the case that it had presumably much to do with the fact as to which, at the present day, I am at a loss for a different explanation: I allude to my unnatural composure on the subject of another school for Miles. What I remember is that I was content not, for the time, to open the question, and that contentment must have sprung from the sense of his perpetually striking show of cleverness. He was too clever for a bad governess, for a parson's daughter, to spoil; and the strangest if not the brightest thread in the pensive embroidery I just spoke of was the impression I might have got, if I had dared to work it out, that he was under some influence operating in his small intellectual life as a tremendous incitement.

If it was easy to reflect, however, that such a boy could postpone school, it was at least as marked that for such a boy to have been 'kicked out' by a schoolmaster was a mystification without end. Let me add that in their company now – and I was careful almost never to be out of it – I could follow no scent very far. We lived in a cloud of music and love and success and private theatricals. The musical sense in each of the children was of the quickest, but the elder in especial had a marvellous knack of catching and repeating. The schoolroom piano broke into all gruesome fancies; and when that failed there were confabulations in corners with a sequel of one of them going out in the highest spirits in order to 'come in' as something new. I had had brothers myself, and it was no revelation to me that little girls could be slavish idolaters of little boys. What surpassed everything was that there was a little boy in the world who could have for the inferior age, sex and intelligence so fine a consideration. They were extraordinarily at one, and to say that they never either quarrelled or complained is to make the note of praise coarse for their quality of sweetness. Sometimes indeed, when I dropped into coarseness, I perhaps came across traces of little understandings between them by which one of them should keep me occupied while the other slipped away. There is a *naïf* side, I suppose, in all diplomacy; but if my pupils practised upon me it was surely with the minimum of grossness. It was all in the other quarter that, after a lull, the grossness broke out.

I find that I really hang back; but I must take my plunge. In going on with the record of what was hideous at Bly I not only challenge the most liberal faith – for which I little care; but – and this is another matter – I renew what I myself suffered, I again push my way through it to the end. There came suddenly an hour after which, as I look back, the affair seems to me to have been all pure suffering; but I have at least reached the heart of it, and the straightest road out is doubtless to advance. One evening – with nothing to lead up or to prepare it – I felt the cold touch of the impression that had breathed on me the night of my arrival and which, much lighter then, as I have mentioned, I should probably have made little of in memory had my subsequent sojourn been less agitated. I had not gone to bed; I sat reading by a couple of candles. There was a roomful of old books at Bly – last-century fiction, some of it, which, to the extent of a distinctly deprecated renown, but never to so much as that of a stray specimen, had reached the sequestered home and appealed to the unavowed curiosity of my youth. I remember that the book I had in my hand was Fielding's *Amelia*; also that I was wholly awake. I recall further both a general conviction that it was horribly late and a particular objection to looking at my watch. I figure, finally, that the white curtain draping, in the fashion of those days, the head of Flora's little bed, shrouded, as I had assured myself long before, the perfection of childish rest. I recollect in short that, though I was deeply interested in my author, I found myself, at the turn of a page and with his spell all scattered, looking straight up from him and hard at the door of my room. There was a moment during which I listened, reminded of the faint sense I had had, the first night, of there being something undefinably astir in the house, and noted the soft breath of the open casement just move the half-drawn blind. Then, with all the marks of a deliberation that must have seemed magnificent had there been anyone to admire it, I laid down my book, rose to my feet and, taking a candle, went straight out of the room and, from the passage, on which my light made little impression, noiselessly closed and locked the door.

I can say now neither what determined nor what guided me, but I went straight along the lobby, holding my candle high, till I came within sight of the tall window that presided over the great turn of the staircase. At this point I precipitately found myself aware of three things. They were practically simultaneous, yet they had flashes of succession. My candle, under a bold flourish, went out, and I perceived, by the uncovered window, that the yielding dusk of earliest morning rendered it unnecessary. Without it, the next instant, I saw that there was someone on the stair. I speak of sequences, but I required no lapse of seconds to stiffen myself for a third encounter with Quint. The apparition had reached the landing half way up and was therefore on the spot nearest the window, where, at sight of me, it stopped short and fixed me exactly as it had fixed me from the tower and from the garden. He knew me as well as I knew him; and so, in the cold, faint twilight, with a glimmer in the high glass and another on the polish of the oak stair below, we faced each other in our common intensity. He was absolutely, on this occasion, a living, detestable, dangerous presence. But that was not the wonder of wonders; I reserve this distinction for quite another circumstance: the circumstance that dread had unmistakably quitted me and that there was nothing in me there that didn't meet and measure him.

I had plenty of anguish after that extraordinary moment, but I had, thank God, no terror. And he knew I had not – I found myself at the end of an instant magnificently aware of this. I felt, in a fierce rigour of confidence, that if I stood my ground a minute I should cease – for the time, at least – to have him to reckon with; and during the minute, accordingly, the thing was as human and hideous as a real interview; hideous just because it *was* human, as human as to have met alone, in the small hours, in a sleeping house, some enemy, some adventurer, some criminal. It was the dead silence of our long gaze at such close quarters that gave the whole horror, huge as it was, its only note of the unnatural. If I had met a murderer in such a place and at such an hour we still at least would have spoken. Something would have passed, in life, between us; if nothing had passed one of us would have moved. The moment was so prolonged that it would have taken but little more to make me doubt if even *I* were in life. I can't express what followed it save by saying that the silence itself – which was indeed in a manner an attestation of my strength – became the element into which I saw the figure disappear; in which I definitely saw it turn, as I might have seen the low wretch to which it had once belonged turn on receipt of an order, and pass, with my eyes on the villainous back that no hunch could have more disfigured, straight down the staircase and into the darkness in which the next bend was lost.

10

I remained a while at the top of the stair, but with the effect presently of understanding that when my visitor had gone, he had gone: then I returned to my room. The foremost thing I saw there by the light of the candle I had left burning was that Flora's little bed was empty; and on this I caught my breath with all the terror that, five minutes before, I had been able to resist. I dashed at the place in which I had left her lying and over which (for the small silk counterpane and the sheets were disarranged), the white curtains had been deceivingly pulled forward; then my step, to my unutterable relief, produced an answering sound: I perceived an agitation of the window-blind, and the child, ducking down, emerged rosily from the other side of it. She stood there in so much of her candour and so little of her nightgown, with her pink bare feet and golden glow of her curls. She looked intensely grave, and I had never had such a sense of losing an advantage acquired (the thrill of which had just been prodigious), as on my consciousness that she addressed me with reproach. 'You naughty: where *have* you been?' – instead of challenging her own irregularity I found myself arraigned and explaining. She herself explained, for that matter, with the loveliest, eagerest simplicity. She had known suddenly, as she lay there, that I was out of the room, and had jumped up to see what had become of me. I had dropped, with the joy of her reappearance, back into my chair – feeling then, and then only, a little faint; and she had pattered straight over to me, thrown herself upon my knee, given herself to be held with the flame of the candle full in the wonderful little face that was still flushed with sleep. I remember closing my eyes an instant, yieldingly, consciously, as before the excess of something beautiful that shone out of the blue of her own. 'You were looking for me out of the window?' I said. 'You thought I might be walking in the grounds?'

'Well, you know, I thought someone was' – she never blanched as she smiled out that at me.

O, how I looked at her now! 'And did you see anyone?'

'Ah, *no!*' she returned, almost, with the full privilege of childish inconsequence, resentfully, though with a long sweetness in her little drawl of the negative.

At that moment, in the state of my nerves, I absolutely believed she lied; and if I once more closed my eyes it was before the dazzle of the three or four possible ways in which I might take this up. One of these, for a moment, tempted me with such singular intensity that, to withstand it, I must have gripped my little girl with a spasm that, wonderfully, she submitted to without a cry or a sign of fright. Why not break out at her on the spot and have it all over? – give it to her straight in her lovely little lighted face? 'You see, you see, you *know* that you do and that you already quite suspect I believe it; therefore why not frankly confess it to me, so that we may at least live with it together and learn perhaps, in the strangeness of our fate, where we are and what it means?' This solicitation dropped, alas, as it came: if I could immediately have succumbed to it I might have spared myself – well, you'll see what. Instead of succumbing I sprang again to my feet, looked at her bed and took a helpless middle way. 'Why did you pull the curtain over the place to make me think you were still there?'

Flora luminously considered; after which, with her little divine smile: 'Because I don't like to frighten you!'

'But if I had, by your idea, gone out—?'

She absolutely declined to be puzzled; she turned her eyes to the flame of the candle as if the question were as irrelevant, or at any rate as impersonal, as Mrs Marcet or nine-times-nine. 'Oh, but you know,' she quite adequately answered, 'that you might come back, you dear, and that you *have!*' And after a little, when she had got into bed, I had, for a long time, by almost sitting on her to hold her hand, to prove that I recognized the pertinence of my return.

You may imagine the general complexion, from that moment, of my nights. I repeatedly sat up till I didn't know when; I selected moments when my room-mate unmistakably slept, and, stealing out, took noiseless turns in the passage and even pushed as far as to where I had last met Quint. But I never met him there again; and I may as well say at once that I on no other occasion saw him in the house. I just missed, on the staricase, on the other hand, a different adventure. Looking down it from the top I once recognized the presence of a woman seated on one of the lower steps with her back presented to me, her body half bowed and her head, in an attitude of woe, in her hands. I had been there but an instant, however, when she vanished without looking round at me. I knew, none the less, exactly what dreadful face she had to show; and I wondered whether, if instead of being above I had been below, I should have had, for going up, the same nerve I had lately shown Quint. Well, there continued to be plenty of chance for nerve. On the eleventh night after my latest encounter with that gentleman – they were all numbered now – I had an alarm that perilously skirted it and that indeed, from the particular quality of its unexpectedness, proved quite my sharpest shock. It was precisely the first night during this series that, weary with watching, I had felt that I might again without laxity lay myself down at my old hour. I slept immediately, and, as I afterwards knew, till about one o'clock; but when I woke it was to sit straight up, as completely roused as if a hand had shook me. I had left a light burning, but it was now out, and I felt an instant certainty that Flora had extinguished it. This brought me to my feet and straight, in the darkness, to her bed, which I found she had left. A glance at the window enlightened me further, and the striking of a match completed the picture.

The child had again got up – this time blowing out the taper, and had again, for some purpose of observation or response, squeezed in behind the blind and was peering out into the night. That she now saw – as she had not, I had satisfied myself, the previous time – was proved to me by the fact that she was disturbed neither by my re-illumination nor by the haste I made to get into slippers and into a wrap. Hidden, protected, absorbed, she evidently rested on the sill – the casement opened forward – and gave herself up. There was a great still moon to help her, and this fact had counted in my quick decision. She was face to face with the apparition we had met at the lake, and could now communicate with it as she had not then been able to do. What I, on my side, had to care for was, without disturbing her, to reach, from the corridor, some other window in the same quarter. I got to the door without her hearing me; I got out of it, closed it and listened, from the other side, for some sound from her. While I stood in the passage I had my eyes on her brother's door, which was but ten steps off and which, indescribably, produced in me a renewal of the strange impulse that I lately spoke of as my temptation. What if I should go straight in and march to *his* window? – what if, by risking to his boyish bewilderment a revelation of my motive, I should throw across the rest of the mystery the long halter of my boldness?

This thought held me sufficiently to make me cross to his threshold and pause again. I preternaturally listened; I figured to myself what might portentously be; I wondered if his bed were also empty and he too were secretly at watch. It was a deep, soundless minute, at the end of which my impulse failed. He was quiet; he might be innocent; the risk was hideous; I turned away. There was a figure in the grounds – a figure prowling for a sight, the visitor with whom Flora was engaged; but it was not the visitor most concerned with my boy. I hesitated afresh, but on other grounds and only a few seconds; then I had made my choice. There were empty rooms at Bly, and it was only a question of choosing the right one. The right one suddenly presented itself to me as the lower one – though high above the gardens – in the solid corner of the house that I have spoken of as the old tower. This was a large, square chamber, arranged with some state as a bedroom, the extravagant size of which made it so inconvenient that it had not for years, though kept by Mrs Grose in exemplary order, been occupied. I had often admired it and I knew my way about in it; I had only, after just faltering at the first chill gloom of its disuse, to pass across it and unbolt as quietly as I could one of the shutters. Achieving this transit, I uncovered the glass without a sound and, applying my face to the pane, was able, the darkness without being much less than within, to see that I commanded the right direction. Then I saw something more. The moon made the night extraordinarily penetrable and showed me on the lawn a person, diminished by distance, who stood there motionless and as if fascinated, looking up to where I had appeared – looking, that is, not so much straight at me as at something that was apparently above me. There was clearly another person above me – there was a person on the tower; but the presence on the lawn was not in the least what I had conceived and had confidently hurried to meet. The presence on the lawn – I felt sick as I made it out – was poor little Miles himself.

11

It was not till late next day that I spoke to Mrs Grose; the rigour with which I kept my pupils in sight making it often difficult to meet her privately, and the more as we each felt the importance of not provoking – on the part of the servants quite as much as on that of the children – any suspicion of a secret flurry or of a discussion of mysteries. I drew a great security in this particular from her mere smooth aspect. There was nothing in her fresh face to pass on to others my horrible confidences. She believed me, I was sure, absolutely: if she hadn't I don't know what would have become of me, for I couldn't have borne the business alone. But she was a magnificent monument to the blessing of a want of imagination, and if she could see in our little charges nothing but their beauty and amiability, their happiness and cleverness, she had no direct communication with the sources of my trouble. If they had been at all visibly blighted or battered she would doubtless have grown, on tracing it back, haggard enough to match them, as matters stood, however, I could feel her, when she surveyed them with her large white arms folded and the habit of serenity in all her look, thank the Lord's mercy that if they were ruined the pieces would still serve. Flights of fancy gave place, in her mind, to a steady fireside glow, and I had already begun to perceive how, with the development of the conviction that – as time went on without a public accident – our young things could, after all, look out for themselves, she addressed her greatest solicitude to the sad case presented by their instructress. That, for myself, was a sound simplification: I could engage that, to the world, my face should tell no tales, but it would have been, in the conditions, an immense added strain to find myself anxious about hers.

At the hour I now speak of she had joined me, under pressure, on the terrace, where, with the lapse of the season, the afternoon sun was now agreeable; and we sat there together while, before us, at a distance, but within call if we wished, the children strolled to and fro in one of their most manageable moods. They moved slowly, in unison, below us, over the lawn, the boy, as they went, reading aloud from a storybook and passing his arm round his sister to keep her quite in touch. Mrs Grose watched them with positive placidity; then I caught the supressed intellectual creak with which she conscientiously turned to take from me a view of the back of the tapestry. I had made her a receptacle of lurid things, but there was an odd recognition of my superiority – my accomplishments and my function – in her patience under my pain. She offered her mind to my disclosures as, had I wished to mix a witch's broth and proposed it with assurance, she would have held out a large clean saucepan. This had become thoroughly her attitude by the time that, in my recital of the events of the night, I reached the point of what Miles had said to me when, after seeing him, at such a monstrous hour, almost on the very spot where he happened now to be, I had gone down to bring him in; choosing then, at the window, with a concentrated need of not alarming the house, rather that method than a signal more resonant. I had left her meanwhile in little doubt of my small hope of representing with success even to her actual sympathy my sense of the real splendour of the little inspiration with which, after I had got him into the house, the boy met my final articulate challenge. As soon as I appeared in the moonlight on the terrace he had come to me as straight as possible; on which I had taken his hand without a word and led him, through the dark spaces, up the staircase where Quint had so hungrily hovered for him, along the lobby where I had listened and trembled, and so to his forsaken room.

Not a sound, on the way, had passed between us, and I had wondered – oh, *how* I had wondered! – if he were groping about in his little mind for something plausible and not too grotesque. It would tax his invention, certainly, and I felt, this time, over his real embarrassment, a curious thrill of triumph. It was a sharp trap for the inscrutable! He couldn't play any longer at innocence; so how the deuce would he get out of it? There beat in me indeed, with the passionate throb of this question, an equal dumb appeal as to how the deuce *I* should. I was confronted at last, as never yet, with all the risk attached even now to sounding my own horrid note. I remember in fact that as we pushed into his little chamber, where the bed had not been slept in at all and the window, uncovered to the moonlight, made the place so clear that there was no need of striking a match – I remember how I suddenly dropped, sank upon the edge of the bed from the force of the idea that he must know how he really, as they say, 'had' me. He could do what he liked, with all his cleverness to help him, so long as I should continue to defer to the old tradition of the criminality of those caretakers of the young who minister to superstitions and fears. He 'had' me indeed, and in a cleft stick; for who would ever absolve me, who would consent that I should go unhung, if, by the faintest tremor of an overture, I were the first to introduce into our perfect intercourse an element so dire? No, no: it was useless to attempt to convey to Mrs Grose, just as it is scarcely less so to attempt to suggest here, how, in our short, stiff brush in the dark, he fairly shook me with admiration. I was of course thoroughly kind and merciful; never, never yet had I placed on his little shoulders hands of such tenderness as those with which, while I rested against the bed, I held him there well under fire. I had no alternative but, in form at least, to put it to him.

'You must tell me now – and all the truth. What did you go out for? What were you doing there?'

I can still see his wonderful smile, the whites of his beautiful eyes and the uncovering of his little teeth, shine to me in the dusk. 'If I tell you why, will you understand?' My heart, at this, leaped into my mouth. *Would* he tell me why? I found no sound on my lips to press it, and I was aware of replying only with a vague, repeated, grimacing nod. He was gentleness itself, and while I wagged my head at him he stood there more than ever a little fairy prince. It was his brightness indeed that gave me a respite. Would it be so great if he were really going to tell me? 'Well,' he said at last, 'just exactly in order that you should do this.'

'Do what?'

'Think me - for a change – *bad*!' I shall never forget the sweetness and gaiety with which he brought out the word, nor how, on top of it, he bent forward and kissed me. It was practically the end of everything. I met his kiss and I had to make, while I folded him for a minute in my arms, the most stupendous effort not to cry. He had given exactly the account of himself that permitted least of my going behind it, and it was only with the effect of confirming my acceptance of it that, as I presently glanced about the room, I could say—

'Then you didn't undress at all?'

He fairly glittered in the gloom. 'Not at all. I sat up and read.'

'And when did you go down?'

'At midnight. When I'm bad I *am* bad!'

'I see, I see – it's charming. But how could you be sure I would know it?'

'Oh, I arranged it with Flora.' His answers rang out with a readiness! 'She was to get up and look out.'

'Which is what she did do.' It was I who fell into the trap!

'So she disturbed you, and, to see what she was looking at, you also looked – you saw.'

'While you,' I concurred, 'caught your death in the night air!'

He literally bloomed so from his exploit that he could afford radiantly to assent. 'How otherwise should I have been bad enough?' he asked. Then, after another embrace, the incident and our interview closed on my recognition of all the reserves of goodness that, for his joke, he had been able to draw upon.

12

The particular impression I had received proved in the morning light, I repeat, not quite successfully presentable to Mrs Grose, though I reinforced it with the mention of still another remark that he had made before we separated. 'It all lies in half-a-dozen words,' I said to her, 'words that really settle the matter. "Think, you know, what I *might* do!" He threw that off to show me how good he is. He knows down to the ground what he "might" do. That's what he gave them a taste of at school.'

'Lord, you do change!' cried my friend.

'I don't change – I simply make it out. The four, depend upon it, perpetually meet. If on either of these last nights you had been with either child you would clearly have understood. The more I've watched and waited the more I've felt that if there were nothing else to make it sure it would be made so by the systematic silence of each. *Never*, by a slip of the tongue, have they so much as alluded to either of their old friends, any more than Miles has alluded to his expulsion. Oh yes, we may sit here and look at them, and they may show off to us there to their fill; but even while they pretend to be lost in their fairy-tale they're steeped in their vision of the dead restored. He's not reading to her,' I declared; 'they're talking of *them* – they're talking horrors! I go on, I know, as if I were crazy; and it's a wonder I'm not. What I've seen would have made *you* so; but it has only made me more lucid, made me get hold of still other things.'

My lucidity must have seemed awful, but the charming creatures who were victims of it, passing and repassing in their interlocked sweetness, gave my colleague something to hold on by; and I felt how tight she held as, without stirring in the breath of my passion, she covered them still with her eyes. 'Of what other things have you got hold?'

'Why, of the very things that have delighted, fascinated and yet, at bottom, as I now so strangely see, mystified and troubled me. Their more than earthly beauty, the absolutely unnatural goodness. It's a game.' I went on; 'it's a policy and a fraud!'

'On the part of little darlings—?'

'As yet mere lovely babies? Yes, mad as that seems!' The very act of bringing it out really helped me to trace it – follow it all up and piece it all together. 'They haven't been good – they've only been absent. It has been easy to live with them, because they're simply leading a life of their own. They're not mine – they're not ours. They're his and they're hers!'

'Quint's and that woman's?'

'Quint's and that woman's. They want to get to them.'

Oh, how, at this, poor Mrs Grose appeared to study them! 'But for what?'

'For the love of all the evil that, in those dreadful days, the pair put into them. And to ply them with that evil still, to keep up the work of demons, is what brings the others back.'

'Laws!' said my friend under her breath. The exclamation was homely, but it revealed a real acceptance of my further proof of what, in the bad time – for there had been a worse even than this! – must have occurred. There could have been no justification for me as the plain assent of her experience to whatever depth of depravity I found credible in our brace of scoundrels. It was in obvious submission of memory that she brought out after a moment: 'They *were* rascals! But what can they now do?' she pursued.

'Do?' I echoed so loud that Miles and Flora, as they passed at their distance, paused an instant in their walk and looked at us. 'Don't they do enough?' I demanded in a lower tone, while the children, having smiled and nodded and kissed hands to us, resumed their exhibition. We were held by it a minute; then I answered: 'They can destroy them!' At this my companion did turn, but the inquiry she launched was a silent one, the effect of which was to make me more explicit. 'They don't know, as yet, quite how – but they're trying hard. They're seen only across, as it were, and beyond – in strange places and on high places, the top of towers, the roof of houses, the outside of windows, the further edge of pools; but there's a deep design, on either side, to shorten the distance and overcome the obstacle; and the success of the tempters is only a question of time. They've only to keep to their suggestions of danger.'

'For the children to come?'

'And perish in the attempt!' Mrs Grose slowly got up, and I scrupulously added: 'Unless, of course, we can prevent!'

Standing there before me while I kept my seat, she visibly turned things over. 'Their uncle must do the preventing. He must take them away.'

'And who's to make him?'

She had been scanning the distance, but she now dropped on me a foolish face. 'You, Miss.'

'By writing to him that his house is poisoned and his little nephew and niece mad?'

'But if they *are*, Miss?'

'And if I am myself, you mean? That's charming news to be sent him by a governess whose prime undertaking was to give him no worry.'

Mrs Grose considered, following the children again. 'Yes, he do hate worry. That was the great reason—'

'Why those fiends took him in so long? No doubt, though his indifference must have been awful. As I'm not a fiend, at any rate, I shouldn't take him in.'

My companion after an instant and for all answer, sat down again and grasped my arm. 'Make him at any rate come to you.'

I stared. 'To *me*?' I had a sudden fear of what she might do. '"Him"?'

'He ought to *be* here – he ought to help.'

I quickly rose, and I think I must have shown her a queerer face than ever yet. 'You see me asking him for a visit?' No, with her eyes on my face she evidently couldn't. Instead of it even – as a woman reads another – she could see what I myself saw: his derision, his amusement, his contempt for the breakdown of my resignation at being left alone and for the fine machinery I had set in motion to attract his attention to my slighted charms. She didn't know – no one knew – how proud I had been to serve him and to stick to our

terms; yet she none the less took the measure, I think, of the warning I now
gave her. 'If you should so lose your head as to appeal to him for me—'

She was really frightened. 'Yes, Miss?'

'I would leave, on the spot, both him and you.'

13

It was all very well to join them, but speaking to them proved as much as
ever an effort beyond my strength – offered, in close quarters, difficulties as
insurmountable as before. This situation continued a month, and with new
aggravations and particular notes, the note above all, sharper and sharper, of
the small ironic consciousness on the part of my pupils. It was not, I am as
sure today as I was sure then, my mere infernal imagination: it was
absolutely traceable that they were aware of my predicament and that this
strange relation made, in a manner, for a long time, the air in which we
moved. I don't mean that they had their tongues in their cheeks or did
anything vulgar, for that was not one of their dangers: I do mean, on the
other hand, that the element of the unnamed and untouched became,
between us, greater than any other, and that so much avoidance could not
have been so successfully effected without a great deal of tacit arrangement.
It was as if, at moments, we were perpetually coming into sight of subjects
before which we must stop short, turning suddenly out of alleys that we
perceived to be blind, closing with a little bang that made us look at each
other – for, like all bangs, it was something louder than we had intended –
the doors we had indiscreetly opened. All roads lead to Rome, and there were
times when it might have struck us that almost every branch of study or
subject of conversation skirted forbidden ground. Forbidden ground was the
question of the return of the dead in general and of whatever, in especial,
might survive, in memory, of the friends little children had lost. There were
days when I could have sworn that one of them had, with a small invisible
nudge, said to the other: 'She thinks she'll do it this time – but she *won't*!' To
'do it' would have been to indulge for instance – and for once in a way – in
some direct reference to the lady who had prepared them for my discipline.
They had a delightful endless appetite for passages in my own history, to
which I had again and again treated them; they were in possession of
everything that had ever happened to me, had had, with every circumstance,
the story of my smallest adventures and of those of my brothers and sisters
and of the cat and the dog at home, as well as many particulars of the
eccentric nature of my father, of the furniture and arrangement of our house
and of the conversation of the old women of our village. There were things
enough, taking one with another, to chatter about, if one went very fast and
knew by instinct when to go round. They pulled with an art of their own the
strings of my invention and my memory; and nothing else perhaps, when I
thought of such occasions afterwards, gave me so the suspicion of being
watched from under cover. It was in any case over *my* life, *my* past and *my*
friends alone that we could take anything like our ease; a state of affairs that
led them sometimes without the least pertinence to break out into sociable
reminders. I was invited – with no visible connexion – to repeat afresh Goody
Gosling's celebrated *mot* or to confirm the details already supplied as to the

cleverness of the vicarage pony.

It was partly at such junctures as these and partly at quite different ones that, with the turn my matters had now taken, my predicament, as I have called it, grew more sensible. The fact that the days passed for me without another encounter ought, it would have appeared, to have done something towards soothing my nerves. Since the light brush, that second night on the upper landing, of the presence of a woman at the foot of the stair, I had seen nothing, whether in or out of the house, that one had better not have seen. There was many a corner round which I expected to come upon Quint, and many a situation that, in a merely sinister way, would have favoured the appearance of Miss Jessel. The summer had turned, the summer had gone; the autumn had dropped upon Bly and had blown out half our lights. The place, with its grey sky and withered garlands, its bared spaces and scattered dead leaves, was like a theatre after the performance – all strewn with crumpled playbills. They were exactly states of the air, conditions of sound and of stillness, unspeakable impressions of the *kind* of ministering moment, that brought back to me, long enough to catch it, the feeling of the medium in which, that June evening out-of-doors, I had had my first sight of Quint, and in which, too, at those other instants, I had, after seeing him through the window, looked for him in vain in the circle of shrubbery. I recognized the signs, the portents – I recognized the moment, the spot. But they remained unaccompanied and empty, and I continued unmolested; if unmolested one could call a young woman whose sensibility had, in the most extraordinary fashion, not declined but deepened. I had said in my talk with Mrs Grose on that horrid scene of Flora's by the lake – and had perplexed her by so saying – that it would from that moment distress me much more to lose my power than to keep it. I had then expressed what was vividly in my mind the truth that, whether the children really saw or not – since, that is, it was not yet definitely proved – I greatly preferred, as a safeguard, the fullness of my own exposure. I was ready to know the very worst that was to be known. What I had then had an ugly glimpse of was that my eyes might be sealed just while theirs were most opened. Well, my eyes *were* sealed, it appeared, at present – a consummation for which it seemed blasphemous not to thank God. There was, alas, a difficulty about that: I would have thanked him with all my soul had I not had in a proportionate measure this conviction of the secret of my pupils.

How can I retrace today the strange steps of my obsession? There were times of our being together when I would have been ready to swear that, literally, in my presence, but with my direct sense of it closed, they had visitors who were known and were welcome. Then it was that, had I not been deterred by the very chance that such an injury might prove greater than the injury to be averted, my exaltation would have broken out. 'They're here, they're here, you little wretches,' I would have cried, 'and you can't deny it now!' The little wretches denied it with all the added volume of their sociability and their tenderness, in just the crystal depths of which – like the flash of a fish in a stream – the mockery of their advantage peeped up. The shock, in truth, had sunk into me still deeper than I knew on the night when, looking out to see either Quint or Miss Jessel under the stars, I had beheld the boy over whose rest I watched and who had immediately brought in with him – had straightway, there, turned it on me – the lovely upward look with which, from the battlements above me, the hideous apparition of Quint had played. If it was a question of a scare, my discovery on this occasion had scared me more than any other, and it was in the condition of nerves produced by it that I made my actual inductions. They harassed me so that sometimes, at odd moments, I shut myself up audibly to rehearse – it was at once a fantastic relief and a renewed despair – the manner in which I might come to the point. I approached it from one side and the other while, in my room, I flung myself about, but I always broke down in the monstrous utterance of names. As they died away on my lips I said to myself that I should indeed help them to represent something infamous if, by pronouncing them, I should violate as rare a little case of instinctive delicacy as any schoolroom, probably, had ever known. When I said to myself: '*They* have the manners to be silent, and you, trusted as you are, the baseness to speak!' I felt myself crimson and I covered my face with my hands. After these secret scenes I chattered more than ever, going on volubly enough till one of our prodigious, palpable hushes occurred – I can call them nothing else – the strange, dizzy lift or swim (I try for terms!) into a stillness, a pause of all life, that had nothing to do with the more or less noise that at the moment we might be engaged in making and that I could hear through any deepened exhilaration or quickened recitation or louder strum of the piano. Then it was that the others, the outsiders, were there. Though they were not angels, they 'passed', as the French say, causing me, while they stayed, to tremble with the fear of their addressing to their younger victims some yet more infernal message or more vivid image than they had thought good enough for myself.

What it was most impossible to get rid of was the cruel idea that, whatever I had seen, Miles and Flora saw *more* – things terrible and unguessable and that sprang from dreadful passages of intercourse in the past. Such things naturally left on the surface, for the time, a chill which we vociferously denied that we felt; and we had, all three, with repetition, got into such splendid training that we went, each time, almost automatically, to mark the close of the incident, through the very same movements. It was striking of the children, at all events, to kiss me inveterately with a kind of wild irrelevance and never to fail – one or the other – of the precious question that has helped us through many a peril. 'When do you think he *will* come? Don't you think we *ought* to write?' – there was nothing like that inquiry, we found by experience, for carrying off an awkwardness. 'He' of course was their uncle in Harley Street; and we lived in much profusion of theory that he might at any moment arrive to mingle in our circle. It was impossible to have given less encouragement than he had done to such a doctrine, but if we had not had the doctrine to fall back upon we should have deprived each other of some of our finest exhibitions. He never wrote to them – that may have been selfish, but it was a part of the flattery of his trust of me; for the way in which a man pays his highest tribute to a woman is apt to be but by the more festal celebration of one of the sacred laws of his comfort; and I held that I carried out the spirit of the pledge given not to appeal to him when I let my charges understand that their own letters were but charming literary exercises. They were too beautiful to be posted; I kept them myself; I have them all to this hour. This was a rule indeed which only added to the satiric effect of my being plied with the supposition that he might at any moment be among us.

It was exactly as if my charges knew how almost more awkward than anything else might be for me. There appears to me, moreover, as I look back, no note in all this more extraordinary than the mere fact that, in spite of my tension and of their triumph, I never lost patience with them. Adorable they must in truth have been, I now reflect, that I didn't in these days hate them! Would exasperation, however, if relief had longer been postponed, finally have betrayed me? It little matters, for relief arrived. I call it relief though it was only the relief that a snap brings to a strain or the burst of a thunderstorm to a day of suffocation. It was at least change, and it came with a rush.

14

Walking to church a certain Sunday morning, I had little Miles at my side and his sister, in advance of us and at Mrs Grose's, well in sight. It was a crisp, clear day, the first of its order for some time; the night had brought a touch of frost, and the autumn air, bright and sharp, made the church-bells almost gay. It was an odd accident of thought that I should have happened at such a moment to be particularly and very gratefully struck with the obedience of my little charges. Why did they never resent my inexorable, my perpetual society? Something or other had brought nearer home to me that I had all but pinned the boy to my shawl and that, in the way our companions were marshalled before me, I might have appeared to provide against some danger of rebellion. I was like a gaoler with an eye to possible surprises and escapes. But all this belonged – I mean their magnificent little surrender – just to the special array of the facts that were most abysmal. Turned out for Sunday by his uncle's tailor, who had had a free hand and a notion of pretty waistcoats and of his grand little air, Miles's whole title to independence, the rights of his sex and situation, were so stamped upon him that if he had suddenly struck for freedom I should have had nothing to say. I was by the strangest of chances wondering how I should meet him when the revolution unmistakably occurred. I call it a revolution because I now see how, with the word he spoke, the curtain rose on the last act of my dreadful drama and the catastrophe was precipitated. 'Look here, my dear, you know,' he charmingly said, 'when in the world, please, am I going back to school?'

Transcribed here the speech sounds harmless enough, particularly as uttered in the sweet, high, casual pipe with which, at all interlocutors, he threw off intonations as if he were tossing roses. There was something in them that always made one 'catch', and I caught, at any rate, now so effectually that I stopped as short as if one of the trees of the park had fallen across the road. There was something new, on the spot, between us, and he was perfectly aware that I recognized it, though, to enable me to do so, he had no need to look a whit less candid and charming than usual. I could feel in him how he already, from my at first finding nothing to reply, perceived the advantage he had gained. I was so slow to find anything that he had plenty of time, after a minute, to continue with his suggestive but inconclusive smile: 'You know, my dear, that for a fellow to be with a lady *always*—!' His 'my dear' was constantly on his lips for me, and nothing could have expressed more the exact shade of the sentiment with which I desired to inspire my pupils than its fond familiarity. It was so respectfully easy.

But, oh, how I felt that at present I must pick my own phrases! I remember that, to gain time, I tried to laugh, and I seemed to see in the beautiful face with which he watched me how ugly and queer I looked. 'And always with the same lady?' I returned.

He neither blenched nor winked. The whole thing was virtually out between us. 'Ah, of course she's a jolly, "perfect" lady; but, after all, I'm a fellow, don't you see? that's – well, getting on.'

I lingered there with him an instant ever so kindly. 'Yes, you're getting on.' Oh, but I felt helpless!

I have kept to this day the heartbreaking little idea of how he seemed to know that and to play with it. 'And you can't say I've not been awfully good, can you?'

I laid my hand on his shoulder, for, though I felt how much better it would have been to walk on, I was not yet quite able. 'No, I can't say that, Miles.'

'Except just that one night, you know—!'

'That one night?' I couldn't look as straight as he.

'Why, when I went down – went out of the house.'

'Oh yes. But I forget what you did it for.'

'You forget?' – he spoke with the sweet extravagance of childish reproach. 'Why, it was to show you I could!'

'Oh yes, you could.'

'And I can again.'

I felt that I might, perhaps, after all, succeed in keeping my wits about me. 'Certainly. But you won't.'

'No, not *that* again. It was nothing.'

He resumed our walk with me, passing his hand into my arm. 'Then when *am* I going back?'

I wore, in turning it over, my most responsible air. 'Were you very happy at school?'

He just considered. 'Oh, I'm happy enough anywhere!'

'Well then,' I quavered, 'if you're just as happy here—!'

'Ah, but that isn't everything! Of course *you* know a lot—'

'But you hint that you know almost as much?' I risked as he paused.

'Not half I want to!' Miles honestly professed. 'But it isn't so much that.'

'What is it then?'

'Well – I want to see more life.'

'I see; I see.' We had arrived within sight of the church and of various persons, including several of the household of Bly, on their way to it and clustered about the door to see us go in. I quickened our step; I wanted to get there before the question between us opened up much further; I reflected hungrily that, for more than an hour, he would have to be silent; and I thought with envy of the comparative dusk of the pew and of the almost spiritual help of the hassock on which I might bend my knees. I seemed literally to be running a race with some confusion to which he was about to reduce me, but I felt that he had got in first when, before we even entered the churchyard, he threw out—

'I want my own sort!'

It literally made me bound forward. 'There are not many of your own sort,

Miles!' I laughed. 'Unless perhaps dear little Flora!'

'You really compare me to a baby girl?'

This found me singularly weak. 'Don't you, then, *love* our sweet Flora?'

'If I didn't – and you too; if I didn't—!' he repeated as if retreating for a jump, yet leaving his thought so unfinished that, after we had come into the gate, another stop, which he imposed on me by the pressure of his arm, had become inevitable. Mrs Grose and Flora had passed into the church, the other worshippers had followed, and we were, for the minute, alone among the old, thick graves. We had paused, on the path from the gate, by a low, oblong, table-like tomb.

'Yes, if you didn't—?'

He looked, while I waited, about at the graves. 'Well, you know what!' But he didn't move, and he presently produced something that made me drop straight down on the stone slab, as if suddenly to rest. 'Does my uncle think what *you* think?'

I markedly rested. 'How do you know what I think?'

'Ah well, of course I don't; for it strikes me you never tell me. But I mean does *he* know?'

'Know what, Miles?'

'Why, the way I'm going on.'

I perceived quickly enough that I could make, to this inquiry, no answer that would not involve something of a sacrifice of my employer. Yet it appeared to me that we were all, at Bly, sufficiently sacrificed to make that venial. 'I don't think your uncle much cares.'

Miles, on this, stood looking at me. 'Then don't you think he can be made to?'

'In what way?'

'Why, by his coming down.'

'But who'll get him to come down?'

'*I* will!' the boy said with extraordinary brightness and emphasis. He gave me another look charged with that expression and then marched off alone into church.

15

The business was practically settled from the moment I never followed him. It was a pitiful surrender to agitation, but my being aware of this had somehow no power to restore me. I only sat there on my tomb and read into what my little friend had said to me the fullness of its meaning; by the time I had grasped the whole of which I had also embraced, for absence, the pretext that I was ashamed to offer my pupils and the rest of the congregation such an example of delay. What I said to myself above all was that Miles had got something out of me and that the proof of it, for him, would be just this awkward collapse. He had got out of me that there was something I was much afraid of and that he should probably be able to make use of my fear to gain, for his own purpose, more freedom. My fear was of having to deal with the intolerable question of the grounds of his dismissal from school, for that was really but the question of the horrors gathered behind. That his uncle should arrive to treat with me of these things was a solution that, strictly speaking, I ought now to have desired to bring on; but I could so little face the ugliness and the pain of it that I simply procrastinated and lived from hand to mouth. The boy, to my deep discomposure, was immensely in the right, was in a position to say to me: 'Either you clear up with my guardian the mystery of this interruption of my studies, or you cease to expect me to lead with you a life that's so unnatural for a boy.' What was so unnatural for the particular boy I was concerned with was this sudden revelation of a consciousness and a plan.

That was what really overcame me, what prevented my going in. I walked round the church, hesitating, hovering; I reflected that I had already, with him, hurt myself beyond repair. Therefore I could patch up nothing, and it was too extreme an effort to squeeze beside him into the pew: he would be so much more sure than ever to pass his arm into mine and make me sit there for an hour in close, silent contact with his commentary on our talk. For the first minute since his arrival I wanted to get away from him. As I paused beneath the high east window and listened to the sounds of worship I was taken with an impulse that might master me, I felt, completely should I give it the least encouragament. I might easily put an end to my predicament by getting away altogether. Here was my chance; there was no one to stop me; I could give the whole thing up – turn my back and retreat. It was only a question of hurrying again, for a few preparations, to the house which the attendance at church of so many of the servants would practically have left unoccupied. No one, in short, could blame me if I should just drive desperately off. What was it to get away if I got away only till dinner? That would be in a couple of hours, at the end of which – I had the acute prevision – my little pupils would play at innocent wonder about my non-appearance in their train.

'What *did* you do, you naughty, bad thing? Why in the world, to worry us so – and take our thoughts off too, don't you know? – did you desert us at the very door?' I couldn't meet such questions nor, as they asked them, their false little lovely eyes; yet it was all so exactly what I should have to meet that, as the prospect grew sharp to me, I at last let myself go.

I got, so far as the immediate moment was concerned, away; I came straight out of the churchyard and, thinking hard, retraced my steps through the park. It seemed to me that by the time I reached the house I had made up my mind I would fly. The Sunday stillness both of the approaches and of the interior, in which I met no one, fairly excited me with a sense of opportunity. Were I to get off quickly, this way, I should get off without a scene, without a word. My quickness would have to be remarkable, however, and the question of a conveyance was the great one to settle. Tormented, in the hall, with difficulties and obstacles, I remember sinking down at the foot of the staircase – suddenly collapsing there on the lowest step and then, with a revulsion, recalling that it was exactly where, more than a month before, in the darkness of night and just so bowed with evil things, I had seen the spectre of the most horrible of women. At this I was able to straighten myself; I went the rest of the way up; I made, in my bewilderment, for the schoolroom, where there were objects belonging to me that I should have to take. But I opened the door to find again, in a flash, my eyes unsealed. In the presence of what I saw I reeled straight back upon my resistance.

Seated at my own table in the clear noonday light I saw a person whom, without my previous experience, I should have taken at the first blush for some housemaid who might have stayed at home to look after the place and who, availing herself of rare relief from observation and of the schoolroom table and my pens, ink and paper, had applied herself to the considerable effort of a letter to her sweetheart. There was an effort in the way that, while her arms rested on the table, her hands, with evident weariness, supported her head; but at the moment I took this in I had already become aware that, in spite of my entrance, her attitude strangely persisted. Then it was – with the very act of announcing itself – that her identity flared up in a change of posture. She rose, not as if she had heard me, but with an indescribable grand melancholy of indifference and detachment, and, within a dozen feet of me, stood there as my vile predecessor. Dishonoured and tragic, she was all before me; but even as I fixed and, for memory, secured it, the awful image passed away. Dark as midnight in her black dress, her haggard beauty and her unutterable woe, she had looked at me long enough to appear to say that her right to sit at my table was as good as mine to sit at hers. While these instants lasted indeed I had the extraordinary chill of a feeling that it was I who was the intruder. It was as a wild protest against it that, actually addressing her – 'You terrible, miserable woman!' – I heard myself break into a sound that, by the open door, rang through the long passage and the empty house. She looked at me as if she heard me, but I had recovered myself and cleared the air. There was nothing in the room the next minute but the sunshine and a sense that I must stay.

16

I had so perfectly expected that the return of my pupils would be marked by a demonstration that I was freshly upset at having to take into account that they were dumb about my absence. Instead of gaily denouncing and caressing me they made no allusion to my having failed them, and I was left, for the time, on perceiving that she too said nothing, to study Mrs Grose's odd face. I did this to such purpose that I made sure they had in some way bribed her to silence; a silence that, however, I would engage to break down on the first private opportunity. This opportunity came before tea: I secured five minutes with her in the houskeeper's room, where, in the twilight, amid a smell of lately-baked bread, but with the place all swept and garnished, I found her sitting in pained placidity before the fire. So I see her still, so I see her best: facing the flame from her straight chair in the dusky, shining room, a large clean image of the 'put away' – of drawers closed and locked and rest without a remedy.

'Oh yes, they asked me to say nothing; and to please them – so long as they were there – of course I promised. But what had happened to you?'

'I only went with you for a walk,' I said. 'I had then to come back to meet a friend.'

She showed her surprise. 'A friend – *you*?'

'Oh yes, I have a couple!' I laughed. 'But did the children give you a reason?'

'For not alluding to your leaving us? Yes; they said you would like it better. Do you like it better?'

My face had made her rueful. 'No, I like it worse!' But after an instant I added: 'Did they say why I should like it better?'

'No; Master Miles only said "We must do nothing but what she likes!"'

'I wish indeed he would! And what did Flora say?'

'Miss Flora was too sweet. She said "Oh, of course, of course!" – and I said the same.'

I thought a moment. 'You were too sweet too – I can hear you all. But none the less, between Miles and me, it's now all out.'

'All out?' My companion stared. 'But what, Miss?'

'Everything. It doesn't matter. I've made up my mind. I came home, my dear,' I went on, 'for a talk with Miss Jessel.'

I had by this time formed the habit of having Mrs Grose literally well in hand in advance of my sounding that note; so that even now, as she bravely blinked under the signal of my word, I could keep her comparatively firm. 'A talk! Do you mean she spoke?'

'It came to that. I found her, on my return, in the schoolroom.'

'And what did she say?' I can hear the good woman still, and the candour of her stupefaction.

'That she suffers the torments—!'

It was this, of a truth, that made her, as she filled out my picture, gape. 'Do you mean,' she faltered, '—of the lost?'

'Of the lost. Of the damned. And that's why, to share them—' I faltered myself with the horror of it.

But my companion, with less imagination, kept me up. 'To share them—?'

'She wants Flora.' Mrs Grose might, as I gave it to her, fairly have fallen away from me had I not been prepared. I still held her there, to show I was. 'As I've told you, however, it doesn't matter.'

'Because you've made up your mind? But to what?'

'To everything.'

'And what do you call "everything"?'

'Why, sending for their uncle.'

'Oh Miss, in pity do,' my friend broke out.

'Ah, but I will, I *will*! I see it's the only way. What's "out", as I told you, with Miles is that if he thinks I'm afraid to – and has ideas of what he gains by that – he shall see he's mistaken. Yes, yes; his uncle shall have it here from me on the spot (and before the boy himself if necessary), that if I'm to be reproached with having done nothing again about more school—'

'Yes Miss—' my companion pressed me.

'Well, there's that awful reason.'

There were now clearly so many of these for my poor colleague that she was excusable for being vague. 'But – a – which?'

'Why, the letter from his old place.'

'You'll show it to the master?'

'I ought to have done so on the instant.'

'Oh no!' said Mrs Grose with decision.

'I'll put it before him,' I went on inexorably, 'that I can't undertake to work the question on behalf of a child who has been expelled—'

'For we've never in the least known what!' Mrs Grose declared.

'For wickedness. For what else – when he's so clever and beautiful and perfect? Is he stupid? Is he untidy? Is he infirm? Is he ill-natured? He's exquisite – so it can be only *that*; and that would open up the whole thing. After all,' I said, 'it's their uncle's fault. If he left here such people—!'

'He didn't really in the least know them. The fault's mine.' She had turned quite pale.

'Well, you shan't suffer,' I answered.

'The children shan't!' she emphatically returned.

I was silent a while; we looked at each other. 'Then what am I to tell him?'

'You needn't tell him anything. *I'll* tell him.'

I measured this. 'Do you mean you'll write—?' Remembering she couldn't, I caught myself up. 'How do you communicate?'

'I tell the bailiff. *He* writes.'

'And should you like him to write our story?'

My question had a sarcastic force that I had not fully intended, and it made her, after a moment, inconsequently break down. The tears were again in her eyes. 'Ah, Miss, *you* write!'

'Well – tonight,' I at last answered; and on this we separated.

17

I went so far, in the evening, as to make a beginning. The weather had changed back, a great wind was abroad, and beneath the lamp, in my room, with Flora at peace beside me, I sat for a long time before a blank sheet of paper and listened to the lash of the rain and the batter of the gusts. Finally I went out, taking a candle; I crossed the passage and listened a minute at Miles's door. What, under my endless obsession, I had been impelled to listen for was some betrayal of his not being at rest, and I presently caught one, but not in the form I had expected. His voice tinkled out. 'I say, you there – come in.' It was a gaiety in the gloom!

I went in with my light and found him, in bed, very wide awake, but very much at his ease. 'Well, what are *you* up to?' he asked with a grace of sociability in which it occurred to me that Mrs Grose, had she been present, might have looked in vain for proof that anything was 'out'.

I stood over him with my candle. 'How did you know I was there?'

'Why, of course I heard you. Did you fancy you made no noise? You're like a troop of cavalry!' he beautifully laughed.

'Then you weren't asleep?'

'Not much! I lie awake and think.'

I had put my candle, designedly, a short way off, and then, as he held out his friendly old hand to me, had sat down on the edge of his bed. 'What is it,' I asked, 'that you think of?'

'What in the world, my dear, but *you*?'

'Ah, the pride I take in your appreciation doesn't insist on that! I had so far rather you slept.'

'Well, I think also, you know, of this queer business of ours.'

I marked the coolness of his firm little hand. 'Of what queer business, Miles?'

'Why, the way you bring me up. And all the rest!'

I fairly held my breath a minute, and even from my glimmering taper there was light enough to show how he smiled up at me from his pillow.

'What do you mean by all the rest?'

'Oh, you know, you know!'

I could say nothing for a minute, though I felt, as I held his hand and our eyes continued to meet, that my silence had all the air of admitting his charge and that nothing in the whole world of reality was perhaps at that moment so fabulous as our actual relation. 'Certainly you shall go back to school,' I said, 'if it be that that troubles you. But not to the old place – we must find another, a better. How could I know it did trouble you, this question, when you never told me so, never spoke of it at all?' His clear, listening face, framed in its smooth whiteness, made him for the minute as appealing as some wistful patient in a children's hospital; and I would have given, as the resemblance came to me, all I possessed on earth really to be the nurse or the sister of charity who might have helped to cure him. Well, even as it was, I perhaps might help! 'Do you know you've never said a word to me about your school – I mean the old one; never mentioned it in any way?'

He seemed to wonder; he smiled with the same loveliness. But he clearly gained time; he waited, he called for guidance. 'Haven't I?' It wasn't for *me* to help him – it was for the thing I had met!

Something in his tone and the expression of his face, as I got this from him, set my heart aching with such a pang as it had never yet known; so unutterably touching was it to see his little brain puzzled and his little resources taxed to play, under the spell laid on him, a part of innocence and consistency. 'No, never – from the hour you came back. You've never mentioned to me one of your masters, one of your comrades, nor the least little thing that ever happened to you at school. Never, little Miles – no never – have you given me an inkling of anything that *may* have happened there. Therefore you can fancy how much I'm in the dark. Until you came out, that way, this morning, you had, since the first hour I saw you, scarce even made a reference to anything in your previous life. You seemed so perfectly to accept the present.' It was extraordinary how my absolute conviction of his secret precocity (or whatever I might call the poison of an influence that I dared but half to phrase), made him, in spite of the faint breath of his inward trouble, appear as accessible as an older person – imposed him almost as an intellectual equal. 'I thought you wanted to go on as you are.'

It struck me that at this he just faintly coloured. He gave, at any rate, like a convalescent slightly fatigued, a languid shake of his head. 'I don't – I don't. I want to get away.'

'You're tired of Bly?'

'Oh no, I like Bly.'

'Well, then—?'

'Oh, *you* know what a boy wants!'

I felt that I didn't know so well as Miles, and I took temporary refuge. 'You want to go to your uncle?'

Again, at this, with his sweet ironic face, he made a movement on the pillow. 'Ah, you can't get off with that!'

I was silent a little, and it was I, now, I think, who changed colour. 'My dear, I don't want to get off!'

'You can't, even if you do. You can't, you can't!' – he lay beautifully staring. 'My uncle must come down, and you must completely settle things.'

'If we do,' I returned with some spirit, 'you may be sure it will be to take you quite away.'

'Well, don't you understand that that's exactly what I'm working for? You'll have to tell him – about the way you've let it all drop: you'll have to tell him a tremendous lot!'

The exultation with which he uttered this helped me somehow, for the instant, to meet him rather more. 'And how much will *you*, Miles, have to tell him? There are things he'll ask you!'

He turned it over. 'Very likely. But what things?'

'The things you've never told me. To make up his mind what to do with you. He can't send you back—'

'Oh, I don't want to go back!' he broke in. 'I want a new field.'

He said it with admirable serenity, with positive unimpeachable gaiety, and doubtless it was that very note that most evoked for me the poignancy, the unnatural childish tragedy, of his probable reappearance at the end of three months with all his bravado and still more dishonour. It overwhelmed me now that I should never be able to bear that, and it made me let myself go. I threw myself upon him and in the tenderness of my pity I embraced him. 'Dear little Miles, dear little Miles—!'

My face was close to his, and he let me kiss him, simply taking it with indulgent good humour. 'Well, old lady?'

'Is there nothing – nothing at all that you want to tell me?'

He turned off a little, facing round towards the wall and holding up his hand to look at as one had seen sick children look. 'I've told you – I told you this morning.'

Oh, I was sorry for him! 'That you just want me not to worry you?'

He looked round at me now, as if in recognition of my understanding him; then ever so gently, 'To let me alone,' he replied.

There was even a singular little dignity in it, something that made me release him, yet, when I had slowly risen, linger beside him. God knows I never wished to harass him, but I felt that merely, at this, to turn my back on him was to abandon or, to put it more truly, to lose him. 'I've just begun a letter to your uncle,' I said.

'Well then, finish it!'

I waited a minute. 'What happened before?'

He gazed up at me again. 'Before what?'

'Before you came back. And before you went away.'

For some time he was silent, but he continued to meet my eyes. 'What happened?'

It made me, the sound of the words, in which it seemed to me that I caught for the very first time a small faint quaver of consenting consciousness – it made me drop on my knees beside the bed and seize once more the chance of possessing him. 'Dear little Miles, dear little Miles, if you *knew* how I want to help you! It's only that, it's nothing but that, and I'd rather die than give you a pain or do you a wrong – I'd rather die than hurt a hair of you. Dear little Miles' – oh, I brought it out now even if I *should* go too far – 'I just want you to help me to save you!' But I knew in a moment after this that I had gone too far. The answer to my appeal was instantaneous, but it came in the form of an extraordinary blast and chill, a gust of frozen air and a shake of the room as great as if, in the wild wind, the casement had crashed in. The boy gave a loud, high shriek which, lost in the rest of the shock of sound, might have seemed, indistinctly, though I was so close to him, a note either of jubilation or of terror. I jumped to my feet again and was conscious of darkness. So for a moment we remained, while I stared about me and saw that the drawn curtains were unstirred and the window tight. 'Why, the candle's out!' I then cried.

'It was I who blew it, dear!' said Miles.

18

The next day, after lessons, Mrs Grose found a moment to say to me quietly: 'Have you written, Miss?'

'Yes – I've written.' But I didn't add – for the hour – that my letter, sealed and directed, was still in my pocket. There would be time enough to send it before the messenger should go to the village. Meanwhile there had been, on the part of my pupils, no more brilliant, more exemplary morning. It was exactly as if they had both had at heart to gloss over any recent little friction. They performed the dizziest feats of arithmetic, soaring quite out of my feeble range, and perpetrated, in higher spirits than ever, geographical and historical jokes. It was conspicuous of course in Miles in particular that he appeared to wish to show how easily he could let me down. This child, to my memory, really lives in a setting of beauty and misery that no words can translate; there was a distinction all his own in every impulse he revealed; never was a small natural creature, to the uninitiated eye all frankness and freedom, a more ingenious, a more extraordinary little gentleman. I had perpetually to guard against the wonder of contemplation into which my initiated view betrayed me; to check the irrelevant gaze and discouraged sigh in which I constantly both attacked and renounced the enigma of what such a little gentleman could have done that deserved a penalty. Say that, by the dark prodigy I knew, the imagination of all evil *had* been opened up to him: all the justice within me ached for the proof that it could ever have flowered into an act.

He had never, at any rate, been such a little gentleman as when, after our early dinner on this dreadful day, he came round to me and asked if I shouldn't like him, for half an hour, to play to me. David playing to Saul could never have shown a finer sense of the occasion. It was literally a charming exhibition of tact, of magnanimity, and quite tantamount to his saying outright: 'The true knights we love to read about never push an advantage too far. I know what you mean now: you mean that – to be left alone yourself and not followed up – you'll cease to worry and spy upon me, won't keep me so close to you, will let me go and come. Well, I "come", you see – but I don't go! There'll be plenty of time for that. I do really delight in your society, and I only want to show you that I contended for a principle.' It may be imagined whether I resisted this appeal or failed to accompany him again, hand in hand, to the schoolroom. He sat down at the old piano and played as he had never played; and if there are those who think he had better have been kicking a football I can only say that I wholly agree with them. For at the end of a time that under his influence I had quite ceased to measure I started up with a strange sense of having literally slept at my post. It was after luncheon, and by the schoolroom fire, and yet I hadn't really, in the least, slept: I had only done something much worse – I had forgotten. Where, all this time, was Flora? When I put the question to Miles he played on a minute before answering, and then could only say: 'Why, my dear, how do *I* know?' – breaking moreover into a happy laugh which immediately after, as if it were a vocal accompaniment, he prolonged into incoherent, extravagant song.

I went straight to my room, but his sister was not there; then, before going downstairs, I looked into several others. As she was nowhere about she would surely be with Mrs Grose, whom, in the comfort of that theory, I accordingly proceeded in the quest of. I found her where I had found her the evening before, but she met my quick challenge with blank, scared ignorance. She had only supposed that, after the repast, I had carried off both the children; as to which she was quite in her right, for it was the very first time I had allowed the little girl out of my sight without some special provision. Of course now indeed she might be with the maids, so that the immediate thing was to look for her without an air of alarm. This we promptly arranged between us; but when, ten minutes later and in pursuance of our arrangement, we met in the hall, it was only to report on either side that after guarded inquiries we had altogether failed to trace her. For a minute there, apart from observation, we exchanged mute alarms, and I could feel with what high interest my friend returned me all those I had from the first given her.

'She'll be above,' she presently said – 'in one of the rooms you haven't searched.'

'No; she's at a distance.' I made up my mind. 'She has gone out.'

Mrs Grose started. 'Without a hat?'

I naturally also looked volumes. 'Isn't that woman always without one?'

'She's with *her*?'

'She's with *her*!' I declared. 'We must find them.'

My hand was on my friend's arm, but she failed for the moment, confronted with such an account of the matter, to respond to my pressure. She communed, on the contrary, on the spot, with her uneasiness. 'And where's Master Miles?'

'Oh, *he's* with Quint. They're in the schoolroom.'

'Lord, Miss!' My view, I was myself aware – and therefore I suppose my tone – had never yet reached so calm an assurance.

'The trick's played,' I went on; 'they've successfully worked their plan. He found the most divine little way to keep me quiet while she went off.'

'"Divine"?' Mrs Grose bewilderedly echoed.

'Infernal, then!' I almost cheerfully rejoined. 'He has provided for himself as well. But come!'

She had helplessly gloomed at the upper regions. 'You leave him—?'

'So long with Quint? Yes – I don't mind that now.'

She always ended, at these moments, by getting posession of my hand, and in this manner she could at present still stay me. But after grasping an instant at my sudden resignation, 'Because of your letter?' she eagerly brought out.

I quickly, by way of answer, felt for my letter, drew it forth, held it up, and then, freeing myself, went and laid it on the great hall-table. 'Luke will take it,' I said as I came back. I reached the house-door and opened it; I was already on the steps.

My companion still demurred: the storm of the night and the early morning had dropped, but the afternoon was damp and grey. I came down to the drive while she stood in the doorway. 'You go with nothing on?'

'What do I care when the child has nothing? I can't wait to dress,' I cried, 'and if you must do so I leave you. Try meanwhile, yourself, upstairs.'

'With *them?*' Oh, on this, the poor woman promptly joined me!

19

We went straight to the lake, as it was called at Bly, and I dare say rightly called, though I reflect that it may in fact have been a sheet of water less remarkable than it appeared to my untravelled eyes. My acquaintance with sheets of water was small, and the pool of Bly, at all events on the few occasions of my consenting, under the protection of my pupils, to affront its surface in the old flat-bottomed boat moored there for our use, had impressed me both with its extent and its agitation. The usual place of embarkation was half a mile from the house, but I had an intimate conviction that wherever Flora might be, she was not near home. She had not given me the slip for any small adventure, and, since the day of the very great one that I had shared with her by the pond, I had been aware, in our walks, of the quarter to which she most inclined. This was why I had now given to Mrs Grose's steps so marked a direction – a direction that made her, when she perceived it, oppose a resistance that showed me she was freshly mystified. 'You're going to the water, Miss? – you think she's *in*—?'

'She may be, though the depth is, I believe, nowhere very great. But what I judge most likely is that she's on the spot from which, the other day, we saw together when I told you.'

'When she pretended not to see—?'

'With that astounding self-possession! I've always been sure she wanted to go back alone. And now her brother has managed it for her.'

Mrs Grose still stood where she had stopped. 'You suppose they really *talk* of them?'

I could meet this with confidence! 'They say things that, if we heard them, would simply appal us.'

'And if she *is* there—?'

'Yes?'

'Then Miss Jessel is?'

'Beyond a doubt. You shall see.'

'Oh, thank you!' my friend cried, planted so firm that, taking it in, I went straight on without her. By the time I reached the pool, however, she was close behind me, and I knew that, whatever, to her apprehension, might befall me, the exposure of my society struck her as her least danger. She exhaled a moan of relief as we at last came in sight of the greater part of the water without a sight of the child. There was no trace of Flora on that nearer side of the bank where my observation of her had been most startling, and none on the opposite edge, where, save for a margin of some twenty yards, a thick copse came down to the water. The pond, oblong in shape, had a width so scant compared to its length that, with its ends out of view, it might have been taken for a scant river. We looked at the empty expanse, and then I felt the suggestion of my friend's eyes. I knew what she meant and I replied with a negative headshake.

'No, no; wait! she has taken the boat.'

My companion stared at the vacant mooring-place and then again across the lake. 'Then where is it?'

'Our not seeing it is the strongest of proofs. She has used it to go over, and then has managed to hide it.'

'All alone – that child?'

'She's not alone, and at such times she's not a child: she's an old, old woman.' I scanned all the visible shore while Mrs Grose took again, into the queer element I offered her, one of her plunges of submission; then I pointed out that the boat might perfectly be in a small refuge formed by one of the recesses of the pool, an indentation masked, for the hither side, by a projection of the bank and by a clump of trees growing close to the water.

'But if the boat's there, where on earth's *she*?' my colleague anxiously asked.

'That's exactly what we must learn.' And I started to walk further.

'By going all the way round?'

'Certainly, far as it is. It will take us but ten minutes, but it's far enough to have made the child prefer not to walk. She went straight over.'

'Laws!' cried my friend again; the chain of my logic was ever too much for her. It dragged her at my heels even now, and when we had got half way round – a devious, tiresome process, on ground much broken and by a path choked with overgrowth – I paused to give her breath. I sustained her with a grateful arm, assuring her that she might hugely help me; and this started us afresh, so that in the course of but few minutes more we reached a point from which we found the boat to be where I had supposed it. It had been intentionally left as much as possible out of sight and was tied to one of the stakes of a fence that came, just there, down to the brink and that had been an assistance to disembarking. I recognized, as I looked at the pair of short, thick oars, quite safely drawn up, the prodigious character of the feat for a little girl; but I had lived, by this time, too long among wonders and had panted to too many livelier measures. There was a gate in the fence, through which we passed, and that brought us, after a trifling interval, more in the open. Then 'There she is!' we both exclaimed at once.

Flora, a short way off, stood before us on the grass and smiled as if her performance was now complete. The next thing she did, however, was to stoop straight down and pluck – quite as if it were all she was there for – a big, ugly spray of withered fern. I instantly became sure she had just come out of the copse. She waited for us, not herself taking a step, and I was conscious of the rare solemnity with which we presently approached her. She smiled and smiled, and we met; but it was all done in a silence by this time flagrantly ominous. Mrs Grose was the first to break the spell: she threw herself on her knees and, drawing the child to her breast, clasped in a long embrace the little tender, yielding body. While this dumb convulsion lasted I could only watch it – which I did the more intently when I saw Flora's face peep at me over our companion's shoulder. It was serious now – the flicker had left it; but it strengthened the pang with which I at that moment envied Mrs Grose the simplicity of *her* relation. Still, all this while, nothing more passed between us save that Flora had let her foolish fern again drop to the ground. What she and I had virtually said to each other was that pretexts were useless now. When Mrs Grose finally got up she kept the child's hand, so that the two were still before me; and the singular reticence of our communion was even more marked in the frank look she launched me. 'I'll be hanged,' it said, 'if *I'll* speak!'

It was Flora who, gazing all over me in candid wonder, was the first. She was struck with our bareheaded aspect. 'Why, where are your things?'

'Where yours are, my dear!' I promptly returned.

She had already got back her gaiety and appeared to take this as an answer quite sufficient, 'And where's Miles?' she went on.

There was something in the small valour of it that quite finished me: these three words from her were, in a flash like the glitter of a drawn blade, the jostle of the cup that my hand, for weeks and weeks, had held high and full to the brim and that now, even before speaking, I felt overflow in a deluge. 'I'll tell you if you'll tell *me*—' I heard myself say, then heard the tremor in which it broke.

'Well, what?'

Mrs Grose's suspense blazed at me, but it was too late now, and I brought the thing out handsomely. 'Where, my pet, is Miss Jessel?'

20

Just as in the churchyard with Miles, the whole thing was upon us. Much as I had made of the fact that this name had never once, between us, been sounded, the quick, smitten glare with which the child's face now received it fairly likened my breach of the silence to the smash of a pane of glass. It added to the interposing cry, as if to stay the blow, that Mrs Grose, at the same instant, uttered over my violence – the shriek of a creature scared, or rather wounded, which, in turn, within a few seconds, was completed by a gasp of my own. I seized my colleague's arm. 'She's there, she's there!'

Miss Jessel stood before us on the opposite bank exactly as she had stood the other time, and I remember, strangely, as the first feeling now produced in me, my thrill of joy of having brought on a proof. She was there, and I was justified; she was there, and I was neither cruel nor mad. She was there for poor scared Mrs Grose, but she was there most for Flora; and no moment of my monstrous time was perhaps so extraordinary as that in which I consciously threw out to her, with the sense that – pale and ravenous demon as she was, she would catch and understand it – an inarticulate message of gratitude. She rose erect on the spot my friend and I had lately quitted, and there was not, in all the long reach of her desire, an inch of her evil that fell short. This first vividness of vision and emotion were things of a few seconds during which Mrs Grose's dazed blink across to where I pointed struck me as a sovereign sign that she too at last saw, just as it carried my own eyes precipitately to the child. The revelation then of the manner in which Flora was affected startled me, in truth, far more that it would have done to find her also merely agitated, for direct dismay was of course not what I had expected. Prepared and on our guard as our pursuit had actually made her, she would repress every betrayal; and I was therefore shaken, on the spot, by my first glimpse of the particular one for which I had not allowed. To see her, without a convulsion of her small pink face, not even feign to glance in the direction of the prodigy I announced, but only, instead of that, turn at *me* an expression of hard, still gravity, an expression absolutely new and unprecedented and that appeared to read and accuse and judge me – this was a stroke that somehow converted the little girl herself into the very presence that could make me quail. I quailed even though my certitude that she thoroughly saw was never greater than at that instant, and in the immediate need to defend myself I called it passionately to witness. 'She's there, you little unhappy thing – there, there, *there*, and you see her as well as you see me!' I had said shortly before to Mrs Grose that she was not at these times a child, but an old, old woman, and that description of her could not have been more strikingly confirmed than in the way in which, for all answer to this, she simply showed me, without a concession, an admission, of her eyes, a countenance of deeper and deeper, of indeed suddenly quite fixed reprobation. I was by this time – if I can put the whole thing at all together – more appalled at what I may properly call her manner than at anything else, though it was simultaneously with this that I became aware of having Mrs Grose also, and very formidably, to reckon with. My elder companion, the next moment, at any rate, blotted out everything but her own flushed face and her loud, shocked protest, a burst of high disapproval. 'What a dreadful turn, to be sure, Miss! Where on earth do you see anything?'

I could only grasp her more quickly yet, for even while she spoke the hideous plain presence stood undimmed and undaunted. It had already lasted a minute, and it lasted while I continued, seizing my colleague, quite thrusting her at it and presenting her to it, to insist with my pointing hand. 'You don't see her exactly as *we* see? – you mean to say you don't now – *now*? She's as big as a blazing fire! Only look, dearest woman, *look*—!' She looked, even as I did, and gave me, with her deep groan of negation, repulsion, compassion – the mixture with her pity of her relief at her exemption – a sense, touching to me even then, that she would have backed me up if she could. I might well have needed that, for with this hard blow of the proof that her eyes were hopelessly sealed I felt my own situation horribly crumble, I felt – I saw – my livid predecessor press, from her position, on my defeat, and I was conscious, more than all, of what I should have from this instant to deal with in the astounding little attitude of Flora. Into this attitude Mrs Grose immediately and violently entered, breaking, even while there pierced through my sense of ruin a prodigious private triumph, into breathless reassurance.

'She isn't there, little lady, and nobody's there – and you never see nothing, my sweet! How can poor Miss Jessel – when poor Miss Jessel's dead and buried? *We* know, don't we, love?' – and she appealed, blundering in, to the child. 'It's all a mere mistake and a worry and a joke – and we'll go home as fast as we can!'

Our companion, on this, had responded with a strange, quick primness of propriety, and they were again, with Mrs Grose on her feet, united, as it were, in pained opposition to me. Flora continued to fix me with her small mask of reprobation, and even at that minute I prayed God to forgive me for seeming to see that, as she stood there holding tight to our friend's dress, her incomparable childish beauty had suddenly failed, had quite vanished. I've said it already – she was literally, she was hideously hard; she had turned common and almost ugly. 'I don't know what you mean. I see nobody. I see nothing. I never *have*. I think you're cruel. I don't like you!' Then, after this deliverance, which might have been that of a vulgarly pert little girl in the street, she hugged Mrs Grose more closely and buried in her skirts the dreadful little face. In this position she produced an almost furious wail. 'Take me away, take me away – oh, take me away from *her*!'

'From *me*?' I panted.

'From *you* – from you!' she cried.

Even Mrs Grose looked across at me dismayed; while I had nothing to do but communicate again with the figure that, on the opposite bank, without a movement, as rigidly still as if catching, beyond the interval, our voices, was as vividly there for my disaster as it was not there for my service. The wretched child had spoken exactly as if she had got from some outside source each of her stabbing little words, and I could therefore, in the full despair of all I had to accept, but sadly shake my head at her. 'If I had ever doubted all my doubt would at present have gone, I've been living with the miserable truth, and now it has only too much closed round me. Of course I've lost you: I've interfered, and you've seen – under *her* dictation' – with which I faced, over the pool again, our infernal witness – 'the easy and perfect way to meet it. I've done my best, but I've lost you. Good-bye.' For Mrs Grose I had an imperative, an almost frantic 'Go, go!' before which, in infinite distress, but mutely possessed of the little girl and clearly convinced, in spite of her blindness, that something awful had occurred and some collapse engulfed us, she retreated, by the way we had come, as fast as she could move.

Of what first happened when I was left alone I had no subsequent memory. I only knew that at the end of, I suppose, a quarter of an hour, an odorous dampness and roughness, chilling and piercing my trouble, had made me understand that I must have thrown myself, on my face, on the ground and given way to a wildness of grief. I must have lain there long and cried and sobbed, for when I raised my head the day was almost done. I got up and looked a moment, through the twilight, at the grey pool and its blank, haunted edge, and then I took, back to the house, my dreary and difficult course. When I reached the gate in the fence the boat, to my surprise, was gone, so that I had a fresh reflection to make on Flora's extraordinary command of the situation. She passed that night, by the most tacit, and I should add, were not the word so grotesque a false note, the happiest of arrangements, with Mrs Grose. I saw neither of them on my return, but, on the other hand, as by an ambiguous compensation, I saw a great deal of Miles. I saw – I can use no other phrase – so much of him that it was as if it were more than it had ever been. No evening I had passed at Bly had the portentous quality of this one; in spite of which – and in spite also of the deeper depths of consternation that had opened beneath my feet – there was literally, in the ebbing actual, an extraordinarily sweet sadness. On reaching the house I had never so much as looked for the boy; I had simply gone straight to my room to change what I was wearing and to take in, at a glance, much material testimony to Flora's rupture. Her little belongings had all been removed. When later, by the schoolroom fire, I was served with tea by the usual maid, I indulged, on the article of my other pupil, in no inquiry whatever. He had his freedom now – he might have it to the end! Well, he did have it; and it consisted – in part at least – of his coming in at about eight o'clock and sitting down with me in silence. On the removal of the tea-things I had blown out the candles and drawn my chair closer: I was conscious of a mortal coldness and felt as if I should never again be warm. So, when he appeared, I was sitting in the glow with my thoughts. He paused a moment by the door as if to look at me; then – as if to share them – came to the other side of the hearth and sank into a chair. We sat there in absolute stillness; yet he wanted, I felt, to be with me.

21

Before a new day, in my room, had fully broken, my eyes opened to Mrs Grose, who had come to my bedside with worse news. Flora was so markedly feverish that an illness was perhaps at hand; she had passed a night of extreme unrest, a night agitated above all by fears that had for their subject not in the least her former, but wholly her present governess. It was not against the possible re-entrance of Miss Jessel on the scene that she protested – it was conspicuously and passionately against mine. I was promptly on my feet of course, and with an immense deal to ask; the more that my friend had discernibly now girded her loins to meet me once more. This I felt as soon as I had put to her the question of her sense of the child's sincerity as against my own. 'She persists in denying to you that she saw, or has ever seen, anything?'

My visitor's trouble, truly, was great. 'Ah, Miss, it isn't a matter on which I can push her! Yet it isn't either, I must say, as if I much needed to. It has made her, every inch of her, quite old.'

'Oh, I see her perfectly from here. She resents, for all the world like some high little personage, the imputation on her truthfulness and, as it were, her respectability. "Miss Jessel indeed – *she*!" Ah, she's "respectable", the chit! The impression she gave me there yesterday was, I assure you, the very strangest of all; it was quite beyond any of the others. I *did* put my foot in it! She'll never speak to me again.'

Hideous and obscure as it all was, it held Mrs Grose briefly silent; then she granted my point with a frankness which, I made sure, had more behind it. 'I think indeed, Miss, she never will. She do have a grand manner about it!'

'And that manner' – I summed it up – 'is practically what's the matter with her now.'

Oh, that manner, I could see in my visitor's face, and not a little else besides! 'She asks me every three minutes if I think you're coming in.'

'I see – I see.' I too, on my side, had so much more than worked it out. 'Has she said to you since yesterday – except to repudiate her familiarity with anything so dreadful – a single word about Miss Jessel?'

'Not one, Miss. And of course you know,' my friend added, 'I took it from her, by the lake that, just then and there at least, there *was* nobody.'

'Rather! and, naturally, you take it from her still.'

'I don't contradict her. What else can I do?'

'Nothing in the world! You've the cleverest little person to deal with. They've made them – their two friends, I mean – still cleverer even than nature did; for it was wondrous material to play on! Flora has now her grievance, and she'll work it to the end.'

'Yes, Miss; but to *what* end?'

'Why, that of dealing with me to her uncle. She'll make me out to him the lowest creature—!'

I winced at the fair show of the scene in Mrs Grose's face; she looked for a minute as if she sharply saw them together. 'And him who thinks so well of you!'

'He has an odd way – it comes over me now,' I laughed, '—of proving it! But that doesn't matter. What Flora wants, of course, is to get rid of me!'

My companion bravely concurred. 'Never again to so much as look at you.'

'So that what you've come to me now for,' I asked, 'is to speed me on my way?' Before she had time to reply, however, I had her in check. 'I've a better idea – the result of my reflections. My going *would* seem the right thing, and on Sunday I was terribly near it. Yet that won't do. It's *you* who must go. You must take Flora.'

My visitor, at this, did speculate. 'But where in the world—?'

'Away from here. Away from *them*. Away, even most of all, now, from me. Straight to her uncle.'

'Only to tell on you—?'

'No, not "only!" To leave me, in addition, with my remedy.'

She was still vague. 'And what *is* your remedy?'

'Your loyalty, to begin with. And then Miles's.'

She looked at me hard. 'Do you think he—?'

'Won't, if he has the chance, turn on me? Yes, I venture still to think it. At all events, I want to try. Get off with his sister as soon as possible and leave me with him alone.' I was amazed, myself, at the spirit I had still in reserve, and therefore perhaps a trifle the more disconcerted at the way in which, in spite of this fine example of it, she hesitated. 'There's one thing, of course,' I went on: 'they mustn't, before she goes, see each other for three seconds.' Then it came over me that, in spite of Flora's presumable sequestration from the instant of her return from the pool, it might already be too late. 'Do you mean,' I anxiously asked, 'that they *have* met?'

At this she quite flushed. 'Ah, Miss, I'm not such a fool as that! If I've been obliged to leave her three or four times, it has been each time with one of the maids, and at present, though she's alone, she's locked in safe. And yet – and yet!' There were too many things.

'And yet what?'

'Well, are you so sure of the little gentleman?'

'I'm not sure of anything but *you*. But I have, since last evening, a new hope. I think he wants to give me an opening. I do believe that – poor little exquisite wretch! – he wants to speak. Last evening, in the firelight and the silence, he sat with me for two hours as if it were just coming.'

Mrs Grose looked hard, through the window, at the grey, gathering day. 'And did it come?'

'No, though I waited and waited, I confess it didn't, and it was without a breach of the silence or so much as a faint allusion to his sister's condition and absence that we at last kissed for good night. All the same,' I continued, 'I can't, if her uncle sees her, consent to his seeing her brother without my having given the boy – and most of all because things have got so bad – a little more time.'

My friend appeared on this ground more reluctant than I could quite understand. 'What do you mean by more time?'

'Well, a day or two – really to bring it out. He'll then be on *my* side – of which you see the importance. If nothing comes, I shall only fail, and you will, at the worst, have helped me by doing, on your arrival in town, whatever you may have found possible.' So I put it before her, but she continued for a little so inscrutably embarrassed that I came again to her aid. 'Unless indeed,' I wound up, 'You really want *not* to go.'

I could see it, in her face, at last clear itself; she put out her hand to me as a pledge. 'I'll go – I'll go. I'll go this morning.'

I wanted to be very just. 'If you *should* wish still to wait, I would engage she shouldn't see me.'

'No, no: it's the place itself. She must leave it.' She held me a moment with heavy eyes, then brought out the rest. 'Your idea's the right one. I myself, Miss—'

'Well?'

'I can't stay.'

The look she gave me with it made me jump at possibilities. 'You mean that, since yesterday, you *have* seen—?'

She shook her head with dignity. 'I've *heard*—!'

'Heard?'

'From that child – horrors! There!' she sighed with tragic relief. 'On my honour, Miss, she says things—!' But at this evocation she broke down; she dropped, with a sudden sob, upon my sofa and, as I had seen her do before, gave way to all the grief of it.

It was quite in another manner that I, for my part, let myself go. 'Oh, thank God!'

She sprang up again at this, drying her eyes with a groan. '"Thank God?"'

'It so justifies me!'

'It does that, Miss!'

I couldn't have desired more emphasis, but I just hesitated, 'She's so horrible?'

I saw my colleague scarce knew how to put it. 'Really shocking.'

'And about me?'

'About you, Miss – since you must have it. It's beyond everything, for a young lady; and I can't think wherever she must have picked up—'

'The appalling language she applied to me? I can, then!' I broke in with a laugh that was doubtless significant enough.

It only, in truth, left my friend still more grave. 'Well, perhaps I ought to also – since I've heard some of it before! Yet I can't bear it,' the poor woman went on while, with the same movement, she glanced, on my dressing-table, at the face of my watch. 'But I must go back.'

I kept her, however. 'Ah, if you can't bear it—!'

'How can I stop with her, you mean? Why, just *for* that: to get her away. Far from this,' she pursued, 'far from *them*—'

'She may be different? she may be free?' I seized her almost with joy. 'Then, in spite of yesterday, you *believe*—'

'In such doings?' Her simple description of them required, in the light of her expression, to be carried no further, and she gave me the whole thing as she had never done. 'I believe.'

Yes, it was a joy, and we were still shoulder to shoulder: if I might continue sure of that I should care but little what else happened. My support in the presence of disaster would be the same as it had been in my early need of confidence, and if my friend would answer for my honesty I would answer for all the rest. On the point of taking leave of her, none the less, I was to some extent embarrassed. 'There's one thing of course – it occurs to me – to remember. My letter, giving the alarm, will have reached town before you.'

I now perceived still more how she had been beating about the bush and how weary at last it had made her. 'Your letter won't have got there. Your letter never went.'

'What then became of it?'

'Goodness knows! Master Miles—'

'Do you mean *he* took it?' I gasped.

She hung fire, but she overcame her reluctance. 'I mean that I saw yesterday, when I came back with Miss Flora, that it wasn't where you had put it. Later in the evening I had the chance to question Luke, and he declared that he had neither noticed nor touched it.' We could only exchange on this, one of our deeper mutual soundings, and it was Mrs Grose who first brought up the plumb with an almost elate 'You see!'

'Yes, I see that if Miles took it instead he probably will have read it and destroyed it.'

'And don't you see anything else?'

I faced her a moment with a sad smile. 'It strikes me that by this time your eyes are open even wider than mine.'

They proved to be so indeed, but she could still blush, almost, to show it. 'I make out now what he must have done at school.' And she gave, in her simple sharpness, an almost droll disillusioned nod. 'He stole!'

I turned it over – I tried to be more judicial. 'Well – perhaps.'

She looked as if she found me unexpectedly calm. 'He stole *letters*!'

She couldn't know my reasons for a calmness after all pretty shallow; so I showed them off as I might. 'I hope then it was to more purpose than in this case! The note, at any rate, that I put on the table yesterday,' I pursued, 'will have given him so scant an advantage – for it contained only the bare demand for an interview – that he is already much ashamed of having gone so far for so little, and that what he had on his mind last evening was precisely the need of confession.' I seemed to myself, for the instant, to have mastered it, to see it all. 'Leave us, leave us' – I was already, at the door, hurrying her off. 'I'll get it out of him. He'll meet me – he'll confess. If he confesses, he's saved. And if he's saved—'

'Then *you* are?' The dear woman kissed me on this, and I took her farewell. 'I'll save you without him!' she cried as she went.

22

Yet it was when she had got off – and I missed her on the spot – that the great pinch really came. If I had counted on what it would give me to find myself alone with Miles I speedily perceived, at least, that it would give me a measure. No hour of my stay in fact was so assailed with apprehensions as that of my coming down to learn that the carriage containing Mrs Grose and my younger pupil had already rolled out of the gates. Now I *was*, I said to myself, face to face with the elements, and for much of the rest of the day, while I fought my weakness, I could consider that I had been supremely rash. It was a tighter place still than I had yet turned round in; all the more that, for the first time, I could see in the aspect of others a confused reflection of the crisis. What had happened naturally caused them all to stare; there was too little of the explained, throw out whatever we might, in the suddenness of my colleague's act. The maids and the men looked blank; the effect of which on my nerves was an aggravation until I saw the necessity of making it a positive aid. It was precisely, in short, by just clutching the helm that I avoided total wreck; and I daresay that, to bear up at all, I became, that morning, very grand and very dry. I welcomed the consciousness that I was charged with much to do, and I caused it to be known as well that, left thus to myself, I was quite remarkably firm. I wandered with that manner, for the next hour or two, all over the place and looked, I have no doubt, as if I were ready for any onset. So, for the benefit of whom it might concern, I paraded with a sick heart.

The person it appeared least to concern proved to be, till dinner, little Miles himself. My perambulations had given me, meanwhile, no glimpse of him, but they had tended to make more public the change taking place in our relation as a consequence of his having at the piano, the day before, kept me, in Flora's interest, so beguiled and befooled. The stamp of publicity had of course been fully given by her confinement and departure, and the change itself was now ushered in by our non-observance of the regular custom of the schoolroom. He had already disappeared when, on my way down, I pushed open his door, and I learned below that he had breakfasted – in the presence of a couple of maids – with Mrs Grose and his sister. He had then gone out, as he said, for a stroll; than which nothing, I reflected, could better have expressed his frank view of the abrupt transformation of my office. What he would now permit this office to consist of was yet to be settled: there was a queer relief, at all events – I mean for myself in especial – in the renouncement of one pretension. If so much had sprung to the surface I scarce put it too strongly in saying that what had perhaps sprung highest was the absurdity of our prolonging the fiction that I had anything more to teach him. It sufficiently stuck out that, by tacit little tricks in which even more than myself he carried out the care of my dignity, I had had to appeal to him to let me off straining to meet him on the ground of his true capacity. He had at any rate his freedom now; I was never to touch it again, as I had amply shown, moreover, when, on his joining me in the schoolroom the previous night, I had uttered, on the subject of the interval just concluded, neither challenge nor hint. I had too much, from this moment, my other ideas. Yet when he at last arrived the difficulty of applying them, the accumulations of my problem, were brought straight home to me by the beautiful little presence on which what had occurred had as yet, for the eye, dropped neither stain nor shadow.

To mark, for the house, the high state I cultivated I decreed that my meals with the boy should be served, as we called it, downstairs; so that I had been awaiting him in the ponderous pomp of the room outside of the window of which I had had from Mrs Grose, that first scared Sunday, my flash of something it would scarce have done to call light. Here at present I felt afresh – for I had felt it again and again – how my equilibrium depended on the success of my rigid will, the will to shut my eyes as tight as possible to the truth that what I had to deal with was, revoltingly, against nature. I could only get on at all by taking 'nature' into my confidence and my account, by treating my monstrous ordeal as a push in a direction unusual, of course, and unpleasant, but demanding, after all, for a fair front, only another turn of the screw of ordinary human virtue. No attempt, none the less, could well require more tact than just this attempt to supply, one's self, *all* the nature. How could I put even a little of that article into a suppression of reference to what had occurred? How, on the other hand, could I make a reference without a new plunge into the hideous obscure? Well, a sort of answer, after a time, had come to me, and it was so far confirmed as that I was met, incontestably, by the quickened vision of what was rare in my little companion. It was indeed as if he had found even now – as he had so often found at lessons – still some other delicate way to ease me off. Wasn't there light in the fact which, as we shared our solitude, broke out with a specious glitter it had never yet quite worn? – the fact that (opportunity aiding, precious opportunity which had now come), it would be preposterous, with a child so endowed, to forego the help one might wrest from absolute intelligence? What had his intelligence been given him for but to save him? Mightn't one, to reach his mind, risk the stretch of an angular arm over his character? It was as if, when we were face to face in the dining-room, he had literally shown me the way. The roast mutton was on the table, and I had dispensed with attendance. Miles, before he sat down, stood a moment with his hands in his pockets and looked at the joint, on which he seemed on the point of passing some humorous judgement. But what he presently produced was: 'I say, my dear, is she really very awfully ill?'

'Little Flora? Not so bad but that she'll presently be better. London will set her up. Bly had ceased to agree with her. Come here and take your mutton.'

He alertly obeyed me, carried the plate carefully to his seat and, when he was established, went on. 'Did Bly disagree with her so terribly suddenly?'

'Not so suddenly as you might think. One had seen it coming on.'

'Then why didn't you get her off before?'

'Before what?'

'Before she became too ill to travel.'

I found myself prompt. 'She's *not* too ill to travel: she only might have become so if she had stayed. This was just the moment to seize. The journey will dissipate the influence' – oh, I was grand! – 'and carry it off.'

'I see, I see' – Miles, for that matter, was grand too. He settled to his repast with the charming little 'table manner' that, from the day of his arrival, had relieved me of all grossness of admonition. Whatever he had been driven from school for, it was not for ugly feeding. He was irreproachable, as always, today; but he was unmistakably more conscious. He was discernibly trying to take for granted more things than he found, without assistance, quite easy; and he dropped into peaceful silence while he felt his situation. Our meal was of the briefest – mine a vain pretence, and I had the things immediately removed. While this was done Miles stood again with his hands in his little pockets and his back to me – stood and looked out of the wide window through which, that other day, I had seen what pulled me up. We continued silent while the maid was with us – as silent, it whimsically occurred to me, as some young couple who, on their wedding-journey, at the inn, feel shy in the presence of the waiter. He turned round only when the waiter had left us. 'Well – so we're alone!'

23

'Oh, more or less.' I fancy my smile was pale. 'Not absolutely. We shouldn't like that!' I went on.

'No – I suppose we shouldn't. Of course we have the others.'

'We have the others – we have indeed the others,' I concurred.

'Yet even though we have them,' he returned, still with his hands in his pockets and planted there in front of me, 'they don't much count, do they?'

I made the best of it, but I felt wan. 'It depends on what you call "much"!'

'Yes' – with all accommodation – 'everything depends!' On this, however, he faced to the window again and presently reached it with his vague, restless, cogitating step. He remained there a while, with his forehead against the glass, in contemplation of the stupid shrubs I knew and the dull things of November. I had always my hypocrisy of 'work', behind which, now, I gained the sofa. Steadying myself with it there as I had repeatedly done at those moments of torment that I have described as the moments of my knowing the children to be given to something from which I was barred, I sufficiently obeyed my habit of being prepared for the worst. But an extraordinary impression dropped on me as I extracted a meaning from the boy's embarrassed back – none other than the impression that I was not barred now. This inference grew in a few minutes to sharp intensity and seemed bound up with the direct perception that it was positively *he* who was. The frames and squares of the great window were a kind of image, for him, of a kind of failure. I felt that I saw him, at any rate, shut in or shut out. He was admirable, but not comfortable: I took it in with a throb of hope. Wasn't he looking, through the haunted pane, for something he couldn't see? – and wasn't it the first time in the whole business that he had known such a lapse? The first, the very first: I found it a splendid portent. It made him anxious, though he watched himself; he had been anxious all day and, even while in his usual sweet little manner he sat at table, had needed all his small strange genius to give it a gloss. When he at last turned round to meet me it was almost as if this genius had succumbed. 'Well, I think I'm glad Bly agrees with *me!*'

'You would certainly seem to have seen, these twenty-four hours, a good deal more of it than for some time before. I hope,' I went on bravely, 'that you've been enjoying yourself.'

'Oh yes, I've been ever so far; all round about – miles and miles away. I've never been so free.'

He had really a manner of his own, and I could only try to keep up with him. 'Well, do you like it?'

He stood there smiling; then at last he put into two words – 'Do *you?*' – more discrimination than I had ever heard two words contain. Before I had time to deal with that, however, he continued as if with the sense that this

was an impertinence to be softened. 'Nothing could be more charming than
the way you take it, for of course if we're alone together now it's you that are
alone most. But I hope,' he threw in, 'you don't particularly mind!'

'Having to do with you?' I asked. 'My dear child, how can I help minding?
Though I've renounced all claim to your company – you're so beyond me – I
at least greatly enjoy it. What else should I stay on for?'

He looked at me more directly, and the expression of his face, graver now,
struck me as the most beautiful I had ever found in it. 'You stay on just for
that?'

'Certainly. I stay on as your friend and from the tremendous interest I take
in you till something can be done for you that may be more worth your while.
That needn't surprise you.' My voice trembled so that I felt it impossible to
suppress the shake. 'Don't you remember how I told you, when I came and
sat on your bed the night of the storm, that there was nothing in the world I
wouldn't do for you?'

'Yes, yes!' He, on his side, more and more visibly nervous, had a tone to
master; but he was so much more successful than I that, laughing out
through his gravity, he could pretend we were pleasantly jesting. 'Only that,
I think, was to get me to do something for *you*!'

'It was partly to get you to do something,' I conceded. 'But, you know, you
didn't do it.'

'Oh yes,' he said with the brightest superficial eagerness, 'you wanted me
to tell you something.'

'That's it. Out, straight out. What you have on your mind, you know.'

'Ah then, is *that* what you've stayed over for?'

He spoke with a gaiety through which I could still catch the finest little
quiver of resentful passion; but I can't begin to express the effect upon me of
an implication of surrender even so faint. It was as if what I had yearned for
had come at last only to astonish me. 'Well, yes – I may as well make a clean
breast of it. It was precisely for that.'

He waited so long that I supposed it for the purpose of repudiating the
assumption on which my action had been founded; but what he finally said
was: 'Do you mean now – here?'

'There couldn't be a better place or time.' He looked round him uneasily,
and I had the rare – oh, the queer! – impression of the very first symptom I
had seen in him of the approach of immediate fear. It was as if he were
suddenly afraid of me – which struck me indeed as perhaps the best thing to
make him. Yet in the very pang of the effort I felt it vain to try sternness, and
I heard myself the next instant so gentle as to be almost grotesque. 'You want
so to go out again?'

'Awfully!' He smiled at me heroically, and the touching little bravery of it
was enhanced by his actually flushing with pain. He had picked up his hat,
which he had brought in, and stood twirling it in a way that gave me, even as
I was just nearly reaching port, a perverse horror of what I was doing. To do
it in *any* way was an act of violence, for what did it consist of but the
obtrusion of the idea of grossness and guilt on a small helpless creature who
had been for me a revelation of the possibilities of beautiful intercourse?
Wasn't it base to create for a being so exquisite a mere alien awkwardness? I
suppose I now read into our situation a clearness it couldn't have had at the
time, for I seem to see our poor eyes already lighted with some spark of a

prevision of the anguish that was to come. So we circled about, with terrors and scruples, like fighters not daring to close. But it was for each other we feared! That kept us a little longer suspended and unbruised. 'I'll tell you everything,' Miles said – 'I mean I'll tell you anything you like. You'll stay on with me, and we shall both be all right and I *will* tell you – I *will*. But not now.'

'Why not now?'

My insistence turned him from me and kept him once more at his window in a silence during which, between us, you might have heard a pin drop. Then he was before me again with the air of a person for whom, outside, someone who had frankly to be reckoned with was waiting. 'I have to see Luke.'

I had not yet reduced him to quite so vulgar a lie, and I felt proportionately ashamed. But, horrible as it was, his lies made up my truth. I achieved thoughfully a few loops of my knitting. 'Well then, go to Luke, and I'll wait for what you promise. Only, in return for that, satisfy, before you leave me, one very much smaller request.'

He looked as if he felt he had succeeded enough to be able still a little to bargain. 'Very much smaller—?'

'Yes, a mere fraction of the whole. Tell me' – oh, my work preoccupied me, and I was off-hand! – 'if, yesterday afternoon, from the table in the hall, you took, you know, my letter.'

24

My sense of how he received this suffered for a minute from something that I can describe only as a fierce split of my attention – a stroke that at first, as I sprang straight up, reduced me to the mere blind movement of getting hold of him, drawing him close and, while I just fell for support against the nearest piece of furniture, instinctively keeping him with his back to the window. The appearance was full upon us that I had already had to deal with here: Peter Quint had come into view like a sentinel before a prison. The next thing I saw was that, from outside, he had reached the window, and then I knew that, close to the glass and glaring in through it, he offered once more to the room his white face of damnation. It represents but grossly what took place within me at the sight to say that on the second my decision was made; yet I believe that no woman so overwhelmed ever in so short a time recovered her grasp of the *act*. It came to me in the very horror of the immediate presence that the act would be, seeing and facing what I saw and faced, to keep the boy himself unaware. The inspiration – I can call it by no other name – was that I felt how voluntarily, how transcendently, I *might*. It was like fighting with a demon for a human soul, and when I had fairly so appraised it I saw how the human soul – held out, in the tremor of my hands, at arms' lengh – had a perfect dew of sweat on a lovely childish forehead. The face that was close to mine was as white as the face against the glass, and out of it presently came a sound, not low nor weak, but as if from much farther away, that I drank like a waft of fragrance.

'Yes – I took it.'

At this, with a moan of joy, I enfolded, I drew him close; and while I held him to my breast, where I could feel in the sudden fever of his little body the tremendous pulse of his little heart, I kept my eyes on the thing at the window and saw it move and shift its posture. I have likened it to a sentinel, but its slow wheel, for a moment, was rather the prowl of a baffled beast. My present quickened courage, however, was such that, not too much to let it through, I had to shade, as it were, my flame. Meanwhile the glare of the face was again at the window, the scoundrel fixed as if to watch and wait. It was the very confidence that I might now defy him, as well as the positive certitude, by this time, of the child's unconsciousness, that made me go on. 'What did you take it for?'

'To see what you said about me.'

'You opened the letter?'

'I opened it.'

My eyes were now, as I held him off a little again, on Miles's own face, in which the collapse of mockery showed me how complete was the ravage of uneasiness. What was prodigious was that at last, by my success, his sense was sealed and his communication stopped: he knew that he was in presence, but knew not of what, and knew still less that I also was and that I did know. And what did this strain of trouble matter when my eyes went back to the window only to see that the air was clear again and – by my personal triumph – the influence quenched? There was nothing there. I felt that the cause was mine and that I should surely get *all*. 'And you found nothing!' – I let my elation out.

He gave the most mournful, thoughtful little headshake. 'Nothing.'

'Nothing, nothing!' I almost shouted in my joy.

'Nothing, nothing,' he sadly repeated.

I kissed his forehead; it was drenched. 'So what have you done with it?'

'I've burnt it.'

'Burnt it?' It was now or never. 'Is that what you did at school?'

Oh, what this brought up! 'At school?'

'Did you take letters? – or other things?'

'Other things?' He appeared now to be thinking of something far off and that reached him only through the pressure of his anxiety. Yet it did reach him. 'Did I *steal*?'

I felt myself redden to the roots of my hair as well as wonder if it were more strange to put to a gentleman such a question or to see him take it with allowances that gave the very distance of his fall in the world. 'Was it for that you mightn't go back?'

The only thing he felt was rather a dreary little surprise. 'Did you know I mightn't go back?'

'I know everything.'

He gave me at this the longest and strangest look. 'Everything?'

'Everything. Therefore *did* you—?' But I couldn't say it again.

Miles could, very simply. 'No. I didn't steal.'

My face must have shown him I believed him utterly; yet my hands – but it was for pure tenderness – shook him as if to ask him why, if it was all for nothing, he had condemned me to months of torment. 'What then did you do?'

He looked in vague pain all round the top of the room and drew his breath, two or three times over, as if with difficulty. He might have been standing at

the bottom of the sea and raising his eyes to some faint green twilight. 'Well –
I said things.'

'Only that?'

'They thought it was enough!'

'To turn you out for?'

Never, truly, had a person 'turned out' shown so little to explain it as this
little person! He appeared to weigh my question, but in a manner quite
detached and almost helpless. 'Well, I suppose I oughtn't.'

'But to whom did you say them?'

He evidently tried to remember, but it dropped – he had lost it. 'I don't
know!'

He almost smiled at me in the desolation of his surrender, which was
indeed practically, by this time, so complete that I ought to have left it there.
But I was infatuated – I was blind with victory, though even then the very
effect that was to have brought him so much nearer was already that of
added separation. 'Was it to everyone?' I asked.

'No; it was only to—' But he gave a sick little headshake. 'I don't
remember their names.'

'Were they then so many?'

'No – only a few. Those I liked.'

Those he liked? I seemed to float not into clearness, but into a darker
obscure, and within a minute there had come to me out of my very pity the
appalling alarm of his being perhaps innocent. It was for the instant
confounding and bottomless, for if he *were* innocent, what then on earth was
I? Paralysed, while it lasted, by the mere brush of the question, I let him go a
little, so that, with a deep-drawn sigh, he turned away from me again; which,
as he faced towards the clear window, I suffered, feeling that I had nothing
now there to keep him from. 'And did they repeat what you said?' I went on
after a moment.

He was soon at some distance from me, still breathing hard and again with
the air, though now without anger for it, of being confined against his will.
Once more, as he had done before, he looked up at the dim day as if, of what
had hitherto sustained him, nothing was left but an unspeakable anxiety.
'Oh yes,' he nevertheless replied – 'they must have repeated them. To those
they liked,' he added.

There was, somehow, less of it than I had expected; but I turned it over.
'And these things came round—?

'To the masters? Oh yes!' he answered very simply. 'But I didn't know
they'd tell.'

'The masters? They didn't – they've never told. That's why I ask you.'

He turned to me again his little beautiful fevered face. 'Yes, it was too
bad.'

'Too bad?'

'What I suppose I sometimes said. To write home.'

I can't name the exquisite pathos of the contradiction given to such a
speech by such a speaker; I only know that the next instant I heard myself
throw off with homely force: 'Stuff and nonsense!' But the next after that I
must have sounded stern enough. 'What *were* these things?'

My sternness was all for his judge, his executioner; yet it made him avert
himself again, and that movement made *me*, with a single bound and an

irrepressible cry, spring straight upon him. For there again, against the glass, as if to blight his confession and stay his answer, was the hideous author of our woe – the white face of damnation. I felt a sick swim at the drop of my victory and all the return of my battle, so that the wildness of my veritable leap only served as a great betrayal. I saw him, from the midst of my act, meet it with a divination, and on the perception that even now he only guessed, and that the window was still to his own eyes free, I let the impulse flame up to convert the climax of his dismay into the very proof of his liberation. 'No more, no more, no more!' I shrieked, as I tried to press him against me, to my visitant.

'Is she *here*?' Miles panted as he caught with his sealed eyes the direction of my words. Then as his strange 'she' staggered me and, with a gasp, I echoed it, 'Miss Jessel, Miss Jessel!' he with a sudden fury gave me back.

I seized, stupefied, his supposition – some sequel to what we had done to Flora, but this made me only want to show him that it was better still than that. 'It's not Miss Jessel! But it's at the window – straight before us. It's *there* – the coward horror, there for the last time!'

At this, after a second in which his head made the movement of a baffled dog's on a scent and then gave a frantic little shake for air and light, he was at me in a white rage, bewildered, glaring vainly over the place and missing wholly, though it now, to my sense, filled the room like the taste of poison, the wide, overwhelming presence. 'It's *he*?'

I was so determined to have all my proof that I flashed into ice to challenge him. 'Whom do you mean by "he"?'

'Peter Quint – you devil!' His face gave again, round the room, its convulsed supplication. '*Where*?'

They are in my ears still, his supreme surrender of the name and his tribute to my devotion. 'What does he matter now, my own? – what will he *ever* matter? *I* have you,' I launched at the beast, 'but he has lost you for ever!' Then, for the demonstration of my work, 'There, *there*!' I said to Miles.

But he had already jerked straight round, stared, glared again, and seen but the quiet day. With the stroke of the loss I was so proud of he uttered the cry of a creature hurled over an abyss, and the grasp with which I recovered him might have been that of catching him in his fall. I caught him, yes, I held him – it may be imagined with what a passion; but at the end of a minute I began to feel what it truly was that I held. We were alone with the quiet day, and his little heart, dispossessed, had stopped.

The Jolly Corner

1

'EVERY ONE ASKS ME WHAT I "think" of everything,' said Spencer Brydon; 'and I make answers as I can — begging or dodging the question, putting them off with any nonsense. It wouldn't matter to any of them really,' he went on, 'for, even were it possible to meet in that stand-and-deliver way so silly a demand on so big a subject, my "thoughts" would still be almost altogether about something that concerns only myself.' He was talking to Miss Staverton, with whom for a couple of months now he had availed himself of every possible occasion to talk; this disposition and this resource, this comfort and support, as the situation in fact presented itself, having promptly enough taken the first place in the considerable array of rather unattenuated surprises attending his so strangely belated return to America. Everything was somehow a surprise; and that might be natural when one had so long and so consistently neglected everything, taken pains to give surprises so much margin for play. He had given them more than thirty years — thirty-three, to be exact; and they now seemed to him to have organized their performance quite on the scale of that license. He had been twenty-three on leaving New York — he was fifty-six today: unless indeed he were to reckon as he had sometimes, since his repatriation, found himself feeling; in which case he would have lived longer than is often allotted to man. It would have taken a century, he repeatedly said to himself, and said also to Alice Staverton, it would have taken a longer absence and a more averted mind than those even of which he had been guilty, to pile up the differences, the newnesses, the queernesses, above all the bignesses, for the better or the worse, that at present assaulted his vision wherever he looked.

The great fact all the while however had been the incalculability; since he *had* supposed himself, from decade to decade, to be allowing, and in the most liberal and intelligent manner, for brilliancy of change. He actually saw that he had allowed for nothing; he missed what he would have been sure of finding, he found what he would never have imagined. Proportions and values were upside-down; the ugly things he had expected, the ugly things of his far-away youth, when he had too promptly waked up to a sense of the ugly — these uncanny phenomena placed him rather, as it happened, under the charm; whereas the 'swagger' things, the modern, the monstrous, the famous things, those he had more particularly, like thousands of ingenuous enquirers every year, come over to see, were exactly his sources of dismay. They were as so many set traps for displeasure, above all for reaction, of which his restless tread was constantly pressing the spring. It was interesting, doubtless, the whole show, but it would have been too disconcerting hadn't a certain finer truth saved the situation. He had distinctly not, in this steadier light, come over *all* for the monstrosities; he had come, not only in the last analysis but quite on the face of the act, under an impulse with which they had nothing to do. He had come – putting the thing pompously – to look at his 'property,' which he had thus for a third of a century not been within four thousand miles of; or, expressing it less sordidly, he had yielded to the humour of seeing again his house on the jolly corner, as he usually, and quite fondly, described it – the one in which he had first seen the light, in which various members of his family had lived and had died, in which the holidays of his overschooled boyhood had been passed and the few social flowers of his chilled adolescence gathered, and which, alienated then for so long a period, had, through the successive deaths of his two brothers and the termination of old arrangements, come wholly into his hands. He was the owner of another, not quite so 'good' – the jolly corner having been, from far back, superlatively extended and consecrated; and the value of the pair represented his main capital, with an income consisting, in these later years, of their respective rents which (thanks precisely to their original excellent type) had never been depressingly low. He could live in 'Europe,' as he had been in the habit of living, on the product of these flourishing New York leases, and all the better since that of the second structure, the mere number of its long row, having within a twelvemonth fallen in, renovation at a high advance had proved beautifully possible.

These were items of property indeed, but he had found himself since his arrival distinguishing more than ever between them. The house within the street, two bristling blocks westward, was already in course of reconstruction as a tall mass of flats; he had acceded, some time before, to overtures for this conversion – in which, now that it was going forward, it had been not the least of his astonishments to find himself able, on the spot, and though without a previous ounce of such experience, to participate with a certain intelligence, almost with a certain authority. He had lived his life with his back so turned to such concerns and his face addressed to those of so different an order that he scarce knew what to make of this lively stir, in a compartment of his mind never yet penetrated, of a capacity for business and a sense for construction. These virtues, so common all round him now, had been dormant in his own organism – where it might be said of them perhaps that they had slept the sleep of the just. At present, in the splendid autumn weather – the autumn at least was a pure boon in the terrible place – he loafed about his 'work' undeterred, secretly agitated; not in the least 'minding' that the whole proposition, as they said, was vulgar and sordid, and ready to climb ladders, to walk the plank, to handle materials and look wise about them, to ask questions, in fine, and challenge explanations and really 'go into' figures.

It amused, it verily quite charmed him; and, by the same stroke, it amused, and even more, Alice Staverton, though perhaps charming her perceptibly less. She wasn't however going to be better off for it, as *he* was – and so astonishingly much: nothing was now likely, he knew, ever to make her better off than she found herself, in the afternoon of life, as the delicately frugal possessor and tenant of the small house in Irving Place to which she had subtly managed to cling through her almost unbroken New York career. If he knew the way to it now better than to any other address among the dreadful multiplied numberings which seemed to him to reduce the whole place to some vast ledger-page, overgrown, fantastic, of ruled and criss-crossed lines and figures – if he had formed, for his consolation, that habit, it was really not a little because of the charm of his having encountered and recognized, in the vast wilderness of the wholesale, breaking through the mere gross generalization of wealth and force and success, a small still scene where items and shades, all delicate things, kept the sharpness of the notes of a high voice perfectly trained, and where economy hung about like the scent of a garden. His old friend lived with one maid and herself dusted her relics and trimmed her lamps and polished her silver; she stood off, in the awful modern crush, when she could, but she sallied forth and did battle when the challenge was really to 'spirit,' the spirit she after all confessed to, proudly and a little shyly, as to that of the better time, that of *their* common, their quite far-away and antediluvian social period and order. She made use of the street-cars when need be, the terrible things that people scrambled for as the panic-stricken at sea scramble for the boats; she affronted, inscrutably, under stress, all the public concussions and ordeals; and yet, with that slim mystifying grace of her appearance, which defied you to say if she were a fair young woman who looked older through trouble, or a fine smooth older one who looked young through successful indifference; with her precious reference, above all, to memories and histories into which he could enter, she was as exquisite for him as some pale pressed flower (a rarity to begin with), and, failing other sweetnesses, she was a sufficient reward of his effort. They had communities of knowledge, 'their' knowledge (this discriminating possessive was always on her lips) of presences of the other age, presences all overlaid, in his case, by the experience of a man and the freedom of a wanderer, overlaid by pleasure, by infidelity, by passages of life that were strange and dim to her, just by 'Europe' in short, but still unobscured, still exposed and cherished, under that pious visitation of the spirit from which she had never been diverted.

She had come with him one day to see how his 'apartment-house' was rising; he had helped her over gaps and explained to her plans, and while they were there had happened to have, before her, a brief but lively discussion with the man in charge, the representative of the building-firm that had undertaken his work. He had found himself quite 'standing-up' to this personage over a failure on the latter's part to observe some detail of one of their noted conditions, and had so lucidly urged his case that, besides ever so prettily flushing, at the time, for sympathy in his triumph, she had afterwards said to him (though to a slightly greater effect of irony) that he had clearly for too many years neglected a real gift. If he had but stayed at home he would have anticipated the inventor of the sky-scraper. If he had but stayed at home he would have discovered his genius in time really to start some new variety of awful architectural hare and run it till it burrowed in a gold-mine. He was to remember these words, while the weeks elapsed, for the small silver ring they had sounded over the queerest and deepest of his own lately most disguised and most muffled vibrations.

It had begun to be present to him after the first fortnight, it had broken out with the oddest abruptness, this particular wanton wonderment: it met him there – and this was the image under which he himself judged the matter, or at least, not a little, thrilled and flushed with it – very much as he might have been met by some strange figure, some unexpected occupant, at a turn of one of the dim passages of an empty house. The quaint analogy quite hauntingly remained with him, when he didn't indeed rather improve it by a still intenser form: that of his opening a door behind which he would have made sure of finding nothing, a door into a room shuttered and void, and yet so coming, with a great suppressed start, on some quite erect confronting presence, something planted in the middle of the place and facing him through the dusk. After that visit to the house in construction he walked with his companion to see the other and always so much the better one, which in the eastward direction formed one of the corners, the 'jolly' one precisely, of the street now so generally dishonoured and disfigured in its westward reaches, and of the comparatively conservative Avenue. The Avenue still had pretensions, as Miss Staverton said, to decency; the old people had mostly gone, the old names were unknown, and here and there an old association seemed to stray, all vaguely, like some very aged person, out too late, whom you might meet and feel the impulse to watch or follow, in kindness, for safe restoration to shelter.

They went in together, our friends; he admitted himself with his key, as he kept no one there, he explained, preferring, for his reasons, to leave the place empty, under a simple arrangement with a good woman living in the neighbourhood and who came for a daily hour to open windows and dust and sweep. Spencer Brydon had his reasons and was growingly aware of them; they seemed to him better each time he was there, though he didn't name them all to his companion, any more than he told her as yet how often, how quite absurdly often, he himself came. He only let her see for the present, while they walked through the great blank rooms, that absolute vacancy reigned and that, from top to bottom, there was nothing but Mrs Muldoon's broomstick, in a corner, to tempt the burglar. Mrs Muldoon was then on the premises, and she loquaciously attended the visitors, preceding them from room to room and pushing back shutters and throwing up sashes – all to show them, as she remarked, how little there was to see. There was little indeed to see in the great gaunt shell where the main dispositions and the general apportionment of space, the style of an age of ampler allowances, had nevertheless for its master their honest pleading message, affecting him as some good old servant's, some lifelong retainer's appeal for a character, or even for a retiring-pension; yet it was also a remark of Mrs Muldoon's that, glad as she was to oblige him by her noonday round, there was a request she greatly hoped he would never make of her. If he should wish her for any reason to come in after dark she would just tell him, if he 'plased,' that he must ask it of somebody else.

The fact that there was nothing to see didn't militate for the worthy woman against what one *might* see, and she put it frankly to Miss Staverton that no lady could be expected to like, could she? 'craping up to thim top storeys in the ayvil hours.' The gas and the electric light were off the house, and she fairly evoked a gruesome vision of her march through the great grey rooms – so many of them as there were too! – with her glimmering taper. Miss Staverton met her honest glare with a smile and the profession that she herself certainly would recoil from such an adventure. Spencer Brydon meanwhile held his peace – for the moment; the question of the 'evil' hours in his old home had already become too grave for him. He had begun some time since to 'crape,' and he knew just why a packet of candles addressed to that pursuit had been stowed by his own hand, three weeks before, at the back of a drawer of the fine old sideboard that occupied, as a 'fixture,' the deep recess in the dining-room. Just now he laughed at his companions – quickly however changing the subject; for the reason that, in the first place, his laugh struck him even at that moment as starting the odd echo, the conscious human resonance (he scarce knew how to qualify it) that sounds made while he was there alone sent back to his ear or his fancy; and that, in the second, he imagined Alice Staverton for the instant on the point of asking him, with a divination, if he ever so prowled. There were divinations he was unprepared for, and he had at all events averted enquiry by the time Mrs Muldoon had left them, passing on to other parts.

There was happily enough to say, on so consecrated a spot, that could be said freely and fairly; so that a whole train of declarations was precipitated by his friend's having herself broken out, after a yearning look round: 'But I hope you don't mean they want you to pull *this* to pieces!' His answer came, promptly, with his reawakened wrath: it was of course exactly what they wanted, and what they were 'at' him for, daily, with the iteration of people who couldn't for their life understand a man's liability to decent feelings. He had found the place, just as it stood and beyond what he could express, an interest and a joy. There were values other than the beastly rent-values, and in short, in short—! But it was thus Miss Staverton took him up. 'In short you're to make so good a thing of your sky-scraper that, living in luxury on *those* ill-gotten gains, you can afford for a while to be sentimental here!' Her smile had for him, with the words, the particular mild irony with which he found half her talk suffused; an irony without bitterness and that came, exactly, from her having so much imagination – not, like the cheap sarcasms with which one heard most people, about the world of 'society,' bid for the reputation of cleverness, from nobody's really having any. It was agreeable to him at this very moment to be sure that when he had answered, after a brief demur, 'Well yes: so, precisely, you may put it!' her imagination would still do him justice. He explained that even if never a dollar were to come to him from the other house he would nevertheless cherish this one; and he dwelt, further, while they lingered and wandered, on the fact of the stupefaction he was already exciting, the positive mystification he felt himself create.

He spoke of the value of all he read into it, into the mere sight of the walls, mere shapes of the rooms, mere sound of the floors, mere feel, in his hand, of the old silver-plated knobs of the several mahogany doors, which suggested the pressure of the palms of the dead; the seventy years of the past in fine that these things represented, the annals of nearly three generations, counting his grandfather's, the one that had ended there, and the impalpable ashes of his long-extinct youth, afloat in the very air like microscopic motes. She listened to everything; she was a woman who answered intimately but who utterly didn't chatter. She scattered abroad therefore no cloud of words; she could assent, she could agree, above all she could encourage, without doing that. Only at the last she went a little further than he had done himself. 'And then how do you know? You may still, after all, want to live here.' It rather indeed pulled him up, for it wasn't what he had been thinking, at least in her sense of the words. 'You mean I may decide to stay on for the sake of it?'

'Well, *with* such a home—' But, quite beautifully, she had too much tact to dot so monstrous an *i*, and it was precisely an illustration of the way she didn't rattle. How could any one – of any wit – insist on any one else's 'wanting' to live in New York?

'Oh,' he said, 'I *might* have lived here (since I had my opportunity early in life); I might have put in here all these years. Then everything would have been different enough – and, I dare say, "funny" enough. But that's another matter. And then the beauty of it – I mean of my perversity, of my refusal to agree to a "deal" – is just in the total absence of a reason. Don't you see that if I had a reason about the matter at all it would *have* to be the other way, and would then be inevitably a reason of dollars? There are no reasons here *but* of dollars. Let us therefore have none whatever – not the ghost of one.'

They were back in the hall then for departure, but from where they stood the vista was large, through an open door, into the great square main saloon, with its almost antique felicity of brave spaces between windows. Her eyes came back from that reach and met his own a moment. 'Are you very sure the "ghost" of one doesn't, much rather, serve—?'

He had a positive sense of turning pale. But it was as near as they were then to come. For he made answer, he believed, between a glare and a grin: 'Oh ghosts – of course the place must swarm with them! I should be ashamed of it if it didn't. Poor Mrs Muldoon's right, and it's why I haven't asked her to do more than look in.'

Miss Staverton's gaze again lost itself, and things she didn't utter, it was clear, came and went in her mind. She might even for the minute, off there in the fine room, have imagined some element dimly gathering. Simplified like the death-mask of a handsome face, it perhaps produced for her just then an effect akin to the stir of an expression in the 'set' commemorative plaster. Yet whatever her impression may have been she produced instead a vague platitude. 'Well, if it were only furnished and lived in—!'

She appeared to imply that in case of its being still furnished he might have been a little less opposed to the idea of a return. But she passed straight into the vestibule, as if to leave her words behind her, and the next moment he had opened the house-door and was standing with her on the steps. He closed the door and, while he re-pocketed his key, looking up and down, they took in the comparatively harsh actuality of the Avenue, which reminded him of the assault of the outer light of the Desert on the traveller emerging from an Egyptian tomb. But he risked before they stepped into the street his gathered answer to her speech. 'For me it *is* lived in. For me it *is* furnished.' At which it was easy for her to sigh 'Ah yes—!' all vaguely and discreetly; since his parents and his favourite sister, to say nothing of other kin, in numbers, had run their course and met their end there. That represented, within the walls, ineffaceable life.

It was a few days after this that, during an hour passed with her again, he had expressed his impatience of the too flattering curiosity – among the people he met – about his appreciation of New York. He had arrived at none at all that was socially producible, and as for that matter of his 'thinking' (thinking the better or the worse of anything there) he was wholly taken up with one subject of thought. It was mere vain egoism, and it was moreover, if she liked, a morbid obsession. He found all things come back to the question of what he personally might have been, how he might have led his life and 'turned out,' if he had not so, at the outset, given it up. And confessing for the first time to the intensity within him of this absurd speculation – which but proved also, no doubt, the habit of too selfishly thinking – he affirmed the impotence there of any other source of interest, any other native appeal. 'What would it have made of me, what would it have made of me? I keep for ever wondering, all idiotically; as if I could possibly know! I see what it has made of dozens of others, those I meet, and it positively aches within me, to the point of exasperation, that it would have made something of me as well. Only I can't make out *what*, and the worry of it, the small rage of curiosity never to be satisfied, brings back what I remember to have felt, once or twice, after judging best, for reasons, to burn some important letter unopened. I've been sorry, I've hated it – I've never known what was in the letter. You may of course say it's a trifle—!'

'I don't say it's a trifle,' Miss Staverton gravely interrupted.

She was seated by her fire, and before her, on his feet and restless, he turned to and fro between this intensity of his idea and a fitful and unseeing inspection, through his single eye-glass, of the dear little old objects on her chimney-piece. Her interruption made him for an instant look at her harder. 'I shouldn't care if you did!' he laughed, however; 'and it's only a figure, at any rate, for the way I now feel. *Not* to have followed my perverse young course – and almost in the teeth of my father's curse, as I may say; not to have kept it up, so, "over there," from that day to this, without a doubt or a pang; not, above all, to have liked it, to have loved it, so much, loved it, no doubt, with such an abysmal conceit of my own preference: some variation from *that*, I say, must have produced some different effect for my life and for my "form." I should have stuck here – if it had been possible; and I was too young, at twenty-three, to judge, *pour deux sous*, whether it *were* possible. If I had waited I might have seen it was, and then I might have been, by staying here, something nearer to one of these types who have been hammered so hard and made so keen by their conditions. It isn't that I admire them so much – the question of any charm in them, or of any charm, beyond that of the rank money-passion, exerted by their conditions *for* them, has nothing to do with the matter: it's only a question of what fantastic, yet perfectly possible, development of my own nature I mayn't have missed. It comes over me that I had then a strange *alter ego* deep down somewhere within me, as the full-blown flower is in the small tight bud, and that I just took the course, I just transferred him to the climate, that blighted him for once and for ever.'

'And you wonder about the flower,' Miss Staverton said. 'So do I, if you want to know; and so I've been wondering these several weeks. I believe in the flower,' she continued, 'I feel it would have been quite splendid, quite huge and monstrous.'

'Monstrous above all!' her visitor echoed; 'and I imagine, by the same stroke, quite hideous and offensive.'

'You don't believe that,' she returned; 'if you did you wouldn't wonder. You'd know, and that would be enough for you. What you feel – and what I feel *for* you – is that you'd have had power.'

'You'd have liked me that way?' he asked.

She barely hung fire. 'How should I not have liked you?'

'I see. You'd have liked me, have preferred me, a billionaire!'

'How should I not have liked you?' she simply again asked.

He stood before her still – her question kept him motionless. He took it in, so much there was of it; and indeed his not otherwise meeting it testified to that. 'I know at least what I am,' he simply went on; 'the other side of the medal's clear enough. I've not been edifying – I believe I'm thought in a hundred quarters to have been barely decent. I've followed strange paths and worshipped strange gods; it must have come to you again and again – in fact you've admitted to me as much – that I was leading, at any time these thirty years, a selfish frivolous scandalous life. And you see what it has made of me.'

She just waited, smiling at him. 'You see what it has made of *me*.'

'Oh you're a person whom nothing can have altered. You were born to be what you are, anywhere, anyway: you've the perfection nothing else could have blighted. And don't you see how, without my exile, I shouldn't have been waiting till now—?' But he pulled up for the strange pang.

'The great thing to see,' she presently said, 'seems to me to be that it has spoiled nothing. It hasn't spoiled your being here at last. It hasn't spoiled this. It hasn't spoiled your speaking—' She also however faltered.

He wondered at everything her controlled emotion might mean. 'Do you believe then – too dreadfully! that I *am* as good as I might ever have been?'

'Oh no! Far from it!' With which she got up from her chair and was nearer to him. 'But I don't care,' she smiled.

'You mean I'm good enough?'

She considered a little. 'Will you believe it if I say so? I mean will you let that settle your question for you?' And then as if making out in his face that he drew back from this, that he had some idea which, however absurd, he couldn't yet bargain away: 'Oh you don't care either – but very differently: you don't care for anything but yourself.'

Spencer Brydon recognized it – it was in fact what he had absolutely professed. Yet he importantly qualified. '*He* isn't myself. He's the just so totally other person. But I do want to see him,' he added. 'And I can. And I shall.'

Their eyes met for a minute while he guessed from something in hers that she divined his strange sense. But neither of them otherwise expressed it, and her apparent understanding, with no protesting shock, no easy derision, touched him more deeply than anything yet, constituting for his stifled perversity, on the spot, an element that was like breatheable air. What she said however was unexpected. 'Well, *I've* seen him.'

'You—?'

'I've seen him in a dream.'

'Oh a "dream"—!' It let him down.

'But twice over,' she continued. 'I saw him as I see you now.'

'You've dreamed the same dream—'

'Twice over,' she repeated. 'The very same.'

This did somehow a little speak to him, as it also gratified him. 'You dream about me at that rate?'

'Ah about *him*!' she smiled.

His eyes again sounded her. 'Then you know all about him.' And as she said nothing more: 'What's the wretch like?'

She hesitated, and it was as if he were pressing her so hard that, resisting for reasons of her own, she had to turn away. 'I'll tell you some other time!'

2

It was after this that there was most of a virtue for him, most of a cultivated charm, most of a preposterous secret thrill, in the particular form of surrender to his obsession and of address to what he more and more believed to be his privilege. It was what in these weeks he was living for – since he really felt life to begin but after Mrs Muldoon had retired from the scene and, visiting the ample house from attic to cellar, making sure he was alone, he knew himself in safe possession and, as he tacitly expressed it, let himself go. He sometimes came twice in the twenty-four hours; the moments he liked best were those of gathering dusk, of the short autumn twilight; this was the time of which, again and again, he found himself hoping most. Then he could, as seemed to him, most intimately wander and wait, linger and listen, feel his fine attention, never in his life before so fine, on the pulse of the great vague place: he preferred the lampless hour and only wished he might have prolonged each day the deep crepuscular spell. Later – rarely much before midnight, but then for a considerable vigil – he watched with his glimmering light; moving slowly, holding it high, playing it far, rejoicing above all, as much as he might, in open vistas, reaches of communication between rooms and by passages; the long straight chance or show, as he would have called it, for the revelation he pretended to invite. It was practice he found he could perfectly 'work' without exciting remark; no one was in the least the wiser for it; even Alice Staverton, who was moreover a well of discretion, didn't quite fully imagine.

He let himself in and let himself out with the assurance of calm proprietorship; and accident so far favoured him that, if a fat Avenue 'officer' had happened on occasion to see him entering at eleven-thirty, he had never yet, to the best of his belief, been noticed as emerging at two. He walked there on the crisp November night, arrived regularly at the evening's end; it was as easy to do this after dining out as to take his way to a club or to his hotel. When he left his club, if he hadn't been dining out, it was ostensibly to go to his hotel; and when he left his hotel, if he had spent a part of the evening there, it was ostensibly to go to his club. Everything was easy in fine; everything conspired and promoted: there was truly even in the strain of his experience something that glossed over, something that salved and simplified, all the rest of consciousness. He circulated, talked, renewed, loosely and pleasantly, old relations – met indeed, so far as he could, new expectations and seemed to make out on the whole that in spite of the career, of such different contacts, which he had spoken of to Miss Staverton as ministering so little, for those who might have watched it, to edification, he was positively rather liked than not. He was a dim secondary social success – and all with people who had truly not an idea of him. It was all mere surface sound, this murmur of their welcome, this popping of their corks – just as his gestures of response were the extravagant shadows, emphatic in proportion as they meant little, of some game of *ombres chinoises*. He projected himself all day, in thought, straight over the bristling line of hard unconscious heads and into the other, the real, the waiting life; the life that, as soon as he had heard behind him the click of his great house-door, began for him, on the jolly corner, as beguilingly as the slow opening bars of some rich music follows the tap of the conductor's wand.

He always caught the first effect of the steel point of his stick on the old marble of the hall pavement, large black-and-white squares that he remembered as the admiration of his childhood and that had then made in him, as he now saw, for the growth of an early conception of style. This effect was the dim reverberating tinkle as of some far-off bell hung who should say where? – in the depths of the house, of the past, of that mystical other world that might have flourished for him had he not, for weal or woe, abandoned it. On this impression he did ever the same thing; he put his stick noiselessly away in a corner – feeling the place once more in the likeness of some great glass bowl, all precious concave crystal, set delicately humming by the play of a moist finger round its edge. The concave crystal held, as it were, this mystical other world, and the indescribably fine murmur of its rim was the sigh there, the scarce audible pathetic wail to his strained ear, of all the old baffled forsworn possibilities. What he did therefore by this appeal of his hushed presence was to wake them into such measure of ghostly life as they might still enjoy. They were shy, all but unappeasably shy, but they weren't really sinister; at least they weren't as he had hitherto felt them – before they had taken the Form he so yearned to make them take, the Form he at moments saw himself in the light of fairly hunting on tiptoe, the points of his evening-shoes, from room to room and from storey to storey.

That was the essence of his vision – which was all rank folly, if one would, while he was out of the house and otherwise occupied, but which took on the last verisimilitude as soon as he was placed and posted. He knew what he meant and what he wanted; it was as clear as the figure on a cheque presented in demand for cash. His *alter ego* 'walked' – that was the note of his image of him, while his image of his motive for his own odd pastime was the desire to waylay him and meet him. He roamed, slowly, warily, but all restlessly, he himself did – Mrs Muldoon had been right, absolutely, with her figure of their 'craping'; and the presence he watched for would roam restlessly too. But it would be as cautious and as shifty; the conviction of its probable, in fact its already quite sensible, quite audible evasion of pursuit grew for him from night to night, laying on him finally a rigour to which nothing in his life had been comparable. It had been the theory of many superficially-judging persons, he knew, that he was wasting that life in a surrender to sensations, but he had tasted of no pleasure so fine as his actual tension, had been introduced to no sport that demanded at once the patience and the nerve of this stalking of a creature more subtle, yet at bay perhaps more formidable, than any beast of the forest. The terms, the comparisons, the very practices of the chase positively came again into play; there were even moments when passages of his occasional experience as a sportsman, stirred memories, from his younger time, of moor and mountain and desert, revived for him – and to the increase of his keenness – by the tremendous force of analogy. He found himself at moments – once he had placed his single light on some mantel-shelf or in some recess – stepping back into shelter or shade, effacing himself behind a door or in an embrasure, as he had sought of old the vantage of rock and tree; he found himself holding his breath and living in the joy of the instant, the supreme suspense created by big game alone.

He wasn't afraid (though putting himself the question as he believed gentlemen on Bengal tiger-shoots or in close quarters with the great bear of

the Rockies had been known to confess to having put it); and this indeed –
since here at least he might be frank! – because of the impression, so intimate
and so strange, that he himself produced as yet a dread, produced certainly a
strain, beyond the liveliest he was likely to feel. They fell for him into
categories, they fairly became familiar, the signs, for his own perception, of
the alarm his presence and his vigilance created; though leaving him always
to remark, portentously, on his probably having formed a relation, his
probably enjoying a consciousness, unique in the experience of man. People
enough, first and last, had been in terror of apparitions, but who had ever
before so turned the tables and become himself, in the apparitional world, an
incalculable terror? He might have found this sublime had he quite dared to
think of it; but he didn't too much insist, truly, on that side of his privilege.
With habit and repetition he gained to an extraordinary degree the power to
penetrate the dusk of distances and the darkness of corners, to resolve back
into their innocence the treacheries of uncertain light, the evil-looking forms
taken in the gloom by mere shadows, by accidents of the air, by shifting
effects of perspective; putting down his dim luminary he could still wander
on without it, pass into other rooms and, only knowing it was there behind
him in case of need, see his way about, visually project for his purpose a
comparative clearness. It made him feel, this acquired faculty, like some
monstrous stealthy cat; he wondered if he would have glared at these
moments with large shining yellow eyes, and what it mightn't verily be, for
the poor hard-pressed *alter ego*, to be confronted with such a type.

He liked however the open shutters; he opened everywhere those Mrs
Muldoon had closed, closing them as carefully afterwards, so that she
shouldn't notice: he liked – oh this he did like, and above all in the upper
rooms! – the sense of the hard silver of the autumn stars through the window-
panes, and scarcely less the flare of the street-lamps below, the white electric
lustre which it would have taken curtains to keep out. This was human
actual social; this was of the world he had lived in, and he was more at his
ease certainly for the countenance, coldly general and impersonal, that all
the while and in spite of his detachment it seemed to give him. He had
support of course mostly in the rooms at the wide front and the prolonged
side; it failed him considerably in the central shades and the parts at the
back. But if he sometimes, on his rounds, was glad of his optical reach, so
none the less often the rear of the house affected him as the very jungle of his
prey. The place was there more subdivided; a large 'extension' in particular,
where small rooms for servants had been multiplied, abounded in nooks and
corners, in closets and passages, in the ramifications especially of an ample
back staircase over which he leaned, many a time, to look far down – not
deterred from his gravity even while aware that he might, for a spectator,
have figured some solemn simpleton playing at hide-and-seek. Outside in
fact he might himself make that ironic *rapprochement*; but within the walls, and
in spite of the clear windows, his consistency was proof against the cynical
light of New York.

It had belonged to that idea of the exasperated consciousness of his victim
to become a real test for him; since he had quite put it to himself from the first
that, oh distinctly! he could 'cultivate' his whole perception. He had felt it as
above all open to cultivation – which indeed was but another name for his
manner of spending his time. He was bringing it on, bringing it to perfection,

by practice; in consequence of which it had grown so fine that he was now aware of impressions, attestations of his general postulate, that couldn't have broken upon him at once. This was the case more specifically with a phenomenon at last quite frequent for him in the upper rooms, the recognition – absolutely unmistakable, and by a turn dating from a particular hour, his resumption of his campaign after a diplomatic drop, a calculated absence of three nights – of his being definitely followed, tracked at a distance carefully taken and to the express end that he should the less confidently, less arrogantly, appear to himself merely to pursue. It worried, it finally quite broke him up, for it proved, of all the conceivable impressions, the one least suited to his book. He was kept in sight while remaining himself – as regards the essence of his position – sightless, and his only recourse then was in abrupt turns, rapid recoveries of ground. He wheeled about, retracing his steps, as if he might so catch in his face at least the stirred air of some other quick revolution. It was indeed true that his fully dislocalized thought of these manœuvres recalled to him Pantaloon, at the Christmas farce, buffeted and tricked from behind by ubiquitous Harlequin; but it left intact the influence of the conditions themselves each time he was re-exposed to them, so that in fact this association, had he suffered it to become constant, would on a certain side have but ministered to his intenser gravity. He had made, as I have said, to create on the premises the baseless sense of a reprieve, his three absences; and the result of the third was to confirm the after-effect of the second.

On his return, that night – the night succeeding his last intermission – he stood in the hall and looked up the staircase with a certainty more intimate than any he had yet known. 'He's *there*, at the top, and waiting – not, as in general, falling back for disappearance. He's holding his ground, and it's the first time – which is a proof, isn't it? that something has happened for him.' So Brydon argued with his hand on the banister and his foot on the lowest stair; in which position he felt as never before the air chilled by his logic. He himself turned cold in it, for he seemed of a sudden to know what now was involved. 'Harder pressed? – yes, he takes it in, with its thus making clear to him that I've come, as they say, "to stay." He finally doesn't like and can't bear it, in the sense, I mean, that his wrath, his menaced interest, now balances with his dread. I've hunted him till he has "turned": that, up there, is what has happened – he's the fanged or the antlered animal brought at last to bay.' There came to him, as I say – but determined by an influence beyond my notation! – the acuteness of this certainty; under which however the next moment he had broken into a sweat that he would as little have consented to attribute to fear as he would have dared immediately to act upon it for enterprise. It marked none the less a prodigious thrill, a thrill that represented sudden dismay, no doubt, but also represented, and with the selfsame throb, the strangest, the most joyous, possibly the next minute almost the proudest, duplication of consciousness.

'He has been dodging, retreating, hiding, but now, worked up to anger, he'll fight!' – this intense impression made a single mouthful, as it were, of terror and applause. But what was wondrous was that the applause, for the felt fact, was so eager, since, if it was his other self he was running to earth, this ineffable identity was thus in the last resort not unworthy of him. It bristled there – somewhere near at hand, however unseen still – as the

hunted thing, even as the trodden worm of the adage *must* at last bristle; and
Brydon at this instant tasted probably of a sensation more complex than had
ever before found itself consistent with sanity. It was as if it would have
shamed him that a character so associated with his own should triumphantly
succeed in just skulking, should to the end not risk the open, so that the drop
of this danger was, on the spot, a great lift of the whole situation. Yet with
another rare shift of the same subtlety he was already trying to measure by
how much more he himself might now be in peril of fear; so rejoicing that he
could, in another form, actively inspire that fear, and simultaneously
quaking for the form in which he might passively know it.

The apprehension of knowing it must after a little have grown in him, and
the strangest moment of his adventure perhaps, the most memorable or
really most interesting, afterwards, of his crisis, was the lapse of certain
instants of concentrated conscious *combat*, the sense of a need to hold on to
something, even after the manner of a man slipping and slipping on some
awful incline; the vivid impulse, above all, to move, to act, to charge,
somehow and upon something – to show himself, in a word, that he wasn't
afraid. The state of 'holding-on' was thus the state to which he was
momentarily reduced; if there had been anything, in the great vacancy, to
seize, he would presently have been aware of having clutched it as he might
under a shock at home have clutched the nearest chairback. He had been
surprised at any rate – of this he *was* aware – into something unprecedented
since his original appropriation of the place; he had closed his eyes, held
them tight, for a long minute, as with that instinct of dismay and that terror
of vision. When he opened them the room, the other contiguous rooms,
extraordinarily, seemed lighter – so light, almost, that at first he took the
change for day. He stood firm, however that might be, just where he had
paused; his resistance had helped him – it was as if there were something he
had tided over. He knew after a little what this was – it had been in the
imminent danger of flight. He had stiffened his will against going; without
this he would have made for the stairs, and it seemed to him that, still with
his eyes closed, he would have descended them, would have known how,
straight and swiftly, to the bottom.

Well, as he had held out, here he was – still at the top, among the more
intricate upper rooms and with the gauntlet of the others, of all the rest of the
house, still to run when it should be his time to go. He would go at his time –
only at his time: didn't he go every night very much at the same hour? He
took out his watch – there was light for that: it was scarcely a quarter past
one, and he had never withdrawn so soon. He reached his lodgings for the
most part at two – with his walk of a quarter of an hour. He would wait for
the last quarter – he wouldn't stir till then; and he kept his watch there with
his eyes on it, reflecting while he held it that this deliberate wait, a wait with
an effort, which he recognized, would serve perfectly for the attestation he
desired to make. It would prove his courage – unless indeed the latter might
most be proved by his budging at last from his place. What he mainly felt
now was that, since he hadn't originally scuttled, he had his dignities – which
had never in his life seemed so many – all to preserve and to carry aloft. This
was before him in truth as a physical image, an image almost worthy of an
age of greater romance. That remark indeed glimmered for him only to glow
the next instant with a finer light; since what age of romance, after all, could

have matched either the state of his mind or, 'objectively,' as they said, the wonder of his situation? The only difference would have been that, brandishing his dignities over his head as in a parchment scroll, he might then – that is in the heroic time – have proceeded downstairs with a drawn sword in his other grasp.

At present, really, the light he had set down on the mantel of the next room would have to figure his sword; which utensil, in the course of a minute, he had taken the requisite number of steps to possess himself of. The door between the rooms was open, and from the second another door opened to a third. These rooms, as he remembered, gave all three upon a common corridor as well, but there was a fourth, beyond them, without issue save through the preceding. To have moved, to have heard his step again, was appreciably a help; though even in recognizing this he lingered once more a little by the chimney-piece on which his light had rested. When he next moved, just hesitating where to turn, he found himself considering a circumstance that, after his first and comparatively vague apprehension of it, produced in him the start that often attends some pang of recollection, the violent shock of having ceased happily to forget. He had come into sight of the door in which the brief chain of communication ended and which he now surveyed from the nearer threshold, the one not directly facing it. Placed at some distance to the left of this point, it would have admitted him to the last room of the four, the room without other approach or egress, had it not, to his intimate conviction, been closed *since* his former visitation, the matter probably of a quarter of an hour before. He stared with all his eyes at the wonder of the fact, arrested again where he stood and again holding his breath while he sounded its sense. Surely it had been *subsequently* closed – that is it had been on his previous passage indubitably open!

He took it full in the face that something had happened between – that he couldn't not have noticed before (by which he meant on his original tour of all the rooms that evening) that such a barrier had exceptionally presented itself. He had indeed since that moment undergone an agitation so extraordinary that it might have muddled for him any earlier view; and he tried to convince himself that he might perhaps then have gone into the room and, inadvertently, automatically, on coming out, have drawn the door after him. The difficulty was that this exactly was what he never did; it was against his whole policy, as he might have said, the essence of which was to keep vistas clear. He had them from the first, as he was well aware, quite on the brain: the strange apparition, at the far end of one of them, of his baffled 'prey' (which had become by so sharp an irony so little the term now to apply!) was the form of success his imagination had most cherished, projecting into it always a refinement of beauty. He had known fifty times the start of perception that had afterwards dropped; had fifty times gasped to himself 'There!' under some fond brief hallucination. The house, as the case stood, admirably lent itself; he might wonder at the taste, the native architecture of the particular time, which could rejoice so in the multiplication of doors – the opposite extreme to the modern, the actual almost complete proscription of them; but it had fairly contributed to provoke this obsession of the presence encountered telescopically, as he might say, focused and studied in diminishing perspective and as by a rest for the elbow.

It was with these considerations that his present attention was charged – they perfectly availed to make what he saw portentous. He *couldn't*, by any lapse, have blocked that aperture; and if he hadn't, if it was unthinkable, why what else was clear but that there had been another agent? Another agent? – he had been catching, as he felt, a moment back, the very breath of him; but when had he been so close as in this simple, this logical, this completely personal act? It was so logical, that is, that one might have *taken* it for personal; yet for what did Brydon take it, he asked himself, while softly panting, he felt his eyes almost leave their socket. Ah this time at last they *were*, the two, the opposed projections of him, in presence; and this time, as much as one would, the question of danger loomed. With it rose, as not before, the question of courage – for what he knew the blank face of the door to say to him was 'Show us how much you have!' It stared, it glared back at him with that challenge; it put to him the two alternatives: should he just push it open or not? Oh to have this consciousness was to *think* – and to think, Brydon knew, as he stood there, was, with the lapsing moments, not to have acted! Not to have acted – that was the misery and the pang – was even still not to act; was in fact *all* to feel the thing in another, in a new and terrible way. How long did he pause and how long did he debate? There was presently nothing to measure it; for his vibration had already changed – as just by the effect of its intensity. Shut up there, at bay, defiant, and with the prodigy of the thing palpably provably *done*, thus giving notice like some stark signboard – under that accession of accent the situation itself had turned; and Brydon at last remarkably made up his mind on what it had turned to.

It had turned altogether to a different admonition; to a supreme hint, for him, of the value of Discretion! This slowly dawned, no doubt – for it could take its time; so perfectly, on his threshold, had he been stayed, so little as yet had he either advanced or retreated. It was the strangest of all things that now when, by his taking ten steps and applying his hand to a latch, or even his shoulder and his knee, if necessary, to a panel, all the hunger of his prime need might have been met, his high curiosity crowned, his unrest assuaged – it was amazing, but it was also exquisite and rare, that insistence should have, at a touch, quite dropped from him. Discretion – he jumped at that; and yet not, verily, at such a pitch, because it saved his nerves or his skin, but because, much more valuably, it saved the situation. When I say he 'jumped' at it I feel the consonance of this term with the fact that – at the end indeed of I know not how long – he did move again, he crossed straight to the door. He wouldn't touch it – it seemed now that he might *if* he would: he would only just wait there a little, to show, to prove, that he wouldn't. He had thus another station, close to the thin partition by which revelation was denied him; but with his eyes bent and his hands held off in a mere intensity of stillness. He listened as if there had been something to hear, but this attitude, while it lasted, was his own communication. 'If you won't then – good: I spare you and I give up. You affect me as by the appeal positively for pity: you convince me that for reasons rigid and sublime – what do I know? – we both of us should have suffered. I respect them then, and, though moved and privileged as, I believe, it has never been given to man, I retire, I renounce – never, on my honour, to try again. So rest for ever – and let *me*!'

That, for Brydon, was the deep sense of this last demonstration – solemn, measured, directed, as he felt it to be. He brought it to a close, he turned away; and now verily he knew how deeply he had been stirred. He retraced his steps, taking up his candle, burnt, he observed, well-nigh to the socket, and marking again, lighten it as he would, the distinctness of his footfall; after which, in a moment, he knew himself at the other side of the house. He did here what he had not yet done at these hours – he opened half a casement, one of those in the front, and let in the air of the night; a thing he would have taken at any time previous for a sharp rupture of his spell. His spell was broken now, and it didn't matter – broken by his concession and his surrender, which made it idle henceforth that he should ever come back. The empty street – its other life so marked even by the great lamplit vacancy – was within call, within touch; he stayed there as to be in it again, high above it though he was still perched; he watched as for some comforting common fact, some vulgar human note, the passage of a scavenger or a thief, some night-bird however base. He would have blessed that sign of life; he would have welcomed positively the slow approach of his friend the policeman, whom he had hitherto only sought to avoid, and was not sure that if the patrol had come into sight he mightn't have felt the impulse to get into relation with it, to hail it, on some pretext, from his fourth floor.

The pretext that wouldn't have been too silly or too compromising, the explanation that would have saved his dignity and kept his name, in such a case, out of the papers, was not definite to him: he was so occupied with the thought of recording his Discretion – as an effect of the vow he had just uttered to his intimate adversary – that the importance of this loomed large and something had overtaken all ironically his sense of proportion. If there had been a ladder applied to the front of the house, even one of the vertiginous perpendiculars employed by painters and roofers and sometimes left standing overnight, he would have managed somehow, astride of the window-sill, to compass by outstretched leg and arm that mode of descent. If there had been some such uncanny thing as he had found in his room at hotels, a workable fire-escape in the form of notched cable or a canvas shoot, he would have availed himself of it as a proof – well, of his present delicacy. He nursed that sentiment, as the question stood, a little in vain, and even – at the end of he scarce knew, once more, how long – found it, as by the action on his mind of the failure of response of the outer world, sinking back to vague anguish. It seemed to him he had waited an age for some stir of the great grim hush; the life of the town was itself under a spell – so unnaturally, up and down the whole prospect of known and rather ugly objects, the blankness and the silence lasted. Had they ever, he asked himself, the hard-faced houses, which had begun to look livid in the dim dawn, had they ever spoken so little to any need of his spirit? Great builded voids, great crowded stillnesses put on, often, in the heart of cities, for the small hours, a sort of sinister mask, and it was of this large collective negation that Brydon presently became conscious – all the more that the break of day was, almost incredibly, now at hand, proving to him what a night he had made of it.

He looked again at his watch, saw what had become of his time-values (he had taken hours for minutes – not, as in other tense situations, minutes for hours) and the strange air of the streets was but the weak, the sullen flush of a dawn in which everything was still locked up. His choked appeal from his own open window had been the sole note of life, and he could but break off at last as for a worse despair. Yet while so deeply demoralized he was capable again of an impulse denoting – at least by his present measure – extraordinary resolution; of retracing his steps to the spot where he had turned cold with the extinction of his last pulse of doubt as to there being in the place another presence than his own. This required an effort strong enough to sicken him; but he had his reason, which overmastered for the moment everything else. There was the whole of the rest of the house to traverse, and how should he screw himself to that if the door he had seen closed were at present open? He could hold to the idea that the closing had practically been for him an act of mercy, a chance offered him to descend, depart, get off the ground and never again profane it. This conception held together, it worked; but what it meant for him depended now clearly on the amount of forbearance his recent action, or rather his recent inaction, had engendered. The image of the 'presence,' whatever it was, waiting there for him to go – this image had not yet been so concrete for his nerves as when he stopped short of the point at which certainty would have come to him. For, with all his resolution, or more exactly with all his dread, he did stop short – he hung back from really seeing. The risk was too great and his fear too definite: it took at this moment an awful specific form.

He knew – yes, as he had never known anything – that, *should* he see the door open, it would all too abjectly be the end of him. It would mean that the agent of his shame – for his shame was the deep abjection – was once more at large and in general possession; and what glared him thus in the face was the act that this would determine for him. It would send him straight about to the window he had left open, and by that window, be long ladder and dangling rope as absent as they would, he saw himself uncontrollably insanely fatally take his way to the street. The hideous chance of this he at least could avert; but he could only avert it by recoiling in time from assurance. He had the whole house to deal with, this fact was still there; only he now knew that uncertainty alone could start him. He stole back from where he had checked himself – merely to do so was suddenly like safety – and, making blindly for the greater staircase, left gaping rooms and sounding passages behind. Here was the top of the stairs, with a fine large dim descent and three spacious landings to mark off. His instinct was all for mildness, but his feet were harsh on the floors, and, strangely, when he had in a couple of minutes become aware of this, it counted somehow for help. He couldn't have spoken, the tone of his voice would have scared him, and the common conceit or resource of 'whistling in the dark' (whether literally or figuratively) have appeared basely vulgar; yet he liked none the less to hear himself go, and when he had reached his first landing – taking it all with no rush, but quite steadily – that stage of success drew from him a gasp of relief.

The house, withal, seemed immense, the scale of space again inordinate; the open rooms to no one of which his eyes deflected, gloomed in their shuttered state like mouths of caverns; only the high skylight that formed the crown of the deep well created for him a medium in which he could advance, but which might have been, for queerness of colour, some watery under-world. He tried to think of something noble, as that his property was really grand, a splendid possession; but this nobleness took the form too of the clear delight with which he was finally to sacrifice it. They might come in now, the builders, the destroyers – they might come as soon as they would. At the end of two flights he had dropped to another zone, and from the middle of the third, with only one more left, he recognized the influence of the lower windows, of half-drawn blinds, of the occasional gleam of street-lamps, of the glazed spaces of the vestibule. This was the bottom of the sea, which showed an illumination of its own and which he even saw paved – when at the last moment he drew up to sink a long look over the banisters – with the marble squares of his childhood. By that time indubitably he felt, as he might have said in a commoner cause, better; it had allowed him to stop and draw breath, and the ease increased with the sight of the old black-and-white slabs. But what he most felt was that now surely, with the element of impunity pulling him as by hard firm hands, the case was settled for what he might have seen above had he dared that last look. The closed door, blessedly remote now, was still closed – and he had only in short to reach that of the house.

He came down further, he crossed the passage forming the access to the last flight; and if here again he stopped an instant it was almost for the sharpness of the thrill of assured escape. It made him shut his eyes – which opened again to the straight slope of the remainder of the stairs. Here was impunity still, but impunity almost excessive; inasmuch as the side-lights and the high fan-tracery of the entrance were glimmering straight into the hall; an appearance produced, he the next instant saw, by the fact that the vestibule gaped wide, that the hinged halves of the inner door had been thrown far back. Out of that again the *question* sprang at him, making his eyes, as he felt, half-start from his head, as they had done, at the top of the house, before the sign of the other door. If he had left that one open, hadn't he left this one closed, and wasn't he now in *most* immediate presence of some inconceivable occult activity? It was as sharp, the question, as a knife in his side, but the answer hung fire still and seemed to lose itself in the vague darkness to which the thin admitted dawn, glimmering archwise over the whole outer door, made a semi-circular margin, a cold silvery nimbus that seemed to play a little as he looked – to shift and expand and contract.

It was as if there had been something within it, protected by indistinctness and corresponding in extent with the opaque surface behind, the painted panels of the last barrier to his escape, of which the key was in his pocket. The indistinctness mocked him even while he stared, affected him as somehow shrouding or challenging certitude, so that after faltering an instant on his step he let himself go with the sense that here *was* at last something to meet, to touch, to take, to know – something all unnatural and dreadful, but to advance upon which was the condition for him either of liberation or of supreme defeat. The penumbra, dense and dark, was the virtual screen of a figure which stood in it as still as some image erect in a niche or as some black-vizored sentinel guarding a treasure. Brydon was to know afterwards, was to recall and make out, the particular thing he had believed during the rest of his descent. He saw, in its great grey glimmering margin, the central vagueness diminish, and he felt it to be taking the very form toward which, for so many days, the passion of his curiosity had yearned. It gloomed, it loomed, it was something, it was somebody, the prodigy of a personal presence.

Rigid and conscious, spectral yet human, a man of his own substance and stature waited there to measure himself with his power to dismay. This only could it be – this only till he recognized, with his advance, that what made the face dim was the pair of raised hands that covered it and in which, so far from being offered in defiance, it was buried as for dark deprecation. So Brydon, before him, took him in; with every fact of him now, in the higher light, hard and acute – his planted stillness, his vivid truth, his grizzled bent head and white masking hands, his queer actuality of evening-dress, of dangling double eye-glass, of gleaming silk lappet and white linen, of pearl button and gold watch-guard and polished shoe. No portrait by a great modern master could have presented him with more intensity, thrust him out of his frame with more art, as if there had been 'treatment,' of the consummate sort, in his every shade and salience. The revulsion, for our friend, had become, before he knew it, immense – this drop, in the act of apprehension, to the sense of his adversary's inscrutable manœuvre. That meaning at least, while he gaped, it offered him; for he could but gape at his other self in this other anguish, gape as a proof that *he*, standing there for the achieved, the enjoyed, the triumphant life, couldn't be faced in his triumph. Wasn't the proof in the splendid covering hands, strong and completely spread? – so spread and so intentional that, in spite of a special verity that surpassed every other, the fact that one of these hands had lost two fingers, which were reduced to stumps, as if accidentally shot away, the face was effectually guarded and saved.

'Saved,' though, *would* it be? – Brydon breathed his wonder till the very impunity of his attitude and the very insistence of his eyes produced, as he felt, a sudden stir which showed the next instant as a deeper portent, while the head raised itself, the betrayal of a braver purpose. The hands, as he looked, began to move, to open; then, as if deciding in a flash, dropped from the face and left it uncovered and presented. Horror, with the sight, had leaped into Brydon's throat, gasping there in a sound he couldn't utter; for the bared identity was too hideous as *his*, and his glare was the passion of his protest. The face, *that* face, Spencer Brydon's? – he searched it still, but looking away from it in dismay and denial, falling straight from his height of sublimity. It was unknown, inconceivable, awful, disconnected from any possibility—! He had been 'sold,' he inwardly moaned, stalking such game as this: the presence before him was a presence, the horror within him a horror, but the waste of his nights had been only grotesque and the success of his adventure an irony. Such an identity fitted his at *no* point, made its alternative monstrous. A thousand times yes, as it came upon him nearer now – the face was the face of a stranger. It came upon him nearer now, quite as one of those expanding fantastic images projected by the magic lantern of childhood; for the stranger, whoever he might be, evil, odious, blatant, vulgar, had advanced as for aggression, and he knew himself give ground. Then harder pressed still, sick with the force of his shock, and falling back as under the hot breath and the roused passion of a life larger than his own, a rage of personality before which his own collapsed, he felt the whole vision turn to darkness and his very feet give way. His head went round; he was going; he had gone.

3

What had next brought him back, clearly – though after how long? – was Mrs Muldoon's voice, coming to him from quite near, from so near that he seemed presently to see her as kneeling on the ground before him while he lay looking up at her; himself not wholly on the ground, but half-raised and upheld – conscious, yes, of tenderness of support and, more particularly, of a head pillowed in extraordinary softness and faintly refreshing fragrance. He considered, he wondered, his wit but half at his service; then another face intervened, bending more directly over him, and he finally knew that Alice Staverton had made her lap an ample and perfect cushion to him, and that she had to this end seated herself on the lowest degree of the staircase, the rest of his long person remaining stretched on his old black-and-white slabs. They were cold, these marble squares of his youth; but *he* somehow was not, in this rich return of consciousness – the most wonderful hour, little by little, that he had ever known, leaving him, as it did, so gratefully, so abysmally passive, and yet as with a treasure of intelligence waiting all round him for quiet appropriation; dissolved, he might call it, in the air of the place and producing the golden glow of a late autumn afternoon. He had come back, yes – come back from further away than any man but himself had ever travelled; but it was strange how with this sense what he had come back *to* seemed really the great thing, and as if his prodigious journey had been all for the sake of it. Slowly but surely his consciousness grew, his vision of his state thus completing itself: he had been miraculously *carried* back – lifted and carefully borne as from where he had been picked up, the uttermost end of an interminable grey passage. Even with this he was suffered to rest, and what had now brought him to knowledge was the break in the long mild motion.

It had brought him to knowledge, to knowledge – yes, this was the beauty of his state; which came to resemble more and more that of a man who has gone to sleep on some news of a great inheritance, and then, after dreaming it away, after profaning it with matters strange to it, has waked up again to serenity of certitude and has only to lie and watch it grow. This was the drift of his patience – that he had only to let it shine on him. He must moreover, with intermissions, still have been lifted and borne; since why and how else should he have known himself, later on, with the afternoon glow intenser, no longer at the foot of his stairs – situated as these now seemed at that dark other end of his tunnel – but on a deep window-bench of his high saloon, over which had been spread, couch-fashion, a mantle of soft stuff lined with grey fur that was familiar to his eyes and that one of his hands kept fondly feeling as for its pledge of truth. Mrs Muldoon's face had gone, but the other, the second he had recognized, hung over him in a way that showed how he was still propped and pillowed. He took it all in, and the more he took it the more it seemed to suffice: he was as much at peace as if he had had food and drink. It was the two women who had found him, on Mrs Muldoon's having plied, at her usual hour, her latchkey – and on her having above all arrived while Miss Staverton still lingered near the house. She had been turning away, all anxiety, from worrying the vain bell-handle – her calculation having been of the hour of the good woman's visit; but the latter, blessedly, had come up while she was still there, and they had entered together. He had then lain, beyond the vestibule, very much as he was lying now – quite, that is, as he appeared to have fallen, but all so wondrously without bruise or gash; only in a depth of stupor. What he most took in, however, at present, with the steadier clearance, was that Alice Staverton had for a long unspeakable moment not doubted he was dead.

'It must have been that I *was*.' He made it out as she held him. 'Yes – I can only have died. You brought me literally to life. Only,' he wondered, his eyes rising to her, 'only, in the name of all the benedictions, how?'

It took her but an instant to bend her face and kiss him, and something in the manner of it, and in the way her hands clasped and locked his head while he felt the cool charity and virtue of her lips, something in all this beatitude somehow answered everything. 'And now I keep you,' she said.

'Oh keep me, keep me!' he pleaded while her face still hung over him: in response to which it dropped again and stayed close, clingingly close. It was the seal of their situation – of which he tasted the impress for a long blissful moment in silence. But he came back. 'Yet how did you know—?'

'I was uneasy. You were to have come, you remember – and you had sent no word.'

'Yes, I remember – I was to have gone to you at one today.' It caught on to their 'old' life and relation – which were so near and so far. 'I was still out there in my strange darkness – where was it, what was it? I must have stayed there so long.' He could but wonder at the depth and the duration of his swoon.

'Since last night?' she asked with a shade of fear for her possible indiscretion.

'Since this morning – it must have been: the cold dim dawn of today. Where have I been,' he vaguely wailed, 'where have I been?' He felt her hold him close, and it was as if this helped him now to make in all security his mild moan. 'What a long dark day!'

All in her tenderness she had waited a moment. 'In the cold dim dawn?' she quavered

But he had already gone on piecing together the parts of the whole prodigy. 'As I didn't turn up you came straight—?'

She barely cast about. 'I went first to your hotel – where they told me of your absence. You had dined out last evening and hadn't been back since. But they appeared to know you had been at your club.'

'So you had the idea of *this*?'

'Of what?' she asked in a moment.

'Well – of what has happened.'

'I believed at least you'd have been here. I've known, all along,' she said, 'that you've been coming.'

'"Known" it—?'

'Well, I've believed it. I said nothing to you after that talk we had a month ago – but I felt sure. I knew you *would*,' she declared.

'That I'd persist, you mean?'

'That you'd see him.'

'Ah but I didn't!' cried Brydon with his long wail. 'There's somebody – an awful beast; whom I brought, too horribly, to bay. But it's not me.'

At this she bent over him again, and her eyes were in his eyes. 'No – it's not you.' And it was as if, while her face hovered, he might have made out in it, hadn't it been so near, some particular meaning blurred by a smile. 'No, thank heaven,' she repeated – 'it's not you! Of course it wasn't to have been.'

'Ah but it *was*,' he gently insisted. And he stared before him now as he had been staring for so many weeks. 'I was to have known myself.'

'You couldn't!' she returned consolingly. And then reverting, and as if to account further for what she had herself done, 'But it wasn't only *that*, that you hadn't been at home,' she went on. 'I waited till the hour at which we had found Mrs Muldoon that day of my going with you; and she arrived, as I've told you, while, failing to bring any one to the door, I lingered in my despair on the steps. After a little, if she hadn't come, by such a mercy, I should have found means to hunt her up. But it wasn't,' said Alice Staverton, as if once more with her fine intention – 'it wasn't only that.'

His eyes, as he lay, turned back to her. 'What more then?'

She met it, the wonder she had stirred. 'In the cold dim dawn, you say? Well, in the cold dim dawn of this morning I too saw you.'

'Saw *me*?'

'Saw *him*,' said Alice Staverton. 'It must have been at the same moment.'

He lay an instant taking it in – as if he wished to be quite reasonable. 'At the same moment?'

'Yes – in my dream again, the same one I've named to you. He came back to me. Then I knew it for a sign. He had come to you.'

At this Brydon raised himself; he had to see her better. She helped him when she understood his movement, and he sat up, steadying himself beside her there on the window-bench and with his right hand grasping her left. '*He* didn't come to me.'

'You came to yourself,' she beautifully smiled.

'Ah I've come to myself now – thanks to you, dearest. But this brute, with his awful face – this brute's a black stranger. He's none of *me*, even as I *might* have been,' Brydon sturdily declared.

But she kept the clearness that was like the breath of infallibility. 'Isn't the whole point that you'd have been different?'

He almost scowled for it. 'As different as *that*—?'

Her look again was more beautiful to him than the things of this world. 'Haven't you exactly wanted to know *how* different? So this morning,' she said, 'you appeared to me.'

'Like *him*?'

'A black stranger!'

'Then how did you know it was I?'

'Because, as I told you weeks ago, my mind, my imagination, had worked so over what you might, what you mightn't have been – to show you, you see, how I've thought of you. In the midst of that you came to me – that my wonder might be answered. So I knew,' she went on; 'and believed that, since the question held you too so fast, as you told me that day, you too would see for yourself. And when this morning I again saw I knew it would be because you had – and also then, from the first moment, because you somehow wanted me. *He* seemed to tell me of that. So why,' she strangely smiled, 'shouldn't I like him?'

It brought Spencer Brydon to his feet. 'You "like" that horror—?'

'I *could* have liked him. And to me,' she said, 'he was no horror. I had accepted him.'

'"Accepted"—?' Brydon oddly sounded.

'Before, for the interest of his difference – yes. And as *I* didn't disown him, as *I* knew him – which you at last, confronted with him in his difference, so cruelly didn't, my dear – well, he must have been, you see, less dreadful to me. And it may have pleased him that I pitied him.'

She was beside him on her feet, but still holding his hand – still with her arm supporting him. But though it all brought for him thus a dim light, 'You "pitied" him?' he grudgingly, resentfully asked.

'He has been unhappy; he has been ravaged,' she said.

'And haven't I been unhappy? Am not I – you've only to look at me! – ravaged?'

'Ah I don't say I like him *better*,' she granted after a thought. 'But he's grim, he's worn – and things have happened to him. He doesn't make shift, for sight, with your charming monocle.'

'No' – it struck Brydon: 'I couldn't have sported mine "down-town." They'd have guyed me there.'

'His great convex pince-nez – I saw it, I recognized the kind – is for his poor ruined sight. And his poor right hand—!'

'Ah!' Brydon winced – whether for his proved identity or for his lost fingers. Then, 'He has a million a year,' he lucidly added. 'But he hasn't you.'

'And he isn't – no, he isn't – *you*!' she murmured as he drew her to his breast.

SARAH ORNE JEWETT
1849-1909

Born in South Berwick, Maine in 1849, Sarah Orne Jewett had had her first story published by the time she was nineteen. A keen observer and able describer of her native surroundings and contemporaries, she went on to publish six volumes of short stories, many of which were much admired by pundits of the day, including the novelist Henry James, and, at a later date, Willa Cather.

One of the greatest of America's regional writers, Sarah Orne Jewett's tales of New England life are characterized by an attention to detail, a precision of language and a sensitivity both to natural beauty and to human frailties and strengths which makes stories like those which follow as vivid and full of life today as they were in the 1870s and 80s when they were written.

The Courting of Sister Wisby

ALL THE MORNING THERE HAD been an increasing temptation to take an out-door holiday, and early in the afternoon the temptation outgrew my power of resistance. A far-away pasture on the long southwestern slope of a high hill was persistently present to mind, yet there seemed to be no particular reason why I should think of it. I was not so sure that I wanted anything from the pasture, and there was no sign, except the temptation, that the pasture wanted anything from me. But I was on the farther side of as many as three fences before I stopped to think again where I was going, and why.

There is no use in trying to tell another person about that afternoon unless he distinctly remembers weather exactly like it. No number of details concerning an Arctic ice-blockade will give a single shiver to a child of the tropics. This was one of those perfect New England days in late summer, when the spirit of autumn takes a first stealthy flight, like a spy, through the ripening countryside, and, with feigned sympathy for those who droop with August heat, puts her cool cloak of bracing air about leaf and flower and human shoulders. Every living thing grows suddenly cheerful and strong; it is only when you catch sight of a horror-stricken little maple in swampy soil, – a little maple that has second sight and foreknowledge of coming disaster to her race, – only then does a distrust of autumn's friendliness dim your joyful satisfaction.

In midwinter there is always a day when one has the first foretaste of spring; in late August there is a morning when the air is for the first time autumnlike. Perhaps it is a hint to the squirrels to get in their first supplies for the winter hoards, or a reminder that summer will soon end, and everybody had better make the most of it. We are always looking forward to the passing and ending of winter, but when summer is here it seems as if summer must always last. As I went across the fields that day, I found myself half lamenting that the world must fade again, even that the best of her budding and bloom was only a preparation for another spring-time, for an awakening beyond the coming winter's sleep.

The sun was slightly veiled; there was a chattering group of birds, which had gathered for a conference about their early migration. Yet, oddly enough, I heard the voice of a belated bobolink, and presently saw him rise from the grass and hover leisurely, while he sang a brief tune. He was much behind time if he were still a housekeeper; but as for the other birds, who listened, they cared only for their own notes. An old crow went sagging by, and gave a croak at his despised neighbor, just as a black reviewer croaked at Keats: so hard it is to be just to one's contemporaries. The bobolink was indeed singing out of season, and it was impossible to say whether he really belonged most to this summer or to the next. He might have been delayed on his northward journey; at any rate, he had a light heart now, to judge from his song, and I wished that I could ask him a few questions, – how he liked being the last man among the bobolinks, and where he had taken singing lessons in the South.

Presently I left the lower fields, and took a path that led higher, where I could look beyond the village to the nothern country mountainward. Here the sweet fern grew, thick and fragrant, and I also found myself heedlessly treading on pennyroyal. Nearby, in a field corner, I long ago made a most comfortable seat by putting a stray piece of board and bit of rail across the angle of the fences. I have spent many a delightful hour there, in the shade and shelter of a young pitch-pine and a wild-cherry tree, with a lovely outlook toward the village, just far enough away beyond the green slopes and tall elms of the lower meadows. But that day I still had the feeling of being outward bound, and did not turn aside nor linger. The high pasture land grew more and more enticing.

I stopped to pick some blackberries that twinkled at me like beads among their dry vines, and two or three yellow-birds fluttered up from the leaves of a thistle, and then came back again, as if they had complacently discovered that I was only an overgrown yellow-bird, in strange disguise but perfectly harmless. They made me feel as if I were an intruder, though they did not offer to peck at me, and we parted company very soon. It was good to stand at last on the great shoulder of the hill. The wind was coming in from the sea, there was a fine fragrance from the pines, and the air grew sweeter every moment. I took new pleasure in the thought that in a piece of wild pasture land like this one may get closest to Nature, and subsist upon what she gives of her own free will. There have been no drudging, heavy-shod ploughmen to overturn the soil, and vex it into yielding artificial crops. Here one has to take just what Nature is pleased to give, whether one is a yellow-bird or a human being. It is very good entertainment for a summer wayfarer, and I am asking my reader now to share the winter provision which I harvested that day. Let us hope that the small birds are also faring well after their fashion, but I give them an anxious thought while the snow goes hurrying in long waves across the buried fields, this windy winter night.

I next went farther down the hill, and got a drink of fresh cool water from the brook, and pulled a tender sheaf of sweet flag beside it. The mossy old fence just beyond was the last barrier between me and the pasture which had sent an invisible messenger earlier in the day, but I saw that somebody else had come first to the rendezvous: there was a brown gingham cape-bonnet and a sprigged shoulder-shawl bobbing up and down, a little way off among the junipers. I had taken such uncommon pleasure in being alone that I instantly felt a sense of disappointment; then a warm glow of pleasant satisfaction rebuked my selfishness. This could be no one but dear old Mrs Goodsoe, the friend of my childhood and fond dependence of my maturer years. I had not seen her for many weeks, but here she was, out on one of her famous campaigns for herbs, or perhaps just returning from a blueberrying expedition. I approached with care, so as not to startle the gingham bonnet; but she heard the rustle of the bushes against my dress, and looked up quickly, as she knelt, bending over the turf. In that position she was hardly taller than the luxuriant junipers themselves.

'I'm a-gittin' in my mulleins,' she said briskly, 'an' I've been thinking o' you these twenty times since I come out o' the house. I begun to believe you must ha' forgot me at last.'

'I have been away from home,' I explained. 'Why don't you get in your pennyroyal too? There's a great plantation of it beyond the next fence but one.'

'Pennyr'yal!' repeated the dear little old woman, with an air of compassion for inferior knowledge; "t ain't the right time, darlin'. Pennyr'yal's too rank now. But for mulleins this day is prime. I've got a dreadful graspin' fit for 'em this year; seems if I must be goin' to need 'em extry. I feel like the squirrels must when they know a hard winter's comin'.' And Mrs Goodsoe bent over her work again, while I stood by and watched her carefully cut the best full-grown leaves with a clumsy pair of scissors, which might have served through at least half a century of herb-gathering. They were fastened to her apron-strings by a long piece of list.

'I'm going to take my jack-knife and help you,' I suggested, with some fear of refusal. 'I just passed a flourishing family of six or seven heads that must have been growing on purpose for you.'

'Now be keerful, dear heart,' was the anxious response; 'choose 'em well. There's odds in mulleins same's there is in angels. Take a plant that's all run up to stalk, and there ain't but little goodness in the leaves. This one I'm at now must ha' been stepped on by some creatur' and blighted of its bloom, and the leaves is han'some! When I was small I used to have a notion that Adam an' Eve must a took mulleins fer their winter wear. Ain't they just like flannel, for all the world? I've had experience, and I know there's plenty of sickness might be saved to folks if they'd quit horse-radish and such fiery, exasperating things, and use mullein drarves in proper season. Now I shall spread these an' dry 'em nice on my spare floor in the garrit, an' come to steam 'em for use along in the winter there'll be the vally of the whole summer's goodness in 'em, sartin.' And she snipped away with the dull scissors, while I listened respectfully, and took great pains to have my part of the harvest present a good appearance.

'This is most too dry a head,' she added presently, a little out of breath. 'There! I can tell you there's win'rows o' young doctors, bilin' over with book-larnin', that is truly ignorant of what to do for the sick, or how to p'int out those paths that well people foller toward sickness. Book-fools I call 'em, them young men, an' some on 'em never'll live to know much better, if they git to be Methuselahs. In my time every middle-aged woman, who had brought up a family, had some proper ideas o' dealing with complaints. I won't say but there was some fools amongst *them*, but I'd rather take my chances, unless they'd forsook herbs and gone to dealin' with patent stuff. Now my mother really did sense the use of herbs and roots. I never see anybody that come up to her. She was a meek-looking woman, but very understandin', mother was.'

'Then that's where you learned so much yourself, Mrs Goodsoe,' I ventured to say.

'Bless your heart, I don't hold a candle to her; 't is but little I can recall of what she used to say. No, her l'arnin' died with her,' said my friend, in a self-depreciating tone. 'Why, there was as many as twenty kinds of roots alone that she used to keep by her, that I forget the use of; an' I'm sure I shouldn't know where to find the most of 'em, any. There was an herb' – *airb*, she called it – 'an herb called masterwort, that she used to get way from Pennsylvany; and she used to think everything of noble liverwort, but I never could seem to get the right effects from it as she could. Though I don't know as she ever really did use masterwort where somethin' else wouldn't a served. She had a cousin married out in Pennsylvany that used to take pains to get it to her every year or two, and so she felt 't was important to have it. Some set more by such things as come from a distance, but I rec'lect mother always used to maintain that folks was meant to be doctored with the stuff that grew right about 'em; 't was sufficient, an' so ordered. That was before the whole population took to livin' on wheels, the way they do now. 'T was never my idee that we was meant to know what's goin' on all over the world to once. There's goin' to be some sort of a set-back one o' these days with these telegraphs an' things, an' letters comin' every hand's turn, and folks leavin' their proper work to answer 'em. I may not live to see it. 'T was allowed to be difficult for folks to git about in old times, or to git work across the country, and they stood in their lot an' place, and weren't all just alike, either, same as pine-spills.'

We were kneeling side by side now, as if in penitence for the march of progress, but we laughed as we turned to look at each other.

'Do you think it did much good when everybody brewed a cracked quart mug of herb-tea?' I asked, walking away on my knees to a new mullein.

'I've always lifted my voice against the practice, far 's I could,' declared Mrs Goodsoe; 'an' I won't deal out none o' the herbs I save for no such nonsense. There was three houses along our road, – I call no names, – where you couldn't go into the livin' room without findin' a mess o' herb-tea drorin' on the stove or side o' the fireplace, winter or summer, sick or well. One was thoroughwut, one would be camomile, and the other, like as not, yellow docks; but they all used to put in a little new rum to git out the goodness, or keep it from spilin'.' (Mrs Goodsoe favored me with a knowing smile.) 'Land, how mother used to laugh! But, poor creaturs, they had to work hard, and I guess it never done 'em a mite o' harm; they was all good herbs. I wish you could hear the quawkin' there used to be when they was indulged with a real case o' sickness. Everybody would collect from far an' near; you'd see 'em coming along the road and across the pastures then; everybody clamorin' that nothin' wouldn't do no kind o' good but her choice o' teas or drarves to the feet. I wonder there was a babe lived to grow up in the whole lower part o' the town; an' if nothin' else 'peared to ail 'em, word was pasted about that 't was likely Mis' So-and-So's last young one was goin' to be foolish. Land, how they'd gather! I know one day the doctor come to Widder Peck's and the house was crammed so 't he could scercely git inside the door; and he says, just as polite, 'Do send for some of the neighbors!' as if there wa'n't a soul to turn to, right or left. You'd ought to seen 'em begin to scatter.'

'But don't you think the cars and telegraphs have given people more to interest them, Mrs Goodsoe? Don't you believe people's lives were narrower then, and more taken up with little things?' I asked, unwisely, being a product of modern times.

'Not one mite, dear,' said my companion stoutly. 'There was as big thoughts then as there is now; these times was born o' them. The difference is in folks themselves; but now, instead o' doin' their own housekeepin' and watchin' their own neighbors, – though that was carried to excess, – they git word that a niece's child is ailin' the other side o' Massachusetts, and they drop everything and git on their best clothes, and off they jiggit in the cars. 'T is a bad sign when folks wears out their best clothes faster 'n they do their every-day ones. The other side o' Massachusetts has got to look after itself by rights. An' besides that, Sunday-keepin' 's all gone out o' fashion. Some lays it to one thing an' some another, but some o' them old ministers that folks are all a-sighin' for did preach a lot o' stuff that wa'n't nothin' but chaff; 't wa'n't the word o' God out o' either Old Testament or New. But everybody went to meetin' and heard it, and come home, and was set to fightin' with their next door neighbor over it. Now I'm a believer, and I try to live a Christian life, but I'd as soon hear a surveyor's book read out, figgers an' all, as try to get any simple truth out o' most sermons. It's them as is most to blame.'

'What was the matter that day at Widow Peck's?' I hastened to ask, for I knew by experience that the good, clear-minded soul beside me was apt to grow unduly vexed and distressed when she contemplated the state of religious teaching.

'Why, there wa'n't nothin' the matter, only a gal o' Miss Peck's had met with a dis'pointment and had gone into screechin' fits. 'T was a rovin' creatur' that had come along hayin' time, and he'd gone off an' forsook her betwixt two days; nobody ever knew what become of him. Them Pecks was "Good Lord, anybody!" kind o' gals, and took up with whoever they could get. One of 'em married Heron, the Irishman; they lived in that little house that was burnt this summer, over on the edge o' the plains. He was a good-hearted creatur', with a laughin' eye and a clever word for everybody. He was the first Irishman that ever came this way, and we was all for gettin' a look at him, when he first used to go by. Mother's folks was what they call Scotch-Irish, though; there was an old race of 'em settled about here. They could foretell events, some on 'em, and had the second sight. I know folks used to say mother's grandmother had them gifts, but mother was never free to speak about it to us. She remembered her well, too.'

'I suppose that you mean old Jim Heron, who was such a famous fiddler?' I asked with great interest, for I am always delighted to know more about that rustic hero, parochial Orpheus that he must have been!

'Now, dear heart, I suppose you don't remember him, do you?' replied Mrs Goodsoe, earnestly. 'Fiddle! He'd about break your heart with them tunes of his, or else set your heels flying up the floor in a jig, though you was minister o' the First Parish and all wound up for a funeral prayer. I tell ye there ain't no tunes sounds like them used to. It used to seem to me summer nights when I was comin' along the plains road, and he set by the window playin', as if there was a bewitched human creatur' in that old red fiddle o' his. He could make it sound just like a woman's voice tellin' somethin' over and over, as if folks could help her out o' sorrows if she could only make 'em understand. I've set by the stone-wall and cried as if my heart was broke, and dear knows it wa'n't in them days. How he would twirl off them jigs and dance tunes! He used to make somethin' han'some out of 'em in fall an' winter, playin' at huskins and dancin' parties; but he was unstiddy by spells, as he got along in years, and never knew what it was to be forehanded. Everybody felt bad when he died; you couldn't help likin' the creatur'. He'd got the gift – that's all you could say about it.

'There was a Mis' Jerry Foss, that lived over by the brook bridge, on the plains road, that had lost her husband early, and was left with three child'n. She set the world by 'em, and was a real pleasant, ambitious little woman, and was workin' on as best she could with that little farm, when there come a rage o' scarlet fever, and her boy and two girls was swept off and laid dead within the same week. Every one o' the neighbors did what they could, but she'd had no sleep since they was taken sick, and after the funeral she set there just like a piece o' marble, and would only shake her head when you spoke to her. They all thought her reason would go; and 't would certain, if she couldn't have shed tears. An' one o' the neighbors – 't was like mother's sense, but it might have been somebody else – spoke o' Jim Heron. Mother an' one or two o' the women that knew her best was in the house with her. 'T was right in the edge of the woods and some of us younger ones was over by the wall on the other side of the road where there was a couple of old willows, – I remember just how the brook damp felt; and we kept quiet 's we could, and some other folks come along down the road, and stood waitin' on the little bridge, hopin' somebody 'd come out, I suppose, and they'd git news. Everybody was wrought up, and felt a good deal for her, you know. By an' by Jim Heron come stealin' right out o' the shadows an' set down on the doorstep, an' 't was a good while before we heard a sound; then, oh, dear me! 't was what the whole neighborhood felt for that mother all spoke in the notes, an' they told me afterwards that Mis' Foss's face changed in a minute, and she come right over an' got into my mother's lap, – she was a little woman, – an' laid her head down, and there she cried herself into a blessed sleep. After awhile one o' the other other women stole out an' told the folks, and we all went home. He only played that one tune.

'But there!' resumed Mrs Goodsoe, after a silence, during which my eyes were filled with tears. 'His wife always complained that the fiddle made her nervous. She never 'peared to think nothin' o' poor Heron after she'd once got him.'

'That's often the way,' said I, with harsh cynicism, though I had no guilty person in my mind at the moment; and we went straying off, not very far apart, up through the pasture. Mrs Goodsoe cautioned me that we must not get so far off that we could not get back the same day. The sunshine began to feel very hot on our backs, and we both turned toward the shade. We had already collected a large bundle of mullein leaves, which were carefully laid into a clean, calico apron, held together by the four corners, and proudly carried by me, though my companion regarded them with anxious eyes. We sat down together at the edge of the pine woods, and Mrs Goodsoe proceeded to fan herself with her limp cape-bonnet.

'I declare, how hot it is! The east wind's all gone again,' she said. 'It felt so cool this forenoon that I overburdened myself with as thick a petticoat as any I've got. I'm despri't afeared of having a chill, now that I ain't so young as once. I hate to be housed up.'

'It's only August, after all,' I assured her unnecessarily, confirming my statement by taking two peaches out of my pocket, and laying them side by side on the brown pine needles between us.

'Dear sakes alive!' exclaimed the old lady, with evident pleasure. 'Where did you get them, now? doesn't anything taste twice better out-o'-doors? I ain't had such a peach for years. Do le's keep the stones, an' I'll plant 'em; it only takes four year for a peach pit to come to bearing, an' I guess I'm good for four year, 'thout I meet with some accident.'

I could not help agreeing, or taking a fond look at the thin little figure, and her wrinkled brown face and kind, twinkling eyes. She looked as if she had properly dried herself, by mistake, with some of her mullein leaves, and was likely to keep her goodness, and to last the longer in consequence. There never was a truer, simple-hearted soul made out of the old-fashioned country dust than Mrs Goodsoe. I thought, as I looked away from her across the wide country, that nobody was left in any of the farm-houses so original, so full of rural wisdom and reminiscence, so really able and dependable, as she. And nobody had made better use of her time in a world foolish enough to sometimes undervalue medicinal herbs.

When we had eaten our peaches we still sat under the pines, and I was not without pride when I had poked about in the ground with a little twig, and displayed to my crony a long fine root, bright yellow to the eye, and a wholesome bitter to the taste.

'Yis, dear, goldthread,' she assented indulgently. 'Seems to me there's more of it than anything except grass an' hardhack. Good for canker, but no better than two or three other things I can call to mind; but I always lay in a good wisp of it, for old times' sake. Now, I want to know why you should a bit it, and took away all the taste o' your nice peach? I was just thinkin' what a han'some entertainment we've had. I've got so I 'sociate certain things with certain folks, and goldthread was somethin' Lizy Wisby couldn't keep house without, no ways whatever. I believe she took so much it kind o' puckered her disposition.'

'Lizy Wisby?' I repeated inquiringly.

'You knew her, if ever, by the name of Mis' Deacon Brimblecom,' answered my friend, as if this were only a brief preface to further information, so I waited with respectful expectation. Mrs Goodsoe had grown tired out in the sun, and good story would be an excuse for sufficient rest. It was a most lovely place where we sat, halfway up the long hillside; for my part, I was perfectly contented and happy. 'You've often heard of Deacon Brimblecom?' she asked, as if a great deal depended upon his being properly introduced.

'I remember him,' said I. 'They called him Deacon Brimfull, you know, and he used to go about with a witch-hazel branch to show people where to dig wells.'

'That's the one,' said Mrs Goodsoe, laughing. 'I didn't know's you could go so far back. I'm always divided between whether you can remember everything I can, or are only a babe in arms.'

'I have a dim recollection of there being something strange about their marriage,' I suggested, after a pause, which began to appear dangerous. I was so much afraid the subject would be changed.

'I can tell you all about it,' I was quickly answered. 'Deacon Brimblecom was very pious accordin' to his lights in his early years. He lived way back in the country then, and there come a rovin' preacher along, and set everybody up that way all by the ears. I've heard the old folks talk it over, but I forget most of his doctrine, except some of his followers was persuaded they could dwell among the angels while yet on airth, and this Deacon Brimfull, as you call him, felt sure he was called by the voice of a spirit bride. So he left a good, deservin' wife he had, an' four children, and built him a new house over to the other side of the land he'd had from his father. They didn't take much pains with the buildin', because they expected to be translated before long, and then the spirit brides and them folks was goin' to appear and divide up the airth amongst 'em, and the world's folks and onbelievers was goin' to serve 'em or be sent to torments. They had meetins about in the schoolhouses, an' all sorts o' goins on; some on 'em went crazy, but the deacon held on to what wits he had, an' by an' by the spirit bride didn't turn out to be much of a housekeeper, an' he had always been used to good livin', so he sneaked home ag'in. One o' mother's sisters married up to Ash Hill, where it all took place; that's how I come to have the particulars.'

'Then how did he come to find his Eliza Wisby?' I inquired. 'Do tell me the whole story; you've got mullein leaves enough.'

'There's all yesterday's at home, if I haven't,' replied Mrs Goodsoe.

'The way he come a-courtin' o' Sister Wisby was this: she went a-courtin' o' him.

'There was a spell he lived to home, and then his poor wife died, and he had a spirit bride in good earnest, an' the child'n was placed about with his folks and hers, for they was both out o' good families; and I don't know what come over him, but he had another pious fit that looked for all the world like the real thing. He hadn't no family cares, and he lived with his brother's folks, and turned his land in with theirs. He used to travel to every meetin' an' conference that was within reach of his old sorrel hoss's feeble legs; he j'ined the Christian Baptists that was just in their early prime, and he was a great exhorter, and got to be called deacon, though I guess he wa'n't deacon, 'less it was for a spare hand when deacon timber was scercer 'n usual. An' one time there was a four days' protracted meetin' to the church in the lower part of the town. 'T was a real solemn time; something more'n usual was goin' forward, an' they collected from the whole country round. Women folks liked it, an' the men too; it give 'em a change an' they was quartered round free, same as conference folks now. Some on 'em, for a joke, sent Silas Brimblecom up to Lizy Wisby's, though she'd give out she couldn't accommodate nobody, because of expectin' her cousin's folks. Everybody knew 't was a lie; she was amazin' close considerin' she had plenty to do with. There was a streak that wa'n't just right somewheres in Lizy's wits, I always thought. She was very kind in case o' sickness, I'll say that for her.

'You know where the house is, over there on what they call Windy Hill? There the deacon went, all unsuspectin', and 'stead o' Lizy's resentin' of him she put in her own hoss, and they come back together to evenin' meetin'. She was prominent among the sect herself, an' he bawled and talked, and she bawled and talked, an' took up more 'n the time allotted in the exercises, just as if they was showin' off to each other what they was able to do at expoundin'. Everybody was laughin' at 'em after the meetin' broke up, and that next day an' the next, an' all through, they was constant, and seemed to be havin' a beautiful occasion. Lizy had always give out she scorned the men, but when she got a chance at a particular one 't was altogether different, and the deacon seemed to please her somehow or 'nother, and – There! you don't want to listen to this old stuff that's past an' gone?'

'Oh yes, I do,' said I.

'I run on like a clock that's onset her striking hand,' said Mrs Goodsoe mildly. 'Sometimes my kitchen timepiece goes on half the forenoon, and I says to myself the day before yisterday I would let it be a warnin', and keep it in mind for a check on my own speech. The next news that was heard was that the deacon an' Lizy – well, opinions differed which of 'em spoke first, but them fools settled it before the protracted meetin' was over, and give away their hearts before they started for home. They considered 't would be wise, though, considerin' their short acquaintance, to take one another on trial a spell; 't was Lizy's notion, and she asked him why he would n't come over and stop with her till spring, and then, if they both continued to like, they could git married any time 't was convenient. Lizy, she come and talked it over with mother, and mother disliked to offend her, but she spoke pretty plain and Lizy felt hurt, and thought they was showin' excellent judgment, so much harm come from hasty unions and folks comin' to a realizin' sense of each other's failin's when 't was too late.

'So one day our folks saw Deacon Brimfull a-ridin' by with a gre't coopful of hens in the back o' his wagon, and bundles o' stuff tied on top and hitched to the exes underneath; and he riz a hymn just as he passed the house, and was speedin' the old sorrel with a willer switch. 'T was 'most Thanksgivin' time, an' sooner 'n she expected him. New Year's was the time she set; but he thought he'd better come while the roads was fit for wheels. They was out to meetin' together Thanksgivin' Day, an' that used to be a gre't season for marryin'; so the young folks nudged each other, and some on 'em ventured to .speak to the couple as they come down the aisle. Lizy carried it off real well; she wa'n't afraid o' what nobody said or thought, and so home they went. They'd got out her yaller sleigh and her hoss; she never would ride after the deacon's poor old creatur', and I believe it died long o' the winter from stiffenin' up.

'Yes,' said Mrs Goodsoe emphatically, after we had silently considered the situation for a short space of time, – 'yes, there was consider'ble talk, now I tell you! The raskil boys pestered 'em just about to death for a while. They used to collect up there an' rap on the winders, and they'd turn out all the deacon's hens 'long at nine o'clock o' night, and chase 'em all over the dingle; an' one night they even lugged the pig right out o' the sty, and shoved it into the back entry, an' run for their lives. They'd stuffed its mouth full o' somethin', so it couldn't squeal till it got there. There wa'n't a sign o' nobody to be seen when Lizy hasted out with the light, and she an' the deacon had to persuade the creatur' back as best they could; 't was a cold night, and they said it took 'em till towards mornin'. You see the deacon was just the kind of man that a hog wouldn't budge for; it takes a masterful man to deal with a hog. Well, there was no end to the works nor the talk, but Lizy left 'em pretty much alone. She did 'pear kind of dignified about it, I must say!'

'And then, were they married in the spring?'

'I was tryin' to remember whether it was just before Fast Day or just after,' responded my friend, with a careful look at the sun, which was nearer the west than either of us had noticed. 'I think likely 't was along in the last o' April, any way some of us looked out o' the window one Monday mornin' early, and says, "For goodness' sake! Lizy's sent the deacon home again!" His old sorrel havin' passed away, he was ridin' in Ezry Welsh's hoss-cart, with his hen-coop and more bundles than he had when he come, and he looked as meechin' as ever you see. Ezry was drivin', and he let a glance fly swiftly round to see if any of us was lookin' out; an' then I declare if he didn't have the malice to turn right in towards the barn, where he see my oldest brother, Joshuay, an' says he real natural, "Joshuay, just step out with your wrench. I believe I hear my kingbolt rattlin' kind o' loose." Brother, he went out an' took in the sitooation, an' the deacon bowed kind of stiff. Joshuay was so full o' laugh, and Ezry Welsh, that they couldn't look one another in the face. There wa'n't nothing ailed the kingbolt, you know, an' when Josh riz up he says, "Goin' up country for a spell, Mr Brimblecom?"

'"I be," says the deacon, lookin' dreadful mortified and cast down.

'"Ain't things turned out well with you an' Sister Wisby?" says Joshuay. "You had ought to remember that the woman is the weaker vessel."

'"Hang her, let her carry less sail, then!" the deacon bu'st out, and he stood right up an' shook his fist there by the hen-coop, he was so mad; an' Ezry's hoss was a young creatur', an' started up an set the deacon right over backwards into the chips. We didn't know but he'd broke his neck; but when he see the women folks runnin' out, he jumped up quick as a cat, an' clim' into the cart, an' off they went. Ezry said he told him that he couldn't git along with Lizy, she was so fractious in thundery weather; if there was a rumble in the daytime she must go right to bed an' screech, and if 't was night she must git right up an' go an' call him out of a sound sleep. But everybody knew he'd never a gone home unless she'd sent him.

'Somehow they made it up agin right away, him an' Lizy, and she had him back. She'd been countin' all along on not havin' to hire nobody to work about the gardin an' so on, an' she said she wa'n't goin' to let him have a whole winter's board for nothin'. So the old hens was moved back, and they was married right off fair an' square, an' I don't know but they got along well as most folks. He brought his youngest girl down to live with 'em after a while, an' she was a real treasure to Lizy; everybody spoke well o' Phebe Brimblecom. The deacon got over his pious fit, and there was consider'ble work in him if you kept right after him. He was an amazin' cider-drinker, and he airn't the name you know him by in his latter days. Lizy never trusted him with nothin', but she kep' him well. She left everything she owed to Phebe, when she died, 'cept somethin' to satisfy the law. There, they're all gone now: seems to me sometimes, when I get thinkin', as if I'd lived a thousand years!'

I laughed, but I found that Mrs Goodsoe's thoughts had taken a serious turn.

'There, I come by some old graves down here in the lower edge of the pasture,' she said as we rose to go. 'I couldn't help thinking how I should like to be laid right out in the pasture ground, when my time comes; it looked sort o' comfortable, and I have ranged these slopes so many summers. Seems as if I could see right up through the turf and tell when the weather was pleasant and get the goodness o' the sweet fern. Now, dear, just hand me my apernful o' mulleins out o' the shade. I hope you won't come to need none this winter, but I'll dry some special for you.'

'I'm going home by the road,' said I, 'or else by the path across the meadows, and I will walk as far as the house with you. Aren't you pleased with my company?' for she demurred at my going the least bit out of the way.

So we strolled toward the little gray house, with our plunder of mullein leaves slung on a stick which we carried between us. Of course I went in to make a call, as if I had not seen my hostess before; she is the last maker of muster-gingerbread, and before I came away I was kindly measured for a pair of mittens.

'You'll be sure to come an' see them two peach-trees after I get 'em well growin'!' Mrs Goodsoe called after me when I had said good-by, and was almost out of hearing down the road.

The Hiltons' Holiday

1

THERE WAS A BRIGHT, full moon in the clear sky, and the sunset was still shining faintly in the west. Dark woods stood all about the old Hilton farmhouse, save down the hill, westward, where lay the shadowy fields which John Hilton, and his father before him, had cleared and tilled with much toil – the small fields to which they had given the industry and even affection of their honest lives.

John Hilton was sitting on the doorstep of his house. As he moved his head in and out of the shadows, turning now and then to speak to his wife, who sat just within the doorway, one could see his good face, rough and somewhat unkempt, as if he were indeed a creature of the shady woods and brown earth, instead of the noisy town. It was late in the long spring evening, and he had just come from the lower field as cheerful as a boy, proud of having finished the planting of his potatoes.

'I had to do my last row mostly by feelin',' he said to his wife. 'I'm proper glad I pushed through an' went back an' ended off after supper. 'Twould have taken me a good part o' tomorrow mornin', an' broke my day.'

''Tain't no use for ye to work yourself all to pieces, John,' answered the woman, quickly. 'I declare it does seem harder than ever that we couldn't have kep' our boy; he'd been comin' fourteen years old this fall, most a grown man, and he'd work right 'longside of ye now the whole time.'

''Twas hard to lose him; I do seem to miss little John,' said the father, sadly. 'I expect there was reasons why 'twas best. I feel able an' smart to work; my father was a girt strong man, an' a monstrous worker afore me. 'Tain't that; but I was thinkin' myself today what a sight o' company the boy would ha' been. You know, small's he was, how I could trust him to leave anywheres with the team, and how he'd beseech to go with me wherever I was goin'; always right in my tracks I used to tell 'em. Poor little John, for all he was so young he had a great deal o' judgment; he'd ha' made a likely man.'

The mother sighed heavily as she sat within the shadow.

'But then there's the little girls, a sight o' help an' company,' urged the father, eagerly, as if it were wrong to dwell upon sorrow and loss. 'Katy, she's most as good as a boy, except that she ain't very rugged. She's a real little farmer, she's helped me a sight this spring; an' you've got Susan Ellen, that makes a complete little housekeeper for ye as far as she's learnt. I don't see but we're better off than most folks, each on us having a workmate.'

'That's so, John,' acknowledged Mrs Hilton, wistfully, beginning to rock steadily in her straight splint-bottom chair. It was always a good sign when she rocked.

440

'Where be the little girls so late?' asked their father. ''Tis gettin' long past eight o'clock. I don't know when we've all set up so late, but it's so kind o' summerlike an' pleasant. Why, where be they gone?'

'I've told ye; only over to Becker's folks,' answered the mother. 'I don't see myself what keeps 'em so late; they beseeched me after supper till I let 'em go. They're all in a dazzle with the new teacher; she asked 'em to come over. They say she's unusual smart with 'rethmetic, but she has a kind of gorpen look to me. She's goin' to give Katy some pieces for her doll, but I told Katy she ought to be ashamed wantin' dolls' pieces, big as she's gittin' to be. I don't know's she ought, though; she ain't but nine this summer.'

'Let her take her comfort,' said the kind-hearted man. 'Them things draws her to the teacher, an' makes them acquainted. Katy's shy with new folks, more so'n Susan Ellen, who's of the business kind. Katy's shy-feelin' and wishful.'

'I don't know but she is,' agreed the mother slowly. 'Ain't it sing'lar how well acquainted you be with that one, an' I with Susan Ellen? 'Twas always so from the first. I'm doubtful sometimes our Katy ain't one that'll be like to get married – anyways not about here. She lives right with herself, but Susan Ellen ain't nothin' when she's alone, she's always after company; all the boys is waitin' on her a'ready. I ain't afraid but she'll take her pick when the time comes. I expect to see Susan Ellen well settled – she feels grown up now – but Katy don't care one mite 'bout none o' them things. She wants to be rovin' out o' doors. I do believe she'd stand an' hark to a bird the whole forenoon.'

'Perhaps she'll grow up to be a teacher,' suggested John Hilton. 'She takes to her books more'n the other one. I should like one on 'em to be a teacher same's my mother was. They're good girls as anybody's got.'

'So they be,' said the mother, with unusual gentleness, and the creak of her rocking-chair was heard, regular as the ticking of a clock. The night breeze stirred in the great woods, and the sound of a brook that went falling down the hillside grew louder and louder. Now and then one could hear the plaintive chirp of a bird. The moon glittered with whiteness like a winter moon, and shone upon the low-roofed house until its small window-panes gleamed like silver, and one could almost see the colours of a blooming bush of lilac that grew in a sheltered angle by the kitchen door. There was an incessant sound of frogs in the lowlands.

'Be you sound asleep, John?' asked the wife presently.

'I don't know but what I was a'most,' said the tired man, starting a little. 'I should laugh if I was to fall sound asleep right here on the step; 'tis the bright night, I expect, makes my eyes feel heavy, an' 'tis so peaceful. I was up an' dressed a little past four an' out to work. Well, well!' and he laughed sleepily and rubbed his eyes. 'Where's the little girls? I'd better step along an' meet 'em.'

'I wouldn't just yet; they'll get home all right, but 'tis late for 'em certain. I don't want 'em keepin' Mis' Becker's folks up neither. There, le's wait a few minutes,' urged Mrs Hilton.

'I've be'n a-thinkin' all day I'd like to give the child'n some kind of a treat,' said the father, wide awake now. 'I hurried up my work 'cause I had it so in mind. They don't have the opportunities some do, an' I want 'em to know of the world, an' not stay right here on the farm like a couple o' bushes.'

'They're a sight better off not to be so full o' notions as some is,' protested the mother, suspiciously.

'Certain,' answered the farmer; 'but they're good, bright child'n, an' commencin' to take a sight o' notice. I want 'em to have all we can give 'em. I want 'em to see how other folks does things.'

'Why, so do I' – here the rocking-chair stopped ominously – 'but so long's they're contented—'

'Contented ain't all in this world; hopper-toads may have that quality an' spend all their time a-blinkin'. I don't know's bein' contented is all there is to look for in a child. Ambition's somethin' to me.'

'Now you've got your mind on some plot or other.' (The rocking-chair began to move again.) 'Why can't you talk right out?'

''Tain't nothin' special,' answered the good man, a little ruffled; he was never prepared for his wife's mysterious powers of divination. 'Well there, you do find things out the master! I only thought perhaps I'd take 'em tomorrow, an' go off somewhere if 'twas a good day. I've been promisin' for a good while I'd take 'em to Topham Corners; they've never been there since they was very small.'

'I believe you want a good time yourself. You ain't never got over bein' a boy.' Mrs Hilton seemed much amused. 'There, go if you want to an' take 'em; they've got their summer hats an' new dresses. I don't know o' nothin' that stands in the way. I should sense it better if there was a circus or anythin' to go to. Why don't you wait an' let the girls pick 'em some strawberries or nice ros'berries, and then they could take an' sell 'em to the stores?'

John Hilton reflected deeply. 'I should like to get me some good yellow-turnip seed to plant late. I ain't more'n satisfied with what I've been gettin' o' late years o' Ira Speed. An' I'm goin' to provide me with a good hoe; mine's gettin' wore out an' all shackly. I can't seem to fix it good.'

'Them's excuses,' observed Mrs Hilton, with friendly tolerance. 'You just cover up the hoe with somethin', if you get it – I would. Ira Speed's so jealous he'll remember it of you this twenty year, your goin' an' buyin' a new hoe o' anybody but him.'

'I've always thought 'twas a free country,' said John Hilton, soberly. 'I don't want to vex Ira neither; he favours us all he can in trade. 'Tis difficult for him to spare a cent, but he's as honest as daylight.'

At this very moment there was a sudden sound of young voices, and a pair of young figures came out from the shadow of the woods into the moon-lighted open space. An old cock crowed loudly from his perch in the shed, as if he were a herald of royalty. The little girls were hand in hand, and a brisk young dog capered about them as they came.

'Wa'n't it dark gittin' home through the woods this time o' night?' asked the mother, hastily, and not without reproach.

'I don't love to have you gone so late; mother an' me was timid about ye, and you've kep' Mis' Becker's folks up, I expect,' said their father, regretfully. 'I don't want to have it said that my little girls ain't got good manners.'

'The teacher had a party,' chirped Susan Ellen, the elder of the two children. 'Goin' home from school she asked the Grover boys, an' Mary an' Sarah Speed. An' Mis' Becker was real pleasant to us: she passed round some cake, an' handed us sap sugar on one of her best plates, an' we played games an' sung some pieces too. Mis' Becker thought we did real well. I can pick out most of a tune on the cabinet organ; teacher says she'll give me lessons.'

'I want to know, dear!' exclaimed John Hilton.

'Yes, an' we played Copenhagen, an' took sides spellin', an' Katy beat everybody spellin' there was there.'

Katy had not spoken, she was not so strong as her sister, and while Susan Ellen stood a step or two away addressing her eager little audience, Katy had seated herself close to her father on the doorstep. He put his arm round her shoulder, and drew her close to his side, where she stayed.

'Ain't you got nothin' to tell, daughter?' he asked, looking down fondly, and Katy gave a pleased little sigh for answer.

'Tell 'em what's goin' to be the last day o' school, and about our trimmin' the schoolhouse,' she said, and Susan Ellen gave the programme in most spirited fashion.

''Twill be a great time,' said the mother, when she had finished. 'I don't see why folks want to go trapesin' off to strange places when such things is happenin' right about 'em.' But the children did not observe her mysterious air. 'Come, you must step yourselves right to bed.'

They all went into the dark, warm house, the bright moon shone upon it steadily all night, and the lilac flowers were shaken by no breath of wind until the early dawn.

2

The Hiltons always waked early. So did their neighbours, the crows and song-sparrows and robins, the light-footed foxes and squirrels in the woods. When John Hilton waked, before five o'clock, an hour later than usual because he had sat up so late, he opened the house door and came out into the yard, crossing the short green turf hurriedly as if the day were too far spent for any loitering. The magnitude of the plan for taking a whole day of pleasure confronted him seriously, but the weather was fair, and his wife, whose disapproval could not have been set aside, had accepted and even smiled upon the great project. It was inevitable now that he and the children should go to Topham Corners. Mrs Hilton had the pleasure of waking them, and telling the news.

In a few minutes they came frisking out to talk over the great plans. The cattle were already fed, and their father was milking. The only sign of high festivity was the wagon pulled out into the yard, with both seats put in as if it were Sunday; but Mr Hilton still wore his everyday clothes, and Susan Ellen suffered instantly from disappointment.

'Ain't we goin', father?' she asked, complainingly, but he nodded and smiled at her, even though the cow, impatient to get to pasture, kept whisking her rough tail across his face. He held his head down and spoke cheerfully, in spite of this vexation.

'Yes, sister, we're goin' certain, an' goin' to have a great time, too.' Susan Ellen thought that he seemed like a boy at that delightful moment, and felt new sympathy and pleasure at once. 'You go an' help mother about breakfast an' them things; we want to get off quick's we can. You coax mother now, both on ye, an' see if she won't go with us.'

'She said she wouldn't be hired to,' responded Susan Ellen. 'She says it's goin' to be hot, an' she's laid out to go over an' see how her aunt Tamsen Brooks is this afternoon.'

The father gave a little sigh; then he took heart again. The truth was that his wife made light of the contemplated pleasure, and, much as he usually valued her companionship and approval, it was sure that they should have a better time without her. It was impossible, however, not to feel guilty of disloyalty at the thought. Even though she might be completely unconscious of his best ideals, he only loved her and the ideals the more, and bent his energies to satisfying her indefinite expectations. His wife still kept much of that youthful beauty which Susan Ellen seemed likely to reproduce.

An hour later the best wagon was ready, and the great expedition set forth. The little dog sat apart, and barked as if it fell entirely upon him to voice the general excitement. Both seats were in the wagon, but the empty place testified to Mrs Hilton's unyielding disposition. She had wondered why one broad seat would not do, but John Hilton meekly suggested that the wagon looked better. The little girls sat on the back seat dressed alike in their Sunday hats of straw with blue ribbons, and their little plaid shawls pinned neatly about their small shoulders. They wore grey thread gloves, and sat very straight. Susan Ellen was half a head the taller, but otherwise, from behind, they looked much alike. As for their father, he was in his Sunday best – a plain black coat, and a winter hat of felt, which was heavy and rusty-looking for that warm early-summer day. He had it in mind to buy a new straw hat at Topham, so that this with the turnip-seed and the hoe made three important reasons for going.

'Remember an' lay off your shawls when you get there, an' carry them over your arms,' said the mother, clucking like an excited hen to her chickens. 'They'll do to keep the dust off your new dresses goin' and comin'. An' when you eat your dinners don't get spots on you, an' don't point at folks as you ride by, an' stare, or they'll know you came from the country. An' John, you call into Cousin Ad'line Marlow's an' see how they all be, an' tell her I expect her over certain to stop a while before hayin'. It always eases her phthisic to git up here on the highland, an' I've got a new notion about doin' over her best-room carpet sence I see her that'll save rippin' one breadth. An' don't come home all wore out; an', John, don't you go an' buy me no kickshaws to fetch home. I ain't a child, an' you ain't got no money to waste. I expect you'll go, like's not, an' buy you some kind of a foolish boy's hat; do look an' see if it's reasonable good straw, an' won't splinter all off round the edge. An' you mind, John—'

'Yes, yes, hold on!' cried John, impatiently; then he cast a last affectionate, reassuring look at her face, flushed with the hurry and responsibility of starting them off in proper shape. 'I wish you was goin' too,' he said, smiling. 'I do so!' Then the old horse started, and they went out at the bars, and began the careful long descent of the hill. The young dog, tethered to the lilac bush, was frantic with piteous appeals; the little girls piped their eager good-byes again and again, and their father turned many times to look back and wave his hand. As for their mother, she stood alone and watched them out of sight.

There was one place far out on the high road where she could catch a last glimpse of the wagon, and she waited what seemed a very long time until it appeared and then was lost to sight again behind a low hill. 'They're nothin' but a pack o' child'n together,' she said aloud, and then felt lonelier than she expected. She even stooped and patted the unresigned little dog as she passed him, going into the house.

The occasion was so much more important than anyone had foreseen that both the little girls were speechless. It seemed at first like going to church in new clothes, or to a funeral; they hardly knew how to behave at the beginning of a whole day of pleasure. They made grave bows at such persons of their acquaintance as happened to be straying in the road. Once or twice they stopped before a farmhouse, while their father talked an inconsiderately long time with someone about the crops and the weather and even dwelt upon town business and the doings of the selectmen, which might be talked of at any time. The explanations that he gave of their excursion seemed quite unnecessary. It was made entirely clear that he had a little business to do at Topham Corners, and thought he had better give the little girls a ride; they had been very steady at school, and he had finished planting, and could take the day as well as not. Soon, however, they all felt as if such an excursion were an everyday affair, and Susan Ellen began to ask eager questions, while Katy silently sat apart enjoying herself as she never had done before. She liked to see the strange houses, and the children who belonged to them; it was delightful to find flowers that she knew growing all along the road, no matter how far she went from home. Each small homestead looked its best and pleasantest, and shared the exquisite beauty that early summer made, shared the luxury of greenness and floweriness that decked the rural world. There was an early peony or a late lilac in almost every dooryard.

It was seventeen miles to Topham. After a while they seemed very far from home, having left the hills far behind, and descended to a great level country with fewer tracts of woodland, and wider fields where the crops were much more forward. The houses were all painted, and the roads were smoother and wider. It had been so pleasant driving along that Katy dreaded going into the strange town when she first caught sight of it, though Susan Ellen kept asking with bold fretfulness if they were not almost there. They counted the steeples of four churches, and their father presently showed them the Topham Academy, where their grandmother once went to school, and told them that perhaps some day they would go there too. Katy's heart gave a strange leap; it was such a tremendous thing to think of, but instantly the suggestion was transformed for her into one of the certainties of life. She looked with solemn awe at the tall belfry, and the long rows of windows in front of the academy, there where it stood high and white among the clustering trees. She hoped that they were going to drive by, but something forbade her taking the responsibility of saying so.

Soon the children found themselves among the crowded village houses. Their father turned to look at them with affectionate solicitude.

'Now sit up straight and appear pretty,' he whispered to them. 'We're among the best people now, an' I want folks to think well of you.'

'I guess we're just as good as they be,' remarked Susan Ellen, looking at some innocent passers-by with dark suspicion, but Katy tried indeed to sit straight, and folded her hands prettily in her lap, and wished with all her heart to be pleasing for her father's sake. Just then an elderly woman saw the wagon and the sedate party it carried, and smiled so kindly that it seemed to Katy as if Topham Corners had welcomed and received them. She smiled back again as if this hospitable person were an old friend, and entirely forgot that the eyes of all Topham had been upon her.

'There, now we're coming to an elegant house that I want you to see; you'll never forget it,' said John Hilton. 'It's where Judge Masterson lives, the great lawyer; the handsomest house in the county, everybody says.'

'Do you know him, father?' asked Susan Ellen.

'I do,' answered John Hilton, proudly. 'Him and my mother went to school together in their young days, and were always called the two best scholars of their time. The judge called to see her once; he stopped to our house to see her when I was a boy. An' then, some years ago — you've heard me tell how I was on the jury, an' when he heard my name spoken he looked at me sharp, and asked if I wa'n't the son of Catharine Winn, an' spoke most beautiful of your grandmother, an' how well he remembered their young days together.'

'I like to hear about that,' said Katy.

'She had it pretty hard, I'm afraid, up on the old farm. She was keepin' school in our district when father married her — that's the main reason I backed 'em down when they wanted to tear the old schoolhouse all to pieces,' confided John Hilton, turning eagerly. 'They all say she lived longer up here on the hill than she could anywhere, but she never had her health. I wa'n't but a boy when she died. Father an' me lived alone afterward till the time your mother come; 'twas a good while, too; I wa'n't married so young as some. 'Twas lonesome, I tell you; father was plumb discouraged losin' of his wife, an' her long sickness an' all set him back, an' we'd work all day on the land an' never say a word. I s'pose 'tis bein' so lonesome early in life that makes me so pleased to have some nice girls growin' up around me now.'

There was a tone in her father's voice that drew Katy's head toward him with new affection. She dimly understood, but Susan Ellen was less interested. They had often heard this story before, but to one child it was always new and to the other old. Susan Ellen was apt to think it tiresome to hear about her grandmother, who, being dead, was hardly worth talking about.

'There's Judge Masterson's place,' said their father in an everyday manner, as they turned a corner, and came into full view of the beautiful old white house standing behind its green trees and terraces and lawns. The children had never imagined anything so stately and fine, and even Susan Ellen exclaimed with pleasure. At that moment they saw an old gentleman, who carried himself with great dignity, coming slowly down the wide, box-bordered path toward the gate.

'There he is now, there's the judge!' whispered John Hilton, excitedly, reining his horse quickly to the green roadside. 'He's goin' downtown to his office; we can wait right here an' see him. I can't expect him to remember me; it's been a good many years. Now you are goin' to see the great Judge Masterson!'

There was a quiver of expectation in their hearts. The judge stopped at his gate, hesitating a moment before he lifted the latch, and glanced up the street at the country wagon with its two prim little girls on the back seat, and the eager man who drove. They seemed to be waiting for something; the old horse was nibbling at the fresh roadside grass. The judge was used to being looked at with interest, and responded now with a smile as he came out to the sidewalk, and unexpectedly turned their way. Then he suddenly lifted his hat with grave politeness, and came directly toward them.

'Good morning, Mr Hilton,' he said. 'I am very glad to see you, sir,' and Mr Hilton, the little girls' own father, took off his hat with equal courtesy, and bent forward to shake hands.

Susan Ellen cowered and wished herself away, but little Katy sat straighter than ever, with joy in her father's pride and pleasure shining in her pale, flowerlike little face.

'These are your daughters, I am sure,' said the old gentleman, kindly, taking Susan Ellen's limp and reluctant hand; but when he looked at Katy, his face brightened. 'How she recalls your mother!' he said with great feeling. 'I am glad to see this dear child. You must come to see me with your father, my dear,' he added, still looking at her. 'Bring both little girls, and let them run about the old garden; the cherries will soon be getting ripe,' said Judge Masterson, hospitably. 'Perhaps you will have time to stop this afternoon as you go home?'

'I should call it a great pleasure if you would come and see us again some time. You may be driving our way, sir,' said John Hilton.

'Not very often in these days,' answered the old judge. 'I thank you for the kind invitation. I should like to see the fine view again from your hill westward. Can I serve you in any way while you are in town? Good-bye, my little friends!'

Then they parted, but not before Katy, the shy Katy, whose hand the judge still held unconsciously while he spoke, had reached forward as he said good-bye and lifted her face to kiss him. She could not have told why, except that she felt drawn to something in the serious worn face. For the first time in her life the child had felt the charm of manners; perhaps she owned a kinship between that which made him what he was, and the spark of nobleness and unity in her own simple soul. She turned again and again to look back at him as they drove away.

'Now you have seen one of the first gentlemen in the country,' said their father. 'It was worth comin' twice as far—' But he did not say any more, nor turn as usual to look in the children's faces.

In the chief business street of Topham a great many country wagons like the Hiltons' were fastened to the posts, and there seemed to our holiday-makers to be a great deal of noise and excitement.

'Now I've got to do my errands, and we can let the horse rest and feed,' said John Hilton. 'I'll slip his headstall right off, an' put on his halter. I'm going to buy him a real good treat o' oats. First we'll go an' buy me my straw hat; I feel as if this one looked a little past to wear in Topham. We'll buy the things we want, an' then we'll walk all along the street, so you can look in the windows an' see the han'some things, same's your mother likes to. What was it mother told you about your shawls?'

'To take 'em off an' carry 'em over our arms,' piped Susan Ellen, without comment, but in the interest of alighting and finding themselves afoot upon the pavement the shawls were forgotten. The children stood in the doorway of a shop while their father went inside, and they tried to see what the

Topham shapes of bonnets were like, as their mother had advised them; but everything was exciting and confusing, and they could arrive at no decision. When Mr Hilton came out with a hat in his hand to be seen in a better light, Katy whispered that she wished he would buy a shiny one like Judge Masterson's; but her father only smiled and shook his head, and said that they were plain folks, he and Katy. There were dry-goods for sale in the same shop, and a young clerk who was measuring linen kindly pulled off some pretty labels with gilded edges and gay pictures, and gave them to the little girls, to their exceeding joy. He may have had small sisters at home, this friendly lad, for he took pains to find two pretty blue boxes besides, and was rewarded by their beaming gratitude.

It was a famous day; they even became used to seeing so many people pass. The village was full of its morning activity, and Susan Ellen gained a new respect for her father, and an increased sense of her own consequence, because even in Topham several persons knew him and called him familiarly by name. The meeting with an old man who had once been a neighbour seemed to give Mr Hilton the greatest pleasure. The old man called to them from a house doorway as they were passing, and they all went in. The children seated themselves wearily on the wooden step, but their father shook his old friend eagerly by the hand, and declared that he was delighted to see him so well and enjoying the fine weather.

'Oh, yes,' said the old man, in a feeble, quavering voice, 'I'm astonishin' well for my age. I don't complain, John, I don't complain.'

They talked long together of people whom they had known in the past, and Katy, being a little tired, was glad to rest, and sat still with her hands folded, looking about the front yard. There were some kinds of flowers that she never had seen before.

'This is the one that looks like my mother,' her father said, and touched Katy's shoulder to remind her to stand up and let herself be seen. 'Judge Masterson saw the resemblance; we met him at his gate this morning.'

'Yes, she certain does look like your mother, John,' said the old man, looking pleasantly at Katy, who found that she liked him better than at first. 'She does, certain; the best of young folks is, they remind us of the old ones. 'Tis nateral to cling to life, folks say, but for me, I git impatient at times. Most everybody's gone now, an' I want to be goin'. 'Tis somethin' before me, an' I want to have it over with. I want to be there 'long o' the rest o' the folks. I expect to last quite a while though; I may see ye couple o' times more, John.'

John Hilton responded cheerfully, and the children were urged to pick some flowers. The old man awed them with his impatience to be gone. There was such a townful of people about him and he seemed as lonely as if he were the last survivor of a former world. Until that moment they had felt as if everything was just beginning.

'Now I want to buy somethin' pretty for your mother,' said Mr Hilton, as they went soberly away down the street, the children keeping fast hold of his hands. 'By now the old horse will have eat his dinner and had a good rest, so pretty soon we can jog along home. I'm goin' to take you round by the academy, and the old North meeting-house where Dr Barstow used to preach. Can't you think o' somethin' that your mother 'd want?' he asked suddenly, confronted by a man's difficulty of choice.

'She was talkin' about wantin' a new pepper-box, one day; the top o' the old one won't stay on,' suggested Susan Ellen, with delightful readiness. 'Can't we have some candy, father?'

'Yes, ma'am,' said John Hilton, smiling and swinging her hand to and fro as they walked. 'I feel as if some would be good myself. What's all this?' They were passing a photographer's doorway with its enticing array of portraits. 'I do declare!' he exclaimed, excitedly, 'I'm goin' to have our pictures taken; 'twill please your mother more'n a little.'

This was perhaps, the greatest triumph of the day, except the delightful meeting with the judge; they sat in a row, with the father in the middle, and there was no doubt as to the excellence of the likeness. The best hats had to be taken off because they cast a shadow, but they were not missed, as their owners had feared. Both Susan Ellen and Katy looked their brightest and best; their eager young faces would forever shine there; the joy of the holiday was mirrored in the little picture. They did not know why their father was so pleased with it; they would not know until age had dowered them with the riches of association and remembrance.

Just at nightfall the Hiltons reached home again, tired out and happy. Katy had climbed over into the front seat beside her father, because that was always her place when they went to church on Sundays. It was a cool evening, there was a fresh sea wind that brought a light mist with it, and the sky was fast growing cloudy. Somehow the children looked different; it seemed to their mother as if they had grown older and taller since they went away in the morning, and as if they belonged to the town now as much as to the country. The greatness of their day's experience had left her far behind, the day had been silent and lonely without them, and she had had their supper ready, and been watching anxiously, ever since five o'clock. As for the children themselves they had little to say at first – they had eaten their luncheon early on the way to Topham. Susan Ellen was childishly cross, but Katy was pathetic and wan. They could hardly wait to show the picture, and their mother was as much pleased as everybody had expected.

'There, what did make you wear your shawls?' she exclaimed a moment afterward, reproachfully. 'You ain't been an' wore 'em all day long? I wanted folks to see how pretty your new dresses was, if I did make 'em. Well, well! I wish more'n ever now I'd gone an seen to ye!'

'An' here's the pepper-box!' said Katy, in a pleased, unconscious tone.

'That really is what I call beautiful,' said Mrs Hilton, after a long and doubtful look. 'Our other one was only tin. I never did look so high as a chiny one with flowers, but I can get us another any time for every day. That's a proper hat, as good as you could have got, John. Where's your new hoe?' she asked, as he came toward her from the barn, smiling with satisfaction.

'I declare to Moses if I didn't forget all about it,' meekly acknowledged the leader of the great excursion. 'That an' my yellow-turnip seed, too; they went clean out o' my head, there was so many other things to think of. But 'tain't no sort o' matter; I can get a hoe just as well to Ira Speed's.'

His wife could not help laughing. 'You an' the little girls have had a great time. They was full o' wonder to me about everythin', and I expect they'll talk about it for a week. I guess we was right about havin' 'em see somethin' more o' the world.'

'Yes,' answered John Hilton, with humility, 'yes, we did have a beautiful day. I didn't expect so much. They looked as nice as anybody, and appeared so modest an' pretty. The little girls will remember it perhaps by an' by. I guess they won't never forget this day they had 'long o' father.'

It was evening again, the frogs were piping in the lower meadows, and in the woods, higher up the great hill, a little owl began to hoot. The sea air, salt and heavy, was blowing in over the country at the end of the hot, bright day. A lamp was lighted in the house, the happy children were chatting together, and supper was waiting. The father and mother lingered for a moment outside and looked down over the shadowy fields; then they went in, without speaking. The great day was over, and they shut the door.

O. HENRY
1862-1910

The eventful and chequered life of William Sydney Porter, alias popular short story writer O. Henry, began in Greensboro, North Carolina in 1862. After a series of unsuccessful jobs, he went to Texas, where he worked on a ranch before becoming a bank clerk. Charged with embezzlement, O. Henry was imprisoned for three years during which time he wrote some of the stories later collected in his first published book, *Cabbages and Kings* (1904). Drawing on his wide range of experience, O. Henry's humorously ironic stories of conmen, hucksters, ranchhands and waitresses, became immensely popular overnight. An amazingly prolific writer, he produced over ten volumes of short stories in the hectic seven-year period before his death.

Of the stories included in this volume, 'Fox-in-the-Morning' first appeared in 1904 in *Cabbages and Kings*; the remaining stories, including 'The Gift of the Magi', which is widely regarded as a miniature masterpiece, are all from *The Four Million* (1906).

The Love-Philtre of Ikey Schoenstein

THE BLUE LIGHT DRUG STORE is downtown, between the Bowery and First Avenue, where the distance between the two streets is the shortest. The Blue Light does not consider that pharmacy is a thing of bric-à-brac, scent and ice-cream soda. If you ask it for pain-killer it will not give you a bonbon.

The Blue Light scorns the labor-saving arts of modern pharmacy. It macerates its opium and percolates its own laudanum and paregoric. To this day pills are made behind its tall prescription desk – pills rolled out on its own pill-tile, divided with a spatula, rolled with the finger and thumb, dusted with calcined magnesia and delivered in little round pasteboard pill-boxes. The store is on a corner about which coveys of ragged-plumed, hilarious children play and become candidates for the cough drops and soothing syrups that wait for them inside.

Ikey Schoenstein was the night clerk of the Blue Light and the friend of his customers. Thus it is on the East Side, where the heart of pharmacy is not glacé. There, as it should be, the druggist is a counsellor, a confessor, an adviser, an able and willing missionary and mentor whose learning is respected, whose occult wisdom is venerated and whose medicine is often poured, untasted, into the gutter. Therefore Ikey's corniform, bespectacled nose and narrow, knowledge-bowed figure was well known in the vicinity of the Blue Light, and his advice and notice were much desired.

Ikey roomed and breakfasted at Mrs Riddle's two squares away. Mrs Riddle had a daughter named Rosy. The circumlocution has been in vain – you must have guessed it – Ikey adored Rosy. She tinctured all his thoughts; she was the compound extract of all that was chemically pure and officinal – the dispensatory contained nothing equal to her. But Ikey was timid, and his hopes remained insoluble in the menstruum of his backwardness and fears. Behind his counter he was a superior being, calmly conscious of special knowledge and worth; outside he was a weak-kneed, purblind, motorman-cursed rambler, with ill-fitting clothes stained with chemicals and smelling of socotrine aloes and valerianate of ammonia.

The fly in Ikey's ointment (thrice welcome, pat trope!) was Chunk McGowan.

Mr McGowan was also striving to catch the bright smiles tossed about by Rosy. But he was no out-fielder as Ikey was; he picked them off the bat. At the same time he was Ikey's friend and customer, and often dropped in at the Blue Light Drug Store to have a bruise painted with iodine or get a cut rubber-plastered after a pleasant evening spent along the Bowery.

One afternoon McGowan drifted in in his silent, easy way, and sat, comely, smooth-faced, hard, indomitable, good-natured, upon a stool.

'Ikey,' said he, when his friend had fetched his mortar and sat opposite,

453

grinding gum benzoin to a powder, 'get busy with your ear. It's drugs for me if you've got the line I need.'

Ikey scanned the countenance of Mr McGowan for the usual evidence of conflict, but found none.

'Take your coat off,' he ordered. 'I guess already that you have been stuck in the ribs with a knife. I have many times told you those Dagoes would do you up.'

Mr McGowan smiled. 'Not them,' he said. 'Not any Dagoes. But you've located the diagnosis all right enough – it's under my coat, near the ribs. Say! Ikey – Rosy and me are goin' to run away and get married tonight.'

Ikey's left forefinger was doubled over the edge of the mortar, holding it steady. He gave it a wild rap with the pestle, but felt it not. Meanwhile Mr McGowan's smile faded to a look of perplexed gloom.

'That is,' he continued, 'if she keeps in the notion until the time comes. We've been layin' pipes for the getaway for two weeks. One day she says she will; the same evenin' she says nixy. We've agreed on tonight, and Rosy's stuck to the affirmative this time for two whole days. But it's five hours yet till the time, and I'm afraid she'll stand me up when it comes to the scratch.'

'You said you wanted drugs,' remarked Ikey.

Mr McGowan looked ill at ease and harassed – a condition opposed to his usual line of demeanor. He made a patent-medicine almanac into a roll and fitted it with unprofitable carefulness about his finger.

'I wouldn't have this double handicap make a false start tonight for a million,' he said. 'I've got a little flat up in Harlem all ready, with chrysanthemums on the table and a kettle ready to boil. And I've engaged a pulpit pounder to be ready at his house for us at 9.30. It's got to come off. And if Rosy don't change her mind again!' – Mr McGowan ceased, a prey to his doubts.

'I don't see then yet,' said Ikey, shortly, 'what makes it that you talk of drugs, or what I can be doing about it.'

'Old man Riddle don't like me a little bit,' went on the uneasy suitor, bent upon marshalling his arguments. 'For a week he hasn't let Rosy step outside the door with me. If it wasn't for losin' a boarder they'd have bounced me long ago. I'm makin' $20 a week and she'll never regret flyin' the coop with Chunk McGowan.'

'You will excuse me, Chunk,' said Ikey. 'I must make a prescription that is to be called for soon.'

'Say,' said McGowan, looking up suddenly, 'say, Ikey, ain't there a drug of some kind – some kind of powders that'll make a girl like you better if you give 'em to her?'

Ikey's lip beneath his nose curled with the scorn of superior enlightenment; but before he could answer, McGowan continued:

'Tim Lacy told me he got some once from a croaker uptown and fed 'em to his girl in soda water. From the very first dose he was ace-high and everybody else looked like thirty cents to her. They was married in less than two weeks.'

Strong and simple was Chunk McGowan. A better reader of men than Ikey was could have seen that his tough frame was strung upon fine wires. Like a good general who was about to invade the enemy's territory he was seeking to guard every point against possible failure.

'I thought,' went on Chunk, hopefully, 'that if I had one of them powders to give Rosy when I see her at supper tonight it might brace her up and keep her from reneging on the proposition to skip. I guess she don't need a mule team to drag her away, but women are better at coaching than they are at running bases. If the stuff'll work just for a couple of hours it'll do the trick.'

'When is this foolishness of running away to be happening?' asked Ikey.

'Nine o'clock,' said Mr McGowan. 'Supper's at seven. At eight Rosy goes to bed with a headache, at nine old Parvenzano lets me through to his backyard, where there's a board off Riddle's fence, next door. I go under her window and help her down the fire-escape. We've got to make it early on the preacher's account. It's all dead easy if Rosy don't balk when the flag drops. Can you fix me one of them powders, Ikey?'

Ikey Schoenstein rubbed his nose slowly.

'Chunk,' said he, 'it is of drugs of that nature that pharmaceutists must have much carefulness. To you alone of my acquaintance would I intrust a powder like that. But for you I shall make it, and you shall see how it makes Rosy to think of you.'

Ikey went behind the prescription desk. There he crushed to a powder two soluble tablets, each containing a quarter of a grain of morphia. To them he added a little sugar of milk to increase the bulk, and folded the mixture neatly in a white paper. Taken by an adult this powder would insure several hours of heavy slumber without danger to the sleeper. This he handed to Chunk McGowan, telling him to administer it in a liquid if possible, and received the hearty thanks of the backyard Lochinvar.

The subtlety of Ikey's action becomes apparent upon recital of his subsequent move. He sent a messenger for Mr Riddle and disclosed the plans of Mr McGowan for eloping with Rosy. Mr Riddle was a stout man, brick-dusty of complexion and sudden in action.

'Much obliged,' he said, briefly, to Ikey. 'The lazy Irish loafer! My own room's just above Rosy's. I'll just go up there myself after supper and load the shot-gun and wait. If he comes in my backyard he'll go away in a ambulance instead of a bridal chaise.'

With Rosy held in the clutches of Morpheus for a many-hours deep slumber, and the blood-thirsty parent waiting, armed and forewarned, Ikey felt that his rival was close, indeed, upon discomfiture.

All night in the Blue Light Drug Store he waited at his duties for chance news of the tragedy, but none came.

At eight o'clock in the morning the day clerk arrived and Ikey started hurriedly for Mrs Riddle's to learn the outcome. And, lo! as he stepped out of the store who but Chunk McGowan sprang from a passing street car and grasped his hand – Chunk McGowan with a victor's smile and flushed with joy.

'Pulled it off,' said Chunk with Elysium in his grin. 'Rosy hit the fire-escape on time to a second, and we was under the wire at the Reverend's at 9.30¼. She's up at the flat – she cooked eggs this mornin' in a blue kimono – Lord! how lucky I am! You must pace up some day, Ikey, and feed with us. I've got a job down near the bridge, and that's where I'm heading for now.'

'The – the – powder?' stammered Ikey.

'Oh, that stuff you gave me!' said Chunk, broadening his grin; 'well, it was this way. I sat down at the supper table last night at Riddle's, and I looked at

Rosy, and I says to myself, "Chunk, if you get the girl get her on the square –
don't try any hocus-pocus with a thoroughbred like her." And I keeps the
paper you give me in my pocket. And then my lamps fall on another party
present, who, I says to myself, is failin' in a proper affection toward his
comin' son-in-law, so I watches my chance and dumps that powder in old
man Riddle's coffee – see?'

The Gift of the Magi

ONE DOLLAR AND EIGHTY-SEVEN CENTS. That was all. And sixty cents of it was in pennies. Pennies saved one and two at a time by bulldozing the grocer and the vegetable man and the butcher until one's cheeks burned with the silent imputation of parsimony that such close dealing implied. Three times Della counted it. One dollar and eighty-seven cents. And the next day would be Christmas.

There was clearly nothing to do but flop down on the shabby little couch and howl. So Della did it. Which instigates the moral reflection that life is made up of sobs, sniffles, and smiles, with sniffles predominating.

While the mistress of the home is gradually subsiding from the first stage to the second, take a look at the home. A furnished flat at $8 per week. It did not exactly beggar description, but it certainly had that word on the lookout for the mendicancy squad.

In the vestibule below was a letter-box into which no letter would go, and an electric button from which no mortal finger could coax a ring. Also appertaining thereunto was a card bearing the name 'Mr James Dillingham Young.'

The 'Dillingham' had been flung to the breeze during a former period of prosperity when its possessor was being paid $30 per week. Now, when the income was shrunk to $20, the letters of 'Dillingham' looked blurred, as though they were thinking seriously of contracting to a modest and unassuming D. But whenever Mr James Dillingham Young came home and reached his flat above he was called 'Jim' and greatly hugged by Mrs James Dillingham Young, already introduced to you as Della. Which is all very good.

Della finished her cry and attended to her cheeks with the powder rag. She stood by the window and looked out dully at a gray cat walking a gray fence in a gray backyard. Tomorrow would be Christmas Day, and she had only $1.87 with which to buy Jim a present. Her Jim. She had been saving every penny she could for months, with this result. Twenty dollars a week doesn't go far. Expenses had been greater than she had calculated. They always are. Only $1.87 to buy a present for Jim. Many a happy hour she had spent planning for something nice for him. Something fine and rare and sterling – something just a little bit near to being worthy of the honor of being owned by Jim.

There was a pier-glass between the windows of the room. Perhaps you have seen a pier-glass in an $8 flat. A very thin and very agile person may, by observing his reflection in a rapid sequence of longitudinal strips, obtain a fairly accurate conception of his looks. Della, being slender, had mastered the art.

Suddenly she whirled from the window and stood before the glass. Her eyes were shining brilliantly, but her face had lost it color within twenty seconds. Rapidly she pulled down her hair and let it fall to its full length.

Now, there were two possessions of the James Dillingham Youngs in which they both took a mighty pride. One was Jim's gold watch that had been his father's and his grandfather's. The other was Della's hair. Had the Queen of Sheba lived in the flat across the airshaft, Della would have let her hair hang out the window some day to dry just to depreciate Her Majesty's jewels and gifts. Had King Solomon been the janitor, with all his treasures piled up in the basement, Jim would have pulled out his watch every time he passed, just to see him pluck at his beard from envy.

So now Della's beautiful hair fell about her rippling and shining like a cascade of brown waves. It reached below her knee and made itself almost a garment for her. And then she did it up again nervously and quickly. Once she faltered for a minute and stood still while a tear or two splashed on the worn red carpet.

On went her old brown jacket; on went her old brown hat. With a whirl of skirts and with the brilliant sparkle still in her eyes, she fluttered out the door and down the stairs to the street.

Where she stopped the sign read: 'Mme. Sofronie. Hair Goods of All Kinds.' One flight up Della ran, and collected herself, panting. Madame, large, too white, chilly, hardly looked the 'Sofronie.'

'Will you buy my hair?' asked Della.

'I buy hair,' said Madame. 'Take yer hat off and let's have a sight at the looks of it.'

Down rippled the brown cascade.

'Twenty dollars,' said Madame, lifting the mass with a practised hand.

'Give it to me quick,' said Della.

Oh, and the next two hours tripped by on rosy wings. Forget the hashed metaphor. She was ransacking the stores for Jim's present.

She found it at last. It surely had been made for Jim and no one else. There was no other like it in any of the stores, and she had turned all of them inside out. It was a platinum fob chain simple and chaste in design, properly proclaiming its value by substance alone and not by meretricious ornamentation – as all good things should do. It was even worthy of The Watch. As soon as she saw it she knew that it must be Jim's. It was like him. Quietness and value – the description applied to both. Twenty-one dollars they took from her for it, and she hurried home with the 87 cents. With that chain on his watch Jim might be properly anxious about the time in any company. Grand as the watch was, he sometimes looked at it on the sly on account of the old leather strap that he used in place of a chain.

When Della reached home her intoxication gave way a little to prudence and reason. She got out her curling irons and lighted the gas and went to work repairing the ravages made by generosity added to love. Which is always a tremendous task, dear friends – a mammoth task.

Within forty minutes her head was covered with tiny, close-lying curls that made her look wonderfully like a truant schoolboy. She looked at her reflection in the mirror long, carefully, and critically.

'If Jim doesn't kill me,' she said to herself, 'before he takes a second look at me, he'll say I look like a Coney Island chorus girl. But what could I do – oh! what could I do with a dollar and eighty-seven cents?'

At 7 o'clock the coffee was made and the frying-pan was on the back of the stove hot and ready to cook the chops.

Jim was never late. Della doubled the fob chain in her hand and sat on the corner of the table near the door that he always entered. Then she heard his step on the stair away down on the first flight, and she turned white for just a moment. She had a habit of saying little silent prayers about the simplest everyday things, and now she whispered: 'Please God, make him think I am still pretty.'

The door opened and Jim stepped in and closed it. He looked thin and very serious. Poor fellow, he was only twenty-two – and to be burdened with a family! He needed a new overcoat and he was without gloves.

Jim stopped inside the door, as immovable as a setter at the scent of quail. His eyes were fixed upon Della, and there was an expression in them that she could not read, and it terrified her. It was not anger, nor surprise, nor disapproval, nor horror, nor any of the sentiments that she had been prepared for. He simply stared at her fixedly with that peculiar expression on his face.

Della wriggled off the table and went for him.

'Jim, darling,' she cried, 'don't look at me that way. I had my hair cut off and sold it because I couldn't have lived through Christmas without giving you a present. It'll grow out again – you won't mind, will you? I just had to do it. My hair grows awfully fast. "Merry Christmas!" Jim, and let's be happy. You don't know what a nice – what a beautiful, nice gift I've got for you.'

'You've cut off your hair?' asked Jim, laboriously, as if he had not arrived at that patent fact yet even after the hardest mental labor.

'Cut it off and sold it,' said Della. 'Don't you like me just as well, anyhow? I'm me without my hair, ain't I?'

Jim looked about the room curiously.

'You say your hair is gone?' he said, with an air almost of idiocy.

'You needn't look for it,' said Della. 'It's sold, I tell you – sold and gone, too. It's Christmas Eve, boy. Be good to me, for it went for you. Maybe the hairs on my head were numbered,' she went on with a sudden serious sweetness, 'but nobody could ever count my love for you. Shall I put the chops on, Jim?'

Out of his trance Jim seemed quickly to wake. He enfolded his Della. For ten seconds let us regard with discreet scrutiny some inconsequential object in the other direction. Eight dollars a week or a million a year – what is the difference? A mathematician or a wit would give you the wrong answer. The Magi brought valuable gifts, but that was not among them. This dark assertion will be illuminated later on.

Jim drew a package from his overcoat pocket and threw it upon the table.

'Don't make any mistake, Dell,' he said, 'about me. I don't think there's anything in the way of a haircut or a shave or a shampoo that could make me like my girl any less. But if you'll unwrap that package you may see why you had me going a while at first.'

White fingers and nimble tore at the string and paper. And then an ecstatic scream of joy; and then, alas! a quick feminine charge to hysterical tears and wails, necessitating the immediate employment of all the comforting powers of the lord of the flat.

For there lay The Combs – the set of combs, side and back, that Della had worshipped for long in a Broadway window. Beautiful combs, pure tortoise shell, with jewelled rims – just the shade to wear in the beautiful vanished hair. They were expensive combs, she knew, and her heart had simply craved and yearned over them without the least hope of possession. And now, they were hers, but the tresses that should have adorned the coveted adornments were gone.

But she hugged them to her bosom, and at length she was able to look up with dim eyes and smile and say: 'My hair grows so fast, Jim!'

And then Della leaped up like a little singed cat and cried, 'Oh, oh!'

Jim had not yet seen his beautiful present. She held it out to him eagerly upon her open palm. The dull precious metal seemed to flash with a reflection of her bright and ardent spirit.

'Isn't it a dandy, Jim? I hunted all over town to find it. You'll have to look at the time a hundred times a day now. Give me your watch. I want to see how it looks on it.'

Instead of obeying, Jim tumbled down on the couch and put his hands under the back of his head and smiled.

'Dell,' said he, 'let's put our Christmas presents away and keep 'em a while. They're too nice to use just at present. I sold the watch to get the money to buy your combs. And now suppose you put the chops on.'

The Magi, as you know, were wise men – wonderfully wise men – who brought gifts to the Babe in the manger. They invented the art of giving Christmas presents. Being wise, their gifts were no doubt wise ones, possibly bearing the privilege of exchange in case of duplication. And here I have lamely related to you the uneventful chronicle of two foolish children in a flat who most unwisely sacrificed for each other the greatest treasures of their house. But in a last word to the wise of these days let it be said that of all who give gifts these two were the wisest. Of all who give and receive gifts, such as they are wisest. Everywhere they are wisest. They are the Magi.

Tobin's Palm

TOBIN AND ME, THE TWO OF US, went down to Coney one day, for there was four dollars between us, and Tobin had need of distractions. For there was Katie Mahorner, his sweetheart, of County Sligo, lost since she started for America three months before with two hundred dollars, her own savings, and one hundred dollars from the sale of Tobin's inherited estate, a fine cottage and pig on the Bog Shannaugh. And since the letter that Tobin got saying that she had started to come to him not a bit of news had he heard or seen of Katie Mahorner. Tobin advertised in the papers, but nothing could be found of the colleen.

So, to Coney me and Tobin went, thinking that a turn at the chutes and the smell of the popcorn might raise the heart in his bosom. But Tobin was a hard-headed man, and the sadness stuck in his skin. He ground his teeth at the crying balloons; he cursed the moving pictures; and, though he would drink whenever asked, he scorned Punch and Judy, and was for licking the tintype men as they came.

So I gets him down a side way on a board walk where the attractions were some less violent. At a little six by eight stall Tobin halts, with a more human look in his eye.

' 'Tis here,' says he, 'I will be diverted. I'll have the palm of me hand investigated by the wonderful palmist of the Nile, and see if what is to be will be.'

Tobin was a believer in signs and the unnatural in nature. He possessed illegal convictions in his mind along the subjects of black cats, lucky numbers and the weather predictions in the papers.

We went into the enchanted chicken coop, which was fixed, mysterious with red cloth and pictures of hands with lines crossing 'em like a railroad centre. The sign over the door says it is Madame Zozo the Egyptian Palmist. There was a fat woman inside in a red jumper with pothooks and beasties embroidered upon it. Tobin gives her ten cents and extends one of his hands. She lifts Tobin's hand, which is own brother to the hoof of a drayhorse, and examines it to see whether 'tis a stone in the frog or a cast shoe he has come for.

'Man,' says this Madame Zozo, 'the line of your fate shows—'

' 'Tis not me foot at all,' says Tobin, interrupting. 'Sure, 'tis no beauty but ye hold the palm of me hand.'

'The line shows,' says the Madame, 'that ye've not arrived at your time of life without bad luck. And there's more to come. The mount of Venus – or is that a stone bruise? – shows that ye've been in love. There's been trouble in your life on account of your sweetheart.'

' 'Tis Katie Mahorner she has references with,' whispers Tobin to me in a loud voice to one side.

'I see,' says the palmist, 'a great deal of sorrow and tribulation with one whom ye cannot forget. I see the lines of designation point to the letter K and the letter M in her name.'

'Whist!' says Tobin to me; 'do ye hear that?'

'Look out,' goes on the palmist, 'for a dark man and a light woman; for they'll both bring ye trouble. Ye'll make a voyage upon the water very soon, and have a financial loss. I see one line that brings good luck. There's a man coming into your life who will fetch ye good fortune. Ye'll know him when ye see him by his crooked nose.'

'Is his name set down?' asks Tobin. ''Twill be convenient in the way of greeting when he backs up to dump off the good luck.'

'His name,' says the palmist, thoughtful looking, 'is not spelled out by the lines, but they indicate 'tis a long one, and the letter "o" should be in it. There's no more to tell. Good-evening. Don't block up the door.'

''Tis wonderful how she knows,' says Tobin as we walk to the pier.

As we squeezed through the gates a nigger man sticks his lighted segar against Tobin's ear, and there is trouble. Tobin hammers his neck, and the women squeal, and by presence of mind I drag the little man out of the way before the police comes. Tobin is always in an ugly mood when enjoying himself.

On the boat going back, when the man calls 'Who wants the good-looking waiter?' Tobin tried to plead guilty, feeling the desire to blow the foam off a crock of suds, but when he felt in his pocket he found himself discharged for lack of evidence. Somebody had disturbed his change during the commotion. So we sat, upon the stools, listening to the Dagoes fiddling on deck. If anything, Tobin was lower in spirits and less congenial with his misfortunes than when we started.

On a seat against the railing was a young woman dressed suitable for red automobiles, with hair the color of an unsmoked meerschaum. In passing by Tobin kicks her foot without intentions, and, being polite to ladies when in drink, he tries to give his hat a twist while apologizing. But he knocks it off, and the wind carries it overboard.

Tobin came back and sat down, and I began to look out for him, for the man's adversities were becoming frequent. He was apt, when pushed so close by hard luck, to kick the best dressed man he could see, and try to take command of the boat.

Presently Tobin grabs my arm and says, excited: 'Jawn,' says he, 'do ye know what we're doing? We're taking a voyage upon the water.'

'There now,' says I; 'subdue yeself. The boat'll land in ten minutes more.'

'Look,' says he, 'at the light lady upon the bench. And have ye forgotten the nigger man that burned me ear? And isn't the money I had gone – a dollar sixty-five it was?'

I thought he was no more than summing up his catastrophes so as to get violent with good excuse, as men will do, and I tried to make him understand such things was trifles.

'Listen,' says Tobin. 'Ye've no ear for the gift of prophecy or the miracles of the inspired. What did the palmist lady tell ye out of me hand? 'Tis coming true before your eyes. "Look out," says she, "for a dark man and a light woman; they'll bring ye trouble." Have ye forgot the nigger man, though he got some of it back from me fist? Can ye show me a lighter woman than the blonde lady that was. the cause of me hat falling in the water? And where's the dollar sixty-five I had in me vest when we left the shooting gallery?'

The way Tobin put it, it did seem to corroborate the art of prediction, though it looked to me that these accidents could happen to any one at Coney without the implication of palmistry.

Tobin got up and walked around on deck, looking close at the passengers out of his little red eyes. I asked him the interpretation of his movements. Ye never know what Tobin has in his mind until he begins to carry it out.

'Ye should know,' says he, 'I'm working out the salvation promised by the lines in me palm. I'm looking for the crooked-nosed man that's to bring the good luck. 'Tis all that will save us. Jawn, did ye ever see a straighter-nosed gang of hellions in the days of your life?'

'Twas the nine-thirty boat, and we landed and walked up-town through Twenty-second Street, Tobin being without his hat.

On a street corner, standing under a gas-light and looking over the elevated road at the moon, was a man. A long man he was, dressed decent, with a segar between his teeth, and I saw that his nose made two twists from bridge to end, like the wriggle of a snake. Tobin saw it at the same time, and I heard him breathe hard like a horse when you take the saddle off. He went straight up to the man, and I went with him.

'Good-night to ye,' Tobin says to the man. The man takes out a segar and passes the compliments, sociable.

'Would ye hand us your name,' asks Tobin, 'and let us look at the size of it? It may be our duty to become acquainted with ye.'

'My name,' says the man, polite, 'is Friedenhausman – Maximus G. Friedenhausman.'

'	'Tis the right length,' says Tobin. 'Do you spell it with an "o" anywhere down the stretch of it?'

'I do not,' says the man.

'*Can ye* spell it with an "o"?' inquires Tobin, turning anxious.

'If your conscience,' says the man with the nose, 'is indisposed toward foreign idioms ye might, to please yourself, smuggle the letter into the penultimate syllable.'

'	'Tis well,' says Tobin. 'Ye're in the presence of Jawn Malone and Daniel Tobin.'

'	'Tis highly appreciated,' says the man, with a bow. 'And now since I cannot conceive that ye would hold a spelling bee upon the street corner, will ye name some reasonable excuse for being at large?'

'By the two signs,' answers Tobin, trying to explain, 'which ye display according to the reading of the Egyptian palmist from the sole of me hand, ye've been nominated to offset with good luck the lines of trouble leading to the nigger man and the blonde lady with her feet crossed in the boat, besides the financial loss of a dollar sixty-five, all so far fulfilled according to Hoyle.'

The man stopped smoking and looked at me.

'Have ye any amendments,' he asks, 'to offer to that statement, or are ye one too? I thought by the looks of ye ye might have him in charge.'

'None,' says I to him, 'except that as one horseshoe resembles another so are ye the picture of good luck as predicted by the hand of me friend. If not, then the lines of Danny's hand may have been crossed, I don't know.'

'There's two of ye,' says the man with the nose, looking up and down for the sight of a policeman. 'I've enjoyed your company immense. Goodnight.'

With that he shoves his segar in his mouth and moves across the street, stepping fast. But Tobin sticks close to one side of him and me at the other.

'What!' says he, stopping on the opposite sidewalk and pushing back his hat; 'do ye follow me? I tell ye,' he says, very loud, 'I'm proud to have met ye. But it is my desire to be rid of ye. I am off to me home.'

'Do,' says Tobin, leaning against his sleeve. 'Do be off to your home. And I will sit at the door of it till ye come out in the morning. For the dependence is upon ye to obviate the curse of the nigger man and the blonde lady and the financial loss of the one-sixty-five.'

''Tis a strange hallucination,' says the man, turning to me as a more reasonable lunatic. 'Hadn't ye better get him home?'

'Listen, man,' says I to him. 'Daniel Tobin is as sensible as he ever was. Maybe he is a bit deranged on account of having drink enough to disturb but not enough to settle his wits, but he is no more than following out the legitimate path of his superstitions and predicaments, which I will explain to you.' With that I relates the facts about the palmist lady and how the finger of suspicion points to him as an instrument of good fortune. 'Now, understand,' I concludes, 'my position in this riot. I am the friend of me friend Tobin, according to me interpretations. 'Tis easy to be a friend to the prosperous, for it pays; 'tis not hard to be friend to the poor, for ye get puffed up by gratitude and have your picture printed standing in front of a tenement with a scuttle of coal and an orphan in each hand. But it strains the art of friendship to be true friend to a born fool. And that's what I'm doing,' says I, 'for, in my opinion, there's no fortune to be read from the palm of me hand that wasn't printed there with the handle of a pick. And, though ye've got the crookedest nose in New York City, I misdoubt that all the fortune-tellers doing business could milk good luck from ye. But the lines of Danny's hand pointed to ye fair, and I'll assist him to experiment with ye until he's convinced ye're dry.'

After that the man turns, sudden, to laughing. He leans against a corner and laughs considerable. Then he claps me and Tobin on the backs of us and takes us by an arm apiece.

''Tis my mistake,' says he. 'How could I be expecting anything so fine and wonderful to be turning the corner upon me? I came near being found unworthy. Hard by,' says he, 'is a café, snug and suitable for the entertainment of idiosyncrasies. Let us go there and have a drink while we discuss the unavailability of the categorical.'

So saying, he marched me and Tobin to the back room of a saloon, and ordered the drinks, and laid the money on the table. He looks at me and Tobin like brothers of his, and we have the segars.

'Ye must know,' says the man of destiny, 'that me walk in life is one that is called the literary. I wander abroad be night seeking idiosyncrasies in the masses and truth in the heavens above. When ye came upon me I was in contemplation of the elevated road in conjunction with the chief luminary of night. The rapid transit is poetry and art: the moon but a tedious, dry body, moving by rote. But these are private opinions, for, in the business of literature, the conditions are reversed. 'Tis me hope to be writing a book to explain the strange things I have discovered in life.'

'Ye will put me in a book,' says Tobin, disgusted; 'will ye put me in a book?'

'I will not,' says the man, 'for the covers will not hold ye. Not yet. The best I can do is to enjoy ye meself, for the time is not ripe for destroying the limitations of print. Ye would look fantastic in type. All alone by meself must I drink this cup of joy. But, I thank ye, boys; I am truly grateful.'

'The talk of ye,' says Tobin, blowing through his moustache and pounding the table with his fist, 'is an eyesore to me patience. There was good luck promised out of the crook of your nose, but ye bear fruit like a bag of a drum. Ye resemble, with your noise of books, the wind blowing through a crack. Sure, now, I would be thinking the palm of me hand lied but for the coming true of the nigger man and the blonde lady and—'

'Whist!' says the long man; 'would ye be led astray by physiognomy? Me nose will do what it can within bounds. Let us have these glasses filled again, for 'tis good to keep idiosyncrasies well moistened, they being subject to deterioration in a dry moral atmosphere.'

So, the man of literature makes good, to my notion, for he pays, cheerful, for everything, the capital of me and Tobin being exhausted by prediction. But Tobin is sore, and drinks quiet, with the red showing in his eye.

By and by we moved out, for 'twas eleven o'clock, and stands a bit upon the sidewalk. And then the man says he must be going home, and invites me and Tobin to walk that way. We arrives on a side street two blocks away where there is a stretch of brick houses with high stoops and iron fences. The man stops at one of them and looks up at the top windows which he finds dark.

''Tis me humble dwelling,' says he, 'and I begin to perceive by the signs that me wife has retired to slumber. Therefore I will venture a bit in the way of hospitality. 'Tis me wish that ye enter the basement room, where we dine, and partake of a reasonable refreshment. There will be some fine cold fowl and cheese and a bottle or two of ale. Ye will be welcome to enter and eat, for I am indebted to ye for diversions.'

The appetite and conscience of me and Tobin was congenial to the proposition, though 'twas sticking hard in Danny's superstitions to think that a few drinks and a cold lunch should represent the good fortune promised by the palm of his hand.

'Step down the steps,' says the man with the crooked nose, 'and I will enter by the door above and let ye in. I will ask the new girl we have in the kitchen,' says he, 'to make ye a pot of coffee to drink before ye go. 'Tis fine coffee Katie Mahorner makes for a green girl just landed three months. Step in,' says the man, 'and I'll send her down to ye.'

Springtime à la Carte

IT WAS A DAY IN MARCH.

Never, never begin a story this way when you write one. No opening could possibly be worse. It is unimaginative, flat dry, and likely to consist of mere wind. But in this instance it is allowable. For the following paragraph which should have inaugurated the narrative, is too wildly extravagant and preposterous to be flaunted in the face of the reader without preparation.

Sarah was crying over her bill of fare.

Think of a New York girl shedding tears on the menu card!

To account for this you will be allowed to guess that the lobsters were all out, or that she had sworn ice-cream off during Lent, or that she had ordered onions, or that she had just come from a Hackett matinée. And then, all these theories being wrong, you will please let the story proceed.

The gentleman who announced that the world was an oyster which he with his sword would open made a larger hit than he deserved. It is not difficult to open an oyster with a sword. But did you ever notice any one try to open the terrestrial bivalve with a typewriter? Like to wait for a dozen raw opened that way?

Sarah had managed to pry apart the shells with her unhandy weapon far enough to nibble a wee bit at the cold and clammy world within. She knew no more shorthand than if she had been a graduate in stenography just let slip upon the world by a business college. So, not being able to stenog, she could not enter that bright galaxy of office talent. She was a freelance typewriter and canvassed for odd jobs of copying.

The most brilliant and crowning feat of Sarah's battle with the world was the deal she made with Schulenberg's Home Restaurant. The restaurant was next door to the old red brick in which she hall-roomed. One evening after dining at Schulenberg's 40-cent, five-course *table d'hôte* (served as fast as you throw the five baseballs at the colored gentleman's head) Sarah took away with her the bill of fare. It was written in an almost unreadable script neither English nor German, and so arranged that if you were not careful you began with a toothpick and rice pudding and ended with soup and the day of the week.

The next day Sarah showed Schulenberg a neat card on which the menu was beautifully typewritten with the viands temptingly marshalled under their right and proper heads from 'hors d'oeuvre' to 'not responsible for over-coats and umbrellas.'

Schulenberg became a naturalized citizen on the spot. Before Sarah left him she had him willingly committed to an agreement. She was to furnish typewritten bills of fare for the twenty-one tables in the restaurant – a new bill for each day's dinner, and new ones for breakfast and lunch as often as changes occurred in the food or as neatness required.

In return for this Schulenberg was to send three meals per diem to Sarah's hall room by a waiter – an obsequious one if possible – and furnish her each afternoon with a pencil draft of what Fate had in store for Schulenberg's customers on the morrow.

Mutual satisfaction resulted from the agreement. Schulenberg's patrons now knew what the food they ate was called even if its nature sometimes puzzled them. And Sarah had food during a cold, dull winter, which was the main thing with her.

And then the almanac lied, and said that spring had come. Spring comes when it comes. The frozen snows of January still lay adamant in the cross-town streets. The hand-organs still played 'In the Good Old Summer-time,' with their December vivacity and expression. Men began to make thirty-day notes to buy Easter dresses. Janitors shut off steam. And when these things happen one may know that the city is still in the clutches of winter.

One afternoon Sarah shivered in her elegant hall bedroom; 'house heated; scrupulously clean; conveniences; seen to be appreciated.' She had no work to do except Schulenberg's menu cards. Sarah sat in her squeaky willow rocker, and looked out the window. The calendar on the wall kept crying to her: 'Springtime is here, Sarah – springtime is here, I tell you. Look at me, Sarah, my figures show it. You've got a neat figure yourself, Sarah – a – nice springtime figure – why do you look out the window so sadly?'

Sarah's room was at the back of the house. Looking out the window she could see the windowless rear brick wall of the box factory on the next street. But the wall was clearest crystal; and Sarah was looking down a grassy lane shaded with cherry trees and elms and bordered with raspberry bushes and Cherokee roses.

Spring's real harbingers are too subtle for the eye and ear. Some must have the flowering crocus, the wood-starring dogwood, the voice of bluebird – even so gross a reminder as the farewell handshake of the retiring buckwheat and oyster before they can welcome the Lady in Green to their dull bosoms. But to old earth's choicest kind there come straight, sweet messages from his newest bride, telling them they shall be no stepchildren unless they choose to be.

On the previous summer Sarah had gone into the country and loved a farmer.

(In writing your story never hark back thus. It is bad art, and cripples interest. Let it march, march.)

Sarah stayed two weeks at Sunnybrook Farm. There she learned to love old Farmer Franklin's son Walter. Farmers have been loved and wedded and turned out to grass in less time. But young Walter Franklin was a modern agriculturist. He had a telephone in his cow house, and he could figure up exactly what effect next year's Canada wheat crop would have on potatoes planted in the dark of the moon.

It was in this shaded and raspberried lane that Walter had wooed and won her. And together they had sat and woven a crown of dandelions for her hair. He had immoderately praised the effect of the yellow blossoms against her brown tresses; and she had left the chaplet there, and walked back to the house swinging her straw sailor in her hands.

They were to marry in the spring – at the very first signs of spring, Walter said. And Sarah came back to the city to pound her typewriter.

A knock at the door dispelled Sarah's vision of that happy day. A waiter had brought the rough pencil draft of the Home Restaurant's next day fare in old Schulenberg's angular hand.

Sarah sat down at her typewriter and slipped a card between the rollers. She was a nimble worker. Generally in an hour and a half the twenty-one menu cards were written and ready.

Today there were more changes on the bill of fare than usual. The soups were lighter; pork was eliminated from the entrées, figuring only with Russian turnips among the roasts. The gracious spirit of spring pervaded the entire menu. Lamb, that lately capered on the greening hillsides, was becoming exploited with the sauce that commemorated its gambols. The song of the oyster, though not silenced, was *dimuendo con amore*. The frying-pan seemed to be held, inactive, behind the beneficent bars of the broiler. The pie list swelled; the richer puddings had vanished; the sausage, with his drapery wrapped about him, barely lingered in a pleasant thanatopsis with the buckwheats and the sweet but doomed maple.

Sarah's fingers danced like midgets above a summer stream. Down through the courses she worked, giving each item its position according to its length with an accurate eye.

Just above the desserts came the list of vegetables. Carrots and peas, asparagus on toast, the perennial tomatoes and corn and succotash, lima beans, cabbage – and then—

Sarah was crying over her bill of fare. Tears from the depths of some divine despair rose in her heart and gathered to her eyes. Down went her head on the little typewriter stand; and the keyboard rattled a dry accompaniment to her moist sobs.

For she had received no letter from Walter in two weeks, and the next item on the bill of fare was dandelions – dandelions with some kind of egg – but bother the egg! – dandelions, with whose golden blooms Walter had crowned her his queen of love and future bride – dandelions, the harbingers of spring, her sorrow's crown of sorrow – reminder of her happiest days.

Madam, I dare you to smile until you suffer this test: Let the Marechal Niel roses that Percy brought you on the night you gave him your heart be served as a salad with French dressing before your eyes at a Schulenberg *table d'hôte*. Had Juliet so seen her love tokens dishonored the sooner would she have sought the Lethean herbs of the good apothecary.

But what witch is Spring! Into the great cold city of stone and iron a message had to be sent. There was none to convey it but the little hardy courier of the fields with his rough green coat and modest air. He is a true soldier of fortune, this *dent-de-lion* – this lion's tooth, as the French chefs call him. Flowered, he will assist at love-making, wreathed in my lady's nut-brown hair; young and callow and unblossomed, he goes into the boiling pot and delivers the word of his sovereign mistress.

By and by Sarah forced back her tears. The cards must be written. But, still in a faint, golden glow from her dandelion dream, she fingered the typewriter keys absently for a little while, with her mind and heart in the meadow lane with her young farmer. But soon she came swiftly back to the rock-bound lanes of Manhattan, and the typewriter began to rattle and jump like a strike-breaker's motor car.

At 6 o'clock the waiter brought her dinner and carried away the typewritten bill of fare. When Sarah ate she set aside, with a sigh, the dish of dandelions with its crowning ovarious accompaniment. As this dark mass had been transformed from a bright and love-indorsed flower to be an ignominious vegetable, so had her summer hopes wilted and perished. Love may, as Shakespeare said, feed on itself: but Sarah could not bring herself to eat the dandelions that had graced, as ornaments, the first spiritual banquet of her heart's true affection.

At 7.30 the couple in the next room began to quarrel: the man in the room above sought for A on his flute; the gas went a little lower; three coal wagons started to unload – the only sound of which the phonograph is jealous; cats on the back fences slowly retreated toward Mukden. By these signs Sarah knew that it was time for her to read. She got out 'The Cloister and the Hearth,' the best non-selling book of the month, settled her feet on her trunk, and began to wander with Gerard.

The front door bell rang. The landlady answered it. Sarah left Gerard and Denys treed by a bear and listened. Oh, yes; you would, just as she did!

And then a strong voice was heard in the hall below, and Sarah jumped for her door, leaving the book on the floor and the first round easily the bear's.

You have guessed it. She reached the top of the stairs just as her farmer came up, three at a jump, and reaped and garnered her, with nothing left for the gleaners.

'Why haven't you written – oh, why?' cried Sarah.

'New York is a pretty large town,' said Walter Franklin. 'I came in a week ago to your old address. I found that you went away on a Thursday. That consoled some; it eliminated the possible Friday bad luck. But it didn't prevent my hunting for you with police and otherwise ever since!'

'I wrote!' said Sarah, vehemently.

'Never got it!'

'Then how did you find me?'

The young farmer smiled a springtime smile.

'I dropped into that Home Restaurant next door this evening,' said he. 'I don't care who knows it; I like a dish of some kind of green at this time of the year. I ran my eye down that nice typewritten bill of fare looking for something in that line. When I got below cabbage I turned my chair over and hollered for the proprietor. He told me where you lived.'

'I remember,' sighed Sarah, happily. 'That was dandelions below cabbage.'

'I'd know that cranky capital W 'way above the line that your typewriter makes anywhere in the world,' said Franklin.

'Why, there's no W in dandelions,' said Sarah in surprise.

The young man drew the bill of fare from his pocket and pointed to a line.

Sarah recognized the first card she had typewritten that afternoon. There was still the rayed splotch in the upper right-hand corner where a tear had fallen. But over the spot where one should have read the name of the meadow plant, the clinging memory of the golden blossoms had allowed her fingers to strike strange keys.

Between the red cabbage and the stuffed green peppers was the item:

'DEAREST WALTER, WITH HARD-BOILED EGG.'

The Furnished Room

RESTLESS, SHIFTING, FUGACIOUS as time itself is a certain vast bulk of the population of the red brick district of the lower West Side. Homeless they have a hundred homes. They flit from furnished room to furnished room, transients forever – transients in abode, transients in heart and mind. They sing 'Home, Sweet Home' in ragtime; they carry their *lares et penates* in a bandbox; their vine is entwined about a picture hat; a rubber plant is their fig tree.

Hence the houses of this district, having had a thousand dwellers, should have a thousand tales to tell, mostly dull ones, no doubt; but it would be strange if there could not be found a ghost or two in the wake of all these vagrant guests.

One evening after dark a young man prowled among these crumbling red mansions, ringing their bells. At the twelfth he rested his lean hand-baggage upon the step and wiped the dust from his hatband and forehead. The bell sounded faint and far away in some remote, hollow depths.

To the door of this, the twelfth house whose bell he had rung, came a housekeeper who made him think of an unwholesome, surfeited worm that had eaten its nut to a hollow shell and now sought to fill the vacancy with edible lodgers.

He asked if there was a room to let.

'Come in,' said the housekeeper. Her voice came from her throat; her throat seemed lined with fur. 'I have the third-floor back, vacant since a week back. Should you wish to look at it?'

The young man followed her up the stairs. A faint light from no particular source mitigated the shadows of the halls. They trod noiselessly upon a stair carpet that its own loom would have forsworn. It seemed to have become vegetable; to have degenerated in that rank, sunless air to lush lichen or spreading moss that grew in patches to the stair-case and was viscid under the foot like organic matter. At each turn of the stairs were vacant niches in the wall. Perhaps plants had once been set within them. If so they had died in that foul and tainted air. It may be that statues of the saints had stood there, but it was not difficult to conceive that imps and devils had dragged them forth in the darkness and down to the unholy depths of some furnished pit below.

'This is the room,' said the housekeeper, from her furry throat. 'It's a nice room. It ain't often vacant. I had some most elegant people in it last summer – no trouble at all, and paid in advance to the minute. The water's at the end of the hall. Sprowls and Mooney kept it three months. They done a vaudeville sketch. Miss B'retta Sprowls – you may have heard of her – Oh, that was just the stage names – right there over the dresser is where the marriage certificate hung, framed. The gas is here, and you see there is plenty of closet room. It's a room everybody likes. It never stays idle long.'

'Do you have many theatrical people rooming here?' asked the young man.

'They comes and goes. A good proportion of my lodgers is connected with the theatres. Yes, sir, this is the theatrical district. Actor people never stays long anywhere. I get my share. Yes, they comes and they goes.'

He engaged the room, paying for a week in advance. He was tired, he said, and would take possession at once. He counted out the money. The room had been made ready, she said, even to towels and water. As the housekeeper moved away he put, for the thousandth time, the question that he carried at the end of his tongue.

'A young girl – Miss Vashner – Miss Eloise Vashner – do you remember such a one among your lodgers? She would be singing on the stage, most likely. A fair girl, of medium height and slender, with reddish, gold hair and dark mole near her left eyebrow.'

'No, I don't remember the name. Them stage people has names they change as often as their rooms. They comes and they goes. No, I don't call that one to mind.'

No. Always no. Five months of ceaseless interrogation and the inevitable negative. So much time spent by day in questioning managers, agents, schools and choruses; by night among the audiences of theatres from all-star casts down to music halls so low that he dreaded to find what he most hoped for. He who had loved her best had tried to find her. He was sure that since her disappearance from home this great, water-girt city held her somewhere, but it was like a monstrous quicksand, shifting its particles constantly, with no foundation, its upper granules of today buried tomorrow in ooze and slime.

The furnished room received its latest guest with a first glow of pseudo-hospitality, a hectic, haggard, perfunctory welcome like the specious smile of a demirep. The sophistical comfort came in reflected gleams from the decayed furniture, the ragged brocade upholstery of a couch and two chairs, a foot-wide cheap pier glass between the two windows, from one or two gilt picture frames and a brass bedstead in the corner.

The guest reclined, inert, upon a chair, while the room, confused in speech as though it were an apartment in Babel, tried to discourse to him of its divers tenantry.

A polychromatic rug like some brilliant-flowered, rectangular, tropical islet lay surrounded by a billowy sea of soiled matting. Upon the gay papered wall were those pictures that pursue the homeless one from house to house – The Huguenot Lovers, The First Quarrel, The Wedding Breakfast, Psyche at the Fountain. The mantel's chastely severe outline was ingloriously veiled behind some pert drapery drawn rakishly askew like the sashes of the Amazonian ballet. Upon it was some desolate flotsam cast aside by the room's marooned when a lucky sail had borne them to a fresh port – a trifling vase or two, pictures of actresses, a medicine bottle, some stray cards out of a deck.

One by one, as the characters of a cryptograph became explicit, the little signs left by the furnished rooms' procession of guests developed a significance. The threadbare space in the rug in front of the dresser told that lovely women had marched in the throng. The tiny fingerprints on the wall spoke of little prisoners trying to feel their way to sun and air. A splattered stain, raying like the shadow of a bursting bomb, witnessed where a hurled glass or bottle had splintered with its contents against the wall. Across the pier glass had been scrawled with a diamond in staggering letters the name 'Marie.' It seemed that the succession of dwellers in the furnished room had turned in fury – perhaps tempted beyond forbearance by its garish coldness – and wreaked upon it their passions. The furniture was chipped and bruised; the couch, distorted by bursting springs, seemed a horrible monster that had been slain during the stress of some grotesque convulsion. Some more potent unheaval had cloven a great slice from the marble mantel. Each plank in the floor owned its particular cant and shriek as from a separate and individual agony. It seemed incredible that all this malice and injury had been wrought upon the room by those who had called it for a time their home; and yet it may have been the cheated home instinct surviving blindly, the resentful rage at false household gods that had kindled their wrath. A hut that is our own we can sweep and adorn and cherish.

The young tenant in the chair allowed these thoughts to file, soft-shod, through his mind, while there drifted into the room furnished sounds and furnished scents. He heard in one room a tittering and incontinent, slack laughter; in others the monologue of a scold, the rattling of dice, a lullaby, and one crying dully; above him a banjo tinkled with spirit. Doors banged somewhere; the elevated trains roared intermittently; a cat yowled miserably upon a back fence. And he breathed the breath of the house – a dank savor rather than a smell – a cold, musty effluvium as from underground vaults mingled with the reeking exhalations of linoleum and mildewed and rotten woodwork.

Then suddenly, as he rested there, the room was filled with the strong, sweet odor of mignonette. It came as upon a single buffet of wind with such sureness and fragrance and emphasis that it almost seemed a living visitant. And the man cried aloud: 'What, dear?' as if he had been called, and sprang up and faced about. The rich odor clung to him and wrapped him around. He reached out his arms for it, all his senses for the time confused and commingled. How could one be peremptorily called by an odor? Surely it must have been a sound. But, was it not the sound that had touched, that had caressed him?

'She has been in this room,' he cried, and he sprang to wrest from it a token, for he knew he would recognize the smallest thing that had belonged to her or that she had touched. This enveloping scent of mignonette, the odor that she had loved and made her own – whence came it?

The room had been but carelessly set in order. Scattered upon the flimsy dresser scarf were half a dozen hairpins – those discreet, indistinguishable friends of womankind, feminine of gender, infinite of mood and uncommunicative of tense. These he ignored, conscious of their triumphant lack of identity. Ransacking the drawers of the dresser he came upon a discarded, tiny, ragged handkerchief. He pressed it to his face. It was racy and insolent with heliotrope; he hurled it to the floor. In another drawer he found odd buttons, a theatre programme, a pawnbroker's card, two lost marshmallows, a book on the divination of dreams. In the last was a woman's black satin hair bow, which halted him, poised between ice and fire. But the black satin hair bow also is femininity's demure, impersonal common ornament and tells no tales.

And then he traversed the room like a hound on the scent, skimming the walls, considering the corners of the bulging matting on his hands and knees, rummaging mantel and tables, the curtains and hangings, the drunken cabinet in the corner, for a visible sign, unable to perceive that she was there beside, around, against, within, above him, clinging to him, wooing him, calling him so poignantly through the finer senses that even his grosser ones became cognizant of the call. Once again he answered loudly: 'Yes, dear!' and turned, wild-eyed, to gaze on vacancy, for he could not yet discern form and color and love and outstretched arms in the odor of mignonette. Oh, God! whence that odor, and since when have odors had a voice to call? Thus he groped.

He burrowed in crevices and corners, and found corks and cigarettes. These he passed in passive contempt. But once he found in a fold of the matting a half-smoked cigar, and this he ground beneath his heel with a green and trenchant oath. He sifted the room from end to end. He found dreary and ignoble small records of many a peripatetic tenant; but of her whom he sought, and who may have lodged there, and whose spirit seemed to hover there, he found no trace.

And then he thought of the housekeeper.

He ran from the haunted room downstairs and to a door that showed a crack of light. She came out to his knock. He smothered his excitement as best he could.

'Will you tell me, madam,' be besought her, 'who occupied the room I have before I came?'

'Yes, sir. I can tell you again. 'Twas Sprowls and Mooney, as I said. Miss B'retta Sprowls it was in the theatres, but Missis Mooney she was. My house is well known for respectability. The marriage certificate hung, framed, on the nail over—'

'What kind of a lady was Miss Sprowls – in looks, I mean?'

'Why, black-haired, sir, short, and stout, with a comical face. They left a week ago Tuesday.'

'And before they occupied it?'

'Why, there was a single gentleman connected with the draying business. He left owing me a week. Before him was Missis Crowder and her two children, that stayed four months; and back of them was old Mr Doyle, whose sons paid for him. He kept the room six months. That goes back a year, sir, and further I do not remember.'

He thanked her and crept back to his room. The room was dead. The essence that had vivified it was gone. The perfume of mignonette had departed. In its place was the old, stale odor of mouldy house furniture, of atmosphere in storage.

The ebbing of his hope drained his faith. He sat staring at the yellow, singing gaslight. Soon he walked to the bed and began to tear the sheets into strips. With the blade of his knife he drove them tightly into every crevice around windows and door. When all was snug and taut he turned out the light, turned the gas full on again and laid himself gratefully upon the bed.

It was Mrs McCool's night to go with the can for beer. So she fetched it and sat with Mrs Purdy in one of those subterranean retreats where housekeepers forgather and the worm dieth seldom.

'I rented out my third-floor this evening,' said Mrs Purdy, across a fine circle of foam. 'A young man took it. He went up to bed two hours ago.'

'Now, did ye, Mrs Purdy, ma'am?' said Mrs McCool, with intense admiration. 'You do be a wonder for rentin' rooms of that kind. And did ye tell him, then?' she concluded in a husky whisper laden with mystery.

'Rooms,' said Mrs Purdy, in her furriest tones, 'are furnished for to rent. I did not tell him, Mrs McCool.'

''Tis right ye are, ma'am; 'tis by renting rooms we kape alive. Ye have the rale sense for business, ma'am. There be many people will rayjict the rentin' of a room if they be tould a suicide has been after dyin' in the bed of it.'

'As you say, we has our living to be making,' remarked Mrs Purdy.

'Yis, ma'am; 'tis true. 'Tis just one wake ago this day I helped ye lay out the third-floor-back. A pretty slip of a colleen she was to be killin' herself wid the gas – a swate little face she had, Mrs Purdy, ma'am.'

'She'd a-been called handsome, as you say,' said Mrs Purdy, assenting but critical, 'but for that mole she had a-growin' by her left eyebrow. Do fill up your glass again, Mrs McCool.'

'Fox-in-the-Morning'

CORALIO RECLINED, IN THE MIDDAY HEAT, like some vacuous beauty lounging in a guarded harem. The town lay at the sea's edge on a strip of alluvial coast. It was set like a little pearl in an emerald band. Behind it, and seeming almost to topple, imminent, above it, rose the sea-following range of the Cordilleras. In front the sea was spread, a smiling jailer, but even more incorruptible than the frowning mountains. The waves swished along the smooth beach; the parrots screamed in the orange and ceiba-trees; the palms waved their limber fronds foolishly like an awkward chorus at the prima donna's cue to enter.

Suddenly the town was full of excitement. A native boy dashed down a grass-grown street, shrieking: '*Busca el Señor* Goodwin. *Ha venido un telegrama por él!*'

The word passed quickly. Telegrams do not often come to anyone in Coralio. The cry of Señor Goodwin was taken up by a dozen officious voices. The main street running parallel to the beach became populated with those who desired to expedite the delivery of the despatch. Knots of women with complexions varying from palest olive to deepest brown gathered at street corners and plaintively carolled: '*Un telegrama por Señor* Goodwin!' The *comandante*, Don Señor el Coronel Encarnación Rios, who was loyal to the Ins and suspected Goodwin's devotion to the Outs, hissed: 'Aha!' and wrote in his secret memorandum book the accusive fact that Señor Goodwin had on that momentous date received a telegram.

In the midst of the hullabaloo a man stepped to the door of a small wooden building and looked out. Above the door was a sign that read 'Keogh and Clancy' – a nomenclature that seemed not to be indigenous to that tropical soil. The man in the door was Billy Keogh, scout of fortune and progress and latter-day rover of the Spanish Main. Tintypes and photographs were the weapons with which Keogh and Clancy were at that time assailing the hopeless shores. Outside the shop were set two large frames filled with specimens of their art and skill.

Keogh leaned in the doorway, his bold and humorous countenance wearing a look of interest at the unusual influx of life and sounded into the street. When the meaning of the disturbance became clear to him he placed a hand beside his mouth and shouted: 'Hey! Frank!' in such a robustious voice that the feeble clamor of the natives was drowned and silenced.

Fifty yards away, on the seaward side of the street, stood the abode of the consul for the United States. Out from the door of this building tumbled Goodwin at the call. He had been smoking with Willard Geddie, the consul, on the back porch of the consulate, which was conceded to be the coolest spot in Coralio.

475

'Hurry up,' shouted Keogh. 'There's a riot in town on account of a telegram that's come for you. You want to be careful about these things, my boy. It won't do to trifle with the feelings of the public this way. You'll be getting a pink note some day with violet scent on it; and then the country'll be steeped in the throes of a revolution.'

Goodwin had strolled up the street and met the boy with the message. The ox-eyed women gazed at him with shy admiration, for his type drew them. He was big, blond, and jauntily dressed in white linen, with buckskin *zapatos*. His manner was courtly, with a sort of kindly truculence in it tempered by a merciful eye. When the telegram had been delivered, and the bearer of it dismissed with a gratuity, the relieved populace returned to the contiguities of shade from which curiosity had drawn it – the women to their baking in the mud ovens under the orange-trees, or to the interminable combing of their long, straight hair; the men to their cigarettes and gossip in the cantinas.

Goodwin sat on Keogh's doorstep and read his telegram. It was from Bob Englehart, an American, who lived in San Mateo, the capital city of Anchuria, eighty miles in the interior. Englehart was a gold miner, an ardent revolutionist and 'good people.' That he was a man of resource and imagination was proven by the telegram he had sent. It had been his task to send a confidential message to his friend in Coralio. This could not have been accomplished in either Spanish or English, for the eye politic in Anchuria was an active one. The Ins and Outs were perpetually on their guard. But Englehart was a diplomatist. There existed but one code upon which he might make requisition with promise of safety – the great and potent code of Slang. So, here is the message that slipped, unconstrued, through the fingers of curious officials, and came to the eye of Goodwin:

His Nibs skedaddled yesterday per jack-rabbit line with all the coin in the kitty and the bundle of muslin he's spoony about. The boodle is six figures short. Our crowd in good shape, but we need the spondulicks. You collar it. The main guy and the dry goods are headed for the briny. You know what to do.

Bob

This screed, remarkable as it was, had no mystery for Goodwin. He was the most successful of the small advance-guard of speculative Americans that had invaded Anchuria, and he had not reached that enviable pinnacle without having well exercised the arts of foresight and deduction. He had taken up political intrigue as a matter of business. He was acute enough to wield a certain influence among the leading schemers, and he was prosperous enough to be able to purchase the respect of the petty office-holders. There was always a revolutionary party; and to it he had always allied himself; for the adherents of a new administration received the rewards of their labors. There was now a Liberal party seeking to overturn President Miraflores. If the wheel successfully revolved, Goodwin stood to win a concession to 30,000 manzanas of the finest coffee lands in the interior. Certain incidents in the recent career of President Miraflores had excited a shrewd suspicion in Goodwin's mind that the government was near a dissolution from another cause than that of a revolution, and now Englehart's telegram had come as a corroboration of his wisdom.

The telegram, which had remained unintelligible to the Anchurian linguists who had applied to it in vain their knowledge of Spanish and elemental English, conveyed a stimulating piece of news to Goodwin's understanding. It informed him that the president of the republic had decamped from the capital city with the contents of the treasury. Furthermore, that he was accompanied in his flight by that winning adventuress Isabel Guilbert, the opera singer, whose troupe of performers had been entertained by the president at San Mateo during the past month on a scale less modest than that with which royal visitors are often content. The reference to the 'jack rabbit line' could mean nothing else than the mule-back system of transport that prevailed between Coralio and the capital. The hint that the 'boodle' was 'six figures short' made the condition of the national treasury lamentably clear. Also it was convincingly true that the ingoing party – its way now made a pacific one – would need the 'spondulicks.' Unless its pledges should be fulfilled, and the spoils held for the delectation of the victors, precarious indeed would be the position of the new government. Therefore it was exceeding necessary to 'collar the main guy,' and recapture the sinews of war and government.

Goodwin handed the message to Keogh.

'Read that, Billy,' he said. 'It's from Bob Englehart. Can you manage the cipher?'

Keogh sat in the other half of the doorway, and carefully perused the telegram.

''Tis not a cipher,' he said, finally. ''Tis what they call literature, and that's a system of language put in the mouths of people that they've never been introduced to by writers of imagination. The magazines invented it, but I never knew before that President Norvin Green had stamped it with the seal of his approval. 'Tis now no longer literature, but language. The dictionaries tried, but they couldn't make it go for anything but dialect. Sure, now that the Western Union indorses it, it won't be long till a race of people will spring up that speaks it.'

'You're running too much to philology, Billy,' said Goodwin. 'Do you make out the meaning of it?'

'Sure,' replied the philosopher of Fortune. 'All languages come easy to the man who must know 'em. I've even failed to misunderstand an order to evacuate in classical Chinese when it was backed up by the muzzle of a breech-loader. This little literary essay I hold in my hands means a game of "Fox-in-the-Morning". Ever play that, Frank, when you was a kid?'

'I think so,' said Goodwin, laughing. 'You join hands all 'round, and—'

'You do not,' interrupted Keogh. 'You've got a fine sporting game mixed up in your head with "All Around the Rosebush." The spirit of "Fox-in-the-Morning" is opposed to the holding of hands. I'll tell you how it's played. This president man and his companion in play, they stand up over in San Mateo, ready for the run, and shout: "Fox-in-the-Morning!" Me and you, standing here, we say: "Goose and the Gander!" They say: "How many miles is it to London Town?" We say: "Only a few, if your legs are long enough. How many comes out?" They say: "More than you're able to catch." And then the game commences.'

'I catch the idea,' said Goodwin. 'It won't do to let the goose and gander slip through our fingers, Billy; their feathers are too valuable. Our crowd is prepared and able to step into the shoes of the government at once; but with the treasury empty we'd stay in power about as long as a tenderfoot would stick on an untamed bronco. We must play the fox on every foot of the coast to prevent their getting out of the country.'

'By the mule-back schedule,' said Keogh, 'it's five days down from San Mateo. We've got plenty of time to set out outposts. There's only three places on the coast where they can hope to sail from – here and Solitas and Alazan. They're the only points we'll have to guard. It's as easy as a chess problem – fox to play, and mate in three moves. Oh, goosey, goosey, gander, whither do you wander? By the blessing of the literary telegraph the boodle of this benighted fatherland shall be preserved to the honest political party that is seeking to overthrow it.'

The situation had been justly outlined by Keogh. The down trail from the capital was at all times a weary road to travel. A jiggety-joggety journey it was; ice-cold and hot, wet and dry. The trail climbed appalling mountains, wound like a rotten string about the brows of breathless precipices, plunged through chilling snow-fed streams, and wriggled like a snake through sunless forests teeming with menacing insect and animal life. After descending to the foothills it turned to a trident, the central prong ending at Alazan. Another branched off to Coralio; the third penetrated to Solitas. Between the sea and the foothills stretched the five miles' breadth of alluvial coast. Here was the flora of the tropics in its rankest and most prodigal growth. Spaces here and there had been wrested from the jungle and planted with bananas and cane and orange groves. The rest was a riot of wild vegetation, the home of monkeys, tapirs, jaguars, alligators and prodigious reptiles and insects. Where no road was cut a serpent could scarcely make its way through the tangle of vines and creepers. Across the treacherous mangrove swamps few things without wings could safely pass. Therefore the fugitives could hope to reach the coast only by one of the routes named.

'Keep the matter quiet, Billy,' advised Goodwin. 'We don't want the Ins to know that the president is in flight. I suppose Bob's information is something of a scoop in the capital as yet. Otherwise he would not have tried to make his message a confidential one; and besides, everybody would have heard the news. I'm going around now to see Dr Zavalla, and start a man up the trail to cut the telegraph wire.'

As Goodwin rose, Keogh threw his hat upon the grass by the door and expelled a tremendous sigh.

'What's the trouble, Billy?' asked Goodwin, pausing. 'That's the first time I ever heard you sigh.'

''Tis the last,' said Keogh. 'With that sorrowful puff of wind I resign myself to a life of praiseworthy but harassing honesty. What are tintypes, if you please, to the opportunities of the great and hilarious class of ganders and geese? Not that I would be president, Frank – and the boodle he's got is too big for me to handle – but in some ways I feel my conscience hurting me for addicting myself to photographing a nation instead of running away with it. Frank, did you ever see the "Bundle of muslin" that His Excellency has wrapped up and carried off?'

'Isabel Guilbert?' said Goodwin, laughing. 'No, I never did. From what

I've heard of her, though, I imagine that she wouldn't stick at anything to carry her point. Don't get romantic, Billy. Sometimes I begin to fear that there's Irish blood in your ancestry.'

'I never saw her either,' went on Keogh; 'but they say she's got all the ladies of mythology, sculpture, and fiction reduced to chromos. They say she can look at a man once, and he'll turn monkey and climb trees to pick cocoanuts for her. Think of that president man with Lord knows how many hundreds of thousands of dollars in one hand, and this muslin siren in the other, galloping down hill on a sympathetic mule amid song-birds and flowers! And here is Billy Keogh, because he is virtuous, condemned to the unprofitable swindle of slandering the faces of missing links on tin for an honest living! 'Tis an injustice of nature.'

'Cheer up,' said Goodwin. 'You are a pretty poor fox to be envying a gander. Maybe the enchanting Guilbert will take a fancy to you and your tintypes after we impoverish her royal escort.'

'She could do worse,' reflected Keogh; 'but she won't. 'Tis not a tintype gallery, but the gallery of the gods that she's fitted to adorn. She's a very wicked lady, and the president man is in luck. But I hear Clancy swearing in the back room for having to do all the work.' And Keogh plunged for the rear of the 'gallery,' whistling gaily in a spontaneous way that belied his recent sigh over the questionable good luck of the flying president.

Goodwin turned from the main street into a much narrower one that intersected it at a right angle.

These side streets were covered by a growth of thick, rank grass, which was kept to a navigable shortness by the machetes of the police. Stone sidewalks, little more than a ledge in width, ran along the base of the mean and monotonous adobe houses. At the outskirts of the village these streets dwindled to nothing; and here were set the palm-thatched huts of the Caribs and the poorer natives, and the shabby cabins of negroes from Jamaica and the West India islands. A few structures raised their heads above the red-tiled roofs of the one-story houses – the bell tower of the *Calaboza*, the Hotel de los Estranjeros, the residence of the Vesuvius Fruit Company's agent, the store and residence of Bernard Brannigan, a ruined cathedral in which Columbus had once set foot, and, most imposing of all, the Casa Morena – the summer 'White House' of the President of Anchuria. On the principal street running along the beach – the Broadway of Coralio – were the larger stores, the government *bodega* and post-office, the *cuartel*, the rum-shops and the market place.

On his way Goodwin passed the house of Bernard Brannigan. It was a modern wooden building, two stories in height. The ground floor was occupied by Brannigan's store, the upper one contained the living apart-ments. A wide cool porch ran around the house half-way up its outer walls. A handsome, vivacious girl neatly dressed in flowering white leaned over the railing and smiled down upon Goodwin. She was no darker than many an Andalusian of high descent, and she sparkled and glowed like a tropical moonlight.

'Good evening, Miss Paula,' said Goodwin, taking off his hat, with his ready smile. There was little difference in his manner whether he addressed women or men. Everybody in Coralio like to receive the salutation of the big American.

'Is there any news, Mr Goodwin? Please don't say no. Isn't it warm? I feel just like Mariana in her moated grange – or was it a range? – it's hot enough.'

'No, there's no news to tell, I believe,' said Goodwin, with a mischievous look in his eye, 'except that old Geddie is getting grumpier and crosser every day. If something doesn't happen to relieve his mind I'll have to quit smoking on his back porch – and there's no other place available that is cool enough.'

'He isn't grumpy,' said Paula Brannigan, impulsively, 'when he—'

But she ceased suddenly, and drew back with a deepening color; for her mother had been a *mestizo* lady, and the Spanish blood had brought to Paula a certain shyness that was an adornment to the other half of her demonstrative nature.

EDITH
WHARTON
1862-1937

Edith Wharton (née Jones) was born in New York in 1862.
After her marriage in 1885, she published some short
stories and a novella, *The Touchstone*, before achieving
critical acclaim as a writer of genuine originality and charm
with her first novel *The Valley of Decision* (1902) and her
major work, *The House of Mirth* (1905).

Much influenced by Henry James, Edith Wharton's
precise and witty style enables her to create sharply
observed comedies of manners in miniature. The stories
which follow, all originally published in a collection
entitled *Crucial Instances* in 1901, display her clear, elegantly
disciplined and ironic narrative gifts at their best.

The Rembrandt

1

'YOU'RE *so* artistic,' my cousin Eleanor Copt began.

Of all Eleanor's exordiums it is the one I most dread. When she tells me I'm so clever I know this is merely the preamble to inviting me to meet the last literary obscurity of the moment: a trial to be evaded or endured, as circumstances dictate; whereas her calling me artistic fatally connotes the request to visit, in her company, some distressed gentlewoman whose future hangs on my valuation of her old Saxe or of her grandfather's Marc Antonios. Time was when I attempted to resist these compulsions of Eleanor's; but I soon learned that, short of actual flight, there was no refuge from her beneficent despotism. It is not always easy for the curator of a museum to abandon his post on the plea of escaping a pretty cousin's importunities; and Eleanor, aware of my predicament, is none too magnanimous to take advantage of it. Magnanimity is, in fact, not in Eleanor's line. The virtues, she once explained to me, are like bonnets: the very ones that look best on other people may not happen to suit one's own particular style; and she added, with a slight deflection of metaphor, that none of the ready-made virtues ever *had* fitted her: they all pinched somewhere, and she'd given up trying to wear them.

Therefore when she said to me, 'You're *so* artistic,' emphasizing the conjunction with a tap of her dripping umbrella (Eleanor is out in all weathers: the elements are as powerless against her as man), I merely stipulated, 'It's not old Saxe again?'

She shook her head reassuringly. 'A picture – a Rembrandt!'

'Good Lord! Why not a Leonardo?'

'Well' – she smiled – 'that, of course, depends on *you*.'

'On me?'

'On your attribution. I dare say Mrs Fontage would consent to the change – though she's very conservative.'

A gleam of hope came to me and I pronounced: 'One can't judge of a picture in this weather.'

'Of course not. I'm coming for you tomorrow.'

'I've an engagement tomorrow.'

'I'll come before or after your engagement.'

The afternoon paper lay at my elbow and I contrived a furtive consultation of the weather-report. It said, 'Rain tomorrow,' and I answered briskly: 'All right, then; come at ten' – rapidly calculating that the clouds on which I counted might lift by noon.

My ingenuity failed of its due reward; for the heavens, as if in league with my cousin, emptied themselves before morning, and punctually at ten Eleanor and the sun appeared together in my office.

I hardly listened, as we descended the Museum steps and got into Eleanor's hansom, to her vivid summing-up of the case. I guessed beforehand that the lady we were about to visit had lapsed by the most distressful degrees from opulence to a 'hall-bedroom'; that her grandfather, if he had not been Minister to France, had signed the Declaration of Independence; that the Rembrandt was an heirloom, sole remnant of disbanded treasures; that for years its possessor had been unwilling to part with it, and that even now the question of its disposal must be approached with the most diplomatic obliquity.

Previous experience had taught me that all Eleanor's 'cases' presented a harrowing similarity of detail. No circumstance tending to excite the spectator's sympathy and involve his action was omitted from the history of her beneficiaries; the lights and shades were indeed so skilfully adjusted that any impartial expression of opinion took on the hue of cruelty. I could have produced closetfuls of 'heirlooms' in attestation of this fact; for it is one more mark of Eleanor's competence that her friends usually pay the interest on her philanthropy. My one hope was that in this case the object, being a picture, might reasonably be rated beyond my means; and as our cab drew up before a blistered brown-stone door-step I formed the self-defensive resolve to place an extreme valuation on Mrs Fontage's Rembrandt. It is Eleanor's fault if she is sometimes fought with her own weapons.

The house stood in one of those shabby provisional-looking New York streets that seem resignedly awaiting demolition. It was the kind of house that, in its high days, must have had a bow-window with a bronze in it. The bow-window had been replaced by a plumber's *devanture*, and one might conceive the bronze to have gravitated to the limbo where Mexican onyx tables and bric-à-brac in buffalo horn await the first signs of our next æsthetic reaction.

Eleanor swept me through a hall that smelled of poverty, up unlit stairs to a bare slit of a room. 'And she must leave this in a month!' she whispered across her knock.

I had prepared myself for the limp widow's weed of a woman that one figures in such a setting; and confronted abruptly with Mrs Fontage's white-haired erectness I had the disconcerting sense that I was somehow in her presence at my own solicitation. I instinctively charged Eleanor with this reversal of the situation; but a moment later I saw it must be ascribed to a something about Mrs Fontage that precluded the possibility of her asking any one a favour. It was not that she was of forbidding, or even majestic, demeanour; but that one guessed, under her aquiline prettiness, a dignity nervously on guard against the petty betrayal of her surroundings. The room was unconcealably poor; the little faded 'relics,' the high-stocked ancestral silhouettes, the steel engravings after Raphael and Correggio, grouped in a vain attempt to hide the most obvious stains on the wall-paper, served only to accentuate the contrast of a past evidently diversified by foreign travel and the enjoyment of the arts. Even Mrs Fontage's dress had the air of being a last expedient, the ultimate outcome of a much-taxed ingenuity in darning and turning. One felt that all the poor lady's barriers were falling save that of her impregnable manner.

To this manner I found myself conveying my appreciation of being admitted to a view of the Rembrandt.

Mrs Fontage's smile took my homage for granted. 'It is always,' she conceded, 'a privilege to be in the presence of the great masters.' Her slim wrinkled hand waved me to a dusky canvas near the window.

'It's *so* interesting, dear Mrs Fontage,' I heard Eleanor exclaiming, 'and my cousin will be able to tell you exactly—' Eleanor, in my presence, always admits that she knows nothing about art; but she gives the impression that this is merely because she hasn't had time to look into the matter – and has had me to do it for her.

Mrs Fontage seated herself without speaking, as though fearful that a breath might disturb my communion with the masterpiece. I felt that she thought Eleanor's reassuring ejaculations ill-timed; and in this I was of one mind with her; for the impossibility of telling her exactly what I thought of her Rembrandt had become clear to me at a glance.

My cousin's vivacities began to languish, and the silence seemed to shape itself into a receptacle for my verdict. I stepped back, affecting a more distant scrutiny; and as I did so my eye caught Mrs Fontage's profile. Her lids trembled slightly. I took refuge in the familiar expedient of asking the history of the picture, and she waved me brightly to a seat.

This was indeed a topic on which she could dilate. The Rembrandt, it appeared, had come into Mr Fontage's possession many years ago, while the young couple were on their wedding-tour, and under circumstances so romantic that she made no excuse for relating them in all their parenthetic fulness. The picture belonged to an old Belgian Countess of redundant quarterings, whom the extravagances of an ungovernable nephew had compelled to part with her possessions (in the most private manner) about the time of the Fontages' arrival. By a really remarkable coincidence, it happened that their courier (an exceptionally intelligent and superior man) was an old servant of the Countess's, and had thus been able to put them in the way of securing the Rembrandt under the very nose of an English Duke, whose agent had been sent to Brussels to negotiate for its purchase. Mrs Fontage could not recall the Duke's name, but he was a great collector, and had a famous Highland castle, where somebody had been murdered, and which she herself had visited (by moonlight) when she had travelled in Scotland as a girl. The episode had in short been one of the most interesting 'experiences' of a tour, almost chromo-lithographic in vivacity of impression; and they had always meant to go back to Brussels for the sake of re-living so picturesque a moment. Circumstances (of which the narrator's surroundings declare the nature) had persistently interfered with the projected return to Europe, and the picture had grown doubly valuable as representing the high-water mark of their artistic emotions. Mrs Fontage's moist eye caressed the canvas. 'There is only,' she added with a perceptible effort, 'one slight drawback: the picture is not signed. But for that the Countess, of course, would have sold it to a museum. All the connoisseurs who have seen it pronounce it an undoubted Rembrandt, in the artist's best manner; but the museums' – she arched her brows in smiling recognition of a well-known weakness – 'give the preference to signed examples—'

Mrs Fontage's words evoked so touching a vision of the young tourists of fifty years ago, entrusting to an accomplished and versatile courier the direction of their helpless zeal for art, that I lost sight for a moment of the point at issue. The old Belgian Countess, the wealthy Duke with a feudal castle in Scotland, Mrs Fontage's own maiden pilgrimage to Arthur's Seat and Holyrood, all the accessories of the *naïf* transaction, seemed a part of that vanished Europe to which our young race carried its indiscriminate ardours, its tender romantic credulity: the legendary castellated Europe of keepsakes, brigands and old masters, that compensated, by one such 'experience' as Mrs Fontage's, for an after-life of æsthetic privation.

I was restored to the present by Eleanor's looking at her watch. The action mutely conveyed that something was expected of me. I risked the temporizing statement that the picture was very interesting; but Mrs Fontage's polite assent revealed the poverty of the expedient. Eleanor's impatience overflowed.

'You would like my cousin to give you an idea of its value?' she suggested.

Mrs Fontage grew more erect. 'No one,' she corrected with great gentleness, 'can know its value quite as well as I, who live with it—'

We murmured our hasty concurrence.

'But it might be interesting to hear' – she addressed herself to me – 'as a mere matter of curiosity – what estimate would be put on it from the purely commercial point of view – if such a term may be used in speaking of a work of art.'

I sounded a note of deprecation.

'Oh, I understand, of course,' she delicately anticipated me, 'that that could never be *your* view, your personal view; but since occasions *may* arise – do arise – when it becomes necessary to – to put a price on the priceless, as it were – I have thought – Miss Copt has suggested—'

'Some day,' Eleanor encouraged her, 'you might feel that the picture ought to belong to some one who has more – more opportunity of showing it – letting it be seen by the public – for educational reasons—'

'I have tried,' Mrs Fontage admitted, 'to see it in that light.'

The crucial moment was upon me. To escape the challenge of Mrs Fontage's brilliant composure I turned once more to the picture. If my courage needed reinforcement, the picture amply furnished it. Looking at that lamentable canvas seemed the surest way of gathering strength to denounce it; but behind me, all the while, I felt Mrs Fontage's shuddering pride drawn up in a final effort of self-defence. I hated myself for my sentimental perversion of the situation. Reason argued that it was more cruel to deceive Mrs Fontage than to tell her the truth; but that merely proved the inferiority of reason to instinct in situations involving any concession to the emotions. Along with her faith in the Rembrandt I must destroy not only the whole fabric of Mrs Fontage's past, but even that life-long habit of acquiescence in untested formulas that makes the best part of the average feminine strength. I guessed the episode of the picture to be inextricably interwoven with the traditions and convictions which served to veil Mrs Fontage's destitution not only from others but from herself. Viewed in that light the Rembrandt had perhaps been worth its purchase-money; and I regretted that works of art do not commonly sell on the merit of the moral support they may have rendered.

From this unavailing flight I was recalled by the sense that something must be done. To place a fictitious value on the picture was at best a provisional measure; while the brutal alternative of advising Mrs Fontage to sell it for a hundred dollars at least afforded an opening to the charitably disposed purchaser. I intended, if other resources failed, to put myself forward in that light; but delicacy of course forbade my coupling my unflattering estimate of the Rembrandt with an immediate offer to buy it. All I could do was to inflict the wound: the healing unguent must be withheld for later application.

I turned to Mrs Fontage, who sat motionless, her finely-lined cheeks touched with an expectant colour, her eyes averted from the picture which was so evidently the one object they beheld.

'My dear madam—' I began. Her vivid smile was like a light held up to dazzle me. It shrouded every alternative in darkness, and I had the flurried sense of having lost my way among the intricacies of my contention. Of a sudden I felt the hopelessness of finding a crack in her impenetrable conviction. My words slipped from me like broken weapons. 'The picture,' I faltered, 'would of course be worth more if it were signed. As it is, I – I hardly think – on a conservative estimate – it can be valued at – at more – than – a thousand dollars, say—'

My deflected argument ran on somewhat aimlessly till it found itself plunging full tilt against the barrier of Mrs Fontage's silence. She sat as impassive as though I had not spoken. Eleanor loosed a few fluttering words of congratulation and encouragement, but their flight was suddenly cut short. Mrs Fontage had risen with a certain solemnity.

'I could never,' she said gently – her gentleness was adamantine – 'under any circumstance whatever, consider, for a moment even, the possibility of parting with the picture at such a price.'

2

Within three weeks a tremulous note from Mrs Fontage requested the favour of another visit. If the writing was tremulous, however, the writer's tone was firm. She named her own day and hour, without the conventional reference to her visitor's convenience.

My first impulse was to turn the note over to Eleanor. I had acquitted myself of my share in the ungrateful business of coming to Mrs Fontage's aid, and if, as her letter denoted, she had now yielded to the closer pressure of need, the business of finding a purchaser for the Rembrandt might well be left to my cousin's ingenuity. But here conscience put in the uncomfortable reminder that it was I who, in putting a price on the picture, had raised the real obstacle in the way of Mrs Fontage's rescue. No one would give a thousand dollars for the Rembrandt; but to tell Mrs Fontage so had become as unthinkable as murder. I had, in fact, on returning from my first inspection of the picture, refrained from imparting to Eleanor my opinion of its value. Eleanor is porous, and I knew that sooner or later the unnecessary truth would exude through the loose texture of her dissimulation. Not infrequently she thus creates the misery she alleviates; and I have sometimes suspected her of paining people in order that she might be sorry for them. I had, at all events, cut off retreat in Eleanor's direction; and the remaining alternative carried me straight to Mrs Fontage.

She received me with the same commanding sweetness. The room was even barer than before – I believe the carpet was gone – but her manner built up about her a palace to which I was welcomed with high state; and it was as a mere incident of the ceremony that I was presently made aware of her decision to sell the Rembrandt. My previous unsuccess in planning how to deal with Mrs Fontage had warned me to leave my farther course to chance; and I listened to her explanation with complete detachment. She had resolved to travel for her health; her doctor advised it, and as her absence might be indefinitely prolonged she had reluctantly decided to part with the picture in order to avoid the expense of storage and insurance. Her voice drooped at the admission, and she hurried on, detailing the vague itinerary of a journey that was to combine long-promised visits to impatient friends with various 'interesting opportunities' less definitely specified. The poor lady's skill in rearing a screen of verbiage about her enforced avowal had distracted me from my own share in that situation, and it was with dismay that I suddenly caught the drift of her assumptions. She expected me to buy the Rembrandt for the Museum; she had taken my previous valuation as a tentative bid, and when I came to my senses she was in the act of accepting my offer.

Had I had a thousand dollars of my own to dispose of, the bargain would have been concluded on the spot; but I was in the impossible position of being materially unable to buy the picture, and morally unable to tell her that it was not worth acquiring for the Museum.

I dashed into the first evasion in sight. I had no authority, I explained, to purchase pictures for the Museum without the consent of the Committee.

Mrs Fontage coped for a moment in silence with the incredible fact that I had rejected her offer; then she ventured, with a kind of pale precipitation: 'But I understood – Miss Copt tells me that you practically decide such matters for the Committee.' I could guess what the effort had cost her.

'My cousin is given to generalizations. My opinion may have some weight with the Committee—'

'Well then—' she timidly prompted.

'For that very reason I can't buy the picture.'

She said, with a drooping note, 'I don't understand.'

'Yet you told me,' I reminded her, 'that you knew museums didn't buy unsigned pictures.'

'Not for what they are worth! Every one knows that. But I – I understood – the price you named—' Her pride shuddered back from the abasement. 'It's a misunderstanding then,' she faltered.

To avoid looking at her, I glanced desperately at the Rembrandt. Could I—? But reason rejected the possibility. Even if the Committee had been blind – and they all *were* but Crozier – I simply shouldn't have dared to do it. I stood up, feeling that to cut the matter short was the only alleviation within reach.

Mrs Fontage had summoned her indomitable smile; but its brilliancy dropped, as I opened the door, like a candle blown out by a draught.

'If there's any one else – if you knew any one who would care to see the picture, I should be most happy—' She kept her eyes on me, and I saw that, in her case, it hurt less than to look at the Rembrandt. 'I shall have to leave here, you know,' she panted, 'if nobody cares to have it—'

3

That evening at my club I had just succeeded in losing sight of Mrs Fontage in the fumes of an excellent cigar, when a voice at my elbow evoked her harassing image.

'I want to talk to you,' the speaker said, 'about Mrs Fontage's Rembrandt.'

'There isn't any,' I was about to growl; but looking up I recognized the confiding countenance of Mr Jefferson Rose.

Mr Rose was known to me chiefly as a young man suffused with a vague enthusiasm for Virtue and my cousin Eleanor.

One glance at his glossy exterior conveyed the assurance that his morals were as immaculate as his complexion and his linen. Goodness exuded from his moist eye, his liquid voice, the warm damp pressure of his trustful hand. He had always struck me as one of the most uncomplicated organisms I had ever met. His ideas were as simple and inconsecutive as the propositions in a primer, and he spoke slowly, with a kind of uniformity of emphasis that made his words stand out like the raised type for the blind. An obvious incapacity for abstract conceptions made him peculiarly susceptible to the magic of generalization, and one felt he would have been at the mercy of any Cause that spelled itself with a capital letter. It was hard to explain how, with such a superabundance of merit, he managed to be a good fellow: I can only say that he performed the astonishing feat as naturally as he supported an invalid mother and two sisters on the slender salary of a banker's clerk. He sat down beside me with an air of bright expectancy.

'It's a remarkable picture, isn't it?' he said.

'You've seen it?'

'I've been so fortunate. Miss Copt was kind enough to get Mrs Fontage's permission; we went this afternoon.'

I inwardly wished that Eleanor had selected another victim; unless indeed the visit were part of the plan whereby some third person, better equipped for the cultivation of delusions, was to be made to think the Rembrandt remarkable. Knowing the limitations of Mr Rose's resources I began to wonder if he had any rich aunts.

'And her buying it in that way, too,' he went on with his limpid smile, 'from that old Countess in Brussels, makes it all the more interesting, doesn't it? Miss Copt tells me it's very seldom old pictures can be traced back for more than a generation. I suppose the fact of Mrs Fontage's knowing its history must add a good deal to its value?'

Uncertain as to his drift, I said: 'In her eyes it certainly appears to.'

Implications are lost on Mr Rose, who glowingly continued: 'That's the reason why I wanted to talk to you about it – to consult you. Miss Copt tells me you value it at a thousand dollars.'

There was no denying this, and I grunted a reluctant assent.

'Of course,' he went on earnestly, 'your valuation is based on the fact that the picture isn't signed – Mrs Fontage explained that; and it *does* make a difference, certainly. But the thing is – if the picture's really good – ought one to take advantage—? I mean – one can see that Mrs Fontage is in a tight place, and I wouldn't for the world—'

My astonished stare arrested him.

'*You* wouldn't—'

'I mean – you see, it's just this way'; he coughed and blushed: 'I can't give more than a thousand dollars myself – it's as big a sum as I can manage to scrape together – but before I make the offer I want to be sure I'm not standing in the way of her getting more money.'

My astonishment lapsed to dismay. 'You're going to buy the picture for a thousand dollars?'

His blush deepened. 'Why, yes. It sounds rather absurd, I suppose. It isn't much in my line, of course. I can see the picture's very beautiful, but I'm no judge – it isn't the kind of thing, naturally, that I could afford to go in for; but in this case I'm very glad to do what I can; the circumstances are so distressing; and knowing what you think of the picture I feel it's a pretty safe investment—'

'I don't think!' I blurted out.

'You—?'

'I don't think the picture's worth a thousand dollars; I don't think it's worth ten cents; I simply lied about it, that's all.'

Mr Rose looked as frightened as though I had charged him with the offence.

'Hang it, man, can't you see how it happened? I saw the poor woman's pride and happiness hung on her faith in that picture. I tried to make her understand that it was worthless – but she wouldn't; I tried to tell her so – but I couldn't. I behaved like a maudlin ass, but you shan't pay for my infernal bungling – you mustn't buy the picture.'

Mr Rose sat silent, tapping one glossy boot-tip with another. Suddenly he turned on me a glance of stored intelligence. 'But you know,' he said good-humouredly, 'I rather think I must.'

'You haven't – already?'

'Oh no; the offer's not made.'

'Well, then—'

His look gathered a brighter significance.

'But if the picture's worth nothing, nobody will buy it—'

I groaned.

'Except,' he continued, 'some fellow like me, who doesn't know anything. *I* think it's lovely, you know; I mean to hang it in my mother's sitting-room.' He rose and clasped my hand in his adhesive pressure. 'I'm awfully obliged to you for telling me this; but perhaps you won't mind my asking you not to mention our talk to Miss Copt? It might bother her, you know, to think the picture isn't exactly up to the mark; and it won't make a rap of difference to me.'

4

Mr Rose left me to a sleepless night. The next morning my resolve was formed, and it carried me straight to Mrs Fontage's. She answered my knock by stepping out on the landing, and as she shut the door behind her I caught a glimpse of her devastated interior. She mentioned, with a careful avoidance of the note of pathos on which our last conversation had closed, that she was preparing to leave that afternoon; and the trunks obstructing the threshold showed that her preparations were nearly complete. They were, I felt certain, the same trunks that, strapped behind a rattling vettura, had accompanied the bride and groom on that memorable voyage of discovery of which the booty had till recently adorned her walls; and there was a dim consolation in the thought that those early 'finds' in coral and Swiss wood-carving, in lava and alabaster, still lay behind the worn locks, in the security of worthlessness.

Mrs Fontage, on the landing, among her strapped and corded treasures, maintained the same air of stability that made it impossible, even under such conditions, to regard her flight as anything less dignified than a departure. It was the moral support of what she tacitly assumed that enabled me to set forth with proper deliberation the object of my visit; and she received my announcement with an absence of surprise that struck me as the very flower of tact. Under cover of these mutual assumptions the transaction was rapidly concluded; and it was not till the canvas passed into my hands that, as though the physical contact had unnerved her, Mrs Fontage suddenly faltered. 'It's the giving it up—' she stammered, disguising herself to the last; and I hastened away from the collapse of her splendid effrontery.

I need hardly point out that I had acted impulsively, and that reaction from the most honourable impulses is sometimes attended by moral perturbation. My motives had indeed been mixed enough to justify some uneasiness, but this was allayed by the instinctive feeling that it is more venial to defraud an institution than a man. Since Mrs Fontage had to be kept from starving by means not wholly defensible, it was better that the obligation should be borne by a rich institution than an impecunious youth. I doubt, in fact, if my scruples would have survived a night's sleep, had they not been complicated by some uncertainty as to my own future. It was true that, subject to the purely formal assent of the Committee, I had full power to buy for the Museum, and that the one member of the Committee likely to dispute my decision was opportunely travelling in Europe; but the picture once in place I must face the risk of any expert criticism to which chance might expose it. I dismissed this contingency for future study, stored the Rembrandt in the cellar of the Museum, and thanked Heaven that Crozier was abroad.

Six months later he strolled into my office. I had just concluded, under conditions of exceptional difficulty, and on terms unexpectedly benign, the purchase of the great Bartley Reynolds; and this circumstance, by relegating the matter of the Rembrandt to a lower stratum of consciousness, enabled me to welcome Crozier with unmixed pleasure. My security was enhanced by his appearance. His smile was charged with amiable reminiscences, and I inferred that his trip had put him in the humour to approve of everything, or at least to ignore what fell short of his approval. I had therefore no uneasiness in accepting his invitation to dine that evening. It is always pleasant to dine with Crozier, and never more so than when he is just back from Europe. His conversation gives even the food a flavour of the Café Anglais.

The repast was delightful, and it was not till we had finished a Camembert, which he must have brought over with him, that my host said, in a tone of after-dinner perfunctoriness: 'I see you've picked up a picture or two since I left.'

I assented. 'The Bartley Reynolds seemed too good an opportunity to miss, especially as the French Government was after it. I think we got it cheap—'

'*Connu, connu,*' said Crozier pleasantly. 'I know all about the Reynolds. It was the biggest kind of a haul, and I congratulate you. Best stroke of business we've done yet. But tell me about the other picture – the Rembrandt.'

'I never said it was a Rembrandt.' I could hardly have said why, but I felt distinctly annoyed with Crozier.

'Of course not. There's "Rembrandt" on the frame, but I saw you'd modified it to "Dutch School"; I apologize.' He paused, but I offered no explanation. 'What about it?' he went on. 'Where did you pick it up?' As he leaned to the flame of the cigar-lighter his face seemed ruddy with enjoyment.

'I got it for a song,' I said.

'A thousand, I think?'

'Have you seen it?' I asked abruptly.

'Went over the place this afternoon and found it in the cellar. Why hasn't it been hung, by the way?'

I paused a moment. 'I'm waiting—'

'To—?'

'To have it varnished.'

'Ah!' He leaned back and poured himself a second glass of Chartreuse. The smile he confided to its golden depths provoked me to challenge him with—

'What do you think of it?'

'The Rembrandt?' He lifted his eyes from the glass. 'Just what you do.'

'It isn't a Rembrandt.'

'I apologize again. You call it, I believe, a picture of the same period?'

'I'm uncertain of the period.'

'H'm.' He glanced appreciatively along his cigar. 'What are you certain of?'

'That it's a damned bad picture,' I said savagely.

He nodded. 'Just so. That's all we wanted to know.'

'*We?*'

'We – I – the Committee, in short. You see, my dear fellow, if you hadn't been certain it was a damned bad picture our position would have been a little awkward. As it is, my remaining duty – I ought to explain that in this matter I'm acting for the Committee – is as simple as it's agreeable.'

'I'll be hanged,' I burst out, 'if I understand one word you're saying!'

He fixed me with a kind of cruel joyousness. 'You will – you will,' he assured me; 'at least you'll begin to, when you hear that I've seen Miss Copt.'

'Miss Copt?'

'And that she has told me under what conditions the picture was bought.'

'She doesn't know anything about the conditions! That is,' I added, hastening to restrict the assertion, 'she doesn't know my opinion of the picture.' I thirsted for five minutes with Eleanor.

'Are you quite sure?' Crozier took me up. 'Mr Jefferson Rose does.'

'Ah – I see.'

'I thought you would,' he reminded me. 'As soon as I'd laid eyes on the Rembrandt – I beg your pardon! – I saw that it – well, required some explanation.'

'You might have come to me.'

'I meant to; but I happened to meet Miss Copt, whose encyclopaedic information has often before been of service to me. I always go to Miss Copt when I want to look up anything: and I found she knew all about the Rembrandt.'

'*All?*'

'Precisely. The knowledge was in fact causing her sleepness nights. Mr Rose, who was suffering from the same form of insomnia, had taken her into his confidence, and she, ultimately, took me into hers.'

'Of course!'

'I must ask you to do your cousin justice. She didn't speak till it became evident to her uncommonly quick perceptions that your buying the picture on its merits would have been infinitely worse for – for everybody – than your diverting a small portion of the Museum's funds to philanthropic uses. Then she told me the moving incident of Mr Rose. Good fellow, Rose. And the old lady's case was desperate. Somebody had to buy that picture.' I moved uneasily in my seat. 'Wait a moment, will you? I haven't finished my cigar. There's a little head of Il Fiammingo's that you haven't seen, by the way; I picked it up the other day in Parma. We'll go in and have a look at it presently. But meanwhile what I want to say is, that I've been charged in the most informal way to express to you the Committee's appreciation of your admirable promptness and energy in capturing the Bartley Reynolds. We shouldn't have got it at all if you hadn't been uncommonly wide-awake, and to get it at such a price is a double triumph. We'd have thought nothing of a few more thousands—'

'I don't see,' I impatiently interposed, 'that, as far as I'm concerned, that alters the case.'

'The case—?'

'Of Mrs Fontage's Rembrandt. I bought the picture because, as you say, the situation was desperate, and I couldn't raise a thousand myself. What I did was of course, indefensible; but the money shall be refunded tomorrow—'

Crozier raised a protesting hand. 'Don't interrupt me when I'm talking *ex cathedrâ*. The money's been refunded already. The fact is, the Museum has sold the Rembrandt.'

I stared at him wildly. 'Sold it? To whom?'

'Why – to the Committee. Hold on a bit, please. Won't you take another cigar? Then perhaps I can finish what I've got to say. Why, my dear fellow, the Committee's under no obligation to you – that's the way we look at it. I've investigated Mrs Fontage's case, and, well, the picture had to be bought. She's eating meat now, I believe, for the first time in a year. And they'd have turned her out into the street that very day, your cousin tells me. Something had to be done at once, and you've simply given a number of well-to-do and self-indulgent gentlemen the opportunity of performing, at very small individual expense, a meritorious action in the nick of time. That's the first thing I've got to thank you for. And then you'll remember, please, that I have the floor – that I'm still speaking for the Committee – and secondly, as a slight recognition of your services in securing the Bartley Reynolds at a very much lower figure than we were prepared to pay, we beg you – the Committee begs you – to accept the gift of Mrs Fontage's Rembrandt. Now we'll go in and look at that little head...'

The Moving Finger

1

THE NEWS OF MRS GRANCY's death came to me with the shock of an immense blunder – one of fate's most irretrievable acts of vandalism. It was as though all sorts of renovating forces had been checked by the clogging of that one wheel. Not that Mrs Grancy contributed any perceptible momentum to the social machine: her unique distinction was that of filling to perfection her special place in the world. So many people are like badly-composed statues, over-lapping their niches at one point and leaving them vacant at another. Mrs Grancy's niche was her husband's life; and if it be argued that the space was not large enough for its vacancy to leave a very big gap, I can only say that, at the last resort, such dimensions must be determined by finer instruments than any ready-made standard of utility. Ralph Grancy's was, in short, a kind of disembodied usefulness: one of those constructive influences that, instead of crystallizing into definite forms, remain as it were a medium for the development of clear thinking and fine feeling. He faithfully irrigated his own dusty patch of life, and the fruitful moisture stole far beyond his boundaries. If, to carry on the metaphor, Grancy's life was a sedulously cultivated enclosure, his wife was the flower he had planted in its midst – the embowering tree, rather, which gave him rest and shade at its foot and the wind of dreams in its upper branches.

We had all – his small but devoted band of followers – known a moment when it seemed likely that Grancy would fail us. We had watched him pitted against one stupid obstacle after another – ill-health, poverty, misunder-standing, and, worst of all for a man of his texture, his first wife's soft insidious egotism. We had seen him sinking under the leaden embrace of her affection like a swimmer in a drowning clutch; but just as we despaired he had always come to the surface again, blinded, panting, but striking out fiercely for the shore. When at last her death released him it became a question as to how much of the man she had carried with her. Left alone, he revealed numb withered patches, like a tree from which a parasite has been stripped. But gradually he began to put out new leaves; and when he met the lady who was to become his second wife – his one *real* wife, as his friends reckoned – the whole man burst into flower.

The second Mrs Grancy was past thirty when he married her, and it was clear that she had harvested that crop of middle joy which is rooted in young despair. But if she had lost the surface of eighteen she had kept its inner light; if her cheek lacked the gloss of immaturity her eyes were young with the stored youth of half a life-time. Grancy had first known her somewhere in the East – I believe she was the sister of one of our consuls out there – and when he brought her home to New York she came among us as a stranger. The

494

idea of Grancy's remarriage had been a shock to us all. After one such calcining most men would have kept out of the fire; but we agreed that he was predestined to sentimental blunders, and we awaited with resignation the embodiment of his latest mistake. Then Mrs Grancy came – and we understood. She was the most beautiful and the most complete of explanations. We shuffled our defeated omniscience out of sight, and gave it hasty burial under a prodigality of welcome. For the first time in years we had Grancy off our minds. 'He'll do something great now!' the least sanguine of us prophesied; and our sentimentalist emended: 'He *has* done it – in marrying her!'

It was Claydon, the portrait-painter, who risked this hyperbole; and who soon afterward, at the happy husband's request, prepared to defend it in a portrait of Mrs Grancy. We were all – even Claydon – ready to concede that Mrs Grancy's unwontedness was in some degree a matter of environment. Her graces were complementary, and it needed the mate's call to reveal the flash of colour beneath her neutral-tinted wings. But if she needed Grancy to interpret her, how much greater was the service she rendered him! Claydon professionally described her as the right frame for him; but if she defined she also enlarged, if she threw the whole into perspective she also cleared new ground, opened fresh vistas, reclaimed whole areas of activity that had run to waste under the harsh husbandry of privation. This interaction of sympathies was not without its visible expression. Claydon was not alone in maintaining that Grancy's presence – or indeed the mere mention of his name – had a perceptible effect on his wife's appearance. It was as though a light were shifted, a curtain drawn back, as though, to borrow another of Claydon's metaphors, Love the indefatigable artist were perpetually seeking a happier 'pose' for his model. In this interpretative light Mrs Grancy acquired the charm which makes some women's faces like a book of which the last page is never turned. There was always something new to read in her eyes. What Claydon read there – or at least such scattered hints of the ritual as reached him through the sanctuary doors – his portrait in due course declared to us. When the picture was exhibited it was at once acclaimed as his masterpiece; but the people who knew Mrs Grancy smiled and said it was flattered. Claydon, however, had not set out to paint *their* Mrs Grancy – or ours even – but Ralph's; and Ralph knew his own at a glance. At the first confrontation he saw that Claydon had understood. As for Mrs Grancy, when the finished picture was shown to her, she turned to the painter and said simply: 'Ah, you've done me facing the east!'

The picture, then, for all its value, seemed a mere incident in the unfolding of their double destiny, a footnote to the illuminated text of their lives. It was not till afterward that it acquired the significance of last words spoken on a threshold never to be recrossed. Grancy, a year after his marriage, had given up his town house and carried his bliss an hour's journey away, to a little place among the hills. His various duties and interests brought him frequently to New York, but we necessarily saw him less often than when his house had served as the rallying-point of kindred enthusiasms. It seemed a pity that such an influence should be withdrawn, but we all felt that his long arrears of happiness should be paid in whatever coin he chose. The distance from which the fortunate couple radiated warmth on us was not too great for friendship to traverse; and our conception of a glorified leisure took the form of Sundays spent in the Grancys' library, with its sedative rural outlook, and the portrait of Mrs Grancy illuminating its studious walls. The picture was at its best in that setting; and we used to accuse Claydon of visiting Mrs Grancy in order to see her portrait. He met this by declaring that the portrait *was* Mrs Grancy; and there were moments when the statement seemed unanswerable. One of us, indeed – I think it must have been the novelist – said that Claydon had been saved from falling in love with Mrs Grancy only by falling in love with his picture of her; and it was noticeable that he, to whom his finished work was no more than the shed husk of future effort, showed a perennial tenderness for this one achievement. We smiled afterward to think how often, when Mrs Grancy was in the room, her presence reflecting itself in our talk like a gleam of sky in the hurrying current, Claydon, averted from the real woman, would sit as it were listening to the picture. His attitude, at the time, seemed only a part of the unusualness of those picturesque afternoons, when the most familiar combinations of life underwent a magical change. Some human happiness is a landlocked lake; but the Grancys' was an open sea, stretching a buoyant and illimitable surface to the voyaging interests of life. There was room and to spare on those waters for all our separate ventures; and always, beyond the sunset, a mirage of the fortunate isles toward which our prows were bent.

2

It was in Rome that, three years later, I heard of her death. The notice said 'suddenly.' I was glad of that. I was glad too – basely perhaps – to be away from Grancy at a time when silence must have seemed obtuse and speech derisive.

I was still in Rome when, a few months afterward, he suddenly arrived there. He had been appointed Secretary of Legation at Constantinople, and was on the way to his post. He had taken the place, he said frankly, 'to get away.' Our relations with the Porte held out a prospect of hard work, and that, he explained, was what he needed. He could never be satisfied to sit down among the ruins. I saw that, like most of us in moments of extreme moral tension, he was playing a part, behaving as he thought it became a man to behave in the eye of disaster. The instinctive posture of grief is a shuffling compromise between defiance and prostration; and pride feels the need of striking a worthier attitude in face of such a foe. Grancy, by nature musing and retrospective, had chosen the *rôle* of the man of action, who answers blow for blow and opposes a mailed front to the thrusts of destiny; and the completeness of the equipment testified to his inner weakness. We talked only of what we were not thinking of, and parted, after a few days, with a sense of relief that proved the inadequacy of friendship to perform, in such cases, the office assigned to it by tradition.

Soon afterward my own work called me home, but Grancy remained several years in Europe. International diplomacy kept its promise of giving him work to do, and during the year in which he acted as *chargé d'affaires* he acquitted himself, under trying conditions, with conspicuous zeal and discretion. A political redistribution of matter removed him from office just as he had proved his usefulness to the Government; and the following summer I heard that he had come home and was down at his place in the country.

On my return to town I wrote him, and his reply came by the next post. He answered as it were in his natural voice, urging me to spend the following Sunday with him, and suggesting that I should bring down any of the old set who could be persuaded to join me. I thought this a good sign, and yet – shall I own it? – I was vaguely disappointed. Perhaps we are apt to feel that our friends' sorrows should be kept like those historic monuments from which the encroaching ivy is periodically removed.

That very evening at the club I ran across Claydon. I told him of Grancy's invitation, and proposed that we should go down together; but he pleaded an engagement. I was sorry, for I had always felt that he and I stood nearer Ralph than the others, and if the old Sundays were to be renewed, I should have preferred that we two should spend the first alone with him. I said as much to Claydon, and offered to fit my time to his; but he met this by a general refusal.

'I don't want to go to Grancy's,' he said bluntly. I waited a moment, but he appended no qualifying clause.

'You've seen him since he came back?' I finally ventured.

Claydon nodded.

'And he is so awfully bad?'

'Bad? No: he's all right.'

'All right? How can he be, unless he's changed beyond all recognition?'

'Oh, you'll recognize *him*,' said Claydon, with a puzzling deflection of emphasis.

His ambiguity was beginning to exasperate me, and I felt myself shut out from some knowledge to which I had as good a right as he.

'You've been down there already, I suppose?'

'Yes; I've been down there.'

'And you've done with each other – the partnership is dissolved?'

'Done with each other? I wish to God we had!' He rose nervously and tossed aside the review from which my approach had diverted him. 'Look here,' he said, standing before me, 'Ralph's the best fellow going, and there's nothing under Heaven I wouldn't do for him – short of going down there again.' And with that he walked out of the room.

Claydon was incalculable enough for me to read a dozen different meanings into his words; but none of my interpretations satisfied me. I determined, at any rate, to seek no farther for a companion; and the next Sunday I travelled down to Grancy's alone. He met me at the station, and I saw at once that he had changed since our last meeting. Then he had been in fighting array, but now if he and grief still housed together it was no longer as enemies. Physically, the transformation was as marked but less reassuring. If the spirit triumphed the body showed its scars. At five-and-forty he was grey and stooping, with the tired gait of an old man. His serenity, however, was not the resignation of age. I saw that he did not mean to drop out of the game. Almost immediately he began to speak of our old interests; not with an effort, as at our former meeting, but simply and naturally, in the tone of a man whose life has flowed back into its normal channels. I remembered, with a touch of self-reproach, how I had distrusted his reconstructive powers; but my admiration for his reserved force was now tinged by the sense that, after all, such happiness as his ought to have been paid with his last coin. The feeling grew as we neared the house, and I found how inextricably his wife was interwoven with my remembrance of the place: how the whole scene was but an extension of that vivid presence.

Within doors nothing was changed, and my hand would have dropped without surprise into her welcoming clasp. It was luncheon-time, and Grancy led me at once to the dining-room, where the walls, the furniture, the very plate and porcelain, seemed a mirror in which a moment since her face had been reflected. I wondered whether Grancy, under the recovered tranquillity of his smile, concealed the same sense of her nearness, saw perpetually between himself and the actual her bright unappeasable ghost. He spoke of her once or twice, in an easy incidental way, and her name seemed to hang in the air after he had uttered it like a chord that continues to vibrate. If he felt her presence it was evidently as an enveloping medium, the moral atmosphere in which he breathed. I had never before known how completely the dead may survive.

After luncheon we went for a long walk through the autumnal fields and woods, and dusk was falling when we re-entered the house. Grancy led the way to the library, where, at this hour, his wife had always welcomed us back to a bright fire and a cup of tea. The room faced the west, and held a clear light of its own after the rest of the house had grown dark. I remembered how young she had looked in this pale gold light, which irradiated her eyes and hair, or silhouetted her girlish outline as she passed before the windows. Of all the rooms the library was most peculiarly hers; and here I felt that her nearness might take visible shape. Then, all in a moment, as Grancy opened the door, the feeling vanished and a kind of resistance met me on the threshold. I looked about me. Was the room changed? Had some desecrating hand effaced the traces of her presence? No; here too the setting was undisturbed. My feet sank into the same deep-piled Daghestan; the book-shelves took the firelight on the same rows of rich subdued bindings; her armchair stood in its old place near the tea-table; and from the opposite wall her face confronted me.

Her face – but *was* it hers? I moved nearer and stood looking up at the portrait. Grancy's glance had followed mine, and I heard him move to my side.

'You see a change in it?' he said.

'What does it mean?' I asked.

'It means – that five years have passed.'

'Over *her*?'

'Why not? Look at me!' He pointed to his grey hair and furrowed temples. 'What do you think kept *her* so young? It was happiness! But now—' he looked up at her with infinite tenderness. 'I like her better so,' he said. 'It's what she would have wished.'

'Have wished?'

'That we should grow old together. Do you think she would have wanted to be left behind?'

I stood speechless, my gaze travelling from his worn grief-beaten features to the painted face above. It was not furrowed like his; but a veil of years seemed to have descended on it. The bright hair had lost its elasticity, the cheek its clearness, the brow its light: the whole woman had waned.

Grancy laid his hand on my arm. 'You don't like it?' he said sadly.

'Like it? I – I've lost her!' I burst out.

'And I've found her,' he answered.

'In *that*?' I cried with a reproachful gesture.

'Yes; in that.' He swung round on me almost defiantly. 'The other had become a sham, a lie! This is the way she would have looked – does look, I mean. Claydon ought to know, oughtn't he?'

I turned suddenly. 'Did Claydon do this for you?'

Grancy nodded.

'Since your return?'

'Yes. I sent for him after I'd been back a week—' He turned away and gave a thrust to the smouldering fire. I followed, glad to leave the picture behind me. Grancy threw himself into a chair near the hearth, so that the light fell on his sensitive, variable face. He leaned his head back, shading his eyes with his hand, and began to speak.

3

'You fellows knew enough of my early history to guess what my second marriage meant to me. I say guess, because no one could understand – really. I've always had a feminine streak in me, I suppose: the need of a pair of eyes that should see with me, of a pulse that should keep time with mine. Life is a big thing, of course; a magnificent spectacle; but I got so tired of looking at it alone! Still it's always good to live, and I had plenty of happiness – of the evolved kind. What I'd never had a taste of was the simple inconscient sort that one breathes in like the air...

'Well – I met her. It was like finding the climate in which I was meant to live. You know what she was – how indefinitely she multiplied one's points of contact with life, how she lit up the caverns and bridged the abysses! Well, I swear to you (though I suppose the sense of all that was latent in me) that what I used to think of on my way home at the end of the day was simply that when I opened this door she'd be sitting over there, with the lamplight falling in a particular way on one little curl in her neck ... When Claydon painted her he caught just the look she used to lift to mine when I came in – I've wondered, sometimes, at his knowing how she looked when she and I were alone.—How I rejoiced in that picture! I used to say to her, "You're my prisoner now – I shall never lose you. If you grew tired of me and left me you'd leave your real self there on the wall!" It was always one of our jokes that she was going to grow tired of me—

'Three years of it – and then she died. It was so sudden that there was no change, no diminution. It was as if she had suddenly become fixed, immovable, like her own portrait: as if time had ceased at its happiest hour, just as Claydon had thrown down his brush one day and said, "I can't do better than that."

'I went away, as you know, and stayed over there five years. I worked as hard as I knew how, and after the first black months a little light stole in on me. From thinking that she would have been interested in what I was doing I came to feel that she *was* interested – that she was there and that she knew.

I'm not talking any psychical jargon – I'm simply trying to express the sense I had that an influence so full, so abounding as hers, couldn't pass like a spring shower. We had so lived into each other's hearts and minds that the consciousness of what she would have thought and felt illuminated all I did. At first she used to come back shyly, tentatively, as though not sure of finding me; then she stayed longer and longer, till at last she became again the very air I breathed ... There were bad moments, of course, when her nearness mocked me with the loss of the real woman; but gradually the distinction between the two was effaced and the mere thought of her grew warm as flesh and blood.

'Then I came home. I landed in the morning and came straight down here. The thought of seeing her portrait possessed me, and my heart beat like a lover's as I opened the library door. It was in the afternoon and the room was full of light. It fell on her picture – the picture of a young and radiant woman. She smiled at me coldly across the distance that divided us. I had the feeling that she didn't even recognize me. And then I caught sight of myself in the mirror over there – a grey-haired broken man whom she had never known!

'For a week we two lived together – the strange woman and the strange man. I used to sit night after night and question her smiling face; but no answer ever came. What did she know of me, after all? We were irrevocably separated by the five years of life that lay between us. At times, as I sat here, I almost grew to hate her; for her presence had driven away my gentle ghost, the real wife who had wept, aged, struggled with me during those awful years ... It was the worst loneliness I've ever known. Then, gradually, I began to notice a look of sadness in the picture's eyes; a look that seemed to say: "Don't you see that *I* am lonely too?" And all at once it came over me how she would have hated to be left behind! I remembered her comparing life to a heavy book that could not be read with ease unless two people held it together; and I thought how impatiently her hand would' have turned the pages that divided us! – So the idea came to me: "It's the picture that stands between us; the picture that is dead, and not my wife. To sit in this room is to keep watch beside a corpse." As this feeling grew on me the portrait became like a beautiful mausoleum in which she had been buried alive: I could hear her beating against the painted walls and crying to me faintly for help ...

'One day I found I couldn't stand it any longer and I sent for Claydon. He came down and I told him what I'd been through, and what I wanted him to do. At first he refused point-blank to touch the picture. The next morning I went off for a long tramp, and when I came home I found him sitting here alone. He looked at me sharply for a moment, and then he said: "I've changed my mind; I'll do it." I arranged one of the north rooms as a studio, and he shut himself up there for a day; then he sent for me. The picture stood there as you see it now – it was as though she'd met me on the threshold and taken me in her arms! I tried to thank him, to tell him what it meant to me, but he cut me short.

'"There's an up-train at five, isn't there?" he asked. "I'm booked for a dinner tonight. I shall just have time to make a bolt for the station, and you can send my traps after me." I haven't seen him since.

'I can guess what it cost him to lay hands on his masterpiece; but, after all, to him it was only a picture lost, to me it was my wife regained!'

4

After that, for ten years or more, I watched the strange spectacle of a life of hopeful and productive effort based on the structure of a dream. There could be no doubt to those who saw Grancy during this period that he drew his strength and courage from the sense of his wife's mystic participation in his task. When I went back to see him a few months later I found the portrait had been removed from the library and placed in a small study upstairs, to which he had transferred his desk and a few books. He told me he always sat there when he was alone, keeping the library for his Sunday visitors. Those who missed the portrait of course made no comment on its absence, and the few who were in his secret respected it. Gradually all his old friends had gathered about him, and our Sunday afternoons regained something of their former character; but Claydon never reappeared among us.

As I look back now I see that Grancy must have been failing from the time of his return home. His invincible spirit belied and disguised the signs of weakness that afterward asserted themselves in my remembrance of him. He seemed to have an inexhaustible fund of life to draw on, and more than one of us was a pensioner on his superfluity.

Nevertheless, when I came back one summer from my European holiday and heard that he had been at the point of death, I understood at once that we had believed him well only because he wished us to.

I hastened down to the country and found him midway in a slow convalescence. I felt then that he was lost to us, and he read my thought at a glance.

'Ah,' he said, 'I'm an old man now, and no mistake. I suppose we shall have to go half-speed after this; but we shan't need towing just yet!'

The plural pronoun struck me, and involuntarily I looked up at Mrs Grancy's portrait. Line by line I saw my fear reflected in it. It was the face of a woman *who knows that her husband is dying*. My heart stood still at the thought of what Claydon had done.

Grancy had followed my glance. 'Yes, it's changed her,' he said quietly. 'For months, you know, it was touch and go with me – we had a long fight of it, and it was worse for her than for me.' After a pause he added: 'Claydon has been very kind; he's so busy nowadays that I seldom see him, but when I sent for him the other day he came down at once.'

I was silent, and we spoke no more of Grancy's illness; but when I took leave it seemed like shutting him in alone with his death-warrant.

The next time I went down to see him he looked much better. It was a Sunday, and he received me in the library, so that I did not see the portrait again. He continued to improve, and towards spring we began to feel that, as he had said, he might yet travel a long way without being towed.

One evening, on returning to town after a visit which had confirmed my sense of reassurance, I found Claydon dining alone at the club. He asked me to join him, and over the coffee our talk turned to his work.

'If you're not too busy,' I said at length, 'you ought to make time to go down to Grancy's again.'

He looked up quickly. 'Why?' he asked.

'Because he's quite well again,' I returned, with a touch of cruelty. 'His wife's prognostications were mistaken.'

Claydon stared at me a moment. 'Oh, *she* knows,' he affirmed, with a smile that chilled me.

'You mean to leave the portrait as it is then?' I persisted.

He shrugged his shoulders. 'He hasn't sent for me yet!'

A waiter came up with the cigars, and Claydon rose and joined another group.

It was just a fortnight later that Grancy's housekeeper telegraphed for me. She met me at the station with the news that he had been 'taken bad,' and that the doctors were with him. I had to wait for some time in the deserted library before the medical men appeared. They had the baffled manner of empirics who have been superseded by the great Healer; and I lingered only long enough to hear that Grancy was not suffering, and that my presence could do him no harm.

I found him seated in his armchair in the little study. He held out his hand with a smile.

'You see she was right after all,' he said.

'She?' I repeated, perplexed for the moment.

'My wife.' He indicated the picture 'Of course I knew she had no hope from the first. I saw that' – he lowered his voice – 'after Claydon had been here. But I wouldn't believe it at first!'

I caught his hands in mine. 'For God's sake don't believe it now!' I adjured him.

He shook his head gently. 'It's too late,' he said. 'I might have known that she knew.'

'But, Grancy, listen to me,' I began; and then I stopped. What could I say that would convince him? There was no common ground of argument on which we could meet; and after all it would be easier for him to die feeling that she *had* known. Strangely enough, I saw that Claydon had missed his mark...

5

Grancy's will named me as one of his executors; and my associate, having other duties on his hands, begged me to assume the task of carrying out our friend's wishes. This placed me under the necessity of informing Claydon that the portrait of Mrs Grancy had been bequeathed to him; and he replied by the next post that he would send for the picture at once. I was staying in the deserted house when the portrait was taken away; and as the door closed on it I felt that Grancy's presence had vanished too. Was it his turn to follow her now, and could one ghost haunt another?

After that, for a year or two, I heard nothing more of the picture, and though I met Claydon from time to time we had little to say to each other. I had no definable grievance against the man, and I tried to remember that he had done a fine thing in sacrificing his best picture to a friend; but my resentment had all the tenacity of unreason.

One day, however, a lady whose portrait he had just finished begged me to go with her to see it. To refuse was impossible, and I went with the less reluctance that I knew I was not the only friend she had invited. The others were all grouped around the easel when I entered, and after contributing my share to the chorus of approval I turned away and began to stroll about the studio. Claydon was something of a collector, and his things were generally worth looking at. The studio was a long tapestried room with a curtained archway at one end. The curtains were looped back, showing a smaller apartment, with books and flowers and a few fine bits of bronze and porcelain. The tea-table standing in this inner room proclaimed that it was open to inspection, and I wandered in. A *bleu poudré* vase first attracted me; then I turned to examine a slender bronze Ganymede, and in so doing found myself face to face with Mrs Grancy's portrait. I stared up at her blankly and she smiled back at me in all the recovered radiance of youth. The artist had effaced every trace of his later touches and the original picture had reappeared. It throned alone on the panelled wall, asserting a brilliant supremacy over its carefully chosen surroundings. I felt in an instant that the whole room was tributary to it: that Claydon had heaped his treasures at the feet of the woman he loved. Yes – it was the woman he had loved and not the picture; and my instinctive resentment was explained.

Suddenly I felt a hand on my shoulder.

'Ah, how could you?' I cried, turning on him.

'How could I?' he retorted. 'How could I *not*? Doesn't she belong to me now?'

I moved away impatiently.

'Wait a moment,' he said with a detaining gesture. 'The others have gone, and I want to say a word to you – Oh, I know what you've thought of me – I can guess! You think I killed Grancy, I suppose?'

I was startled by his sudden vehemence. 'I think you tried to do a cruel thing,' I said.

'Ah – what a little way you others see into life!' he murmured. 'Sit down a moment – here, where we can look at her – and I'll tell you.'

He threw himself on the ottoman beside me and sat gazing up at the picture, with his hands clasped about his knee.

'Pygmalion,' he began slowly, 'turned his statue into a real woman; *I* turned my real woman into a picture. Small compensation, you think – but you don't know how much of a woman belongs to you after you've painted her! – Well, I made the best of it, at any rate – I gave her the best I had in me; and she gave me in return what such a woman gives by merely being. And after all, she rewarded me enough by making me paint as I shall never paint again! There was one side of her, though, that was mine alone, and that was her beauty; for no one else understood it. To Grancy even it was the mere expression of herself – what language is to thought. Even when he saw the picture he didn't guess my secret – he was so sure she was all his! As though a man should think he owned the moon because it was reflected in the pool at his door—

'Well – when he came home and sent for me to change the picture it was like asking me to commit murder. He wanted me to make an old woman of her – of her who had been so divinely, unchangeably young! As if any man who really loved a woman would ask her to sacrifice her youth and beauty for his sake! At first I told him I couldn't do it – but afterward, when he left me alone with the picture, something queer happened. I suppose it was because I was always so confoundedly fond of Grancy that it went against me to refuse what he asked. Anyhow, as I sat looking up at her, she seemed to say, "I'm not yours but his, and I want you to make me what he wishes." And so I did it, I could have cut my hand off when the work was done – I daresay he told you I never would go back and look at it. He thought I was too busy – he never understood...

'Well – and then last year he sent for me again – you remember. It was after his illness, and he told me he'd grown twenty years older, and that he wanted her to grow older too – he didn't want her to be left behind. The doctors all thought he was going to get well at that time and he thought so too; and so did I when I first looked at him. But when I turned to the picture – ah, now I don't ask you to believe me; but I swear it was *her* face that told me he was dying, and that she wanted him to know it! She had a message for him, and she made me deliver it.'

He rose abruptly and walked toward the portrait; then he sat down beside me again.

'Cruel? Yes, it seemed so, to me at first; and this time, if I resisted, it was for *his* sake and not for mine. But all the while I felt her eyes drawing me, and gradually she made me understand. If she'd been there in the flesh (she seemed to say) wouldn't she have seen before any of us that he was dying? Wouldn't he have read the news first in her face? And wouldn't it be horrible if now he should discover it instead in strange eyes? – Well – that was what she wanted of me and I did it – I kept them together to the last!' He looked up at the picture again. 'But now she belongs to me,' he repeated...

The Recovery

1

TO THE VISITING STRANGER, Hillbridge's first question was, 'Have you seen Keniston's things?'

Keniston took precedence of the Colonial State House, the Gilbert Stuart Washington, and the Ethnological Museum; nay, he ran neck and neck with the President of the University, a pre-historic relic who had known Emerson, and who was still sent about the country in cotton-wool to open educational institutions with a toothless oration on Brook Farm.

Keniston was sent about the country too: he opened art exhibitions, laid the foundation of academies, and acted in a general sense as the spokesman and apologist of art. Hillbridge was proud of him in his peripatetic character, but his fellow-townsmen let it be understood that to 'know' Keniston one must come to Hillbridge. Never was work more dependent for its effect on 'atmosphere,' on *milieu*. Hillbridge was Keniston's *milieu*, and there was one lady, a devotee of his art, who went so far as to assert that once, at an exhibition in New York, she had passed a Keniston without recognizing it. 'It simply didn't want to be seen in such surroundings; it was hiding itself under an incognito,' she declared.

It was a source of special pride to Hillbridge that it contained all the artist's best works. Strangers were told that Hillbridge had discovered him. The discovery had come about in the simplest manner. Professor Driffert, who had a reputation for 'collecting,' had one day hung a sketch on his drawing-room wall, and thereafter Mrs Driffert's visitors (always a little flurried by the sense that it was the kind of house in which one might be suddenly called upon to distinguish between a dry-point and an etching, or between Raphael Mengs and Raphael Sanzio) were not infrequently subjected to the Professor's off-hand inquiry, 'By the way, have you seen my Keniston?' The visitors, perceptibly awed, would retreat to a critical distance and murmur the usual guarded generalities, while they tried to keep the name in mind long enough to look it up in the Encyclopædia. The name was not in the Encyclopædia; but, as a compensating fact, it became known that the man himself was in Hillbridge. Hillbridge, then, owned an artist whose celebrity it was the proper thing to take for granted! Some one else, emboldened by the thought, bought a Keniston; and the next year, on the occasion of the President's golden jubilee, the Faculty, by unanimous consent, presented him with a Keniston. Two years later there was a Keniston exhibition, to which the art-critics came from New York and Boston; and not long afterward a well-known Chicago collector vainly attempted to buy Professor Driffert's sketch, which the art journals cited as a rare example of the painter's first or silvery manner. Thus there gradually

505

grew up a small circle of connoisseurs known in artistic circles as men who collected Kenistons.

Professor Wildmarsh, of the chair of Fine Arts and Archæology, was the first critic to publish a detailed analysis of the master's methods and purpose. The article was illustrated by engravings which (though they had cost the magazine a fortune) were declared by Professor Wildmarsh to give but an imperfect suggestion of the esoteric significance of the originals. The Professor, with a tact that contrived to make each reader feel himself included among the exceptions, went on to say that Keniston's work would never appeal to any but exceptional natures; and he closed with the usual assertion that to apprehend the full meaning of the master's 'message,' it was necessary to see him in the surroundings of his own home at Hillbridge.

Professor Wildmarsh's article was read one spring afternoon by a young lady just speeding eastward on her first visit to Hillbridge, and already flushed with anticipation of the intellectual opportunities awaiting her. In East Onondaigua, where she lived, Hillbridge was looked on as an Oxford. Magazine writers, with the easy American use of the superlative, designated it as 'the venerable *alma mater*,' the 'antique seat of learning,' and Claudia Day had been brought up to regard it as the fountain-head of knowledge, and of that mental distinction which is so much rarer than knowledge. An innate passion for all that was thus distinguished and exceptional made her revere Hillbridge as the native soil of those intellectual amenities that were of such difficult growth in the thin air of East Onondaigua. At the first suggestion of a visit to Hillbridge – whither she went at the invitation of a girl friend who (incredible apotheosis!) had married one of the University professors – Claudia's spirit dilated with the sense of new possibilities. The vision of herself walking under the 'historic elms' toward the Memorial Library, standing rapt before the Stuart Washington, or drinking in, from some obscure corner of an academic drawing-room, the President's reminiscences of the Concord group – this vividness of self-projection into the emotions awaiting her made her glad of any delay that prolonged so exquisite a moment.

It was in this mood that she opened the article on Keniston. She knew about him, of course; she was wonderfully 'well up,' even for East Onondaigua. She had read of him in the magazines; she had met, on a visit to New York, a man who collected Kenistons, and a photogravure of a Keniston in an 'artistic' frame hung above her writing-table at home. But Professor Wildmarsh's article made her feel how little she really knew of the master; and she trembled to think of the state of relative ignorance in which, but for the timely purchase of the magazine, she might have entered Hillbridge. She had, for instance, been densely unaware that Keniston had already had three 'manners,' and was showing symptoms of a fourth. She was equally ignorant of the fact that he had founded a school and 'created a formula;' and she learned with a thrill that no one could hope to understand him who had not seen him in his studio at Hillbridge surrounded by his own works. 'The man and the art interpret each other,' their exponent declared; and Claudia Day, bending a brilliant eye on the future, wondered if she were ever to be admitted to the privilege of that double initiation.

Keniston, to his other claims to distinction, added that of being hard to know. His friends always hastened to announce the fact to strangers –

adding, after a pause of suspense, that they 'would see what they could do.'
Visitors in whose favour he was induced to make an exception were further
warned that he never spoke unless he was interested – so that they mustn't
mind if he remained silent. It was under these reassuring conditions that,
some ten days after her arrival at Hillbridge, Miss Day was introduced to the
master's studio. She found him a tall listless-looking man, who appeared
middle-aged to her youth, and who stood before his own pictures with a
vaguely interrogative gaze, leaving the task of their interpretation to the lady
who had courageously contrived the visit. The studio, to Claudia's surprise,
was bare and shabby. It formed a rambling addition to the small cheerless
house in which the artist lived with his mother and a widowed sister. For
Claudia it added the last touch to his distinction to learn that he was poor,
and that what he earned was devoted to the maintenance of the two limp
women who formed a neutral-tinted background to his impressive outline.
His pictures, of course, fetched high prices; but he worked slowly –
'painfully,' as his devotees preferred to phrase it – with frequent intervals of
ill-health and inactivity, and the circle of Keniston connoisseurs was still as
small as it was distinguished. The girl's fancy instantly hailed in him that
favourite figure of imaginative youth, the artist who would rather starve than
paint a pot-boiler. It is known to comparatively few that the production of
successful pot-boilers is an art in itself, and that such heroic abstentions as
Keniston's are not always purely voluntary.

On the occasion of her first visit the artist said so little that Claudia was
able to indulge to the full the harrowing sense of her inadequacy. No wonder
she had not been one of the few that he cared to talk to; every word she
uttered must so obviously have diminished the inducement! She had been
cheap, trivial, conventional; at once gushing and inexpressive, eager and
constrained. She could feel him counting the minutes till the visit was over,
and as the door finally closed on the scene of her discomfiture she almost
shared the hope with which she confidently credited him – that they might
never meet again.

                                      2

Mrs Davant glanced reverentially about the studio. 'I have always said,' she
murmured, 'that they ought to be seen in Europe.'

Mrs Davant was young, credulous, and emotionally extravagant: she
reminded Claudia of her earlier self – the self that, ten years before, had first
set an awestruck foot on that very threshold.

'Not for *his* sake,' Mrs Davant continued, 'but for Europe's.'

Claudia smiled. She was glad that her husband's pictures were to be
exhibited in Paris. She concurred in Mrs Davant's view of the importance of
the event; but she thought her visitor's way of putting the case a little
overcharged. Ten years spent in an atmosphere of Keniston-worship had
insensibly developed in Claudia a preference for moderation of speech. She
believed in her husband, of course; to believe in him, with an increasing
abandonment and tenacity, had become one of the necessary laws of being;
but she did not believe in his admirers. Their faith in him was perhaps as
genuine as her own; but it seemed to her less able to give an account of itself.

Some few of his appreciators doubtless measured him by their own standards; but it was difficult not to feel that in the Hillbridge circle, where rapture ran the highest, he was accepted on what was at best but an indirect valuation; and now and then she had a frightened doubt as to the independence of her own convictions. That innate sense of relativity, which even East Onondaigua had not been able to check in Claudia Day, had been fostered in Mrs Keniston by the artistic absolutism of Hillbridge, and she often wondered that her husband remained so uncritical of the quality of admiration accorded him. Her husband's uncritical attitude toward himself and his admirers had in fact been one of the surprises of her marriage. That an artist should believe in his potential powers seemed to her at once the incentive and the pledge of excellence: she knew there was no future for a hesitating talent. What perplexed her was Keniston's satisfaction in his achievement. She had alway imagined that the true artist must regard himself as the imperfect vehicle of the cosmic emotion – that beneath every difficulty overcome a new one lurked, the vision widening as the scope enlarged. To be initiated into these creative struggles, to shed on the toiler's path the consolatory ray of faith and encouragement, had seemed the chief privilege of her marriage. But there is something supererogatory in believing in a man obviously disposed to perform that service for himself; and Claudia's ardour gradually spent itself against the dense surface of her husband's complacency. She could smile now at her vision of an intellectual communion which should admit her to the inmost precincts of his inspiration. She had learned that the creative processes are seldom self-explanatory, and Keniston's inarticulateness no longer discouraged her; but she could not reconcile her sense of the continuity of all high effort to his unperturbed air of finishing each picture as though he had despatched a masterpiece to posterity. In the first recoil from her disillusionment she even allowed herself to perceive that, if he worked slowly, it was not because he mistrusted his powers of expression, but because he had really so little to express.

'It's for Europe,' Mrs Davant vaguely repeated; and Claudia noticed that she was blushingly intent on tracing with the tip of her elaborate sunshade the pattern of the shabby carpet.

'It will be a revelation to them,' she went on provisionally, as though Claudia had missed her cue and left an awkward interval to fill.

Claudia had in fact a sudden sense of deficient intuition. She felt that her visitor had something to communicate which required, on her own part, an intelligent cooperation; but what it was her insight failed to suggest. She was, in truth, a little tired of Mrs Davant, who was Keniston's latest worshipper, who ordered pictures recklessly, who paid for them regally in advance, and whose gallery was, figuratively speaking, crowded with the artist's unpainted masterpieces. Claudia's impatience was perhaps complicated by the uneasy sense that Mrs Davant was too young, too rich, too inexperienced; that somehow she ought to be warned. Warned of what? That some of the pictures might never be painted? Scarcely that, since Keniston, who was scrupulous in business transactions, might be trusted not to take any material advantage of such evidence of faith. Claudia's impulse remained undefined. She merely felt that she would have liked to help Mrs Davant, and that she did not know how.

'You'll be there to see them?' she asked, as her visitor lingered.

'In Paris?' Mrs Davant's blush deepened. 'We must all be there together.'

Claudia smiled. 'My husband and I meant to go abroad some day – but I don't see any chance of it at present.'

'But he *ought* to go – you ought both to go this summer!' Mrs Davant persisted. 'I know Professor Wildmarsh and Professor Driffert and all the other critics think that Mr Keniston's never having been to Europe has given his work much of its wonderful individuality, its peculiar flavour and meaning – but now that his talent is formed, that he has full command of his means of expression' (Claudia recognized one of Professor Driffert's favourite formulas), 'they all think that he ought to see the work of the *other* great masters – that he ought to visit the home of his ancestors, as Professor Wildmarsh says!' She stretched an impulsive hand to Claudia. 'You ought to let him go, Mrs Keniston!'

Claudia accepted the admonition with the philosophy of the wife who is used to being advised on the management of her husband. 'I shan't interfere with him,' she declared; and Mrs Davant instantly caught her up with a cry of 'Oh, it's too lovely of you to say that!' With this exclamation she left Claudia to a silent renewal of wonder.

A moment later Keniston entered: to a mind curious in combinations it might have occurred that he had met Mrs Davant on the doorstep. In one sense he might, for all his wife cared, have met fifty Mrs Davants on the doorstep: it was long since Claudia had enjoyed the solace of resenting such coincidences. Her only thought now was that her husband's first words might not improbably explain Mrs Davant's last; and she waited for him to speak.

He paused with his hands in his pockets before an unfinished picture on the easel; then, as his habit was, he began to stroll tourist-like from canvas to canvas, standing before each in a musing ecstasy of contemplation that no readjustment of view ever seemed to disturb. Her eye instinctively joined his in its inspection; it was the one point where their natures merged. Thank God, there was no doubt about the pictures! She was what she had always dreamed of being – the wife of a great artist. Keniston dropped into an armchair and filled his pipe. 'How should you like to go to Europe?' he asked.

His wife looked up quickly. 'When?'

'Now – this spring, I mean.' He paused to light the pipe. 'I should like to be over there while these things are being exhibited.'

Claudia was silent.

'Well?' he repeated after a moment.

'How can we afford it?' she asked.

Keniston had always scrupulously fulfilled his duty to the mother and sister whom his marriage had dislodged; and Claudia, who had the atoning temperament which seeks to pay for every happiness by making it a source of fresh obligations, had from the outset accepted his ties with an exaggerated devotion. Any disregard of such a claim would have vulgarized her most delicate pleasures; and her husband's sensitiveness to it in great measure extenuated the artistic obtuseness that often seemed to her like a failure of the moral sense. His loyalty to the dull women who depended on him was, after all, compounded of finer tissues than any mere sensibility of ideal demands.

'Oh, I don't see why we shouldn't,' he rejoined. 'I think we might manage it.'

'At Mrs Davant's expense?' leaped from Claudia. She could not tell why she had said it; some inner barrier seemed to have given way under a confused pressure of emotions.

He looked up at her with frank surprise. 'Well, she *has* been very jolly about it – why not? She has a tremendous feeling for art – the keenest I ever knew in a woman.' Claudia imperceptibly smiled. 'She wants me to let her pay in advance for the four panels she has ordered for the Memorial Library. That would give us plenty of money for the trip, and my having the panels to do is another reason for my wanting to go abroad just now.'

'Another reason?'

'Yes; I've never worked on such a big scale. I want to see how those old chaps did the trick; I want to measure myself with the big fellows over there. An artist ought to, once in his life.'

She gave him a wondering look. For the first time his words implied a sense of possible limitation; but his easy tone seemed to retract what they conceded. What he really wanted was fresh food for his self-satisfaction: he was like an army that moves on after exhausting the resources of the country.

Womanlike, she abandoned the general survey of the case for the consideration of a minor point.

'Are you sure you can do that kind of thing?' she asked.

'What kind of thing?'

'The panels.'

He glanced at her indulgently: his self-confidence was too impenetrable to feel the pin-prick of such a doubt.

'Immensely sure,' he said with a smile.

'And you don't mind taking so much money from her in advance?'

He stared. 'Why should I? She'll get it back – with interest!' He laughed and drew at his pipe. 'It will be an uncommonly interesting experience. I shouldn't wonder if it freshened me up a bit.'

She looked at him again. This second hint of self-distrust struck her as a sign of a quickened sensibility. What if, after all, he was beginning to be dissatisfied with his work? The thought filled her with a renovating sense of his sufficiency.

3

They stopped in London to see the National Gallery.

It was thus that, in their inexperience, they had narrowly put it; but in reality every stone of the streets, every trick of the atmosphere, had its message of surprise for their virgin sensibilities. The pictures were simply the summing up, the final interpretation, of the cumulative pressure of an unimagined world; and it seemed to Claudia that long before they reached the doors of the gallery she had some intuitive revelation of what awaited them within.

They moved about from room to room without exchanging a word. The vast noiseless spaces seemed full of sound, like the roar of a distant multitude heard only by the inner ear. Had their speech been articulate their language would have been incomprehensible; and even that far-off murmur or meaning pressed intolerably on Claudia's nerves. Keniston took the onset without outward sign of disturbance. Now and then he paused before a canvas, or prolonged from one of the benches his silent communion with some miracle of line or colour; but he neither looked at his wife or spoke to her. He seemed to have forgotten her presence.

Claudia was conscious of keeping a furtive watch on him; but the sum total of her impressions was negative. She remembered thinking when she first met him that his face was rather expressionless; and he had the habit of self-engrossed silences.

All that evening, at the hotel, they talked about London, and he surprised her by an acuteness of observation that she had sometimes inwardly accused him of lacking. He seemed to have seen everything, to have examined, felt, compared, with nerves as finely adjusted as her own; but he said nothing of the pictures. The next day they returned to the National Gallery, and he began to study the paintings in detail, pointing out differences of technique, analyzing and criticizing, but still without summing up his conclusions. He seemed to have a sort of provincial dread of showing himself too much impressed. Claudia's own sensations were too complex, too overwhelming, to be readily classified. Lacking the craftsman's instinct to steady her, she felt herself carried off her feet by the rush of incoherent impressions. One point she consciously avoided, and that was the comparison of her husband's work with what they were daily seeing. Art, she inwardly argued, was too various, too complex, dependent on too many inter-relations of feeling and environment, to allow of its being judged by any provisional standard. Even the subtleties of technique must be modified by the artist's changing purpose, as this in turn is acted on by influences of which he is himself unconscious. How, then, was an unprepared imagination to distinguish between such varied reflections of the elusive vision? She took refuge in a passionate exaggeration of her own ignorance and insufficiency.

After a week in London they went to Paris. The exhibition of Keniston's pictures had been opened a few days earlier; and as they drove through the streets on the way to the station an 'impressionist' poster here and there invited them to the display of the American artist's work. Mrs Davant, who had been in Paris for the opening, had already written rapturously of the impression produced, enclosing commendatory notices from one or two papers. She reported that there had been a great crowd on the first day, and that the critics had been 'immensely struck.'

The Kenistons arrived in the evening, and the next morning Claudia, as a matter of course, asked her husband at what time he meant to go and see the pictures.

He looked up absently from his guidebook.

'What pictures?'

'Why – yours,' she said, surprised.

'Oh, they'll keep,' he answered; adding with a slightly embarrassed laugh, 'We'll give the other chaps a show first.' Presently he laid down his book and proposed that they should go to the Louvre.

They spent the morning there, lunched at a restaurant near by, and returned to the gallery in the afternoon. Keniston had passed from inarticulateness to an eager volubility. It was clear that he was beginning to coordinate his impressions, to find his way about in a corner of the great imaginative universe. He seemed extraordinarily ready to impart his discoveries; and Claudia felt that her ignorance served him as a convenient buffer against the terrific impact of new sensations.

On the way home she asked when he meant to see Mrs Davant.

His answer surprised her. 'Does she know we're here?'

'Not unless you've sent her word,' said Claudia, with a touch of harmless irony.

'That's all right, then,' he returned simply. 'I want to wait and look about a day or two longer. She'd want us to go sight-seeing with her; and I'd rather get my impressions alone.'

The next two days were hampered by the necessity of eluding Mrs Davant. Claudia, under different circumstances, would have scrupled to share in this somewhat shabby conspiracy; but she found herself in a state of suspended judgment, wherein her husband's treatment of Mrs Davant became for the moment merely a clue to larger meanings.

They had been four days in Paris when Claudia, returning one afternoon from a parenthetical excursion to the Rue de la Paix, was confronted on her threshold by the reproachful figure of their benefactress. It was not to her, however, that Mrs Davant's reproaches were addressed. Keniston, it appeared, had borne the brunt of them; for he stood leaning against the mantelpiece of their modest *salon* in that attitude of convicted negligence when, if ever, a man is glad to take refuge behind his wife.

Claudia had however no immediate intention of affording him such shelter. She wanted to observe and wait.

'He's too impossible!' cried Mrs Davant, sweeping her at once into the central current of her grievance.

Claudia looked from one to the other.

'For not going to see you?'

'For not going to see his pictures!' cried the other nobly.

Claudia coloured and Keniston shifted his position uneasily.

'I can't make her understand,' he said, turning to his wife.

'I don't care about myself!' Mrs Davant interjected.

'*I* do, then; it's the only thing I do care about,' he hurriedly protested. 'I meant to go at once – to write – Claudia wanted to go, but I wouldn't let her.' He looked helplessly about the pleasant red-curtained room, which was rapidly burning itself into Claudia's consciousness as a visible extension of Mrs Davant's claims.

'I can't explain,' he broke off.

Mrs Davant in turn addressed herself to Claudia.

'People think it's so odd,' she complained. 'So many of the artists here are anxious to meet him; they've all been so charming about the pictures; and several of our American friends have come over from London expressly for the exhibition. I told every one that he would be here for the opening – there was a private view, you know – and they were so disappointed – they wanted to give him an ovation; and I didn't know what to say. What *am* I to say?' she abruptly ended.

'There's nothing to say,' said Keniston slowly.

'But the exhibition closes the day after tomorrow.'

'Well, *I* shan't close – I shall be here,' he declared, with an effort at playfulness. 'If they want to see me – all these people you're kind enough to mention – won't there be other chances?'

'But I wanted them to see you *among* your pictures – to hear you talk about them, explain them in that wonderful way. I wanted you to interpret each other, as Professor Wildmarsh says!'

'Oh, hang Professor Wildmarsh!' said Keniston, softening the commination with a smile. 'If my pictures are good for anything they oughtn't to need explaining.'

Mrs Davant stared. 'But I thought that was what made them so interesting!' she exclaimed.

Keniston looked down. 'Perhaps it was,' he murmured.

There was an awkward silence, which Claudia broke by saying, with a glance at her husband: 'But if the exhibition is to remain open tomorrow, could we not meet you there? And perhaps you could send word to some of our friends.'

Mrs Davant brightened like a child whose broken toy is glued together. 'Oh, *do* make him!' she implored. 'I'll ask them to come in the afternoon – we'll make it into a little tea – a *five o'clock*. I'll send word at once to everybody!' she gathered up her beruffled boa and sunshade, settling her plumage like a reassured bird. 'It will be too lovely!' she ended in a self-consoling murmur.

But in the doorway a new doubt assailed her. 'You won't fail me?' she said, turning plaintively to Keniston. 'You'll make him come, Mrs Keniston?'

'I'll bring him!' Claudia promised.

4

When, the next morning, she appeared equipped for their customary ramble, her husband surprised her by announcing that he meant to stay at home.

'The fact is, I'm rather surfeited,' he said, smiling. 'I suppose my appetite isn't equal to such a plethora. I think I'll write some letters and join you somewhere later.'

She detected the wish to be alone, and responded to it with her usual readiness.

'I shall sink to my proper level and buy a bonnet, then,' she said. 'I haven't had time to take the edge off that appetite.'

They agreed to meet at the Hôtel Cluny at midday, and she set out alone with a vague sense of relief. Neither she nor Keniston had made any direct reference to Mrs Davant's visit; but its effect was implicit in their eagerness to avoid each other.

Claudia accomplished some shopping in the spirit of perfunctoriness that robs even new bonnets of their bloom; and this business despatched, she turned aimlessly into the wide inviting brightness of the streets. Never had she felt more isolated amid that ordered beauty which gives a social quality to the very stones and mortar of Paris. All about her were evidences of an artistic sensibility pervading every form of life like the nervous structure of the huge frame – a sensibility so delicate, alert, and universal, that it seemed to leave no room for obtuseness or error. In such a medium the faculty of plastic expression must develop as unconsciously as any organ in its normal surroundings; to be 'artistic' must cease to be an attitude and become a natural function. To Claudia the significance of the whole vast revelation was centred in the light it shed on one tiny spot of consciousness – the value of her husband's work. There are moments when, to the groping soul, the world's accumulated experiences are but stepping-stones across a private difficulty.

She stood hesitating at a street corner. It was barely eleven, and she had an hour to spare before going to the Hôtel Cluny. She seemed to be letting her inclination float as it would on the cross-currents of suggestion emanating from the brilliant complex scene before her; but suddenly, in obedience to an impulse that she became aware of only in acting on it, she called a cab and drove to the gallery where her husband's pictures were exhibited.

A magnificent official in gold braid sold her a ticket, and pointed the way up the empty crimson-carpeted stairs. His duplicate, on the upper landing, held out a catalogue with an air of recognizing the futility of the offer; and a moment later she found herself in the long, noiseless impressive room, full of velvet-covered ottomans and exotic plants. It was clear that the public ardour on which Mrs Davant had expatiated had spent itself earlier in the week; for Claudia had this luxurious apartment to herself. Something about its air of rich privacy, its diffusion of that sympathetic quality in other countries so conspicuously absent from the public showroom, seemed to emphasize its present emptiness. It was as though the flowers, the carpet, the lounges, surrounded their visitor's solitary advance with the mute assurance that they had done all they could toward making the thing 'go off,' and that if they had failed it was simply for lack of cooperation. She stood still and looked about her. The pictures struck her instantly as odd gaps in the general harmony; it was self-evident that they had not cooperated. They had not been pushing, aggressive, discordant: they had merely effaced themselves. She swept a startled eye from one familiar painting to another. The canvases were all there – and the frames – but the miracle, the mirage of life and meaning, had vanished like some atmospheric illusion. What was it that had happened? And had it happened to *her* or to the pictures? She tried to rally her frightened thoughts; to push or coax them into semblance of resistance; but argument was swept off its feet by the huge rush of a single conviction – the conviction that the pictures were bad. There was no standing up against that: she felt herself submerged

The stealthy fear that may have been following her all these days had her by the throat now. The great vision of beauty through which she had been moving, as one enchanted, was turned to a phantasmagoria of evil-mocking shapes. She hated the past; she hated its splendour, its power, its wicked magical vitality . . . She dropped into a seat and continued to stare at the wall before her. Gradually, as she stared, there stole out to her from the dimmed humbled canvases a reminder of what she had once seen in them, a spectral appeal to her faith to call them back to life. What proof had she that the present estimate of them was less subjective than the other? The confused impressions of the last few days were hardly to be pleaded as a valid theory of art. How, after all, did she know that the pictures were bad? On what suddenly acquired technical standard had she thus decided the case against them? It seemed as though it were a standard outside of herself, as though some unheeded inner sense were gradually making her aware of the presence, in that empty room, of a critical intelligence that was giving out a subtle effluence of disapproval. The fancy was so vivid that, to shake it off, she rose and began to move about again. In the middle of the room stood a monumental divan surmounted by a *massif* of palms and azaleas. As Claudia's muffled wanderings carried her round the angle of this seat, she saw that its further side was occupied by the figure of a man, who sat with his hands resting on his stick and his head bowed upon them. She gave a little cry, and her husband rose and faced her.

Instantly the live point of consciousness was shifted, and she became aware that the quality of the pictures no longer mattered. It was what *he* thought of them that counted: her life hung on that.

They looked at each other a moment in silence; such concussions are not apt to flash into immediate speech. At length he said simply, 'I didn't know you were coming here.'

She coloured as though he had charged her with something underhand.

'I didn't mean to,' she stammered; 'but I was too early for our appointment—'

Her words cast a revealing glare on the situation. Neither of them looked at the pictures; but to Claudia those unobtruding presences seemed suddenly to press upon them and force them apart.

Keniston glanced at his watch. 'It's twelve o'clock,' he said, 'shall we go on?'

5

At the door he called a cab and put her in it; then, drawing out his watch again, he said abruptly: 'I believe I'll let you go alone. I'll join you at the hotel in time for luncheon.' She wondered for a moment if he meant to return to the gallery; but, looking back as she drove off, she saw him walk rapidly away in the opposite direction.

The cabman had carried her half-way to the Hôtel Cluny before she realized where she was going, and cried out to him to turn home. There was an acute irony in this mechanical prolongation of the quest of beauty. She had had enough of it, too much of it; her one longing was to escape, to hide herself away from its all-suffusing implacable light.

At the hotel, alone in her room, a few tears came to soften her seared vision; but her mood was too tense to be eased by weeping. Her whole being was centred in the longing to know what her husband thought. Their short exchange of words had, after all, told her nothing. She had guessed a faint resentment at her unexpected appearance; but that might merely imply a dawning sense, on his part, of being furtively watched and criticized. She had sometimes wondered if he was never conscious of her observation; there were moments when it seemed to radiate from her in visible waves. Perhaps, after all, he was aware of it, on his guard against it, as a lurking knife behind the thick curtain of his complacency; and today he must have caught the gleam of the blade.

Claudia had not reached the age when pity is the first chord to vibrate in contact with any revelation of failure. Her one hope had been that Keniston should be clear-eyed enough to face the truth. Whatever it turned out to be, she wanted him to measure himself with it. But as his image rose before her she felt a sudden half-maternal longing to thrust herself between him and disaster. Her eagerness to see him tested by circumstances seemed now like a cruel scientific curiosity. She saw in a flash of sympathy that he would need her most if he fell beneath his fate.

He did not, after all, return for luncheon; and when she came upstairs from her solitary meal their *salon* was still untenanted. She permitted herself no sensational fears; for she could not, at the height of apprehension, figure Keniston as yielding to any tragic impulse; but the lengthening hours brought an uneasiness that was fuel to her pity. Suddenly she heard the clock strike five. It was was the hour at which they had promised to meet Mrs Davant at the gallery – the hour of the 'ovation.' Claudia rose and went to the window, straining for a glimpse of her husband in the crowded street. Could it be that he had forgotten her, had gone to the gallery without her? Or had something happened – that veiled 'something' which, for the last hour, had grimly hovered on the outskirts of her mind?

She heard a hand on the door and Keniston entered. As she turned to meet him her whole being was swept forward on a great wave of pity: she was so sure, now, that he must know.

But he confronted her with a glance of preoccupied brightness; her first impression was that she had never seen him so vividly, so expressively pleased. If he needed her it was not to bind up his wounds.

He gave her a smile which was clearly the lingering reflection of some inner light. 'I didn't mean to be so late,' he said, tossing aside his hat and the little red volume that served as a clue to his explorations. 'I turned in to the Louvre for a minute after I left you this morning, and the place fairly swallowed me up – I couldn't get away from it. I've been there ever since.' He threw himself into a chair and glanced about for his pipe.

'It takes time,' he continued musingly, 'to get at them, to make out what they're saying – the big fellows, I mean. They're not a communicative lot. At first I couldn't make much out of their lingo – it was too different from mine! But gradually, by picking up a hint here and there, and piecing them together, I've begun to understand; and today, by Jove, I got one or two of the old chaps by the throat and fairly turned them inside out – made them deliver up their last drop.' He lifted a brilliant eye to her. 'Lord, it was tremendous!' he declared.

He had found his pipe and was musingly filling it. Claudia waited in silence.

'At first,' he began again, 'I was afraid their language was too hard for me – that I should never quite know what they were driving at; they seemed to cold-shoulder me, to be bent on shutting me out. But I was bound I wouldn't be beaten, and now, today –' he paused a moment to strike a match – 'when I went to look at those things of mine it all came over me in a flash. By Jove! it was as if I'd made them all into a big bonfire to light me on my road!'

His wife was trembling with a kind of sacred terror. She had been afraid to pray for light for him, and he was joyfully casting his whole past upon the pyre!

'Is there nothing left?' she faltered.

'Nothing left? There's everything!' he exulted. 'Why, here I am, not much over forty, and I've found out already – already!' He stood up and began to move excitedly about the room. 'My God! Suppose I'd never known! Suppose I'd gone on painting things like that for ever! Why, I feel like those chaps at revivalist meetings when they get up and say they're saved! Won't somebody please start a hymn?'

Claudia, with a tremulous joy was letting herself go on the strong current of his emotion; but it had not yet carried her beyond her depth, and suddenly she felt hard ground underfoot.

'Mrs Davant—' she exclaimed.

He stared, as though suddenly recalled from a long distance. 'Mrs Davant?'

'We were to have met her – this afternoon – now—'

'At the gallery? Oh, that's all right. I put a stop to that; I went to see her after I left you; I explained it all to her.'

'All?'

'I told her I was going to begin all over again.'

Claudia's heart gave a forward bound and then sank back hopelessly.

'But the panels—?'

'That's all right too. I told her about the panels,' he reassured her.

'You told her—?'

'That I can't paint them now. She doesn't understand, of course; but she's the best little woman and she trusts me.'

She could have wept for joy at his exquisite obtuseness. 'But that isn't all,' she wailed. 'It doesn't matter how much you've explained to her. It doesn't do away with the fact that we're living on those panels!'

'Living on them?'

'On the money that she paid you to paint them. Isn't that what brought us here? And – if you mean to do as you say – to begin all over again – how in the world are we ever to pay her back?'

Her husband turned on her an inspired eye. 'There's only one way that I know of,' he imperturbably declared, 'and that's to stay out here till I learn how to paint them.'

STEPHEN CRANE
1817-1900

Stephen Crane was born in New Jersey in 1871. During his short life (he died of tuberculosis at only 29) he wrote two novels and a quantity of short stories which reveal him as a writer of exceptional talent. His first work, a long short story, *Maggie: A Girl of the Streets*, a realistic evocation of a life shaped and moulded by a harsh environment, was rejected by publishers as being too depressing and was printed privately. His masterpiece, based on the experiences related to him as a child by survivors of the Civil War, *The Red Badge of Courage*, was published in 1895 and at once established Crane as a major literary figure.

Apart from *Maggie*, the stories included here were first published in *The Open Boat and Other Tales* in 1898. All show an impressive narrative power and gently observant characterization which serve to suggest the extent of the loss to literature constituted by Crane's early death.

Maggie: A Girl of the Streets

1

A VERY LITTLE BOY stood upon a heap of gravel for the honor of Rum Alley. He was throwing stones at howling urchins from Devil's Row, who were circling madly about the heap and pelting him.

His infantile countenance was livid with the fury of battle. His small body was writhing in the delivery of oaths.

'Run, Jimmie, run! Dey'll git yehs!' screamed a retreating Rum Alley child.

'Naw,' responded Jimmie with a valiant roar, 'dese mugs can't make me run.'

Howls of renewed wrath went up from Devil's Row throats. Tattered gamins on the right made a furious assault on the gravel heap. On their small convulsed faces shone the grins of true assassins. As they charged, they threw stones and cursed in shrill chorus.

The little champion of Rum Alley stumbled precipitately down the other side. His coat had been torn to shreds in a scuffle and his hat was gone. He had bruises on twenty parts of his body, and blood was dripping from a cut in his head. His wan features looked like those of a tiny insane demon.

On the ground, children from Devil's Row closed in on their antagonist. He crooked his left arm defensively about his head and fought with madness. The little boys ran to and fro, dodging, hurling stones, and swearing in barbaric trebles.

From a window of an apartment house that uprose from amid squat ignorant stables there leaned a curious woman. Some laborers, unloading a scow at a dock at the river, paused for a moment and regarded the fight. The engineer of a passive tugboat hung lazily over a railing and watched. Over on the island a worm of yellow convicts came from the shadow of a gray ominous building and crawled slowly along the river's bank.

A stone had smashed in Jimmie's mouth. Blood was bubbling over his chin and down upon his ragged shirt. Tears made furrows on his dirt-stained cheeks. His thin legs had begun to tremble and turn weak, causing his small body to reel. His roaring curses of the first part of the fight had changed to a blasphemous chatter.

In the yells of the whirling mob of Devil's Row children there were notes of joy like songs of triumphant savagery. The little boys seemed to leer gloatingly at the blood upon the other child's face.

Down the avenue came boastfully sauntering a lad of sixteen years, although the chronic sneer of an ideal manhood already sat upon his lips. His hat was tipped over his eyes with an air of challenge. Between his teeth a cigar stump was tilted at the angle of defiance. He walked with a certain swing of the shoulders which appalled the timid. He glanced over into the vacant lot in which the little raving boys from Devil's Row seethed about the shrieking and tearful child from Rum Alley.

'Gee!' he murmured with interest, 'a scrap. Gee!'

He strode over to the cursing circle, swinging his shoulders in a manner which denoted that he held victory in his fists. He approached at the back of one of the most deeply engaged of the Devil's Row children.

'Ah, what d' hell,' he said, and smote the deeply engaged one on the back of the head. The little boy fell to the ground and gave a tremendous howl. He scrambled to his feet, and perceiving, evidently, the size of his assailant, ran quickly off, shouting alarms. The entire Devil's Row party followed him. They came to a stand a short distance away and yelled taunting oaths at the boy with the chronic sneer. The latter, momentarily, paid no attention to them.

'What's wrong wi'che, Jimmie?' he asked of the small champion.

Jimmie wiped his blood-wet features with his sleeve.

'Well, it was dis way, Pete, see! I was goin' teh lick dat Riley kid and dey all pitched on me.'

Some Rum Alley children now came forward. The party stood for a moment exchanging vainglorious remarks with Devil's Row. A few stones were thrown at long distances, and words of challenge passed between small warriors. Then the Rum Alley contingent turned slowly in the direction of their home street. They began to give, each to each, distorted versions of the fight. Causes of retreat in particular cases were magnified. Blows dealt in the fight were enlarged to catapultian power, and stones thrown were alleged to have hurtled with infinite accuracy. Valor grew strong again, and the little boys began to brag with great spirit.

'Ah, we blokies kin lick d' hull damn Row,' said a child, swaggering.

Little Jimmie was trying to stanch the flow of blood from his cut lips. Scowling, he turned upon the speaker.

'Ah, where was yehs when I was doin' all deh fightin'?' he demanded. 'Youse kids makes me tired.'

'Ah, go ahn!' replied the other argumentatively.

Jimmie replied with heavy contempt. 'Ah, youse can't fight, Blue Billie! I kin lick yeh wid one han'.'

'Ah, go ahn!' replied Billie again.

'Ah!' said Jimmie threateningly.

'Ah!' said the other in the same tone.

They struck at each other, clinched, and rolled over on the cobblestones.

'Smash 'im Jimmie, kick d' face off 'im!' yelled Pete, the lad with the chronic sneer, in tones of delight.

The small combatants pounded and kicked, scratched and tore. They began to weep and their curses struggled in their throats with sobs. The other little boys clasped their hands and wriggled their legs in excitement. They formed a bobbing circle about the pair.

A tiny spectator was suddenly agitated.

'Cheese it, Jimmie, cheese it! Here comes yer fader,' he yelled.

The circle of little boys instantly parted. They drew away and waited in ecstatic awe for that which was about to happen. The two little boys, fighting in the modes of four thousand years ago, did not hear the warning.

Up the avenue there plodded slowly a man with sullen eyes. He was carrying a dinner pail and smoking an apple-wood pipe. As he neared the spot where the little boys strove, he regarded them listlessly. But suddenly he roared an oath and advanced upon the rolling fighters.

'Here, you Jim, git up, now, while I belt yer life out, yeh disorderly brat.'

He began to kick into the chaotic mass on the ground. The boy Billie felt a heavy boot strike his head. He made a furious effort and disentangled himself from Jimmie. He tottered away.

Jimmie arose painfully from the ground and, confronting his father, began to curse him. His parent kicked him. 'Come home, now,' he cried, 'an' stop yer jawin', er I'll lam the everlasting head off yehs.'

They departed. The man paced placidly along with the apple-wood emblem of serenity between his teeth. The boy followed a dozen feet in the rear. He swore luridly, for he felt that it was degradation for one who aimed to be some vague kind of soldier, or a man of blood with a sort of sublime licence, to be taken home by a father.

2

Eventually they entered a dark region where, from a careening building, a dozen gruesome doorways gave up loads of babies to the street and the gutter. A wind of early autumn raised yellow dust from cobbles and swirled it against a hundred windows. Long streamers of garments fluttered from fire-escapes. In all unhandy places there were buckets, brooms, rags, and bottles. In the street infants played or fought with other infants or sat stupidly in the way of vehicles. Formidable women, with uncombed hair and disordered dress, gossiped while leaning on railings, or screamed in frantic quarrels. Withered persons, in curious postures of submission to something, sat smoking pipes in obscure corners. A thousand odors of cooking food came forth to the street. The building quivered and creaked from the weight of humanity stamping about in its bowels.

A small ragged girl dragged a red, bawling infant along the crowded ways. He was hanging back, babylike, bracing his wrinkled, bare legs.

The little girl cried out: 'Ah, Tommie, come ahn. Dere's Jimmie and fader. Don't be a-pullin' me back.'

She jerked the baby's arm impatiently. He fell on his face, roaring. With a second jerk she pulled him to his feet, and they went on. With the obstinacy of his order, he protested against being dragged in a chosen direction. He made heroic endeavors to keep on his legs, denounced his sister, and consumed a bit of orange peeling which he chewed between the times of his infantile orations.

As the sullen-eyed man, followed by the blood-covered boy, drew near, the little girl burst into reproachful cries. 'Ah, Jimmie, youse bin fightin' agin.'

The urchin swelled disdainfully.

'Ah, what d' hell, Mag. See?'

The little girl upbraided him. 'Youse allus fightin', Jimmie, an' yeh knows it puts mudder out when yehs come home half dead, an' it's like we'll all get a poundin'.'

She began to weep. The babe threw back his head and roared at his prospects.

'Ah,' cried Jimmie, 'shut up er I'll smack yer mout'. See?'

As his sister continued her lamentations, he suddenly struck her. The little girl reeled and, recovering herself, burst into tears and quaveringly cursed him. As she slowly retreated, her brother advanced, dealing her cuffs. The father heard, and turned about.

'Stop that, Jim, d'yeh hear? Leave yer sister alone on the street. It's like I can never beat any sense into yer wooden head.'

The urchin raised his voice in defiance to his parent and continued his attacks. The babe bawled tremendously, protesting with great violence. During his sister's hasty manoeuvres he was dragged by the arm.

Finally the procession plunged into one of the gruesome doorways. They crawled up dark stairways and along cold, gloomy halls. At last the father pushed open a door and they entered a lighted room in which a large woman was rampant.

She stopped in a career from a seething stove to a pan-covered table. As the father and children filed in she peered at them.

'Eh, what? Been fightin' agin!' She threw herself upon Jimmie. The urchin tried to dart behind the others, and in the scuffle the babe, Tommie, was knocked down. He protested with his usual vehemence, because they had bruised his tender shins against a table leg.

The mother's massive shoulders heaved with anger. Grasping the urchin by the neck and shoulder she shook him until he rattled. She dragged him to an unholy sink, and, soaking a rag in water, began to scrub his lacerated face with it. Jimmie screamed in pain and tried to twist his shoulders out of the clasp of the huge arms.

The babe sat on the floor watching the scene, his face in contortions like that of a woman at a tragedy. The father, with a newly ladened pipe in his mouth, sat in a backless chair near the stove. Jimmie's cries annoyed him. He turned about and bellowed at his wife:

'Let the kid alone for a minute, will yeh, Mary? Yer allus poundin' 'im. When I come home nights I can't git no rest 'cause yer allus poundin' a kid. Let up, d'yeh hear? Don't be allus poundin' a kid.'

The woman's operations on the urchin instantly increased in violence. At last she tossed him to a corner where he limply lay weeping.

The wife put her immense hands on her hips, and with a chieftainlike stride approached her husband.

'Ho!' she said, with a great grunt of contempt. 'An' what in the devil are you stickin' your nose for?'

The babe crawled under the table and, turning, peered out cautiously. The ragged girl retreated, and the urchin in the corner drew his legs carefully beneath him.

The man puffed his pipe calmly and put his great muddied boots on the back part of the stove.

'Go t' hell,' he said tranquilly.

The woman screamed and shook her fists before her husband's eyes. The rough yellow of her face and neck flared suddenly crimson. She began to howl.

He puffed imperturbably at his pipe for a time, but finally arose and went to look out of the window into the darkening chaos of back yards.

'You've been drinkin', Mary,' he said. 'You'd better let up on the bot', ol' woman, or you'll git done.'

'You're a liar. I ain't had a drop,' she roared in reply. They had a lurid altercation.

The babe was staring out from under the table, his small face working in his excitement. The ragged girl went stealthily over to the corner where the urchin lay.

'Are yehs hurted much, Jimmie?' she whispered timidly.

'Not a little bit, See?' growled the little boy.

'Will I wash d'blood?'

'Naw!'

'Will I –'

'When I catch dat Riley kid I'll break 'is face! Dat's right, See?'

He turned his face to the wall as if resolved grimly to bide his time.

In the quarrel between husband and wife the woman was victor. The man seized his hat and rushed from the room, apparently determined upon a vengeful drunk. She followed to the door and thundered at him as he made his way downstairs.

She returned and stirred up the room until her children were bobbing about like bubbles.

'Git outa d'way,' she bawled persistently, waving feet with their dishevelled shoes near the heads of her children. She shrouded herself, puffing and snorting, in a cloud of steam at the stove, and eventually extracted a frying-pan full of potatoes that hissed.

She flourished it. 'Come t' yer suppers, now,' she cried with sudden exasperation. 'Hurry up, now, er I'll help yeh!'

The children scrambled hastily. With prodigious clatter they arranged themselves at table. The babe sat with his feet dangling high from a precarious infant's chair and gorged his small stomach. Jimmie forced, with feverish rapidity, the grease-enveloped pieces between his wounded lips. Maggie, with side glances of fear of interruption, ate like a small pursued tigress.

The mother sat blinking at them. She delivered reproaches, swallowed potatoes, and drank from a yellow-brown bottle. After a time her mood changed and she wept as she carried little Tommie into another room and laid him to sleep, with his fists doubled, in an old quilt of faded red and green grandeur. Then she came and moaned by the stove. She rocked to and fro upon a chair, shedding tears and crooning miserably to the two children about their 'poor mother' and 'yer fader, damn 'is soul.'

The little girl plodded between the table and the chair with a dish pan on it. She tottered on her small legs beneath burdens of dishes.

Jimmie sat nursing his various wounds. He cast furtive glances at his mother. His practised eye perceived her gradually emerge from a mist of muddled sentiment until her brain burned in drunken heat. He sat breathless.

Maggie broke a plate.

The mother started to her feet as if propelled.

'Good Gawd!' she howled. Her glittering eyes fastened on her child with sudden hatred. The fervent red of her face turned almost to purple. The little boy ran to the halls, shrieking like a monk in an earthquake.

He floundered about in darkness until he found the stairs. He stumbled, panic-stricken, to the next floor. An old woman opened a door. A light behind her threw a flare on the urchin's face.

'Eh, child, what is it dis time? Is yer fader beatin' yer mudder, or yer mudder beatin' yer fader?'

3

Jimmie and the old woman listened long in the hall. Above the muffled roar of conversation, the dismal wailings of babies at night, the thumping of feet in unseen corridors and rooms, and the sound of varied hoarse shoutings in the street and the rattling of wheels over cobbles, they heard the screams of the child and the roars of the mother die away to a feeble moaning and a subdued bass muttering.

The old woman was a gnarled and leathery personage who could don, at will, an expression of great virtue. She possessed a small music-box capable of one tune, and a collection of 'God bless yeh's' pitched in assorted keys of fervency. Each day she took a position upon the stones of Fifth Avenue, where she crooked her legs under her and crouched, immovable and hideous, like an idol. She received daily a small sum in pennies. It was contributed, for the most part, by persons who did not make their homes in that vicinity.

Once, when a lady had dropped her purse on the sidewalk, the gnarled woman had grabbed it and smuggled it with great dexterity beneath her cloak. When she was arrested she had cursed the lady into a partial swoon, and with her aged limbs, twisted from rheumatism, had kicked the breath out of a huge policeman whose conduct upon that occasion she referred to when she said, 'The police, damn 'em!'

'Eh, Jimmie, it's a shame,' she said. 'Go, now, like a dear, an' buy me a can, an' if yer mudder raises 'ell all night yehs can sleep here.'

Jimmie took a tendered tin pail and seven pennies and departed. He passed into the side door of a saloon and went to the bar. Straining up on his toes he raised the pail and pennies as high as his arms would let him. He saw two hands thrust down to take them. Directly the same hands let down the filled pail and he left.

In front of the gruesome doorway he met a lurching figure. It was his father, swaying about on uncertain legs.

'Give me deh can. See?' said the man.

'Ah, come off! I got dis can fer dat ol' woman, an' it 'ud be dirt teh swipe it. See?' cried Jimmie.

The father wrenched the pail from the urchin. He grasped it in both hands and lifted it to his mouth. He glued his lips to the under edge and tilted his head. There was a tremendous gulping movement and the beer was gone.

The man caught his breath and laughed. He hit his son on the head with the empty pail. As it rolled clanging into the street, Jimmie began to scream, and kicked repeatedly at his father's shins.

'Look at deh dirt what yeh done me,' he yelled. 'Deh ol' woman'll be t'rowin' fits.'

He retreated to the middle of the street, but the old man did not pursue. He staggered towards the door.

'I'll paste yeh when I ketch yeh!' he shouted, and disappeared.

During the evening he had been standing against a bar drinking whiskies, and declaring to all comers confidentially: 'My home reg'lar livin' hell! Why do I come an' drin' whisk' here thish way?' 'Cause home reg'lar livin' hell!'

Jimmie waited a long time in the street and then crept warily up through the building. He passed with great caution the door of the gnarled woman, and finally stopped outside his home and listened.

He could hear his mother moving heavily about among the furniture of the room. She was chanting in a mournful voice, occasionally interjecting bursts of volcanic wrath at the father, who, Jimmie judged, had sunk down on the floor or in a corner.

'Why deh blazes don' chere try teh keep Jim from fightin'? I'll break yer jaw!' she suddenly bellowed.

The man mumbled with drunken indifference. 'Ah, w'at's bitin' yeh? W'a's odds? Wha' makes kick?'

'Because he tears 'is clothes, yeh fool!' cried the woman in supreme wrath.

The husband seemed to become aroused. 'Go chase yerself!' he thundered fiercely in reply. There was a crash against the door and something broke into clattering fragments. Jimmie partially suppressed a yell and darted down the stairway. Below he paused and listened. He heard howls and curses, groans and shrieks – a confused chorus as if a battle were raging. With it all there was the crash of splintering furniture. The eyes of the urchin glared in his fear that one of them would discover him.

Curious faces appeared in doorways, and whispered comments passed to and fro. 'Ol' Johnson's playin' horse agin.'

Jimmie stood until the noises ceased and the other inhabitants of the tenement had all yawned and shut their doors. Then he crawled upstairs with the caution of an invader of a panther's den. Sounds of labored breathing came through the broken door-panels. He pushed the door open and entered, quaking.

A glow from the fire threw red hues over the bare floor, the cracked and soiled plastering, and the overturned and broken furniture.

In the middle of the floor lay his mother asleep. In one corner of the room his father's limp body hung across the seat of a chair.

The urchin stole forward. He began to shiver in dread of awakening his parents. His mother's great chest was heaving painfully. Jimmie paused and looked down at her. Her face was inflamed and swollen from drinking. Her yellow brows shaded eyelids that had grown blue. Her tangled hair tossed in waves over her forehead. Her mouth was set in the same lines of vindictive hatred that it had, perhaps, borne during the fight. Her bare, red arms were thrown out above her head in an attitude of exhaustion, something, mayhap, like that of a sated villain.

The urchin bent over his mother. He was fearful lest she should open her eyes, and the dread within him was so strong that he could not forbear to stare, but hung as if fascinated over the woman's grim face.

Suddenly her eyes opened. The urchin found himself looking straight into an expression which, it would seem, had the power to change his blood to salt. He howled piercingly and fell backward.

The woman floundered for a moment, tossed her arms about her head as if in combat, and again began to snore.

Jimmie crawled back into the shadows and waited. A noise in the next room had followed his cry at the discovery that his mother was awake. He grovelled in the gloom, his eyes riveted upon the intervening door.

He heard it creak, and then the sound of a small voice came to him. 'Jimmie! Jimmie! Are yehs dere?' it whispered. The urchin started. The thin, white face of his sister looked at him from the doorway of the other room. She crept to him across the floor.

The father had not moved, but lay in the same deathlike sleep. The mother writhed in an uneasy slumber, her chest wheezing as if she were in the agonies of strangulation. Out at the window a florid moon was peering over dark roofs, and in the distance the waters of a river glimmered pallidly.

The small frame of the ragged girl was quivering. Her features were haggard from weeping, and her eyes gleamed with fear. She grasped the urchin's arm in her little trembling hands and they huddled in a corner. The eyes of both were drawn, by some force, to stare at the woman's face, for they thought she need only to awake and all the fiends would come from below.

They crouched until the ghost mists of dawn appeared at the window, drawing close to the panes, and looking in at the prostrate, heaving body of the mother.

4

The babe, Tommie died. He went away in an insignificant coffin, his small waxen hand clutching a flower that the girl, Maggie, had stolen from an Italian.

She and Jimmie lived.

The inexperienced fibres of the boy's eyes were hardened at an early age. He became a young man of leather. He lived some red years without laboring. During that time his sneer became chronic. He studied human nature in the gutter, and found it no worse than he thought he had reason to believe it. He never conceived a respect for the world, because he had begun with no idols that it had smashed.

He clad his soul in armor by means of happening hilariously in at a mission church where a man composed his sermons of 'you's.' Once a philosopher asked this man why he did not say 'we' instead of 'you.' The man replied, 'What?'

While they got warm at the stove he told his hearers just where he calculated they stood with the Lord. Many of the sinners were impatient over the pictured depths of their degradation. They were waiting for soup tickets.

A reader of the words of wind demons might have been able to see the portions of a dialogue pass to and fro between the exhorter and his hearers.

'You are damned,' said the preacher. And the reader of sounds might have seen the reply go forth from the ragged people: 'Where's our soup?'

Jimmie and a companion sat in a rear seat and commented upon the things that didn't concern them, with all the freedom of English tourists. When they grew thirsty and went out, their minds confused the speaker with Christ.

Momentarily, Jimmie was sullen with thoughts of a hopeless altitude where grew fruit. His companion said that if he should ever go to heaven he would ask for a million dollars and a bottle of beer.

Jimmie's occupation for a long time was to stand on street corners and watch the world go by, dreaming blood-red dreams at the passing of pretty women. He menaced mankind at the intersections of streets.

On the corners he was in life and of life. The world was going on and he was there to perceive it.

He maintained a belligerent attitude towards all well-dressed men. To him fine raiment was allied to weakness, and all good coats covered faint hearts. He and his order were kings, to a certain extent, over the men of untarnished clothes, because these latter dreaded, perhaps, to be either killed or laughed at.

Above all things he despised obvious Christians and ciphers with the chrysanthemums of aristocracy in their buttonholes. He considered himself above both of these classes. He was afraid of nothing.

When he had a dollar in his pocket his satisfaction with existence was the greatest thing in the world. So, eventually, he felt obliged to work. His father died, and his mother's years were divided up into periods of thirty days.

He became a truck driver. There was given to him the charge of a painstaking pair of horses and a large rattling truck. He invaded the turmoil and tumble of the downtown streets, and learned to breathe maledictory defiance at the police, who occasionally used to climb up, drag him from his perch, and punch him.

In the lower part of the city he daily involved himself in hideous tangles. If he and his team chanced to be in the rear he preserved a demeanor of serenity, crossing his legs and bursting forth into yells when foot passengers took dangerous dives beneath the noses of his champing horses. He smoked his pipe calmly, for he knew that his pay was marching on.

If his charge was in the front and if it became the key-truck of chaos, he entered terrifically into the quarrel that was raging to and fro among the drivers on their high seats, and sometimes roared oaths and violently got himself arrested.

After a time his sneer grew so that it turned its glare upon all things. He became so sharp that he believed in nothing. To him the police were always actuated by malignant impulses, and the rest of the world was composed, for the most part, of despicable creatures who were all trying to take advantage of him, and with whom, in defence, he was obliged to quarrel on all possible occasions. He himself occupied a down-trodden position, which had a private but distinct element of grandeur in its isolation.

The greatest cases of aggravated idiocy were, to his mind, rampant upon the front platforms of all the street-cars. At first his tongue strove with these beings, but he eventually became superior. In him grew a majestic contempt for those strings of street-cars that followed him like intent bugs.

He fell into the habit, when starting on a long journey, of fixing his eyes on a high and distant object, commanding his horses to start and then going into a trance of oblivion. Multitudes of drivers might howl in his rear, and passengers might load him with opprobrium, but he would not awaken until some blue policeman turned red and began frenziedly to seize bridles and beat the soft noses of the responsible horses.

When he paused to contemplate the attitude of the police towards himself and his fellows, he believed that they were the only men in the city who had no rights. When driving about, he felt that he was held liable by the police for anything that might occur in the streets, and that he was the common prey of all energetic officials. In revenge, he resolved never to move out of the way of anything, until formidable circumstances or a much larger man than himself forced him to it.

Foot passengers were mere pestering flies with an insane disregard for their legs and his convenience. He could not comprehend their desire to cross the streets. Their madness smote him with eternal amazement. He was continually storming at them from his throne. He sat aloft and denounced their frantic leaps, plunges, dives, and straddles.

When they would thrust at, or parry, the noses of his champing horses, making them swing their heads and move their feet, and thus disturbing a stolid, dreamy repose, he swore at the men as fools, for he himself could perceive that Providence had caused it to be clearly written that he and his team had the inalienable right to stand in the proper path of the sun chariot and, if they so minded, to obstruct its mission or take a wheel off.

And if the god driver had had a desire to step down, put up his flame-colored fists, and manfully dispute the right of way, he would have probably been immediately opposed by a scowling mortal with two sets of hard knuckles.

It is possible, perhaps, that this young man would have derided, in an axle-wide alley, the approach of a flying ferryboat. Yet he achieved a respect for a fire engine. As one charged towards his truck, he would drive fearfully upon a sidewalk, threatening untold people with annihilation. When an engine struck a mass of blocked trucks, splitting it into fragments as a blow annihilates a cake of ice, Jimmie's team could usually be observed high and safe, with whole wheels, on the sidewalk. The fearful coming of the engine could break up the most intricate muddle of heavy vehicles at which the police had been storming for half an hour.

A fire engine was enshrined in his heart as an appalling thing that he loved with a distant, dog-like devotion. It had been known to overturn a street-car. Those leaping horses, striking sparks from the cobbles in their forward lunge, were creatures to be ineffably admired. The clang of the gong pierced his breast like a noise of remembered war.

When Jimmie was a little boy, he began to be arrested. Before he reached a great age, he had a fair record.

He developed too great a tendency to climb down from his truck and fight with other drivers. He had been in quite a number of miscellaneous fights, and in some general bar-room rows that had become known to the police. Once he had been arrested for assaulting a Chinaman. Two women in different parts of the city, and entirely unknown to each other, caused him considerable annoyance by breaking forth, simultaneously, at fateful intervals, into wailings about marriage and support and infants.

Nevertheless, he had, on a certain star-lit evening, said wonderingly and quite reverently, 'Deh moon looks like hell, don't it?'

5

The girl, Maggie, blossomed in a mud puddle. She grew to be a most rare and wonderful production of a tenement district, a pretty girl.

None of the dirt of Rum Alley seemed to be in her veins. The philosophers, upstairs, downstairs, and on the same floor, puzzled over it.

When a child, playing and fighting with gamins in the street, dirt disguised her. Attired in tatters and grime, she went unseen.

There came a time, however, when the young men of the vicinity said 'Dat Johnson goil is a putty good looker.' About this period her brother remarked to her: 'Mag, I'll tell yeh dis! See? Yeh've eeder got t' go on d' toif er go t' work!' Whereupon she went to work, having the feminine aversion to the alternative.

By a chance, she got a position in an establishment where they made collars and cuffs. She received a stool and a machine in a room where sat twenty girls of various shades of yellow discontent. She perched on the stool and treadled at her machine all day, turning out collars with a name which might have been noted for its irrelevancy to anything connected with collars. At night she returned home to her mother.

Jimmie grew large enough to take the vague position of head of the family. As incumbent of that office, he stumbled upstairs late at night, as his father had done before him. He reeled about the room, swearing at his relations, or went to sleep on the floor.

The mother had gradually risen to such a degree of fame that she could bandy words with her acquaintances among the police justices. Court officials called her by her first name. When she appeared they pursued a course which had been theirs for months. They invariably grinned, and cried out, 'Hello, Mary, you here again?' Her grey head wagged in many courts. She always besieged the bench with voluble excuses, explanations, apologies, and prayers. Her flaming face and rolling eyes were a familiar sight on the island. She measured time by means of sprees, and was eternally swollen and dishevelled.

One day the young man Pete, who as a lad had smitten the Devil's Row urchin in the back of the head and put to flight the antagonists of his friend Jimmie, strutted upon the scene. He met Jimmie one day on the street, promised to take him to a boxing match in Williamsburg, and called for him in the evening.

Maggie observed Pete.

He sat on a table in the Johnson home, and dangled his checked legs with an enticing nonchalance. His hair was curled down over his forehead in an oiled bang. His pugged nose seemed to revolt from contact with a bristling moustache of short, wirelike hairs. His blue double-breasted coat, edged with black braid, was buttoned close to a red puff tie, and his patent leather shoes looked like weapons.

His mannerisms stamped him as a man who had a correct sense of his personal superiority. There were valor and contempt for circumstances in the glance of his eye. He waved his hands like a man of the world who dismisses religion and philosophy, and says 'Rats!' He had certainly seen everything, and with each curl of his lip he declared that it amounted to nothing. Maggie thought he must be a very 'elegant' bartender.

He was telling tales to Jimmie.

Maggie watched him furtively, with half-closed eyes lit with vague interest.

'Hully gee! Dey makes me tired,' he said. 'Mos' e'ry day some farmer comes in an' tries t' run d' shop. See? But d' gits t'rowed right out. I jolt dem right out in d' street before dey knows where dey is. See?'

'Sure,' said Jimmie.

'Dere was a mug come in d' place d' odder day wid an idear he was goin' t' own d' place. Hully gee! he was goin' t' own d' place. I see he had a still on, and' I didn' wanna giv 'im no stuff, so I says, "Git outa here an' don' make no trouble," I says like dat. See? "Git outa here an' don' make no trouble"; like dat. "Git outa here," I says. See?'

Jimmie nodded understandingly. Over his features played an eager desire to state the amount of his valor in a similar crisis, but the narrator proceeded.

'Well, deh blokie he says: "T' blazes wid it! I ain' lookin' for no scrap," he says – see? – "but," he says, "I'm 'spectable cit'zen an' I wanna drink, an' quick, too." See? "Aw, go ahn!" I says, like dat. "Aw, go ahn," I says. See? "Don' make no trouble," I says, like dat. "Don' make no trouble." See? Den d' mug, he squared off an' said he was fine as silk wid his dukes – see? an' he wan'ed a drink – quick. Dat's what he said. See?'

'Sure,' repeated Jimmie.

Pete continued. 'Say, I jes' jumped d' bar, an' d' way I plunked dat blokie was outa sight. See? Dat's right! In d' jaw! See? Hully gee! he t'rowed a spittoon t'rough d' front windee. Say, I tau't I'd drop dead. But d' boss, he comes in after, an' he says: "Pete, yehs done jes' right! Yeh've gotta keep order, an' it's all right." See? "It's all right," he says. Dat's what he said.'

The two held a technical discussion.

'Dat bloke was a dandy,' said Pete in conclusion, 'but he hadn't oughta made no trouble. Dat's what I says t' dem: "Don' come in here an' make no trouble," I says, like dat. "Don' make no trouble." See?'

As Jimmie and his friend exchanged tales descriptive of their prowess, Maggie leaned back in the shadow. Her eyes dwelt wonderingly and rather wistfully upon Pete's face. The broken furniture, grimy walls, and general disorder and dirt of her home of a sudden appeared before her and began to take a potential aspect. Pete's aristocratic person looked as if it might soil. She looked keenly at him, occasionally wondering if he was feeling contempt. But Pete seemed to be enveloped in reminiscence.

'Hully gee!' said he, 'dose mugs can't phase me. Dey knows I kin wipe up d' street wid any tree of dem.'

When he said, 'Ah, what d' hell!' his voice was burdened with disdain for the inevitable and contempt for anything that fate might compel him to endure.

Maggie perceived that here was the ideal man. Her dim thoughts were often searching for far away lands where the little hills sing together in the morning. Under the trees of her dream-gardens there had always walked a lover.

6

Pete took note of Maggie.

'Say, Mag, I'm stuck on yer shape. It's outa sight,' he said, parenthetically, with an affable grin.

As he became aware that she was listening closely, he grew still more eloquent in his description of various happenings in his career. It appeared that he was invincible in fights.

'Why,' he said, referring to a man with whom he had had a misunderstanding, 'dat mug scrapped like a dago. Dat's right. He was dead easy. See? He tau't he was a scrapper. But he foun' out diff'ent. Hully gee!'

He walked to and fro in the small room, which seemed then to grow even smaller and unfit to hold his dignity, the attribute of a supreme warrior. That swing of the shoulders which had frozen the timid when he was but a lad had increased with his growth and education in the ratio of ten to one. It, combined with the sneer upon his mouth, told mankind that there was nothing in space which could appal him. Maggie marveled at him and surrounded him with greatness. She vaguely tried to calculate the altitude of the pinnacle from which he must have looked down upon her.

'I met a chump deh odder day way up in deh city,' he said. 'I was goin' teh see a frien' of mine. When I was a-crossin' deh street deh chump runned plump inteh me, an' den he turns aroun' an' says, "Yer insolen' ruffin!" he says, like dat. "Oh, gee!" I says, "oh, gee! git off d' eart'!" I says, like dat. See? "Git off d' eart'!" like dat. Den deh blokie he got wild. He says I was a contempt'ble scoun'el, er somethin' like dat, an' he says I was doom' teh everlastin' pe'dition, er somethin' like dat. "Gee!" I says, "Gee! Yer joshin' me." I says, "Yer joshin' me." An' den I slugged 'im. See?'

With Jimmie in his company, Pete departed in a sort of blaze of glory from the Johnson home. Maggie, leaning from the window, watched him as he walked down the street.

Here was a formidable man who disdained the strength of a world full of fists. Here was one who had contempt for brass-clothed power; one whose knuckles could ring defiantly against the granite of law. He was a knight.

The two men went from under the glimmering street lamp and passed into shadows.

Turning, Maggie contemplated the dark, dust-stained walls, and the scant and crude furniture of her home. A clock, in a splintered and battered oblong box of varnished wood, she suddenly regarded as an abomination. She noted that it ticked raspingly. The almost vanished flowers in the carpet pattern, she conceived to be newly hideous. Some faint attempts which she had made with blue ribbon to freshen the appearance of a dingy curtain, she now saw to be piteous.

She wondered what Pete dined on.

She reflected upon the collar-and-cuff factory. It began to appear to her mind as a dreary place of endless grinding. Pete's elegant occupation brought him, no doubt, into contact with people who had money and manners. It was probable that he had a large acquaintance with pretty girls. He must have great sums of money to spend.

To her the earth was composed of hardships and insults. She felt instant admiration for a man who openly defied it. She thought that if the grim angel of death should clutch his heart, Pete would shrug his shoulders and say, 'Oh, ev'ryt'ing goes.'

She anticipated that he would come again shortly. She spent some of her week's pay in the purchase of flowered cretonne for a lambrequin. She made it with infinite care, and hung it to the slightly careening mantel over the stove in the kitchen. She studied it with painful anxiety from different points in the room. She wanted it to look well on Sunday night when, perhaps, Jimmie's friend would come. On Sunday night, however, Pete did not appear.

Afterwards the girl looked at it with a sense of humiliation. She was now convinced that Pete was superior to admiration for lambrequins.

A few evenings later Pete entered with fascinating innovations in his apparel. As she had seen him twice and he wore a different suit each time, Maggie had a dim impression that his wardrobe was prodigious.

'Say, Mag,' he said, 'put on yer bes' duds Friday night an' I'll take yehs t' d' show. See?'

He spent a few moments in flourishing his clothes, and then vanished without having glanced at the lambrequin.

Over the eternal collars and cuffs in the factory Maggie spent the most of three days in making imaginary sketches of Pete and his daily environment. She imagined some half-dozen women in love with him, and thought he must lean dangerously towards an indefinite one whom she pictured as endowed with great charms of person, but with an altogether contemptible disposition.

She thought he must live in a blare of pleasure. He had friends and people who were afraid of him.

She saw the golden glitter of the place where Pete was to take her. It would be an entertainment of many hues and many melodies, where she was afraid she might appear small and mouse-colored.

Her mother drank whiskey all Friday morning. With lurid face and tossing hair she cursed and destroyed furniture all Friday afternoon. When Maggie came home at half-past six her mother lay asleep amid the wreck of chairs and a table. Fragments of various household utensils were scattered about the floor. She had vented some phase of drunken fury upon the lambrequin. It lay in a bedraggled heap in the corner.

'Hah!' she snorted, sitting up suddenly, 'where yeh been? Why don' yeh come home earlier? Been loafin' 'round d' streets. Yer gettin' t' be a regular devil.'

When Pete arrived, Maggie, in a worn black dress, was waiting for him in the midst of a floor strewn with wreckage. The curtain at the window had been pulled by a heavy hand and hung by one tack, dangling to and fro in the draught through the cracks at the sash. The knots of blue ribbons appeared like violated flowers. The fire in the stove had gone out. The displaced lids and open doors showed heaps of sullen gray ashes. The remnants of a meal, ghastly, lay in a corner. Maggie's mother, stretched on the floor, blasphemed and gave her daughter a bad name.

7

An orchestra of yellow silk women and bald-headed men, on an elevated stage near the centre of a great green-hued hall, played a popular waltz. The place was crowded with people grouped about little tables. A battalion of waiters slid among the throng, carrying trays of beer glasses, and making change from the inexhaustible vaults of their trousers pockets. Little boys, in the costumes of French chefs, paraded up and down the irregular aisles vending fancy cakes. There was a low rumble of conversation and a subdued clinking of glasses. Clouds of tobacco smoke rolled and wavered high in air above the dull gilt of the chandeliers.

The vast crowd had an air throughout of having just quitted labor. Men with callused hands, and attired in garments that showed the wear of an endless drudging for a living, smoked their pipes contentedly and spent five, ten, or perhaps fifteen cents for beer. There was a mere sprinkling of men who smoked cigars purchased elsewhere. The great body of the crowd was composed of people who showed that all day they strove with their hands. Quiet Germans, with maybe their wives and two or three children, sat listening to the music, with the expressions of happy cows. An occasional party of sailors from a warship, their faces pictures of sturdy health, spent the earlier hours of the evening at the small round tables. Very infrequent tipsy men, swollen with the value of their opinions, engaged their companions in earnest and confidential conversation. In the balcony, and here and there below, shone the impassive faces of women. The nationalities of the Bowery beamed upon the stage from all directions.

Pete walked aggressively up a side aisle and took seats with Maggie at a table beneath the balcony.

'Two beehs!'

Leaning back, he regarded with eyes of superiority the scene before them. This attitude affected Maggie strongly. A man who could regard such a sight with indifference must be accustomed to very great things.

It was obvious that Pete had visited this place many times before, and was very familiar with it. A knowledge of this fact made Maggie feel little and new.

He was extremely gracious and attentive. He displayed the consideration of a cultured gentleman who knew what was due. 'Say, what's eatin' yeh? Bring d' lady a big glass! What use is dat pony?'

'Don't be fresh, now,' said the waiter, with some warmth, as he departed.

'Ah, git off d' eart'!' said Pete, after the other's retreating form.

Maggie perceived that Pete brought forth all his elegance and all his knowledge of high-class customs for her benefit. Her heart warmed as she reflected upon his condescension.

The orchestra of yellow silk women and bald-headed men gave vent to a few bars of anticipatory music, and a girl, in a pink dress with short skirts, galloped upon the stage. She smiled upon the throng as if in acknowledgment of a warm welcome, and began to walk to and fro, making profuse gesticulations, and singing, in brazen soprano tones, a song the words of which were inaudible. When she broke into the swift rattling measures of a chorus some half-tipsy men near the stage joined in the rollicking refrain, and glasses were pounded rhythmically upon the tables. People leaned forward to watch her and to try to catch the words of the song. When she vanished there were long rollings of applause.

Obedient to more anticipatory bars, she reappeared among the half-suppressed cheering of the tipsy men. The orchestra plunged into dance music, and the laces of the dancer fluttered and flew in the glare of gas jets. She divulged the fact that she was attired in some half-dozen skirts. It was patent that any one of them would have proved adequate for the purpose for which skirts are intended. An occasional man bent forward, intent upon the pink stockings. Maggie wondered at the splendor of the costume and lost herself in calculations of the cost of the silks and laces.

The dancer's smile of enthusiasm was turned for ten minutes upon the faces of her audience. In the finale she fell into some of those grotesque attitudes which were at the time popular among the dancers in the theatres uptown, giving to the Bowery public the diversions of the aristocratic theatre-going public at reduced rates.

'Say, Pete,' said Maggie, leaning forward, 'dis is great.'

'Sure!' said Pete, with proper complacence.

A ventriloquist followed the dancer. He held two fantastic dolls on his knees. He made them sing mournful ditties and say funny things about geography and Ireland.

'Do dose little men talk?' asked Maggie.

'Naw,' said Pete, 'it's some big jolly. See?'

Two girls, set down on the bills as sisters, came forth and sang a duet which is heard occasionally at concerts given under church auspices. They supplemented it with a dance, which, of course, can never be seen at concerts given under church auspices.

After they had retired, a woman of debatable age sang a negro melody. The chorus necessitated some grotesque waddlings supposed to be an imitation of a plantation darky, under the influence, probably, of music and the moon. The audience was just enthusiastic enough over it to have her return and sing a sorrowful lay, whose lines told of a mother's love, and a sweetheart who waited, and a young man who was lost at sea under harrowing circumstances. From the faces of a score or so in the crowd the self-contained look faded. Many heads were bent forward with eagerness and sympathy. As the last distressing sentiment of the piece was brought forth, it was greeted by the kind of applause which rings as sincere.

As a final effort, the singer rendered some verses which described a vision of Britain annihilated by America, and Ireland bursting her bonds. A carefully prepared climax was reached in the last line of the last verse, when the singer threw out her arms and cried, 'The star-spangled banner.' Instantly a great cheer swelled from the throats of this assemblage of the masses, most of them of foreign birth. There was a heavy rumble of booted feet thumping the floor. Eyes gleamed with sudden fire, and callused hands waved frantically in the air.

After a few moments' rest, the orchestra played noisily, and a small fat man burst out upon the stage. He began to roar a song and to stamp back and forth before the footlights, wildly waving a silk hat and throwing leers broadcast. He made his face into fantastic grimaces until he looked like a devil on a Japanese kite.

The crowd laughed gleefully. His short, fat legs were never still a moment. He shouted and roared and bobbed his shock of red wig until the audience broke out in excited applause.

Pete did not pay much attention to the progress of events upon the stage. He was drinking beer and watching Maggie.

Her cheeks were blushing with excitement and her eyes were glistening. She drew deep breaths of pleasure. No thoughts of the atmosphere of the collar-and-cuff factory came to her.

With the final crash of the orchestra they jostled their way to the sidewalk in the crowd. Pete took Maggie's arm and pushed a way for her, offering to fight with a man or two. They reached Maggie's home at a late hour and stood for a moment in front of the gruesome doorway.

'Say, Mag,' said Pete, 'give us a kiss for takin' yeh t' d' show, will yer?'

Maggie laughed, as if startled, and drew away from him.

'Naw, Pete,' she said, 'dat wasn't in it.'

'Ah, why wasn't it?' urged Pete.

The girl retreated nervously.

'Ah, go ahn!' repeated he.

Maggie darted into the hall and up the stairs. She turned and smiled at him, then disappeared.

Pete walked slowly down the street. He had something of an astonished expression upon his features. He paused under a lamppost and breathed a low breath of surprise.

'Gee!' he said, 'I wonner if I've been played for a duffer.'

8

As thoughts of Pete came to Maggie's mind, she began to have an intense dislike for all of her dresses.

'What ails yeh? What makes ye be allus fixin' and fussin'?' her mother would frequently roar at her.

She began to note with more interest the well-dressed women she met on the avenues. She envied elegance and soft palms. She craved those adornments of person which she saw every day on the street, conceiving them to be allies of vast importance to women.

Studying faces, she thought many of the women and girls she chanced to meet smiled with serenity as though for ever cherished and watched over by those they loved.

The air in the collar-and-cuff establishment strangled her. She knew she was gradually and surely shrivelling in the hot, stuffy room. The begrimed windows rattled incessantly from the passing of elevated trains. The place was filled with a whirl of noises and odors.

She became lost in thought as she looked at some of the grizzled women in the room, mere mechanical contrivances sewing seams and grinding out, with heads bent over their work, tales of imagined or real girlhood happiness, or of past drunks, or the baby at home, and unpaid wages. She wondered how long her youth would endure. She began to see the bloom upon her cheeks as something of value.

She imagined herself, in an exasperating future, as a scrawny woman with an eternal grievance. She thought Pete to be a very fastidious person concerning the appearance of women.

She felt that she would love to see somebody entangle their fingers in the oily beard of the fat foreigner who owned the establishment. He was a detestable creature. He wore white socks with low shoes. He sat all day delivering orations in the depths of a cushioned chair. His pocket-book deprived them of the power of retort.

'What do you sink I pie fife dolla a week for? Play? No, py tamn!'

Maggie was anxious for a friend to whom she could talk about Pete. She would have liked to discuss his admirable mannerisms with a reliable mutual friend. At home, she found her mother often drunk and always raving. It seemed that the world had treated this woman very badly, and she took a deep revenge upon such portions of it as came within her reach. She broke furniture as if she were at last getting her rights. She swelled with virtuous indignation as she carried the lighter articles of household use, one by one, under the shadows of the three gilt balls, where Hebrews chained them with chains of interest.

Jimmie came when he was obliged to by circumstances over which he had no control. His well-trained legs brought him staggering home and put him to bed some nights when he would rather have gone elsewhere.

Swaggering Pete loomed like a golden sun to Maggie. He took her to a dime museum, where rows of meek freaks astonished her. She contemplated their deformities with awe and thought them a sort of chosen tribe.

Pete, racking his brains for amusement, discovered the Central Park Menagerie and the Museum of Arts. Sunday afternoons would sometimes find them at these places. Pete did not appear to be particularly interested in what he saw. He stood around looking heavy, while Maggie giggled in glee.

Once at the menagerie he went into a trance of admiration before the spectacle of a very small monkey threatening to thrash a cageful because one of them had pulled his tail and he had not wheeled about quickly enough to discover who did it. Ever after Pete knew that monkey by sight, and winked at him, trying to induce him to fight with other and larger monkeys.

At the museum, Maggie said, 'Dis is outa sight!'

'Aw, rats!' said Pete; 'wait till next summer an' I'll take yehs to a picnic.'

While the girl wandered in the vaulted rooms, Pete occupied himself in returning, stony stare for stony stare, the appalling scrutiny of the watchdogs of the treasures. Occasionally he would remark in loud tones, 'Dat jay has got glass eyes,' and sentences of the sort. When he tired of this amusement he would go to the mummies and moralize over them.

Usually he submitted with silent dignity to all that he had to go through, but at times he was goaded into comment.

'Aw!' he demanded once. 'Look at all dese little jugs! Hundred jugs in a row! Ten rows in a case, an' 'bout a t'ousand cases! What d' blazes use is dem?'

In the evenings of week days he often took her to see plays in which the dazzling heroine was rescued from the palatial home of her treacherous guardian by the hero with the beautiful sentiments. The latter spent most of his time out at soak in pale-green snow-storms, busy with a nickel-plated revolver rescuing aged strangers from villains.

Maggie lost herself in sympathy with the wanderers swooning in snow-storms beneath happy-hued church windows, while a choir within sang 'Joy to the World.' To Maggie and the rest of the audience this was transcendental realism. Joy always within, and they, like the actor, inevitably without. Viewing it, they hugged themselves in ecstatic pity of their imagined or real condition.

The girl thought the arrogance and granite-heartedness of the magnate of the play were very accurately drawn. She echoed the maledictions that the occupants of the gallery showered on this individual when his lines compelled him to expose his extreme selfishness.

Shady persons in the audience revolted from the pictured villainy of the drama. With untiring zeal they hissed vice and applauded virtue. Unmistakably bad men evinced an apparently sincere admiration for virtue. The loud gallery was overwhelmingly with the unfortunate and the oppressed. They encouraged the struggling hero with cries, and jeered the villain, hooting and calling attention to his whiskers. When anybody died in the pale-green snow-storms, the gallery mourned. They sought out the painted misery and hugged it as akin.

In the hero's erratic march from poverty in the first act to wealth and triumph in the final one, in which he forgives all the enemies that he has left, he was assisted by the gallery, which applauded his generous and noble sentiments and confounded the speeches of his opponents by making irrelevant but very sharp remarks. Those actors who were cursed with the parts of villains were confronted at every turn by the gallery. If one of them rendered lines containing the most subtle distinctions between right and wrong, the gallery was immediately aware that the actor meant wickedness, and denounced him accordingly.

The last act was a triumph for the hero, poor and of the masses, the representative of the audience, over the villain and the rich man, his pockets stuffed with bonds, his heart packed with tyrannical purposes, imperturbable amid suffering.

Maggie always departed with raised spirits from these melodramas. She rejoiced at the way in which the poor and virtuous eventually overcame the wealthy and wicked. The theatre made her think. She wondered if the culture and refinement she had seen imitated, perhaps grotesquely, by the heroine on the stage, could be acquired by a girl who lived in a tenement house and worked in a shirt factory.

9

A group of urchins were intent upon the side door of a saloon. Expectancy gleamed from their eyes. They were twisting their fingers in excitement.

'Here she comes!' yelled one of them suddenly.

The group of urchins burst instantly asunder and its individual fragments were spread in a wide, respectable half-circle about the point of interest. The saloon door opened with a crash, and the figure of a woman appeared upon the threshold. Her gray hair fell in knotted masses about her shoulders. Her face was crimsoned and wet with perspiration. Her eyes had a rolling glare.

'Not a cent more of me money will yehs ever get – not a red! I spent me money here for t'ree years, an' now yehs tells me yeh'll sell me no more stuff! Go fall on yerself, Johnnie Murckre! 'Disturbance?' Disturbance be blowed! Go fall on yerself, Johnnie—'

The door received a kick of exasperation from within, and the woman lurched heavily out on the sidewalk.

The gamins in the half-circle became violently agitated. They began to dance about and hoot and yell and jeer. A wide dirty grin spread over each face.

The woman made a furious dash at a particularly outrageous cluster of little boys. They laughed delightedly, and scampered off a short distance, calling out to her over their shoulders. She stood tottering on the curbstone and thundered at them.

'Yeh devil's kids!' she howled, shaking her fists. The little boys whooped in glee. As she started up the street they fell in behind and marched uproariously. Occasionally she wheeled about and made charges on them. They ran nimbly out of reach and taunted her.

In the frame of a gruesome doorway she stood for a moment cursing them. Her hair straggled, giving her red features a look of insanity. Her great fists quivered as she shook them madly in the air.

The urchins made terrific noises until she turned and disappeared. Then they filed off quietly in the way they had come.

The woman floundered about in the lower hall of the tenement house, and finally stumbled up the stairs. On an upper hall a door was opened and a collection of heads peered curiously out, watching her. With a wrathful snort the woman confronted the door, but it was slammed hastily in her face and the key was turned.

She stood for a few minutes, delivering a frenzied challenge at the panels. 'Come out in deh hall, Mary Murphy, if yehs want a scrap! Come ahn! yeh overgrown terrier, come ahn!'

She began to kick the door. She shrilly defied the universe to appear and do battle. Her cursing trebles brought heads from all doors save the one she threatened. Her eyes glared in every direction. The air was full of her tossing fists.

'Come ahn! deh hull gang of yehs, come ahn!' she roared at the spectators. An oath or two, catcalls, jeers, and bits of facetious advice were given in reply. Missiles clattered about her feet.

'What's wrong wi'che?' said a voice in the gathered gloom, and Jimmie came forward. He carried a tin dinner pail in his hand and under his arm a truckman's brown apron done in a bundle. 'What's wrong?' he demanded.

'Come out! all of yehs, come out,' his mother was howling. 'Come ahn an' I'll stamp yer faces tru d' floor.'

'Shet yer face, an' come home, yeh old fool!' roared Jimmie at her. She strode up to him and twirled her fingers in his face. Her eyes were darting flames of unreasoning rage, and her frame trembled with eagerness for a fight.

'An' who are youse? I ain't givin' a snap of me fingers fer youse!' she bawled at him. She turned her huge back in tremendous disdain and climbed the stairs to the next floor.

Jimmie followed, and at the top of the flight he seized his mother's arm and started to drag her towards the door of their room.

'Come home!' he gritted between his teeth.

'Take yer hands off me! Take yer hands off me!' shrieked his mother.

She raised her arm and whirled her great fist at her son's face. Jimmie dodged his head, and the blow struck him in the back of the neck. 'Come home!' he gritted again. He threw out his left hand and writhed his fingers about her middle arm. The mother and the son began to sway and struggle like gladiators.

'Whoop!' said the Rum Alley tenement house. The hall filled with interested spectators.

'Hi, ol' lady, dat was a dandy!'

'T'ree t' one on d' red!'

'Ah, quit yer scrappin'!'

The door of the Johnson home opened and Maggie looked out. Jimmie made a supreme cursing effort and hurled his mother into the room. He quickly followed and closed the door. The Rum Alley tenement swore disappointedly and retired.

The mother slowly gathered herself up from the floor. Her eyes glittered menacingly upon her children.

'Here now,' said Jimmie, 'we've had enough of dis. Sit down, an' don' make no trouble.'

He grasped her arm and, twisting it, forced her into a creaking chair.

'Keep yer hands off me!' roared his mother again.

'Say, yeh ol' bat! Quit dat!' yelled Jimmie, madly. Maggie shrieked and ran into the other room. To her there came the sound of a storm of crashes and curses. There was a great final thump and Jimmie's voice cried: 'Dere, now! Stay still.' Maggie opened the door now, and went warily out. 'Oh, Jimmie!'

He was leaning against the wall and swearing. Blood stood upon bruises on his knotty forearms where they had scraped against the floor or the wall in the scuffle. The mother lay screeching on the floor, the tears running down her furrowed face.

Maggie, standing in the middle of the room, gazed about her. The usual upheaval of the tables and chairs had taken place. Crockery was strewn broadcast in fragments. The stove had been disturbed on its legs, and now leaned idiotically to one side. A pail had been upset and water spread in all directions.

The door opened and Pete appeared. He shrugged his shoulders. 'Oh, gee!' he observed.

He walked over to Maggie and whispered in her ear: 'Ah, what d' hell, Mag? Come ahn and we'll have a outa-sight time.'

The mother in the corner upreared her head and shook her tangled locks.

'Aw, yer bote no good, needer of yehs,' she said, glowering at her daughter in the gloom. Her eyes seemed to burn balefully. 'Yeh've gone t' d' devil, Mag Johnson, yehs knows yehs have gone t' d' devil. Yer a disgrace t' yer people. An' now, git out an' go ahn wid dat doe-faced jude of yours. Go wid him, curse yeh, an' a good riddance. Go, an' see how yeh likes it.'

Maggie gazed long at her mother.

'Go now, an' see how yeh likes it. Git out. I won't have sech as youse in me house! Git out, d' yer hear! Damn yeh, git out!'

The girl began to tremble.

At this instant Pete came forward. 'Oh, what d' hell Mag, see?' whispered he softly in her ear. 'Dis all blows over. See? D' ol' woman 'ill be all right in d' mornin'. Come ahn out wid me! We'll have a outa-sight time.'

The woman on the floor cursed. Jimmie was intent upon his bruised forearms. The girl cast a glance about the room filled with a chaotic mass of *débris*, and at the writhing body of her mother.

'Git th' devil outa here.'

Maggie went.

10

Jimmie had an idea it wasn't common courtesy for a friend to come to one's home and ruin one's sister. But he was not sure how much Pete knew about the rules of politeness.

The following night he returned home from work at a rather late hour in the evening. In passing through the halls he came upon the gnarled and leathery old woman who possessed the music box. She was grinning in the dim light that drifted through dust-stained panes. She beckoned to him with a smudged forefinger.

'Ah, Jimmie, what do yehs tink I tumbled to, las' night! It was deh funnies' t'ing I ever saw,' she cried, coming close to him and leering. She was trembling with eagerness to tell her tale. 'I was by me door las' night when yer sister and her jude feller came in late, oh, very late. An' she, the dear, she was a-cryin' as if her heart would break, she was. It was deh funnies' t'ing I ever saw. An' right out here by me door she asked him did he love her, did he. An' she was a-crying as if her heart would break, poor t'ing. An' him, I could see be deh way what he said it dat she had been askin' orften; he says, "Oh, gee, yes," he says, says he. "Oh, gee, yes."'

Storm-clouds swept over Jimmie's face, but he turned from the leathery old woman and plodded on upstairs.

'"Oh, gee, yes,"' she called after him. She laughed a laugh that was like a prophetic croak.

There was no one in at home. The rooms showed that attempts had been made at tidying them. Parts of the wreckage of the day before had been repaired by an unskilful hand. A chair or two and the table stood uncertainly upon legs. The floor had been newly swept. The blue ribbons had been restored to the curtains, and the lambrequin, with its immense sheaves of yellow wheat and red roses of equal size, had been returned, in a worn and sorry state, to its place at the mantel. Maggie's jacket and hat were gone from the nail behind the door.

Jimmie walked to the window and began to look through the blurred glass. It occurred to him to wonder vaguely, for an instant, if some of the women of his acquaintance had brothers.

Suddenly, however, he began to swear.

'But he was me frien'! I brought 'im here! Dat's d' devil of it!'

He fumed about the room, his anger gradually rising to the furious pitch. 'I'll kill deh jay! Dat's what I'll do! I'll kill deh jay!'

He clutched his hat and sprang towards the door. But it opened, and his mother's great form blocked the passage.

'What's d' matter wid yeh?' exclaimed she, coming into the room.

Jimmie gave vent to a sardonic curse and then laughed heavily.

'Well, Maggie's gone teh d' devil! Dat's what! See?'

'Eh?' said his mother.

'Maggie's gone teh d' devil! Are yehs deaf?' roared Jimmie, impatiently.

'Aw, git out!' murmured the mother, astounded.

Jimmie grunted, and then began to stare out the window. His mother sat down in a chair, but a moment later sprang erect and delivered a maddened whirl of oaths. Her son turned to look at her as she reeled and swayed in the middle of the room, her fierce face convulsed with passion, her blotched arms raised high in imprecation.

'May she be cursed for ever!' she shrieked. 'May she eat nothin' but stones and deh dirt in deh street. May she sleep in deh gutter an' never see deh sun shine again. D' bloomin'—'

'Here now,' said her son. 'Go fall on yerself, an' quit dat.'

The mother raised lamenting eyes to the ceiling.

'She's d' devil's own chil', Jimmie,' she whispered. 'Ah, who would t'ink such a bad girl could grow up in our fambly, Jimmie, me son. Many d' hour I've spent in talk wid dat girl an' tol' her if she ever went on d' streets I'd see her damned. An' after all her bringin' up, an' what I tol' her and talked wid her, she goes teh d' bad, like a duck teh water.'

The tears rolled down her furrowed face. Her hands trembled.

'An' den when dat Sadie MacMallister next door to us was sent teh d' devil by dat feller what worked in d' soap factory, didn't I tell our Mag dat if she—'

'Ah, dat's anudder story,' interrupted the brother. 'Of course, dat Sadie was nice an' all dat – but – see – it ain't dessame if – see – she was diff'ent.'

He was trying to formulate a theory that he had always unconsciously held, that all sisters excepting his own could, advisedly, be ruined.

He suddenly broke out again. 'I'll go t'ump d' mug what done her d' harm. I'll kill 'im! He t'inks he kin scrap, but when he gits me a-chasin' 'im he'll fin' out where he's wrong, d' big stiff! I'll wipe up d' street wid 'im.'

In a fury he plunged out the doorway. As he vanished the mother raised her head and lifted both hands, entreating.

'May she be cursed for ever!' she cried.

In the darkness of the hallway Jimmie discerned a knot of women talking volubly. When he strode by they paid no attention to him.

'She allus was a bold thing,' he heard one of them cry in an eager voice. 'Dere wasn't a feller come teh deh house but she'd try teh mash 'im. My Annie says deh shameless t'ing tried teh ketch her feller, her own feller, what we useter know his fader.'

'I could 'a tol' yehs dis two years ago,' said a woman, in a key of triumph. 'Yes, sir, it was over two years ago dat I says teh my ol' man, I says, "Dat Johnson girl ain't straight," I says. "Oh, rats!" he says. "Oh, hell!" "Dat's all right," I says, "but I know what I knows," I says, "an' it'll come out later. You wait an' see," I says, "you see."'

'Anybody what had eyes could see dat dere was somethin' wrong wid dat girl. I didn't like her actions.'

On the street Jimmie met a friend. 'What's wrong?' asked the latter.

Jimmie explained. 'An' I'll t'ump 'im till he can't stand.'

'Oh, go ahn!' said the friend. 'What's deh use! Yeh'll git pulled in! Everybody'ill be on to it! An' ten plunks! Gee!'

Jimmie was determined. 'He t'inks he kin scrap, but he'll fin' out diff'ent.'

'Gee,' remonstrated the friend, 'what's d' use?'

11

On a corner a glass-fronted building shed a yellow glare upon the pavements. The open mouth of a saloon called seductively to passengers to enter and annihilate sorrow or create rage.

The interior of the place was papered in olive and bronze tints of imitation leather. A shining bar of counterfeit massiveness extended down the side of the room. Behind it a great mahogany-imitation sideboard reached the ceiling. Upon its shelves rested pyramids of shimmering glasses that were never disturbed. Mirrors set in the face of the sideboard multiplied them. Lemons, oranges, and paper napkins, arranged with mathematical precision, sat among the glasses. Many-hued decanters of liquor perched at regular intervals on the lower shelves. A nickel-plated cash-register occupied a place in the exact centre of the general effect. The elementary senses of it all seemed to be opulence and geometrical accuracy.

Across from the bar a smaller counter held a collection of plates upon which swarmed frayed fragments of crackers, slices of boiled ham, dishevelled bits of cheese, and pickles swimming in vinegar. An odor of grasping, begrimed hands and munching mouths pervaded all.

Pete, in a white jacket, was behind the bar bending expectantly toward a quiet stranger. 'A beeh,' said the man. Pete drew a foam-topped glassful and set it dripping upon the bar.

At this moment the light bamboo doors at the entrance swung open and crashed against the wall. Jimmie and a companion entered. They swaggered unsteadily but belligerently towards the bar and looked at Pete with bleared and blinking eyes.

'Gin,' said Jimmie.

'Gin,' said the companion.

Pete slid a bottle and two glasses along the bar. He bent his head sideways as he assiduously polished away with a napkin at the gleaming wood. He wore a look of watchfulness.

Jimmie and his companion kept their eyes upon the bartender and conversed loudly in tones of contempt.

'He's a dandy masher, ain't he?' laughed Jimmie.

'Well, ain't he!' said the companion, sneering. 'He's great, he is. Git on to deh mug on deh blokie. Dat's enough to make a feller turn handsprings in 'is sleep.'

The quiet stranger moved himself and his glass a trifle farther away and maintained an attitude of obliviousness.

'Gee! ain't he hot stuff?'

'Git onto his shape!'

'Hey,' cried Jimmie, in tones of command. Pete came along slowly, with a sullen dropping of the under lip.

'Well,' he growled, 'what's eatin' yehs?'

'Gin,' said Jimmie.

'Gin,' said the companion.

As Pete confronted them with the bottle and the glasses they laughed in his face. Jimmie's companion, evidently overcome with merriment, pointed a grimy forefinger in Pete's direction.

'Say, Jimmie,' demanded he, 'what's dat behind d' bar?'

'Looks like some chump,' replied Jimmie. They laughed loudly. Pete put down a bottle with a bang and turned a formidable face towards them. He disclosed his teeth and his shoulders heaved restlessly.

'You fellers can't guy me,' he said. 'Drink yer stuff an' git out an' don' make no trouble.'

Instantly the laughter faded from the faces of the two men, and expressions of offended dignity immediately came. 'Aw, who has said anyt'ing t' you?' cried they in the same breath.

The quiet stranger looked at the door calculatingly.

'Ah, come off,' said Pete to the two men. 'Don't pick me up fer no jay. Drink yer rum an' git out an' don' make no trouble.'

'Aw, go ahn!' airily cried Jimmie.

'Ah, go ahn!' airily repeated his companion.

'We goes when we git ready! See?' continued Jimmy.

'Well,' said Pete in a threatening voice, 'don' make no trouble.'

Jimmie suddenly leaned forward with his head on one side. He snarled like a wild animal.

'Well, what if we does? See?' said he.

Hot blood flushed into Pete's face, and he shot a lurid glance at Jimmie. 'Well, den we'll see who's d' bes' man, you or me,' he said.

The quiet stranger moved modestly towards the door. Jimmie began to swell with valor.

'Don' pick me up fer no tenderfoot. When yeh tackles me yeh tackles one of d' bes' men in d' city. See? I'm a scrapper, I am. Ain't dat right, Billie?'

'Sure, Mike,' responded his companion in tones of conviction.

'Aw!' said Pete, easily. 'Go fall on yerself.'

The two men again began to laugh.

'What is dat talking?' cried the companion.

'Don' ast me,' replied Jimmie with exaggerated contempt.

Pete made a furious gesture. 'Git outa here now, an' don' make no trouble. See? Youse fellers er lookin' fer a scrap, an' it's like yeh'll fin' one if yeh keeps on shootin' off yer mout's. I know yehs! See? I kin lick better men dan yehs ever saw in yer lifes. Dat's right! See? Don' pick me up fer no stiff, er yeh might be jolted out in d' street before yeh knows where yeh is. When I comes from behind dis bar, I t'rows yehs boat inteh d' street. See?'

'Ah, go ahn!' cried the two men in chorus.

The glare of a panther came into Pete's eyes. 'Dat's what I said! Unnerstan'?'

He came through a passage at the end of the bar and swelled down upon the two men. They stepped promptly forward and crowded close to him.

They bristled like three roosters. They moved their heads pugnaciously and kept their shoulders braced. The nervous muscles about each mouth twitched with a forced smile of mockery.

'Well, what yer goin' t' do?' gritted Jimmie.

Pete stepped warily back, waving his hands before him to keep the men from coming too near.

'Well, what yer goin' t' do?' repeated Jimmie's ally. They kept close to him, taunting and leering. They strove to make him attempt the initial blow.

'Keep back now! Don' crowd me,' said Pete ominously.

Again they chorused in contempt. 'Aw, go ahn!'

In a small, tossing group, the three men edged for positions like frigates contemplating battle.

'Well, why don' yeh try t' t'row us out?' cried Jimmie and his ally with copious sneers.

The bravery of bulldogs sat upon the faces of the men. Their clenched fists moved like eager weapons.

The allied two jostled the bartender's elbows, glaring at him with feverish eyes and forcing him towards the wall.

Suddenly Pete swore furiously. The flash of action gleamed from his eyes. He threw back his arm and aimed a tremendous, lightning-like blow at Jimmie's face. His foot swung a step forward and the weight of his body was behind his fist. Jimmie ducked his head, Bowery-like, with the quickness of a cat. The fierce answering blows of Jimmie and his ally crushed on Pete's bowed head.

The quiet stranger vanished.

The arms of the combatants whirled in the air like flails. The faces of the men, at first flushed to flame-colored anger, now began to fade to the pallor of warriors in the blood and heat of a battle. Their lips curled back and stretched tightly over the gums in ghoul-like grins. Through their white, gripped teeth struggled hoarse whisperings of oaths. Their eyes glittered with murderous fire.

Each head was huddled between its owner's shoulders, and arms were swinging with marvellous rapidity. Feet scraped to and fro with a loud scratching sound upon the sanded floor. Blows left crimson blotches upon the pale skin. The curses of the first quarter-minute of the fight died away. The breaths of the fighters came wheezing from their lips and the three chests were straining and heaving. Pete at intervals gave vent to low, labored hisses, that sounded like a desire to kill. Jimmie's ally gibbered at times like a wounded maniac. Jimmie was silent, fighting with the face of a sacrificial priest. The rage of fear shone in all their eyes, and their blood-colored fists whirled.

At a critical moment a blow from Pete's hand struck the ally, and he crashed to the floor. He wriggled instantly to his feet and, grasping the quiet stranger's beer-glass from the bar, hurled it at Pete's head.

High on the wall it burst like a bomb, shivering fragments flying in all directions. Then missiles came to every man's head. The place had heretofore appeared free of things to throw, but suddenly glasses and bottles went singing through the air. They were thrown point-blank at bobbing heads. The pyramids of shimmering glasses, that had never been disturbed, changed to cascades as heavy bottles were flung into them. Mirrors splintered to nothing.

The three frothing creatures on the floor buried themselves in a frenzy for blood. There followed in the wake of missiles and fists some unknown prayers, perhaps for death.

The quiet stranger had sprawled very pyrotechnically out on the sidewalk. A laugh ran up and down the avenue for the half of a block. 'Dey've t'rowed a bloke inteh deh street.'

People heard the sound of breaking glass and shuffling feet within the saloon and came running. A small group, bending down to look under the bamboo doors, and watching the fall of glass and three pairs of violent legs, changed in a moment to a crowd.

A policeman came charging down the sidewalk and bounced through the doors into the saloon. The crowd bent and surged in absorbing anxiety to see.

Jimmie caught the first sight of the oncoming interruption. On his feet he had the same regard for a policeman that, when on his truck, he had for a fire-engine. He howled and ran for the side door.

The officer made a terrific advance, club in hand. One comprehensive sweep of the long night-stick threw the ally to the floor and forced Pete to a corner. With his disengaged hand he made a furious effort at Jimmie's coat tails. Then he regained his balance and paused.

'Well, well, you are a pair of pictures. What have ye been up to?'

Jimmie, with his face drenched in blood, escaped up a side street, pursued a short distance by some of the more law-loving, or excited individuals of the crowd.

Later, from a safe dark corner, he saw the policeman, the ally, and the bartender emerge from the saloon. Pete locked the doors and then followed up the avenue in the rear of the crowd-encompassed policeman and his charge.

At first Jimmie, with his heart throbbing at battle heat, started to go desperately to the rescue of his friend, but he halted.

'Ah, what's d' use?' he demanded of himself.

12

In a hall of irregular shape sat Pete and Maggie drinking beer. A submissive orchestra dictated to by a spectacled man with frowsy hair and in soiled evening dress, industriously followed the bobs of his head and the waves of his baton. A ballad singer, in a gown of flaming scarlet, sang in the inevitable voice of brass. When she vanished, men seated at the tables near the front applauded loudly, pounding the polished wood with their beer-glasses. She returned attired in less gown, and sang again. She received another enthusiastic encore. She reappeared in still less gown and danced. The deafening rumble of glass and clapping of hands that followed her exit indicated an overwhelming desire to have her come on for the fourth time, but the curiosity of the audience was not gratified.

Maggie was pale. From her eyes had been plucked all look of self-reliance. She leaned with a dependent air towards her companion. She was timid, as if fearing his anger or displeasure. She seemed to beseech tenderness of him.

Pete's air of distinguished valor had grown upon him until it threatened to reach stupendous dimensions. He was infinitely gracious to the girl. It was apparent to her that his condescension was a marvel.

He could appear to strut even while sitting still, and he showed that he was a lion of lordly characteristics by the air with which he spat.

With Maggie gazing at him wonderingly, he took pride in commanding the waiters, who were, however, indifferent or deaf.

'Hi, you, git a russle on yehs! What yehs lookin' at? Two more beehs,' d' yeh hear?'

He leaned back and critically regarded the person of a girl with a straw-colored wig who was flinging her heels about upon the stage in somewhat awkward imitation of a well-known *danseuse*.

At times Maggie told Pete long confidential tales of her former home life, dwelling upon the escapades of the other members of the family and the difficulties she had had to combat in order to obtain a degree of comfort. He responded in the accents of philanthropy. He pressed her arm with an air of reassuring proprietorship.

'Dey was cursed jays,' he said, denouncing the mother and brother.

The sound of the music which, through the efforts of the frowsy-headed leader, drifted to her ears in the smoke-filled atmosphere, made the girl dream. She thought of her former Rum Alley environment and turned to regard Pete's strong protecting fists. She thought of a collar-and-cuff manufactory and the eternal moan of the proprietor: 'What een hale do you sink I pie fife dolla a week for? Play? No, py tamn!' She contemplated Pete's man-subduing eyes and noted that wealth and prosperity were indicated by his clothes. She imagined a future rose-tinted because of its distance from all that she had experienced before.

As to the present she perceived only vague reasons to be miserable. Her life was Pete's and she considered him worthy of the charge. She would be disturbed by no particular apprehensions so long as Pete adored her as he now said he did. She did not feel like a bad woman. To her knowledge she had never seen any better.

At times men at other tables regarded the girl furtively. Pete, aware of it, nodded at her and grinned. He felt proud.

'Mag, yer a bloomin' good looker,' he remarked, studying her face through the haze. The men made Maggie fear, but she blushed at Pete's words as it became apparent to her that she was the apple of his eye.

Gray-headed men, wonderfully pathetic in their dissipation, stared at her through clouds. Smooth-cheeked boys, some of them with faces of stone and mouths of sin, not nearly so pathetic as the gray heads, tried to find the girl's eyes in the smoke-wreaths. Maggie considered she was not what they thought her. She confined her glances to Pete and the stage.

The orchestra played negro melodies, and a versatile drummer pounded, whacked, clattered, and scratched on a dozen machines to make noise.

Those glances of the men, shot at Maggie from under half-closed lids, made her tremble. She thought them all to be worse men than Pete.

'Come, let's go,' she said.

As they went out Maggie perceived two women seated at a table with some men. They were painted, and their cheeks had lost their roundness. As she passed them the girl, with a shrinking movement, drew back her skirts.

13

Jimmie did not return home for a number of days after the fight with Pete in the saloon. When he did, he approached with extreme caution.

He found his mother raving. Maggie had not returned home. The parent continually wondered how her daughter could come to such a pass. She had never considered Maggie as a pearl dropped unstained into Rum Alley from Heaven, but she could not conceive how it was possible for her daughter to fall so low as to bring disgrace upon her family. She was terrific in denunciation of the girl's wickedness.

The fact that the neighbors talked of it maddened her. When women came in, and in the course of their conversation casually asked, 'Where's Maggie dese days?' the mother shook her fuzzy head at them and appalled them with curses. Cunning hints inviting confidence she rebuffed with violence.

'An' wid all d' bringin' up she had, how could she?' moaningly she asked of her son. 'Wid all d' talkin' wid her I did an' d' t'ings I tol' her to remember. When a girl is bringed up d' way I bringed up Maggie, how kin she go teh d' devil?'

Jimmie was transfixed by the questions. He could not conceive how, under the circumstances, his mother's daughter and his sister could have been so wicked.

His mother took a drink from a bottle that sat on the table. She continued her lament.

'She had a bad heart, dat girl did, Jimmie. She was wicked t' d' heart an' we never knowed it.'

Jimmie nodded, admitting the fact.

'We lived in d' same house wid her an' I brought her up, an' we never knowed how bad she was.'

Jimmie nodded again.

'Wid a home like dis an' a mudder like me, she went teh d' bad,' cried the mother, raising her eyes.

One day Jimmie came home, sat down in a chair, and began to wriggle about with a new and strange nervousness. At last he spoke shamefacedly.

'Well, look-a-here, dis t'ing queers us! See? We're queered! An' maybe it 'ud be better if I – well, I t'ink I kin look 'er up an' – maybe it 'ud be better if I fetched her home an'—'

The mother started from her chair and broke forth into a storm of passionate anger.

'What! Let 'er come an' sleep under deh same roof wid her mudder agin? Oh, yes, I will, won't I! Sure! Shame on yehs, Jimmie Johnson, fer sayin' such a t'ing teh yer own mudder – teh yer own mudder! Little did I t'ink when yehs was a baby playin' about me feet dat ye'd grow up teh say sech a t'ing teh yer mudder – yer own mudder. I never taut—'

Sobs choked her and interrupted her reproaches.

'Dere ain't nothin' teh make sech trouble about,' said Jimmie. 'I on'y says it 'ud be better if we keep dis t'ing dark, see? It queers us! See?'

His mother laughed a laugh that seemed to ring through the city and be echoed and re-echoed by countless other laughs. 'Oh, yes, I will, won't I? Sure!'

'Well, yeh must take me fer a damn fool,' said Jimmie, indignant at his mother for mocking him. 'I didn't say we'd make 'er inteh a little tin angel, ner nottin', but deh way it is now she can queer us! Don' che see?'

'Ay, she'll git tired of deh life atter a while, an' den she'll wanna be a-comin' home, won' she, deh beast! I'll let 'er in den, won't I?'

'Well, I didn't mean none of dis prod'gal bus'ness anyway,' explained Jimmie.

'It wa'n't no prod'gal daughter, yeh fool,' said the mother. 'It was prod'gal son, anyhow.'

'I know dat,' said Jimmie.

For a time they sat in silence. The mother's eyes gloated on the scene which her imagination called before her. Her lips were set in a vindictive smile.

'Ay, she'll cry, won' she, an' carry on, an' tell how Pete, or some odder feller, beats 'er, an' she'll say she's sorry an' all dat, an' she ain't happy, she ain't, an' she wants to come home agin, she does.'

With grim humor the mother imitated the possible wailing notes of the daughter's voice.

'Den I'll take 'er in, won't I? She kin cry 'er two eyes out on deh stones of deh street before I'll dirty d' place wid her. She abused an' ill-treated her own mudder – her own mudder what loved her, an' she'll never git anodder chance.'

Jimmie thought he had a great idea of women's frailty, but he could not understand why any of his kin should be victims.

'Curse her!' he said fervidly.

Again he wondered vaguely if some of the women of his acquaintance had brothers. Nevertheless, his mind did not for an instant confuse himself with those brothers nor his sister with theirs. After the mother had, with great difficulty, suppressed the neighbors, she went among them and proclaimed her grief. 'May Heaven forgive dat girl,' was her continual cry. To attentive ears she recited the whole length and breadth of her woes.

'I bringed 'er up deh way a daughter oughta be bringed up, an' dis is how she served me! She went teh deh devil deh first chance she got! May Heaven forgive her.'

When arrested for drunkenness she used the story of her daughter's downfall with telling effect upon the police justices. Finally one of them said to her, peering down over his spectacles: 'Mary, the records of this and other courts show that you are the mother of forty-two daughters who have been ruined. The case is unparalleled in the annals of this court, and this court thinks—'

The mother went through life shedding large tears of sorrow. Her red face was a picture of agony.

Of course Jimmie publicly damned his sister that he might appear on a higher social plane. But, arguing with himself, stumbling about in ways that he knew not, he, once, almost came to a conclusion that his sister would have been more firmly good had she better known why. However, he felt that he could not hold such a view. He threw it hastily aside.

14

In a hilarious hall there were twenty-eight tables and twenty-eight women and a crowd of smoking men. Valiant noise was made on a stage at the end of the hall by an orchestra composed of men who looked as if they had just happened in. Soiled waiters ran to and fro, swooping down like hawks on the unwary in the throng; clattering along the aisles with trays covered with glasses; stumbling over women's skirts and charging two prices for every-thing but beer, all with a swiftness that blurred the view of the coconut palms and dusty monstrosities painted upon the walls of the room. A 'bouncer,' with an immense load of business upon his hands, plunged about in the crowd, dragging bashful strangers to prominent chairs, ordering waiters here and there, and quarrelling furiously with men who wanted to sing with the orchestra.

The usual smoke cloud was present, but so dense that heads and arms seemed entangled in it. The rumble of conversation was replaced by a roar. Plenteous oaths heaved through the air. The room rang with the shrill voices of women bubbling over with drink laughter. The chief element in the music of the orchestra was speed. The musicians played in intent fury. A woman was singing and smiling upon the stage, but no one took notice of her. The rate at which the piano, cornet, and violins were going seemed to impart wildness to the half-drunken crowd. Beer glasses were emptied at a gulp and conversation became a rapid chatter. The smoke eddied and swirled like a shadowy river hurrying towards some unseen falls. Pete and Maggie entered the hall and took chairs at a table near the door. The woman who was seated there made an attempt to occupy Pete's attention, and, failing, went away.

Three weeks had passed since the girl had left home. The air of spaniel-like dependence had been magnified and showed its direct effect in the peculiar off-handedness and ease of Pete's ways towards her.

She followed Pete's eyes with hers, anticipating with smiles gracious looks from him.

A woman of brilliance and audacity, accompanied by a mere boy, came into the place and took a seat near them.

At once Pete sprang to his feet, his face beaming with glad surprise.

'Hully gee, dere's Nellie!' he cried.

He went over to the table and held out an eager hand to the woman.

'Why, hello, Pete, me boy, how are you?' said she, giving him her fingers.

Maggie took instant note of the woman. She perceived that her black dress fitted her to perfection. Her linen collar and cuffs were spotless. Tan gloves were stretched over her well-shaped hands. A hat of a prevailing fashion perched jauntily upon her dark hair. She wore no jewellery and was painted with no apparent paint. She looked clear-eyed through the stares of the men.

'Sit down, and call your lady friend over,' she said to Pete. At his beckoning Maggie came and sat between Pete and the mere boy.

'I t'ought yeh was gone away fer good,' began Pete, at once. 'When did yeh git back? How did dat Buff'lo business turn out?'

The woman shrugged her shoulders. 'Well, he didn't have as many stamps as he tried to make out, so I shook him, that's all.'

'Well, I'm glad teh see yehs back in deh city,' said Pete with gallantry.

He and the woman entered into a long conversation, exchanging reminiscences of days together. Maggie sat still, unable to formulate an intelligent sentence as her addition to the conversation and painfully aware of it.

She saw Pete's eyes sparkle as he gazed upon the handsome stranger. He listened smilingly to all she said. The woman was familiar with all his affairs, asked him about mutual friends, and knew the amount of his salary.

She paid no attention to Maggie, looking towards her once or twice and apparently seeing the wall beyond.

The mere boy was sulky. In the beginning he had welcomed the additions with acclamations. 'Let's all have a drink! What'll you take, Nell? And you, Miss What's-your-name. Have a drink, Mr – you, I mean.'

He had shown a sprightly desire to do the talking for the company and tell all about his family. In a loud voice he declaimed on various topics. He assumed a patronizing air towards Pete. As Maggie was silent, he paid no attention to her. He made a great show of lavishing wealth upon the woman of brilliance and audacity.

'Do keep still, Freddie! You talk like a clock,' said the woman to him. She turned away and devoted her attention to Pete.

'We'll have many a good time together again, eh?'

'Sure, Mike,' said Pete, enthusiastic at once.

'Say,' whispered she, leaning forward, 'let's go over to Billie's and have a time.'

'Well, it's dis way! See?' said Pete. 'I got dis lady frien' here.'

'Oh, g'way with her,' argued the woman.

Pete appeared disturbed.

'All right,' said she, nodding her head at him. 'All right for you! We'll see the next time you ask me to go anywheres with you.'

Pete squirmed.

'Say,' he said, beseechingly, 'come wid me a minit an' I'll tell yer why.'

The woman waved her hand. 'Oh, that's all right, you needn't explain, you know. You wouldn't come merely because you wouldn't come, that's all.'

To Pete's visible distress she turned to the mere boy, bringing him speedily out of a terrific rage. He had been debating whether it would be the part of a man to pick a quarrel with Pete, or would he be justified in striking him savagely with his beer glass without warning. But he recovered himself when the woman turned to renew her smilings. He beamed upon her with an expression that was somewhat tipsy and inexpressibly tender.

'Say, shake that Bowery jay,' requested he, in a loud whisper.

'Freddie, you are so funny,' she replied.

Pete reached forward and touched the woman on the arm.

'Come out a minit while I tells yeh why I can't go wid yer. Yer doin' me dirt, Nell! I never taut ye'd do me dirt, Nell. Come on, will yer?' He spoke in tones of injury.

'Why, I don't see why I should be interested in your explanations,' said the woman, with a coldness that seemed to reduce Pete to a pulp.

His eyes pleaded with her. 'Come out a minit while I tells yeh. On d' level, now.'

The woman nodded slightly at Maggie and the mere boy, saying, ''Scuse me.'

The mere boy interrupted his loving smile and turned a shrivelling glare upon Pete. His boyish countenance flushed and he spoke in a whine to the woman: 'Oh, I say, Nellie, this ain't a square deal, you know. You aren't goin' to leave me and go off with that duffer, are you? I should think—'

'Why, you dear boy, of course I'm not,' cried the woman, affectionately. She bent over and whispered in his ear. He smiled again and settled in his chair as if resolved to wait patiently.

As the woman walked down between the rows of tables, Pete was at her shoulder talking earnestly, apparently in explanation. The woman waved her hands with studied airs of indifference. The doors swung behind them, leaving Maggie and the mere boy seated at the table.

Maggie was dazed. She could dimly perceive that something stupendous had happened. She wondered why Pete saw fit to remonstrate with the woman, pleading forgiveness with his eyes. She thought she noted an air of submission about her leonine Pete. She was astounded.

The mere boy occupied himself with cocktails and a cigar. He was tranquilly silent for half an hour. Then he bestirred himself and spoke.

'Well,' he said, sighing, 'I knew this was the way it would be. They got cold feet.' There was another stillness. The mere boy seemed to be musing.

'She was pulling m' leg. That's the whole amount of it,' he said, suddenly. 'It's a bloomin' shame the way that girl does. Why, I've spent over two dollars in drinks tonight. And she goes off with that plug-ugly, who looks as if he had been hit in the face with a coin die. I call it rocky treatment for a fellah like me. Here, waiter, bring me a cocktail, and make it strong.'

Maggie made no reply. She was watching the doors. 'It's a mean piece of business,' complained the mere boy. He explained to her how amazing it was that anybody should treat him in such a manner. 'But I'll get square with her, you bet. She won't get far ahead of yours truly, you know,' he added, winking. 'I'll tell her plainly that it was bloomin' mean business. And she won't come it over me with any of her "now-Freddie-dear's." She thinks my name is Freddie, you know, but of course it ain't. I always tell these people some name like that, because if they got on to your right name they might use it sometime. Understand? Oh, they don't fool me much.'

Maggie was paying no attention, being intent upon the doors. The mere boy relapsed into a period of gloom, during which he exterminated a number of cocktails with a determined air, as if replying defiantly to fate. He occasionally broke forth into sentences composed of invectives joined together in a long chain.

The girl was still staring at the doors. After a time the mere boy began to see cobwebs just in front of his nose. He spurred himself into being agreeable and insisted upon her having a charlotte russe and a glass of beer.

'They's gone,' he remarked, 'they's gone.' He looked at her through the smoke wreaths. 'Shay, lil' girl, we mightish well make bes' of it. You ain't such bad-lookin' girl, y' know. Not half bad. Can't come up to Nell, though. No, can't do it! I should shay not! Nell fine-lookin' girl! F-i-ine. You look bad longsider her, but by y'self ain't so bad. Have to do, anyhow. Nell gone. O'ny you left. Not half bad, though.'

Maggie stood up.

'I'm going home,' she said.

The mere boy started. 'Eh? What? Home!' he cried, struck with amazement. 'I beg pardon, did hear say home?'

'I'm going home,' she repeated.

'Great heavens!' what hav' a struck?' demanded the mere boy of himself, stupefied.

In a semicomatose state he conducted her on board an uptown car, ostentatiously paid her fare, leered kindly at her through the rear window, and fell off the steps.

15

A forlorn woman went along a lighted avenue. The street was filled with people desperately bound on missions. An endless crowd darted at the elevated station stairs, and the horse-cars were thronged with owners of bundles.

The pace of the forlorn woman was slow. She was apparently searching for some one. She loitered near the doors of saloons and watched men emerge from them. She furtively scanned the faces in the rushing stream of pedestrians. Hurrying men, bent on catching some boat or train, jostled her elbows, failing to notice her, their thoughts fixed on distant dinners.

The forlorn woman had a peculiar face. Her smile was no smile. But when in repose her features had a shadowy look that was like a sardonic grin, as if some one had sketched with cruel forefinger indelible lines about her mouth.

Jimmie came strolling up the avenue. The woman encountered him with an aggrieved air. 'Oh, Jimmie, I've been lookin' all over for yehs—' she began.

Jimmie made an impatient gesture and quickened his pace.

'Ah, don't bodder me!' he said, with the savageness of a man whose life is pestered.

The woman followed him along the sidewalk in somewhat the manner of a suppliant.

'But, Jimmie,' she said, 'yehs told me ye'd—'

Jimmie turned upon her fiercely as if resolved to make a last stand for comfort and peace.

'Say, Hattie, don' foller me from one end of deh city teh deh odder. Let up, will yehs! Give me a minute's res', can't yehs? Yehs makes me tired, allus, taggin' me. See? Ain' yehs got no sense? Do yehs want people teh get on to me? Go chase yerself.'

The woman stepped closer and laid her fingers on his arm. 'But, look-a here—'

Jimmie snarled. 'Oh, go teh blazes.'

He darted into the front door of a convenient saloon and a moment later came out into the shadows that surrounded the side door. On the brilliantly lighted avenue he perceived the forlorn woman dodging about like a scout. Jimmie laughed with an air of relief and went away.

When he returned home he found his mother clamoring. Maggie had returned. She stood shivering beneath the torrent of her mother's wrath.

'Well, I'm damned!' said Jimmie in greeting.

His mother, tottering about the room, pointed a quivering forefinger.

'Lookut her, Jimmie, lookut her. Dere's yer sister, boy. Dere's yer sister. Lookut her! Lookut her!'

She screamed at Maggie with scoffing laughter.

The girl stood in the middle of the room. She edged about as if unable to find a place on the floor to put her feet.

'Ha, ha, ha!' bellowed the mother. 'Dere she stands! Ain' she purty? Lookut her! Ain' she sweet, deh beast? Lookut her! Ha, ha! lookut her!'

She lurched forward and put her red and seamed hands upon her daughter's face. She bent down and peered keenly up into the eyes of the girl.

'Oh, she's jes' dessame as she ever was, ain't she? She's her mudder's putty darlin' yit, ain' she? Lookut her, Jimmie. Come here and lookut her.'

The loud, tremendous railing of the mother brought the denizens of the Rum Alley tenement to their doors. Women came in the hallways. Children scurried to and fro.

'What's up? Dat Johnson party on anudder tear?'

'Naw. Young Mag's come home!'

'Git out!'

Through the open doors curious eyes stared in at Maggie. Children ventured into the room and ogled her as if they formed the front row at a theatre. Women, without, bent towards each other and whispered, nodding their heads with airs of profound philosophy.

A baby, overcome with curiosity concerning this object at which all were looking, sidled forward and touched her dress, cautiously, as if investigating a red-hot stove. Its mother's voice rang out like a warning trumpet. She rushed forward and grabbed her child, casting a terrible look of indignation at the girl.

Maggie's mother paced to and fro, addressing the doorful of eyes, expounding like a glib showman. Her voice rang through the building.

'Dere she stands,' she cried, wheeling suddenly and pointing with dramatic finger. 'Dere she stands! Lookut her! Ain' she a dindy? An' she was so good as to come home teh her mudder, she was! Ain' she a beaut'? Ain't she a dindy?'

The jeering cries ended in another burst of shrill laughter.

The girl seemed to awaken. 'Jimmie—'

He drew hastily back from her.

'Well, now, yer a t'ing, ain' yeh?' he said, his lips curling in scorn. Radiant virtue sat upon his brow, and his repelling hands expressed horror of contamination.

Maggie turned and went.

The crowd at the door fell back precipitately. A baby falling down in front of the door wrenched a scream like that of a wounded animal from its mother. Another woman sprang forward and picked it up with a chivalrous air, as if rescuing a human being from an oncoming express train.

As the girl passed down through the hall, she went before open doors framing more eyes strangely microscopic, and sending broad beams of inquisitive light into the darkness of her path. On the second floor she met the gnarled old woman who possessed the music-box.

'So,' she cried, ''ere yehs are back again, are yehs? An' dey've kicked yehs out? Well, come in an' stay wid me t'night. I ain' got no moral standin'.'

From above came an unceasing babble of tongues, over all of which rang the mother's derisive laughter.

16

Pete did not consider that he had ruined Maggie. If he had thought that her soul could never smile again, he would have believed the mother and brother, who were pyrotechnic over the affair, to be responsible for it.

Besides, in his world, souls did not insist upon being able to smile. 'What d' hell?'

He felt a trifle entangled. It distressed him. Revelations and scenes might bring upon him the wrath of the owner of the saloon, who insisted upon respectability of an advanced type.

'What do dey wanna raise such a smoke about it fer?' demanded he of himself, disgusted with the attitude of the family. He saw no necessity that people should lose their equilibrium merely because their sister or their daughter had stayed away from home.

Searching about in his mind for possible reasons for their conduct, he came upon the conclusion that Maggie's motives were correct, but that the two others wished to snare him. He felt pursued.

The woman whom he had met in the hilarious hall showed a disposition to ridicule him.

'A little pale thing with no spirit,' she said. 'Did you note the expression of her eyes? There was something in them about pumpkin pie and virtue. That is a peculiar way the left corner of her mouth has of twitching, isn't it? Dear, dear, Pete, what are you coming to?'

Pete asserted at once that he never was very much interested in the girl. The woman interrupted him, laughing.

'Oh, it's not of the slighest consequence to me, my dear young man. You needn't draw maps for my benefit. Why should I be concerned about it?'

But Pete continued with his explanations. If he was laughed at for his tastes in women, he felt obliged to say that they were only temporary or indifferent ones.

The morning after Maggie had departed from home Pete stood behind the bar. He was immaculate in white jacket and apron, and his hair was plastered over his brow with infinite correctness. No customers were in the place. Pete was twisting his napkined fist slowly in a beer glass, softly whistling to himself, and occasionally holding the object of his attention between his eyes and a few weak beams of sunlight that found their way over the thick screens and into the shaded rooms.

With lingering thoughts of the woman of brilliance and audacity, the bartender raised his head and stared through the varying cracks between the swaying bamboo doors. Suddenly the whistling pucker faded from his lips. He saw Maggie walking slowly past. He gave a great start, fearing for the previously mentioned eminent respectability of the place.

He threw a swift, nervous glance about him, all at once feeling guilty. No one was in the room.

He went hastily over to the side door. Opening it and looking out, he perceived Maggie standing, as if undecided, at the corner. She was searching the place with her eyes.

As she turned her face towards him, Pete beckoned to her hurriedly, intent upon returning with speed to a position behind the bar, and to the atmosphere of respectability upon which the proprietor insisted.

Maggie came to him, the anxious look disappearing from her face and a smile wreathing her lips.

'Oh, Pete—' she began brightly.

The bartender made a violent gesture of impatience.

'Oh, say,' cried he vehemently. 'What d' yeh wanna hang aroun' here fer?' Do yer wanna git me inteh trouble?' he demanded with an air of injury.

Astonishment swept over the girl's features. 'Why, Pete! yehs tol' me—'

Pete's glance expressed profound irritation. His countenance reddened with the anger of a man whose respectability is being threatened.

'Say, yehs makes me tired! See? What d' yeh wanna tag aroun' atter me fer? Yeh'll do me dirt wid d' ol' man an' dey'll be trouble! If he sees a woman roun' here he'll go crazy an' I'll lose me job! See? Ain' yehs got no sense? Don' be allus bodderin' me. See? Yer brudder came in here an' made trouble an' d' ol' man hadda put up fer it! An' now I'm done! See? I'm done.'

The girl's eyes stared into his face. 'Pete, don' yeh remem—'

'Oh, go ahn!' interrupted Pete, anticipating.

The girl seemed to have a struggle with herself. She was apparently bewildered and could not find speech. Finally she asked in a low voice, 'But where kin I go?'

The question exasperated Pete beyond the powers of endurance. It was a direct attempt to give him some responsibility in a matter that did not concern him. In his indignation he volunteered information.

'Oh, go t' hell!' cried he. He slammed the door furiously and returned, with an air of relief, to his respectability.

Maggie went away.

She wandered aimlessly for several blocks. She stopped once and asked aloud a question of herself: 'Who?'

A man who was passing near her shoulder humorously took the questioning word as intended for him.

'Eh! What? Who? Nobody! I didn't say anything,' he laughingly said, and continued his way.

Soon the girl discovered that if she walked with such apparent aimlessness, some men looked at her with calculating eyes. She quickened her step, frightened. As a protection, she adopted a demeanor of intentness as if going somewhere.

After a time she left rattling avenues and passed between rows of houses with sternness and stolidity stamped upon their features. She hung her head, for she felt their eyes grimly upon her.

Suddenly she came upon a stout gentleman in a silk hat and a chaste black coat, whose decorous row of buttons reached from his chin to his knees. The girl had heard of the grace of God and she decided to approach this man.

His beaming, chubby face was a picture of benevolence and kind-heartedness. His eyes shone good will.

But as the girl timidly accosted him he made a convulsive movement and saved his respectability by a vigorous side-step. He did not risk it to save a soul. For how was he to know that there was a soul before him that needed saving?

17

Upon a wet evening, several months after the last chapter, two interminable rows of cars, pulled by slipping horses, jangled along a prominent side street. A dozen cabs, with coat-enshrouded drivers, clattered to and fro. Electric lights, whirring softly, shed a blurred radiance. A flower dealer, his feet tapping impatiently, his nose and his wares glistening with raindrops, stood behind an array of roses and chrysanthemums. Two or three theatres emptied a crowd upon the stormswept sidewalks. Men pulled their hats over their eyebrows and raised their collars to their ears. Women shrugged impatient shoulders in their warm cloaks and stopped to arrange their skirts for a walk through the storm. People who had been constrained to comparative silence for two hours burst into a roar of conversation, their hearts still kindling from the glowings of the stage.

The pavements became tossing seas of umbrellas. Men stepped forth to hail cabs or cars, raising their fingers in varied forms of polite request or imperative demand. An endless procession wended towards elevated stations. An atmosphere of pleasure and prosperity seemed to hang over the throng, born, perhaps, of good clothes and of two hours in a place of forgetfulness.

In the mingled light and gloom of an adjacent park, a handful of wet wanderers, in attitudes of chronic dejection, were scattered among the benches.

A girl of the painted cohorts of the city went along the street. She threw changing glances at men who passed her, giving smiling invitations to those of rural or untaught pattern and usually seeming sedately unconscious of the men with a metropolitan seal upon their faces.

Crossing glittering avenues, she went into the throng emerging from the places of forgetfulness. She hurried forward through the crowd as if intent upon reaching a distant home, bending forward in her handsome cloak, daintly lifting her skirts, and picking for her well-shod feet the dryer spots upon the sidewalks.

The restless doors of saloons, clashing to and fro, disclosed animated rows of men before bars and hurrying barkeepers.

A concert hall gave to the street faint sounds of swift, machine-like music, as if a group of phantom musicians were hastening.

A tall young man, smoking a cigarette with a sublime air, strolled near the girl. He had on evening dress, a moustache, a chrysanthemum, and a look of *ennui*, all of which he kept carefully under his eye. Seeing the girl walk on as if such a young man as he was not in existence, he looked back transfixed with interest. He stared glassily for a moment, but gave a slight convulsive start when he discerned that she was neither new, Parisian, nor theatrical. He wheeled about hastily and turned his stare into the air, like a sailor with a searchlight.

A stout gentleman, with pompous and philanthropic whiskers, went stolidly by, the broad of his back sneering at the girl.

A belated man in business clothes, and in haste to catch a car, bounced against her shoulder. 'Hi, there, Mary, I beg your pardon! Brace up, old girl.' He grasped her arm to steady her, and then was away running down the middle of the street.

The girl walked on out of the realm of restaurants and saloons. She passed more glittering avenues and went into darker blocks than those where the crowd travelled.

A young man in light overcoat and Derby hat received a glance shot keenly from the eyes of the girl. He stopped and looked at her, thrusting his hands into his pockets and making a mocking smile curl his lips. 'Come, now, old lady,' he said, 'you don't mean to tell me that you sized me up for a farmer?'

A laboring man marched along with bundles under his arms. To her remarks he replied, 'It's a fine evenin', ain't it?'

She smiled squarely into the face of a boy who was hurrying by with his hands buried in his overcoat pockets, his blond locks bobbing on his youthful temples, and a cheery smile of unconcern upon his lips. He turned his head and smiled back at her, waving his hands. 'Not this eve – some other eve.'

A drunken man, reeling in her pathway, began to roar at her. 'I ain' ga no money!' he shouted, in a dismal voice. He lurched on up the street, wailing to himself: 'I ain' ga no money. Ba' luck. Ain' ga no more money.'

The girl went into gloomy districts near the river, where the tall black factories shut in the street and only occasional broad beams of light fell across the sidewalks from saloons. In front of one of these places, whence came the sound of a violin vigorously scraped, the patter of feet on boards, and the ring of loud laughter, there stood a man with blotched features.

Farther on in the darkness she met a ragged being with shifting, bloodshot eyes and grimy hands.

She went into the blackness of the final block. The shutters of the tall buildings were closed like grim lips. The structures seemed to have eyes that looked over them, beyond them, at other things. Afar off the lights of the avenues glittered as if from an impossible distance. Street-car bells jingled with a sound of merriment.

At the feet of the tall buildings appeared the deathly black hue of the river. Some hidden factory sent up a yellow glare, that lit for a moment the waters lapping oilily against timbers. The varied sounds of life, made joyous by distance and seeming unapproachableness, came faintly and died away to a silence.

18

In a partitioned-off section of a saloon sat a man with a half-dozen women, gleefully laughing, hovering about him. The man had arrived at that stage of drunkenness where affection is felt for the universe.

'I'm good f'ler, girls,' he said, convincingly. 'I'm good f'ler. An'body trea's me all right, I allus trea's zem right! See?'

The women nodded their heads approvingly. 'To be sure,' they cried in hearty chorus. 'You're the kind of a man we like, Pete. You're outa sight! What yeh goin' to buy this time, dear?'

'An't'ing yehs wants!' said the man in an abandonment of good will. His countenance shone with the true spirit of benevolence. He was in a proper mood of missionaries. He would have fraternized with obscure Hottentots. And above all he was overwhelmed in tenderness for his friends, who were all illustrious.

'An't'ing yehs wants!' repeated he, waving his hands with beneficent recklessness. 'I'm good f'ler, girls, an' if an'body trea's me right I – here,' called he through an open door to a waiter, 'bring girls drinks. What 'ill yehs have, girls? An't'ing yehs want.'

The waiter glanced in with the disgusted look of the man who serves intoxicants for the man who takes too much of them. He nodded his head shortly at the order from each individual, and went.

'W' 're havin' great time,' said the man. 'I like you girls! Yer right sort! See?'

He spoke at length and with feeling concerning the excellences of his assembled friends.

'Don' try pull man's leg, but have a good time! Das right! Das way teh do! Now, if I s'ought yehs tryin' work me fer drinks, wouldn't buy not'ing. But yer right sort! Yehs know how ter treat a f'ler, an' I stays by yehs till spen' las' cent! Das right! I'm good f'ler and I knows when an'body trea's me right!'

Between the times of the arrival and departure of the waiter, the man discoursed to the women on the tender regard he felt for all living things. He laid stress upon the purity of his motives in all dealings with men in the world, and spoke of the fervor of his friendship for those who were amiable. Tears welled slowly from his eyes. His voice quavered when he spoke to his companions.

Once when the waiter was about to depart with an empty tray, the man drew a coin from his pocket and held it forth.

'Here,' said he, quite magnificently, 'here's quar'.'

The waiter kept his hands on his tray.

'I don't want yer money,' he said.

The other put forth the coin with tearful insistence.

'Here's quar'!' cried he, 'take 't! Yer goo' f'ler an' I wan' yehs take 't!'

'Come, come, now,' said the waiter, with the sullen air of a man who is forced into giving advice. 'Put yer mon in yer pocket! Yer loaded an' yehs on'y makes a fool of yerself.'

As the waiter passed out of the door the man turned pathetically to the women.

'He don' know I'm goo' f'ler,' cried he, dismally.

'Never you mind, Pete, dear,' said the woman of brilliance and audacity, laying her hand with great affection upon his arm. 'Never you mind, old boy! We'll stay by you, dear!'

'Das ri'!' cried the man, his face lighting up at the soothing tones of the woman's voice. 'Das ri'; I'm goo' f'ler, an' w'en any one trea's me ri', I trea's zem ri'! Shee?'

'Sure!' cried the women. And we're not goin' back on you, old man.'

The man turned appealing eyes to the woman. He felt that if he could be convicted of a contemptible action he would die.

'Shay, Nell, I allus trea's yehs shquare, didn' I? I allus been goo' f'ler wi' yehs, ain't I, Nell?'

'Sure you have, Pete,' assented the woman. She delivered an oration to her companions. 'Yessir, that's a fact. Pete's a square fellah, he is. He never goes back on a friend. He's the right kind an' we stay by him, don't we, girls?'

'Sure!' they exclaimed. Looking lovingly at him they raised their glasses and drank his health.

'Girlsh,' said the man, beseechingly, 'I allus trea's yehs ri', didn' I? I'm goo' f'ler, ain' I, girlsh?'

'Sure!' again they chorused.

'Well,' said he finally, 'Le's have nozzer drink, zen.'

'That's right,' hailed a woman, 'that's right. Yer no bloomin' jay! Yer spends yer money like a man. Dat's right.'

The man pounded the table with his quivering fists.

'Yessir,' he cried, with deep earnestness, as if some one disputed him. 'I'm goo' f'ler, an' w'en any one trea's me ri', I allus trea's – le's have nozzer drink.'

He began to beat the wood with his glass.

'Shay!' howled he, growing suddenly impatient. As the waiter did not then come, the man swelled with wrath.

'Shay!' howled he again.

The waiter appeared at the door.

'Bringsh drinksh,' said the man.

The waiter disappeared with the orders.

'Zat f'ler fool!' cried the man. 'He insul' me! I'm ge'man! Can' stan' be insul'! I'm goin' lickim when comes!'

'No, no!' cried the women, crowding about and trying to subdue him. 'He's all right! He didn't mean anything! Let it go! He's a good fellah!'

'Di'n' he insul' me?' asked the man earnestly.

'No,' said they. 'Of course he didn't! He's all right!'

'Sure he didn't insul' me?' demanded the man, with deep anxiety in his voice.

'No, no! We know him! He's a good fellah. He didn't mean anything.'

'Well, zen,' said the man resolutely, 'I'm go' 'pol'gize!'

When the waiter came, the man struggled to the middle of the floor. 'Girlsh shed you insul' me! I shay – lie! I 'pol'gize!'

'All right,' said the waiter.

The man sat down. He felt a sleepy but strong desire to straighten things out and have a perfect understanding with everybody. 'Nell, I allus trea's yeh shquare, din' I? Yeh likes me, don' yehs, Nell? I'm goo' f'ler?'

'Sure!' said the woman.

'Yeh knows I'm stuck on yehs, don' yehs, Nell?'

'Sure!' she repeated carelessly.

Overwhelmed by a spasm of drunken adoration, he drew two or three bills from his pocket and, with the trembling fingers of an offering priest, laid them on the table before the woman.

'Yehs knows yehs kin have all I got, 'cause I'm stuck on yehs, Nell, I – I'm stuck on yehs, Nell – buy drinksh – we're havin' grea' time – w'en any one trea's me ri' – I – Nell – we're havin' heluva – time.'

Presently he went to sleep with his swollen face fallen forward on his chest.

The women drank and laughed, not heeding the slumbering man in the corner. Finally he lurched forward and fell groaning on the floor.

The women screamed in disgust and drew back their skirts. 'Come ahn!' cried one, starting up angrily, 'let's get out of here.'

The woman of brilliance and audacity stayed behind, taking up the bills and stuffing them into a deep, irregularly shaped pocket. A guttural snore from the recumbent man caused her to turn and look down at him.

She laughed, 'What a fool!' she said, and went.

The smoke from the lamps settled heavily down in the little compartment, obscuring the way out. The smell of oil, stifling in its intensity, pervaded the air. The wine from an overturned glass dripped softly down upon the blotches on the man's neck.

19

In a room a woman sat at a table eating like a fat monk in a picture.

A soiled, unshaven man pushed open the door and entered.

'Well,' said he, 'Mag's dead.'

'What?' said the woman, her mouth filled with bread.

'Mag's dead,' repeated the man.

'Deh blazes she is!' said the woman. She continued her meal.

When she finished her coffee she began to weep. 'I kin remember when her two feet was no bigger dan yer t'umb, and she weared worsted boots,' moaned she.

'Well, what a' dat?' said the man.

'I kin remember when she weared worsted boots,' she cried.

The neighbors began to gather in the hall, staring in at the weeping woman as if watching the contortions of a dying dog. A dozen women entered and lamented with her. Under their busy hands the room took on that appalling appearance of neatness and order with which death is greeted.

Suddenly the door opened and a woman in a black gown rushed in with outstretched arms. 'Ah, poor Mary!' she cried, and tenderly embraced the moaning one.

'Ah, what ter'ble affliction is dis!' continued she. Her vocabulary was derived from mission churches. 'Me poor Mary, how I feel fer yehs! Ah, what a ter'ble affliction is a disobed'ent chile.'

Her good, motherly face was wet with tears. She trembled in eagerness to express her sympathy. The mourner sat with bowed head, rocking her body heavily to and fro, and crying out in a high strained voice that sounded like a dirge on some forlorn pipe.

'I kin remember when she weared worsted boots, an' her two feets was no bigger dan yer t'umb, an' she weared worsted boots, Miss Smith,' she cried, raising her streaming eyes.

'Ah, me poor Mary!' sobbed the woman in black. With low, coddling cries, she sank on her knees by the mourner's chair, and put her arms about her. The other women began to groan in different keys.

'Yer poor misguided chil' is gone now, Mary, an' let us hope it's fer deh bes'. Yeh'll fergive her now, Mary, won't yehs, dear, all her disobed'ence? All her t'ankless behaviour to her mudder an' all her badness? She's gone where her ter'ble sins will be judged.'

The woman in black raised her face and paused. The inevitable sunlight came streaming in at the window and shed a ghastly cheerfulness upon the faded hues of the room. Two or three of the spectators were sniffing, and one was weeping loudly. The mourner arose and staggered into the other room. In a moment she emerged with a pair of faded baby shoes held in the hollow of her hand.

'I kin remember when she used to wear dem!' cried she. The women burst anew into cries as if they had all been stabbed. The mourner turned to the soiled and unshaven man.

'Jimmie, boy, go git yer sister! Go git yer sister an' we'll put deh boots on her feets!'

'Dey won't fit her now, yeh fool,' said the man.

'Go git yer sister, Jimmie!' shrieked the woman, confronting him fiercely.

The man swore sullenly. He went over to a corner and slowly began to put on his coat. He took his hat and went out, with a dragging, reluctant step.

The woman in black came forward and again besought the mourner.

'Yeh'll fergive her, Mary! Yeh'll fergive yer bad, bad chil'! Her life was a curse an' her days were black, an' yeh'll fergive yer bad girl? She's gone where her sins will be judged.'

'She's gone where her sins will be judged!' cried the other women, like a choir at a funeral.

'Deh Lord gives and deh Lord takes away,' said the woman in black, raising her eyes to the sunbeams.

'Deh Lord gives and deh Lord takes away,' responded the others.

'Yeh'll fergive her, Mary?' pleaded the woman in black. The mourner essayed to speak, but her voice gave way. She shook her great shoulders frantically, in an agony of grief. The tears seemed to scald her face. Finally her voice came and arose in a scream of pain.

'Oh, yes, I'll fergive her! I'll fergive her!'

The Open Boat

A TALE INTENDED TO BE AFTER THE FACT: BEING THE EXPERIENCE OF
FOUR MEN FROM THE SUNK STEAMER COMMODORE

1

NONE OF THEM KNEW THE color of the sky. Their eyes glanced level, and were fastened upon the waves that swept toward them. These waves were of the hue of slate, save for the tops, which were of foaming white, and all of the men knew the colours of the sea. The horizon narrowed and widened, and dipped and rose, and at all times its edge was jagged with waves that seemed thrust up in points like rocks.

Many a man ought to have a bathtub larger than the boat which here rode upon the sea. These waves were most wrongfully and barbarously abrupt and tall, and each froth-top was a problem in small-boat navigation.

The cook squatted in the bottom, and looked with both eyes at the six inches of gunwale which separated him from the ocean. His sleeves were rolled over his fat forearms, and the two flaps of his unbuttoned vest dangled as he bent to bail out the boat. Often he said, 'Gawd! that was a narrow clip.' As he remarked it he invariably gazed eastward over the broken sea.

The oiler, steering with one of the two oars in the boat, sometimes raised himself suddenly to keep clear of water that swirled in over the stern. It was a thin little oar, and it seemed often ready to snap.

The correspondent, pulling at the other oar, watched the waves and wondered, why he was there.

The injured captain, lying in the bow, was at this time buried in that profound dejection and indifference which comes, temporarily at least, to even the bravest and most enduring when, willy-nilly, the firm fails, the army loses, the ship goes down. The mind of the master of a vessel is rooted deep in the timbers of her, though he command for a day or a decade; and this captain had on him the stern impression of a scene in the greys of dawn of seven turned faces, and later a stump of a topmast with a white ball on it, that slashed to and fro at the waves, went low and lower, and down. Thereafter there was something strange in his voice. Although steady, it was deep with mourning, and of a quality beyond oration or tears.

'Keep 'er a little more south, Billie,' said he.

'A little more south, sir,' said the oiler in the stern.

A seat in his boat was not unlike a seat upon a bucking bronco, and by the same token a bronco is not much smaller. The craft pranced and reared and plunged like an animal. As each wave came, and she rose for it, she seemed like a horse making at a fence outrageously high. The manner of her scramble over these walls of water is a mystic thing, and, moreover, at the top of them were ordinarily these problems in white water, the foam racing down from the summit of each wave requiring a new leap, and a leap from the air. Then, after scornfully bumping a crest, she would slide and race and splash down a long incline, and arrive bobbing and nodding in front of the next menace.

A singular disadvantage of the sea lies in the fact that after successfully surmounting one wave you discover that there is another behind it just as important and just as nervously anxious to do something effective in the way of swamping boats. In a ten-foot dinghy one can get an idea of the resources of the sea in the line of waves that is not probable to the average experience which is never at sea in a dinghy. As each slaty wall of water approached, it shut all else from the view of the men in the boat, and it was not difficult to imagine that this particular wave was the final outburst of the ocean, the last effort of the grim water. There was a terrible grace in the move of the waves, and they came in silence, save for the snarling of the crests.

In the wan light the faces of the men must have been grey. Their eyes must have glinted in strange ways as they gazed steadily astern. Viewed from a balcony, the whole thing would doubtless have been weirdly picturesque. But the men in the boat had no time to see it, and if they had had leisure, there were other things to occupy their minds. The sun swung steadily up the sky, and they knew it was broad day because the colour of the sea changed from slate to emerald green streaked with amber lights, and the foam was like tumbling snow. The process of the breaking day was unknown to them. They were aware only of this effect upon the colour of the waves that rolled toward them.

In disjointed sentences the cook and the correspondent argued as to the difference between a life-saving station and a house of refuge. The cook had said: 'There's a house of refuge just north of the Mosquito Inlet Light, and as soon as they see us they'll come off in their boat and pick us up.'

'As soon as who sees us?' said the correspondent.

'The crew,' said the cook.

'Houses of refuge don't have crews,' said the correspondent. 'As I understand them, they are only places where clothes and grub are stored for the benefit of ship-wrecked people. They don't carry crews.'

'Oh, yes, they do,' said the cook.

'No, they don't,' said the correspondent.

'Well, we're not there yet, anyhow,' said the oiler, in the stern.

'Well,' said the cook, 'perhaps it's not a house of refuge that I'm thinking of as being near Mosquito Inlet Light; perhaps it's a life-saving station.'

'We're not there yet,' said the oiler in the stern.

2

As the boat bounced from the top of each wave the wind tore through the hair of the hatless men, and as the craft plopped her stern down again the spray slashed past them. The crest of each of these waves was a hill, from the top of which the men surveyed for a moment a broad tumultuous expanse, shining and wind-riven. It was probably splendid, it was probably glorious, this play of the free sea, wild with lights of emerald and white and amber.

'Bully good thing it's an on-shore wind,' said the cook. 'If not, where would we be? Wouldn't have a show.'

'That's right,' said the correspondent.

The busy oiler nodded his assent.

Then the captain, in the bow, chuckled in a way that expressed humour, contempt, tragedy, all in one. 'Do you think we've got much of a show now, boys?' said he.

Whereupon the three were silent, save for a trifle of hemming and hawing. To express any particular optimism at this time they felt to be childish and stupid, but they all doubtless possessed this sense of the situation in their minds. A young man thinks doggedly at such times. On the other hand, the ethics of their condition was decidedly against any open suggestion of hopelessness. So they were silent.

'Oh, well,' said the captain, soothing his children, 'we'll get ashore all right.'

But there was that in his tone which made them think; so the oiler quoth, 'Yes! if this wind holds.'

The cook was bailing. 'Yes! if we don't catch hell in the surf.'

Canton-flannel gulls flew near and far. Sometimes they sat down on the sea, near patches of brown seaweed that rolled over the waves with a movement like carpets on a line in a gale. The birds sat comfortably in groups, and they were envied by some in the dinghy, for the wrath of the sea was no more to them than it was to a covey of prairie chickens a thousand miles inland. Often they came very close and stared at the men with black bead-like eyes. At these times they were uncanny and sinister in their unblinking scrutiny, and the men hooted angrily at them, telling them to be gone. One came, and evidently decided to alight on the top of the captain's head. The bird flew parallel to the boat and did not circle, but made short sidelong jumps in the air in chicken-fashion. His black eyes were wistfully fixed upon the captain's head. 'Ugly brute,' said the oiler to the bird. 'You look as if you were made with a jackknife.' The cook and the correspondent swore darkly at the creature. The captain naturally wished to knock it away with the end of the heavy painter, but he did not dare do it, because anything resembling an emphatic gesture would have capsized this freighted boat; and so, with his open hand, the captain gently and carefully waved the gull away. After it had been discouraged from the pursuit the captain breathed easier on account of his hair, and others breathed easier because the bird struck their minds at this time as being somehow gruesome and ominous.

In the meantime the oiler and the correspondent rowed. And also they rowed. They sat together in the same seat, and each rowed an oar. Then the oiler took both oars; then the correspondent took both oars; then the oiler; then the correspondent. They rowed and they rowed. The very ticklish part of the business was when the time came for the reclining one in the stern to take his turn at the oars. By the very last star of truth, it is easier to steal eggs from under a hen than it was to change seats in the dinghy. First the man in the stern slid his hand along the thwart and moved with care, as if he were of Sèvres. Then the man in the rowing-seat slid his hand along the other thwart. It was all done with the most extraordinary care. As the two sidled past each other, the whole party kept watchful eyes on the coming wave, and the captain cried: 'Look out, now! Steady, there!'

The brown mats of seaweed that appeared from time to time were like islands, bits of earth. They were traveling, apparently, neither one way nor the other. They were, to all intents, stationary. They informed them in the boat that it was making progress slowly toward the land.

The captain, rearing cautiously in the bow after the dinghy soared on a great swell, said that he had seen the lighthouse at Mosquito Inlet. Presently the cook remarked that he had seen it. The correspondent was at the oars then, and for some reason he too wished to look at the lighthouse; but his back was toward the far shore, and the waves were important, and for some time he could not seize an opportunity to turn his head. But at last there came a wave more gently than the others, and when at the crest of it he swiftly scoured the western horizon.

'See it?' said the captain.

'No,' said the correspondent, slowly; 'I didn't see anything.'

'Look again,' said the captain. He pointed. 'It's exactly in that direction.'

At the top of another wave the correspondent did as he was bid, and this time his eyes chanced on a small, still thing on the edge of the swaying horizon. It was precisely like the point of a pin. It took an anxious eye to find a lighthouse so tiny.

'Think we'll make it, Captain?'

'If this wind holds and the boat don't swamp, we can't do much else,' said the captain.

The little boat, lifted by each towering sea and splashed viciously by the crests, made progress that in the absence of seaweed was not apparent to those in her. She seemed just a wee thing wallowing, miraculously top up, at the mercy of five oceans. Occasionally a great spread of water, like white flames, swarmed into her.

'Bail her, cook,' said the captain, serenely.

'All right, Captain,' said the cheerful cook.

3

It would be difficult to describe the subtle brotherhood of men that was here established on the seas. No one said that it was so. No one mentioned it. But it dwelt in the boat, and each man felt it warm him. They were a captain, an oiler, a cook, and a correspondent, and they were friends – friends in a more curiously iron-bound degree than may be common. The hurt captain, lying against the water-jar in the bow, spoke always in a low voice and calmly; but he could never command a more ready and swiftly obedient crew than the motley three of the dinghy. It was more than a mere recognition of what was best for the common safety. There was surely in it a quality that was personal and heart-felt. And after this devotion to the commander of the boat, there was this comradeship, that the correspondent, for instance, who had been taught to be cynical of men, knew even at the time was the best experience of his life. But no one said that it was so. No one mentioned it.

'I wish we had a sail,' remarked the captain. 'We might try my overcoat on the end of an oar, and give you two boys a chance to rest.' So the cook and the correspondent held the mast and spread wide the overcoat; the oiler steered; and the little boat made good way with her new rig. Sometimes the oiler had to scull sharply to keep a sea from breaking into the boat, but otherwise sailing was a success.

Meanwhile the lighthouse had been growing slowly larger. It had now almost assumed colour, and appeared like a little grey shadow on the sky. The man at the oars could not be prevented from turning his head rather often to try for a glimpse of this little grey shadow.

At last, from the top of each wave, the men in the tossing boat could see land. Even as the lighthouse was an upright shadow on the sky, this land seemed but a long black shadow on the sea. It certainly was thinner than paper. 'We must be about opposite New Smyrna,' said the cook, who had coasted this shore often in schooners. 'Captain, by the way, I believe they abandoned that life-saving station there about a year ago.'

'Did they?' said the captain.

The wind slowly died away. The cook and the correspondent were not now obliged to slave in order to hold high the oar. But the waves continued their old impetuous swooping at the dinghy, and the little craft, no longer under way, struggled woundily over them. The oiler or the correspondent took the oars again.

Shipwrecks are apropos of nothing. If men could only train them and have them occur when the men had reached pink condition, there would be less drowning at sea. Of the four in the dinghy none had slept any time worth mentioning for two days and two nights previous to embarking in the dinghy, and in the excitement of clambering about the deck of a foundering ship they had also forgotten to eat heartily.

For these reasons, and for others, neither the oiler nor the correspondent was fond of rowing at this time. The correspondent wondered ingenuously how in the name of all that was sane could there be people who thought it amusing to row a boat. It was not an amusement; it was a diabolical punishment, and even a genius of mental aberrations could never conclude that it was anything but a horror to the muscles and a crime against the back. He mentioned to the boat in general how the amusement of rowing struck him, and the weary-faced oiler smiled in full sympathy. Previously to the foundering, by the way, the oiler had worked a double watch in the engine-room of the ship.

'Take her easy now, boys,' said the captain. 'Don't spend yourselves. If we have to run a surf you'll need all your strength, because we'll sure have to swim for it. Take your time.'

Slowly the land arose from the sea. From a black line it became a line of black and a line of white – trees and sand. Finally the captain said that he could make out a house on the shore. 'That's the house of refuge, sure,' said the cook. 'They'll see us before long, and come out after us.'

The distant lighthouse reared high. 'The keeper ought to be able to make us out now, if he's looking through a glass,' said the captain. 'He'll notify the life-saving people.'

'None of those other boats could have got ashore to give word of this wreck,' said the oiler, in a low voice, 'else the life-boat would be out hunting us.'

Slowly and beautifully the land loomed out of the sea. The wind came again. It had veered from the north-east to the south-east. Finally a new sound struck the ears of the men in the boat. It was the low thunder of the surf on the shore. 'We'll never be able to make the lighthouse now,' said the captain. 'Swing her head a little more north, Billie.'

'A little more north, sir,' said the oiler.

Whereupon the little boat turned her nose once more down the wind, and all but the oarsman watched the shore grow. Under the influence of this expansion doubt and direful apprehension were leaving the minds of the men. The management of the boat was still more absorbing, but it could not prevent a quiet cheerfulness. In an hour, perhaps, they would be ashore.

Their backbones had become thoroughly used to balancing in the boat, and they now rode this wild colt of a dinghy like circus men. The correspondent thought that he had been drenched to the skin, but happening to feel in the top pocket of his coat, he found therein eight cigars. Four of them were soaked with sea-water; four were perfectly scatheless. After a search, somebody produced three dry matches; and thereupon the four waifs rode impudently in their little boat and, with an assurance of an impending rescue shining in their eyes, puffed at the big cigars, and judged well and ill of all men. Everybody took a drink of water.

4

'Cook,' remarked the captain, 'there don't seem to be any signs of life about your house of refuge.'

'No,' replied the cook. 'Funny they don't see us!'

A broad stretch of lowly coast lay before the eyes of the men. It was of low dunes topped with dark vegetation. The roar of the surf was plain, and sometimes they could see the white lip of a wave as it spun up the beach. A tiny house was blocked out black upon the sky. Southward, the slim lighthouse lifted its little grey length.

Tide, wind, and waves were swinging the dinghy northward. 'Funny they don't see us,' said the men.

The surf's roar was here dulled, but its tone was nevertheless thunderous and mighty. As the boat swam over the great rollers the men sat listening to this roar. 'We'll swamp sure,' said everybody.

It is fair to say here that there was not a life-saving station within twenty miles in either direction; but the men did not know this fact, and in consequence they made dark and opprobrious remarks concerning the eyesight of the nation's life-savers. Four scowling men sat in the dinghy and surpassed records in the invention of epithets.

'Funny they don't see us.'

The light-heartedness of a former time had completely faded. To their sharpened minds it was easy to conjure pictures of all kinds of incompetency and blindness and, indeed, cowardice. There was the shore of the populous land, and it was bitter and bitter to them that from it came no sign.

'Well,' said the captain, ultimately, 'I suppose we'll have to make a try for ourselves. If we stay out here too long, we'll none of us have strength left to swim after the boat swamps.'

And so the oiler, who was at the oars, turned the boat straight for the shore. There was a sudden tightening of muscles. There was some thinking.

'If we don't all get ashore,' said the captain – 'if we don't all get ashore, I suppose you fellows know where to send news of my finish?'

They then briefly exchanged some addresses and admonitions. As for the reflections of the men, there was a great deal of rage in them. Perchance they might be formulated thus: If I am going to be drowned – if I am going to be drowned – if I am going to be drowned, why, in the name of the seven mad gods who rule the sea, was I allowed to come thus far and contemplate sand and trees? Was I brought here merely to have my nose dragged away as I was about to nibble the sacred cheese of life? It is preposterous. If this old ninny-woman, Fate, cannot do better than this, she should be deprived of the management of men's fortunes. She is an old hen who knows not her intention. If she has decided to drown me, why did she not do it in the beginning and save me all this trouble? The whole affair is absurd. – But no; she cannot mean to drown me. She dare not drown me. She cannot drown me. Not after all this work.' Afterward the man might have had an impulse to shake his fist at the clouds. 'Just you drown me, now, and then hear what I call you!'

The billows that came at this time were more formidable. They seemed always just about to break and roll over the little boat in a turmoil of foam. There was a preparatory and long growl in the speech of them. No mind unused to the sea would have concluded that the dinghy could ascend these sheer heights in time. The shore was still afar. The oiler was a wily surfman. 'Boys,' he said swiftly, 'she won't live three minutes more, and we're too far out to swim. Shall I take her to sea again, Captain?'

'Yes; go ahead!' said the captain.

This oiler, by a series of quick miracles and fast and steady oarsmanship, turned the boat in the middle of the surf and took her safely to sea again.

There was a considerable silence as the boat bumped over the furrowed sea to deeper water. Then somebody in gloom spoke: 'Well, anyhow, they must have seen us from the shore by now.'

The gulls went in slanting flight up the wind toward the grey, desolate east. A squall, marked by dingy clouds and clouds brick-red like smoke from a burning building, appeared from the south-east.

'What do you think of those life-saving people? Ain't they peaches?'

'Funny they haven't seen us.'

'Maybe they think we're out here for sport! Maybe they think we're fishin'. Maybe they think we're damned fools.'

It was a long afternoon. A changed tide tried to force them southward, but wind and wave said northward. Far ahead, where coast-line, sea, and sky formed their mighty angle, there were little dots which seemed to indicate a city on the shore.

'St Augustine?'

The captain shook his head. 'Too near Mosquito Inlet.'

And the oiler rowed, and then the correspondent rowed; then the oiler rowed. It was a weary business. The human back can become the seat of more aches and pains than are registered in books for the composite anatomy of a regiment. It is a limited area, but it can become the theatre of innumerable muscular conflicts, tangles, wrenches, knots, and other comforts.

'Did you ever like to row, Billie?' asked the correspondent.

'No,' said the oiler; 'hang it!'

When one exchanged the rowing-seat for a place in the bottom of the boat, he suffered a bodily depression that caused him to be careless of everything save an obligation to wiggle one finger. There was cold sea-water swashing to and fro in the boat, and he lay in it. His head, pillowed on a thwart, was within an inch of the swirl of a wave-crest, and sometimes a particularly obstreperous sea came inboard and drenched him once more. But these matters did not annoy him. It is almost certain that if the boat had capsized he would have tumbled comfortably out upon the ocean as if he felt sure that it was a great soft mattress.

'Look! There's a man on the shore!'

'Where?'

'There! See 'im? See 'im?'

'Yes, sure! He's walking along.'

'Now he's stopped. Look! He's facing us!'

'He's waving at us!'

'So he is! By thunder!'

'Ah, now we're all right! Now we're all right! There'll be a boat out here for us in half an hour.'

'He's going on. He's running. He's going up to that house there.'

The remote beach seemed lower than the sea, and it required a searching glance to discern the little black figure. The captain saw a floating stick, and they rowed to it. A bath towel was by some weird chance in the boat, and, trying this on the stick, the captain waved it. The oarsman did not dare turn his head, so he was obliged to ask questions.

'What's he doing now?'

'He's standing still again. He's looking, I think. – There he goes again – toward the house. – Now he's stopped again.'

'Is he waving at us?'

'No, not now; he was, though.'

'Look! There comes another man!'

'He's running.'

'Look at him go, would you!'

'Why, he's on a bicycle. Now he's met the other man. They're both waving at us. Look!'

'There comes something up the beach.'

'What the devil is that thing?'

'Why, it looks like a boat.'

'Why, certainly, it's a boat.'

'No; it's on wheels.'

'Yes, so it is. Well, that must be the life-boat. They drag them along shore on a wagon.'

'That's the life-boat, sure.'

'No, by God, it's – it's an omnibus.'

'I tell you it's a life-boat.'

'It is not! It's an omnibus. I can see it plain. See? One of these big hotel omnibuses.'

'By thunder, you're right. It's an omnibus, sure as fate. What do you suppose they are doing with an omnibus? Maybe they are going around collecting the life-crew, hey?'

'That's it, likely. Look! There's a fellow waving a little black flag. He's standing on the steps of the omnibus. There come those other two fellows. Now they're all talking together. Look at the fellow with the flag. Maybe he ain't waving it!'

'That ain't a flag, is it? That's his coat. Why, certainly, that's his coat.'

'So it is; it's his coat. He's taken it off and is waving it around his head. But would you look at him swing it!'

'Oh, say, there isn't any life-saving station there. That's just a winter-resort hotel omnibus that has brought over some of the boarders to see us drown.'

'What's that idiot with the coat mean? What's he signalling, anyhow?'

'It looks as if he were trying to tell us to go north. There must be a life-saving station up there.'

'No; he thinks we're fishing. Just giving us a merry hand. See? Ah, there, Willie!'

'Well, I wish I could make something out of those signals. What do you suppose he means?'

'He don't mean anything; he's just playing.'

'Well, if he'd just signal us to try the surf again, or to go to sea and wait, or go north, or go south, or go to hell, there would be some reason in it. But look at him! He just stands there and keeps his coat revolving like a wheel. The ass!'

'There come more people.'

'Now there's quite a mob. Look! Isn't that a boat?'

'Where? Oh, I see where you mean. No, that's no boat.'

'That fellow is still waving his coat.'

'He must think we like to see him do that. Why don't he quit it? It don't mean anything.'

'I don't know. I think he is trying to make us go north. It must be that there's a life-saving station there somewhere.'

'Say, he ain't tired yet. Look at 'im wave!'

'Wonder how long he can keep that up. He's been revolving his coat ever since he caught sight of us. He's an idiot. Why aren't they getting men to bring a boat out? A fishing-boat – one of those big yawls – could come out here all right. Why don't he do something?'

'Oh, it's all right now.'

'They'll have a boat out here for us in less than no time, now that they've seen us.'

A faint yellow tone came into the sky over the low land. The shadows on the sea slowly deepened. The wind bore coldness with it, and the men began to shiver.

'Holy smoke!' said one, allowing his voice to express his impious mood, 'if we keep on monkeying out here! If we've got to flounder out here all night!'

'Oh, we'll never have to stay here all night! Don't you worry. They've seen us now, and it won't be long before they'll come chasing out after us.'

The shore grew dusky. The man waving a coat blended gradually into this gloom, and it swallowed in the same manner the omnibus and the group of people. The spray, when it dashed uproariously over the side, made the voyagers shrink and swear like men who were being branded.

'I'd like to catch the chump who waved the coat. I feel like socking him one, just for luck.'

'Why? What did he do?'

'Oh, nothing, but then he seemed so damned cheerful.'

In the meantime the oiler rowed, and then the correspondent rowed, and then the oiler rowed. Grey-faced and bowed forward, they mechanically, turn by turn, plied the leaden oars. The form of the lighthouse had vanished from the southern horizon, but finally a pale star appeared, just lifting from the sea. The streaked saffron in the west passed before the all-merging darkness, and the sea to the east was black. The land had vanished, and was expressed only by the low and drear thunder of the surf.

'If I am going to be drowned – if I am going to be drowned – if I am going to be drowned, why, in the name of the seven mad gods who rule the sea, was I allowed to come thus far and contemplate sand and trees? Was I brought here merely to have my nose dragged away as I was about to nibble the sacred cheese of life?'

The patient captain, drooped over the water-jar, was sometimes obliged to speak to the oarsman.

'Keep her head up! Keep her head up!'

'Keep her head up, sir.' The voices were weary and low.

This was surely a quiet evening. All save the oarsman lay heavily and listlessly in the boat's bottom. As for him, his eyes were just capable of noting the tall black waves that swept forward in a most sinister silence, save for an occasional subdued growl of a crest.

The cook's head was on a thwart, and he looked without interest at the water under his nose. He was deep in other scenes. Finally he spoke. 'Billie,' he murmured, dreamfully, 'what kind of pie do you like best?'

5

'Pie!' said the oiler and the correspondent, agitatedly. 'Don't talk about those things, blast you!'

'Well,' said the cook, 'I was just thinking about ham sandwiches and—'

A night on the sea in an open boat is a long night. As darkness settled finally, the shine of the light, lifting from the sea in the south, changed to full gold. On the northern horizon a new light appeared, a small bluish gleam on the edge of the waters. These two lights were the furniture of the world. Otherwise there was nothing but waves.

Two men huddled in the stern, and distances were so magnificent in the dinghy that the rower was enabled to keep his feet partly warm by thrusting them under his companions. Their legs indeed extended far under the rowing-seat until they touched the feet of the captain forward. Sometimes, despite the efforts of the tired oarsman, a wave came piling into the boat, an icy wave of the night, and the chilling water soaked them anew. They would twist their bodies for a moment and groan, and sleep the dead sleep once more, while the water in the boat gurgled about them as the craft rocked.

The plan of the oiler and the correspondent was for one to row until he lost the ability, and then arouse the other from his sea-water couch in the bottom of the boat.

The oiler plied the oars until his head drooped forward and the overpowering sleep blinded him; and he rowed yet afterward. Then he touched a man in the bottom of the boat, and called his name. 'Will you spell me for a little while?' he said, meekly.

'Sure, Billie,' said the correspondent, awaking and dragging himself to a sitting position. They exchanged places carefully, and the oiler, cuddling down in the sea-water at the cook's side, seemed to go to sleep instantly.

The particular violence of the sea had ceased. The waves came without snarling. The obligation of the man at the oars was to keep the boat headed so that the tilt of the rollers would not capsize her, and to preserve her from filling when the crests rushed past. The black waves were silent and hard to be seen in the darkness. Often one was almost upon the boat before the oarsman was aware.

In a low voice the correspondent addressed the captain. He was not sure that the captain was awake, although this iron man seemed to be always awake. 'Captain, shall I keep her making for that light north, sir?'

The same steady voice answered him. 'Yes. Keep it about two points off the port bow.'

The cook had tied a life-belt around himself in order to get even the warmth which this clumsy cork contrivance could donate, and he seemed almost stove-like when a rower, whose teeth invariably chattered wildly as soon as he ceased his labour, dropped down to sleep.

The correspondent, as he rowed, looked down at the two men sleeping underfoot. The cook's arm was around the oiler's shoulders, and, with their fragmentary clothing and haggard faces, they were the babes of the sea – a grotesque rendering of the old babes in the wood.

Later he must have grown stupid at his work, for suddenly there was a growling of water, and a crest came with a roar and a swash into the boat, and it was a wonder that it did not set the cook afloat in his lifebelt. The cook continued to sleep, but the oiler sat up, blinking his eyes and shaking with the new cold.

'Oh, I'm awfully sorry, Billie,' said the correspondent, contritely.

'That's all right, old boy,' said the oiler, and lay down again and was asleep.

Presently it seemed that even the captain dozed, and the correspondent thought that he was the one man afloat on all the oceans. The wind had a voice as it came over the waves, and it was sadder than the end.

There was a long, loud swishing astern of the boat, and a gleaming trail of phosphorescence, like blue flame, was furrowed on the black waters. It might have been made by a monstrous knife.

Then there came a stillness, while the correspondent breathed with open mouth and looked at the sea.

Suddenly there was another swish and another long flash of bluish light, and this time it was alongside the boat, and might almost been reached with an oar. The correspondent saw an enormous fin speed like a shadow through the water, hurling the crystalline spray and leaving the long glowing trail.

The correspondent looked over his shoulder at the captain. His face was hidden, and he seemed to be asleep. He looked at the babes of the sea. They certainly were asleep. So, being bereft of sympathy, he leaned a little way to one side and swore softly into the sea.

But the thing did not then leave the vicinity of the boat. Ahead or astern, on one side or the other, at intervals long or short, fled the long sparkling streak, and there was to be heard the *whirroo* of the dark fin. The speed and power of the thing was greatly to be admired. It cut the water like a gigantic and keen projectile.

The presence of this biding thing did not affect the man with the same horror that it would if he had been a picnicker. He simply looked at the sea dully and swore in an undertone.

Nevertheless, it is true that he did not wish to be alone with the thing. He wished one of his companions to awake by chance and keep him company with it. But the captain hung motionless over the water-jar, and the oiler and the cook in the bottom of the boat were plunged in slumber.

6

'If I am going to be drowned – if I am going to be drowned – if I am going to be drowned, why, in the name of the seven mad gods who rule the sea, was I allowed to come thus far and contemplate sand and trees?'

During this dismal night, it may be remarked that a man would conclude that it was really the intention of the seven mad gods to drown him, despite the abominable injustice of it. For it was certainly an abominable injustice to drown a man who had worked so hard, so hard. The man felt it would be a crime most unnatural. Other people had drowned at sea since galleys swarmed with painted sails, but still—

When it occurs to a man that nature does not regard him as important, and that she feels she would not maim the universe by disposing of him, he at first wishes to throw bricks at the temple, and he hates deeply the fact that there are no bricks and no temples. Any visible expression of nature would surely be pelleted with his jeers.

Then, if there be no tangible thing to hoot, he feels, perhaps, the desire to confront a personification and indulge in pleas, bowed to one knee, and with hands supplicant, saying, 'Yes, but I love myself.'

A high cold star on a winter's night is the word he feels that she says to him. Thereafter he knows the pathos of his situation.

The men in the dinghy had not discussed these matters, but each had, no doubt, reflected upon them in silence and according to his mind. There was seldom any expression upon their faces save the general one of complete weariness. Speech was devoted to the business of the boat.

To chime the notes of his emotion, a verse mysteriously entered the correspondent's head. He had even forgotten that he had forgotten this verse, but it suddenly was in his mind.

> A soldier of the Legion lay dying in Algiers;
> There was lack of woman's nursing, there was dearth
>   of woman's tears;
> But a comrade stood beside him, and he took that
>   comrade's hand.
> And he said, 'I never more shall see my own, my
>   native land.'

In his childhood the correspondent had been made acquainted with the fact that a soldier of the Legion lay dying in Algiers, but he had never regarded the fact as important. Myriads of his school-fellows had informed him of the soldier's plight, but the dinning had naturally ended by making him perfectly indifferent. He had never considered it his affair that a soldier of the Legion lay dying in Algiers, nor had it appeared to him as a matter for sorrow. It was less to him than the breaking of a pencil's point.

Now, however, it quaintly came to him as a human, living thing. It was no longer merely a picture of a few throes in the breast of a poet, meanwhile drinking tea and warming his feet at the grate; it was an actuality – stern, mournful, and fine.

The correspondent plainly saw the soldier. He lay on the sand with his feet out straight and still. While his pale left hand was upon his chest in an attempt to thwart the going of his life, the blood came between his fingers. In the far Algerian distance, a city of low square forms was set against a sky that was faint with the last sunset hues. The correspondent, plying the oars and dreaming of the slow and slower movements of the lips of the soldier, was moved by a profound and perfectly impersonal comprehension. He was sorry for the soldier of the Legion who lay dying in Algiers.

The thing which had followed the boat and waited had evidently grown bored at the delay. There was no longer to be heard the slash of the cutwater, and there was no longer the flame of the long trail. The light in the north still glimmered, but it was apparently no nearer to the boat. Sometimes the boom of the surf rang in the correspondent's ears, and he turned the craft seaward then and rowed harder. Southward, some one had evidently built a watch-fire on the beach. It was too low and too far to be seen, but it made a shimmering, roseate reflection upon the bluff in back of it, and this could be discerned from the boat. The wind came stronger, and sometimes a wave suddenly raged out like a mountain cat, and there was to be seen the sheen and sparkle of a broken crest.

The captain, in the bow, moved on his water-jar and sat erect. 'Pretty long night,' he observed to the correspondent. He looked at the shore. 'Those life-saving people take their time.'

'Did you see that shark playing around?'

'Yes, I saw him. He was a big fellow, all right.'

'Wish I had known you were awake.'

Later the correspondent spoke into the bottom of the boat. 'Billie!' There was a slow and gradual disentanglement. 'Billie, will you spell me?'

'Sure,' said the oiler.

As soon as the correspondent touched the cold, comfortable sea-water in the bottom of the boat and had huddled close to the cook's life-belt he was deep in sleep, despite the fact that his teeth played all the popular airs. This sleep was so good to him that it was but a moment before he heard a voice call his name in a tone that demonstrated the last stages of exhaustion. 'Will you spell me?'

'Sure, Billie.'

The light in the north had mysteriously vanished, but the correspondent took his course from the wide-awake captain.

Later in the night they took the boat farther out to sea, and the captain directed the cook to take one oar at the stern and keep the boat facing the seas. He was to call out if he should hear the thunder of the surf. This plan enabled the oiler and the correspondent to get respite together. 'We'll give those boys a chance to get into shape again,' said the captain. They curled down and, after a few preliminary chatterings and trembles, slept once more the dead sleep. Neither knew they had bequeathed to the cook the company of another shark, or perhaps the same shark.

As the boat caroused on the waves, spray occasionally bumped over the side and gave them a fresh soaking, but this had no power to break their repose. The ominous slash of the wind and the water affected them as it would have affected mummies.

'Boys,' said the cook, with the notes of every reluctance in his voice, 'she's drifted in pretty close. I guess one of you had better take her to sea again.' The correspondent, aroused, heard the crash of the toppled crests.

As he was rowing, the captain gave him some whisky-and-water, and this steadied the chills out of him. 'If I ever get ashore and anybody shows me even a photograph of an oar—'

At last there was a short conversation.

'Billie! – Billie, will you spell me?'

'Sure,' said the oiler.

7

When the correspondent again opened his eyes, the sea and the sky were each of the grey hue of the dawning. Later, carmine and gold was painted upon the waters. The morning appeared finally, in its splendour, with a sky of pure blue, and the sunlight flamed on the tips of the waves.

On the distant dunes were set many little black cottages, and a tall white windmill reared above them. No man, nor dog, nor bicycle appeared on the beach. The cottages might have formed a deserted village.

The voyagers scanned the shore. A conference was held in the boat. 'Well,' said the captain, 'if no help is coming, we might better try a run through the surf right away. If we stay out here much longer we will be too weak to do anything for ourselves at all.' The others silently acquiesced in this reasoning. The boat was headed for the beach. The correspondent wondered if none ever ascended the tall wind-tower, and if then they never looked seaward. This tower was a giant, standing with its back to the plight of the ants. It represented in a degree, to the correspondent, the serenity of nature amid the struggles of the individual – nature in the wind, and nature in the vision of men. She did not seem cruel to him then, nor beneficent, nor treacherous, nor wise. But she was indifferent, flatly indifferent. It is, perhaps, plausible that a man in this situation, impressed with the unconcern of the universe, should see the innumerable flaws of his life, and have them taste wickedly in his mind, and wish for another chance. A distinction between right and wrong seems absurdly clear to him, then, in this new ignorance of the grave-edge, and he understands that if he were given another opportunity he would mend his conduct and his words, and be better and brighter during an introduction or at a tea.

'Now, boys,' said the captain, 'she is going to swamp sure. All we can do is to work her in as far as possible, and then when she swamps, pile out and scramble for the beach. Keep cool now, and don't jump until she swamps sure.'

The oiler took the oars. Over his shoulder he scanned the surf. 'Captain,' he said, 'I think I'd better bring her about and keep her head-on to the seas and back her in.'

'All right, Billie,' said the captain. 'Back her in.' The oiler swung the boat then, and, seated in the stern, the cook and the correspondent were obliged to look over their shoulders to contemplate the lonely and indifferent shore.

The monstrous inshore rollers heaved the boat high until the men were again enabled to see the white sheets of water scudding up the slanted beach. 'We won't get in very close,' said the captain. Each time a man could wrest his attention from the rollers, he turned his glance toward the shore, and in the expression of the eyes during this contemplation there was a singular quality. The correspondent, observing the others, knew that they were not afraid, but the full meaning of their glances was shrouded.

As for himself, he was too tired to grapple fundamentally with the fact. He tried to coerce his mind into thinking of it, but the mind was dominated at this time by the muscles, and the muscles said they did not care. It merely occurred to him that if he should drown it would be a shame.

There were no hurried words, no pallor, no plain agitation. The men simply looked at the shore. 'Now, remember to get well clear of the boat when you jump,' said the captain.

Seaward the crest of a roller suddenly fell with a thunderous crash, and the long white comber came roaring down upon the boat.

'Steady now,' said the captain. The men were silent. They turned their eyes from the shore to the comber and waited. The boat slid up the incline, leaped at the furious top, bounced over it, and swung down the long back of the wave. Some water had been shipped, and the cook bailed it out.

But the next crest crashed also. The tumbling, boiling flood of white water caught the boat and whirled it almost perpendicular. Water swarmed in from all sides. The correspondent had his hands on the gunwale at this time, and when the water entered at that place he swiftly withdrew his fingers, as if he objected to wetting them.

The little boat, drunken with this weight of water, reeled and snuggled deeper into the sea.

'Bail her out, cook! Bail her out!' said the captain.

'All right, Captain,' said the cook.

'Now, boys, the next one will do for us sure,' said the oiler. 'Mind to jump clear of the boat.'

The third wave moved forward, huge, furious, implacable. It fairly swallowed the dinghy, and almost simultaneously the men tumbled into the sea. A piece of life-belt had lain in the bottom of the boat, and as the correspondent went overboard he held this to his chest with his left hand.

The January water was icy, and he reflected immediately that it was colder than he had expected to find it off the coast of Florida. This appeared to his dazed mind as a fact important enough to be noted at the time. The coldness of the water was sad; it was tragic. This fact was somehow mixed and confused with his opinion of his own situation, so that it seemed almost a proper reason for tears. The water was cold.

When he came to the surface he was conscious of little but the noisy water. Afterward he saw his companions in the sea. The oiler was ahead in the race. He was swimming strongly and rapidly. Off to the correspondent's left, the cook's great white and corked back bulged out of the water; and in the rear the captain was hanging with his one good hand to the keel of the overturned dinghy.

There is a certain immovable quality to a shore, and the correspondent wondered at it amid the confusion of the sea.

It seemed also very attractive; but the correspondent knew that it was a long journey, and he paddled leisurely. The piece of life-preserver lay under him, and sometimes he whirled down the incline of a wave as if he were on a hand-sled.

But finally he arrived at a place in the sea where travel was beset with difficulty. He did not pause swimming to inquire what manner of current had caught him, but there his progress ceased. The shore was set before him like a bit of scenery on a stage, and he looked at it and understood with his eyes each detail of it.

As the cook passed, much farther to the left, the captain was calling to him. 'Turn over on your back, cook! Turn over on your back and use the oar.'

'All right, sir.' The cook turned on his back, and, paddling with an oar, went ahead as if he were a canoe.

Presently the boat also passed to the left of the correspondent, with the captain clinging with one hand to the keel. He would have appeared like a man raising himself to look over a board fence if it were not for the extraordinary gymnastics of the boat. The correspondent marvelled that the captain could still hold to it.

They passed on nearer to shore – the oiler, the cook, the captain – and following them went the water-jar, bouncing gaily over the seas.

The correspondent remained in the grip of this strange new enemy – a current. The shore, with its white slope of sand and its green bluff topped with little silent cottages, was spread like a picture before him. It was very near to him then, but he was impressed as one who, in a gallery, looks at a scene from Brittany or Algiers.

He thought: 'I am going to drown? Can it be possible? Can it be possible? Can it be possible?' Perhaps an individual must consider his own death to be the final phenomenon of nature.

But later a wave perhaps whirled him out of this small deadly current, for he found suddenly that he could again make progress toward the shore. Later still he was aware that the captain, clinging with one hand to the keel of the dinghy, had his face turned away from the shore and toward him, and was calling his name. 'Come to the boat! Come to the boat!'

In his struggle to reach the captain and the boat, he reflected that when one gets properly wearied drowning must really be a comfortable arrangement – a cessation of hostilities accompanied by a large degree of relief; and he was glad of it, for the main thing in his mind for some moments had been horror of the temporary agony. He did not wish to be hurt.

Presently he saw a man running along the shore. He was undressing with most remarkable speed. Coat, trousers, shirt, everything flew magically off him.

'Come to the boat!' called the captain.

'All right, Captain.' As the correspondent paddled, he saw the captain let himself down to bottom and leave the boat. Then the correspondent performed his one little marvel of the voyage. A large wave caught him and flung him with ease and supreme speed completely over the boat and far beyond it. It struck him even then as an event in gymnastics and a true miracle of the sea. An overturned boat in the surf is not a plaything to a swimming man.

The correspondent arrived in water that reached only to his waist, but his condition did not enable him to stand for more than a moment. Each wave knocked him into a heap, and the undertow pulled at him.

Then he saw the man who had been running and undressing, and undressing and running, come bounding into the water. He dragged ashore the cook, and then waded toward the captain; but the captain waved him away and sent him to the correspondent. He was naked – naked as a tree in winter; but a halo was about his head, and he shone like a saint. He gave a strong pull, and a long drag, and a bully heave at the correspondent's hand. The correspondent, schooled in the minor formulae, said, 'Thanks, old man.' But suddenly the man cried, 'What's that?' He pointed a swift finger. The correspondent said, 'Go.'

In the shallows, face downward, lay the oiler. His forehead touched sand that was periodically, between each wave, clear of the sea.

The correspondent did not know all that transpired afterward. When he achieved safe ground he fell, striking the sand with each particular part of his body. It was as if he had dropped from a roof, but the thud was grateful to him.

It seemed that instantly the beach was populated with men with blankets, clothes, and flasks, and women with coffee-pots and all the remedies sacred to their minds. The welcome of the land to the men from the sea was warm and generous; but a still and dripping shape was carried slowly up the beach, and the land's welcome for it could only be the different and sinister hospitality of the grave.

When it came night, the white waves paced to and fro in the moonlight, and the wind brought the sound of the great sea's voice to the men on the shore, and they felt that they could then be interpreters.

The Upturned Face

'WHAT WILL WE DO NOW?' said the adjutant, troubled and excited.

'Bury him,' said Timothy Lean.

The two officers looked down close to their toes where lay the body of their comrade. The face was chalk-blue; gleaming eyes stared at the sky. Over the two upright figures was a windy sound of bullets, and on the top of the hill Lean's prostrate company of Spitzbergen infantry was firing measured volleys.

'Don't you think it would be better—' began the adjutant. 'We might leave him until tomorrow.'

'No,' said Lean. 'I can't hold that post an hour longer. I've got to fall back, and we've got to bury old Bill.'

'Of course,' said the adjutant, at once. 'Your men got entrenching tools?'

Lean shouted back to his little line, and two men came slowly, one with a pick, one with a shovel. They started in the direction of the Rostina sharpshooters. Bullets cracked near their ears. 'Dig here,' said Lean gruffly. The men, thus caused to lower their glances to the turf, became hurried and frightened, merely because they could not look to see whence the bullets came. The dull beat of the pick striking the earth sounded amid the swift snap of close bullets. Presently the other private began to shovel.

'I suppose,' said the adjutant, slowly, 'we'd better search his clothes for – things.'

Lean nodded. Together in curious abstraction they looked at the body. Then Lean stirred his shoulders suddenly, arousing himself.

'Yes,' he said, 'we'd better see what he' got.' He dropped to his knees, and his hands approached the body of the dead officer. But his hands wavered over the buttons of the tunic. The first button was brick-red with drying blood, and he did not seem to dare touch it.

'Go on,' said the adjutant, hoarsely.

Lean stretched his wooden hand, and his fingers fumbled the bloodstained buttons. At last he rose with ghastly face. He had gathered a watch, a whistle, a pipe, a tobacco-pouch, a handkerchief, a little case of cards and papers. He looked at the adjutant. There was a silence. The adjutant was feeling that he had been a coward to make Lean do all the grisly business.

'Well,' said Lean, 'that's all, I think. You have his sword and revolver?'

'Yes,' said the adjutant, his face working, and then he burst out in a sudden strange fury at the two privates. 'Why don't you hurry up with that grave? What are you doing, anyhow? Hurry, do you hear? I never saw such stupid—'

Even as he cried out in his passion the two men were labouring for their lives. Ever overhead the bullets were spitting.

The grave was finished. It was not a masterpiece – a poor little shallow thing. Lean and the adjutant again looked at each other in a curious silent communication.

Suddenly the adjutant croaked out a weird laugh. It was a terrible laugh, which had its origin in that part of the mind which is first moved by the singing of the nerves. 'Well,' he said humorously to Lean, 'I suppose we had best tumble him in.'

'Yes,' said Lean. The two privates stood waiting, bent over their implements. 'I suppose,' said Lean, 'it would be better if we laid him in ourselves.'

'Yes,' said the adjutant. Then, apparently remembering that he had made Lean search the body, he stooped with great fortitude and took hold of the dead officer's clothing. Lean joined him. Both were particular that their fingers should not feel the corpse. They tugged away; the corpse lifted, heaved, toppled, flopped into the grave, and the two officers, straightening, looked again at each other – they were always looking at each other. They sighed with relief.

The adjutant said, 'I suppose we should – we should say something. Do you know the service, Tim?'

'They don't read the service until the grave is filled in,' said Lean, pressing his lips to an academic expression.

'Don't they?' said the adjutant, shocked that he had made the mistake. 'Oh, well,' he cried, suddenly, 'let us – let us say something – while he can hear us.'

'All right,' said Lean. 'Do you know the service?'

'I can't remember a line of it,' said the adjutant.

Lean was extremely dubious. 'I can repeat two lines, but—'

'Well, do it,' said the adjutant. 'Go as far as you can. That's better than nothing. And the beasts have got our range exactly.'

Lean looked at his two men. 'Attention,' he barked. The privates came to attention with a click, looking much aggrieved. The adjutant lowered his helmet to his knee. Lean, bareheaded, he stood over the grave. The Rostina sharpshooters fired briskly.

'O Father, our friend has sunk in the deep waters of death, but his spirit has leaped toward Thee as the bubble arises from the lips of the drowning. Perceive, we beseech, O Father, the little flying bubble, and—'

Lean, although husky and ashamed, had suffered no hesitation up to this point, but he stopped with a hopeless feeling and looked at the corpse.

The adjutant moved uneasily. 'And from Thy superb heights—' he began, and then he too came to an end.

'And from they superb heights,' said Lean.

The adjutant suddenly remembered a phrase in the back of the Spitzbergen burial service, and he exploited it with the triumphant manner of a man who has recalled everything, and can go on.

'O God, have mercy—'

'O God, have mercy—' said Lean.

'Mercy,' repeated the adjutant, in quick failure.

'Mercy,' said Lean. And then he was moved by some violence of feeling, for he turned upon his two men and tigerishly said, 'Throw the dirt in.'

The fire of the Rostina sharpshooters was accurate and continuous.

One of the aggrieved privates came forward with his shovel. He lifted his first shovel-load of earth, and for a moment of inexplicable hesitation it was held poised above this corpse, which from its chalk-blue face looked keenly out from the grave. Then the soldier emptied his shovel on – on the feet.

Timothy Lean felt as if tons had been swiftly lifted from off his forehead. He had felt that perhaps the private might empty the shovel on – on the face. It had been emptied on the feet. There was a great point gained there – ha, ha! – the first shovelful had been emptied on the feet. How satisfactory!

The adjutant began to babble. 'Well, of course – a man we've messed with all these years – impossible – you can't, you know, leave your intimate friends rotting on the field. Go on, for God's sake, and shovel, you.'

The man with the shovel suddenly ducked, grabbed his left arm with his right hand, and looked at his officer for orders. Lean picked the shovel from the ground. 'Go to the rear,' he said to the wounded man. He also addressed the other private. 'You get under cover, too; I'll finish this business.'

The wounded man scrambled hard still for the top of the ridge without devoting any glances to the direction from whence the bullets came, and the other man followed at an equal pace; but he was different, in that he looked back anxiously three times.

This is merely the way – often – of the hit and unhit.

Timothy Lean filled the shovel, hesitated, and then, in a movement which was like a gesture of abhorrence, he flung the dirt into the grave, and as it landed it made a sound – plop. Lean suddenly stopped and mopped his brow – a tired labourer.

'Perhaps we have been wrong,' said the adjutant. His glanced wavered stupidly. 'It might have been better if we hadn't buried him just at this time. Of course, if we advance tomorrow the body would have been—'

'Damn you,' said Lean, 'shut your mouth.' He was not the senior officer.

He again filled the shovel and flung the earth. Always the earth made that sound – plop. For a space Lean worked frantically, like a man digging himself out of danger.

Soon there was nothing to be seen but the chalk-blue face. Lean filled the shovel. 'Good God,' he cried to the adjutant. 'Why didn't you turn him somehow when you put him in? This—' Then Lean began to stutter.

The adjutant understood. He was pale to the lips. 'Go on, man,' he cried, beseechingly, almost in a shout.

Lean swung back the shovel. It went forward in a pendulum curve. When the earth landed it made a sound – plop.

WILLA CATHER
1876-1947

Born in Winchester, Virginia in 1876, Willa Cather grew
up, among the immigrant farm labourers and pioneer stock
of Nebraska, to become one of America's major twentieth
century writers. Although she had poems and stories
published regularly throughout the first decade of this
century, it was with *O Pioneers!* (1913) that she took the
literary establishment by storm.

Willa Cather was an extremely gifted short story
writer, as the two collections *The Troll Garden* (1905) and
Youth and the Bright Medusa (1920) reveal. The three stories
collected here were all published in literary periodicals
during the 1890s and are an interesting record of the germs
of talent in an exceptionally gifted lady of letters.

The Clemency of the Court

'DAMN YOU! WHAT DO YOU mean by giving me hooping like that?'

Serge Povolitchky folded his big, workworn hands and was silent. That helpless, doglike silence of his always had a bad effect on the guard's temper, and he turned on him afresh.

'What do you mean by it, I say? Maybe you think you are some better than the rest of us; maybe you think you are too good to work. We'll see about that.'

Serge still stared at the ground, muttering in a low, husky voice, 'I could make some broom, I think. I would try much.'

'O, you would, would you? So you don't try now? We will see about that. We will send you to a school where you can learn to hoop barrels. We have a school here, a little, dark school, a night school, you know, where we teach men a great many things.'

Serge looked up appealingly into the man's face and his eyelids quivered with terror, but he said nothing, so the guard continued:

'Now I'll sit down here and watch you hoop them barrels, and if you don't do a mighty good job, I'll report you to the warden and have you strung up as high as a rope can twist.'

Serge turned to his work again. He did wish the guard would not watch him; it seemed to him that he could hoop all right if he did not feel the guard's eye on him all the time. His hands had never done anything but dig and plow and they were so clumsy he could not make them do right. The guard began to swear and Serge trembled as he could scarcely hold his hammer. He was very much afraid of the dark cell. His cell was next to it and often at night he had heard the men groaning and shrieking when the pain got bad, and begging the guards for water. He heard one poor fellow get delirious when the rope cut and strangled him, and talk to his mother all night long, begging her not to hug him so hard, for she hurt him.

The guard went out and Serge worked on, never even stopping to wipe the sweat from his face. It was strange he could not hoop as well as the other men, for he was as strong and stalwart as they, but he was so clumsy at it. He thought he could work in the broom room if they would only let him. He had handled straw all his life, and it would seem good to work at the broom corn that had the scent of outdoors about it. But they said the broom room was full. He felt weak and sick all over, someway. He could not work in the house, he had never been indoors a whole day in his life until he came here.

Serge was born in the western part of the State, where he did not see many people. His mother was a handsome Russian girl, one of a Russian colony that a railroad had brought West to build grades. His father was supposed to be a railroad contractor, no one knew surely. At any rate by no will of his own or wish of his own, Serge existed. When he was a few months old, his mother had drowned herself in a pond so small that no one ever quite saw how she managed to do it.

Baba Skaldi, an old Russian woman of the colony, took Serge and brought him up among her own children. A hard enough life he had of it with her. She fed him what her children would not eat, and clothed him in what her children would not wear. She used to boast to *baba* Konach that she got a man's work out of the young rat. There was one pleasure in Serge's life with her. Often at night after she had beaten him and he lay sobbing on the floor in the corner, she would tell her children stories of Russia. They were beautiful stories, Serge thought. In spite of all her cruelty he never quite disliked *baba* Skaldi because she could tell such fine stories. The story told oftenest was one about her own brother. He had done something wrong, Serge could never make out just what, and had been sent to Siberia. His wife had gone with him. The *baba* told all about the journey to Siberia as she had heard it from returned convicts; all about the awful marches in the mud and ice, and how on the boundary line the men would weep and fall down and kiss the soil of Russia. When her brother reached the prison, he and his wife used to work in the mines. His wife was too good a woman to get on well in the prison, the *baba* said, and one day she had been knouted to death at the command of an officer. After that her husband tried in many ways to kill himself, but they always caught him at it. At last, one night, he bit deep into his arm and tore open the veins with his teeth and bled to death. The officials found him dead with his teeth still in his lacerated arm. When she finished the little boys used to cry out at the awfulness of it, but their mother would soothe them and tell them that such things could not possibly happen here, because in this country the State took care of people. In Russia there was no State, only the great Tzar. Ah, yes, the State would take care of the children! The *baba* had heard a Fourth-of-July speech once, and she had great ideas about the State.

Serge used to listen till his eyes grew big, and play that he was that brother of the *baba's* and that he had been knouted by the officials and that was why his little legs smarted so. Sometimes he would steal out in the snow in his bare feet and take a sunflower stalk and play he was hunting bears in Russia, or would walk about on the little frozen pond where his mother had died and think it was the Volga. Before his birth his mother used to go off alone and sit in the snow for hours to cool the fever in her head and weep and think about her own country. The feeling for the snow and the love for it seemed to go into the boy's blood, somehow. He was never so happy as when he saw the white flakes whirling.

When he was twelve years old a farmer took him to work for his board and clothes. Then a change came into Serge's life. That first morning he stood, awkward and embarrassed, in the Davis kitchen, holding his hands under his hat and shuffling his bare feet over the floor, a little yellow cur came up to him and began to rub its nose against his leg. He held out his hand and the dog licked it. Serge bent over him, stroking him and calling him Russian pet names. For the first time in his lonely, loveless life, he felt that something liked him.

The Davises gave him enough to eat and enough to wear and they did not beat him. He could not read or talk English, so they treated him very much as they did the horses. He stayed there seven years because he did not have sense enough to know that he was utterly miserable and could go somewhere else, and because the Slavonic instinct was in him to labor and keep silent. The dog was the only thing that made life endurable. He called the dog Matushka, which was the name by which he always thought of his mother. He used to go to town sometimes, but he did not enjoy it, people frightened him so. When the town girls used to pass him dressed in their pretty dresses with their clean, white hands, he thought of his bare feet and his rough, tawny hair and his ragged overalls, and he would slink away behind his team with Matushka. On the coldest winter nights he always slept in the barn with the dog for a bedfellow. As he and the dog cuddled up to each other in the hay, he used to think about things, most often about Russia and the State. Russia must be a fine country but he was glad he did not live there, because the State was much better. The State was so very good to people. Once a man came there to get Davis to vote for him, and he asked Serge who his father was. Serge said he had none. The man only smiled and said, 'Well, never mind, the State will be a father to you, my lad, and a mother.'

Serge had a vague idea that the State must be an abstract thing of some kind, but he always thought of her as a woman with kind eyes, dressed in white with a yellow light about her head, and a little child in her arms, like the picture of the virgin in the church. He always took off his hat when he passed the court house in town, because he had an idea that it had something to do with the State someway. He thought he owed the State a great deal for something, he did not know what; that the State would do something great for him some day, because he had no one else. After his chores he used to go and sit down in the corral with his back against the wire fence and his chin on his knees and look at the sunset. He never got much pleasure out of it, it was always like watching something die. It made him feel desolate and lonesome to see so much sky, yet he always sat there, irresistibly fascinated. It was not much wonder that his eyes grew dull and his brain heavy, sitting there evening after evening with his dog, staring across the brown, windswept prairies that never lead anywhere, but always stretch on and on in a great yearning for something they never reach. He liked the plains because he thought they must be like the Russian steppes, and because they seemed like himself, always lonely and empty-handed.

One day when he was helping Davis top a hay stack, Davis got angry at the dog for some reason and kicked at it. Serge threw out his arm and caught the blow himself. Davis, angrier than before, caught the hatchet and laid the dog's head open. He threw down the bloody hatchet and telling Serge to go clean it, he bent over his work. Serge stood motionless, as dazed and helpless as if he had been struck himself. The dog's tail quivered and its legs moved weakly, its breath came through its throat in faint, wheezing groans and from its bleeding head its two dark eyes, clouded with pain, still looked lovingly up at him. He dropped on his knees beside it and lifted its poor head against his heart. It was only for a moment. It laid its paw upon his arm and then was still. Serge laid the dog gently down and rose. He took the bloody hatchet and went up behind his master. He did not hurry and he did not falter. He raised the weapon and struck down, clove through the man's skull from crown to chin, even as the man had struck the dog. Then he went to the barn to get a shovel to bury the dog. As he passed the house, the woman called out to him to tell her husband to come to dinner. He answered simply, 'He will not come to dinner today. I killed him behind the haystack.'

She rushed from the house with a shriek and when she caught sight of what lay behind the haystack, she started for the nearest farm house. Serge went to the barn for the shovel. He had no consciousness of having done wrong. He did not even think about the dead man. His heart seemed to cling to the side of his chest, the only thing he had ever loved was dead. He went to the haystack where he and Matushka slept every night and took a box from under the hay from which he drew a red silk handkerchief, the only 'pretty thing,' and indeed, the only handkerchief he had ever possessed. He went back to the haystack and never once glancing at the man, took the dog in his arms.

There was one spot on the farm that Serge liked. He and Matushka used often to go there on Sundays. It was a little, marshy pool, grown up in cattails and reeds with a few scraggy willows on the banks. The grass used to be quite green there, not red and gray like the buffalo grass. There he carried Matushka. He laid him down and began to dig a grave under the willows. The worst of it was that the world went on just as usual. The winds were laughing away among the rushes, sending the water slapping against the banks. The meadow larks sang in the corn field and the sun shone just as it did yesterday and all the while Matushka was dead and his own heart was breaking in his breast. When the hole was deep enough, he took the handkerchief from his pocket and tied it neatly about poor Matushka's mangled head. Then he pulled a few wild roses and laid them on its breast and fell sobbing across the body of the little yellow cur. Presently he saw the neighbors coming over the hill with Mrs Davis, and he laid the dog in the grave and covered him up.

About his trial Serge remembered very little, except that they had taken him to the court house and he had not found the State. He remembered that the room was full of people, and some of them talked a great deal, and that the young lawyer who defended him cried when his sentence was read. That lawyer seemed to understand it all, about Matushka and the State, and everything. Serge thought he was the handsomest and most learned man in the world. He had fought day and night for Serge, without sleeping and almost without eating. Serge could always see him as he looked when he paced up and down the platform, shaking the hair back from his brow and trying to get it through the heads of the jurymen that love was love, even if it was for a dog. The people told Serge that his sentence had been commuted from death to imprisonment for life by the clemency of the court, but he knew well enough that it was by the talk of that lawyer. He had not deserted Serge after the trial even, he had come with him to the prison and had seen him put on his convict clothing.

'It's the State's badge of knighthood, Serge,' he said, bitterly, touching one of the stripes. 'The old emblem of the royal garter, to show that your blood is royal.'

Just as the six o'clock whistle was blowing, the guard returned.

'You are to go to your cell tonight, and if you don't do no better in the morning, you are to be strung up in the dark cell, come along.'

Serge laid down his hammer and followed him to his cell. Some of the men made little book shelves for their cells and pasted pictures on the walls. Serge had neither books nor pictures, and he did not know how to ask for any, so his cell was bare. The cells were only six by four, just a little larger than a grave.

As a rule, the prisoners suffered from no particular cruelty, only from the elimination of all those little delicacies that make men men. The aim of the prison authorities seemed to be to make everything unnecessarily ugly and repulsive. The little things in which fine feeling is most truly manifest received no respect at all. Serge's bringing up had been none of the best, but it took him some time to get used to eating without knife or fork the indifferent food thrust in square tin bowls under the door of his cell. Most of the men read at night, but he could not read, so he lay tossing on his iron bunk, wondering how the fields were looking. His greatest deprivation was that he could not see the fields. The love of the plains was strong in him. It had always been so, ever since he was a little fellow, when the brown grass was up to his shoulders and the straw stacks were the golden mountains of fairyland. Men from the cities on the hills never understand this love, but the men from the plain country know what I mean. When he had tired himself out with longing, he turned over and fell asleep. He was never impatient, for he believed that the State would come some day and explain, and take him to herself. He watched for her coming every day, hoped for it every night.

In the morning the work went no better. They watched him all the time and he could do nothing. At noon they took him into the dark cell and strung him up. They put his arms behind him and tied them together, then passed the rope about his neck, drawing arms up as high as they could be stretched, so that if he let them 'sag' he would strangle, and so they left him. The cell was perfectly bare and was not long enough for a man to lie at full length in. The prisoners were told to stand up, so Serge stood. At night his arms were let down long enough for him to eat his bread and water, then he was roped up again. All night long he stood there. By the end of the next day the pain in his arms was almost unendurable. They were paralyzed from the shoulder down so that the guard had to feed him like a baby. The next day and the next night and the next day he lay upon the floor of the cell, suffering as though every muscle were being individually wrenched from his arms. He had not been out of the bare cell for four days. All the ventilation came through some little augur holes in the door and the heat and odor were becoming unbearable. He had thought on the first night that the pain would kill him before morning, but he had endured over eighty-four hours of it and when the guard came in with his bread and water he found him lying with his eyes closed and his teeth set on his lip. He roused him with a kick and held the bread and water out to him, but Serge took only the water.

'Rope too tight?' growled the guard. Serge said nothing. He was almost dead now and he wanted to finish for he could not hoop barrels.

'Gittin so stuck up you can't speak, are you? Well, we'll just stretch you up a bit tighter.' And he gave the stick in the rope another vicious twist that almost tore the arms from their sockets and sent a thrill of agony through the man's whole frame. Then Serge was left alone. The fever raged in his veins and about midnight his thirst was intolerable. He lay with his mouth open and his tongue hanging out. The pain in his arms made his whole body tremble like a man with a chill. He could no longer keep his arms up and the ropes were beginning to strangle him. He did not call for help. He had heard poor devils shriek for help all night long and get no relief. He suffered, as the people of his mother's nation, in hopeless silence. The blood of the serf was in him, blood that has cowered beneath the knout for centuries and uttered no complaint. Then the State would surely come soon, she would not let them kill him. His mother, the State!

He fell into a half stupor. He dreamed about what the *baba* used to tell about the bargemen in their bearskin coats coming down the Volga in the spring when the ice had broken up and gone out; about how the wolves used to howl and follow the sledges across the snow in the starlight. That cold, white snow, that lay in ridges and banks! He thought he felt it in his mouth and he awoke and found himself licking the stone floor. He thought how lovely the plains would look in the morning when the sun was up; how the sunflowers would shake themselves in the wind, how the corn leaves would shine and how the cobwebs would sparkle all over the grass and the air would be clear and blue, the birds would begin to sing, the colts would run and jump in the pasture and the black bull would begin to bellow for his corn.

The rope grew tighter and tighter. The State must come soon now. He thought he felt the dog's cold nose against his throat. He tried to call its name, but the sound only came in an inarticulate gurgle. He drew his knees up to his chin and died.

And so it was that this great mother, the State, took this willful, restless child of hers and put him to sleep in her bosom.

Lou, the Prophet

IT HAD BEEN A VERY trying summer to every one, and most of all to Lou. He had been in the West for seven years, but he had never quite gotten over his homesickness for Denmark. Among the northern people who emigrate to the great West, only the children and the old people ever long much for the lands they have left over the water. The men only know that in this new land their plow runs across the field tearing up the fresh, warm earth, with never a stone to stay its course. That if they dig and delve the land long enough, and if they are not compelled to mortgage it to keep body and soul together, some day it will be theirs, their very own. They are not like the southern people; they loose their love for their fatherland quicker and have less of sentiment about them. They have to think too much about how they shall get bread to care much what soil gives it to them. But among even the most blunted, mechanical people, the youths and the aged always have a touch of romance in them.

Lou was only twenty-two; he had been but a boy when his family left Denmark, and had never ceased to remember it. He was a rather simple fellow, and was always considered less promising than his brothers; but last year he had taken up a claim of his own and made a rough dug-out upon it and he lived there all alone. His life was that of many another young man in our country. He rose early in the morning, in the summer just before daybreak; in the winter, long before. First he fed his stock, then himself, which was a much less important matter. He ate the same food at dinner that he ate at breakfast, and the same at supper that he ate at dinner. His bill of fare never changed the year round; bread, coffee, beans and sorghum molasses, sometimes a little salt pork. After breakfast he worked until dinner time, ate, and then worked again. He always went to bed soon after the sun set, for he was always tired, and it saved oil. Sometimes, on Sundays, he would go over home after he had done his washing and house cleaning, and sometimes he hunted. His life was as sane and as uneventful as the life of his plow horses, and it was as hard and thankless. He was thrifty for a simple, thick-headed fellow, and in the spring he was to have married Nelse Sorenson's daughter, but he had lost all his cattle during the winter, and was not so prosperous as he had hoped to be; so, instead she married her cousin, who had an 'eighty' of his own. That hurt Lou more than anyone ever dreamed.

A few weeks later his mother died. He had always loved his mother. She had been kind to him and used to come over to see him sometimes, and shake up his hard bed for him, and sweep, and make his bread. She had a strong affection for the boy, he was her youngest, and she always felt sorry for him; she had danced a great deal before his birth, and an old woman in Denmark had told her that was the cause of the boy's weak head.

Perhaps the greatest calamity of all was the threatened loss of his corn crop. He had bought a new corn planter on time that spring, and had intended that his corn should pay for it. Now, it looked as though he would not have corn enough to feed his horses. Unless rain fell within the next two weeks, his entire crop would be ruined; it was half gone now. All these things together were too much for poor Lou, and one morning he felt a strange loathing for the bread and sorghum which he usually ate as mechanically as he slept. He kept thinking about the strawberries he used to gather on the mountains after the snows were gone, and the cold water in the mountain streams. He felt hot someway, and wanted cold water. He had no well, and he hauled his water from a neighbor's well every Sunday, and it got warm in the barrels those hot summer days. He worked at his haying all day; at night, when he was through feeding, he stood a long time by the pig stye with a basket on his arm. When the moon came up, he sighed restlessly and tore the buffalo pea flowers with his bare toes. After a while, he put his basket away, and went into his hot, close, little dug-out. He did not sleep well, and he dreamed a horrible dream. He thought he saw the Devil and all his angels in the air holding back the rain clouds, and they loosed all the damned in Hell, and they came, poor tortured things, and drank up whole clouds of rain. Then he thought a strange light shown from the south, just over the river bluffs, and the clouds parted, and Christ and all his angels were descending. They were coming, coming, myriads and myriads of them, in a great blaze of glory. Then he felt something give way in his poor, weak head, and with a cry of pain he awoke. He lay shuddering a long time in the dark, then got up and lit his lantern and took from the shelf his mother's bible. It opened of itself at Revelations, and Lou began to read, slowly indeed, for it was hard work for him. Page by page, he read those burning, blinding, blasting words, and they seemed to shrivel up his poor brain altogether. At last the book slipped from his hands and he sank down upon his knees in prayer, and stayed so until the dull gray dawn stole over the land and he heard the pigs clamoring for their feed.

He worked about the place until noon, and then prayed and read again. So he went on several days, praying and reading and fasting, until he grew thin and haggard. Nature did not comfort him any, he knew nothing about nature, he had never seen her; he had only stared into a black plow furrow all his life. Before, he had only seen in the wide, green lands and the open blue the possibilities of earning his bread; now, he only saw in them a great world ready for the judgment, a funeral pyre ready for the torch.

One morning, he went over to the big prairie dog town, where several little Danish boys herded their fathers' cattle. The boys were very fond of Lou; he never teased them as the other men did, but used to help them with their cattle, and let them come over to his dug-out to make sorghum taffy. When they saw him coming, they ran to meet him and asked him where he had been all these days. He did not answer their questions, but said: 'Come into the cave, I want to see you.'

Some six or eight boys herded near the dog town every summer, and by their combined efforts they had dug a cave in the side of a high bank. It was large enough to hold them all comfortably, and high enough to stand in. There the boys used to go when it rained or when it was cold in the fall. They followed Lou silently and sat down on the floor. Lou stood up and looked tenderly down into the little faces before him. They were old-faced little fellows, though they were not over twelve or thirteen years old; hard work matures boys quickly.

'Boys,' he said earnestly, 'I have found out why it don't rain, it's because of the sins of the world. You don't know how wicked the world is, it's all bad, all, even Denmark. People have been sinning a long time, but they won't much longer. God has been watching and watching for thousands of years, and filling up the phials of wrath, and now he is going to pour out his vengeance and let Hell loose upon the world. He is burning up our corn now, and worse things will happen; for the sun shall be as sack-cloth, and the moon shall be like blood, and the stars of heaven shall fall, and the heavens shall part like a scroll, and the mountains shall be moved out of their places, and the great day of his wrath shall come, against which none may stand. Oh, boys! the floods and the flames shall come down upon us together and the whole world shall perish.' Lou paused for breath, and the little boys gazed at him in wonder. The sweat was running down his haggard face, and his eyes were staring wildly. Presently, he resumed in a softer tone, 'Boys, if you want rain, there is only one way to get it, by prayer. The people of the world won't pray, perhaps if they did God would not hear them, for they are so wicked; but he will hear you, for you are little children and are likened unto the kingdom of heaven, and he loved ye.'

Lou's haggard, unshaven face bent toward them and his blue eyes gazed at them with terrible earnestness.

'Show us how, Lou,' said one little fellow in an awed whisper. Lou knelt down in the cave, his long, shaggy hair hung down over his face, and his voice trembled as he spoke:

'Oh God, they call thee many long names in thy book, thy prophets; but we are only simple folk, the boys are all little and I am weak headed ever since I was born, therefore, let us call thee Father, for thy other names are hard to remember. O Father, we are so thirsty, all the world is thirsty; the creeks are all dried up, and the river is so low that the fishes die and rot in it; the corn is almost gone; the hay is light; and even the little flowers are no more beautiful. O God! our corn may yet be saved. O, give us rain! Our corn means so much to us, if it fails, all our pigs and cattle will die, and we ourselves come very near it; but if you do not send rain, O Father, and if the end is indeed come, be merciful to thy great, wicked world. They do many wrong things, but I think they forget thy word, for it is a long book to remember, and some are little, and some are born weak headed, like me, and some are born very strong headed, which is near as bad. Oh, forgive them their abominations in all the world, both in Denmark and here, for the fire hurts so, O God! Amen.'

The little boys knelt and each said a few blundering words. Outside, the sun shone brightly and the cattle nibbled at the short, dry grass, and the hot wind blew through the shriveled corn; within the cave, they knelt as many another had knelt before them, some in temples, some in prison cells, some in the caves of earth, and One, indeed, in the garden, praying for the sin of the world.

The next day, Lou went to town, and prayed in the streets. When the people saw his emaciated frame and wild eyes, and heard his wild words, they told the sheriff to do his duty, the man must be mad. Then Lou ran away; he ran for miles, then walked and limped and stumbled on, until he reached the cave; there the boys found him in the morning. The officials hunted him for days, but he hid in the cave, and the little Danes kept his secret well. They shared their dinners with him, and prayed with him all day long. They had always liked him, but now they would have gone straight through fire for him, any one of them, they almost worshipped him. He had about him that mysticism which always appeals so quickly to children. I have always thought that bear story which the Hebrews used to tell their children very improbable. If it was true, then I have my doubts about the prophet; no one in the world will hoot at insincere and affected piety sooner than a child, but no one feels the true prophetic flame quicker, no one is more readily touched by simple goodness. A very young child can tell a sincere man better than any phrenologist.

One morning, he told the boys that he had had another 'true dream.' He was not going to die like other men, but God was going to take him to himself as he was. The end of the world was close at hand, too very close. He prayed more than usual that day, and when they sat eating their dinner in the sunshine, he suddenly sprang to his feet and stared wildly south, crying, 'See, see, it is the great light! the end comes!! and they do not know it; they will keep on sinning, I must tell them, I must!'

'No, no, Lou, they will catch you; they are looking for you, you must not go!'

'I must go, my boys; but first let me speak once more to you. Men would not heed me, or believe me, because my head is weak, but you have always believed in me, that God has revealed his word to me, and I will pray God to take you to himself quickly, for ye are worthy. Watch and pray always, boys, watch the light over the bluffs, it is breaking, breaking, and shall grow brighter. Good bye, my boys, I must leave ye in the world yet awhile.' He kissed them all tenderly and blessed them, and started south. He walked at first, then he ran, faster and faster he went, all the while shouting at the top of his voice, 'The sword of the Lord and of Gideon!'

The police officers heard of it, and set out to find him. They hunted the country over and even dragged the river, but they never found him again, living or dead. It is thought that he was drowned and the quicksands of the river sucked his body under. But the little Dane boys in our country firmly believe that he was translated like Enoch of old. On stormy nights, when the great winds sweep down from the north they huddle together in their beds and fancy that in the wind they still hear the wild cry, 'The sword of the Lord and of Gideon.'

A Night at Greenway Court

I, RICHARD MORGAN, OF the town of Winchester, county of Frederick, of the Commonwealth of Virginia, having been asked by my friend Josiah Goodrich, who purports making a history of this valley, to set down all I know concerning the death of M. Philip Marie Maurepas, a gentleman, it seems, of considerable importance in his own country, will proceed to do so briefly and with what little skill I am master of.

The incident which I am about to relate occurred in my early youth, but so deeply did it fix itself upon my memory that the details are as clear as though it had happened but yesterday. Indeed, of all the stirring events that have happened in my time, those nights spent at Greenway Court in my youth stand out most boldly in my memory. It was, I think, one evening late in October, in the year 1752, that my Lord Fairfax sent his man over to my father's house at Winchester to say that on the morrow his master desired my company at the Court. My father, a prosperous tobacco merchant, greatly regretted that I should be brought up in a new country, so far from the world of polite letters and social accomplishments, and contrived that I should pass much of my leisure in the company of one of the most gracious gentlemen and foremost scholars of his time, Thomas, Lord Fairfax. Accordingly, I was not surprised at my lord's summons. Late in the afternoon of the following day I rode over to the Court, and was first shown into my lord's private office, where for some time we discussed my lord's suit, then pending with the sons of Joist Hite, concerning certain lands beyond the Blue Ridge, then held by them, which my lord claimed through the extension of his grant from the crown. Our business being dispatched, he said:

'Come, Richard, in the hall I will present you to some gentlemen who will entertain you until supper time. There is a Frenchman stopping here, M. Maurepas, a gentleman of most engaging conversation. The Viscount Chillingham you will not meet until later, as he has gone out with the hounds.'

We crossed the yard and entered the hall where the table was already laid with my lord's silver platters and thin glass goblets, which never ceased to delight me when I dined with him, and though since, in London, I have drunk wine at a king's table, I have seen none finer. At the end of the room by the fireplace sat two men over their cards. One was a clergyman, whom I had met before, the other a tall spare gentleman whom my lord introduced as M. Philip Marie Maurepas. As I sat down, the gentleman addressed me in excellent English. The bright firelight gave me an excellent opportunity for observing this man, which I did, for with us strangers were too few not to be of special interest, and in a way their very appearance spoke to us of an older world beyond the seas for which the hearts of all of us still hungered.

He was, as I have said, a tall man, narrow chested and with unusually long arms. His forehead was high and his chin sharp, his skin was dark, tanned, as I later learned, by his long service in the Indes. He had a pair of restless black eyes and thin lips shaded by a dark mustache. His hair was coal black and grew long upon his shoulders; later I noticed that it was slightly touched with gray. His dress had once been fine, but had seen considerable service and was somewhat the worse for the weather. He wore breeches of dark blue velvet and leather leggins. His shirt and vest were of dark red and had once been worked with gold.

In his belt he wore a long knife with a slender blade and a handle of gold curiously worked in the form of a serpent, with eyes of pure red stones which sparkled mightily in the firelight. I must confess that in the very appearance of this man there was something that both interested and attracted me, and I fell to wondering what strange sights those keen eyes of his had looked upon.

'M. Maurepas intends spending the winter in our wilderness, Richard, and I fear he will find that our woods offer a cold welcome to a stranger.'

'Well, my lord, all the more to my taste. Having seen how hot the world can be, I am willing to see how cold.'

'To see that, sir,' said I, 'you should go to Quebeck where I have been with trappers. There I have thrown a cup full of water in the air and seen it descend solid ice.'

'I fear it will be cold enough here for my present attire,' said he laughing, 'yet it may be that I will taste the air of Quebeck before quitting this wilderness of yours.'

My lord then excused himself and withdrew, leaving me alone with the gentlemen.

'Come join me in a game of hazard, Master Morgan; it is yet half an hour until supper time,' said the clergyman, who had little thought for anything but his cards and his dinner.

'And I will look at the portraits; you have fleeced me quite enough for one day, good brother of the Church. I have nothing left but my diamond that I cut from the hand of a dead Rajpoot, finger and all, and it is a lucky stone, and I have no mind to lose it.'

'With your permission, M. Maurepas, I will look at the portraits with you, as I have no mind to play tonight; beside I think this is the hour of Mr Courtney's devotions,' said I, for I had no liking for the fat churchman. He, like so many of my lord's guests, was in a sense a refugee from justice; having fallen into disgrace with the heads of the English church, he had fled to our country and sought out Lord Halifax, whose door was closed against no man. He had been there then three months, dwelling in shameful idleness, one of that band of renegades who continually ate at my lord's table and hunted with his dogs and devoured his substance, waiting for some turn of fortune, like the suitors in the halls of Penelope. So we left the clergyman counting his gains and repaired to the other end of the hall, where, above the mahogany bookcases, the portraits hung. Of these there were a considerable number, and I told the Frenchman the names of as many as I knew. There was my lord's father and mother, and his younger brother, to whom he had given his English estate. There was his late majesty George I., and old Firnando Fairfax. Hanging under the dark picture of the king he had deposed and yet loved was Firnando's son, fighting Thomas Fairfax, third Lord and Baron of

Cameron, the great leader of the commoners with Cromwell, who rode after Charles at Heyworth Moore and thrust the people's petition in the indignant monarch's saddle bow; who defeated the king's forces at Naseby, and after Charles was delivered over to the commissioners of Parliament, met him at Nottingham and kissed his fallen sovereign's hand, refusing to sit in judgment over God's anointed.

Among these pictures there was one upon which I had often gazed in wonderment. It was the portrait of a lady, holding in her hand a white lily. Some heavy instrument had been thrust through the canvas, marring the face beyond all recognition, but the masses of powdered hair, and throat and arms were enough to testify to the beauty of the original. The hands especially were of surpassing loveliness, and the thumb was ornamented with a single emerald, as though to call attention to its singular perfection. The costume was the court dress of the then present reign, and with the eagerness of youthful imagination I had often fancied that could that picture speak it might tell something of that upon which all men wondered; why, in the prime of his manhood and success at court, Lord Fairfax had left home and country, friends, and all that men hold dear, renounced the gay society in which he had shone and his favorite pursuit of letters, and buried himself in the North American wilderness. Upon this canvas the Frenchman's eye was soon fixed.

'And this?' he asked.

'I do not know, sir; of that my lord has never told me.'

'Well, let me see; what is a man's memory good for, if not for such things? I must have seen those hands before, and that coronet.'

He looked at it closely and then stood back and looked at it from a distance. Suddenly an exclamation broke from him, and a sharp light flashed over his features.

'Ah, I thought so! So your lord has never told you of this, *parbleau, il a beaucoup de cause!* Look you, my boy, that emerald is the only beautiful thing that ever came out of Herrenhausen – that, and she who wears it. Perhaps you will see that emerald, too, some day; how many and how various they will yet be, God alone knows. How long, O Lord, how long? as your countrymen say.'

So bitter was his manner that I was half afraid, yet had a mind to question him, when my lord returned. He brought with him a young man of an appearance by no means distinguished, yet kindly and affable, whom he introduced as the Viscount Chillingham.

'You've a good country here, Master Norton, and better sport than we, for all our game laws. Hang laws, I say, they're naught but a trouble to them that make 'em and them that break 'em, and it's little good they do any of us. My lord, you must sell me your deer hound, Fanny, I want to take her home with me, and show 'em what your dogs are made of over here.'

'You are right welcome to her, or any of the pack.'

At this juncture my lord's housekeeper, Mistress Crawford, brought in the silver candlesticks, and the servants smoking dishes of bear's meat and venison, and many another delicacy for which my lord's table was famous, besides French wines and preserved cherries from his old estates in England.

The viscount flung himself into his chair, still flushed from his chase after the hounds, and stretched his long limbs.

'This is a man's life you have here, my lord. I tell you, you do well to be away from London now; it's as dull there as Mr Courtney's church without its spiritual pastor.'

The clergyman lifted his eyes from his venison long enough to remark slyly, 'Or as Hampton Court without its cleverest gamester,' at which the young man reddened under his fresh coat of tan, for he had been forced to leave England because of some gaming scandal which cast grave doubts upon his personal honor.

The talk drifted to the death of the queen of Denmark, the king's last visit to Hanover, and various matters of court gossip. Of these the gentlemen spoke freely, more freely, perhaps, than they would have dared to do at home. As I have said, my lord's guests were too often gentlemen who had left dark histories behind them, and had fled into the wilds where law was scarce more than a name and man had to contend only with the savage condition of nature, and a strong arm stood in better stead than a tender conscience. I have met many a strange man at Greenway Court, men who had cheated at play, men who had failed in great political plots, men who fled from a debtor's prison, and men charged with treason, and with a price upon their heads. For in some respects Lord Fairfax was a strangely conservative man, slow to judge and slow to anger, having seen much of the world, and thinking its conditions hard and its temptations heavy, deeming, I believe, all humanity more sinned against than sinning. And yet I have seldom known his confidence to be misplaced or his trust to be ill repaid. Whatever of information I may have acquired in my youth, I owe to the conversation of these men, for about my lord's board exiles and outlaws of all nations gathered, and unfolded in the friendly solitude of the wilderness plots and intrigues then scarce known in Europe.

On all the matters that were discussed the Frenchman seemed the best versed man present, even touching the most minute details of the English court. At last the viscount, who was visibly surprised, turned upon him sharply.

'Have you been presented at court, monsieur?'

'Not in England, count, but I have seen something of your king in Hanover; there, I think, on the banks of the stupid Leine, is his proper court, and 'tis there he sends the riches of your English. But in exchange I hear that he has brought you his treasure of Herrenhausen in her private carriage with a hundred postilions to herald her advent.'

His eyes were fixed keenly on my lord's face, but Fairfax only asked coldly:

'And where, monsieur, have you gained so perfect a mastery of the English tongue?'

'At Madras, your lordship, under Bourdonnais, where I fought your gallant countrymen, high and low, for the empire of the Indes. They taught me the sound of English speech well enough, and the music of English swords.'

'Faith,' broke in the viscount, 'then they taught you better than they know themselves, though it's their mother tongue. You've seen hot service there, I warrant?'

'Well, what with English guns sweeping our decks by sea, and the Indian sun broiling our skin by land, and the cholera tearing our entrails, we saw hot service indeed.'

'Were you in the Indian service after the return of Governor Bourdonnais to France, M. Maurepas?'

'After his return to the Bastile, you mean, my lord. Yes, I was less fortunate than my commander. There are worse prisons on earth than the Bastile, and Madras is one of them. When France sends a man to the Indes she has no intention he shall return alive. How I did so is another matter. Yes, I served afterward under Duplix, who seized Bourdonnais' troops as well as his treasure. I was with him in the Deccan when he joined his troops with Murzapha Jung against the Nabob of the Carnatic, and white men were set to fight side by side with heathen. And I say to you, gentlemen, that the bravest man in all that mêlée was the old Nabob himself. He was a hundred and seven years old, and he had been a soldier from his mother's knee. He was mounted on the finest elephant in the Indian army, and he led his soldiers right up into the thick of the fight in full sweep of the French bullets, ordering his bodyguard back and attended only by his driver. And when he saw his old enemy, Tecunda Sahib in the very midst of the French guards, he ordered his driver to up and at him, and he prodded the beast forward with his own hand. When the beast came crashing through our lines a bullet struck the old man in the breast, but still he urged him on. And when the elephant was stopped the driver was gone and the old Nabob was stone dead, sitting bolt upright in his curtained cage with a naked scimitar in his hand, ready for his vengeance. And I tell ye now, gentlemen, that I for one was right sorry that the bullet went home, for I am not the man who would see a brave soldier balked of his revenge.'

It is quite impossible with the pen to give any adequate idea of the dramatic manner in which he related this. I think it stirred the blood of more than one of us. The viscount struck the table with his hand and cried:

'That's talking, sir; you see the best of life, you French. As for us, we are so ridden by king-craft and state-craft we are as good as dead men. Between Walpole and the little German we have forgot the looks of a sword, and we never hear a gun these times but at the christening of some brat or other.'

The clergyman looked up reproachfully from his preserved cherries, and Lord Fairfax, who seldom suffered any talk that savored of disloyalty, rose to his feet and lifted his glass.

'Gentlemen, the king's health.'

'The king's health,' echoed we all rising. But M. Maurepas sat stiff in his chair, and his glass stood full beside him. The viscount turned upon him fiercely.

'Monsieur, you do not drink the king's health?'

'No, sir; your king, nor my king, nor no man's king. I have no king. May the devil take them one and all! and that's my health to them.'

'Monsieur,' cried my lord sternly, 'I am surprised to hear a soldier of the king of France speak in this fashion.'

'Yes, my lord, I have been a soldier of the king, and I know the wages of kings. What were they for Bourdonnais, the bravest general who ever drew a sword? The Bastile! What were they for all my gallant comrades? Cholera, massacre, death in the rotting marshes of Pondicherry. *Le Diable!* I know them well; prison, the sword, the stake, the recompense of kings.' He laughed terribly and struck his forehead with his hand.

'Monsieur,' said my lord, 'It may be that you have suffered much, and for that reason only do I excuse much that you say. Human justice is often at fault, and kings are but human. Nevertheless, they are ordained of heaven, and so long as there is breath in our bodies we owe them loyal service.'

The Frenchman rose and stood, his dark eyes flashing like coals of fire and his hands trembling as he waved them in the air. And methought the prophets of Israel must have looked so when they cried out unto the people, though his words were as dark blasphemy as ever fell from human lips.

'I tell you, sir, that the day will come and is now at hand when there will be no more kings. When a king's blood will be cheaper than pothouse wine and flow as plentifully. When crowned heads will pray for a peasant's cap, and princes will hide their royal lineage as lepers hide their sores. Ordained of God! Look you, sir, there is a wise man of France, so wise indeed that he dares not dwell in France, but hides among the Prussians, who says that there is no God! No Jehovah with his frying pan of lost souls! That it is all a tale made up by kings to terrify their slaves; that instead of God making kings, the kings made God.'

We were all struck with horror and the viscount rose to his feet again and threw himself into an attitude of attack, while Mr Courtney, whose place it was to speak, cowered in his seat and continued to look wistfully at the cherries.

'Stop, sir,' bawled the viscount, 'we have not much faith left in England, thanks to such as Mr Courtney here, but we've enough still to fight for. Little George may have his faults, but he's a brave man and a soldier. Let us see whether you can be as much.'

But the Frenchman did not so much as look at him. He was well sped with wine, and in his eyes there was a fierce light as of some ancient hatred woke anew. Staggering down the hall he pointed to the canvas which had so interested him in the afternoon.

'My lord, I wonder at you, that you should dare to keep that picture here, though three thousands miles of perilous sea, and savagery, and forests, and mountains impassable lie between you and Hampton Court. If you are a man, I think you have no cause to love the name of king. Yet, is not your heart as good as any man's, and will not your money buy as many trinkets? I tell you, this wilderness is not dark enough to hide that woman's face! And she carries a lily in her hand, the lilies of Herrenhausen! *Justice de Dieu*—' but he got no further, for my lord's hand had struck him in the mouth.

It all came about so quickly that even then it was but a blur of sudden action to me. We sprang between them, but Fairfax had no intention of striking twice.

'We can settle this in the morning, sir,' he said quietly. As he turned away M. Maurepas drew himself together with the litheness of a cat, and before I could catch his arm he had seized the long knife from his belt and thrown it after his host. It whizzed past my lord and stuck quivering in the oak wainscoating, while the man who threw it sank upon the floor, a pitiable heap of intoxication. My lord turned to his man, who still stood behind his chair. 'Henry, call me at five; at six I shall kill a scoundrel.'

With that he left us to watch over the drunken slumbers of the Frenchman.

In the morning they met on the level stretch before the court. At my lord's request I stood as second to M. Maurepas. My principal was much shaken by his debauch of last night, and I thought when my lord looked upon him he was already dead. For in Lord Fairfax's face was a purpose which it seemed no human will could thwart. Never have I seen him look the noble, Christian gentleman as he looked it then. Just as the autumn mists were rising from the hills, their weapons crossed, and the rising sun shot my lord's blade with fire until it looked the sword of righteousness indeed. It lasted but a moment. M. Maurepas, so renowned in war and gallantry, who had been the shame of two courts and the rival of two kings, fell, unknown and friendless, in the wilderness.

Two years later, after I had been presented and, through my father, stood in favor at court, I once had the honor to dine with his majesty at Hampton Court. At his right sat a woman known to history only too well; still brilliant, still beautiful, as she was unto the end. By her side I was seated. When the dishes were removed, as we sat over our wine, the king bade me tell him some of the adventures that had befallen in my own land.

'I can tell you, your majesty, how Lord Fairfax fought and killed M. Maurepas about a woman's picture.'

'That sounds well, tell on,' said the monarch in his heavy accent.

Then upon my hand under the table I felt a clasp, cold and trembling. I glanced down and saw there a white hand of wondrous beauty, the thumb ornamented with a single emerald. I sat still in amazement, for the lady's face was smiling and gave no sign.

The king clinked his glass impatiently with his nail.

'Well, go on with your story. Are we to wait on you all day?'

Again I felt that trembling pressure in mute entreaty on my hand.

'I think there is no story to tell, your majesty.'

'And I think you are a very stupid young man,' said his majesty testily, as he rose from the table.

'Perhaps he is abashed,' laughed my lady, but her bosom heaved with a deep sigh of relief.

So my day of royal favor was a short one, nor was I sorry, for I had kept my friend's secret and shielded a fair lady's honor, which are the two first duties of a Virginian.

JACK
LONDON
1876-1916

Born in San Francisco in 1876, Jack London left school at fourteen and scrounged a living selling stolen oysters in Oakland Bay. In 1897 he joined a seal-hunting ship bound for Japan and, on his return, became a vagabond. His life was short-lived and eventful and many of his works are based on his own extraordinary experiences. A remarkable journalist of his day, and an even more remarkable writer, Jack London acted as correspondent for the Hearst Newspaper group in the Russian/Japanese war, and he was a reporter in Mexico, the South Seas and the Caribbean. Constantly hounded by the horror of his own observations he was, nevertheless, an unhappy man and died aged forty.

The stories which follow are all taken from the collection *The Son of the Wolf* (1902). Evoking the rigors and excitements of seal-hunting, their powerful imaginative appeal and narrative skill first established London's reputation as a fine short story writer.

The White Silence

'CARMEN WON'T LAST MORE than a couple of days.' Mason spat out a chunk of ice and surveyed the poor animal ruefully, then put her foot in his mouth and proceeded to bite out the ice which clustered cruelly between the toes.

'I never saw a dog with a highfalutin' name that ever was worth a rap,' he said, as he concluded his task and shoved her aside. 'They just fade away and die under the responsibility. Did ye ever see one go wrong with a sensible name like Cassiar, Siwash, or Husky? No, sir! Take a look at Shookum here, he's—'

Snap! The lean brute flashed up, the white teeth just missing Mason's throat.

'Ye will, will ye?' A shrewd clout behind the ear with the butt of the dog whip stretched the animal in the snow, quivering softly, a yellow slaver dripping from its fangs.

'As I was saying, just look at Shookum here – he's got the spirit. Bet ye he eats Carmen before the week's out.'

'I'll bank another proposition against that,' replied Malemute Kid, reversing the frozen bread placed before the fire to thaw. 'We'll eat Shookum before the trip is over. What d'ye say, Ruth?'

The Indian woman settled the coffee with a piece of ice, glanced from Malemute Kid to her husband, then at the dogs, but vouchsafed no reply. It was such a palpable truism that none was necessary. Two hundred miles of unbroken trail in prospect, with a scant six days' grub for themselves and none for the dogs, could admit no other alternative. The two men and the woman grouped about the fire and began their meager meal. The dogs lay in their harnesses for it was a midday halt, and watched each mouthful enviously.

'No more lunches after today,' said Malemute Kid. 'And we've got to keep a close eye on the dogs – they're getting vicious. They'd just as soon pull a fellow down as not, if they get a chance.'

'And I was president of an Epworth once, and taught in the Sunday school.' Having irrelevantly delivered himself of this, Mason fell into a dreamy contemplation of his steaming moccasins, but was aroused by Ruth filling his cup. 'Thank God, we've got slathers of tea! I've seen it growing, down in Tennessee. What wouldn't I give for a hot corn pone just now! Never mind, Ruth; you won't starve much longer, nor wear moccasins either.'

The woman threw off her gloom at this, and in her eyes welled up a great love for her white lord – the first white man she had ever seen – the first man whom she had known to treat a woman as something better than a mere animal or beast of burden.

'Yes, Ruth,' continued her husband, having recourse to the macaronic jargon in which it was alone possible for them to understand each other, 'wait till we clean up and pull for the Outside. We'll take the White Man's canoe and go to the Salt Water. Yes, bad water, rough water, great mountains dance up and down all the time. And so big, so far, so far away – you travel ten sleep, twenty sleep, forty sleep' – he graphically enumerated the days on his fingers – 'all the time water, bad water. Then you come to great village, plenty people, just the same mosquitoes next summer. Wigwams oh, so high – ten, twenty pines. Hi-yu skookum!'

He paused impotently, cast an appealing glance at Malemute Kid, then laboriously placed the twenty pines, end on end, by sign language. Malemute Kid smiled with cheery cynicism; but Ruth's eyes were wide with wonder and with pleasure; for she half believed he was joking, and such condescension pleased her poor woman's heart.

'And then you step into a – a box, and pouf! up you go.' He tossed his empty cup in the air by way of illustration and, as he deftly caught it, cried, 'And biff! down you come. Oh, great medicine men! You go Fort Yukon. I go Arctic City – twenty-five sleep – big string, all the time – I catch him string – I say, "Hello, Ruth! How are ye?" – and you say, "Is that my good husband?" – and I say, "Yes" – and you say, "No can bake good bread, no more soda" – then I say, "Look in cache, under flour; good-by." You look and catch plenty soda. All the time you Fort Yukon, me Arctic City. Hi-yu medicine man!'

Ruth smiled so ingenuously at the fairy story that both men burst into laughter. A row among the dogs cut short the wonders of the Outside, and by the time the snarling combatants were separated, she had lashed the sleds and all was ready for the trail.

'Mush! Baldy! Hi! Mush on!' Mason worked his whip smartly and, as the dogs whined low in the traces, broke out the sled with the gee pole. Ruth followed with the second team, leaving Malemute Kid, who had helped her start, to bring up the rear. Strong man, brute that he was, capable of felling an ox at a blow, he could not bear to beat the poor animals, but humored them as a dog driver rarely does – nay, almost wept with them in their misery.

'Come, mush on there, you poor sore-footed brutes!' he murmured, after several ineffectual attempts to start the load. But his patience was at last rewarded, and though whimpering with pain, they hastened to join their fellows.

No more conversation; the toil of the trail will not permit such extravagance. And of all deadening labors, that of the Northland trail is the worst. Happy is the man who can weather a day's travel at the price of silence, and that on a beaten track.

And of all heartbreaking labors, that of breaking trail is the worst. At every step the great webbed shoe sinks till the snow is level with the knee. Then up, straight up, the deviation of a fraction of an inch being a certain precursor of disaster, the snowshoe must be lifted till the surface is cleared; then forward, down, and the other foot is raised perpendicularly for the matter of half a yard. He who tries this for the first time, if haply he avoids bringing his shoes in dangerous propinquity and measures not his length on the treacherous footing, will give up exhausted at the end of a hundred yards; he who can keep out of the way of the dogs for a whole day may well crawl into his sleeping bag with a clear conscience and a pride which passeth all understanding; and he who travels twenty sleeps on the Long Trail is a man whom the gods may envy.

The afternoon wore on, and with the awe, born of the White Silence, the voiceless travelers bent to their work. Nature has many tricks wherewith she convinces man of his finity – the ceaseless flow of the tides, the fury of the storm, the shock of the earthquake, the long roll of heaven's artillery – but the most tremendous, the most stupefying of all, is the passive phase of the White Silence. All movement ceases, the sky clears, the heavens are as brass; the slightest whisper seems sacrilege, and man becomes timid, affrighted at the sound of his own voice. Sole speck of life journeying across the ghostly wastes of a dead world, he trembles at his audacity, realizes that his is a maggot's life, nothing more. Strange thoughts arise unsummoned, and the mystery of all things strives for utterance. And the fear of death, of God, of the universe, comes over him – the hope of the Resurrection and the Life, the yearning for immortality, the vain striving of the imprisoned essence – it is then, if ever, man walks alone with God.

So wore the day away. The river took a great bend, and Mason headed his team for the cutoff across the narrow neck of land. But the dogs balked at the high bank. Again and again, though Ruth and Malemute Kid were shoving on the sled, they slipped back. Then came the concerted effort. The miserable creatures, weak from hunger, exerted their last strength. Up – up – the sled poised on the top of the bank; but the leader swung the string of dogs behind him to the right, fouling Mason's snowshoes. The result was grievous. Mason was whipped off his feet; one of the dogs fell in the traces; and the sled toppled back, dragging everything to the bottom again.

Slash! the whip fell among the dogs savagely, especially upon the one which had fallen.

'Don't, Mason,' entreated Malemute Kid; 'the poor devil's on its last legs. Wait and we'll put my team on.'

Mason deliberately withheld the whip till the last word had fallen, then out flashed the long lash, completely curling about the offending creature's body. Carmen – for it was Carmen – cowered in the snow, cried piteously, then rolled over on her side.

It was a tragic moment, a pitiful incident of the trail – a dying dog, two comrades in anger. Ruth glanced solicitously from man to man. But Malemute Kid restrained himself, though there was a world of reproach in his eyes, and, bending over the dog, cut the traces. No word was spoken. The teams were double-spanned and the difficulty overcome; the sleds were under way again, the dying dog dragging herself along in the rear. As long as an animal can travel, it is not shot, and this last chance is accorded it – the crawling into camp, if it can, in the hope of a moose being killed.

Already penitent for his angry action, but too stubborn to make amends, Mason toiled on at the head of the cavalcade, little dreaming that danger hovered in the air. The timber clustered thick in the sheltered bottom, and through this they threaded their way. Fifty feet or more from the trail towered a lofty pine. For generations it had stood there, and for generations destiny had had this one end in view – perhaps the same had been decreed of Mason.

He stooped to fasten the loosened thong of his moccasin. The sleds came to a halt, and the dogs lay down in the snow without a whimper. The stillness was weird; not a breath rustled the frost-encrusted forest; the cold and silence of outer space had chilled the heart and smote the trembling lips of nature. A sigh pulsed through the air – they did not seem to actually hear it, but rather felt it, like the premonition of movements in a motionless void. Then the great tree, burdened with its weight of years and snow, played its last part in the tragedy of life. He heard the warning crash and attempted to spring up but, almost erect, caught the blow squarely on the shoulder.

The sudden danger, the quick death – how often had Malemute Kid faced it! The pine needles were still quivering as he gave his commands and sprang into action. Nor did the Indian girl faint or raise her voice in idle wailing, as might many of her white sisters. At his order, she threw her weight on the end of a quickly extemporized handspike, easing the pressure and listening to her husband's groans, while Malemute Kid attacked the tree with his ax. The steel rang merrily as it bit into the frozen trunk, each stroke being accompanied by a forced, audible respiration, the 'Huh!' 'Huh!' of the woodsman.

At last the Kid laid the pitiable thing that was once a man in the snow. But worse than his comrade's pain was the dumb anguish in the woman's face, the blended look of hopeful, hopeless query. Little was said; those of the Northland are early taught the futility of words and the inestimable value of deeds. With the temperature at sixty-five below zero, a man cannot lie many minutes in the snow and live. So the sled lashings were cut, and the sufferer, rolled in furs, laid on a couch of boughs. Before him roared a fire, built of the very wood which wrought the mishap. Behind and partially over him was stretched the primitive fly – a piece of canvas, which caught the radiating heat and threw it back and down upon him – a trick which men may know who study physics at the fount.

And men who have shared their bed with death know when the call is sounded. Mason was terribly crushed. The most cursory examination revealed it. His right arm, leg, and back were broken; his limbs were paralyzed from the hips; and the likelihood of internal injuries was large. An occasional moan was his only sign of life.

No hope; nothing to be done. The pitiless night crept slowly by – Ruth's portion, the despairing stoicism of her race, and Malemute Kid adding new lines to his face of bronze. In fact, Mason suffered least of all, for he spent his time in eastern Tennessee, in the Great Smoky Mountains, living over the scenes of his childhood. And most pathetic was the melody of his long-forgotten Southern vernacular, as he raved of swimming holes and coon hunts and watermelon raids. It was as Greek to Ruth, but the Kid understood and felt – felt as only one can feel who has been shut out for years from all that civilization means.

Morning brought consciousness to the stricken man, and Malemute Kid bent closer to catch his whispers.

'You remember when we foregathered on the Tanana, four years come next ice run? I didn't care so much for her then. It was more like she was pretty, and there was a smack of excitement about it, I think. But d'ye know, I've come to think a heap of her. She's been a good wife to me, always at my shoulder in the pinch. And when it comes to trading, you know there isn't her equal. D'ye recollect the time she shot the Moosehorn Rapids to pull you and me off that rock, the bullets whipping the water like hailstones? – and the time of the famine at Nuklukyeto? – when she raced the ice run to bring the news? Yes, she's been a good wife to me, better'n that other one. Didn't know I'd been there? Never told you, eh? Well, I tried it once, down in the States. That's why I'm here. Been raised together, too. I came away to give her a chance for divorce. She got it.

'But that's got nothing to do with Ruth. I had thought of cleaning up and pulling for the Outside next year – her and I – but it's too late. Don't send her back to her people, Kid. It's beastly hard for a woman to go back. Think of it! – nearly four years on our bacon and beans and flour and dried fruit, and then to go back to her fish and caribou. It's not good for her to have tried our ways, to come to know they're better'n her people's, and then return to them. Take care of her, Kid – why don't you – but no, you always fought shy of them – and you never told me why you came to this country. Be kind to her, and send her back to the States as soon as you can. But fix it so she can come back – liable to get homesick, you know.

'And the youngster – it's drawn us closer, Kid. I only hope it is a boy. Think of it! – flesh of my flesh, Kid. He mustn't stop in this country. And if it's a girl, why, she can't. Sell my furs; they'll fetch at least five thousand, and I've got as much more with the company. And handle my interests with yours. I think that bench claim will show up. See that he gets a good schooling; and Kid, above all, don't let him come back. This country was not made for white men.

'I'm a gone man, Kid. Three or four sleeps at the best. You've got to go on. You must go on! Remember, it's my wife, it's my boy – O God! I hope it's a boy! You can't stay by me – and I charge you, a dying man, to pull on.'

'Give me three days,' pleaded Malemute Kid. 'You may change for the better; something may turn up.'

'No.'

'Just three days.'

'You must pull on.'

'Two days.'

'It's my wife and my boy, Kid. You would not ask it.'

'One day.'

'No, no! I charge—'

'Only one day. We can shave it through on the grub, and I might knock over a moose.'

'No – all right; one day, but not a minute more. And, Kid, don't – don't leave me to face it alone. Just a shot, one pull on the trigger. You understand. Think of it! Think of it! Flesh of my flesh, and I'll never live to see him!

'Send Ruth here. I want to say good-by and tell her that she must think of the boy and not wait till I'm dead. She might refuse to go with you if I didn't. Good-by, old man; good-by.

'Kid! I say – a – sink a hole above the pup, next to the slide. I panned out forty cents on my shovel there.

'And, Kid!' He stooped lower to catch the last faint words, the dying man's surrender of his pride. 'I'm sorry – for – you know – Carmen.'

Leaving the girl crying softly over her man, Malemute Kid slipped into his parka and snowshoes, tucked his rifle under his arm, and crept away into the forest. He was no tyro in the stern sorrows of the Northland, but never had he faced so stiff a problem as this. In the abstract, it was a plain, mathematical proposition – three possible lives as against one doomed one. But now he hesitated. For five years, shoulder to shoulder, on the rivers and trails, in the camps and mines, facing death by field and flood and famine, had they knitted the bonds of their comradeship. So close was the tie that he had often been conscious of a vague jealousy of Ruth, from the first time she had come between. And now it must be severed by his own hand.

Though he prayed for a moose, just one moose, all game seemed to have deserted the land, and nightfall found the exhausted man crawling into camp, lighthanded, heavyhearted. An uproar from the dogs and shrill cries from Ruth hastened him.

Bursting into the camp, he saw the girl in the midst of the snarling pack, laying about her with an ax. The dogs had broken the iron rule of their masters and were rushing the grub. He joined the issue with his rifle reversed, and the hoary game of natural selection was played out with all the ruthlessness of its primeval environment. Rifle and ax went up and down, hit or missed with monotonous regularity; lithe bodies flashed, with wild eyes and dripping fangs; and man and beast fought for supremacy to the bitterest conclusion. Then the beaten brutes crept to the edge of the firelight, licking their wounds, voicing their misery to the stars.

The whole stock of dried salmon had been devoured, and perhaps five pounds of flour remained to tide them over two hundred miles of wilderness. Ruth returned to her husband, while Malemute Kid cut up the warm body of one of the dogs, the skull of which had been crushed by the ax. Every portion was carefully put away, save the hide and offal, which were cast to his fellows of the moment before.

Morning brought fresh trouble. The animals were turning on each other. Carmen, who still clung to her slender thread of life, was downed by the pack. The lash fell among them unheeded. They cringed and cried under the blows, but refused to scatter till the last wretched bit had disappeared – bones, hide, hair, everything.

Malemute Kid went about his work, listening to Mason, who was back in Tennessee, delivering tangled discourses and wild exhortations to his brethren of other days.

Taking advantage of neighboring pines, he worked rapidly, and Ruth watched him make a cache similar to those sometimes used by hunters to preserve their meat from the wolverines and dogs. One after the other, he bent the tops of two small pines toward each other and nearly to the ground, making them fast with thongs of moosehide. Then he beat the dogs into submission and harnessed them to two of the sleds, loading the same with everything but the furs which enveloped Mason. These he wrapped and lashed tightly about him, fastening either end of the robes to the bent pines. A single stroke of his hunting knife would release them and send the body high in the air.

Ruth had received her husband's last wishes and made no struggle. Poor girl, she had learned the lesson of obedience well. From a child, she had bowed, and seen all women bow, to the lords of creation, and it did not seem in the nature of things for woman to resist. The Kid permitted her one outburst of grief, as she kissed her husband – her own people had no such custom – then led her to the foremost sled and helped her into her snowshoes. Blindly, instinctively, she took the gee pole and whip, and 'mushed' the dogs out on the trail. Then he returned to Mason, who had fallen into a coma, and long after she was out of sight crouched by the fire, waiting, hoping, praying for his comrade to die.

It is not pleasant to be alone with painful thoughts in the White Silence. The silence of gloom is merciful, shrouding one as with protection and breathing a thousand intangible sympathies; but the bright White Silence, clear and cold, under steely skies, is pitiless.

An hour passed – two hours – but the man would not die. At high noon the sun, without raising its rim above the southern horizon, threw a suggestion of fire athwart the heavens, then quickly drew back. Malemute Kid roused and dragged himself to his comrade's side. He cast one glance about him. The White Silence seemed to sneer, and a great fear came upon him. There was a sharp report; Mason swung into his aerial sepulcher, and Malemute Kid lashed the dogs into a wild gallop as he fled across the snow.

The Son of the Wolf

MAN RARELY PLACES A PROPER valuation upon his womankind, at least not until deprived of them. He has no conception of the subtle atmosphere exhaled by the sex feminine, so long as he bathes in it; but let it be withdrawn, and an ever-growing void begins to manifest itself in his existence, and he becomes hungry, in a vague sort of way, for a something so indefinite that he cannot characterize it. If his comrades have no more experience than himself, they will shake their heads dubiously and dose him with strong physic. But the hunger will continue and become stronger; he will lose interest in the things of his everyday life and wax morbid; and one day, when the emptiness has become unbearable, a revelation will dawn upon him.

In the Yukon country, when this comes to pass, the man usually provisions a poling boat, if it is summer, and if winter, harnesses his dogs, and heads for the Southland. A few months later, supposing him to be possessed of a faith in the country, he returns with a wife to share with him in that faith, and incidentally in his hardships. This but serves to show the innate selfishness of man. It also brings us to the trouble of 'Scruff' Mackenzie, which occurred in the old days, before the country was stampeded and staked by a tidal-wave of the *che-cha-quas*, and when the Klondike's only claim to notice was its salmon fisheries.

'Scruff' Mackenzie bore the earmarks of a frontier birth and a frontier life. His face was stamped with twenty-five years of incessant struggle with Nature in her wildest moods, – the làst two, the wildest and hardest of all, having been spent in groping for the gold which lies in the shadow of the Arctic Circle. When the yearning sickness came upon him, he was not surprised, for he was a practical man and had seen other men thus stricken. But he showed no sign of his malady, save that he worked harder. All summer he fought mosquitoes and washed the sure-thing bars of the Stuart River for a double grubstake. Then he floated a raft of houselogs down the Yukon to Forty Mile, and put together as comfortable a cabin as any the camp could boast of. In fact, it showed such cozy promise that many men elected to be his partner and to come and live with him. But he crushed their aspirations with rough speech, peculiar for its strength and brevity, and bought a double supply of grub from the trading-post.

As has been noted, 'Scruff' Mackenzie was a practical man. If he wanted a thing he usually got it, but in doing so, went no farther out of his way than was necessary. Though a son of toil and hardship, he was averse to a journey of six hundred miles on the ice, a second of two thousand miles on the ocean, and still a third thousand miles or so to his last stamping-grounds, – all in the mere quest of a wife. Life was too short. So he rounded up his dogs, lashed a curious freight to his sled, and faced across the divide whose westward slopes were drained by the head-reaches of the Tanana.

He was a sturdy traveler, and his wolf-dogs could work harder and travel farther on less grub than any other team in the Yukon. Three weeks later he strode into a hunting-camp of the Upper Tanana Sticks. They marveled at his temerity; for they had a bad name and had been known to kill white men for as trifling a thing as a sharp ax or a broken rifle. But he went among them single-handed, his bearing being a delicious composite of humility, familiarity, *sang-froid*, and insolence. It required a deft hand and deep knowledge of the barbaric mind effectually to handle such diverse weapons; but he was a past-master in the art, knowing when to conciliate and when to threaten with Jove-like wrath.

He first made obeisance to the Chief Thling-Tinneh, presenting him with a couple of pounds of black tea and tobacco, and thereby winning his most cordial regard. Then he mingled with the men and maidens, and that night gave a *potlach*. The snow was beaten down in the form of an oblong, perhaps a hundred feet in length and quarter as many across. Down the center a long fire was built, while either side was carpeted with spruce boughs. The lodges were forsaken, and the fivescore or so members of the tribe gave tongue to their folk-chants in honor of their guest.

'Scruff' Mackenzie's two years had taught him the not many hundred words of their vocabulary, and he had likewise conquered their deep gutturals, their Japanese idioms, constructions, and honorific and agglutinative particles. So he made oration after their manner, satisfying their instinctive poetry-love with crude flights of eloquence and metaphorical contortions. After Thling-Tinneh and the Shaman had responded in kind, he made trifling presents to the menfolk, joined in their singing, and proved an expert in their fifty-two-stick gambling game.

And they smoked his tobacco and were pleased. But among the younger men there was a defiant attitude, a spirit of braggadocio, easily understood by the raw insinuations of the toothless squaws and the giggling of the maidens. They had known few white men, 'Sons of the Wolf,' but from those few they had learned strange lessons.

Nor had 'Scruff' Mackenzie, for all his seeming carelessness, failed to note these phenomena. In truth, rolled in his sleeping-furs, he thought it all over, thought seriously, and emptied many pipes in mapping out a campaign. One maiden only had caught his fancy, – none other than Zarinska, daughter to the chief. In features, form, and poise, answering more nearly to the white man's type of beauty, she was almost an anomaly among her tribal sisters. He would possess her, make her his wife, and name her – ah, he would name her Gertrude! Having thus decided, he rolled over on his side and dropped off to sleep, a true son of his all-conquering race, a Samson among the Philistines.

It was slow work and a stiff game; but 'Scruff' Mackenzie maneuvered cunningly, with an unconcern which served to puzzle the Sticks. He took great care to impress the men that he was a sure shot and a mighty hunter, and the camp rang with his plaudits when he brought down a moose at six hundred yards. Of a night he visited in Chief Thling-Tinneh's lodge of moose and cariboo skins, talking big and dispensing tobacco with a lavish hand. Nor did he fail to likewise honor the Shaman; for he realized the medicine-man's influence with his people, and was anxious to make of him an ally. But that worthy was high and mighty, refused to be propitiated, and was unerringly marked down as a prospective enemy.

Though no opening presented for an interview with Zarinska, Mackenzie stole many a glance to her, giving fair warning of his intent. And well she knew, yet coquettishly surrounded herself with a ring of women whenever the men were away and he had a chance. But he was in no hurry; besides he knew she could not help but think of him, and a few days of such thought would only better his suit.

At last, one night, when he deemed the time to be ripe, he abruptly left the chief's smoky dwelling and hastened to a neighboring lodge. As usual, she sat with squaws and maidens about her, all engaged in sewing moccasins and beadwork. They laughed at his entrance, and badinage, which linked Zarinska to him, ran high. But one after the other they were unceremoniously bundled into the outer snow, whence they hurried to spread the tale through all the camp.

His cause was well pleaded, in her tongue, for she did not know his, and at the end of two hours he rose to go.

'So Zarinska will come to the White Man's lodge? Good! I go now to have talk with thy father, for he may not be so minded. And I will give him many tokens; but he must not ask too much. If he say no? Good! Zarinska shall yet come to the White Man's lodge.'

He had already lifted the skin flap to depart, when a low exclamation brought him back to the girl's side. She brought herself to her knees on the bearskin mat, her face aglow with true Eve-light, and shyly unbuckled his heavy belt. He looked down, perplexed, suspicious, his ears alert for the slightest sound without. But her next move disarmed his doubt, and he smiled with pleasure. She took from her sewing bag a moosehide sheath, brave with bright beadwork, fantastically designed. She drew his great hunting-knife, gazed reverently along the keen edge, half tempted to try it with her thumb, and shot it into place in its new home. Then she slipped the sheath along the belt to its customary resting-place, just above the hip.

For all the world, it was like a scene of olden time, – a lady and her knight. Mackenzie drew her up full height and swept her red lips with his moustache, – the, to her, foreign caress of the Wolf. It was a meeting of the stone age and the steel; but she was none the less a woman, as her crimson cheeks and the luminous softness of her eyes attested.

There was a thrill of excitement in the air as 'Scruff' Mackenzie, a bulky bundle under his arm, threw open the flap of Thling-Tinneh's tent. Children were running about in the open, dragging dry wood to the scene of the *potlach*, a babble of women's voices was growing in intensity, the young men were consulting in sullen groups, while from the Shaman's lodge rose the eerie sounds of an incantation.

The chief was alone with his blear-eyed wife, but a glance sufficed to tell Mackenzie that the news was already told. So he plunged at once into the business, shifting the beaded sheath prominently to the fore as advertisement of the betrothal.

'O Thling-Tinneh, mighty chief of the Sticks and the land of the Tanana, ruler of the salmon and the bear, the moose and the cariboo! The White Man is before thee with a great purpose. Many moons has his lodge been empty, and he is lonely. And his heart has eaten itself in silence, and grown hungry for a woman to sit beside him in his lodge, to meet him from the hunt with warm fire and good food. He has heard strange things, the patter of baby moccasins and the sound of children's voices. And one night a vision came upon him, and he beheld the Raven, who is thy father, the great Raven, who is the father of all the Sticks. And the Raven spoke to the lonely White Man, saying: "Bind thou thy moccasins upon thee, and gird thy snow-shoes on, and lash thy sled with food for many sleeps and fine tokens for the Chief Thling-Tinneh. For thou shalt turn thy face to where the midspring sun is wont to sink below the land and journey to this great chief's hunting-grounds. There thou shalt make big presents, and Thling-Tinneh, who is my son, shall become to thee as a father. In his lodge there is a maiden into whom I breathed the breath of life for thee. This maiden shalt thou take to wife."

O Chief, thus spake the great Raven; thus do I lay many presents at thy feet; thus am I come to take thy daughter!'

The old man drew his furs about him with crude consciousness of royalty, but delayed reply while a youngster crept in, delivered a quick message to appear before the council, and was gone.

'O White Man, whom we have named Moose-Killer, also known as the Wolf, and the Son of the Wolf! We know thou comest of a mighty race; we are proud to have thee our *potlach*-guest; but the king-salmon does not mate with the dog-salmon, nor the Raven with the Wolf.'

'Not so!' cried Mackenzie. 'The daughters of the Raven have I met in the camps of the Wolf, – the squaw of Mortimer, the squaw of Tregidgo, the squaw of Barnaby, who came two ice-runs back, and I have heard of other squaws, though my eyes beheld them not.'

'Son, your words are true; but it were evil mating, like the water with the sand, like the snow-flake with the sun. But met you one Mason and his squaw? No? He came ten ice-runs ago, – the first of all the Wolves. And with him there was a mighty man, straight as a willow-shoot, and tall; strong as the bald-faced grizzly, with a heart like the full summer moon; his—'

'Oh!' interrupted Mackenzie, recognizing the well-known Northland figure, – 'Malemute Kid!'

'The same, – a mighty man. But saw you aught of the squaw? She was full sister to Zarinska.'

'Nay, Chief; but I have heard. Mason – far, far to the north, a spruce-tree, heavy with years, crushed out his life beneath. But his love was great, and he had much gold. With this, and her boy, she journeyed countless sleeps toward the winter's noonday sun, and there she yet lives, – no biting frost, no snow, no summer's midnight sun, no winter's noonday night.'

A second messenger interrupted with imperative summons from the council. As Mackenzie threw him into the snow, he caught a glimpse of the swaying forms before the council-fire, heard the deep basses of the men in rhythmic chant, and knew the Shaman was fanning the anger of his people. Time passed. He turned upon the chief.

'Come! I wish thy child. And now, see! Here are tobacco, tea, many cups of sugar, warm blankets, handkerchiefs, both good and large; and here, a true rifle, with many bullets and much powder.'

'Nay,' replied the old man, struggling against the great wealth spread before him. 'Even now are my people come together. They will not have this marriage.'

'But thou art chief.'

'Yet do my young men rage because the Wolves have taken their maidens so that they may not marry.'

'Listen, O Thling-Tinneh! Ere the night has passed into the day, the Wolf shall face his dogs to the Mountains of the East and fare forth to the Country of the Yukon. And Zarinska shall break trail for his dogs.'

'And ere the night has gained its middle, my young men may fling to the dogs the flesh of the Wolf, and his bones be scattered in the snow till the springtime lay them bare.'

It was threat and counter-threat. Mackenzie's bronzed face flushed darkly. He raised his voice. The old squaw, who till now had sat an impassive spectator, made to creep by him for the door. The song of the men broke suddenly and there was a hubbub of many voices as he whirled the old woman roughly to her couch of skins.

'Again I cry – listen, O Thling-Tinneh! The Wolf dies with teeth fast-locked, and with him there shall sleep ten of thy strongest men, – men who are needed, for the hunting is not begun, and the fishing is not many moons away. And again, of what profit should I die? I know the custom of thy people; thy share of my wealth shall be very small. Grant me thy child, and it shall all be thine. And yet again, my brothers will come, and they are many, and their maws are never filled; and the daughters of the Raven shall bear children in the lodges of the Wolf. My people are greater than thy people. It is destiny. Grant, and all this wealth is thine.'

Moccasins were crunching the snow without. Mackenzie threw his rifle to cock, and loosened the twin Colts in his belt.

'Grant, O Chief!'

'And yet will my people say no.'

'Grant, and the wealth is thine. Then shall I deal with thy people after.'

'The Wolf will have it so. I will take his tokens, – but I would warn him.'

Mackenzie passed over the goods, taking care to clog the rifle's ejector, and capping the bargain with a kaleidoscopic silk kerchief. The Shaman and half a dozen young braves entered, but he shouldered boldly among them and passed out.

'Pack!' was his laconic greeting to Zarinska as he passed her lodge and hurried to harness his dogs. A few minutes later he swept into the council at the head of the team, the woman by his side. He took his place at the upper end of the oblong, by the side of the chief. To his left, a step to the rear, he stationed Zarinska, – her proper place. Besides, the time was ripe for mischief, and there was need to guard his back.

On either side, the men crouched to the fire, their voices lifted in a folk-chant out of the forgotten past. Full of strange, halting cadences and haunting recurrences, it was not beautiful. 'Fearful' may inadequately express it. At the lower end, under the eye of the Shaman, danced half a score of women. Stern were his reproofs of those who did not wholly abandon themselves to the ecstasy of the rite. Half hidden in their heavy masses of raven hair, all dishevelled and falling to their waists, they slowly swayed to and fro, their forms rippling to an ever-changing rhythm.

It was a weird scene; an anachronism. To the south, the nineteenth century was reeling off the few years of its last decade; here flourished man primeval, a shade removed from the prehistoric cave-dweller, forgotten fragment of the Elder World. The tawny wolf-dogs sat between their skin-clad masters or fought for room, the firelight cast backward from their red eyes and dripping fangs. The woods, in ghostly shroud, slept on unheeding. The White Silence, for the moment driven to the rimming forest, seemed ever crushing inward; the stars danced with great leaps, as is their wont in the time of the Great Cold; while the Spirits of the Pole trailed their robes of glory athwart the heavens.

'Scruff' Mackenzie dimly realized the wild grandeur of the setting as his eyes ranged down the fur-fringed sides in quest of missing faces. They rested for a moment on a newborn babe, suckling at its mother's naked breast. It was forty below, – seven and odd degrees of frost. He thought of the tender women of his own race and smiled grimly. Yet from the loins of some such tender woman had he sprung with a kingly inheritance, – an inheritance which gave to him and his dominance over the land and sea, over the animals and the peoples of all the zones. Single-handed against fivescore, girt by the Arctic winter, far from his own, he felt the prompting of his heritage, the desire to possess, the wild danger-love, the thrill of battle, the power to conquer or to die.

The singing and the dancing ceased, and the Shaman flared up in rude eloquence. Through the sinuosities of their vast mythology, he worked cunningly upon the credulity of his people. The case was strong. Opposing the creative principles as embodied in the Crow and the Raven, he stigmatized Mackenzie as the Wolf, the fighting and the destructive principle. Not only was the combat of these forces spiritual, but men fought, each to his totem. They were the children of Jelchs, the Raven, the Promethean fire-bringer; Mackenzie was the child of the Wolf, or in other words, the Devil. For them to bring a truce to this perpetual warfare, to marry their daughters to the arch-enemy, were treason and blasphemy of the highest order. No phrase was harsh nor figure vile enough in branding Mackenzie as a sneaking interloper and emissary of Satan. There was a subdued, savage roar in the deep chests of his listeners as he took the swing of his peroration.

'Aye, my brothers, Jelchs is all-powerful! Did he not bring heaven-borne fire that we might be warm? Did he not draw the sun, moon, and stars, from their holes that we might see? Did he not teach us that we might fight the Spirits of Famine and of Frost? But now Jelchs is angry with his children, and they are grown to a handful, and he will not help. For they have forgotten him, and done evil things, and trod bad trails, and taken his enemies into their lodges to sit by their fires. And the Raven is sorrowful at the wickedness of his children; but when they shall rise up and show they have come back, he will come out of the darkness to aid them. O brothers! the Fire-Bringer has whispered messages to thy Shaman; the same shall ye hear. Let the young men take the young women to their lodges; let them fly at the throat of the Wolf; let them be undying in their enmity! Then shall their women become fruitful and they shall multiply into a mighty people! And the Raven shall lead great tribes of their fathers and their fathers' fathers from out the North; and they shall beat back the Wolves till they are as last year's campfires; and they shall again come to rule over all the land! 'Tis the message of Jelchs, the Raven.'

This foreshadowing of the Messiah's coming brought a hoarse howl from the Sticks as they leaped to their feet. Mackenzie slipped the thumbs of his mittens and waited. There was a clamor for the 'Fox,' not to be stilled till one of the young men stepped forward to speak.

'Brothers! The Shaman has spoken wisely. The Wolves have taken our women, and our men are childless. We are grown to a handful. The Wolves have taken our warm furs and given for them evil spirits which dwell in bottles, and clothes which come not from the beaver or the lynx, but are made from the grass. And they are not warm, and our men die of strange sicknesses. I, the Fox, have taken no woman to wife; and why? Twice have the maidens which pleased me gone to the camps of the Wolf. Even now have I laid by skins of the beaver, of the moose, of the cariboo, that I might win favor in the eyes of Thling-Tinneh, that I might marry Zarinska, his daughter. Even now are her snow-shoes bound to her feet, ready to break trail for the dogs of the Wolf. Nor do I speak for myself alone. As I have done, so has the Bear. He, too, had fain been the father of her children, and many skins has he cured thereto. I speak for all the young men who know not wives. The Wolves are ever hungry. Always do they take the choice meat at the killing. To the Ravens are left the leavings.

'There is Gugkla,' he cried, brutally pointing out one of the women, who was a cripple. 'Her legs are bent like the ribs of a birch canoe. She cannot gather wood nor carry the meat of the hunters. Did the Wolves choose her?'

'Ai! ai!' vociferated his tribesmen.

'There is Moyri, whose eyes are crossed by the Evil Spirit. Even the babes are affrighted when they gaze upon her, and it is said the bald-face gives her the trail. Was she chosen?'

Again the cruel applause rang out.

'And there sits Pischet. She does not hearken to my words. Never has she heard the cry of the chit-chat, the voice of her husband, the babble of her child. She lives in the White Silence. Cared the Wolves aught for her? No! Theirs is the choice of the kill; ours is the leavings.

'Brothers, it shall not be! No more shall the Wolves slink among our campfires. The time is come.'

A great streamer of fire, the aurora borealis, purple, green, and yellow, shot across the zenith, bridging horizon to horizon. With head thrown back and arms extended, he swayed to his climax.

'Behold! The spirits of our fathers have arisen and great deeds are afoot this night!'

He stepped back, and another young man somewhat diffidently came forward, pushed on by his comrades. He towered a full head above them, his broad chest defiantly bared to the frost. He swung tentatively from one foot to the other. Words halted upon his tongue, and he was ill at ease. His face was horrible to look upon, for it had at one time been half torn away by some terrific blow. At last he struck his breast with his clenched fist, drawing sound as from a drum, and his voice rumbled as does the surf from an ocean cavern.

'I am the Bear, – the Silver-Tip and the Son of the Silver-Tip! When my voice was yet as a girl's, I slew the lynx, the moose, and the cariboo; when it whistled like the wolverines from under a cache, I crossed the Mountains of the South and slew three of the White Rivers; when it became as the roar of the Chinook, I met the bald-faced grizzly, but gave no trail.'

At this he paused, his hand significantly sweeping across his hideous scars.

'I am not as the Fox. My tongue is frozen like the river. I cannot make great talk. My words are few. The Fox says great deeds are afoot this night. Good! Talk flows from his tongue like the freshets of the spring, but he is chary of deeds. This night shall I do battle with the Wolf. I shall slay him, and Zarinska shall sit by my fire. The Bear has spoken.'

Though pandemonium raged about him, 'Scruff' Mackenzie held his ground. Aware how useless was the rifle at close quarters, he slipped both holsters to the fore, ready for action, and drew his mittens till his hands were barely shielded by the elbow gauntlets. He knew there was no hope in attack *en masse*, but true to his boast, was prepared to die with teeth fast-locked. But the Bear restrained his comrades, beating back the more impetuous with his terrible fist. As the tumult began to die away. Mackenzie shot a glance in the direction of Zarinska. It was a superb picture. She was leaning forward on her snow shoes, lips apart and nostrils quivering, like a tigress about to spring. Her great black eyes were fixed upon her tribesmen, in fear and defiance. So extreme the tension, she had forgotten to breathe. With one hand pressed spasmodically against her breast and the other as tightly gripped about the dog-whip, she was as turned to stone. Even as he looked, relief came to her. Her muscles loosened; with a heavy sigh she settled back, giving him a look of more than love – of worship.

Thling-Tinneh was trying to speak, but his people drowned his voice. Then Mackenzie strode forward. The Fox opened his mouth to a piercing yell, but so savagely did Mackenzie whirl upon him that he shrank back, his larynx all agurgle with suppressed sound. His discomfiture was greeted with roars of laughter, and served to soothe his fellows to a listening mood.

'Brothers! The White Man, whom ye have chosen to call the Wolf, came among you with fair words. He was not like the Innuit; he spoke not lies. He came as a friend, as one who would be a brother. But your men have had their say, and the time for soft words is past. First, I will tell you that the Shaman has an evil tongue and is a false prophet, that the messages he spake are not those of the Fire-Bringer. His ears are locked to the voice of the Raven, and out of his own head he weaves cunning fancies, and he has made fools of you. He has no power. When the dogs were killed and eaten, and your stomachs were heavy with untanned hide and strips of moccasins; when the old men died, and the old women died, and the babes at the dry dugs of the mothers died; when the land was dark, and ye perished as do the salmon in the fall; aye, when the famine was upon you, did the Shaman bring reward to your hunters? did the Shaman put meat in your bellies? Again I say, the Shaman is without power. Thus I spit upon his face!'

Though taken aback by the sacrilege, there was no uproar. Some of the women were even frightened, but among the men there was an uplifting, as though in preparation or anticipation of the miracle. All eyes were turned upon the two central figures. The priest realized the crucial moment, felt his power tottering, opened his mouth in denunciation, but fled backward before the truculent advance, upraised fist, and flashing eyes, of Mackenzie. He sneered and resumed.

'Was I stricken dead? Did the lightning burn me? Did the stars fall from the sky and crush me? Pish! I have done with the dog. Now will I tell you of my people, who are the mightiest of all the peoples, who rule in all the lands. At first we hunt as I hunt, alone. After that we hunt in packs; and at last, like the cariboo-run, we sweep across all the land. Those whom we take into our lodges live; those who will not come die. Zarinska is a comely maiden, full and strong, fit to become the mother of Wolves. Though I die, such shall she become; for my brothers are many, and they will follow the scent of my dogs. Listen to the Law of the Wolf: *Whoso taketh the life of one Wolf, the forfeit shall ten of his people pay.* In many lands has the price been paid; in many lands shall it yet be paid.

'Now will I deal with the Fox and the Bear. It seems they have cast eyes upon the maiden. So? Behold, I have bought her! Thling-Tenneh leans upon the rifle; the goods of purchase are by his fire. Yet will I be fair to the young men. To the Fox, whose tongue is dry with many words, will I give of tobacco five long plugs. Thus will his mouth be wetted that he may make much noise in the council. But to the Bear, of whom I am well proud, will I give of blankets two; of flour, twenty cups; of tobacco, double that of the Fox; and if he fare with me over the Mountains of the East, then will I give him a rifle, mate to Thling-Tinneh's. If not? Good! The Wolf is weary of speech. Yet once again will he say the Law: *Whoso taketh the life of one Wolf, the forfeit shall ten of his people pay.*'

Mackenzie smiled as he stepped back to his old position, but at heart he was full of trouble. The night was yet dark. The girl came to his side, and he listened closely as she told of the Bear's battletricks with the knife.

The decision was for war. In a trice, scores of moccasins were widening the space of beaten snow by the fire. There was much chatter about the seeming defeat of the Shaman; some averred he had but withheld his power, while others conned past events and agreed with the Wolf. The Bear came to the center of the battleground, a long naked hunting-knife of Russian make in his hand. The Fox called attention to Mackenzie's revolvers; so he stripped his belt, buckling it about Zarinska, into whose hands he also entrusted his rifle. She shook her head that she could not shoot, – small chance had a woman to handle such precious things.

'Then, if danger come by my back, cry aloud, "My husband!" No; thus, "My husband!"'

He laughed as she repeated it, pinched her cheek, and reentered the circle. Not only in reach and stature had the Bear the advantage of him, but his blade was longer by a good two inches. 'Scruff' Mackenzie had looked into the eyes of men before, and he knew it was a man who stood against him; yet he quickened to the glint of light on the steel, to the dominant pulse of his race.

Time and again he was forced to the edge of the fire or the deep snow, and time and again, with the foot tactics of the pugilist, he worked back to the center. Not a voice was lifted in encouragement, while his antagonist was heartened with applause, suggestions, and warnings. But his teeth only shut the tighter as the knives clashed together, and he thrust or eluded with a coolness born of conscious strength. At first he felt compassion for his enemy; but this fled before the primal instinct of life, which in turn gave way to the lust of slaughter. The ten thousand years of culture fell from him, and he was a cave-dweller, doing battle for his female.

Twice he pricked the Bear, getting away unscathed; but the third time caught, and to save himself, free hands closed on fighting hands, and they came together. Then did he realize the tremendous strength of his opponent. His muscles were knotted in painful lumps, and cords and tendons threatened to snap with the strain; yet nearer and nearer came the Russian steel. He tried to break away, but only weakened himself. The fur-clad circle closed in, certain of and anxious to see the final stroke. But with wrestler's trick, swinging partly to the side, he struck at his adversary with his head. Involuntarily the Bear leaned back, disturbing his center of gravity. Simultaneous with this, Mackenzie tripped properly and threw his whole weight forward, hurling him clear through the circle into the deep snow. The Bear floundered out and came back full tilt.

'O my husband!' Zarinska's voice rang out, vibrant with danger.

To the twang of a bow-string, Mackenzie swept low to the ground, and a bone-barbed arrow passed over him into the breast of the Bear, whose momentum carried him over his crouching foe. The next instant Mackenzie was up and about. The Bear lay motionless, but across the fire was the Shaman, drawing a second arrow.

Mackenzie's knife leaped short in the air. He caught the heavy blade by the point. There was a flash of light as it spanned the fire. Then the Shaman, the hilt alone appearing without his throat, swayed and pitched forward into the glowing embers.

Click! Click! – the Fox had possessed himself of Thling-Tinneh's rifle and was vainly trying to throw a shell into place. But he dropped it at the sound of Mackenzie's laughter.

'So the Fox has not learned the way of the plaything? He is yet a woman. Come! Bring it, that I may show thee!'

The Fox hesitated.

'Come, I say!'

He slouched forward like a beaten cur.

'Thus, and thus; so the thing is done.' A shell flew into place and the trigger was at cock as Mackenzie brought it to shoulder.

'The Fox has said great deeds were afoot this night, and he spoke true. There have been great deeds, yet least among them were those of the Fox. Is he still intent to take Zarinska to his lodge? Is he minded to tread the trail already broken by the Shaman and the Bear? No? Good!'

Mackenzie turned contemptuously and drew his knife from the priest's throat.

'Are any of the young men so minded? If so, the Wolf will take them by two and three till none are left. No? Good! Thling-Tinneh, I now give thee this rifle a second time. If, in the days to come, thou shouldst journey to the Country of the Yukon, know thou that there shall always be a place and much food by the fire of the Wolf. The night is now passing into the day. I go, but I may come again. And for the last time, remember the Law of the Wolf!'

He was supernatural in their sight as he rejoined Zarinska. She took her place at the head of the team, and the dogs swung into motion. A few moments later they were swallowed up by the ghostly forest. Till now the Fox had waited; he slipped into his snow-shoes to follow.

'Has the Wolf forgotten the five long plugs?'

Mackenzie turned upon the Fox angrily; then the humor of it struck him. 'I will give thee one short plug.'

'As the Wolf sees fit,' meekly responded the Fox, stretching out his hand.

The Men of Forty-Mile

WHEN BIG JIM BELDEN ventured the apparently innocuous proposition that mush-ice was 'rather pecooliar,' he little dreamed of what it would lead to. Neither did Lon McFane, when he affirmed that anchor-ice was even more so; nor did Bettles, as he instantly disagreed, declaring the very existence of such a form to be a bugaboo.

'An' ye'd be tellin' me this,' cried Lon, 'after the years ye've spint in the land! An' we atin' out the same pot this many's the day!'

'But the thing's agin reasin,' insisted Bettles. 'Look you, water's warmer than ice—'

'An' little the difference, once ye break through.'

'Still it's warmer, because it ain't froze. An' you say it freezes on the bottom?'

'Only the anchor-ice, David, only the anchor-ice. An' have ye niver drifted along, the water clear as glass, whin suddin, belike a cloud over the sun, the mushy-ice comes bubblin' up an' up, till from bank to bank an' bind to bind it's drapin' the river like a first snowfall?'

'Unh, hunh! more'n once when I took a doze at the steering-oar. But it allus come out the nighest side-channel, an' not bubblin' up an' up.'

'But with niver a wink at the helm?'

'No; nor you. It's agin reason. I'll leave it to any man!'

Bettles appealed to the circle about the stove, but the fight was on between himself and Lon McFane.

'Reason or no reason, it's the truth I'm tellin' ye. Last fall, a year gone, 'twas Sitka Charley and meself saw the sight, droppin' down the riffle ye'll remember below Fort Reliance. An' regular fall weather it was – the glint o' the sun on the golden larch an' the quakin' aspens; an' the glister of light on ivery ripple; an' beyand, the winter an' the blue haze of the North comin' down hand in hand. It's well ye know the same, with a fringe to the river an' the ice formin' thick in the eddies – an' a snap an' sparkle to the air, an' ye a-feelin' it through all yer blood, a-takin' new lease of life with ivery suck of it. 'Tis then, me boy, the world grows small an' the wandtherlust lays ye by the heels.

'But it's meself as wandthers. As I was sayin', we a-paddlin', with niver a sign of ice, barrin' that by the eddies, when the Injun lifts his paddle an' sings out, "Lon McFane! Look ye below! So have I heard, but niver thought to see!" As ye know, Sitka Charley, like meself, niver drew first breath in the land; so the sight was new. Then we drifted, with a head over ayther side, peerin' down through the sparkly water. For the world like the days I spint with the pearlers, watchin' the coral banks a-growin' the same as so many gardens under the sea. There it was, the anchor-ice, clingin' an' clusterin' to ivery rock, after the manner of the white coral.

'But the best of the sight was to come. Just after clearin' the tail of the riffle, the water turns quick the color of milk, an' the top of it in wee circles, as when the graylin' rise in the spring, or there's a splatter of wet from the sky. 'Twas the anchor-ice comin' up. To the right, to the lift, as far as iver a man cud see, the water was covered with the same. An' like so much porridge it was, slickin' along the bark of the canoe, stickin' like glue to the paddles. It's many's the time I shot the self-same riffle before, and it's many the time after, but niver a wink of the same have I seen. 'Twas the sight of a lifetime.'

'Do tell!' dryly commented Bettles. 'D'ye think I'd b'lieve such a yarn? I'd ruther say the glister of light'd gone to your eyes, and the snap of the air to your tongue.'

''Twas me own eyes that beheld it, an' if Sitka Charley was here, he'd be the lad to back me.'

'But facts is facts, an' they ain't no gettin' round 'em. It ain't in the nature of things for the water furtherest away from the air to freeze first.'

'But me own eyes—'

'Don't git het up over it,' admonished Bettles, as the quick Celtic anger began to mount.

'Then yer not after belavin' me?'

'Sence you're so blamed forehanded about it, no; I'd b'lieve nature first, and facts.'

'Is it the lie ye'd be givin' me?' threatened Lon. 'Ye'd better be askin' that Siwash wife of yours. I'll lave it to her, for the truth I spake.'

Bettles flared up in sudden wrath. The Irishman had unwittingly wounded him; for his wife was the half-breed daughter of a Russian fur-trader, married to him in the Greek Mission of Nulato, a thousand miles or so down the Yukon, thus being of much lighter caste than the common Siwash, or native, wife. It was a mere Northland nuance, which none but the Northland adventurer may understand.

'I reckon you kin take it that way,' was his deliberate affirmation.

The next instant Lon McFane had stretched him on the floor, the circle was broken up, and half a dozen men had stepped between.

Bettles came to his feet, wiping the blood from his mouth. 'It hain't new, this takin' and payin' of blows, and don't you never think but that this will be squared.'

'An' niver in me life did I take the lie from mortal man,' was the retort courteous. 'An' it's an avil day I'll not be to hand, waitin' an' willin' to help ye lift yer debts, barrin' no manner of way.'

'Still got that 38-55?'

Lon nodded.

'But you'd better git a more likely caliber. Mine'll rip holes through you the size of walnuts.'

'Niver fear; it's me own slugs smell their way with soft noses, an' they'll spread like flapjacks against the coming out beyond. An' when'll I have the pleasure of waitin' on ye? The waterhole's a strikin' locality.'

''Tain't bad. Jest be there in an hour, and you won't set long on my coming.'

Both men mittened and left the Post, their ears closed to the remonstrances of their comrades. It was such a little thing; yet with such men, little things, nourished by quick tempers and stubborn natures, soon blossomed into big things. Besides, the art of burning to bedrock still lay in the womb of the future, and the men of Forty-Mile, shut in by the long Arctic winter, grew high-stomached with overeating and enforced idleness, and became as irritable as do the bees in the fall of the year when the hives are overstocked with honey.

There was no law in the land. The mounted police was also a thing of the future. Each man measured an offense, and meted out the punishment inasmuch as it affected himself. Rarely had combined action been necessary, and never in all the dreary history of the camp had the eighth article of the Decalogue been violated.

Big Jim Belden called an impromptu meeting. Scruff Mackenzie was placed as temporary chairman, and a messenger dispatched to solicit Father Roubeau's good offices. Their position was paradoxical, and they knew it. By the right of might could they interfere to prevent the duel; yet such action, while in direct line with their wishes, went counter to their opinions. While their rough-hewn, obsolete ethics recognized the individual prerogative of wiping out blow with blow, they could not bear to think of two good comrades, such as Bettles and McFane, meeting in deadly battle. Deeming the man who would not fight on provocation a dastard, when brought to the test it seemed wrong that he should fight.

But a scurry of moccasins and loud cries, rounded off with a pistol-shot, interrupted the discussion. Then the storm-doors opened and Malemute Kid entered, a smoking Colt's in his hand, and a merry light in his eye.

'I got him.' He replaced the empty shell, and added, 'Your dog, Scruff.'

'Yellow Fang?' Mackenzie asked.

'No; the lop-eared one.'

'The devil! Nothing the matter with him.'

'Come out and take a look.'

'That's all right after all. Buess he's got 'em, too. Yellow Fang came back this morning and took a chunk out of him, and came near to making a widower of me. Made a rush for Zarinska, but she whisked her skirts in his face and escaped with the loss of the same and a good roll in the snow. Then he took to the woods again. Hope he don't come back. Lost any yourself?'

'One – the best one of the pack – Shookum. Started amuck this morning, but didn't get very far. Ran foul of Sitka Charley's team, and they scattered him all over the street. And now two of them are loose, and raging mad; so you see he got his work in. The dog census will be small in the spring if we don't do something.'

'And the man census, too.'

'How's that? Who's in trouble now?'

'Oh, Bettles and Lon McFane had an argument, and they'll be down by the waterhole in a few minutes to settle it.'

The incident was repeated for his benefit, and Malemute Kid, accustomed to an obedience which his fellow men never failed to render, took charge of the affair. His quickly formulated plan was explained, and they promised to follow his lead implicitly.

'So you see,' he concluded, 'we do not actually take away their privilege of fighting; and yet I don't believe they'll fight when they see the beauty of the scheme. Life's a game and men the gamblers. They'll stake their whole pile on the one chance in a thousand. Take away that one chance, and – they won't play.'

He turned to the man in charge of the Post. 'Storekeeper, weight out three fathoms of your best half-inch manila.

'We'll establish a precedent which will last the men of Forty-Mile to the end of time,' he prophesied. Then he coiled the rope about his arm and led his followers out of doors, just in time to meet the principals.

'What danged right'd he to fetch my wife in?' thundered Bettles to the soothing overtures of a friend. ''Twa'n't called for,' he concluded decisively. ''Twa'n't called for,' he reiterated again and again, pacing up and down and waiting for Lon McFane.

And Lon McFane – his face was hot and tongue rapid as he flaunted insurrection in the face of the Church. 'Then, father,' he cried, 'it's with an aisy heart I'll roll in me flamy blankets, the broad of me back on a bed of coals. Niver shall it be said that Lon McFane took a lie 'twixt the teeth without iver liftin' a hand! An' I'll not ask a blessin'. The years have been wild, but it's the heart was in the right place.'

'But it's not the heart, Lon,' interposed Father Roubeau; 'it's pride that bids you forth to slay your fellow man.'

'Yer Frinch,' Lon replied. And then, turning to leave him, 'An' will ye say a mass if the luck is against me?'

But the priest smiled, thrust his moccasined feet to the fore, and went out upon the white breast of the silent river. A packed trail, the width of a sixteen-inch sled, led out to the waterhole. On either side lay the deep, soft snow. The men trod in single file, without conversation; and the black-stoled priest in their midst gave to the function the solemn aspect of a funeral. It was a warm winter's day for Forty-Mile – a day in which the sky, filled with heaviness, drew closer to the earth, and the mercury sought the unwonted level of twenty below. But there was no cheer in the warmth. There was little air in the upper strata, and the clouds hung motionless, giving sullen promise of an early snowfall. And the earth, unresponsive, made no preparation, content in its hibernation.

When the waterhole was reached, Bettles, having evidently reviewed the quarrel during the silent walk, burst out in a final ''Twa'n't called for,' while Lon McFane kept grim silence. Indignation so choked him that he could not speak.

Yet deep down, whenever their own wrongs were not uppermost, both men wondered at their comrades. They had expected opposition, and this tacit acquiescence hurt them. It seemed more was due them from the men they had been so close with, and they felt a vague sense of wrong, rebelling at the thought of so many of their brothers coming out, as on a gala occasion, without one word of protest, to see them shoot each other down. It appeared their worth had diminished in the eyes of the community. The proceedings puzzled them.

'Back to back, David. An' will it be fifty paces to the man, or double the quantity?'

'Fifty,' was the sanguinary reply, grunted out, yet sharply cut.

But the new manila, not prominently displayed, but casually coiled about Malemute Kid's arm, caught the quick eye of the Irishman, and thrilled him with a suspicious fear.

'An' what are ye doin' with the rope?'

'Hurry up!' Malemute Kid glanced at his watch. 'I've a batch of bread in the cabin, and I don't want it to fall. Besides, my feet are getting cold.'

The rest of the men manifested their impatience in various suggestive ways.

'But the rope, Kid? It's bran' new, an' sure yer bread's not that heavy it needs raisin' with the like of that?'

Bettles by this time had faced around. Father Roubeau, the humor of the situation just dawning on him, hid a smile behind his mittened hand.

'No, Lon; this rope was made for a man.' Malemute Kid could be very impressive on occasion.

'What man?' Bettles was becoming aware of a personal interest.

'The other man.'

'An' which is the one ye'd mane by that?'

'Listen, Lon – and you, too, Bettles! We've been talking this little trouble of yours over, and we've come to one conclusion. We know we have no right to stop your fighting—'

'True for ye, me lad!'

'And we're not going to. But this much we can do, and shall do – make this the only duel in the history of Forty-Mile, set an example for every *che-cha-qua* that comes up or down the Yukon. The man who escapes killing shall be hanged to the nearest tree. Now, go ahead!'

Lon smiled dubiously, then his face lighted up. 'Pace her off, David – fifty paces, wheel, an' niver a cease firin' till a lad's down for good. 'Tis their hearts'll niver let them do the deed, an' it's well ye should know it for a true Yankee bluff.'

He started off with a pleased grin on his face, but Malemute Kid halted him.

'Lon! It's a long while since you first knew me?'

'Many's the day.'

'And you, Bettles?'

'Five year next June high water.'

'And have you once, in all that time, known me to break my word? Or heard of me breaking it?'

Both men shook their heads, striving to fathom what lay beyond.

'Well, then, what do you think of a promise made by me?'

'As good as your bond,' from Bettles.

'The thing to safety sling yer hopes of heaven by,' promptly endorsed Lon McFane.

'Listen! I, Malemute Kid, give you my word – and you know what that means – that the man who is not shot stretches rope within ten minutes after the shooting.' He stepped back as Pilate might have done after washing his hands.

A pause and a silence came over the men of Forty-Mile. The sky drew still closer, sending down a crystal flight of frost – little geometric designs, perfect, evanescent as a breath, yet destined to exist till the returning sun had covered half its northern journey. Both men had led forlorn hopes in their time – led with a curse or a jest on their tongues, and in their souls an unswerving faith in the God of Chance. But that merciful deity had been shut out from the present deal. They studied the face of Malemute Kid, but they studied as one might the Sphinx. As the quiet minutes passed, a feeling that speech was incumbent on them began to grow. At last the howl of a wolf-dog cracked the silence from the direction of Forty-Mile. The weird sound swelled with all the pathos of a breaking heart, then died away in a long-drawn sob.

'Well I be danged!' Bettles turned up the collar of his mackinaw jacket and stared about him helplessly.

'It's a gloryus game yer runnin', Kid,' cried Lon McFane. 'All the percentage of the house an' niver a bit to the man that's buckin'. The Devil himself'd niver tackle such a cinch – and damned if I do.'

There were chuckles, throttled in gurgling throats, and winks brushed away with the frost which rimed the eyelashes, as the men climbed the ice-notched bank and started across the street to the Post. But the long howl had drawn nearer, invested with a new note of menace. A woman screamed round the corner. There was a cry of, 'Here he comes!' Then an Indian boy, at the head of half a dozen frightened dogs, racing with death, dashed into the crowd. And behind came Yellow Fang, a bristle of hair and a flash of gray. Everybody but the Yankee fled. The Indian boy had tripped and fallen. Bettles stopped long enough to grip him by the slack of his furs, then headed for a pile of cordwood already occupied by a number of his comrades. Yellow Fang, doubling after one of the dogs, came leaping back. The fleeing animal, free of the rabies, but crazed with fright, whipped Bettles off his feet and flashed on up the street. Malemute Kid took a flying shot at Yellow Fang. The mad dog whirled a half airspring, came down on his back, then, with a single leap, covered half the distance between himself and Bettles.

But the fatal spring was intercepted. Lon McFane leaped from the woodpile, countering him in midair. Over they rolled, Lon holding him by the throat at arm's length, blinking under the fetid slaver which sprayed his face. Then Bettles, revolver in hand and coolly waiting a chance, settled the combat.

''Twas a square game, Kid,' Lon remarked, rising to his feet and shaking the snow from out his sleeves; 'with a fair percentage to meself that bucked it.'

That night, while Lon McFane sought the forgiving arms of the Church in the direction of Father Roubeau's cabin, Malemute Kid talked long to little purpose.

'But would you,' persisted Mackenzie, 'supposing they had fought?'

'Have I ever broken my word?'

'No; but that isn't the point. Answer the question. Would you?'

Malemute Kid straightened up. 'Scruff, I've been asking myself that question ever since, and—'

'Well?'

'Well, as yet, I haven't found the answer.'

In a Far Country

WHEN A MAN JOURNEYS into a far country, he must be prepared to forget many of the things he has learned, and to acquire such customs as are inherent with existence in the new land; he must abandon the old ideals and the old gods, and oftentimes he must reverse the very codes by which his conduct has hitherto been shaped. To those who have the protean faculty of adaptability, the novelty of such change may even be a source of pleasure; but to those who happen to be hardened to the ruts in which they were created, the pressure of the altered environment is unbearable, and they chafe in body and in spirit under the new restrictions which they do not understand. This chafing is bound to act and react, producing divers evils and leading to various misfortunes. It were better for the man who cannot fit himself to the new groove to return to his own country; if he delay too long, he will surely die.

The man who turns his back upon the comforts of an elder civilization, to face the savage youth, the primordial simplicity of the North, may estimate success at an inverse ratio to the quantity and quality of his hopelessly fixed habits. He will soon discover, if he be a fit candidate, that the material habits are the less important. The exchange of such things as a dainty menu for rough fare, of the stiff leather shoe for the soft, shapeless moccasin, of the feather bed for a couch in the snow, is after all a very easy matter. But his pinch will come in learning properly to shape his mind's attitude toward all things, and especially toward his fellow man. For the courtesies of ordinary life, he must substitute unselfishness, forbearance, and tolerance. Thus, and thus only, can he gain that pearl of great price – true comradeship. He must not say 'Thank you'; he must mean it without opening his mouth, and prove it by responding in kind. In short, he must substitute the deed for the word, the spirit for the letter.

When the world rang with the tale of Arctic gold, and the lure of the North gripped the heartstrings of men, Carter Weatherbee threw up his snug clerkship, turned the half of his savings over to his wife, and with the remainder bought an outfit. There was no romance in his nature – the bondage of commerce had crushed all that; he was simply tired of the ceaseless grind, and wished to risk great hazards in view of corresponding returns. Like many another fool, disdaining the old trails used by the Northland pioneers for a score of years, he hurried to Edmonton in the spring of the year; and there, unluckily for his soul's welfare, he allied himself with a party of men.

There was nothing unusual about this party, except its plans. Even its goal, like that of all the other parties, was the Klondike. But the route it had mapped out to attain that goal took away the breath of the hardiest native, born and bred to the vicissitudes of the Northwest. Even Jacques Baptiste, born of a Chippewa woman and a renegade *voyageur* (having raised his first whimpers in a deerskin lodge north of the sixty-fifth parallel, and had the same hushed by blissful sucks of raw tallow), was surprised. Though he sold his services to them and agreed to travel even to the never-opening ice, he shook his head ominously whenever his advice was asked.

Percy Cuthfert's evil star must have been in the ascendant, for he, too, joined this company of argonauts. He was an ordinary man, with a bank account as deep as his culture, which is saying a good deal. He had no reason to embark on such a venture – no reason in the world, save that he suffered from an abnormal development of sentimentality. He mistook this for the true spirit of romance and adventure. Many another man has done the like, and made as fatal a mistake.

The first break-up of spring found the party following the ice-run of Elk River. It was an imposing fleet, for the outfit was large, and they were accompanied by a disreputable contingent of half-breed *voyageurs* with their women and children. Day in and day out, they labored with the bateaux and canoes, fought mosquitoes and other kindred pests, or sweated and swore at the portages. Severe toil like this lays a man naked to the very roots of his soul, and ere Lake Athabasca was lost in the south, each member of the party had hoisted his true colors.

The two shirks and chronic grumblers were Carter Weatherbee and Percy Cuthfert. The whole party complained less of its aches and pains than did either of them. Not once did they volunteer for the thousand and one petty duties of the camp. A bucket of water to be brought, an extra armful of wood to be chopped, the dishes to be washed and wiped, a search to be made through the outfit for some suddenly indispensable article – and these two effete scions of civilization discovered sprains or blisters requiring instant attention. They were the first to turn in at night, with score of tasks yet undone; the last to turn out in the morning, when the start should be in readiness before the breakfast was begun. They were the first to fall to at mealtime, the last to have a hand in the cooking; the first to dive for a slim delicacy, the last to discover they had added to their own another man's share. If they toiled at the oars, they slyly cut the water at each stroke and allowed the boat's momentum to float up the blade. They thought nobody noticed; but their comrades swore under their breaths and grew to hate them, while Jacques Baptiste sneered openly and damned them from morning till night. But Jacques Baptiste was no gentleman.

At the Great Slave, Hudson Bay dogs were purchased, and the fleet sank to the guards with its added burden of dried fish and pemican. Then canoe and bateau answered to the swift current of the Mackenzie, and they plunged into the Great Barren Ground. Every likely-looking 'feeder' was prospected, but the elusive 'pay-dirt' danced ever to the north. At the Great Bear, overcome by the common dread of the Unknown Lands, their *voyageurs* began to desert, and Fort of Good Hope saw the last and bravest bending to the towlines as they bucked the current down which they had so treacherously glided. Jacques Baptiste alone remained. Had he not sworn to travel even to the never-opening ice?

The lying charts, compiled in main from hearsay, were now constantly consulted. And they felt the need of hurry, for the sun had already passed its northern solstice and was leading the winter south again. Skirting the shores of the bay, where the Mackenzie disembogues into the Arctic Ocean, they entered the mouth of the Little Peel River. Then began the arduous up-stream toil, and the two Incapables fared worse than ever. Towline and pole, paddle and tumpline, rapids and portages – such tortures served to give the one a deep disgust for great hazards, and printed for the other a fiery text on the true romance of adventure. One day they waxed mutinous, and being vilely cursed by Jacques Baptiste, turned, as worms sometimes will. But the half-breed thrashed the twain, and sent them, bruised and bleeding, about their work. It was the first time either had been manhandled.

Abandoning their river craft at the headwaters of the Little Peel, they consumed the rest of the summer in the great portage over the Mackenzie watershed to the West Rat. This little stream fed the Porcupine, which in turn joined the Yukon where that mighty highway of the North counter-marches on the Arctic Circle. But they had lost in the race with winter, and one day they tied their rafts to the thick eddy-ice and hurried their goods ashore. That night the river jammed and broke several times; the following morning it had fallen asleep for good.

'We can't be more'n four hundred miles from the Yukon,' concluded Sloper, multiplying his thumb nails by the scale of the map. The council, in which the two Incapables had whined to excellent disadvantage, was drawing to a close.

'Hudson Bay Post, long time ago. No use um now.' Jacques Baptiste's father had made the trip for the Fur Company in the old days, incidentally marking the trail with a couple of frozen toes.

'Sufferin' cracky!' cried another of the party. 'No whites?'

'Nary white,' Sloper sententiously affirmed; 'but it's only five hundred more up the Yukon to Dawson. Call it a rough thousand from here.'

Weatherbee and Cuthfert groaned in chorus.

'How long'll that take, Baptiste?'

The half-breed figured for a moment. 'Workum like hell, no man play out, ten – twenty – forty – fifty days. Um babies come' (designating the Incapables), 'no can tell. Mebbe when hell freeze over; mebbe not then.'

The manufacture of snowshoes and moccasins ceased. Somebody called the name of an absent member, who came out of an ancient cabin at the edge of the campfire and joined them. The cabin was one of the many mysteries which lurk in the vast recesses of the North. Built when and by whom, no man could tell. Two graves in the open, piled high with stones, perhaps contained the secret of those early wanderers. But whose hand had piled the stones?

The moment had come. Jacques Baptiste paused in the fitting of a harness and pinned the struggling dog in the snow. The cook made mute protest for delay, threw a handful of bacon into a noisy pot of beans, then came to attention. Sloper rose to his feet. His body was a ludicrous contrast to the healthy physiques of the Incapables. Yellow and weak, fleeing from a South American fever-hole, he had not broken his flight across the zones, and was still able to toil with men. His weight was probably ninety pounds, with the heavy hunting knife thrown in, and his grizzled hair told of a prime which had ceased to be. The fresh young muscles of either Weatherbee or Cuthfert were equal to ten times the endeavor of his; yet he could walk them into the

earth in a day's journey. And all this day he had whipped his stronger
comrades into venturing a thousand miles of the stiffest hardship man can
conceive. He was the incarnation of the unrest of his race, and the old
Teutonic stubbornness, dashed with the quick grasp and action of the
Yankee, held the flesh in the bondage of the spirit.

'All those in favor of going on with the dogs as soon as the ice sets, say ay.'

'Ay!' rang out eight voices – voices destined to string a trail of oaths along
many a hundred miles of pain.

'Contrary minded?'

'No!' For the first time the Incapables were united without some
compromise of personal interests.

'And what are you going to do about it?' Weatherbee added belligerently.

'Majority rule! Majority rule!' clamored the rest of the party.

'I know the expedition is liable to fall through if you don't come,' Sloper
replied sweetly; 'but I guess, if we try real hard, we can manage to do without
you. What do you say, boys?'

The sentiment was cheered to the echo.

'But I say, you know,' Cuthfert ventured apprehensively; 'what's a chap
like me to do?'

'Ain't you coming with us?'

'No-o.'

'Then do as you damn well please. We won't have nothing to say.'

'Kind o' calkilate yuh might settle it with that canoodlin' pardner of
yourn,' suggested a heavy-going Westerner from the Dakotas, at the same
time pointing out Weatherbee. 'He'll be shore to ask yuh what yur a-goin' to
do when it comes to cookin' an' gatherin' the wood.'

'Then we'll consider it all arranged,' concluded Sloper. 'We'll pull out
tomorrow, if we camp within five miles – just to get everything in running
order and remember if we've forgotten anything.'

The sleds groaned by on their steel-shod runners, and the dogs strained low
in the harnesses in which they were born to die. Jacques Baptiste paused by
the side of Sloper to get a last glimpse of the cabin. The smoke curled up
pathetically from the Yukon stovepipe. The two Incapables were watching
them from the doorway.

Sloper laid his hand on the other's shoulder.

'Jacques Baptiste, did you ever hear of the Kilkenny cats?'

The half-breed shook his head.

'Well, my friend and good comrade, the Kilkenny cats fought till neither
hide, nor hair, nor yowl, was left. You understand? – till nothing was left.
Very good. Now, these two men don't like work. They'll be all alone in that
cabin all winter – a mighty long, dark winter. Kilkenny cats – well?'

The Frenchman in Baptiste shrugged his shoulders, but the Indian in him
was silent. Nevertheless, it was an eloquent shrug, pregnant with prophecy.

Things prospered in the little cabin at first. The rough badinage of their
comrades had made Weatherbee and Cuthfert conscious of the mutual
responsibility which had devolved upon them; besides, there was not so
much work after all for two healthy men. And the removal of the cruel
whiphand, or in other words the bulldozing half-breed, had brought with it a

joyous reaction. At first, each strove to outdo the other, and they performed petty tasks with an unction which would have opened the eyes of their comrades who were now wearing out bodies and souls on the Long Trail.

All care was banished. The forest, which shouldered in upon them from three sides, was an inexhaustible woodyard. A few yards from their door slept the Porcupine, and a hole through its winter robe formed a bubbling spring of water, crystal clear and painfully cold. But they soon grew to find fault with even that. The hole would persist in freezing up, and thus gave them many a miserable hour of ice-chopping. The unknown builders of the cabin had extended the sidelogs so as to support a cache at the rear. In this was stored the bulk of the party's provisions. Food there was, without stint, for three times the men who were fated to live upon it. But the most of it was the kind which built up brawn and sinew, but did not tickle the palate. True, there was sugar in plenty for two ordinary men; but these two were little else than children. They early discovered the virtues of hot water judiciously saturated with sugar, and they prodigally swam their flapjacks and soaked their crusts in the rich, white syrup. Then coffee and tea, and especially the dried fruits, made disastrous inroads upon it. The first words they had were over the sugar question. And it is a really serious thing when two men, wholly dependent upon each other for company, begin to quarrel.

Weatherbee loved to discourse blatantly on politics, while Cuthfert, who had been prone to clip his coupons and let the commonwealth jog on as best it might, either ignored the subject or delivered himself of startling epigrams. But the clerk was too obtuse to appreciate the clever shaping of thought, and this waste of ammunition irritated Cuthfert. He had been used to blinding people by his brilliancy, and it worked him quite a hardship, this loss of an audience. He felt personally aggrieved and unconsciously held his mutton-head companion responsible for it.

Save existence, they had nothing in common – came in touch on no single point. Weatherbee was a clerk who had known naught but clerking all his life; Cuthfert was a master of arts, a dabbler in oils, and had written not a little. The one was a lower-class man who considered himself a gentleman, and the other was a gentleman who knew himself to be such. From this it may be remarked that a man can be a gentleman without possessing the first instinct of true comradeship. The clerk was as sensuous as the other was aesthetic, and his love adventures, told at great length and chiefly coined from his imagination, affected the supersensitive master of arts in the same way as so many whiffs of sewer gas. He deemed the clerk a filthy, uncultured brute, whose place was in the muck with the swine, and told him so; and he was reciprocally informed that he was a milk-and-water sissy and a cad. Weatherbee could not have defined 'cad' for his life; but it satisfied its purpose, which after all seems the main point in life.

Weatherbee flatted every third note and sang such songs as 'The Boston Burglar' and 'The Handsome Cabin Boy,' for hours at a time, while Cuthfert wept with rage, till he could stand it no longer and fled into the outer cold. But there was no escape. The intense frost could not be endured for long at a time, and the little cabin crowded them – beds, stove, table, and all – into a space of ten by twelve. The very presence of either became a personal affront to the other, and they lapsed into sullen silences which increased in length and strength as the days went by. Occasionally, the flash of an eye or the curl of a lip got the better of them, though they strove to wholly ignore each other during these mute periods. And a great wonder sprang up in the breast of each, as to how God had ever come to create the other.

With little to do, time became an intolerable burden to them. This naturally made them still lazier. They sank into a physical lethargy which there was no escaping, and which made them rebel at the performance of the smallest chore. One morning when it was his turn to cook the common breakfast, Weatherbee rolled out of his blankets, and to the snoring of his companion, lighted first the slush-lamp and then the fire. The kettles were frozen hard, and there was no water in the cabin with which to wash. But he did not mind that. Waiting for it to thaw, he sliced the bacon and plunged into the hateful task of bread-making. Cuthfert had been slyly watching through his half-closed lids. Consequently there was a scene, in which they fervently blessed each other, and agreed, henceforth, that each do his own cooking. A week later, Cuthfert neglected his morning ablutions, but none the less complacently ate the meal which he had cooked. Weatherbee grinned. After that the foolish custom of washing passed out of their lives.

As the sugar-pile and other little luxuries dwindled, they began to be afraid they were not getting their proper shares, and in order that they might not be robbed, they fell to gorging themselves. The luxuries suffered in this gluttonous contest, as did also the men. In the absence of fresh vegetables and exercise, their blood became impoverished, and a loathsome, purplish rash crept over their bodies. Yet they refused to heed the warning. Next, their muscles and joints began to swell, the flesh turning black, while their mouths,. gums, and lips took on the color of rich cream. Instead of being drawn together by their misery, each gloated over the other's symptoms as the scurvy took its course.

They lost all regard for personal appearance, and for that matter, common decency. The cabin became a pigpen, and never once were the beds made or fresh pine boughs laid underneath. Yet they could not keep to`their blankets, as they would have wished; for the frost was inexorable, and the fire box consumed much fuel. The hair of their heads and faces grew long and shaggy, while their garments would have disgusted a ragpicker. But they did not care. They were sick, and there was no one to see; besides, it was very painful to move about.

To all this was added a new trouble – the Fear of the North. This Fear was the joint child of the Great Cold and the Great Silence, and was born in the darkness of December, when the sun dipped below the horizon for good. It affected them according to their natures. Weatherbee fell prey to the grosser superstitions, and did his best to resurrect the spirits which slept in the forgotten graves. It was a fascinating thing, and in his dreams they came to him from out of the cold, and snuggled into his blankets, and told him of their toils and troubles ere they died. He shrank away from the clammy contact as they drew closer and twined their frozen limbs about him, and when they whispered in his ear of things to come, the cabin rang with his frightened shrieks. Cuthfert did not understand – for they no longer spoke – and when thus awakened he invariably grabbed for his revolver. Then he would sit up in bed, shivering nervously, with the weapon trained on the unconscious dreamer. Cuthfert deemed the man going mad, and so came to fear for his life.

His own malady assumed a less concrete form. The mysterious artisan who had laid the cabin, log by log, had pegged a wind-vane to the ridgepole. Cuthfert noticed it always pointed south, and one day, irritated by its steadfastness of purpose, he turned it toward the east. He watched eagerly, but never a breath came by to disturb it. Then he turned the vane to the north, swearing never again to touch it till the wind did blow. But the air frightened him with its unearthly calm, and he often rose in the middle of the night to see if the vane had veered – ten degrees would have satisfied him. But no, it poised above him as unchangeable as fate. His imagination ran riot, till it became to him a fetish. Sometimes he followed the path it pointed across the dismal dominions, and allowed his soul to become saturated with the Fear. He dwelt upon the unseen and the unknown till the burden of eternity appeared to be crushing him. Everything in the Northland had that crushing effect – the absence of life and motion; the darkness; the infinite peace of the brooding land; the ghastly silence, which made the echo of each heartbeat a sacrilege; the solemn forest which seemed to guard an awful, inexpressible something, which neither word nor thought could compass.

The world he had so recently left, with its busy nations and great enterprises, seemed very far away. Recollections occasionally obtruded – recollections of marts and galleries and crowded thoroughfares, of evening dress and social functions, of good men and dear women he had known – but they were dim memories of a life he had lived long centuries agone, on some other planet. This phantasm was the Reality. Standing beneath the wind-vane, his eyes fixed on the polar skies, he could not bring himself to realize that the Southland really existed, that at that very moment it was a-roar with life and action. There was no Southland, no men being born of women, no giving and taking in marriage. Beyond his bleak skyline there stretched vast solitudes, and beyond these still vaster solitudes. There were no lands of sunshine, heavy with the perfume of flowers. Such things were only old dreams of paradise. The sunlands of the West and the spicelands of the East, the smiling Arcadias and blissful Islands of the Blest – ha! ha! His laughter split the void and shocked him with its unwonted sound. There was no sun. This was the Universe, dead and cold and dark, and he its only citizen. Weatherbee? At such moments Weatherbee did not count. He was a Caliban, a monstrous phantom, fettered to him for untold ages, the penalty of some forgotten crime.

He lived with Death among the dead, emasculated by the sense of his own insignificance, crushed by the passive mastery of the slumbering ages. The magnitude of all things appalled him. Everything partook of the superlative save himself – the perfect cessation of wind and motion, the immensity of the snow-covered wildness, the height of the sky and the depth of the silence. That wind-vane – if it would only move. If a thunderbolt would fall, or the forest flare up in flame. The rolling up of the heavens as a scroll, the crash of Doom – anything, anything! But no, nothing moved; the Silence crowded in, and the Fear of the North laid icy fingers on his heart.

Once, like another Crusoe, by the edge of the river he came upon a track – the faint tracery of a snowshoe rabbit on the delicate snow-crust. It was a revelation. There was life in the Northland. He would follow it, look upon it, gloat over it. He forgot his swollen muscles, plunging through the deep snow in an ecstasy of anticipation. The forest swallowed him up, and the brief midday twilight vanished; but he pursued his quest till exhausted nature asserted itself and laid him helpless in the snow. There he groaned and cursed his folly, and knew the track to be the fancy of his brain; and late that night he dragged himself into the cabin on hands and knees, his cheeks frozen and a strange numbness about his feet. Weatherbee grinned malevolently, but made no offer to help him. He thrust needles into his toes and thawed them out by the stove. A week later mortification set in.

But the clerk had his own troubles. The dead men came out of their graves more frequently now, and rarely left him, waking or sleeping. He grew to wait and dread their coming, never passing the twin cairns without a shudder. One night they came to him in his sleep and led him forth to an appointed task. Frightened into inarticulate horror, he awoke between the heaps of stones and fled wildly to the cabin. But he had lain there for some time, for his feet and cheeks were also frozen.

Sometimes he became frantic at their insistent presence, and danced about the cabin, cutting the empty air with an axe, and smashing everything within reach. During these ghostly encounters, Cuthfert huddled into his blankets and followed the madman about with a cocked revolver, ready to shoot him if he came too near. But, recovering from one of these spells, the clerk noticed the weapon trained upon him. His suspicions were aroused, and thenceforth he, too, lived in fear of his life. They watched each other closely after that, and faced about in startled fright whenever either passed behind the other's back. The apprehensiveness became a mania which controlled them even in their sleep. Through mutual fear they tacitly let the slush-lamp burn all night, and saw to a plentiful supply of bacon-grease before retiring. The slightest movement on the part of one was sufficient to arouse the other, and many a still watch their gazes countered as they shook beneath their blankets with fingers on the trigger-guards.

What with the Fear of the North, the mental strain, and the ravages of the disease, they lost all semblance of humanity, taking on the appearance of wild beasts, hunted and desperate. Their cheeks and noses, as an aftermath of the freezing, had turned black. Their frozen toes had begun to drop away at the first and second joints. Every movement brought pain, but the fire box was insatiable, wringing a ransom of torture from their miserable bodies. Day in, day out, it demanded its food – a veritable pound of flesh – and they dragged themselves into the forest to chop wood on their knees. Once, crawling thus in search of dry sticks, unknown to each other they entered a thicket from opposite sides. Suddenly, without warning, two peering death's-heads confronted each other. Suffering had so transformed them that recognition was impossible. They sprang to their feet, shrieking with terror, and dashed away on their mangled stumps; and falling at the cabin's door, they clawed and scratched like demons till they discovered their mistake.

Occasionally they lapsed normal, and during one of these sane intervals, the chief bone of contention, the sugar, had been divided equally between them. They guarded their separate sacks, stored up in the cache, with jealous eyes; for there were but a few cupfuls left, and they were totally devoid of faith in each other. But one day Cuthfert made a mistake. Hardly able to move, sick with pain, with his head swimming and eyes blinded, he crept into the cache, sugar canister in hand, and mistook Weatherbee's sack for his own.

January had been born but a few days when this occurred. The sun had some time since passed its lowest southern declination, and at meridian now threw flaunting streaks of yellow light upon the northern sky. On the day following his mistake with the sugarbag, Cuthfert found himself feeling better, both in body and in spirit. As noontime drew near and the day brightened, he dragged himself outside to feast on the evanescent glow, which was to him an earnest of the sun's future intentions. Weatherbee was also feeling somewhat better, and crawled out beside him. They propped themselves in the snow beneath the moveless wind-vane, and waited.

The stillness of death was about them. In other climes, when nature falls into such moods, there is a subdued air of expectancy, a waiting for some small voice to take up the broken strain. Not so in the North. The two men had lived seeming eons in this ghostly peace. They could remember no song of the past; they could conjure no song of the future. This unearthly calm had always been – the tranquil silence of eternity.

Their eyes were fixed upon the north. Unseen, behind their backs, behind the towering mountains to the south, the sun swept toward the zenith of another sky than theirs. Sole spectators of the mighty canvas, they watched the false dawn slowly grow. A faint flame began to glow and smoulder. It deepened in intensity, ringing the changes of reddish-yellow, purple, and saffron. So bright did it become that Cuthfert thought the sun must surely be behind it – a miracle, the sun rising in the north! Suddenly, without warning and without fading, the canvas was swept clean. There was no color in the sky. The light had gone out of the day. They caught their breaths in half-sobs. But lo! the air was aglint with particles of scintillating frost, and there, to the north, the wind-vane lay in vague outline of the snow. A shadow! A shadow! It was exactly midday. They jerked their heads hurriedly to the south. A golden rim peeped over the mountain's snowy shoulder, smiled upon them an instant, then dipped from sight again.

There were tears in their eyes as they sought each other. A strange softening came over them. They felt irresistibly drawn toward each other. The sun was coming back again. It would be with them tomorrow, and the next day, and the next. And it would stay longer every visit, and a time would come when it would ride their heaven day and night, never once dropping below the skyline. There would be no night. The ice-locked winter would be broken; the winds would blow and the forests answer; the land would bathe in the blessed sunshine, and life renew. Hand in hand, they would quit this horrid dream and journey back to the Southland. They lurched blindly forward, and their hands met – their poor maimed hands, swollen and distorted beneath their mittens.

But the promise was destined to remain unfulfilled. The Northland is the Northland, and men work out their souls by strange rules, which other men, who have not journeyed into far countries, cannot come to understand.

An hour later, Cuthfert put a pan of bread into the oven, and fell to speculating on what the surgeons could do with his feet when he got back. Home did not seem so very far away now. Weatherbee was rummaging in the cache. Of a sudden, he raised a whirlwind of blasphemy, which in turn ceased with startling abruptness. The other man had robbed his sugar-sack. Still, things might have happened differently, had not the two dead men come out from under the stones and hushed the hot words in his throat. They led him quite gently from the cache, which he forgot to close. That consummation was reached; that something they had whispered to him in his dreams was about to happen. They guided him gently, very gently, to the woodpile, where they put the axe in his hands. Then they helped him shove open the cabin door, and he felt sure they shut it after him – at least he heard it slam and the latch fall sharply into place. And he knew they were waiting just without, waiting for him to do his task.

'Carter! I say, Carter!'

Percy Cuthfert was frightened at the look on the clerk's face, and he made haste to put the table between them.

Carter Weatherbee followed, without haste and without enthusiasm. There was neither pity nor passion in his face, but rather the patient, stolid look of one who has certain work to do and goes about it methodically.

'I say, what's the matter?'

The clerk dodged back, cutting off his retreat to the door, but never opening his mouth.

'I say, Carter, I say; let's talk. There's a good chap.'

The master of arts was thinking rapidly, now, shaping a skillful flank movement on the bed where his Smith & Wesson lay. Keeping his eyes on the madman, he rolled backward on the bunk, at the same time clutching the pistol.

'Carter!'

The powder flashed full in Weatherbee's face, but he swung his weapon and leaped forward. The axe bit deeply at the base of the spine, and Percy Cuthfert felt all consciousness of his lower limbs leave him. Then the clerk fell heavily upon him, clutching him by the throat with feeble fingers. The sharp bite of the axe had caused Cuthfert to drop the pistol, and as his lungs panted for release, he fumbled aimlessly for it among the blankets. Then he remembered. He slid a hand up the clerk's belt to the sheath-knife; and they drew very close to each other in that last clinch.

Percy Cuthfert felt his strength leave him. The lower portion of his body was useless. The inert weight of Weatherbee crushed him – crushed him and pinned him there like a bear under a trap. The cabin became filled with a familiar odor, and he knew the bread to be burning. Yet what did it matter? He would never need it. And there were all of six cupfuls of sugar in the cache – if he had foreseen this he would not have been so saving the last several days. Would the wind-vane ever move? Why not? Had he not seen the sun today? He would go and see. No; it was impossible to move. He had not thought the clerk so heavy a man.

How quickly the cabin cooled! The fire must be out. The cold was forcing in. It must be below zero already, and the ice creeping up the inside of the door. He could not see it, but his past experience enabled him to gauge its progress by the cabin's temperature. The lower hinge must be white ere now. Would the tale of this ever reach the world? How would his friends take it? They would read it over their coffee, most likely, and talk it over at the clubs. He could see them very clearly, 'Poor Old Cuthfert,' they murmured; 'not such a bad sort of a chap, after all.' He smiled at their eulogies, and passed on in search of a Turkish bath. It was the same old crowd upon the streets. Strange, they did not notice his moosehide moccasins and tattered German socks! He would take a cab. And after the bath a shave would not be bad. No; he would eat first. Steak, and potatoes, and green things, how fresh it all was! And what was that? Squares of honey, streaming liquid amber! But why did they bring so much? Ha! ha! he could never eat it all. Shine! Why certainly. He put his foot on the box. The bootblack looked curiously up at him, and he remembered his moosehide moccasins and went away hastily.

Hark! The wind-vane must be surely spinning. No; a mere singing in his ears. That was all – a mere singing. The ice must have passed the latch by now. More likely the upper hinge was covered. Between the moss-chinked roof-poles, little points of frost began to appear. How slowly they grew! No; not so slowly. There was a new one, and there another. Two – three – four; they were coming too fast to count. There were two growing together. And there, a third had joined them. Why, there was no more spots. They had run together and formed a sheet.

Well, he would have company. If Gabriel ever broke the silence of the North, they would stand together, hand in hand, before the great White Throne. And God would judge them, God would judge them!

Then Percy Cuthfert closed his eyes and dropped off to sleep.

F. SCOTT FITZGERALD
1896-1940

Born in 1896 in St Paul, Minnesota, Scott Fitzgerald's rise
to fame matched a rise in fortunes in America. Made
famous by his novel, *This Side of Paradise* (1920) and a
collection of short stories, *Flappers and Philosophers* (1920)
his satirical descriptions of the rich and prosperous and
their fond preoccupations with money were to make
Fitzgerald's name legendary. He tragically died of a heart
attack in 1940 in Hollywood having made an outstanding
contribution to the American short story.

    The story reprinted here from *Taps at Reveille* (1935), a
fascinating survey of the decay and decadence of the 1920s
through the eyes of a man caught up in that raffish decade,
provides ample evidence of why Fitzgerald is widely
regarded as the greatest fictional recorder of the Jazz Age
and a brilliant social observer and critic.

Babylon Revisited

1

'AND WHERE'S MR CAMPBELL?' Charlie asked.

'Gone to Switzerland. Mr Campbell's a pretty sick man, Mr Wales.'

'I'm sorry to hear that. And George Hardt?' Charlie inquired.

'Back in America, gone to work.'

'And where is the Snow Bird?'

'He was here last week. Anyway, his friend, Mr Schaeffer, is in Paris.'

Two familiar names from the long list of a year and a half ago. Charlie scribbled an address in his notebook and tore out the page.

'If you see Mr Schaeffer, give him this,' he said. 'It's my brother-in-law's address. I haven't settled on a hotel yet.'

He was not really disappointed to find Paris was so empty. But the stillness in the Ritz bar was strange and portentous. It was not an American bar any more – he felt polite in it, and not as if he owned it. It had gone back into France. He felt the stillness from the moment he got out of the taxi and saw the doorman, usually in a frenzy of activity at this hour, gossiping with a *chasseur* by the servants' entrance.

Passing through the corridor, he heard only a single, bored voice in the once-clamorous women's room. When he turned into the bar he travelled the twenty feet of green carpet with his eyes fixed straight ahead by old habit; and then, with his foot firmly on the rail, he turned and surveyed the room, encountering only a single pair of eyes that fluttered up from a newspaper in the corner. Charlie asked for the head barman, Paul, who in the latter days of the bull market had come to work in his own custom-built car – disembarking, however, with due nicety at the nearest corner. But Paul was at his country house today and Alix giving him information.

'No, no more,' Charlie said, 'I'm going slow these days.'

Alix congratulated him: 'You were going pretty strong a couple of years ago.'

'I'll stick to it all right,' Charlie assured him. 'I've stuck to it for over a year and a half now.'

'How do you find conditions in America?'

'I haven't been to America for months. I'm in business in Prague, representing a couple of concerns there. They don't know about me down there.'

Alix smiled.

'Remember the night of George Hardt's bachelor dinner here?' said Charlie. 'By the way, what's become of Claude Fessenden?'

Alix lowered his voice confidentially: 'He's in Paris, but he doesn't come here any more. Paul doesn't allow it. He ran up a bill of thirty thousand francs, charging all his drinks and his lunches, and usually his dinner, for more than a year. And when Paul finally told him he had to pay, he gave him a bad check.'

Alix shook his head sadly.

'I don't understand it, such a dandy fellow. Now he's all bloated up—' He made a plump apple of his hands.

Charlie watched a group of strident queens installing themselves in a corner.

'Nothing affects them,' he thought. 'Stocks rise and fall, people loaf or work, but they go on forever.' The place oppressed him. He called for the dice and shook with Alix for the drink.

'Here for long, Mr Wales?'

'I'm here for four or five days to see my little girl.'

'Oh-h! You have a little girl?'

Outside, the fire-red, gas-blue, ghost-green signs shone smokily through the tranquil rain. It was late afternoon and the streets were in movement; the *bistros* gleamed. At the corner of the Boulevard des Capucines he took a taxi. The Place de la Concorde moved by in pink majesty; they crossed the logical Seine, and Charlie felt the sudden provincial quality of the Left Bank.

Charlie directed his taxi to the Avenue de l'Opéra, which was out of his way. But he wanted to see the blue hour spread over the magnificent façade, and imagine that the cab horns, playing endlessly the first few bars of *Le Plus que Lent*, were the trumpets of the Second Empire. They were closing the iron grill in front of Brentano's Book-store, and people were already at dinner behind the trim little bourgeois hedge of Duval's. He had never eaten at a really cheap restaurant in Paris. Five-course dinner, four francs fifty, eighteen cents, wine included. For some odd reason he wished that he had.

As they rolled on to the Left Bank and he felt its sudden provincialism, he thought, 'I spoiled this city for myself. I didn't realize it, but the days came along one after another, and then two years were gone, and everything was gone, and I was gone.'

He was thirty-five, and good to look at. The Irish mobility of his face was sobered by a deep wrinkle between his eyes. As he rang his brother-in-law's bell in the Rue Palatine, the wrinkle deepened till it pulled down his brows; he felt a cramping sensation in his belly. From behind the maid who opened the door darted a lovely little girl of nine who shrieked 'Daddy!' and flew up, struggling like a fish, into his arms. She pulled his head around by one ear and set her cheek against his.

'My old pie,' he said.

'Oh, daddy, daddy, daddy, daddy, dads, dads, dads!'

She drew him into the salon, where the family waited, a boy and girl his daughter's age, his sister-in-law and her husband. He greeted Marion with his voice pitched carefully to avoid either feigned enthusiasm or dislike, but her response was more frankly tepid, though she minimized her expression of unalterable distrust by directing her regard toward his child. The two men clasped hands in a friendly way and Lincoln Peters rested his for a moment on Charlie's shoulder.

The room was warm and comfortably American. The three children moved intimately about, playing through the yellow oblongs that led to other rooms; the cheer of six o'clock spoke in the eager smacks of the fire and the sounds of French activity in the kitchen. But Charlie did not relax; his heart sat up rigidly in his body and he drew confidence from his daughter, who from time to time came close to him, holding in her arms the doll he had brought.

'Really extremely well,' he declared in answer to Lincoln's question. 'There's a lot of business there that isn't moving at all, but we're doing even better than ever. In fact, damn well. I'm bringing my sister over from America next month to keep house for me. My income last year was bigger than it was when I had money. You see, the Czechs—'

His boasting was for a specific purpose; but after a moment, seeing a faint restiveness in Lincoln's eye, he changed the subject:

'Those are fine children of yours, well brought up, good manners.'

'We think Honoria's a great little girl too.'

Marion Peters came back from the kitchen. She was a tall woman with worried eyes, who had once possessed a fresh American loveliness. Charlie had never been sensitive to it and was always surprised when people spoke of how pretty she had been. From the first there had been an instinctive antipathy between them.

'Well, how do you find Honoria?' she asked.

'Wonderful. I was astonished how much she's grown in ten months. All the children are looking well.'

'We haven't had a doctor for a year. How do you like being back in Paris?'

'It seems very funny to see so few Americans around.'

'I'm delighted,' Marion said vehemently. 'Now at least you can go into a store without their assuming you're a millionaire. We've suffered like everybody, but on the whole it's a good deal pleasanter.'

'But it was nice while it lasted,' Charlie said. 'We were a sort of royalty, almost infallible, with a sort of magic around us. In the bar this afternoon' – he stumbled, seeing his mistake – 'there wasn't a man I knew.'

She looked at him keenly. 'I should think you'd have had enough of bars.'

'I only stayed a minute. I take one drink every afternoon, and no more.'

'Don't you want a cocktail before dinner?' Lincoln asked.

'I take only one drink every afternoon, and I've had that.'

'I hope you keep to it,' said Marion.

Her dislike was evident in the coldness with which she spoke, but Charlie only smiled; he had larger plans. Her very aggressiveness gave him an advantage, and he knew enough to wait. He wanted them to initiate the discussion of what they knew had brought him to Paris.

At dinner he couldn't decide whether Honoria was most like him or her mother. Fortunate if she didn't combine the traits of both that had brought them to disaster. A great wave of protectiveness went over him. He thought he knew what to do for her. He believed in character; he wanted to jump back a whole generation and trust in character again as the eternally valuable element. Everything wore out.

He left soon after dinner, but not to go home. He was curious to see Paris by night with clearer and more judicious eyes than those of other days. He bought a *strapontin* for the Casino and watched Josephine Baker go through her chocolate arabesques.

After an hour he left and strolled toward Montmartre, up the Rue Pigalle into the Place Blanche. The rain had stopped and there were a few people in evening clothes disembarking from taxis in front of cabarets, and *cocottes* prowling singly or in pairs, and many Negroes. He passed a lighted door from which issued music, and stopped with the sense of familiarity; it was Bricktop's, where he had parted with so many hours and so much money. A few doors farther on he found another ancient rendezvous and incautiously put his head inside. Immediately an eager orchestra burst into sound, a pair of professional dancers leaped to their feet and a maître d'hôtel swooped towards him, crying, 'Crowd just arriving, sir!' but he withdrew quickly.

'You have to be damn drunk,' he thought.

Zelli's was closed, the bleak and sinister cheap hotels surrounding it were dark; up in the Rue Blanche there was more light and a local, colloquial French crowd. The Poet's Cave had disappeared, but the two great mouths of the Café of Heaven and the Café of Hell still yawned – even devoured, as he watched, the meagre contents of a tourist bus – a German, a Japanese, and an American couple who glanced at him with frightened eyes.

So much for the effort and ingenuity of Montmartre. All the catering to vice and waste was on an utterly childish scale, and he suddenly realized the meaning of the word 'dissipate' – to dissipate into thin air; to make nothing out of something. In the little hours of the night every move from place to place was an enormous human jump, an increase of paying for the privilege of slower and slower motion.

He remembered thousand-franc notes given to an orchestra for playing a single number, hundred-franc notes tossed to a doorman for calling a cab.

But it hadn't been given for nothing.

It had been given, even the most wildly squandered sum, as an offering to destiny that he might not remember the things most worth remembering, the things that now he would always remember – his child taken from his control, his wife escaped to a grave in Vermont.

In the glare of a *brasserie* a woman spoke to him. He bought her some eggs and coffee, and then, eluding her encouraging stare, gave her a twenty-franc note and took a taxi to his hotel.

2

He woke upon a fine fall day – football weather. The depression of yesterday was gone and he liked the people on the streets. At noon he sat opposite Honoria at Le Grand Vatel, the only restaurant he could think of not reminiscent of champagne dinners and long luncheons that began at two and ended in a blurred and vague twilight.

'Now, how about vegetables? Oughtn't you to have some vegetables?'

'Well, yes.'

'Here's *épinards* and *chou-fleur* and carrots and *haricots*.'

'I'd like *chou-fleur*.'

'Wouldn't you like to have two vegetables?'

'I usually only have one at lunch.'

The waiter was pretending to be inordinately fond of children. '*Qu'elle est mignonne la petite! Elle parle exactement comme une française.*'

'How about dessert? Shall we wait and see?'

The waiter disappeared. Honoria looked at her father expectantly.

'What are we going to do?'

'First, we're going to that toy store in the Rue Saint-Honoré and buy you anything you like. And then we're going to the vaudeville at the Empire.'

She hesitated. 'I like it about the vaudeville, but not the toy store.'

'Why not?'

'Well, you brought me this doll.' She had it with her. 'And I've got lots of things. And we're not rich any more, are we?'

'We never were. But today you are to have anything you want.'

'All right,' she agreed resignedly.

When there had been her mother and a French nurse he had been inclined to be strict; now he extended himself, reached out for a new tolerance; he must be both parents to her and not shut any of her out of communication.

'I want to get to know you,' he said gravely. 'First let me introduce myself. My name is Charles J. Wales, of Prague.'

'Oh, daddy!' her voice cracked with laughter.

'And who are you, please?' he persisted, and she accepted a rôle immediately: 'Honoria Wales, Rue Palatine, Paris.'

'Married or single?'

'No, not married. Single.'

He indicated the doll. 'But I see you have a child, madame.'

Unwilling to disinherit it, she took it to her heart and thought quickly: 'Yes, I've been married, but I'm not married now. My husband is dead.'

He went on quickly, 'And the child's name?'

'Simone. That's after my best friend at school.'

'I'm very pleased that you're doing so well at school.'

'I'm third this month,' she boasted. 'Elsie' – that was her cousin – 'is only about eighteenth, and Richard is about at the bottom.'

'You like Richard and Elsie, don't you?'

'Oh, yes. I like Richard quite well and I like her all right.'

Cautiously and casually he asked: 'And Aunt Marion and Uncle Lincoln – which do you like best?'

'Oh, Uncle Lincoln, I guess.'

He was increasingly aware of her presence. As they came in, a murmur of '... adorable' followed them, and now the people at the next table bent all their silences upon her, staring as if she were something no more conscious than a flower.

'Why don't I live with you?' she asked suddenly. 'Because mama's dead?'

'You must stay here and learn more French. It would have been hard for daddy to take care of you so well.'

'I don't really need much taking care of any more. I do everything for myself.'

Going out of the restaurant, a man and a woman unexpectedly hailed him!

'Well, the old Wales!'

'Hello there, Lorraine. ... Dunc.'

Sudden ghosts out of the past: Duncan Schaeffer, a friend from college. Lorraine Quarrles, a lovely, pale blonde of thirty; one of a crowd who had helped them make months into days in the lavish times of three years ago.

'My husband couldn't come this year,' she said, in answer to his question. 'We're poor as hell. So he gave me two hundred a month and told me I could do my worst on that. ... This your little girl?'

'What about coming back and sitting down?' Duncan asked.

'Can't do it.' He was glad for an excuse. As always, he felt Lorraine's passionate, provocative attraction, but his own rhythm was different now.

'Well, how about dinner?' she asked.

'I'm not free. Give me your address and let me call you.'

'Charlie, I believe you're sober,' she said judicially. 'I honestly believe he's sober, Dunc. Pinch him and see if he's sober.'

Charlie indicated Honoria with his head. They both laughed.

'What's your address?' said Duncan sceptically.

He hesitated, unwilling to give the name of his hotel.

'I'm not settled yet. I'd better call you. We're going to see the vaudeville at the Empire.'

'There! That's what I want to do,' Lorraine said. 'I want to see some clowns and acrobats and jugglers. That's just what we'll do, Dunc.'

'We've got to do an errand first,' said Charlie. 'Perhaps we'll see you there.'

'All right, you snob. ... Good-by, beautiful little girl.'

'Good-by.'

Honoria bobbed politely.

Somehow, an unwelcome encounter. They liked him because he was functioning, because he was serious; they wanted to see him, because he was stronger than they were now, because they wanted to draw a certain sustenance from his strength.

At the Empire, Honoria proudly refused to sit upon her father's folded coat. She was already an individual with a code of her own, and Charlie was more and more absorbed by the desire of putting a little of himself into her before she crystallized utterly. It was hopeless to try to know her in so short a time.

Between acts they came upon Duncan and Lorraine in the lobby where the band was playing.

'Have a drink?'

'All right, but not up at the bar. We'll take a table.'

'The perfect father.'

Listening abstractedly to Lorraine, Charlie watched Honoria's eyes leave their table, and he followed them wistfully about the room, wondering what they saw. He met her glance and she smiled.

'I like that lemonade,' she said.

What had she said? What had he expected? Going home in a taxi afterward, he pulled her over until her head rested against his chest.

'Darling, do you ever think about your mother?'

'Yes, sometimes,' she answered vaguely.

'I don't want you to forget her. Have you got a picture of her?'

'Yes, I think so. Anyhow, Aunt Marion has. Why don't you want me to forget her?'

'She loved you very much.'

'I loved her too.'

They were silent for a moment.

'Daddy, I want to come and live with you,' she said suddenly.

His heart leaped; he had wanted it to come like this.

'Aren't you perfectly happy?'

'Yes, but I love you better than anybody. And you love me better than anybody, don't you, now that mummy's dead?'

'Of course I do. But you won't always like me best, honey. You'll grow up and meet somebody your own age and go marry him and forget you ever had a daddy.'

'Yes, that's true,' she agreed tranquilly.

He didn't go in. He was coming back at nine o'clock and he wanted to keep himself fresh and new for the thing he must say then.

'When you're safe inside, just show yourself in that window.'

'All right. Good-by, dads, dads, dads, dads.'

He waited in the dark street until she appeared, all warm and glowing, in the window above and kissed her fingers out into the night.

3

They were waiting. Marion sat behind the coffee service in a dignified black dinner dress that just faintly suggested mourning. Lincoln was walking up and down with the animation of one who had already been talking. They were as anxious as he was to get into the question. He opened it almost immediately:

'I suppose you know what I want to see you about – why I really came to Paris.'

Marion played with the black stars on her necklace and frowned.

'I'm awfully anxious to have a home,' he continued. 'And I'm awfully anxious to have Honoria in it. I appreciate your taking in Honoria for her mother's sake, but things have changed now' – he hesitated and then continued more forcibly – 'changed radically with me, and I want to ask you to reconsider the matter. It would be silly for me to deny that about three years ago I was acting badly—'

Marion looked up at him with hard eyes.

'—but all that's over. As I told you, I haven't had more than a drink a day for over a year, and I take that drink deliberately, so that the idea of alcohol won't get too big in my imagination. You see the idea?'

'No,' said Marion succinctly.

'It's a sort of stunt I set myself. It keeps the matter in proportion.'

'I get you,' said Lincoln. 'You don't want to admit it's got any attraction for you.'

'Something like that. Sometimes I forget and don't take it. But I try to take it. Anyhow, I couldn't afford to drink in my position. The people I represent are more than satisfied with what I've done, and I'm bringing my sister over from Burlington to keep house for me, and I want awfully to have Honoria too. You know that even when her mother and I weren't getting along well we never let anything that happened touch Honoria. I know she's fond of me and I know I'm able to take care of her and – well, there you are. How do you feel about it?'

He knew that now he would have to take a beating. It would last an hour or two hours, and it would be difficult, but if he modulated his inevitable resentment to the chastened attitude of the reformed sinner, he might win his point in the end.

Keep your temper, he told himself. You don't want to be justified. You want Honoria.

Lincoln spoke first: 'We've been talking it over ever since we got your letter last month. We're happy to have Honoria here. She's a dear little thing, and we're glad to be able to help her, but of course that isn't the question—'

Marion interrupted suddenly. 'How long are you going to stay sober, Charlie?' she asked.

'Permanently, I hope.'

'How can anybody count on that?'

'You know I never did drink heavily until I gave up business and came over here with nothing to do. Then Helen and I began to run around with—'

'Please leave Helen out of it. I can't bear to hear you talk about her like that.'

He stared at her grimly; he had never been certain how fond of each other the sisters were in life.

'My drinking only lasted about a year and a half – from the time we came over until I – collapsed.'

'It was time enough.'

'It was time enough,' he agreed.

'My duty is entirely to Helen,' she said. 'I try to think what she would have wanted me to do. Frankly, from the night you did that terrible thing you haven't really existed for me. I can't help that. She was my sister.'

'Yes.'

'When she was dying she asked me to look out for Honoria. If you hadn't been in a sanitarium then, it might have helped matters.'

He had no answer.

'I'll never in my life be able to forget the morning when Helen knocked at my door, soaked to the skin and shivering, and said you'd locked her out.'

Charlie gripped the sides of the chair. This was more difficult than he expected; he wanted to launch out into a long expostulation and explanation, but he only said: 'The night I locked her out—' and she interrupted, 'I don't feel up to going over that again.'

After a moment's silence Lincoln said: 'We're getting off the subject. You want Marion to set aside her legal guardianship and give you Honoria. I think the main point for her is whether she has confidence in you or not.'

'I don't blame Marion,' Charlie said slowly, 'but I think she can have entire confidence in me. I had a good record up to three years ago. Of course, it's within human possibilities I might go wrong any time. But if we wait much longer I'll lose Honoria's childhood and my chance for a home.' He shook his head, 'I'll simply lose her, don't you see?'

'Yes, I see,' said Lincoln.

'Why didn't you think of all this before?' Marion asked.

'I suppose I did, from time to time, but Helen and I were getting along badly. When I consented to the guardianship, I was flat on my back in a sanitarium and the market had cleaned me out. I knew I'd acted badly, and I thought if it would bring any peace to Helen, I'd agree to anything. But now it's different. I'm functioning, I'm behaving damn well, so far as—'

'Please don't swear at me,' Marion said.

He looked at her, startled. With each remark the force of her dislike became more and more apparent. She had built up all her fear of life into one wall and faced it toward him. This trivial reproof was possibly the result of some trouble with the cook several hours before. Charlie became increasingly alarmed at leaving Honoria in this atmosphere of hostility against himself; sooner or later it would come out, in a word here, a shake of the head there, and some of that distrust would be irrevocably implanted in Honoria. But he pulled his temper down out of his face and shut it up inside him; he had won a point, for Lincoln realized the absurdity of Marion's remark and asked her lightly since when she had objected to the word 'damn.'

'Another thing,' Charlie said: 'I'm able to give her certain advantages now. I'm going to take a French governess to Prague with me. I've got a lease on a new apartment—'

He stopped, realizing that he was blundering. They couldn't be expected to accept with equanimity the fact that his income was again twice as large as their own.

'I suppose you can give her more luxuries than we can,' said Marion. 'When you were throwing away money we were living along watching every ten francs. ... I suppose you'll start doing it again.'

'Oh, no,' he said. 'I've learned. I worked hard for ten years, you know – until I got lucky in the market, like so many people. Terribly lucky. It didn't seem any use working any more, so I quit. It won't happen again.'

There was a long silence. All of them felt their nerves straining, and for the first time in a year Charlie wanted a drink. He was sure now that Lincoln Peters wanted him to have his child.

Marion shuddered suddenly; part of her saw that Charlie's feet were planted on the earth now, and her own maternal feeling recognized the naturalness of his desire; but she had lived for a long time with a prejudice – a prejudice founded on a curious disbelief in her sister's happiness, and which, in the shock of one terrible night, had turned to hatred for him. It all happened at a point in her life where the discouragement of ill health and adverse circumstances made it necessary for her to believe in tangible villainy and a tangible villain.

'I can't help what I think!' she cried out suddenly. 'How much you were responsible for Helen's death, I don't know. It's something you'll have to square with your own conscience.'

An electric current of agony surged through him; for a moment he was almost on his feet, an unuttered sound echoing in his throat. He hung on to himself for a moment, another moment.

'Hold on there,' said Lincoln uncomfortably. 'I never thought you were responsible for that.'

'Helen died of heart trouble,' Charlie said dully.

'Yes, heart trouble.' Marion spoke as if the phrase had another meaning for her.

Then, in the flatness that followed her outburst, she saw him plainly and she knew he had somehow arrived at control over the situation. Glancing at her husband, she found no help from him, and as abruptly as if it were a matter of no importance, she threw up the sponge.

'Do what you like!' she cried, springing up from her chair. 'She's your child. I'm not the person to stand in your way. I think if it were my child I'd rather see her—' She managed to check herself. 'You two decide it. I can't stand this. I'm sick. I'm going to bed.'

She hurried from the room; after a moment Lincoln said:

'This has been a hard day for her. You know how strongly she feels—' His voice was almost apologetic: 'When a women gets an idea in her head.'

'Of course.'

'It's going to be all right. I think she sees now that you – can provide for the child, and so we can't very well stand in your way or Honoria's way.'

'Thank you, Lincoln.'

'I'd better go along and see how she is.'

'I'm going.'

He was still trembling when he reached the street, but a walk down the Rue Bonaparte to the quais set him up, and as he crossed the Seine, fresh and new by the quai lamps, he felt exultant. But back in his room he couldn't sleep. The image of Helen haunted him. Helen whom he had loved so until they had senselessly begun to abuse each other's love, tear it into shreds. On that terrible February night that Marion remembered so vividly, a slow quarrel had gone on for hours. There was a scene at the Florida, and then he attempted to take her home, and then she kissed young Webb at a table; after that there was what she had hysterically said. When he arrived home alone he turned the key in the lock in wild anger. How could he know she would arrive an hour later alone, that there would be a snowstorm in which she wandered about in slippers, too confused to find a taxi? Then the aftermath, her escaping pneumonia by a miracle, and all the attendant horror. They were 'reconciled,' but that was the beginning of the end, and Marion, who had seen with her own eyes and who imagined it to be one of many scenes from her sister's martyrdom, never forgot.

Going over it again brought Helen nearer, and in the white, soft light that steals upon half sleep near morning he found himself talking to her again. She said that he was perfectly right about Honoria and she wanted Honoria to be with him. She said she was glad he was being good and doing better. She said a lot of other things – very friendly things – but she was in a swing in a white dress, and swinging faster and faster all the time, so that at the end he could not hear clearly all that she said.

4

He woke up feeling happy. The door of the world was open again. He made plans, vistas, futures for Honoria and himself, but suddenly he grew sad, remembering all the plans he and Helen had made. She had not planned to die. The present was the thing – work to do and someone to love. But not to love too much, for he knew the injury that a father can do to a daughter or a mother to a son by attaching them too closely; afterward, out in the world, the child would seek in the marriage partner the same blind tenderness and, failing probably to find it, turn against love and life.

It was another bright, crisp day. He called Lincoln Peters at the bank where he worked and asked if he could count on taking Honoria when he left for Prague. Lioncoln agreed that there was no reason for delay. One thing – the legal guardianship. Marion wanted to retain that a while longer. She was upset by the whole matter, and it would oil things if she felt that the situation was still in her control for another year. Charlie agreed, wanted only the tangible, visible child.

Then the question of a governess. Charlie sat in a gloomy agency and talked to a cross Bernaise and to a buxom Breton peasant, neither of whom he could have endured. There were others whom he would see tomorrow.

He lunched with Lincoln Peters at Griffons, trying to keep down his exultation.

'There's nothing quite like your own child,' Lincoln said. 'But you understand how Marion feels too.'

'She's forgotten how hard I worked for seven years there,' Charlie said. 'She just remembers one night.'

'There's another thing.' Lincoln hesitated. 'While you and Helen were tearing around Europe throwing money away, we were just getting along. I didn't touch any of the prosperity because I never got ahead enough to carry anything but my insurance. I think Marion felt there was some kind of injustice in it – you not even working toward the end, and getting richer and richer.'

'It went just as quick as it came,' said Charlie.

'Yes, a lot of it stayed in the hands of *chasseurs* and saxophone players and maîtres d'hôtel – well, the big party's over now. I just said that to explain Marion's feeling about those crazy years. If you drop in about six o'clock tonight before Marion's too tired, we'll settle the details on the spot.'

Back at his hotel, Charlie found a *pneumatique* that had been redirected from the Ritz bar where Charlie had left his address for the purpose of finding a certain man.

DEAR CHARLIE: You were so strange when we saw you the other day that I wondered if I did something to offend you. If so, I'm not conscious of it. In fact, I have thought about you too much for the last year, and it's always been in the back of my mind that I might see you if I came over here. We *did* have such good times that crazy spring, like the night you and I stole the butcher's tricycle, and the time we tried to call on the president and you had the old derby rim and the wire cane. Everybody seems so old lately, but I don't feel old a bit. Couldn't we get together some time today for old time's sake? I've got a vile hang-over for the moment, but will be feeling better this afternoon and will look for you about five in the sweat-shop at the Ritz.

Always devotedly,
LORRAINE

His first feeling was one of awe that he had actually, in his mature years, stolen a tricycle and pedalled Lorraine all over the Étoile between the small hours and dawn. In retrospect it was a nightmare. Locking out Helen didn't fit in with any other act of his life, but the tricycle incident did – it was one of many. How many weeks or months of dissipation to arrive at that condition of utter irresponsibility?

He tried to picture how Lorraine had appeared to him then – very attractive; Helen was unhappy about it, though she said nothing. Yesterday, in the restaurant, Lorraine had seemed trite, blurred, worn away. He emphatically did not want to see her, and he was glad Alix had not given away his hotel address. It was a relief to think, instead, of Honoria, to think of Sundays spent with her and of saying good morning to her and of knowing she was here in his house at night, drawing her breath in the darkness.

At five he took a taxi and bought presents for all the Peters – a piquant cloth doll, a box of Roman soldiers, flowers for Marion, big linen handkerchiefs for Lincoln.

He saw, when he arrived in the department, that Marion had accepted the inevitable. She greeted him now as though he were a recalcitrant member of the family, rather than a menacing outsider. Honoria had been told she was going; Charlie was glad to see that her tact made her conceal her excessive happiness. Only on his lap did she whisper her delight and the question 'When?' before she slipped away with the other children.

He and Marion were alone for a minute in the room, and on an impulse he spoke out boldly:

'Family quarrels are bitter things. They don't go according to any rules. They're not like aches or wounds; they're more like splits in the skin that won't heal because there's not enough material. I wish you and I could be on better terms.'

'Some things are hard to forget,' she answered. 'It's a question of confidence.' There was no answer to this and presently she asked, 'When do you propose to take her?'

'As soon as I can get a governess. I hoped the day after tommorow.'

'That's impossible. I've got to get her things in shape. Not before Saturday.'

He yielded. Coming back into the room, Lincoln offered him a drink.

'I'll take my daily whisky,' he said.

It was warm here, it was a home, people together by a fire. The children felt safe and important; the mother and father were serious, watchful. They had things to do for the children more important than his visit here. A spoonful of medicine was, after all, more important that the strained relations between Marion and himself. They were not dull people, but they were very much in the grip of life and circumstances. He wondered if he couldn't do something to get Lincoln out of his rut at the bank.

A long peal at the door-bell; the *bonne á toute faire* passed through and went down the corridor. The door opened upon another long ring, and then voices, and the three in the salon looked up expectantly; Richard moved to bring the corridor within his range of vision, and Marion rose. Then the maid came back along the corridor, closely followed by the voices, which developed under the light into Duncan Schaeffer and Lorraine Quarrles.

They were gay, they were hilarious, they were roaring with laughter. For a moment Charlie was astounded; unable to understand how they ferreted out the Peters' address.

'Ah-h-h!' Duncan wagged his finger roguishly at Charlie. 'Ah-h-h!'

They both slid down another cascade of laughter. Anxious and at a loss, Charlie shook hands with them quickly and presented them to Lincoln and Marion. Marion nodded, scarcely speaking. She had drawn back a step toward the fire; her little girl stood beside her, and Marion put an arm about her shoulder.

With growing annoyance at the intrusion, Charlie waited for them to explain themselves. After some concentration Duncan said:

'We came to invite you out to dinner. Lorraine and I insist that all this shishi, cagy business 'bout your address got to stop.'

Charlie came closer to them, as if to force them backward down the corridor.

'Sorry, but I can't. Tell me where you'll be and I'll phone you in half an hour.'

This made no impression. Lorraine sat down suddenly on the side of a chair, and focussing her eyes on Richard, cried, 'Oh, what a nice little boy! Come here, little boy.' Richard glanced at his mother, but did not move. With a perceptible shrug of her shoulder, Lorraine turned back to Charlie:

'Come and dine. Sure your cousins won' mine. See you so sel'om. Or solemn.'

'I can't,' said Charlie sharply. 'You two have dinner and I'll phone you.'

Her voice became suddenly unpleasant. 'All right, we'll go. But I remember once when you hammered on my door at 4 AM I was enough of a good sport to give you a drink. Come on, Dunc.'

Still in slow motion, with blurred, angry faces, with uncertain feet, they retired along the corridor.

'Good night,' Charlie said.

'Good night!' responded Lorraine emphatically.

When he went back into the salon Marion had not moved, only now her son was standing in the circle of her other arm. Lincoln was still swinging Honoria back and forth like a pendulum from side to side.

'What an outrage!' Charlie broke out. 'What an absolute outrage!'

Neither of them answered. Charlie dropped into an armchair, picked up his drink, set it down again and said:

'People I haven't seen for two years having the colossal nerve—'

He broke off. Marion had made the sound 'Oh!' in one swift, furious breath, turned her body from him with a jerk and left the room.

Lincoln set down Honoria carefully.

'You children go in and start your soup,' he said, and when they obeyed, he said to Charlie:

'Marion's not well and she can't stand shocks. That kind of people make her really physically sick.'

'I didn't tell them to come here. They wormed your name out of somebody. They deliberately—'

'Well, it's too bad. It doesn't help matters. Excuse me a minute.'

Left alone, Charlie sat tense in his chair. In the next room he could hear the children eating, talking in monosyllables, already oblivious to the scene between their elders. He heard a murmur of conversation from a farther room and then the ticking bell of a telephone receiver picked up, and in a panic he moved to the other side of the room and out of earshot.

In a minute Lincoln came back. 'Look here, Charlie. I think we'd better call off dinner for tonight. Marion's in bad shape.'

'Is she angry with me?'

'Sort of,' he said, almost roughly. 'She's not strong and—'

'You mean she's changed her mind about Honoria?'

'She's pretty bitter right now. I don't know. You phone me at the bank tomorrow.'

'I wish you'd explain to her I never dreamed these people would come here. I'm just as sore as you are.'

'I couldn't explain anything to her now.'

Charlie got up. He took, his coat and hat and started down the corridor. Then he opened the door of the dining room and said in a strange voice, 'Good night, children.'

Honoria rose and ran around the table to hug him.

'Good night, sweetheart,' he said vaguely, and then trying to make his voice more tender, trying to conciliate something, 'Good night, dear children.'

5

Charlie went directly to the Ritz bar with the furious idea of finding Lorraine and Duncan, but they were not there, and he realized that in any case there was nothing he could do. He had not touched his drink at the Peters', and now he ordered a whisky-and-soda. Paul came over to say hello.

'It's a great change,' he said sadly. 'We do about half the business we did. So many fellows I hear about back in the States lost everything, maybe not in the first crash, but then in the second. Your friend George Hardt lost every cent, I hear. Are you back in the States?'

'No, I'm in business in Prague.'

'I heard that you lost a lot in the crash.'

'I did,' and he added grimly, 'but I lost everything I wanted in the boom.'

'Selling short.'

'Something like that.'

Again the memory of those days swept over him like a nightmare – the people they had met travelling; the people who couldn't add a row of figures or speak a coherent sentence. The little man Helen had consented to dance with at the ship's party, who had insulted her ten feet from the table; the women and girls carried screaming with drink or drugs out of public places –

– The men who locked their wives out in the snow, because the snow of twenty-nine wasn't real snow. If you didn't want it to be snow, you just paid some money.

He went to the phone and called the Peters' apartment; Lincoln answered.

'I called up because this thing is on my mind. Has Marion said anything definite?'

'Marion's sick,' Lincoln answered shortly. 'I know this thing isn't altogether your fault, but I can't have her go to pieces about it. I'm afraid we'll have to let it slide for six months; I can't take the chance of working her up to this state again.'

'I see.'

'I'm sorry, Charlie.'

He went back to his table. His whisky glass was empty, but he shook his head when Alix looked at it questionably. There wasn't much he could do now except send Honoria some things; he would send her a lot of things tomorrow. He thought rather angrily that this was just money – he had given so many people money...

'No, no more,' he said to another waiter. 'What do I owe you?'

He would come back some day; they couldn't make him pay forever. But he wanted his child, and nothing was much good now, beside that fact. He wasn't young any more, with a lot of nice thoughts and dreams to have by himself. He was absolutely sure Helen wouldn't have wanted him to be so alone.

WILLIAM FAULKNER
1897-1962

Awarded the Nobel Prize in 1950, William Faulkner's works about the unsavory aspects of American life have won him worldwide acclaim. Born in 1897 in New Albany, Mississippi, he was 39 when his first novel was published. *Soldier's Pay* launched him as a novelist and is the trenchant story of a soldier's return after World War I. Several successes followed including *The Sound and The Fury* (1929), *As I Lay Dying* (1930) and *Light in August* (1932), also his collection of short stories which focuses on the American South and its unrelenting prejudices.

A Rose for Emily (1931) is one of Faulkner's best short stories. Its precision and economy of language, its haunting and unusual theme mark the work of one of the great innovative writers of the twentieth century.

WILLIAM FAULKNER
1897-1962

A Rose for Emily

WHEN MISS EMILY GRIERSON died, our whole town went to her funeral: the men through a sort of respectful affection for a fallen monument, the women mostly out of curiosity to see the inside of her house, which no one save an old manservant – a combined gardener and cook – had seen in at least ten years.

It was a big, squarish frame house that had once been white, decorated with cupolas and spires and scrolled balconies in the heavily lightsome style of the seventies, set on what had once been our most select street. But garages and cotton gins had encroached and obliterated even the august names of that neighbourhood; only Miss Emily's house was left, lifting its stubborn and coquettish decay above the cotton wagons and the petrol pumps – an eyesore among eyesores. And now Miss Emily had gone to join the representatives of those august names where they lay in the cedar-demused cemetery among the ranked and anonymous graves of Union and Confederate soldiers who fell at the battle of Jefferson.

Alive, Miss Emily had been a tradition, a duty, and a care; a sort of hereditary obligation upon the town, dating from that day in 1894 when Colonel Sartoris, the mayor – he who fathered the edict that no Negro woman should appear on the streets without an apron – remitted her taxes, the dispensation dating from the death of her father on into perpetuity. Not that Miss Emily would have accepted charity. Colonel Sartoris invented an involved tale to the effect that Miss Emily's father had loaned money to the town, which the town, as a matter of business, preferred this way of repaying. Only a man of Colonel Sartoris's generation and thought could have invented it, and only a woman could have believed it.

When the next generation, with its more modern ideas, became mayors and aldermen, this arrangement created some little dissatisfaction. On the first of the year they mailed her a tax notice. February came, and there was no reply. They wrote her a formal letter asking her to call at the sheriff's office at her convenience. A week later the mayor wrote her himself, offering to call or to send his car for her, and received in reply a note on paper of an archaic shape, in a thin, flowing calligraphy in faded ink, to the effect that she no longer went out at all. The tax notice was also enclosed, without comment.

They called a special meeting of the Board of Aldermen. A deputation waited upon her, knocked at the door through which no visitor had passed since she ceased giving china-painting lessons eight or ten years earlier. They were admitted by the old Negro into a dim hall from which a stairway mounted into still more shadow. It smelled of dust and disuse – a close, dank smell. The Negro led them into the parlour. It was furnished in heavy, leather-covered furniture. When the Negro opened the blinds of one window, they could see that the leather was cracked; and when they sat down, a faint dust rose sluggishly about their thighs, spinning with slow notes in the single sunray. On a tarnished gilt easel before the fireplace stood a crayon portrait of Miss Emily's father.

They rose when she entered – a small, fat woman in black, with a thin gold chain descending to her waist, and vanishing into her belt, leaning on an ebony cane with a tarnished gold head. Her skeleton was small and spare; perhaps that was why what would have been merely plumpness in another was obesity in her. She looked bloated, like a body long submerged in motionless water, and of that pallid hue. Her eyes, lost in the fatty ridges of her face, looked like two small pieces of coal pressed into a lump of dough as they moved from one face to another while the visitors stated their errand.

She did not ask them to sit. She just stood in the doorway and listened quietly until the spokesman came to a stumbling halt. Then they could hear the invisible watch ticking at the end of the gold chain.

Her voice was dry and cold. 'I have no taxes in Jefferson. Colonel Sartoris explained it to me. Perhaps one of you can gain access to the city records and satisfy yourselves.'

'But we have. We are the city authorities, Miss Emily. Didn't you get a notice from the sheriff, signed by him?'

'I received a paper, yes,' Miss Emily said. 'Perhaps he considers himself the sheriff . . . I have no taxes in Jefferson.'

'But there is nothing on the books to show that, you see. We must go by the—'

'See Colonel Sartoris. I have no taxes in Jefferson.'

'But Miss Emily—'

'See Colonel Sartoris.' (Colonel Sartoris had been dead almost ten years.) 'I have no taxes in Jefferson. Tobe!' The Negro appeared. 'Show these gentlemen out.'

2

So she vanquished them, horse and foot, just as she had vanquished their fathers thirty years before about the smell. That was two years after her father's death and a short time after her sweetheart – the one we believed would marry her – had deserted her. After her father's death she went out very little; after her sweetheart went away, people hardly saw her at all. A few of the ladies had the temerity to call, but were not received, and the only sign of life about the place was the Negro man – a young man then – going in and out with a market basket.

'Just as if a man – any man – could keep a kitchen properly,' the ladies said; so they were not surprised when the smell developed. It was another link between the gross, teeming world and the high and mighty Griersons.

A neighbour, a woman, complained to the mayor, Judge Stevens, eighty years old.

'But what will you have me to do about it, madam?' he said.

'Why, send her word to stop it,' the woman said. 'Isn't there a law?'

'I'm sure that won't be necessary,' Judge Stevens said. 'It's probably just a snake or a rat that nigger of hers killed in the yard. I'll speak to him about it.'

The next day he received two more complaints, one from a man who came in diffident deprecation. 'We really must do something about it, Judge. I'd be the last one in the world to bother Miss Emily, but we've got to do something.' That night the Board of Aldermen met – three greybeards and one younger man, a member of the rising generation.

'It's simple enough,' he said. 'Send her word to have her place cleaned up. Give her a certain time to do it in, and if she don't...'

'Dammit, sir,' Judge Stevens said, 'will you accuse a lady to her face of smelling bad?'

So the next night, after midnight, four men crossed Miss Emily's lawn and slunk about the house like burglars, sniffing along the base of the brickwork and at the cellar openings, while one of them performed a regular sowing motion with his hand out of a sack slung from his shoulder. They broke open the cellar door and sprinkled lime there, and in all the outbuildings. As they recrossed the lawn, a window that had been dark was lighted and Miss Emily sat in it, the light behind her, and her upright torso motionless as that of an idol. They crept quietly across the lawn and into the shadow of the locusts that lined the street. After a week or two the smell went away.

That was when people had begun to feel really sorry for her. People in our town, remembering how Old Lady Wyatt, her great-aunt, had gone completely crazy at last, believed that the Griersons held themselves a little too high for what they really were. None of the young men was quite good enough to Miss Emily and such. We had long thought of them as a tableau: Miss Emily a slender figure in white in the background, her father a spraddled silhouette in the foreground, his back to her and clutching a horsewhip, the two of them framed by the back-flung front door. So when she got to be thirty and was still single, we were not pleased exactly, but vindicated; even with insanity in the family she wouldn't have turned down all of her chances if they had really materialized.

When her father died, it got about that the house was all that was left to her; and in a way, people were glad. At last they could pity Miss Emily. Being left alone, and a pauper, she had become humanized. Now she too would know the old thrill and the old despair of a penny more or less.

The day after his death all the ladies prepared to call at the house and offer condolence and aid, as is our custom. Miss Emily met them at the door, dressed as usual and with no trace of grief on her face. She told them that her father was not dead. She did that for three days, with the ministers calling on her, and the doctors, trying to persuade her to let them dispose of the body. Just as they were about to resort to law and force, she broke down, and they buried her father quickly.

We did not say she was crazy then. We believed she had to do that. We remembered all the young men her father had driven away, and we knew that, with nothing left, she would have to cling to that which had robbed her, as people will.

3

She was sick for a long time. When we saw her again, her hair was cut short, making her look like a girl, with a vague resemblance to those angels in coloured church windows – sort of tragic and serene.

The town had just let the contracts for paving the sidewalks, and in the summer after her father's death they began the work. The construction company came with niggers and mules and machinery, and a foreman named Homer Barron, a Yankee – a big, dark, ready man, with a big voice and eyes lighter than his face. The little boys would follow in groups to hear him cuss the niggers, and the niggers singing in time to the rise and fall of picks. Pretty soon he knew everybody in town. Whenever you heard a lot of laughing anywhere about the square, Homer Barron would be in the centre of the group. Presently we began to see him and Miss Emily on Sunday afternoons driving in the yellow-wheeled buggy and the matched team of bays from the livery stable.

At first we were glad that Miss Emily would have an interest, because the ladies all said, 'Of course a Grierson would not think seriously of a Northerner, a day labourer.' But there were still others, older people, who said that even grief could not cause a real lady to forget *noblesse oblige* – without calling it *noblesse oblige*. They just said, 'Poor Emily. Her kinsfolk should come to her.' She had some kin in Alabama; but years ago her father had fallen out with them over the estate of Old Lady Wyatt, the crazy woman, and there was no communication between the two families. They had not even been represented at the funeral.

And as soon as the old people said, 'Poor Emily,' the whispering began. 'Do you suppose it's really so?' they said to one another.

'Of course it is. What else could . . .' This behind their hands; rustling of craned silk and satin behind jalousies closed upon the sun of Sunday afternoon as the thin, swift clop-clop-clop of the matched team passed: 'Poor Emily.'

She carried her head high enough – even when we believed that she was fallen. It was as if she demanded more than ever the recognition of her dignity as the last Grierson; as if it had wanted that touch of earthiness to reaffirm her imperviousness. Like when she bought the rat poison, the arsenic. That was over a year after they had begun to say 'Poor Emily', and while the two female cousins were visiting her.

'I want some poison,' she said to the druggist. She was over thirty then, still a slight woman, though thinner than usual, with cold haughty black eyes in a face the flesh of which was strained across the temples and about the eye-sockets as you imagine a lighthouse-keeper's face ought to look. 'I want some poison,' she said.

'Yes, Miss Emily. What kind? For rats and such? I'd recom—'

'I want the best you have. I don't care what kind.'

The druggist named several. 'They'll kill anything up to an elephant. But what you want is—'

'Arsenic,' Miss Emily said. 'Is that a good one?'

'Is . . . arsenic? Yes, ma'am. But what you want—'

'I want arsenic.'

The druggist looked down at her. She looked back at him, erect, her face like a strained flag. 'Why, of course,' the druggist said. 'If that's what you want. But the law requires you to tell what you are going to use it for.'

Miss Emily just stared at him, her head tilted back in order to look him eye for eye, until he looked away and went and got the arsenic and wrapped it up. The Negro delivery boy brought her the package; the druggist didn't come back. When she opened the package at home there was written on the box, under the skull and bones: 'For rats.'

4

So the next day we all said, 'She will kill herself'; and we said it would be the best thing. When she had first begun to be seen with Homer Barron, we had said, 'She will marry him.' Then we said, 'She will persuade him yet,' because Homer himself had remarked – he liked men, and it was known that he drank with the younger men in the Elks' Club – that he was not a marrying man. Later we said, 'Poor Emily' behind the jalousies as they passed on Sunday afternoon in the glittering buggy, Miss Emily with her head high and Homer Barron with his hat cocked and a cigar in his teeth, reins and whip in a yellow glove.

Then some of the ladies began to say that it was a disgrace to the town and a bad example to the young people. The men did not want to interfere, but at last the ladies forced the Baptist minister – Miss Emily's people were Episcopal – to call upon her. He would never divulge what happened during that interview, but he refused to go back again. The next Sunday they again drove about the streets, and the following day the minister's wife wrote to Miss Emily's relations in Alabama.

So she had blood-kin under her roof again and we sat back to watch developments. At first nothing happened. Then we were sure that they were to be married. We learned that Miss Emily had been to the jeweller's and ordered a man's toilet set in silver, with the letters H.B. on each piece. Two days later we learned that she had bought a complete outfit of men's clothing including a night-shirt, and we said, 'They are married.' We were really glad. We were glad because the two female cousins were even more Grierson than Miss Emily had ever been.

So we were not surprised when Homer Barron – the streets had been finished some time since – was gone. We were a little disappointed that there was not a public blowing-off, but we believed that he had gone on to prepare for Miss Emily's coming, or to give her a chance to get rid of the cousins. (By that time it was a cabal, and we were all Miss Emily's allies to help circumvent the cousins.) Sure enough, after another week they departed. And, as we had expected all along, within three days Homer Barron was back in town. A neighbour saw the Negro man admit him at the kitchen door at dusk one evening.

And that was the last we saw of Homer Barron. And of Miss Emily for some time. The Negro man went in and out with the market basket, but the front door remained closed. Now and then we would see her at a window for a moment, as the men did that night when they sprinkled the lime, but for almost six months she did not appear on the streets. Then we knew that this was to be expected too; as if that quality of her father which had thwarted her woman's life so many times had been too virulent and too furious to die.

When we next saw Miss Emily, she had grown fat and her hair was turning grey. During the next few years it grew greyer and greyer until it attained an even pepper-and-salt iron-grey, when it ceased turning. Up to the day of her death at seventy-four it was still that vigorous iron-grey, like the hair of an active man.

From that time on her front door remained closed, save for a period of six or seven years, when she was about forty, during which she gave lessons in china-painting. She fitted up a studio in one of the downstairs rooms, where the daughters and grand-daughters of Colonel Sartoris's contemporaries were sent to her with the same regularity and in the same spirit that they were sent to church on Sundays with a twenty-five cent piece for the collection plate. Meanwhile her taxes had been remitted.

Then the newer generation became the backbone and the spirit of the town, and the painting pupils grew up and fell away and did not send their children to her with boxes of colour and tedious brushes and pictures cut from the ladies' magazines. The front door closed upon the last one and remained closed for good. When the town got free postal delivery, Miss Emily alone refused to let them fasten the metal numbers above her door and attach a mail-box to it. She would not listen to them.

Daily, monthly, yearly we watched the Negro grow greyer and more stooped, going in and out with the market basket. Each December we sent her a tax notice, which would be returned by the post office a week later, unclaimed. Now and then we would see her in one of the downstairs windows – she had evidently shut up the top floor of the house – like the carven torso of an idol in a niche, looking or not looking at us, we could never tell which. Thus she passed from generation to generation – dear, inescapable, impervious, tranquil, and perverse.

And so she died. Fell ill in the house filled with dust and shadows, with only a doddering Negro man to wait on her. We did not even know she was sick; we had long since given up trying to get any information from the Negro. He talked to no one, probably not even to her, for his voice had grown harsh and rusty, as if from disuse.

She died in one of the downstairs rooms, in a heavy walnut bed with a curtain, her grey head propped on a pillow yellow and mouldy with age and lack of sunlight.

5

The Negro met the first of the ladies at the front door and let them in, with their hushed, sibilant voices, and their quick curious glances, and then he disappeared. He walked right through the house and out the back and was not seen again.

The two female cousins came at once. They held the funeral on the second day, with the town coming to look at Miss Emily beneath a mass of bough flowers, with the crayon face of her father musing profoundly above the bier and the ladies sibilant and macabre; and the very old men – some in their brushed Confederate uniforms – on the porch and the lawn, talking of Miss Emily as if she had been a contemporary of theirs, believing that they had danced with her and courted her perhaps, confusing time with its mathematical progression, as the old do, to whom all the past is not a diminishing road but, instead, a huge meadow which no winter ever quite touches, divided from them now by the narrow bottle-neck of the most recent decade of the years.

Already we knew that there was one room in that region above the stairs which no one had seen in forty years, and which would have to be forced. They waited until Miss Emily was decently in the ground before they opened it.

The violence of breaking down the door seemed to fill this room with pervading dust. A thin, acrid pall as of the tomb seemed to lie everywhere upon this room decked and furnished as for a bridal: upon the valance curtains of faded rose colour, upon the rose-shaded lights, upon the dressing-table, upon the delicate array of crystal and the man's toilet things backed with tarnished silver, silver so tarnished that the monogram was obscured. Among them lay a collar and tie, as if they had just been removed, which, lifted, left upon the surface a pale crescent in the dust. Upon a chair hung the suit, carefully folded; beneath it the two mute shoes and the discarded socks.

The man himself lay in the bed.

For a long while we just stood there, looking down at the profound fleshless grin. The body had apparently once lain in the attitude of an embrace, but now the long sleep that outlasts love, that conquers even the grimace of love, had cuckolded him. What was left of him, rotted beneath what was left of the night-shirt, had become inextricable from the bed in which he lay; and upon him and upon the pillow beside him lay that even coating of the patient and biding dust.

Then we noticed that in the second pillow was the indentation of a head. One of us lifted something from it, and leaning forward, that faint and invisible dust dry and acrid in the nostrils, we saw a long strand of iron-grey hair.

ERNEST HEMINGWAY
1899-1961

The poignant works of Ernest Hemingway have assured him a leading place in the ranks of twentieth century American writers. He won the Nobel Prize in 1954 for his narrative powers and descriptive abilities, which have in turn made his style particularly suited to the short story. Hemingway was born in Illinois in 1898 and took to journalism on leaving school.

The story 'Big Two-Hearted River' is reprinted from *In Our Time* (1925), Hemingway's first collection of fifteen stories, which concern the boyhood of Nick Adams in the region of the Great Lakes. The story itself, about a trout-fishing trip, explores Nick's feeling of renewal and rebirth after the horrors of World War 1 among the haunts of his youth.

Big Two-Hearted River

THE TRAIN WENT ON UP THE track out of sight, around one of the hills of burnt timber. Nick sat down on the bundle of canvas and bedding the baggage man had pitched out of the door of the baggage car. There was no town, nothing but the rails and the burned-over country. The thirteen saloons that had lined the one street of Seney had not left a trace. The foundations of the Mansion House hotel stuck up above the ground. The stone was chipped and split by the fire. It was all that was left of the town of Seney. Even the surface had been burned off the ground.

Nick looked at the burned-over stretch of hillside, where he had expected to find the scattered houses of the town and then walked down the railroad track to the bridge over the river. The river was there. It swirled against the log spiles of the bridge. Nick looked down into the clear, brown water, colored from the pebbly bottom, and watched the trout keeping themselves steady in the current with wavering fins. As he watched them they changed their positions by quick angles, only to hold steady in the fast water again. Nick watched them a long time.

He watched them holding themselves with their noses into the current, many trout in deep, fast moving water, slightly distorted as he watched far down through the glassy convex surface of the pool, its surface pushing and swelling smooth against the resistance of the log-driven piles of the bridge. At the bottom of the pool were the big trout. Nick did not see them at first. Then he saw them at the bottom of the pool, big trout looking to hold themselves on the gravel bottom in a varying mist of gravel and sand, raised in spurts by the current.

Nick looked down into the pool from the bridge. It was a hot day. A kingfisher flew up the stream. It was a long time since Nick had looked into a stream and seen trout. They were very satisfactory. As the shadow of the kingfisher moved up the stream, a big trout shot upstream in a long angle, only his shadow marking the angle, then lost his shadow as he came through the surface of the water, caught the sun, and then, as he went back into the stream under the surface, his shadow seemed to float down the stream with the current, unresisting, to his post under the bridge where he tightened facing up into the current.

Nick's heart tightened as the trout moved. He felt all the old feeling.

He turned and looked down the stream. It stretched away, pebbly-bottomed with shallows and big boulders and a deep pool as it curved away around the foot of a bluff.

Nick walked back up the ties to where his pack lay in the cinders beside the railway track. He was happy. He adjusted the pack harness around the bundle, pulling straps tight, slung the pack on his back, got his arms through the shoulder straps and took some of the pull off his shoulders by leaning his forehead against the wide band of the tump-line. Still, it was too heavy. It was much too heavy. He had his leather rod-case in his hand and leaning forward to keep the weight of the pack high on his shoulders he walked along the road that paralleled the railway track, leaving the burned town behind in the heat, and then turned off around a hill with a high, fire-scarred hill on either side onto a road that went back into the country. He walked along the road feeling the ache from the pull of the heavy pack. The road climbed steadily. It was hard work walking up-hill. His muscles ached and the day was hot, but Nick felt happy. He felt he had left everything behind, the need for thinking, the need to write, other needs. It was all back of him.

From the time he had gotten down off the train and the baggage man had thrown his pack out of the open car door things had been different. Seney was burned, the country was burned over and changed, but it did not matter. It could not all be burned. He knew that. He hiked along the road, sweating in the sun, climbing to cross the range of hills that separated the railway from the pine plains.

The road ran on, dipping occasionally, but always climbing. Nick went on up. Finally the road after going parallel to the burnt hillside reached the top. Nick leaned back against a stump and slipped out of the pack harness. Ahead of him, as far as he could see, was the pine plain. The burned country stopped off at the left with the range of hills. On ahead islands of dark pine trees rose out of the plain. Far off to the left was the line of the river. Nick followed it with his eye and caught glints of the water in the sun.

There was nothing but the pine plain ahead of him, until the far blue hills that marked the Lake Superior height of land. He could hardly see them, faint and far away in the heat-light over the plain. If he looked too steadily they were gone. But if he only half-looked they were there, the far-off hills of the height of land.

Nick sat down against the charred stump and smoked a cigarette. His pack balanced on the top of the stump, harness holding ready, a hollow molded in it from his back. Nick sat smoking, looking out over the country. He did not need to get his map out. He knew where he was from the position of the river.

As he smoked, his legs stretched out in front of him, he noticed a grasshopper walk along the ground and up onto his woolen sock. The grasshopper was black. As he had walked along the road, climbing, he had started many grasshoppers from the dust. They were all black. They were not the big grasshoppers with yellow and black or red and black wings whirring out from their black wing sheathing as they fly up. These were just ordinary hoppers, but all a sooty black in color. Nick had wondered about them as he walked, without really thinking about them. Now, as he watched the black hopper that was nibbling at the wool of his sock with its fourway lip, he realized that they had all turned black from living in the burned-over land. He realized that the fire must have come the year before, but the grasshoppers were all black now. He wondered how long they would stay that way.

Carefully he reached his hand down and took hold of the hopper by the wings. He turned him up, all his legs walking in the air, and looked at his jointed belly. Yes, it was black too, iridescent where the back and head were dusty.

'Go on, hopper,' Nick said, speaking out loud for the first time. 'Fly away somewhere.'

He tossed the grasshopper up into the air and watched him sail away to a charcoal stump across the road.

Nick stood up. He leaned his back against the weight of his pack where it rested upright on the stump and got his arms through the shoulder straps. He stood with the pack on his back on the brow of the hill looking out across the country, toward the distant river and then struck down the hillside away from the road. Underfoot the ground was good walking. Two hundred yards down the hillside the fire line stopped. Then it was sweet fern, growing ankle high, to walk through, and clumps of jack pines; a long undulating country with frequent rises and descents, sandy underfoot and the country alive again.

Nick kept his direction by the sun. He knew where he wanted to strike the river and he kept on through the pine plain, mounting small rises to see other rises ahead of him and sometimes from the top of a rise a great solid island of pines off to his right or his left. He broke off some sprigs of the heathery sweet fern, and put them under his pack straps. The chafing crushed it and he smelled it as he walked.

He was tired and very hot, walking acros the uneven, shadeless pine plain. At any time he knew he could strike the river by turning off to his left. It could not be more than a mile away. But he kept on toward the north to hit the river as far upstream as he could go in one day's walking.

For some time as he walked Nick had been in sight of one of the big islands of pine standing out above the rolling high ground he was crossing. He dipped down and then as he came slowly up to the crest of the bridge he turned and made toward the pine trees.

There was no underbrush in the island of pine trees. The trunks of the trees went straight up or slanted toward each other. The trunks were straight and brown without branches. The branches were high above. Some interlocked to make a solid shadow on the brown forest floor. Around the grove of trees was a bare space. It was brown and soft underfoot as Nick walked on it. This was the over-lapping of the pine needle floor, extending out beyond the width of the high branches. The trees had grown tall and the branches moved high, leaving in the sun this bare space they had once covered with shadow. Sharp at the edge of this extension of the forest floor commenced the sweet fern.

Nick slipped off his pack and lay down in the shade. He lay on his back and looked up into the pine trees. His neck and back and the small of his back rested as he stretched. The earth felt good against his back. He looked up at the sky, through the branches, and then shut his eyes. He opened them and looked up again. There was a wind high up in the branches. He shut his eyes again and went to sleep.

Nick woke stiff and cramped. The sun was nearly down. His pack was heavy and the straps painful as he lifted it on. He leaned over with the pack on and picked up the leather rod-case and started out from the pine trees across the sweet fern swale, toward the river. He knew it could not be more than a mile.

He came down a hillside covered with stumps into a meadow. At the edge of the meadow flowed the river. Nick was glad to get to the river. He walked upstream through the meadow. His trousers were soaked with the dew as he walked. After the hot day, the dew had come quickly and heavily. The river made no sound. It was too fast and smooth. At the edge of the meadow, before he mounted to a piece of high ground to make camp, Nick looked down the river at the trout rising. They were rising to insects come from the swamp on the other side of the stream when the sun went down. The trout jumped out of water to take them. While Nick walked through the little stretch of meadow alongside the stream, trout had jumped high out of water. Now as he looked down the river, the insects must be settling on the surface, for the trout were feeding steadily all down the stream. As far down the long stretch as he could see, the trout were rising, making circles all down the surface of the water, as though it were starting to rain.

The ground rose, wooded and sandy, to overlook the meadow, the stretch of river and the swamp. Nick dropped his pack and rod-case and looked for a level piece of ground. He was very hungry and he wanted to make his camp before he cooked. Between two jack pines, the ground was quite level. He took the ax out of the pack and chopped out two projecting roots. That leveled a piece of ground large enough to sleep on. He smoothed out the sandy soil with his hand and pulled all the sweet fern bushes by their roots. His hands smelled good from the sweet fern. He smoothed the uprooted earth. He did not want anything making lumps under the blankets. When he had the ground smooth, he spread his three blankets. One he folded double, next to the ground. The other two he spread on top.

With the ax he slit off a bright slab of pine from one of the stumps and split it into pegs for the tent. He wanted them long and solid to hold in the ground. With the tent unpacked and spread on the ground, the pack, leaning against a jack pine, looked much smaller. Nick tied the rope that served the tent for a ridge-pole to the trunk of one of the pine trees and pulled the tent up off the ground with the other end of the rope and tied it to the other pine. The tent hung on the rope like a canvas blanket on a clothesline. Nick poked a pole he had cut up under the back peak of the canvas and then made it a tent by pegging out the sides. He pegged the sides out taut and drove the pegs deep, hitting them down into the ground with the flat of the ax until the rope loops were buried and the canvas was drum tight.

Across the open mouth of the tent Nick fixed cheesecloth to keep out mosquitoes. He crawled inside under the mosquito bar with various things from his pack to put at the head of the bed under the slant of the canvas. Inside the tent the light came through the brown canvas. It smelled pleasantly of canvas. Already there was something mysterious and homelike. Nick was happy as he crawled inside the tent. He had not been unhappy all day. This was different though. Now things were done. There had been this to do. Now it was done. It had been a hard trip. He was very tired. That was done. He had made his camp. He was settled. Nothing could touch him. It was a good place to camp. He was there, in the good place. He was in his home where he had made it. Now he was hungry.

He came out, crawling under the cheesecloth. It was quite dark outside. It was lighter in the tent.

Nick went over to the pack and found, with his fingers, a long nail in a paper sack of nails, in the bottom of the pack. He drove it into the pine tree, holding it close and hitting it gently with the flat of the ax. He hung the pack up on the nail. All his supplies were in the pack. They were off the ground and sheltered now.

Nick was hungry. He did not believe he had ever been hungrier. He opened and emptied a can of pork and beans and a can of spaghetti into the frying pan.

'I've got a right to eat this kind of stuff, if I'm willing to carry it,' Nick said. His voice sounded strange in the darkening woods. He did not speak again.

He started a fire with some chunks of pine he got with the ax from a stump. Over the fire he stuck a wire grill, pushing the four legs down into the ground with his boot. Nick put the frying pan on the grill over the flames. He was hungrier. The beans and spaghetti warmed. Nick stirred them and mixed them together. They began to bubble, making little bubbles that rose with difficulty to the surface. There was a good smell. Nick got out a bottle of tomato catchup and cut four slices of bread. The little bubbles were coming faster now. Nick sat down beside the fire and lifted the frying pan off. He poured about half the contents out into the tin plate. It spread slowly on the plate. Nick knew it was too hot. He poured on some tomato catchup. He knew the beans and spaghetti were still too hot. He looked at the fire, then at the tent, he was not going to spoil it all by burning his tongue. For years he had never enjoyed fried bananas because he had never been able to wait for them to cool. His tongue was very sensitive. He was very hungry. Across the river in the swamp, in the almost dark, he saw a mist rising. He looked at the tent once more. All right. He took a full spoonful from the plate.

'Chrise,' Nick said, 'Geezus Chrise,' he said happily.

He ate the whole plateful before he remembered the bread. Nick finished the second plateful with the bread, mopping the plate shiny. He had not eaten since a cup of coffee and a ham sandwich in the station restaurant at St Ignace. It had been a very fine experience. He had been that hungry before, but had not been able to satisfy it. He could have made camp hours before if he had wanted to. There were plenty of good places to camp on the river. But this was good.

Nick tucked two big chips of pine under the grill. The fire flared up. He had forgotten to get water for the coffee. Out of the pack he got a folding canvas bucket and walked down the hill, across the edge of the meadow, to the stream. The other bank was in the white mist. The grass was wet and cold as he knelt on the bank and dipped the canvas bucket into the stream. It bellied and pulled hard in the current. The water was ice cold. Nick rinsed the bucket and carried it full up to the camp. Up away from the stream it was not so cold.

Nick drove another big nail and hung up the bucket full of water. He dipped the coffee pot half full, put some more chips under the grill onto the fire and put the pot on. He could not remember which way he made coffee. He could remember an argument about it with Hopkins, but not which side he had taken. He decided to bring it to a boil. He remembered now that was Hopkins's way. He had once argued about everything with Hopkins. While he waited for the coffee to boil, he opened a small can of apricots. He liked to open cans. He emptied the can of apricots out into a tin cup. While he watched the coffee on the fire, he drank the juice syrup of the apricots, carefully at first to keep from spilling, then meditatively, sucking the apricots down. They were better than fresh apricots.

The coffee boiled as he watched. The lid came up and coffee and grounds ran down the side of the pot. Nick took it off the grill. It was a triumph for Hopkins. He put sugar in the empty apricot cup and poured some of the coffee out to cool. It was too hot to pour and he used his hat to hold the handle of the coffee pot. He would not let it steep in the pot at all. Not the first cup. It should be straight Hopkins all the way. Hop deserved that. He was a very serious coffee drinker. He was the most serious man Nick had ever known. Not heavy, serious. That was a long time ago. Hopkins spoke without moving his lips. He had played polo. He made millions of dollars in Texas. He had borrowed carfare to go to Chicago, when the wire came that his first big well had come in. He could have wired for money. That would have been too slow. They called Hop's girl the Blonde Venus. Hop did not mind because she was not his real girl. Hopkins said very confidently that none of them would make fun of his real girl. He was right. Hopkins went away when the telegram came. That was on the Black River. It took eight days for the telegram to reach him. Hopkins gave away his .22 caliber Colt automatic pistol to Nick. He gave his camera to Bill. It was to remember him always by. They were all going fishing again next summer. The Hop Head was rich. He would get a yacht and they would all cruise along the north shore of Lake Superior. He was excited but serious. They said good-bye and all felt bad. It broke up the trip. They never saw Hopkins again. That was a long time ago on the Black River.

Nick drank the coffee, the coffee according to Hopkins. The coffee was bitter. Nick laughed. It made a good ending to the story. His mind was starting to work. He knew he could choke it because he was tired enough. He spilled the coffee out of the pot and shook the grounds loose into the fire. He lit a cigarette and went inside the tent. He took off his shoes and trousers, sitting on the blankets, rolled the shoes up inside the trousers for a pillow and got in between the blankets.

Out through the front of the tent he watched the glow of the fire, when the night wind blew on it. It was a quiet night. The swamp was perfectly quiet. Nick stretched under the blanket comfortably. A mosquito hummed close to his ear. Nick sat up and lit a match. The mosquito was on the canvas, over his head. Nick moved the match quickly up to it. The mosquito made a satisfactory hiss in the flame. The match went out. Nick lay down again under the blanket. He turned on his side and shut his eyes. He was sleepy. He felt sleep coming. He curled up under the blanket and went to sleep.

PART II

In the morning the sun was up and the tent was starting to get hot. Nick crawled out under the mosquito netting stretched across the mouth of the tent, to look at the morning. The grass was wet on his hands as he came out. The sun was just up over the hill. There was the meadow, the river and the swamp. There were birch trees in the green of the swamp on the other side of the river.

The river was clear and smoothly fast in the early morning. Down about two hundred yards were three logs all the way across the stream. They made the water smooth and deep above them. As Nick watched, a mink crossed the river on the logs and went into the swamp. Nick was excited. He was excited by the early morning and the river. He was really too hurried to eat breakfast, but he knew he must. He built a little fire and put on the coffee pot.

While the water was heating in the pot he took an empty bottle and went down over the edge of the high ground to the meadow. The meadow was wet with dew and Nick wanted to catch grasshoppers for bait before the sun dried the grass. He found plenty of good grasshoppers. They were at the base of the grass stems. Sometimes they clung to a grass stem. They were cold and wet with the dew, and could not jump until the sun warmed them. Nick picked them up, taking only the medium-sized brown ones, and put them into the bottle. He turned over a log and just under the shelter of the edge were several hundred hoppers. It was a grasshopper lodging house. Nick put about fifty of the medium browns into the bottle. While he was picking up the hoppers the others warmed in the sun and commenced to hop away. They flew when they hopped. At first they made one flight and stayed stiff when they landed, as though they were dead.

Nick knew that by the time he was through with breakfast they would be as lively as ever. Without dew in the grass it would take him all day to catch a bottle full of good grasshoppers and he would have to crush many of them, slamming at them with his hat. He washed his hands at the stream. He was excited to be near it. Then he walked up to the tent. The hoppers were already jumping stiffly in the grass. In the bottle, warmed by the sun, they were jumping in a mass. Nick put in a pine stick as a cork. It plugged the mouth of the bottle enough, so the hoppers could not get out and left plenty of air passage.

He had rolled the log back and knew he could get grasshoppers there every morning.

Nick laid the bottle full of jumping grasshoppers against a pine trunk. Rapidly he mixed some buckwheat flour with water and stirred it smooth, one cup of flour, one cup of water. He put a handful of coffee in the pot and dipped a lump of grease out of a can and slid it sputtering across the hot skillet. On the smoking skillet he poured smoothly the buckwheat batter. It spread like lava, the grease spitting sharply. Around the edges the buckwheat cake began to firm, then brown, then crisp. The surface was bubbling slowly to porousness. Nick pushed under the browned under surface with a fresh pine chip. He shook the skillet sideways and the cake was loose on the surface. I won't try and flop it, he thought. He slid the chip of clean wood all the way under the cake, and flopped it over onto its face. It sputtered in the pan.

When it was cooked Nick regreased the skillet. He used all the batter. It made another big flapjack and one smaller one.

Nick ate a big flapjack and a smaller one, covered with apple butter. He put apple butter on the third cake, folded it over twice, wrapped it in oiled paper and put it in his shirt pocket. He put the apple butter jar back in the pack and cut bread for two sandwiches.

In the pack he found a big onion. He sliced it in two and peeled the silky outer skin. Then he cut one half into slices and made onion sandwiches. He wrapped them in oiled paper and buttoned them in the other pocket of his khaki shirt. He turned the skillet upside down on the grill, drank the coffee, sweetened and yellow brown with the condensed milk in it, and tidied up the camp. It was a good camp.

Nick took his fly rod out of the leather rod-case, jointed it, and shoved the rod-case back into the tent. He put on the reel and threaded the line through the guides. He had to hold it from hand to hand, as he threaded it, or it would slip back through its own weight. It was a heavy, double tapered fly line. Nick had paid eight dollars for it a long time ago. It was made heavy to lift back in the air and come forward flat and heavy and straight to make it possible to cast a fly which has no weight. Nick opened the aluminium leader box. The leaders were coiled between the damp flannel pads. Nick had wet the pads at the water cooler on the train up to St Ignace. In the damp pads the gut leaders had softened and Nick unrolled one and tied it by a loop at the end to the heavy fly line. He fastened a hook on the end of the leader. It was a small hook; very thin and springy.

Nick took it from his hook book, sitting with the rod across his lap. He tested the knot and the spring of the rod by pulling the line taut. It was a good feeling. He was careful not to let the hook bite into his finger.

He started down to the stream, holding his rod, the bottle of grasshoppers hung from his neck by a thong tied in half hitches around the neck of the bottle. His landing net hung by a hook from his belt. Over his shoulder was a long flour sack tied at each corner into an ear. The cord went over his shoulder. The sack flapped against his legs.

Nick felt awkward and professionally happy with all his equipment hanging from him. The grasshopper bottle swung against his chest. In his shirt the breast pockets bulged against him with the lunch and his fly book.

He stepped into the stream. It was a shock. His trousers clung tight to his legs. His shoes felt the gravel. The water was a rising cold shock.

Rushing, the current sucked against his legs. Where he stepped in, the water was over his knees. He waded with the current. The gravel slid under his shoes. He looked down at the swirl of water below each leg and tipped up the bottle to get a grasshopper.

The first grasshopper gave a jump in the neck of the bottle and went out into the water. He was sucked under in the whirl by Nick's right leg and came to the surface a little way down stream. He floated rapidly, kicking. In a quick circle, breaking the smooth surface of the water, he disappeared. A trout had taken him.

Another hopper poked his face out of the bottle. His antennæ wavered. He was getting his front legs out of the bottle to jump. Nick took him by the head and held him while he threaded the slim hook under his chin, down through his thorax and into the last segments of his abdomen. The grasshopper took hold of the hook with his front feet, spitting tobacco juice on it. Nick dropped him into the water.

Holding the rod in his right hand he let out line against the pull of the grasshopper in the current. He stripped off line from the reel with his left hand and let it run free. He could see the hopper in the little waves of the current. It went out of sight.

There was a tug on the line. Nick pulled against the taut line. It was his first strike. Holding the now living rod across the current, he brought in the line with his left hand. The rod bent in jerks, the trout pumping against the current. Nick knew it was a small one. He lifted the rod straight up in the air. It bowed with the pull.

He saw the trout in the water jerking with his head and body against the shifting tangent of the line in the stream.

Nick took the line in his left hand and pulled the trout, thumping tiredly against the current, to the surface. His back was mottled the clear, water-over-gravel color, his side flashing in the sun. The rod under his right arm, Nick stooped, dipping his right hand into the current. He held the trout, never still, with his moist right hand, while he unhooked the barb from his mouth, then dropped him back into the stream.

He hung unsteadily in the current, then settled to the bottom beside a stone. Nick reached down his hand to touch him, his arm to the elbow under water. The trout was steady in the moving stream, resting on the gravel, beside a stone. As Nick's fingers touched him, touched his smooth, cool, underwater feeling he was gone, gone in a shadow across the bottom of the stream.

He's all right, Nick thought. He was only tired.

He had wet his hand before he touched the trout, so he would not disturb the delicate mucus that covered him. If a trout was touched with a dry hand, a white fungus attacked the unprotected spot. Years before when he had fished crowded streams, with fly fishermen ahead of him and behind him, Nick had again and again come on dead trout, furry with white fungus, drifted against a rock, or floating belly up in some pool. Nick did not like to fish with other men on the river. Unless they were of your party, they spoiled it.

He wallowed down the stream, above his knees in the current, through the fifty yards of shallow water above the pile of logs that crossed the stream. He did not rebait his hook and held it in his hand as he waded. He was certain he could catch small trout in the shallows, but he did not want them. There would be no big trout in the shallows this time of day.

Now the water deepened up his thighs sharply and coldly. Ahead was the smooth dammed-back flood of water above the logs. The water was smooth and dark; on the left, the lower edge of the meadow; on the right the swamp.

Nick leaned back against the current and took a hopper from the bottle. He threaded the hopper on the hook and spat on him for good luck. Then he pulled several yards of line from the reel and tossed the hopper out ahead onto the fast, dark water. It floated down towards the logs, then the weight of the line pulled the bait under the surface. Nick held the rod in his right hand, letting the line run out through his fingers.

There was a long tug. Nick struck and the rod came alive and dangerous, bent double, the line tightening, coming out of water, tightening, all in a heavy, dangerous, steady pull. Nick felt the moment when the leader would break if the strain increased and let the line go.

The reel ratcheted into a mechanical shriek as the line went out in a rush. Too fast. Nick could not check it, the line rushing out, the reel note rising as the line ran out.

With the core of the reel showing, his heart feeling stopped with the excitement, leaning back against the current that mounted icily his thighs, Nick thumbed the reel hard with his left hand. It was awkward getting his thumb inside the fly reel frame.

As he put on pressure the line tightened into sudden hardness and beyond the logs a huge trout went high out of water. As he jumped, Nick lowered the tip of the rod. But he felt, as he dropped the tip to ease the strain, the moment when the strain was too great; the hardness too tight. Of course, the leader had broken. There was no mistaking the feeling when all spring left the line and it became dry and hard. Then it went slack.

His mouth dry, his heart down, Nick reeled in. He had never seen so big a trout. There was a heaviness, a power not to be held, and then the bulk of him, as he jumped. He looked as broad as a salmon.

Nick's hand was shaky. He reeled in slowly. The thrill had been too much. He felt, vaguely, a little sick, as though it would be better to sit down.

The leader had broken where the hook was tied to it. Nick took it in his hand. He thought of the trout somewhere on the bottom, holding himself steady over the gravel, far down below the light, under the logs, with the hook in his jaw. Nick knew the trout's teeth would cut through the snell of the hook. The hook would imbed itself in his jaw. He'd bet the trout was angry. Anything that size would be angry. That was a trout. He had been solidly hooked. Solid as a rock. He felt like a rock, too, before he started off. By God, he was a big one. By God, he was the biggest one I ever heard of.

Nick climbed out onto the meadow and stood, water running down his trousers and out of his shoes, his shoes squelchy. He went over and sat on the logs. He did not want to rush his sensations any.

He wriggled his toes in the water, in his shoes, and got out a cigarette from his breast pocket. He lit it and tossed the match into the fast water below the logs. A tiny trout rose at the match, as it swung around in the fast current. Nick laughed. He would finish the cigarette.

He sat on the logs, smoking, drying in the sun, the sun warm on his back, the river shallow ahead entering the woods, curving into the woods, shallows, light glittering, big water-smooth rocks, cedars along the bank and white birches, the logs warm in the sun, smooth to sit on, without bark, gray to the touch; slowly the feeling of disappointment left him. It went away slowly, the feeling of disappointment that came sharply after the thrill that made his shoulders ache. It was all right now. His rod lying out on the logs, Nick tied a new hook on the leader, pulling the gut tight until it grimped into itself in a hard knot.

He baited up, then picked up the rod and walked to the far end of the logs to get into the water, where it was not too deep. Under and beyond the logs was a deep pool. Nick walked around the shallow shelf near the swamp shore until he came out on the shallow bed of the stream.

On the left, where the meadow ended and the woods began, a great elm tree was uprooted. Gone over in a storm, it lay back into the woods, its roots clotted with dirt, grass growing in them, rising a solid bank beside the stream. The river cut to the edge of the uprooted tree. From where Nick stood he could see deep channels, like ruts, cut in the shallow bed of the stream by the flow of the current. Pebbly where he stood and pebbly and full of boulders beyond; where it curved near the tree roots, the bed of the stream was marly and between the ruts of deep water green weed fronds swung in the current.

Nick swung the rod back over his shoulder and forward, and the line, curving forward, laid the grasshopper down on one of the deep channels in the weeds. A trout struck and Nick hooked him.

Holding the rod far out toward the uprooted tree and sloshing backward in the current, Nick worked the trout, plunging, the rod bending alive, out of the danger of the weeds into the open river. Holding the rod, pumping alive against the current, Nick brought the trout in. He rushed, but always came, the spring of the rod yielding to the rushes, sometimes jerking under water, but always bringing him in. Nick eased downstream with the rushes. The rod above his head he led the trout over the net, then lifted.

The trout hung heavy in the net, mottled trout back and silver sides in the meshes. Nick unhooked him; heavy sides, good to hold, big undershot jaw, and slipped him, heaving and big sliding, into the long sack that hung from his shoulders in the water.

Nick spread the mouth of the sack against the current and it filled, heavy with water. He held it up, the bottom in the stream, and the water poured out through the sides. Inside at the bottom was the big trout, alive in the water.

Nick moved downstream. The sack out ahead of him sunk heavy in the water, pulling from his shoulders.

It was getting hot, the sun hot on the back of his neck.

Nick had one good trout. He did not care about getting many trout. Now the stream was shallow and wide. There were trees along both banks. The trees of the left bank made short shadows on the current in the forenoon sun. Nick knew there were trout in each shadow. In the afternoon, after the sun had crossed toward the hills, the trout would be in the cool shadows on the other side of the stream.

The very biggest ones would lie up close to the bank. You could always pick them up there on the Black. When the sun was down they all moved out into the current. Just when the sun made the water blinding in the glare before it went down, you were liable to strike a big trout anywhere in the current. It was almost impossible to fish then, the surface of the water was blinding as a mirror in the sun. Of course, you could fish upstream, but in a stream like the Black, or this, you had to wallow against the current and in a deep place, the water piled up on you. It was no fun to fish upstream with this much current.

Nick moved along through the shallow stretch watching the banks for deep holes. A beech tree grew close beside the river, so that the branches hung down into the water. The stream went back in under the leaves. There were always trout in a place like that.

Nick did not care about fishing that hole. He was sure he would get hooked in the branches.

It looked deep though. He dropped the grasshopper so the current took it under water, back in under the overhanging branch. The line pulled hard and Nick struck. The trout threshed heavily, half out of water in the leaves and branches. The line was caught. Nick pulled hard and the trout was off. He reeled in and holding the hook in his hand, walked down the stream.

Ahead, close to the left bank, was a big log. Nick saw it was hollow; pointing up river the current entered it smoothly, only a little ripple spread each side of the log. The water was deepening. The top of the hollow log was gray and dry. It was partly in the shadow.

Nick took the cork out of the grasshopper bottle and a hopper clung to it. He picked him off, hooked him and tossed him out. He held the rod far out so that the hopper on the water moved into the current flowing into the hollow log. Nick lowered the rod and the hopper floated in. There was a heavy strike. Nick swung the rod against the pull. It felt as though he were hooked into the log itself, except for the live feeling.

He tried to force the fish out into the current. It came, heavily.

The line went slack and Nick thought the trout was gone. Then he saw him, very near, in the current, shaking his head, trying to get the hook out. His mouth was clamped shut. He was fighting the hook in the clear flowing current.

Looping in the line with his left hand, Nick swung the rod to make the line taut and tried to lead the trout toward the net, but he was gone, out of sight, the line pumping. Nick fought him against the current, letting him thump in the water against the spring of the rod. He shifted the rod to his left hand, worked the trout upstream, holding his weight, fighting on the rod, and then let him down into the net. He lifted him clear of the water, a heavy half circle in the net, the net dripping, unhooked him and slid him into the sack.

He spread the mouth of the sack and looked down in at the two big trout alive in the water.

Through the deepening water, Nick waded over to the hollow log. He took the sack off, over his head, the trout flopping as it came out of water, and hung it so the trout were deep in the water. Then he pulled himself up on the log and sat, the water from his trousers and boots running down into the stream. He laid his rod down, moved along to the shady end of the log and took the sandwiches out of his pocket. He dipped the sandwiches in the cold water. The current carried away the crumbs. He ate the sandwiches and dipped his hat full of water to drink, the water running out through his hat just ahead of his drinking.

It was cool in the shade, sitting on the log. He took a cigarette out and struck a match to light it. The match sunk into the gray wood, making a tiny furrow. Nick leaned over the side of the log, found a hard place and lit the match. He sat smoking and watching the river.

Ahead the river narrowed and went into a swamp. The river became smooth and deep and the swamp looked solid with cedar trees, their trunks close together, their branches solid. It would not be possible to walk through a swamp like that. The branches grew so low. You would have to keep almost level with the ground to move at all. You could not crash through the branches. That must be why the animals that lived in swamps were built the way they were, Nick thought.

He wished he had brought something to read. He felt like reading. He did not feel like going on into the swamp. He looked down the river. A big cedar slanted all the way across the stream. Beyond that the river went into the swamp.

Nick did not want to go in there now. He felt a reaction against deep wading with the water deepening up under his armpits, to hook big trout in places impossible to land them. In the swamp the banks were bare, the big cedars came together overhead, the sun did not come through, except in patches; in the fast deep water, in the half light, the fishing would be tragic. In the swamp fishing was a tragic adventure. Nick did not want it. He did not want to go down the stream any further today.

He took out his knife, opened it and stuck it in the log. Then he pulled up the sack, reached into it and brought out one of the trout. Holding him near the tail, hard to hold, alive, in his hand, he whacked him against the log. The trout quivered, rigid. Nick laid him on the log in the shade and broke the neck of the other fish the same way. He laid them side by side on the log. They were fine trout.

Nick cleaned them, slitting them from the vent to the tip of the jaw. All the insides and the gills and tongue came out in one piece. They were both males; long gray-white strips of milt, smooth and clean. All the insides clean and compact, coming out all together. Nick tossed the offal ashore for the minks to find.

He washed the trout in the stream. When he held them back up in the water they looked like live fish. Their color was not gone yet. He washed his hands and dried them on the log. Then he laid the trout on the sack spread out on the log, rolled them up in it, tied the bundle and put it in the landing net. His knife was still standing, blade stuck in the log. He cleaned it on the wood and put it in his pocket.

Nick stood up on the log, holding his rod, the landing net hanging heavy, then stepped into the water and splashed ashore. He climbed the bank and cut up into the woods, toward the high ground. He was going back to camp. He looked back. The river just showed through the trees. There were plenty of days coming when he could fish the swamp.

JOHN
STEINBECK
1902-1968

John Steinbeck stands amongst the great writers of the short story. He is probably best remembered for *The Grapes of Wrath* (1939) for which he was awarded the Pulitzer Prize. Steinbeck was born in California and began his writing career at the age of twenty-seven in 1929. One topic which concerned him greatly was the life of the rural working class. He examines this in many of his stories including *The Pastures of Heaven* (1932), *To a God Unknown* (1933), *Tortilla Flat* (1935) and *Of Mice and Men* (1937). He also wrote volumes of non-fiction works and was awarded the Nobel Prize in 1962.

The story which follows is reprinted from *The Long Valley* (1938) and is concerned with the archetypal times of Steinbeck's greatness – life-and-death struggles, fierce loyalty and the pioneering spirit – and confirms him as himself a major pioneering figure in the modern development of the great American short story.

Flight

ABOUT FIFTEEN MILES BELOW Monterey, on the wild coast, the Torres family had their farm, a few sloping acres above a cliff that dropped to the brown reefs and to the hissing white waters of the ocean. Behind the farm the stone mountains stood up against the sky. The farm buildings huddled like little clinging aphids on the mountain skirts, crouched low to the ground as though the wind might blow them into the sea. The little shack, the rattling, rotting barn were gray-bitten with sea salt, beaten by the damp wind until they had taken on the color of the granite hills. Two horses, a red cow and a red calf, half a dozen pigs and a flock of lean, multicolored chickens stocked the place. A little corn was raised on the sterile slope, and it grew short and thick under the wind, and all the cobs formed on the landward sides of the stalks.

Mama Torres, a lean, dry woman with ancient eyes, had ruled the farm for ten years, ever since her husband tripped over a stone in the field one day and fell full length on a rattlesnake. When one is bitten on the chest there is not much that can be done.

Mama Torres had three children, two undersized black ones of twelve and fourteen, Emilio and Rosy, whom Mama kept fishing on the rocks below the farm when the sea was kind and when the truant officer was in some distant part of Monterey County. And there was Pepé, the tall smiling son of nineteen, a gentle, affectionate boy, and very lazy. Pepé had a tall head, pointed at the top, and from its peak, coarse black hair grew down like a thatch all around. Over his smiling little eyes Mama cut a straight bang so he could see. Pepé had sharp Indian cheek bones and an eagle nose, but his mouth was as sweet and shapely as a girl's mouth, and his chin was fragile and chiseled. He was loose and gangling, all legs and feet and wrists, and he was very lazy. Mama thought him fine and brave, but she never told him so. She said, 'Some lazy cow must have got into thy father's family, else how could I have a son like thee.' And she said, 'When I carried thee, a sneaking lazy coyote came out of the brush and looked at me one day. That must have made thee so.'

Pepé smiled sheepishly and stabbed at the ground with his knife to keep the blade sharp and free from rust. It was his inheritance, that knife, his father's knife. The long heavy blade folded back into the black handle. There was a button on the handle. When Pepé pressed the button, the blade leaped out ready for use. The knife was with Pepé always, for it had been his father's knife.

One sunny morning when the sea below the cliff was glinting and blue and the white surf creamed on the reef, when even the stone mountains looked kindly, Mama Torres called out the door of the shack, 'Pepé, I have a labor for thee.'

There was no answer. Mama listened. From behind the barn she heard a burst of laughter. She lifted her full long skirt and walked in the direction of the noise.

Pepé was sitting on the ground with his back against a box. His white teeth glistened. On either side of him stood the two black ones, tense and expectant. Fifteen feet away a redwood post was set in the ground. Pepé's right hand lay limply in his lap, and in the palm the big black knife rested. The blade·was closed back into the handle. Pepé looked smiling at the sky.

Suddenly Emilio cried, 'Ya!'

Pepé's wrist flicked like the head of a snake. The blade seemed to fly open in mid-air, and with a thump the point dug into the redwood post, and the black handle quivered. The three burst into excited laughter. Rosy ran to the post and pulled out the knife and brought it back to Pepé. He closed the blade and settled the knife carefully in his listless palm again. He grinned self-consciously at the sky.

'Ya!'

The heavy knife lanced out and sunk into the post again. Mama moved forward like a ship and scattered the play.

'All day you do foolish things with the knife, like a toy-baby,' she stormed. 'Get up on thy huge feet that eat up shoes. Get up!' She took him by one loose shoulder and hoisted at him. Pepé grinned sheepishly and came half-heartedly to his feet. 'Look!' Mama cried. 'Big lazy, you must catch the horse and put on him thy father's saddle. You must ride to Monterey. The medicine bottle is empty. There is no salt. Go thou now, Peanut! Catch the horse.'

A revolution took place in the relaxed figure of Pepé. 'To Monterey, me? Alone? *Sí*, Mama.'

She scowled at him. 'Do not think, big sheep, that you will buy candy. No, I will give you only enough for the medicine and the salt.'

Pepé smiled. 'Mama, you will put the hatband on the hat?'

She relented then. 'Yes, Pepé. You may wear the hatband.'

His voice grew insinuating, 'And the green handkerchief, Mama?'

'Yes, if you go quickly and return with no trouble, the silk green handkerchief will go. If you make sure to take off the handkerchief when you eat so no spot may fall on it...'

'*Sí*, Mama. I will be careful. I am a man.'

'Thou? A man? Thou art a peanut.'

He went into the rickety barn and brought out a rope, and he walked agilely enough up the hill to catch the horse.

When he was ready and mounted before the door, mounted on his father's saddle that was so old that the oaken frame showed through torn leather in many places, then Mama brought out the round black hat with the tooled leather band, and she reached up and knotted the green silk handkerchief about his neck. Pepé's blue denim coat was much darker than his jeans, for it had been washed much less often.

Mama handed up the big medicine bottle and the silver coins. 'That for the medicine,' she said, 'and that for the salt. That for a candle to burn for the papa. That for *dulces* for the little ones. Our friend Mrs Rodriguez will give you dinner and maybe a bed for the night. When you go to the church say only ten Paternosters and only twenty-five Ave Marias. Oh! I know, big coyote. You would sit there flapping your mouth over Aves all day while you looked at the candles and the holy pictures. That is not good devotion to stare at the pretty things.'

The black hat, covering the high pointed head and black thatched hair of Pepé, gave him dignity and age. He sat the rangy horse well. Mama thought how handsome he was, dark and lean and tall. 'I would not send thee now alone, thou little one, except for the medicine,' she said softly. 'It is not good to have no medicine, for who knows when the toothache will come, or the sadness of the stomach. These things are.'

'Adios, Mama,' Pepé cried. 'I will come back soon. You may send me often alone. I am a man.'

'Thou art a foolish chicken.'

He straightened his shoulders, flipped the reins against the horse's shoulder and rode away. He turned once and saw that they still watched him, Emilio and Rosy and Mama. Pepé grinned with pride and gladness and lifted the tough buckskin horse to a trot.

When he had dropped out of sight over a little dip in the road, Mama turned to the black ones, but she spoke to herself. 'He is nearly a man now,' she said. 'It will be a nice thing to have a man in the house again.' Her eyes sharpened on the children. 'Go to the rocks now. The tide is going out. There will be abalones to be found.' She put the iron hooks into their hands and saw them down the steep trail to the reefs. She brought the smooth stone *metate* to the doorway and sat grinding her corn to flour and looked occasionally at the road over which Pepé had gone. The noonday came and then the afternoon, when the little ones beat the abalones on a rock to make them tender and Mama patted the tortillas to make them thin. They ate their dinner as the red sun was plunging down toward the ocean. They sat on the doorsteps and watched the big white moon come over the mountain tops.

Mama said, 'He is now at the house of our friend Mrs Rodriguez. She will give him nice things to eat and maybe a present.'

Emilio said, 'Some day I too will ride to Monterey for medicine. Did Pepé come to be a man today?'

Mama said wisely, 'A boy gets to be a man when a man is needed. Remember this thing. I have known boys forty years old because there was no need for a man.'

Soon afterwards they retired, Mama in her big oak bed on one side of the room, Emilio and Rosy in their boxes full of straw and sheepskins on the other side of the room.

The moon went over the sky and the surf roared on the rocks. The roosters crowed the first call. The surf subsided to a whispering surge against the reef. The moon dropped toward the sea. The roosters crowed again.

The moon was near down to the water when Pepé rode on a winded horse to his home flat. His dog bounded out and circled the horse yelping with pleasure. Pepé slid off the saddle to the ground. The weathered little shack was silver in the moonlight and the square shadow of it was black to the north and east. Against the east the piling mountains were misty with light; their tops melted into the sky.

Pepé walked wearily up the three steps and into the house. It was dark inside. There was a rustle in the corner.

Mama cried out from her bed. 'Who comes? Pepé, is it thou?'

'*Sí*, Mama.'

'Did you get the medicine?'

'*Sí*, Mama.'

'Well, go to sleep, then. I thought you would be sleeping at the house of Mrs Rodriguez.' Pepé stood silently in the dark room. 'Why do you stand there, Pepé? Did you drink wine?'

'*Sí*, Mama.'

'Well, go to bed then and sleep out the wine.'

His voice was tired and patient, but very firm. 'Light the candle, Mama. I must go away into the mountains.'

'What is this, Pepé? You are crazy.' Mama struck a sulphur match and held the little blue burr until the flame spread up the stick. She set light to the candle on the floor beside her bed. 'Now, Pepé, what is this you say?' She looked anxiously into his face.

He was changed. The fragile quality seemed to have gone from his chin. His mouth was less full than it had been, the lines of the lips were straighter, but in his eyes the greatest change had taken place. There was no laughter in them any more, nor any bashfulness. They were sharp and bright and purposeful.

He told her in a tired monotone, told her everything just as it had happened. A few people came into the kitchen of Mrs Rodriguez. There was wine to drink. Pepé drank wine. The little quarrel – the man started toward Pepé and then the knife – it went almost by itself. It flew, it darted before Pepé knew it. As he talked, Mama's face grew stern, and it seemed to grow more lean. Pepé finished. 'I am a man now, Mama. The man said names to me I could not allow.'

Mama nodded. 'Yes, thou art a man, my poor little Pepé. Thou art a man. I have seen it coming on thee. I have watched you throwing the knife into the post, and I have been afraid.' For a moment her face had softened, but now it grew stern again. 'Come! We must get you ready. Go. Awaken Emilio and Rosy. Go quickly.'

Pepé stepped over to the corner where his brother and sister slept among the sheepskins. He leaned down and shook them gently. 'Come, Rosy! Come, Emilio! The mama says you must arise.'

The little black ones sat up and rubbed their eyes in the candlelight. Mama was out of bed now, her long black skirt over her nightgown. 'Emilio,' she cried. 'Go up and catch the other horse for Pepé. Quickly, now! Quickly.' Emilio put his legs in his overalls and stumbled sleepily out the door.

'You heard no one behind you on the road?' Mama demanded.

'No, Mama. I listened carefully. No one was on the road.'

Mama darted like a bird about the room. From a nail on the wall she took a canvas water bag and threw it on the floor. She stripped a blanket from her bed and rolled it into a tight tube and tied the ends with a string. From a box beside the stove she lifted a flour sack half full of black stringy jerky. 'Your father's black coat, Pepé. Here, put it on.'

Pepé stood in the middle of the floor watching her activity. She reached behind the door and brought out the rifle, a long 38-56, worn shiny the whole length of the barrel. Pepé took it from her and held it in the crook of his elbow. Mama brought a little leather bag and counted the cartridges into his hand. 'Only ten left,' she warned. 'You must not waste them.'

Emilio put his head in the door. ''*Qui 'st 'l caballo*, Mama.'

'Put on the saddle from the other horse. Tie on the blanket. Here, tie the jerky to the saddle horn.'

Still Pepé stood silently watching his mother's frantic activity. His chin looked hard, and his sweet mouth was drawn and thin. His little eyes followed Mama about the room almost suspiciously.

Rosy asked softly, 'Where goes Pepé?'

Mama's eyes were fierce. 'Pepé goes on a journey. Pepé is a man now. He has a man's thing to do.'

Pepé straightened his shoulders. His mouth changed until he looked very much like Mama.

At last the preparation was finished. The loaded horse stood outside the door. The water bag dripped a line of moisture down the bay shoulder.

The moonlight was being thinned by the dawn and the big white moon was near down to the sea. The family stood by the shack. Mama confronted Pepé. 'Look, my son! Do not stop until it is dark again. Do not sleep even though you are tired. Take care of the horse in order that he may not stop of weariness. Remember to be careful with the bullets – there are only ten. Do not fill thy stomach with jerky or it will make thee sick. Eat a little jerky and fill thy stomach with grass. When thou comest to the high mountains, if thou seest any of the dark watching men, go not near to them nor try to speak to them. And forget not thy prayers.' She put her lean hands on Pepé's shoulders, stood on her toes and kissed him formally on both cheeks, and Pepé kissed her on both cheeks. Then he went to Emilio and Rosy and kissed both of their cheeks.

Pepé turned back to Mama. He seemed to look for a little softness, a little weakness in her. His eyes were searching, but Mama's face remained fierce. 'Go now,' she said. 'Do not wait to be caught like a chicken.'

Pepé pulled himself into the saddle. 'I am a man,' he said.

It was the first dawn when he rode up the hill toward the little canyon which let a trail into the mountains. Moonlight and daylight fought with each other, and the two warring qualities made it difficult to see. Before Pepé had gone a hundred yards, the outlines of his figure were misty; and long before he entered the canyon, he had become a gray, indefinite shadow.

Mama stood stiffly in front of her doorstep, and on either side of her stood Emilio and Rosy. They cast furtive glances at Mama now and then.

When the gray shape of Pepé melted into the hillside and disappeared, Mama relaxed. She began the high, whining keen of the death wail. 'Our beautiful – our brave,' she cried. 'Our protector, our son is gone.' Emilio and Rosy moaned beside her. 'Our beautiful – our brave, he is gone.' It was the formal wail. It rose to a high piercing whine and subsided to a moan. Mama raised it three times and then she turned and went into the house and shut the door.

Emilio and Rosy stood wondering in the dawn. They heard Mama whimpering in the house. They went out to sit on the cliff above the ocean. They touched shoulders. 'When did Pepé come to be a man?' Emilio asked.

'Last night,' said Rosy. 'Last night in Monterey.' The ocean clouds turned red with the sun that was behind the mountains.

'We will have no breakfast,' said Emilio. 'Mama will not want to cook.' Rosy did not answer him. 'Where is Pepé gone?' he asked.

Rosy looked around at him. She drew her knowledge from the quiet air. 'He has gone on a journey. He will never come back.'

'Is he dead? Do you think he is dead?'

Rosy looked back at the ocean again. A little steamer, drawing a line of smoke sat on the edge of the horizon. 'He is not dead,' Rosy explained. 'Not yet.'

Pepé rested the big rifle across the saddle in front of him. He let the horse walk up the hill and he didn't look back. The stony slope took on a coat of short brush so that Pepé found the entrance to a trail and entered it.

When he came to the canyon opening, he swung once in his saddle and looked back, but the houses were swallowed in the misty light. Pepé jerked forward again. The high shoulder of the canyon closed in on him. His horse stretched out its neck and sighed and settled to the trail.

It was a well-worn path, dark soft leaf-mould earth strewn with broken pieces of sandstone. The trail rounded the shoulder of the canyon and dropped steeply into the bed of the stream. In the shallows the water ran smoothly, glinting in the first morning sun. Small round stones on the bottom were as brown as rust with sun moss. In the sand along the edges of the stream the tall, rich wild mint grew, while in the water itself the cress, old and tough, had gone to heavy seed.

The path went into the stream and emerged on the other side. The horse sloshed into the water and stopped. Pepé dropped his bridle and let the beast drink of the running water.

Soon the canyon sides became steep and the first giant sentinel redwoods guarded the trail, great round red trunks bearing foliage as green and lacy as ferns. Once Pepé was among the trees, the sun was lost. A perfumed and purple light lay in the pale green of the underbrush. Gooseberry bushes and blackberries and tall ferns lined the stream, and overhead the branches of the redwoods met and cut off the sky.

Pepé drank from the water bag, and he reached into the flour sack and brought out a black string of jerky. His white teeth gnawed at the string until the tough meat parted. He chewed slowly and drank occasionally from the water bag. His little eyes were slumberous and tired, but the muscles of his face were hard set. The earth of the trail was black now. It gave up a hollow sound under the walking hoofbeats.

The stream fell more sharply. Little waterfalls splashed on the stones. Five-fingered ferns hung over the water and dripped spray from their fingertips. Pepé rode half over in his saddle, dangling one leg loosely. He picked a bay leaf from a tree beside the way and put it into his mouth for a moment to flavor the dry jerky. He held the gun loosely across the pommel.

Suddenly he squared in his saddle, swung the horse from the trail and kicked it hurriedly up behind a big redwood tree. He pulled up the reins tight against the bit to keep the horse from whinnying. His face was intent and his nostrils quivered a little.

A hollow pounding came down the trail, and a horseman rode by, a fat man with red cheeks and a white stubble beard. His horse put down its head and blubbered at the trail when it came to the place where Pepé had turned off. 'Hold up!' said the man and he pulled up his horse's head.

When the last sound of the hoofs died away, Pepé came back into the trail again. He did not relax in the saddle any more. He lifted the big rifle and swung the lever to throw a shell into the chamber, and then he let down the hammer to half cock.

The trail grew very steep. Now the redwood trees were smaller and their tops were dead, bitten dead where the wind reached them. The horse plodded on; the sun went slowly overhead and started down toward the afternoon.

Where the stream came out of a side canyon, the trail left it. Pepé dismounted and watered his horse and filled up his water bag. As soon as the trail had parted from the stream, the trees were gone and only the thick brittle sage and manzanita and chaparral edged the trail. And the soft black earth was gone, too, leaving only the light tan broken rock for the trail bed. Lizards scampered away into the brush as the horse rattled over the little stones.

Pepé turned in his saddle and looked back. He was in the open now: he could be seen from a distance. As he ascended the trail the country grew more rough and terrible and dry. The way wound about the bases of great square rocks. Little gray rabbits skittered in the brush. A bird made a monotonous high creaking. Eastward the bare rock mountaintops were pale and powder-dry under the dropping sun. The horse plodded up and up the trail toward a little V in the ridge which was the pass.

Pepé looked suspiciously back every minute or so, and his eyes sought the tops of the ridges ahead. Once, on a white barren spur, he saw a black figure for a moment, but he looked quickly away, for it was one of the dark watchers. No one knew who the watchers were, nor where they lived, but it was better to ignore them and never to show interest in them. They did not bother one who stayed on the trail and minded his own business.

The air was parched and full of light dust blown by the breeze from the eroding mountains. Pepé drank sparingly from his bag and corked it tightly and hung it on the horn again. The trail moved up the dry shale hillside, avoiding rocks, dropping under clefts, climbing in and out of old water scars. When he arrived at the little pass he stopped and looked back for a long time. No dark watchers were to be seen now. The trail behind was empty. Only the high tops of the redwoods indicated where the stream flowed.

Pepé rode on through the pass. His little eyes were nearly closed with weariness, but his face was stern, relentless and manly. The high mountain wind coasted sighing through the pass and whistled on the edges of the big blocks of broken granite. In the air, a red-tailed hawk sailed over close to the ridge and screamed angrily. Pepé went slowly through the broken jagged pass and looked down on the other side.

The trail dropped quickly, staggering among broken rock. At the bottom of the slope there was a dark crease, thick with brush, and on the other side of the crease a little flat, in which a grove of oak trees grew. A scar of green grass cut across the flat. And behind the flat another mountain rose, desolate with dead rocks and starving little black bushes. Pepé drank from the bag again for the air was so dry that it encrusted his nostrils and burned his lips. He put the horse down the trail. The hooves slipped and struggled on the steep way, starting little stones that rolled off into the brush. The sun was gone behind the westward mountain now, but still it glowed brilliantly on the oaks and on the grassy flat. The rocks and the hillsides still sent up waves of the heat they had gathered from the day's sun.

Pepé looked up to the top of the next dry withered ridge. He saw a dark form against the sky, a man's figure standing on top of a rock, and he glanced away quickly not to appear curious. When a moment later he looked up again, the figure was gone.

Downward the trail was quickly covered. Sometimes the horse floundered for footing, sometimes set his feet and slid a little way. They came at last to the bottom where the dark chaparral was higher than Pepé's head. He held up his rifle on one side and his arm on the other to shield his face from the sharp brittle fingers of the brush.

Up and out of the crease he rode, and up a little cliff. The grassy flat was before him, and the round comfortable oaks. For a moment he studied the trail down which he had come, but there was no movement and no sound from it. Finally he rode over the flat, to the green streak, and at the upper end of the damp he found a little spring welling out of the earth and dropping into a dug basin before it seeped out over the flat.

Pepé filled his bag first, and then he let the thirsty horse drink out of the pool. He led the horse to the clump of oaks, and in the middle of the grove, fairly protected from sight on all sides, he took off the saddle and the bridle and laid them on the ground. The horse stretched his jaws sideways and yawned. Pepé knotted the lead rope about the horse's neck and tied him to a sapling among the oaks, where he could graze in a fairly large circle.

When the horse was gnawing hungrily at the dry grass, Pepé went to the saddle and took a black string of jerky from the sack and strolled to an oak tree on the edge of the grove, from under which he could watch the trail. He sat down in the crisp dry oak leaves and automatically felt for his big black knife to cut the jerky, but he had no knife. He leaned back on his elbow and gnawed at the tough strong meat. His face was blank, but it was a man's face.

The bright evening light washed the eastern ridge, but the valley was darkening. Doves flew down from the hills to the spring, and the quail came running out of the brush and joined them, calling clearly to one another.

Out of the corner of his eye Pepé saw a shadow grow out of the bushy crease. He turned his head slowly. A big spotted wildcat was creeping toward the spring, belly to the ground, moving like thought.

Pepé cocked his rifle and edged the muzzle slowly around. Then he looked apprehensively up the trail and dropped the hammer again. From the ground beside him he picked an oak twig and threw it toward the spring. The quail flew up with a roar and the doves whistled away. The big cat stood up: for a long moment he looked at Pepé with cold yellow eyes, and then fearlessly walked back into the gulch.

The dusk gathered quickly in the deep valley. Pepé muttered his prayers, put his head down on his arm and went instantly to sleep.

The moon came up and filled the valley with cold blue light, and the wind swept rustling down from the peaks. The owls worked up and down the slopes looking for rabbits. Down in the brush of the gulch a coyote gabbled. The oak trees whispered softly in the night breeze.

Pepé started up, listening. His horse had whinnied. The moon was just slipping behind the western ridge, leaving the valley in darkness behind it.

Pepé sat tensely gripping his rifle. From far up the trail he heard an answering whinny and the crash of shod hooves on the broken rock. He jumped to his feet, ran to his horse and led it under the trees. He threw on the saddle and cinched it tight for the steep trail, caught the unwilling head and forced the bit into the mouth. He felt the saddle to make sure the water bag and the sack of jerky were there. Then he mounted and turned up the hill.

It was velvet dark. The horse found the entrance to the trail where it left the flat, and started up, stumbling and slipping on the rocks. Pepé's hand rose up to his head. His hat was gone. He had left it under the oak tree.

The horse had struggled far up the trail when the first change of dawn came into the air, a steel grayness as light mixed thoroughly with dark. Gradually the sharp snaggled edge of the ridge stood out above them, rotten granite tortured and eaten by the winds of time. Pepé had dropped his reins on the horn, leaving direction to the horse. The brush grabbed at his legs in the dark until one knee of his jeans was ripped.

Gradually the light flowed down over the ridge. The starved brush and rocks stood out in the half light, strange and lonely in high perspective. Then there came warmth into the light. Pepé drew up and looked back, but he could see nothing in the darker valley below. The sky turned blue over the coming sun. In the waste of the mountainside, the poor dry brush grew only three feet high. Here and there, big outcroppings of unrotted granite stood up like mouldering houses. Pepé relaxed a little. He drank from his water bag and bit off a piece of jerky. A single eagle flew over, high in the light.

Without warning Pepé's horse screamed and fell on its side. He was almost down before the rifle crash echoed up from the valley. From a hole behind the struggling shoulder, a stream of bright crimson blood pumped and stopped and pumped and stopped. The hooves threshed on the ground. Pepé lay half stunned beside the horse. He looked slowly down the hill. A piece of sage clipped off beside his head and another crash echoed up from side to side of the canyon. Pepé flung himself frantically behind a bush.

He crawled up the hill on his knees and one hand. His right hand held the rifle up off the ground and pushed it ahead of him. He moved with the instinctive care of an animal. Rapidly he wormed his way toward one of the big outcroppings of granite on the hill above him. Where the brush was high he doubled up and ran, but where the cover was slight he wriggled forward on his stomach, pushing the rifle ahead of him. In the last little distance there was no cover at all. Pepé poised and then he darted across the space and flashed around the corner of the rock.

He leaned panting against the stone. When his breath came easier he moved along behind the big rock until he came to a narrow split that offered a thin section of vision down the hill. Pepé lay on his stomach and pushed the rifle barrel through the slit and waited.

The sun reddened the western ridges now. Already the buzzards were settling down toward the place where the horse lay. A small brown bird scratched in the dead sage leaves directly in front of the rifle muzzle. The coasting eagle flew back toward the rising sun.

Pepé saw a little movement in the brush far below. His grip tightened on the gun. A little brown doe stepped daintily out on the trail and crossed it and disappeared into the brush again. For a long time Pepé waited. Far below he could see the little flat and the oak trees and the slash of green.

Suddenly his eyes flashed back at the trail again. A quarter of a mile down there had been a quick movement in the chaparral. The rifle swung over. The front sight nestled in the v of the rear sight. Pepé studied for a moment and then raised the rear sight a notch. The little movement in the brush came again. The sight settled on it. Pepé squeezed the trigger. The explosion crashed down the mountain and up the other side, and came rattling back. The whole side of the slope grew still. No more movement. And then a white streak cút into the granite of the slit and a bullet whined away and a crash sounded up from below. Pepé felt a sharp pain in his right hand. A sliver of granite was sticking out from between his first and second knuckles and the point protruded from his palm. Carefully he pulled out the sliver of stone. The wound bled evenly and gently. No vein nor artery was cut.

Pepé looked into a little dusty cave in the rock and gathered a handful of spider web, and he pressed the mass into the cut, plastering the soft web into the blood. The flow stopped almost at once.

The rifle was on the ground. Pepé picked it up, levered a new shell into the chamber. And then he slid into the brush on his stomach. Far to the right he crawled, and then up the hill, moving slowly and carefully, crawling to cover and resting and then crawling again.

In the mountains the sun is high in its arc before it penetrates the gorges. The hot face looked over the hill and brought instant heat with it. The white light beat on the rocks and reflected from them and rose up quivering from the earth again, and the rocks and bushes seemed to quiver behind the air.

Pepé crawled in the general direction of the ridge peak, zig-zagging for cover. The deep cut between his knuckles began to throb. He crawled close to a rattlesnake before he saw it, and when it raised its dry head and made a soft beginning whirr, he backed up and took another way. The quick gray lizards flashed in front of him, raising a tiny line of dust. He found another mass of spider web and pressed it against his throbbing hand.

Pepé was pushing the rifle with his left hand now. Little drops of sweat ran to the ends of his coarse black hair and rolled down his cheeks. His lips and tongue were growing thick and heavy. His lips writhed to draw saliva into his mouth. His little dark eyes were uneasy and suspicious. Once when a gray lizard paused in front of him on the parched ground and turned its head sideways he crushed it flat with a stone.

When the sun slid past noon he had not gone a mile. He crawled exhaustedly a last hundred yards to a patch of high sharp manzanita, crawled desperately, and when the patch was reached he wriggled in among the tough gnarly trunks and dropped his head on his left arm. There was little shade in the meager brush, but there was cover and safety. Pepé went to sleep as he lay and the sun beat on his back. A few little birds hopped close to him and peered and hopped away. Pepé squirmed in his sleep and he raised and dropped his wounded hand again and again.

The sun went down behind the peaks and the cool evening came, and then the dark. A coyote yelled from the hillside, Pepé started awake and looked about with misty eyes. His hand was swollen and heavy; a little thread of pain ran up the inside of his arm and settled in a pocket in his armpit. He peered about and then stood up, for the mountains were black and the moon had not yet risen. Pepé stood up in the dark. The coat of his father pressed on his arm. His tongue was swollen until it nearly filled his mouth. He wriggled out of the coat and dropped it in the brush, and then he struggled up the hill, falling over rocks and tearing his way through the brush. The rifle knocked against stones as he went. Little dry avalanches of gravel and shattered stone went whispering down the hill behind him.

After a while the old moon came up and showed the jagged ridge top ahead of him. By moonlight Pepé traveled more easily. He bent forward so that his throbbing arm hung away from his body. The journey uphill was made in dashes and rests, a frantic rush up a few yards and then a rest. The wind coasted down the slope rattling the dry stems of the bushes.

The moon was at meridian when Pepé came at last to the sharp backbone of the ridge top. On the last hundred yards of the rise no soil had clung under the wearing winds. The way was on solid rock. He clambered to the top and looked down on the other side. There was a draw like the last below him, misty with moonlight, brushed with dry struggling sage and chaparral. On the other side the hill rose up sharply and at the top the jagged rotten teeth of the mountain showed against the sky. At the bottom of the cut the brush was thick and dark.

Pepé stumbled down the hill. His throat was almost closed with thirst. At first he tried to run, but immediately he fell and rolled. After that he went more carefully. The moon was just disappearing behind the mountains when he came to the bottom. He crawled into the heavy brush feeling with his fingers for water. There was no water in the bed of the stream, only damp earth. Pepé laid his gun down and scooped up a handful of mud and put it in his mouth, and then he spluttered and scraped the earth from his tongue with his finger, for the mud drew at his mouth like a poultice. He dug a hole in the stream bed with his fingers, dug a little basin to catch water; but before it was very deep his head fell forward on the damp ground and he slept.

The dawn came and the heat of the day fell on the earth, and still Pepé slept. Late in the afternoon his head jerked up. He looked slowly around. His eyes were slits of wariness. Twenty feet away in the heavy brush a big tawny mountain lion stood staring at him. Its long thick tail waved gracefully, its ears were erect with interest, not laid back dangerously. The lion squatted down on its stomach and watched him.

Pepé looked at the hole he had dug in the earth. A half inch of muddy water had collected in the bottom. He tore the sleeve from his hurt arm, with his teeth ripped out a little square, soaked it in the water and put it in his mouth. Over and over he filled the cloth and sucked it.

Still the lion sat and watched him. The evening came down but there was no movement on the hills. No birds visited the dry bottom of the cut. Pepé looked occasionally at the lion. The eyes of the yellow beast dropped as though he were about to sleep. He yawned and his long thin red tongue curled out. Suddenly his head jerked round and his nostrils quivered. His big tail lashed. He stood up and slunk like a tawny shadow into the thick brush.

A moment later Pepé heard the sound, the faint far crash of horses' hooves on gravel. And he heard something else, a high whining yelp of a dog.

Pepé took his rifle in his left hand and he glided into the brush almost as quietly as the lion had. In the darkening evening he crouched up the hill toward the next ridge. Only when dark came did he stand up. His energy was short. Once it was dark he fell over the rocks and slipped to his knees on the steep slope, but he moved on and on up the hill, climbing and scrabbling over the broken hillside.

When he was far up toward the top, he lay down and slept for a little while. The withered moon, shining on his face, awakened him. He stood up and moved up the hill. Fifty yards away he stopped and turned back, for he had forgotten his rifle. He walked heavily down and poked about in the brush, but he could not find his gun. At last he lay down to rest. The pocket of pain in his armpit had grown more sharp. His arm seemed to swell out and fall with every heartbeat. There was no position lying down where the heavy arm did not press against his armpit.

With the effort of a hurt beast, Pepé got up and moved again toward the top of the ridge. He held his swollen arm away from his body with his left hand. Up the steep hill he dragged himself, a few steps and a rest, and a few more steps. At last he was nearing the top. The moon showed the uneven sharp back of it against the sky.

Pepé's brain spun in a big spiral up and away from him. He slumped to the ground and lay still. The rock ridge top was only a hundred feet above him.

The moon moved over the sky. Pepé half turned on his back. His tongue tried to make words, but only a thick hissing came from between his lips.

When the dawn came, Pepé pulled himself up. His eyes were sane again. He drew his great puffed arm in front of him and looked at the angry wound. The black line ran up from his wrist to his armpit. Automatically he reached in his pocket for the big black knife, but it was not there. His eyes searched the ground. He picked up a sharp blade of stone and scraped at the wound, sawed at the proud flesh and then squeezed the green juice out in big drops. Instantly he threw back his head and whined like a dog. His whole right side shuddered at the pain, but the pain cleared his head.

In the gray light he struggled up the last slope to the ridge and crawled over and lay down behind a line of rocks. Below him lay a deep canyon exactly like the last, waterless and desolate. There was no flat, no oak trees, not even heavy brush in the bottom of it. And on the other side a sharp ridge stood up, thinly brushed with starving sage, littered with broken granite. Strewn over the hill there were giant outcroppings, and on the top the granite teeth stood out against the sky.

The new day was light now. The flame of the sun came over the ridge and fell on Pepé where he lay on the ground. His coarse black hair was littered with twigs and bits of spider web. His eyes had retreated back into his head. Between his lips the tip of his black tongue showed.

He sat up and dragged his great arm into his lap and nursed it, rocking his body and moaning in his throat. He threw back his head and looked up into the pale sky. A big black bird circled nearly out of sight, and far to the left another was sailing near.

He lifted his head to listen, for a familiar sound had come to him from the valley he had climbed out of; it was the crying yelp of hounds, excited and feverish, on a trail.

Pepé bowed his head quickly. He tried to speak rapid words but only a thick hiss came from his lips. He drew a shaky cross on his breast with his left hand. It was a long struggle to get to his feet. He crawled slowly and mechanically to the top of a big rock on the ridge peak. Once there, he arose slowly, swaying to his feet, and stood erect. Far below he could see the dark brush where he had slept. He braced his feet and stood there, black against the morning sky.

There came a ripping sound at his feet. A piece of stone flew up and a bullet droned off into the next gorge. The hollow crash echoed up from below. Pepé looked down for a moment and then pulled himself straight again.

His body jarred back. His left hand fluttered helplessly toward his breast. The second crash sounded from below. Pepé swung forward and toppled from the rock. His body struck and rolled over and over, starting a little avalanche. And when at last he stopped against a bush the avalanche slid slowly down and covered up his head.

Acknowledgements

The editor wishes to acknowledge the permission of the following copyright holders to reprint material reproduced in this volume.

Babylon Revisited by F. Scott Fitzgerald. Reprinted from *Taps at Reveille* with the permission of Charles Scribner's Sons. Copyright 1931 The Curtis Publishing Company; copyright renewed 1959 Frances S. F. Hanahan.

A Rose for Emily by William Faulkner. Reprinted from *Collected Stories of William Faulkner* by permission of Random House, Inc. Copyright 1930 and renewed 1958 by William Faulkner.

Big Two-Hearted River by Ernest Hemingway. Reprinted from *In Our Time* with the permission of Charles Scribner's Sons. Copyright 1925 Charles Scribner's Sons; copyright renewed 1953 Ernest Hemingway.

Flight by John Steinbeck. Reprinted from *The Long Valley* by permission of Viking Penguin Inc. Copyright 1938, renewed © 1966 by John Steinbeck.

Every effort has been made to clear the copyrights in these stories and the editor apologizes to copyright holders for any errors or omissions that may have occurred inadvertently.